GOTREK & FELIX
THE FOURTH OMNIBUS

More Warhammer from Black Library

· GOTREK & FELIX ·

GOTREK & FELIX: THE FIRST OMNIBUS
William King
(Contains books 1-3 in the series: *Trollslayer*, *Skavenslayer*
and *Daemonslayer*)

GOTREK & FELIX: THE SECOND OMNIBUS
William King
(Contains books 4-6 in the series: *Dragonslayer*, *Beastslayer*
and *Vampireslayer*)

GOTREK & FELIX: THE THIRD OMNIBUS
William King & Nathan Long
(Contains books 7-9 in the series: *Giantslayer*, *Orcslayer*
and *Manslayer*)

GOTREK & FELIX: THE FOURTH OMNIBUS
Nathan Long
(Contains books 10-12 in the series: *Elfslayer*, *Shamanslayer* and
Zombieslayer)

BOOK 13: ROAD OF SKULLS
Josh Reynolds

SLAYER OF THE STORM GOD
An audio drama by Nathan Long

CURSE OF THE EVERLIVING
An audio drama by David Guymer

· ULRIKA THE VAMPIRE ·
Nathan Long

Book 1: BLOODBORN
Book 2: BLOODFORGED
Book 3: BLOODSWORN

· THANQUOL & BONERIPPER ·
C.L. Werner

Book 1: GREY SEER
Book 2: TEMPLE OF THE SERPENT
Book 3: THANQUOL'S DOOM

A WARHAMMER OMNIBUS

NATHAN LONG

GOTREK & FELIX

THE FOURTH OMNIBUS

BLACK LIBRARY

A Black Library Publication

Elfslayer copyright © 2008 Games Workshop Ltd.
Shamanslayer copyright © 2009 Games Workshop Ltd.
Zombieslayer copyright © 2010 Games Workshop Ltd.
Slayer of the Storm God copyright © 2011 Games Workshop Ltd.
The Funeral of Gotrek Gurnisson first appeared in *Gotrek & Felix Anthology*
copyright © 2012 Games Workshop Ltd.
Slayer's Honour first appeared in *Gotrek & Felix Anthology*
copyright © 2012 Games Workshop Ltd.
All rights reserved.

Updated Gotrek & Felix Gazetteer by Lindsey D le Doux Priestley.

With thanks to Rob Clarke and Angela McIntosh for the
original version of the Gotrek & Felix Gazetteer.

This omnibus edition published in Great Britain in 2013 by
Black Library,
Games Workshop Ltd.,
Willow Road,
Nottingham, NG7 2WS, UK.

10 9 8 7 6 5 4 3 2 1

Cover illustration by Winona Nelson.
Map by Nuala Kinrade.

© Games Workshop Limited 2013. All rights reserved.

Black Library, the Black Library logo, Warhammer, the Warhammer Logo, Time of Legends, the Time of Legends logo, Games Workshop, the Games Workshop logo and all associated brands, names, characters, illustrations and images from the Warhammer universe are either ®, TM and/or © Games Workshop Ltd 2000-2013, variably registered in the UK and other countries around the world. All rights reserved.

A CIP record for this book is available from the British Library.

UK ISBN13: 978 1 84970 327 7
US ISBN13: 978 1 84970 328 4

No part of this publication may be reproduced, stored in a retrieval system, or transmitted in any form or by any means, electronic, mechanical, photocopying, recording or otherwise, without the prior permission of the publishers.

This is a work of fiction. All the characters and events portrayed in this book are fictional, and any resemblance to real people or incidents is purely coincidental.

See Black Library on the internet at
www.blacklibrary.com

Find out more about Games Workshop
and the world of Warhammer at
www.games-workshop.com

Printed and bound by CPI Group (UK) Ltd, Croydon, CR0 4YY

This is a dark age, a bloody age, an age of daemons
and of sorcery. It is an age of battle and death, and of the
world's ending. Amidst all of the fire, flame and fury
it is a time, too, of mighty heroes, of bold deeds
and great courage.

At the heart of the Old World sprawls the Empire, the
largest and most powerful of the human realms. Known for
its engineers, sorcerers, traders and soldiers, it is
a land of great mountains, mighty rivers, dark forests
and vast cities. And from his throne in Altdorf reigns
the Emperor Karl Franz, sacred descendant of the
founder of these lands, Sigmar, and wielder
of his magical warhammer.

But these are far from civilised times. Across the length
and breadth of the Old World, from the knightly palaces
of Bretonnia to ice-bound Kislev in the far north, come
rumblings of war. In the towering Worlds Edge Mountains,
the orc tribes are gathering for another assault. Bandits and
renegades harry the wild southern lands of
the Border Princes. There are rumours of rat-things, the
skaven, emerging from the sewers and swamps across the
land. And from the northern wildernesses there is the
ever-present threat of Chaos, of daemons and beastmen
corrupted by the foul powers of the Dark Gods.
As the time of battle draws ever near,
the Empire needs heroes
like never before.

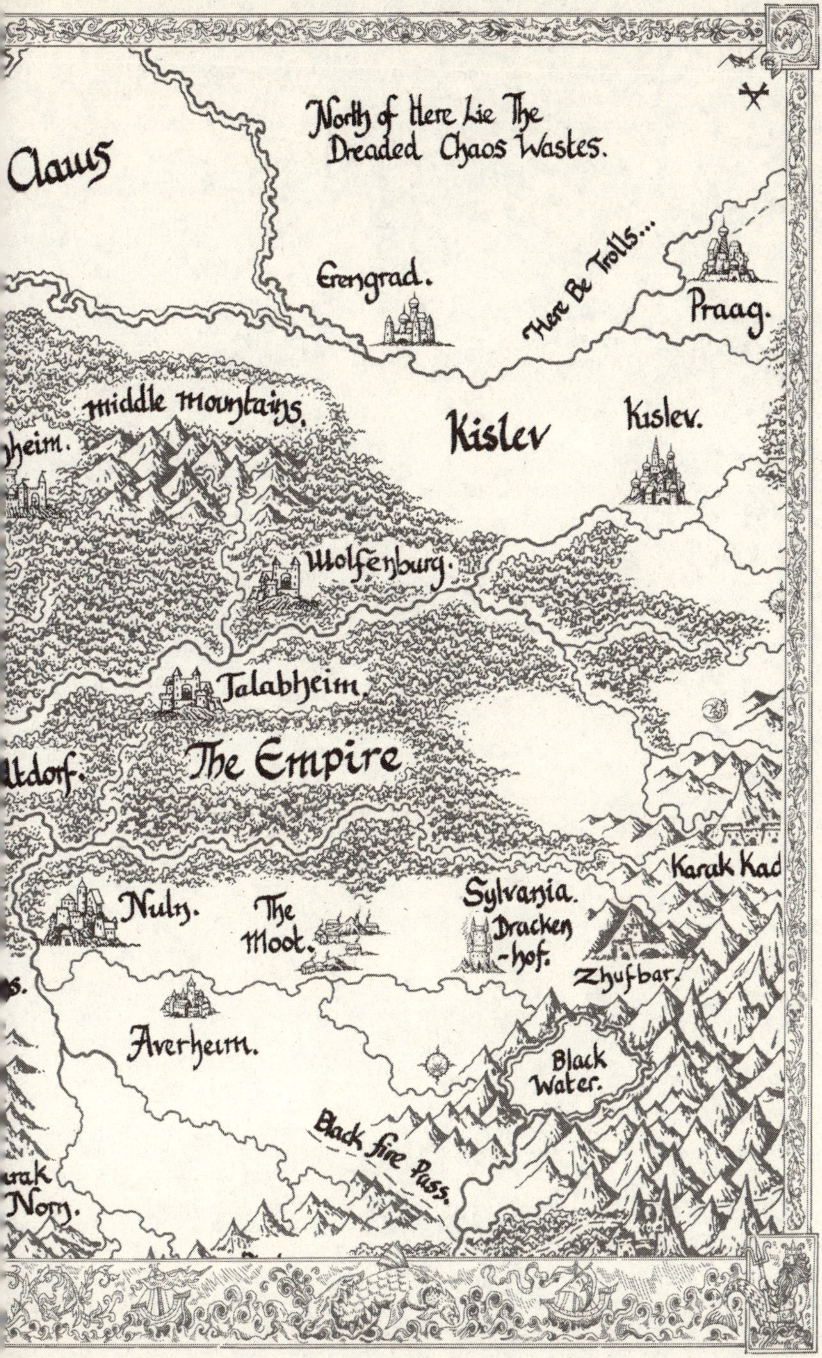
North of Here Lie The
Dreaded Chaos Wastes.
Erengrad.
Here Be Trolls...
Praag.
middle mountains.
Kislev
Kislev.
Wolfenburg.
Talabheim.
The Empire
Sylvania.
Nuln.
The
Moot.
Dracken
-hof.
Zhufbar.
Averheim.
Black
Water.
Black fire Pass.

CONTENTS

INTRODUCTION *by Nathan Long* 11

ELFSLAYER *by Nathan Long* 15

SLAYER OF THE STORM GOD *by Nathan Long* 273

SHAMANSLAYER *by Nathan Long* 299

ZOMBIESLAYER *by Nathan Long* 549

OTHER TALES
The Funeral of Gotrek Gurnisson *by Richard Salter* 823
Slayer's Honour *by Nathan Long* 839

A GOTREK & FELIX GAZETTEER 913

INTRODUCTION

In a way, you can look at the three books in this anthology as the world's longest 'assemble-the-team' montage. You know what I'm talking about, right? That's the part in the movie where the hero is given a new assignment and has to go round up the old team for one last job, and we see quick cuts of what they've all been doing since they last went their separate ways. And that – elves, beastman shamans, necromancers and zombies aside – is a lot of what I did in these 80-odd pages. Within them, I brought back to the story many of the characters from William King's original books and reintroduced them in what I hoped were new and interesting ways, while at the same time catching the reader up on what they'd all been doing, and also giving them new challenges to conquer.

And I didn't just do it because the fans asked for it, though I have a folder full of e-mails to prove they did, but because while Gotrek and Felix are perfect foils for each other, and do very well on their own, in my opinion they work best when they have some recurring friends and enemies to play against, and to stir things up a bit.

Nothing defines Gotrek and Felix's contrasting personalities better than how they deal with the people around them. A reunion that brings great joy to Felix might instill in Gotrek only distrust or disgust. A reunion that Gotrek welcomes might make Felix squirm with embarrassment or bring back unwelcome memories. And how our two heroes travel and work together – or not – with these old friends in times of crisis can not only add depth to the story, it can sometimes *become* the story. One returning character in *Elfslayer* literally sails them towards the plot. Another forces their final showdown with the main villains. One old character in *Shamanslayer* reawakens Felix's heart and sets him to wondering if there might just be a life for him after Gotrek. Another causes Gotrek to contemplate, for the first time in more than twenty years, releasing Felix from his vow.

And all that is in addition to the way each new returnee changes the dynamics of the party as it travels from battle to battle. Every new person adds a new twist to the unspoken tension that always exists just below the surface between Gotrek and Felix, and helps keep their relationship interesting and fresh. This is one of the great things with working in a long established series – *twelve books now, yikes!* – the characters all have history, and as a writer, I can use that history to add depth to their interactions and to the stories they're living through now.

One of my writerly mottos is, 'All action should have consequence,' so it was a lot of fun to go through the old books and look at what Gotrek and Felix had done back in the day and think about what the upshot would be now. Did they save a village from a Chaos champion twenty years ago? What would a survivor think of them today? Did Felix loot a magic sword once? What would happen if the original owners came looking for it? Was Felix once romantic rivals with an old friend? How would they feel about each other now? How would Felix deal with his family obligations twenty years on? How would Gotrek deal with being the world's least successful Slayer after all this time?

With these three books, *Elfslayer*, *Shamanslayer*, and *Zombieslayer*, I really felt I could finally start bringing more depth and detail to the series. *Orcslayer* and *Manslayer* were introductory books where I did my best to set the stage for their further adventures. In *Orcslayer* I brought our heroes back to the Old World and reestablished their characters. In *Manslayer* I returned them to the Empire and got them up to date in the current Warhammer timeline.

Now that I had those books under my belt and the fans weren't actively calling for my head on a stake well, mostly I felt like I could loosen up a bit and start telling stories that focused as much on character as carnage. The plots didn't have to be all action all the time. Though there was still more battle than you could shake a stick at, there was also time for moments of contemplation, sidetracks into stories of family and friends, and the lives of the ordinary people of the Empire. There was time for comedy, drama, heartbreak and even a little romance.

It was exciting to show Gotrek as more than an unstoppable killing machine, to force him to face problems that an axe and a bad attitude couldn't solve. It was a blast to show Felix as more than just a faithful but anxious rememberer, to give him a chance to be the brave one or the bright one or the honourable one, the lover or the prodigal son, and to let him think about someday being his own man. It was exciting to explore parts of the Empire that hadn't been visited before, and tell the stories of the kinds of people who are too often ignored in the rush of narrative, or trampled in the heat of battle. It was exciting to advance the plot, and bring changes and new elements to the ongoing epic. It was exciting, in other words, to finally get to the meat of the story that I had always wanted to tell.

But...

On the other hand, now that I think about it, maybe these last three books are still part of the introduction. Maybe things are just getting started. After all, as I said at the beginning, *Elfslayer*, *Shamanslayer* and *Zombieslayer* could be thought of as the world's longest 'assemble-the-team' montage. Well, now, after all those hundreds of thousands of words, the team is finally assembled. All the major characters from Bill's original books have been brought back to their proper places, and are standing in the wings, waiting for the call to action. Everything is in readiness for the next chapter in the saga. All that is necessary is to dim the lights, cue the orchestra and raise the curtain.

I can't wait to see what they do next.

Nathan Long
May 2012

ELFSLAYER

'And so, for the first time since that long ago night when I made my vow to the Slayer, I returned to the city of my birth, to find neither the welcome I had hoped for, nor that which I had feared, but a reality more strange and terrible than either.

'Our failure to reach Middenheim in time to take part in its defence precipitated the Slayer into the most prolonged despondency of our acquaintance. Indeed, I feared for a time that he might never recover from it. But then a chance meeting with an old ally drew us into one of the maddest, most desperate adventures we ever shared, and the Slayer's spirits revived, though it seemed on many occasions during those days that we might pay for his recovery with our lives.'

– From *My Travels With Gotrek*, Vol VII, by Herr Felix Jaeger
(Altdorf Press, 2528)

ONE

Felix Jaeger looked at himself in the gilt-framed mirror in the grand entry hall of his father's Altdorf mansion as he smoothed his new grey doublet and fixed the collar of his shirt for the tenth time. The deep gash in his forehead that he had received when the *Spirit of Grungni* exploded was now just a curving pink scar above his left eyebrow. The other smaller cuts and scrapes were gone entirely. The physicians who were caring for him were astonished. Less than two months had passed since the crash, and he was fully recovered. The sprains in both ankles from hitting the ground while wearing Makaisson's 'reliable' no longer hurt. The headaches and the double vision had cleared up. Even the multitude of burns had left no marks, and the cultist's sword cut that had opened him to the ribs under his left arm was no more than a fading line.

He sighed. It was of course a very good thing to be fit and healthy again, but it also meant he'd had no more excuses not to visit his father.

There was a discreet cough from behind him. He turned. His father's butler stood on the marble stair that led to the upper floors.

'He'll see you now.'

Right, thought Felix, this is it. Can't be worse than facing down a daemon, can it?

He swallowed, then started up the stairs after the butler.

Gustav Jaeger was a shrivelled manikin drowning in a sea of white bedclothes. His withered hands lay still and pink on the top of an eiderdown quilt. A gaudy gold ring, set with sapphires surrounding the letter 'J' picked out in rubies, hung loose on one shrunken finger. His face sagged from his bones like wet laundry on a line. He looked like he was already dead. Felix barely recognised him as the man he still thought of as towering over him. Only his eyes were as he remembered – alive and angry, and capable of turning Felix's insides to water with a single steel-blue glance.

'Forty-two years,' came a voice like steam. 'Forty-two years and nothing to show for it. Pathetic.'

'I've travelled the world, Father,' said Felix. 'I've written books. I…'

'I've read 'em,' snapped his father. 'Or tried to. Rubbish. The lot of them. Didn't make a crown, I'll warrant.'

'Actually, Otto says…'

'Have you any savings? Any property? A wife? Children?'

'Uh…'

'I thought not. Thank the gods Otto's pupped. There'd be no one left to carry on the Jaeger name if I'd left it to you.' Gustav lifted his feeble head from the pillow and fixed Felix with an acid glare. 'I suppose you've come back to beg for your inheritance.'

Felix was offended. He hadn't come for money. He had come to make peace. 'No, Father. I…'

'Well, you will beg in vain,' the old man sneered. 'Wasting all the advantages I offered you – the education, the position in the family business, the money I earned by the sweat of my brow, all to become a *poet*.' He spat the word out like another man might say 'orc' or 'mutant'. 'Tell me when a poet has ever done anything useful in the world!'

'Well, the great Detlef…'

'*Don't* tell me, you idiot! You think I want to hear your milk-sop prattle?'

'Father, don't excite yourself,' said Felix, alarmed as he saw Gustav's pink face turning a blotchy red. 'You're not well. Shall I fetch your nurse?'

His father sank back onto his pillow, his breath coming in whistling wheezes. 'Keep that… fat poisoner… away from me.' He turned his head and looked at Felix again. His eyes looked clouded now – troubled. One of his claws beckoned Felix closer. 'Come here.'

Felix shifted forwards on his chair, heart thudding. 'Yes, Father?' Perhaps his father was finally going to soften. Perhaps they would heal the old wounds at last. Perhaps he was going to tell him that in his heart of hearts he had actually always loved him.

'There is… one way you may regain my favour and… your inheritance.'

'But, I don't want an inheritance. I only want your–'

'Don't interrupt, damn you! Did they teach you nothing at university?'

'Sorry, Father.'

Gustav lay back and looked up at the ceiling. He was silent and still for so long that Felix began to be afraid he had died then and there – and with his words of reconciliation unspoken and Felix to blame for interrupting.

'I…' said Gustav, his voice almost inaudible.

Felix leaned forwards eagerly. 'Yes, father?'

'I am in danger of losing Jaeger and Sons… to a villainous pirate by the name of Hans Euler.'

Felix blinked. Those were not the words he expected. 'Losing…? Who is this man? How did this happen?'

'His father Ulfgang was an old associate of mine, an honourable man of Marienburg who dealt in… er, tariff-free merchandise.'

'A smuggler.'

'Call him what you will – he always dealt fairly with me.' Gustav's face darkened. 'His son, however, is another matter. Ulfgang died last year, and Hans, the black-hearted little extortionist, has come into possession of a private letter I wrote to his father thirty years ago which he claims proves I imported contraband into the Empire and avoided Imperial tariffs. He says he will show the letter to the Emperor and the board of the Altdorf Merchants' Guild if I do not give him a controlling interest in Jaeger and Sons before the end of next month.'

Felix frowned. '*Did* you import contraband and avoid Imperial tariffs?'

'Eh? Of course I did. Everybody does. How do you think I paid for your wasted education, boy?'

'Ah.' Felix was quietly shocked. He had always known that his father was a ruthless man of business, but he hadn't realised he had actually broken the law. 'And what will happen if this Euler brings the letter to the authorities?'

Gustav began to turn red again. 'Are you a lawyer suddenly? Are you weighing the merits of my case? I'm your father, damn your eyes! It should be enough that I ask.'

'I was only…'

'The Guild will blackball me and the Imperial Fisc will seize my assets, is what will happen,' said Gustav. 'That corrupt old bitch Hochsvoll will take away my charter and give it to one of her cronies. It will mean prison for me, and no inheritance for Otto, or for you. Is that enough to move your pity?'

Felix flushed. 'I didn't mean…'

'Euler awaits my answer at his house in Marienburg,' continued the old man, lying back again. 'I want you to go there and recover the letter from him, by any means that you see fit. Bring it to me and you shall have your inheritance. Otherwise you can die in poverty as you deserve.'

Felix frowned. He wasn't sure what he had expected from this meeting, but this wasn't it. 'You want me to rob him?'

'I don't want to know how you do it! Just do it!'

'But…'

'What is the difficulty?' rasped Gustav. 'I read your books. You go about the world, killing all and sundry and taking their treasure. Will you baulk to do the same for your father?'

Felix hesitated to answer. Why should he do this? He didn't want his inheritance, he didn't care enough for his brother Otto to be concerned that he wouldn't get his, and he doubted that his father would live long enough to serve any time in prison. He certainly didn't feel he owed the old man anything. Gustav had cast him out without a pfennig twenty years ago and hadn't asked after him since, and he had been a harsh, uncaring father before that. There had been numerous times over the years when Felix had hoped that the old man would choke on his morning porridge and die, and yet…

And yet, hadn't Felix come here to put an end to the old anger? Hadn't he wanted to tell his father that he at last understood that, in his way, he had tried? Gustav might have scolded his sons unmercifully, and held them to impossibly high standards, but he had also given them a childhood free from want, paid for the best schools and tutors, spent untold amounts of money trying to buy them titles, and offered them positions in his thriving business. He might not have been able to express himself except with curses and slaps and insults, but he had wanted his sons to have good lives – and Felix had come to thank him for that, and to put the past behind them. How, then, could he refuse what might well be his father's last request?

He couldn't.

Felix sighed and lowered his head. 'Very well, Father. I will get the letter back.'

So anxious had Felix been before meeting his father that he had looked neither left nor right on the way to his house, but now, as he walked back towards the Griffon, clutching his cloak about him in the chill of a late autumn morning, his eyes roamed hither and thither and the crowded Altdorf streets became streets of memory.

There on the right, with the green wall of the Jade College looming behind them, were the apartments of Herr Klampfert, the tutor who had taught him his alphabet and his history and who had smelled strongly of rosewater. There was the house of Mara Gosthoff who, at the tender age of fourteen, had let him kiss her at a Sonnstill Day dance. Off to the west, as he turned and pushed south down the bustling Austauschstrasse, he could just see the towers of the University of Altdorf, where he had studied literature and poetry and had fallen in with the young rabble-rousers who had preached abolishment of the ruling classes and equality for all.

The further he walked, the faster the memories came, rushing towards the moment when his life had changed forever and there had been no going back. Just down that street was the courtyard where he had fought his duel with Krassner and killed him when he had only meant to wound. Now he was entering the Konigsplatz, where he and his fellow agitators had lit their bonfires and led the crowds in their grand protest against the injustice of the Window Tax. There was the statue of Emperor

Wilhelm that Gotrek had dragged him behind when the Reiksguard cavalry had charged the protesters, slashing indiscriminately with their swords. Those were the cobbles on which half a dozen lancers had died by Gotrek's axe, their blood soaking into the filth and black ash of the bonfires. And here, just before the Reiksbruck bridge, was the tiny alley that led to the tavern where he and Gotrek had got blind drunk together, and where, in the wee hours of the morning, Felix had pledged to follow the Slayer and record in an epic poem his great quest to die in battle.

He stopped in the mouth of the alley, staring into its shadowed depths as a stew of conflicting emotions bubbled up inside him. Part of him wished he could walk down it and back into time to tap his younger self on the shoulder and tell him not to make the pledge. Another part of him imagined the life he would have had had he not made it – a life of marriage and property, and responsibility – and thought he should stay right where he was.

He shook himself and continued on. It was very strange to be back in Altdorf. It was full of ghosts.

Felix paused and looked up as he reached the low-lintelled door of the Griffon, a faint scrabbling sound drawing his attention towards the roof, four storeys above. He saw nothing but closed shutters and birds' nests. Pigeons fighting under the eaves, no doubt. He went in.

A few late risers still lingered over their breakfasts in the inn's warm, flagstoned taproom. He nodded to Irmele, who was clearing away plates and cups, and saluted Rudgar, the landlord, who was rolling a fresh keg of Mootland ale into place behind the bar.

'Has he come down?' Felix asked.

Rudgar nodded towards the back of the room. 'He never went up. Kept Janse up all night, filling and refilling his stein. He was there when you left this morning. You didn't see him?'

Felix shook his head. He had been too preoccupied with his visit to his father to notice anything on his way out. Now he peered into the shadows at the far end of the taproom. Half hidden in a nook behind the inn's enormous fireplace was Gotrek, slumped unmoving in a low chair, his bearded chin on his chest and a stein of ale held loose in one massive hand. Felix shook his head. The Slayer looked terrible.

It wasn't Gotrek's wounds that gave Felix pause. For the most part they were gone – healing as they always did – cleanly and completely. Except for the bulky cast on his right arm, he was good as new. What concerned Felix was that the Slayer had stopped taking care of himself. The roots of his crest showed an inch of brown where he hadn't bothered to dye them. Patchy stubble furred his scalp, obscuring his faded blue tattoos, and his face looked bloated and slack. There was dried food in his beard and the once-white plaster of the cast was grimed with filth and stained with beer. His single eye stared half closed at the wall in front of him. Felix couldn't tell if he was awake or asleep. He grimaced. This was becoming an all too common occurrence.

'Has he paid you?'

'Oh aye,' said Rudgar. 'Gave us one of his gold bracelets. He's paid up 'til Sigmar comes back.'

Felix frowned. That was bad. Gotrek had no vault to carry the treasure he had amassed during their adventures, so he wore it on his wrists. The golden bracelets and bands that circled his powerful forearms were as precious to him as the hoard of any dwarf king. He parted with them only in the direst emergencies. Felix had known him to go hungry for weeks rather than use one to buy food. Now he had paid his drinks bill with one.

The Slayer would never have done that in the past. But these days the Slayer was as morose as Felix had ever seen him, and had been since they had come to Altdorf after the destruction of the *Spirit of Grungni* – since they had missed the siege of Middenheim.

It had been the strangest waking in a life of strange wakings, that day when Felix had opened his eyes after falling from the sky. At first he could see nothing but white, and he wondered if he was lying in a cloud, or had died and gone to some strange world of mist. Then a trio of Malakai's students had pulled the silk canopy of Malakai's 'air catcher' off him and crowded above him, their heads silhouetted against a crimson sunset sky as they checked him for broken bones.

Things remained strange when they sat him up, for he found that he was in the middle of some farmer's field with the massive shapes of the corrupted cannons that Magus Lichtmann had hoped to bring to Middenheim jutting up at odd angles from the furrows all around him, like the iron menhirs of some long-forgotten cult. In an adjacent field, the smoking remains of the gondola of the *Spirit of Grungni* lay half-buried, a shattered metal leviathan seemingly about to dive beneath a sea of earth.

Then, to his left, the strangest sight of all – Gotrek, high up in a tree, dangling from the silk cords of his air catcher as more of Malakai's students climbed the branches to cut him down.

Malakai himself was by a split-rail fence, trying to convince a group of pitchfork-wielding farmers that he and his companions weren't daemons or northmen or orcs, and not having much luck.

When all had been sorted out, the crew of the *Grungni* discovered that they had crashed in the heart of the Reikland, not far north of Altdorf. With no fit cannons or supplies to bring to the front, there was no more reason for them to continue on to Middenheim, and something had to be done with the tainted guns. The evil things couldn't be left where they were. Their influence would corrupt the land and the people for miles around. Malakai decided he must take them back to Nuln in order to find a way to dispose of them safely. He hired carts to take them back, and another to take Gotrek and Felix to Altdorf, as their wounds were too severe for them to make the long journey all the way back to Nuln.

Though Gotrek protested mightily that he would go on to Middenheim broken arm or no, in the end, even he admitted that he wouldn't be much use in a fight with a bone sticking out through his skin. So, two of Malakai's students escorted him and Felix to the capital and used Gunnery School funds to pay for their lodgings and for the care of proper physicians. Malakai had said it was the least the school could do for them after they had stopped the cursed cannons from reaching Middenheim and possibly bringing about the downfall of the Empire. 'And it would ha' been the school's fault, an' mine, had it happened,' the engineer had said morosely, 'Fer nae seeing that the puir wee things had been cursed in the first place. I'd ha' shaved my heid all over again.'

And so, for the last two months, Gotrek and Felix had stewed in Altdorf, waiting for their wounds to heal, with nothing to do but sit in the taproom of the Griffon. The enforced inaction wouldn't have been so bad except that, ten days after they arrived, news had come from the north that Archaon had retreated from Middenheim and the siege was lifted.

The war was over.

Gotrek hadn't stopped drinking since.

Felix couldn't blame him, really. From the moment they had arrived in Barak Varr that spring and learned of the invasion, the Slayer had had his heart set on facing a daemon on the field of battle, and once again his doom had been denied him. It had put him in a mood so bleak that Felix was concerned he might die from it.

Felix had seen Gotrek in the depths of despair before, but never like this. Always before, no matter how low he sank, anger or insult could rouse him. Now the jibes of peevish drunks and the threats of swaggering bullies didn't even raise his head. He just continued to stare straight ahead, as if there was nothing in the world except him and his ale stein.

It made Felix heartsick to see it. One couldn't say of a Slayer that he had lost his will to live, since his whole life was a search for death, but it was a sad thing indeed to see a Slayer who had lost his will to seek a good doom.

Felix sat down across from Gotrek in the alcove behind the fireplace. The Slayer didn't seem to notice.

'Gotrek.'

Gotrek continued staring into the middle distance.

'Gotrek, are you awake?'

Gotrek didn't turn his head. 'What is it, manling?' he said at last. 'You're interrupting my drinking.' His voice sounded like someone grinding stones against each other in a tomb.

'I... I want to go to Marienburg.'

Gotrek contemplated this news for a long moment before answering. 'Taverns there are the same as here. Why bother?'

'I have something to do for my father there. You're welcome to stay here if you like, though a change of scenery might be refreshing. It should only take three weeks or so.'

Gotrek gave this some more thought, then at last shrugged his massive shoulders. 'One place is as good as another.' He raised his stein for another drink.

Felix was just trying to work out if that was a yes or a no, when something flashed past his nose and shattered Gotrek's stein, spilling beer all over the Slayer's beard and lap.

Gotrek looked up slowly as Felix turned in the direction from which the dart had come. Something long and narrow poked through a missing pane in a mullioned window. A dart flashed from it. Felix flung himself aside. Gotrek lifted his arm, and the dart stuck in the plaster of his cast. He glared with cold, one-eyed fury at the window as he reached down for his axe, which was propped against his chair.

'That was a waste of beer,' he said.

TWO

Gotrek and Felix ran out of the Griffon and thumped down the shadowed alley beside it, their weapons out. Gotrek swayed and stumbled as he ran, but considering he had been stone drunk for a solid month, his progress was remarkable.

Halfway around to the stable yard from which the dart had come, a flicker of movement above them caught Felix's eye. He looked up, still running. Something indistinct dropped past his eyes and hit his collarbone. He looked down. A slim grey rope lay across his chest. He reached for it.

It snapped tight, biting deep into his neck, and he jerked to a stop like a dog at the end of its chain, losing his sword and almost losing his footing. The cord pulled higher, forcing him onto tiptoes as he gagged and clawed at it. A slurred curse came from beside him, and he saw the Slayer staggering in a drunken circle with his cast raised over his head like he was waving it, a rope noose tight around his wrist, tugging it upwards violently.

'Cowards!' shouted Gotrek. 'Come down and fight!'

The Slayer aimed his axe at the rope, but before he could swing, a cobblestone hit him in the face. He snarled and turned, blood dripping from his forehead. Felix swung around, his vision darkening as he fought for air. Out of the shadows rushed a crowd of crouching men holding cudgels, nets and sacks. Gotrek lashed out at them with his axe, but a jerk on the rope that held his cast ruined his aim, and the men surged all around him, throwing ropes and nets at him.

A cudgel struck Felix a glancing blow on the back of the head as he scrabbled at his belt for his dagger. Another hit his shoulder. He kicked at his attackers but overbalanced and fell to one side, the rope around his neck taking all his weight. The pain and lack of air made black spots dance before his eyes. Fists and sticks pummelled him from all sides. The men's eyes were wild and wide, their lips black and wet with drool. There seemed to be scores of them.

Three men with an open sack were calling to some others. 'Lift him up! Hurry!'

Felix heard heavy thuds and cracks, and men flew back from Gotrek, bloody and maimed, but more closed around him, beating him and wrapping him up like a cocoon. His axe was pinned to his side.

'Loose me, you damned silkworms!' the Slayer roared, then threw both feet up and dropped right on his rump in the alley filth, knocking his tormentors back and pulling sharply on the rope holding his cast. There was a squeal from above and a black shape plummeted from the Griffon's top storey to land with a thud on a lower roof on the opposite side of the alley. The rope went slack.

The crowd of men closed in on Gotrek again as their companions lifted Felix towards the mouth of the sack, but the Slayer had a hand free now. The grimy cast flashed out, cracking men across the shins and knees. Gotrek surged up, struggling out of the entangling nets as they stumbled back.

They leapt at him again, trying to pin him before he got his axe free, but the razor-sharp rune blade tore through the last ropes and gutted the first man in. He fell back, his entrails spilling through his clutching hands, and crashed into the men lowering Felix into the sack.

The one holding Felix's left arm stumbled aside, letting go as he fought for balance. Felix took the opportunity and snatched his dagger from his belt. His captors flinched back and cried out, but they weren't his targets. Instead he swiped the blade over his head, severing the slim cord that choked him. The men dropped him as they took his full weight unexpectedly, and he slapped hard on the wet muck of the alley.

'I have him!' cried a man as he dived on Felix's dagger hand, trying to hold it down.

But Felix's other hand found his sword, half-submerged in alley sludge, and he hacked him with it. The man shrieked as the blade gashed his shoulder, and he rolled away, blood soaking his ragged clothes. The others swung their sticks and clubs at Felix, but he laid about him with Karaghul and they leapt back, bleeding from grievous wounds.

Felix staggered to his feet, his vision swimming and his balance gone. He waved the sword weakly in front of him as he dropped his dagger and clawed at the grey rope, which still bit deeply into his neck. It came free at last and he sucked in a beautiful, painful breath.

His vision cleared a little as blood pumped throbbingly back into his head. He looked around. Bloody corpses lay everywhere, some missing hands or arms. The remaining attackers were running for both ends of the alley. Gotrek was chasing the dozen or so heading for the inn yard, shouting at them to turn and fight. Felix stumbled after him, trying to make his legs obey his commands. They felt like they were made of custard.

Who were these men? And what did they want with them? It couldn't possibly be just some random attack. Were they cultists of the Cleansing Flame looking for revenge? Were they thralls of the Lahmian vampiresses who had sworn vengeance on them? If so, why had they tried to capture them and not kill them? Felix shivered as he imagined what those three harpies would do to him if they had him helpless. A bloody death in a back alley would be infinitely preferable.

Felix skidded into the Griffon's yard, a muddy dirt lot with the stables and privies on one side and an empty ale-cart on the other. Gotrek was just disappearing through the back gate into the alley behind, still trailing a length of rope from his cast.

Felix ran through the gate after him. Their mysterious attackers were fleeing around a corner ahead of him, into a narrower alley.

'Come back here, vermin!' roared Gotrek.

The men failed to obey.

'Do you know what this is about?' asked Felix as they charged into the alley after them. 'Who are they?'

'The ones who spilled my beer,' rasped Gotrek.

They chased their attackers through a maze of alleys – night-dark though it was almost noon, because the buildings that rose above them were so tall. Felix was surprised to find that, despite his shortness of breath and Gotrek's short legs, they kept up with the men easily. They appeared in terrible shape – weak and confused, staggering and wailing and colliding with each other as they ran.

Unfortunately they were not the only danger. As Felix and Gotrek turned a further corner, another dart parted the Slayer's crest and glanced off the alley wall beside them. They looked up. A dark shape blurred from one roof to another and vanished behind a chimney. Visions of Ulrika dancing across the rooftops of Nuln echoed through Felix's mind. Was it her? Another of the Lahmians? They were the only foes he could think of who could leap like that.

Gotrek and Felix burst out of the narrow alley into a crowded market. Felix remembered the place from his youth, the Huhnmarkt, a poultry market where his father's cook had bought chickens and ducks for the larder. Their attackers were shoving through the press of shopping servants and shouting poultry-sellers, and leaving a trail of chaos in their wake. Cages of chickens and geese were overturned, and egg men and butchers were shaking fists and cleavers at them. Gotrek ploughed after the fleeing men, heedless – trampling fallen cages and shouldering more to the ground in his single-minded pursuit. Felix gritted his teeth and started after him, ears burning at the angry shouts that followed them.

'The watch!' shouted a woman. 'Someone call the watch!'

The cry echoed all around them.

Halfway across the square, the ragged men slowed, trapped between a wall of chicken cages and a cart that was unloading more. Before they could squeeze through, Gotrek was on them, burying his axe in the last one's back and grabbing the next. Cornered, they turned to fight, lashing out with their crude weapons and throwing anything they could get their hands on.

Mostly, this was chickens. Chickens in cages, chickens out of cages, dead chickens, live chickens and chickens that had been reduced to their component parts all flew towards Gotrek and Felix in a squawking, flapping storm. Felix and the Slayer batted them aside with sword and axe and cast, smashing cages and butchering birds as they tried to close with their foes. Blood, feathers and splintering wood flew everywhere.

Felix ducked a cage of angry geese and impaled a man armed with a studded club, then hacked at another who had taken up a butcher's cleaver and flailed wildly with it. This was the first time since the noose had settled around his neck that he had been able to get a clear look at his attackers, and he found that they were very strange men indeed.

To a man they were as ragged and degenerate as any beggar Felix had ever encountered, with matted hair and beards, grimy skin and greasy, tattered clothes – but what truly alarmed him were their faces. Their eyes glittered with an unnatural excitement, and they drooled constantly – ropey black strands of spit that stained their lips and gums and spattered their clothes.

Though weak and spindle-thin, they fought with a feverish excitement and a twitchy quickness that made their attacks hard to predict. Was it a drug that made them this way? Zealotry for some god? Were they enslaved to some evil master? Felix might have felt pity for their miserable state except for the fact that they had nearly strangled him and were even now trying to beat him senseless. He cut the man with the cleaver across the knuckles. Though the wound went to the bone the man barely seemed to feel it, and swung again.

Felix blocked then thrust, stabbing deep into the man's shoulder. He screamed and fell aside. Felix looked to Gotrek. The Slayer was surrounded by bodies, and two more men were falling away from him, trailing streamers of blood from calamitous wounds. Three more madmen leapt at him from behind, wailing like the damned. Gotrek spun and split one from neck to nape, then caught a second by the belt and threw him over his shoulder into another. The men crashed through a butcher's stall, bringing down the canvas roof and landing upon sacks of plucked feathers as the butcher and his apprentices dived away. An explosion of feathers filled the air.

Two more men charged through the whirling cloud at Felix. He chopped easily through their clubs with his rune sword, then just as easily cut through their muscle and bone on his backswing. They fell screaming before him.

He looked around, wary, but the fight was over. In the middle of a ruined poultry stand, Gotrek was rising from decapitating the last of the men. He wiped his bloody forehead with the back of his bloody hand.

'Interrupt my drinking, will you?' he growled at a corpse.

The Slayer was covered from head to toe in blood, sweat and feathers. They clung to the gore that clotted his axe. They stuck to his face and shoulders and were matted in his beard, crest and eyebrows. Felix looked down at his hands and realised he must look the same. They were furred with patchy clumps of white and brown feathers. He had feathers in his mouth and up his nose. There were feathers stuck to his eyelashes.

'What's all this then?' came a voice behind him.

Felix and Gotrek turned. Stepping through the settling feathers was a patrol of the city watch, a tall, stringy captain at their head, looking around at the wreckage like a disapproving headmaster.

'Sigmar's blood!' he said, as he found the body of one of the strange men. 'There's been murder done! Who's responsible for this?'

Everyone in the square pointed at Gotrek and Felix.

'It was them!' cried a big woman in an apron and rolled sleeves. 'They chased them poor beggars in here and chopped 'em to pieces!'

'The villains smashed up my stand!' called a vendor.

'They killed my chickens!' complained another.

'All my eggs is broken!' wailed a third.

'Captain, I can explain,' said Felix, stepping forwards.

But the captain stepped back and signalled his men to go on guard. Suddenly Felix was facing a thicket of swords.

'You'll stay where you are, murderer,' the captain said. He shook his head. 'Nine, ten, eleven dead. By all the gods, what a massacre.'

'We were attacked,' said Felix. 'We defended ourselves.'

The captain didn't look as if he believed it. 'You can make your defence to Commander Halstig at the watch house. Now surrender your weapons and put your wrists behind your backs.'

Gotrek's head lowered menacingly. 'No man takes my axe.'

'Gotrek...' said Felix.

The captain sneered. 'Resistance will only make it harder on you, dwarf.' He motioned his troops forwards. 'Take it from him.'

Gotrek dropped into a fighting stance as the swordsmen edged forwards. 'Try and you die.'

'Gotrek,' said Felix, desperate, 'We can't fight the watch. They're not our enemies.'

'If they try to take my axe they are,' the Slayer growled.

Felix stepped between Gotrek and the watchmen, holding up his hands. 'Gentlemen, please. If you allow us to keep our weapons we will come peacefully, I promise you.'

'And what is the promise of a murderer worth?' asked the captain. 'Surrender your weapons immediately.'

Felix backed away as the watchmen advanced. He looked over his shoulder. 'Gotrek, please.'

'Step aside, manling.'

A young watchman raised his sword at Felix, his eyes nervous. 'Your sword. Now.'

Felix stepped back again. 'I... I cannot.'

The watchmen took another step, closing ranks.

'Don't be a fool...' said the young watchman, then gasped and clutched at his neck. A black dart sprouted from it, just above the collar of his breastplate. His eyes rolled up in his head and he dropped to the ground.

The other watchmen jumped back, shouting, unsure what had happened. Felix stepped back too, crouching and scanning the roofs around the square. Another dart flashed past him. Gotrek deflected it with his axe. It thudded against the canvas of the collapsed stall, its tip glistening, black and wet.

'What's happening?' shouted the captain.

'There!' said Felix, pointing to the roof of an exchange on the far side of the square.

The watchmen followed his gaze just in time to see a dark shape scurrying over the peak of the roof.

'And there!' said another watchman, pointing to the left.

A dart caught him on the cheek and he collapsed on top of his comrade. Another shadowy form ducked back behind the lip of a townhouse roof.

'Down!' shouted the captain.

His men dived for cover.

'Come on, manling,' said Gotrek, starting through the smashed stalls in the direction of the townhouse.

Felix shot a look at the watchmen, then followed, keeping low.

'Stop!' cried the captain. 'After them!' he called to his men.

They hesitated, wary eyes on the rooftops.

'Go!' the captain shouted.

The watchmen started after them, but slowly, keeping in cover. Gotrek turned and twisted through the maze of stalls, trailing feathers and leaving bloody footprints. His eye never left the roof of the townhouse.

'We'll never catch them,' said Felix, falling in with him.

Gotrek said nothing, walking through a stall full of complaining chickens and out the back as the owner cowered behind a chopping block. They were on the edge of the square now. The townhouse was to their left. Behind them Felix heard a babble of voices, as the watchmen trailed reluctantly after them.

A silhouetted head popped up on the townhouse roof. Gotrek swung his axe in an arc before him and knocked another dart to the ground.

'Cowards,' he rumbled.

'He's moving,' said Felix, pointing to where the silhouette had appeared briefly again at the top of the roof.

Gotrek ran into the alley between the townhouse and another building. The dark form blurred as it leapt from roof to roof further down the alley – an impossible jump – then disappeared over a gable.

Gotrek grunted and hurried on.

'Gotrek, it's useless!' called Felix. 'He's too fast.'

The Slayer ignored him.

Seven blocks later, Gotrek stopped and glared around at the roofs above him. Felix caught his breath, relieved. He was hot and sticky, and the feathers he was covered with itched horribly.

They had seen no sign of the dart shooter for four blocks, and he was just going to suggest to Gotrek that they give up, when the Slayer grunted, disgusted, then turned and started shuffling slowly down a side street. Felix stared after him. One moment he had been angry and determined and nearly his old self, the next his eye had gone dull and far-away again, like it had been for the last month. It was like someone had pulled his spine out.

'Gotrek? Where are we going?' asked Felix, trailing after him.

'I need a drink.'

'At the Griffon? But, uh, the watch will ask around. They'll find us there.'

'Let them.'

Felix hemmed uneasily. 'Listen, Gotrek, I have no interest in fighting the watch. Nor do I wish to live the life of an outlaw again. Why don't we go to another inn? Say in Marienburg.'

Gotrek said nothing, only plodded on dully.

Just then, three watchmen ran out of an alley ahead of them. They saw Gotrek and Felix and skidded to a stop in surprise.

'Halt!' said the first, the oldest of the three, though no more than twenty at the most. The watch recruited young these days, with so many older men dead in the war.

The boys went on guard. Gotrek didn't slow, only lowered his head and readied his axe. Felix groaned. This was just what they needed.

'Gotrek, they're only doing their job,' he murmured.

'They're in my way.'

'Gotrek, please!'

'Hand over your weapons,' said the young watchman. His voice quavered, but he stood firm.

Still stumping forwards, Gotrek raised his head and looked the watchman in the face. Felix saw the boy's eyes widen with fear. Felix didn't blame him. He'd taken the full brunt of that piercing, one-eyed glare before. It had shrivelled his guts every time.

'Step aside,' the Slayer said calmly. 'Tell your captain you didn't find us.'

The watchmen shot nervous glances at each other, hesitating.

Gotrek kept coming. He raised his axe, still crusted with blood and feathers and filth. Felix held his breath, not wanting to look.

The young men fled.

Felix let out a sigh of relief.

Gotrek grunted and walked on. 'Marienburg,' he said, nodding. 'One place is as good as another.'

An hour later, after a wash at a bathhouse of less than sterling repute, Felix slipped through the back door of the Griffon while Rudgar and Irmele were busy serving dinner, changed into his old clothes and his old red Sudenland cloak, collected his and Gotrek's few belongings, slipped back out again, and walked with the Slayer to the Reikside docks. He left a stack of coins on the dresser to pay for the room, and the bloodstained grey doublet as well, cursing the ruination of yet another set of good clothes. He decided that he would never again buy clothes of any quality for himself. He always managed to destroy them almost instantly.

At the docks he enquired about services to Marienburg and learned that the *Jilfte Bateau*, a Marienburg passenger boat, was leaving in two hours, so he and Gotrek settled into the Broken Anchor to wait. Though the Anchor was far from the Griffon and the Huhnmarkt, and there was little likelihood of the watch coming to look for them there, Felix still picked the table in the darkest corner of the room and looked up nervously every time someone walked through the door.

He spent the rest of the time looking to the diamond-paned windows, expecting drugged darts to come whistling from missing panes again at any moment. He still didn't know who their strange attackers had been. His money was on the Lahmians, but he couldn't rule out the Cleansing Flame either. Did they have any other enemies in the Empire? They had been away for so long, how could they? Whoever they were, would the men find them again? Would they follow them to Marienburg? From things Ulrika and the countess said, he had the impression that the Lahmians had agents everywhere. If it was them, he and Gotrek might never escape their reach.

Despite Felix's worry, their wait at the Anchor passed without incident and they made their way through the twilit Altdorf streets to the bustling docks just as the *Jilfte Bateau's* purser dropped the rope and waved the passengers aboard.

Gotrek grumbled and spat as he climbed the gangplank to the foredeck of the long low boat. 'Slopping about on the water in a leaky wooden bucket,' he muttered. 'Makes me sick. I'm going below.'

Felix smiled to himself. Every time they travelled by water Gotrek made the same complaints, but it never stopped him from boarding.

'You'll feel better if you stay above,' he said. 'Seeing the shore pass helps, I'm told.'

'Man wisdom,' said Gotrek contemptuously, and stumped for the door to the staterooms.

Felix shook his head, bemused, then turned to the rail. He wasn't going to share a cramped cabin with the Slayer when he was in such a foul mood. Better by far to watch his fellow passengers board the boat and enjoy the warmth of the late autumn sun.

The people making their way up the gangplank were a mixed lot: poor folk who had obviously paid their last coin for a berth in steerage, merchants in broadcloth on their way to trade in Bretonnia or Marienburg, their bullies carrying their baggage for them, a full company of Hochland handgunners under a bellowing captain, nobles and their retinues in silks and velvets being ushered aboard by fawning stewards, tanned and bearded sailors with packs on their backs, and fat merchant princes of Marienburg, dressed more gaudily than the nobles, returning home after signing trade agreements with wholesalers and distributors of the Empire.

It was all so normal and mundane that Felix felt an unaccustomed longing for a regular life. These people weren't attacked by strange, drooling madmen in taverns. These people weren't on a first-name basis with vampire countesses. These people didn't know anybody who had vowed to die a glorious death in battle. They'd never fought a troll. They most likely had never even seen a troll.

Maybe his father was right. Maybe he should have followed the path the old man had set out for him. Things certainly would have been more comfortable. But also more boring. Not that boredom was the worst fate that could happen to a man. It was certainly preferable to finding oneself covered in blood and chicken feathers and being hunted by the watch.

A richly appointed coach rolled up the dock and stopped near the gangplank. Though it had no insignia, it was obvious that someone important was inside. The coach was flanked by eight Reiksguard knights in steel breastplates and blue and red uniforms, and the purser ran out to meet it, bringing a low step and setting it before the door while stewards hurried to take the luggage handed down to them by the coachmen.

Felix watched with interest as the coach door opened, wondering who would emerge. First to step out was an older man in long, cream-coloured robes, over which he wore a darker travelling cloak, the voluminous hood pulled up to hide his features. Felix marked him for a wizard, not just because of his clothes and the long amber-tipped staff that he carried, but also for the fear and awe that he inspired in the purser and the stewards who waited upon him. The purser seemed torn between showing him every courtesy and bolting like a scared rabbit. The stewards handled his luggage as if it might explode at any moment.

The wizard turned back to the coach and offered a hand to its other occupant. Felix raised his head for a better look, for the woman who stepped delicately down to the dock was striking to say the least.

She was dressed in silk robes of a deep, rich blue, like a summer sky just after sunset, embroidered all over with sigils of the stars, planets and moons – a seeress of the Celestial College then – but no wizened crone, weighed down with the burden of foreknowledge that came from years of divination. This woman was young, hardly more than twenty by Felix's estimate, and as slim and graceful as a cat. Long straight hair the colour of honey fell down her back, almost to her waist, and she carried her fine-featured head high, looking about her with alert interest, her lips quirked into a permanent half-smile, as if she knew a secret no one else did, which, considering her college, she undoubtedly did.

The older wizard walked her to the boat, his head bent to talk to her as they went, while the purser bowed and scraped before them and their Reiksguard escort marched on either side of them.

Felix's fellow passengers whispered and muttered amongst themselves as the pair started up the gangplank.

'Sigmar preserve us, they're not travelling with us?' asked an Altdorf matron.

'Oh, they're all right,' said her husband. 'They're from the Colleges. Reikers wouldn't be travelling with 'em if they weren't.'

'Still warlocks all the same,' said another man. 'Can't trust 'em.'

'And even if they're good 'uns, what're they doing here? Nothing good happens around a wizard,' said a third man.

'Aye,' said the matron. 'I'm not travelling with 'em. Henrich, talk to the purser.'

'But, Hieke, my love. There isn't another boat for two days. And we must get to Carroburg by Aubentag.'

And on and on. Felix didn't blame them. Even the best of wizards made him nervous. Like any weapon in the Empire's arsenal they could be as dangerous to friend as to foe if something went wrong – powder could explode, cannons could crack, a sword could be turned against its owner, and wizards could go mad or bad, as he knew from recent personal experience.

He turned with the other passengers as the sorcerous pair reached the top of the gangplank and allowed themselves to be led towards the door to the staterooms. Felix gave the young seeress another look now that she was nearer. She was as beautiful close up as she had been far away, with high cheekbones, full lips and bright eyes that matched the deep blue of her robe.

She smiled at him as they passed, and the older wizard looked up to see who she was looking at.

Felix blinked in recognition as they made eye contact. There was a beard now where there once had been none, and grey hair where there had once been brown, but the eyes that looked at him from the lean, lined face were the same, as was the sad, slow smile that broke through the man's solemn expression.

'Felix Jaeger,' said Maximilian Schreiber. 'You haven't aged a day.'

THREE

In a chamber far beneath the deepest cellars of Altdorf, Grey Seer Thanquol hand-fed his personal rat ogre Boneripper, the thirteenth of that name. It was important with such beasts to make sure that their food – and their punishment – came only from their master. In that way was meek devotion and savage loyalty won. In that way were they his and his alone.

With some effort he lifted a fat man-leg from the basket of scraps his servants had brought and tossed into the corner where the massive rat ogre crouched, devouring another choice niblet. This incarnation of Boneripper was particularly impressive, for it was milk-white from its thick-clawed feet to its misshapen, blunt-horned head, and had the viscera-pink eyes of an albino. Thanquol had picked him from the litter Clan Moulder had offered him, particularly for his colour, which matched his own.

He looked up from watching Boneripper suck the marrow from a femur as his simpering, tailless servant, Issfet Loptail, pulled back the manskin door curtain and bowed in a lean skaven in the black garb and mask of a night runner. The skaven, an accomplished assassin known only as Shadowfang, who Thanquol had hired from Clan Eshin at great expense, knelt before him, head down, tail flat and meek. He only flinched a little as he heard Boneripper crack the leg bone with his teeth.

'I return, oh sage of the underdark,' whispered the assassin.

'Yes-yes,' said the seer impatiently. Wasn't it obvious he had returned? 'Speak-speak! Do you have them? Are they mine at last?'

Shadowfang hesitated. 'I… I crave your pardon, grey seer. The kidnap did not go as planned.'

Thanquol slammed his bony claw on the table, almost upsetting his inkpot. Boneripper rumbled ominously. 'You promised me success! You promised you had anticipated every contingency!'

'I thought I had, your supremacy,' said the assassin.

'You thought? You thought incorrectly then, yes? What happened? Tell me, quick-quick!' Thanquol's tail lashed with impatience.

'Yes-yes, grey seer. I begin,' said Shadowfang, touching his snout to the floor and casting a nervous glance at the rat ogre. 'The crested one blocked Mao Shing's sleep darts – he has been punished for his incompetence, I assure you – then, as I foresaw, the crested one and the yellow fur ran, fast-fast, out of the drinking place to fight. There they fell into my second trap, and success was nearly ours.'

'Nearly?' asked Thanquol, sneering.

The assassin's tail quivered at his devastating disdain. 'The fault is not mine, most benevolent of seers!' he shrilled. 'Had I been able to employ brave, proud gutter runners instead of sickly man-slaves, the targets would be even now in your noble claws. But outside in the day-sun in the over-burrow, skaven might have been discovered, so man-slaves must suffice.'

'But suffice they did not,' snarled Thanquol.

'No, grey seer,' said Shadowfang, swallowing nervously. 'They failed. The dwarf and the human kill-maimed them all, then escaped.'

'Escaped?' said Thanquol. 'Where-where?'

'I… I know not.'

'You know not?' Thanquol's voice was quickly rising to an imperious squeak. Boneripper sensed his distress and lowed unhappily. 'You know not? You, who I was told could sniff-sniff the trail of a crow through a swamp seven days after it had flown past? You know not?'

'Mercy-mercy, your eminence,' whined Shadowfang. 'I… I made a strategic withdrawal after the man-slaves died, and when I returned to the drinking place, they had vanished.'

'A strategic withdrawal,' said Thanquol dryly. 'You skitter-ran. You squirted the musk of fear.'

'No-no, your magnificence,' insisted Shadowfang. 'I merely redeployed to a rearwards position.'

Thanquol closed his eyes, so that he would not have to see the miserable excuse for an assassin that knelt before him. He was tempted to blast the worthless incompetent with a bolt of sorcerous fire, or feed him to Boneripper, but then he recalled how many long-hoarded warp tokens he had spent procuring the fool's services, and resisted the urge. He would get his money's worth out of him, and *then* he would let the rat ogre eat him.

'If I might speak, your fearsomeness,' said Shadowfang.

Thanquol sighed and opened his eyes. 'Oh yes, pray speak, enlightened one. Speak-speak. Let your wisdom shine upon us.'

Behind his mask, the assassin's red eyes blinked, confused. He was apparently a stranger to sarcasm. 'Er, had you allowed me to kill-maim the overdwellers instead of snare-catching them, even lowly man-slaves might have succeeded...'

'No-no!' shrieked Thanquol, causing Boneripper to bellow and Shadowfang and Issfet to curl their tails around them in fear. 'No! It must be I that take-takes their lives. It must be I that wreaks my vengeance upon their helpless bodies for all the pain-shame they have caused me. Only I can have that joy. Only I! You hear?'

He scrabbled among his papers until he found a stoppered bottle, then uncorked it and stuffed it up one cankered nostril. He inhaled deeply, shivering to the tip of his tail as the powdered warpstone began to spread throughout his system. Issfet and Shadowfang took a further step back as the seer's eyes glowed a malefic green.

'They will die,' Thanquol said, after he had at last controlled his trembling. 'Yes-yes, but only at my whim, and long after they have beg-cried to be free of life.' His glowing eyes snapped back to the assassin. 'Find them! Find them! And this time you must not fail to take them!'

'Yes, grey seer,' said Shadowfang, touching his snout again to the floor. 'At once, grey seer. I go, grey seer.'

'Master,' said Issfet, wobbling unsteadily on his hind paws. 'A man-spy tells me that the crested one and the yellow fur have left the drinking burrow, taking their hoardings with them. It may be that they journey again.'

'They have left?' said Thanquol, turning on him. 'Why did you not tell me this before?'

'I only just learned of it, your malfeasance,' said Issfet. 'I was coming to say when Master Shadowfang arrived.'

'But how will I find them?' whined Thanquol. 'They might vanish again for another twenty years.'

'I will send my gutter runners to every corner of the over-burrow,' said Shadowfang.

'I will question my man-spies,' said Issfet.

'No,' said Thanquol, raising a yellowed claw. 'I have it!' The powdered warpstone was once again clearing his head and allowing his genius to blossom. 'The yellow fur spoke with its brood sire today, yes-yes?'

'Yes-yes, your excellence,' said Shadowfang. 'It was from there I followed him.'

'Then to there you return,' said Thanquol, baring his teeth to admit a squeal of triumph. 'To learn what the man-sire knows of its offspring.'

Max raised a glass of wine in one beringed hand. 'To fond reunions,' he said, then took a drink.

Felix raised his glass and drank in turn. 'To fond reunions.'

Gotrek just drank.

They sat in Max's handsome stateroom on board the *Jilfte Bateau*, only slightly larger, but several steps more luxurious, than Gotrek and Felix's little cabin, with mahogany panelling on the walls and coloured glass in the windows. An iron stove against one wall radiated a pleasant warmth. If it weren't for the motion of the boat upon the river, Felix would have thought himself in some tidy study.

'We all thought you dead, you know,' said Max. 'When you failed to return from that strange portal in Sylvania we lost all hope.'

Felix nodded. 'Malakai said the same thing.'

Max raised his greying eyebrows. 'You've seen him?'

'We were on the *Spirit of Grungni* when it crashed,' said Felix. 'You hadn't heard about that?'

'I heard, yes,' said Max. 'But your names weren't mentioned.'

Max had aged well, Felix thought. He was still handsome, and the grey streaks in his neatly trimmed beard added to the air of grave dignity he had always projected. His hair was mostly grey now and flowed down past his shoulders in a kingly mane.

'I have only recently returned from Middenheim,' he said. 'There was much to be done after the final battle. Much cleansing.'

Gotrek gave an angry grunt at the mention of Middenheim.

'How did the *Grungni* come to crash?' Max asked.

Felix paused. Where to begin? It was a story that could take an evening to tell. Before he could start, there was a knock on the door.

'Come,' called Max.

The door opened and in stepped the young seeress, dressed now in a much less ostentatious robe of dark blue wool with no embroidery. She inclined her head to Max. 'Good evening, magister,' she said, smiling. 'I hope I'm not intruding.'

'Not at all,' said Max as he and Felix stood.

Gotrek didn't look up.

'Let me make the introductions we were too rushed to make on deck,' said Max. 'Felix, Gotrek, may I present Fraulein Claudia Pallenberger, a journeyman of the Celestial College, and a seeress of great perception.'

Felix bowed. Gotrek grunted.

'Fraulein Pallenberger,' continued Max. 'May I introduce to you Felix Jaeger, poet, adventurer and swordsman of renown, and Gotrek Gurnisson, Slayer of trolls, dragons and daemons, and the most dangerous companion with whom I have ever had the honour of travelling.'

Gotrek snorted at that.

Claudia curtseyed and smiled at Felix and Gotrek. 'I'm pleased to make your acquaintance, Herr Jaeger, and you Herr Gurnisson.'

'The pleasure is all mine,' said Felix, bowing again. 'Are you travelling to Marienburg, fraulein?'

'To Marienburg and beyond,' said Claudia as she crossed to a chair next to the stove and sat down. She raised her chin and looked mysterious. 'I've had premonitions.'

Max almost dropped the glass of wine he was pouring for her. 'This *is* a secret mission, fraulein,' he murmured.

Claudia blushed and her mysterious look collapsed. She suddenly looked closer to seventeen than twenty. 'I'm sorry, magister. I didn't think. I…'

Max smiled and handed Claudia her wine. 'Don't worry, we're among friends. But please try to be more cautious in the future.' She nodded her head, sheepish.

Max turned to Felix and Gotrek. 'You'll not speak of this.'

'Of course not,' said Felix.

Gotrek shook his head and drank again.

'Thank you,' said Max. 'Then you may tell the rest of it, seeress.'

Claudia nodded again, then looked solemnly at Felix. 'I have seen Altdorf destroyed in fire and flood. I have seen Marienburg swept from the face of the earth by a towering wave. I have seen death and ruin on an unimaginable scale, and the coming of a great dark age.'

'Ah,' said Felix. 'I see.' There didn't seem to be anything else to say.

'And I am drawn to the north by the feeling that the prevention of these events may be found there.'

'Fraulein Pallenberger's visions have been confirmed as true divinations by the magisters of her College,' said Max. 'They have also determined that she is particularly attuned to these strands of possibility, and have sent her to follow them to their source. I accompany her as mentor and, ah, protector.'

Felix frowned, confused. 'You are with the Celestial College, Max? I always thought…'

Max smiled and took another drink. 'No, I am of the Order of Light. But it was felt that, er, that a man who had seen something of the world…'

'The magisters of my College,' interrupted Claudia, her eyes flaring, 'are a lot of dusty old greybeards who never leave their rooms. Their eyes are always at their telescopes and their minds are always in the clouds. They hid behind their doors like old biddies when I asked who would accompany me.'

Max coughed to hide a laugh. 'I was chosen because, in my youthful wanderings before I found employment with the Graf of Middenheim, I had spent some time in Marienburg and came to know some of the leaders of the magical fraternity there, such as they are.'

'And because you have actually cast a spell in battle,' added Claudia hotly.

Max nodded. 'That too. Although I hope that this will be nothing more than a reconnaissance mission and that there will be no reason for violence.'

Felix frowned at Max. 'Forgive me, Max, but I'm confused now. When Makaisson said that you were at the Colleges I didn't think anything of it, but weren't you…? That is, how did it come about? I seem to remember you telling me that you had, ah, broken with them. Wasn't that the cause of your "youthful wanderings"?'

Max smiled wistfully. 'There comes a time in a man's life–' He shot a sharp glance at Felix here. 'At least in some men's lives – when he puts wandering behind him, and wants some security.' He had another sip of wine. 'I was honoured by the Tsarina for my help in the defence of Praag that year. This won me the grudging acceptance of the Colleges, and a few years later, after some hemming and hawing, they offered me a teaching position, and a chance to continue my studies – within reason.' He cast a look at Gotrek, who continued to stare dully into his mug. 'Adventuring wasn't the same after you two vanished anyway, so I took the job. Been there ever since.'

Claudia smiled over the rim of her glass. 'Have you all shared adventures before, then? Is that how you know each other? Were you brave friends on some noble quest?'

Felix and Max exchanged an uncomfortable glance. They had certainly shared numerous adventures, but they had not always been the best of friends.

'Herr Jaeger, Herr Gurnisson and I travelled together into the Chaos Wastes once,' said Max. 'On an airship.'

'And we fought a dragon,' said Felix.

'And the hordes of Chaos,' said Max.

'And defeated a… a vampire.' Felix stammered, wishing as soon as he said it that he hadn't spoken. He remembered the outcome of that nightmarish episode and how Max had reacted to the news of Ulrika's undeath. Should he tell Max he had seen her? Would Ulrika want him to know? What would Max do if he knew? Would he seek her out? Would she fall in love with him again? The bitter bile of jealousy suddenly welled up in Felix's heart as if the hurt had happened yesterday instead of nearly twenty years before. He fought it down, angry with himself for being ridiculous. What did he possibly have to be jealous about? Ulrika had said that love between the living and the unliving was impossible. She could no more betray him with Max than with anyone else, and yet still the wound burned. He cursed himself. Men truly were fools.

Max was looking at him curiously.

Felix flushed and turned back to Claudia, forcing a smile. 'So, yes, we have had a few adventures together, I suppose, but all many, many years ago.'

Claudia's full lips curved into a smile. 'You don't look old enough to have had adventures many, many years ago, Herr Jaeger.'

'Ah, well, I…'

'Yes,' said Max, eyeing Felix with a bemused frown. 'Herr Jaeger is remarkably well preserved.'

'Mm, yes,' said Claudia, looking at Felix from under a curtain of golden tresses. 'Remarkably.'

Felix started like he had been goosed. The girl found him attractive! That was no good at all. He shot a look at Max. The wizard was scowling. He had seen it too. Felix swallowed. This could all get very awkward. 'I think perhaps it is time for us to retire,' he said, standing quickly. 'You no doubt have many things to speak of regarding your mission. Ready, Gotrek?'

'There's no need,' said the seeress. 'Really.'

'No no,' Felix insisted, stepping to the door. 'The Slayer and I have had an exhausting day, thank you all the same.' He nodded respectfully to Max. 'Max, a pleasure to see you again.' Then he turned to Claudia. 'Fraulein Pallenberger, an honour to make your acquaintance. I bid you both a very good night.'

Gotrek stood and downed the last of his beer in one long swallow, then put the mug down and stumped out after Felix.

'Thanks for the beer,' he said.

The journey down the Reik from Altdorf to Marienburg took twelve days, according to the ship's pilot, but by the end of the second day, Felix was convinced it was more like twelve years. It seemed as if it would never be over.

Gotrek, never the most effervescent of travelling companions, had become a monosyllabic lump that sat in the dark in their cabin and stared at the wall, never leaving except to find food and beer. Without the Slayer's company, Felix had little to do but pace the decks and try to avoid the attentions of Fraulein Pallenberger, which proved no easy task.

She seemed to be everywhere: on the stairs coming down when he was coming up, stepping out of her cabin just as he was stepping out of his, walking on the foredeck just when he wanted to stretch his legs, and sipping tea in the taproom just when he was in the mood for a drink. And always, somewhere in the background, like a hovering grey owl, was Max, glaring at Felix as if it were he who was instigating things.

Felix always excused himself as quickly and politely as possible, and Claudia never made any fuss, just exchanged pleasantries and moved on, but there was something in her smile, and in the gleam of her dancing eyes, that suggested that, like a cat who waits at a mouse hole, she knew that her patience would eventually win out over his reticence.

On the third evening, when Felix had scurried to the aft deck after seeing Claudia engrossed in a book on the foredeck, Max finally sought him out, joining him as he leaned on the stern rail and looked out at the trees and fields that glided by on either side of them. The wizard filled a long clay pipe with tobacco, lit it with a flame from his finger, then exhaled a long plume of smoke.

'You would do well to keep your roving eye to yourself, Felix,' he said at last.

Felix felt his hackles raise. The accusation was unfair. And even if it weren't, who was Max to tell him what to do? 'I have no intention of allowing my eye to rove,' he said sharply. 'Nor any other part of my anatomy, for that matter.'

'I am glad to hear it,' said Max. Then he sighed. 'I'm sorry, Felix. She is a bright girl, but very sheltered. She entered the College at eleven, and has seen nothing of the world except its cloisters since. Recently, according to her masters, this has begun to chafe.'

'That's hardly surprising, is it?' said Felix. 'An energetic, inquisitive girl, coming to maturity in a monastery of – what did she call them – dusty old greybeards? You can't blame her for wanting to experience something of life while she's young.'

'No, I can't,' said Max sadly. 'I certainly wanted to see the world when I was her age. Nevertheless, I have been charged by her College to keep her safe from any entanglements or embarrassments while she undertakes this journey, and if I fail… well there will be some unpleasant political repercussions.' He looked up at Felix with a rueful smile. 'So, as a favour to your old travelling companion…?' He let the question hang.

Felix sighed and looked down the river winding away south and east behind them, as if he could see all the way back to Nuln. 'Trust me, Max. I've no interest in her, nor any woman, at the moment. My heart is locked in an iron box and I've lost the key.'

Max raised his eyebrows. 'It must be a terrible melancholy indeed to cause you to resort to metaphor.' He nodded and stood. 'Well, no matter the cause, I appreciate your understanding and restraint. I will do my best to keep her occupied, but remember what you have said here if she escapes me.'

'I will,' said Felix.

Max tapped his pipe on the rail, knocking the ash into the river, then turned to go. Felix looked after him, hesitant, then spoke.

'Max.'

The wizard looked back. 'Yes?'

'I've seen Ulrika.'

Max looked at him, his face growing still. He returned to the rail. 'She still lives?'

Felix nodded. 'If it can be called living.'

'Is she… is she well?'

'As well as can be expected, I suppose. She is still under the patronage of the Countess Gabriella. She is her bodyguard. In Nuln.'

Max twisted his pipe in his hands, his eyes far away. 'I have often thought of seeking her out, but I never had the courage.'

'I wish *I* hadn't found her,' said Felix, with unexpected bitterness.

'No?' asked Max, turning to look at him. 'Is she so changed then?'

'Not nearly enough,' said Felix. He found he had a lump in his throat. He fought to swallow it. 'Not nearly enough.'

'Ah,' said Max. 'Ah, I see.' He pressed his lips together and stared hard over the rail into the swirling waters of the river. 'Then I think that I shall not seek her out after all.' He turned away, then, after a step, turned back and looked at Felix. 'Thank you for telling me.'

Felix shrugged. 'I'm not sure it was a kindness.'

'Nor am I,' said Max. 'But I am glad to know nonetheless. Good day, Felix.' Then he turned and walked towards the main deck.

Claudia caught Felix at last on the afternoon of the fifth day.

Except for light fare in the taproom, the *Jilfte Bateau* did not serve meals. Instead, it had arrangements with inns at various towns along the Reik that would provide food and drink for its passengers. It stopped only twice a day, once in the morning and once in the afternoon, meaning that those who were inclined to be peckish at other times of day were advised to buy extra food for later. This afternoon, the riverboat had docked in the small town of Schilderheim, and the passengers had disembarked – all but Felix.

Finding himself more in need of solitude than sustenance, and seeing Max and Fraulein Pallenberger making their way down the gangplank, he had decided to remain on board, settling down in the empty taproom with a pint and the first volume of the *My Travels With Gotrek* books that his brother Otto had published during his absence. Felix had hesitated to read them these last two months, fearing that he would find that his journals had been clumsily fleshed out, or imperfectly edited, or worse, that his own youthful prose would not stand up to his scrutiny, but he could resist no longer, and at last opened the leather-bound, gilt-stamped cover and began.

He was not reassured by the title page, for there was an error even there. The publishing date was wrong – 2505. He hadn't even sent the first journal to his brother then. Someone must have used the date he had written on the inside cover of his original journal as the publishing date. But even that wasn't right, was it? It had been a few years before that. It was baffling. Out of curiosity, he pulled the other books out of his satchel and checked them. The publishing date in every one of them was the same! Whoever had typeset the books had been lazy in the extreme and left the title page untouched in each edition. Felix shook his head, then shrugged. What did he expect from a penny-pincher like Otto? He wouldn't have gone to a first-rate printer, would he?

Just as he began the first chapter, and shivered as it recalled to his mind the horrors of that long past Geheimnisnacht, a shadow fell across the page and he looked up. Fraulein Pallenberger was smiling down at him. Felix jumped in surprise.

'Herr Jaeger,' she said, curtseying and smiling at his unease.

Felix stood and bowed. 'Fraulein Pallenberger, how unexpected to find you here. I thought I saw you leave for the inn.'

'Nothing is unexpected to one of the Celestial Order, Herr Jaeger,' she said, taking the seat next to his. 'May I?'

'Certainly,' said Felix, cursing himself for not having the courage to refuse her.

He watched Claudia out of the corner of his eye as she signalled to the barman to bring her some tea. In truth, he wished he could find it within him to succumb to her charms, if only to annoy Max, but also to try to find some balm for the pain in his heart. His last view of Ulrika, running into the darkness of the skaven tunnels beneath Nuln, had been more than two months ago, and still not a day went by – not an hour! – when he did not think of her and feel the stab of regret rip through him.

Part of him wanted that never to change. The pain was all he had left of her, and that made it precious, and yet, another part of him wanted to be free of it. He longed to drown himself in the solace of loving – or at least lustful – arms. What had Ulrika said? We must find happiness among our own kind? It seemed impossible.

Claudia was beautiful, there was no denying it, and alluring as well, with her knowing glances and gleaming fall of honey-coloured hair, but though he tried his best not to, he could not stop himself from comparing her to Ulrika, and in each instance finding her wanting. Her blue eyes were bright and beautiful, but not as alive as Ulrika's – not even in her undeath. Her smile was sultry, but not as forthright as Ulrika's, her curves were lovely, even under her seeress's robes, but seemed to him girlish and unformed when compared to Ulrika's clean-limbed martial grace. Her nose... ah, but it was useless! No matter how beautiful Claudia was, and how beguiling her attraction to him, it was not *her* arms he wanted to find solace in, it was Ulrika's, and though he knew that could never be, that didn't stop him wanting it with all his heart.

'What are you reading, Herr Jaeger?' Claudia asked, leaning in to look at the cover of the book.

Felix flushed. There really was nothing more embarrassing than to be caught reading one's own memoirs. 'Ah, my brother published my journals without my knowledge. I... I'm checking to see that he didn't change them too much.'

She read the title. *'My Travels With Gotrek.'* She looked up at him. 'You and Herr Gurnisson seem an odd pairing. How did you come to travel together?'

Felix groaned inwardly. It was a long story and he didn't particularly feel like telling it just now. He held out the book. 'Would you like to read about it?'

Claudia laughed. 'I would much rather hear it from the lips of the man that lived it.'

Felix sighed. 'Well, if you insist.'

And so he told her about his student days, and the Window Tax riots, and how Gotrek had saved him from the swords of the Reiksguard – though he downplayed the slaughter somewhat – and how he and Gotrek had retired to the inn and got abysmally drunk, and how he had sworn to follow Gotrek and record his death in an epic poem.

When he finished, Claudia looked at him strangely. 'And for how many years have you followed the Slayer?' she asked.

'More than twenty,' he said.

'That seems a long time to continue honouring a vow made while in one's cups,' she said.

Felix nodded. 'Yes, it is.'

'It's a wonder you continue.'

'A vow is still a vow, no matter how long ago it was made,' said Felix.

'But what about your life!' cried Claudia, suddenly overwhelmed by emotion. 'Did you not have plans of your own? Did you not have dreams? How could you give up your life to follow another?'

Felix frowned. It was rare that he talked about these things out loud. 'I did have plans. I meant to be a poet. Possibly a playwright. I believed I would spend my life among the inns and theatres of Altdorf. But as I said, a vow is a vow.'

'But you were drunk!'

'It was still a vow.'

She shook her head, seeming truly upset. 'It must be more than that. Surely Herr Gurnisson would have forgiven you your duty if you had gone to him and asked to be released from it. I cannot believe that anyone would ask someone to hold to a promise made when they were too young or too drunk to know what it meant – when they had no idea of all the wonders that life offers for someone who is free to see them. Have you no regrets? Did you never want to leave?'

Felix wasn't sure Gotrek *would* have released him from his vow. Like all dwarfs, the Slayer was a stickler when it came to honouring pledges, but still she was right, it had been more than the vow. 'I do have regrets,' he said at last. 'And I did want to leave. Many times. I even agreed to abandon him once.' A shiver went through him as he remembered the circumstances. 'Though I didn't in the end. On the other hand, I have seen more of the world following the Slayer than I ever would have writing poems in Altdorf, and though it has often been dangerous, and I have come close to losing my life more times than I can count, I don't think I could trade it for a safer life. Not any more. I believe I have become addicted to excitement.'

'Well, I envy you that part of it, at least,' said the seeress. 'But to not be able to call your life your own. To not be able to say, "I want to go this way", or "I want to try this", or "I want to talk to this person", because you have pledged to make your life beholden to someone else for all time seems... unbearable! I don't know how you can stand it!'

Felix blinked at her. Was she talking about him any more, or herself? 'It is indeed a hard thing,' he said at last, 'to make a vow that one regrets later, but a man of honour – or a woman of honour, for that matter…'

'Fraulein Pallenberger,' said a voice.

They looked up.

Max Schreiber stood in the door, his eyes cold. 'I thought you had returned to the boat for your gloves.'

Claudia smiled brightly at him. 'And I found them, Magister Schreiber,' she said, holding up a pair of long fawn gloves. 'But then I saw Herr Jaeger here alone and thought I would take some tea with him.'

'You've missed your dinner,' said Max, sounding very much like an out-of-sorts schoolmaster.

'Sometimes a conversation can be more filling than a meal, magister,' she said, standing. She turned to Felix and held out her hand to him, smirking conspiratorially as she did so. 'Thank you for your company, Herr Jaeger,' she said. 'It is very refreshing to speak now and then to someone who still understands the yearning of youth for knowledge and experience.'

'The pleasure was all mine, fraulein.' Felix glanced at Max as he bent over her hand. The wizard was glaring daggers at him. Claudia squeezed Felix's fingers warmly before she let go.

He sighed as she rejoined Max and they turned to go. Would this journey never end? He sat down and returned to his travels with Gotrek.

FOUR

Seven days later the journey did end, and not before time, as far as Felix was concerned. With Claudia popping out at him from every corner and Max scowling at him from every doorway, he felt a haunted man by the time the riverboat reached Marienburg, and he disembarked onto the fog-shrouded docks of the Suiddock with a sigh of relief.

He and Gotrek took lodging in an inn that his father had recommended called the Three Bells, in the bustling Handelaarmarkt district – a place of shipping offices, guild halls and trade associations – and had sent word to Hans Euler that he wished to meet with him on a matter of business. While he waited for a response, he continued to read through the first volume of *My Travels With Gotrek*, which was proving better than he had feared. Every now and then he would find himself nodding at a particularly neat turn of phrase and thinking that his younger self was a better writer than he had given him credit for.

Gotrek had immediately installed himself at a table at the back of the Three Bells' long, narrow taproom and proceeded to drink himself into a stupor, just as he had at the Griffon in Altdorf. Felix sighed to see it. It was as if all the life had been sucked out of the Slayer, and all that was left was an empty husk that remembered nothing of its former life except how to drink. With Archaon's invasion repelled, was there anything now that could stir Gotrek from his melancholy? Or would he spend the rest of his days travelling from tavern to tavern, as miserable in one as he was in another?

Though he often complained when he was forced to follow the Slayer into danger, Felix didn't fancy that prospect either. It certainly wouldn't make a very exciting epic.

The next morning, when Felix came down from his room to look for breakfast, the landlord brought him a note. It was from Hans Euler. Felix opened it and read,

> *Herr Jaeger,*
> *Warmest regards, and I would be very pleased to meet you today, two hours after noon, at my house on the Kaasveltstraat in the Noordmuur district.*
> *Yours,*
> *Hans Euler*

Felix was pleased, if a little surprised, at the speed and politeness of the reply. From what his father had said of the man, he had expected to be put off or outright refused. He sent a messenger with a reply saying that he would be there at two, then went to find Gotrek.

He didn't have far to look. The Slayer was at the same table Felix had left him at the night before, staring into nothingness with a huge mug in one fist. It looked as if, once again, he had not returned to their room. Felix asked the barmaid to bring him some breakfast, then went and joined the Slayer at the table. Gotrek remained staring straight ahead.

Felix cleared his throat. 'Euler agreed to meet with me today,' he said.

'Who?' rumbled Gotrek, not turning.

'Hans Euler. The man I'm here to see.'

'Ah.' Gotrek drained the mug, then made a face. 'Grungni, that's terrible. Tastes like fish.' He signalled the barman for another.

'I was hoping you would come with me.'

'Why?'

'Well, Euler might be difficult. I might need some help convincing him to hand over the letter.'

Gotrek's single eye looked up at Felix, dim interest stirring behind it. 'A fight?'

'I hope not, but possibly. Mainly I just want him to see you, and your axe, while I talk to him.'

Gotrek pondered this, then shrugged. 'Sounds like too much bother. I'll just stay here and drink.'

Felix nearly choked. The Slayer turning away from the possibility of violence? The end times truly had come. 'But you don't like the beer. It tastes like fish.'

'It's still beer,' said Gotrek, and turned back to stare at the wall.

Felix sighed. He really wanted Gotrek along. There were few things more intimidating than a Slayer, and Gotrek was a particularly impressive example of the breed. It might mean the difference between success or failure in his negotiations. He leaned forwards. 'Listen Gotrek, I can't leave Marienburg until I resolve this matter. If you don't help me, it might take weeks – weeks of drinking fishy beer. On the other hand, if you come with me, I could have the letter today, and we could be on our way back to Altdorf, where the beer *doesn't* taste like fish. What do you think?'

As Gotrek thought this through, the barmaid brought him his next round and Felix his breakfast. Gotrek took up the fresh mug as she set it in front of him, raised it to his lips, then paused, his nose wrinkling. He grunted, drank anyway, then set the mug down again, swallowing with effort. 'All right, manling. I'll come.'

Kaasveltstraat was a wealthy street in the middle of the quietly prosperous Noordmuur district, lined on both sides with tidy stone-and-brick three-storey townhouses, each with a white marble stoop leading up to a sturdy wooden front door, and fronted with diamond-paned windows that glittered in the chilly afternoon sun. Hans Euler's house was on the east side of the street, which butted up against a canal, and its upper storeys hung out over the water at the back. It all looked very solid and respectable, not how Felix had imagined the den of a pirate's son to look at all.

Gotrek stood behind him on the cobbled street, trying to reach an itch under his cast, as Felix stepped up to the door to knock – and hesitated. He was not looking forward to what was to follow. These sorts of situations always made him squirm. Why was he even doing this? He had never cared about his father's business. It didn't matter to him if the old man lost a portion of it to someone else. As far as Felix was concerned the whole enterprise could go up in flames. He had half a mind to go back to the Three Bells and forget the whole thing.

But he didn't. Instead, he cursed under his breath and knocked. Family was a stickier trap than any spider's web.

After a moment, a prim little butler in a high-collared black doublet opened the door. He had a spit-curl of oiled black hair plastered to his forehead, and his mouth pursed with disdain as he looked Felix up and down.

'*Oui?*' he said.

'Felix Jaeger to see Hans Euler,' said Felix. 'And my companion, Gotrek Gurnisson.'

The butler's eyes widened a fraction as he saw Gotrek, then he regained his composure. He made a bow that had more moves in it than a chess game. 'Please to enter, messieurs. Monsieur Euler is expecting you.'

Felix and Gotrek stepped through the door into a wood-panelled entryway with a tight spiral staircase on one side and a door that opened into a large parlour at the back. A bay window in the parlour looked out over the canal. Felix sized up the house as the butler closed the door behind them. It was small, but richly furnished with heavy tables and chairs.

Dark oil paintings of men in tight ruffs crowded the walls and expensive Estalian rugs covered the polished wooden floors. It all told Felix that Herr Euler wasn't in his father's league, but he was still a wealthy man.

'Your sword, monsieur?' said the butler, clicking his heels together as he bowed.

Felix unbuckled his sword belt and handed his rune sword to him.

The butler bowed again and turned to Gotrek. 'And ze axe, monsieur dwarf?'

Gotrek just stared at him with his single, expressionless eye.

The butler held his gaze for a brief moment, and looked about to speak again, but then thought better of it. He bowed convulsively and turned away, his face pale. 'It is of no matter,' he stuttered. 'With only ze one arm, how is it possible that you might use it?'

Felix could have informed him otherwise, but let it go.

The butler put Felix's sword in a small cupboard by the door, then bowed them towards the stairs. 'If messieurs will come this way?'

They followed him up to the first floor, where he stopped at a door just at the top of the spiral stair and knocked. A muffled voice called and he opened the door.

'Felix Jaeger and companion, monsieur,' he said into the room, then bowed and edged aside, allowing Felix and Gotrek to enter.

They stepped into the middle of a long room with tall diamond-paned windows along one wall. It was in every way a much lighter room than the one below it. A fire crackled in a small fireplace opposite the door. To the left, a set of graceful Bretonnian chairs was arranged around a low table, and to the right was a grand desk with, behind it, mounted on a cherrywood sideboard, an ironbound safe of dwarf make, that seemed a bit brusque and business-like in the otherwise cultured surroundings.

Standing by the desk with an expression of welcome on his mild round face was the least piratical-looking man Felix had ever seen. He was thick and short and balding, with a shapeless lump of a nose and mild blue eyes. His conservatively tailored clothes were of the most expensive Middenland broadcloth, and he held a silver-headed cane in one pudgy hand. He looked much more merchant than pirate. Perhaps, thought Felix, in these modern times there isn't much difference.

'Messieurs, Herr Euler,' said the butler.

Herr Euler's warm smile faltered when he saw Felix in his rough travelling clothes, and fell entirely when Gotrek's half-naked, tattooed bulk sidled through the narrow door.

He turned to the butler. 'Guiot! The dwarf has his axe!' Felix decided Euler's eyes weren't quite so mild after all.

The butler turned pink and bowed vigorously. 'I apologise, monsieur, but he did not wish, and I did not think… er, that is, crippled as he is, he cannot…'

'It is you who are crippled, Guiot,' Euler snapped. 'With cowardice.'

He sighed and waved a dismissive hand. 'Very well, send up Harald and Jochen with food and drink for our guests. You may go.'

'Oui, monsieur. I am sorry, monsieur.' The butler bowed again and withdrew.

Euler reassembled his smile as he turned to Felix. 'Herr Jaeger,' he said, stepping forwards and holding out a hand. 'It is good to meet you at last.'

'The pleasure is mine, Herr Euler,' said Felix, shaking his hand.

'My apologies for my outburst,' Euler continued. 'And to you, master dwarf. Your presence surprised me, that is all. Please, will you sit?'

He motioned to the fragile-looking chairs. Felix sat down with care, making sure his boots and buckles didn't scrape anything. Gotrek plopped down on another as though the exquisite thing was a tavern bench. Euler winced as it creaked in complaint, but maintained his smile.

'I must say, Herr Jaeger,' he said. 'I am surprised to see you here, and before time too. From your father's letters, I expected to be visited by solicitors or assassins, not family members.' He chuckled. 'Ah well, I suppose the old gentleman finally saw the wisdom of my offer at last.'

'Your offer?' Felix frowned. 'Your pardon, Herr Euler. What offer is this? My father said nothing of an offer.'

Herr Euler's broad brow puckered. 'Why, I offered to buy a share in Jaeger and Sons and, as he is getting on, help him with the running of the main office, as well as setting up a new office in Marienburg to facilitate his dealings with overseas merchants.'

Felix raised his eyebrows at this, then glanced over at Gotrek. If things got difficult, he was going to want his support. The Slayer was staring at the floor, paying not the least attention, his cast laying limp in his lap. Felix hoped he was paying enough attention to know when it was time to look menacing.

'My father put it slightly differently,' Felix said at last. 'He called it blackmail, rather than an offer. He said you had a letter that you meant to show the authorities in Altdorf if he failed to give you a controlling interest in Jaeger and Sons.'

There were footsteps in the hall and two men entered, one carrying a silver coffee service, and the other a tray of jam tarts. Though they were dressed in black doublets and breeches with lace at the cuffs and ribbons at the knees, Felix thought he had never seen two more unlikely footmen. They were massive men, each well over six feet tall, with bulging muscles that strained the velvet of their uniforms, hair pulled back in tarred queues, and faces that wore the scars of lifetimes of battle. The hands of the man who carried the coffee service were nearly as large as the tray he balanced it upon.

Felix looked again at Gotrek. He continued to stare at the floor, seemingly unaware as the two behemoths moved with extreme care through the room's maze of featherweight furniture and set down the refreshments on the table between Felix and Euler. Guiot the butler hovered at the door.

'It was not blackmail, Herr Jaeger,' said Euler patiently as he picked up a jam tart. 'I have no love for the dirty dealings our fathers once engaged in, and only want to make things right. What I suggested was that if your father allowed me to purchase part of Jaeger and Sons, we would, together, make amends for our mutual criminal past. But that if he refused my offer and remained in breach of imperial law, I would have no choice, as a law-abiding citizen, but to report him to the proper authorities.'

Felix pursed his lips, Euler's sanctimonious tone grating on him. It appeared his first impression of the man had been incorrect. He was a pirate after all. 'I see.'

The two giants retreated to either side of the fireplace and remained there in attendance.

'But all this is beside the point, since you are here,' said Euler, smiling. 'Have you brought the documents? Have you decided the value of the shares?'

Felix coughed, cursing his father for putting him in such a situation. He hated this sort of venal confrontation. His brother Otto would have been much better suited for the job. He would have known exactly the sort of veiled threats to use. 'Herr Euler. You misunderstand the purpose of my visit. I have not come to sell you any part of my father's company. I have come to get the letter back.'

Euler's smile disappeared as if it had never been. He shot a look at the safe on the table behind his desk, then put down his jam tart in a cold sort of way.

Felix pushed on. 'Before you say anything, I should tell you that my father has authorised me to offer you a very generous price for the letter.'

Euler barked a laugh. 'What is a one-time payment compared to the continual revenue that owning part of the company will bring me? No thank you, Herr Jaeger. There is only one way that your father may resolve this difficulty, and that is *my* way. He has seventeen days left. Until he is prepared to sell, we have nothing further to discuss. You may go.'

Felix sighed. It was at this point in the proceedings that his father undoubtedly expected him to start smashing things up until Euler gave him the letter, but he really didn't have the heart for it. The man was vile, but no more vile than his father, and Felix had never bullied anyone for anything in his life. He wasn't a robber, and that's what he felt like here. It was embarrassing. If only he had some other kind of leverage. If only he could play the same sort of trick on Euler that Euler had played on his father.

Felix paused. Well, why couldn't he? 'I am sorry to hear you say it, Herr Euler,' he said at last. 'For I was hoping that I wouldn't have to resort to blackmail of my own.'

'What nonsense is this?' asked Euler.

Felix swallowed, and plunged in. 'Well, correspondence goes both ways. My father also has a letter from your father, in which he admits engaging in the same activities as my father did, and also, that he introduced you to the business as well.'

'What activities does he mean?' cried Euler.

Felix had no idea. 'It's best not to name them aloud, don't you think?' he said. 'Even after so many years.' He smiled at Euler with what he hoped looked like malevolent guile. 'My father wishes to assure you that, if you drag him down, you will find yourself drowning in the same sewer – and you have much more life to lose than he. But, if you are prepared to give up your letter, he is prepared to give up his. We can make an exchange, and conclude the matter peacefully.'

Euler's eyes blazed. He stroked his round chin with chubby fingers. 'The cunning old goat. I believe he would be willing to die in shame and poverty just so that he could see me ruined as well.' A sudden thought seemed to come to him. He looked at his hulking serving men, then back to Felix. 'Have you this letter here?'

Felix's eyes widened. It hadn't occurred to him that Euler would resort to violence. Despite the size of his servants, he was still a respectable man on a respectable street. He wasn't going to try anything in his own home, was he?

'Er, not on me,' said Felix. 'I left it at the inn, thinking you would be reasonable and I wouldn't need it. If it must come to this, I will go and fetch it.'

Euler smiled. 'No need to trouble yourself. I will have a servant fetch it while you wait here.'

Felix shot a look at Gotrek. He still didn't appear to be paying attention. Couldn't he feel the tension thickening the air? 'It is no trouble, Herr Euler,' he said, standing. 'We will return in an hour, shall we say?'

'I'm sorry, Herr Jaeger,' said Euler, standing as well. 'I must insist that you stay.' He gave a nod to the two massive footmen and they began to cross to the door.

Felix grunted, angry now. He was about to get into a fight over something he hadn't wanted anything to do with from the beginning. Damn Euler and damn his father both. 'You will regret holding us against our will, mein herr,' he said. 'My companion is not to be trifled with lightly.'

Euler looked at Gotrek, and Felix followed his gaze. The Slayer was a sight to instil fear and respect, his massive frame and corded muscles completely eclipsing the tiny chair he sat in, and his fearsome crest and swirling tattoos exuding exotic menace. Of course, he would have been more impressive still had he not chosen that moment to open his mouth and snore like a chain rattling through a pulley.

Euler laughed. 'Terrifying.' He turned away from him, waving a hand at the footmen. 'Take them to the cellar.'

The brutes stepped forwards. Felix nudged Gotrek with his elbow. The Slayer mumbled under his breath, but didn't wake. 'You will force me to release the letter, Herr Euler,' he said, nudging Gotrek harder.

Euler snorted. 'How can you release what you no longer have?'

The footmen loomed closer.

'Now then, sir,' said the one on the left, whose right ear was missing. 'Come quietly and we won't have to break anything.'

'Gotrek!' barked Felix, and jabbed the Slayer in the shoulder with his elbow.

The Slayer woke with a start, instinctively grabbing for his axe. The sudden motion was too much for his delicate chair. It snapped in a dozen places and Gotrek thumped to the floor in a splay of spindly kindling.

'Vandalism!' shouted Euler. 'Your father will get a bill for that!'

Gotrek was up in an instant, fists balled and turning his head from side to side like a sleepy bear. 'Who pushed me off my seat?' he growled.

'They did!' said Felix, backing up and pointing at the looming footmen.

Gotrek turned towards them, glaring and blinking.

'Come along, tipsy,' said the one on the right, who had an oft-broken nose. 'Sleep it off in the nice dark cellar, eh?' He put an enormous hand on Gotrek's shoulder.

Gotrek swung his cast and re-broke the man's nose. The footman staggered back, howling and clutching his face, and fell backwards over the low table, smashing it to flinders.

'Here, now!' said One-Ear, swinging at Gotrek.

The punch snapped Gotrek's head around, but only seemed to make him mad. He growled and doubled the footman up with a fist to the guts, then shoved him back into a side table. It exploded under his weight.

'Pillagers!' cried Euler. 'Guiot! Call Uwe and the others! Call the Black Caps! Hurry!'

The Bretonnian butler bowed and turned for the door. Felix ran for him. The last thing they needed was the watch showing up. Euler leapt in his path, twisting the head of his cane and drawing forth a slim blade.

'No, Herr Jaeger,' he said, levelling the sword-cane at Felix's chest.

Felix stepped back, then cuffed an Estalian vase off a table, right at Euler's face. When he raised his sword to block it, Felix dived forwards and tackled him to the ground, pinning his sword arm with a knee and punching him in the face. The merchant bucked and twisted under him, surprisingly strong.

'Harald! Jochen!' Euler called, struggling to get his sword free.

But the two footmen were otherwise engaged. Out of the corner of his eye, Felix could see that Broken-Nose was up again, blood streaming down his face, swinging the remains of the low table at Gotrek. Beyond him, One-Ear was holding his stomach and puking all over a set of marble chessmen.

'Gotrek,' Felix shouted, elbowing Euler in the eye. 'Forget them! Get the safe! Open it!' If Euler was going to stoop to outright villainy, Felix had no more compunctions about robbing him.

Gotrek headbutted Broken-Nose on the broken nose and pushed him aside. He turned and looked at the safe as the big man slumped peacefully to the floor behind him. 'There's no cracking that,' the Slayer said, frowning. 'It's dwarf work. You'll need a key.'

Euler wrenched his sword hand free of Felix's knee, but Felix caught it again and slammed it against the ground. Euler lost his grip and the blade bounced across the carpet. As he stretched for it, Felix saw a ring of keys on the belt at his waist. He ripped them free and tossed them to Gotrek.

'Try these!'

Gotrek caught the key ring, but as he started around the desk towards the safe, there was a thunder of boots from the passage and a flood of large bodies burst into the room.

Gotrek and Felix turned towards them. There were six of them, all dressed in the same beribboned footmen's uniforms that Harald and Jochen wore, and all apparently born of the same breed as well – huge, lumbering bashers with lantern jaws and scarred scalps, all armed with clubs and cudgels. One had a hook for a hand. Guiot peered nervously into the room behind them.

'Take yer hands off the captain,' said one with a milky left eye.

That wasn't necessary, for, distracted by their entrance, Felix had let his grip slip, and Euler crashed a fist into his jaw with a hard-knuckled hand. Felix swayed back, and Euler pushed him off, shouting at his men.

'Get them! Hold them! Keep them away from the safe!'

The six footmen waded forwards, pushing the broken furniture out of the way. Gotrek reached over his shoulder for his axe.

'Not the axe,' gasped Felix from the floor. 'No murder, Gotrek, please.'

The Slayer snarled like a thwarted badger, then lowered his hand, roared a wordless challenge at the approaching men and charged, swinging his fist and his cast with equal abandon. He disappeared in a storm of flailing, velvet-clad limbs.

Felix shook his head, trying to reseat his jaw, and pulled himself to his feet. Euler beat him to it. He scooped up his sword-cane and turned on him, raising the blade. The eye Felix had elbowed was purpling rapidly.

'I believe I've changed my mind,' he said, smiling through bloody lips. 'Perhaps the watch should find you dead when they arrive. A man must defend his home, mustn't he?'

Euler lunged, extending his arm with the grace of an Estalian diestro. Felix dived aside, alarmed. For all his padding and his bland burgher's clothes the man had been well trained in the sword. Felix rolled up and ran for the door, passing the scrum in the middle of the floor. Two of the big men were down, one with an arm bent at a sickening angle, but the rest continued to rain blows upon the squat struggling figure in their midst. Guiot, the butler, stood wide-eyed in the door, then dived sensibly out of the way.

Felix barrelled down the stairs, slipping once on the well-worn treads and nearly falling head first. He heard Euler pounding down right behind him.

At the bottom, he charged across the foyer for the cupboard next to the front door. As he threw it open, Euler careened out after him, cane sword extended in a fencer's lunge.

Felix snatched up his scabbard and leapt away as Euler's blade impaled the cupboard door. He ran for the back parlour, drawing as he went. Euler lurched after him.

The room was darker than Euler's office, and filled with sturdy, more liveable furniture. The ceiling was low and ribbed with heavy, widely spaced beams. Felix cracked his head on one as he vaulted a long red brocade couch. He turned to face Euler, his rune sword held out with one hand while he rubbed vigorously at a lump like half an onion that was forming on the crown of his skull with the other. His eyes were tearing.

Euler edged around the couch, sword high, shaking his head and unbuttoning his doublet so that he had more mobility. 'Poorly played, Herr Jaeger.' Felix could barely hear him over the thuds and bangs and crashes coming from the fight upstairs. The ceiling vibrated with them. 'Had you left the letter in Altdorf I would have been checkmated – a threat I couldn't reach. Your father would never have made such a mistake.'

'You sound like you admire him,' said Felix.

'I do,' said Euler. 'He plays the game very well.' He sneered. 'But this time he has picked a very poor pawn.'

Euler lunged, extending his sword-cane with blurring swiftness. Felix blocked it, but the lighter blade came at him again instantly. He jumped back, wishing for more space to swing his bigger sword. Euler had him at a disadvantage in the low room.

Then a horrendous thump and chorus of wild shouts from above made Felix look up. Euler's blade snaked for his throat. Felix backpedalled furiously. Unfortunately there was a footstool behind him and he toppled backwards over it, slamming his breath out as his back hit the fine Estalian carpet.

Euler stepped over him, white flakes of plaster floating down around him from the ceiling. 'I will send your body back to your father,' said Euler, shouting to be heard over the rumpus coming from above, 'as a token of my admiration.'

Felix struggled to get his limbs to respond as Euler put his sword-cane to his throat. Then, suddenly, the shouts from above became screams, and there was a horrendous crashing from the stairs.

Euler and Felix looked towards the noise and saw a large square object bounce down out of the stairwell in a shower of wood, plaster and dust, and hit the entryway floor with an impact that shook the house. It was quickly followed by a rain of flying footmen, all spinning down and slapping loosely on the floor around it.

'My safe,' said Euler, blinking.

After the footmen tumbled Gotrek, landing shoulders first on a heaving velvet-clad stomach. He staggered up and shook his fist up the stairwell. 'Come down here, you cowards!' He was bleeding freely from the back of his skull.

Felix took advantage of Euler's distraction to roll out from under the point of his sword and stand.

Euler was beside himself. 'My floor!' he cried. 'My panelling! Manann's scales, the expense!' He turned on Felix, eyes blazing. 'I'll send your corpse back to your father with a bill for damages!'

He thrust at Felix with his cane-sword and Felix blocked and kicked the footstool at him.

'Gotrek!' he called. 'Here!'

The Slayer swung around and started towards him. One of the fallen men tried to rise, lifting a dagger at him. Gotrek backhanded his face with his cast and kept walking. The strike sounded like a pistol shot, and Felix thought for a moment that he had shattered the man's skull. But it was the cast that had split, a zigzag crack that ran the length of the thing. With a grunt of satisfaction Gotrek tore it off and flexed and shook out his arm.

'About time,' he growled, stepping into the back parlour and starting around the red brocade couch towards Euler. The merchant danced back, trying to keep both Felix and Gotrek in front of him. Just then, there was a rumble of boots from the spiral stair and two men ran into the room, then skidded to a stop behind the couch when they saw Gotrek.

'Sigmar's hammer, he lives!' said the one on the left, who held a blood-spattered fireplace poker.

Gotrek growled in his throat and beckoned them forwards. 'Try that again,' he rasped. 'I dare you.'

'Kill them!' screeched Euler, backing behind an elegant Tilean harpsichord.

'I'm not going near him,' said the one with the poker. 'He's mad!'

'He threw the safe at Uwe!' said the other, who was none other than One-Ear, still on his feet and now carrying a sailor's cutlass.

'Kill them or all your back pay is forfeit!' Euler shouted.

Felix stepped beside Gotrek as the two towering footmen eyed them warily.

'Can I use my axe now?' rumbled Gotrek.

'Now would be a good time, yes,' said Felix.

'Good,' said the Slayer, and drew it off his back.

One-Ear leaned towards his companion and said something out of the side of his mouth that Felix couldn't hear.

'What are you waiting for?' called Euler.

Then, before Felix could understand what they meant to do, the two giants threw aside their weapons, picked up the massive couch as if it weighed nothing, and charged Gotrek and Felix with it.

Felix stumbled back, surprised. But Gotrek roared and hacked at the brocade barrier with his axe as it raced towards them. The rune weapon bit deep, smashing through the wooden frame and the horsehair depths of the upholstery, but not deep enough.

The couch hit Felix and the Slayer amidships and drove them back towards the rear wall of the house. They tried to push back, but it was no use, the loose carpet under their boots slid across the polished floorboards and gave them no purchase. Felix's heels hit the baseboard and then, with an enormous explosion of diamond-paned glass, he and Gotrek flew backwards out of the window, trailing velvet curtains and a few red brocade couch cushions.

There was a frozen moment when Felix took in the beauty of the flying shards of glass glittering in the afternoon sun, the intricacy of the decorative brickwork on Euler's back wall, and the fluffy white clouds above it all, then the canal smacked him in the back and the water closed over his head in a freezing, silty rush.

The shock of it drove sense from his head for a moment, then he was kicking back to the surface, fighting the heavy pull of his saturated clothes. He broke the surface, gasping and kicking to stay afloat, and saw Gotrek to his left, his crest plastered down over his good eye, shaking his axe over his head.

'Craven humans!' he roared as he and Felix were drawn down the canal by the slow current. 'A couch is a coward's weapon!'

Felix looked up. From the shattered window, Euler was shouting back, his two remaining footmen at his sides, glaring murder down at them.

'This vandalism will cost you, Jaeger!' he cried. 'I will no longer settle for half of Jaeger and Sons! I will have it all!'

Gotrek returned his axe to his shoulder and struck for the side of the canal. 'Come on, manling, let's finish these furniture-throwers.'

Felix made to follow, but just then Euler and his men were joined at the window by men in the black-capped uniforms of the Marienburg city watch. Euler shouted and pointed at Felix. 'That's the man! He and the dwarf did all this!'

Felix sighed. He was almost ready to cry 'enough' and let his father take care of his own dirty business. But he *had* promised, and Euler had made him mad. The man had tried to murder him. Well, Felix wasn't going to respond in kind, but he'd find some other way to get the letter. It was a matter of pride now.

'We'll come back later,' he said. 'I need to think.'

Gotrek grunted, but then nodded. 'I could use a drink anyway.' He turned, and he and Felix swam for the far bank.

FIVE

They made their way circuitously back to the Three Bells, taking alleys and lesser bridges to avoid the watch. Felix was miserable the whole way, wet and cold in the windy Marienburg sunshine, with his drenched clothes hanging off him like they were made of lead and his boots squishing with every step. Gotrek, annoyingly, didn't seem bothered in the least.

Felix slowed as they reached the last corner before the inn, worried that there would be a company of the watch waiting for them at the door. He leaned his head out to have a look, and felt a different sort of chill as he saw that there were indeed Black Caps milling outside the door of the inn. He pulled back instinctively, but then looked again, frowning. If the watch was there for them, what were they doing carrying people out of the inn on stretchers? And why were the landlord and the serving women all talking to them at once?

'Something's happened,' he said.

Gotrek had a look too, then shrugged. 'As long as they're still serving.'

He tromped forwards single-mindedly. Felix followed more cautiously, keeping his head down, but the Black Caps didn't seem interested in him or the Slayer in the slightest. They were too busy helping sickly-looking people out onto the street and interviewing the owner of the Bells. More sick people sat on the cobbles, coughing and retching. A few were weeping. People from neighbouring businesses clustered outside their doorways, talking in hushed tones.

As they neared the inn, Felix staggered, hit by a wave of horrible odour, like rotting eggs and attar of rose mixed together. He covered his nose and mouth, and continued on. Gotrek did the same. The stench was making him dizzy.

A Black Cap held up a hand at the door. 'You don't want to go in, mein herr.' His eyes were streaming and he had a kerchief over his mouth.

'What happened?' Felix asked.

'Something in the cellar,' said the watchman. 'Came up like smoke, they say, and everybody who got a good whiff fell down like they was dead.'

'They died?' Felix was shocked.

'No, sir,' said the Black Cap. 'Only fainted like, and very sick with it.'

'But what was it?'

'That's what the captain is trying to find out.'

'Sewer gas is what it was!' said a prosperous-looking merchant who appeared to have been hurried out of the inn in the middle of dressing. 'Damned city hasn't fixed those channels in decades. Manann knows what's growing down there.'

'It were cultists!' gasped a barman, looking up with bloodshot eyes from where he sat. He had flecks of bloody foam around his mouth. Felix remembered him from earlier when he had served them in the taproom. 'Cut a hole in the cask cellar floor. I saw it. Like a green fog it was. Then it got me.'

Could it have been only sewer gas? Felix looked at Gotrek. The Slayer's expression said he didn't think so.

'When did this happen?' he asked the barman.

'Just after lunch, sir,' he said. 'Right after you left in fact. I remember, because it was when I went down to bring up a new keg after you finished the old one that I saw the smoke.'

Felix exchanged another uneasy glance with Gotrek. He was willing to bet that their room had been broken into, and he wanted to see if there were any clues as to who had done it, but he didn't want to poison himself to do it.

'How long before we can go in?' asked Felix.

The Black Cap shrugged. 'Not until the captain blows the all-clear.'

It was an uneasy wait, with Felix watching the ends of the street constantly for Euler's Black Caps, and Gotrek grumbling about being thirsty, but fortunately, Felix wasn't the only one who wanted to go back in and get his things, and finally the captain gave in to the besieging guests who clamoured around him in various states of undress and distress, and said that they could all enter to retrieve their belongings, but that the inn would be closed immediately afterwards until it could be searched more thoroughly. The innkeeper looked sullen about this, but everyone else cheered and rushed in.

Gotrek and Felix followed the flow up to the second floor. The interior of the inn still smelled horrible, and the stink was worse in the confines of the narrow upper halls. Felix covered his mouth with his handkerchief, but he still felt the corridor swim around him, and had to brace himself against the wall for balance as they went along. They slowed and drew their weapons as they approached their room. Then Felix stopped altogether. The door was ajar. Had the Black Caps forced it? He certainly hadn't left it that way.

They crept to it and listened. Felix looked to Gotrek. He shook his head. The lack of noise did nothing to allay Felix's fears. It might only mean that their enemies were lying in wait. Gotrek raised his axe, then nodded.

As one, they jumped forwards and kicked the door in. It banged open and Gotrek leapt in, slashing left and right. He struck nothing. The tiny room was empty but for the expected furnishings, a bed along each wall, a wash stand and a clothes trunk. The beds had been smashed, the wash stand overturned, and the trunk had been opened and their few belongings strewn about.

Felix followed after Gotrek and closed the door behind them. Things would be awkward should the landlord come by and see the damage. He looked around. The window that was the room's only source of light was open and there were fresh splinters on the sill, as if someone had gone in or out that way. It would have had to have been a very small and agile someone, for the window was tiny, and high up on the wall. A child might have done it – or a slim woman.

He pushed that thought away and searched through his few clothes. Everything had been ripped and cut, and he feared that his armour was stolen, but then he found it thrown in a corner, still whole, but reeking like everything else from the poisonous stink. Perhaps the vandals had been unable to tear it. The Slayer's bedroll had been hacked up too, but he had no clothes to ruin. He owned no other possessions that he didn't carry on his person at all times.

'Darts, nets, poison gas,' said Gotrek. 'Only cowards use such things.'

Felix looked at him. 'You think it was the same ones who attacked us in Altdorf?'

Gotrek nodded. 'And whoever they are, they want us alive.'

Once again the image of Lady Hermione and Mistress Wither looking down at him while he was bound and helpless came unbidden to his mind, and he shivered convulsively.

On their way out, Felix paid the landlord double what they owed him for the room. It was his father's money, and the least he could do for the trouble they had brought upon his establishment.

As they started down the street, Felix wondered if they might not need to sleep in the open, just so they wouldn't bring a similar fate to another hostelry. He was beginning to feel like he was the carrier of some deadly plague, and that he should keep away from human society until it had run its course. They needed to face these foes and finish them, but they didn't even know who they were.

A block away from the inn, someone called their names.

'Felix! Gotrek!'

Felix and Gotrek turned, their hands drifting towards their weapons. A coach was heading towards them and Max was leaning out the window.

'I was just coming to find you,' he said, then noticed that Felix was carrying his armour. 'Have you left your inn?'

'Uh...' Felix paused, uncertain how much to tell him. 'Our room was burgled,' he said at last. 'We decided to look for other lodgings.'

Max shook his head, bemused. 'Trouble follows you two like a stray dog.'

'More like a bat,' said Felix under his breath, then spoke up. 'What did you want to see us about?'

'I have an urgent matter to discuss with you,' said Max, opening the door to his coach. 'Will you join me?'

Max said not a word about the urgent matter in the coach as they crossed the many bridges and islands of the city to the Suiddock wharfs.

'Are we going back to the *Jilfte Bateau*?' asked Felix as the coach's wheels boomed on the wooden planks of the docks.

'No,' said Max. 'Our new companion waits for us at the Pike and Pike.'

'New companion?'

But Max would say no more.

The coach came to a stop on a busy commercial wharf, with stevedores unloading goods from merchant ships flying the colours of Bretonnia, Estalia and Tilea, as well as dozens of Imperial and Marienburg vessels. They stepped down from the coach and Max led the way to a small tavern with a river pike impaled on a spear over the door. The place smelled, unsurprisingly, of fish, but the odour lessened as they made their way through the noisy taproom to a stair that led up to a small, but neatly furnished private dining room on the first floor.

Felix nodded politely to Claudia, who sat sideways on a cushioned bench by the fire on the left wall, her feet curled underneath her, then stopped dead as he saw the other occupant of the room, sitting ram-rod straight at the head of the table that filled the centre of the room. Gotrek grunted like he'd smelled something foul. It was an elf. Felix understood suddenly why Max hadn't mentioned this earlier. He wouldn't have got Gotrek in the coach.

'Felix Jaeger,' said Max, 'Gotrek Gurnisson, may I present Aethenir Whiteleaf, student of the White Tower of Hoeth and son of the fair land of Eataine.'

The elf rose, inclining his head respectfully. He was tall, and as slender as a willow branch in his flowing white robes, but there was an air of youth and nervousness about him that made him look more awkward than graceful. He had the long, haughty features of his kind, but the nervousness showed also in his cobalt-blue eyes, which flicked about the room as he spoke. 'I am honoured, friends. Your acquaintance enriches me.'

'An elf,' Gotrek spat. He turned back to the door. 'Come on, manling.'

'Wait, Slayer,' said Max. 'If you still seek your doom, hear him out.'

'We go into the gravest danger, with you or without you,' added Claudia.

Gotrek paused at the door, his fists clenching. Felix looked from him to Max to the elf to the seeress, all waiting for the Slayer's decision.

At last the Slayer turned back around. 'Speak your piece, beard-cutter.'

'That is a myth,' snapped the elf. 'It never happened. You–'

Max held up a hand. 'Friends, please. This is perhaps not the time to bring up old arguments. We have little time.'

'You are right, magister,' said Aethenir. 'Forgive me.'

Gotrek just grunted.

Max offered Gotrek and Felix seats at the table and took one himself. Felix sat, but Gotrek remained standing, arms crossed, glaring at the elf.

'We met Scholar Aethenir last night,' said Max, 'when he came to a gathering of Marienburg magisters seeking their knowledge of the region of the Wasteland to the north and west of here.'

'The same region that my visions are leading me to,' said Claudia, leaning forwards meaningfully.

'A book was stolen from the library of the Tower of Hoeth,' said Aethenir. 'A book containing maps and descriptions of the area you call the Wasteland, and the elven cities that once graced it, as it was before the Sundering ravaged both land and sea and changed the coastline forever. I must recover this book.'

'And…?' said Gotrek when the elf didn't continue.

'And?' asked Aethenir.

'Where is my doom in this?'

'Don't you see, Slayer?' said Claudia, speaking up. 'The book details exactly the same area that my visions have told me will be the birth of the destruction of Marienburg and Altdorf. This is not coincidence. Some great evil is brewing there. We must go and prevent it.'

'It is my belief,' said Aethenir, 'that those who stole the book are agents of the Dark Powers, and seek some ancient elven artefact in one of the ruined cities. I know not what it might be, but an item of great power in the hands of the pawns of Chaos can only spell ruin and despair for the peoples of Ulthuan and the Old World.'

'I don't understand,' said Felix. 'If this is such a grave threat, why are the elves not going in force? No disrespect to you, high one, or to Herr Schreiber and Fraulein Pallenberger, but why have you come to us? Why haven't you brought the navy of Ulthuan with you?'

Aethenir hesitated, looking down at the table, then spoke. 'As I explained to the magisters last night, the Tower of Hoeth is the centre of magical learning in Ulthuan. There, the greatest mages of the world are taught the one true art. The tomes and scrolls housed within its white walls make up the most complete, and most dangerous, library that exists in the world. The tower itself is reputed to be unreachable and unbreachable. Never has anything been stolen from it before.' Colour came into the high elf's cheeks. 'The loremasters of the tower are proud of this reputation, and do not wish it to be known that this shame has befallen them, so they have dispatched me, a mere humble initiate, to retrieve the book in secret before any know that it is missing. I have come with no escort except a few of my father's household guard, all sworn to secrecy, on the pretext of examining some pre-Sundering ruins in the pursuit of my field of study. It was felt that any larger force would call attention to the theft.'

Gotrek snorted. 'Typical elven shiftiness.'

Felix frowned. 'How soon would you be leaving on this journey?' he asked.

'Immediately,' said Max. 'Scholar Aethenir has hired a ship, and its captain is prepared to sail on the evening tide.'

Felix turned to Gotrek. 'Slayer, I still must retrieve Euler's letter.'

Gotrek nodded. 'Aye. And I've no time for elf snotling chases. I'll pass.'

He turned to the door. Felix rose to follow him, bowing to Max, Aethenir and Claudia. 'I'm sorry, but…'

'I dreamed of you, Slayer,' called Claudia, as Gotrek pushed open the door. 'I saw you in the bowels of a black mountain, fighting foes without number. I saw blood rise like a tide to drown you. I saw a towering abomination crushing you in its claws.'

Gotrek paused in the doorway. Felix stopped behind him, shooting a dirty look back at Claudia. Had she really seen these things, or was she just wooing the Slayer with the only lure that could sway him?

Gotrek looked to Max. 'Do you vouch for this girl's seeing, wizard?'

Max nodded gravely. 'Yes, Gotrek. She has been judged to have true powers of divination by the Lord Magisters of her order.'

'Gotrek,' Felix said. 'I cannot go.'

Gotrek nodded, but a light had kindled in his single eye that Felix hadn't seen since he had fought Magus Lichtmann and his cannon daemon. 'Do what you have to, manling,' Gotrek said. 'I won't stop you. But I must fulfil my doom.' He turned to face Claudia, Max and Aethenir. 'Right,' he said. 'I'll come. But keep the elf away from me.'

Felix fought with his conscience as he walked with Gotrek, Max and the others to the wharf where their hired ship was docked. What should he do? Did he wish them a good voyage and have another go at Hans Euler tomorrow, or did he go with them and forget retrieving the incriminating letter? To whom was he more beholden, Gotrek or his father? Which vow came first? He had followed Gotrek for twenty years, and had never taken another vow that contradicted the one he had made to the Slayer. But Gotrek wasn't family. He wasn't on his death bed. On the other hand, what if the Slayer met his doom at last and he wasn't there to witness it? That would invalidate their whole reason for travelling together. It would be a terribly anti-climactic ending to such a grand adventure.

At last he sighed and dropped back to Gotrek, who had fallen a little behind.

'Slayer,' he said. 'I can't make the decision to stay or go.'

Gotrek shrugged. 'A dwarf's first loyalty is to family. I will not begrudge you this.'

Felix nodded, but continued pondering. Gotrek's permission to leave didn't actually make his decision any easier. Mad as it sounded, he would still rather go with Gotrek towards his doom. He didn't really care what happened to Euler. It was his father who had forced him into conflict with him. It would serve the old buzzard right if Felix just sat on his hands for the next seventeen days and let Euler send his letter to the authorities. And yet, he had promised. Hadn't he just told Claudia that a vow was a vow, no matter–

Seventeen days! Felix's heart lurched. That was it! That was the solution.

He turned to Gotrek. 'I've made up my mind,' he said. 'I have seventeen days to recover the letter, so I will go with you. It can't be more than a week up the coast and a week back. So we will have a day or two once we return, to take the letter back from Euler.'

'We may not return, manling,' said Gotrek.

'Then it will be fate that kept me from fulfilling my promise,' said Felix, insistent. 'Not lack of will.'

Gotrek raised an eyebrow at this but said nothing as Felix went to tell Max of his decision.

The hospitality of Clan Skryre Warleader Riskin Tatter-Ear, commander of the skaven burrows under the fish-stinking man-warren the humans called Marienburg, amounted to a single damp room at the far end of an unused tunnel, barely large enough to house Thanquol, let alone all his retinue and Boneripper, and for which the impertinent young pup expected to be paid a fortune in warp tokens! The gross disrespect of it astounded Thanquol. Did he not know who he was? In the old days a mere warleader would have bowed and licked his hind paws in his eagerness to serve a grey seer of his renown.

The cold welcome had done nothing to improve Thanquol's mood, already befouled by the slow, miserable journey that had brought him here. In his day the palanquin-bearers had been speedy and subservient. They had known their place and how to get one to one's destination without colliding with every skaven coming the other way. Now it seemed more than they could do to all move in the same direction at once. It was therefore with little patience that he listened to his overpaid, under-successful assassin make yet more excuses.

'My abject apologies, oh most forgiving of skaven,' said Shadowfang from the floor where he knelt before him. 'But though our sleep-smoke missed them at the drinking place, all is not lost.'

'No?' said Thanquol. 'Have you managed to poison yourself in the process, then?'

Issfet tittered fawningly at that, and Thanquol nodded approvingly. He liked his servants servile and obsequious.

'No, grey seer,' said Shadowfang. 'But we have sneak-followed the pair to a ship, and have tortured one of the sailors to reveal its destination.'

'And…?'

The assassin squirmed uncomfortably. 'They have no destination, sagacious one. They hunt-seek something in the stink-swamp, but know not where it is.'

Thanquol turned this information over in his head. It was unfortunate that Shadowfang had once again been unable to capture his two nemeses, but it would not be the most terrible of plans to follow them into the Wasteland where there would be no one to interfere or come to their rescue. Yes, perhaps it was for the best. Now he only needed some way of following them there.

He turned to Issfet. 'What manners of conveyance does this fool Riskin have at his disposal?' he asked. 'Quick-quick.'

The tailless skaven bowed and once again nearly lost his balance. 'I shall enquire, oh most effluent of masters.'

SIX

The Pride of SKINTSTAAD was a two-masted trading ship out of Marienburg that Aethenir had hired with elven gold. She was a pot-bellied little barque, slow but sea-worthy, with a grizzled, vulture-beaked captain by the name of Ulberd Breda, and a crew from every corner of the Old World.

Though happy to take Aethenir's money, Captain Breda seemed a bit uneasy about their voyage, and Felix didn't blame him. Max's instructions had been to sail north and west through the Manaspoort Sea and on into the Sea of Chaos until Fraulein Pallenberger called a halt. They might sail all the way to the Sea of Ice if she failed to receive any vision, and a journey into those barbarous climes was not to be made lightly by a little ship with winter coming on. Storms, Norse raiders and icebergs were the least they could expect if they went that far.

Felix shivered at the idea of all those days at sea, and not because of the cold or the danger. Being cooped up on the tiny ship with such a volatile mix of personalities for any length of time was sure to be a miserable experience. In fact, even before they had left the dock there had been conflict. Aethenir had come on board with seven elf warriors, taken one look at his cabin and come back out again, saying he refused to stay there until it had been thoroughly cleaned.

'It's filthy,' he said with a shudder. 'It stinks of urine and vermin. There was a rat on my bed.'

The crew snorted at that.

'Ain't a ship that sails that doesn't have rats, yer worship,' said Captain Breda.

'You've never sailed on a ship of Ulthuan, then,' said Aethenir, sniffing.

'No, yer worship, I never has. But if we was to try to chase off all the rats on *this* ship we'd never leave the dock.' He turned to one of his crewmen, an Estalian by his look. 'Doso, go and clean his worship's cabin.'

'But I swabbed it this morning,' complained Doso.

'Then swab it again,' growled the captain. 'And use clean water this time.'

Doso grumbled, but did as he was told.

It was clear that, even after this extra cleaning, Aethenir was less than satisfied, but Max whispered a few words in the high elf's ear and he dropped the matter. Unfortunately, the damage was done. The high elf had earned the ill will of the crew – men that might have treated him with the awe and respect that humans generally reserved for the elder races were, in one stroke, sneering at him behind his back and spitting on his shadow.

His warriors fared better, for unlike their master, they seemed hardened veterans – cold, silent elves who wore scarred scale mail under the green and white surcoats of Aethenir's livery, and asked for no special favours. They found a place near the aft rail and talked quietly amongst themselves, and that was that.

Gotrek did what he always did on any voyage over water. He went directly to his cabin and stayed there. Felix hoped he continued this way, for that would lessen the probability that he and Aethenir would meet during the voyage, a situation to be avoided at all costs if blood was not to be spilled and the War of the Beard not to be rekindled.

Max and Claudia spoke briefly with the captain and also retired to their cabins, but Felix feared that there would be trouble from that quarter ere long, for as she started down the stairs to her quarters, the seeress cast a look back at him from under her golden fall of hair that made the hair stand up on the back of his neck.

Max's Reiksguard escort found a place for themselves along the port rail and lounged there, chatting and smoking pipes and spitting over the side, as the crew made ready to make way.

At last, with a heavy mist freshening into a light rain, they cast off the lines and were towed out of the Brynwater into the centre of the Rijksweg by boats of the Marienburg port authority. Then the sails were unfurled, and they were away, sailing past the grim fortifications of Rijker's Isle and out into the Manaanspoort Sea.

And a less breathtaking beginning to a voyage Felix could not have imagined. The sky was a dull, uninterrupted grey. The air was wet and chilly, the rain not even strong enough to be called a drizzle, and the scenery left much to be desired. The east coast of the sea, which ran almost due north towards the Sea of Chaos, was known as the Cursed Marshes, but Felix, after the fifth hour of watching them slide slowly by, was ready to rename them the Dull Marshes, because he had never seen a more uninteresting landscape in all his life – nothing but saw grass and cat-tails and stunted trees for as far as the eye could see, mile after mile after mile. Occasionally a stork would fly past, or a chevron of geese, gabbling like noisy children, or there would come the rustle and plop of some hidden swamp-dweller sliding into the still water, but that was all. It was little wonder, thought Felix, that the Empire had let Marienburg claim the marshes and the wastelands for their own. Who would want them?

There was more trouble with Aethenir at lunch – trouble with far-reaching repercussions for Felix's peace of mind – though at its beginning, it had only been an argument about food.

Before he had even tasted the bowl of stew that one of his warriors had brought him, Aethenir had thrown it overboard. He had come up from his cabin already agitated – presumably from the lack of cleanliness – and the smell of the food appeared to be the last straw.

'This is unacceptable!' he said in a high, clear voice. 'I may be forced to sleep in filth, but I refuse to eat it.'

Felix took another sniff of his stew. It smelled fine to him, if a little strong on the garlic.

Captain Breda glared at the high elf over the lip of his bowl, his mouth full. 'You got what we all got,' he said.

'And I wonder you don't die from it!' cried Aethenir. He turned to Max. 'Is it too much to ask for fresh vegetables and fresh meat, cleanly prepared?'

Max glanced around uneasily, but before he could speak, the cook, a peg-legged Tilean with a pot belly and a black beard that would have done a dwarf proud, popped out of the galley, glaring around. 'Who say my meat is bad? I kill that pig myself, last week!'

'Last week?' Aethenir blanched. He put a hand to his forehead. 'How is it possible that humanity has risen to such heights while the noble asur have fallen? How have they even survived? Their ships are slow, their knowledge of the world contemptible, their hygiene appalling, their food poisonous...'

Max stood, trying to stem the tide. 'High one, please, calm yourself. Conditions could be better, I admit, but...'

The cook turned on Aethenir, shaking his spit-fork angrily. 'I know not what this hygiene is, but...'

'By the Everqueen, *that's* obvious,' said Aethenir as his warriors went on guard behind him. 'Look at yourself. When was the last time you washed your hands? Why did learned Teclis ever decide to grant such shaven apes the blessing of–'

'Lord Aethenir!' Max yelped, stepping between him and the begrimed cook. 'I think perhaps you would find it more congenial to dine in your cabin.' He took the elf gently by the elbow and steered him towards the door to the underdecks. 'I will have new food made for you, and I will oversee its preparation myself. It is part of the learning of my College to cleanse and purify. You need have no fears for your health.'

The high elf allowed himself to be led below with further placating murmurings. Everyone let out a held breath and returned to their meal, though there was much muttering from the crew and from Max's Reiksguard swords.

'Called our boat slow,' said a sailor.

'He throw my food off the ship,' said the cook.

'And one of my bowls,' said Captain Breda. 'That'll go on the bill.'

'Shaved apes, did he call us?' asked the captain of the Reiksguard, a knight by the name of Rudeger Oberhoff. 'Hope he doesn't think we'll be watching his back for him after that.'

His men laughed at that, but Felix didn't see anything particularly funny about the situation. If the elf got the crew too worked up, there might be mutiny or violence, and Aethenir's warriors looked like capable fellows. He was just glad that Gotrek had elected to stay below and drink instead of joining the others for lunch. Things could have gone much worse if he'd been there.

When Max returned to the main deck to oversee the preparation of Aethenir's meal, Captain Breda pulled him aside and had a few words in his ear. Felix happened to be nearby, and overheard, little knowing then how those words would affect him later.

'Magister, sir,' said the captain. 'Er, it might be best, milord, if yon high one was to stay off the deck as much as possible for the remainder. Out of sight, out of mind, if you get my meaning, sir.'

'Perfectly, captain,' said Max. 'And I apologise for Scholar Aethenir's behaviour. He is young, for an elf, and has never left Ulthuan before. I'm afraid it's been a bit of a shock.'

'That's as may be,' said Captain Breda. 'But he's in for a ruder shock if he spouts off like that again, elder race or no. The men won't stand for it.'

'I understand completely, captain,' said Max. 'I will see to it personally that he stays below as much as can possibly be managed.'

'Thank you, magister,' said the captain, bowing. 'You ease my mind.'

Not exactly the most doom-laden exchange of words, but that is exactly what they were for Felix, because what keeping Aethenir below decks entailed was keeping him company. For the rest of the journey, Max spent night and day in Aethenir's cabin, discussing magic, philosophy and the nature of the world, as well as playing endless games of chess. And it was in this caretaking that the far-reaching repercussions of the 'stew incident' made themselves apparent, for with Max made nursemaid to Aethenir he was no longer able to keep an eye on Fraulein Pallenberger, and finding herself unchaperoned, she made a beeline for the target she had had her eye on since boarding the *Jilfte Bateau* – Felix.

* * *

The battle recommenced on the morning of their second day out of Marienburg. At first it seemed that it would be nothing more than a skirmish, but soon it escalated into a full-on assault, with Felix fighting a desperate rearguard action in order to get away unscathed.

The morning had begun peacefully enough, settling into what was to be the daily routine of the voyage – wake, dress, have a breakfast of oat mash, grilled flounder or pike and Tilean coffee, then watch the Wasteland go by until lunch, and then more of the same until sunset. Felix would have welcomed almost any interruption of the monotony, but not this one.

'You look sad, Herr Jaeger,' said Claudia, appearing at his side.

Felix jumped, startled. 'Sad?' he said. 'Not at all.' He had actually been in the middle of a reverie about what he might do with his father's inheritance if he did manage to get Euler's letter for him. Not that he wanted the money, of course. But if he did inherit some, what would he do with it? Visions of exquisite leather-bound volumes of his poetry dissipated into smoke as he turned to the seeress. 'Just musing.'

'Musing,' she asked, sliding closer to him along the rail. 'About what?'

'Oh, ah, nothing really. Just, well, just musing.' He looked around him for an excuse to escape, but could see none.

She touched his arm and looked at him with her deep blue eyes. 'You hide a secret grief, don't you, Herr Jaeger.'

'Eh? Oh no, not really. No more than anybody else, I should think.'

'I don't believe it,' she said.

Felix didn't have any response to that except for a keen desire to push her over the side, so he said nothing, just watched the reeds go by and hoped she would go away. Unfortunately, she did not.

'Have you ever loved, Herr Jaeger?'

Felix choked, and had to cover his mouth as he was wracked with sudden coughs. 'Once or twice, I suppose,' he said, when he had recovered.

She turned and faced him, leaning her shapely hip against the rail. 'Tell me about them.'

'You don't want to hear about that,' he said.

'Oh, but I do,' the seeress said, her eyes never leaving his. 'You fascinate me, Herr Jaeger.'

'Ah,' said Felix. And in spite of his best efforts, he found himself thinking back to the women he had shared a bed with throughout his wanderings. There had been a fair number over the years, mostly half-remembered tavern girls and harlots in lonely ports scattered from the Old World to Ind, and a few who stood out above the rest; Elissa, the barmaid at the Blind Pig, who had stolen his money, and for a time his heart, Siobhain of Albion, who had travelled with him and Gotrek in the dark lands of the east, and the Veiled One, spy and assassin for the Old Man of the Mountain, whose true name he had never learned. But there were only two he had ever truly loved: Kirsten, with whom he had thought to settle down and raise a family, murdered by the mad playwright Manfred von Diehl in a little outpost in the Border Princes, and Ulrika, with whom he had thought to travel the world, worse-than-murdered by the vampire Adolphus Krieger. The memories, one long buried and one still as raw as an open wound, brought a lump to his throat. Damn the woman. Why had she asked such a vile question? He turned away from her so she wouldn't see the pain in his eyes.

'I have only ever loved two women,' he said at last. 'And they are both dead. Is that fascinating enough?'

Perhaps he hadn't done a very good job masking his pain after all, for when he turned to look at her, she stepped back, eyes wide and face pale, and put a hand to her heart.

'I... I'm sorry, Herr Jaeger,' she said. 'I did not think... That is, I did not mean...' Her face went suddenly from white to pink, and she turned and hurried away, almost running for the door to the underdecks in her haste.

Felix turned back to the rail, cursing her for digging so thoughtlessly into his heart, but then a cheerier thought came into his mind. Perhaps this meant that she would leave him alone from now on.

Suddenly the day looked a little brighter.

Alas, it was not to be. She said nothing to him at lunch, only spooned dully at her stew and glanced at him guiltily when she thought he wasn't looking, but later in the afternoon, just when he was getting another few hours of marsh-watching in, she reappeared at his side, eyes downcast and lip out-thrust.

'I want to apologise to you, Herr Jaeger,' she said. 'I was awful to you earlier today and I feel terrible about it.'

'Forget it,' said Felix, wishing she really would. Unfortunately she persisted.

She took another step closer to him. 'Sometimes I forget that men are not books, to be opened and read like... er, books. I should not have pried and I am truly sorry for it.'

'Never mind,' said Felix, throwing a splinter from the rail into the water. 'No harm done.'

He felt a soft pressure on his arm and turned to see that she was leaning against him. The swell of her breast under her dark blue robe pressed against his elbow. 'If there is any way...' she said, looking up at him from under her long lashes, 'any way that I could make it up to you, I would be grateful for the opportunity.'

Felix stood, rolling his eyes, then turned to face her. 'I am beginning to wonder, fraulein, if you didn't use your visions to convince the Slayer to come on this journey just so that you would be able to get me alone on a ship.'

The seeress blinked at that, then drew herself up haughtily as the full meaning of what he had said sank in. 'The oath of the Celestial Order is very clear, Herr Jaeger,' she said. 'We will not use our powers for personal gain, nor will we announce false visions or predictions for any reason whatsoever!'

'Well, I won't tell if you won't,' said Felix, a little meaner than he had intended.

'Oh!' she said. Then 'Oh!' again. Then she turned and stomped away just as quickly as she had before, but with much more noise. Felix hoped this time it would stick, but he very much doubted it.

On the afternoon of the third day, he sat down on the aft deck with his journal to fill in the so far thrilling events of their journey up the Sea of Manann. Apparently, his last insult had done the trick, for he was able to get in nearly a full hour of scribbling without any interruptions from Fraulein Pallenberger. It was very refreshing.

When he was finished he closed the journal, sighed contentedly and sat back, thinking that a little dinner would be in order shortly. But then the feeling that he was being watched crept over him and he turned, expecting to find Claudia peeking out from behind a mast. Instead, it was Max, leaning against the opposite rail and observing him with furrowed intensity as he puffed on his pipe.

Felix raised an eyebrow. What had he done this time? Hadn't he given Claudia the cold shoulder? Surely Max couldn't be unhappy about that.

He nodded politely and began to cap his ink and put away his pen. Before he finished, Max had tapped his pipe out on the rail and crossed to him, sitting down next to him on an overturned bucket. Felix hid a sigh. Was he going to get another lecture?

'Good afternoon, Max,' he said, as pleasantly as he could.

Max continued to look at him, saying nothing for long enough that Felix began to feel uncomfortable.

At last, just as Felix was about to ask what the matter was, he spoke. 'You really haven't aged a day, Felix.'

Felix sighed. 'Everyone says that. I'm getting a little tired of–'

'I do not mean it as a compliment,' said Max. 'I mean it as a fact. It is impossible that you should look this young and vigorous.' He frowned and pointed at Felix's cheek. 'You used to have a scar, just there. Do you remember?'

Felix reached up and touched his cheek – the duelling scar, taken when he had fought his schoolmate Krassner at university, and killed him.

'It's gone now,' said Max.

'Scars fade,' said Felix.

'Not a scar like that. Not completely. And yet it has.'

Felix frowned. He didn't like this scrutiny. 'But isn't that good?'

'Good?' Max shrugged. 'Yes, I suppose. But mysterious as well. Something unnatural is affecting your body – keeping it young, keeping it free from disease, allowing you to recover from wounds faster and more completely than you should. I know other hardy warriors of your age, Felix. They are strong and fit, but their knees still creak and their hands are scarred. Their faces are lined and creased. Yours is not. You no longer look a youth of twenty, it's true, but you look ten years younger than your true age and well cared for besides.'

'I think you're exaggerating, Max. But if what you say is true, what…' Felix swallowed, uncertain he wanted to know the answer. 'What do you think has caused it?'

Max leaned back, stroking his neat beard and considering. 'I don't know, but I can think of several possibilities. You will note,' he said, adopting a professorial tone, 'that Gotrek is affected in the same way. More so, in fact. There is no dwarf stronger or more massive than he. I'll wager he has the strength of ten of his kind. And he too is virtually unscarred, but for his missing eye. Perhaps something the two of you encountered during your journey to the Chaos Wastes has caused this effect. Or it might be some consequence of entering that portal through which you disappeared when I saw you last. Perhaps it is some property of Gotrek's axe. It is a weapon of great power. Perhaps it is keeping him, and you, fit for some important purpose, though what that might be, I couldn't say. Whatever it is, it is possible it could keep you alive indefinitely.'

'Indefinitely? You mean I might be…' He laughed at the ridiculousness of it. 'Immortal?'

'Or as near as makes no difference,' said Max, nodding. 'But be aware that it is not an unmixed blessing. We of the Empire are not tolerant of the unusual or the unnatural, Felix. If you continue to look as you do for another ten or twenty years, people will talk. You might be accused of being some sort of mutant, or a master of the dark arts, or even one of the undead.'

Felix blanched. He had never considered that his good health might be seen as the taint of Chaos. What was he supposed to do, get sick?

Max sighed and stood. 'I must go hold Scholar Aethenir's hand again, but think on what I have said, Felix. I believe it would be wise to face your true nature, instead of pretending you have not changed.'

'Thank you, Max,' said Felix, softly. 'I will.'

He barely noticed Max as he turned and left, so confounded was he by what the wizard had said. He didn't want to believe it. How could it be true? If something had happened to him, wouldn't he have noticed? He felt no different than he ever had. But perhaps that is what Max had meant. He should have felt different – achy, more run down, older.

What if he *was* immortal? Should he be happy about it? It was every man's dream to live forever, wasn't it? But to be made immortal without his consent by some force he didn't understand – that was more unnerving than thrilling. And did he really want to be following the Slayer into danger for ever and ever without end? Even the wildest journey must come to an end sometime, mustn't it?

A sudden thought came to him and made his heart lurch. Could he be some sort of vampire, as Max suggested? That would mean that he and Ulrika could be together after all! But no, he decided with a sigh, he doubted very much he was a vampire. He was sitting in the sun, wasn't he? And he had not, as far as he could remember, ever drunk anyone's blood. And besides, if he were a vampire, he would never have the chance to be with Ulrika, because Gotrek would kill him first.

'Sail ho!' called a voice from above. 'To the stern on our heading.'

Felix looked up. This sort of cry had been frequent on the first two days of their journey, when the *Pride of Skintstaad* had been at the narrow end of the Manannspoort Sea and in the major shipping lane, but as they had continued to hug the east coast while most of the traders hugged the west, heading for Bretonnia, Estalia and Tilea, other ships had become fewer and fewer.

He rose and joined Captain Breda at the aft rail. Far in the distance, between the iron sea and the pewter sky, was a sharp fleck of white, like a tooth sticking up over the horizon.

'What sort of ship is it?' asked Felix.

The captain shrugged. 'Hard to tell, this far out,' he said. 'Three masts. Square rigged. Marienburg, most likely, possibly Imperial. Don't know what she's doing going north. Not much trade with the Norse this late in the year. Wouldn't be doing it myself, if it weren't for the high one's gold.'

The ship remained on the horizon for the rest of the day, not gaining and not falling back. Captain Breda left instructions for the night watch to keep an eye on its lights and wake him if it got closer, but it never did.

The fourth day dawned grey and misty, with gusts of intermittent rain, and it was impossible to tell if the ship with the white sail was still behind them or not.

Just before noon, the *Pride of Skintstaad* sailed past the last headland of the Manaanspoort Sea and out into the great black expanse of the Sea of Chaos. The north wind, which had been softened somewhat by its passage over the Wasteland, was here a cold wet slap in the face. All the sailors donned oiled leather jerkins and shivered at their stations. Felix pulled his red cloak closer around him and looked in all directions. For all his travels, he had never sailed these waters before. Directly north was Norsca, land of longships, snow-topped mountains and furclad reavers. East was Erengrad and Kislev and the Sea of Claws. West was fabled Albion, the mist-shrouded isle that he and Gotrek had once visited, but never travelled to. Adventure awaited in every direction, but on the whole, it all seemed a bit chilly and unappealing.

It was a few hours later that the inevitable finally happened, and Gotrek and Aethenir crossed paths. Such a confrontation had so far been avoided because both the elf and the dwarf had spent most of their time in their cabins, and generally came up only to use the privy. Thus, it was at the privy that the meeting occurred.

The privy of the *Pride of Skintstaad* was nothing more than a round hole in a bench that hung out over the prow of the ship, directly under the bowsprit and screened off from the rest of the ship by a leather curtain. The path to it was very narrow, a little wedge of space between the looming bowsprit and the starboard rail, which had spare sails and spars and other nautical debris lashed to it.

Though Felix was not there for the beginning of the argument, it started, apparently, when Aethenir stepped out of the privy and found Gotrek waiting impatiently to go in.

The first Felix and the rest of the crew heard of it was Gotrek's rasp rising above the sounds of wind and wave.

'I'll not step aside for any honourless, tree-worshipping elf! You step aside!'

'Do you dare make demands of me, dwarf? I have paid for this ship, and you are upon it at my pleasure. Now step aside, I say.'

Felix sprang up from where he had been reading more of his travels with Gotrek, and ran for the prow. This was just what was needed. Max too was hurrying to the scene. Aethenir's household guard was not far behind. When they all reached the tiny space, they found the elf and the dwarf face to face – or face to chest, to be more accurate – and barking at each other like dogs.

'I go where I please, when I please, and no pompous, prick-eared pantywaist is going to bar my way. Now step aside before I throw you overboard!'

'Stubborn son of earth. I do not bar your way. You bar mine!'

'Gotrek,' called Felix. 'Leave off. What is the point of this?'

'Yes, Slayer,' said Max. 'Give way and have done.'

'Give way to an elf?' said Gotrek, with a dangerous edge to his voice. 'I would die first.'

'By Asuryan,' said Aethenir. 'There would be no need for this argument were you to shave that monstrous filthy beard. There would be room enough for both of us then.'

Gotrek froze, his one eye blazing. His hand slowly reached up and caught the haft of his axe. 'What did you say?'

Felix heard the scrape of steel as the high elf's warriors all drew their swords at once.

Aethenir looked up to them. 'Captain Rion! Brothers! Defend me! Save me from this mad rock hewer!'

The elves pushed forwards through the other onlookers.

'Coward,' snarled Gotrek, bringing his axe before him and ignoring the elves at his rear. 'Would you have others fight your battles for you? Draw your sword!'

'I carry no sword,' said Aethenir, backing against the privy curtain. 'I am a scholar.'

'Ha!' barked Gotrek. 'A scholar should be wise enough not to start with his mouth what he can't finish with his hands.' He took another step towards the elf.

'Turn, dwarf,' said Captain Rion, a weathered-looking elf with cold grey eyes. 'I would not slay even a tunnel-digger from behind.'

Gotrek turned and grinned at the thicket of sharp steel that faced him. 'All right,' he said. 'You first, then the "scholar".'

Felix squeezed in beside him. 'Gotrek, listen to me. You can't do this.'

'Step back, manling,' growled Gotrek. 'You're crowding my arm.'

Felix stayed where he was. 'Gotrek, please. He might deserve it, but he paid for the ship. This voyage ends if you kill him or his friends. Remember the seeress's vision? The black mountain? The tide of blood? The towering abomination? If this argument ends in slaughter we all go back to Marienburg and that doom fades away like all the others. Is that what you want?'

Gotrek stood rigid for a long moment, breathing heavily. Felix could see his jaw muscles clenching under his beard as he ground his teeth. At last he put up his axe and turned, shouldering roughly past Aethenir as the elf flattened against the rail.

Gotrek slapped aside the curtain, then looked back. 'This had better be a damned good doom!'

He turned and disappeared into the privy. There was a noise like an explosion in a brewery.

Everybody hurried quickly away.

Felix retired to his cramped cabin that night well pleased. Though Gotrek's altercation with Aethenir had been a terrifying near-massacre that had almost ended their journey before it had really begun, afterwards, Felix had been heartened at the thought of how angry and alive the Slayer had been – trading spirited insults with the elf and challenging his whole retinue to a fight. Such a contrast to the somnambulant lump that had sat glumly in the Griffon with barely the energy to lift his tankard to his lips. The seeress's vision seemed to have worked upon him like an elixir, raising him from the living death of his depression and giving him purpose again.

As he lay down in the tiny cupboard bed and pulled the heavy quilt over him, Felix hoped that, for the Slayer's sake, the premonition wasn't a lie. After that his thoughts became scattered, and he let the swell of the waves and the creaks and groans of the ship timbers lull him into a deep, dreamless sleep.

When he woke again, it was to a soft noise. Long years of experience in dangerous awakenings had taught him not to make any sudden noises or movements. Instead he moved only his eyes, passing them slowly over the small area of dark room that he could see without turning his head. Nothing. Had he imagined it? No. The soft noise was repeated, and followed by quiet rustlings and shiftings. Someone, or some thing, was most definitely in the room with him.

He could make out the corners and edges of things now, illuminated in a dim glow of moonlight from the small, thick-glassed window. He eased his head a few inches around, as quietly as he could.

Yes, there was someone in his room, and she was stark naked, the pale light highlighting her slim, youthful curves as she dropped her robe to the deck.

'What are you doing here?' Felix asked.

'I couldn't sleep,' said Fraulein Pallenberger.

'And so you decided that I shouldn't either.'

She sighed and sat on the bed, shivering a little in the chill as she lay a hand on the covers that draped over his legs. 'You use harsh humour to hide your misery, Herr Jaeger, but I know that, beneath your cruel words, you long for solace. You drive me away so that you will not have to share your pain, but in your mind you are calling, "come back, come back".' She lay down on top of the covers and brought her face close to his. 'And so, I have.'

She closed her eyes and leaned in to kiss him. Felix turned his head so that her lips fell awkwardly on his ear.

'Fraulein,' he said, then struggled with the bedclothes and sat up. 'Fraulein, you cannot be here.'

She rolled over and looked up at him, stretching as she raised an eyebrow in what he was sure she thought was a sultry expression. He swallowed. Despite her overplaying, she did look rather fetching sprawled out like that.

'And why not?' she said. 'You long for it. I long for it. Surely you are not some prudish…'

'I do not long for it!' snapped Felix. 'And you… This has more to do with putting one over on Magister Schreiber and rebelling against your order than any attraction you have to me.'

Her languid look vanished in an angry flash of eyes and she sat up too, all semblance of desire gone. 'Why shouldn't it?' she hissed. 'Don't you see that this might be my last chance? Herr Jaeger, I am young! Young! I want to taste the world before it is taken away from me! I want to live before I die! It is my gift – my curse! – to predict the future, and I predict that the rest of my life will be a long, grey corridor, full of dust and charts and telescopes and pale, wrinkled old men!' She covered her face with one hand. 'I know I cannot leave the Colleges. The Empire does not suffer a witch to live. I know I have to go back and shuffle along with the rest of them, but for now – for these few days…' She looked up at Felix with eyes that burned with a shimmering fire. 'I want to live!'

Felix sat back, torn between heartbreak and laughter. 'Fraulein

Pallenberger, this is all very moving, but the Celestial Order is not a celibate order. You may marry. You may take your pleasure as you like.'

'Not until I become a magister,' said Claudia sullenly. 'And that might take until I am thirty! I will be old then. No one will want to look at me. My youth will be behind me.'

This time Felix did chuckle. 'And how old do you think I am?'

'It's different for men!' she cried, then started to weep in earnest. 'Oh, I've made a terrible mistake!' she bawled. 'I didn't want to join the order! I don't want to be a seeress!'

'Shhhh, shhhh,' said Felix, taking her hands. 'You'll wake the ship.' He groaned as he imagined Max finding them like this. 'Please, fraulein. Calm down.'

She muffled her sobs with her hands and fell heavily against his chest, nestling her head against his shoulder. He folded her in his arms and stroked her hair – not in any romantic way, he told himself – purely to comfort and quieten her. But when her hands crept around his torso and she pressed herself against him, he found desire stirring within him despite himself.

He fought it down and pried her off, but she clung again as soon as he let go.

'Do not cast me out, Herr Jaeger,' she murmured in his ear. 'Let me live. I beg you.'

'Fraulein – Claudia,' he said, trying to disentangle himself. 'You really overstate your case. Thirty, even for a woman, is not…'

Her lips found his, and then her tongue. He responded before he could remember not to.

'Claudia, please,' he said, pushing away from her at last. This wasn't right. He loved Ulrika. Her memory was still fresh in his heart. He doubted it would ever die. He didn't want anyone else but her. And since he could not have her, then he would have no one at all. It would be sacrilege to defile the memory of their love with some petty animal flailing.

Claudia's hands trailed down his torso and gripped his legs as she kissed his neck. He shivered. On the other hand, there was something to be said, in this world of trouble and pain, for taking pleasure where one could find it. Ulrika's words came back to him again. 'We must find happiness among our own kind.' He still wasn't certain that happiness was possible, but comfort might be.

With a sigh and a silent apology to Ulrika, wherever she might be, he lowered his lips to Claudia's and kissed her, long and deep. The seeress whimpered and pressed harder against him. He pulled his nightshirt off over his head and moved his lips to her throat, kissing and nibbling tenderly. She shivered and groaned. Felix chuckled to himself. It had been a while, but he appeared not to have forgotten what to do. He pressed her back against the bed and kissed her clavicle, then down between her breasts. She moaned and clutched him, trembling as if with fever. 'Here,' she said. 'Here!'

By Taal and Rhya, thought Felix, delving lower, no wonder the girl regrets her apprenticeship, she's as enflamed as a rutting cat.

'Here!' the seeress shrieked, and scrambled up out of the bed, kneeing him in the cheek in her haste.

'Claudia, what…?' he said, then stared.

She stood in the centre of the tiny cabin, her arms thrust wide and her eyes rolled up in their sockets, shaking like she was bracing against a high wind.

'Here!' she screamed. 'Here is the source of the visions! I can feel it! It is from here that the ruin of Marienburg will spring!'

Felix heard the thumps and questioning cries of his fellow passengers through the walls all around him. He jumped out of bed and snatched her robe up off the floor where she had dropped it. He had to get her dressed and back to her own cabin. But it was impossible. She continued to stand with arms outstretched, as rigid as a sword, and he could not get both of her sleeves on her at once.

'Here!' she wailed in his ear as he tried to wrap the robe around her nakedness. 'Here is where we will find Altdorf's doom!'

It was in this tableau that the others found them when they slammed open the door – Max, Aethenir, Captain Breda, Gotrek and assorted swordsmen, sailors and elves – all staring at Felix and Claudia struggling and naked in the centre of the room, with the seeress's robe fluttering once again to the deck.

'Could you be quieter about it, manling?' rumbled Gotrek. 'Some of us are trying to sleep.'

SEVEN

Captain Breda dropped anchor there and then, but there was little point in looking around in the dark, so they waited until first light before lowering the boats and rowing them to shore to see if they could find the source of Claudia's vision.

Gotrek and Felix set out in the boat that carried Max and Claudia and their eight Reiksguard knights, Aethenir and his elf warriors were rowed in another, and Captain Breda sent another party of sailors to look for fresh water to replenish the stores. As they all left the ship, Felix could see the sailors at the rail looking at him and elbowing each other lasciviously. His face burned crimson. They had been laughing behind his back since word had spread of how he and Claudia had been discovered. He didn't know what they had to snicker about. She had come to his cabin and not theirs after all.

The sailors' mirth was unfortunately not the only fallout. Max had not spoken to him since. Nor had Claudia. She seemed too embarrassed to look at him. The ride to the shore was therefore silent and uncomfortable.

They pulled the boats up onto a rocky beach hemmed in on three sides by high sand dunes. A cold wind whistled through the saw grass that topped them, and clouds scudded by above them in a steely autumn sky. A few raindrops fell. Max and Aethenir turned to Claudia, expectant, while the Reiksguard and the elf warriors prepared to march and Felix shrugged into his chainmail and strapped on his sword.

'Have you further insight as to where this evil lies, seeress?' asked Max, who had grown very formal with her since the previous night. 'Or what it might be?'

Claudia shook her head, unable to meet his eyes. 'The vision has passed and I have not had another. I'm sorry, magister. It is near here, but I don't know where, or what it is, precisely.'

Max nodded. 'Very well, then we will split up and look for it. You and I will go south with Reikscaptain Oberhoff and his men along the shore. High one, will you take your kin inland and look there?'

'Of course,' said Aethenir.

Max turned to Gotrek, pointedly ignoring Felix. 'Slayer, will you and Herr Jaeger walk the coast to the north? We will search until mid-morning, then return here and compare notes. And whatever you find, let it lie until we may all examine it together.'

Gotrek nodded.

Felix stiffened at the snub, but said nothing. He had, after all, all but promised Max that he would have nothing to do with Claudia, and he had gone back on that promise – however unwillingly – so he supposed he deserved a snubbing. Still, it felt a bit petty. Maybe Max was jealous that Claudia had chased Felix instead of him. The thought sparked others. Was Max married? Did he have a mistress? Did he even care about such worldly matters any more? Felix didn't know.

As they took packs and waterskins out of the boats, Felix found himself for a moment alone next to Claudia. He leaned in and lowered his voice. 'I hope Max hasn't scolded you too much for last night's–'

'You might have covered me,' she snapped, cutting him off. 'I've never been so embarrassed.'

'I tried!' said Felix, defensive. Then he got angry. What right did she have to criticise his actions? 'And you might have stayed in your own cabin and saved us both a lot of bother!'

'Oh!' she said, and turned away without another word.

He watched her walk away and found Max giving him the evil eye again. Felix cursed silently and turned away, shouldering his pack.

Rain began to spit intermittently from the sky as Felix and Gotrek set off to the north, staying within sight of the water. This was not as easy as one might have thought. The shore was not all beaches and dunes. In fact, most of it was swampy, foul-smelling wetlands, an endless flat swamp with the occasional scrawny, leafless tree sticking up out of it like a witch's claw reaching up from a drowning pool. They slogged through brittle, knife-sharp grass – waist high for Felix, chest high for Gotrek – that grew out of rank, spongy ground, their footprints filling in with water behind them. The muck exhaled a low, foetid mist that swirled around their ankles, and clouds of midges and mosquitoes rose from it continually, getting in their eyes and noses and biting them unmercifully on every inch of exposed skin. Weird cries echoed through the humid silence, and once something big splashed heavily into a stream nearby, but they didn't see what it was.

Gotrek took the flies and the mud and the smell and the unnerving noises without apparent discomfort, but Felix was slapping and cursing and stumbling and walking into enormous spiderwebs the whole way. It seemed all of a piece with his vile mood. He couldn't get over Claudia's unfair anger at him. It wasn't his fault she had been found naked in his cabin. He had tried to get her to leave, repeatedly. It was she who had come uninvited and tried to seduce him. It was she who had decided that the best time to have a vision of the future was during love-making. Even more galling was the fact that Max seemed to think that he had lured her there, that he was some sort of low lothario that preyed upon young, inexperienced girls. It made him want to go back and shout the truth in their faces. It made him forget to look where he was going and step into a puddle that filled his boots to the top with freezing, green-scummed water.

His cursing startled a flock of ducks who flew over their heads, complaining querulously, and started a racket of strange shrieks off to the west that made his skin crawl. He cursed them too.

If only he had some idea what they were looking for, it might have made the journey more bearable. That was Claudia's fault too. Did she have to be so vague? What good was an ability that only gave half-answers? Should they be on the look-out for some ruined tower? A ring of stones? A weird tree with tentacles for branches? A fissure in the earth that radiated a ghastly glow? Without some goal in mind it all felt like some wild goose chase. Maybe Claudia had no powers of foresight at all. He had seen nothing conclusive to prove to the contrary. Maybe she made all of it up just so that she would have an excuse to leave the confines of the Celestial College. He wouldn't put it past her.

Gotrek discovered the footprints just as they were about to turn back and report their failure. They had trudged up out of the marshland onto a hillocky plain that was covered in bramble bushes and scrub pine, and had found, carving through the brush to the sea, a narrow, clear-running stream with high, undercut banks. Below one of these banks was a line of bootprints, paralleling the stream and heading inland.

They drew their weapons and followed the prints as they weaved in and out of the water for perhaps a quarter of a mile. They stopped at last at a place where the stream widened into a pool and the banks drew back to make a muddy little beach. Here the first prints were joined by many others, and also the imprint of the keels of small boats at the waterline and the circular imprints of barrels, sunk heavily into the mud. It was clear that a landing party had been here recently and refilled their water barrels, just as Captain Breda's men were doing now further south. And the narrowness of the prints also made it clear – at least to Gotrek – who had collected the water.

'More elves,' Gotrek growled.

Felix nodded, and they turned back. It had been a discovery, but it didn't seem to be the portent of doom they had been looking for.

The rain chose that moment to begin sheeting down like a waterfall. Felix sighed. Of course it was raining. A day like today wouldn't be complete without being soaked to the skin.

As the sky grew darker and the downpour got heavier, they turned inland, partly to be good scouts and search new ground, but mostly to avoid the marshes during the rain. It appeared that Max and Claudia and their Reiksguard escort had done the same, for they met them coming north about a quarter of a mile inland from the beach where they had landed. The two wizards were much the worse for wear, their cloaks and long robes muddied to the waist, their hands and faces scratched by brambles and dotted with insect bites. Felix felt a warm glow at the thought that Claudia had shared his misery. It served her right.

'Anything to report?' asked Max, raising his voice over the hiss of the rain as he mopped his face with a handkerchief. Despite the chill wind and the downpour, he and Claudia were beetroot-red and boiling from their exertions, as were their swordsmen, who were steaming slightly, and appeared to be regretting having worn breastplates and pauldrons for the march.

'Not much,' Felix shouted in return. 'We found signs of an elf watering party at the limit of our march.'

'A watering party?' asked Captain Oberhoff. 'In this godforsaken place? Must have been desperate.'

'Or searching for something,' said Max. 'Like us.'

The clink of scale mail brought their heads up and they saw, coming over a hill to the east, Aethenir and his escort, marching in perfect double file. Felix was annoyed to see that, though wet, their surcoats were still pristine, and their boots clean. And not one of them seemed to have been bitten by mosquitoes.

'A disappointing search,' said Aethenir as the elves joined them. 'We found nothing.' He looked to Max. 'I hope you have had more success.'

Max shook his head. 'Nothing. Gotrek and Herr Jaeger have found signs of a recent elf watering party to the north, but nothing else.'

'Elves?' said Aethenir, his eyes narrowing. He turned to Captain Rion and asked him a question in the elven tongue. The captain shook his head and Aethenir looked troubled. 'I pray it was only elves,' he said to Max, then turned to look at Claudia. 'And has Fraulein Pallenberger experienced any new revelations about our goal?'

'No,' said Max. 'Not yet.'

Claudia hung her head. 'I wish I could call them forth, high one,' she said glumly. 'But they come when they come.'

The elf smiled slyly. 'So I have observed.'

Claudia turned crimson at that, and Max's eyes blazed. Even Felix felt angry. The girl might be a young fool who needed to learn restraint, but there was no need to make her feel worse about last night's embarrassment.

Aethenir turned towards the beach again, oblivious to their anger, his escort following. Max opened his mouth to speak, but Claudia grabbed his arm and shook her head, pleading silently. Felix could see her point. Protesting would only make her the centre of more excruciating attention. Max relented and they all followed the elves as they trudged up the hill into the driving rain.

Felix was slipping and stumbling down the far side and thinking that perhaps stealing his father's letter from Euler might have been the better option after all, when suddenly Claudia gasped and staggered into him.

He caught her but then lost his footing and they both went down together. It took all his will to be polite.

'Are you all right, fraulein?' he asked. 'Have you trodden on something?'

But Claudia's eyes were wide and unseeing, and she clutched her robes with spasming, white-knuckled hands. 'The flames! The sea crawls with flames!'

'Back to the boats!' snapped Max, and he motioned for two of the stronger Reiksguarders to take Claudia from Felix as he and Gotrek and the rest of the party raced towards the shore.

It was difficult to see for more than ten paces in the freezing torrent and the gathering dark. Even so, all could see the flickering glow that silhouetted the last dune before the beach, and they hurried up the shifting sandy slope with anxious speed.

Felix was one of the first to the top, just behind Aethenir's elves, and he looked towards the source of the light. Out on the sea, the *Pride of Skintstaad* was a roaring pyre of sallow green flames – too far gone to even think of trying to save it.

The others joined him on the crest, Max, Claudia and the men gasping and wheezing from their run. Gotrek just stared, the green fire reflected in his single eye.

Claudia choked and wept. 'No! Why didn't I see it sooner?'

Felix was wondering the same thing.

Max pointed down to the beach. 'To our boats. We must go help the survivors.'

Felix and the others nodded and started trotting quickly down to the boats, calling for the sailors to take up their oars, but though the boats were there, the men who had rowed them ashore were nowhere to be seen.

'Where in Sigmar's name have they run off to?' growled Reikscaptain Oberhoff.

Then one of his Reiksguard pointed to the water. 'Look!' he said. 'The crew! They're swimming ashore!'

Felix looked where he pointed. It was hard to see through the rain, but he could make out the lumpy shapes of heads bobbing in the water, moving closer to the beach. Some of them were crawling through the surf.

'Praise Manann,' said one of the other Reiksguard.

But Felix frowned. Had there been so many crewmen? He only remembered a score at the most. There seemed to be twice that many heads in the water. 'Wait,' he said. 'Aren't there too many?'

The others looked again, blinking in the downpour.

Aethenir stepped back. 'Those aren't men,' he said. 'They are...'

With a feral hiss, the first wave of swimmers rose from the breaking waves and ran at the party on the beach – dark, crouching forms with water dripping from their piecemeal armour and their matted fur. Dagger teeth flashed bone-white in the gloom. Red eyes glowed. Rust-grimed spearheads glinted green in the light of the burning ship.

'Skaven!' roared Gotrek. He charged into the surf, drawing his axe from his back and sweeping it around him savagely. Skaven heads and limbs and tails spun away from skaven bodies to splash in the water.

The men and elves did not follow the Slayer's example. They fell back, shouting and drawing swords as dozens of the horrible creatures rose from the sea and scrabbled towards them, swinging wide around Gotrek and up the beach like a black tide. Felix backed off and fought alongside the others, separated from the Slayer by the seething wall of fur, filth and fangs. Spearheads flashed out of the glistening gloom, invisible until almost too late. Felix parried desperately, and slashed back, but it was like striking at shadows. A hoarse cry of pain came from his left – a curse from his right.

Felix was having a hard time getting his bearings as he fell in with the Reiksguard. Why skaven? Why now? What did they want? And where had they come from?

Then, with a shout of strange words, Max thrust up a hand and a ball of brilliant white light crackled into existence above his head. The skaven cringed back in the harsh illumination, chittering fearfully.

The Reiksguarders, hardened veterans of the recent Chaos invasion, did not flinch from this magic, nor did the elves. The Reiksguard fell in shoulder to shoulder, their swords and shields working in unison, while beside them, the elves attacked in a spinning, whirling fury, their long blades chopping through spears and furred limbs with equal ease as further spells from Max's hands shot past them and blasted the ranks of skaven with orbs of scintillating light that made them shriek and fall and writhe on the ground. But though the glowing ball made the vermin easier to see and kill, it also showed just how many there were. Felix's heart thudded as he looked out over the milling carpet of ratmen that covered the beach, while still more rose from the waves. There seemed no end to them.

The harsh light illuminated all their most hideous attributes – the patchy, scrofulous fur, the pustule-plagued snouts, the soulless black-marble eyes, the horrible, hissing mouths, the revolting trophies that dangled from their necks and belts. Nausea constricted his throat as he slashed viciously at them, all his disgust and fear of the vile creatures turning into a seething rage. His first stroke opened a ratman's stomach in a spray of blood and viscera, then he removed another's arm on the back swing. He buried the blade in the skull of a third, kicked it free and spun to face more.

On the far side of the skaven, Gotrek was doing the same, or trying to. The Slayer was as angry as Felix had ever seen him, for though he was surrounded by foes, he had no one to fight. The skaven scampered away from him like – well, like rats – and on his short legs he could not close with them. 'Stand and fight, vermin!' he raged as he ran backwards and forwards in the centre of an empty circle of sand.

Felix quickly found himself having the same problem. The skaven were staying behind their spears, prodding at him from a distance, but making no attempt to kill him. He lunged at a cluster of them, but they only parted before him, like water around a stone. He could not understand the behaviour. Skaven either fought with maddened fury or fled. There had never in his experience been anything in between.

Roaring with frustration, Gotrek gave up trying to close with passing ratmen and charged the back of the skaven line, cutting a hole through it with his axe. He only killed a few, for, as before, they jumped out of his way. The Slayer halted beside Felix, shaking his axe, his crest hanging limp from the pelting rain as he bellowed at their foes. 'Craven ratkin! Give me a proper fight!'

But they did not. The skaven continued to shy away from them. Gotrek and Felix had almost no enemies facing them at their portion of the line.

The Reiksguarders and the high elves were not so fortunate. The swordsman beside Felix crumpled, impaled by a spear, and another lay face-down on the sand. One of the high elves was stepping back behind his comrades, his left leg a bloody ruin. Though the men and the elves seemed to be killing ten skaven for every one that fell on their side, there were so many of the beasts that it didn't matter. The sheer mass of the vermin pressed the whole party back towards the dunes, step by inexorable step, and threatened to encircle it as well.

Behind the thin line of Reiksguard and elf warriors, Max wove trails of light in the air that expanded into a shimmering bubble of energy that encircled himself, Claudia and Aethenir. Within the circle, Aethenir motioned the wounded elf into the bubble and began making gestures in the air over his leg, while Claudia, looking terrified but determined, mouthed a spell and let loose a blast of lightning from her hands that caused the skaven front line to twitch and fall. So the girl had a use after all, thought Felix, uncharitably.

Just as he thought it, Claudia screamed. He looked back again. Gotrek did too. Bursting from the sawgrass at the base of the dune to their rear were black shadows, throwing metal stars and glass globes. Men and elves alike cried out as the stars bit into their limbs and torsos.

An elf warrior instinctively knocked a globe out of the air with his sword and it shattered. He and another elf went down as if shot, as green mist blossomed from the glass ball and enveloped them. The skaven hacked them savagely as they fell. Captain Rion and the other elves dodged back and covered their noses and mouths. The mist drifted into the skaven ranks and half a dozen collapsed. Two of the globes landed with a soft thud on the wet sand at Felix's feet. He picked them up in one hand and hurled them towards the sea. They left a faint familiar odour on his fingers.

Gotrek snarled and ran at the star-hurling shadows.

'Protect the wizards,' cried Felix to the swordsmen, then raced after the Slayer.

But just as they were about to close with the murky shapes, a deep bellow rose above the noise of the rain. Gotrek stopped in his tracks and looked around. A massive black-furred, rat-headed creature, nearly twice Felix's height and thick with mutated muscle, was bounding down the dune towards Max, Aethenir and Claudia. Max spun and shot a blast of light at it. The creature howled but did not slow. Claudia sent a bolt of lightning at it. It hardly seemed to notice.

The wounded high elf pushed away from Aethenir's ministrations and limped to intercept it, his teeth clenched but his sword at the ready. Captain Rion and the other elf warriors looked back, but they were engaged with the skaven front line and could not break away.

Gotrek sprinted to get between the wounded elf and the rat ogre, his one eye blazing. 'Mine, you chalk-faced thief!' he roared. 'Leave off!'

Felix ran behind the Slayer, but suddenly, with a jerk at his chest, he wasn't running any more. He was flat on his back.

He looked down at himself. There was a noose of thin grey cord wrapped around his chest. His heart thudded with sudden recognition, even as he picked himself up and turned to look where the noose led. The attack in Altdorf! It had been the skaven! And the attack in Marienburg as well! The globes smelled the same as the gas that had knocked out everyone at the Three Bells! But why did the skaven want to capture them?

'Loose me, you damned rope twirlers!' bawled Gotrek beside him.

Felix chopped through the line with his sword and turned to see that the Slayer was similarly infested with nooses. One was around his neck, another looped around his left wrist and another around his right ankle. They did not stop him by any means, but they did slow him, and the wounded elf reached the rat ogre first, his shining blade parrying the monster's massive claws with a deafening clang.

Enraged, Gotrek gathered up all the ropes that held him in one hand and pulled savagely. Black-clad skaven stumbled out of the shadows at the end of the ropes. Gotrek roared and charged them – then vanished into a pit that opened up in the sand below his feet.

Felix stared. One moment, the Slayer had been running full tilt, axe raised, the next moment he was gone, to be replaced by a dark hole in the ground with wet sand trickling down into it.

'Gotrek!' Felix ran to the edge of the hole and nearly fell in himself as the edge crumbled and fell down on the Slayer below. Gotrek clawed at the sides of the pit, half-buried in wet sand, as he tried to climb out, but the sand broke apart under his fingers and he sank back.

'Hang on, Gotrek!' cried Felix. 'I'll get you out!'

Just then a chittering from beyond the hole brought his head up. The black-clad skaven were running at him, holding what looked like a big leather bag. Felix grabbed the rope that was wrapped around Gotrek's wrist and hauled on it one-handed while lashing out at the skaven with his blade, but the Slayer was too heavy and the sand too loose. The skaven danced back out of reach, then darted in at his back and cut the cord.

He fell back as the cord snapped, then rolled to his feet, on guard, panic rising in his chest. There was no pulling Gotrek out. Not with the skaven ambushers trying to stuff him in a sack. And with the Slayer out of the fight the vermin might win, and he and Felix would be taken prisoner. He shivered at the thought. That was an unthinkable outcome. He had to get Gotrek out, but how?

Then he saw the way. Unfortunately, it meant putting himself in the path of a marauding monster. Felix hacked around at the assassins, fanning them back, then raced through the rain towards the wounded elf and the rat ogre. The skaven scampered after him. To one side, the remaining Reiksguard and elf warriors had surrounded Max, Claudia and Aethenir, and were fighting desperately to keep the skaven horde from breaking through their circle.

Felix ran past them and hacked into the side of the massive rat beast as it swung again at the elf. It roared and turned to him, and the elf staggered back in relief. He was in bad shape, barely able to move on his maimed leg, and three fingers of his left hand were missing.

'Fall back!' Felix shouted, taking a step back and slashing at the assassins behind him. 'Let me lead it away!'

The high elf nodded and stumbled aside as Felix waved his sword in the brute's face. It bellowed and lumbered forwards, swiping at him with its massive claws. Felix ducked, then turned and ran, hacking down two of the bag-wielding skaven who were creeping up behind him, and looking back to be sure the thing was following. It was – too fast! Felix sprang ahead as the monster's fists pounded the sand just inches from his heels, almost jarring him off his feet. The assassins scampered out of its path.

As he reached the hole, Felix bent down and scooped up another of Gotrek's noose ropes, then dived forwards as the rat ogre's claws whooshed over his head. He rolled to his feet and faced the towering rat ogre. It raised its arms and charged. Felix dodged aside, holding the rope and swiping at the ambushers, who were scurrying around the outskirts of the fight, still trying to put him in the bag. The beast stumbled into the rope. Felix quickly ran behind it, wrapping the cord around its legs, then got in front of it again, jerking the cord tight.

'Come on, you overgrown sewer rat!' he shouted, waving his sword. 'Come and die!'

The monster obliged, striding forwards with a savage bellow as Felix dodged back. The rope around the rat ogre's waist pulled taut behind him, and with an explosion of sand, Gotrek was dragged from the hole – by the neck!

Felix gaped, and nearly had his head taken off. He'd grabbed the wrong rope! Sigmar, had he strangled the Slayer?

Felix ducked to the side, forcing the rat ogre to stop and change direction. Its tail of rope went slack, and to Felix's great relief, he saw Gotrek stagger to his feet, cursing and clawing at the noose that had cinched his beard to his neck.

The giant beast swung its claws again. Felix dodged back, then darted in under its massive arm and stabbed it between the ribs. The point sank deep. The thing roared and twisted, wrenching the sword from Felix's hands and clubbing him to the sand with a flailing elbow.

It raised its fists over its head to deliver the death blow. Felix crabbed feebly backwards, weaponless and stunned, knowing he was dead. But suddenly the rat ogre was toppling sideways as its right leg fell away from its body in a shower of blood. It crashed down onto its back, thrashing and screaming. Gotrek stood behind it, his axe dripping gore. He raised his axe high, then chopped down through the beast's bony skull with a sickening crunch. The muscle-bloated body went slack and Felix breathed a sigh of relief.

Gotrek levered his axe out of the rat ogre's skull and ran at the skaven assassins, who were creeping in again. 'You've got a funny sense of humour, manling.'

'I grabbed the wrong rope!' said Felix, staggering up and joining. 'I didn't mean to.'

It seemed, however, that the assassins had had enough. They scattered before Gotrek and Felix like cockroaches, whistling shrilly as they ran.

The whistle appeared to be a signal, for the mob of skaven that were still pressing the Reiksguard swordsmen and Aethenir's retinue broke away from the battle and raced back towards the shore. The men and elves chased them, but the ratmen dived into the waves and swam strongly out to sea, their long snouts making streaming bow waves in the black water.

Felix stared after them as he and Gotrek strode down to the surf. 'Where are they going?' he asked. 'Do they have a ship?'

Gotrek shrugged. There was no ship to be seen except the *Pride of Skintstaad*, now burnt to the waterline and sinking fast. 'I hope they drown.'

Felix said a silent prayer for Captain Breda and his crew as he took a final look at the dying ship and turned back and surveyed the aftermath of the battle. Skaven bodies littered the beach, misshapen lumps of fur surrounded by clotted red sand. There were too many men and elves lying among the horrors, however. Two of the high elves were dead, gutted while knocked out by the skaven's sleep gas. Four of the Reikland swordsmen were dead as well, impaled by skaven spears, and a fifth was dying, a river of blood pouring from a deep gash on his inner thigh. Captain Oberhoff and two others were all that were left, and even they bled from numerous wounds. They knelt by the dying man, holding his hands and speaking comforting words to him as his face drained white and his head began to nod. Captain Rion prayed over the two elves that had fallen.

Max, Claudia and Aethenir were untouched. Their guards had done their job, and had paid for it. Aethenir cast spells of healing on the wounded elves, and Max waited for the Reiksguarders to finish saying goodbye to their companion so that he could do the same to them. Claudia knelt on the wet sand, soaked to the bone, staring around at all the carnage, blank with shock. Felix almost asked her how she was enjoying her freedom, but decided that was too cruel and held his tongue.

Max eyed Gotrek and Felix as they neared. 'They were after you,' he said, bitterly. 'I should have remembered that you two always bring trouble with you.'

Felix shook his head. 'I don't understand it. What do they want with us? We've fought them before, but that was twenty years ago. These can't possibly be the same ones, can they?'

Max shrugged. 'Nonetheless, they want you, and they want you alive. You were the only ones they didn't try to kill. I only hope they don't come for you again until we have parted company.'

Felix nodded, fighting down a wave of guilt. Max was right. The skaven attacks had hurt everyone but their intended targets. He was about to tell Max about the attacks in Altdorf and Marienburg, when a glint of red and blue on the chest of one of the skaven assassins caught Felix's attention. It seemed out of place amidst the rest of the ratman's filthy possessions.

He stepped closer and toed aside the vermin's ragged black garment. Threaded onto a dirty string around its neck was a collection of odd trinkets – bones, coins, a human ear, bits of amber and tin, and, in the middle of this trash, a gaudy gold ring, set with sapphires surrounding the letter 'J' picked out in rubies.

Felix blinked at it for several seconds, uncomprehending. He recognised it, but it was so out of place in its current surroundings that for a moment he couldn't place it. Then he knew it, and his heart turned to a fist of ice.

It was his father's ring.

EIGHT

'We must go back to Altdorf!' Felix cried, ripping the ring from the slimy cord around the skaven's neck. 'Immediately!'

The others turned towards him, curious.

Felix held up the ring. 'This vile creature has my father's ring! It must have... It must have...' Felix found that he could not bring himself to voice what he feared the skaven must have done. 'I don't know what it has done. But I must return to Altdorf at once to find out!'

Gotrek's eyes narrowed as he looked at the ring.

Max stepped forwards, concerned. 'Felix, this is terrible. Are you certain it is your father's ring?'

'Of course I'm certain,' snapped Felix, holding it out. 'Look at it. It has the Jaeger J. The last I saw it, it was on his hand. The skaven have been in his house! I must go back as soon as possible!'

'No!' cried Claudia from behind them. 'You will not!'

They turned. She was struggling to her feet, encumbered by her wet robes.

Felix glared at her. 'Are you ordering me?' he asked, hotly.

'No,' she said again, staring sightlessly past him towards the sea, her eyes rolled up in her head. 'We will not leave.' She thrust out a trembling finger, pointing past the drifting column of black smoke that was all that was left now of the *Pride of Skintstaad*. 'We will go there! That is where the evil lies!'

Felix cursed under his breath. Damn the woman and her inconvenient visions. He was really beginning to think she did it on purpose.

The others looked out over the water in the direction she pointed. Felix reluctantly joined them, hoping against hope that there would be nothing there. Unfortunately, there was.

About a mile out, a distance they had not been able to see when the rain was at its heaviest, there was a break in the thick clouds that blanketed the sky from horizon to horizon, and the ragged edges of the hole were slowly circling like porridge being stirred by a spoon. A shaft of bleak sunshine streamed straight down through the hole. Felix shivered at the unnatural sight. It was hard to tell through all the mist and rain, but it looked like the water below the opening was swirling in exactly the same way that the clouds were.

'No, curse it! I refuse!' he said, the blood pounding strongly in his temples. 'Ancient evils from the dawn of time can wait for once! My father might be... might be *harmed*, and I intend to return to his side at once!'

'We haven't got a ship, manling,' said Gotrek.

'I don't care! I'll walk!'

'Certainly we will walk, Felix,' said Max, in the sort of patient voice one would use to speak to a pouty child. 'We have no choice now. But as we're here, we should do what we came to do. One day out of twenty won't make a difference.'

'It could make all the difference in the world!' shouted Felix, glaring around at them all. Didn't they understand? His father could be dying. The skaven might have done anything to him.

Gotrek knelt and cleaned the blood from his axe with a handful of sand. 'The rats have already done what they have done, manling,' he said without looking up. 'No matter how fast we return, we can't turn back time.'

Felix bit back an angry reply, trying to find some fault in the Slayer's cold logic, but at last, with a final kick at the dead skaven, he let out a breath. 'All right, fine. Let's go have a look at where the evil lies, but then I'm going back to Altdorf, with you or without you.'

'Thank you, Felix,' said Max.

The others turned away and began preparing to row out to the cloudbreak. Felix stepped to the dead rat ogre and began wrenching his sword out from between its ribs.

'Manling,' said Gotrek.

Felix looked around to find the Slayer fixing him with his one hard eye. 'Yes?'

'Revenge is patient,' Gotrek said, then sheathed his axe and turned away.

Half an hour later, after Max and Aethenir had seen to the survivors' wounds as well as they could, and after the bodies of the slain had been buried in the sand and the grave marked so that they could be retrieved later, the remains of the landing party set out towards the swirling clouds in a single boat. Gotrek, Felix, Captain Rion, his three unwounded elves and the two remaining Reiksguard swordsmen manned the oars while Aethenir, Max, the wounded elf and Reikscaptain Oberhoff sat in the back and Claudia stood at the front, staring ahead into the wind and rain like a living figurehead. Felix once again fought the urge to push her in.

Several times during the journey he got the distinct feeling that they were being watched, but when he looked back, he could see no one on the shore, and no skaven snouts bobbing in the water, so he decided it was his imagination, though it was still a mystery where the swimming ratmen had gone.

The closer they got to the opening in the swirling clouds, the more the rain let up until, about half a mile from it, they reached the eye of the bizarre storm and all became bright and clear, with the autumn sun slanting down through the ragged aperture and shining on the dark blue water – and something else.

Standing in the prow, Claudia was the first to see it. 'There... there's a hole. In the water.'

Felix stopped rowing and turned around with the others. 'A hole?'

Max stood, shielding his eyes and looking ahead. 'A whirlpool.'

'It's... it's huge!' said Captain Oberhoff.

Gotrek grunted, as if to say that this was just the sort of thing he would expect from water.

Felix stood and looked ahead. There was indeed a whirlpool, and it was indeed huge – almost half a mile across – an exact mirror of the hole in the clouds that roiled above it. The sea around it swirled and frothed like water going down a drain, and a noise like an endlessly crashing wave reached their ears now that they were out of the rain. Felix swallowed, terrified. It was a great maw in the sea, hungry to swallow them.

'Well, there it is then,' he said nervously. 'Now we've seen it we can go back. We'll tell the Marienburg High Council a whirlpool is coming their way and they can, ah, take measures.'

'It is not the whirlpool that is the threat,' said Claudia. 'It is what's within it. I can feel it, but we must get closer.'

Felix cursed. The woman's visions kept leading them into trouble. Shouldn't prophecy warn one away from danger, not drag one towards it? 'You can't be serious! We'll be sucked in! We'll die!'

'I too can feel it,' said Aethenir. 'There is great evil here. Row on.'

Felix looked to Max for support. The wizard hesitated, but Felix could see the lust for knowledge in his eyes.

'I can't protect you from that, lord magister,' said Oberhoff, piping up. 'Best to turn back.'

'Aye, lord,' said Captain Rion to Aethenir. 'Our swords are useless against such a threat.'

Finally some voices of reason, thought Felix.

'Nevertheless,' said Aethenir. 'We must get closer so that we may try to sense what is causing it. Row on.'

Max looked from Felix to Oberhoff to Aethenir. 'Perhaps a little closer,' he said at last. 'Only be careful.'

Captain Oberhoff sighed. Rion's jaw clenched. They exchanged a look of comradely suffering. Felix and the others reluctantly picked up their oars again and rowed slowly closer. There was a visible line between the choppy waves of the sea and the fast rippling current that raced around the great vortex. They edged towards the line, measuring every stroke. At last they began to feel the fatal tug of the current upon the keel of the boat.

'It's pulling now!' said Felix, louder than he meant to.

'Then retreat slightly and hold,' said Aethenir calmly, and stepped towards the front of the boat.

Felix cast a glance at his comrades as they worked together to reverse their strokes and bring the boat to a halt. The swordsmen looked nervous, Gotrek furious, and the elves as calm as milk. At last the boat came to a shaky stop, wavering restlessly in the water as the current drew it one way and their oar-work pulled it the other. It felt like they were balancing on a teetering rock. One slip and they would all go down. Felix wiped the sweat from his brow with his shoulder and kept back-stroking.

Claudia and Max joined Aethenir in the prow of the boat and closed their eyes, mumbling under their breath. A glow of light began to shimmer around Max's grey-haired head. Ripples distorted the air around Aethenir. Claudia looked up at the patch of sky that showed through the clouds, whispering fiercely.

Felix, Gotrek and the others kept pushing slowly but steadily on the oars, keeping the boat in place as the wizards' incantations grew louder and more droning. The three different spells weaved in and out of each other like some unearthly melody, and Felix felt weird pressures and unexpected emotions pushing at him from within and without. Claudia began to sway in place, and Felix feared – or perhaps hoped – she would fall out of the boat.

In the middle of it all, Reikscaptain Oberhoff raised a shout. 'A ship!'

Max broke off instantly – Claudia and Aethenir more reluctantly. Gotrek, Felix and the others turned, following the captain's finger. On the far side of the storm's eye, a dark shape was moving, just within the curtain of the rain.

'Keep pulling, human,' said Captain Rion.

Felix hastily returned to his oar, but his quick glance had shown him a black-hulled ship, small, but with a prow like a knife, with black sails and rows of long oars on both sides.

'Asuryan preserve thy noble sons,' said Aethenir, his pale skin turning even whiter. 'It is as I feared. The corsairs of Naggaroth.'

'The what?' asked Oberhoff.

'The dark elves,' said Max.

'We'd better get back to shore,' said Felix.

Max nodded. 'That would be wisest, yes.'

'But the source of the prophecy!' said Claudia.

No one listened to her. Even Aethenir, staring in frozen terror at the black ship, seemed no longer interested in the whirlpool. Gotrek, Felix, and the human and elf warriors bent to their oars and began backing them again, much more quickly now. Even so, they were only barely moving away from the vortex.

'Lord Aethenir, Fraulein Pallenberger, sit down,' said Max. 'We must stay as low as possible and hope they don't see us.'

Claudia and Aethenir crouched down; she petulantly, he like a tent collapsing. He looked back at the rowers.

'Can we go no faster?' he asked.

'If you want to go faster,' said Gotrek, 'row.'

The high elf looked with horror at the last pair of oars in the bottom of the boat. 'Impossible. I have never…'

'Let me,' said Oberhoff, stepping forwards and picking up one of the oars.

'And I'll take the other,' said Max as he lifted the second.

The Reiksguard captain and the magister sat on the last bench, slotted the oars into the oarlocks and began to row with the others.

Gotrek snorted at Aethenir with disgust. 'Letting an old man pull an oar. Weak-wristed little…'

His muttering drifted off as he put his back into it again. They rowed on, pulling as hard as they could while the dark elf ship continued its circular route around the eye of the storm, but even with the added help of Max and Rion they went very slowly indeed.

'What is it doing?' asked Claudia, watching the ship.

'Staying a sensible distance from that hole,' said Felix, gloomily.

'We should have tried that,' muttered Oberhoff under his breath.

The black ship sailed closer, moving like the sweep hand of a watch around the edge of the circle. Felix found himself hunching down over his oars, trying to stay as low as possible. The druchii craft was soon near enough that, even through the curtain of rain, he could pick out the individual ropes that rose to the black sails and the elves climbing them. He saw the burnished helmet of an officer glinting on the aft deck, and the cruel emblems emblazoned on the banners that fluttered at the tops of the masts.

The ship was nearly parallel with them now. Felix held his breath. Sail on, he thought, closing his eyes. Sail on. Pass us by and continue around the circle. Another revolution and we will be gone.

Alas, it worked as well as most other childish incantations. A harsh cry echoed over the water and Felix opened his eyes again. A druchii sailor was pointing at them from the weather top and calling to the deck below.

'That's torn it,' said Captain Oberhoff with a curse.

With a swiftness that spoke of a decisive captain and a well-trained crew, the black ship arced off its course and aimed straight at them, its wet black sails gleaming like beetle shells as it broke into the sunshine of the storm's eye. It cut an oblique angle towards them across the open circle of sea, like a man laying a knife across the top of his dinner plate, and moved at an alarming speed.

'Row!' cried Aethenir. 'Row harder!'

'Why don't you use that hot air and blow?' said Gotrek, pulling powerfully at his oar.

'Don't any of you have any spells that could help?' asked Felix, before the elf could return the insult.

'All my spells are of healing and divination,' said Aethenir.

'Rowing is more helpful than anything I could muster at the moment,' said Max.

Felix turned his gaze towards the seeress. 'Claudia?'

'I... I don't know,' she said helplessly.

Felix ground his teeth as he and Gotrek and the others pulled for all they were worth. Still the little boat only crawled, while the druchii ship loomed closer with every second. It was like one of those bad dreams where one ran in place seemingly never to escape a monstrous pursuer.

'He means to ram us!' cried Aethenir. 'Does he not fear to go into the vortex himself?'

'He has enough speed and sailpower to pull out,' said Max. 'We do not.'

The little boat was moving faster now, as it moved further from the whirlpool's insidious grip, but still it was not fast enough. The black ship was only fifty yards away now. There was no way they could escape it.

'It's useless,' wailed Aethenir. 'We are doomed.'

'Good,' said Gotrek, throwing down his oar and drawing his axe off his back. He stepped to the prow and beckoned to the onrushing ship with one meaty hand. 'Come on, you beardless skeletons, I'll smash that floating toothpick to driftwood!'

Everyone else braced for impact. The druchii captain, however, did not attack them directly. Instead, at the last moment, he turned hard to port and shaved past them just out of reach.

But though the ship did not touch them, its bow wave did, nearly capsizing them and pushing them up and back on a mountain of white froth that threw Felix and the other rowers from their benches. Gotrek flew head over heels into the water and only prevented himself from disappearing beneath the waves by grabbing one of the rowlocks as he went over and holding on for dear life. Felix could hear haughty laughter coming from the black ship as its tall hull hissed by only yards away from them.

As the others recovered themselves, Felix scrambled to his knees and grabbed the Slayer's arm, helping him pull himself back in.

'What were those villains laughing about?' said Captain Oberhoff, climbing back to his oar. 'They missed.'

'No,' said Aethenir, looking towards the whirlpool. 'They did not.'

Felix and the others turned to see what he was looking at. Felix's heart sank. The little boat was now deep within the band of rushing current that surrounded the hole. He could feel it pulling at them like an insistent lover.

'Bugger,' said Captain Oberhoff.

'Row,' cried Max. 'Quickly, friends!'

Gotrek, Felix, and the elves and men clambered back to their oars and tried to pull in unison. It was hopeless. The current dragged them sideways around the whirlpool faster than a man could run, and always a little closer to the centre. Their oars did nothing but jerk the boat this way and that. Felix's blood ran cold in his veins. There was no way out. They would die here, not beaten by some great monster or devious enemy, but by simple gravity. The vortex would pull them down into its gullet and they would drown.

The glistening slope was getting closer, so smooth and glossy that it seemed almost motionless. Felix looked around at his companions. Gotrek, Captain Oberhoff and his Reiksguard, Rion and his warriors, all bent grimly to their oars, trying to the last. Max rowed too, but his eyes seemed far-away, as if searching for some solution. Claudia stared towards the whirlpool, eyes wide, crouching in the prow of the boat and mumbling under her breath. Aethenir seemed to be praying as well, his eyes closed and his delicate hands clamped together in supplication.

Reikscaptain Oberhoff murmured, 'Sigmar, welcome me to your hall,' over and over again, his eyes closed, and Felix found he was repeating the prayer with him.

Then they were tipping backwards down into the maw, sweeping down it at an angle like a marble spiralling down a funnel made of glittering green bottle glass. The angle of the slope steepened every second, and everyone shrank down into the boat, clinging to the sides. At last the slope became entirely vertical and they plummeted down in free fall.

Claudia screamed, and Felix was afraid he might have too. The others cursed and shouted, starting to fall faster than the boat as the drag of the hull against the watery walls slowed it. Felix clutched instinctively at one of the oar benches to hold himself in, then looked down into the green well, terrified, but determined to face his death head-on. The shock of what he saw there almost knocked the fear right out of him. Firstly, the walls of the whirlpool did not taper, as he expected, but went straight down, leaving a half-mile-wide circle of ocean floor exposed to the sky. Secondly, rising from that muddy floor were the shattered white towers and ruined buildings of an ancient city.

'By the Everqueen!' said Aethenir.

'A city,' said Max, in awe.

A city that would be their final resting place in a matter of seconds, thought Felix.

Claudia's murmuring rose in pitch and volume. Felix could not tell what god or goddess she was praying to, but it seemed that whichever it was, they weren't listening.

'This is a bad doom,' said Gotrek, glaring down at the rapidly approaching sea floor.

'I agree,' said Felix, a lump of helpless rage rising in his throat. Now he would never find out what had happened to his father. Now he would never resolve things with Ulrika. Now he would never finish the epic of Gotrek's death. He put the blame squarely on Claudia. It was her damned visions that had brought them out here in the first place. The woman had seemed determined to ruin his life and his peace of mind since the first moment she laid eyes on him. This calamity was exactly what she deserved for her foolishness. He would have laughed at her demise if he hadn't been about to share it.

Suddenly, the seeress rose from her crouch, throwing out her arms and diving from the boat. Felix stared. Had she gone mad at last? Was she giving in to the inevitable?

But then she rose above them – or rather they dropped faster than she – while at the same time she turned in the air and swept an arm towards them. Felix felt himself buffeted by an impossible wind – a wind that came from below them, a wind that grabbed at his sleeves and his cloak and tried to tear his grip from the boat.

'What is it?' cried one of the Reiksguard. 'What is the witch doing?'

'Let go!' called Max. 'She cannot support the boat as well.'

Felix's eyes bulged, and shame flooded his heart. The girl was trying to save them, using some sort of wind spell. He fought his natural inclination to cling for safety and forced his fingers to let go of the boat.

'Push off!' Max cried.

Felix kicked away from the floor of the boat, trying to tell himself it didn't matter how he fell. It would all end the same. The others did likewise. Even Gotrek pushed off, muttering about the untrustworthiness of magic all the while.

Felix looked down as the wind blew up at him from below, and his heart dropped faster than his body. The seeress had left it too late. The ground was rushing up at them too fast. They were too close. She would never stop their descent in time.

But then the wind from below increased tenfold, blasting him like an icy furnace and beating at his face like a living thing. His clothes flapped around him deafeningly. He was slowing! They all were! She was doing it! The wind was stopping them. They were hanging in the air, almost as if they were attached to Makaisson's air catchers. Claudia floated in the midst of them, her eyes closed tight, her arms out rigidly to her sides, her lips moving furiously.

'It's a miracle,' breathed Oberhoff, looking around him in terrified wonder.

It was indeed a miracle, but they were still going the wrong way. Lift us up, Felix wanted to call, but he didn't dare break Claudia's concentration. Get us out of this hole!

They continued to drift down. Was she mad? It was all very well to save them from smashing into a pulp on the ocean floor, but this unnatural whirlpool could collapse any moment.

Twenty feet above the sea floor, Gotrek dropped like a stone. He barked in surprise and fell away from the rest, landing with a wet smack in the mud.

Claudia whimpered and Felix dropped too. He yelped and flailed his arms as the wind that had been supporting him weakened to nothing, and he slammed into the mud a few feet from Gotrek. He bent his knees as he hit and found himself kneeling waist deep in blue-grey silt the consistency of wet plaster. His body rang with shock from the impact, but he didn't think anything had been broken or sprained. The others plopped down all around him, cursing and crying out, with the last being Claudia, landing ungracefully on her posterior.

Felix looked around as he tried to free himself from the sucking mud. They had landed very close to the shimmering, humming wall of water, on the very outskirts of the ruined city. The shattered remains of their boat stuck out of the muck not far away, and to their left he could see low walls, now little more than piles of seaweed-covered rubble, that might once have been a grand house. The city rose high and white and broken in the distance beyond them, like a collection of impossibly slim and delicate porcelain vases that had been smashed with a mattock. And beyond the ruined spires, lay the towering green cliff of water that was the other side of the whirlpool going up and up and up. The weight of all that water was palpable. It crushed him just looking at it. He didn't know what was keeping it up, but whatever it was, it certainly couldn't last. At some point the impossible walls would collapse and the water would come crashing back down to smash and drown them all. It made Felix want to curl up and cover his head.

Around him, the others were struggling to stand, mired to the knees or deeper in the mud, but apparently unhurt. Only Claudia remained motionless, sagging sideways, half-conscious, knee-deep in the muck. Gotrek was in the worst straits, buried up to his chest. He spat out a mouthful of mud.

'Magic,' he said, like a curse.

'Stupid woman,' snapped Aethenir as he tried to pull the hem of his robes free of the mud. 'Why did you not lift us out! We are stuck here now!'

Felix felt like punching the elf on the nose, even though he had thought the same thing just seconds before. It was different to say it out loud.

'High one, control your tongue!' said Max sharply. 'She did the best she could.'

'I'm sorry. I was too weak,' said Claudia, clutching her head as she came out of her faint. 'You were too many. I have never tried so complex an incantation before.' She turned to Gotrek, frowning. 'You were very slippery, master dwarf. Very hard to hold.'

'Dwarfs are very resistant to magic,' said Max. 'And the Slayer more so than most, I would think.'

Felix extricated himself at last and crossed to Gotrek to offer him a hand. Two of the Reiksguard joined him.

Behind them, Aethenir inclined his head briefly towards Claudia. 'My apologies, seeress. I spoke harshly out of distress. I see you have done as much as a human can do.' He looked to Max as she glared at his back. 'But what now, magister?' he asked. 'We are still stuck here. We have only delayed our death.'

'I will try again,' said Claudia, seething. 'But I will need some time to gather my paltry human energies.'

'Let us pray then that there is time enough,' said the high elf nodding politely to her again, and apparently oblivious to her sarcasm.

'Lord magister,' called Captain Oberhoff. Max and the others turned. He was pointing to the mud a short distance away from him. 'Look, milord. Footprints.'

Max and Aethenir's eyes widened.

Max slogged forwards, the mud sucking at his feet with every step. 'Are you certain?'

'Aye, sir,' said the captain.

With Felix and the Reiksguarders' help, Gotrek pulled himself free of the muck at last, and he and Felix joined Max and Aethenir beside the captain. The holes in the mud were definitely footprints – many pairs of them – and all leading further into the city. Because the wet mud had oozed back into the holes, it was impossible to tell who or what had left them, but whatever they were, there appeared to be about twenty of them.

'Someone else has fallen down this hole,' said the captain.

'Or caused it to be created,' said Max, ominously. He turned to Aethenir. 'Do you know what place this is, high one?'

Aethenir looked around, frowning at the distant buildings. 'It is one of the elven cities that sank during the Sundering, perhaps Lothlakh, or Ildenfane. Without maps and books I cannot be sure.' He returned his gaze to the mud. 'But of one thing I can be certain. Whoever has exposed it like this, whoever has come seeking within it, can be up to no good.'

Claudia stood upright, swaying only slightly. 'Yes. This is the place.

This is the heart of it. There is where the evil will be found that will destroy Marienburg and Altdorf.'

Of course it is, thought Felix, stifling a groan.

Max stroked his muddy beard and sighed. 'I suppose we better go have a look then, hadn't we?'

It was hard going, at least at first, each step a strenuous effort as the mud sucked at their feet and clung to their cloaks and robes. It got easier nearer to the city when they found the remains of a paved road. It too was covered with silt, but not nearly as deep.

It was one of the strangest environments Felix had ever travelled through – the delicate white walls of the elven buildings and the slender, jutting towers, now crumbled and covered in a wild phantasmagoria of ornament – shells, starfish and draperies of kelp, baroque filigree of dull-coloured coral, mossy algae, colonies of clinging clams, and stranger, tentacled things that looked like trees from the Chaos Wastes in miniature. Dead fish and feebly gesturing lobsters lay in the mud of ancient alleyways while water dripped from gutters that had known no rain for centuries. And above it all, the impossible green walls of seawater.

Felix couldn't help but look back at them nervously every few steps, afraid they might drop when he wasn't looking. At the gates of the city, a high white arch the wooden doors of which had long ago rotted away, he turned one last time and saw something within the water, a strange black shape bigger than a whale, gliding slowly past like a fish within a fishbowl.

'Gotrek! Max!' he cried, pointing, but by the time everyone turned around, the shape was gone, vanished back into the green murk beyond the whirlpool.

'What is it, Felix?' said Max.

'A shape,' he said. 'In the water. Like a whale.'

Max looked at the wall, waiting for something to appear, then shrugged. 'Perhaps it was a whale.' He turned and entered the gate.

The others followed. Felix scowled, feeling foolish, and took up the rear.

Within the walls, the full glory of the elven architecture became apparent. Though much of it had fallen, much more still stood, and it was glorious. The doors and windows were all tall and thin and topped with graceful arches. The columns were delicate and fluted. The streets were wide and well laid out, so that every corner was a new and breathtaking vista.

The party followed the footprints into the heart of the city, where the buildings became even taller and more ostentatious. These were obviously temples and palaces and places of public entertainment, and those that still stood were awe-inspiring in their scale and delicacy – at least to Felix.

'Flimsy elf rubbish,' grumbled Gotrek as he looked at it. 'No wonder it sank.'

Felix expected a retort of some kind from Aethenir, but he was too busy staring at the city. The elf was so fascinated by what he was seeing that he seemed to have lost all fear. 'Yes,' he said, more to himself than anyone else. 'It is just as my studies said it would be. This is definitely Lothlakh. The *Diary of Selyssin* describes the tower of the loremasters just so, but... no, if this is Lothlakh, then surely the Temple of Khaine is meant to be just to the left of the baths. Perhaps it is Ildenfane after all.'

At last the footprints led them to a sprawling, symmetrical palace with high, buttressed towers at each end and a pair of golden doors in the centre, flanked on either side by tall golden statues of regal elves holding swords and staffs. The gold of both the doors and the statues was filthy with black mud and crusted with barnacles and mussels, but they were all still whole.

Gotrek nodded approvingly. 'That's dwarf work,' he said. 'Made before the elves attacked and insulted us.'

Even that failed to raise a response from Aethenir. He was walking towards the palace like a sleepwalker, his hands waving vaguely at the various details of architecture and placement. 'It *is* Lothlakh!' he said. 'It must be. This is the palace of Lord Galdenaer, ruler of Lothlakh, described exactly in Oraine's *Book of the East*. To think that I have lived to see this.'

'It is indeed beautiful,' said Max. 'But we should perhaps approach it with more caution. It appears that those we seek may be within.'

Aethenir looked down at the footsteps leading to the golden doors, and a nervous look appeared in his eyes as he awoke from his scholar's dream. 'Yes,' he said. 'Yes of course.' He turned to the captain of his house guard. 'Rion, take the lead.'

The elf captain bowed and his elves moved towards the broad, muck-covered marble steps to the golden doors. The others followed. Gotrek and Felix and the Reiksguard took up the rear, watching all around.

The doors had been pulled open – by what means Felix couldn't guess – just enough to allow them passage one at a time. The first of the elves slipped through the opening while the others waited. After a moment he reappeared and beckoned the others through. The party followed him into an enormous entry hall. Felix and the rest looked with wonder upon the gold-chased columns, the crumbling obsidian statues, and the high arched ceiling. Windows that had once been filled with coloured glass were now gaping holes, through which watery green sunshine streamed in, giving the impression that the palace was still under the sea.

The mysterious footprints led across the silt-covered marble floor to a wide stairway that descended into darkness. Max created a small light – less bright than a candle – that he sent ahead of the elf warriors so they could follow the footprints. The silt was heavier here, making the stairs treacherous. Felix gripped the marble banister to steady himself. One flight down, Captain Rion held up his hand and everyone stopped. From below came the faint sounds of movement and conversation, and a bright noise of metal rubbing on metal, like someone endlessly scraping a dagger around the inside of a bell. Felix strained his ears, but could not make out the words or the language that was being spoken. The high elves looked at each other, but said nothing. They continued down the stairs, as silent as cats. Felix and the others tried to do the same.

At the base of the stairway there was an archway that glowed with a strange purple light. The high elves crept to one side of the archway, keeping out of sight, then leaned their heads out cautiously. Felix, Max and Gotrek followed their example.

Through the arch was a moderately large chamber with decorative pillars running down both sides and, at the far end, at the top of three wide marble stairs, a pair of enormous steel, granite and brass doors. Standing on the broad dais before the doors were a number of tall, thin figures, silhouetted in the glow of a purple light that hovered over the head of the one nearest the door – an elven woman in long black robes with black hair to her waist. Her hands were raised towards the door, and weird words poured from her lips in a sinuous melody. Five other robed women surrounded her, while surrounding them were twelve warriors in black enamelled scale mail and helms that were faced with silver skull masks. The tallest of the women wore an elaborate headdress and held a metal wand aloft, spinning a silver hoop on it. It was from this that the metallic ringing sound came.

Aethenir shrunk back behind the arch. 'Druchii!' he hissed.

'Sorceresses of Morathi's cult,' said Rion, his hand tightening convulsively on the hilt of his sword. 'And Endless, the Witch King's personal guard.'

'At last,' rumbled Gotrek. 'Elves I *can* kill.'

Rion turned to Aethenir. 'Lord, we humble house guards are no match for such as these. Even swordmasters of Hoeth would find themselves in difficulty here.'

Aethenir returned his attention to the room, biting his noble lip. 'We may have no choice,' he said, his voice quavering.

At the vault, the sorceress with the waist-length hair finished her incantation on a high, sustained note and then stepped back. With a rumble of hidden counterweights and a grinding of stone on stone, the massive doors began to swing out. She turned and smiled at her black-clad companions, motioning them to enter.

When he saw her face, Aethenir gasped and staggered back. 'Belryeth!' he whispered. 'It can't be!'

NINE

Max turned and looked at the high elf, raising a questioning eyebrow. 'You know this dark elf?'

Captain Rion was looking at Aethenir with a much colder look on his face.

Aethenir looked from one to the other, stepping back. 'I didn't know she was druchii.'

Captain Rion's gaze got colder yet. 'I believe that requires explanation, Lord Aethenir.' He motioned the elf back up the stairs, out of sight of the door.

'Yes,' said Max, following. 'I believe it does.'

The others crept back up to the first landing with them, then everybody turned to face the high elf.

'Now, my lord,' said Rion. 'Pray continue. How do you know this druchii?'

Aethenir swallowed. 'Ah, yes, well, you see, when last she came to me, she claimed to be a maiden in distress. Belryeth Eldendawn she called herself, and she told me–'

'You mistook one of the fallen ones for a true elf?' asked Rion, his voice like ice.

'She didn't look like she does now!' squealed Aethenir. 'Her hair was blonde and she had a beautiful, noble face, and a voice like the sweetest, saddest song ever sung by...'

The high elf caught Captain Rion's eye and faltered. Felix had never seen an elf blush before. From down the stairs came crashings and smashings and the tinkling of broken crystal. It sounded like the druchii were tearing the contents of the vault apart.

'Go on, my lord,' said the elf captain.

Aethenir nodded. 'She came to me,' he said, 'begging for help. She said that her family was in disgrace and could not approach the tower directly, but she must learn something hidden in one of the volumes in the library. Her grandfather, it seemed, had lost a precious family heirloom during the Sundering when he was stationed in one of the cities of the Old World. Recovering it was the only way she could fend off an odious marriage, now that her father had lost the family's fortune and all honour in a disastrous trading scandal. Her misfortunes moved me to tears.'

Felix rolled his eyes. The poor sheltered elf had obviously never seen a Detlef Sierck melodrama.

'She swore that all she wanted was the information contained in one book,' Aethenir continued. 'A book that told of that time and of those cities.'

'Do you mean the book that was stolen from the tower?' asked Max. 'Did she learn its location from you? Is she the thief?'

Aethenir hung his head. 'It was not stolen from the tower. As I said before, none may find the tower if the loremasters do not wish them to.' He hesitated, then went on. 'I borrowed it from the tower, and she stole it from me.'

Rion went rigid, his eyes blazing. '*What?*'

Aethenir shrunk before that terrible gaze. 'I swear I didn't know until now! She promised me that we would always look at the book together and it would never leave my sight, but the night I brought the book to her we were assaulted by masked assassins. I saw her killed! Then they leapt at me, knocking me out. When I awoke from my swoon, her body was gone, and so was the book.' He looked down the stairs towards the vault. 'All this time I thought her dead.'

Max coughed. 'I had always read that no books were allowed to be borrowed from the Tower of Hoeth. That they were never to leave the premises.'

Neither Rion or Aethenir acknowledged that he had spoken. They seemed to have forgotten that anyone else was there.

'My lord,' said Rion, with a dangerous softness. 'You told me that you had discovered that the book was missing, and that the loremasters had sent you to find it as a test of your worthiness to be taught the arts of Saphery. You told your *father* this.'

Aethenir covered his face with a shaking hand. 'I lied,' he whispered, so low Felix almost couldn't hear him.

'So the loremasters of Hoeth know nothing of the truth?' Rion asked.

Aethenir shook his head. 'I ran away from the tower. It has been my hope that I might, with your help, find the book and return it to the library before they know it is missing.'

Captain Rion's head sank and his fists clenched. 'My lord,' he said, 'were it not my sworn duty to protect your life, I would kill you here and now.'

Aethenir paled and stepped back at that, but Rion made no move against him.

'You have not only compromised your own honour,' the elf captain continued, 'but by asking your father for money and assistance in this misbegotten quest, you have compromised his honour, and the honour of all House Whiteleaf. Not to mention jeopardising the safety of our beloved homeland.'

Aethenir hung his head. It looked like he was sobbing.

Rion carried on mercilessly. 'Recovering the book will not win back House Whiteleaf's honour, my lord. The crime is too great. But it must be recovered even so, for to leave it in enemy hands would be an even greater crime.'

'Yes,' said Aethenir, still looking at the ground. 'It must be done. It is the least that I can do.'

'I am pleased that you think so, my lord,' said Rion, stepping closer to him. 'Because if you swerve from the path of honour – if you fail in the duty to your father and your house,' he curled the front of Aethenir's robe in his fist and jerked it up so that the young elf's jaw came up and he was forced to look the captain in the eye, 'I *will* kill you.'

'I won't fail, Rion,' said Aethenir, trembling. 'I promise you.'

Rion stepped back and bowed, very formal. 'Thank you, lord. That is all I ask.'

'Just a moment,' said Max. 'I wish to be clear. Ulthuan has no knowledge of this quest? You are not here by the authority of the Tower of Hoeth, as you previously implied? You are not an initiate?'

'No, magister. I am the merest novice.'

'And you are entirely on your own in this?'

'Yes, magister.'

Max sighed. 'Had I known this, I would not have so blithely...' He paused, then shook his head. 'Never mind. What's done is done. The danger is still the same and we must still face it.'

Gotrek grunted. 'Are you through? Can we kill some elves?'

Captain Rion turned and glared at him, seemingly displeased with his turn of phrase, but then nodded. 'Aye,' he said. 'Whatever these fiends mean to do, it can only mean dark days for Ulthuan if they succeed.'

'Good,' said Gotrek. He turned on his heel and started down the stairs again.

'Slayer,' whispered Max after him. 'We must be cautious! It is the sorceresses who maintain the whirlpool. If they die...'

But Gotrek was already striding through the arch into the antechamber. Felix and the others trailed in his wake, whispering after him urgently, as the sounds of smashing and shifting continued from the vault.

'Wait, Gotrek,' said Felix.

'Stop, dwarf,' hissed Captain Rion. 'We need a strategy.'

'Bring him back,' cried Aethenir.

'Here's your strategy,' rumbled Gotrek. 'We kill everyone except the one with the stick and the hoop, then force her to take us out the way she got in.'

'Very good,' said Max, trotting along beside him. 'But how?'

'Like this,' said Gotrek and strode up the low stairs to the half-open vault doors. 'Come on, you corpse-faced scarecrows!' he roared. 'Show me you've got more courage than your white-livered cousins!' Then he charged into the vault.

Aethenir gasped. Max groaned. The Reiksguard and Rion's elves exchanged grim glances and prepared to follow him in.

'Wait!' hissed Felix. For once he had an idea of how to take advantage of the Slayer's bullheadedness. 'Hide. Let them think he's alone. Max, Claudia, Lord Aethenir, prepare your most deadly spells. Captain Rion, be ready to attack. Reikscaptain Oberhoff, protect the magisters.'

Oberhoff and his men obeyed, as did Max and Aethenir. Rion looked at Felix like he was a dog who had suddenly begun to sing opera, but then motioned his elves to the left of the vault door as Felix peered into the vault.

'Firandaen,' Rion said to the elf whose leg had been maimed by the skaven. 'You will stay with the magisters.'

The skull-masked Endless were charging Gotrek from all sides, swerving around overturned chests and mounds of dumped treasure. Beyond them, the sorceresses stared at the Slayer, shocked. The only person who seemed entirely undisturbed was the sorceress who spun the silver hoop on the metal wand, a tall, ageless, hard-faced beauty who watched coolly as Gotrek and the Endless met in the centre of the room with a deafening crash and a flurry of flashing steel.

The Slayer disappeared as his taller foes swarmed around him, hacking and stabbing with their long slim swords. One of them fell back, a scarlet trench dug through the armour and flesh of his chest, spraying blood everywhere.

'Magisters! Captain Rion! Now!' cried Felix.

Max and Claudia stepped to the gap between the doors, thrusting their hands through and propelling streams of light and crackling lightning into the room. Felix, Rion and his three unwounded warriors ran in right behind the blasts. The masked druchii screamed and fell back as the blue fire and blinding light attacked their bodies, then Felix and the high elves slammed into them and five more went down, Gotrek killing two, Rion and the elves killing two more between them, and one dying fried to a crisp by Claudia's lightning. Half of them dead already! Felix rejoiced. This might be easier than he had expected.

Felix lunged at his bedazzled opponent, but the dark elf recovered with alarming speed and Felix's sword only scraped his armour as he blocked and whipped his blade into a blurring riposte. Felix barely brought his sword up in time. The next attack came almost before the first had finished, aiming straight for his eyes. Felix back-pedalled desperately, panic sweat prickling his skin. In two seconds Felix knew the dark elf was the best swordsman he had ever faced. There was no question of going on the offensive. Felix couldn't keep up with his attacks. He counted himself a better than average swordsman, but he was only human. He had only been fighting with a sword for twenty-five years or so. The dark elf, on the other hand, had probably been studying the blade for two hundred years, and was of a race naturally more agile than mankind to begin with.

Felix blocked again, but the druchii slipped under his guard and stabbed him at the crux of his right shoulder and chest. Felix's chainmail stopped most of it, but still the point sank an inch into meat before striking bone, driving links of mail with it. Felix fell back, barking with pain, and landed gasping on his back. The world dimmed and throbbed before his eyes. He waved his sword weakly above him with his off hand, but the druchii had turned away from him and was attacking Rion's warriors.

The arrogance of it cut through Felix's pain. Was he really so negligible a threat that the dark elf would turn away without finishing him off? He had never felt more dismissed. Felix struggled to get up and go on guard, then understood the druchii's confidence. The attack had been a carefully calculated crippling blow, goring the muscle that allowed him to lift his sword. He couldn't use it.

Beyond the melee, the woman with the wand and the silver hoop called out an order in a slithery voice, and two of her five sorceresses began scribing spells in the air. The others, Aethenir's Belryeth included, returned to searching through the stacks of treasure chests, as they had been doing before Gotrek's interruption – casually dumping them and kicking through their contents.

Determined to stay in the fight, if only to prove to the dark elf that he was still a threat, Felix switched his sword to his barely competent left hand, and charged him again. The Endless didn't even look back, just threw his leg out behind him in the middle of a lunge and kicked Felix precisely on the wound.

Felix smashed to the ground, hissing and curling up in a ball. By the gods, I'm useless, he thought as he fought to remain conscious through the pain.

His eye was caught by a cloud of boiling blackness that roiled towards the combat from the two druchii sorceresses. The pain of the wound was instantly eclipsed by a greater one as the black cloud enveloped him, and a burning like red-hot brands seared through him, seeming to cook him from the inside. He screamed and beat at himself like he was on fire, though there were no flames. The high elves were affected in the same way. They fell back, cursing and wailing and blocking desperately as the

Endless lunged in to take advantage. Only Gotrek fought on unaffected.

But almost as quickly as the black cloud was upon them, a bubble of light pushed it back, dissolving it in its radiance. The pain receded from Felix's limbs as the bubble expanded beyond him. He looked to the door and saw Max and Aethenir standing within it and working in tandem, sending pulses of white and golden energy into the room as Claudia shot more lightning at the sorceresses.

The bubble of light expanded to surround the high elves, allowing them to recover, but for one it was too late. He was crumbling, blood pouring down his white and green surcoat as Captain Rion and the other two elves fought on at Gotrek's side, surrounded by five skull-masked Endless.

Felix rolled out of the way of the combatants and staggered to his feet, while all around him invisible forces flexed and strained as the sorceresses and the magisters cast and countered each other's spells. With one arm useless, he couldn't hope to fight the dark elves directly, but he could at least take up his old position and guard Gotrek's sides. He limped behind the Slayer and immediately put his sword in the way of a slashing druchii sword. It was amazing to see how much trouble the Slayer was having. He who had fought armies of orcs and hordes of skaven single-handed, and who had faced down daemons and vampires, wasn't able to get a single strike in on the three druchii he held at bay. Though his axe was everywhere and his face was red with effort, he could not touch them, and shallow gashes covered his chest and arms.

The three druchii that fought him looked the same, blooded and winded. Their eyes, barely seen through the eye holes of their skull masks, were wide with offended surprise that any foe could last so long before them.

Rion and his remaining elves were drenched in sweat and blood, and fought their opponents with doomed desperation, for though, being elves, they might best any man alive at the sword, compared to the Endless, they were fumbling beginners. There was no question what the outcome of their fights would be, and Felix shuddered at what would happen when they had died and all the Endless were able to turn their attention on Gotrek. Against five such enemies, even the Slayer could not hope to prevail.

Suddenly, from atop a stack of treasure chests to the right of the door, Belryeth cried out in triumph and raised a sinuously curved black object over her head. The other sorceresses cheered. She turned towards the door of the chamber and smiled at Aethenir. 'Look, beloved, the Harp of Ruin, which you have helped us find!'

Aethenir shouted something back at her in the elvish tongue, but she laughed at him.

'No,' she said. 'I will speak so these fools can understand and know your humiliation. Bewitched and beglamoured, you have given into the hands of your enemies the greatest weapon of a lost age. One pluck of these strings can cause earthquakes that raise mountains from valleys or sink highlands lower than the sea bed. With this will the druchii create a wave that will sweep all the asur from Ulthuan. With this will we raise lost Nagarythe and rule the world again from our true homeland! You have doomed your people, and all for a love that never was!'

She reached into her robe and drew out something thick and square, then threw it so that it skidded across the floor to stop at Aethenir's feet. It was a book. Aethenir stared at it, then stooped and picked it up.

'Please thank your masters for the loan,' called Belryeth, laughing. 'It was everything I'd hoped it would be.'

The sorceress who spun the silver ring on the wand barked something that sounded to Felix suspiciously like 'enough gloating', and Belryeth and the other druchii women began making their way towards the door of the vault as they began new incantations.

With five of the sorceresses turning their attentions on them now, Max, Aethenir and Claudia were overwhelmed. Beams of darkness, like shafts from a black sun, smashed through their protective bubble. Felix saw Max stagger and Aethenir fall back, clutching his throat. Claudia wailed and tore at her face as if she were staring into the abyss. The Reiksguarders fell to the floor, screaming. Firandaen, the wounded elf who had stayed back to guard the spellcasters, pulled Aethenir and the magisters behind the vault door as blood poured from his nose, mouth, ears and eyes.

Gotrek and the elf warriors glanced towards the women, but could not disengage from the Endless, who would have cut them down the instant they lowered their guard to run. Only Felix was free. Though he knew it was death, he sprinted towards the women, his shoulder screaming with every jarring step. Belryeth turned casually and waved her free hand at him. A ripple of air rushed from her fingers and blew over him. It was as cold as death. He dropped, frozen to the bone, his teeth chattering. He couldn't move. His very blood seemed to have turned to ice. Frost rimmed his eyelashes.

Belryeth paused, smiling, as her sisters filed out the vault door. 'You are fools helping a fool on a fool's errand, and you will die a fool's death as a result.' And with a merry laugh, she turned and followed the others out.

Though the cold would not let him turn his head, Felix could hear screams and raving from the antechamber and he knew that the Reiksguard were trying, and failing, to prevent the sorceresses from leaving. He willed his limbs to move, wanting to go to their aid, but they would not. They were frozen stiff.

After a moment the cries fell silent and all that he could hear was the clashing of sword on sword and axe, and the heavy breathing and stamping of the fight behind him. And that will end soon enough, he thought, miserably.

But then, to Felix's surprise, Max appeared in the gap between the doors of the vault, clutching them for support and looking near death. He raised a feeble shout over the clamour of the battle. 'Your mistresses have left you to die, warriors. Will you still fight for them?'

A cold voice came from the depths of the skull helmet of one of the Endless. 'For the ruin of Ulthuan and the rebirth of Nagarythe, we are proud to die.'

'Then die you shall,' said Max. He forced himself upright and summoned his sorcerous energies, though it seemed to age him to do so. With a grunt of pain and effort, he unleashed a stream of swirling lights at the druchii. It was weak compared to his earlier attacks, but it was enough. With the sorceresses gone, the Endless could not defend themselves from it. The lights danced in front of their eyes, blinding and confusing them.

It was their end. Gotrek and Rion and his warriors beat down their swords and chopped through their armour with brutal ease. Gotrek dismembered the three who had defied him, as the others fell to the elves.

'Damned dancers wouldn't stay still,' growled the Slayer as he and the three elves stood over the pile of limbs and heads, breathing heavily.

Felix uncurled slowly as the effects of the unnatural cold faded and the stab wound in his shoulder throbbed to prominence again. He bit his cheeks against the pain.

Max sagged against the vault doors. 'No time to rest,' he said. 'We must go after the sorceresses.'

Aethenir appeared behind him, swaying like an aspen. 'Yes, hurry. They carry the doom of the asur in their hands.'

'Then let them go,' said Gotrek, shrugging.

'Vile dwarf,' said Aethenir. 'Would you doom the rest of the world to satisfy your grudge against the elves?'

'Why not?' said Gotrek. 'You doomed it for a druchii kiss.'

'I told you,' cried Aethenir. 'I did not know that she–'

'Their leader holds the key to escaping this trap alive,' said Max, interrupting their sniping angrily.

Suddenly not even Gotrek had any objections to going after the sorceresses.

Felix, Gotrek, Rion, and his elves followed Max and Aethenir out of the vault and found a bloodless massacre. Firandaen was dead, a look of wide-eyed horror on his noble face. Captain Oberhoff and the last of the Reiksguard were dead too, icicles like daggers growing out of their mouths and eyes, and stabbing through their breastplates from within.

Felix for a moment thought Claudia was dead too, her little body huddled in a ball at the base of the low stairs, but then he saw her twitch. He and one of Rion's remaining warriors helped her up and supported her between them as the party moved towards the stairs. She whimpered and flinched at their touch, and her face was shredded where she had clawed at herself after the sorceress's attack.

As they hurried across the antechamber, Aethenir turned to Rion, holding up the stolen book. 'I know this is not enough,' he said. 'Not any more. I vow that I will not rest until I recover the harp and prevent the sorceresses' plan.'

Rion nodded, but did not look around. 'That is the path of honour, my lord,' he said coldly.

Aethenir's eyes were downcast as they entered the stairwell.

The two flights to the entry hall was one of the most terrifying distances Felix had ever travelled, for he expected at every moment for a roaring torrent of water to pour down them and bury them beneath the sea. It was also one of the most painful, for with every step the wound in his shoulder staggered him afresh. The blood from it was soaking his shirt and padded jerkin and turning the rings of his mail red. He nearly lost his grip on Claudia several times as the pain made him faint.

The others were in equally bad shape. Max's face was pale and drawn, as if he had aged twenty years since the beginning of the battle. Aethenir was shaking as if with fever, sweat standing out on his pale skin. Rion and his last two elves moved with grim precision, staring fixedly ahead of them as their wounds bled into their surcoats. Only Gotrek seemed fit and ready for another battle. Though he bled from a score of wounds, his step was firm and his eye was clear and angry.

They reached the silt-filled entry hall and ran to the golden doors, then slipped through them onto the wide porch at the top of the marble steps, looking around anxiously for the sorceresses. Felix didn't see them, and it looked as if it would be impossible to follow them, for the streets of the city were flooded with water, and it was rising swiftly, already halfway up the palace's grand marble steps.

'The water!' wailed Aethenir. 'She has loosed the walls!'

'If she had loosed the walls, scholar,' said Max, with barely concealed impatience, 'we would be dead by now. They are whole, you see? She is losing concentration, that is all.'

'And that is better?' asked Aethenir.

Over their voices Felix thought he still heard the now familiar chime of the sorceress's silver hoop, faint, but still audible. 'Shhh!' he said. 'The ringing. Listen!'

Everyone listened, but it was hard to pinpoint where the sound was coming from, and it was getting fainter, lost in the deep distant roar of the whirlpool's spinning sides.

'Where is it?' said Aethenir.

'There,' said Claudia, looking straight up at the sky with dull eyes.

Everyone followed her gaze. At first Felix could see nothing – only the glare of the sky shining down into the gloomy green well of the whirlpool. But then, as his eyes accustomed themselves to the light, he saw them – six black dots, levitating up towards the top of the well like they were being drawn up on ropes – the sorceresses. They rose in a circle, with one of their number in the centre.

'Bring them down!' cried Aethenir. 'Stop them!'

'But we'll die,' said Felix.

'Still I think I must,' said Max. 'For the safety of the world.' He took a deep breath and began an incantation, pulling power from the air around him with his hands.

He was too late.

Before he was halfway through his droning, the shrill ringing stopped, like a chiming glass pinched silent.

There was a short pause in which Felix could hear half a dozen frightened gasps – one of them his – then, with a sound like the world ending, the whirlpool collapsed, the green walls caving in and an avalanche of water thundering towards the centre to fill the unnatural hole in the sea.

TEN

Aethenir screamed.
Gotrek cursed.
Claudia stared.
Felix turned to her, shouting though she was right next to him. 'Seeress! Lift us up! Levitate us!'
Claudia didn't appear to hear.
The titanic waves were already crashing into the city, smashing buildings and toppling towers in their wake, and the shallow water in the street began rising much more rapidly.
'Back to the vault,' rasped Gotrek.
'Back to the vault?' cried Felix. 'But that's suicide!' The Slayer was insane! They would be trapped underground, under water. They would die!
Gotrek was already pushing through the narrow gap between the doors. 'It's the only thing that isn't,' he shouted.
'Follow him!' said Max, and hurried in with Aethenir and his escort.
Felix and the elf who was helping him support Claudia hustled her through the door as quick as they could, but she was still too slow. The water from the street was already spilling into the palace. She would never make it to the vault, and neither would they. With a curse, Felix scooped Claudia up, slung her over his unwounded shoulder and raced across the entry hall after the others. The pain was still almost more than he could bear.
'Thank you, Felix,' said Max, then turned back and held out his hands towards the palace doors.

Felix heard them grind shut as he plunged into the stairway. A useless gesture, he thought. Even if they held, the palace was full of broken windows. As Max caught up with him, the roar of the approaching water drowned out every other noise. The party splashed breakneck down the last flight, slipping and clutching at the walls as water pushed at the back of their legs and rained down from above.

Then, just as they reached the bottom, with a noise like the world ending, a cataclysmic impact shook the palace, knocking them all off their feet and sending huge blocks of masonry crashing down from the ceiling all around them. Felix landed on top of Claudia, his shoulder screaming and his ears nearly bursting as a horrible pressure slammed them.

The whirlpool had closed.

Gotrek picked himself up from the knee-high water as rocks and dust continued to splash down. 'Run!' he roared.

Felix found his feet and pulled Claudia up after him, slinging her over his shoulder again and slogging across the antechamber after the Slayer, dizzy from the pain and weaving drunkenly. A deafening thunder roared behind them. The palace doors? Felix didn't dare look back.

After several endless seconds Felix trudged up the three steps to the vault with Claudia and stumbled through the half-open doors. Water was lapping over the raised threshold and spreading out in a puddle towards the treasures.

'To the side!' called Gotrek.

The elves and humans splashed to the right. Felix started to follow but tripped over the body of a dead elf and dropped Claudia again. The pain as he crashed down almost made him black out. He tried to rise, but his head was swimming too much. Then Gotrek's powerful fingers grabbed his collar and pulled him across the floor. Rion was doing the same to Claudia. The whole room was shaking.

Felix looked back towards the vault doors as the Slayer dragged him aside. A frothing wall of water was blasting out of the stairwell towards the vault faster than stampeding horses. It's over, he thought, cringing away from the sight. This is the end.

But then, just as he expected the full weight of the sea to burst in and batter them all to death against the walls of the vault, the doors slammed shut with a deafening boom, closed by the force of the water, and there was silence.

The elves and humans all looked at the doors in shock. They had held. Gotrek looked smug.

'We... we're alive,' said Aethenir, as if he didn't quite believe it.

'Good thinking, Slayer,' said Max.

'Dwarf work,' Gotrek grunted with a nod towards the doors. 'The only doors I could trust not to break in this elf hovel.'

Aethenir sniffed. 'That's all very well, dwarf, but now you've trapped us under the sea. How am I to honour my pledge to Rion and make recompense for my crimes if we all die of asphyxiation down here?'

'Not asphyxiation, my lord,' said Rion, looking towards the doors. 'Drowning.'

Everyone turned. The doors had held perfectly, but there was a knife-thin arc of water spraying through the narrow gap between them. The puddle on the floor continued to spread.

'Shallya's mercy,' moaned Claudia, staring with dull eyes. 'You've made it worse. We might have been dead already. Now we must wait for it.'

Gotrek snorted. 'You can all die down here if you like, but this will not be my doom. I'm getting out.'

'How?' asked Aethenir, in a voice tinged with hysteria.

'I'm still working that out,' said the Slayer, sitting down on a treasure chest and looking thoughtfully around the room.

Felix looked around with him. He had been too busy fighting or running until now to take in its details. Though the druchii had made a mess of it during their search for the harp, it was still a place filled with beauty. Below the witchlight chandeliers hanging above were neatly stacked treasure chests, ranks of statues carved from marble, alabaster and obsidian, jewelled suits of armour, beautiful swords, spears and axes, so delicate and exquisite that it seemed impossible that they could be used in battle, paintings, rugs, a throne of gold, complete with a deep blue canopy, and in one corner, a gilded war chariot – and all of it as bright and clean and unweathered as if the doors of the vault had closed yesterday and it had not spent the last four thousand years under the sea. Some elven magic, no doubt.

Aethenir threw up his hands. 'He's still working it out? You ordered us down here and you didn't have a plan?'

'Would you have rather stayed above?' snarled Gotrek.

'I would rather you had waited for us to form some strategy before charging impetuously into battle with the druchii, dwarf,' snapped Aethenir.

'High one, please,' said Felix, trying to be a voice of reason so that he wouldn't succumb to panic too. 'We cannot change the past. Do you have any spells that might help us? Can you make us able to breathe water? Can you create a bubble of air?'

Aethenir blinked. 'I... I can do none of those things. My few skills, as I said before, are in healing and divination.'

Felix turned to Max. 'Max?'

The wizard shook his head. 'Such spells exist, but they are not the purview of my college.'

Felix looked to Claudia. 'Fraulein Pallenberger? You can make the wind blow. Can you not make air?'

She shook her head dully. 'I require air to make a breeze. I cannot make it out of nothing.'

Felix sagged. No air. They were doomed. Even if they could get out of the sealed vault, their lungs would burst long before they reached the surface. Damn magic and damn all magicians too! All they seemed to be able to do was kill people and predict disaster. Never anything useful.

'Ha!' said Gotrek, standing.

Everyone, even the stoic Rion, turned to him with the eager light of hope in their eyes.

Gotrek strode past them towards the vault's treasures. 'Collect nine of the largest wooden chests, the biggest rug, as much rope as you can find and the chains from those chandeliers.'

The others stared after him, dumbfounded.

'But, Slayer,' said Max, struggling for calm. 'What do you intend to do? How will this get us to the surface?'

'Just do it!' snapped Gotrek, upending a casket the size of a courtesan's bathtub and spilling golden treasure in every direction. 'We don't have much time.'

By the time Felix, Rion and his elves had assembled the nine largest wooden treasure chests they could find, the water in the vault was up to their ankles. Gotrek collected the chandelier chains by the simple expedient of chopping through the winches mounted on the walls by which the chandeliers could be raised and lowered. They crashed to the ground in an explosion of delicate silver and crystal as the witchlights shattered. Aethenir wailed at this and the hundreds of priceless lost treasures uncaringly dumped on the floor, but the vandalism continued.

While Felix and Gotrek and the elves worked, Aethenir and Max called them over one at a time and used their healing arts on them. Felix bit a piece of leather against the pain while Max used a pair of tweezers to tug bits of cloth and broken links of chainmail from the wound Felix had received from the druchii swordsman, all the while murmuring spells of cleansing. Then Aethenir attended to him, and though by this time Felix was of the general opinion that the elf needed his neck wrung at the earliest opportunity, in this at least he was a useful addition to the party. Felix watched amazed as his long, slim fingers weaved over the wound and seemed to sew it up without touching it. The skin around the puncture glowed from within and the wound began to knit together at the ends, and then gradually close towards the centre, until finally there was nothing left but a pink scar and a deep ache.

'It is still weak,' said the high elf when he had finished. 'You must rest it for a few days.'

Felix looked around at where they were. 'I don't know if I'll have the opportunity, high one.'

Nonetheless he did his best not to tire it – leaving most of the heavy lifting to Gotrek and the elves, and instead pulling the gold tasselled ropes from the canopy of the throne and coiling them. The elves stripped the ropes and leather straps from the gilded war chariot. Claudia, recovering slowly from the druchii sorceresses' mind blasts, sat cross-legged on a chest and untied the cords that held ancient war banners to their poles. Max searched the vault and determined that the largest rug was rolled up in the back right corner, but by the time they found it, it was half-soaked in the rising water and it took Gotrek, Felix and Rion's elves to carry it out to the corner into the open. Felix's head spun with every step, his shoulder aching like a hammer blow.

When everything was brought together, Gotrek laid three of the gold tasselled ropes parallel on the ground near the door, each about a long pace apart – actually they floated in the water, but there was no dry space left to lay them now, so it had to do. Then he hacked the lids of the chests off with his axe and set the chests upside down on top of the ropes in three rows of three, wedged as close to each other and the door as possible. They bobbled and bumped a bit in the water, floating. Gotrek nailed the ends of the ropes to the sides of the chests with gold-headed nails pried from the golden throne.

'Now unroll the rug over the chests,' said Gotrek.

Felix, Rion and the elf warriors did as he asked, pushing and lifting the heavy rug until it covered the nine chests completely. Felix was still unsure what Gotrek was up to, but at least staying busy kept his mind off their impending drowning.

'Now the chains.' Gotrek picked up the end of one of the chains and started pulling it around the covered chests. Felix grabbed the other end and pulled the other way. They met on the far side of the chests with several feet of chain to spare. The elves did the same with the second chain.

'Tuck the carpet as close to the chests as you can while I pull,' said Gotrek, taking the two ends of one of the chains.

The rest of the party stepped to the chests, folding and pushing down on the carpet all around the edges of the chests as if trying to tuck in the sheets of a bed. All the while, Gotrek hauled on the ends of the chains, taking in the slack.

'I think I begin to see what you intend, Slayer,' said Max as they were at it. 'The wooden chests will float, and also hold air, and binding them together keeps *us* together, and makes it harder for any of the chests to flip over and spill its air.'

'Aye,' grunted Gotrek, heaving again. 'And the ropes underneath are to hold on to.'

'But I don't understand,' said Aethenir. 'Even if this bizarre contraption works, we will never get out of the vault. There are hundreds of thousands of pounds of water holding the doors shut!'

Gotrek snorted. 'And you call yourself a scholar. When the vault fills with water it will equalise the pressure.'

'When the vault fills with water we will drown!' cried Aethenir.

Gotrek didn't dignify this with a reply, though Felix wished he had, because he wanted to know the answer too.

When the carpet and the first chain were as tight to the sides of the chests as they could make them, Gotrek attached a jewelled, dwarf-made crossbow to one end of the chain and hooked the cleat into the other end, then used the ratchet to winch the chain even tighter. When it was so tight Felix feared that a link would break, Gotrek lashed the crossbow in place with a length of the leather chariot reins and did the whole thing again with the second chain and another crossbow. By the time he was finished, he was cranking the crossbow's handle under a foot of water, and the nine chests were floating like a raft.

Max looked at the raft uneasily. 'Slayer, I foresee a problem. When the water rises so will this. And the roof is far above the top of the vault doors. It will press against the ceiling. How will we get it out?'

Gotrek didn't answer, only stepped to the nearest full treasure chest, picked it up as if it weighed nothing, then carried it to a corner of the raft and set it down. The raft dipped down into the water at that end.

'Ah!' said Max. 'Excellent.'

'Space them evenly,' said Gotrek. 'The raft must be just heavier than the air and wood.'

'How do you think of these things, dwarf?' asked Aethenir, shaking his head as Rion and his elves lifted a single chest between them and staggered with it to the raft.

'Dwarfs are practical,' said Gotrek. 'They look at the ground. Not the sky.'

'Which is why they so rarely soar,' sneered the high elf.

'They don't drown much either,' said Gotrek dryly.

Felix scratched his head, still not quite understanding. 'I assume we'll float up on other chests as the water rises in here, but then how will we swim down to the raft? I'm not sure I can dive so deep, and I doubt Fraulein Pallenberger can.'

'I have never swum at all,' she said in a small voice.

Gotrek grinned and nodded towards the ranks of beautiful ceremonial armour along the left wall. 'We will carry armour for weight,' he said. 'Though you should put your own armour on top of the raft, or you won't be light enough to float when we rise.'

As Felix struggled out of his armour and threw it onto the raft with the treasure, he marvelled once again at the change that had come over the Slayer. Only two weeks ago he had been slumped in the Three Bells, unable to string more than three words together, and now he was solving problems of engineering and survival of which Felix would never have been able to conceive. It was an amazing transformation.

The waiting was the hardest part. With all the work done, there was nothing to do but watch the water rise. They sat inside empty treasure chests, rising slowly with the water, hour after hour, inch by incremental inch, with the elven armour that Gotrek had insisted they use for weight belted around themselves so that they could swiftly drop it when they needed to later.

'What do you know of this Harp of Ruin, Lord Aethenir?' asked Max as they rose. His voice echoed strangely in the enclosed space.

Aethenir looked guilty at the mention of the thing. 'Nothing more than Belryeth said,' he replied. 'I believe I might have read the name in some old texts, but I remember nothing else. There were many weapons created out of desperation during the first rise of Chaos that were later deemed too dangerous to use safely, and also too dangerous to destroy.' He looked around the flooded room. 'Thus they were locked away and often forgotten.' He sighed. 'One would have thought that this harp was doubly safe, hidden in this vault and buried as it was beneath the sea.'

'Yes,' said Rion bitterly. 'One would have thought.'

Aethenir hung his head in shame.

After that, conversation faltered and they all just stared at the walls, glum and silent. With the water of the deep sea all around them, the vault, which had been chilly to begin with, now grew painfully cold, and they all shivered and hugged their knees. Only Gotrek, shirtless though he was, bore it without any sign of discomfort.

When it got too much to bear, Max cast a further spell of light which gave off a mild pleasant warmth as well. It wasn't nearly enough.

Eventually the water rose above the doors, and its climb slowed even further. Still Gotrek told them they must wait, saying that the pressure must be completely equal or the doors wouldn't budge. Now that the air wasn't escaping through the crack that the water was coming in through, it started to become compressed, and Felix could feel it pushing on his eardrums and his chest. A while later it seemed to be pressing against his eyes. His head ached terribly, and the others were similarly affected. Aethenir got a spontaneous nosebleed that he had difficulty stopping.

Finally, after an hour where Felix's pulse pounded in his temples like an orc war drum and they had to hunch down in their floating chests to avoid knocking their heads against the carved and gilded beams of the vault's ceiling, Gotrek nodded.

'Right,' he said. 'Into the water. When you're on the floor, lift the raft over your heads and set it down over your shoulders. Walk forwards and push the chests against the door. When we're free of the palace, drop the armour. I'll shift some of the treasure off the top too so we'll rise.' He looked around at them all. 'Ready?'

Everyone nodded, though they didn't look particularly ready.

'Go,' said Gotrek, and, taking a deep breath, he leaned to the side, tipped out of his chest and sank like a stone.

Rion and his warriors followed his example instantly, but Felix, Claudia, Max and Aethenir all hesitated a moment, looking around at each other with unhappy eyes, then they too took deep breaths, capsized their chests and plunged into the icy water.

The cold shock of it was like a blow to the head, and Felix fought a desperate urge to flail back to the surface. He opened his eyes. Max's magical ball of light shone just as well under the water as above it, and suffused the sunken vault with an eerie greenish light, suspended silt sparkling like diamond dust in the murky water. Gotrek was already on the floor, the elves landing with dreamlike slowness all around him. Felix saw Max, Claudia and Aethenir sinking as well, their robes billowing around them like living flowers, then they too were on the floor and stepping with strange, bouncing strides to the treasure-laden raft, which hovered at about knee height.

Felix touched down a second later, his slow impact raising a puff of silt. His lungs were now crying for air, and the pressure on his chest was like a crushing fist. He bounced to the front of the raft and grabbed for an edge. Gotrek's hand stopped him and he looked up.

The Slayer held up a hand and looked around at everyone, then, when he had their attention, motioned for them to lift all at once. The raft, which not even Gotrek would have been able to lift by himself on dry land, came up with ease and they raised it above their heads, then shuffled around until they were all under one of the upside-down chests – Felix, Gotrek and Rion in the first rank, Aethenir and the two remaining elf warriors in the middle rank, and Max and Claudia in the corner chests of the last rank.

Felix's blood was beating in his throat now, and black spots danced in front of his eyes, so it was a great relief when they pulled on the underslung ropes and lowered the strange contraption down over themselves. Felix gasped in great gulps of air as his head broke the surface, then he tried to slow his breathing as he realised how little air was within the inverted chest. Though it might save his life, the little cubicle was terrifyingly small, and he felt more closed in here than he had pressing against the roof of the vault. He hoped that none of the others suffered from a fear of small spaces.

There was a loud rap from Gotrek's side of the chest and Felix started walking forwards. He looked down through the water and saw that Rion was doing the same, but Gotrek's short legs were pedalling uselessly above the floor. He heard a muffled dwarf curse through the wood.

Another step and the raft boomed hollowly against the vault's lefthand door. Felix placed his hands on the front wall of his chest and pushed with all his might. His feet scraped and slipped, struggling to gain purchase against the slick marble floor. Through the water he could see Rion doing the same, and the chests creaked as the others behind him applied pressure too.

The doors didn't move. Felix strained harder. Still nothing. Panic began to rise in his chest. He heard another curse from his right, then a small splash. He looked down into the water again and saw Gotrek, out of his chest, pushing at the door with both hands. Still nothing happened, and

Felix's panic grew worse. Had the doors locked when they closed? Was the pressure still too unequal? Were the doors just too heavy to move without magic?

Then, with agonising slowness, Felix saw the bottom edge of the door inch forwards. He let out a breath he hadn't known he had been holding, loud in the confines of the chest, and pressed all the harder. Slowly, but then more swiftly, the door began to swing open. Gotrek gave a final push, then leapt back up to his chest, and Felix heard hoarse breathing coming through the wood.

The door opened all the way with a shuddering thud that reverberated through the water and they were free. The raft shot ahead, the momentum almost dragging them across the antechamber towards the archway. They slowed by the time they reached the stairs, and began to ascend. After the first few steps, Felix noticed that the front of the raft started to angle up – only natural as they were on stairs – but alarming, as he heard the heaps of treasure above him shift, and a stream of bubbles escaped under the leading edge of his chest.

He heard another curse from Gotrek's chest, then an angry slap.

'Crouch down, manling!' came Gotrek's blunted voice. 'Crawl! Tell the elf!'

Felix rapped at the left side of the chest. 'Crouch down!' he shouted. 'Crawl!' Then he started pulling down on the rope that underslung the chest. To his relief, the elf did the same, and the raft's angle slowly evened out again. Felix, Gotrek and the elf began crawling up the stairs like turtles sharing the same shell.

At the first landing, Felix cautiously rose again. Fortunately, both the stairs and the landings were built on a grand scale, and they had no trouble manoeuvring around to start crawling up the next flight.

By the time they reached the entry chamber, the air inside the chest was rank and humid and thin. Felix tried to stop his heart from pumping in panic. It would be the cruellest of jokes if, after all of Gotrek's genius invention, they died of asphyxiation just short of the surface.

They pushed quickly across the entry hall. Felix had a momentary flash of panic as he remembered that Max had closed the palace doors, and he ducked down into the water to look ahead. He needn't have worried. The doors lay, splintered and bent on the marble floor, ripped off their hinges by the wall of water that had rocked the palace. Felix and the others walked over their twisted remains, then out onto the wide front steps, where Gotrek banged on the chests for them to stop.

'Drop the armour!' he called. 'Pass it on!'

Felix rapped on the high elf's side of his chest. 'Drop the armour! Pass it on!' He reached down into the water and undid the belt that held the elaborate elven ceremonial armour around his waist. It dropped away and he felt his toes rise off the steps.

Beside him, the Slayer's thick legs disappeared again and he heard heavy thuds and clunks above him. He looked up, then down as something bumped his boot. One of the treasure chests was settling down sideways on the steps, spilling bubbles and golden treasures.

A thud to the rear of the raft told him that Gotrek was being careful to dump their ballast in a way that wouldn't raise one side of the raft before the others.

And the raft was indeed rising. Felix was busy thinking how much treasure was being lost forever, and didn't notice at first, but then he was up to his chin in the water instead of his chest. He caught at the underslung rope and pulled himself up into the chest again as his feet floated off the steps. After another second he heard a splash and a gasp and a smug chuckle from Gotrek's chest. The Slayer had reason to be proud. Everything he had planned seemed to be working.

Felix tried to look down at the city as they rose, but couldn't see any distance through the ripples on the surface of the water in the chest, so he took a breath and ducked his head under again.

The sight below him was an eerie wonderland. What had looked like a sad, crumbling relic of lost glory when exposed to the air and the harsh light of day was, by the light of Max's glowing globe, a beautiful blue dream of ruined towers and swaying seaweed taller than cedars. The coral and the strange undersea plants which had looked so dull and dry out of the water were now bright and lurid. Things like jewels glowed in the shadows with their own luminescence. It was a city where mermaids should live.

He pulled himself back into the air of the chest, gasping as his lungs burned, and found that the air within was hardly enough to give him relief. The spots in front of his eyes remained, and the blood pounded against the roof of his mouth, demanding to be fed.

He clung to the rope, trying to breathe as shallowly as possible and praying for the raft to rise faster. How deep was the city below the waves? A hundred feet? A hundred yards? A hundred fathoms? He had no idea. Deep enough that no sailor had ever seen or suspected the elven towers below.

The black spots began to crowd his eyes. His fingers tingled with pins and needles. He couldn't feel the rope and had to look to be sure he was holding it. Then his heart leapt with hope. The sea around them was becoming brighter and Max's light paler. They must be nearing the surface. He could hold on a little longer knowing that.

Then something heavy pushed past his legs. At first he thought it was Gotrek, heading for the back of the raft for some reason, but when he looked down he saw a thick grey trunk and a sharp tail. His air-starved mind took a second to put those things together, and then he gasped.

A shark!

Just as the realisation came to him, he heard a muffled scream from behind. He dropped his head down into the water and looked back.

Beyond the kicking, dangling limbs of his companions, a shark the size of the *Pride of Skintstaad's* long boat had an elf warrior in its jaws and was shaking him back and forth violently. The elf's limbs flopped like a doll's as plumes of red billowed from his body.

Felix fumbled for his sword, holding on to the rope with one hand. He looked towards Gotrek. The Slayer was in the water too, readying his axe and kicking towards the shark as Rion and the other warrior drew their swords and guarded Aethenir. Max and Claudia looked like they were trying to crawl up into their chests. Then Felix saw something beyond and below them that stopped his heart. Rising up from the murky, tower-pierced depths were more moving shadows – a whole school of sharks. Manann preserve us, he thought, we're all dead.

Gotrek caught the shark by the tail and swung his axe, burying it in the creature's slate-coloured side. Blood blossomed into the water and the shark flinched and spun, dropping its mangled prey to face this new threat. It lunged at Gotrek with a mouth the size of a rain barrel. Gotrek kicked up, trying to get out of the way, and the thing butted him in the stomach with its snout, smashing him back twenty feet. Felix slashed at it uselessly as it rushed past, and saw, to his horror, that a smaller snout was growing from the side of the shark's head, complete with eyes and mouth, and its needle teeth were clamped down on the golden bracelets on the Slayer's left wrist. Was not even the sea free from the taint of Chaos?

Through a storm of black spots, Felix watched as the Slayer rained blow after blow on the head of the massive grey monster. The other sharks were close enough now that Felix could see their beady eyes gleaming through the murk. Rion and his last elf stayed close to Aethenir and turned towards the monsters as their dead comrade spun lazily down and away, red blood and white and green surcoat trailing gracefully behind him. Some of the sharks turned towards him, but most came on.

Suddenly Felix felt the rope go slack in his hand. He looked up, frightened. The raft had stopped rising. Had they hit some obstruction? Was something holding it down? Then he saw the dapple and shine of sunlight on water. They were at the surface!

Every fibre of his body screamed for him to climb to the air, but he couldn't leave the others to the mercy of the sharks. He looked back and saw Rion and his last elf pushing Aethenir to the edge of the raft. Max was doing the same for Claudia. Felix clambered hand under hand to them and caught the seeress's other arm. He and Max reached the side and lifted her up so that her head broke the surface. Felix's face hit the air a second later. He took one gasping, glorious breath, saw that Claudia was doing the same, then ducked back down and grabbed her left leg as Max grabbed her right. Together they raised her up until her torso flopped on top of the raft.

Felix looked back towards Gotrek. The Slayer had hit some vital spot on the shark and it was flipping and flailing down through the water, a curling column of blood erupting from its side, while Gotrek frog-kicked back towards the surface, his left arm also spewing blood.

Half the oncoming sharks turned towards their wounded cousin but the rest still came on. Felix looked around. All he could see were the flailing legs of the others clambering onto the raft. He joined them, kicking up out of the water and gripping the soggy carpet with desperate fingers. He could feel the wound Aethenir had just healed ripping internally as he humped himself up. Max was crawling out beside him, hampered by his waterlogged robes. Rion and the other elf were rolling Aethenir up onto the chests by brute force. Felix flopped himself out at last and immediately turned back to the water. Gotrek's head broke the surface and he sucked air as he kicked forwards, chopping his axe into top of the raft to try to pull himself up. Felix saw deep gashes in the Slayer's left wrist as he rushed to help. Half the gold bracelets upon it had been crushed so badly by the shark's bite that they pressed deep into his flesh. Felix grabbed Gotrek by the shoulder, and hauled at him. The Slayer surged up and crashed to the carpet, breathing deeply.

'Friends, help me!' called Aethenir.

Felix and Max crawled to where the high elf and the last elf warrior were trying to pull Rion out of the water. Felix caught him under the left arm, while Max grabbed his right.

But suddenly the elf captain jerked down in the water, nearly torn from their hands. He gasped, his eyes bulging.

'Rion!' cried Aethenir.

Gotrek joined them and all pulled desperately at Rion as something below tried to drag him down in the water. Then, with a horrible scream, the elf captain came up all at once and they fell back in a heap.

'Rion!' cried Aethenir again, scrambling up. 'Are you...?' His words ended in a cry of horror and he collapsed again.

Felix sat up to see what had happened. Rion's right leg was covered in blood. His left leg was... gone. The ragged stump pumped gore all over the wet carpet in thick gouts. Max and Gotrek cursed. Claudia looked away.

Aethenir crawled to Rion and cradled his head. 'Rion, I... I am sorry. I never...'

The dying captain reached up and clutched at Aethenir's sleeve. He looked hard into his eyes. 'Follow... the path of honour.'

'I will,' wept Aethenir. 'I promise you. By Asuryan and Aenarion, I promise.'

Rion nodded, apparently satisfied, then closed his eyes and sank back, dead. Aethenir sobbed. His last elf hung his head. Felix found a lump blocking his throat, and fought down the unworthy thought that he would rather that it had been Aethenir who had died and Rion who had lived, for the captain had been the epitome of elven virtue that Aethenir should have been.

The last elf warrior began to pull Rion's body to the centre of the carpet, but before he could take a step, a huge grey snout full of picket-fence teeth surged up out of the water and smashed the little raft, raising it out of the water and sending everyone flying. Felix crashed down on his wounded shoulder and nearly rolled off. Only Max's sprawled body stopped him. The wizard tottered at the edge. Felix grabbed him and pulled him back. Nearby, Gotrek and the elf warrior were doing the same for Claudia and Aethenir.

'Thank you, Felix,' Max gasped.

The survivors crawled to the centre of the pitifully small raft, while all around cruel triangular fins circled them and hidden predators bumped them from beneath.

Gotrek surged up, shaking his axe and beckoning towards the water. 'Come on, you skulking cowards!' he roared. 'I'll kill the lot of you!'

But then Claudia saw something that the others had been too preoccupied to notice.

'A... a ship,' she breathed.

Everyone looked up. Felix's heart pounded with fear that it was the dark elves' black galley swooping in to ram them again, but it was a different ship altogether – a fat merchant ship flying the flag of Marienburg, not half a mile away from them, its white sails a reddish gold in the late afternoon sun.

Felix jumped up, waving his arms. 'Ahoy!' he cried. 'Ahoy! Save us!'

Another bump from the sharks knocked him flat again, but the ship was turning their way.

'Praise be to Manann and Shallya,' whispered Claudia with tears in her eyes.

But suddenly Felix wasn't so sure the ship was salvation. The covers were being raised from the forward gun ports and the black muzzles of cannons were pushing into the sun.

'Oh come,' wailed Aethenir. 'This beggars belief! Does everyone in the world seek to kill us?'

'Bring 'em on,' said Gotrek.

Twin puffs of smoke obscured the prow of the ship. Everyone but Gotrek ducked. A second later, the boom of the guns reached them and two huge plumes of water shot up about a dozen yards away.

Felix let out a sigh of relief. 'They missed.'

'No,' said Max, looking around. 'I believe they hit what they intended.'

Felix followed the wizard's gaze. The shark fins were gone from the water, vanished as if they had never been.

'You think they mean to save us?' asked Aethenir.

'I hope so,' said Max.

And so it seemed, for no more shots came from the approaching ship, and it banked its sails and eased in gently to their side. Ropes dropped down to them. Felix and Gotrek and the elves grabbed them and pulled themselves tight to the ship's towering hull.

Felix called up to the deck above. 'Have you a ladder? We have women and wounded.'

A short round man leaned on the rail and smiled down at them as several dozen large and unsmiling men appeared at either side of him and aimed a profusion of pistols and long guns in their direction.

'Good evening, Herr Jaeger,' said Hans Euler. 'What a pleasure to once again make your acquaintance.'

ELEVEN

'So it's guns now, is it?' Gotrek growled at Euler. 'Couches weren't cowardly enough?'

Felix stepped quickly in front of the Slayer. 'Herr Euler. How unexpected.' He recognised some of the gun-wielding crewmen as Euler's massive footmen, who had since traded their black velvet doublets for leather jerkins and red bandanas.

'Yes, I suppose you would think so,' said Euler, pleasantly. 'But some friends of mine in the Suiddock overheard the sailors of your hired ship say you were going north seeking treasure, and I decided to come along and learn if this was true.'

'It isn't treasure we seek,' said Aethenir. 'It is—'

Max trod heavily on his foot.

'It had better be treasure, high one,' said Euler. 'Herr Jaeger owes me considerable recompense for the damage he and his uncouth friend did to my house. I intend to collect from him one way or the other.'

'Come down here,' said Gotrek, 'and you'll get more of the same.'

'Is it wise to threaten me, dwarf?' said Euler, raising an eyebrow. 'I can easily leave you here. There is blood in the water now. The sharks will soon return.'

'Herr Euler,' said Felix. 'There is indeed treasure. Look.' Felix turned and searched the rug they stood on. As he had hoped, a few spilled treasures remained. He picked up a gold and silver ewer of elven design that lay next to Rion's corpse, then turned and tossed it up to Hans. The merchant caught it and examined it with the practiced eye of the connoisseur. 'We had a holdful of it, but it was stolen from us.'

'Stolen by whom?' asked Euler. 'Where have they taken it?'

Aethenir opened his mouth to speak, but Max once again crushed his foot. The high elf glared at him.

'That,' said Felix carefully, 'I will not tell you until you allow us to come aboard. But they are not far away.'

Euler paused, greed warring with caution behind his eyes. He ran his hands over the fine filigree of the elven ewer and sighed. 'Very well, Herr Jaeger, but I must first receive vows from every member of your party that you will not harm me, my property or my crew, if you come aboard – particularly the dwarf,' he added, glaring at Gotrek.

Max, Claudia and the elves swore quickly enough, but Gotrek growled under his breath. Felix knew it was no small thing for a dwarf to make an oath.

'Make oath with a liar and a blackmailer?' he said. 'I won't.'

'Gotrek,' said Felix. 'We can't stay on this raft. We must follow your prophesied doom, remember?'

Gotrek grunted, annoyed. 'Very well, manling.' He turned and looked up at Euler. 'I will swear to do no harm to you, your property and your crew, unless harm is done to us first.'

'I swear to that as well,' said Felix.

Euler glared down at them, but finally sighed and waved a hand. 'Fine. I agree to those terms.' He motioned to his men. 'Throw down a ladder.'

A few minutes later they were all aboard, standing on the deck and shivering in the cold breeze. Claudia leaned against Max, her lips blue and her limbs shaking, but Euler had yet to offer them any food or shelter or dry clothes.

He stood in front of them with his arms crossed above his round belly. 'Now then,' he said. 'Who stole this treasure and where did they go?'

Felix looked at Max and Aethenir. They nodded.

'It was dark elves. They sank our ship and headed...' Actually he couldn't be sure where they had headed, but Euler had come from the south and would have seen them if they had gone that way, so north was a safe bet. 'They headed north. Our seeress can divine their location if,' he said pointedly, 'she doesn't die from exposure first.'

'Dark elves?' said Hans, hesitant.

His men looked uneasily at each other.

'Not a war ship,' said Felix hastily. 'A scout, smaller than your own ship.' He coughed, then lied through his teeth. 'They carry enough elven gold to repay you for your house and buy another just like it, as well as provide handsome shares for us and your men.'

Euler fingered his chin, thinking. 'One ship?' he asked.

'One ship,' agreed Felix.

'Any wizards?'

'Not a one,' said Felix. It wasn't technically a lie. Sorceresses were different than wizards, weren't they?

After another second, Euler nodded. 'Very well, Herr Jaeger, but if you have deceived me in this, I will find some other way to make you pay.' He turned to his men. 'Find quarters and food for them.' He turned away, then glared back at Felix. 'Bring me the word of the seeress as soon as she learns their location.'

Felix bowed. 'Of course, Herr Euler.'

When evening mess was served, Gotrek, Felix and Claudia brought their plates to Max and Aethenir's lantern-lit cabin to discuss their plans. Only the elves and the wizards had been given private quarters, probably more out of fear than hospitality. Gotrek and Felix had had to find places on deck to sleep, for none of Euler's surly crew would give up an inch of hammock space below.

Now they were all wedged into a cramped little cabin with two narrow cots along the side walls. Felix sat on an overturned bucket by the bulkhead. Gotrek stood near the door, legs braced wide.

'I don't believe,' said Max, between mouthfuls of beef stew and peas, 'that Herr Euler will be very pleased when he learns we have deceived him.'

Felix ate greedily as well. Whatever his shortcomings as a human being, Euler did not skimp when feeding his crew. The food was easily among the best Felix had ever had on board a ship.

'Who cares?' grunted Gotrek.

'*I* do, dwarf,' said Aethenir with a sniff. 'If this man is our only way home once we have wrested the harp from the druchii, then we cannot afford to anger him.'

Gotrek sneered as he shovelled a hunk of beef into his mouth. 'After what you did, you should be ashamed to go home. A dwarf would have shaved his head and sworn to die.'

'I am prepared to die,' replied Aethenir, raising his head and trying his best to look noble. 'But I am also prepared to live, and continue to make recompense for my crime.'

'Such a shame demands death,' said Gotrek.

Aethenir shook his head pityingly. 'That is why the dwarfs have fallen. Their greatest warriors are always shaving their heads and killing themselves.'

Gotrek lowered his wooden spoon, glaring dangerously at the high elf.

Max coughed. 'Friends, please, if we could return to the matter of Captain Euler. Some of us have no great shame to be expunged and would like to return from this journey alive. Have you any suggestions?'

For a moment there was nothing but the sound of chewing.

'We can't fight his crew without casualties,' said Max at last. 'And we can afford no more casualties.'

'Could we take the druchii ship?' asked Felix.

Max shook his head. 'There are too few of us to crew it.'

Claudia looked up from the bowl of stew that she cupped in both hands. Her eyes were still dull, but the colour had returned to her cheeks. 'Could... could we make sure the druchii ship sank?' she asked. 'So that Captain Euler would think the treasure sank with the ship, and would not know we lied?'

Felix nodded, approving. The girl was quick – mad, of course – but quick. 'It would be surer than facing them hand to hand.'

Aethenir, however, was frowning. 'Sink the ship? And lose the harp?'

'Isn't that the general idea?' growled Gotrek.

'Are you mad, dwarf?' cried Aethenir. 'A treasure like that cannot be lost again. There would be much we could learn from it.'

'Being a student of history, scholar,' said Max to the high elf, 'you must certainly know that treasures like that have a way of being used for terrible things, no matter the intentions of those who preserve them. Perhaps it would be best to let it sink.'

'But what guarantee is that?' the high elf asked. 'The druchii raised it from the sea once. What is to stop them from doing it again?'

'You won't tell them where it is next time,' said Gotrek dryly.

'Will you be silent, dwarf!' snapped Aethenir. 'I am doing what I can to amend the fault.'

'How would we do it, though?' asked Max, forestalling Gotrek's reply. 'Euler would be suspicious if he saw any of us deliberately trying to sink it.'

'Some spell, perhaps?' asked Felix.

Max's brow wrinkled as he thought. Claudia pursed her lips, but in the end they shook their heads and the others returned to thinking.

'Well,' said Max when no one came forwards with a suggestion. 'We will think more upon it. Go and sleep. Perhaps the answer will come to us in the morning.'

As he was following Gotrek up the stairs to the deck, Felix felt a hand on his arm and turned. It was Claudia. She looked up at him, biting her lip.

'I seem always to be apologising to you, Herr Jaeger,' she said finally.

'Er, there's no need,' said Felix, edging back.

'But there is,' she insisted. 'I was vile to you this morning, and I feel terrible about it. I snapped at you when you were only asking about my welfare.'

'Oh, it was nothing,' said Felix, taking another backwards step up the stairs.

'But it was. I could see how I had hurt you. And yet...' Her voice caught in her throat. 'And yet, when the waters came crashing in, you picked me up and carried me to safety, though you were grievously wounded. Such selflessness, such charity in the face of my rude behaviour...'

'Well, I couldn't let you drown, could I...?' Felix tripped as the next step caught his heel. He stopped himself as Claudia reached to catch him. They ended up very close.

She looked up at him with her wide blue eyes, smiling shyly. 'I have caused you considerable anger, pain and embarrassment, Herr Jaeger, but I believe you were beginning to warm to me before all this. Captain Euler has given me a private cabin. If you would like a more comfortable berth than the deck...'

'Ah, I wouldn't actually,' said Felix, sweat breaking out on his brow as he backed up onto the first step. 'Thank you all the same. As delightful as I find your company, I don't think that either of our reputations would survive a repeat of last night's events. Now, if you will excuse me...'

'It doesn't happen every night,' said Claudia, pouting.

'Yes, but if it did,' said Felix, still backing up. 'All in all, I think the risk is too great.'

Claudia's eyes began to burn into him with an unsettling keenness.

'Not that I don't appreciate the honour,' he continued. 'But, er, it's for the best, I think, don't you? Good night.'

And with that he fled to the main deck, feeling her angry gaze upon his back all the way.

Gotrek and Felix bedded down on the foredeck, laying out their bedrolls on either side of the cages that held the ship's goat and chickens. The barnyard stench was enough to make Felix's eyes water, but they were out of the way of the crew and, more importantly, for Felix anyway, out of Claudia's reach.

Felix stretched his cloak across the rail and the cages to make a little tent over his bedroll before he lay down, for the night was cloudy and cold and there was a chilling drizzle wetting the deck. The goat stared reproachfully out of its cage at Felix for a while, but then lost interest and curled up in its nest of hay.

Felix found it difficult to sleep. The day had been so full of terror and danger that he hadn't had a moment to think, but as he lay there, all the thoughts that fighting for his life had pushed from his mind now flooded back and preyed upon him. Was his father unharmed? Did he still live? What had the skaven done to him? He wanted desperately to get back and learn the answers to these questions, and yet, in the heat of the moment, he had convinced Euler to go the other way, chasing after the dark elf ship. Knowing the scope of what the sorceresses intended to do, he knew it was the right thing to do. The needs of the many outweighed his need to discover his father's fate, but it was still agony to be sailing in the opposite direction from Altdorf.

Part of his concern for his father was undoubtedly guilt. He had wished the old man dead on many occasions, and now that it was possible that he actually might be, Felix felt responsible, as if one of his petty wishes had come true. But it wasn't just that. He truly *was* responsible, for the skaven had undoubtedly visited his father while hunting for him and Gotrek. Gustav Jaeger – if he was indeed dead or hurt – was just another victim of the plague of vermin that had been trailing Felix since Altdorf – which was only a lesser strain of the epidemic of mayhem and bloodshed which followed Gotrek and Felix wherever they went. Truly, he thought, it was probably best for the Empire that we stayed away for twenty years. The land would likely have half its current population had we remained.

At last exhaustion won out over worry and guilt, and dragged him down into a dark and anxiety-haunted sleep.

He woke again, as he had the morning before, to nearby rustling in the dark, and at first his foggy mind thought that it must be Claudia again.

'Really, Fraulein Pallenberger,' he mumbled. 'Your tenacity is alarming.'

The rustling stopped and he heard a grunt that sounded very little like Claudia. He froze and opened his eyes. It was still night, and very dark, but a faint yellow flicker reached him from the lanterns hung on the main deck, giving him just enough light to see by.

The first thing that he saw was the goat, almost eye to eye with him, and staring at him again. Felix let out a relieved breath. It had only been the goat. Then he paused. The goat had not blinked. And it was lying on its side. And it had a rusted metal star sticking out of its throat. And blood was soaking the straw beneath it. From somewhere nearby came another muffled grunt and then thrashing and thumping sounds.

'Gotrek?'

Through the goat cage he could see flashes of violent movement on the far side. He heard hoarse cries of surprise from the main deck and looked that way. A crewman was slumped across the taffrail, three metal stars sticking from his back.

'Gotrek!'

Then he heard the rustling again, directly behind him. He twisted around. A black shape with glittering black eyes crouched by the rail, clutching something in its bony little hands. The hands darted forwards and the something was jerked down over Felix's head.

Felix gasped and inhaled a horrible smell – the smell from the glass globes the skaven had used. Immediately his head started to swim and his limbs began going numb. A horrible seasick nausea made his stomach roil. He cried out and swung his scabbarded sword. There was an impact and he heard a squeak and a thud. He snatched the bag off his head and staggered up, falling against the goat cage. His hands and face were sticky with the foul, narcotic paste.

The skaven assassin was up as well, and reaching towards him with hooked metal claws curling out over its true hands.

Felix threw an unsteady foot out and booted the creature in its narrow chest. It squealed and toppled backwards over the side of the ship. But three more skaven took its place, carrying ropes with what looked like fish hooks on the ends. The vermin seemed to distort and stretch as they approached. In fact, the whole ship was twisting and melting around him like it was made of hot wax.

Felix stumbled back, his gorge rising, as the world swam around him. On the far side of the goat cage, Gotrek was on his feet, legs braced wide, slashing around with his gore-smeared axe and struggling to pull a bag from his head while scrawny black shadows capered around him, swinging the barbed ropes at him. Unfortunately for the Slayer, one of the ropes was wound around his neck, pulling the bag tight. Incoherent roaring came from within. Three black forms lay dead at his feet, their guts spilling across the deck.

Sharp pains stabbed Felix's arms and legs, bringing him back to his own predicament. Fish hooks pierced his clothes. Another bit into his bare wrist as he tried to lift his sword to cut them away. The dancing black shapes wobbled and oozed like they were behind warped glass as they wrapped him up in a cocoon of ropes.

Felix surged towards them with the slowness of a dream, the acrid smell of the drug paste filling his nose. Pain erupted all over his body as the hooks dug deep into his flesh, but it felt like it was happening to someone else. The shadows squirmed out of the way, wrapping him tighter and dragging him towards the rail. He struggled feebly, fading in and out of conciousness, and seeing the chaos around him in a series of long blinks, surrounded by moments of blackness.

In one blink, he saw Euler's crew running in panic from skittering black shapes as big as dogs. In another blink, he saw spindly shadows carrying something wrapped in a bed sheet as the last elf warrior fought towards them through a crowd of spear-wielding ratkin. In a third blink he saw Gotrek drop to one knee, using his axe to hold himself up, the leather bag still tight around his head. In a fourth blink, he saw Claudia running out onto the decks in a nightdress, anguish in her eyes as Max tried to hold her back.

'I saw it!' she wailed, fighting to get free of him. 'I saw it! Oh, gods, forgive me!'

In the next blink the night clouds were above Felix, and he felt his feet go out from under him. The disorientation made him vomit all down the front of his chest. Hard little hands were lifting him over the rail, and he saw more rising to take him as he was lowered, upside down, towards the waves.

The last thing he saw before unconsciousness swallowed him was a glinting green shape humping up out of the water like the back of a verdigrised brass whale. The beast had a huge black blowhole in the centre of its back, and skaven were crawling in and out of it like ants.

* * *

Felix puked himself awake, the rising of his gorge so painful in his raw throat that it tore him from the leaden grip of unnatural sleep. It was the worst waking of his life.

The first thing he was aware of, beyond the dripping of sputum down his chin, was the throbbing in his head. It felt like someone was slowly and methodically cutting into the back of his skull with a carpenter's saw. His vision pulsed in time with the throbbing, going from dim to painfully bright with each thud of his heart. His mouth tasted like an orc's armpit, and his body ached from head to foot – most particularly his arms, which seemed to be drawn back so far behind his back that he could barely breathe. His ankles throbbed too, and he couldn't feel his feet at all. The pain of it all made him wish he had stayed unconscious.

When his vision cleared somewhat, he saw a puddle of filthy water below him, floating with what looked like a film of fur. The view did not improve when he raised his head. He was in some sort of low-roofed metal room, the walls and ceiling crawling with grimy pipes and strange brass reservoirs that sprouted taps and spigots from every surface. Every bit of it looked like it had been salvaged from a dwarf engineer's rubbish tip. Rats fought over something in one corner.

The room was nearly as hot as the pouring room at the Imperial Gunnery School at Nuln, but as humid as a jungle of the Southlands. Water sweated from the pipes and dripped from the ceiling, and from all around came a howling, booming roar that made the room – and Felix's head – vibrate horribly.

Then Felix heard a familiar grunt to his left. He turned his head and nearly vomited again, for the movement had triggered what felt like an avalanche of boulders inside his skull. When he could breathe and think again, he blinked away the tears and looked left.

Gotrek was beside him, his huge arms bound tightly behind him around a heavy, corroded brass pipe. His ankles had been bound as well, in such a way that his feet did not touch the ground. There were deep cuts and gouges all over the Slayer's body, and his beard was clotted with blood and filth. His head hung low, but Felix could see that he was conscious, and looking around the room with his single eye.

A third figure hung limply from another pipe beyond Gotrek – Aethenir. He was less battered and bloody than Gotrek, but just as covered in filth, and with a purple bruise on his left cheek that bled at its centre.

None of them had their weapons.

'So, you live, manling?' said Gotrek.

'Aye,' said Felix.

Gotrek looked up at him. Trails of bright green mucus ran from his nose and the corners of his mouth. 'I'm sorry to hear it.'

Flashes of the fight on Euler's ship returned to Felix's mind as he tried to work out why Gotrek would say such a thing – rat faces and ropes,

Max and Claudia shouting, the elf warrior fighting shadows, claws pulling Felix over the side.

'The others,' he said. 'What happened to them? Do they live?'

Gotrek shrugged. 'Alive or dead, they're better off than we are.'

'Eh? Why?'

'Because this will be worse than death.'

Aethenir jerked awake with a cry of fear, then lifted his head and blinked around. 'Mercy of Isha,' he moaned as he took in their surroundings. 'What hell is this?'

'It's a skaven submersible,' said Gotrek.

'A... a what?' asked Aethenir.

'A ship that travels underwater.' Gotrek snorted contemptuously. 'Damned vermin stole the idea from the dwarfs, and got it wrong, naturally – powered by warpstone instead of black water. I'm surprised it hasn't exploded.'

'Skaven again?' said Aethenir. 'But what do they want?'

Before Gotrek or Felix could answer, splashing footsteps made them all look up. Through a circular opening on the far side of the metal chamber came a figure out of a nightmare. It was a skaven – the oldest Felix had ever seen – and decrepit beyond imagining. Felix had seen undead who looked healthier. It was skeletally gaunt, with gnarled hands and matchstick arms sticking from the sleeves of its dirty grey robes. Its paper-thin flesh was stretched skeletally across its angular, spade-shaped skull, and its snout seemed to have rotted away, the area around its nostrils nothing more than a gaping hole of black, corrupted meat. Horrible cysts and warts grew from shrivelled, scabrous skin gone mostly bald with mange. Only a few clumps of wispy white fur clung to its head and arms.

It limped towards them with the aid of a tall metal staff topped with a glittering green stone. A retinue of other skaven followed it. Four big white brutes in polished brass armour, a crouching, scurrying ratman clad head to toe in black, a round, pop-eyed skaven that tottered unsteadily after the rest and seemed to have no tail, and behind them all, ducking to pass through the room's low round opening, a huge albino monster of the kind that Felix and Gotrek had fought when the skaven had attacked them on the beach. It went and sat in a corner, scratching itself. Aethenir moaned when he saw the thing.

The ancient skaven glanced at the high elf and paused. It muttered a question to the skaven in black. The assassin bowed obsequiously and replied in kind, motioning from Felix and Aethenir and back with nervous paws and pointing to their hair.

The old skaven raised its head and hissed a laugh, then snapped its gaze back to Gotrek and Felix. Its laughter ceased as if it had never been. It limped forwards and looked them up and down with glittering black eyes that contained all the life the rest of its body seemed to have been drained of.

'So long,' it crooned in a voice like a broken flute, as it smiled at them both with cracked yellow fangs turned brown with decay. 'So long I have waited for this day.'

TWELVE

Gotrek lunged forwards, snarling savagely, the violence of his motion making the pipe creak at its joins.

Felix strained forwards too, shouting as fury boiled within him. 'What have you done to my father, you filth?'

The ancient skaven leapt back from them, squeaking with alarm, and the rat ogre stood, rumbling dangerously and looking around. The seer turned to its minions and screeched in its own language, pointing a trembling claw at Gotrek.

'Answer me!' shouted Felix. 'What did you do to my father?'

One of the armoured guards backhanded Felix across the cheek with a mailed gauntlet as the black-clad assassin hurried towards Gotrek, taking a coil of thin, grey rope from its belt. The blow snapped Felix's head around and made his head ring with agony. He could feel blood trickling down past his ear. He decided he would wait to ask any more questions about his father until he had the ancient skaven at sword's point.

'Loose me, you skull-faced bag of sticks!' Gotrek grated.

He snapped at the assassin with his teeth as it wound the rope tightly around his chest and shoulders and the pipe, and the old skaven squealed orders from a safe distance. Aethenir stared around at all this as if it might be some strange nightmare.

The assassin hauled at Gotrek's ropes until Felix saw the thin strands bite deep into the Slayer's flesh, drawing blood in places, then it tied them off and backed away. Gotrek struggled but couldn't move an inch. With a grunt he seemed to resign himself to his situation, conserving his strength.

The old skaven breathed a phlegmy sigh of relief, and stepped forwards again, gazing at them triumphantly.

'My nemeses,' it whispered. 'At last I have you in my claws. At last you will pay for all the indignities you have heaped upon me.' It hissed, like steam from a kettle. 'Horribly, you will die, yes-yes, but slowly, slowly. First, you will pay for all the long years I have suffered by your cruel schemes.' The mad ratman's eyes shone with wild glee. 'For every defeat, a snip-cut. For every setback, a blood-bruise. For every misery, a bone break.' It stepped closer, its tail and its frail limbs twitching with fevered excitement, until Felix could smell its acrid breath with each whispered word. 'You will beg-beg for mercy, my nemeses – but to no avail.'

'But...' said Felix, completely at a loss. 'But, who are you?'

The ancient skaven stopped. It blinked and stepped back. 'You... you know me not?'

Felix looked to Gotrek questioningly.

The Slayer shrugged. 'They all look alike to me.'

Felix turned back to the skaven and shook his head.

The ratman staggered back, eyes rolling, and collided with its tailless servant. The servant squeaked and the ancient whirled on it, swiping at it with its staff and spitting shrill abuse. The servant cringed back, then scurried unsteadily out of the chamber, leaving the old skaven screeching after it. The rat ogre lowed anxiously and thumped the deck with its huge paws.

The skaven spun back towards its captives again, shaking with rage and tearing at the few tufts of fur on its skeletal head. 'Madness! Madness! Can it be possible that you do not remember me? Can it be possible that you have masterminded my failure-fall by accident? Did you not destroy my works in the Nuln warren, oh those many years gone by? Kill-killing my plague priests, burn-smashing my gutter runners and my engineers, killing even my first gift of Moulder?' It clenched its paws in rage. 'Close-close I came to killing you then, in the brood queen's burrow. But for that cursed man-mage, my torment would have ended before it had begun!'

Felix gaped, wide-eyed, remembering. This was that skaven? The ratkin sorcerer who had attacked them during Countess Emmanuelle's costume ball twenty years ago? The one Doctor Drexler had saved them from? It was impossible! Surely skaven didn't live that long. It had been ancient then. How old must it be now? And what sustained it?

Felix glanced at Gotrek. The Slayer was glaring at the skaven with new loathing, and straining harder against the cruel ropes.

The skaven paid neither of them any attention. It continued gibbering away, pacing back and forth before them, its limbs and tail atremble, lost in its memories. 'Did you not then follow me north, foiling my every attempt to capture the earth diggers' flying machine? Did you not twist-taint my servant-slave and turn him against me when you flew to the Wastes? Did you not rip-take the machine from me when my magic had it in its grip?' The creature clutched its forehead. 'Impossible! Impossible that you do not know me! Impossible that all is by chance! My whole life! My whole *life*!'

With a whimpering wail, the old skaven began to scrabble furiously at its robes, checking pockets and sleeves, and finally raised a small stone bottle in its shaking paws. It pried out the stopper, tapped a mound of glittering powder in the hollow between its thumb and foreclaw, then inhaled it through the ragged wet hole that served it as a nose.

For a moment after it had ingested the stuff, the skaven shook even worse than it had before, and its escort of armoured troopers took a nervous step back, but then, with a final seismic shake, the tremors stopped and it stood straight, taking a deep, if thready, breath.

It turned back to them, calm and composed, a stream of blood and mucus trickling unnoticed from its nose-hole as it glared at them with eyes that blazed with green fire. 'If that is the case, then my shame-rage is even greater, and therefore so will be your suffering. You will know agony-fear that no overdweller has ever endured, and yet by my magic you will heal to be tortured again-again, until you share all of my torture despair–'

'Ah, your pardon, ratkin,' said Aethenir, his voice quavering. 'But, does this mean that you have captured me by acci–'

'You dare to interrupt?' squealed the skaven, snapping around. 'I am speak-speaking, miserable prick-ear!'

'Indeed,' said Aethenir. 'But, er, as your feud appears to be with my companions and not myself, perhaps you could be so gracious as to let me return to the ship upon which–'

'What do I care for your wishes?' screamed the seer. 'You are mine-mine to do with as I please!' It limped to the elf, looking him up and down and stroking its cankered chin. 'It was an accident that you were taken, yes-yes. Your misfortune to have yellow fur like the tall one. But never-never have I experimented on a prick-ear. Never have I put one through my mazes, or fed one with poisons. Never have I cut-snipped its flesh and examined its organs.' It leaned in, its ruined nose almost touching the elf's high-bridged one. 'You will be the first.'

Aethenir flinched away, gagging, as the skaven turned from him and chittered furiously at its escort.

'Just like an elf,' snarled Gotrek out of the side of his mouth. 'Only thinking of himself.'

'I do not think of myself,' said Aethenir, as one of the armoured guards scampered out of the room on the old skaven's orders. 'But of my duty. Did I not promise Rion that I would let nothing stop me from righting the wrong I have caused?' He ground his teeth. 'I must recover that terrible weapon or the destruction of Ulthuan will be upon my head. Surely a dwarf will not begrudge me doing all that I can to restore my honour?'

'Elves have no honour to restore,' snarled Gotrek.

Just then the old skaven turned back to Aethenir, its eyes gleaming. 'What-what? Terrible weapon? What is this?'

The elf's eyes went wide as the ratman advanced on him. 'I... I know not what you mean. I said nothing of any weapon. You misheard me.'

'I did not mishear,' said the skaven. 'No-no. I heard perfectly.'

Just then the tailless skaven returned, a box under one arm which appeared to be made entirely of bone, etched all over with crude-looking glyphs. The little creature hurried to the ancient, making trembling obeisances, and held out the bone box with quivering paws.

The old skaven turned the clasp of the box, which looked to have been fashioned from a human finger bone, and opened the lid. Inside it, Felix could see a terrifying collection of steel and brass tools, none of them very clean. The ancient ran a claw over them, then selected one and held it up. It looked like a scalpel, but with a serrated edge, and it was orange with rust. The skaven turned towards the high elf, showing its teeth in a travesty of a smile.

'Now, prick-ear,' it hissed. 'Now you will tell-tell what I misheard.'

Felix had to admit that Aethenir held out much longer than he expected, but in the end he cracked, just as Felix had feared he would. He remained strong through the knives and the saws and flames and the collar that fit over a finger and increased pressure on it with a screw until it snapped. He had even kept silent when they had fixed a cage around his head and filled it with diseased rats, murmuring only some endlessly repeated elven cantrip that allowed him to remove himself into some interior chamber of the mind so that the excruciations of his flesh did not reach him.

Felix looked away when torture began, though hearing the sounds was nearly as bad as watching. The clever skaven was serving a dual purpose with its treatment of the elf, extracting information while at the same time attempting to build terror in the hearts of those who would next face its ministrations. Felix couldn't speak for Gotrek, but the ploy was working on him. With every moan and scream that came from the elf, cold dread dripped into Felix's heart. He could feel every cut, anticipate every twist of the screw. He wanted to scream, 'Tell him! Tell him!' to make it stop.

Of course, it would be worse when the skaven started on him and Gotrek, for the seer wanted no information from them. There would be nothing they could tell it to make it stop. Their torture itself was the creature's goal, and Felix could think of no way to escape it.

It was when the wizened ratkin attacked Aethenir's mind directly, dabbing a glowing paste of warpstone in his held-open eyes and then blasting him with spells that brought the poor elf screaming out of his mental stronghold, that he finally broke, whispering and weeping words in the elven tongue that Felix was glad he couldn't understand.

'Make them stop,' he whimpered finally to the skaven sorcerer. 'Make them go away. They are eating my knowledge... eating it.'

'I will banish them if you speak-speak,' said the skaven.

And at last Aethenir spoke, weeping as he did. 'It is called the Harp of Ruin,' he moaned, as Gotrek snarled curses at him. 'A weapon that can cause earthquakes... tidal waves... raise valleys and lower mountains. The druchii mean to use it on fair Ulthuan.'

The old skaven stared past the elf as it digested this information, scratching distractedly at a patch of scaly skin on its withered neck as it mused. 'A great weapon indeed,' it said at last. 'What the skaven might do with such a weapon. What *I* might do with such a weapon! The warrens of the overdwellers I would crash low, and raise-lift skaven cities in their place! I would show the council the greatness of my power! They would bow-scrape before me! At last I would rise-return to my true stature!'

Its eye refocused on Aethenir. 'Where is this harp?' it snapped. 'Quick-quick! I must have it!'

The high elf looked like he was going to resist again, but the ancient had only to raise a hand that glowed with green fire and he spoke again, babbling in his fear. 'A druchii ship takes it north. Six powerful sorceresses guard it. Their destination may be Naggaroth, or Ulthuan itself.'

The skaven nodded and began to pace. 'The ship I spied. Small-small, easily taken. But six sorceresses.' It looked hesitant. 'The prick-ears are great in the ways of magic. Equals nearly of the skaven. The whirlpool. Could even I have created such a...?' It shook its head, as if banishing the thought. 'How to accomplish this without risk-pain to myself. There must some trick weapon I could deploy that...' its eye fell suddenly on Gotrek and Felix. It paused, looking at them appraisingly, then turned away again, angry.

'No,' it said. 'Never-never! Not when I have them at last. I have waited for this too long. They are mine, mine, to do with as I wish.' It looked at Aethenir. 'And yet... and yet will vengeance win me power? Is it better to use them as tools to reclaim my former position? Better, isn't it, to set them against my enemies as my enemies once turned them against me? Yes-yes! That is the skaven way! They will smash-kill the tainted prick-ears, and I will pluck pick the harp from the wreckage.' It looked at its captives and a hissing giggle escaped it. 'You will be the cheese in the trap!'

It turned to its guards and chittered something to them in its own tongue. They bowed and went to a metal locker in one corner of the room.

When they turned back to the prisoners they held leather sacks, crusted on the edges with green muck.

* * *

Felix opened his eyes, then blinked with shock. There were white clouds above him, drifting across a blue sky. He felt a cool breeze on his cheek, and a gentle rocking as if he were in a hammock. This was a decided improvement on the humid skaven torture chamber he had woken in last. Were they free? Had some incredible miracle happened? Had it all been a dream?

All at once the pain returned, worse than ever, blinding him with its savagery, and he nearly blacked out again. When he had mastered it, he raised his head like a man might raise a brimming mug, afraid the slightest motion would cause some of the contents to slop out. Again his vision was distorted, as if he was seeing the world through an imperfect mirror, and nausea and vertigo threatened to overwhelm him with each turn of his head.

He tried to sit up and realised that his hands and feet were still bound. With a lot of grunting and cursing he finally managed to get up on one elbow and look around. His heart sank.

They were indeed free. The gentle rocking he felt was waves, lapping at the sides of a small wooden rowboat. There were no skaven in sight. In fact there was nothing in sight. All he could see, in every direction, was endless cold grey ocean. Aethenir lay in the bottom of the boat, his head down, trussed as Felix was, but with Gotrek the skaven had taken no chances. He was still cocooned to the pipe that he had awoken on. It had been freed from its moorings and now lay across the rowing bench. The Slayer hung from it like a meaty, but particularly ugly, chicken on a spit.

'The knife,' the Slayer rasped.

'Eh?' said Felix, looking around. 'What knife?'

A curved dagger, rusted and filthy, had been stabbed, point first, into the edge of the boat. It pinned a piece of vellum to the wood.

Felix flopped over painfully and began wiggling it from the wood.

'Don't drop it,' said Gotrek.

'I won't,' said Felix, then dropped it. Fortunately it clattered into the boat instead of out. The folded vellum fluttered down next to it. Felix picked up the vellum and unfolded it. He frowned.

'What is it?' asked Gotrek.

'A note.' Felix struggled to read the jagged script. 'Druchii… coming. Fight… well.'

Felix groaned, then scooped the dagger up and started towards Gotrek. Humping across a wobbling boat with one's wrists and ankles tied and a knife in one's hands was no easy task, and more than once he fell forwards and nearly impaled himself before he reached Gotrek and began sawing.

'Cowards,' he said as the strands of rope began to part. 'Wouldn't free us even though we were unconscious.'

'Aye,' said Gotrek. 'They lead from the back.'

'This time they lead from under the water.'

After another minute of sawing, the heavy ropes came free, and Felix moved to the thin grey cord. This parted more quickly and soon Gotrek thudded heavily to the bottom of the boat. He grunted, then closed his eye and lay where he had fallen, massaging his cruelly abraded arms and flexing his fingers to get the blood back into them.

Felix turned to Aethenir and began sawing at the ropes that encircled his wrists. He winced when he looked at the elf's injuries. Aethenir looked as if he should be dead. The old skaven had robbed him of his beauty and done terrible things to him. His face was a mass of cuts, his nose was broken and both eyes blackened, the skin of his right forearm was black and blistered from fire, the pinkies and middle fingers of both hands bent at unnatural angles, and Felix knew that more atrocities were hidden beneath the elf's blood-smeared robes.

Aethenir twitched and whimpered as his last rope fell away, then opened his eyes. 'The fiend has killed me,' he moaned.

'He would have if you had any honour,' said Gotrek from where he lay. 'Instead, you talked.'

Felix scowled at that. Gotrek's words seemed a bit unfair. The elf had held out a long time – longer than he would have. He wasn't sure he could have stood half what the elf had endured, but he hesitated to say anything. Gotrek would just think him weak.

Though he was free, Aethenir continued to lay in a stupor, so Felix put the knife between his knees and tried to saw through his own wrist cords.

'I'll do that, manling,' said Gotrek.

Felix looked around. The Slayer was sitting up and rolling his shoulders. The marks the ropes had left on his arms, chest and wrists looked like deep scars, but there was colour in his hands again.

He crawled to Felix and took the knife, then cut swiftly through his bonds. Felix hissed in agony as the blood rushed back into his fingers. The pins and needles were more like daggers and spikes. He couldn't imagine how much pain Gotrek must have been in when all his ropes had come off, and yet the Slayer had shown no emotion or discomfort at all.

'Where are we?' murmured Aethenir, blinking up at the sky.

'You got your wish, high one,' said Felix. 'We are free.'

Aethenir raised his head and looked around. He moaned and lay back. 'But... where are the druchii? Where are the skaven?'

Felix reached a tingling hand to the vellum note and handed it to the elf. Aethenir took it with his three unbroken fingers and read it. He sighed, disgusted.

'And do they think we will win their battle for them like this?' he asked. 'Have they even given us weapons?'

'You're lying on them,' said Gotrek.

Aethenir and Felix looked down. There was a lumpy canvas sack under the elf, also tied up securely.

'Not taking any chances, were they?' said Felix.

He took the knife from Gotrek and cut open the sack. Inside it were Karaghul, Felix's chainmail and Gotrek's rune axe, as well as all their belts, clothes and packs. There was also a slim elven dagger that Felix had never seen Aethenir draw.

After that there was little to do but prepare themselves for the arrival of the druchii. Aethenir summoned his magic and did his best to cleanse and heal his and Felix's wounds. When he took off his robe and shirt to attend to the wounds the skaven seer had given him during its interrogation, Felix had to look away, and found he had to reappraise once again his estimate of the elf's fortitude.

Aethenir's spells of healing were not as powerful as before, but they closed up most of the open wounds and burns on his face and torso, and eased Felix's aches considerably. The elf's four mangled fingers however were too badly broken for him to fix with spells, so Felix helped him set and bind them with canvas from the sack that had held their weapons. The elf took the manipulation of his bones with closed eyes and gritted teeth, but neither cursed nor wept. Gotrek refused to be magicked and just washed his cuts and bruises in the ocean.

Felix mopped his face clean the same way, hissing as the salt water attacked his wounds. He rinsed out his doublet and cloak too, as they were filthy with muck from the skaven ship, then put them on and pulled his chainmail over them, so that he would be ready when the druchii came.

Then they settled in to wait.

And wait.

After an hour of nothing, they discovered that the skaven had not provided them with water or food, nor oars. Felix had a little water in the skin he'd had when the vermin had captured him, but that was all.

'So,' said Aethenir, sighing. 'We will go into battle hungry and athirst, and if the druchii fail to see us and sail by, there will be no battle at all, and we will float here until we die of starvation.'

'I'll kill you long before that,' muttered Gotrek, then turned away and stared out to sea as the high elf glared at his back.

Felix had nothing to add, so he looked off in the other direction and tried to pretend he wasn't thirsty.

It had been mid-afternoon when they had regained consciousness on the boat, and still no ship had appeared from any direction as they watched the sun set in the west and a thick fog roll in from the north on the back of a cold breeze. An hour later, with the light fading to purple, the fog wrapped its cold, clammy arms around them and they could see no more than twenty feet from the boat. Then darkness fell completely and they couldn't see at all. The druchii ship could have passed within spitting distance of them and they would never have known it.

Gotrek took first watch, and Felix and Aethenir curled up to sleep as best they could in the bottom of the boat.

After a surprisingly deep sleep, Felix woke to Gotrek tapping his shoulder. 'Your watch, manling,' he said.

Felix grunted and pushed himself up, hissing at the stiffness in his limbs. He felt miserable. Every part of his body ached. His muscles were sore from the fighting and the swimming and from being tied up for so long, his head still hurt from the skaven's horrible sleep drug, his lips were cracked and bleeding, his tongue thick from lack of water, and he was starving.

He pulled the cork from his waterskin and took a sip, but only a small one. There was less than two cupfuls left, and it might have to last, well, forever.

He looked around him as Gotrek lay down in the back of the boat. The fog had thinned somewhat, becoming a fine mist that he could see into for nearly forty feet, with thicker drifts roiling slowly by in patches that glowed a sickly green in the dim light of Morrslieb, shining almost full above them. The sea was dead calm, as if the fog had pressed it flat, and the silence was eerie, just the soft slap of wavelets on the hull of the boat and, after a few moments, Gotrek's snores.

Felix sat on the oar bench and put his sword on his knees, ready, and tried not to think about how hungry he was. It was impossible. His mind drifted back to grilled chops in taverns, to pheasant in noble houses, to rabbit stew and wild vegetables on the march, to grilled sea bass in Barak Varr, to strange spiced dishes in the lands to the east. He cursed as his stomach growled.

It had only been a day since he'd eaten last. He had gone longer than that. Much longer. And longer without water too. Now his mind flashed back to a less savoury time – the brutal brazen sun, the sea of sand, hiding in the shade of the ancient statues and waiting for the cool of night.

He cursed again. Now he wanted a drink! His hand reached for his water skin. Just one more sip, just to rinse the taste of hot sand from his mouth. But no, he mustn't. He must save it for morning when the sun would rise again.

He leaned forwards on his knees and stared out into the misty nothingness. The curls of fog suggested menacing shapes in the darkness, but then dissolved into nothing again. He sighed. It was going to be a long night.

Felix jerked his head up and blinked around, instantly angry with himself as he realised that he'd fallen asleep. It couldn't have been for long. The sea hadn't changed, the mist hadn't changed, and Morrslieb was still in the sky. But something had woken him up. What had it been?

He turned on the bench, checking behind him. Gotrek and Aethenir were both asleep, and there was no black ship prow looming behind the little boat.

Then he heard it again – a quiet splash somewhere far off in the fog. He looked in the direction he thought the sound had come from, but he could see nothing, just the drifts of mist billowing silently by. What was it? It could have been anything – a wave, a fish breaking the surface. A…

'Hoog!'

Felix froze. That had not been a fish. A seal perhaps, but not a fish. Once again he tried to pinpoint the far-off sound, but he could not. It had seemed to echo from every direction at once. He stood, drawing his sword. At least it had been far away. Perhaps whatever it was would miss them in the fog and pass on.

The hooting came again, closer now! Much closer! He stepped over the oar bench to Gotrek and Aethenir and shook them, whispering in their ears.

'Gotrek, high one, wake up. Something said "hoog".'

Gotrek grimaced and yawned. 'What's that, manling?' He scratched his chin through his beard.

Aethenir rubbed his eyes with his splinted fingers and groaned. 'Something said what?' he murmured.

'Hoog!'

Gotrek and Aethenir leapt up at the sound, almost capsizing the boat. Gotrek had his axe in his hands. Aethenir clutched his delicate dagger. Felix gripped his sword. They stared out at the fog.

The high elf swallowed, his eyes wide. 'I know that sound,' he hissed. 'I have read a description of it in the diaries of Captain Riabbrin, hero of the Lothern Sea Guard. It is the hunting cry of the menlui-sarath, used as scout beasts by the druchii corsairs.'

'The what?' asked Felix. Was that something moving in the fog? He couldn't be sure. He strove to listen, but the pounding of his heart was too loud.

'The menlui-sarath,' repeated Aethenir. 'The hunter of the deep. A sea dragon. If such a thing is abroad, then the black ships cannot be far behind.'

'HOOG!'

They spun around. Out of the fog loomed a towering silhouette, a supple swaying trunk like a swan's neck, but as thick around as a tree and rising higher than a house.

'By Sigmar, it's enormous,' said Felix.

'And still only a juvenile,' breathed Aethenir. 'The adults are large enough to pull ships.'

Perched on top of the supple trunk was an angular, asymmetrical mass that Felix at first mistook for some gigantic misshapen head. Then it drifted closer and he could see that the silhouette was not just a beast, but a beast and rider.

The beast was a sleek silver-green serpent with a blunt reptilian head the size of a cask of ale, and a chin full of dangling, tentacle-like feelers. Its glistening hide was made of thick overlapping plates, and rippling ribbons of fin ran down its flanks. Felix hated it on sight. The rider was a dark elf in black plate armour, sitting on an elaborate saddle strapped just behind the monster's head. She carried a long curved sword in one hand, and a strange conical shield in the other, like the pointed roof of a castle tower, made of polished steel.

The rider saw them at the same moment as they saw her, and her reaction was instantaneous. She shouted a harsh cry and jabbed her spurred boots into the sea dragon's neck.

With another deafening hoot, the beast's head shot down like a fist, straight at the boat. Felix and Aethenir leapt aside, yelping. Gotrek swung as he dived the other way. Felix couldn't tell if he connected, because the dragon smashed its huge skull into the boat and sent them all flying in an explosion of water and spinning timbers.

Felix came down on something hard, then bounced off it into the water. His armour and heavy clothes dragged him down and he grabbed desperately at what he had hit. He caught it and held on. It was the boat – half the boat, rather – the prow end, upside down in the water. He sucked in a gulp of air as he tried to pull himself on top of it. Aethenir thrashed and coughed in the water beside him. Felix caught him by the collar and pulled him to the broken boat. The elf clung desperately, panting and wheezing. A few yards away, Gotrek clawed up onto the stern half of the boat.

Of the sea dragon and its rider, there was no sign except the ever-widening ripple where it had plunged beneath the sea.

'Where is it?' snarled Felix. 'I must kill it!' He found himself boiling with rage and righteous fury. 'On land or sea, dragons are the bane of mankind!'

'Herr Jaeger,' said Aethenir, still breathing hard. 'The runes of your sword are glowing.'

Felix looked down. Aethenir was right. The dwarf runes engraved along Karaghul's length, which Felix hardly noticed most of the time, were glowing with an inner light. He cursed. This was the source of his sudden hatred of the sea dragon. Once again, the sword was trying to take over his will, trying to force its purpose upon him. It hadn't happened often, but when it did, it infuriated him. His mind and his will were his own, and any attempt to wrest control from him was an intimate violation of his self.

On the other hand, he never fought better than when the sword awakened and he surrendered his will to it. He had killed the Chaos-twisted dragon Skjalandir with it, had he not? Of course, he had nearly died in the doing of that mighty deed, something that he didn't think the sword cared about in the least.

The sea dragon had still not reappeared. Felix, Gotrek and Aethenir looked around warily, dripping with freezing water. Had the dragon rider left them to drown? Had it decided they were too insignificant to fight?

'Gotrek,' called Felix. 'Are you all–'

With no warning, the end of the boat Felix and Aethenir clung to exploded upwards as the dragon's head smashed up through it from below. Felix and Aethenir pinwheeled through the air as the long neck shot up like a geyser. Felix came down hard, still clutching a splintered plank, and bobbed to the surface, gasping for breath, in time to see the massive beast looping back on itself to plunge at Gotrek, who balanced, legs bent, on the capsized stern of the boat, roaring a dwarfish challenge.

'Over here, damn you!' Felix cried, filled with the sword's purpose, but to no avail.

The rider tucked herself behind her conical shield, and dug her spurs into the dragon's flanks. The beast's battering-ram head rocketed down towards the Slayer. At the last second, he dived to the side, swinging his axe behind him.

Dragon and rider smashed down through the stern and disappeared into the water. Now Felix understood what the conical shield was for. It pushed the water aside so that the rider wasn't punched off the back of its mount every time it dived beneath the waves.

Then he noticed that the dragon seemed to have taken Gotrek with it. The Slayer had vanished.

'Gotrek?'

The serpent and rider shot up again. Gotrek came with them, his axe hooked behind the rider's leg. The rider slashed down at him with her curved sword and the Slayer blocked with his armful of gold bracelets, then grabbed the rider's leg and freed his axe.

The rider hacked down at him again, but Gotrek's weight on his leg ruined her balance and she missed. Gotrek swung the axe over his head and buried it in the rider's gut, punching through her armour with a bright clang.

The rider screamed and tumbled from the saddle. She and Gotrek splashed down in a spinning tangle and disappeared under the waves. The sea dragon plunged after them, roaring its anger.

Felix waved his sword at it. 'Face me, dragon!' he shouted.

The serpent ignored him, intent on killing he who had killed its master. It dived down into the water, then came up again, looking around. Gotrek bobbed up behind him, one arm over the remains of the rowing bench.

'Down here, sea wyrm!' he roared. 'My axe thirsts!'

The sea dragon howled and lunged down at him, jaws agape. Gotrek kicked aside, letting go of the bench and swinging his axe two-handed. There was a crack of impact and then both dragon and Slayer vanished beneath the water in a violent splash.

'Damn you, Slayer!' called Felix. 'The dragon was mine.'

Only echoes returned to him. The sea was quiet. The ripples were spreading and fading.

'Perhaps they have slain each other,' said Aethenir, looking around with worried eyes.

But then Felix noticed that the runes on his sword were glowing brighter. 'It's coming back!'

The sea dragon surged out of the sea right beside them, its scales flashing by so fast that they blurred. It thrashed its head back and forth like a terrier trying to kill a rat, and Felix feared the worst, but when he got a good look, he saw that Gotrek was not in its mouth, but hanging from the beast's back, one leg caught in a loop of its bridle, and flopping about like a banner in a high wind. The Slayer's axe was buried in the side of the sea dragon's snout, and it was this that was causing it to writhe so wildly.

It weaved towards Felix and Aethenir, and Felix kicked towards it, clinging to his plank.

'Yes! To me!' he cried, then slashed at it as it collided with him. Karaghul bit deep, cutting through the dragon's protective scales as if they were made of cheese, and opening it to the bone. Blood and black bile spilled from the gaping wound and the serpent howled in pain, turning to face its new attacker.

Felix roared up at it as it rose above him, its eyes meeting his for the first time. 'Come, drake! Your death awaits!'

Beside him Aethenir screamed. 'No, you lunatic! You'll be killed!'

Felix didn't care, as long as his blade got another chance to strike. The serpent reared back. Felix saw Gotrek catch its reins and begin to pull himself upright.

'HOOG!'

The head shot down at Felix like a ball from a cannon. He raised his sword, howling in anticipation. A hand grabbed his collar and jerked him back. The head smashed down into the water an inch from his chest. Even so, the momentum of the beast pulled him under and he spun in a jumble of water, bubbles and whirling timber.

The hand still had a hold of him when he came back, sputtering, to the surface. He turned to find Aethenir gripping him and a section of the broken rowboat.

'Interfering elf!' he spat, water shooting painfully from his nose. 'I nearly had it!'

'I saved your life,' said Aethenir.

'Did I ask for it?'

The elf shook his head, wonderingly. 'You're both mad.'

Just then, with an enraged 'HOOG!' the sea dragon exploded from the waves again, twisting and snapping at something on its back. Felix and Aethenir could see that it was Gotrek, his short, powerful legs clamped around the serpent's neck just behind its head, his axe raised high, roaring a wordless battle cry as water flew from his crest and beard.

Just as the sea dragon rose to its highest height, the Slayer slashed down and buried the axe's blade deep into its brain-pan, spraying blood in all directions.

With a last soft 'hoog', the fires died in the sea dragon's eyes. For a brief moment, as Gotrek struggled to wrench his axe free, it hung motionless in the air, then toppled, Gotrek still clinging to it, as slow and inevitable as a tree falling in a forest, right for Felix and Aethenir.

'Flee! Swim!' cried the elf, and kicked wildly while clinging to the timber.

Felix kicked with him. The serpent slapped down beside them with a smack that hurt the ears and pushed them forwards on a surging swell. Its huge body slipped swiftly beneath the waves, leaving little eddies and whirlpools in its passing. It also seemed to have taken Gotrek with it, for he was nowhere to be seen.

Felix turned in a circle as the seconds ticked past. Had the Slayer not managed to free his axe? Was he still caught in the beast's bridle straps? Had he found his doom at last?

But then, after it seemed that there could no longer be any hope, a familiar head broke the waves, gasping and choking and flipping its crest out of its eye.

'Gotrek! You live!' said Felix as he reached a hand out.

'Aye,' said Gotrek catching his hand. 'Worse luck.'

Felix pulled him to the floating plank and the three of them clung to it and just breathed for a while. With the death of the sea dragon, Karaghul's runes faded out, and so too did Felix's all-consuming hatred for dragonkind, to be replaced by sick fear at all the suicidal risks he had just taken. Had he really shouted in the dragon's face and waited for its attack?

He turned to Aethenir. 'Thank you, high one, for pulling me aside. And I apologise for insulting you.'

Aethenir waved a dismissive hand. 'You were ridden by the sword. I took no offence.'

Around them, the grey light of pre-dawn was beginning to push back the darkness. The mist continued to lift and the sea remained calm. The miserable night was over. Not that it mattered. Though they had survived the fight with the sea dragon, they were as dead as if it had eaten them, for without a boat, the cold of the sea would kill them long before their thirst or hunger ever did.

'Perhaps the skaven will save us,' said Aethenir. 'Perhaps they've been watching all along.'

Gotrek spat into the water. 'Saved by skaven. I'd die first.'

Then little more than a mile away, silhouetted against the pearl-grey horizon, Felix saw jutting black crags rising from the sea. 'An island!' he cried, pointing. 'Look! We're saved!'

The others followed his gaze and peered into the half-light.

Beside him Aethenir moaned. 'No, Herr Jaeger, that is no island, and we are not saved.' He shivered and lowered his forehead to the shattered plank. 'We are doomed.'

THIRTEEN

Felix turned to Aethenir, confused. 'What do you mean? Certainly it's an island. Look at it.'

The high elf shook his head. 'It is a Black Ark. A floating city, a piece of sunken Nagarythe held above the water by the profane magics of the druchii. It is a moving fortress from which the black ships of the corsairs spill to pillage and enslave. And it is coming our way.'

Felix blinked at Aethenir, aghast, then turned back to the island. Fear gripped his heart. It was closer now, much closer, and he had a sudden understanding of its scale. It rose hundreds of yards out of the sea, and must have been nearly a mile across. Towers and thick-walled fortifications jutted up all along the tall crags, and palaces and temples and citadels climbed steeply towards the centre, where a massive black keep glowered down on the rest of the island like a black dragon surveying its chosen domain.

Felix turned in the water, looking around for some escape. There was none. 'This is madness,' he said. 'We were after one tiny ship! The cursed skaven put us in the way of the wrong druchii!' He lowered himself again so that only his head showed above the water. 'Perhaps they won't see us. Perhaps they will think we are dead and pass us by.'

'No, manling,' said Gotrek. 'They will not.'

Felix looked at him. The Slayer's single eye blazed.

'This is what I have been waiting for,' Gotrek said, never looking away from the ark. 'This is the black mountain the seeress promised. This is my doom.'

And mine too, thought Felix. For if Gotrek met his death on that floating rock there was no way Felix would ever make it off alive.

As they watched, a piece of darkness broke off from the craggy island and became a black ship with a lateen sail.

'Are they looking for us?' asked Felix, swallowing.

'They are looking for the rider,' said Aethenir. 'They will have heard the beast's battle cries, and are coming to investigate.'

And so it seemed, for the sleek ship rowed straight for them while Gotrek chuckled under his breath.

'Once we kill these,' he said, 'we sail it back to the island. Then the real slaying begins.'

Felix looked at Gotrek agog. The Dwarf was serious. 'Putting aside that it may be difficult to kill a whole ship full of druchii, not to mention an island,' he said. 'Three men aren't enough to sail us there.'

'The galley slaves will row us back,' said Gotrek.

'And why would they do that?' asked Aethenir.

'To see their masters die.'

The ship was getting close now, slowing and arcing towards the wreckage. Gotrek watched it like a wolf eyeing an approaching sheep, seemingly unaware that he was the prey and the ship was the predator.

'Closer,' he murmured. 'Closer.'

Aethenir, on the other hand, seemed to be praying. Felix joined him.

The ship heaved to a considerable distance from them and sat in the water, drifting slowly. It was a low, evil-looking craft, with a blood-red sail, rows of sweeps and giant, bow-like bolt-throwers lining both rails. Felix saw a flash of reflection from the deck. Someone was observing them with a spyglass.

A muffled command echoed across the water and one of the bolt-throwers turned their way.

'They're going to fire!' cried Aethenir.

'Dive!' said Gotrek, and disappeared below the water.

Aethenir dived, but before Felix could follow there was a sharp clack, and something shot from the weapon. It wasn't a bolt. Halfway through ducking down, he paused to watch the strange, amorphous shape come towards them, twisting and blossoming as it came. A net!

Panicked, he let go of the floating timber and dropped under the water, then panicked again as he remembered he was wearing chainmail, and was starting to sink. He kicked and flailed desperately with his arms, clawing his way back to the surface, and finally caught a hold of something, but it wasn't the wreck. It was the net. He grabbed it gratefully anyway and pulled his face up to the air, sticking his head up through the weave of ropes.

Gotrek and Aethenir had risen too, and were also clinging to the net.

'To the edge,' said Gotrek. 'Before they draw it in.'

But as they tried to pull themselves along the underside of the net, they realised that their hands were stuck fast to the ropes they had first touched. They pulled and yanked, but it was no good. It was worse than tar, and it wasn't just their hands that were trapped. The strands that lay upon Felix's shoulders were stuck to his chainmail. A strand that had fallen across Gotrek's head was stuck to his scalp and his crest. Aethenir's long blond hair was caught in it, as were the sleeves of his robes.

Gotrek growled a curse as he tried to pull his hand away from the stickum. He could not. He brought a foot up and hooked it in the rope for leverage, then heaved mightily. After much straining and grunting, his hand tore free, leaving a patch of skin, but then his boot was stuck.

'Grimnir take all tricksy elves!' he cursed as he tried to free his foot. Without thinking, he grabbed the net for leverage and was back where he started. He roared with frustration.

The black hull of the corsair ship suddenly loomed up beside them, and ropes and grapnels snaked out from the deck and splashed in the water. The grapnels hooked the net and winches lifted it slowly clear of the water.

Felix, Gotrek and Aethenir came up with it, hanging at awkward angles and getting more entangled as more of the net touched their bodies and their clothes. Gotrek was the most tightly held, for he had struggled the most, and by the time the net had been swung over the deck, he was covered from head to toe in the sticky ropes.

As the winches lowered them to the deck, figures in ragged clothes spread out a canvas tarpaulin that shone greasily, and it was onto this that they were dropped – none too gently – on their faces.

A chorus of laughter rang out as they crashed down, and Felix turned his head to see that they were surrounded by tall dark elves in close-fitting grey surcoats, over which they wore heavy cloaks that looked as if they had been made from the hide of the sea dragon Felix and Gotrek had just fought. The corsairs looking down at them with sneering smiles on their long, gaunt faces.

'You'll be laughing with your necks when I get free,' snarled Gotrek from where he lay.

A pair of red-heeled boots strode through the crowd of legs and stood before them. Felix looked up. A tall druchii with an amused smirk on his lips looked down at him. He wore a red sash belted around his surcoat and his long, braided hair was pulled back with silver wire.

'What strange fish my net has caught,' he said in heavily accented Reikspiel. 'An Old World flounder, a cave-dwelling rock fish and an Ulthuan minnow – and none of them market fresh by the smell of them.'

'Free me and face me, you corpse-faced coward,' said Gotrek.

The dark elf's eyes widened in mock amazement. 'By the Dark Mother, a talking fish! And with such an ill-favoured tongue.' He stepped forwards delicately to the edge of the oiled tarpaulin and kicked Gotrek savagely in the cheek with his high heel.

Gotrek snarled and lunged, blood welling from a deep gouge, but trussed as he was, he could do nothing.

The druchii stepped back. 'I am almost curious enough to ask how three such strange companions came to be floating out in the middle of the sea alone, but not quite. No matter where you come from, you all go to the same place.' He turned away and said something to his lieutenants, waving a dismissive hand.

One of the lieutenants bowed and, in turn, gave orders to the ragged human slaves who spread the tarp, but then another corsair pointed at Gotrek and said something that caused the druchii captain to turn back and look at him again.

The crouching humans were padding towards the captives, holding strange objects that looked something like oil lamps, but the captain waved them back again. They shrank away as he began to circle the net, staring at Gotrek intently. Felix couldn't figure out what had caught his attention, but Aethenir understood the murmured exchanges between the druchii.

'He is interested in your axe, dwarf,' whispered the high elf. 'And your sword, Herr Jaeger. He recognises them as powerful weapons and knows collectors who will pay well to own them.'

Gotrek snarled at that. 'No one touches my axe. No one.'

But there didn't seem to be much he could do about it at the moment. The axe was on his back, and his arms were so entangled in the sticky ropes that he couldn't reach it.

After circling the net twice, the dark elf stepped back and waved the slaves forwards again. Felix thought he had never seen sadder-looking men in all his life – emaciated, dead-eyed creatures with patchy, close-cropped heads and permanently stooped shoulders. They came and crouched next to Felix, Gotrek and Aethenir, deftly avoiding the sticky ropes while they held up the strange lamps and began smearing black paste into a little metal reservoir above the flames.

'Brothers,' whispered Felix. 'Help us. Free us and we will free you. We will slaughter these slavers and return you to the Old World.'

The men didn't even turn their heads, just kept at their task as if he hadn't spoken. Wisps of smoke began to rise from the black paste as the little pan that held it heated up.

Felix tried again in the few words of Tilean he knew, and then in halting Bretonnian. The men made no response.

'Damn you, are you deaf?' snapped Felix. 'Do you not want to be free?'

'Leave them be, Herr Jaeger,' said Aethenir. 'They have been so long under the druchii lash that they have forgotten what freedom is.'

The smoke was rising thickly now from the black paste, and a sweet, cloying scent reached Felix's nose. His eyes watered. The slaves quickly covered the lamps with ceramic caps that looked like tobacco pipes with two stems. Felix had no idea what the strange devices were for until the slave who knelt next to him put one of the stems to his lips and pointed the other at Felix's face.

A stream of sweet smoke shot from the stem, right at Felix's nose. He pulled back and tried to turn his head, but the ropes held him too tightly. He couldn't get away from it.

'The black lotus,' said Aethenir, choking. 'They seek to drug us!'

Felix held his breath, but a second slave, a little boy of no more than nine or ten, reached forwards and pinched Felix's nostrils shut while the first punched him in the stomach. Felix gasped and sucked in an involuntary gulp of smoke. He choked and sputtered as the resinous poison filled his lungs, but then had to inhale again just to breathe, and took in more smoke. He could hear Aethenir and Gotrek coughing and cursing as well.

The third lungful was easier, and the fourth was actually pleasant, the smoke slipping silkily down his throat and spreading sweet languor through his veins. The cold and the discomfort of the ropes felt far away, cushioned by a delicious warmth that felt like the heat of a summer sun radiating from his lungs. By the fifth lungful he was straining forwards to catch as much of the smoke as he could.

Aethenir's choking protests quietened as well. Only Gotrek continued coughing and cursing. Felix wished he would stop. The Slayer's struggles were disturbing his lovely lethargy.

A moment later, Felix's pipe slave got up and went to blow smoke in Gotrek's face instead, as did Aethenir's. Felix was sad that the smoke was gone, and he was angry with Gotrek for being so greedy, but sadness and anger took too much energy to maintain, and he quickly let go of them, content to relax into the sluggish current of contentment that flowed through his veins.

After a while even Gotrek's struggles subsided, and then more slaves came, this time with buckets of some foul-smelling grease that they rubbed into the ropes to loosen their hold. Felix watched with idle interest as his sword was carried away, followed by Gotrek's axe. There was some sort of seismic convulsion behind him at this, and another when further slaves carried away the Slayer's golden bracelets, but both times the eruptions subsided again in a rumble of slurring curses.

Then the grease was rubbed on the rest of the ropes and Felix, Gotrek and Aethenir were pulled from the net. More slaves helped Felix to his feet and took off his armour, jerkin and shirt, then put shackles on his wrists and his ankles that were connected by a chain so short he couldn't stand upright. He thought the shackles were silly. He didn't want to go anywhere. He just wanted to lie down again. Unfortunately, they wouldn't let him. They locked his chains to a ring on the central mast and left him there with Gotrek and Aethenir. It wasn't comfortable, but he was too happy to care. He just stared ahead as the high crags of the black island loomed closer. It quickly filled his vision from edge to edge.

It must be the size of Nuln, he thought dreamily. He wondered if they had a college of engineering too. That would be nice.

After a time he could differentiate between the island's jagged grey granite cliffs and the towering black basalt walls that topped them. Tall, crenellated watchtowers rose up at every turn of the wall, each crowned with a halo of wind-whipped fire. For a moment Felix thought that they were going to crash right into the granite cliffs, and he giggled at the druchii's foolishness. They would smash their pretty boat. But then he saw that what he had taken for a dark shadow next to a craggy outcropping was actually the mouth of a black cave. Felix's head tipped back and back as the roof of the cave came closer and closer, then swallowed them entirely. For a while all was dark, and he found that restful, but then an orange glow appeared in the darkness before the ship, a flickering light that reflected on rough stone walls and a baroque filigree of stalactites that thrust down from the ceiling high above them.

Then the dark channel opened out into a vast underground bay, at the far end of which great fires blazed in giant braziers mounted on towers that rose above a long line of docks and wharfs. It reminded Felix of Barak Varr – not nearly as big, or as brightly lit, but just as full of ships. There must have been more than thirty low-slung galleys docked in the harbour, as well as many smaller ships and boats, including some that looked like Old World merchantmen. Felix thought the light of the flames dancing on the black water as their ship rowed towards the braziers was the most fascinating thing he had ever seen.

The Clan Skryre skaven at the periscope turned and bowed to Thanquol, who stood in the centre of the bridge of the mighty skaven submersible, trembling with excitement.

'They have been taken into the ark, grey seer,' said the sailor.

Issfet smiled up at Thanquol fawningly. 'It has happened just as you hoped, oh most geriatric of masters,' he shrilled.

'Yes-yes,' said Thanquol, rubbing his paws together. 'Now we must only be patient, for surely, where my nemeses go, ruin and confusion must follow.'

It had better, he thought darkly. For he had paid dearly for the use of the submersible, in oaths of alliance, promises of warp tokens and pledges of future services rendered, none of which he was in any position to deliver. If he failed to recover the Harp of Ruin, he was ruined.

By the time the dark elf ship docked, and Felix, Gotrek and Aethenir were prodded down the gangplank to the busy stone dock by spear-wielding druchii, the lotus smoke's sweet euphoria had soured and gone flat. The warmth that had filled Felix's veins had turned to a dull numbness, and his fascinated gaze had become a blank stare. It was hard to think, hard to remember to move until the butt of a spear thudded into his back. His feet, as he shuffled through the crowded streets of the cave-roofed port with the others, felt encased in mud, and he tripped often on the too-short chains that rattled between them. When his captors stopped to talk to guards who stood at either side of a great arch set in a rock wall, he stopped and stared straight ahead until they pushed him forwards again, too torpid to care about his surroundings.

He passed unseeing through wide, crowded corridors, looking neither right nor left. Only once did he look up, when he heard a garbled mumble from Aethenir and saw the elf staring dully ahead of them. Felix swung his head around heavily and saw, coming up the wide passage that they were shuffling down, a tall, scarred druchii noble in beautiful black and silver armour, accompanying a proud, cold-eyed druchii woman in flowing black robes and an elaborate headdress. They were escorted by a double file of silver-masked warriors who shoved aside anyone who didn't get out of their way.

Felix blinked at the woman. He knew her. His lotus-smothered brain churned as he wondered how. Then he remembered. It was the sorceress who had spun the silver ring on the metal wand. The one who had let the ocean close on top of them. Fear tried to fight through his lethargy, tried to tell him to look away so that she would not see him and recognise him, but the warning reached him much too late, and he didn't look down until the sorceress and her noble companion had already passed him. It hadn't mattered. They had spared not a glance for chained slaves. They hadn't even noticed their existence.

Their guards led them down a long zigzag stairway into the depths of the floating island, which got colder and damper the deeper they descended, until they passed through a gate into a chamber lit with thickly smoking torches, then through another gate, and finally into a low square chamber with iron doors in its walls. A number of wooden railings sectioned the floor of the room off into paths that led to the doors. Felix couldn't think what they reminded him of until a dim memory of his father taking him to a stockyard in Averheim formed in his head. The cows had been forced into runs just like this as they were divided into lots.

Druchii guards in leather armour came out of a room to one side, followed by another in robes who prodded forwards a bent-over slave with what looked like an enormous book strapped to his back. The robed druchii talked with their captors briefly, examined Felix, Gotrek and Aethenir from all sides, then stepped to the slave and opened the book on his back. He made some notations in it, then gave their captors some sort of receipt. The slavers left the way they had come as the guards led Felix, Gotrek and Aethenir to one of the iron doors, unlocked it, and prodded them into a pitch-dark cell, then slammed and locked the door behind them.

Felix could see nothing at first, and could hear nothing but rustling and a constant low buzzing. His nose wasn't so lucky. The reek of human waste hit him like a solid wall, forcing its way through his smoke-deadened senses and making him gag. Then his eyes became accustomed to the dim reflected light of the torches outside, and he saw the source of the smell.

The room was like a tunnel – long, low and dark – with what appeared to be a raised bench running down the centre at knee height, and it was packed with more people than Felix had ever seen in so small a place. Emaciated men, women and children covered the filth-smeared floor like a carpet, sitting, squatting or lying as best they could – the short chains between their wrists and ankles making it impossible to stretch out. Hundreds of dull eyes turned to look at him and Gotrek and Aethenir, blinking at them with empty misery.

Felix, Gotrek and Aethenir stared back at them. They were horrible-looking wretches, dressed in rags, covered in filth and gaunt with starvation. Many of them showed open, untreated wounds and trembled with fever, and Felix realised that the buzzing he had heard was the sound of the thousand, thousand flies that crawled all over them, feasting.

A man halfway down the left wall stood and glared at them. 'Stolen treasure, you said!' he rasped, shaking his chains. 'A tiny druchii scout ship, you said!'

It took a moment for Felix to realise that the haggard wreck who was spitting so venomously at him was Hans Euler.

FOURTEEN

Surprise fought through Felix's drug-induced dullness. 'Herr Euler?'

'Aye, you lying little trickster!' said Euler, as the remnants of his crew began to stand all around him. 'First the damned rats come for you, then an entire fleet of dark elves. By Manann's deeps, I curse the day you walked into my house, you wrecker!'

His men glared at Felix menacingly. Felix saw Broken-Nose and One-Ear among them. He didn't know how much damage they could do with their wrists and ankles shackled, but he didn't want to find out. He shot a glance at Gotrek. The Slayer was still staring straight ahead, apparently oblivious to everything around him.

Felix put his hands as high as the chains would let him. 'Herr Euler, please. I didn't lie. I just didn't know all the facts. I thought the scout ship was alone.'

'A likely story,' sneered Euler.

'But what happened?' asked Felix. 'Are Magister Schreiber and Fraulein Pallenberger with you? Did they survive?'

'Does my guard, Celorael, live? Asked Aethenir.

Euler shrugged. 'The elf died fighting the rats. The magisters were alive when we were brought here, but they were taken away.'

Felix's heart sank at that. Where had they been taken? What had been done to them? Did they still live?

'*They* did well by us at least,' said Euler. 'Didn't sneak off like some I could mention when the going got rough. Although the little seeress is a regular little nutcase, I have to say.'

'How do you mean?' asked Felix.

'Jumped in the sea when she'd found you'd disappeared during the fight with the rats. Thought they had taken you.'

Felix blinked. 'She jumped in the water?'

'Aye,' said Euler. 'We'd chased the rat-things away and found you were missing. Magister Schreiber insisted that we come about and look for you, thinking you had fallen overboard, but the seeress said the rats had you and that we had to swim down to their ship and save you.' He shook his head. 'There was no ship to be seen, but she said it was under the water and that it was all her fault. She dived in with all her clothes on, and we had to get a hook out before she drowned.'

Felix blinked again. 'That... *does* sound peculiar.' What could Claudia have meant, saying it was her fault? Surely she hadn't summoned the skaven. They had been after him and Gotrek all along.

'But she did well when we found the dark elves. She and the magister blasted them with light and lightning like they were sun and storm, but it wasn't enough.' He shook his head. 'We'd nearly chased down your little scout ship when out of the fog came five black galleys. We turned and ran, but we were no match for their sweeps. The magister and the girl loosed their spells over the aft rail as we peppered them with the nine-pounders. Her lightning set one of the galleys alight and it crashed into another, but then the scout ship came to the fore and six elf women stepped into her prow.' He spat. 'That was the end of your friends, and then the end of us. Weird black clouds balled them up and dropped them to the deck, choking and puking – and with them gone, we didn't stand a chance.'

Aethenir muttered something at this, but Felix didn't hear what it was.

'I'm sorry, Herr Euler,' said Felix. 'I had no idea it would end like this.' Much as he disliked the man, he wouldn't wish this fate on anyone. Of course, if the fool hadn't come chasing after them looking for treasure, he would be at home nibbling on jam tarts in his cosy little office.

'Never mind your damned "sorry",' said Euler. 'We'll settle what's between us if we somehow manage to escape this pit.' He sat back down against the wall. 'Until then, just stay away from me and mine. You're bad luck.'

Felix nodded, then picked his way awkwardly through the close-packed bodies of his fellow prisoners towards the opposite wall to find a space to sit. Gotrek and Aethenir clanked dully after him.

Felix woke some unknowable time later, his mouth dry and foul, his head aching, but at last clear of the black smoke's lulling lethargy. He looked around blearily. The torch-tinged darkness of the cell was unchanged, so it was impossible to tell how long he had been asleep. The filthy bodies of other prisoners pressed against him from all sides. Most lay curled up in sleep, though others moaned with pain, or sat and stared straight ahead, or shivered and twitched in the throes of sickness as the flies rose and fell in clouds all around them and the dark shapes of bold rats squirmed through the crowd. Aethenir had his head on his knees next to him, his splinted, fettered hands curled in his lap. Gotrek lay on his side. No one spoke. No one raged. No one tried to free themselves from their fetters.

And why should they? The reality of their situation hadn't truly sunk in for Felix before. The lassitude of the drug, the surprise of seeing Euler there, the story he had told – all had momentarily pushed it aside. But now, waking among the lost and the damned in a slave pen in the depths of a floating dark elf island, no doubt sailing at this moment towards the far shores of Naggaroth, with their weapons taken from them and numberless dark elf warriors and sorceresses between them and the dubious escape of the sea, he could understand their despair. There was no hope. None at all. They would die here, or as slaves in some dark elf city. He wished he had more of the black smoke. Everything would be better with a few whiffs of blissful oblivion.

To his right, Aethenir shifted, then raised his head and opened his eyes. He closed them again with a groan. 'So it wasn't a dream.'

'You aren't pleased?' asked Felix sourly. 'Didn't you want to find the dark elves so we could recover the harp?'

'Do not make jokes, Herr Jaeger,' said the high elf. 'There is no hope for us now. It would have been better for us to have died by the teeth of the sea dragon, for the death the druchii give their slaves is cruel by comparison.' He shivered.

Strangely, though he had been thinking much the same thing only seconds before, hearing Aethenir say it out loud stirred Felix's contrary nature.

'While we have life there is hope,' he said, trying to sound like he meant it.

'We have no life,' said Aethenir. 'We were dead the moment the druchii net settled over our heads. Our corpses still twitch, that is all.'

Gotrek woke with a snort to Felix's left. He blinked his eye and looked around, then instinctively tried to reach over his shoulder for his axe. His chains stopped him. He tugged harder.

'It's gone, Gotrek,' said Felix.

'Where is it?'

'The dark elves took it.'

Gotrek struggled to sit up, fighting the shackles. He stopped as he looked down at his blood-caked bare arms. 'Where is my gold?'

'They took that too.'

Gotrek went still, his hands clenching so tight that the bulging of his thick wrists made his manacles creak. 'I will kill every elf in this place.'

He stood, growling, and gripped the chain that connected his wrist manacles to his ankle fetters, preparing to wrench it.

'Wait, Gotrek,' said Felix. If he was going to pretend to be hopeful, he had to pretend to do his best to turn that hope into a reality. 'We need a plan.'

'Damn all plans,' said Gotrek, wrapping the chain around his bound wrists. 'I will not be chained.'

The other prisoners were looking around sleepily at the Slayer.

'Shut up, can't you?' said a tired voice.

'Gotrek,' Felix whispered quickly. 'If you reveal your strength now, the druchii will kill you before you get a chance to use it. Hide it until we can do something useful with it.'

'What's more useful than killing druchii?'

'How many will you kill unarmed?' Felix asked. 'A few jailors? Is that enough? Wouldn't you like to die with your axe in your hands?'

Gotrek paused and turned to Felix, his eye blazing. 'Aye. I would.'

'Then wait. We may find a way to escape this cell and find it.'

'And if not?' asked Gotrek.

'Then you're more than welcome to break free and kill as many as you can.'

Gotrek grunted and let go of the chains. 'And do you have a plan, manling?'

Felix shrugged. 'Not at the moment. No.'

Aethenir raised his head. 'I know where your weapons are,' he said. 'And your gold.'

They both turned on him. 'Where?' they said, in unison.

The high elf drew back at their attention. 'Ah, that is to say, I know who has them. The corsair captain who took them. His name is Landryol Swiftwing. I overheard him say that he plans to sell your things to a collector in Karond Kar.'

'What good does that do us?' growled Gotrek.

Aethenir shrugged. 'Knowing his name, we might learn where his quarters are, and then...' He paused, then looked around the dank, crowded cell again, and the stout iron door. 'And then...' He sighed and lowered his forehead back to his knees. 'Never mind.'

'Landryol,' rumbled Gotrek, sitting down again. 'He will be the first to die when I take back my axe.'

Suddenly Aethenir's head jerked up again. 'Asuryan! I forgot!'

'What is it, high one?' asked Felix, hoping against hope that the elf had just remembered some magic spell that would miraculously get them out of this situation.

'The high sorceress,' he said, turning to them. 'She is here. I saw her as we were brought to this place!'

'I saw her too,' said Felix, remembering.

'If she is here, the harp is here!' said Aethenir. He turned to Felix. 'Perhaps we *could* recover it.'

'We'd be dead long before we reached her,' said Gotrek. 'There are foes without number between us,' he murmured, his single eye far away.

'Then we must avoid them!' cried Aethenir. 'All that matters is the harp. If we don't take it back, Ulthuan is doomed!'

Gotrek grimaced at the high elf's shrill tone. 'Good riddance,' he rasped.

Aethenir stood, angry, then staggered when his chains caught him as he tried to draw himself up to his full height. 'Dwarf! Your stupidity amazes me. If the druchii destroy us, they will come for you next and, armed with the harp, they will crush your holds one by one until there is nothing left of your race but rotting corpses in buried ruins. You must promise me–'

Gotrek swung his chained hands and knocked Aethenir's legs out from under him, then clamped his fingers around the high elf's throat. 'A dwarf makes no promise he can't keep, elf. I will seek the harp, but I will make no vow. My doom awaits me somewhere on this ark. If it finds me first, then the defenders of Ulthuan will have to fight their own battles for once.'

He shoved the high elf away with an angry grunt. The prisoners around him were looking towards him, frightened by the violent outburst.

'What of Max and Claudia?' Felix asked, trying to calm things down again. 'Do we try to save them? Or do we try only for the harp?'

Aethenir coughed and sat up, massaging his throat and glaring at Gotrek. 'We have no hope of reaching the harp without them. Their magic will help us immeasurably.'

Felix shook his head. It all sounded convoluted and impossible. 'So, let me see if I have it. If we escape the cell, we look for our weapons, then for Max and Claudia, then seek the harp and fight until we reach it or die trying. Yes?'

Aethenir nodded.

Gotrek shrugged. 'If we escape the cell.'

Felix nodded. Nice to have a plan.

They all settled back to wait for an opportunity to escape to present itself.

No such opportunity arose in the next few hours, and Felix drifted between consciousness and sleep, finding it almost impossible to distinguish between the two. The monotony of sitting there with nothing to do but breathe the foul wet air and wave away the flies was the same in either state. After a while Felix had to relieve himself and discovered that there was a narrow gutter that ran along the base of the wall. A thin stream of water trickled through it.

He paused when he saw it, all the thirst that had tormented him in the boat coming back to him now more strongly than ever. He wanted a drink more than anything he had ever wanted in the world, and yet, it was water at the bottom of a piss gutter. It turned his stomach to think of drinking it. Still, if they were going to be ready to fight when the time came – if it ever did – he would need all his strength. Perhaps it wouldn't be so bad.

He finished his business and let the water run on for a moment, then squatted down and reached a tentative hand towards the stream.

'Don't,' murmured a voice beside him.

Felix looked over. A middle-aged woman, horribly gaunt, lay on her side, looking up at him.

'It's salt,' she said. 'All the new ones make that mistake.'

Felix withdrew his hand from the gutter and nodded to her gratefully. 'Thank you.' He sighed. Salt water. The druchii truly were as cruel as they were depicted.

The woman closed her eyes and curled up again. 'They'll come with our food and water soon enough.'

Felix nodded and sat back to wait.

Another unguessable while later, there came voices and a rumble of heavy wheels from outside the door. Everyone looked up or woke up at this and crowded towards the raised bench that ran down the centre of the room, pushing and shoving to be close to it. Those too weak or too injured to move lay behind them, raising quivering hands and moaning to be brought forwards. Some didn't move at all. Felix didn't understand what it was all about, and stayed with Gotrek and Aethenir along the wall.

A key turned in the lock and the door swung open. Four druchii guards, armed with drawn swords, filed in and stood to either side. After them came a whip-wielding overseer leading six strong-looking slaves. Two of them were dwarfs, one gnarled and greying, the other very young, who carried a huge metal cauldron between them, hung from chains hooked to a long metal pole that they bore on their broad shoulders. The other four slaves were human, and they split into pairs and walked down the length of the cell carrying torches and prodding any of the prisoners that didn't move.

Gotrek growled, deep in his throat. Felix looked around to see what the matter was and found the Slayer staring at the dwarfs.

'What's the matter?' whispered Felix.

'Dwarf slaves,' rumbled Gotrek. 'The most despicable creatures in the world. They are without honour.'

Aethenir looked up at that. 'Surely even a dwarf can't blame someone for being captured by slavers.' He smiled sadly. 'We ourselves are guilty of that.'

'A dwarf should die before capture,' Gotrek snarled. 'And no true dwarf should live as a slave. He should kill himself first.'

He spat, then sat with his knees up, glaring at the dwarfs, his single eye glittering balefully. Felix decided it was wisest to keep silent on the subject, and watched them too.

The dwarfs carried the cauldron to the raised bench and then tipped it so that the contents spilled into it. Felix recoiled as he realised what was happening. The bench was in reality a food trough. They were being slopped, like pigs.

A thin grey gruel flowed down the channel and the prisoners scooped at it with their hands as it passed, daubing it into their mouths and gulping it down. Even proud Euler and his crewmen mucked in with the rest, elbowing weaker men and women out of the way. It didn't seem enough to feed them all, and it wasn't. When the dwarfs had emptied the first pot, they went out and carried in a second pot and spilled that down the trough as well.

Felix knew that there would come a time when he would be fighting for a mouthful of the muck just like all the others, but just now it turned his stomach and he stayed where he was. Gotrek and Aethenir seemed similarly disinclined to try it.

As the dwarf slaves finished pouring the slop into the trough, the human slaves continued their examination of the prisoners. If a prisoner didn't respond to their prodding, they kicked him. If there was still no response, they grabbed him by the wrists and dragged him to the door.

Felix's heart leapt when he saw this. Here was the way to escape! All they had to do was play dead and they would be taken out of the cell! His heart sank again when he saw the overseer take out a curved dagger and cut the throat of every prisoner the slaves brought to him, before allowing them to take the body out the door. So, they had thought of that one. He sighed.

The dwarf slaves went out again and returned with a third cauldron on their shoulders, but this one they did not immediately pour. Instead they waited at the end of the trough, and Felix took the time to study them. Both were strong, and both had their hair cropped to patchy stubble. They had beards too, but only just. These had also been trimmed to little more than an inch all over. Not since poor Leatherbeard had Felix seen more naked-looking dwarfs. They wore breeches and filthy aprons, but no shirts or shoes, and their eyes were as dead and emotionless as those of zombies.

After a moment, the overseer cracked the whip over his head. 'Hurry up, you filthy cattle!' he cried in Reikspiel. 'I've twelve more cells to feed!' The prisoners at the trough flinched and scooped faster.

Half a minute later, the overseer decided he had waited long enough and snapped his fingers. The two dwarf slaves lifted the last cauldron and tipped it into the trough. This time it was water that rushed down the trough, and the prisoners stuck their faces down into it and guzzled greedily.

Felix's thirst got the better of him and he shoved forwards. He couldn't yet imagine eating the food, but he needed water desperately. Gotrek and Aethenir joined him, and they squeezed to the trough. Other prisoners whined and complained when he shouldered past them, but he was too thirsty to care. He stuck his head down in the trough and sucked at the thin current of water that ran down the channel. He had never tasted anything so good in his life. Gotrek and Aethenir slurped on either side of him. They sounded like pigs. It didn't matter. Water was all that mattered.

With the last cauldron empty and the last corpse dragged from the cell, the slaves and the overseer went back out through the door, followed by the guards with drawn swords. Then the door swung shut with a clang, and Felix heard the key turn in the lock.

Gotrek raised his head from the trough and glared at the door, and Felix wondered if he was thinking about how difficult it might be to break through, or how many of the guards he could kill before they raised the alarm.

'Filth!' barked Gotrek. 'Kissers of pale arses. Your ancestors disown you.'

After the prisoners had drunk and licked the trough clean and settled back to their places, Felix asked the woman who had told him about the salt water how often they were fed.

'Twice a day,' she mumbled. 'Leastways, it might be. No telling the days now.'

Felix thanked her and turned to his companions. 'We have to talk to the slaves,' he said.

'The dwarfs? Never,' growled Gotrek.

'The dwarfs or the humans,' Felix insisted. 'They're our only way of finding out what's going on beyond the door. They might be able to tell us where the corsair captain lives. Where Max and Fraulein Pallenberger are.'

'And where the Harp of Ruin is,' said Aethenir.

'I'd sooner kiss a troll,' sneered Gotrek.

Felix sighed. 'Well, I'll talk to them.'

A few hours later, Felix began to regret not eating. It wasn't that the cell did anything to arouse the appetite. The reek of unwashed bodies and human waste was nauseating, the cold wet air made him shiver and sweat at the same time, and the constant pestering of the flies was enough to drive him mad. He felt fevered and close to vomiting, yet his stomach wouldn't be denied. He tried to remember the last time he had eaten. It had been before the skaven had captured them. Had that been two days ago? Three days ago? His limbs trembled with weakness just sitting there. He snapped awake several times, never realising that he had fallen asleep.

At last, several hours after Felix had given up hope of the overseer ever coming again, the sound of rumbling wheels woke the prisoners and they rushed to the trough. This time Felix, Gotrek and Aethenir joined them. Felix fought forwards to be the closest to the food slaves. It wasn't easy. Weak as he was, he was stronger than the other prisoners, whose confinement and poor diet had wasted them away, but there were more of them and they were just as desperate as he – a scrabbling mass of frenzied skeletons. Felix was elbowed in the face and kneed in the ribs as he shoved closer. They squirmed around him and under him like sickly wolves.

Then suddenly, his path was cleared. A woman with mottled bruises all over her naked arms and legs was plucked out of his way. A man in the uniform of the Marienburg coastal patrol was dragged back. Felix looked around. Gotrek had entered the fray, picking prisoners up and putting them firmly behind him. The Slayer didn't look at Felix, but he seemed to be making sure that Felix would get an opportunity to talk to the slaves. Felix said nothing. Speaking of it might anger Gotrek and make him change his mind.

With the Slayer's help he bellied up to the trough right at the end, closest to the door, harvesting a crop of dirty looks for his pains. Gotrek and Aethenir were right next to him. Euler and his crewmen, the strongest men on the left side of the pen, were directly across from him.

Euler smiled wickedly at him over the trough. 'Decided to join us for dinner this time, have you?'

Felix opened his mouth to speak, but just then the key turned in the lock and the guard and the overseer filed in, followed by the human and dwarf slaves.

He waited anxiously as the slaves carried the first cauldron to the trough, its chains creaking as it swung from the pole they shouldered. To his relief, the slaves were the same dwarfs as last time. They stepped forwards and tipped the contents of the cauldron into the trough. Felix paused as he reached down to scoop up his first mouthful. Hungry as he was, he almost backed away.

It was thin oat gruel, more water than meal, but had that been its only sin, Felix would have dug in with a will. Unfortunately, it was rotten as well, made with mouldy grain, and a sweet reek of mildew rose from it. In addition, Felix could see fat weevils and rat droppings floating in the gruel.

Felix heard Aethenir retch, but Gotrek began shovelling the stuff into his mouth with both hands. Felix did his best to follow his example, though it was an act of will to put it in his mouth and he wished he could have kept it from touching his tongue. More than once he had to fight down the urge to vomit.

He did not attempt to communicate until the dwarfs had poured the second cauldron and returned to wait by the trough with the cauldron of water. Felix shot a quick look at the overseer, who prowled impatiently near the door as he had before, then, as he bent down and pretended to scrape at the last smears of the porridge in the bottom of the trough, he spoke in low tones.

'My friends, we need your help. The fate of your homelands and holds hangs in the balance. We seek the location of the quarters of Corsair Captain Landryol Swiftwing.' Felix risked a glance up at the slaves. They were staring ahead as if they hadn't heard. He looked down again and continued. 'And also where two recently captured human wizards are being held – a man and a girl. If you have any fondness for your old lands, I beg you, bring us this information and–'

A pain like liquid fire exploded across Felix's back and he reared up, crying out.

The overseer was drawing back his whip for another strike. 'No talking, vermin! I'll have your tongue!'

The prisoners scattered away from Felix like terrified rats. Euler and his men stared at him and backed away.

The overseer lashed out again. Felix put up a hand, but the tip of the whip licked past it and striped his shoulder and neck. The pain made his eyes water, and he instinctively reached out to grab the leather strand and yank it from its wielder's hand.

Gotrek shouldered him hard and he missed.

The druchii laughed. 'That's it, human dog. Take a lesson from the rock-eater. Fight the lash and die. Obey and live.' He cracked the whip over their heads. 'Now back! You've had your fill. For today and tomorrow. Neither of you will eat for the next two feedings.'

Felix clenched his fists with pain and rage, but forced himself to lower his head and turn away from the trough. Gotrek and Aethenir followed him. As they sat, Felix cast another glance at the cauldron slaves. Neither of them had shown any reaction when Felix had been whipped, and they remained stone-faced now, staring straight ahead as they tipped the cauldron full of water into the trough. Had they heard? Had they understood? Did they care? Would they do anything? Or were they too scared or too dulled by their years of captivity to try?

The two dwarfs emptied the cauldron, then turned to the door without a backwards glance. Felix waited until the overseer and guards had followed them out and locked the doors behind them, then let out a long-held breath.

From across the room came a cackling laugh. 'Serves you right, Jaeger! What were you playing at, you fool?'

Felix looked over and saw Euler and his men grinning savagely at them. He grunted and turned away, probing gently at the whip cut on his neck. 'I hope that was worth it.'

Aethenir shook his head. 'The slaves will do nothing. They are too cowed. They have lived too long under the lash.'

'And we will have to wait two feedings to learn one way or the other,' said Felix bitterly. He looked at the high elf. 'At least you will get to eat tomorrow.'

Aethenir made a face. 'A debatable pleasure,' he said.

The Slayer shrugged and motioned for them to return to the trough. 'Water is more important than food. Drink.'

Felix wondered how he was going to survive without eating again for a full day. He had managed to choke down only a few handfuls of the miserable porridge, and he was hungry again almost immediately after he had finished it. The thirst was excruciating as well. His head throbbed with it, the pain a dull counterpoint to the singing agony of his whip cuts, which prevented him from leaning against the wall or lying on his back.

When he heard the rumble of wheels again he almost couldn't bear it. He fought the urge to charge the trough and get as much gruel down his throat as he could before they pulled him away. But he couldn't do that. If they wanted to have any hope of getting information from the slaves, he had to make the overseer forget he existed.

He wondered if that would be possible. The druchii looked his way as soon as he came in the door, then laughed when he saw that Felix and Gotrek were staying away from the trough.

'Good dogs,' he said. 'A slave who is quick to learn can rise high with us. Just ask these fellows.' He turned and slapped the shoulder of the younger dwarf slave as he was pouring the gruel into the trough, causing him to slop some on the ground in surprise.

The druchii hissed and clubbed the dwarf on the back of the head with the brass-pommelled handle of his whip. 'Clumsy cur! Dare you waste food?'

The dwarf lowered his head and said nothing, merely continuing to hold the cauldron steady as he poured, though blood ran down the back of his head to his neck. Felix heard Gotrek growl at this, and his fists clenched, but he remained where he was.

After that, the overseer's anger seemed sated, and he returned to pacing impatiently as the slaves went back for the second cauldron and the prisoners gobbled and slurped noisily at their meal. Felix was disgusted with himself when he realised he was envious of them.

As the dwarf slaves waited with the cauldron of water and the human slaves dragged the morning's bodies away, Gotrek did a strange thing. He hadn't moved or said a word since the overseer had struck the young dwarf, but now he leaned forwards and, without looking up, slapped the filthy floor three times, then twice more.

The noise was hardly loud enough to be heard over the noise of the prisoners feeding, and no one seemed to notice. Felix was about to ask him what he was doing, but the Slayer shook his head. After a few seconds, he slapped the floor again, no louder than before, and in the same pattern. And then once more a few seconds later.

The third time, for the briefest of seconds, the dwarf slaves' eyes flicked up, wide, then dropped again instantly. The older dwarf frowned and stared fixedly at the trough, but the younger dwarf's eyes suddenly looked alive. Felix looked from the two dwarfs to Gotrek, unsure what had just happened. Then he saw the younger dwarf's finger silently tapping on the rim of the cauldron. Was it the same rhythm, or was it just idle motion? Felix glanced nervously at the overseer. The druchii didn't seem to have noticed the exchange.

'Don't look, manling,' Gotrek muttered under his breath.

Felix looked away, though his curiosity was killing him. Gotrek patted the floor again, much softer than before, and in new and different patterns. It reminded Felix of something, but he couldn't quite place it.

A moment later, the overseer snapped his fingers, and the slaves poured the water into the trough and left, followed quickly by the overseer and the guards. Felix waited impatiently until he heard the lock turn and the rumble of wheels fade away, then turned to Gotrek.

'What was that?' he asked. 'What passed between you?'

Gotrek stood and started pushing to the trough. 'Water first,' he said.

Felix grunted with annoyance, but followed Gotrek. Aethenir came too, and they all drank as much as they could, as well as scraping up the few meagre grains of gruel the others had left.

When they had finished, Gotrek sat back down near the wall. 'The mine code,' he said. 'For talking through walls with picks and hammers.'

Felix slapped his forehead. 'Yes! I remember now. Hamnir used it to communicate with the dwarfs inside the lost… hold…' He trailed off as Gotrek turned a cold, angry eye on him, and Felix realised that it was the first time he had mentioned Gotrek's former friend in his presence since they had left Karak Hirn. Apparently the wound was still fresh. Fear and embarrassment made him flush. 'I'm sorry,' he said quickly. 'I didn't mean to interrupt. What did you tell them?'

Gotrek gave an angry snort. 'I told them that they were cowardly oathbreakers who should have taken their own lives rather than become slaves to elves. Then I told them to tell me where our weapons are, and where Max and the girl and the harp are, the next time they come, or I'd return to their holds and let their clans know what had become of them.'

Aethenir sniffed derisively. 'That's sure to get results.'

'You told them all that in a few slaps?' asked Felix, incredulous.

Gotrek shrugged. 'More or less.' He lay down on his side and closed his eye. 'Now we wait and see.'

Felix found it hard to be so calm about it. He was restless and jumpy, hunger gnawing at his belly while impatience gnawed at his mind. He started wondering what they would do with the information if they got it. Could they even break out of the cell? With Gotrek's strength and fighting prowess, he didn't doubt it, but how far would they get after that? He could not remember the way from the harbour to the slave pens or how many guards were beyond the cell door. His brain had been too fogged with the smoke of the black lotus at the time, and none of it linked together.

His restlessness and the pain from his whip cuts wouldn't let him sleep, so he got up and shuffled as quietly as he could to the door. There was a viewing port in it about the size of a playing card. The chain between his wrists and his ankles was so short he could barely lift his head high enough, and he had to twist it at an uncomfortable angle to see out into the area outside the cell.

It was a square room lined with cell doors. At the far end, a narrow area was separated off from the rest by a cage of iron bars that protected the door to the hallway and two smaller doors. The main area was further divided by low wooden walls that were meant to channel prisoners from the cage door to the doors of the various cells. The hallway door was a lattice of bars through which he could see a short hall that led to a larger torchlit area in the distance. That was as far as he could see, but he vaguely remembered that they had come into the torchlit area by coming down some stairs.

He sighed. That stairway might as well have been on Morrslieb. There were at least three locked doors between him and it – the cell door, the cage door and the hallway door – and there were guards to deal with as well. In the left-hand room beyond the cage he could see the office where the robed clerk worked, while in the right-hand room he could see half a dozen guards lounging. The gods only knew how many more might guard the stairway.

He almost gave up and went back to the wall to sit with Gotrek and Aethenir, but if they were going to try something, it would be imperative to know everything they could about the world beyond the cell. He watched a little longer, though it was putting a terrible crick in his neck. Nothing happened. The guards laughed and occasionally walked through the caged area to speak to the clerk in the other room, but that was all.

Felix lowered his head and crouched beside the door. This wasn't telling him enough. He needed to see what happened when the food came, which guards had keys, what doors were opened and when. He sighed and sat down to wait.

He found that the other prisoners were all looking at him, wondering what he was doing. Euler's gang were glaring at him and whispering amongst themselves. But after a while, when he did nothing but sit, they lost interest and returned to sleeping or staring at nothing.

Felix did his fair share of sleeping and staring as well, but finally, after what seemed to his tortured mind to have been several weeks, he heard the rumble of distant wheels and commotion among the guards. He pushed himself back to his feet, groaning at the stiffness in his shackled arms and legs, and raised his eye cautiously to the little port again.

The hallway door was swinging out, and one of the druchii guards was opening the cage door with a key. Eight other guards stepped into the main area of the room, then turned and watched as the overseer and a procession of carts rolled in from the hall. There were three carts, and the first two were enormous – taller than a dark elf and consisting of sturdy wooden frames from which hung the heavy iron cauldrons that held the gruel and the water. Dwarf slaves pushed these, straining mightily. The third cart was an empty box on wheels, pushed by humans, and Felix couldn't think what it was for until he remembered that the human slaves took dead bodies out of the cells.

Once the eight guards and the overseer and the carts were all inside the main area of the room, a guard at the cage door locked it behind them. Four of the guards remained near the door, watching, while the other four travelled with the overseer and the carts as they began to move from cell to cell. Felix watched the whole process unhappily. The druchii weren't taking any chances. The hallway door and the cage door had been locked before any of the cell doors were opened, and the guard with the key to the cage door remained outside it, and Felix wasn't sure who had the key to the exit door or how it was opened.

He sighed and went back to Gotrek and Aethenir. It wouldn't do for the overseer to find him crouching by the door.

'What did you see, manling?' asked Gotrek.

As briefly as he could, Felix sketched out the layout of the central chamber and the guards who stood between them and the exit.

'It's impossible,' moaned Aethenir.

Gotrek stroked his beard thoughtfully.

Then the cart wheels rumbled close and the prisoners rushed to the trough. Aethenir looked as if he meant to stay with Gotrek and Felix, who were still on starvation punishment, but Gotrek pushed him forwards.

'Go,' he said. 'Can't have you weaker than you already are.'

Aethenir made a face, but he went.

Felix waited in anxious anticipation as the key turned in the lock. If Gotrek had got through to the dwarf slaves, they might have brought them information. But when he looked at them, Felix moaned with disappointment. Neither of them looked their way, nor did they betray any signs of nervousness. They weren't tapping their fingers or feet. They weren't doing anything except their job, emptying the cauldron of watery meal into the trough and going back for the second.

'Eyes down, manling,' murmured Gotrek.

Felix forced himself to look at the floor, though it killed him to do it. He wanted to know.

Beside him, Gotrek patted the floor as he had done before, then waited. Felix's ears strained. Had he heard a faint tap-tap in response? With the sounds of shuffling and slobbering that filled the room it was hard to tell. Several times he caught himself in the act of looking up and jerked his head back down.

Finally it was over and the slaves and the guards filed out. Gotrek gave a grunt of satisfaction as the door slammed shut once again and Felix looked up at him.

'Well?' he asked.

Gotrek nodded. 'I know the way to our weapons and to Max and the girl.'

'You know the way?' asked Aethenir. 'You mean you can lead us there?'

'Aye,' said Gotrek.

The high elf looked amazed. 'How is that possible?'

'That is the purpose of the code,' said Gotrek. 'Guiding dwarfs through mines at a distance.'

'But what about the Harp of Ruin?' Aethenir asked. 'Do you know where it lies?'

Gotrek shook his head. 'They didn't know. They hadn't heard of it.'

Aethenir hung his head. 'Of course they wouldn't. They are only slaves after all.' He sighed. 'Well, it is a beginning. Perhaps we can question some druchii along the way.'

Gotrek chuckled evilly. 'Aye. Good idea.'

They all looked up as they heard the rattling of chains coming their way. Euler was shuffling towards them with One-Ear and Broken-Nose at his back. He stopped in front of them and looked down, a suspicious look on his jowly, unshaven face.

'What are you up to, Jaeger?' he asked.

Felix did his best to look uncomprehending. 'What do you mean?'

'Don't think we haven't noticed,' Euler sneered. 'Trying to talk to the slaves. Looking out the window. Whispering to each other. You're thinking about making a break.'

'Doesn't every prisoner?' said Felix.

'It's impossible,' Euler snorted. 'We had a look too, the first day. You'll never get past the cage. Even if you do, the second door will stop you cold. Do you know how it opens?'

'I haven't a clue,' said Felix, trying to sound uninterested, though it would indeed be nice to know.

'There's no key – just a lever inside the clerk's office,' said Euler. 'We saw it when they brought us in. He looks through a little window into the hall and only pulls it if all's well. You haven't a chance.'

'If you didn't think we had a chance,' rumbled Gotrek, 'you wouldn't be pestering us.'

Euler smiled slyly. 'Ah, so you *are* thinking about it.'

Gotrek looked up at him, his face expressionless. 'And if we were?'

Euler exchanged a look with his men, then turned back to him and leaned in. 'If you can get us to the harbour, we can get you away.'

Felix's heart leapt. He had been prepared to die when there didn't seem to be any option, but if Euler could get them off the ark...

'How?' he said, perhaps too eagerly.

Euler glanced at his men again, then shrugged. 'I suppose there's no harm, seeing as you couldn't manage it without us.' He squatted down and began drawing with his fingernail in the filth of the floor. 'That tunnel that leads to the underground harbour,' he said. 'Very clever. Hard to find if you don't know it's there. Keeps the weather out too. But...' He tapped his sketch. 'It's very narrow. If one were to sink a ship in it, all the rest would be bottled up tight.' He smiled up at Felix. 'You help us get to a ship, we'll get you home, Herr Jaeger.'

It could work, thought Felix. We might be able to leave after all! Then he paused. 'Didn't you say you would settle what was between us if we escaped?'

Euler looked embarrassed at that, then shrugged. 'I'm prepared to put that aside if you are, Herr Jaeger. What are petty grievances in a situation like this? We need each other.'

'Well, then I...' Felix paused again and looked over at Gotrek. What would the Slayer think of him leaving? Would he count it as a betrayal? As cowardice?

The Slayer didn't seem to notice his hesitation. He turned to Euler. 'Are you prepared to fight when the time comes?'

'Oh aye,' Euler said. 'If you can get us through the doors we'll fight every long-ear between here and freedom.'

Gotrek nodded. 'Then we have a deal.'

Euler smiled. 'Excellent. Just give us the nod when you're ready.' He inclined his head to Gotrek and Felix, then turned and shuffled away, his men flanking him.

'We can't trust him,' said Felix, when Euler had returned to his own side of the cell. 'He still wants his vengeance, despite all his smiles.'

'We can trust him as far as the harbour,' said Gotrek. 'And we need him no further, unless you mean to go with him.'

Felix paused, his face flushing. 'I... I haven't decided.'

'You swore to record my death, manling,' Gotrek said. 'Not to die with me. I won't stop you.'

Felix bit his lip, still conflicted. Every sensible part of his brain was saying that he should go with Euler, but his loyalty to Gotrek and his desire to see the story to the end were once again making him think twice.

Just then, the key turned in the lock. Everyone looked up, because it had been much too short a time for another feeding and they hadn't heard the rumble of the cauldron carts. The door opened and a double file of uniformed druchii marched in, longswords drawn. There were eight of them, each with a cruel rune stitched into the breast of his dark purple surcoat. They moved with grace and precision, holding themselves erect and alert. Felix marked them as several cuts above the guards who usually visited the cell.

They were followed by two richly dressed druchii who held scented pomanders to their noses. A handful of slaves accompanied them, some carrying witchlight torches and others brooms. The male druchii was shorter than most elves Felix had so far seen, and with a weaker chin. He wore a heavily brocaded black coat over a dark red velvet jerkin and had so many rings on his fingers that Felix was surprised he could lift his hands to his face. The rune the guards wore was stitched into his jerkin as well. The female was beautiful in a heavy-lidded, sleepy sort of way, and wore a massive sable fur coat over a sea-green silk slip that hugged her voluptuous body and seemed more suited for the boudoir than the slave pen. Her hair was piled on top of her head and held in place by what looked like half a dozen miniature stilettos.

The man bowed the woman into the cell and then snapped his fingers. Two of the slaves hurried forwards and swept and scraped the stone floor in front of them clear of filth and then sprinkled what smelled like rosewater on the bare flags. The couple stepped fastidiously into the cleared area, then the man snapped his fingers again, and two larger slaves pushed into the huddled mass of prisoners, shoving a witchlight torch into the dark corners of the cell.

While they waited, the two druchii chatted to each other in their own tongue, occasionally laughing or shaking their heads at something the other had said. Felix looked to Aethenir and saw that the high elf was concentrating very hard on what they were saying.

After a moment, the two big slaves dragged a handful of young girls and boys out of the crowd, shoving back their wailing mothers and fathers, and brought them before the druchii. The man gestured to the children like a horse trader trying to sell a horse, seemingly pointing out height and build and other qualities. The woman ignored the man's words and gave each of the children a thorough going over, pulling back their lips to see their teeth, snapping her fingers in front of their eyes and watching them blink. Then she gestured to the slaves and they tore the children's clothes off one by one and turned them roughly around in front of her. An angry murmur rippled through the cell.

Felix's hands clenched, and his heart thudded in his chest. He heard Gotrek rumbling beside him like an angry bear.

Felix leaned in to Aethenir. 'Is she buying them?' he asked.

Aethenir nodded. 'She is from a brothel. The other druchii owns us.'

'A brothel!' Felix wanted to leap across the cell and strangle both of them, and he must have given in to the urge, because suddenly Gotrek was holding him back.

'Easy, manling,' he murmured. 'Now is not the time.'

'But they're taking children,' whispered Felix.

'And they'll take them just the same after they've killed you,' said Gotrek. 'Save your strength until it can do some good, you said.'

Felix sat back again reluctantly. How was it possible to sit by when he knew what would be done to those children? And yet Gotrek was right, attacking now was futile. He would be cut down and the children still taken. He watched in sullen silence as the druchii woman examined each of them from top to bottom, rejecting more than half of them for various flaws – scars, sickness, deformity or insufficient beauty – the lucky ones.

When she was done with the first batch, another few were brought up, and another, until the slaves had worked their way through the whole room, and the woman had seventeen boys and girls lined up behind her.

Men and women screamed and rushed forwards as the slaver's slaves began leading the children out.

'You won't take my daughter!' roared one man.

'Animals!' cried a woman. 'Beasts! What are you going to do to them?'

The prisoners were kicked back and bludgeoned down by the slaver's guards, who did not bother to use their swords on such weak foes. The parents fell back weeping and cursing as the children were prodded out and the druchii and their guards followed.

Felix shuddered with horror and loathing as the door clanged shut again. He ought to have done something, but he couldn't think what.

Aethenir sighed and ran his broken fingers through his filthy hair. 'Most disturbing.'

Felix nearly hit him. 'Children are sold into prostitution and all you can say is "most disturbing"?'

The high elf shook his head. 'I wasn't speaking of that. I was speaking of what the druchii said.'

Felix snarled. 'What could they have said that would be more disturbing than that?'

Aethenir raised his head and looked at him. 'They are angry with Lord Tarlkhir, the commander of this ark, because he has acquiesced to the wishes of High Sorceress Heshor – the leader of the sorceresses we met in the sunken city – and is sailing the ark to the Sea of Manann, instead of home to Naggaroth. They fear the delay will cause them to be frozen out of the Sea of Chill and unable to return until spring, something that will lose them both much business.'

Felix raised an eyebrow. 'We are sailing back to the Sea of Manann? Why?'

Aethenir shrugged. 'The slaver didn't know, but the whore had heard a rumour from one of her customers that High Sorceress Heshor intended to somehow close off the sea. She didn't know how this would be done, but I believe I can guess. It appears the sorceress wants to test her new toy.'

Felix's eyes widened with horror. 'She's going to use the harp to raise the land at the mouth of the sea! By Sigmar, it's...' His mind boggled at the consequences of such an act. Blocking the Sea of Manann would cut off Marienburg from all trade, which would in turn cut off the Empire from all trade. The country would be landlocked. 'She will have destroyed the economy of the Empire in one blow,' he said when he could speak again. 'She will do more damage than even Archaon did!'

'And it won't be just trade she destroys,' said Aethenir. 'The tidal waves and earthquakes created when so much land suddenly thrusts up out of the sea will undoubtedly swamp and shatter Marienburg, and the storm surge could travel up the Reik all the way to Altdorf and beyond, flooding as it goes.'

Felix stared at him. 'Fraulein Pallenberger's prophecy.'

'Indeed,' said the elf.

FIFTEEN

'We have to destroy the harp,' said Felix, his heart racing. 'It is no longer a matter of fighting our way out and hoping. We *must* reach it.'

'Aye,' said Gotrek.

'How quickly one's attitude changes when one's own lands are in danger,' said Aethenir dryly.

'Never mind that,' said Felix impatiently. 'How do we do it?' He looked up at the roof of the cell. 'This high sorceress must surely keep it with her, somewhere above us, but where?'

'She will live among the highest of the high, for in druchii society, her rank is even above that of the commander of this ark.'

'So how do we reach her?' asked Felix.

'We do not,' said Aethenir. 'It is impossible.'

'Nothing is impossible,' growled Gotrek.

'Certainly it could be accomplished by an army,' said Aethenir. 'But not by us. The druchii are often as much at war with each other as they are with the world, and so their houses and palaces are guarded against invasions and assassinations of all kinds. There will be a hundred guarded gates between here and her, and thousands of druchii going about their business on the streets – every one of which will know us for intruders. We will never make it.'

Felix shot him a look. 'I thought you were the one who was urging us to go?'

Aethenir nodded his head. 'It must be tried, if I am to remain on the path of honour, but we have no chance of success.'

'No wonder you're a dying race,' muttered Gotrek.

Felix had to agree. 'Perhaps we'd have a better chance if you put your great scholar's mind to work on a solution instead of bemoaning our fate.'

The elf sniffed. 'I shall think on it.'

'Well, don't take too long,' said Felix. 'Who knows how close we are to the Manannspoort.'

They fell silent as each began mulling the problem over in their heads. Mad ideas came to Felix – schemes out of the worst sort of melodrama.

They would wait until the slaver came back, then kill all his guards, dress Aethenir up in one of their uniforms, then deliver themselves to the high sorceress. No. Could even Gotrek kill eight armed guards bare-handed? And even if he could, what were the odds the slaver would come back before the ark reached the Manannspoort?

They would fake their deaths so well that the overseer wouldn't bother cutting their throats, and escape after they had been wheeled out with the other bodies. No. The overseer cut every corpse's throat, regardless.

They would tell the overseer that Aethenir was a loremaster of Hoeth, who could tell the high sorceress secrets of Ulthuan's magical defences if they brought him before her. No. Even if they were believed, the overseer would take Aethenir away and leave Gotrek and Felix behind.

Felix hung his head in despair. He could think of nothing. Aethenir was right. It was impossible. They had too little knowledge of what was outside their cell. There was no way to make realistic plans. They didn't even know if they could get past the first three gates.

He looked up at Aethenir and Gotrek. They didn't seem to be having any better luck. Aethenir just sat there, running his fingers through his filthy hair and murmuring over and over again. 'I must stay on the path. I must stay on the path.'

Gotrek just stared ahead, his single eye blank and distant, cracking his knuckles absent-mindedly.

Felix sighed and sat back, closing his eyes, determined to go through it again. There had to be some way. There had to be.

Felix woke to Gotrek grunting and sitting up. He opened his eyes and looked around. Nothing appeared to have changed. The prisoners lay coughing and moaning and snoring on the ground as usual. There were no strange sounds from outside the cell. The key was not turning in the lock, and yet Gotrek was looking around, alert and awake.

'What's happened?' Felix mumbled sleepily.

'The ark has stopped,' said Gotrek.

'Stopped?' said Felix. 'How do you know?'

'Trust me, manling,' said Gotrek. 'A dwarf's stomach knows when a ship sails – and when it doesn't.'

Felix's heart dropped. 'Then we've reached the Sea of Manann,' he whispered. 'We're out of time!'

On the other side of Felix, Aethenir raised his head. 'What do you say? The ark has stopped?'

Gotrek nodded as he stood. 'We must act now.'

Felix groaned but nodded, resigned. They had no choice.

Aethenir sat up and pushed the hair out of his eyes. 'You assume much, dwarf. Can we be certain this is why we have stopped? It might be for another reason.'

'It might be,' said Felix, getting to his feet beside Gotrek. 'But can we risk it if it isn't? The sorceress might play the harp at any moment. We may already be too late.'

'But we still have no plan,' said the high elf, querulous. 'It won't work.'

'Then we will die gloriously,' said Gotrek, gathering his chains in his hands. 'There are two hours to the evening feeding. We will go then, and fight until they kill us.'

Felix looked at him. 'You'll wait two hours?'

Gotrek looked towards the cell door. 'It would take me more than two hours to get through that door with no tools, and they would stop me in two minutes. We have to wait.' He stood up sharply and the chain that connected his wrists to his ankles snapped like it was made of dry biscuit.

Aethenir sighed. 'I had hoped for a chance to rectify my sin. This will only be pointless death.'

Gotrek glared at him as he strained to snap the chains between his wrists. 'Better a pointless death than a life of shame.' The chains parted with a bright ping. He turned to Felix and broke his chains for him in a matter of seconds. 'Tell Euler to bring his men and I'll do the same for them.'

Felix nodded, but first he stood tall and stretched, raising his arms over his head. It felt glorious! Then he walked through the crowd and around the trough to the other side of the room. Taking long strides was another joy. He felt like he had been living like an old man for the last few days, hunched over and eating gruel. He felt more optimistic already.

Euler and some of his men were playing a game with pebbles and a circle scratched in the floor. The others slept or stared at the walls.

The balding pirate looked up at him as he approached, noting his dangling chains. 'So it's time then, Jaeger?'

'Yes,' said Felix. 'We go when the cart comes again. Go to Gotrek and he'll break your chains.'

Euler's men cheered at this and started to stand. Felix was about to turn and go back to Gotrek when he paused and faced Euler again.

'Uh, Euler.'

'Aye?' said the merchant, struggling to his feet.

'Listen to me a moment,' said Felix. 'The druchii sorceresses you fought. They have a weapon – the Harp of Ruin – a magical instrument that can raise and lower mountains. They mean to use it to close off the Manannspoort.'

'Eh?' said Euler. 'What's this?'

Some of his men were turning to listen.

'They're going to raise the sea floor and block the mouth of the sea,' said Felix. 'It will cause a tidal wave that will destroy Marienburg and possibly Altdorf, not to mention stop all ship trade.'

'Is this a joke, Jaeger?' said Euler. 'Because I don't find it amusing.'

Felix shook his head. 'It's no joke. It is the reason we tricked you into going after the sorceresses in the first place – to try to wrest it from them before they could use it.' He looked Euler in the eye. 'They are going to use it now, unless we stop them. Will you help us? Will you fight with us to the top of the ark and find the sorceress and the harp?'

'What?' Euler snorted. 'That's suicide.'

'Yes,' said Felix.

Euler held up a hand and turned away. 'Sorry, Herr Jaeger. No heroes here. We part at the harbour as planned.'

'Can you really stand by and watch Marienburg destroyed?' asked Felix angrily. 'That is what will happen if the sorceress unleashes the power of the harp. Your city will be swept away. Your precious trading empire will be no more.'

Euler shrugged. 'What will I care if I die helping you?'

'Have you no family there? Will you allow them to die by your cowardice?'

The pirate looked up, glaring, his chains rattling as he balled his fists. 'You fooled me once with your lies, you wrecker, but I won't be fooled again. If you want to go above decks looking for treasure, or whatever it is you're after, that's your business, but you won't drag me into it again. I'm not going to sacrifice my life and my men for the sake of your greed.' He laughed, sharp and angry. 'A harp that raises mountains. You couldn't think of a better lie than that?'

He shouldered past Felix and started around the trough towards Gotrek, his men following, though some of them looked back, frowning thoughtfully.

Felix sighed, wondering if he should try one more time to convince Euler. There didn't seem to be any point. The man's heart was so larcenous that he could not believe that everyone else wasn't larcenous at heart as well.

He shuffled back towards Gotrek behind the pirates. The Slayer had snapped Aethenir's chains and was now surrounded by a crowd of prisoners, amazed by this feat of strength. They pushed in on all sides, men and women holding out their wrists towards him. Gotrek snapped them as they came, untiring – three sharp pulls freeing each one.

Then Euler's men pushed through the weaker prisoners and stepped up to Gotrek, grinning. Gotrek snapped their chains too, not even looking up to see who he was freeing.

Felix looked around at the throng of prisoners pushing forwards. Most of them were so malnourished and weak that they could barely stand. Only a few were better than animated corpses. They would be worth hardly anything in a fight. Still, without Euler and his men, Felix, Aethenir and Gotrek were only three, and three wouldn't get far alone.

Felix pushed through the crowd and stood beside Gotrek to address them. 'The dark elves mean to destroy Marienburg and the Empire,' he said. 'If you can swing a sword, we need volunteers to help stop them. It will be death, but you will be saving your families back home.'

Only a very few came forwards. Most seemed too numbed to understand what he was saying, and only wanted to be able to move their arms and legs.

Felix sighed and let it go. He had tried.

The key turned in the lock and the four guards filed in, swords drawn as usual. Felix looked nervously at his fellow prisoners, hoping they wouldn't jump too soon. If anything, they hesitated too long, watching nervously as human slaves started through the room, looking for bodies, and the dwarf slaves trudged in, the heavy cauldron hanging by its chains from the iron pole between them. Gotrek, Felix and Aethenir started for the trough, shuffling and holding their wrists together to hide that their chains were broken as, on the other side of the trough, Euler and his biggest men did the same, taking the positions closest to the cauldron. The rest of the prisoners surged in behind them. Most of them remembered to keep their wrists and ankles together.

Felix exchanged nervous nods with Euler and Aethenir as the dwarf slaves stepped up to the trough and started to tip the cauldron. This was it. Much as he would have liked to, they could not wait to eat. Their deception would be discovered as soon as they tried to dip their hands in the gruel.

With an animal roar, Gotrek leapt up and shoved the young dwarf back. The slave staggered back, the iron pole slipping off his shoulders and the cauldron slamming to the floor, splashing gruel. Before the overseer or the guards understood what was happening, Gotrek grabbed the big pot by its chains and swung it around him as the dwarfs dived away, alarmed. The overseer shouted, running in, only to be smashed to the floor by the thing, his knees a shattered ruin.

The guards cried out, raising their swords, but Felix, Euler and the others were moving and mobbed two of them, dragging them to the floor and smashing their heads on the flagstones. The other two foolishly stepped into the arc of Gotrek's spinning cauldron and were knocked flat, arms and ribs broken. Gruel slopped everywhere. The corpse collectors also turned, calling out in surprise, but the prisoners jumped them and dragged them down.

Aethenir wisely stayed out of the way.

Felix rose again and saw that the overseer was trying to push himself off the floor, scrabbling for his sword. Felix leapt on him and slammed him back down with all his weight, then snatched the druchii's dagger from his belt and stabbed it into his stomach, jerking it up under his ribs.

'That's for the whip cut,' he hissed in his ear as he died.

He took the overseer's sword and tore the key ring from his belt. He tossed it to one of the other prisoners. 'Open the other pens when we go.'

He looked around. Euler and the others were finishing off the two guards they had dragged down, and Gotrek was raising the cauldron and dropping it on the head of the second guard he had flattened. The druchii's skull cracked with a sickening pop. The other one's brains were already oozing across the flagstones. The prisoners had killed the corpse collectors.

Felix shook his head, amazed. They had done it! No more than thirty seconds had passed and the guards and the overseer were dead. But now there were shouted questions from the room outside – the four backup guards. Felix turned to the door as Euler, One-Ear, Broken-Nose and one of the other crewmen armed themselves with the dead guards' swords. Gotrek took up the iron pole that the slaves had used to carry the cauldron. Felix swallowed, afraid of what came next. This fight had only been the beginning, and already his limbs were trembling from exhaustion and hunger. He felt too weak to lift the sword.

'Slayer,' said the young dwarf slave, standing and bowing before Gotrek. 'Let me come with you. I can help you find your way.'

'Farnir, you fool!' said the older dwarf. 'The masters will kill you!'

Gotrek pushed the young dwarf aside. 'You already told me the way, oathbreaker,' he said, then gathered up the chains of the cauldron in his left hand and started for the door, holding the iron pole in his right hand and dragging the heavy pot behind him with his left like it was the head of some giant's flail.

Felix and Euler pushed out into the big room after him, the pirate crew hard behind and Aethenir timidly bringing up the rear. The four backup guards were advancing warily towards the open cell, swords out, while three more guards and the clerk watched and cried questions from behind the cage. The two huge carts sat near the cell doors, each loaded with giant cauldrons. Two well-muscled dwarf slaves stood by one, staring in amazement.

The four guards shouted and charged forwards, raising their swords. Gotrek roared in response and again swung the mighty cauldron around himself, then let go of the chains. It flew towards the guards, bowling one over and sending the others leaping over the low wooden rails that divided up the room. Felix, Euler and the others rushed forwards to attack them before they recovered.

Felix hacked one of them in the neck as he tried to rise, then parried a wild slash from another. His arm was so weak the second druchii's blow almost drove his sword back into his face. He fell back, blocking another stronger attack by a hair's breadth. Felix cursed. It seemed even lowly druchii prison guards were better, faster swords than he. He made a desperate chop at the guard's flickering blade and knew it wouldn't be enough, but then an iron pole slashed down and crushed the druchii's head like an egg.

Felix looked around. Gotrek was roaring past him to where Euler and three of his men were trying to bring down the last guard, who fought them furiously.

One of the pirates stumbled back, screaming, his guts spilling from a tear in his belly. Gotrek shoved him aside and slammed the yoke down on the druchii's arm, snapping it and knocking his sword to the ground. The pirates ran the druchii through, then hacked him to pieces in a release of pent-up fury.

Behind the melee, the prisoners were stumbling out of the cell and blinking around in somnambulant wonder. The prisoner Felix had given the ring of keys to opened another cell door and waved his arms at those within.

'Free! You're free!' he cried.

Felix wondered for a brief second if he was doing the poor, half-starved wretches any favours freeing them. They would probably be killed by the guards for escaping. There was no time to think about it.

The pirates took the swords and daggers from the dead guards and advanced on the cage. Gotrek and Felix joined them, pushing to the fore, just in time to see the three guards spill from the guard room holding odd-looking crossbows. The clerk had vanished into the other room, and Felix heard the brazen clangour of an alarm bell.

Gotrek, Felix and the others slammed into the cage bars, stabbing through them at the guards, who jumped back out of reach and fired their crossbows. One missed Felix by a hair's breadth, and one of the pirates fell back, screaming and clutching his face. Felix's stomach dropped when he saw new bolts appear in the slots of the bows and the bowstrings draw back by themselves. They would be slaughtered!

Felix and the pirates swiped at the guards with their swords, but only Gotrek, with the length of the iron pole, could touch them. He knocked the crossbow out of one guard's hands and struck another on the shoulder, ruining his aim.

The guard with the keys on his belt fired at the Slayer, but Gotrek ducked and the bolt struck a prisoner. The Slayer stabbed at the key guard again, but missed. He dodged back, turning for the guard room door with his companions, who were realising too late that they should have stayed back. Gotrek flailed after him with the pole, but hit another instead, knocking him to the floor.

Cursing, Felix shoved up to the bars, reversed the overseer's dagger in his hand and flung it end over end. The knife struck the key guard pommel-first on the back of the head and he careened off the wall to fall to the floor next to the other fallen guard.

'Good work, manling,' said Gotrek.

Unfortunately, the blows hadn't been enough to knock either guard out. They started picking themselves up again instantly, but they had fallen too close to the bars of the cage and the pirates ran them through as they stood. The key guard collapsed to the floor again, his left foot tantalisingly within reach.

Felix shot an arm through the bars, reaching for the druchii's ankle as the last guard grabbed him under the arms and tried to pull him back into the guard room. Felix pulled the other way, grunting with effort, the guard's ankle slipping from his grip. Then Gotrek's yoke shot forwards and poked the last guard in the chest. He fell back, winded.

Felix pulled for all he was worth – which wasn't much just then – and dragged the dead guard an arm's length closer to the bars. He let go and reached for the keys. They were just an inch from his fingertips.

The last guard sat up, gasping, and crawled forwards to grab his dead comrade's arms again, but with a thwack that made Felix's ears ring, Gotrek's yoke came down across the druchii's shoulders and dropped him to the floor.

Felix pulled again on the dead guard's ankle and brought him another foot closer. He thrust out his hand and this time closed his fingers around the key ring. It had two keys. He ripped it off the guard's belt and pulled it through the bars, then tossed it to Aethenir, who hovered anxiously behind the pirates.

The high elf stepped to the cage door as Felix, Gotrek and the pirates kept their eyes on the doors. He tried one key. It didn't work. Euler cursed.

He tried the other and there was a satisfying click. Euler and Felix shoved past him, slamming the door open and stabbing all the fallen guards again just to be sure.

As the pirates stripped the dead guards of their swords and crossbows and pushed past to loot the guard room, Gotrek stumped to the exit door, a lattice of heavy iron slats, and shook it. It barely rattled. Through it Felix could see worrying movement at the end of a short corridor.

'Come on, dwarf,' snapped Euler uneasily. 'Don't tell me we're finished before we've begun. I thought you had a plan.'

Gotrek examined the edges of the door with care, ignoring him. Both the lock and the hinges were hidden behind the fitted stone of the door frame.

'Damned dwarf slaves built too well for their masters,' the Slayer growled. 'Might be tougher than I thought.'

A black-shafted bolt glanced off a slat and rattled into the room. A few more clattered off the lattice, but did not come in. Felix jerked back and looked through the door again. Half a dozen guards were lined up at the end of the short corridor, aiming repeating crossbows at them.

'Manann's depths,' groaned Euler. 'We're done for.'

'Not yet. Come on.' Gotrek turned away from the door and jogged back into the larger portion of the room, pushing through the milling crowd of freed prisoners and striding for the massive cauldron carts. 'And clear the door!' he called.

Felix, Euler and his pirates trotted after the Slayer, curious. Gotrek checked both carts. Each was taller than a man, and each carried twelve of the cauldrons – six below and six above – all hanging by their chains from stout wooden racks built into a heavy frame. On the first cart – the one that had fed their cell – all but two of the cauldrons were empty, but on the second cart, all were full.

'This one,' said the Slayer, slapping it. 'Turn it round.'

Felix and a few of the pirates inched the heavily laden cart until it faced the door as Gotrek stepped to the other cart and lifted one of the empty cauldrons off its rack. He carried it to the full cart and used the chains to hook it to the front, like the nose of a battering ram, then came around the back and joined the rest at the push bar.

Farnir, the young dwarf slave, and the two dwarfs who had pushed the cart approached them.

'Let us help,' said Farnir. 'Please.'

Gotrek turned his back on them without a word.

From the cell door, the old dwarf slave cried to the others. 'Don't! Stay here! Wait for the masters!'

'Clear the way!' called Felix, waving at the aimlessly wandering prisoners.

'Now!' said Gotrek, and shoved at the bar. Felix and the pirates joined him. The cart started rolling, swiftly picking up speed as it rumbled across the flagstones. They ran faster. The hanging cauldrons swung back a little, creaking and sloshing.

If the door doesn't open, thought Felix, this is going to hurt.

The cart hurtled through the open cage door with inches to spare on either side, and slammed into the outer door with a sound like dwarf ironclads colliding. The twelve full cauldrons swung forwards, adding a second impact and sending gruel and water splashing everywhere. The racks cracked and splintered, and some of the cauldrons jumped their hooks and crashed to the floor.

The lattice door, unfortunately, didn't open. Felix and the others crashed into the back of the cart. Felix's cheek smashed against the wooden frame, loosening teeth, and his ribs were crushed against the push bar as the pirate behind him slammed into him. He had been right. It hurt.

Groaning and cursing, Gotrek, Felix and the pirates stepped out from behind the cart to survey the damage to the door. The lattice of slats bulged out in the centre where the nose-cauldron had smashed into them, and the door's iron frame was bowed in, but the hinges still held, and the bolt of the lock had not quite slipped its collar.

'Again!' called Gotrek, and began pulling back on the push bar.

It was clear, as they hauled it back into the big room, that the cart had lost much of its structural integrity. The wheels wobbled and some of the cauldrons hung off it at odd angles, nevertheless it still rolled. When they had it in position, Gotrek fitted it with another nose-cauldron – the first one had cracked and was squashed nearly flat – and they pushed at it again.

This time it rattled and shuddered as it bounced across the floor, and they had to fight to keep it going straight. One of the cauldrons banged off the edge of the cage door as they charged through, but they made it, and slammed into the outer door again. The noise was even worse this time, and cauldrons and timbers flew everywhere, but with a deafening clang, the outer door flew open and they were through and staggering into the wide corridor after the rapidly disintegrating cart.

'Keep on!' shouted Gotrek.

Felix and the others obeyed the order and sprinted down the corridor towards the thin line of archers as arrows ricocheted off the swinging cauldrons and stuck in the shattered spars. The rest of the pirates followed in their wake, crouching in ragged double file behind the cart's bulk, some of them holding more cauldrons in front of them like shields, others firing back with crossbows purloined from the guards and the guard room.

Felix heard a shouted order and the archers fell back before them, disappearing to the left. Then, about ten strides from the end of the hallway, the front right wheel of the cart fell off and wobbled away as the cart slammed down on its axle end, scraping a groove in the flagstones. Gotrek and Felix and the other pushers unfortunately didn't stop pushing in time, and the cart swerved wildly, pivoting on the dragging axle, then toppled slowly forwards to crash on its side. It skidded noisily to a stop as cauldrons and bits of wood bounced away ahead of it, and a tide of water and mouldy gruel spread out before it.

The escapees halted just before the end of the hallway, not wanting to run into a hail of arrows, and edged forwards. Felix peeked left and right, trying to see the lay of the land.

The room was large and octagonal – the junction of four corridors – all identical to the one they were in. The archers had retreated to the mouth of the corridor to their left. In the angled wall to their right was another iron gate – this one guarding a broad stairway that led up into darkness. Six guards stood at the ready behind it, armed with swords and crossbows.

'A crossfire,' said Felix, his heart sinking.

'And another gate for which we have no key,' said Aethenir.

'Don't think the cart is going to be much use this time,' said Euler.

Gotrek was glaring at the gate with his single eye, edging out further than Felix thought safe to have a good look. It was not a lattice this time, but a line of close-set iron bars that stretched from floor to ceiling, with a wide, vertically barred door in the centre. Much easier to shoot through, thought Felix, swallowing nervously.

But Gotrek didn't seem daunted. 'Easy,' he said at last, then turned to Euler. 'Cauldrons for shields around me and crossbows in the middle.'

Euler nodded and whistled up four of his pirates. They took up four of the cauldrons, wrapping the chains around their arms so they could hold them like shields, then clutched crossbows in their opposite hands. Felix grabbed a fifth cauldron, groaning with the weight. Even when empty the things were staggeringly heavy, and yet Gotrek had swung a full one around like it was a mace. Then Felix and the four pirates formed up in a tight circle around Gotrek, as the rest of the pirates and prisoners made ready to run for it the instant the door was opened. Felix noticed that the three young dwarf slaves had joined with the rest.

'Now,' said Gotrek.

Felix and the others ran out and right, aiming for the gate. Crossbow bolts immediately began spanging off the cauldrons and skittering past their feet and Felix was hard pressed to slow his pace to Gotrek's. The temptation to run from the shooting was almost overwhelming.

As they reached the gate, the pirates fired their crossbows through the bars at the guards behind it, forcing them back towards the stairs. Gotrek stabbed forwards with the iron pole. The frame of the door was nothing but four long iron bars, forged into a rectangle, and the space between it and the door was about two fingers wide. Plenty of room for Gotrek to wedge the end of the iron pole and pull, which is what he did. He jammed the end into the gap just above the square plate that hid the deadbolt, and began to pry sideways, trying to bend the door frame out far enough that the deadbolt would pop out of its socket and the door would spring open.

Gotrek crouched down and heaved mightily. The frame shrieked. Felix and the other shield carriers crouched with the Slayer, trying to hide as much of their bodies behind the cauldrons as they could as they fired over them at the druchii behind the gate. The archers backed up the stairs and fired back. More bolts clanged off Felix's cauldron. The tip of one punched through. One of the pirates howled as another pierced his naked foot and he almost fell.

Gotrek kept pulling. The door frame was bending out, but not enough. The pole was bending more than the frame. Felix was afraid it was going to snap.

'I thought you said this one would be easier,' said Felix.

'Shut up, manling,' Gotrek rasped.

A guard tumbled to the ground, a bolt through his chest. Another turned and fled up the stairs, out of bolts, but the other four kept firing. A hot stripe of pain burned across Felix's shin as a bolt tore a trench in it. Another skipped off the stone floor and buried itself in Gotrek's calf. He grunted, but kept pulling.

'Hurry, dwarf,' gritted one of the pirates.

Felix heard the slap of bare feet rushing towards them, but before he could turn to look, someone shoved through two of the cauldrons. Felix almost struck out with his sword, but checked when he saw that it was the young dwarf Farnir. A bolt stuck from his back.

Without a word, the slave grasped the pole about mid-way along its length and added his strength to Gotrek's. The door frame groaned. Felix readied his sword in anticipation. The pirates fired the last of their bolts at the guards.

'One, two, THREE!' rasped Gotrek, and he and Farnir heaved together. The metal screamed and suddenly Gotrek and Farnir were staggering sideways as the door sprang open.

The guards on the stairs dropped their crossbows and rushed down to hold it shut, but they were too late. Felix and a pirate slammed through behind their cauldron shields, knocking them back and slashing at them before they could draw their swords. Gotrek and the others charged in behind. The Slayer swept the legs out from under two of the guards with the pole, and Felix bowled another down with his cauldron. He stabbed the dark elf in the throat as he stepped over him, then turned to face another. There were none left to face. The pirates had finished them all off.

Felix threw aside the cauldron with a relieved sigh. His shoulder felt broken from carrying it. There was a thunder of running feet. Felix turned to see Aethenir, Euler and the rest of the pirates, as well as a mob of prisoners, breaking cover and running towards them. A handful fell to the arrows of the druchii in the far corridor, but the rest kept coming.

Gotrek pulled out the bolt that had pierced his calf as the first pirates pushed through the door and armed themselves with the weapons of the dead guards. Aethenir selected a crossbow.

'Well done, dwarf,' called Euler.

The Slayer shrugged and turned to the stairs. 'This is only the beginning.'

Felix and Aethenir joined him and they started up the stairs into darkness with Euler and his pirates and the rest following behind.

Felix feared that they would find the ark's entire garrison waiting for them at the top of the stairs, but though they heard alarm drums booming in every direction, the reinforcements were apparently still on their way. He was glad of it. It had been six flights. His legs were like jelly from the climb and he was soaked with sweat.

Aethenir leaned against the wall, his eyes half-closed. Beside him,

Euler was gasping for breath, hands on his knees, as his pirates recovered around them, looking anxiously up and down the wide, high-ceilinged corridor.

After a moment Euler collected himself and stood. 'Right,' he said. 'Which way is the harbour?'

'You certain you won't change your mind, Euler?' asked Felix.

Euler laughed. 'Very.'

Gotrek pointed left down the hall.

Euler bowed to him. 'Thank you, Herr dwarf. You've done us a great service.' He turned to Felix, smiling. 'Well, Herr Jaeger. It seems this is goodbye.'

Felix nodded, not about to join the pirate in his false bonhomie. 'Goodbye, Euler. Good luck, I suppose.'

Euler's smile broadened. 'You don't understand, Herr Jaeger. This is *goodbye*!'

And with that, Euler and his pirates attacked.

SIXTEEN

Felix fell back, throwing up his sword in a desperate parry, and barely turned aside Euler's blade. Beside him, Gotrek roared as a sword lashed him across his back, then spun in a circle, swinging his iron pole and fanning the pirates back. To one side Aethenir cowered against the wall.

'Euler!' cried Felix, turning another attack. 'What is this?'

'After all you've done to me,' snarled Euler, 'do you think I would let the long-ears have the satisfaction of killing you?' He laughed, harsh and breathless. 'I meant to wait until I had you on my ship, but since you've chosen suicide, it was now or never.'

He pressed in, attacking feverishly, his breathing ragged, his eyes wild. As Felix blocked the crazed stabs, he saw one of Euler's men fall back from Gotrek, screaming, his arm bent at an unnatural angle. Two others were on the floor, clutching their shins.

'This is madness, Euler,' said Felix, as the alarm drums continued to boom. 'You're ruining your chance to escape. The druchii are coming. Leave off and go!'

'Not until I've finished you!' Euler beat Felix's sword aside and did a running lunge, straight at his naked chest, but the pirate was winded and weak from captivity, and the attack was slow. Felix knocked it away and shoved him past.

Euler turned, roaring and weaving, and slashed down wildly. Felix thrust over his arm and ran him through the heart. Euler gasped, his eyes going wide.

His sword dropped to his side and he looked Felix in the eye. 'You really are a curse, Jaeger.'

He sank to his knees, then fell back and collapsed, sliding off Felix's blade. Felix looked pityingly at him for a brief moment. Haggard and scruffily bearded, his corpse looked nothing like the plump, proud man Felix had met in the study of his prosperous Marienburg townhouse.

Felix turned to help Gotrek, but found that the pirates were stepping back from him and holding up their hands. Five lay on the ground around the Slayer, legs and arms broken.

Gotrek snarled at the rest, beckoning them forwards. 'Come on, you cowards. Finish what you started.'

One-Ear backed up, shaking his head. 'It was the captain that wanted this. Now he's dead, we only want to leave.'

'Then go,' growled Gotrek. 'And good riddance.'

The pirates let out relieved breaths and turned and ran towards the harbour – at least most of them did. About a dozen of them hesitated, looking uncertainly from their departing comrades to Gotrek, Felix and Aethenir. Broken-Nose was among them.

One of the other pirates nudged him forwards. 'Ask him, Jochen.'

Broken-Nose turned to Felix. 'It is true what you said about Marienburg?'

'It's true,' said Felix, who then suddenly looked up, his blood freezing. In the distance he heard the steady tramp of marching feet. The druchii were answering the alarm at last. The others heard it too. Aethenir whimpered. Gotrek growled.

'I have a wife and two boys there,' Jochen said. 'They will die?'

Felix nodded, anxious to be away. The marching was getting closer every second. It was just around the next corner. 'They will if we don't stop the sorceress.'

Jochen looked at the other pirates who had hesitated. They nodded. He turned back to Felix. 'We might be pirates, but we are Marienburg pirates. We will come with you.'

'Then hurry,' said Gotrek. 'This way.' He turned to the right.

'Master Slayer, don't,' said the young dwarf slave. 'You won't make it that way now.' He stepped to a small door in the wall where the two other dwarfs waited. 'The slave corridors. No druchii goes here.'

Gotrek hesitated, his brow lowering, then turned and followed the slaves through the door. Felix, Aethenir and the pirates followed.

The slave corridors were quite a contrast to all else that Felix had seen of the black ark. Even in the slave pen area, filthy as it was, the stone had been cleanly cut and finished, and the corridors broad. Not so here. These passages were little more than clawed out tunnels, narrow, low and choking with smoke from the torches that were used to light them. No witchlights for the slaves. The floors were uneven and damp, and littered with trash and the stubs of old torches. They branched and weaved this way and that in a bewildering maze, with steps and ramps in unexpected places and doors everywhere from which one could hear kitchen or laundry noises or smell sawdust or manure or food or perfume.

Felix, Gotrek, Aethenir and the dozen pirates who Jochen had brought with him followed the dwarf slave through the tunnels uneasily. Felix couldn't stop looking over his shoulder, expecting to hear shouts and the rumble of running boots behind them at any moment, but they never came. Whatever consternation the escape of the prisoners was generating in the main corridors had not penetrated here. The only sign that anything unusual was happening was the faint pounding of the alarm drums, pulsing though the rock walls, but the passing slaves – almost all human – paid it no mind. They hurried past on various errands – carrying baskets of food or clothing, trundling barrows full of trash, loaded down with heavy tomes or chests, or shuffling along in work details, armed with mops or brooms or shovels, eyes down and arms close to their sides.

As they hurried on, young Farnir fell back and bowed respectfully to Gotrek. 'Can you tell me, master Slayer, what is this threat to the holds? Is it the same thing that you say will destroy the city of Marienburg?'

'I will not speak to you, coward,' said Gotrek, staring straight ahead. 'You are a disgrace. You should have died before allowing yourself to be captured.'

The young dwarf flushed. 'Forgive me, Slayer,' he said, 'but I was captured when I was yet a beardling. I was raised here.'

Felix had never seen Gotrek brought up so short in all the time he had travelled with him. The Slayer turned on the slave, his eye bulging. 'What?'

Farnir cringed before his gaze. 'But my father has taught me much about the old ways and our noble ancestors. The mine code, the book of–'

Gotrek cut him off with a curse. 'Your *father*? Your father is a–' He bit off what he had begun to say and returned his gaze to the way ahead, his fists clenching and a thick vein pulsing in his temple as they continued on.

Without exception, the slaves they passed were pale, miserable things, with close-cropped heads and downcast eyes, gaunt from undernourishment and hunched as if they expected to be whipped at any moment. It made Felix's heart sick just to see them. Many times in his life he had seen men and women in much more miserable straits – chained, starved, diseased, wounded, mad or suffering from horrific mutations, but the look of hopelessness in the eyes of the slaves, the dull acceptance that their life would never change, that salvation would never come, was almost more than he could bear. These people had sunk below despair to an empty blankness that made them more like the undead than any living, breathing thing. Here they were, in a part of the ark that the druchii never visited, and still the slaves did not talk to each other or allow themselves to relax. They just hurried on, eyes fixed on the path ahead and glancing neither left or right. They hardly gave Gotrek and Felix a second look.

At the intersection with a slightly larger corridor, Farnir paused and turned to his dwarf companions. He whispered in their ears and sent them off in different directions, then turned and beckoned the escapees on.

After another few minutes, they came to a straight corridor that had evenly spaced doors all along its left side.

Farnir stopped at the third one and turned to them. 'Captain Landryol's house.' He said. 'This is the kitchen.'

Gotrek strode forwards, raising the iron pole.

'Wait, master Slayer,' said the slave. 'No need.' He motioned them out of sight.

'Betraying us will be the last thing you do,' said Gotrek.

Farnir nodded, cowed, then stepped to the door and knocked as Felix, Gotrek and the pirates stood against the wall.

After a moment a slot opened in the door.

The dwarf slave bowed. 'A delivery for Master Landryol. Wine from Bretonnia. Three casks.'

'One minute,' said a flat voice.

The slot closed, and then a latch clacked and the door swung out.

'Who sent it?' said a human cook in an apron, stepping out. 'I don't remember–'

The dwarf slave wrenched the door out of the cook's hands and slammed it open. Gotrek, Felix, Aethenir and the pirates shoved quickly past them and into a dark, low-roofed kitchen.

'Hoy! What are you–' said the cook, but the young dwarf clamped a big hand over his mouth and shoved him inside. Felix closed it behind them.

The kitchen was lit by torches and the fires that burned in ovens and hearths. Gape-mouthed kitchen slaves stared at them from long work tables, where they were preparing trays of food and drink. A serving man almost dropped a tray of silverware. But all these details were overwhelmed and obliterated by the delicious, overpowering smell of cooked food. Felix's stomach rumbled and growled like a caged lion at the scent of it.

'Who are you?' asked the cook, looking wide-eyed at them and their weapons. 'What do you want?'

'Nothing of you,' said Felix, fighting down his hunger and returning to the business at hand. 'We only want a word with your master.'

The serving man yelped at that and ran for a set of stairs, but Jochen leapt after him and shoved him down, then stood in front of the stairs with his sword drawn.

'We'd rather we were unannounced,' said Felix. He turned to the cook. 'Is the captain in?'

The cook said nothing, only stared at him, trembling, until Gotrek grabbed him by the shirt front and pulled him down so he could speak in his ear. 'Answer him,' he said softly.

'Y-yes,' said the cook. 'He's in.'

'Does he live alone?' asked Felix.

'Yes. Alone.'

'Any guards?'

'Two men from his crew. They live above stairs.'

Gotrek shook him again. 'Where?'

'At the back. Left at the top of the stairs.'

'Any other slaves?' continued Felix.

'The master's body slaves. Four girls.'

'Where are they?' demanded Gotrek.

'Usually in his chambers.'

'Right,' said Gotrek. He turned to Jochen. 'You'll stay here and keep these quiet.' He looked at Aethenir. 'You too, elf. The manling and I will deal with this corsair.'

The pirates nodded.

'But first,' said Gotrek, turning to the tables where the food was being prepared, 'we eat.'

Felix's heart leapt at the prospect. The pirates laughed. They advanced like wolves towards a downed deer.

'You mustn't!' said the cook. 'That is Master Landryol's food. We'll be whipped.'

'He won't be wanting it,' said Gotrek, and tore the leg off a roasted chicken. 'And bring more.'

Felix and the others attacked the platters ravenously as the servants backed away to obey Gotrek's demand. Even Aethenir ate like an animal, shoving food into his mouth with both hands and guzzling down wine and ale like all the rest.

'You're going to kill him!' said the serving man. 'We must raise the alarm! They kill slaves who fail to protect their masters!'

'And we kill slaves that warn their masters,' said Jochen.

After that, the servants watched in silence as the intruders ravaged their master's meal, and then his larder.

Felix moaned with pleasure as he choked down bread and meat and fruit and washed it down with something that he suspected was Averland wine. Never in his life had food tasted so good. After the days of rotten gruel and filthy water it was like ambrosia. He practically wept as the smell and the taste filled his mouth, and he had to force himself to remember to chew and not just gulp it down like a snake.

Then, only a minute after they had begun, Gotrek stepped back and wiped his mouth with the back of his hand.

'That's enough,' he said. 'We can't waste time.'

Felix groaned. He was only getting started. He never wanted to stop.

His stomach was still howling for more. With aching reluctance, he stuffed one last piece of ham into his mouth and turned away, wiping his hands on his filthy breeches and taking up his curved sword as Aethenir and the pirates continued to feast.

'Coming,' he said with a sigh.

Gotrek grabbed the serving man by the front of his jerkin and shoved him towards the stairs. 'You lead us,' he said. 'And no tricks.'

The slave whimpered and started up the stairs. Gotrek and Felix followed, their weapons at the ready. They came up into a dark hallway between, on one side, a dark-panelled dining area filled with small round tables and low chaises, and on the other, what appeared to be some sort of study. Maps covered its stone walls, and a large desk with scrolls, books and more maps sat in its centre. On this floor, they could better hear the alarm drums, still sounding faintly in the distance.

The slave led them to the far end of the hallway, where it opened out into a high-ceilinged entry chamber, an ironbound oak door at its front, and a straight, iron-railinged stairway rising up to the second floor.

They went up the stairs to a second floor, passing closed doors, and then up another stair to a third, but before they had reached the top, they heard a terrific explosion, far off, but still very loud.

Felix exchanged a glance with Gotrek.

'Euler's men are putting up a fight,' he said.

'Aye.'

The third floor was a single corridor, very dark, with doors on either side.

The slave stepped to a door on the left, then hesitated, shaking. He looked back at Gotrek and Felix, eyes wide with fear. 'Have mercy, sirs,' he murmured. 'If you kill him, we will die. They will kill us.'

'Step aside, craven,' sneered Gotrek.

He pushed past the quivering slave to the door and turned the handle. It was unlocked. He readied his weapon and looked over his shoulder. Felix gripped his stolen sword and nodded. They pushed in.

'Is that you, Mechlin?' came a voice speaking sibilant Reikspiel from within the dark chamber. 'Where in the name of the Dark Mother is our dinner? And what was that damned noise?' Felix recognised the voice as if from a dream.

The entrance was curtained off from the rest of the room by heavy brocade drapes, but Felix could see through a gap hints of panelled walls and dark wood furniture glinting red in the light of a banked fire.

Gotrek drew the drapery aside a few inches to get the lay of the land, and they saw their quarry sprawled naked on a fur-covered sleeping platform with his head propped up on a tasselled bolster and his arms draped around the sleeping forms of four beautiful young human girls, completely bald, and clad only in delicate silver fetters at throat, wrists and ankles. They curled like cats around him. The scent of black lotus smoke hung heavy in the air, and Felix could see enamelled pipes and braziers glinting by the bed.

'Stop cowering and come in, Mechlin,' drawled Landryol. 'I won't bite.' He chuckled and looked at his bedmates. 'Not you, anyway.'

'They seek to kill you, master!' shrieked the slave from the corridor. 'Protect yourself!'

Gotrek cursed and ripped aside the curtain, then charged across the dark room with Felix beside him as Landryol struggled to sit up and the four beauties raised sleepy heads.

Gotrek leapt up onto the sleeping platform and caught the druchii captain around the neck with one massive hand. Felix stood beside him and put his sword to Landryol's chest. The pleasure slaves shrieked and spilled off the bed in all directions.

Gotrek raised the iron pole over his head. 'Where is my axe?'

'And my sword,' said Felix.

'How do you come here?' asked Landryol, blinking drug-fogged eyes and looking back and forth between them. 'No one escapes the pens.'

Gotrek shook him like a doll. 'My axe!'

The druchii raised a trembling hand and pointed to a curtained alcove on the far side of the room. 'Under the floor.'

Gotrek shoved Landryol back down and sprang from the bed, looking back at Felix. 'Watch him.'

Felix nodded and moved the tip of his sword to the druchii's throat as the Slayer disappeared behind the curtain.

Footsteps thudded somewhere below them. Felix glanced to the door.

'Guards coming!' Felix called.

'Good,' said Gotrek from behind the curtain.

'You will never leave here alive,' said Landryol.

'We know that already,' said Felix, looking towards the door again. The footsteps were thundering up the stairs now.

There was a sound of splitting wood from the alcove and then a grunt of satisfaction. The curtain jerked aside and Gotrek strode out brandishing his axe in one hand and carrying Felix's scabbarded sword in the other.

'My arm is complete,' the Slayer said.

With a clatter of boots, two druchii corsairs ran in, swords drawn, and skidded to a stop at the scene that met their eyes.

'Kill them!' said Landryol.

The corsairs needed no encouragement. One charged Gotrek while the other leapt onto the bed and lunged at Felix. Felix whipped his stolen sword around and parried a blade aimed straight at his face, but Landryol kicked him behind the knee and he crashed down on the bed. The corsair slashed down at him. Felix rolled off onto the floor, sending one of the bed slaves scurrying for a corner. He scrambled up as the corsair came after him.

'Manling,' called Gotrek.

Felix looked up just in time to see his sword arcing towards him, thrown by the Slayer as he blocked the other druchii's attacks.

Felix's opponent knocked Karaghul out of the air and stabbed at him again. Felix cursed and hopped back, then kicked the table with the pipe and brazier at him. The corsair stumbled back, trying to avoid the hot coals, and Felix flung his stolen sword after him then dived for Karaghul, drawing the blade as he rolled to his feet. The corsair charged and they clashed again.

On the other side of the bed, Gotrek blocked another blow by the second druchii, then kicked him in the stomach. The druchii curled up, retching and exposing his neck, but Gotrek only cracked him in the face with the heel of the axe and stepped back as he fell. 'You will not die yet,' he said.

He turned to Landryol, who had caught up a jewelled sword, and stood at the foot of the bed, entirely naked.

'I vowed that you would be the first to die when I recovered my axe,' said the Slayer, striding towards him.

Landryol's lip curled in derision as he dropped into a guard and extended his blade. 'You may try, dwarf. But I am a formidable–'

Gotrek's axe hacked the slender sword in two and buried itself in the dark elf's breastbone, and the rest of the boast went unsaid.

The corsair facing Felix gaped at his master's sudden death. Felix ran him through before he recovered.

Gotrek wrenched his axe from Landryol's chest, then turned on the corsair he had cracked over the head. The druchii was still struggling to stand.

'*Now* you die,' said Gotrek, and beheaded him with a casual backhand.

The room was suddenly silent, the only noise Felix and Gotrek's breathing, and the soft weeping of the bed slaves. Felix wiped his sword clean on the bed furs and returned it to its scabbard. It felt good to have it again, but this was only the first part of what they must do.

He turned to Gotrek. 'Are you ready?'

'One moment, manling.'

The Slayer crossed back to the alcove and disappeared, then came back with an open wooden chest. The contents glinted in the dim firelight. He lifted out a heavy shirt of chainmail and handed it to Felix. It was his!

Under it was a profusion of golden bracelets, armbands and chains.

'Your gold,' said Felix.

'Aye,' said Gotrek, obviously pleased. 'Besmirched by elven hands, but all here, Grungni be praised.'

Gotrek slipped it all back on his meaty wrists while Felix pulled his mail on over his head, then they strode back out into the hall. The slave who had brought them there still cowered by the door. Gotrek glared at him for a second, as if contemplating killing him for his betrayal, but then snorted and continued to the stairs.

'The druchii will do worse to him,' he said.

* * *

The kitchen slaves, all pushed into one corner by the pirates, stared in horror as Gotrek and Felix came back down the stairs to the kitchen holding their weapons.

'You killed him,' said the cook.

Felix nodded.

The slaves moaned in misery. A scullery girl burst into tears. 'We'll be sold off now! To who knows who! How could you be so cruel?'

Another patted her on the shoulder, comforting her. Felix glared, angry, though he knew not at whom. Shouldn't slaves be happy that their master was killed?

Jochen stepped up to them, looking grim. 'We were right to come with you, it seems. The others didn't make it out of the harbour. Blown up with their own powder.'

'Where did you hear this?' asked Gotrek.

Jochen nodded towards the dark end of the room, where the slaves' meal table was. Farnir sat with the two dwarfs he had sent off earlier there, as well as two other dwarfs, a grizzled elder with a stiff brush of short grey hair, and a youngster with downcast eyes and a balding horseshoe of ginger hair. The newcomers' beards were little more than grown out stubble. They rose in silent awe as the Slayer turned to face them.

'What is this?' asked Gotrek.

Farnir opened his mouth to speak, but the grey-haired dwarf spoke first, stepping forwards. 'Farnir sent word to us that you'd broken the pens, and we came to see it for ourselves.'

'Never would have believed it,' said the balding dwarf, shaking his head.

'Never would have tried it,' grunted Gotrek.

The older dwarf bowed his head respectfully to Gotrek. 'I am Birgi, father of Farnir. And this is Skalf. It is an honour to meet a true follower of Grimnir.'

Gotrek glared at him with cold contempt. 'Your shame is twice that of the others. You live as a slave, and you raised a son into slavery. You are lower than grobi.'

Birgi hung his head, 'Aye, Slayer. We know what you think of us, but you'd be crest-deep in druchii at the moment if it weren't for Farnir bringing you through the slave corridors, and it was us who told him the way to this house and to where the wizards are held, when you asked, so you might be polite.'

Gotrek snorted, and looked about to retort, but then Jochen stepped forwards.

'The dwarfs say the magister and the seeress are locked up downstairs in the druchii barracks,' he said. 'Is that true?'

Gotrek nodded. Felix sighed at this news.

'I want to save Marienburg,' Jochen continued, 'but is it necessary to walk into the middle of the whole damned dark elf army? Can't we leave them?'

'We won't stand a chance against the sorceresses without them,' Aethenir said, looking up from where he was cleaning himself fastidiously at the kitchen's pump.

'We can lead you there,' said Birgi. 'There are service tunnels down to the barracks level, but you can't enter the barracks themselves without passing through a guarded gate.'

'We don't need a guide,' snapped Gotrek.

Everyone looked to him.

'I will not be in the debt of honourless dwarfs,' he growled.

'Slayer, they want to help,' said Felix. 'And we need help.'

Birgi nodded. 'We'll do anything we can,' he said.

'Except put your lives at risk,' growled Gotrek.

The balding dwarf raised his head at that, angry, but Birgi put a hand on his arm.

'Easy, Skalf,' he said, then turned to Gotrek. 'If our deaths would make a difference, Slayer, we would die. But if we rose up, if all the slaves on this ark rose up, the druchii would only kill us and replace us with new slaves. They are too strong.'

Gotrek snorted at that. 'The death of one elf is difference enough.'

The old slave continued, undaunted. 'We will gladly help you stop this threat to our old holds – for it is there that our hearts lie – but even if you succeed, this ark will go on, the few druchii you kill forgotten when the next fleet of hakseer corsairs comes to reinforce it. Nothing will change. Nothing has ever changed, for four thousand years.'

'Where are the wizards inside the barracks area?' Felix asked before Gotrek could respond. There was no time for argument.

Birgi coughed and turned to him. 'Er, well, they're being held by the Endless, the cold bastards that High Sorceress Heshor brought with her. We had to fix up a pair of old barracks for them. Refitted one for new officers' quarters, new rooms carved, fine furniture – only the best for our guests from the mainland.'

'Why have they held them? Why weren't they locked up with the rest of us?' asked Felix.

Birgi shrugged. 'I don't know about that, only the Temple of Khaine don't allow wizards as slaves. Kill 'em as soon as they're taken. So I'd guess the Endless are hiding them from the witches. No guess as to why.'

Felix couldn't quite understand all that. Weren't the sorceresses witches? What was the difference? It didn't matter now. What mattered was how they were going to get past the barracks guards.

'Does this Heshor have a lot of power here?' he asked.

Birgi and the other dwarfs laughed.

'She's turned the ark upside down since she's come,' said Skalf, the balding dwarf. 'Making us sail this way and that like she owned the place. Twisted old Tarlkhir around her finger like a ribbon.'

'Orders from Naggarond,' said Birgi. 'Whatever she's here for, she's doing it on the authority of the Witch King himself.'

'So things done in her name would carry weight?' Felix asked.

The old dwarf nodded. 'Aye, but...'

Felix turned to Aethenir and Gotrek. 'If we dress the high one as a druchii and pretend to be his prisoners, and if he says that he is bringing slaves captured during the pirates' attack on the harbour to the Endless by Heshor's orders...'

'It won't work,' interrupted Aethenir. 'I look nothing like a druchii!'

The others gave him a look.

He groaned. 'Well, I *sound* nothing like a druchii. My accent...'

'Then you'd better start practising,' said Gotrek. 'And go find some clothes.'

Aethenir sighed, but reluctantly went up the stairs to look through the dead druchii's closets as Gotrek and Felix fell on the remains of the food.

Not long after, they wound through the tunnels again, following Aethenir, who wore Landryol's armour, helm and sea dragon cloak, as Birgi trotted at his side, telling him the name of the captain of the Endless and other important names a corsair would know. Felix wondered if it was all for naught. The ark had stopped hours ago – at least two hours before they had made their break – and it seemed hours more since they had fought Euler's pirates, though in fact it was probably no more than half an hour. Could it be possible that Heshor hadn't plucked the harp yet? Did harnessing its terrible power require more than just playing it? Was there some ceremony involved? He expected at every step to feel the ark shake or sway and hear the far-off rumble of land being born from the waves. But perhaps he wouldn't have felt a thing. Perhaps Heshor had already done it!

He sighed to himself. If it had already happened, then they would take what revenge they could, though it could never be enough.

At last they neared the door that Birgi said opened near the front gates of the druchii barracks. They stopped some distance from it and made their final preparations, putting all their weapons and mail in a sack Felix and Gotrek would carry between them, and manacling themselves to a long slave chain that they had found among Landryol's belongings. Felix and the pirates didn't like this measure, and Gotrek hated it, for it meant that he would not be able to get to his axe quickly if anything went wrong, and also that he was putting all his trust in Aethenir, who, as their 'captor', held the only key to unlock them. But it was a necessary measure, for no captured prisoners would be allowed to keep their weapons, and if they were to get through the gate, they must be able to pass an inspection by the guards. Simply looping the chains around their wrists and pretending to be locked up wouldn't do.

As Aethenir struggled to get a pair of manacles around Gotrek's massive wrists, Birgi gave them detailed instructions for finding their way through the barracks area to the lodgings of the Endless, then he and the other dwarfs gave them a dwarfen salute.

'Good luck, Slayer,' said the old dwarf. 'Good luck to you all.'

Gotrek sneered and said nothing.

Suddenly Farnir stepped to Birgi. 'Father, I'm going with them.' He turned and offered his wrists to Aethenir.

Birgi blinked, stunned. 'Farnir, you have already risked much. Don't be...'

'Did the stories you told me about brave dwarf heroes of old mean nothing?' asked Farnir insistently.

'Of course they did,' said Birgi. 'But...'

'This is for the holds of our homeland,' said the young dwarf, backing away. 'This is for the honour you told me we once had.'

'But... but it will fail, Farnir,' called Birgi, his face sagging with despair. 'It won't make any difference.'

'I'm sorry, Father. I must.' Farnir turned away, stone-faced, and allowed Aethenir to add him to the line of 'prisoners'.

Gotrek laughed over his shoulder, scornful. 'Ha! A beardling shames them. They should all shave their heads, the lot of them.' He turned away as Aethenir stepped to the head of the coffle. 'Lead us out, elf. It stinks in here.'

Aethenir took a deep breath then stepped to the door and opened it. As Felix shuffled out after him with the others he cast a last look back at the four dwarfs who had stayed behind. They stood with their heads hung low, unable to look towards Gotrek or each other. He felt for them. Offered the choice of death and torture or serving as a slave, he wasn't sure what he would have done, either.

Aethenir looked back at Felix and his other 'prisoners' as they approached the gate. 'Put your heads down, curse you,' he hissed. 'Look defeated.'

Felix did as he was told, although the temptation to look forwards and see what was transpiring was hard to fight. He could tell by the tremor in the high elf's voice that he was terrified – which made Felix terrified, for if Aethenir betrayed his fear to the guards they would be exposed, and that would be the end. They would be killed here, unable to defend themselves, and never find Max and Claudia or stop the sorceresses.

They were crossing a broad, cave-roofed plaza in front of the barracks area. Druchii spear and sword companies hurried past towards the gate, some bearing the wounded behind them on stretchers – casualties from fighting the pirates, Felix thought. Other companies marched out in quickstep behind their captains – looking for them, perhaps?

The barracks gate was a wide portcullised doorway with defensive towers on either side. It looked like the front of a castle built into the end of a cave. A double rank of well-armoured guards stood outside it, their captain passing companies in and out, and a dozen archers walked an artillery platform above. As Aethenir and his line of slaves approached, the captain held up a hand and asked a question in the druchii tongue.

Aethenir answered, keeping his voice clipped and hard and, thankfully, remarkably steady. Felix couldn't understand a word of the exchange, but he heard the high elf mention the names the old dwarf had give him – High Sorceress Heshor and Istultair, the captain of the Endless – and seem to make demands in their names. Felix had hoped that the magic of their exalted influence would usher them smoothly through the gate, but this did not happen. The guard captain seemed unimpressed, and walked down their line with his hands folded behind his back, examining them one at a time. He paid particular attention to Gotrek, and stopped at him again when he came back up the line. Gotrek's fists clenched at the attention and Felix held his breath.

The guard captain turned away and said something to Aethenir in a sly tone. Aethenir answered haughtily, but Felix could hear a tremor at the edges of his voice. It's all going wrong, Felix thought, and sweat began to pour down his sides. The guard captain came back with a jovial yet menacing reply. Aethenir repeated his refusal, and the guard just shrugged and waved him away.

Aethenir paused, in what appeared to be angry indecision, then finally stepped to Gotrek. 'Do not kill me, dwarf,' he murmured. 'He requires a bribe.'

He reached out and began to tug on two of Gotrek's smaller golden bracelets. Gotrek growled and jerked away. Aethenir cursed in the druchii tongue and slapped the Slayer hard on the ear. 'Insolent cur,' he shouted in Reikspiel. 'Dare you resist? You have no possessions! All that you are and own belongs to High Sorceress Heshor now!'

Felix nearly fainted. The Slayer was going to kill the high elf, and then they would be chopped to pieces by the guards. But amazingly, Gotrek held his temper, doing nothing more than grinding his teeth and balling his fists as the high elf pried the two bracelets from his wrists. Felix could see that the self-restraint required to keep still was nearly killing Gotrek. A vein pulsed dangerously in his forehead and his face was blood-red.

Aethenir tossed the bracelets to the guard captain as if they meant nothing to him, and the druchii bowed them through the gate.

'I will take the price of that gold out of your hide, elf,' growled Gotrek when they had passed out of earshot.

'I had no choice,' whimpered the high elf. 'Surely you can see that.'

'You could have bargained better,' said Gotrek.

Inside the gate, they came into a large open parade square with a high roof and rows of doors and windows cut into the stone walls on either side – the barracks themselves – and passages leading off in every direction. The place was a swirl of activity – companies forming up in the square under the barked orders of baton-wielding captains, and other companies falling out and laying their wounded in neat ranks along one side as surgeons and healers and slaves moved among them. It reminded Felix of what one saw when one stirred up an ant hill, only much more orderly.

Birgi had told them that the barracks he and his crew had refitted for the use of the Endless was in a left-hand passage that opened off the far end of the parade ground. Felix swallowed nervously at the idea of walking shackled and unarmed through so many of the enemy, but thankfully, the druchii paid them no mind, except to shove them aside if they got in their way. Felix held his breath again, afraid that Gotrek would explode into violence at such treatment, but he kept his head down, muttering Khazalid curses all the while.

At the end of the square, Aethenir found the left-hand passage and they entered it. There was no one in it, and the noise of the parade ground fell away behind them as they turned a second corner into another row of barracks. Aethenir paused in the shadow of the passage and they looked out, examining the long corridor. Most of the barracks appeared to be unoccupied – the windows boarded up and the steps that led up to the doors dusty. The first two on the right, however, were freshly scrubbed, with new doors and open windows but, unsettlingly, no sign of activity.

'Strange,' said Aethenir. 'I expected to see guards, or at least slaves.'

'Maybe they're all inside,' said Jochen.

'Let's have a look,' said Felix.

Aethenir got to work with his key and they all shucked their manacles. Gotrek opened the sack full of weapons and drew his axe from it while Felix pulled on his mail and buckled Karaghul around his waist. The pirates followed suit and they all crept forwards, only this time with Aethenir taking up the rear.

Felix and Jochen raised their heads and looked through the first window they came to. Inside was a barracks room like any other – except that the walls were carved from solid rock. Cots ran down each wall, each with a small iron-bound chest at its foot. There was one door at the back of the room and another in the side wall. A few slaves were cleaning the floor, and a few young druchii were sitting on the cots and polishing armour, boots and belts. The Endless were not there.

'Yer wizards might be behind one of them doors,' said Jochen when they had crouched down again.

'Let's check the other barracks first,' said Felix.

They crossed to the second barracks and looked through those windows. These were clearly the officers' quarters. There was a well-appointed entry way, the stone walls covered with ebony panelling and mounted with witchlights, and a central corridor leading away into darkness. No one was in sight.

'This one first,' said Felix.

Gotrek stepped to the door. It was unlocked. He pushed it open and stepped through. Felix, Aethenir, Farnir and Jochen's pirates followed him in. They padded silently down the corridor. It had two lavishly carved doors on each side and a plain one at the far end. Felix and Aethenir listened at each of the carved doors in turn, but heard nothing. They continued on.

Gotrek listened at the door at the end of the hall, then tried it. It too was unlocked. A feeling of unease crept over Felix. They should have been challenged by now. They should have met some resistance.

On the other side of the door was a narrow set of stairs going down into darkness. Aethenir made a tiny ball of light with a snap of his fingers and Gotrek started down. Felix and the others followed.

They came down into a supply room, bedding and candles and sundries stacked in crates along the walls. At the far end of the room was a heavy door. There was a chair and a table outside it, and the remains of a meal drawing flies.

'That's it,' said Gotrek, and started forwards.

Felix and the others crept along behind him, weapons at the ready. Felix held his breath, expecting hidden druchii to leap out of the shadows at every step. No attack came.

Gotrek put his hand on the latch and turned it. It opened easily. He threw the door wide, revealing blackness beyond.

Aethenir sent his light in before them. The room was small and bare but for two piles of filthy straw. Gotrek and Felix stepped cautiously inside. It smelled of urine and sweat and rotting food. There were grimy, blood-spattered rags on the floor. Some of them might have once been deep blue, others might have once been gold and white, but of Max and Claudia there was no sign.

SEVENTEEN

A druchii voice called a question behind them and they turned. A young dark elf stood upon the stairs, a witchlight torch in one hand.

Aethenir called to him, beckoning him forwards, but the youth, seeing them all with their weapons, sensed something wrong and ran back up the stairs, shouting warnings.

Felix cursed and sprinted after him, pounding up the stairs and into the hall. A door opened halfway down, and the youth, looking back towards Felix, ran smack into it and fell reeling to the ground. A slave looked out from the open door, then shrieked and darted back, slamming it behind him.

Felix pounced on the young druchii before he could recover himself and pinned him to the floor, putting his sword across his throat.

'The mages!' he hissed. 'Where are they? Where have you taken them?'

The youth babbled in the druchii tongue. Felix shook him. 'Reikspiel, damn you!'

There were footsteps behind him and Gotrek and Aethenir joined him, followed closely by the pirates.

Aethenir asked something in the elf tongue and the youth stared at him, then spat on his boots. Aethenir kicked him in the ribs. Felix pressed his sword harder against the druchii's neck. Gotrek stepped forwards and raised his axe over him, his single eye cold and dead.

The youth blanched at the sight of Gotrek and blurted out something. Aethenir asked a few more questions and got short replies.

He sighed and turned to Felix and Gotrek. 'The sorceresses came and took them away several hours ago. The Endless went with them.'

'Where?' asked Felix. 'Where have they gone?'

'He doesn't know,' said the high elf. 'Only that they took the stairs at the end of this avenue, which go only down.'

'Further down?' said Jochen, looking uneasy. 'Let's give up on these magisters.'

'What is below us?' asked Gotrek, ignoring him.

'The menagerie of the beastmasters,' said Farnir. 'And those flesh houses reserved for officers and the nobility.'

Felix blinked. 'Are they going to feed them to wild beasts? Are they going to…?' he couldn't complete the thought.

The dwarf slave suddenly paled. His eyes widened. 'It is rumoured among the slaves that there is a secret temple in the depths of the ark, with its entrance somewhere inside one of the flesh houses. They say many are taken there, never to return.'

'What sort of temple?' growled Gotrek.

'None dare say,' said the dwarf.

'A temple with an entrance in such a house can only serve one god,' whispered Aethenir, looking sick with fear.

'What house is it in?' Felix asked Farnir.

He shook his head. 'I know not.'

'Then we'll have to check every one,' said Gotrek.

'There are more guards before the stairs,' said Farnir. 'You will need your disguises again.'

'We'll need a new disguise,' said Gotrek, thinking. He turned to Aethenir. 'Trade that armour for Endless kit, elf. And hurry.'

'What do we do with this fool?' asked Jochen, pointing to the young druchii still cowering under Felix's sword.

Gotrek dropped his axe and buried it in the young dark elf's face, shattering his skull and splashing blood everywhere.

'That,' he said, and turned away.

A few minutes later, once more locked to their chain, and with their weapons once more bundled in the sack, they shuffled down the long corridor between the unused barracks towards the menagerie stair gate, trailing behind the trembling figure of Aethenir, dressed as an officer of the Endless and wearing a silver skull mask.

This time there was no bribery required. The guards at the gate seemed awed by the uniform of the Endless, and bowed Aethenir through without question. The high elf led them to a narrow stairwell that zigzagged down into the rock for twelve flights before ending in a broad, low-roofed corridor that reeked of animal dung and rotting meat.

The roars of fierce beasts and the crack of whips echoed all around them as they started down it. The sounds and the smells came from a wide archway on the left-hand wall, sealed by elaborate wrought iron gates, and guarded by druchii in uniforms adorned with leopardskin capes and carrying long, wickedly barbed spears.

Aethenir ignored them and continued on, as he had been instructed to by Farnir, and soon they came to a much smaller archway with no gate and no guard. The sounds and smells that wafted from this arch were of an entirely different sort of wildlife. Felix smelled wine and perfume, incense and the smoke of the black lotus, as well as sweat and sex and death. Raucous laughter and strange discordant singing reached his ears, mixed with far-off shrieks of pain.

They filed through the arch and stopped dead at the scene that opened before them. The street, or tunnel – it was hard to make the distinction – was narrow and tall, with houses carved from the solid rock rising three storeys on either side. The high arched roof of the tunnel was cut back deeply, so that the houses had roofs and rooftop gardens and verandas. Witchlights blazed purple and red in iron lanterns hung from baroque facades, and the sights illuminated by this blood-coloured light were enough to turn Felix's stomach. He had been in the red light districts of cities from Kislev to Araby, but never had he seen a place so dedicated to pleasure, pain and perversion. Usually, even in the loosest of cities, the joy houses kept a somewhat respectable front. Such a pretence was apparently unnecessary here.

Friezes and statues depicting the most lewd and vile acts decorated the fronts of every establishment. Some places had iron cages hung above their doors, within which dull-eyed human slaves flagellated one another or performed listless acts of coitus. In front of every house stood armed guards dressed in fanciful armour that seemed to have more to do with titillation than protection.

Strolling from house to house were the flower of druchii society – tall, cruelly handsome lords, sultry, sway-hipped ladies, swaggering officers, naked, silver-masked courtesans, exquisite persons whose gender it was impossible to tell, and pushing through the crush to the sound of cracking whips, covered palanquins carried by stooped, scarred human slaves, transporting those who wished to keep their identities secret.

'Asuryan protect me,' murmured Aethenir. 'This place is an abomination.'

'For once we agree,' said Gotrek. 'Even for elves this is disgusting.'

Felix concurred, but the thing that concerned him more than the vileness of the place was its vastness. The street curved away into the smoke-shrouded distance before them and more streets branched from it on either side, and every house that they could see was a house of pleasure. They might search for the next three days and not find the house that hid the entrance to the secret temple.

His fear was unfounded, however, for as he and the others stood staring around slack-jawed, Farnir called to a female slave who was displaying herself lewdly in a window cage.

'Sister,' he said. 'Did a troop of Endless and a party of sorceresses pass this way?'

'Aye,' said the woman, not ceasing her gyrations.

'What house did they enter?'

The woman didn't know, but she told them that the procession had turned the corner to the left, a few hours ago.

It was in this way that they proceeded – Aethenir marching along as if he knew where he was going, while Farnir whispered questions to the slaves they passed – and they were legion – to learn where they should go. At last, after several more lefts and rights, they were directed to a house known as the Crucible of Joy.

Just before they reached it, Aethenir marched them into a dark alley between two houses and began unlocking their shackles. 'What am I to say?' he whimpered. 'What if we are turned away?'

'Then we fight at last,' said Gotrek.

'What if it isn't the right place after all?'

'We still fight,' said Gotrek.

'Tell them...' said Felix, trying to think. 'Tell them, "She awaits". If it is the right place, they will lead us to the sorceress. If it isn't, we haven't compromised ourselves.'

They left the unlocked shackles loose around their wrists and followed Aethenir out of the alley and up to the guards that stood before the door of the Crucible of Joy. From the outside at least, it looked little different than any of the other flesh houses. Its sign, if one could call it that, was a bubbling crucible hung over a fire in an alcove cut in the front wall, out of which spilled something that looked – and smelled – very much like blood. The guards were towering druchii women, dressed only in stained leather blacksmiths' aprons, golden greaves and gauntlets, and helmets crested with pink and purple feathers that looked like flames. They came to attention as Aethenir stopped in front of them.

Again, Felix could not understand what passed between them, but the guards seemed to treat him with the utmost deference. They bowed to him, and then one went to the door and spoke to someone within. After a moment, a human slave clad only in a purple loincloth came out, bowed almost to the floor, then motioned for them to follow.

The interior was everything that Felix had feared, and worse. The fire motif continued through a hexagonal entry chamber where braziers blazed with purple flames. A druchii woman, topless, but wearing a black veil, bowed to Aethenir as the slave led them into a corridor painted with black and purple flames. From above and below and all around Felix could hear sounds of ecstasy and excruciation – moans and screams and whimpers of fear. A girl pleaded heartbreakingly for mercy in Bretonnian. A male voice laughed or screamed, Felix couldn't decide which.

Through open archways only partially curtained, Felix saw glimpses of fire and flesh and murder being done. He flinched from brandings and scarrings and knives that glowed a cherry-red. Memories of fighting in the cellars of the Cleansing Flame, and the fires that Lichtmann had attacked them with, came unbidden to his mind and made him shiver. In one room he saw a ring of druchii men and women passing around an enamelled pipe as they watched molten gold being dripped from a crucible onto the face of a bound woman, one drop at a time. They laughed dreamily at each scream and convulsion.

Felix heard Gotrek growling beside him, and realised that he was echoing him with growls of his own.

The house slave led them down a winding iron staircase that was hot to the touch. Three flights later he bowed them into a square black marble chamber with doors on each wall and a chandelier of purple-flamed torches hanging above. Veins in the marble glinted pink in the flickering light. The door directly opposite the stair was grander than the others, framed by fluted columns and topped by a decorative arch, into which was set a white stone face of cold, immaculate beauty. Three Endless stood before the door, rigidly at attention.

Aethenir slowed when he saw them.

'Go on, elf,' muttered Gotrek.

'But surely they will know that I am not one of their fellows,' said the high elf.

'They will if you cower back here,' said Felix. 'Be bold.'

The elf snorted angrily at this, but it seemed to have some effect. He straightened his shoulders and strode towards the guards. Felix held his breath and loosened the mouth of the sack that carried their weapons. The guards eyed Aethenir as he approached, motionless and impassive behind their silver masks. Then the centre one spoke.

Aethenir replied, but apparently the answer was not to the Endless's liking. He asked a second question. This time Aethenir faltered in his response.

The hands of the guards dropped to the hilts of their swords and the centre one motioned for Aethenir to remove his mask.

'Right,' said Gotrek, throwing off his chains and dropping the sack with a clang. 'That's it.'

The Endless turned, drawing their swords as Gotrek and Felix pulled their weapons from the sack. Gotrek roared and charged them, shoving the paralysed Aethenir behind him. Felix followed the Slayer in, though he knew from past experience that it was hopeless. The slave in the loincloth ran shrieking back up the stairs as Farnir, Jochen and the pirates snatched up their weapons and joined the fray.

The Endless in the centre died on the first pass, parrying perfectly, but totally unprepared for the Slayer's strength. The flashing axe drove his blade back into his helm, staggering him, and Gotrek hacked him in the side, cutting through both armour and ribs like they were brittle shale.

Felix's first exchange with the druchii he faced was almost exactly opposite. He slashed with his sword, only to find that the druchii had moved and was stabbing at his chest with an overhand thrust. Felix twisted, and the sword grazed his ribs. He fell back, slashing desperate figure-eights in the air. The druchii followed and he thought he was dead, but then Farnir, Jochen and the pirates came to his rescue, hacking and stabbing and howling.

The druchii didn't bat an eye. He blocked every wild attack and returned with a riposte that skewered a pirate's neck. Felix lunged at him again, but his sword was turned neatly aside in passing as the druchii gashed another man's wrist and turned to face Felix again.

Felix fell back, then felt himself shoved aside, as Gotrek stepped in, swinging his axe up from the floor. The druchii saw him and spun to counter, but Gotrek was faster. The axe split the dark elf from crotch to chest and his guts slapped wetly on the polished floor. He crumpled on top of them.

Felix and the pirates stepped back, looking for the last druchii. He was already dead – his head missing. Another pirate had fallen as well, pierced through the heart.

'Well done, friends,' said Aethenir, stepping forwards.

'You might have helped,' said Jochen, looking around at his dead and wounded comrades.

'Better he didn't,' said Gotrek with a sneer.

The pirate searched the dead dark elves for the key to the door as Felix pulled his mail from the sack and put it on. There was no key. Whoever had entered had locked it behind them.

Gotrek shrugged and stepped to the door. 'Get ready,' he said.

Felix, Aethenir and the remaining pirates lined up behind him. Farnir armed himself with one of the druchii blades and joined them. Felix took a deep breath and got a firmer grip on Karaghul.

The door was of heavy, intricately carved wood. The lock was protected by a sturdy, black iron plate. Gotrek was through it in three swings of his axe, then kicked open the splintered panel and strode in, on his guard.

Inside was a large and entirely empty bedchamber.

Felix stared around him, confused. This was not the secret temple to some foul god that he had been expecting. This was – by druchii flesh house standards at any rate – a perfectly ordinary boudoir. A nightmarish mural of carnal atrocities was painted on the four walls above intricately worked ebony panelling. Fetters, whips and instruments of torture were displayed on racks to the right and left. Against the wall in front of them rose a massive sleeping platform, piled with furs and pillows, all in disarray, and so high that it was reached by a set of shallow black marble steps. At its four corners were hung columns of red velvet drapery, and torches were set into the wall on either side of it. All very grand and nasty, but a dead end.

'This can't be right,' said Jochen.

'We have been led astray somehow,' said Aethenir.

'Is it a trap?' asked Felix, looking back at the door.

Gotrek snorted. 'Men and elves are blind.'

He stumped across the room to the torch on the left-hand side of the sleeping platform and pressed the wood panelling below it. There was a click, and everyone stepped back, wary.

Felix watched the wall beside the torch, expecting to see a secret door open in it, but then movement caught his eye and he turned. The entire sleeping platform was slowly rising like the lid of a treasure chest, and folding back against the wall. The underside of the bed was revealed to be a large marble panel, carved into a bas-relief of a graceful figure that appeared to be both masculine and feminine, and who danced upon a mound of naked copulating bodies, all of them maimed in the most horrible ways. In the flickering torchlight of the room it almost seemed as if the figure and the bodies that it trod on writhed and squirmed lasciviously.

There was a hole in the raised platform where the bed had rested, with marble stairs that led down into darkness.

'Sigmar and Manann preserve us,' said Jochen.

Felix had the sinking suspicion that they would shortly need the help of every god they could call upon.

The stairs went straight down for so long that Felix was afraid they would come out at the bottom of the floating island and be dumped in the sea again. There were no torches mounted on the walls. They felt their way down in utter darkness but for a reddish glow far below them that bobbed and weaved with each step. The further down they went, the thicker the air became – a cloying soup of incense, lotus smoke, and something sharp and bitter.

Then another, closer glow began to light their steps. Felix looked around and saw that the runes on Gotrek's axe were pulsing as if fire was coursing through them.

'Gotrek...' he said.

'Aye, manling.'

As they descended further, the red glow resolved itself into the reflection of crimson light shining upon a black marble floor at the base of the stairs. Gotrek and Felix stepped cautiously down to it and looked along a short corridor that ended at a pair of half-open, unguarded doors, through which came the red light, accompanied by the sound of voices raised in a high, wailing chant that set Felix's teeth on edge.

With the others edging forwards behind them, Gotrek and Felix crept to the doors, a pair of heavy gold panels crusted with rubies, amethysts and lapis lazuli in patterns that depicted thousands of naked bodies entwined in impossible, painful ways. Felix looked through the gap between them, then jerked his head back, startled, for a face was staring directly at them.

'It's only a statue, manling,' said Gotrek.

Felix looked again. The air inside was so hazed with violet smoke that it was hard to make out details, but directly ahead of them, in the middle of a circular, brazier-lit chamber, was a statue of a six-headed snake that reared up twice as high as a man. Each of the heads was fronted with a beautiful white marble druchii face of indeterminate gender, one of them looking directly at the door with eyes that glittered like living onyx. Half-hidden behind the statue, on the far side of the room, was a pillared archway that opened into a further chamber, within which Felix could see shadows of sinuous movement that seemed to follow the rhythms of the chanting.

Gotrek pushed through the obscene doors and entered. Felix tried to follow, but as he put his hand on the door, his mind whirled with unbidden emotions. All in an instant he wanted to weep and rage, laugh and kill, love and torture. A vision of writing the Slayer's story in the Slayer's blood on vellum made from the Slayer's flesh crawled up into his brain, and he found he could not push it away.

'This is an evil place,' said Aethenir, behind him.

The words brought Felix back to himself. He forced the horrid visions back down into his subconscious and followed the Slayer into the chamber. Aethenir, Farnir, Jochen and the pirates edged in even more reluctantly. The pirates huddled together like frightened cattle, and Farnir clutched a stolen sword like it was a lifeline. Under his druchii helm, Aethenir's eyes showed white all around, and he murmured a constant stream of elven prayers.

The chamber was perfectly circular. Walls of pink stone glittered like mica, and it throbbed with low moans of pain and ecstasy, counterpoint to the wailing chant that continued to grate on Felix's ears. Purple flames leapt in golden braziers set at regular intervals around the walls, and the floor was a mosaic of golden tiles with a large offset ring of purple tiles within them, surrounded by strange runes. The six-headed snake sat at the centre of the room, with its pedestal touching the arc of the offset ring.

As they crept across the golden floor towards the far archway, they passed close to the statue, and Felix saw around its base offerings of wine, blood, ink and other intimate liquids shimmered in little golden dishes amidst pink, red and purple candles. The pirates skirted warily around the thing, spitting and making warding signs.

Beyond the archway was the second chamber. Thick purple smoke made it hard to tell just how large it was, but if there was a back wall Felix couldn't see it. It appeared though to be another circle, with pillars ringing a sunken central area in which there was a broad circular platform. Braziers as big as shields were set between the pillars, within which smouldering mounds of incense raised columns of curling smoke that seemed to form into semi-human shapes if Felix looked at them too long.

Behind drifting veils of smoke, High Sorceress Heshor stood facing away from them in the centre of a circle drawn on the marble surface of the raised platform, her arms raised in supplication. The Harp of Ruin sat upon a tall black iron table before her. A much larger circle bordered – but did not intersect – hers. There was a crude stone table within the larger circle, and something – or some things – lay upon it, obscured by the haze.

Strange, many-limbed shapes writhed to either side of Heshor, and it took Felix a moment to see that the shapes were Heshor's five sorceresses, lying along the edge of the platform and coupling wildly with five of the Endless, naked but for their skull masks, and drenched with sweat. The lovers tore at each other constantly with sharpened fingernails, and all bled from long weals that criss-crossed their bodies, yet they moaned in a chorus of rising ecstasy. They looked as if they had been at it for hours. Felix shivered in disgust at the sight, and yet it was impossible to deny a horrible arousal as well.

The participants in the strange ceremony were guarded by seven armoured Endless, standing on the steps that descended to the centre, and watching the proceedings while at attention, their swords drawn and point-down on the floor before them.

'Magister Schreiber,' breathed Aethenir. 'And Fraulein Pallenberger.'

Felix frowned, for he had no idea what the high elf meant, then he followed his gaze and saw that the lumps that lay upon the stone table within the larger circle were indeed Max and Claudia, cruelly strapped down with leather ropes and with their mouths bound and gagged. He choked when he saw them. They were almost unrecognisable. They were naked and emaciated, and both had been shaved entirely bald, even unto the eyebrows. Paint had been applied to their faces and their bodies in purple and red swirls, and runes had been carved into their skin with knives. Max looked a hundred years old, Claudia's ribs stood out through her lacerated skin, and their eyes were shut tight as if in pain.

Gotrek spat, disgusted at the sight.

'Sigmar,' murmured Felix. 'Are they are alive?'

'They are alive,' said Aethenir dully. 'They are sacrifices to the Great Defiler.'

'Sacrifices!' said Felix, horrified.

Aethenir shuddered. 'It appears she intends to raise a daemon, though what purpose that would serve in using the harp I know not.'

Gotrek's eye lit up. 'A daemon!'

'Control your lust for glory, dwarf,' said Aethenir. 'If Heshor succeeds in calling something out of the void, your friends will be killed.' He trembled. 'Though it must surely mean our death, we must strike before the ceremony is finished.'

The moans of pleasure coming from the archway were growing higher and more urgent, as was Heshor's chanting. 'That might be very soon,' Felix said, swallowing.

'Leave the skull-faces to me,' said Gotrek. He turned to Felix and the others. 'Kill the hags and save Max and the girl.'

Jochen and his men looked at him like he had suggested they run into a burning building, but they nodded. Felix nodded too, though he wondered if it would go quite as neatly as that.

Felix, Farnir and the pirates lined up on either side of the archway, weapons at the ready. Aethenir stood further back, readying spells of healing and protection. Felix was finding it difficult to concentrate. The cries of ecstasy were getting louder and wilder, and try as he might, they were stirring dark thoughts and desires in his depths. He could see that the pirates were affected as well, twitching and grunting and shaking their heads like bulls beset by flies.

Gotrek stepped to the centre of the archway, running his thumb along the blade of his axe until it drew blood. The axe's runes blazed like the glow of a furnace. Gotrek raised it over his head and opened his mouth to roar a challenge, but before he could speak, with simultaneous shrieks, the coupling druchii all climaxed together, while in the same instant, Heshor shrieked the final words of her summoning.

There was a crack like thunder and the room shook, nearly knocking them off their feet. Suddenly the air was filled with the cloying scents of roses and ambergris and sweet milk, and Felix felt the presence of a terrifying intelligence looming within his brain. His vague stirrings of desire were suddenly an all-encompassing lust. He wanted to race into the summoning room, not to kill, but to tear off his clothes and join the druchii in their orgy. Only past experience of alien thoughts invading his mind allowed him to resist the urges and understand that they were not his own. He shook like an aspen as he concentrated on hating the intruding emotions and casting them out.

The pirates, unfortunately, had not encountered such violent attacks on their consciousness before, and knew not how to resist. They shrieked and tore at themselves and their clothes. Some of them pawed at each other like lovers, while others stumbled through the arch towards the chamber, their breeches around their ankles.

'Come back!' called Jochen, though it was clear he was only inches from following them.

Felix reached after one to drag him back, and looked into the chamber. He regretted it instantly.

Standing in the large circle before Heshor and wreathed in rose-coloured fog was the most beautiful being Felix had ever seen. She – he? – it? – towered more than twice the height of a man and appeared to be neither male nor female but, unsettlingly, both – a voluptuous icon of lust that looked directly at him and beckoned him hither with violet eyes and luscious lips.

'What do you desire of me?' it asked in a voice like honeyed thunder.

High Sorceress Heshor replied in the druchii tongue, her arms spread wide. Felix cursed her. It was speaking to him, not her! Felix stepped forwards, trying to see the beauty more clearly. He caught glimpses of writhing tentacles, or perhaps swaying snakes, graceful limbs and clawed hands, that seemed to flicker in and out of existence. He couldn't decide if the beauty had two arms or four, if it had breasts or a powerful chest, if its legs were those of a shapely woman or those of a goat.

'Back, manling,' said Gotrek.

Felix was jerked roughly back. He turned, snarling at this intrusion into his luscious dream, then blinked. Gotrek had pulled him behind him. He had been halfway into the summoning chamber though he had no memory of moving forwards. A dozen Endless were streaming up the curved steps towards them, half still naked, swords high, cutting down the enraptured pirates as they passed them.

Gotrek bellowed a challenge and slashed with his axe as three armoured Endless reached him. The first blocked the blow, but the force of it pushed him into another, staggering both of them. Felix ran one through before he recovered, but that was the last blood he drew. The rest of the Endless swarmed around him and Gotrek, Farnir, Jochen and the pirates, swords flickering faster than the eye could follow.

Aethenir huddled in the shadow of the arch, waving his hands, though whether he was casting spells or only flailing in fear Felix couldn't tell.

'Out of my way!' Gotrek roared at the Endless. 'I've a daemon to kill!'

The Slayer lashed about him in a blur of steel, his axe's rune-glow trailing behind it like a comet tail, but he was the only one fast enough to return the dark elves' attacks. Half the pirates were dead in seconds, and Jochen had a gash on his forehead that showed bone. Even firm of mind and in the best of health they would have been no match for the Endless. Starved on gruel and distracted by unnatural lusts, they fell like wheat before the scythe.

Another Endless went down before Gotrek, but the end was inevitable. There were too many of them. It was just Felix, Farnir, Jochen and the Slayer now. Then Jochen died with a foot of steel sticking from his back. Felix took a savage cut on his left forearm and suddenly his sword felt like lead. Two Endless were stabbing at him at the same time. He couldn't block both. He fought to raise his sword, knowing that he was going to die.

The two druchii suddenly stumbled aside, their swords missing him. In fact, all around him the druchii were turning and falling and shouting in confusion. Felix blinked, surprised, but didn't fail to take advantage. He ran one through the neck, then turned to see what had staggered them. He gaped. The chamber was suddenly chest deep in dwarfs, all attacking the Endless.

Gotrek turned as he cut down another masked druchii. 'You,' he said.

'Da!' cried Farnir.

Birgi saluted them with a bloody shovel. Skalf raised a framing maul.

Their heads were bald and bleeding from dozens of little cuts. It looked like they had shaved them with butchers' cleavers. Felix looked around. All the dwarfs in the room had shaved their heads and had armed themselves with what makeshift weapons they could find – picks, hammers, fireplace pokers, frying pans, pitchforks and roasting spits, and they battered the Endless with terrifying fury. Felix was amazed and relieved.

'We've heeded your words, Slayer,' Birgi said. 'Go take your doom. This is ours.'

EIGHTEEN

'About time,' said Gotrek, but his voice was gruff. 'Come on, manling!'

He turned from the newly made Slayers and started towards the summoning chamber. As Felix followed, he saw that the sorceresses had risen and were joining Heshor in a new chant, all calling out an endlessly repeated phrase while extending their arms towards the harp and sending energy pulsing towards it. The daemon too thrust its hands forwards, feeding the harp with its power, and the instrument glowed within a pink and purple aura. Two of the abomination's other appendages were held out towards Max and Claudia, and curls of white and blue vapour rose from their bodies and trailed towards the daemon.

'It's killing them,' said Felix.

'Worse,' said Aethenir, stepping up behind them. 'Much worse.' He trembled as he fell in with them, but he did not falter. He held a druchii sword in his hand.

The sorceresses – still naked – were all facing away from them as Gotrek, Felix and Aethenir strode into the chamber, concentrating their attention and their energies on the harp. The daemon too was fixed on the harp, but Felix could feel its attention everywhere at once, a beacon that charred what it illuminated.

'Your warriors have failed you, daughters,' it said as Felix, Aethenir and the Slayer ran down the stairs into the circle. 'Your enemies draw near.'

Heshor did not turn or slacken the flow of energy she was pouring into the harp, but by some silent command, two of her sorceresses did. One was Belryeth, Aethenir's nemesis, and she laughed when she saw him.

'Dearest, you return to me!' she said as she wove her incantations. 'Love, it seems, conquers all.'

'Honour conquers all,' hissed the high elf, and leapt up onto the platform straight at her, sword high.

She and her sister shot streamers of black mist at him and Gotrek and Felix. Aethenir screamed and dropped his sword as it enveloped him, but pitched himself headlong into Belryeth and they went down together on the platform. The Slayer shrugged off the mist and bulled on, but Felix staggered as it blew over him, every inch of his skin screaming as if he was being both frozen and cooked at the same time. His muscles tensed to the point of snapping and he crashed to the floor before the platform.

Gotrek leapt onto the platform and slashed his axe at the second sorceress in passing, his eye never leaving the daemon. She shrieked and fell as it bit into her side.

With her death, the black cloud dissipated, but the effects of the spell lingered, needles of fire and ice stabbing into Felix, and he could only watch as Gotrek plunged across the platform straight for the daemon.

Heshor and the other sorceresses broke off their chanting and shrieked at this interruption, but the daemon smiled down at Gotrek as he leapt across the warding line that bound it within its circle.

'Ah, little one,' it purred. 'You save me from boredom. Excellent.'

It slashed down at Gotrek with a crab-clawed arm it had not possessed a second before. Gotrek blocked the blow with the flat of his axe and was bowled back like a hedgehog hit with a spade. He bounced twice before he spun off the platform and slammed to the floor of the chamber.

'Come, try again,' laughed the daemon. 'I haven't experienced a wound in millennia.'

Felix fought to his feet. On the platform, Aethenir and Belryeth were rolling back and forth in a parody of ecstasy as they fought for control of her dagger, while Heshor and her coven blasted the Slayer as he pushed himself up to his knees, shaking his head. The spells seemed only to anger Gotrek, and he roared as he rose to his feet.

Felix saw his chance. Though every sane portion of his brain told him to turn and run the other way, he jumped up onto the platform, weaved through the angry sorceresses and ran into the daemon's circle – being careful, even in his mad rush, not to disturb the warding line, which appeared to have been drawn with some kind of purple powder – and aimed for the table upon which Max and Claudia were bound.

He didn't make it. The daemon turned its full attention upon him as he crossed the purple line and he stopped as if he had run into the wall, held by the power of its regard.

'Have you come to steal my sacrifices, beloved?' it murmured, reaching hooked claws out towards him. 'Or to join them?'

Felix's mouth went slack, overwhelmed by the daemon's majesty. He stumbled towards it, spreading his arms to receive its cruel embrace. He had never longed for anything more than he longed to be rent apart by those beautiful glistening claws.

Suddenly the daemon shrieked, and Felix collapsed as its pain broadcast through the chamber, sending waves of searing agony through his mind. He hit the ground screaming and writhing and saw that Aethenir and the sorceresses were too. Even Max and Claudia struggled and spasmed in their bonds. Only Heshor remained upright, shaking and tearing at her hair and gouging her face with her nails.

The daemon was falling back before the Slayer, who had somehow climbed back onto the platform. Purple blood spewed from a deep wound in the daemon's leg, and the edges of it boiled and sizzled as if they had been splashed with acid.

'Exquisite,' rumbled the apparition's beautiful voice, as it slashed at Gotrek with an enormous black sword that it plucked from thin air. The Slayer ducked the blow and chopped at its other leg. A new claw parried the blow, and a suddenly-appearing mace smashed down at him from above.

Felix's waves of pain subsided as the daemon's attention was narrowed to fighting Gotrek, and he found he could move again. He crawled to the stone table and pulled himself up on it. Close to, Max and Claudia looked even worse than they had at a distance. Their cheeks were hollow and their skin slack and filthy. Scrapes and bruises and ritual cuts covered them from head to toe, and their fingernails were cracked and bloody, as if they had tried to dig their way through stone. Max had a black eye and Claudia a split lip. The seeress was unconscious, and Max only a little better. His eyes rolled madly when he saw Felix and he mumbled something behind his gag.

Felix reached trembling hands forwards and sawed through the silk cords that held the gag in place, then pulled it from his lips.

'My hands,' mouthed the wizard, his voice rattling like paper. 'Then I can defend you.'

Felix almost laughed at this. Max didn't look like he could defend himself against a strong wind, let alone daemons and sorceresses. Nonetheless, he went to work on the braided leather that held Max's wrists. He didn't get far, for the daemon wailed again and its pain drove all thought and ability out of Felix's head. The screams of the sorceresses told him that they too were affected.

One of the daemon's arms was effervescing away and it staggered back to the limits of its circle as it defended itself against the Slayer with three other limbs.

'That axe,' it moaned. 'I know it now.' It shifted the weight of its attention to Heshor. 'Release me back to the void, mortal. I crave sensation, not destruction.'

'No!' shrieked the high sorceress, some resonance with the daemon's all-encompassing consciousness allowing Felix to understand her though she spoke in the druchii tongue. 'You must fulfil your bargain! Finish the dwarf and resume!'

'You will hold me to your regret, hag,' it rumbled, as Gotrek attacked it again.

Felix recovered himself and finished cutting through Max's wrist bonds and started on Claudia's. He looked back. The sorceresses were standing again.

'Kill the human!' cried Heshor, pointing a black-nailed finger at him. 'He must not disturb the sacrifices!'

She and the three still-standing sorceresses turned towards him, spouting vile incantations as Max mumbled a protection, moving his hands weakly through the ritual motions.

But then, before either spells or counter-spells could be completed, the daemon smashed Gotrek in the chest with an armoured fist the size of a boulder and sent him flying back again. This time the Slayer hit the platform shoulder-first and skidded backwards towards the edge – straight through the purple powder boundary of the binding circle, wiping it away. Blood welled from the Slayer's nose and mouth as he came to a stop. He didn't move.

Heshor and her sorceresses gasped and faltered in their incantations at this momentous accident. The daemon laughed.

'Did I not say?' it chuckled, then strode out of the circle, straight towards Heshor. 'Come, daughter, I will make you a guest of my realm, as you have welcomed me to yours.'

The sorceress screamed and backed away, snatching up the harp as her remaining sisters stepped before her to guard her retreat, blasting the daemon with their black sorcery.

The daemon appeared to relish the attack, moaning with pleasure but slowing not one whit. It caressed the three sorceresses with probing tentacles and they collapsed in paroxysms of ecstasy so intense that they snapped their own spines.

Heshor turned and ran with the harp, but then a bloody figure rose up and tackled her, stabbing at her with a dagger. Felix was shocked to see that it was Aethenir.

'For Ulthuan and the asur!' he cried as they slammed to the ground, the harp between them. 'For Rion and the path of honour!'

'No, scholar,' shrilled Belryeth as she stood and leapt to defend her mistress. 'You will win no redemption.' She dragged Aethenir off Heshor as the daemon stepped closer.

The high sorceress scrambled to her feet as the high elf and the young sorceress fought once again, and fled for the door.

The daemon came after her, laughing melodiously. 'Do you abandon me now, dear heart? Have you not pledged your undying love to me?'

It trod on Aethenir and Belryeth as it followed her, and they screamed, though whether in pain or delight, it was hard to tell. They continued flailing and fighting as the daemon slashed down at Heshor with an arm like a bone scythe.

Heshor leapt away, but the tip of the appendage gashed her trailing leg and she fell on the steps that led to the outer chamber. The daemon loomed over her, raising new arms, but then, just as her fate seemed sealed, a red-crested figure staggered out of the shadows, then leapt up and buried its axe in the base of the daemon's spine.

'Die, spawn of the abyss!' roared the Slayer, blood bubbling from his mouth with every word.

The daemon shrieked with a thousand tortured voices, and its agony once again crushed Felix to the ground with its vastness. It turned and staggered back from the Slayer, bits of it fading in and out as it bled pink mist. The wound in its lower back grew larger as Felix watched, sharing its agony, the edges eating away like parchment attacked by fire.

The daemon glared down at Gotrek as the Slayer stumped doggedly after it. 'No, little one. I will not fight you. This is not my fate. One greater than I is to die killing you. In the meanwhile, I will relish your disappointment.'

And then, between blinks, it was gone, and the chamber was silent, the sudden vacuum of its absence almost as painful as its presence had been. It felt for a moment as if all the joy and colour and excitement had been bled from the world – as if life wasn't worth living. Felix almost wept.

Gotrek, on the other hand, roared with rage, slamming his axe down and shattering the marble floor. 'Craven hellspawn!' he bellowed. 'Leavings of the void! Will you rob me of my death? Will you rob me of glory? Come back and face me!'

Felix looked up, terrified, but the daemon failed to reappear. Gotrek bent over and coughed blood all over the floor, the glow fading from the runes on his axe.

Recovering, Felix looked around for High Sorceress Heshor. She was gone – and so was the Harp of Ruin.

'The harp,' he said, struggling to stand. 'We…'

'Felix,' came Max's feeble whisper. 'Claudia's bonds.'

Felix returned to the stone table and finished cutting Claudia free. She did not move or open her eyes.

Felix checked her pulse. 'We had hoped to save you before this,' he said. There was a faint flutter beneath his fingers. 'But they moved you.'

Max sat up as if he was made of dry twigs. 'I am frankly surprised to see you at all. The last we saw of you…'

'Friends,' came a weak voice from behind them. 'Help me. Something has happened.'

Max and Felix turned. Aethenir lay where the daemon had stepped upon him and Belryeth. He was under the sorceress and pushing at her.

'Release me, cursed asur,' whined the sorceress, flailing in his grasp.

Max and Felix limped wearily to the two elves, but as they came closer, Felix staggered and nearly vomited. Max choked.

Something had indeed happened. It had appeared from a distance that Belryeth lay on top of Aethenir. This was not the case. In truth, they had become one. The touch of the daemon had fused them in a permanent lovers' embrace. Their bodies were melted together at the torso, Belryeth's head looking forever over Aethenir's shoulder, and their arms and legs intertwined.

'By the gods,' said Felix, gagging.

'Horrible,' agreed Max.

'Please, friends,' said Aethenir, looking up at them with frightened eyes. 'Do something.'

'Take him away,' whimpered Belryeth.

Gotrek stepped up and looked down at them. He snorted. 'A fit punishment for causing all this,' he said.

Felix glared at him.

'Don't be cruel, Slayer,' said Max.

'Taking your example, Slayer,' said Aethenir, 'I had hoped to die to atone for my sin, But this... this is not to be borne.'

Felix looked at Max. 'Is there nothing to be done?'

Max shook his head. 'The unmaking of this would be beyond the greatest of magisters.'

'Do you still wish for death, elf?' asked Gotrek.

Aethenir swallowed, then nodded. 'Aye, dwarf.'

'Then pray and die well.'

Aethenir looked around at them all and spoke. 'Let it be said that, though I strayed from it, I died upon the path of honour.' Then he closed his eyes and murmured a prayer as Gotrek raised his axe.

When the scholar's prayer was finished, the Slayer let the axe fall and beheaded him. Aethenir's face was peaceful when his head rolled to a stop.

Felix silently bade the high elf farewell. He might have been a fool, and perhaps not the bravest of his race, but, as he had said, in the end he had not flinched from doing what he could to rectify his foolishness.

'Come on,' said Gotrek, striding towards the outer chamber. 'There's still the sorceress.'

'Wait!' cried Belryeth. 'You can't leave me like this! Kill me like you killed him.'

They all looked down at her, then at each other.

'It would be much more fitting to spare your life,' said Max.

'Barbarians!' she cried. 'You will pay for this indignity!'

They ignored her. Felix draped one of the naked seeress's discarded black robes around Claudia, picked her up and put her over his shoulder, then hurried after the Slayer. Max donned the surcoat of one of the Endless and joined them.

In the outer chamber the Endless were dead, but so were the dwarf slaves, their bodies strewn about the room with great wounds hacked through them by the Endless's longswords. By contrast, the druchii had been dragged down and bludgeoned to death. Not one of them still had a face. The mosaic floor was a lake of blood.

Kneeling in the middle of the lake was Farnir, cradling the head of his father in his lap. The young dwarf was near death. There was a wound in his chest that made red bubbles when he breathed. Birgi was dead, a wound in his side opening him up to his spine.

Farnir looked up. There were tears in his eyes. 'Have we saved the Old World?' he asked.

Gotrek looked at him, then towards the door that led to the stairs. 'We will, beardling. Rest easy.'

'Aye,' said the slave. 'Aye, good.' He closed his eyes and slumped over the body of his father and died.

Gotrek bowed his head. 'May Grungni welcome you in his halls.'

They hurried on, splashing through the blood to the stairs. Felix found it impossible to dismiss Farnir's face from his mind as they started up the endless flight of stairs. The young dwarf had lived almost his entire life as a slave of the druchii. He had seen nothing of the world except the inside of the black ark, and yet he had died gladly for a homeland and an idea of honour he knew only from a few old stories told to him by his father. He had died to preserve a whole race's freedom, a thing he had never known himself.

By the time they had followed Heshor's trail of blood spatters to the top of the stairs, Max was crawling on his hands and knees, Felix's legs were like jelly, and even Gotrek, suffering from the daemon's last hammer-blow punch to the chest, was wheezing, wiping blood from his mouth with the back of his hand.

A few steps from the top the Slayer paused. Twittering voices and the sound of hurried movement came from the room above.

'Put down the girl and ready your sword, manling.'

Felix did as he was ordered, giving Claudia over to the care of Max, and sucking in deep breaths to strengthen himself. Then, at a nod from Gotrek, they ran up the stairs and into the druchii boudoir.

A crowd of slaves and harlots and pleasure house guards swarmed around what looked like a litter in the centre of the room. Several of them turned as Gotrek and Felix burst in, and Felix saw that the litter was in fact a low divan, and that Heshor lay on it, clutching the Harp of Ruin as a slave tried to bind the wound in her leg.

The guards shouted and charged Gotrek and Felix, while a majordomo cried orders and four burly human slaves picked the divan up at its four corners and ran towards the door as the whores and slaves shrieked after them.

Gotrek hewed through the guards like they were tall grass. Even Felix cut one down – they were hardly the elite fighters the Endless had been. The fight slowed them down nonetheless, and by the time the last guard fell to Gotrek's axe, his head dangling from a string of neck flesh, Heshor's makeshift stretcher was out the door.

Gotrek tramped towards it resolutely. Felix looked behind him. Max was just rising from the opening in the bed platform. Claudia's arm was draped over his shoulder, but she was moving under her own power.

'Go,' said Max. 'We'll catch up.'

Felix nodded and hurried after Gotrek. They ran out into the hallway just in time to see the slaves and the divan disappearing up the iron stairs opposite.

They charged after them, though Gotrek was wheezing and Felix felt like an anvil sat on his chest. At the top of the stairs they saw Heshor's bearers running down the long purple hall to the foyer and started after them, but it was clear that the sorceress would escape the pleasure house before they caught up with her.

Gotrek skidded to a stop, cocked back his arm, and threw his axe. It spun end over end down the hall and bit into the back of the slave holding the back left corner of the divan with a sickening chunk. The slave screamed and fell. The divan dropped at his corner and Heshor squawked and let go of the harp to steady herself. It bounced across the marble floor.

The other slaves screamed in fear and ran on, steadying the divan. Heshor screamed orders and pointed back at the harp, but they didn't heed her and ran out through the open door.

Gotrek and Felix thundered into the hexagonal foyer seconds later. Gotrek wrenched his axe from the dead slave's back and raced with Felix to the door, but as they burst out onto the shallow front porch they drew up sharply. The street was filled in every direction with what appeared to be the black ark's entire complement of spear companies, lined up in orderly ranks and all facing the front door of the pleasure house. In their centre, next to an imperious druchii in elaborate armour who Felix deduced must be Lord Tarlkhir, commander of the ark, Heshor sat up on her divan and pointed a trembling finger at Gotrek.

Gotrek chuckled deep in his throat and readied his dripping axe. 'Foes without number,' he said, grinning savagely.

At an order from Tarlkhir, the druchii lowered their spears and started to advance.

Felix looked back through the door to the harp, which still rang on the marble floor near the middle of the foyer and seemed, strangely, to be getting louder rather than diminishing.

'Gotrek,' he said. 'Wait. Perhaps we should destroy the harp first, just in case they get through us.'

Gotrek grunted, but he could see the logic in this, because he jumped back through the door, then turned and strode for the harp.

'Lock it, manling,' he said.

Felix slammed and locked the door just as the first druchii mounted the house's steps, then crossed to the Slayer, who was looking down at the harp, which was ringing even louder now, dancing on the tiles of the floor. Felix could feel the vibrations through his feet. The foyer moaned with sympathetic overtones that made Felix want to pop his ears.

'Foul thing,' said Gotrek, as the sound of spear butts thudded on the door behind them.

Felix had to agree. Its growing note was a discordant howl that hurt the ears, and its twisted, black, U-shaped body was vibrating so much now that its edges were blurred. Its translucent strings quivered like strands of saliva.

Felix stepped back as Gotrek lifted his axe over his head for a mighty stroke.

A weak voice came from the purple corridor. 'Slayer, no!'

Gotrek and Felix looked around. Max was limping up the corridor towards them with Claudia stumbling along beside him. 'Break it, and the energies released could kill us all!' said Max.

Gotrek raised an eyebrow. 'Truly?' An evil smile spread across his ugly face. 'Good.'

He reached down and grabbed for the harp, but he had trouble reaching it. His thick fingers stopped inches from it, as if blocked by an invisible wall, and his hand and arm shook. He cursed. Dust began sifting down from the roof of the chamber, shaken loose by the harp's vibrations, and the braziers that ringed the room rattled in their alcoves, spitting sparks.

'Filthy magic.'

Max looked at the harp with fear. 'Its strings have been struck. It is releasing its power.'

With bared teeth Gotrek forced his arm forwards, his muscles bulging and the veins popping out on his forearms and neck, then closed his hand around the harp's vibrating frame. It continued to ring, making his fingers blur as he turned to the door, which was shuddering from the blows of the druchii spears.

'Open it, manling,' he said through clenched teeth.

Felix stared at the harp. Pebbles and mortar were now pitter-pattering down along with the dust, and he could feel the vibrations in his chest and heart as if he were standing beside a company of kettle drummers. His knees shook with it. He couldn't imagine how it must feel to hold it.

'Manling!'

Felix snapped out of it and ran to the door. He drew the bolt, then pulled it open and jumped to the side. A wave of druchii spearmen stumbled in, caught off balance, and Gotrek slammed into them, chopping one-handed with his axe as he held the roaring harp in the other.

The druchii soldiers fell back before the savagery of Gotrek's bloodthirsty attack and the instrument's horrible noise, retreating to the bottom of the steps and holding their ears, ten of their fellows dead in as many seconds. Gotrek strode out and looked across to Heshor, who was staring at him from her divan next to Commander Tarlkhir on the far side of the street.

'Here's your harp, witch!' he bellowed, holding it up. It looked like the thing was shaking the meat from his arm. 'Come get it.'

He threw it down on the porch in front of him.

It was possibly not one of the Slayer's better ideas.

The harp clanged off the flagstones, and a shockwave like a mortar impact rocked the building and knocked them all to the ground. The witchlight globes in the foyer's chandelier exploded and rained crystal shards down upon them. Cracks ran up the plastered walls, and the steaming crucible that was the symbol of the house jumped its hooks and clattered to the ground, spilling boiling blood across the cobbles. The street was pelted with falling masonry and black slate roof tiles. Spearmen were clubbed to the ground by stones. The floor Felix lay on split and buckled. The harp rang in his ears like a hundred temple bells. His sword sang as if it was being struck with a mallet, and shook so hard he could barely hold it. His guts churned. His heart hammered in his chest.

'Fool of a dwarf!' shouted Heshor in Reikspiel. 'Surrender it before it buries you in rubble. Only I can stop it. Only I can save you.'

Gotrek picked himself up, laughing as more masonry smashed down all around him. 'Save a Slayer? I'm taking you all with me!' He picked up his axe and started to raise it. Heshor shrieked. The druchii soldiers scrambled back, trying to get away. A block the size of a cow slammed down from above, crushing three of them.

Gotrek cackled maniacally and raised his axe high above his head, but just as he started to slash down, something bright shot down past him from above and jerked the harp aside. Gotrek's axe missed it, and shattered the black marble of the porch instead.

Gotrek ripped his axe from the stone, cursing, and swung again at the harp, but it hopped into the air like a puppet and his axe swished under it. Felix gaped as it rose higher. It was hooked to a crossbow bolt with flanges like a grapnel, swinging at the end of a grey silk cord.

Felix and Gotrek stared after the harp as it shot up towards the rooftops. Heshor and Commander Tarlkhir shouted and pointed. Halfway up, it clanged against the wall of a house, and this time the impact rocked the whole ark, making it boom like a giant drum. The street lurched and dropped, knocking everyone to the cobbles, and the roaring throb that filled the air drowned out even the sounds of half-ton stones tearing from the ceiling and smashing druchii to a pulp in the street. From the depths of the ark came a sound like muffled thunder and a deep tectonic rumbling.

Felix looked up through the rain of debris that was falling from the cave ceiling, searching for the harp. Then he saw it – a glittering, bouncing spark, hanging from the barbed bolt that had whisked it away, dragged, banging and clanging across the shaking, shattering rooftops of the pleasure houses behind a pack of scrawny scampering black shadows.

NINETEEN

'Skaven!' shouted Felix, pointing.

'After them,' roared Gotrek.

Heshor and Commander Tarlkhir were shouting the same thing to their troops, and the druchii spear companies hared off down the street, following the leaping shadows.

Gotrek and Felix ran after them, but it quickly became clear that it was impossible. The skaven were already out of sight, and there were thousands of druchii spears in the way, all trying to do the same thing.

Gotrek stopped when they reached the first intersection, watching Heshor and Tarlkhir's forces hurry away ahead of them. 'This won't work,' he shouted.

'No,' Felix shouted back.

Though they no longer stood beside the harp, the walls and streets around them still throbbed with deafening sympathetic vibrations, and they were getting worse. It was like being inside a snoring giant's nose. Blocks of stone and spear-tip stalactites dropped all around them. Felix had a vision of the harp getting louder and louder and its resonances and reverberations stronger and stronger until at last it shook the whole world apart. The ark would only be the beginning. When it shattered, the harp would fall to the ocean floor and continue vibrating, causing earthquakes and tidal waves that would drown the Old World, the Northlands and Ulthuan alike beneath the waves. The high elves had been right to lock the vile instrument in a vault. Perhaps they had even sunk the city on purpose to hide the horrible thing away for all time.

'They're going out. So we go out,' called the Slayer. 'This way.'

The Slayer turned around and stomped back towards the flesh house, pushing through the crowds of druchii gallants and whores and half-dressed officers who were spilling out of the houses and screaming orders at each other and the jostling throngs of slaves – all so frightened that they ignored Gotrek and Felix entirely.

Max and Claudia stood in the door of the crumbling pleasure house when they returned to it, looking fearfully out at the rain of debris. Gotrek beckoned to them and continued on down the street, back the way they had originally come. The magister and the seeress ducked their heads and limped out after them.

'The skaven have stolen the harp,' said Felix as they fell in beside him. 'We went after them but it was impossible. We're getting out.'

'An admirable idea,' said Max.

Felix took Claudia's arm, hurrying her along and keeping her steady as the ground continued to vibrate beneath their feet.

'Are you well, Fraulein Pallenberger?' he shouted over the din of destruction.

'I... I no longer know,' she said dully. 'But I am glad you live.'

Felix looked at her with concern. Her voice was utterly devoid of life or spark. Had her experiences shattered her mind? Imprisoned and abused by the druchii, attacked by the blackest of magics and exposed to the reality-altering presence of a daemon, it would be little wonder if they had.

Gotrek led them back towards the stair to the barracks, but before they had gone two blocks, another titanic crack rocked the ark, sending everyone lurching sideways as the street tilted violently to the left. Felix caught Claudia before she fell, then almost fell himself. Ahead of them the facade of a building toppled forwards and sloughed to the ground like a spill of gravel, crushing dozens of druchii and their slaves.

Max looked pale. 'The harp's vibrations have disrupted the magics that hold the ark level. I don't think it will survive.'

'Good,' said Gotrek.

Water started to stream down from the ceiling.

They all looked up, as did the druchii and the slaves all around them.

'What's happened?' asked Felix.

'We're under the harbour,' said Gotrek. 'It's sprung a leak. Keep moving.'

'Not again,' murmured Claudia, but when Felix asked her to repeat herself, she had sunk back into dull silence.

Too soon the water was ankle deep and rising steadily. Great columns of it poured down from the cracks in the roof, and carriage-sized stones were breaking away around the rifts and thundering down to smash houses to bits.

They reached the narrow door to the corridor that passed the beastmaster's menagerie and found scores of druchii and slaves running out of it, shouting and waving others back. Gotrek and Felix pushed through against the tide and pulled Max and Claudia in after them.

The crowded corridor echoed with frightened animal roaring and the screams of terrified humans and druchii. In the shadowed distance near the menagerie gates, fur-cloaked druchii were struggling with some mammoth beast that Felix couldn't quite make out. He got the impression of mass and violent movement, and a dark elf flew through the air and smashed against the wall, but it was too dark and congested in the corridor to see what had thrown him.

Felix paused. 'Do we find another way?'

'Any other way will be under water by the time we reach it, manling,' said Gotrek, and pressed on.

Felix looked down. The water was knee deep now. He followed with the others.

As they got closer the shapes became clearer. Druchii with whips were trying to lead a pair of massive reptilian beasts out of the gate towards the stair. Felix quailed at the sight of the monsters. He had never seen the like – lizards that walked on their hind legs, taller at the shoulder than a man. Their sinewy forelegs ended in cruelly hooked claws, and their heads were enormous bony things with spear-tip teeth gnashing in roaring, slavering mouths.

Gotrek chuckled dangerously when he saw them, and stomped forwards eagerly.

'Slayer,' said Felix, following unhappily. 'Now is perhaps not the time.'

'Don't fret, manling,' said Gotrek. 'Get along the wall, and be ready to run.'

Felix led Claudia and Max to the right wall, edging towards the confusion as Gotrek splashed openly down the centre of the corridor, shoving frightened druchii and slaves out of the way. The beastmasters didn't look around. They were too busy trying to control their charges, who seemed to have been driven to a frenzy by the noise, the rising water and the ground shaking and tilting beneath their feet. Already two of the trainers were down, one lying in a broken lump at the foot of the left wall, half-underwater, the other kneeling and holding a crushed arm close to his chest.

The others were hauling on long leads attached to the beasts' saddles and bridles while a few brave souls whipped them and shouted commands at them, trying to make them turn towards the stairwell. The beasts were having none of it, bellowing and whipping their heads around and snapping at anyone who came close.

Ten paces behind them, Gotrek crouched down, axe ready, then looked to Felix, Max and Claudia, continuing to inch along the wall in the shadows of the milling beastmasters. Felix nodded. He still didn't know what the Slayer intended, but they were ready to run from it, whatever it was.

Gotrek grinned in a worrying way, then turned back and charged, silent. The two closest druchii turned at his splashing steps, and died before they could open their mouths to scream. They went down in a spray of blood, the leads slipping from their hands.

By Sigmar, thought Felix. The lunatic is freeing the beasts!

Gotrek swung into two more beastmasters, chopping through their padded leather armour like it wasn't there. They collapsed into the water, screaming.

The giant lizards roared and turned towards the scent of blood, dragging their handlers with them. The beastmasters screamed and shouted. A druchii with a whip lashed at a monster's face. It lunged and snapped him in half.

Gotrek ran between the beasts, ducking under a massive tail, and pounded for the end of the tunnel. 'Now, manling! Now!'

Felix took Claudia's arm and propelled her forwards. Max ran with them, skirting the edge of the chaos as the beastmasters fled and fell before the rampaging monsters. One beast brought down two of them in a terrifying hop, then nosed in the water for their corpses. It came up with a head.

Felix didn't look back to see more, just splashed with Max and Claudia into the shadows again, the roars of the monsters and the shrieks of the eaten echoing in their ears.

'Well… well done, Slayer,' said Max, as they hurried on.

Gotrek snorted. 'I could wish the same for the entire race.'

By the time they reached the stairwell the water was hip deep – rib deep on Gotrek – and rising faster than before.

'The water appears to be sinking the ark,' said Max. 'The druchii's magic cannot support the added weight.'

'Then hurry,' growled Gotrek. 'There are twelve flights to this stair.'

They started up as quickly as they could, Felix half-carrying Claudia along with her arm over his shoulder while Gotrek did the same for Max. Even so it was slow going. The stairwell shook and twisted like a tent in a high wind, the walls and ceiling groaning and cracking and falling apart, making every step a challenge. At the fourth landing they had to climb over a portion of wall that had buckled and filled the landing almost to the roof, on the next flight there was a cavernous booming from above and they flattened themselves to the walls just in time to avoid being crushed by a massive boulder that bounced away down the stairs. Ominously, they heard it splash only a few flights below them.

A little further on, Felix felt Claudia staring at him and turned his head to her as they walked. 'Yes, fraulein?'

She looked away, flushing, but then, after a few more steps, she spoke up.

'Herr Jaeger,' she said. 'I have a confession to make.'

'Oh yes?' he said, as he helped her over a spill of rock.

'It is my fault that you were taken by the ratmen,' she said, and her lower lip trembled.

Felix frowned. 'I think you might be mistaken, fraulein. They had been following us from Altdorf. In fact, you might say they have been following us for twenty years.'

'You don't understand,' she said, hanging her head. 'I... I saw it. I saw the attack, before it happened. I saw you fighting shadows on the deck of a ship. I might have warned you, but...' She sobbed suddenly. 'But because you had... had spurned me, I... I was angry with you, and I decided I wouldn't speak!'

Felix stopped climbing the stairs and stared at her. 'You... you saw that I was to fall into the clutches of the skaven and said nothing?' His heart was pounding in his chest.

Above them Max and Gotrek paused and looked back.

'I didn't see that!' she wailed. 'I didn't see so much! Only that you would be fighting! I thought... I thought you might be hurt a little, or...' She faltered and sobbed again. 'I didn't think you would be taken away! I only wanted you to have a fright, a petty vengeance for your coldness. Oh what a fool I am! I thought I had killed you.'

Felix clenched his fists and started up the stairs again, pulling her more forcefully than necessary. 'You nearly did kill Aethenir,' he snarled. 'In fact he would most likely have preferred it. Those fiends tortured him, broke his fingers, cut into the muscles of his chest and–'

'Felix!' snapped Max, as Claudia went white. 'Enough!'

Felix turned to him. 'Enough? After what she's done? She should be charged with aiding the enemies of mankind! You didn't see what those vermin did–'

'She made a terrible mistake, Felix,' said Max, stepping in his way. 'A terrible mistake. It, more than anything the druchii have done to us, has tortured her mind and driven her to despair.'

'She deserves it,' grunted Gotrek.

'She does deserve it,' said Max. 'For it is part of the charter of her college that its students shall not use their powers for personal gain, or allow someone to come to harm by failing to warn them of danger. If we escape this nightmare and return to Altdorf, I will see to it that she is punished by the Celestial Order, and she has agreed to accept that punishment without complaint.'

'That's all well and good,' said Felix, not at all satisfied. 'But–'

'Did you not tell me once that you killed a man in a duel, Felix?' asked Max evenly.

'Yes, but...'

'Youth is a terrible time, Felix,' Max continued, 'as you may remember. A time when our strength and prowess often outstrip our ability to use them wisely. We may do a thing out of petulance or quick anger that we then regret for the rest of our lives – your duel, Aethenir's Belryeth,

Claudia her silence. But, given a chance, given the gift of forgiveness and a second chance by older, wiser heads, we may live long enough to learn from those mistakes, and make amends for them.'

Felix turned away, unable to let go of his anger. He had certainly done things in his youth that he regretted, but this... this was criminally irresponsible. The girl deserved more than just punishment. He should give her to the skaven. He...

'Come on, manling,' said Gotrek. 'A long way to go yet.'

Felix grunted, angry, but faced the stairs and started up them again, helping Claudia up as before, though he felt like leaving her to drown.

As they reached the seventh flight, there came a deep, muffled crack from the depths of the ark. It was followed by ominous thunderings and crashes that echoed from above and below and all around. Then the stairwell tilted, sending them all slamming into the left wall, and the stone around them groaned and splintered. Everyone froze and looked around, waiting for death to strike.

The howling reverberations that had been shaking the ark lessened slightly, as if some great pressure had been released, and in the relative silence they heard a noise coming from below them that turned Felix's spine into a column of ice – the gurgling, slapping roar of swiftly rising water.

Gotrek stood. 'The cracks have gone through to the bottom of the ark,' he said. 'Hurry.'

He started up the stairs with Max again, practically carrying the magister. Felix pulled Claudia up and they all fled up the stairwell as the water whispered and giggled at their backs, closer and closer with every step.

The water was faster. At the top of the flight, Felix turned and looked back. The dim light of Max's globe of light reflected on the ripples of black water at the bottom of the flight. He could see it moving, inching up the dust-powdered walls.

They ran on. The water closed the gap. At the eighth landing it was half a flight back. Ten steps later it was licking at their heels. At the ninth landing they were wading through it. Halfway to the tenth, it was up to their waists, and bitterly cold. It dragged at Felix's legs, slowing him and numbing his body.

As they rounded onto the eleventh flight, Felix had to keep his chin up, and was lifting Claudia out of the water so she could breathe. Gotrek was paddling as much as walking and Max was floundering weakly.

'We're not going to make it,' said Claudia.

Felix hoped it wasn't a prophecy.

He was on tiptoes as they came around the last landing and saw to his great relief the gate at the top, flung wide and abandoned by its guards. He felt with his toes for the submerged steps and pushed on. They reached the top neck and neck – quite literally – with the water, and slogged up out of it as it crested the top step and spilled through the open gate into the barracks corridor beyond.

Felix set Claudia on her feet and Gotrek helped Max to his.

'Keep moving,' said the Slayer. 'This will fill slower than the stairs, but it'll still fill.'

He strode through the gate and down the sharply tilted corridor towards the barracks like he was walking along the side of a peaked roof. Felix, Max and Claudia shambled after him, moaning with weariness. The rising water chased them as they went, running along the base of the left wall like it was a mill race.

The barracks area was deserted and destroyed, a chalky mist of rock dust still settling as they hurried through. Great portions of the roof had come down, and most of the barracks, cut into the solid rock, had caved in, their fronts fallen away to reveal collapsed floors and ceilings with bunks and chairs all fallen and smashed, the mangled bodies of slaves jumbled into the mess. But the truly terrifying damage was to the parade ground, which slanted away before them like they were walking down a hill. There was a jagged gaping crack running at a diagonal across it, the ground on the near side of the crack a foot higher than the ground on the far side. Out of the crack gurgled more water, racing away down the slanted ground. Felix looked up and saw that there was a corresponding crack running across the roof.

'It's going to split in half,' he murmured, swallowing nervously.

'Might sink first,' said Gotrek.

The Slayer picked up his pace, splashing quickly through the knee-deep water to the front gate – the gate that had cost him two gold bracelets to pass through only hours before. It had collapsed. The massive wooden doors lay shattered and askew between the ruins of the guard towers and gate house, with the cave roof fallen in on top of the lot – a solid mountain of rock. All the water from the crack in the floor was pooling here, rapidly hiding the doors and the bottom-most rubble.

'Trapped again,' said Max dully.

'Bah!' said Gotrek and started towards the right-hand guard tower, which was still semi-whole. There was a wooden door in its base, half-submerged in the water. He tried the handle, but the door was stuck in its frame, twisted from the pressure pushing down on it from above.

'Stay back,' said Gotrek, then slammed his axe into the door. The curved blade bit deep, and he kept chopping, ripping long chunks out of the door near the frame. Felix kept an eye on the tower above, afraid that the door was the only thing holding it up. Finally, Gotrek hacked a hole through it, then reached in and pulled. The door wrenched open with a splintering shriek.

Felix closed his eyes, expecting the whole structure to crash down and bury the Slayer. He should have known better.

'Come on,' said the Slayer, and waded into the tower.

Felix, Max and Claudia followed. The water at the door was up to Felix's waist, and got deeper within. Gotrek was up to his neck in it. Felix looked around. There was no other door in the small room. What was the Slayer doing?

'Up,' said the Slayer, and started up an iron-runged ladder set in the wall. Felix followed him warily up through a hole in the ceiling into another tiny room – this one studded with narrow arrow slots and completely crushed on the left side by the fallen cave roof. The walls that still stood did so only barely, the stones sitting precariously one atop the other with all the mortar turned to powder between them.

As Max and Claudia crawled up through the trap, Gotrek crossed to one of the arrow slots and kicked at the frame. Felix flinched back, expecting the ceiling to come down as the narrow window shifted and the wall around it crumbled, but once again the Slayer seemed to know what he was doing. A few more kicks and the stone frame fell out of the wall in one piece. An avalanche of mortared stone tumbled out after it, but to Felix's great relief, the roof stayed where it was. Gotrek stepped to the V-shaped hole he created and looked out. After a slight hesitation, Felix joined him.

The tower looked out over a lake where the wide plaza that fronted the barracks area had once been. On the far side was a broad arch that opened into the huge central stairwell that led both up and down to the other levels. The plaza was tilted at the same angle as the parade ground, and it was flooded with rapidly rising water – shallow at Gotrek and Felix's end, and deep near the stairwell, and filled with floating corpses. As Felix watched, the two witchlights that flanked the archway to the stairs were swallowed up, and glowed strangely from beneath the waves.

'Throw the seeress down to me, then jump,' said Gotrek. He stepped up into the gap and leapt down into the water with a big splash.

Felix turned to Claudia and motioned her forwards. Max led her to him, and Felix helped her up into the gap. She groped weakly at the edges, trembling and looking down. Felix shoved her. She squeaked and dropped out of sight, and there was a splash.

Felix looked guiltily at Max. 'Sorry,' he said.

Max shrugged. 'It had to be done.'

The magister stepped up into the gap and jumped of his own accord. Felix jumped a second later. Gotrek was already dog-paddling for the stairs. Felix then put Claudia's arms around his shoulders, and he and Max struck out after him.

Only a foot of the archway to the stairs was still above water as they began, and it was being swallowed up more quickly than they were swimming. Gotrek was a slow, awkward swimmer, Max was breathing like a bellows, and Felix, with chainmail on and Claudia clinging to his back, could barely keep his nose up. They had got no more than two-thirds of the way across, shouldering floating corpses out of the way all the while, when the arch vanished under the water.

'We'll have to swim down and back up,' said Felix.

When they reached the wall, Gotrek inhaled and dived. Felix pulled Claudia's arms tight and made her lock her hands around his neck.

'Take a breath and hold on,' he said over his shoulder.

He waited until he heard her suck in air, then plunged down beneath the waves. The glow of witchlights gave the scene a strange beauty. Even the bedraggled corpses that drifted half-submerged in the current looked graceful. Felix kicked down hard towards the submerged arch, and remembered just in time to kick down a little further so that he wouldn't scrape Claudia off his back when he went under it. With a final kick he was through and paddling for the surface again. Instead he cracked his head on a ceiling. He nearly yelped in surprise and terror, and he heard Claudia do just that. She started thrashing and kicking in terror.

He turned his head up and saw what had happened. He had come up in the landing. The ceiling was flat above him. The stairs up were to his left. He clamped down on Claudia's thrashing arms and kicked left as hard as he could, and at last they got out from under the roof and broke the surface, both retching and gasping for air. Gotrek was bobbing beside them.

Felix wiped the water from his eyes and looked around. 'Where's Max?'

Without a word Gotrek ducked back under the water and pushed back towards the submerged landing. He was no swimmer, but he had no fear of being under water either.

Felix paddled for the stairs where they rose up out of the water and helped Claudia out. She sat wearily on a step, her bald head bleeding from a dozen long scrapes.

'I'm sorry, fraulein,' he said. 'It wasn't intentional.'

She huddled over her knees, not looking up. 'You've done more than you should,' she said. 'More than I deserve.'

A moment later, Gotrek reappeared, spitting water and hauling Max to the surface. The wizard came up choking and coughing, and could barely drag himself up the steps when Gotrek pulled him over.

Gotrek climbed out and whipped his crest out of his eyes. 'Come on. Can't stop.'

Felix rose wearily and helped Claudia to her feet. Already the place they had been sitting was two feet under water. Max pushed himself up, swaying like a drunk. Gotrek stepped beside him and put the magister's around his shoulder again.

'On,' he said.

The central stair was broader than the barracks stair, and with higher ceilings, but the water seemed to rise just as fast. Again they were limping and cursing and stumbling with the water coming up behind them like some vast, silent snake, ready to swallow them, while the ark groaned and shuddered around them. At the harbour level they looked towards the docks, wondering if there might be an escape that way, but the corridor tilted down in that direction, and was filling rapidly with black water. Slaves and dark elves clambered up the slope towards them like they were running up a hill.

Gotrek snorted. 'Only elves would build a harbour inside a floating rock.'

They hurried on, joined in their flight by the slaves and the druchii alike – none, in their terror, paying them the slightest attention. More fleeing ark-dwellers poured out of the next level and the stairs were soon filled with a scrambling, surging mob.

Two flights later, as they rounded a landing in the middle of the panicked throng, Felix saw a sight he had never expected to see again – daylight. It shone through a great, columned archway – a warm, golden radiance that made even the cruel faces of the druchii and the gaunt faces of their slaves beautiful as they turned towards it. Felix thought he had never seen anything so wonderful in his life.

The crowd raced towards it like lost children running towards their mother, and Felix, Gotrek, Max and Claudia were borne along with it. At the top, they spilled into a square plaza, dominated by a black statue of a robed and hooded woman, and hemmed in by tall, sharp-roofed buildings. Beyond these Felix could see houses and temples and fortified walls climbing up a central hill towards the massive black keep that perched at the top of the ark – all of it tilted dizzyingly to the left. Streets radiated from the plaza at odd angles, but the druchii and the slaves were all running towards one that rose towards the upper reaches of the city, heading for high ground.

'Follow them!' said Gotrek.

He and Felix helped Max and Claudia to run with the crowd as the water bubbled out of the stairwell behind them and began to spread across the square.

But after only a few uphill turnings, Felix's earlier fears were realised as they came to a locked gate. This appeared to be a barrier between the merchant quarters and the enclaves of the highborn. A huge mob of druchii and slaves pushed at the sturdy iron gates, roaring for entry, while on the far side, guards with repeating crossbows fired into them and shouted at them to fall back. Even nobles and officers were being shot down in the guards' panic.

Felix and Gotrek paused and looked around as Max and Claudia leaned against them, gasping and catching their breath. There had to be another way. Perhaps they could climb to the roofs. As he turned, searching for an escape, he looked down over the lower quarters, spread out below them, and saw something that stopped him dead. Waves were slopping over the city's outer wall, and water was running down the inside. Felix stared. He hadn't thought the ark had sunk so far, but the ocean was spilling into it like water filling a ladle dipped into a bucket.

'Gotrek!' he said, and pointed.

Just as the Slayer looked around, the pressure from the water outside the wall became too much and it buckled exploding inward in a shower of stones and a towering avalanche of foam. The first breach quickly triggered others, and towers and curtain walls came down all along the west-facing side of the city.

The slaves and druchii in the square shrieked as the ground shook and tilted under their feet, then the shrieks became wails of despair as they turned and saw the ocean water surging through the city below them, levelling houses and toppling temples, and rising fast.

The crowd redoubled its efforts at the gates, and they bent inwards, but Gotrek turned away from them.

'Too late for that,' he said, starting down a side street. 'Come on.'

Felix followed after him dumbly. What could the Slayer do now? The water would rise and swallow them no matter where they went. There was no escape. Any high ground they could find would be under water in a matter of minutes. Again the mad plans of High Sorceress Heshor had left them to be drowned in a sunken city.

But the Slayer trotted down the tilted street regardless, looking around, as the thunder of the approaching water got louder and louder and the ground slanted more and more under their feet.

'Ha!' Gotrek said suddenly.

Felix looked up and saw a sturdy wooden cart filled with large casks dragging two terrified dray horses backwards across the sloping street as they bucked and kicked. The cart slid sideways into a house and came to rest as Gotrek ran to it.

'Here,' he shouted.

Gotrek wrenched down the cart's tailgate then climbed up. The casks were nearly as tall as he was. He glared when he saw dwarf runes branded into the wood.

'Filthy thieving elves.'

He stove in the top of one of the casks then tipped it on its side. The heady brew spilled down the street in a golden tide.

'In,' he said, rolling the cask off the cart and setting it on its end. 'Two of you.'

'Are you sure this will work?' asked Felix, hesitating.

'Just get in!' roared the Slayer.

Felix lifted Claudia into the cask, then climbed in awkwardly after her as Gotrek chopped through the top of a second cask and emptied it, then dropped it to the cobbles.

He jumped down into it. 'In, magister!' The sound of the approaching water was so loud now he had to bellow. Felix looked down the street. He could see it coming up the hill faster than a man could run, swallowing houses and carrying dark elves and slaves and tumbling debris with it as it rose.

Max started climbing feebly into the giant barrel.

Gotrek grabbed him by the scruff of the neck and pulled him in head-first. 'Get down!'

'It won't work,' cried Felix. 'We'll be smashed to pieces.'

The black tide reached them.

Felix dropped down into the bottom of the barrel next to Claudia as he felt the water lift them and shove them down the street. The cart horses screamed as they and the cart were carried away. Felix's teeth snapped shut as the barrel smashed into something and rushed on. Another impact, and another. The barrel splintered. Water slopped into it. Claudia's knee cracked him in the jaw. He caught her and held her tight, as much to protect himself as to shelter her as they bounced around like dice in a cup. From all sides he heard shrieks and wails and juddering collisions, and always the water was lifting and throwing them around.

Felix looked up through the opening of the barrel and saw one of the massive walls of the highborn quarter rising above them and coming closer. They were being carried towards it by the water. Then a hand gripped the lip of the barrel. A dark elf face appeared, eyes round with fright. He tried to climb in. He was going to capsize them!

Felix let go of Claudia and punched the druchii in the face. He snarled and caught Felix's wrist. Felix rose up and punched with his other hand. The dark elf wouldn't let go.

Then suddenly the black wall filled his vision and they slammed into it. Felix fell back as the dark elf was mashed flat, his ribs snapping like sticks. He fell away screaming as the great wave receded and the barrel was swept back from the wall again.

Felix peeked over the lip as currents began to pull them this way and that, and saw the rooftops and chimneys of the merchant quarter disappearing below the crashing, spuming waves. Eddies and whirlpools whipped the refuse of the city around in a chaos of clutter. The barrel swirled around nauseatingly. Felix thought he saw the cask with Max and Gotrek in it, but then he was spun around and lost it again.

There was a crack like thunder above him and Felix turned and looked up. A massive castle-sized section of the retaining wall sheered off from the rest and slid down into the water, houses and people and furniture tumbling after it. A huge rolling swell rose up as the black cliff vanished in a towering splash, and Felix and Claudia's barrel was pushed even further away from the city.

Felix couldn't take his eyes off the demise of the ark. It sank more slowly than he expected, as if the dark elf magic that had kept it afloat for four thousand years was still fighting to support it, but it sank all the same, coming to pieces as it did. Knife-sharp towers crumbled and toppled, walls collapsed. Cracks ran up through the once-solid ground, ripping the mansions and palaces built upon it asunder with a sound like an endless cannon barrage. Dark elves and slaves were crushed by

falling masonry or were swallowed by chasms that opened beneath their feet or fell screaming into the water. Felix felt the barrel being pulled back towards the ark by a powerful undertow as more of it was sucked under the waves and his heart raced. They were going to be pulled into the cataclysm and swallowed, and there was nothing he could do.

The temple level disappeared as they swirled closer, explosions of black fire erupting all over it, and great crackling arcs of purple energy leaping from building to building, shivering stone to dust wherever they touched. Felix swore he saw a river of blood pouring from the imploded ruins of a brass-walled temple and staining the water as it sank. An unearthly howling that sounded like neither man nor beast rose up to a hair-raising shriek, and then was cut off as if a door had shut.

The barrel was hit from behind as it rushed towards the sinking ark, then again from the left and the right. All the floating debris from the sinking city was converging towards the sucking centre, crowding the sea with bobbing, bumping junk and knocking Felix and Claudia this way and that.

They were close enough to see the eyes of the black stone dragons that were carved into the eaves of the roof, when waves finally reached the massive black keep, its proud, jutting towers still miraculously whole, but smoke rising in billowing columns from every window. Then, with a crack that Felix felt more than heard, the castle cleaved in half, jagged orange fissures appearing in its basalt flanks as the fire that raged within it was revealed.

The half closer to Felix sank more quickly, its towers toppling as it slid down into the sea to show blazing rooms and corridors and frantic silhouetted figures burning like paper dolls as they leapt into the water. The other half followed immediately, and suddenly Felix and Claudia's barrel was tilting down a surging hill of water as the tallest tower of the keep slipped down into the sea and disappeared into the centre of a swirling whirlpool. Felix saw a glossy black carriage heave up beside them and topple towards them as the vortex sucked them down, and he dropped back down into the barrel and clung to Claudia for dear life.

'Hold on, fraulein!' he shouted.

Then everything became a terrifying jumble of sound, motion and jarring impacts. Water swallowed the cask, whirling and slamming it around like a cork beneath a waterfall. Felix was upside down, then rightside up, crashing into Claudia, then mashed by her, all in the space of a second, unable to see anything but swirling bubbles, crashing water and flashes of waves, refuse and sky, as the cask was sucked under the pummelling waves. Bodies flew past in the water – men, women, druchii, horses, rats. Things slammed into the barrel, knocking it up, down and sideways. A human child caught the edge of it, looking pleadingly into his eyes, then was gone again before he could react.

The barrel filled with water as it went down and down. His lungs screamed for air and the world began to turn black and blurry at the edges. He wondered if they would be pulled all the way to the bottom of the sea, or smashed out of the barrel and crushed to death by whirling debris. He felt himself floating and pressed against the sides to keep himself in.

Then, long after it seemed possible that it could continue, the water began to calm, and he felt the cask slowly rising through the silt-clouded water. They broke the surface miraculously face-up, the top of the barrel almost level with the water. Felix pushed up and sucked air greedily, then realised that Claudia was still in the barrel, under the water. He reached down and hauled her up and she clung to him, choking and puking water down his chest and shivering.

He looked around at the mad scene around them, hoping to see the Slayer and Max. The sea in all directions was cluttered with ships and floating junk – barrels, boxes, planks, carts, wooden spoons, bits of clothing, papers, trash, what appeared to be a wig, and corpses of all races floated everywhere. To his left, three small druchii sloops were entangled, thrown together by the mad whirlpool of the ark's sinking. Further away, more black ships pulled swimming druchii out of the water, or fired crossbows into floating masses of pleading slaves while sea serpents, both mounted and unmounted, breasted through the rubbish and fed indiscriminately upon all.

Felix heard a splash and a familiar cough. He turned. Another barrel floated not far away, upside down! Was it the one?

'Gotrek!' called Felix. 'Max!'

Gotrek's head bobbed up next to the barrel, and he hauled Max up beside him and helped him cling to the cask. The magister was barely conscious, but he was alive. Felix shook his head in wonder. They had made it. They had survived. As impossible as it had seemed, they had escaped the black ark.

Then Felix heard a noise behind the moans, screams and shouts of the survivors and the 'hoog' of the serpents that sent a chill up his spine – the clamouring wail of the Harp of Ruin.

TWENTY

Felix and Gotrek looked around, searching for the hellish instrument amid the chaos of ships and trash and fighting. Then Felix found it. He blinked, confused, for it seemed to be floating about a yard above the water, as if it were somehow levitating. He looked closer and saw that the harp was hooked to a halberd, and that the halberd was strapped to the back of a dog-paddling skaven, who was heading right for them at the head of a cluster of swimming skaven. The water around them frothed with the thing's vibrations.

Gotrek pulled his axe from his back and shook it over his head. 'Come on, you vermin!' He roared.

But it seemed he might not be the first to reach the ratmen. Bearing down on them from behind was a phalanx of sea dragon knights, with High Sorceress Heshor mounted behind Commander Tarlkhir on the first. Heshor looked entirely healed from the wound the daemon had inflicted upon her. Tarlkhir spurred his mount and the serpent scooped a skaven out of the water and choked it down with a single gulp.

'Hoog!'

'Foul serpents!' cried Felix, drawing his sword.

Karaghul's runes were glowing brightly in the presence of so many sea dragons, and Felix could feel the urge to swim towards them welling up in him. His muscles twitched and tingled with barely controlled violence. He fought down his fury with difficulty. He had already fought a sea dragon while bobbing helplessly in the middle of the sea and hadn't cared for it much. Doing so floating precariously in a flooded beer keg with a half-conscious girl beside him was unlikely to be an improvement. Maybe the damned serpent would choke to death on the barrel, he thought.

But then, without warning, the cask rose up under him as if lifted by a hand. He swayed and clutched the lip of the cask. All around them the sea was mounding up into a hill of water.

'What in Sigmar's name?' he said.

Gotrek and Max and their barrel tumbled down the hill of water as it continued to grow, and Felix and Claudia's cask toppled with them, spinning end over end and plunging them under the sea again. Felix pushed and kicked out of the barrel, then took Claudia's arms and pulled her after him. Was the ark rising again? Did they have to do it all over again?

They came gasping to the surface and clung to a raft of debris beside Max and Gotrek as a massive rusted tower burst out of the mounded water, bristling with pipes, tanks and brass guns. Then, below the tower, a great bulk breached the waves – a verdigrised monstrosity like a scrap-metal whale, longer than a druchii galley, with a corroded metal deck and strange weapons jutting from a prow like a rat's snout. It loomed more than a storey above them, a barnacle-covered brass cliff, shedding water and hissing and blowing like a living thing.

The serpents reared back fearfully at the sight of it, fighting their riders' spurs, and in the distance, the cries of the druchii echoed from their ships, alarmed at the appearance of this massive threat in their midst. Felix could see galleys turning towards it, their ranked oars raising and pulling as one.

'What kind of machine is this?' asked Max.

'It is the thing that ate Felix and Herr Gurnisson,' said Claudia miserably. 'The thing that I allowed to take them.'

'A skaven submersible,' said Gotrek, spitting contemptuously.

Max grimaced. 'It reeks of warpstone.'

The swimming skaven clambered up the submersible's tall side as Tarlkhir's sea dragon snapped at them, ripping two away and chewing them in half. The other serpents lunged in behind the first, their heads snaking after the fleeing thieves. Skaven armed with rust-grimed swords poured out of a hatch and raced forwards to defend their brothers, then shied as the submersible began to vibrate like a gong when the black-clad skaven who carried the howling harp set foot on the deck. The water around the edges of the craft simmered and splashed as if it was on the boil.

'The harp is going to shake it apart,' Max said.

'Good,' said Gotrek.

Next out of the hatch was the ancient skaven sorcerer, hobbling forwards with the aid of its staff, and surrounded by a retinue of black-armoured vermin and followed by its albino rat ogre and its tottering tailless minion.

Felix found himself growling in his throat as he watched the black-clad thief hurry the grey seer. He was free, he had his sword, and the vermin that had hurt his father was before him.

'Him,' rumbled Gotrek. 'Come, manling. I owe him much.'

'Not if I get him first,' said Felix, and kicked for the side of the skaven submersible. Gotrek followed. Max did too.

Felix looked back. 'Maybe you should stay behind, Max.'

'There is too much magic there,' said Max. 'You will not prevail without me.'

Felix was more worried about Max prevailing. The magister looked more dead than alive.

'I will come too,' said Claudia, paddling after them.

'Claudia–' said Felix, but she shook her head.

'I must make recompense for my crime,' she said.

Felix was going to protest more, but then he shrugged. Was she really any safer clinging to a barrel in the middle of a sea full of sea dragons?

The black-clad skaven went down on one knee before the grey seer, the halberd strapped to its back extending forwards over its head to put the harp within the sorcerer's reach. Its fellow thieves knelt behind it.

'We did exactly what he wanted,' said Felix angrily as they reached the side of the submersible near its stern. 'We stirred up trouble with the dark elves and allowed his thieves to snatch the harp in the confusion. He's been pulling our strings since he freed us.'

'I am no one's puppet,' growled Gotrek, and began to climb the side of the submersible.

'Nor am I,' said Felix, as he, Max and Claudia followed, pulling themselves up the strange pipes, flanges and poorly fitted plates that made up the behemoth's skin. The metal was vibrating so much that holding it stung the hands.

The ancient skaven stared at the screaming harp, seemingly caught between horror and desire, as his minions edged away from it. The rat ogre moaned unhappily and covered its ears. The seer reached out a tentative claw towards it, but before it could touch it, a cloud of black fire exploded around it, staggering it. The skaven thieves dived away from the black flames with uncanny quickness, while the tailless minion fell back clumsily and the rat ogre howled, but many of the warrior skaven around the seer shrieked and died in the ebony fire, shrinking to charred skeletons within their armour. The seer squealed in agony and rage, but seemed to absorb the fire without damage. It turned towards the front of the submersible, where Heshor and Tarlkhir rode high on their sea dragon, surrounded by the other serpent riders.

The skaven sorcerer swept its staff in a circle and the air rippled before it, travelling out in a spreading arc towards the druchii. The sea dragons went mad, roaring and thrashing as if beset by wasps. They threw their riders and attacked themselves and each other, ripping their scaly hides with dagger teeth. Heshor and Tarlkhir were tossed into the sea as their knights screamed and tried to regain control of their mounts.

Karaghul howled for Felix to run and dive and slaughter them all. He ground his teeth, forcing himself to ignore the insistent call, and instead stepped with Gotrek, Claudia and Max onto the rattling deck of the submersible. There would be a time to unleash the sword's fury, but now wasn't it, and they weren't the targets. It was the ratman sorcerer he wanted to kill.

They crept towards the central tower as the loose plates of the submersible clanged and clattered in deafening harmony to the harp's howl.

The skaven seer returned its attention to the harp, which the thief again held before it at the end of the halberd. It threw its arms wide, shrilling a harsh incantation, and the air around the harp began to thicken, warping light and muffling its whine. Then the old skaven slowly brought its arms closer together, squeaking all the while, and the air between its paws grew thicker still, gelling like aspic, and the harp quietened even more. The seer trembled with the effort.

The rattling metal plate around Felix and the others calmed, and the deck under their feet grew still.

'Such power,' said Max, in wonder, as they watched from the shadow of the central tower. 'To quell so powerful a thing.'

'I'll still kill him,' snarled Felix.

The grey seer brought its paws together and the harp stopped ringing entirely. It reached out and took it from the halberd as easily as if it picked up a book.

The sudden silence was eerie. It felt as if Felix had been hearing the sound of the harp all his life and, with it gone, a weight he had carried since childhood was lifted off his shoulders. The cries of the dying, the slap of the waves, the rumblings from within the submersible, the roars of the sea dragons, all were clear and close, the chittering of the skaven and the shouting of the druchii knights loud in Felix's ears.

There were more distant cries too, and Felix saw that two dark elf galleys were sailing their way, their prows cleaving paths through the floating debris as their sweeps rose and fell.

The grey seer hurried back towards the hatch from which it had emerged, triumphant, surrounded by its remaining guards and followed by the shambling rat ogre and its scampering servant. Gotrek drew his axe and prepared to charge. Felix, enflamed by Karaghul's hate for the sea dragons and his own for the skaven sorcerer, fought the urge to run out ahead of the Slayer.

'Now?' he asked eagerly.

Just then the hatch cover trembled and slammed shut by itself with a loud clang, cutting in half a skaven who was just climbing out.

The other skaven fell back, frightened. The grey seer whipped around. Behind it, at the prow of the submersible, Heshor floated up out of the sea, arms still extended from casting the spell that had closed the hatch, while Tarlkhir and his sea dragon knights clambered out more prosaically and surrounded her.

Still clutching the harp in its right paw, the skaven sorcerer snarled and shot spears of green light towards Heshor with its left. She threw up her hands and a shield of dark air flared into being in front of her and the green spears glanced away. She shot curling snakes of smoke back towards the seer and the battle was joined. Leather-clad sword-rats charged Tarlkhir and his knights. The albino rat ogre and the black-armoured skaven warriors remained at the seer's side.

'Now, manling!' roared Gotrek.

'Wait,' said Max, 'Let me provide you with some protection...'

But Gotrek and Felix were already charging straight at the skaven sorcerer's back, roaring jubilant battle cries. Felix let Karaghul take full control and a red rage consumed him.

The armoured skaven turned at their roar, but not quickly enough. Gotrek's axe took the head of one, carved a trench through the chest of a second and hacked through the legs of a third. Felix cut down two more. The Slayer bellowed for the hulking rat ogre to face him. It obliged, roaring and raising battering-ram fists as it rushed to meet him. Felix leapt at three black-armoured skaven, trying to smash through them towards the grey seer.

The old skaven spun in mid-spell and shrieked at the sight of the carnage behind it. It raised a hand and began a new spell, this time directed at them. Felix felt a tingle and for a moment thought the worst, but then a sphere of golden light enveloped them and he realised that Max had completed his spell.

As Gotrek hacked at the albino monstrosity and Felix fought the armoured skaven, a flash of blinding un-light shot from Heshor and the skaven sorcerer hissed and twitched, blackness crawling over its body and invading every orifice. The seer stumbled, trying to force a counterspell through grinding teeth.

Felix cut down two of the big skaven. To his left, Gotrek was in the grip of the rat ogre, which lifted him high over its head. Felix ducked a slash and parried another. When he looked back, the rat ogre was toppling backwards, Gotrek's axe blade deep in its skull. It hit the metal deck with a hollow boom and Gotrek wrenched his axe free, then bulled on towards the seer, who was still fighting Heshor's web of power. As Gotrek slashed at the ancient skaven, it shrieked and threw itself backwards. Gotrek's axe chopped through its wrist, severing it in a spray of black blood.

The grey seer screamed as the harp clanged away across the deck towards the dark elves, its right claw still gripping it. It fell to the deck, squeaking and clutching the bloody stump of its scrawny wrist as it turned terrified black eyes on Gotrek.

'Your head is next, vermin!' roared the Slayer.

A knot of skaven swarmed in to defend the grey seer. Gotrek charged into them.

'No, Gotrek!' shouted Felix. 'He's mine. He hurt my father!'

Felix hacked through the armour-clad skaven, trying to reach the fallen seer, but just then the black-clad skaven assassin leapt at him, stabbing with gauntlets from which jutted long metal claws.

Felix gutted the assassin as it crashed into him, its claws ripping red grooves in his back and chest. He threw it aside and joined Gotrek just as he decapitated the seer's last guard and loomed over the figure that writhed at the edge of the submersible.

'I would have to kill you a dozen times to cancel my debt with you, vermin,' said Felix.

'Once will have to do,' growled Gotrek.

Together they raised their weapons over the cowering grey seer, but suddenly, with a shrill squeak, its little lop-tailed servant leapt forwards and tackled its master over the side of the submersible and into the sea.

'Come back here!' shouted Felix.

Gotrek roared angrily. 'Face your death, coward!'

'Gotrek! Felix!' shouted Max, from cover. 'The harp! The druchii! The ships are getting closer!'

Gotrek and Felix turned reluctantly. The harp, with the old skaven's severed paw still clutching it, had awoken again, and was dancing and jittering in the middle of a crazed melee as the submersible began to shake anew with its resonance. Tarlkhir and his knights fought a horde of sword-wielding skaven over it, while to port and starboard, the two druchii warships ploughed ever closer. Felix swallowed. If they didn't get the harp now, it would be too late.

He and Gotrek started towards the harp, hewing their way through skaven and dark elves as they went, but Heshor wasn't about to let them close to it. She cried a foul phrase and beams of un-light shot at them. Max's golden sphere absorbed some of their power before popping like a soap bubble. The beams came on.

The Slayer cursed and threw up his axe. The beams parted around him, glancing off the blade and impaling the skaven around them, sending them squealing to the deck with blood pouring from their mouths, noses and eyes. Felix crouched behind the Slayer, but even so, horrible scything pains shot through his lungs and joints and nearly brought him to his knees.

Then a bright bolt of lightning shot past from behind him and struck Heshor. The high sorceress snarled and turned, shooting her black beams towards the tower where Max and Claudia hid.

Felix sent a silent thanks to the seeress as his pain eased slightly. He stumbled on with Gotrek, hacking through the mad scrum of fighting dark elves and skaven after the harp. It was a terrible thing to try to catch, for its vibrations made it impossible to pick up. The skaven that grabbed for it snatched their paws back in pain, only to be cut down by druchii who also could not hold it, and it skittered and slid back and forth across the deck as each side tried to grab it.

At last Gotrek and Felix hacked through a swarm of skaven and found the harp before them. Gotrek strode towards it as Felix defended his sides.

'No, dwarf,' snarled a voice.

Gotrek and Felix looked up. Tarlkhir and a handful of his sea dragon knights were advancing towards them.

'You have sunk our city,' Tarlkhir shouted over the noise of the harp. 'Vengeance demands that we bury yours.'

'You sank your own damned city,' said Gotrek. 'Calling daemons and playing with magic.'

The Slayer charged the druchii commander, axe held out to his side. Felix howled and raced in behind him, as Karaghul sang to him sweet songs of slaughter. He knew the knights were druchii elite. He knew they would kill him. But Karaghul didn't care, and so neither did he.

Fortunately, the sword seemed to lend him some of its arcane fury, and he found himself fighting with an unnatural vigour and speed. Even so, he could not break through the perfect guard of the two hard-eyed dark elves he faced, but neither could they break through his. Gotrek was facing the same difficulty. One on one with Tarlkhir he would undoubtedly have triumphed, but three other druchii knights fought him as well, and his flashing axe could only block as the druchii blades thrust in at him from all sides.

'Damned tricksy elves,' Gotrek rasped.

Felix could barely hear him over the harp's hellish wail. It was tearing the submersible apart. Hot steam was whistling up through ruptured metal plates. Felix fell back from one, scalded. He felt himself faltering. The energy flowing from Karaghul did not flag, but his body was so battered and worn out that it was having difficulty keeping up. His muscles screamed for rest and his lungs felt filled with hot sand.

Behind the knights, Heshor was preparing another spell. That would be the end, Felix knew – at least for him. He was not behind Gotrek's axe now, and Max's protective spells had collapsed. The black energy would rip through him undiluted this time and tear his insides to pieces.

At least, he thought, it was a good ending. At least he and the Slayer were going to die as they should – knee-deep in the slain, surrounded by enemies, fighting for the fate of the world after sending a floating hell of depravity and oppression to the bottom of the sea. At least this was as grand and epic as the Slayer could have wished. The Slayer had done everything Claudia had spoken of in her prophecy. He had fought in the bowels of a black mountain, he had fought foes without number, he had fought a towering abomination, and now he was going to die. It was right. It was fitting. He was content. If only he could have found out what had happened to his father before he died.

A juddering impact knocked him and everyone on the deck to the right. Then another crash threw them to the left. The combatants staggered and looked around. The druchii ships had arrived. On the left, a black galley was scraping against the side of the submersible, tearing up corroded metal plates as it ground to a halt. On the right another galley had crashed nose-first into the skaven craft, beaching itself on its deck and crashing into the tower in the centre. The submersible groaned and shuddered like a dying elephant.

Gangplanks slammed down from the galleys and scores of druchii corsairs poured onto the deck towards the combat.

Tarlkhir roared an order at them as he staggered to his feet, and the corsairs stopped reluctantly.

Tarlkhir faced Gotrek, his eyes blazing, while the Harp of Ruin jigged madly on the deck between them. 'This is not for the likes of them,' he said. 'Your death shall be mine alone.'

Gotrek shrugged. 'Suit yourself.'

The Slayer ran at Tarlkhir, swinging high. The druchii commander whipped his sword into a parry and Gotrek's axe scraped down it in a shower of sparks. Gotrek slashed again, and Tarlkhir circled to the Slayer's left, his blind side. Gotrek had to turn quickly to keep his good right eye on him.

Tarlkhir lunged when Gotrek was on his off foot, and the Slayer had to duck out the way. One of Tarlkhir's knights raised his sword, but the commander shouted him back. Felix rose and went on guard, ready in case any of the other knights got ideas.

Gotrek charged again, his axe a steel blur as he drove Tarlkhir back. The ferocity of the attack stunned the dark elf and he began to lose his composure, parrying desperately and stumbling as he gave ground.

All around, the corsairs and the knights edged in. Felix swallowed, terrified.

'Even now you have failed, dwarf,' sneered Tarlkhir, as he fell back before Gotrek's assault. 'Kill me or no, we will still get the harp.'

'At least there will be one less elf in the world,' said Gotrek, and leapt forwards again, roaring.

Tarlkhir raised his sword to block, but Gotrek's axe sheared right through the black metal and swept on, splitting the commander's breastplate down the middle and burying itself deep in his chest. Blood welled up through the blued armour as Tarlkhir's eyes rolled up in his head.

Heshor wailed from the prow of the submersible. The corsairs cried out as well, then surged forwards to avenge their commander's death. Felix was so weary he almost welcomed the end.

Gotrek didn't even look at them. Instead he laughed and raised his axe above the howling harp. 'Now they all die!' he roared.

Heshor's wail turned into a terrified shriek. 'No!' she cried.

Gotrek slammed the heavy blade down on the hellish instrument with a deafening clang. The harp cracked and danced away, the ancient skaven's hand still gripping it, and weird purple light spilled from hairline fissures in its frame. Gotrek staggered back, covering his single eye, and Felix and the dark elves and the skaven were knocked off their feet. The discordant ringing quickly rose to a daemonic scream. The corsairs and knights scrambled back in fear. Behind them, Heshor shrieked, her face a white mask of terror, then turned and leapt into the sea.

'Felix! Gotrek!' called Max from the submersible's tower. 'Away! Into the water!' Then, following his own suggestion, he turned and ran, dragging Claudia with him.

'Come on, Gotrek!' called Felix, then sprinted after the magister and the seeress. He was joined in his flight by terrified corsairs and skaven, all running for cover from the spinning, spitting harp.

Felix ran towards the submersible's stern, then jumped into the water behind the galley and came up near Max and Claudia and the floating casks. He shook the water out of his eyes and glanced around. Gotrek wasn't with them.

'Gotrek?'

Felix looked back towards the submersible. The Slayer stood alone in the centre of the deck, lit from below by a terrible purple light, his axe raised, his feet braced wide on either side of the dancing harp as druchii and skaven dived away from him in all directions. Then, with a roar, Gotrek swung down again and chopped the harp in half.

'Down!' shouted Max, and shoved Claudia's head under the water as he dived down himself.

Felix ducked, the image of Gotrek vanishing in a flash of blazing purple light that was burned into his retinas as the water closed over his head. He felt a wave of heat and pressure pass through the water, and heard a deafening concussion like a clap of thunder directly overhead.

Seconds later he came gasping back to the surface and looked towards the deck. It was empty but for a raging purple fire where the harp had been, and crackling arcs of purple energy that crawled and leapt across the rupturing, steam-shot metal. Gotrek was nowhere to be seen.

'Did... did he escape?' said Felix, stunned. 'He can't have died.'

'He died,' said Max, looking in terror at the dancing purple energy. 'He has to have done. And killed us as well. The blast has agitated the warpstone on the skaven craft.'

'The aetheric winds are building,' said Claudia staring as well. 'It will not hold.'

Then, from above them, came a familiar groan.

Felix looked up. 'Gotrek?'

The druchii galley loomed over their heads. Gotrek's groan had come from somewhere upon it.

'Gotrek!' Relief flooded Felix's heart, and he began swimming towards the aft gangplank of the druchii ship.

'Felix!' called Max after him. 'We must get away! The submersible will explode!'

Felix swam on, ignoring him. How were they to get away anyway? Fly? There was nothing they could do, but if the Slayer was still alive, Felix knew he should be with him at the end. It was the fitting thing to do. He grabbed the gangplank and pulled himself up onto it, not daring to touch the surface of the glowing, shuddering submersible.

He ran up it onto the broad deck of the black galley, sword out, fully expecting to die fighting a crowd of corsairs as he tried to reach Gotrek, but the few druchii who had clambered back on board lay writhing and clutching themselves obscenely, their eyes mad and blind and their white skins burned pink.

Felix picked his way through them to the sterncastle as the rumbling and hissing from the submersible got louder and more violent, and found Gotrek at last by the aft rail, lying motionless on his side, both hands still holding his axe in a death grip. The Slayer looked ghastly. His one eye was rolled up in his head, his beard, crest and eyebrows were blackened and smoking, and the front of him was as red as a lobster, and steamed slightly. But the most extraordinary thing about him was his axe. It glowed a bright red from blade to pommel, and was as hot as if it had been pulled seconds ago from a forge. Smoke curled from the haft where Gotrek's hands clenched it, and it hissed and popped like fat on a fire. Felix smelled cooked meat.

'Gotrek? Do you still live? Can you stand?'

He looked back towards the skaven craft, then knelt beside the Slayer, to listen for his breathing. He paused when he heard footsteps coming up the steps to the stern deck, then stood. A powerfully built druchii with a short sailor's cutlass and a whip appeared, looking around cautiously.

Felix ran at him, hoping to kill him before he reached the deck, but the druchii lashed out with his whip and cut Felix across the thighs. His chainmail took the brunt of the blow, but it still stung, and he stumbled, nearly impaling himself on the dark elf's cutlass. Felix parried, and what had been a charge quickly became a retreat as the druchii gained the deck and forced him back.

Then a cry and a sudden burst of light made them both cringe. Felix dived away and looked towards the skaven craft, expecting to see it erupting, but it was not the submersible, it was Max, staggering up the gangplank with Claudia and shooting a stream of light at the druchii sailor. He shielded his eyes and swiped blindly at Felix, dazzled by the magical light.

Felix charged in and dispatched him in two quick strokes while he was still defenceless, then collapsed from exhaustion on top of him.

'Get below!' gasped Max. 'It's going to blow.'

'Will that save us?' asked Felix.

'I doubt it,' said Max as he led Claudia across the deck. 'But it's our only chance.'

The seeress trailed behind him, mumbling up towards the sky and pawing at the air.

She's gone truly mad this time, thought Felix, as he hurried back to Gotrek. Heshor's counter-spells must have crushed her mind. He hooked his hands under the Slayer's arms and pulled, but it was like trying to shift a bull. He was so weak, and the Slayer was so heavy. He hauled again, and moved Gotrek perhaps a foot, the glowing rune axe branding a smouldering black line in the deck. It would take him an hour to get him to the door to the lower decks.

He ran back to the rail that looked down to the deck. 'Max!' he called. 'Help me move the Slayer.'

His voice was drowned out by a wrenching crash and once again he flinched and looked towards the skaven craft, expecting the worst. Instead he saw the gangplanks twisting and tearing away from the galley as the submersible slid past, still glowing and shaking and crawling with purple lightning.

Max stared too, stepping towards the rail.

'They're sailing off!' Felix shouted, elated.

'No,' said Max. 'We are.'

The magister turned towards Claudia. Felix followed his gaze. The seeress was still mumbling at the sky, but now her arms were outstretched towards the galley's lateen sail, which was bellied out and straining full of a wind that existed nowhere else. They *were* moving, slowly still, but picking up speed, thumping through the clutter of debris that floated all around them as they went.

Felix ran back to the Slayer and hauled at him again. A moment later Max joined him, though in his weakened state he wasn't much help. Still they had to try. Every yard they sailed gave them a little more hope for survival. And if he could get the Slayer below the decks, his chances might be better still.

At last they got him to the top of the stairs. Max looked down them, then back to the skaven ship. 'There's no way,' he said, panting.

With a curse, Felix heaved Gotrek up and over, and pushed him down the stairs. The Slayer bounced down loosely and sprawled at the bottom, unmoving. Felix hurried down after him with Max close behind, and started dragging him towards the door.

The galley was beyond the swamp of floating garbage now and sailing past other druchii ships, which still circled the mess. There was nothing but open sea before them, and Felix began to hope that they might make it after all, when suddenly, with Gotrek's body still two yards away from the underdecks door, an enormous 'whump' of sound buffeted Felix's ears and a blinding green light blazed off the aft rail.

Max cursed and tackled Claudia to the deck as Felix threw himself down next to Gotrek. The magister shouted a terse incantation and a fragile bubble of golden light sprang into being around them. And just in time, for with an impact like a hammer, a hot wind slammed into the ship, spinning it around and heeling it over on its side.

Felix looked back and saw a huge cloud of glittering smoke racing towards them faster than a cannon ball. Then it was over them, as thick as mud, and pushed by a howling, oven-hot wind, filled with spinning bits of metal, wood and flesh. Bodies and spars and twisted metal plates smashed into the deck and punched holes in the sails and tore away the rigging.

Max's golden bubble kept out the smoke and the rain of glittering powder that skirled across the deck, but heavier things came through. A severed druchii hand slapped Felix in the face and nearly dislocated his jaw. A decorative silver candlestick flew past and smashed into the bulkhead behind them.

'Inside!' cried Max. 'Hurry!' He crawled for the door, the bubble of pure air moving with him.

Claudia dragged herself after him. Felix grabbed Gotrek's body under the arms again and hauled at it.

Max reached the door and threw it open, then shoved Claudia through. With strength born of desperation, Felix dragged the Slayer over the threshold, then collapsed in a heap behind him. Max shouldered the door closed again against the horrible hot wind, turned the latch and slumped against it.

'Are we safe?' asked Felix, raising his head.

Before Max could answer the ship rose beneath them as if it were the *Spirit of Grungni*, and for a moment Felix felt almost weightless. Then they crashed down again with a colossal impact and Felix and the others were thrown about the little corridor like rag dolls. Felix crashed head-first into a cabin door, them slammed back down to the deck as water poured in under the deck door and dripped down from the ceiling.

The last thing he saw before he lost consciousness was Gotrek's massive chest rising and falling. Ah, he thought. So that's all right.

Then all went black.

When he woke again, Felix was still in the cramped, ebony-panelled corridor of the dark elf war galley, and the others were still lying around him as they had been when he had passed out, but some things had changed. The ship was still. Water was no longer coming under the door, and no wind howled around them. In fact, there was hardly any noise at all.

Felix tried to sit up. His body refused, every muscle screaming with agony and his head throbbing and spinning. After several more tries, he finally managed it, then went about the even more complicated process of getting to his feet.

A minute later, with the assistance of the walls, he had done it, and he tottered slowly and painfully to the door, stepping over Max and Claudia's unconscious bodies as he went. He pulled it open and stepped cautiously onto the deck. It was a sight to behold, blackened and shattered and strewn with bodies and wreckage flung there by the submersible's explosion. The mast was snapped off halfway up its length, and the broken end hung over the port rail, the sail drooping into the water.

He stepped past it and looked out over the sea. Except for the climbing pall of smoke blotting out much of the northern horizon, it was a beautiful late autumn afternoon. The sun was setting in the west. There was a light breeze from the south east and the ocean was blue and empty in every direction for as far as he could see.

He shook his head in disbelief. Somehow, incredibly, they had survived – a thing that had seemed impossible almost since they had left Marienburg a thousand years ago. And not only had they survived; through luck, strategy and Gotrek's single-minded determination to die well, they had succeeded in averting the disaster that Claudia had foretold. The Harp of Ruin was destroyed, and the plans that the druchii and the skaven had had for it were foiled. Marienburg would not be swept away. Altdorf would not be flooded. The Empire and the Old World would not fall – at least not from this cause.

Of course, though they had survived and succeeded, many had died too. Around him on the deck, amidst the twisted wreckage, lay dozens of twisted corpses – the remains of the corsairs, their slaves, and the scrawny, furred bodies of skaven – all with their flesh half-eaten away by the glittering poison that had rained down from the smoke of the submersible's explosion.

And these were only a few of the dead. Aethenir, Rion and his house guards, Max's Reiksguard escort, Farnir, his father Birgi, and thousands more. A whole city had died – and not just wicked druchii, but human, dwarf and elf slaves and prisoners, not all of whom had given their lives willingly for the cause. Felix tried not to feel guilty for this horde of ghosts. It certainly hadn't been him who had enslaved them, or who had woken the deadly instrument that had shaken the floating island to pieces, but once again, had he and Gotrek not been present, they would not have died. On the other hand, had he and Gotrek not been present Marienburg *would* have died, and Altdorf drowned – hundreds of thousands dead instead of a few.

And there might be one more dead.

The moment he thought it, his heart thudded in his chest and he wanted instantly to be home. His father. He had to learn what the vile skaven had done to his father. He had to discover if the old man were alive or dead.

The thought brought him out of his reverie and he looked around. The galley drifted quietly, its mast broken, its sails slack and torn. Much of the rigging was hanging in tangled ruins. He stepped to the rail. He could see no land in any direction. They had survived, yes, but how were they to get home? How could two men, a dwarf and a not particularly handy young woman sail a dark elf galley back to the Old World? Even if any of them knew how to sail it would be impossible. There were too many things to do at once. They would need a whole crew.

The thought brought him up short. Perhaps they had one. He turned and climbed painfully to the sterncastle. There he found the druchii with the whip and the cutlass, or what was left of him. He pulled the ring of iron keys from his belt – the corroded leather tore like tissue – then hurried as fast as his battered body would take him back down the stairs and into the bowels of the ship.

He found them in the dank, sweat-grimed hell of the rowers' deck, and for a wonder, most of them were still alive – the only dead being those closest to the oar holes where the poison cloud must have blown in. Those that still lived looked up from their oars as he unlocked the latticed iron door that imprisoned them, and stared when they saw that he was human. They were a gaunt, haggard lot – men and dwarfs with dirt-blackened, whip-scarred skin and dreadlocked hair and beards, all chained at the ankle to the hard wooden benches that rose in tiers along the length of the galley.

'Greetings, friends,' said Felix as he stepped to the first iron padlock and opened it with the key, 'Do any of you know how to sail a ship?'

Grey Seer Thanquol sat chest deep in water in the bottom of a leaky ale cask in the middle of the Sea of Chaos, contemplating the follies of ambition as his servant, Issfet Loptail, bailed water using a druchii helmet for a bucket.

For almost twenty years Thanquol had longed for only one thing, vengeance on the tall yellow-furred human and the mad red-furred dwarf. For almost twenty years he had nursed his hatred for the pair and dreamed of new and more creative ways of dismantling them body and soul. And after twenty years he had had them at last. They had been at his mercy. He might have done anything he pleased with them.

But then the words of that vainglorious prick-ear, the tale of the Harp of Ruin and what it could do, had set his mind to thoughts of position and power and the rightful return to his former rank and privilege. And like a human in a maze who drops one piece of meat for a bigger piece of meat and in the process loses both, he had let go of his nemeses, used them to confound the druchii and steal from them the harp, and just when everything seemed to have gone according to plan, he had lost it all.

The human and the dwarf had escaped him, the harp had been destroyed, the submersible, surely the most glorious invention in the long history of skaven innovation, and which he had hired at great expense and with many promises of political favours from Riskin of Clan Skryre, had been blown to dust, and... and...

He looked at his tied-off right wrist, the ragged stump already healing due to his sorcerous ministrations. The dwarf would pay for this painful, humiliating maiming. He would never stop paying. Though Thanquol had nothing now, having squandered all his coin and influence hiring the submersible and Shadowfang's night runners, he would rise again. He would amass wealth and power and influence, and when he had it, he would reach out his remaining claw and crush the vicious, black-hearted dwarf to a pulp, but not before tearing off his disgusting pink limbs one by one, as if he were a fly.

'What now, oh most bereft of masters?' asked Issfet as he dumped the last of the water out of the cask and leaned, panting, against its rim.

'What now?' snapped Thanquol querulously. 'What else, fool? Start paddling, quick-quick!'

SLAYER OF THE STORM GOD

'Knock again, manling,' said Gotrek Gurnisson.

Felix Jaeger raised his fist and rapped on the door of Hans Euler's Marienburg town house, louder this time.

A window opened in the house next door and a maid in a winged cap leaned out.

'Herr Euler is away, mein Herren,' she said. 'You won't find him home.'

Felix would have been very surprised if he had, for he had stabbed Euler through the heart on the dark elves' black ark more than a week ago, and the treacherous pirate was hopefully rotting at the bottom of the sea at the moment.

He was about to tell the girl some lie about leaving a card, or delivering a letter, but then Gotrek turned towards her and her eyes went wide. She disappeared into the house with a squeak of fright.

Felix didn't blame her. Gotrek was a fearsome sight. He was a dwarf Trollslayer, and ugly even for that ugly breed. Short, broad, and muscled like a jungle ape, his scarred, sun-browned flesh was covered in swirling blue tattoos, and a crest of flame-orange hair rose from his shaved head. Add to this an eye-patch, a face like a weathered boulder, and a rune-inscribed battle-axe in a fist the size of a baked ham, and one had a vision to make a hardened veteran blanch, let alone a Marienburg housemaid.

Felix knocked again. Again there was no answer, but this time he thought he heard faint shufflings and thumpings inside.

'Someone's after your safe,' said Gotrek. 'Stand aside.'

Felix stepped back and the Slayer gripped the doorknob, twisting it with slow, inexorable strength. His biceps bulged. The lock mechanism squealed for a moment in pain, then, with a sharp snap, the knob spun loose and the door creaked open.

There were more thumpings and rustlings from within. Felix drew his sword as Gotrek pushed the door wide and stepped into the dim interior. All was as he remembered it – or nearly all. The wood-paneled entry hall was still dark and stuffy, with a spiral staircase to the left and a door that opened into a richly furnished parlour at the back. The parlour's bay window still had a big hole – now partially boarded up – where Gotrek and Felix had been shoved out of it during their last visit, and the small safe that Gotrek had thrown down the stairs was still half-sunk into the wooden floor where it had smashed through the polished planks.

The dead butler sprawled on the floor was new, however, as were the chisels and hammers and files that were scattered in a puddle of water surrounding the safe. Felix turned away from the butler, whose brains were spilling out of the hole in his head. The thieves must have been hard men indeed to murder the man and then leave him where he fell as they went about their work.

Gotrek snorted as he looked at the safe-cracking tools. 'Cheap human chisels. No match for dwarf workmanship.'

Felix rolled his eyes at this typical dwarfen bias, but had to admit that the safe showed hardly a mark. Beyond it, a trail of wet footprints led from the broken parlour window to the puddle and back again.

'They've gone out the back,' he said.

He and Gotrek strode to the back window and looked out. Euler's back wall dropped straight down to the canal they had plunged into when his bodyguards had thrown them out. If the housebreakers had gone out the window, they'd have had to have gone into the water, but Felix saw no swimmers, only circular ripples spreading out across the calm water.

'Strange,' said Felix.

Gotrek shrugged. 'At least they didn't get into the safe,' he said, and turned away, pulling a ring of keys from his belt pouch.

Felix followed the Slayer to the safe. They had stolen the keys from Euler on their previous visit, but their abrupt exit had prevented them from using them.

The whole business had been distasteful. Not the sort of thing Felix normally cared to do. Euler had been in possession of some incriminating letter with which he'd attempted to blackmail Felix's father, and the old man had asked Felix to get it back. If he hadn't been on his death bed when he'd made the request, Felix would never have done it, but as it was he'd felt obliged, and had come reluctantly to Euler's house to try to intimidate him into giving it up.

Needless to say, it hadn't gone well, and then the business with the dark elves had intervened, with Euler chasing them across the Sea of Chaos, thinking that they were on the trail of great treasure, and Felix had been forced to kill the pirate when he had turned on them in the bowels of the black ark.

That nightmare was over, thankfully, and now he and Gotrek were back in Marienburg until the following morning, when they and their old friend Max Schreiber, a magister of the College of Light, and Claudia Pallenberger, a seeress from the Celestial College, would board a riverboat to Altdorf for the last leg of their journey home.

Max and Claudia were staying the night at the house of an acquaintance of Max's, and Gotrek would have been content to bide his time drinking at their inn, the Pelican's Perch, but Felix still felt an obligation to recover the letter, even though Euler was dead and there was a distinct possibility that his father was as well. So he had asked the Slayer to accompany him back to the smuggler's house for one last try.

The key turned in its lock with a satisfying click, and Felix knelt as Gotrek hauled on the handle and opened the safe's heavy steel door. The walls of it were inches thick, and the space inside hardly big enough to hold a loaf of bread, but what lay within glittered in a way that made Felix's heart race and Gotrek's ugly face split in a terrifying smile.

'You can have the letter, manling,' he said. 'I'll take the rest.'

He pulled out a sheaf of papers and handed them to Felix, then began scooping out the treasure and dumping it on the floor – a small spill of jewellery, loose gems, and gold coins of strange foreign design.

Felix sorted through the papers. There were contracts, promissory notes, articles of incorporation, and, at last, an envelope scrawled upon in his father's scratchy hand. His heart thumping with relief, Felix opened it and made sure there was a letter within, then stuffed it in his belt pouch.

'I have it,' he said.

Gotrek just grunted and kept sorting the treasure, entirely engrossed. He held a thick gold circlet up to his single appraising eye. 'Dwarf gold, human work,' he said. 'Not bad for all that.'

Felix looked at the coil as the Slayer slipped it on his wrist. He thought it might have once been a necklace, but it barely fit around Gotrek's meaty arm. It was made of heavy gold wire – eight braided strands branching from a central bezel set with a sea-green gem the size of a walnut. Though it was undeniably beautiful, Felix found he didn't like the look of the thing. Perhaps he was just sick of anything that reminded him of the sea.

'Are you sure it's not elven?' he asked, hoping to make Gotrek take it off.

Gotrek snorted. 'Not flimsy enough.' He tossed a delicate gold necklace into the puddle. 'That's elven,' he said with a sneer, then began picking through the rest and putting the choicer bits in his belt pouch.

Felix thought the elven necklace was beautiful, but he wasn't going to argue the point with a dwarf. He'd just take it. But as he picked it up, voices reached them from the street.

'Aye, sergeant,' came the housemaid's voice. 'I saw 'em. They broke down Herr Euler's door.'

A man's voice answered her. 'Back inside, miss. We'll take care of this. Swords out, boys.'

'The watch,' whispered Felix.

Gotrek grunted angrily, and for a moment Felix was afraid he meant to stay and fight, but instead he just swept up the treasure in his big hands, stuffed it down his breeches, then stumped towards the spiral staircase, jingling with each step.

'To the roof, manling,' he said. 'While they follow the footprints to the canal.'

Felix followed, surprised and relieved. Apparently Gotrek's lust for gold had momentarily won out over his lust for battle.

As they started up the stairs, Felix paused and looked back at the wet footprints, suddenly wondering why they seemed so wide and splayed. Had the housebreakers used some sort of special shoes to swim the canal?

There was a crash as the front door burst in. Felix hurried after the Slayer.

Gotrek shook another ruby out of his trouser leg and put it on the table with the rest. 'I think that's the last of them.'

Felix looked up from reading his father's letter and glanced askance at the little pile of now-pungent treasure the Slayer had amassed. Showing so much wealth in a tavern like the Pelican's Perch would bring nothing but trouble, but perhaps that was what the Slayer wanted, or perhaps he just didn't care.

Even with the sun still up, the taproom was crowded with rowdy revellers. In fact all Marienburg was crowded with rowdy revellers, piling into town for the Storm Festival, a local holiday that culminated with the priests of the sea god Manann leading their congregations in a prayer to spare their fishing and trading fleets from harsh winter storms. Despite the freezing winter winds that whipped spray off the canals and blew it in their faces, the merry celebrants were singing songs in the streets and carousing from inn to inn, red-cheeked and rubber-legged and praising Manann with every bend of their elbows.

A squad of Black Caps pushed into the tavern. Felix hid his face behind his father's letter, but the watchmen only spoke with the barman, scanned the place cursorily, and headed back out to the street. The watchmen looked on edge – understandable, what with the town full of drunks, and also rumours that some of those drunks were going missing – pulled into the canals by strange assailants, never to be seen again. The Storm Festival Curse, the locals called it, for apparently it happened every year. Felix thought it much more likely that the missing revellers had fallen into the canals after one too many toasts to Manann.

As Gotrek muttered over his glittering hoard, Felix returned to the old letter. So far he hadn't found anything particularly blackmail-worthy. It was a note from his father, acknowledging that he had received some goods from Euler's father – a smuggler just like his son. There were lists of Tilean glass, Bretonnian brandy, Cathayan silk, and other fancy goods that Felix supposed might have been smuggled or stolen. It didn't seem enough somehow. His father had been terrified that this letter would rob him of Jaeger and Sons. Nothing here seemed to merit that terror.

Felix turned the letter over. His heart stopped. He had found it. At the top of the page was a list of six books, with a note scrawled to one side in his father's hand. Felix didn't recognise all the titles, but even the ones he did were enough to tie his stomach in sailors' knots – *The Maelificarium* by Salini, Urbanus's *The Seven Gates*, Sudenberg's *Treatise on the Hidden World*. All were forbidden texts in the eyes of the Temple of Sigmar, and tomes of darkest sorcery. The possession of any one of them would be enough to have a man burned at the stake.

Felix read the note his father had written beside them.

> *Returning the Urbanus and the Bastory.*
> *Estlemann says they are damaged and*
> *unsellable. Will want full refund.*
>   *GJ*

Felix's head swam. His father had dealt, was perhaps still dealing, in forbidden books! This was indeed something that would destroy Jaeger and Sons if exposed. He was filled once again with loathing for the old man's greed. This proved beyond a doubt that Gustav would do *anything* to increase his fortune. Of course, Felix thought with a twinge of guilt, his father might be dead now, and he shouldn't think ill of him, but the old villain certainly made it difficult to be charitable.

A shadow passed over the letter and a voice jarred Felix from his musings. 'How much for the bracelet?'

Felix looked up. A piratical old sailor in a long coat stood at the table, jostled on all sides by the crowd that filled the tap room. He was a barrel-chested man, with a bald head, gold earrings, and a clay pipe that stuck out from an enormous white moustache and beard. He pointed a thick finger at Gotrek's wrist, indicating the bracelet with the sea-green gem.

'Not for sale,' said Gotrek. He pushed a small pile of jewellery towards the man. 'If you want any of that, we can deal. It's elven.'

The old sailor shook his head. 'Just the bracelet.'

'Then you're out of luck,' said Gotrek.

The sailor frowned. 'Double its weight in Altdorf Crowns,' he said.

Gotrek snorted. 'Crowns are cut with copper. This is pure. Ten times its weight wouldn't be enough.'

'So, you're willing to haggle?'

'No,' said the Slayer, and returned his attention to his sorting.

The sailor shrugged. 'Can't say I didn't try.' He stepped back. 'Get 'em, messmates.'

All at once, all the men who had been jostling and laughing and drinking behind the old man turned towards Gotrek and Felix, grinning as they readied cudgels, brass knuckles and saps. Felix had never in his life seen so few teeth among so many men.

Gotrek jumped up, laughing, and snatched up two three-legged stools. 'Come and get it, you wharf rats!'

The wharf rats obliged him, roaring and leaping over the table at him as bracelets and necklaces scattered everywhere. Felix was shouldered to the floor in the rush. Boots stomped his spine as he rolled under the table, covering his head, and the smack of fists on flesh was loud in his ears.

He took the opportunity to stuff his father's letter back into his doublet, then looked around for a suitable weapon. Unfortunately, just then, Gotrek heaved up on the table, overturning it and sending the pirates that fought upon it flying – along with the rest of his treasure.

A pirate crashed down on Felix's ribs, knocking the wind out of him. Felix sucked in a stabbing breath and elbowed the man in the face, then ripped the cudgel from his hands and staggered up, looking around. Pirates were reeling away from Gotrek as he windmilled about him with a stool in each fist, but others still surged in, howling and slashing furiously, as the rest of the tavern-goers pressed to the walls, trying to get away.

Felix waded into the scrum, cracking heads and elbows with his cudgel. The pirates snarled and lashed back at him. He took a punch to the ribs.

Then a woman's voice shrilled over the cacophony. 'Gold! The floor's covered with it!'

Suddenly, all the onlookers, who had been doing their best to keep out of the melee, charged forward, diving under the pirates' feet and bowling them over in their frenzy to reach the spilled treasure.

'Keep back, ye lubbers!' bellowed the old pirate, but no one paid him any heed.

A pirate with a face like a frog leapt on Gotrek's arm, weighing it down and trying to pull off the braided gold bracelet.

'Get it!' roared the old pirate. 'Throw it here.'

Gotrek brained frog-face with one of his stools and heaved him into the others. He held up his left arm, showing them all the bracelet.

'It this what you want?' the Slayer roared. 'Come–!'

He was drowned out by a pair of deafening explosions. The whole room stopped where they were and everyone turned towards the bar. The landlord, a short, round man with sailor's tattoos and a peg leg, stood upon it, two smoking pistols in his hands as plaster rained down all around him. From the look of the ceiling it wasn't the first time such measures had been warranted.

'Right, you wreckers!' he said, dropping the pistols and taking an enormous bell-mouthed blunderbuss from a serving girl behind the bar. 'Outside or I'll give you a volley of shot in yer tender parts!'

The threat worked well enough on most of the patrons – particularly those that already had some of Gotrek's gold clutched in their hands – and they ran for the exits, but the pirates were made of sterner stuff. One of them pulled a pistol of his own and aimed it at the landlord.

'And I'll give you a hole where yer mouth is,' he snarled.

Felix raised his cudgel to beat the man's arm down, but just then the Black Caps ran back in, whistles blowing and truncheons at the ready.

The landlord waved them towards the pirates. 'Them there, Captain Schnell! They're disturbing the peace!'

The old pirate backed away. 'Hard about, messmates!' he croaked, as the watchmen started forward. He shot a glare at Gotrek. 'We'll finish this later.'

The pirates scattered in every direction, and the Black Caps raced after them. The taproom was suddenly empty.

Gotrek glared around at the floor, which was conspicuously bare of treasure. 'All gone,' he said, disgusted. 'The dirty thieves.'

'Serves you right for sorting it in public,' said Felix wearily. He looked around for a place to sit, but before he could right a bench, the landlord turned his blunderbuss their way.

'You too, buckos,' he called, jerking his chin towards the door. 'You were in the middle of it. On yer way.'

'But...' said Felix. 'But we have a room here.'

'You *had* a room here,' said the landlord.

Felix was about to argue the point, but Gotrek grunted and started towards the door. 'Forget it, manling. The beer was terrible anyway.'

As they crossed to the door, Gotrek paused, then bent and picked something up from the floor – a wayward topaz. 'Here,' he said, flipping it to the surprised landlord, who almost dropped his blunderbuss trying to catch it. 'For the damages.'

With the old pirate's vow that he would 'finish this later' still ringing in his ears, Felix was afraid that they would be jumped as soon as they left the inn, but apparently the Black Caps had chased the pirates off, for they made their way through the crowded streets without incident.

Unfortunately, because of those crowds, finding another room was difficult, and they spent more than an hour walking from inn to inn, and being turned away at every one. But finally, at the western-most end of the Suiddock, on a street that reeked of tar and rotting fish, they discovered a place that had a vacancy. Felix didn't wonder why. The Bunk and Binnacle was dreadful. Anyone with any money or sense would never have looked twice at the place.

It was small and cramped and reeked of damp and mildew, and every surface felt like it was covered in a thin layer of slime. Its floors dipped in the centre, its ceilings sagged, and its walls bulged in on either side. Felix was afraid to lean against them for fear they would collapse.

'This place is a deathtrap,' he said as he and Gotrek made their way up the three cockeyed flights of stairs to their room.

Gotrek shrugged. 'No worse than most human places,' he said.

Felix was too tired to argue. They had been walking forever. All he wanted to do was lie down and sleep.

Felix stared around, appalled, as they entered their room. He had been in nicer prison cells. The smell of mildew was even stronger here, and seemed to be coming from the beds. The floor sloped down alarmingly towards the back wall, where the winter wind whistled through a shuttered window. He stepped cautiously down the slippery incline and opened it. One of the shutters tore from its rusty hinges and fell away. Felix looked down and saw it splash into the water of the harbour, directly below him. The inn leaned out over it like a vulture preparing to swoop down on a carcass.

Felix backed cautiously from the drop, wiping his hands on his breeches. 'I really would have preferred to give up the bracelet and keep our room at the Pelican's Perch,' he said.

'It wasn't your bracelet,' said Gotrek, and started laying out his bedroll on the floor.

Felix was dragged from sleep some time later by soft squelching noises and angry dwarfen grunts. He pried open his eyes and peered around at the darkness, feeling for his sword.

'Gotrek?'

'Get off me, you snot-skinned invertebrates!' came the Slayer's voice, followed by the crunch of an axe through bone and a shriek of pain.

Felix jumped to his feet and drew his sword. In the fuzzy dimness of the room he could see a dozen black shapes squirming and thrashing where Gotrek had been lying. The reek of damp, which before had been only unbearable, was now too thick to breathe. 'Hoy!' he choked, then stabbed at the back of a flailing form.

The thing snarled and turned on him, lashing out with long arms. It was wearing breeches and a shirt, but that was Felix's only clue that it had once been human. As his eyes adjusted, he could see that the inner side of its arms and hands were covered with disc-shaped suckers, and it had a head like a trout.

Felix slashed at it, nausea and pity warring within him. The trout-man ducked and caught his blade in a suckered hand. Felix tried to jerk it away, but the discs stuck fast to the smooth steel, and the mutant pulled at it with uncanny strength.

Sounds of terrible violence continued from Gotrek's side of the room as Felix fought the trout-man for the sword. Then two more mutants charge out of the dark. One had a rusty boarding axe clutched in hands like crab claws. The other was a woman – or had been – with hair like a sea anemone and translucent fins running down the length of her forearms. She slashed at him and they sliced through his clothes to his skin. They were razor sharp!

Felix kicked her in the face, then ducked crab-hands' rusty axe. Trout-face tried to catch Felix's neck with his other tentacle. Felix let go of his sword and grabbed the slimy thing, yanking him off his feet and sending him careening into crab-hands. The mutants crashed down on the flimsy bed, collapsing it. Felix stomped on trout-face's wrist. He yelped and let go of the sword. Felix snatched it up and spun just in time to block another swipe from the fin-woman. His sword tore through her right fin and into her arm. She staggered back, wailing, and fell in a heap against the door.

Felix whipped back and gutted crab-hands and trout-face as they tried to stand. They toppled back into the ruin of the bed, gushing black blood.

Felix stumbled over the uneven floor towards Gotrek. The Slayer was in the centre of a whirlwind of crazed mutants. Half a dozen lay dead and dismembered on the floor, but just as many still surrounded him, swinging boathooks, cutlasses and belaying pins at him with wild abandon. One of them, a sleek-skinned, barrel-shaped little runt with flipper arms, had swallowed Gotrek's left arm up to the elbow in its sphincter-like mouth. Gotrek swung him around like a flesh mace, knocking down his comrades with his bulbous body, then cleaving their heads and chests with his axe as they fell.

Felix leapt into the fray and cut down two of Gotrek's attackers from behind. Gotrek clubbed three more to the floor and hacked them to pieces. Only the flipper-man remained, stuck on the end of Gotrek's arm like a living gauntlet.

'Mutant filth!' rasped Gotrek, and slammed him down as hard as he could.

The mutant slapped against the planks like a carp against a cutting board, letting go of Gotrek's arm with a fishy gasp.

Gotrek chopped down at it, but it squirmed wetly down the sloping floor and the Slayer's axe smashed through rotting floorboards. Felix leapt after the thing, but the canted planks were slick with blood and slime and he fell.

'I've got him,' said Gotrek, skating forward on the film of muck with his axe raised.

But he didn't, for before the Slayer could reach him, the flipper-man humped himself upright against the wall and threw himself out the window.

Gotrek slammed into the sill and looked out and down. He cursed as, from far below, there came a splash.

Felix picked himself up, his clothes wet with blood and noxious fluids.

All the remaining mutants seemed to be dead or dying. The battle was over.

'Is everyone out to get us in this miserable town?' he sighed. 'What did *they* want?'

'The bracelet,' said Gotrek. He turned away from the window and held up the arm the flipper-man had been gnawing on. 'And they took it. That thing swallowed it.'

Felix groaned. The damned bracelet again.

From the door came a shrill cackling. They looked around. The wounded fin woman was grinning at them, a demented gleam in her too widely-spaced eyes. 'Though you kill a thousand of us, we will prevail. Stromfels' will shall not be denied.'

Felix hadn't heard that name since he and Gotrek had sailed with the pirates of Sartosa. Stromfels was a sea god – a shark god – the evil mirror of Manann, sworn to by pirates up and down the coast of the Old World.

Gotrek strode towards the woman, his axe raised menacingly. 'Do you know where they took it?'

'Oh yes,' she laughed. 'To the swamps. To the ceremony. To Stromfels' Reach.'

Gotrek put the axe blade to her throat. 'You will take us there, wretch.'

The fin-woman tittered. 'No need for threats, mein Herren. I'll take you. Stromfels welcomes sacrifices.'

By the shifting light of the moons, which peeked occasionally through breaks in the roiling clouds like pale eyes through knotholes, Gotrek and Felix set down their poles and followed the fin-woman as she stepped from the weathered flatboat onto a mist-shrouded mud bank deep in the middle of the Cursed Marshes. Gotrek steadied himself with his axe and spat a fat gob of phlegm.

'The only thing worse than sitting in a boat,' he said, wiping his mouth. 'Is standing in one.'

Felix for once agreed with him. Dwarfs were notoriously unhappy on water, but even for Felix, piloting the wobbly little craft had been a stomach-churning chore.

Something shrieked like a banshee in the middle distance. Felix jumped, heart thudding. Gotrek turned, ready to fight.

The fin-woman paid the noise no attention. 'Hurry, mein Herren,' she said, beckoning them on. 'They will beginning soon. They will want you.'

Felix let out a breath, then glared at Gotrek as they followed the fin-woman into the sea of chest-high sawgrass that rippled and whispered around them in all directions. There was no reason for them to be traipsing through a swamp in the middle of the night. They could have been back in Marienburg, asleep in a comfortable bed – or at least looking for one – if not for Gotrek's stubbornness.

Felix had tried his best to convince him to forget the bracelet and go back to Altdorf, but the Slayer would have none of it.

'No, manling,' he had said. 'A Slayer cannot stand by when there are mutants to be killed, and a dwarf can never forgive a theft.'

'But you stole it from Euler,' Felix had countered.

Gotrek had snorted. 'Stealing from a thief is not stealing.'

After that faultless display of dwarf logic, Felix had given up. Now he wished he had tried harder. Even on a summer's day, the Cursed Marshes were unlikely to have been a pleasant place for a stroll, but now, in winter, in the coldest hours of the morning, with a fitful wind spitting icy swamp-water in Felix's face and the sopping ground sucking at his boots and freezing his toes through the leather, it was a nightmare. Weird rustlings and moanings came from every direction, and writhing arms of mist curled up from the tall grass like looming spectres. He kept looking over his shoulders at things that weren't there.

'Careful, mein Herren,' said the fin-woman as Felix almost stepped into a hidden channel. She giggled. 'Wouldn't want to deny Stromfels' Harbinger his snack.'

Felix backed from the channel and followed more carefully behind her. She might once have been attractive, for she had a shapely figure and piercing blue eyes, but now she was repulsive. In addition to the fins that stuck from her wiry forearms, her mouth hung open in a fishy gape, and her eyes were pushed to the sides of her head, peering slyly from under a mop of tiny, translucent tentacles that writhed with a mind of their own.

'What do your friends want with this bracelet?' he asked her as they swished through the grass.

'Stromfels' Heart?' she said, chuckling. 'Why, it's the centre of the whole thing, mein Herr. It calls the Harbinger. Wakes him, y'might say. Gives him his strength. Without it, there ain't no ceremony.' Her lower lip pushed out in a pout. 'Like last year. Very sad, that was, when that false pirate Euler took it.'

'False pirate?' said Felix. 'He seemed piratical enough to me.'

'A true pirate worships Stromfels,' she sniffed. 'That fat lubber was just a thief with a boat, and we're obliged to you for getting the Heart back from his safe. Most kind of you. Mind the bloodsedge, mein Herr,' she added.

Felix jerked his foot back as a bush in his path rattled to life and extended vine-like tendrils towards him. He hacked at one that tried to snare his ankle, then danced away after Gotrek and the woman. The thing rustled in agitated frustration behind them.

'I hate this place,' said Felix.

'At least were off the cursed boat,' said Gotrek.

They pressed on.

A half hour later, they came to a dense stand of bulrushes growing from the water of a wide, shallow inlet. The plants were taller than Felix's head.

'Just through here, mein Herren,' said the fin-woman, smiling back at them as she stepped down into the water. 'Hurry now.' And with that she disappeared into the towering thicket.

They splashed after her and shouldered into the close set plants. The tall stalks bent aside as they parted them, then sprung back after they had passed. Felix couldn't see more than a few feet ahead, and lost sight of the woman almost immediately. He tried to listen for the slosh of her footsteps, but they were drowned out by their own.

Felix looked over his left shoulder, then his right. 'This is an ambush,' he muttered.

'We can only hope,' said Gotrek.

He lashed out with his axe, hacking a swath through the tall plants. Felix drew his sword and joined him, swinging wide. The bulrushes toppled before them, but didn't reveal hidden assailants, only more bulrushes.

'Quicker, mein Herren!' echoed the fin-woman's voice from far ahead. 'You don't want to be late.'

They pressed on, cursing, and a few minutes later came to the far edge of the stand, and a muddy shore that fringed another sea of sawgrass. They stepped warily up out of the water and looked around. The fin-woman was nowhere to be seen.

'Where are you, woman?' called Felix. 'Come out!'

There was no response. Felix cursed and slashed angrily at the sawgrass. 'She's tricked us. She's led us off into the middle of nowhere. I'll wager the ceremony is miles from here.'

'No, manling,' said Gotrek, pointing. 'It is there.'

Felix turned and followed the Slayer's gaze. Far across the waving grass was a low hill, rising from the marsh like the back of some aquatic behemoth, and behind it, glowing dimly through the shrubs that furred its spine, was an orange flicker of fire.

A short while later, Felix and Gotrek hid among those shrubs and peered at the scene below them. The hill sloped down to a shale beach that curved around a tidal lagoon, hemmed in on all sides by the sawgrass marsh. A bonfire blazed on the beach, illuminating an ancient, sea-weathered standing stone that rose from the shallows. The thing was twice as high as a man and carved to resemble a shark's head, with a crude triangular notch in the front to delineate a mouth. Around this central stone eight smaller stones, man-high and carved all over with saucer-sized circles, also poked from the waves. An altar to Stromfels, Felix was certain, though it wasn't clear to him what the lesser stones might represent.

More than a score of fish-featured mutants stood on the beach and in the water around the stone circle, chanting and raising their misshapen arms in exaltation as their long shadows undulated across the water like black snakes. In their centre, standing knee-deep in front of the shark stone, was the old pirate from the Pelican's Perch, stripped to the waist and holding aloft Gotrek's bracelet as he shouted an invocation to the sky. Felix wasn't surprised to see him, nor his men, who stood and chanted along with the other worshippers. In fact, it made the night's events fall into place. And though it sickened him, he wasn't surprised that they were mutants either.

With their coats flung off in the heat of the fire, the pirates' abnormalities were revealed – scales, fins, gills, webbed fingers, eel-like tails, trailing tendrils like those of a jellyfish. It was as if their god was slowly shaping them in his own image.

The old pirate's mutation was the subtlest, but also the most disturbing. As the man gyrated in his ecstasy, Felix saw what he at first thought were strands from his beard waving in the wind. But a longer look revealed that the strands were actually finger-sized tentacles that ringed his mouth, and which had been hidden within the luxuriousness of his moustaches.

'It seems you were right not to sell to him,' said Felix, chagrined.

'Aye,' said Gotrek, but that was all. The Slayer wasn't one to say 'I told you so.'

Felix looked further down the beach. At the edge of the firelight, a number of longboats were pulled up on the shale, and near them crouched half a dozen pitiful figures, all bound hand and foot, their ropes staked to the ground so they couldn't escape. Felix thought he recognised their guide, the fin-woman, among the guards that watched over them. He could see her peering around into the shadows – looking for him and Gotrek no doubt.

'The vanished revellers?' Felix asked, nodding towards the six prisoners.

Gotrek nodded. 'Sacrifices,' he growled.

Felix feared he was right. He gripped his sword. 'Then we'd better go stop the ceremony before it is complete.'

'No,' said Gotrek. 'We wait.'

Felix turned to him, confused. 'But if we wait, they will call their god, and–'

'Aye,' Gotrek interrupted. 'Mutants are nothing. I want to fight this Harbinger, whatever it is.'

'But, the sacrifices,' said Felix.

'I'll kill it before it comes to that,' said Gotrek dismissively.

Felix shook his head. He sometimes forgot that, though Gotrek generally fought for the good of the Old World, and hated Chaos with a passion, he chose his fights for glory as much as for any other reason.

A rising wail from the mutants returned his attention to the ceremony below. Things seemed to be reaching a climax.

While the mutants writhed and chanted, in the centre of the ring, the old pirate turned to the shore and dropped to his knees in the water, the bracelet raised high over his head.

Felix blinked and squinted at the thing. This far away, it was hard to make out details, but its appearance had definitely changed. The braided gold coil that the central bezel was fixed to seemed to have unwoven itself, the gleaming strands spreading out from the gem like spider legs. They even appeared to be stretching and curling – a grasping hand of yellow wire.

Gotrek edged forward, his single eye glittering eagerly in the firelight.

As the wild chant grew faster and louder, the old pirate lowered the clutching golden thing to his chest and pressed it against his sternum. Felix saw the gold wires clench, digging into his tattooed flesh. The pirate grimaced, but held the jewel in place. The wires gripped harder. He screamed and spasmed, his mouth tentacles trembling. The gold claws dug down into his chest like they were seeking his heart.

The pirate thrashed and convulsed, but made no move to try to pull off the burrowing bracelet. Finally, with a last agonised bellow, he stiffened and pitched face-first into the waves, his head completely submerged.

The mutant worshippers all fell silent, staring, as he floated face down in the water. Felix stared too. Had the old man died? Had the evil jewel killed him?

'Do you think perhaps that didn't go as planned?' he whispered.

'Quiet, manling,' said Gotrek.

Felix turned back to the beach. For a long moment there was no movement at all, and no noise but for the crackle of the bonfire. But then, with a splash and a cry, the old pirate twitched and floundered in the water.

Felix could hear an indrawn breath from the mutants, and then a huge cheer as the pirate pushed himself up and stood, streaming with water.

'The Harbinger!' they cried. 'Stromfels' Harbinger is here!'

Felix did not feel like cheering. He felt like vomiting, for a horrible transformation had come over the old pirate, and was continuing as he watched.

For one thing, he was larger than before, and was growing bigger still. He now towered head and shoulders above his followers, and his body was thickening and turning a dull iron grey. For another, he was distorting hideously. His neck swelled with muscle until it was as wide as his shoulders and his head grew to match. A triangular fin sprouted from his back, and his eyes became black orbs and shifted position, moving above his ears, which shrank into his skull and vanished. His nose widened and lengthened until it took over his whole face, and his mouth stretched along with it, a black, lipless gash filled with razor-sharp teeth. But more horrible still was the transformation of the eight little tentacles that had surrounded his mouth. As he grew and changed, so did they, lengthening and thickening until they were as big around as pythons, while their inner surfaces sprouted cup-sized suckers that clenched and contracted obscenely.

The pirate-turned-monster threw back his head and howled in a voice like a howling winter storm, his arms and tentacles raised in triumph. 'Bring the offerings!' he roared. The gem from the evil bracelet glowed blue-green in the centre of his chest.

Gotrek stood and drew his axe from his back, grinning savagely. 'Now *this* will be a fight,' he said, then charged down the slope towards the beach, roaring a wordless battle-cry.

Felix hesitated as the mutants all turned and stared, then he sighed and ran after the Slayer. It rankled somewhat that Gotrek seemed to assume that he would automatically follow him into battle. That certainly hadn't been their original bargain. Felix had sworn to record Gotrek's doom, not share it. But he had fought so many times at the Slayer's side that it had indeed become second nature, and he did sometimes charge in after him without thinking. Had he, Felix wondered with sudden concern, come to look forward to it?

The pirates and mutants swarmed to meet them as the hulking, shark-mouthed octopoid howled behind them from the water.

'Bring me the trespassers!' it cried. 'They will be first!'

Gotrek ploughed into the horde, driving those at the front back into the rest as his rune axe splintered spears and sheared through swords and arms and stranger appendages in a bloody blur. He didn't slow to fight them, however, only cut a path through them, his attention entirely on Stromfels' Harbinger, who surged out of the lagoon to face him.

Felix fell on the mutants before they had recovered from Gotrek's passage, impaling the wounded and hacking down those who were trying to stand. Not exactly sporting, but then again, they meant to feed him to their god as a snack, so he felt little remorse. The rest turned and leapt at him as, beyond them, Gotrek pounded across the shale at the looming monster.

Now Felix *did* regret following the Slayer, for a dozen weapons were stabbing at him all at once, and he had to whirl like a top with his sword at full extent just to keep them at bay. At least, he thought, there is room enough here to swing and light enough to see, luxuries he hadn't had in his earlier fights against them.

'Get 'im, my darlings!' screeched a familiar female voice from the edges of the mob. 'He ain't nice to ladies!'

Felix cut down a man with gaping fish-heads for hands and dodged past him to the bonfire, then snatched up a burning branch in his left hand and turned to face the rest. A brilliant plan, he thought. With the flames at his back he would only have to defend in front of him.

They charged in, howling, and he stumbled back, nearly falling into the fire as he blocked their blows. A brilliant plan, he thought again, as his backside began to grow unpleasantly warm.

Beyond the mutants, Felix saw Gotrek's fight in brief glimpses – two heavy, suckered tentacles spinning away in a spray of black blood – the Harbinger of Stromfels howling in agony – Gotrek clubbed into the lagoon by another tentacle.

'You are fools,' the fin-backed behemoth shouted as it waded out after him. 'Just like the damned Marienburgers.'

The Slayer jumped up again, axe raised, but to Felix's horror, the monster's two severed tentacles had grown back, as thick and strong as before.

'They think it is their milquetoast prayers to Manann that protect them from the winter gales,' the monster rumbled as it lashed the Slayer with its limbs and drove him back amongst the standing stones. 'Ha! Only appeasing Stromfels will stop the storms. We are the true protectors of Marienburg!'

Gotrek chopped furiously, severing tentacle after tentacle as he tried to reach the monster's shark-like trunk, but no matter how many he cut, by the time he had finished cutting the last, the first had grown back again.

Felix, too, was in desperate straits. A woman with stinging whips growing from her neck lashed them at his face while a dozen more mutants stabbed at him. He hacked wildly around at them all while trying to shield his face from the whips. One burned his cheek and he flinched back, crying out. His heel crunched down on a burning log. He smelled burning wool. He was standing in the fire!

An iron-shod staff rammed him in the chest, knocking him further back. He was falling! Desperate, he snatched at the staff, hauling at it with all his might.

Fortunately, the mutant was pulling too, trying to jerk the staff from Felix's grip. Felix used the momentum to launch himself forward and shouldered the man to the ground, then hurriedly tore off the flaming cloak, his heart pounding, and whirled it over his head.

'Back, damn you!' he gasped, fighting for breath. 'I'll burn you!'

A mutant snagged the cloak on his spear tip and whipped it contemptuously away. The others pressed in again from all sides. Felix cursed and spun around with his sword, his lungs aching as he tried to hold them all away – right back where he'd started. At least he'd gotten away from the fire.

In the water, the Harbinger of Stromfels shouted in triumph and lifted a struggling Gotrek over his gaping mouth, pinning his right arm and axe with a tentacle.

Felix cursed and charged towards it, trying to break through the ring of mutants to reach the Slayer in time.

'Gotrek!' he cried, hacking wildly. 'Hang on!'

The Slayer's left hand scrabbled for the haft his axe, then tore it free and hacked down at the tentacle, severing it. He splashed at the monsters feet and disappeared under the water as it screamed in agony.

It plunged its arms and tentacles below the surface, feeling for him. 'I will tear you apart!'

Gotrek surged up behind the thing, the severed tentacle still wrapped around him, and aimed a left-handed slash at its spine, but the massive beast turned with surprising speed and the axe blade caught it under the ribs instead, sinking deep. The Harbinger roared in pain and fell back into the water, crashing down by the standing stone.

All around Felix, the mutants wailed and spasmed in eerie unison to their leader's agony. Felix lashed out at them, trying to take advantage of their weakness, but they staggered away, shrieking. He was too tired to pursue. He stumbled towards the Slayer.

Gotrek was wading deeper into the water, axe raised for another strike. Felix sloshed in after him, and they strode out past the circle of stones together, looking all around, but the water remained calm and flat.

'He has defeated the Harbinger of Stromfels!' cried the mutants, fleeing into the shadows. 'He'll kill us all!'

Gotrek ignored them, chopping at the water with his axe. 'Come back, you coward!' he bellowed. 'I know you're not dead!'

His voice echoed away across the lagoon, to be answered only with silence. He grunted and spit into the waves, then turned and slogged back to the shore, prying the severed tentacle from his skin with a series of dull pops.

Felix looked around the beach. The mutants had vanished, leaving their dead behind. 'Well done,' he said.

'Bah,' said the Slayer, disgusted. 'It ran away, and took the bracelet with it.'

Felix nodded, knowing the Slayer would accept no sympathy. 'Well, at least we can bring these poor wretches back to safety.' He pointed down the beach. 'They left their boats.'

Gotrek shrugged, not at all consoled. 'I suppose.'

They walked down the beach to the prisoners, keeping their eyes on the shadows, but the mutants remained hidden.

'What have you done, you meddlers?' whined a tired-looking woman in a shopkeeper's apron as Felix knelt to cut her ropes.

'Eh?' said Felix. 'We're saving you.'

'And dooming Marienburg,' said a captured stevedore. 'You should have left well enough alone.'

Felix frowned. 'You came willingly? Then why did they tie you down?'

The stevedore hung his head. 'Some change their minds at the last minute.'

'Now Stromfels will send the storms,' said a third captive, a young man in the uniform of the Black Caps. 'Our deaths would have appeased him, but now....'

Gotrek turned his single baleful eye on him. 'You worship that abomination?'

'No,' said the shop wife. 'Never. But the swamp men are right. It is he who calls the storms, not Manann, and so we give ourselves up to keep our families safe for another winter.'

Gotrek spat, disgusted. 'You're to blame for its power. You make it stronger with your fear.'

'And you've made it angry with your slaughter,' said the stevedore. 'Many ships will sink this winter because of you.'

Gotrek snorted and turned away.

Despite their protestations, the rescued prisoners were quite willing to go back to Marienburg with Gotrek and Felix before the mutants returned, so they stole one of the longboats and set off. Gotrek refused to row, or do anything but sit in the stern looking green at the gills, so Felix and the men took up the oars and poles, with the shop wife at the prow, calling out the hazards.

After a long hour of rowing and poling through weed-choked and winding waterways, then fighting the strong currents of the Manannspoort Sea, they pulled wearily into Marienburg's harbour and rowed through the Brunwasser Kanal just as the first grey light of the day began to tinge the eastern sky.

Already, the big merchant ships that lined the docks were being loaded and unloaded by armies of longshoremen, while huge winches lifted cargo nets full of barrels and burlap sacks from deep holds, and carts and wagons piled to the point of collapse with goods from all over the world creaked away into the city.

It made Felix tired just to look at it all. He was ready to drop. Except for a fitful hour's sleep on the damp floor of the Bunk and Binnacle, the entire night had been spent walking, rowing, fighting, or slogging across swampy ground.

Finally, they nosed the longboat under the prow of a cargo ship and glided towards a little wooden dock that stuck out from a stone bank. Felix reached out to grab a piling and pull them close as the others backed their oars, but just as he touched the post the boat stopped suddenly, and then jerked backward in the water. Felix stumbled and fell on top of the shop wife.

'Easy,' he said, pushing himself upright. 'No need to...'

He paused as he saw the other rowers looking around too.

'Who did that?' Gotrek growled, raising his head.

The boat lurched suddenly down at the stern, and the nose shot up. Felix fell again as the others cried out. Something snaked from the water and curled over the side of the boat. A tentacle.

'Stromfels' Harbinger!' screamed the shop wife.

Felix's heart lurched as he stood again. More tentacles gripped the boat from all sides.

'Off!' roared Gotrek.

'Onto the dock!' Felix shouted.

He tried to run to the side, but the boat tilted and rose out of the water. He fought for balance, then threw himself towards the dock, now a man's height below him. He landed hard on his hands and rolled across the planks. A thud and a curse told him that Gotrek had done the same.

A few splashes told him that others had fallen short.

He rolled on his back and looked up. Eight huge tentacles were lifting the longboat as the rescued sacrifices wailed and clung to it. Then, with a splintering crack, the curling limbs ripped the boat asunder, and the men and women fell into the water, flailing and screaming.

A blunt grey island poked up directly under the shop wife, and she clung to it. The island had a mouth. It yawned open and the woman tumbled in, shrieking. Teeth like elven shields closed, crushing her. The shrieks ceased.

The others floundered desperately for the dock, but the huge tentacles caught them and raised them high.

'Gods,' said Felix, backing away. 'It's grown.'

Gotrek grinned maniacally. 'Good.' He drew his axe.

The Harbinger of Stromfels breached the waves, water streaming down it in sheets – a shark's head and body, twice the height of a man, with tiny, useless arms, but eight tree-trunk tentacles ringing its mouth. The axe wound Gotrek had given it earlier was nothing more than a puckered line on one flank. The gem of the golden bracelet looked as small as a nail head in the centre of its broad grey chest. Felix stared in horrified wonder. The thing could tear down a temple of Sigmar.

'Did you think Stromfels would let the sea be my grave?' it roared, turning eyes like black glass cannonballs on them as the shop wife's blood streamed from its mouth.

All over the docks people ran and screamed. Stevedores abandoned their loads. Merchants and sailors fled their ships. The crew of a winch left a pallet of grain sacks swinging in mid-air as they ran and called for the Black Caps.

'I've come for what is mine!' the Harbinger rumbled, shaking four of its squirming victims at Gotrek as it stuffed a fifth into its maw.

'Let them go, fish!' bellowed Gotrek, sprinting to the end of the dock and swiping at one of the extended tentacles. 'Fight me!'

The beast howled in pain and jerked the tentacle back as Gotrek's axe bit deep. It glared at the Slayer. 'Very well,' it said. 'They will wait.'

It tossed the captives aside and whipped its tentacles at Gotrek, trying to sweep him off the dock.

The Slayer rolled between two sturdy pilings, then lashed out at the Harbinger's limbs from their cover. Felix ran forward to help him, but leapt back again immediately as a tentacle nearly knocked his legs out from under him. He swiped wildly at it as it passed, opening a red groove in it. The monster roared and grabbed for him, but he dodged out of reach.

Gotrek, however, was in the middle of a tentacle hurricane. Some tried to knock him from between the pilings. Some tried to squash him to the dock. Some tried to grab him. He countered them all, making the beast pay for each attack with bloody, trench-deep gashes. It howled at every strike, but kept flailing. Its tentacles were too thick now to be severed with one blow, and to Felix's horror, the wounds grew closed in the time it took for it to draw back and strike again. It seemed impossible that Gotrek could kill it before it found some way to pry him from his cover.

A tentacle slammed into the dock, smashing through the planks at Gotrek's feet. It had found a way.

The Slayer jumped back. Another tentacle slapped down and more planks caved in. Gotrek fell back again. The Harbinger came on, hauling itself out of the water with its tentacles and stomping forward on huge human legs that shook the dock with each step.

Felix backed towards the stone embankment with the Slayer as the tentacles swatted at them, inches away.

'What now?' he asked.

'The fish-woman said the bracelet gives it its power,' Gotrek rasped. 'If I can take it, I wager I can kill it.'

They reached the embankment and ducked behind a wall of crates.

'But how will you get past its tentacles?'

The Slayer shrugged. 'I have no idea.'

The monster tore down the crates and hurled them away. Gotrek and Felix dove to the ground as they bounced over their heads and smashed to pieces beyond them. People fled screaming. Felix and Gotrek picked themselves up and joined them. The Harbinger lumbered after them on its tentacles like an ape on its knuckles.

A handful of sailors appeared at the rail of the ship to their left, all armed with long guns. They fired. The beast writhed as the bullets tore into its body, but kept on, not turning from its prey.

Gotrek looked up at the ship and paused, almost taking a tentacle in the small of the back. He spun and lopped off the tip of the thing, then started up the ramp to the big cargo dock. 'Lead it this way.'

There was no time to wonder what Gotrek's plan was. The Harbinger was pulling itself up the ramp faster than they could run. Felix slashed behind him at a questing tentacle and missed, then had to leap like a scalded cat to avoid being flattened by a barrel it flung after them.

'Faster, manling,' said Gotrek.

Felix grunted, he *was* going faster.

They topped the ramp and stumbled on, weaving through piles of cargo as the towering mutant smashed barrels and crates into the water. Gotrek looked up as they ran under the pallet of grain sacks that dangled high over the dock, and Felix suddenly knew what the Slayer intended.

Gotrek looked over his shoulder. The Harbinger was just ducking under the pallet.

Gotrek chuckled evilly. 'Away, manling!'

The Slayer veered left, sprinting for the winch that held the pallet and raising his axe. Felix dived over a pile of rolled carpets and looked back.

He gaped as Gotrek fell flat on his face, inches from the base of the winch. A tentacle jerked the Slayer up off the ground by the ankles and raised him high.

'You think I'm such a fool?' laughed the monster.

It stepped out from under the dangling pallet, more tentacles wrapping around Gotrek as it lowered him towards its gaping mouth. The Slayer wrenched his axe arm free and slashed around, but the limbs healed as fast as he cut them and didn't let go.

With a grunt, Gotrek threw his axe at the Harbinger of Stromfels's head. The weapon spun through the air and chunked into its shark-like snout, right between its oval nostrils, and stuck.

The beast bellowed and staggered back, cracking its head on the pallet as it blundered under it.

'Manling, get the–' A tentacle clamped over Gotrek's face.

Felix ran for the winch, raising his sword.

The monster saw him and swayed forward unsteadily, shooting a pair of unoccupied tentacles after him. Felix dove, slashing. His sword sliced the rope, making it sing like a harp string, but a few strands still held.

Felix cursed and crashed to the dock. A tentacle wrapped around his leg, lifting him into the air. He swiped at the rope again as he was dragged back.

The last strands parted.

Swinging upside down in the Harbinger's grip, Felix saw the pallet of grain sacks drop as the rope zipped through the pulleys. The monster lurched out of the way, but not fast enough. The pallet hit it on the hip, crushing its right leg and knocking it into a pile of crates. It crashed to the dock on its back, tentacles flailing for balance, and flung Felix away.

He slammed down on the lip of the dock and almost bounced off into the water. Only catching a wooden piling in the ribs stopped him from going over. He gasped as all the air shot out of him and lay there glaze-eyed, clinging feebly to the post.

The monster shoved feebly at the grain sacks with its tentacles, trying to free its legs. For a moment, Felix couldn't see Gotrek amidst all the coiling limbs, but then he appeared, climbing the monster's broad chest and reaching for the bracelet.

'No!' it roared.

The Slayer got his thick fingers around the glowing green gem and pulled as tentacles bludgeoned his shoulders and back. Gotrek only tucked his head and pulled harder.

Felix staggered to his feet, clutching his aching ribs, and stumbled forward. He could see the golden wires of the bracelet pulling from the Harbinger's flesh as Gotrek hauled on it. They stretched and strained, fighting to maintain their grip.

Felix hacked weakly at a flailing tentacle, hoping to divert the monster's attention. It worked. It swatted him across the dock. Unfortunately, the rest of its tentacles were not distracted.

As Felix sat up, dazed, he saw the suckered limbs wrap around Gotrek's arms, legs, torso and head, pulling him in eight directions at once. Felix winced. It was like watching someone being torn apart by horses. The Slayer was so wrapped in tentacles that all Felix could see of him was one foot, a bit of orange crest, and his left arm, pinned fast against his back.

With a howl of frustration, Stromfels' Harbinger pushed Gotrek away from its chest like someone trying to peel off an overly affectionate monkey, but Gotrek was still gripping the gem, and as the monster thrust him away, the bracelet tore from its chest. Felix saw the golden strands waving in the air like the legs of an inverted crab as Gotrek held it high.

The Harbinger screamed and convulsed, whipping its tentacles about in a frenzy and slamming Gotrek down on the deck of a nearby ship like a sack of wet clay. The bracelet spun away from Gotrek's slack fingers and bounced down to the dock as the massive monster pushed up and looked around, the rune axe still sticking from its snout.

'My heart!' the Harbinger roared, as it saw the golden bracelet rolling along the planks.

Felix blanched. The cursed bauble was coming right towards him!

The beast surged up and thundered after it. 'You will pay for this! All will pay!'

Felix scrambled between some crates as the Harbinger loomed over him, but it only snatched up the bracelet in a tentacle and held it high, its black eyes glittering triumphantly.

Felix gripped his sword, preparing to dash out and sever the tip of the tentacle that held the evil thing, but then he saw movement above and behind the monster.

Gotrek was running along the rail of the merchant ship. He leapt and landed on the beast's broad back, clambering up its triangular fin towards its snout. The harbinger spun around, nearly throwing him off, but the Slayer held tight and wrenched his axe free, then hacked down at its skull.

The monster roared and stumbled as the axe struck bone. Its tentacles whipped around, trying to dislodge the Slayer. Gotrek struck again, laughing maniacally, and this time shattered the beast's bony carapace. Blood and ooze soaked his face and beard as he pulled back for another blow.

Felix's heart pounded with sudden hope. The Harbinger's wound was not healing! The bracelet was no longer protecting it!

A third stroke and the monster's tentacles sagged. It weaved on its legs, then toppled to the deck, crushing a pyramid of wine barrels. A pool of red spread out from beneath it as Gotrek rolled off its back and lay panting on the planks. His skin was marked from head to foot with red, saucer-sized rings.

Felix limped out of hiding as the Slayer pulled himself to his feet. They looked down at the massive corpse.

'This time,' said Felix. 'I think it's finished.'

Gotrek shook his head, then turned to scan the dock. 'There's still the bracelet.'

Felix stared at him. 'You're not going to keep it?' he asked, incredulous. 'Not after this!'

'No,' said Gotrek. He crossed to the tentacle that held the jewel and pulled it free. He held it up. The thing had reverted to its original shape – a coil of woven gold holding a sea-green gem. 'It needs to be destroyed. Cleansed.'

The Slayer turned towards the city. 'Come on, manling. There has to be a dwarf smith somewhere in this human swamp.'

Three hours later, as a cold wind whipped whitecaps across the harbour, Gotrek and Felix trudged wearily up the gangplank of the *Jilfte Bateau*, the river boat that would take them up the Reik to Altdorf.

Leaning on the rail at the top of the ramp was their old friend Max Schreiber, smoking a meditative pipe. Beside him was the young seeress, Claudia Pallenberger, still gaunt and weak from their recent adventure on the Sea of Chaos. Max smiled as Felix and the Slayer stepped onto the deck.

'You two look like you visited every taproom in Marienburg,' he said.

'Almost,' answered Felix, too tired to deny his implication.

'You nearly missed the boat,' said Claudia.

'We were busy,' said Gotrek. 'Purifying cursed gold.'

Max smirked and blew a stream of smoke into the air. 'Some euphemism for drinking beer, no doubt,' he said.

'No,' said Felix. 'Not really.'

He shuffled with Gotrek towards the door to the cabins. He would explain later. Right now all he wanted to do was sleep all the way to Altdorf.

Just as he ducked through the door, raindrops spattered across the deck and the wind pushed hard at his back. He turned and looked to the west. The sky over the Manannspoort Sea was black with clouds. Felix's chest tightened as they rolled closer. It looked like a terrible storm was about to hit Marienburg.

SHAMANSLAYER

'After our near-fatal encounter with the dark elves, I returned to Altdorf with the Slayer to discover that my greatest fears concerning my father were true. In my rage and guilt I made a vow then to destroy the shadowy nemesis that had killed him, no matter how long it took, or the cost incurred. But fate did not allow me to pursue this new quest. Instead, because of a long-forgotten pledge, the Slayer and I were swept up into a quest of another sort – one that led us into the darkest depths of the Drakwald to face the oldest and bitterest enemies of mankind, and a new threat of staggering proportions.

'It was as we fought this horror that we were once again reunited with companions from our long ago past, and once again, those reunions were both sweet and bitter, joyous and heartrending, and both would change the nature of my travels with Gotrek for all time.'

– From *My Travels with Gotrek*, Vol VIII, by Herr Felix Jaeger
(Altdorf Press, 2529)

ONE

Felix Jaeger paused as he looked up at his father's Altdorf mansion under the grey winter sky. Did it have an empty, shut-up look to it, or was he just imagining it? Surely the marble steps hadn't been so dirty the last time he had visited. Surely the curtains hadn't been drawn. He climbed the steps to the door, then stopped again.

Ever since he had found his father's ring on a cord around the neck of a skaven assassin on a beach by the Sea of Chaos, Felix had burned with fevered impatience to return to Altdorf to find out what the rat-faced villains had done to the old man. But now, on the doorstep of knowledge, he found it difficult to go on.

For more than a month his heart had been filled with dread and uncertainty. How did the skaven come to have the ring? Had they hurt his father for it? Had they killed him? Had they only stolen it and let him be? The questions had chased their tails inside Felix's head unceasingly as he and his companions had made their too-slow journey back to civilisation. But as much as the helplessness of not knowing had driven him mad, Felix suddenly feared knowing even more. If he knew, he would have to allow the emotions he had been stifling to come to the fore. If he knew, he would have to do something.

He cursed himself and squared his shoulders. He was like a man frightened of having a wound stitched shut – the anticipation was worse than the act. Better to take the pain and close it and heal.

He knocked on the door.

There was no answer. He knocked again, and waited again, trepidation rising in his heart. Then, just as he was wondering if he should find some way to break in, he heard locks turning and bolts drawing back. The door opened and the grave, grey face of his father's butler looked out at him.

'Is he...?' asked Felix hesitantly.

'Your father is dead, sir,' said the butler. 'I'm sorry, sir.'

A hot rush of anger and regret flooded through Felix. He had known it, of course – known it all along – but it was one thing to know it in one's heart and another to hear it spoken as fact.

'And...' he stammered. 'And how did it happen?'

The butler paused, a brief flash of fear disturbing his solemn features, then spoke again. 'Your brother is here, sir. Perhaps you should speak to him.'

Felix blanched. Otto was here? Speaking to him was the last thing he wanted to do! On the other hand, he would have to see him sometime. There were no doubt legalities to be attended to. He sighed. No point in avoiding the inevitable.

'Very well,' he said. 'Show me to him.'

The butler pushed open the door to Felix's father's study, a long dark room lined with ledger-filled bookcases and lit by a small fire in a large fireplace. Near the meagre blaze was a broad desk, almost buried in ledgers, stacks of papers, scrolls and leather folios, and surrounded by chests and strongboxes, all spilling even more papers and books. At the desk, almost entirely obscured by this mountain of paper, sat Otto, quill in one pudgy hand, bald head down, peering myopically at an open ledger by the light of a candle perched on top of the mess and muttering under his breath.

Felix stepped in and the butler closed the door behind him. Otto didn't look up. Felix paused, then cleared his throat and started forwards. Still Otto didn't look up, only kept murmuring and ticking things off with his quill.

Felix reached the foothills of the desk's clutter. He cleared his throat again. There was still no response.

'Ah, Otto...'

'Thirty-two thousand, nine hundred and... and... Damn you! You made me lose my count!' Otto looked up, his bearded jowls quivering with anger. 'Why couldn't you...?' He froze as he saw who he addressed. 'You.' Then again after a few seconds, 'You!'

'Hello, brother,' said Felix. 'I'm sorry to–'

'You dare to show your face here, you... you murderer!' said Otto, recovering.

'I didn't kill him!' exclaimed Felix, though he was suddenly bathed in a guilty sweat.

'Didn't you, by the gods? Didn't you?' cried Otto, rising up and stabbing towards him with his quill. 'You come to see him for the first time in over twenty years and that very night he is found butchered in his bed! Do you count that coincidence? No? You might not have done the cutting, but, by Sigmar, you brought the knives!'

Felix hung his head at that, for he could not deny it. Though he had not known it at the time, the skaven had been tailing him. They must have followed him to his father's house. 'What did they do to him?'

Otto glared at him. 'Schmidt found him in his bed, bound at the wrists and ankles. He... he had been tortured. There was no fatal wound. He seemed to have died of terror.'

Felix shuddered, remembering what the decrepit skaven seer had done to Aethenir and imagining it being done to his frail old father. Gustav Jaeger had not been a good man, but not even the worst of men deserved a death like that.

'I'm sorry, Otto. It was indeed my enemies that–'

'Sorry?' interrupted Otto. 'Do you think an apology will suffice? You caused the death of your father! Sigmar's blood, you're like a curse! I told you once before I never wanted to see you again. Everywhere you go, death and destruction follow. You can take your "sorry" and be damned with it. Now go, before you kill me too.'

Felix sighed. He couldn't blame Otto, really. He was right. He was a curse. He had exposed Otto and his family to danger, had nearly got him killed in an attack on the street in Nuln, and then had come to Altdorf and led his enemies to his father's house, where they had tortured him to death. And it wasn't just his own family Felix's presence had destroyed. He and Gotrek had been in a fight that had burned down an entire neighbourhood in Nuln, the crew of the *Pride of Skintstaad* had been slaughtered, thousands of innocent slaves had drowned with the sinking of the black ark of the dark elves, and there were more – many more – an army of dead who marched behind him, pointing at his back and whispering, 'I would yet live if not for you...'

Felix bowed to Otto sadly, then stepped back from the desk and turned to go. He had learned what he had come to learn. There was no reason to stay. Except...

Felix turned back around. 'There is one last thing–'

Otto's eyes went wide with angry surprise. 'Sigmar, don't tell me you have the brass to ask for an inheritance! After what you've done? You should be paid with a hangman's noose, not the gold of the man you murdered!'

'I don't want his gold!' snapped Felix. 'Would you let me speak?'

Otto crossed his arms over his ponderous belly, glaring, but waiting.

Felix took an envelope from his doublet. 'Father asked me to do him a favour when I saw him. He wanted me to go to Marienburg and get back from Hans Euler an incriminating letter he had once written to Euler's father.'

'Euler,' spat Otto. 'That conniving little crook. I hope he rots.'

'Very likely,' said Felix, remembering his last duel with Euler where he had run him through. He held up the envelope. 'I recovered the letter. But–'

'But it's too late now, as Father is dead,' sneered Otto. 'Well done.'

Felix's hands clenched. He fought the urge to punch his brother in the nose. 'But,' he repeated as patiently as he could. 'When I read the letter, I was very disturbed.'

Otto beckoned impatiently and Felix handed him the envelope. He continued speaking as Otto opened it and unfolded the letter.

'Father said that it contained proof that he had smuggled goods into the Empire without paying the tariff, and that Euler meant to use it as blackmail to force him to sell him Jaeger and Sons.'

'The swine,' said Otto, beginning to read. 'He's ten times the smuggler Father ever was.'

'But that's not the worst of it,' said Felix. 'Look on the reverse. Father says that he has received from Euler's father six rare books from Tilea, but that some of them are in poor condition and he wants his money back.'

'So?' said Otto, holding the letter closer to the candle to read it. 'It wouldn't have been the first time that old pirate tried to pass shoddy goods.'

'The *Maelificarium* is a forbidden book,' said Felix. 'So is Urbanus's *The Seven Gates*. They are tomes of the blackest magic. Men have been burned at the stake just for knowing their names.'

Otto grew still, staring at the letter.

Felix stepped closer. 'This is more than mere smuggling, Otto. This is dangerous business. If Father made a habit of–'

Otto crumpled the letter and threw it into the fire.

Felix yelped. 'What are you doing?' He started towards the fireplace.

Otto stepped in his way, glaring into Felix's eyes. 'The letter was a forgery. A trick of Euler's to try to bring us down. Father never dealt in forbidden books. Never. Do you understand?'

'But how can you be sure?' asked Felix. 'Don't you think we ought to tell someone? The letter names the book dealer that–'

Otto shoved him, snarling. Felix stumbled back, nearly tripping over a satchel full of papers.

'By the gods!' Otto cried. 'Haven't you done enough? You killed the man once already. Do you want to dig him up and kill him all over again? Do you want to kill me? Do you want to ruin me?'

'Of course not,' said Felix. 'But…'

'Do you know what would happen if you were to "tell someone"?' sputtered Otto, limping forwards ponderously. Even in the ruddy light of the fire his skin looked pale. 'The witch hunters would be here before you could snap your fingers, and every book, every ledger, every letter owned by father, and by me, and by Jaeger and Sons, would be impounded and pored over for evidence of more witchery. They'd take me too, and

Annabella, and my son, and you, if they could catch you, and what your "friends" did to Father would be nothing compared to what the witch hunters would do to us. Is that what you want? Do you want to see us racked and flayed?'

'Not at all,' said Felix. 'But–'

'But nothing!' said Otto. 'What Father did or didn't do doesn't matter. Jaeger and Sons is a legitimate company now. We deal in wholesome goods and honest services. Leave the past alone and go away, I beg you, Felix!' He caught at Felix's shirt front and stared pleadingly up at him. 'I beg you!'

Felix blinked, for the anger that had blazed within Otto's eyes was gone. All that was left was fear.

The streets of Altdorf were choked with refugees and soldiers returning from the war. Families with all their belongings on their backs wandered through the Konigsplatz staring up at the tall buildings in awe. Broken men with stumps for legs or hooks for hands begged in the shadow of the Temple of Sigmar. Mothers hugged weeping children to them to try and keep them warm in the winter wind that whistled through canyon-like alleys. Ragged columns of spearmen and crossbowmen shuffled after their sergeants with unshaven faces and thousand-yard stares.

Felix saw none of them as he wandered back from his father's house to the *Oxen's Yoke*, where he and Gotrek had taken a room upon returning to the city. He was still wondering if he had done the right thing by promising Otto not to tell anyone about the letter. As much as Otto seemed to think otherwise, he didn't truly wish his family any harm, but at the same time, books like those named in the letter were harmful to everyone. He wished now that he had shown it to Max. He wasn't the sort to bring the witch hunters into things. He would have taken care of things discreetly. Maybe he could still tell him. They had only said goodbye yesterday, though the magister had made it pretty clear that he hoped they wouldn't see each other again for a good long time.

Felix could understand why. Their sojourn on the Sea of Chaos had aged Max terribly. He had spent most of the trip back to Marienburg lying in a bunk in the captain's quarters of the dark elf galley they had taken, shaking and sweating with some sort of fever, while the flesh melted from his bones at an alarming rate.

Claudia Pallenberger, the seeress from the Celestial College whose premonitions had taken them there in the first place, had fared little better, raving and weeping in her sleep, and dull and unresponsive when awake. Felix had been more nursemaid than captain on that long, painful voyage, and he had feared many times during its course that his inexpert ministrations would kill the two mages, but they proved more resilient than he could have hoped, and by the time the ragged black ship had been accosted by the Marienburg Harbour Patrol they were able to come to the deck and make their way across the gangplank on their own power.

Neither, however, had fully recovered. Though Max's keen wit and his humour had returned to him, he remained terribly gaunt, even after a week of Marienburg chowders and black beer, and his hair, which had been brown streaked with grey before the dark elf sorceresses had shaved him bald, was growing in snow-white. Claudia's scars were more hidden. Except for her shorn hair, she quickly regained her beauty and health, but there was a gravity and sad understanding in her eyes that had not been there at the start of the trip. She had seen the cruelty and depravity of the world, and had been marked by it.

Felix was sorry to see it, for her innocence and youthful arrogance had been charming, but at the same time, it had got them all in a lot of trouble – and this experience, bitter as it might have been for her, had undoubtedly given her wisdom that would make her a better, more responsible seeress in the future.

Max and Claudia had spent the day they'd had to wait for a riverboat to take them to Altdorf recovering at an inn, while Gotrek and Felix went back to Euler's house to recover Felix's father's letter from Euler's safe. That had been an adventure in itself, complete with monsters and mayhem, but they had got it at last, and after a journey of twelve days toiling up the Reik, they had returned to Altdorf the previous evening.

Their leave-taking had been friendly, if a bit subdued. Max and Claudia thanked Felix and Gotrek for getting them through the adventure alive, Felix thanked Max and Claudia for the same thing, Gotrek grunted, and that was that. Max led Claudia away to face charges of misconduct and recklessness at her College, and Gotrek and Felix went to look for drinks and a room.

Felix was a little surprised – and a little disappointed – that Claudia hadn't tried to kiss him as they parted, but perhaps the streak of wild rebellion that had sent her into his arms had been burned out of her when the brand of hard-won wisdom had been burned in. As Max had said, given a second chance and the gift of forgiveness, we may all live long enough to learn from our mistakes, and make amends for them. He hoped it were so for Claudia.

Felix chuckled ruefully at the thought of all his recent goodbyes. It seemed he had only just got back to the Empire and everyone was telling him to leave again. But that wasn't a bad thing, for he had a debt with the skaven to settle that might just get him killed, and it wouldn't do to bring any innocents along for the ride.

Felix pushed through the leather curtain of the *Oxen's Yoke* and strode to the table at the back where Gotrek sat alone, a stein in one fist and another brimming before him, waiting to be consumed. The Slayer too had been changed by their journey into the Sea of Chaos. Like Max and

Claudia he had been scarred, the palms of his powerful hands melted to the smoothness of candle-wax by the arcane power that had coursed through his rune axe when he had chopped the Harp of Ruin in half on the deck of the skaven submersible. But where the wizard and the seeress had been sobered by the danger of the experience, Gotrek had been revived. His single eye was once more bright and alert, his orange crest high and freshly dyed, his beard neatly plaited and his squat, powerful frame fairly vibrating with barely controlled violence.

Felix wasn't sure what had caused the change. The escape from the black ark had been one of the most gruelling challenges they had ever faced, and yet Gotrek seemed fitter and healthier than ever. Perhaps it had been the opportunity to fight the age-old nemesis of his race, the dark elves. Perhaps it had been the prophecy the daemon had spoken in the summoning chamber, that Gotrek was fated to die killing a daemon greater than itself. Whatever it was, Gotrek was in better spirits than he had been since they had left Karak Hirn.

The Slayer looked up as Felix motioned to the serving girl for an ale and sat down beside him.

'What did you learn, manling?' he asked.

Felix sighed. 'Everything I feared. My father is dead. The skaven tortured and killed him.' He clenched his fists and turned to look at the Slayer. 'I vow that I will have my revenge on that vile old rat or die in the attempt.'

Gotrek nodded approvingly. 'Well said.' He took a pull from his stein. 'Though he could already be dead. He fell into the sea.'

Felix shook his head. 'No. He lives. I know it. And I will kill him.'

The serving girl brought Felix's ale.

Gotrek raised his stein. 'To vengeance,' he said.

Felix did the same and they knocked them together. 'To vengeance!'

They both drank deep, then slammed the mugs down on the wooden table. Felix wiped his mouth with the back of his hand. He felt as if, after such a pronouncement, he should get up and stride off manfully towards his enemy, but he had no idea where the evil ratman might be.

'So, er, where do you suppose we find him?' he asked after an awkward minute.

Gotrek belched and started on his second beer. 'I wouldn't worry about it, manling. If he's alive, I'll wager he'll find us. All that is required is that we be ready.'

'Aye,' said Felix. 'Ever vigilant.'

'There he is!' said a high voice from the front of the tavern.

Gotrek and Felix jumped up, almost upsetting their steins as they drew sword and axe, but it was no skaven sorcerer who had cried out, but a youth in squire's livery, who was pointing directly at them.

Felix blinked in confusion. The boy had a bowl haircut, and was dressed in doublet and hose of deep blue, with a red heart haloed by fire emblazoned on the right breast. He stood with a tall, frail-looking old knight with a bald head and a magnificent white beard, whose pale blue eyes shone with the light of fanaticism. Under a heavy wool mantle, the knight wore clothes of the same blue. Felix had never seen either of them before in his life.

'Do you know them?' he asked Gotrek out of the side of his mouth.

'No,' said Gotrek. 'Do you?'

'Haven't a clue.'

The knight made his way across the taproom with stiff dignity, while the youth, who could have been no more than seventeen, followed in his wake.

Gotrek growled a warning as the two approached the table, but the old knight never took his angry eyes away from Felix's face.

'What do you want with me?' Felix asked.

The old knight reached into a pocket within his cloak and pulled out a book. He cast it on the table with a disdainful flick of the wrist. 'Are you he who wrote this dreck?'

Felix looked down at the book. It was the second volume of his travels with Gotrek. He blinked with surprise. It was the last thing he had been expecting.

'Well, I wouldn't call it dreck,' he said at last. 'But, yes. I wrote it.'

'And did you venture 'neath Karak Eight Peaks with the templar Aldred Keppler, of the Order of the Fiery Heart?'

This was getting stranger and stranger. Felix exchanged a glance with Gotrek. The Slayer shrugged.

'We did,' said Felix at last. 'What is this all about?'

'And did you take the sword Karaghul from his corpse, though it was not yours to take?'

'Uh, well…' said Felix.

'Answer not, craven,' cried the old knight. 'For I see it upon your person even now!' He thrust an accusatory finger at Felix, his eyes blazing with righteous fury. 'The sword belongs to the Order of the Fiery Heart! Your twenty-year thievery is at an end, Felix Jaeger. Return it to us at once!'

TWO

Felix stared at the ancient knight, utterly staggered. He had carried Karaghul for so long that he had almost forgotten that there was a time when it wasn't his. He couldn't imagine being parted with it. It was the best sword he had ever owned. Its runic power had once allowed him to slay a dragon, and do mortal harm to a sea serpent more recently. He might not have survived either encounter without it.

'I... I always meant to give it back,' he stuttered.

'A likely tale,' sneered the knight.

'I did,' said Felix. 'Only... only I haven't been to Altdorf in twenty years.' Which wasn't precisely true. He had been here for two months before leaving for Marienburg and the Wasteland, and he hadn't thought once of looking for the Order of the Fiery Heart and giving back the sword. That they had claim on it had slipped his mind long long ago.

That brought another question to Felix's mind. 'How did you know I was here?'

The old knight cast a baleful look at the boy at his side. 'The order's chapter house is nearby. My squire, Ortwin, may Sigmar have mercy on his soul for such a waste of hours, has read your braggart's tale, and recognised your companion in the street from the descriptions therein. Now, return the sword you stole.'

'He didn't steal the sword, knight,' said Gotrek, glaring up at him.

The knight glared back, apparently not one whit intimidated by Gotrek's fierce one-eyed gaze. 'Did he have Templar Keppler's permission to take it?'

Felix shivered, remembering how the troll had ripped Keppler's head clean off at exactly the moment that he had found the sword. 'Ah, he didn't get the chance,' he said. 'He was dead before he could say anything.'

'How can I know this to be true?' asked the knight. 'The whole tale might be false. You might have set upon the noble templar and robbed him of it.'

Gotrek gave him a level look. 'Dwarfs don't lie.'

This seemed to give the old knight pause. He inclined his head respectfully towards Gotrek. 'Your pardon, Herr dwarf. The honesty and honour of your race is well known, and I would not question it under normal circumstances, but to hold something which belongs to another for more than twenty years…'

'I… I will give back the sword,' said Felix, though his heart sank when he said it. It was like saying he would cut off his leg. 'I never meant to keep it, but we were away for so long.' He began to unbuckle his sword belt from his waist. 'It became a part of me.'

'And in your absence, you have denied its power to a generation of Knights of the Fiery Heart. Who knows what prodigies they might have performed armed with such a noble sword. Far greater deeds than you ever assayed, I'll warrant.'

Felix paused as he wrapped the belt around the scabbard. There was no need for the old knight to be insulting. 'I slew a dragon,' he said.

'And scores of orcs and undead,' said Gotrek.

'And turned back the hordes of Chaos,' said Ortwin.

The knight shot the squire an angry look at this.

'It said so in the books,' the boy persisted.

Felix held out the sword, and something, perhaps the dignity of the old knight, or the solemnity of the occasion, compelled him to go down on one knee as he did so. 'Sir knight,' he said, 'I will return this sword to your order as I always meant to, but… you should know that I never dishonoured it, or the memory of Templar Keppler, and… and if there is any way that I might convince you to let me keep it, I promise I will not dishonour it in the future. I have grown so accustomed to it that I don't know what I would do without it.'

The knight raised an incredulous eyebrow. 'You want me to *give* you the sword? Which has been a relic of our order for nigh on five hundred years? No. You have held it long enough.'

'Well, er, perhaps I could, ah, buy it from you, or make some trade for it.'

Out of the corner of his eye Felix saw Gotrek wince at that, and the look on the old knight's face confirmed that he had said the wrong thing.

'Buy it!' cried the knight. 'Buy a holy relic? You might as well ask to purchase the honour of our order. Are you some base merchant? A sword such as this is not to be bought and sold. It is to be passed from templar to templar so that it may be used in the never-ending battle against the forces of darkness.'

Felix flushed, embarrassed, and scrambled for some better argument. 'I'm sorry, sir knight. I…. I mis-spoke. What I meant to say was, ah, could I perform some service for you? Some, uh, deed of honour or quest, that would convince you I was worthy to carry the sword?'

The knight stared down at him for a moment, then snatched the sword from his upraised hands. 'No,' he said. 'I do not believe you mis-spoke. I believe you revealed your true nature in your first statement. The sword will return to the order, and to honour, at last.'

He turned away with a sweep of his heavy cloak and walked, stiff and proud, towards the door.

The squire hesitated, looking at Felix and Gotrek with an appraising eye, then snatched up his book and turned and hurried after the knight, calling to him in a loud whisper, 'Master Teobalt. Wait. Master.'

But the knight did not slow, and the curtain swished closed behind them as they pushed out into the street. Felix stared after them though they were already out of sight.

'Get off your knees, manling,' said Gotrek gruffly. 'They've gone.'

Felix had forgotten he was kneeling. He looked around. People were staring. He scrambled up, embarrassed, then sat back on the bench and patted his empty waist. Karaghul was gone. His sword. He felt naked without it. He didn't know what to do. He would have to get another sword, of course, but how could he replace it? Certainly he had hated Karaghul at times, when its dragon-loathing nature had invaded his mind and urged him into suicidal situations, but it had protected him as well, and defeated many a great and powerful enemy. He had had it so long, and it was so much a part of him, that he wasn't sure he would be himself without it.

'It… it seems I need a sword,' he said.

'Aye,' said Gotrek.

'And a drink,' he said.

'Aye,' said Gotrek. He pounded the table. 'Barkeep! Two more! No, four more!'

The rest of the night passed in a sodden blur of beer and bewilderment. Felix sat benumbed as Gotrek handed him mug after mug and ordered him to drink them down. He did so mechanically, staring into the middle distance as his mind spun in slow circles, like a wobbly cartwheel after the cart has tipped into a ditch.

He tried to focus on how he was going to reap his revenge on the skaven, but visions of bursting in on the grey seer in its lair and cutting its scabrous head off kept bringing him back to Karaghul, and he would mourn its loss all over again.

This grief took on different shades as he moved through the various stages of drunkenness. Sometimes he wanted to weep. Sometimes he laughed at the bitter humour of it. Other times he flushed with anger, and grew determined to stride to the templar's chapter house and demand the sword back. Still other times, he considered throwing himself at the templar's feet and begging.

In the end, he did none of those things, only took the next mug and methodically drank it dry, and the mug after that, on into the night.

The next morning he nearly did weep, for when he awoke at last, still dressed except for one boot, and with his head hammering like a cave full of dwarf smiths, he reached blindly for his sword belt, as he had done every day of his adult life, and found nothing.

He turned and stared at the bedpost, where he always hung his sword when he stayed in inns, and his heart dropped into his guts. It was gone! Someone had stolen Karaghul! He leapt up, about to call to Gotrek in the next room, and rouse him to go after the thief. But just as he filled his lungs to shout, he remembered, and his heart sank even further. The sword wasn't stolen. He had given it away. He would never see it again.

He sank back down on the bed and lowered his throbbing head into his hands. What had he done? What had honour made him do? How could he have been so foolish?

He sat there just breathing for quite a while, his mind drifting in a fugue of pain and regret, but then a sharp rap on the door jarred him awake again.

'Who is it?'

'Wake up, manling,' came Gotrek's voice. 'We must find you a sword today.'

Felix groaned and stood. 'Don't remind me.'

He straightened his clothes and crossed to the door, and even though he knew Karaghul was gone, even though he knew he was going out to look for a new sword, it still made his heart jump when his arms brushed his sides and he didn't feel the familiar shape of the old blade's pommel knocking against his wrist as it always did.

As it always *had*, he corrected himself. As it never would again. He took a deep breath and opened the door. It was going to be a long day.

Felix squinted against the light that streamed through the leaded windows as he and Gotrek shuffled down the stairs to the taproom. The smell of sausage and fritters and stale beer made his gorge rise, and he swallowed with difficulty. He needed fresh air and a walk, and perhaps a nice quiet puke in an alley somewhere.

A pair of fiery blue eyes caught him as he followed Gotrek towards the exit, and he stumbled as if he'd been hit. It was the old templar! The knight sat ramrod straight at the table nearest the door, glaring at Gotrek and Felix from under shaggy white brows. His squire stood behind him, gazing at them with a more anxious expression.

Felix's heart leapt as he saw that Karaghul was resting across the templar's knees. He had come to give it back! He had changed his mind! The sword would be Felix's again! But if that was the case, why was he looking at them so coldly?

'You rise late,' the old knight said as they stopped before him. 'I have waited here since dawn.'

'You just missed us, then,' said Gotrek. 'That's when we went to bed.'

The knight sniffed, disgusted, then turned to cast a baleful glance at his squire, as if it was somehow all his fault. The squire shrank before his displeasure.

Felix stepped forwards and inclined his head respectfully. 'You wanted to see us about something, sir knight?' he asked, trying to keep the pathetic hope out of his voice.

The knight did not look at him. Instead he turned and stared at Gotrek, who stood, arms crossed over his beard before him. 'Swear by the honour of your ancestors and your gods that you will answer me truthfully,' he said at last.

'I so swear,' said Gotrek, without hesitation.

The knight picked up the copy of *My Adventures with Gotrek – Vol II* which lay on the table beside him. 'Are the events in this book, and in the other volumes of your travels, true? Did you and your companion truly perform the deeds written of therein?'

Gotrek nodded. 'We did.'

'And there is no exaggeration, or embroidery in the telling?'

'None that I know of,' said Gotrek.

The knight continued to look hard at the Slayer for a long moment, then at last turned to Felix. The expression on his face said that he would rather be drinking urine. 'I will not give you the sword,' he said. 'But you may earn the right to carry it.'

Felix blinked, shocked but elated. 'H-how?'

'You spoke of doing some service for me,' said the knight. 'My squire assures me that you are a man of honour and valorous deeds, and your companion confirms it. Well, we shall see. If you wish to once again wield the sword, I would have you travel north with me into the Drakwald, to discover what has become of the rest of our order – brave templars who went north to fight Archaon's hordes and did not return. Be they alive, we must save them. Be they dead, we must recover the order's holy banner and regalia. If you prove yourself worthy on this quest, I will grant you the stewardship of Karaghul. If you are unworthy, I will take the sword from you, whether you would return it or not. Do you accept this venture?'

Felix paused, though every fibre of him wanted to scream, 'Yes!'

'What do you mean by "stewardship"?' he asked.

'The sword belongs to the order,' said the knight, raising his bearded chin. 'And always will. But if you show me that you are the hero this book claims, I will grant you the right to carry it until you die or dishonour it, or until the order requires it again, at which time it will be returned to us.'

Felix frowned. As much as he wanted the sword back, that sounded fishy. He had no objection to holding Karaghul as steward. He had no son to pass the sword to, and it was doubtful he ever would. But 'until the order requires it again,' could mean the day after he helped the templar find his fellow knights. It could be a trick.

And there was another consideration. Only last night he had made a vow to hunt down the evil old skaven who had slain his father, and kill it in its lair. Could he let a wild goose chase into the deep woods get in the way of that vow? It didn't seem right, even to win back Karaghul. On the other hand, as Gotrek had said, the skaven were likely to come to him. Perhaps it was better to stay in the wilderness until they did. Fewer innocent people would be endangered that way.

'Archaon's hordes still haunt the Drakwald?' asked Gotrek.

The knight nodded. 'So I have been told,' he said. 'As well as beastmen, orcs, goblins and horrors too strange to be described. It will be a perilous journey.'

Felix glanced at the Slayer, and saw his one eye shining with bloodthirsty anticipation. He sighed. Whatever he might have decided in the end, it didn't matter now. The decision had been made.

Felix turned back to the old knight and nodded. 'Very well,' he said. 'I will take this quest. And I will do my best to prove myself worthy of possessing, er, carrying Karaghul – for however long you are pleased to grant it to me.'

The old knight looked at him, almost disappointed, then after a reluctant pause, picked up the sword and thrust it out. 'Take it, then, and sit. I will tell you my tale.'

Felix bowed, then took the sword and began strapping it around his waist. He was embarrassed at how comforted he was to have it again.

When he was finished, he and Gotrek sat down across the table from the knight, while his squire remained standing at attendance behind him.

'My name,' said the knight, as Gotrek signalled the serving girl, 'is Sir Teobalt von Dreschler, templar and librarian of the Order of the Fiery Heart, and, I fear, its last living representative.'

Young Ortwin coughed at this and Teobalt sighed and corrected himself. 'With the exception, of course, of my squire, Ortwin Wielhaber, who is the last novitiate of the order.'

The serving girl brought steins for Gotrek and Felix. Felix's stomach churned at the smell and he pushed his across to Sir Teobalt.

The old knight nodded his thanks, took a sip, then continued. 'When

Archaon's invasion began,' he said, 'it was decided that, because of my advanced age, I should stay behind and maintain the chapter house while the others went north with the Emperor to do battle. Ortwin remained to assist me. Since then we have waited for our brothers' return, but they have not come home, and I have begun to fear that they will not.'

'I'm sorry to hear it,' said Felix politely.

Sir Teobalt waved that away. 'If they died in battle, fighting bravely for their Emperor and their homeland, then they will have achieved all that a knight may wish. I do not grieve them. I envy them.'

Gotrek grunted approvingly at this.

'Still,' said Teobalt, 'it is my duty to learn what became of them and to recover, if possible, the regalia of the order. We have had word from others who returned that, while many of my brothers fell at the siege of Middenheim, the order as a whole survived to begin the march back to Altdorf in the train of Karl Franz. The last anyone heard of them came to us more than a month ago. They had answered the plea of some peasants from a town near the abandoned fort of Stangenschloss to help defend their village against a herd of beastmen.'

Teobalt took another sip and continued. 'I know not the name of the town, or whether my brothers succeeded in its defence, but we must find it and learn their fate. We shall make our way to Stangenschloss and enquire of them along the way.'

'What is the regalia of the order?' asked Felix.

Teobalt looked about to answer, then smiled slyly and looked at Ortwin. 'Squire, prove that you have been diligent in your studies. What is the regalia of the Order of the Fiery Heart?'

Ortwin snapped to attention and coughed nervously. 'The regalia of the Order of the Fiery Heart consists of two pieces,' he began in a high, clear voice, 'the Banner of Baldemar, made from the cloak of the mighty warrior who founded the order, and bearing the device of a heart surrounded by a halo of flames, and the Sword of Righteous Flame, wielded first by Baron Konrad von Zechlin at the gates of Kislev during the Great War against Chaos. It is said that the blade of the sword bursts into flames in the presence of the unrighteous.'

Teobalt nodded. 'Very good, boy. Very good. You have learned well.' He turned to Gotrek and Felix. 'If my brothers yet live, then time is of the essence. I would therefore start on the morrow at dawn, if that is not *too early* for you,' he said, giving them a sharp look.

Gotrek grunted. 'We'll be ready.'

Felix would have liked another full night's sleep to recover from last night's excesses, but he knew it would never happen. No matter how much he drank, Gotrek would be up and ready to march before the cock crowed if there was any prospect of danger and doom in the offing.

'Aye,' he sighed. 'We'll be ready.'

THREE

It took three days' travel on the riverboat *Magnus the Pious* before Ortwin, the young squire, got up the courage to speak to Felix.

For some reason, Felix had pictured Sir Teobalt making the entire journey from Altdorf to Fort Stangenschloss dressed in full armour and astride his mighty warhorse. It suited his image of Teobalt as a mad old knight, clanking off on adventures far past his prime, but the reality was much more mundane. The old knight travelled by cart, with his armour, lances and instruments of war piled on the back under canvas, and his warhorse hitched to the tailgate along with Ortwin's pony. In the interests of speed, they didn't even take to the road until they were halfway to their destination. Using funds from the coffers of the Order of the Fiery Heart, Sir Teobalt paid for passage on the *Magnus the Pious* up the Talabec from Altdorf to the town of Ahlenhof. Fort Stangenschloss was apparently due north from there, deep within the woods near the head of the Zufuhr river, a tributary of the Talabec that passed by the town.

For the first three days of the voyage, Felix noticed young Ortwin peering at him whenever he thought he wasn't looking. He was always peeking out from behind the mast when Felix was walking the deck, or goggling at him from the door when he was sitting in the common area. It was unnerving. When Ortwin was with Sir Teobalt he kept his eyes to himself, but as soon as they were apart, Ortwin was stalking Felix again. The boy's stare was like an owl's, wide and intense, but whenever Felix turned towards him to ask him what he wanted, he flew off like a frightened sparrow.

Felix didn't understand what the boy wanted. Did he hate Felix for holding Karaghul for so long? Did he suspect he was going to betray his master and run off with it without completing his end of the bargain? Had Sir Teobalt told him to keep an eye on him? If so, he was being less than subtle about it.

Finally, on the third day, as Felix was updating his journal in the common room with a hot brandy to keep out the chill of the day, he noticed the squire hovering nearby, his skullcap in his hands. Felix sighed and looked up, ready for another scurrying retreat, but wonder of wonders, Ortwin didn't dart for the long grass this time, but only swallowed and stood on one foot.

'Yes, Ortwin?' Felix said. 'You want to speak to me?'

'If… if it's not too much trouble, m'lord,' Ortwin stammered.

'Not at all,' said Felix dryly. 'I was only writing. And it isn't, m'lord, I'm a merchant's son.'

'Well, sir,' said Ortwin, swallowing again. 'I… I just wanted to say that… that you are my hero, Herr Jaeger! I have read every book you have published. Sir Teobalt frowns on books that aren't about Sigmar or the knightly virtues, but I think they're wonderful!'

Felix stared, surprised. It wasn't what he had expected to hear. 'Er, thank you,' he said at last. 'I'm glad you liked them.' He felt a bit uncomfortable with the praise, but it felt good too. His chest swelled. Someone liked his work! He hadn't had a favourable review since his poetry days.

'Uh, can you tell me, sir,' the boy continued, nervously. 'Can you tell me how you chose to become an adventurer?'

Felix frowned. 'You did read the books, yes?'

'Oh, yes!' said the squire. 'Many times!'

'Then you know that it wasn't precisely a choice. I swore to follow the Slayer, but… I didn't really know what I was letting myself in for.'

Ortwin laughed as if Felix had told a joke. 'You see,' he said, stuttering a little, 'I intend to become an adventurer too. When I have become a full knight of the order, I am going to go to the ends of the earth, seeking out ancient evils and destroying them, just like you.'

Felix's face fell. Was the boy a complete idiot? He sighed, then closed his journal and looked him right in the eye. 'Listen to me, Ortwin. I think you've got the wrong idea from the books. I have had a lot of exciting adventures, it's true.' Terrifying, near-death experiences, he thought to himself. 'But there's not a day that goes by that I don't regret making that vow. There's not a day that goes by that I don't wish that I had chosen the path of warm beds and regular meals, of a wife and children and a proper job. The books…' He waved a hand, wishing he had read more of them. He still had no idea what was in most of them. 'It's not that I don't enjoy it sometimes. I do. But quite a lot of the time, I don't. I… I don't put everything in the books. I leave out the bits about starving for days, sometimes weeks, at a time, and the bits about getting soaking wet and catching horrible colds.'

'No, that's in,' said Ortwin, smiling.

'Fine,' said Felix. 'What I am trying to say is that it is not a romantic thing to be an adventurer. You are going to have a dangerous enough life as it is, being a member of a knightly order, but you will at least have a home to go to, and a whole company of comrades to watch your back, and some sort of pension set aside for when you get old. An adventurer has none of that. It is a lonely life, uncomfortable, wounding to the body, the mind and the spirit, and more dangerous than you could ever imagine. It is not a thing that any sane man would wish for himself. The adventurers I have known, man, elf and dwarf, were driven, desperate people, either running from something terrible, or chasing something impossible. They were not adventuring for the fun of it, or for some noble purpose, but because life had left them no other option. And they were all, without exception, stark, raving mad. Do you understand what I'm saying?'

'Oh, yes, sir,' said the boy, with the same gleam in his eye he had had when he had first admitted his love for the books. 'Thank you. That is very good advice, sir. I will be sure to keep it in mind.' He looked over his shoulder, then smiled again. 'I have to go tend to Sir Teobalt's corns now. I won't keep you from your writing any further. Thank you, Herr Jaeger. It was an honour to meet you.'

He hurried off with a spring in his step. It was quite clear to Felix that not a single word of what he had said had penetrated the young squire's thick skull. He moaned. How many young idiots were reading his books and making plans to go a-roving? He could just picture Ortwin's snow-covered corpse curled up in his bedroll somewhere in the Worlds Edge Mountains with a goblin spear through his spine, his first adventure over before it had begun. If he died, and all the other idiots with him, was Felix responsible? Would he have set them on the road to a quick death?

The idea of recalling and burning all the copies of the books rose up in his head. He didn't want any more deaths on his conscience. But it would be impossible to get all the books back, and would it really be his fault if some fool ran off after reading his stories? After all, some people – perhaps most people – just laughed at the books. Who was to say that the Ortwins of the world would not have sought adventure anyway? Felix had certainly not read stirring tales of derring-do when he was young. He had read romantic poetry and great philosophical dissertations, and yet here he was, vowing eternal vengeance on vile ratmen, and following a mad old knight into the woods in dead of winter on a wild goose chase after a sword and an old cloak. So perhaps one thing had nothing to do with the other.

They disembarked in the bustling trading town of Ahlenhof four days later and asked about for a boat to take them up the Zufuhr as far as it was possible to go, but there seemed to be no boats to be had, though Teobalt offered double the normal rate.

'I'm sorry, sir,' said the fifth boatman they approached, 'but we are all commandeered. Stangenschloss has been regarrisoned, and is getting in supplies for the winter. Their quartermasters have rented every northbound boat along the Zufuhr for themselves, and the refugees take every southbound one. I wait now for oat fodder bound for the fort and daren't let my boat to any other.'

'Stangenschloss regarrisoned?' said Teobalt, his ears perking up. 'Have you heard aught of the Knights of the Fiery Heart there? Or of who garrisons it?'

'No, m'lord,' said the boatman. 'I have not heard that name, or who commands there.'

And so, with similar answers everywhere they asked, and Sir Teobalt impatient to be started, they put their packs in the cart and began to make their way north by the rutted and muddy forest road that paralleled the little river instead.

With winter coming on, almost no one was going north, but many were coming south. Huddled refugees bundled in rags against the cold, trains of Shallyan hospital wagons, carrying the wounded and diseased down from the northern battlefields, soldiers from every province of the Empire, limping home after fighting all summer and autumn. Some were boisterous and prideful, for the Empire had won a great victory, and they sang jaunty marching songs and bragged amongst themselves about their kills and their conquests, but more were gaunt, sick, maimed or shattered in their minds, for the victory had come at a great cost, and against an enemy so strange and terrible that even to defeat them was to risk madness. It made Felix uneasy to see them.

The way was narrow and hemmed in by trees, and at every meeting, Sir Teobalt had to pull his cart to the side to let the southbound travellers pass. Sometimes they were met by jocularities – 'Off to fight at Middenheim, grandfather? You're a little late,' and, 'He may be old, but his lance is still hard! Just ask his squire!'

Just as often, however, they were met by warnings – 'Turn back, my lord. There is snow and ice north of Leer,' and, 'Beware the beasts! They ate half our party at Trenkenkraag,' and, 'Come back in the spring. Whatever you seek won't be found this winter. You will find only death.'

Sir Teobalt paid no attention to either jests or advice, just set his face in a look of dour disapproval and waited for whomever it might be to pass. Gotrek also made no comment, mostly because after one look at his crest and massive physique, no one was foolish enough to toss any jibes his way.

On the afternoon of the first day they came across a troop of Reikland archers surrounding a plump merchant and his four guards, who perched atop their ale wagon like cats treed by a pack of dogs. The archers were all clamouring to be given a drink, and some were trying to pull down kegs from the back as the guards shouted and banged at their fingers with cudgels.

'It's all spoken for, friends!' cried the merchant, wide-eyed with fear. 'I can't sell you any! I'm sorry!'

'Then give us some!' cried one of the archers. 'Do you want the boys who saved your sorry hide from the Kurgan to go thirsty?'

'Ungrateful lout,' said another. 'Fat while we're starving!'

'Only one barrel!' shouted several others.

Felix didn't like to see such bullying, but he might have passed by without interfering, as he could also see the archers' point of view, but Sir Teobalt, however, was incensed.

'Sergeant! Control your men!' he bellowed as he stood up on the buckboard of their cart.

The sergeant, who had been harrying the merchant just as strongly as his men, turned, sneering, but when he saw that he was addressing a nobleman he paused, then gave a hesitant salute.

'Sorry, m'lord,' he said. 'But the men are sore thirsty, and long on the road.'

'That is no excuse to rob an innocent merchant on the high road. By Sigmar, did you not go north to protect the people of our dear land? You might as well be Kurgan yourselves! Be off with you!'

Some of the archers growled under their breath at this, and none of them moved from the ale wagon.

The sergeant looked nervously from Teobalt to the archers and back. 'M'lord, I don't think they'll listen to me. They'll have my head if they don't have beer.'

Gotrek drew his axe and stood beside the templar. 'And I'll have their heads if they do!' he roared.

The sergeant's eyes bulged, and his men looked around and stared.

'Who wants a drink, then?' snarled Gotrek, slapping the haft of the axe against his palm.

The sergeant looked doleful, but finally sighed and turned to his men. 'All right then, lads. Let's away and leave this honest merchant to his journey. We was only teasing anyway.'

A chorus of 'aye' and 's'right' and 'only a bit of fun' followed this, and the archers formed up reluctantly behind the sergeant and began again to head south.

Teobalt regarded them disdainfully from under his shaggy white brows as they marched by. 'For shame,' he said. 'That soldiers of Karl Franz's Empire must be turned from evil by threat of violence. I despair for the modern age.'

The archers hung their heads as they passed under that penetrating gaze, but as they marched away, Felix thought he heard one of them say, 'Stick it in yer ear, m'lord.'

When they had gone, Teobalt turned to Gotrek and inclined his head. 'My thanks, Herr dwarf. But for your timely interjection, things might have gone very differently.'

Gotrek shrugged. 'Forget it.'

Just then the merchant jumped down from his cart and hurried over to them, his eyes bright. 'My lord! My friends! Herr dwarf! Thank you! How can I ever repay you? I was in desperate danger of losing my stock and perhaps my life. Had you not come along, all would have been taken.'

'Do not trouble yourself, my good man,' said Teobalt. 'It is only what any man of the Empire would do, when faced with such injustice.'

'Not so, m'lord,' said the merchant. 'There are many who would have helped the soldiers against me and shared in the spoils.' He clasped Teobalt's boot upon the buckboard. 'I beg you, m'lord. If we travel the same road, might we not travel it together? This was not the first such trouble, and I fear it may not be the last, but with your presence, I may get my beer all the way to Bauholz in safety.'

'If Bauholz lies on the path to Fort Stangenschloss, then you are welcome to join our train,' said Sir Teobalt.

'It does, m'lord,' said the merchant eagerly. 'It is the town closest to it. The fort is just five days or so north of it, through the woods. And I thank you for your kindness.'

Sir Teobalt waved that aside and they got underway again, Teobalt's cart in the lead and the ale wagon following close behind.

As he walked beside the cart, Felix leaned in towards Gotrek, who sat beside the old knight. 'I've never seen you take such an interest in defending the common man when there wasn't a monster or daemon involved,' he said.

'It wasn't the common man I was defending,' said Gotrek, licking his lips. 'It was his beer.'

'Ah,' said Felix, and they travelled on.

North of the little village of Leer, the road became no more than a track, with the trees drawn in closer on either side, making even high noon dark and full of shadows. Sir Teobalt ordered Ortwin to don his armour and helmet and to keep his sword at the ready. With the squire's help he did the same himself, strapping on his cuirass and vambraces and setting his helmet beside him on the buckboard. The merchant and his guards belted their leather jacks tighter underneath their woollen cloaks and heavy scarves. Felix followed their example, shrugging into his ringmail and loosening Karaghul in its scabbard, then tugging his old red cloak close around his shoulders. Gotrek had no armour to don, but he held his axe across his knees, not on his back.

At the same time it began to grow colder, with a few dry flakes of snow drifting down through the interwoven firs above them, and the thick mud of the track freezing into lumpy ridges and making it hard going for the carts. There were many times when they were obliged to get out and push, or lift their wheels out of some deep depression.

This was no problem with Teobalt's cart, which was almost empty, but the ale wagon was another matter, and the merchant, whose name was Dider Reidle, had many opportunities to thank Gotrek for his strength and Felix for his assistance; and that first night north of Leer, when they made camp, rewarded them all by broaching a cask of his precious cargo as they sat down to their dinner around the fire, and filling their cups and jacks.

Gotrek pronounced it 'not bad,' which was high praise coming from a dwarf.

Felix saluted the merchant. 'Thank you, Herr Reidle,' he said. 'It's very good.'

Reidle bowed his head. 'Thank *you*, sir. Without you I would have none to share.'

'I don't understand why you made the journey if it is so dangerous,' said Felix. 'Can the profit be so great that it's worth the risk?'

Reidle sighed. 'Well, had I been able to take the river, there would have been little risk, but all the boats are spoken for, and since I had already been partly paid for the shipment I felt I must try, dangerous though it may be.'

'Is Bauholz so large that it needs all this beer?' asked Sir Teobalt.

'Only recently, m'lord,' said Reidle. 'It was a tiny little village by all accounts, but since the war it has become a booming place. It is the last good port on the Zufuhr, and so has got a lot of traffic lately, with soldiers going one way, and refugees going the other. Before they had no inn, and only Taal's bower for a tavern. Now they have three inns, and beer and sausages for sale in every shack and tent that can hold two people.'

Sir Teobalt made a face. 'It sounds like a place of sin and depravity.'

'Oh aye,' said Reidle with a smile. 'But good for business.'

For four more days they continued north into the woods towards Bauholz, and with every step Felix felt like he was pushing deeper into some web that he would not be able to walk out of again. He could not shake the feeling that the forest was watching them – that unseen presences were waiting for them to let down their guard so that they might pounce. He never saw anything, or heard anything more than birdcalls and the yelp of foxes or the bay of distant wolves, but always there was the same tingling between his shoulder blades that felt like hungry eyes upon him.

They spent their third night at a lumber camp on the banks of Zufuhr, little more than a few tents and stacks of trimmed tree trunks inside a temporary wooden palisade. The wood cutters knew Reidle from previous trips and welcomed him warmly, particularly after he rolled the broached barrel off the back of his cart and invited them all to share.

'Well worth it,' he whispered to Felix as they were sitting down to eat a hearty venison stew in the camp's mess tent, 'for the security of sleeping inside walls.'

Though he knew the safety of the camp was largely an illusion, Felix was inclined to agree. The feeling of being watched had diminished as soon as they had entered the palisade, and his shoulders had relaxed for the first time since they had left Leer.

'And with luck we'll be in Bauholz and journey's end before dark tomorrow,' Reidle continued. 'As long as the weather holds.'

It was too bad Bauholz was only the beginning of *his* journey, thought Felix. Sigmar only knew where Sir Teobalt's search for the missing templars would lead them. He had a sudden fantasy of finding them all waiting for them at the gates of Bauholz, healthy and happy and ready for Teobalt to lead them home. He chuckled at the foolishness of the vision. It was never that easy.

Never.

The next morning, as they shared a breakfast of river trout, porridge and beer with the camp foreman, Felix watched with interest as the wood cutters laid dozens of tree trunks side by side on the bank of the river, then lashed them together with sturdy ropes.

By the time they'd finished eating and hitched the horses again to the wagons, these log rafts had been pushed out onto the water, and as Felix and Gotrek and the rest rode out of the compound and turned north towards Bauholz, they had begun drifting south down the river towards Ahlenhof, each carrying two men armed with long hook-tipped poles who stood at the forward corners.

They're going the right way, thought Felix, as the flotilla vanished around a bend in the river, and the feeling of being watched settled between his shoulderblades once again, just as strongly as before.

By late afternoon it was clear that, though the weather had held, in all other ways, Reidle's luck had failed him. With the light of the sun turning from red to purple, they were still hours away from Bauholz and trying, for the fifth time that day, to rock the ale cart out of a deep frozen rut.

They were having little success.

Gotrek was under the wagon, muddy to the knees and lifting with his back pressed against the bottom of the bed, while Felix and Reidle hauled at the spokes of the back wheels and the rest pushed at the tail. Squire Ortwin held the leads of the carthorses while Sir Teobalt directed the whole operation from the side.

'Ortwin,' cried the old knight. 'On my mark, lead them forwards while the rest push. Ready? Heave!'

Felix heaved at the wagon along with Gotrek and the others, his feet slipping in the icy muck. It rolled forwards almost to the lip of the rut, then slid back again like it had the last seven times.

'Better,' called Teobalt encouragingly. 'Once more and we shall have it. Ready?'

Felix wiped mud from his eye and put his shoulder to the wagon again with the others, but just as Sir Teobalt was raising his hand to call 'heave,' one of the horses whickered and backed nervously in its traces while the other neighed and plunged ahead.

The wagon jolted forwards. Gotrek was knocked flat as the axle clipped his back and the others staggered and fell. Felix slipped too, banging his shoulder against the wheel and landing in the mud.

He jumped up cursing and rubbing his shoulder as Ortwin tried to calm the horses. 'Damn this cart!' he said. 'Damn these horses! We should take the damned barrels off and roll them to Bauholz!' He kicked the wagon wheel. 'I've had enough of this–'

'Quiet, manling,' said Gotrek, crawling out from under the wagon. He picked up his axe and looked around at the surrounding woods.

Felix stopped and listened as well, though it was hard to hear anything over the worried whickering of the wagon's horses. Their distress seemed to have spread to the other animals as well. Sir Teobalt's carthorses were throwing their heads and rolling their eyes, while Ortwin's pony was pulling at its lead. Only Sir Teobalt's charger remained calm, though its ears turned alertly.

Reidle's guards drew their swords, their heads on swivels.

'What is it?' whispered Reidle. 'Bandits?'

'Wolves?' asked one of his guards.

'Worse,' said Gotrek.

Sir Teobalt clapped on his helmet and took up his shield, then motioned them all to get between the two wagons. 'Face out from the centre. They may come from any side.'

They gathered behind Sir Teobalt's cart, which was in front of the ale wagon, and turned to either side, weapons at the ready. Teobalt began praying and Ortwin and Reidle's guards picked it up. 'Lord Sigmar grant us your strength in this our hour of need. Let us smite our enemies like your hammer. Let us push back the powers of darkness.'

Behind them, Reidle took his horses from Ortwin and did his best to calm them, whispering, 'There now, Bess. Nothing to be afraid of,' and, 'Here, Pommertz, who's a brave boy then.'

For a moment, his murmurs and the shifting of the horses and the harsh breathing of the men was all that could be heard. The silence was unnerving. Felix and the others stared into the murk of shadows under the trees, their breath trailing away in steaming clouds, waiting for Sigmar only knew what. The tension made Felix grind his teeth.

'Which way are they coming from?' murmured Ortwin, adjusting a helmet that looked too big for him.

'Where are they?' asked one of the guards.

'Maybe the horses only spooked themselves,' said another.

'Silence,' said Sir Teobalt. 'Be ready.' A fine old long sword gleamed in his hand.

'Be ready for what?' asked one of the guards querulously.

He was cut off by a bloodcurdling roar from the woods to their left. Everyone jumped. The horses screamed and tore from Reidle's grasp.

'Steady!' cried Sir Teobalt.

With a thunder of hooves, the woods erupted with nightmares made flesh. Felix froze, terror gripping his heart. He had faced them before, but no amount of familiarity could breed contempt for such monsters. Five towering goat-legged, goat-headed monsters led the charge – two to the left of the carts, three on the right – followed by a swarm of smaller, more human horrors, mutated men with short, budding horns and mouths full of filed teeth. The behemoths rushed in, bellowing, their powerful limbs swinging huge spiked clubs and massive iron maces. Their smaller, scrawnier followers spread out behind them, knives and sickles and clubs clutched in their twisted claws.

Two of Reidle's guards died instantly, bodies pulped by a single swing of a beastman's mace. Gotrek leapt forwards before the monster had finished its swing and buried his axe in its stomach. He tore it out again with a spray of blood and was on the next before the first had begun to topple.

Teobalt strode out to meet another of the leaders, crying, 'To me, foul beast! Come face Sigmar's wrath!'

The beastman swung at him with a club that looked like a giant's femur, and Teobalt took it on his shield. The force of it slammed the old knight to the ground and the beast trampled over him and leapt at Reidle's horses, ripping old Bess's throat out with its teeth as the merchant fell back, screaming and throwing up his arms.

A beastman with a third horn sprouting from its forehead charged Felix. He flinched away from its gore-matted mace and crashed against Teobalt's cart to fall in the mud again. Three-Horn came on. Felix backhanded desperately with Karaghul and rolled under the cart as the beastman's sticky mace crashed down, splintering the planks of the cart. Felix hunched down, then lashed out from under the tailgate, hacking at the beastman's backward-bending legs. It jumped back.

All around, Felix could hear the screams of men and horses and the roaring cries of the beastmen and their followers. Quick glances showed him flashes of violence in every direction – the two remaining guards fighting for their lives in the midst of a handful of the lesser beasts, Teobalt's warhorse kicking the brains out of another, a lesser beast on the ale wagon, hacking at the straps that held the barrels tight, Gotrek exchanging clanging blows with a beastman three times his height, Reidle the merchant crawling on his belly, weeping like a baby, Ortwin slashing wildly at a pair of beast-followers as he tried to reach Sir Teobalt, who fought the beastman that had trampled him.

Then, with almost human screams, Teobalt's carthorses bolted as a pair of the scrawny beastlings leapt on their backs. With the horses went the cart, leaving Felix exposed again. The three-horned beastman loomed above him, swinging down with its mace. Felix rolled to the side and felt the ground shake as the massive iron weapon slammed down beside him. He jumped to his feet, slashing blindly around at the beastman's encroaching followers. The smell of them was overpowering. They reeked like a sewer full of dead dogs.

The three-horned beastman leapt at him again, swinging for his head. Felix ducked and lunged, stabbing forwards with all his might. Karaghul's point skidded across the beast's massive belly shield and punched through its ribs.

The monster howled and wrenched away violently. Felix held on, but could not pull his sword loose. Enraged and in pain, the beastman swung down at him. Felix let go of his sword and jumped back, slamming into a lesser beast who was trying to brain him from behind.

He grabbed the thing by its stubby horns and threw it in front of him. The three-horned beastman's mace crushed it, and it slumped to the ground like a bag of wet meat.

Three-Horn came on. Felix turned to run and found himself surrounded by its followers, all closing in on him. A sword! He needed a sword. One of the dead guards held on to one. Felix rolled to him, ducking a handful of attacks, ripped it from the guard's slack hand and lashed out all around. The lesser beasts dodged back then advanced again. There seemed no escape. Or was there?

Screaming he knew not what, Felix charged a man-beast that was between him and the ale wagon. The thing leapt aside and Felix sprang up onto the cart, kicking down the hideous thing that had been cutting at the leather straps. He climbed to the top of the barrels and turned to face his pursuers.

'Now try me!' he cried, triumphant.

The three-horned beastman slammed its mace into the cart so hard that it jumped. Felix staggered and almost lost his footing. His skinny followers started to climb the sides. Perhaps this hadn't been Felix's best idea.

A quick glance around told him that the rest of the wagon train was faring no better. Sir Teobalt and the beastman he had fought were both down, while Ortwin stood over the old knight's body, fighting a handful of lesser beasts. Only one of the guards remained standing, backed up by two more beastlings, and Reidle lay unmoving on the ground next to the ale cart. Only Gotrek was master of his situation, beating back his monstrous opponent with blow after blow.

Felix hacked at a climbing man-beast with his borrowed sword and bit deep into its shoulder. It screamed and fell off. But then Three-Horn swung again and Felix had to leap up to let the mace pass under his feet.

He knew before he landed that it would go wrong. His boot heels slipped on the curve of the barrel and he bounced down the side of the pyramid, knocking the wind from his lungs, and just barely catching himself at the wagon's rail.

The lesser beasts converged towards him, cackling. He kicked one in the chops and lashed out at another, but he was so precariously balanced that if he tried to move more than that he would fall between the barrels and the rail of the cart and be wedged tight.

The three-horned beastman pushed through its followers, Karaghul still sticking out of its ribs. Felix scrambled for purchase on the barrels and could find none. Behind Three-Horn he saw Gotrek running to help Ortwin. Couldn't the damn fool dwarf see that his old friend was in trouble?

'Gotrek! Help!' he called, but he was too winded, and it came out as a whisper. As Three-Horn loomed over him, raising its mace, Felix held up his short sword, knowing it would be like trying to stop an avalanche with a twig.

But then, as he waited cringing for the blow to fall, the beastman bellowed and arched its back in pain. Felix blinked. Karaghul was sticking from Three-Horn's ribs right in front of him. It was like the beastman was offering it to him.

Felix reached forwards with both hands and wrenched with all his might. The blade came free, causing the beastman to howl even louder. It also threw Felix's balance off, and he fell, just as he had feared, on his back between the barrels and the cart rail. He was trapped.

Three-Horn roared above him, blood flowing down its furred side like a river as it raised its mace once again. Felix did the only thing he could do, and thrust up fast and hard with Karaghul, aiming as best he could. The blade punched into the flesh below Three-Horn's lowest rib and sank deep.

With a whistling sigh, the beastman staggered sideways, its knees buckling. The bloody rent in its flesh ripped wider as its weight dragged at the sword, and its guts spilled out and slapped against its belt. It twisted as it fell, and Felix saw something thin and white sticking out of its back – an arrow!

Felix clawed at the rail, struggling up out of the confining space and looking around. The man-beasts that had been climbing the ale cart were on the ground, all writhing with arrows in their backs and necks.

As he turned towards Ortwin and Gotrek, he saw them cutting down the lesser beasts around them, half of which were also impaled with arrows, and as he watched, another arrow shot from the woods to the left and pierced the leg of one of the three beastlings fighting the last standing guard. The man killed it as it lost its balance, then turned on the others.

Felix vaulted the cart rail and ran to help him, but the lesser beastmen, seeing him coming, turned and fled for the woods – straight for where the arrows had come from. A third beastling picked itself up and joined them, squealing in fright.

Felix and the last guard started after them, but before they could take two steps, another arrow shot from the trees and took one of the man-beasts in the eye, dropping it. The other two kept running for the trees.

With a wail like a banshee, the hidden archer burst from the underbrush with a long, narrow-headed hatchet in each hand. He was small and quick and bundled in filthy furs, and ran straight at the escaping beastlings. They dodged right and left, too panicked to fight, but the archer side-armed one of the hatchets at the one on the left, then leapt at the one on the right. The thrown axe spun in a perfect arc and split the forehead of the left-hand man-beast. At the same time the archer kicked the right-hand monster full in the face with both feet, knocking it flat, then landed, turned and buried the second hatchet in its chest. The man-beast shrieked and tried to sit up, but the archer stomped on its throat and levered the axe free, then stepped back and let out a sigh of relief.

Felix looked around in the sudden silence. All the beastmen and their lesser followers were dead or fled, and he and at least some of the others still lived. Such an outcome hadn't seemed possible a moment ago. They had the archer to thank for that.

He and Gotrek started towards the figure as Ortwin knelt beside the fallen templar.

'Nice shooting,' said Gotrek.

'Thank you for the help,' added Felix.

The archer stood from prying the second axe from the other beastling and flipped back dirty, matted hair to peer at them. Felix stopped short, surprised.

Though she was bundled in thick leather armour and furs, with a scarf up to her narrow chin against the cold, and though her face was mottled with grime and scarred from hairline to the corner of her full lips on her left side, there was no mistaking the archer's sex at close range. Her fierce brown eyes flashed keenly under her unruly mass of hair, which was all black but for a lock over her left eye that was as white as snow. 'I… I have sworn an oath to…' Her words faded away as she looked closely at Gotrek for the first time.

'You,' she said, staring.

She turned and looked at Felix. 'And you!'

Felix exchanged a puzzled glance with Gotrek. Gotrek shrugged. He didn't know her either.

Suddenly the filthy girl fell to her knees before them. She grabbed Felix's hand and kissed it.

'My heroes!' she said.

FOUR

Felix stared down at the young woman as she covered his hand with kisses. He felt slightly dizzy. First Ortwin and now this strange forest creature. Had everyone read his books? Was he truly this famous?

'So… so you've read them too?' he asked.

She looked up at him curiously. 'Read? Read what?'

'My books,' he said. 'You've read my books.'

She shook her head. 'I don't know how to read.'

Felix felt even dizzier. 'Then how… uh, that is, why are we your heroes?'

She blinked, confused. 'You… But, I'm Kat. Katerina. You rescued me from the beastmen. You rescued me from… that woman.'

Felix looked at Gotrek again. The Slayer shrugged.

'We… we did?'

'Yes!' said the archer, a slight edge of desperation creeping into her voice. 'In Flensburg! It is because of you that I have become a Slayer of beasts!' She looked worried now. 'You… you don't remember?'

Suddenly, with a flood of images and emotions, he *did* remember. The massacred village. The frightened little girl, hiding in the ruins of the inn. The desperate fight with the beastmen in the woods. The defence of Flensburg. The hideous strength of the woman with the white streak in her hair as she closed her hand around his throat. The little girl again, her eyes wide as she held the sword that had killed the woman, then once more as she begged and pleaded with Felix and Gotrek to take her with them, and then hugged them goodbye.

'You,' he said.

'You,' said Gotrek, and an uncharacteristic smile cracked his hard expression. 'You seem to have become a hero yourself, little one.'

Kat flushed at that, though it barely showed through the patina of dirt on her cheeks. 'I have vowed to rid all of the Drakwald of beastmen,' she said into her scarf.

'A noble ambition,' said Felix, his mind still reeling. 'I… I can't believe, after all this time…'

'Friends!' came Ortwin's voice from behind them. 'Help me. Sir Teobalt is sorely wounded.'

They turned. Ortwin was still kneeling by the old knight, who lay flat on the ground. Gotrek and Felix hurried towards them, Kat tailing behind.

On the way, Felix looked around at the aftermath of the battle and totalled the cost. Two guards dead and the other two wounded, one so badly he couldn't stand. Both of the ale cart horses mauled to death. Sir Teobalt's cart wedged between two trees, its wheels smashed and its horses missing. Ortwin's pony dead with its skull caved in, and Sir Teobalt's charger pacing nervously nearby with deep claw marks in its flanks. It occurred to Felix that if the beastmen hadn't been so hungry for horse-flesh the battle might have gone much worse. At least the beer had been saved – and the beer merchant, it seemed, for Herr Reidle was groaning to his feet behind his wagon and peering around anxiously.

Sir Teobalt looked up as they gathered around him. He had a deep gash across one cheek where the edge of his helmet had cut him, and his armour was covered in dents. 'Right glad I am to see you alive, friends,' he said feebly. 'Valiantly fought.'

'How badly are you hurt, sir?' asked Felix, kneeling beside him.

'Mere inconveniences,' he said. 'My shoulder took a heavy blow, and I cannot at the moment move my left leg. Also, my vision is blurred. I fear I will need some rest.'

Felix turned to Kat. 'Do you know how far it is to Bauholz?'

'About an hour's walk,' she said. 'No more than two.'

Felix looked up at the few patches of purple sky that showed through the thick canopy of needles above them. 'Perhaps we should camp–' he began, but Kat cut him off.

'You must not stay here tonight. There are wolves and other beasts that will smell the blood. You will get no peace.'

Felix looked around, assessing their resources. One horse and a heavily laden wagon – that was all they had in the way of transport. He stood. It would have to do. 'Unload Herr Reidle's wagon and hitch Sir Teobalt's horse to it. We will lay Sir Teobalt and the other wounded men in it.'

Both Reidle and Teobalt erupted at this.

'Leave the beer?' cried the merchant. 'It'll be stolen!'

'Hitch Machtig to a cart!' complained Teobalt. 'Never! He is a war-horse. He has never stooped to such common duty, and never shall.'

'That common duty may save your life,' growled Gotrek.

'And do you expect us to carry your beer to Bauholz?' Felix asked Herr Reidle. 'Not even a warhorse has the strength to pull all that.'

'The horses from the other cart might come back,' insisted Reidle.

'They might,' said Felix. 'But I'm not waiting all night to find out.'

Both the merchant and the knight continued to complain, but there was little they could do. Gotrek, Felix, Ortwin and the less wounded guard set to unloading the beer from the cart and hitching the warhorse to it as Kat bound the wounds of Teobalt and the maimed guard as best she could with a field kit she wore at her belt. The proud charger complained almost as bitterly as its master when they laid the yoke across its neck, but with Ortwin whispering soothing words in his ears it finally acquiesced. Then they laid Sir Teobalt, the wounded guard and his dead companions on the back, and set off for Bauholz as the hidden sky above turned from violet to cobalt, and the shadows of the trees closed in around them.

Felix had a thousand questions he wanted to ask Kat, for her transformation from a scared, sweet little girl to hardened beast-slayer was still a shock to him, but she had insisted on going ahead to scout the way and so he had no opportunity to talk to her. Instead he carried a lantern beside Ortwin as the youth led Machtig down the track. Gotrek took up the rear, keeping an eye out behind them in case more horrors came out of the woods.

After a half an hour or so during which Ortwin remained entirely silent, Felix looked over at him. The poor lad had had his first taste of adventure and it seemed to have stunned him a bit. Felix didn't blame him. Death and mutilation at close range were a far different thing than death and mutilation in a book. Felix had become somewhat inured to it over the years, but he could well remember the feelings of terror and nausea that used to overcome him before and after a fight. Maybe the boy was having second thoughts about a life of adventure. He hoped so.

'Not quite like it is in books, is it?' he said, smiling sadly.

'I'm sorry, sir?' said Ortwin, lifting his head from his thoughts.

'I was just wondering if our fight just now lived up to your expectations.'

Ortwin shook his head, eyes wide and far away. 'It was… it was glorious!'

Felix blinked at him, stunned. 'Uh… glorious?'

'Oh yes, sir!'

Felix frowned, anger stirring inside him. Was the boy bloodthirsty? Was he cold-hearted? 'You weren't frightened of the beasts? You weren't troubled by the slaughter of Reidle's guards, or the horses? Or by poor Sir Teobalt's grievous wounds?'

'Of course I was,' said Ortwin, not appearing to notice Felix's hard tone. 'I have never been so terrified in my life, Herr Jaeger. They were the foulest creatures I have ever set eyes upon, and they did vile, horrible things. My heart was near frozen with fear. But... but we vanquished them! We looked into the face of evil and though we were sorely tested, we did not flinch. We persevered! We have pushed back the forces of Chaos!'

A laugh burst from Felix though he tried to stop it. 'We haven't even given the forces of Chaos a paper-cut. And we didn't persevere over anything. We were about to die defending a wagonload of beer from a bunch of mindless beasts, when a girl with a good eye and a quick draw saved us. And I flinched plenty.'

Ortwin turned and stared at him, his eyes wide in the lantern light, his mouth open. Felix sighed. He shouldn't have been so harsh. He had broken the boy's poor sheltered heart with his hard-won bitterness.

He coughed. 'Listen, Ortwin, I...'

But then Ortwin laughed and grinned at him. 'Oh, but I see! This is the grim humour that I love so much in your books. The self-mocking jokes you use to disguise the true nobility of your acts.' He smiled sheepishly. 'Forgive me, sir. For a moment I almost thought you serious, but I see now that, like all good knights, you are truly humble, and do not wish to be praised for your deeds.'

It was Felix's turn to stare. The boy really thought he was joking. Felix opened his mouth to tell him that he wasn't kidding, and that he actually meant what he said, but then he closed it again. What was the point? Ortwin probably wouldn't believe him anyway, and besides, there was no need to shatter the boy's delusions about the world so quickly. He would find out for himself soon enough.

'Believe what you like, Ortwin,' said Felix, defeated. 'Just keep buying the books.'

Ortwin laughed. 'Very good, sir. Very good!'

Felix sighed and they walked on in silence.

At last, an hour into true night, the wagon came out of the forest into a narrow area of cleared land beside the Zufuhr river, and Felix saw, on its banks, the silhouette of a small, palisaded village in the distance, a faint glow of torchlight illuminating the tops of its squat wooden watchtowers. Felix noted that the fields were patchy with dead weeds and stray stalks of wheat, all gone to seed. It appeared that there had been no planting and no harvest this year. How had the village survived?

He turned away from Ortwin, looking around for Kat, and jumped when he discovered that she was already beside him. It was as if she had stepped out from behind a moonbeam. 'Oh!' he said, then lowered his voice. 'There you are.'

'I must warn you, Fel...' she paused suddenly and looked down. 'I... I'm sorry. I don't know what to call you now.'

Felix smiled as they started towards the town again. What a strange young woman she was, so vicious and yet so demure at the same time. 'You may still call me Felix, Kat,' he said. 'We've known each other for a long time, after all.'

'Thank you, Felix,' she said, smiling shyly.

His heart fluttered uncomfortably in his chest as her smile lanced through him. It seemed wrong to be stirred by someone you last knew as a seven-year-old, but filthy as she was, she was undeniably attractive. 'You're... most welcome,' he mumbled. 'Er, what was it you were saying?'

Her face grew grim and she nodded towards the village. 'Bauholz. I wanted to warn you that it is a bad town.'

'Oh?'

'It was good once,' she said. 'Before the war. It was my home from the woods. But the war killed it, and now the soldiers and bandits are feeding on the corpse.'

'Soldiers?' asked Felix.

'Aye. A man from the south and his men – Captain Ludeker.' She spat on the ground at the name. 'He was like all the others, coming back from the war on his way home, but then he decided to stay and rob all the rest. Now he runs the town.'

Felix frowned. He knew about those kinds of soldiers. They were in every war, and on every side. 'What has he done?'

'He steals from the supply boats going north and sells seats on all the boats going south. All the refugees must pay him to board, and he charges a fortune. He has turned the strong house and the temple of Sigmar into taverns, and he runs dice and card games in them, and keeps women upstairs. Every soldier that comes through town has his pocket picked.' She looked up into Felix's face, her eyes flashing. 'Beware of him, Felix, and tell Gotrek too. He will try to take everything you own.'

Felix chuckled, imagining anyone trying to take anything from Gotrek. 'I will be sure to warn him,' he said. 'But if the town is so bad, why are we going there?'

She pointed across the Zufuhr. 'We're not. We are going to the refugee camp on the other side of the river, but the only bridge is within the town. There is no other way across for miles.'

Felix frowned. 'You're taking us to a refugee camp?'

'Yes,' said Kat. 'To Herr Doktor Vinck. He is my friend. He will doctor your friends.'

Felix nodded, though he wondered how qualified a doctor that lived among refugees would be.

Kat turned to him, biting her lip, as the walls of the town loomed before them. 'Er, do you have any money?' she asked.

'Ah, a little. Why?'

'Ludeker has made a gate tax.'

* * *

'Who's that, then?' said a voice in the darkness.

Felix peered ahead to the big closed gate and saw two men in dirt-grimed uniforms that suggested they were from a company of Streissen handgunners strolling out from a small torchlit side door, naked swords dangling from casual hands.

'Travellers with wounded,' said Felix. 'Please let us in.'

'Wounded?' said the first man suspiciously. He was a thin-faced fellow with lank blond hair. 'What happened to ye?'

'We were attacked by beastmen in the woods,' said Reidle from where he sat on the buckboard. 'I beg you, sirs, be swift.'

The two men looked out into the night at the mention of beastmen, gripping their weapons tighter.

'There's beasts about and you want us to open the gate?' said the second man, a square-built tough with a three-day beard. He took a step back towards the little door.

'Please,' said Ortwin, stepping up beside Felix. 'They have hurt my master. He requires a doctor.'

'Open the gate, Wappler,' sighed Kat. 'The beastmen are dead. You've no need to fear.'

Wappler, the thinner man, peered towards her. 'Is it the she-beast, then? Brought us some more deadbeat refugees?'

The thick man laughed. 'Don't need any more of those. Town's full.'

'What are we waiting for?' asked Gotrek, coming from behind the wagon.

The two guards turned to him, then stared, their eyes drawn to the golden bracelets on his wrists, which gleamed warmly in the torchlight.

Wappler licked his lips. 'We'll open the gates, yer worships,' he said. 'But first there's the matter of the taxes.'

'Aye,' said the other, shouldering his sword. 'We have a foot tax here in Bauholz – for wear and tear on the public way. One pfennig per foot.'

Wappler walked among them, muttering under his breath. 'Two, four, six, eight, ten, twelve, and four for the horse makes sixteen. Now who do we have in the back?' He peered over the side of the beer wagon where Teobalt and the badly wounded guard dozed between the corpses of the others. 'Four more. That makes twenty-four. Two shillings.'

'Two of those men are dead,' said Felix.

'Still got feet, haven't they?'

'But they're not going to make much wear and tear on the public way,' Felix protested.

Wappler shrugged. 'I don't make the laws, mein herr, I just enforce 'em.' He smacked his lips. 'Now, there's also the danger tax – opening the gate when there's hostiles about. That's a shilling.'

'And the wounded tax,' said his companion. 'Four pennies each for each man who can't walk through the gate on his own. That's another eight pennies.'

'Right, that's three shillings and... aw, just round it up to four shillings, then,' said Wappler cheerily. 'That's easier.'

'A wounded tax?' rasped Gotrek menacingly.

'Aye, herr dwarf,' said Wappler. 'A man who's wounded can't work, and is therefore a burden on the community. Got to compensate for that, haven't we?'

Gotrek balled his fists, and his single eye sparked like a lit fuse in the torchlight. 'You can take your taxes and shove them up your skinny little human–'

'I'll pay, sirs!' said Ortwin, stepping forwards hastily. 'I would not argue while my master bleeds.'

He took a purse from his belt and shook out four silver shillings. Wappler took the money and signalled behind him, his eyes never leaving Gotrek. 'Be glad I didn't levy a resisting taxation tax on you, dwarf,' he said.

'You should be glad too,' growled Gotrek.

With a creaking of rope and timber, the big gates swung slowly open and the party started forwards into Bauholz.

Beyond the torches at the gate, the little village was dark, and it was hard to see many details, but Felix could see enough to realise that Bauholz was not a healthy town. The silhouettes of the little houses were lopsided and tumble-down, some with the ribs of their roof timbers naked to the sky. There was rubbish in the street and a stink of excrement, urine and rot all around. Things skittered away from them in the dark.

Towards the centre of the village there was more light – quite a bit of it in fact. Bright lanterns hung outside two large structures on opposite corners of the central intersection. To the right was a squat, stone strong house with a crenellated roof that must have been the town's last line of defence at one time. Now it seemed to be a bawdy house. There was a shield above the door that sported the coat of arms of Countess Emmanuelle von Liebewitz, and drunken songs and women's laughter came from within it. To the left was the old stone temple of Sigmar that Kat had said the soldiers had made into a tavern. The hammer had been taken down from above the door and replaced with a sign that showed a barrel of blackpowder with pyramids of cannon balls piled around it. Roaring laughter and heated argument spilled from its open door, and a man in the uniform of an Ostland spearman was being violently sick on the front steps.

'Ludeker's places,' whispered Kat.

'Lovely,' said Felix.

At the intersection, she led them to the right, down a dirty street that sloped towards the river. A sturdy warehouse – in better repair than any other building in the village – squatted to the left, and beyond it, the town's wall stretched out a little way into the water to guard the end of a wooden bridge. More guards stood before it, barring the way.

Felix raised an eyebrow. 'Don't tell me.'
Kat nodded, embarrassed. 'Aye. Another tax.'

If the village was a garbage dump, the refugee camp was a pigsty – a muddy field by the river with dozens of tents and makeshift shacks sticking up from it like broken kites trampled into a swamp.

'Are you sure this is best?' asked Reidle, looking around uncertainly from the bench of the wagon as he followed them.

'Your men will get no care in the village, mein Herr,' said Kat. 'Not any worth the price, at least.' She looked around at the camp angrily. 'Doktor Vinck was once the mayor of Bauholz, the most respected man in town,' she said. 'Now he lives here. It isn't right.'

'What happened?' asked Ortwin.

Kat sighed. 'Marauders came during the invasion. The people hid in the woods. When they came back, they found it all ruined. Captain Ludeker came a while later with his men. He offered to rebuild the town and protect it. Doktor Vinck said no, they didn't need the help, but the rest of the people were scared. They asked Ludeker to stay, so he did.' She kicked a pebble. 'He tried to charge Doktor Vinck rent on his own house if he wanted to practise medicine there. Doktor Vinck refused. Now he is here and Ludeker lives in his house.'

'This Captain Ludeker sounds like a charming fellow,' said Felix.

Kat snorted and kicked another pebble.

The doctor lived near the centre of the ramshackle encampment, in a tent only slightly grander than those around it – its principal amenity being that it had a plank floor that mostly kept the mud out.

Kat rapped the edge of this floor with the toe of her boot as they drew the wagon up in the narrow street outside it. 'Herr Doktor, are you at home?' she called.

'Just a minute, just a minute,' came a reedy voice from within, and a few moments later the flap of the tent was pushed aside and a thin old man in a night shirt and a scarf looked out at them, wispy white hair floating in the night breeze. 'Ah,' he said. 'Young Kat. You have some business for me?'

Felix winced a little when he saw the man. There was thin and there was gaunt. Herr Doktor Vinck was gaunt. He looked of an age with Sir Teobalt, but he appeared to be starving to death. And maybe this was the case. If it cost so much just to get inside Bauholz, how much would it cost to get food? There was obviously none stored from the harvest. There had been no harvest. All the food in the town would have had to be imported from somewhere else, and Felix could not imagine that prices were cheap.

'These men fought beastmen in the forest,' said Kat. 'All are wounded. Two are dire.'

'Well, bring them in, bring them in,' said the doctor, holding aside the tent flap. 'And we shall see what we can do.'

Felix, Gotrek, Ortwin and the less wounded guard carried in Sir Teobalt and the other guard and laid them on the bare floorboards. There were two makeshift cots at the back of the tent, but they were already occupied, one with a young woman and a baby, the other with a man with a bandage around his head – all asleep. The rest of the tent was hardly better furnished – a small iron stove and a barrel of water on one side, a table and stool on the other, and a chair in the centre with a little tray full of barber and dentistry tools next to it. A curtain hung half-open before the entrance to another room. Felix saw another cot in it.

Doktor Vinck dragged a surgeon's bag out from behind the stove and then examined Teobalt and the unconscious guard, tsking and murmuring as he pulled back Kat's crude bandages and poked and prodded. 'Broken arm. Broken leg. Lacerations. Sigmar, that's a nasty cut.'

Teobalt woke with a hiss as the doctor turned to him and manipulated his shoulder.

'Good evening, sir knight,' said Doktor Vinck. 'Sorry to wake you.'

The templar lay back and composed himself. 'Not at all,' he said. 'Pray continue.'

The doctor smiled. 'Thank you. May I have a look at your eyes? Very good. And if you could move your fingers? Excellent. Well, I shall have a busy night tonight, and no mistake.'

He turned to Felix and the others. 'My friends, we will start with this fellow here,' he said, pointing to the unconscious guard, who had horrible gashes on his chest and arms, and a leg that was bent at an unnatural angle. 'If you would be so kind as to hold his arms and legs while I wash his wounds and sew them up?'

Ortwin spluttered at this. 'My master is a knight, sir. You will attend to him first!'

Doktor Vinck glared at him as he dipped a bucket in the barrel of water. 'Your master has only bruises, minor cuts, a concussion and a dislocated shoulder. He will not die if he waits a while. This man will.'

'But–' began Ortwin.

'Obey the doctor, novitiate,' said Teobalt. 'We are in his domain here.'

Doktor Vinck bowed to the knight, then collected a bottle of vinegar from the table. 'There is no hierarchy here but the hierarchy of need, young sir. Now, if you wish your master to be seen to quickly, then you would do well to assist me with the first.'

Ortwin frowned stubbornly at this and muttered under his breath, but after watching for a while, gave in and joined the others as they helped the doctor with his surgery.

More than two hours later, Felix lay down with the others on the bare floor beside the patched-up men and tried to sleep. The surgery had been long and unpleasant, and in the end the guard that Doktor Vinck had tried to patch first had died. He had lost too much blood. They had put him outside on the wagon with the other bodies and concentrated on saving Sir Teobalt, and then patching the rest of them. Teobalt had survived, at least for now. His arm had been set back in its socket and bound tightly. His lacerations had been bandaged and the hideous bruises on his legs where the beastman had trod on him and crushed his armour had been bled with leeches and salved. Doktor Vinck also gave him a draught of 'elixir of poppy' to help his sleep. Felix noticed that the good doctor had a gulp of it himself before he retired to his room.

Felix wouldn't have minded a sip himself, for the floor was hard and cold, and his aches and cuts and bruises from the fight were less than comfortable. It made it hard to sleep. He shifted, hissing, then rolled over – and found Kat staring at him from her space beside him on the floor.

His heart thudded at the intensity of her stare. 'Uh, hello?' he said uncertainly.

'Where have you been, Felix?' she asked in a whisper. 'And why have you come back again?'

Felix let out a sigh, then chuckled. What a question. 'It's too late in the evening to tell you everywhere I've been, Kat. It's a long story. As to why I've come back to the Drakwald...' He paused, suddenly embarrassed. It sounded silly and old-fashioned to say it. 'I am on a quest,' he said at last, and waited for her to laugh, but she took it without even a smile. 'The sword I carry belongs to Sir Teobalt's knightly order. He has said that I can keep it if I help him find out what happened to his brother templars.'

'What was the name of the order?' Kat asked. 'I served as a scout during the fighting, and guided many knights north through the woods.'

'The Order of the Fiery Heart,' said Felix. 'Sir Teobalt told me he had word of them a month ago, defending a village near Fort Stangenschloss from beastmen.'

Kat nodded, her brow furrowing. 'I remember them, but from the beginning of the war. I did not see them or hear of them the last time I was at Stangenschloss.' She shrugged. 'They may have come and gone again while I was elsewhere. I am mostly in the woods.'

'When were you last there?' asked Felix.

'About two weeks ago,' she said. 'Since the end of the war I have made it my job to guide refugees from Stangenschloss to Bauholz, and supply trains from Bauholz to Stangenschloss.'

'How did you find us, then?' Felix asked, frowning. 'We weren't on your route.'

'There were rumours of beastmen near Bauholz, so I went hunting for them.' Her eyes glittered. 'That is my other job – my true job – finding the camps of the beastmen and leading the soldiers to them so that they can kill them all.'

Felix's eyes widened. He could think of no more dangerous profession. The girl was mad – valiant – but mad. 'That… that is very brave of you.'

'I only follow your example,' she said.

Felix groaned to himself. It was like Ortwin all over again! His was not a life to be emulated, particularly not by a petite young woman. He was about to say this when he saw she was yawning.

'Good night, Felix,' she said, closing her eyes.

'Good night, Kat,' he replied, but it took him a long time to go to sleep, and he looked over at her many times.

The next morning Felix woke so cold that he felt as if he were frozen to the floorboards. The others looked just as miserable – all except Gotrek, who might have been in Tilea in the summer for all the discomfort he showed.

Herr Reidle and the remaining guard went out as soon as they were up to try and find some horses and an escort to help them recover the barrels of beer they had left in the woods the night before, but Kat and Felix huddled around Doktor Vinck's little iron stove and stomped their feet to get their blood moving.

As the doctor made them all willow tea, which was all he had to give them, Sir Teobalt beckoned Felix and Gotrek to his cot, where Ortwin was sitting him up and bundling him with everyone else's blankets.

'Though it pains me, it seems I must stay here for some time until my shoulder heals,' Teobalt said in a tired voice. 'But I would not have the search for my brother templars wait with me. I bid you continue to look for them, and if you find them, return with them to me.'

'We will do our best, sir,' said Felix, though he had secretly hoped that, now that he was injured, the knight would declare the adventure over.

Teobalt inclined his head. 'My squire will accompany you to assist you.'

Felix paused at this. He didn't want to take Ortwin along. The boy was more likely to be a burden than an able assistant. His bright-eyed naïvety and his desperate longing for glory were a sure recipe for disaster, and Felix didn't want to have to keep an eye on him if things got rough. He had enough trouble looking after the Slayer.

'Sir,' he said at last. 'I thank you for your concern, but the search is likely to be hazardous, and I wouldn't like to endanger the life of your squire unnecessarily. The Slayer and I will be more effective on our own.'

The old knight's eyes flashed up at him, recovering something of their old fire. 'I am afraid I must insist, Herr Jaeger. Out of my sight, your enthusiasm for the vow you have made may wane. Ortwin shall be my eyes and ears, to see that you see the thing to its finish.'

Gotrek bristled at this. 'You doubt our honour? We have sworn.'

'You have done nothing yet to make me doubt it,' said Teobalt stiffly. 'But a man is entitled to ask for proof that a deed has been done. If you are truly honourable, you should have no objection to Ortwin's presence. Honesty fears no scrutiny, as the saying goes.'

Felix could see that Gotrek was going to make further objection. He couldn't let him. If they weren't careful the argument could get out of hand and Sir Teobalt could withdraw the quest – and Felix's chance to keep Karaghul.

'If you insist, Sir Teobalt,' Felix said. 'And if Ortwin is willing to take the risk, then we will take him.'

'I do insist,' said Teobalt. 'And I thank you for your acquiescence.'

Gotrek grunted unhappily, but then shrugged, resigned. Felix let out a relieved breath, but felt a pang of guilt as well. He had agreed to take the boy into danger just so he could get his sword back. That seemed a very callous thing to do. Of course, if Teobalt had forbidden them from searching for the templars, he would likely have sent Ortwin on the quest alone, so by bringing the squire along, Felix and Gotrek were actually protecting him. At least that's what Felix told himself.

They decided over their tea that the best course of action was to go back into Bauholz proper and ask the soldiers and southbound refugees there if any of them had heard news of the Order of the Fiery Heart. If they learned nothing, then tomorrow they would set off for Stangenschloss and enquire there.

At that, Kat said that if they could wait another day, she would guide them. 'I am to lead a supply train to the fort. They start the day after tomorrow, once one last supply boat from Ahlenhof arrives.'

Felix and Gotrek readily agreed. Neither of them was adept at navigating through deep woods.

Walking through the refugee camp on their way to the bridge to Bauholz, Felix could see that it was even worse than he had thought the night before. The inhabitants didn't just live in a garbage heap, they lived in garbage itself. Some of the shacks were made from broken carts, or stacks of broken barrels or crates. Some were no more than stained bedsheets draped over a line.

Even in the freezing cold, the smell was abominable, and ice-ringed latrine pits were everywhere. Felix saw men, women and children huddling around small fires, cooking rats and pigeons for their breakfasts. Others seemed to be eating leaves and brown grass. All of them had the near-death gauntness that Doktor Vinck had shown. He wondered how any of them were going to survive the winter.

Even as he thought it, he saw two men carrying a woman out of a tent. She was as stiff as a log, and frosted with ice. One of the men had tears frozen on his face.

Felix shivered, and not from the cold. The true horror of war was not the battlefield, no matter how bloody. It was the aftermath – the disease and famine and displacement that followed when a land was laid waste.

The knights did not suffer. They either died or went home to their plenty. The enemy did the same. It was the poor damned souls in whose fields the battles were fought that suffered, and not for days or weeks, but for years. He hated the iniquity of it.

As they neared the bridge, Kat sucked in a breath and slowed her steps.

Felix looked ahead. 'What's the matter?' he asked.

'Noseless Milo,' she said, pointing with her chin. 'He runs the refugee camp like Ludeker runs the village. He may want to make trouble.'

'Good,' said Gotrek. 'I could use a warm-up.'

Felix looked to where Kat had pointed. A group of men in tattered leather jerkins lounged against the end posts of the bridge, swords and clubs dangling from their belts, watching everybody that passed. The passers-by all hunched their shoulders and ducked their heads as they edged by the men, as if they were afraid they were going to be hit. The men grinned and called out to some. Others they tripped and laughed at. One pinched a young girl on the behind as she went by and giggled as she scurried away across the bridge like a frightened rabbit.

'Scum,' said Gotrek.

'Varlets,' said Ortwin.

'Aye,' agreed Felix. After seeing the misery and deprivation around him, he too was angry enough to want a fight, particularly with anyone who was making life more miserable for these people.

'Please don't fight them,' begged Kat. 'You will only make trouble for Doktor Vinck and the knight if you do. And me,' she added.

Gotrek looked up at her. 'Do these villains have some hold on you, little one?'

She shook her head. 'No. But I cannot live completely in the woods. Sometimes I have to come back here. And I won't be able to if...'

'Aye,' said Gotrek. 'I see.'

The biggest of the men looked up as they approached, and a snag-toothed smile snaked across his face. It was one of the ugliest faces Felix had seen that wasn't on a mutant. The man was balding, with piggy little eyes in a moon face, but his most distinguishing feature was one he didn't have. Just as Kat's name for him suggested, he had no nose. It looked like it had been torn off a long while ago, and he was left now with nothing but two vertical slits in his face and a bit of white cartilage that poked out above them, all surrounded by a puckered sphincter of scar tissue.

"Lo, Kat,' he said, in a pleasant, mocking voice, as his eyes trailed over Gotrek, Felix and Ortwin. 'Looking lovely as always. Who's yer friends?'

His men sidled forwards, grinning and blocking the way.

FIVE

'Let us pass, Milo,' said Kat, sticking out her chin. 'We don't want any trouble.'

'Come in last night, didn't they?' said Milo, ignoring her. 'Stayed with Herr Doktor.' He smiled at her look of alarm. 'You think I wouldn't know? I may not have a nose, but I got eyes everywhere.'

His men laughed at that. Felix noticed that none of them appeared to be starving.

Milo looked from Gotrek's glowering face, to the gold on his wrists, and finally to Felix. 'You and yer mates staying in town long, sir?'

'They're just travellers going up to Stangenschloss, Milo,' said Kat before Felix could answer. 'They're no concern of yours.'

Milo raised his eyebrows. 'Going to Stangenschloss at this time of year? Y'must be hearty men, then. Regular champions, I'll wager.'

'Leave them alone, Milo,' sighed Kat. 'They won't work for you.'

Milo scowled. 'Why don't y'let the gentlemen speak for themselves, Kat?'

'We're not looking for work,' said Felix stiffly.

'Oh come now, sir,' said Milo, smiling. 'Stangenschloss is a hard berth in the winter. Likely to be the death of ye, what with all them northers and beastmen running about. Why slog all the way up there when there's good money to be made right here for a man who can use his fists? Or a dwarf,' he added with a wink to Gotrek.

He shot a sly glance over his shoulder at the walled village just over the bridge. 'And promise of even more money very soon, ain't that right, lads?' He swivelled his ugly head back to Felix as his men laughed evilly. 'So, what do y'say, sir? Spend the winter in comfort in lovely old Bauholz?'

'We already have employment,' said Felix. 'Sorry. Now, please, step aside.'

An angry twitch flickered across Milo's face for the briefest second at this, but it was covered instantly by a shrug and a rueful smile. 'All right, all right, no harm in asking, is there? If y'change yer minds, Kat knows where to find me.'

He stepped aside and shooed his men back so that the bridge was clear, then winked at Kat as she, Gotrek, Felix and Ortwin passed between them. 'Bye now, beloved. And if y'get tired of freezing yer tail off at Herr Doktor's, remember I've always got a warm bed waiting for ye if ye want it.' He chuckled, low and dirty. 'And all the sausage y'can eat.'

Gotrek growled at that, and Felix's fists clenched. Ortwin's eyes blazed. They made to turn around, but Kat shook her head, and they kept walking. She let out a relieved breath as they reached the other side of the bridge and got out of earshot.

'He wouldn't be known as *nose*less Milo when I got through with him,' said Gotrek.

'Don't worry,' said Kat. 'I can take care of myself.'

'The villain,' said Ortwin, outraged. 'Hoarding sausage when all these poor souls are starving!'

Kat stifled a laugh. Felix blinked and almost said something, then let it go. Why dirty a pristine mind?

Instead he turned to Kat. 'What did he want to hire us for?'

Kat looked back over her shoulder. 'Milo wants to run all of Bauholz. He is trying to get enough men and arms together to drive out Ludeker and take over. He makes the same offer to every able-bodied man who comes through town.' She turned to Gotrek. 'Be careful, Gotrek. They were looking at your bracelets.'

Gotrek snorted. 'They can look all they want, little one.'

She grinned at that, and Felix saw lines appear at the corners of her eyes and mouth. He looked her over again, as if seeing her for the first time. He had been thinking of her as a young girl, and with her shyness and her small frame she had appeared so under the shadows of the forest last night. But in the morning sun he could see that she was no longer in the first blush of youth. She would be twenty-six or twenty-seven now, he calculated, and though they looked good on her, they had not been easy years.

They paid another eight pfennig foot tax to get back through Bauholz's village gate, and then they were inside, where everything was a bustle of soldiers and boatmen and wagons being loaded into Ludeker's warehouse.

Kat told Gotrek, Felix and Ortwin that she knew some people in the village who she could ask about the Templars of the Fiery Heart, and it would be better if she went alone. She suggested they ask around in the *Powder and Shot*, the tavern that had once been the Sigmarite temple. It was always full of soldiers, either coming north or going south. 'But watch out,' she said as they parted at the intersection. 'Ludeker's men will try to get money out of you any way they can. And they don't take no for an answer.'

Gotrek snorted again, and Felix smiled.

'Don't worry, Kat,' he said with a chuckle. 'We can take care of ourselves too.'

'Aye,' said Ortwin, puffing up his chest. 'We can take care of ourselves.'

Felix and Gotrek exchanged a private look at that.

'How much?' asked Gotrek, with a dangerous rasp to his voice.

'A shilling a mug, Herr dwarf,' said the barman.

Felix blinked as he fished in his belt pouch. 'Even the best dwarf beer in Altdorf only costs half that,' he said.

'Well, this ain't Altdorf, mein Herr,' said the barman, pouring two pints. 'Costs an arm and a leg to get it up here – sometimes literally. One of our suppliers was just in here, said he lost three men last night trying to bring a shipment in. Now he's hired a cart and some bullies to fetch it out of the woods. You know he's going to add that to the price.'

Felix reluctantly put three shillings down on the bar, and he and Gotrek and Ortwin drank deep from the mugs the barman set in front of them. Felix made a face. It was flat and thin, as if they'd been mixing it with water.

Gotrek choked and set the mug down like he'd found rat droppings in it. 'How much is the good beer?' he asked.

'That's the only beer there is, Herr dwarf,' said the barman.

Gotrek pushed the mug back towards the barman, stone-faced.

Felix did the same. 'We'll wait until Reidle brings the fresh barrels,' he said.

Ortwin kept drinking.

As they stepped away from the bar, two soldiers staggered past them and called for two beers. Felix shook his head as he heard the barman say, 'Here you are, gents. Already poured. I saw you coming. That'll be a shilling each.'

Gotrek and Felix surveyed the taproom. It still retained the shape of a temple of Sigmar, but trestle tables with little three-legged stools around them lined the nave, and the bar was where the altar had once been, with kegs lined up against the back wall, under the place where the golden hammer should have hung.

This early in the morning, the tavern wasn't terribly busy, only about a quarter full, with as many eating food as were drinking. Felix didn't like to think how much the food must cost if the beer was so expensive. He was glad they still had some of their road rations, or they would be broke before they left on the morrow.

On the left a crowd of young men in the colours of the town of Schmiedorf were talking animatedly amongst themselves as they drank and looked around with excited eyes. Beyond them were some river men, talking in low tones to a man in the same uniform as the men who had stopped Felix and the others at the gate the night before. He dismissed both groups. The soldiers were new recruits, just come north, and would have no information, and the river men would know of nothing north of Bauholz.

On the right side of the room was a more promising bunch. Spearmen of Wissenland practically asleep in their seats, with more scars and bandages among them than a Shallyan hospital. These men had been in the north. They might know.

Gotrek was already heading to them. Felix followed him, with Ortwin tailing behind. They sat down beside the weary men at one of the tables and Felix smiled at their sergeant, a red-headed man with only one ear.

'Heading home, sergeant?' he asked.

The sergeant nodded. 'Aye, sir, as soon as there's a space on a boat. Damned harbour master says it'll be a week.'

'Where were you fighting?' asked Ortwin eagerly. 'Did you kill many Kurgan?'

The soldiers turned dead eyes on him, staring in dull wonder.

'Aye,' said the sergeant. 'Plenty. From Middenheim to the Howling Hills. Chased 'em like hounds. Not that it made any difference. There was always more.'

His men murmured in agreement.

'Always more,' repeated one.

'Did you pass by Stangenschloss on your way here?' Felix asked.

The sergeant nodded. 'We was sent home from there. Service done. Pay coming. Go home and wait.'

'Did you by chance happen to see, or to hear of, a group of knights called the Order of the Fiery Heart on your travels?' Felix pressed. 'Their insignia is a heart with a halo of flame.'

The sergeant frowned and turned to his men. 'Any of you lot remember?'

They shrugged and muttered amongst themselves.

'Them jaggers at the Middenstag, was that them?'

'Nah, that were the Knights of the Silver Fist.'

'How about them fellows that got torn up by orcs in the hills?'

'I never heard their name, but they had a bird, didn't they?'

'Aye, a bird, not a heart.'

There was another minute of this, then the sergeant turned back to Felix. 'Sorry, mein Herr. Don't think we saw them.'

Felix shrugged. 'Thank you anyway, sergeant.'

He and Gotrek were just turning to survey the room for someone else to ask when a big man in a barman's apron appeared beside them. They looked up. The man was Milo's height, but thicker in the chest and the arms. He smiled at them.

'Get you gentlemen a drink?' he asked politely.

'No thank you,' said Felix, and continued to look about the room.

The man didn't move. 'Have to have a drink if you want to sit at a table,' he said. 'What can I get you?' He was a little less polite this time.

Gotrek glared up at him.

Felix grunted. 'We paid for drinks less than five minutes ago,' he said. 'We left them at the bar.'

'Still need a drink to sit at a table,' said the man.

'You don't have any drinks worth the name,' said Gotrek. 'Get lost.'

The Wissenland spearmen were starting to take an interest.

'We don't want a drink,' said Felix quickly, before the man could say anything that would make Gotrek stand up. 'We just want to sit here.'

'Then there's a table tax,' said the man. 'Two shillings an hour, paid in advance.'

'A table tax?' said Gotrek dangerously. 'What kind of man-nonsense is that?'

'We're a tavern, sir,' said the man. 'Not a refugee camp. Tables are reserved for paying customers.'

Felix looked around the room again. It was still only a quarter full. There was plenty of room to sit. 'What if we leave when you need these seats?'

The barman crossed his brawny arms. 'I'm not going to argue with you, sir. If you won't drink and won't pay, you'll have to leave.'

Gotrek stood. The man stepped back warily.

'Listen, you clot,' said the Slayer, advancing on him. 'I will pay for a beer when you bring me a beer that doesn't taste like you pissed it into a mouldy rain-barrel!'

Ortwin stared. Felix groaned. The Wissenland spears laughed and applauded.

'That's exactly what it tastes like!' said the sergeant.

'Get out,' said the barman, stepping back again. 'We'll have no violence here.'

'If you want me out,' said Gotrek, still advancing, 'throw me out.'

The barman hesitated, his fists balled at his sides, but then turned and hurried back behind the bar as the soldiers jeered at him. He whispered to the other barman, then disappeared into the back room.

The Wissenland men began to pound the table with their mugs. 'Real beer! Real beer!'

'Come on, manling,' said Gotrek, turning away. 'There are more to talk to.'

He started across the tavern towards a trio of young pistoliers who had been watching the whole episode with amused eyes. Though they were dressed in the latest Altdorf fashions, Felix could see that their boots and clothes were worn, and had been patched extensively – as had they themselves. One had a parting in his hair that had been made with an axe, and another had a hook for a left hand.

He saluted Gotrek with it idly as the Slayer and Felix and Ortwin sat down at their table. 'Well done, Herr dwarf!' he said in a noble accent. 'I've been wanting to express that particular opinion all week.'

'And I as well,' said his scalp-scarred companion. 'Damned busybodies won't give a man a moment's peace. 'Fill your cup, m'lord? Another beer, m'lord. Steal your wallet, m'lord?'

'Damned if I don't think they hold the boats on purpose so they can milk us for our last few crowns before we sail,' said Hook-hand. He smiled at them, then indicated his friends and himself. 'Abelhoff, Kholer, and von Weist. Now, to what do we have the pleasure?'

'You've come from the fighting?' asked Felix.

Von Weist laughed and held up his stump. 'I didn't get this playing euchre, my lad.'

Felix flushed, embarrassed, and a bit irked that a boy twenty years his junior was calling him 'my lad', then let it go. 'We were wondering if, during your travels, you met an order of knights known as the Templars of the Fiery Heart?'

The three pistoliers looked at each other, frowning, then the third, Kholer, who hadn't spoken yet, nodded. He did not appear to have suffered the kind of wounds his companions had, but there was a gravity about him that suggested that he had seen his share of horrors.

'Aye,' he said. 'We met them. They were at Stangenschloss when we came through, about a month ago. Not many of them left as I recall. Lost half their number at Middenheim and Sokh, their bugler told me.'

'Were they still there when you left, m'lords?' asked Ortwin eagerly.

Abelhoff, the one with the scarred scalp, shook his head. 'They got wind of a village on the edge of the Howling Hills being threatened by some great herd of beastmen and went out to defend it.' He shook his head. 'Mad of course. All templars are. Took no support. No foot troops–'

Ortwin stood up hotly at this. 'I am a novitiate of the order, sir. We are not mad!'

'Easy, lad, easy,' said von Weist. 'No offence meant. We'd have been with 'em like a shot if we weren't all returned to store for want of parts.' He grinned like a cat. 'That kind of madness is our bread and butter.'

'And they didn't return?' asked Felix.

Kholer shook his head. 'Not before we continued south. Haven't heard what became of them. Sorry.'

Felix nodded. It looked like a trip to Stangenschloss was inevitable.

'I say,' said von Weist, turning to Gotrek. 'You're a Trollslayer, aren't you?'

Gotrek looked at him with his single eye. 'And if I am?'

Von Weist smiled. 'Oh, nothing. Just an interesting coincidence, that's all. We saw three of your sort at Stangenschloss.' He laughed. 'They were mad too!'

'Aye,' said Abelhoff. 'Fiery fellows. Fight you as soon as look at you.'

'Except the one with the nails in his head,' said von Weist. 'He just drank, mostly.'

Felix and Gotrek both looked up at that.

'Nails in his head?' asked Felix.

Von Weist held up his stump. 'I swear to you it's true. He wore them like Herr Slayer here wears his crest.'

Gotrek and Felix looked at each other, then Felix leaned forwards to question the pistoliers further, but just then there was a commotion in the street and a handful of men ran into the tavern.

Felix, Gotrek and Ortwin looked up with everyone else. Standing inside the door were a half-dozen men in the uniform of Ludeker's men, and with them stood the burly barman who Gotrek had menaced.

'There!' he said, pointing directly at Gotrek. 'Those are the ones! They threatened me and didn't pay the table tax.'

The leader of the guards nodded and swaggered forwards, his men spreading out behind him. He was a big man, with a bulging belly that spoke of three meals a day, with an occasional snack in between. In a starving town like Bauholz, Felix found that obscene.

'These tables are reserved for drinkers, lads,' he said. 'Buy a beer or go.'

His men began to surround them.

'We bought a beer,' said Felix.

'And it wasn't a beer,' said Gotrek.

'You'll have to buy another,' said the guard. 'And while you're digging in your purses, there's a fine for disturbing the peace. Two shillings each.'

He held out his hand.

Gotrek growled in his throat.

Felix and Ortwin shot him a nervous glance.

'Easy, Gotrek,' said Felix. 'We can't make trouble. We've got to stay here another day, and I want to talk to more people about the templars.'

'Then get him away from me,' said Gotrek.

Felix turned to the leader of the guards and opened his belt pouch. 'All right, we'll pay. Four shillings for the fine, and two for two more "beers".'

'It's six shillings for the fine, mein herr,' said the guard.

Felix frowned. 'You said two each.'

The guard pointed a stubby finger at Ortwin. 'Ain't he with you?'

'But he didn't do anything. It was only us.'

'Still a member of your party,' said the guard.

Gotrek stood and faced the guard. 'Take the four shillings and get out, before I throw you out.'

The guard stepped back. His men laid their hands on their truncheons.

'Threatening an officer of the law,' said the guard. 'That's an eight shilling fine.'

'And he's got a naked blade, sir,' said one of his men, pointing to the axe on Gotrek's back.

'Why, so he does,' said the leader. 'That's five shillings.'

Gotrek took a step forwards. 'I'll feed you your five shillings at the end of my–'

'Gotrek!' yelped Felix.

'Threatening again!' cried the guard, backing away. 'The fine's doubled for the second offence. Sixteen shillings! That's… that's…'

'One crown, fifteen shillings total,' said his man helpfully.

'Gotrek, don't,' said Felix as the Slayer raised his fist. 'I'll pay. We can't afford trouble. We…'

He paused as he heard the *shing* of drawn steel beside him. Everybody turned.

Ortwin stood with his sword drawn, glaring at the leader of the guards. 'You are dishonourable men!' he said in his high, clear voice. 'These are not the honest laws of the Empire, and you have no right to enforce–'

One of the guards clubbed him from behind and he fell forwards, his blade gouging the leader of the guards in the leg as he slumped to the ground.

'Committing violence upon an officer of the law!' roared the leader. 'Get them!'

His men charged in from all sides, clubs swinging. Gotrek blocked with his forearms as Felix ducked and snatched up a stool and the three pistoliers scattered away.

'Sorry, lads,' called von Weist. 'Not our fight.'

'Good luck to you!' cried Abelhoff.

Felix parried a club with his stool and kicked a guard in the knee. Gotrek buried his fist up to the wrist in the leader's soft belly, then swung at two more guards as the fat man crashed to the floor, puking. Felix cracked another guard on the helmet with his stool, then turned as a cudgel across the shoulders staggered him. One of the guards stood on the table, raising his arm for another strike.

Felix kicked the edge of the table and the man stumbled forwards. Felix swatted him with the stool as he fell. Gotrek shoved a guard into a stone pillar, then threw another over his shoulder, sending him crashing through another table.

In less than a minute Gotrek and Felix stood panting in the centre of a ring of bruised and fallen men, all groaning and holding various parts of their anatomies. The room burst out into spontaneous applause. The Wissenland spear company whistled and stomped their feet. The pistoliers clapped politely.

'Good show!' cried von Weist.

But before the cheering had died away, another crowd of guards had run through the door – a score at least – all breathing hard and with weapons drawn. At their head was a trim, compact man with a head that thrust forwards like a crow's. He wore a captain's uniform, and four pistols and an expensive rapier at his belt.

'What's all this?' he said, with a voice like a file scraping rusty iron.

SIX

The burly barman hurried out from behind the bar. 'Captain Ludeker! These men–'

'Never mind, Geert,' said Ludeker, his sharp eyes fixing on Gotrek and Felix. 'I see what they've done.' He stepped forwards, his hands behind his back, shaking his head as soldiers and curious citizens of Bauholz began to edge into the tavern to see what was going on.

'Disturbing the peace,' said Ludeker. 'Destroying private property. Drawing a sword within the boundaries of the town. Resisting arrest. Striking officers of the law. Damaging the uniforms and equipment of officers of the law.' He smiled darkly as he stopped in front of Gotrek and Felix. 'Such barbaric behaviour cannot go unpunished. Fifteen days in the strong house, and a fine of…' His eyes slanted to Gotrek's gold bracelets. 'Of twenty gold crowns, or the equivalent.'

Gotrek laughed, harsh and loud. He beckoned Ludeker forwards with a massive hand. 'Come and take it.'

Ludeker drew two of his pistols and aimed them both at the Slayer. 'You're making it worse for yourself, dwarf. Thirty crowns.'

Felix sneered. 'You're not an officer of the law,' he said. 'You're a thief in uniform.'

Ludeker turned one of the pistols towards Felix. 'Forty crowns. Do you want to go higher?'

Just then there was a commotion in the crowd and Kat pushed through to the front, her eyes wide.

'Felix! Gotrek! What happened?' she gasped.

Ludeker glanced at her. 'Take her too,' he said. 'She's the one who brought these troublemakers.'

Felix knew he shouldn't. He knew that the best thing to do was to try to talk their way out of the situation – to bargain with Ludeker, or find a way to buy some breathing room, but somehow he just couldn't help himself. He threw the stool at Ludeker's head.

Ludeker ducked and fired convulsively, his shots going wild.

Gotrek roared a laugh and charged. Felix was right behind him.

Ludeker scrambled back, tossing aside his spent guns and grabbing for the other two. 'Get them! Kill them!' he bellowed.

Gotrek knocked the captain's front teeth out and sent him skidding across the stone floor on his back.

There was a moment of shocked silence as the guards stared at the unmoving body of their leader, then they swarmed in, screaming, holding swords in their hands this time, not cudgels.

Gotrek pulled his axe from his back and swept it at the oncoming men. Felix ripped Karaghul from its scabbard and flashed it around him in a wide arc.

'Stay back!' he shouted. 'Do you want to die for this stupidity?'

They didn't listen. Felix parried and kicked and dodged as the guards mobbed him. Behind him he heard screams and shearing steel and snapping limbs as Gotrek went to work. Felix stabbed a man in the chest and elbowed another in the nose. A third man was coming up fast on his right. Then he fell, and Felix saw Kat standing behind him, holding a crimsoned hand-axe.

Surrounded by a distant wall of mesmerised onlookers, Felix, Gotrek and Kat fought in a whirlwind of Ludeker's men – kicking, swiping, ducking and lunging. Felix took a cut on the back and gave back a gash across the brow. Kat tripped a man and cut off the fingers of his sword hand. Gotrek took off the legs of another man with one swipe.

That was the end of it. The guards had expected a one-sided slaughter, but hadn't thought they would be on the receiving end. Those who could still run ran, shoving through the crowd to escape the terror of Gotrek's bloody axe. Those who couldn't run crawled away, weeping and begging for mercy.

'Blatth you, dwaafff!' lisped a hoarse voice.

Felix and Gotrek turned to see Ludeker, his four front teeth missing, aiming his second pair of pistols at them. Gotrek hurled his axe just as Ludeker fired.

Sparks flashed off the spinning axe and one of bullets ricocheted past Felix's ear, while another shattered a mug behind Gotrek. Ludeker was punched off his feet as the rune weapon caught him in the face and slammed him into the wall, his head split in two halves from crown to chin. He slid down the wall, his guns dropping from his slack hands, and slumped to the ground. Blood pumped from around the edges of the axe like a fountain and poured down Ludeker's neck, turning his uniform from grey to red.

The room was silent for a long moment. People were staring and backing away. Ortwin was sitting up and blinking around at the half-dozen corpses, bafflement and horror in his eyes. Felix felt like the squire looked. His stomach roiled with sudden nausea. No matter how corrupt, these had been Empire men. They had no doubt fought Archaon's hordes. It shouldn't have come to this.

Kat stumbled to him and clutched his arm. 'We'd better go,' she said, glancing towards the door. 'The others will be back before long, and with guns.' She shook her head as she watched Gotrek pull his axe from Ludeker's face. 'Can't wait two days any more. We'll have to leave for Stangenschloss right away.'

'Aye,' said Gotrek. 'I was sick of the place anyway.'

'How did this happen?' murmured Ortwin.

'Just go,' said Felix.

He steered the boy towards the door. Gotrek and Kat went with them. The crowd parted silently before them, frightened. Even the three pistoliers eyed them askance as they passed.

Felix was glad to have the air in his face as they stepped out onto the street, even if it was cold enough to freeze his snot.

As they were running across the bridge to the refugee camp, they came upon Noseless Milo and his gang trotting the other way, all armed to the teeth. The big bandit gave them a grin and a jaunty salute. 'Hear I owe you lads a favour,' he said. 'Ta.'

His men laughed at that.

As they ran on, Milo turned and called after them. 'Herr Doktor's house will be mine now, Kat! A warm bed and a warm fire any time you want it!'

Kat curled her lip, not bothering to look back. 'He should give it back to the doctor,' she muttered.

'Ludeker's dead?' asked Doktor Vinck, shocked. He was giving a shave to a man in the uniform of the Talabheim city guard, and almost nicked his ear.

'Yes, doctor,' said Kat, angrily stuffing her belongings into her pack. 'But we didn't start it. He tried to kill Felix and Gotrek.'

'It was my fault,' said Ortwin, hanging his head where he knelt beside Sir Teobalt. 'Had I not drawn my sword, things might not have come to such a pass.'

Felix, off to one side tying up his bedroll, wished he could have told the boy it wasn't true, but really, it was. If the squire hadn't drawn steel, they might have got out of that tavern for a few shillings.

'My dear boy,' Vinck said, returning to the task at hand with renewed vigour. 'Don't apologise. I would rather Ludeker had faced the hangman's noose after a lawful trial, but he was a cancer upon the heart of this town that has sorely needed excising, and I am not sad to hear of his passing.'

'Milo is already trying to pick up the reins,' said Kat sadly, then looked up, eyes hard, as a thought occurred to her. 'And he might come looking for us afterwards. He might be worried we'll do the same to him.'

Sir Teobalt struggled up onto one elbow, wincing. 'You must leave the village with the others, young Ortwin, and quickly. Go north to Stangenschloss in my name and pursue these rumours you have heard. Perhaps, when you send word to me, I will be well enough to join you.'

'But we must take you with us!' said Ortwin. 'They may try to hurt you when they cannot find us.'

'He cannot be moved,' said Doktor Vinck. 'He must have rest.'

'I see no reason why they would try to hurt me,' said Teobalt. 'And even if they do, my life is not as important as the recovery of the order's regalia. I have said I would recover it or die in the attempt. The danger means nothing to me.'

Gotrek grunted approvingly.

Felix stood and shouldered his pack. 'We better go, then.'

Kat stood too. Her pack and bow were slung across her back. 'Aye,' she said.

'May Taal watch over you,' said Doktor Vinck.

'And Sigmar guide your path,' said Sir Teobalt.

Ortwin bowed low over Sir Teobalt's hand. 'I will not fail you, sir,' he said, then he turned and joined Felix and the others as they ducked through the tent flap and out into the cold white day.

It had begun to snow.

Felix found himself in a black mood as he and the others tramped north along the banks of the Zufuhr and deeper into the Drakwald. As the lazy snowflakes settled on his eyelashes and melted into his red Sudenland wool cloak, his mind turned sourly to the infinite corruptibility of man.

He had sensed no taint of Chaos in Bauholz, had seen nothing that reeked of cult activity, had found no vile altars or eldritch symbols daubed on the walls, and yet it was as foul a pit of villainy as any he had ever seen. Why was it that the corrupt were always strong and the good always weak? Why did the Ludekers and Noseless Milos of the world flourish while good men like Doktor Vinck were crushed and killed and shoved aside?

Felix sighed. He knew the answer, and it depressed him. It was because the good and strong went forth to battle the forces of darkness and died to defend mankind while the cowardly stayed at home and preyed on the weak who were left behind. In that way the corruption of Bauholz *was* the fault of Chaos, for though the vile forces of the Dark Gods had not reached the village, those that would have protected it against corruption from within had gone north and not come back, leaving it defenceless against the depredations of purely human predators who saw opportunity where others saw tragedy.

He wondered if perhaps greed was the unacknowledged fifth god of Chaos – some gold-skinned brother to lust, madness, disease and hate. Certainly greed seemed to do as much evil as the others, seducing men and women to steal from their brothers and sisters, to grind down those weaker than themselves, driving them into mad schemes and desperate gambles, birthing robbery, kidnapping, blackmail and murder.

But perhaps not. The fault might lie within the nature of man himself, for though the greed of the dwarfs was proverbial, Felix had never seen one so degraded by it that he would stoop to murdering one of his own to satisfy his lust for gold. The dwarfs might indulge in sharp dealing, or take advantage of outsiders, but dwarf thieves and murderers were rare, and kidnappers and blackmailers were, as far as he knew, unheard of. It was man – weak-willed, frightened and desperate – that made blood sacrifices to greed, and swore terrible oaths at its glittering altar.

His thoughts flew back again to his father, who, though he'd had a successful business in legitimate trade, and who had more money than he could have spent in two lifetimes, had still felt compelled to consort with smugglers and pirates, and to deal in forbidden books, because he must have more! And Felix's brother Otto looked set to follow his father's example. When Felix had shown him the letter that proved Gustav's crimes, Otto had been more concerned with losing the family business than restoring the family honour.

All his brooding left him with the glum belief that mankind would finally be dragged down into the pit, not by the gods of Chaos, but by its own frail, fallible nature, and that no amount of heroic victories over the marauders and the orcs and the skaven would save it from its self-inflicted demise.

Of course, that didn't mean one stopped fighting them – particularly not those scheming lurkers in the shadows, the skaven. His hand gripped his sword hilt hard as he thought again of what they had done to his father. Revenge would be sweet when he finally–

'Go carefully here, Felix,' said Kat.

Felix looked up, blinking. He had been following behind her blindly, lost in his thoughts, and hadn't been looking where he was going. They had come to a high-banked stream which fed into the Zufuhr. Someone had laid a log across the stream as a crude bridge, but the bark was glassy with ice and covered with a dusting of powdery snow. A false step and he might have plunged into the stream – not wise in weather like this. Being wet in freezing weather was a more certain death than a fight with beastmen.

'Thank you, Kat,' he said, as he picked his way across the log.

Gotrek followed onto the log behind him, stumping along without pause as if he were on solid ground. Ortwin came more hesitantly, but with a little tottering and arm-flapping he was across too, then Kat bounded effortlessly across like a, well, like a cat, and they were on their way again.

Felix looked at her as she took the lead again. She moved down the nearly non-existent path with perfect confidence and grace, her stride light and her head turning to one side and the other as she listened to the forest, her posture relaxed yet ready – a complete contrast to how she had been in Bauholz. There she had been nervous and ill at ease, afraid of Ludeker and Milo, uncertain how to deal with the people she spoke to. All the strength and calm she had shown in the battle with the beastmen had disappeared when they had approached the village gates – now it was back again.

Felix quickened his steps and caught up to her. 'Er, Kat,' he said.

She looked up. 'Yes, Felix?'

'How did you come to this?' he asked. 'Your profession, I mean. My last memory of you is seeing you and the old forester – I forget his name – waving goodbye to us as we left Flensburg for Nuln.'

'Papa,' she said, nodding. 'Herr Messner.' Then she smirked at him. 'I was mad at you when you went away. I wanted to go with you.'

Felix smiled. 'I remember.'

'It just seemed natural to me,' she said. 'Leaving with you, I mean. You saved my life. I saved yours. We'd killed that… that woman together.' She shivered. 'I didn't want to stay in another village. I'd felt safer travelling in the woods with you than when the beasts came to Kleindorf. There was somewhere to run in the woods. There was somewhere to hide.'

Felix paused, uncomfortable at the mention of the woman – the strange, beautiful champion of Chaos who had led the beasts during their pillaging of the two towns – who looked so much like the girl he walked beside now. 'That woman,' he said. 'I… Did anyone ever tell you about her? About who she was?'

Kat's eyes narrowed. 'You mean that she was my mother?'

Felix let out a relieved breath. He hadn't been sure he could have told her even now. He was glad she already knew. 'Messner told you?'

She shook her head. 'I figured it out.' She tugged out the long lock of white hair that grew among her dirty black tresses. 'My witch-lock.' She snorted and pulled off her stocking cap, then smoothed the lock back down and put it back on. 'I don't care about her. Herr Messner and his family were my real family – Magda and Hob and Gus. I'm Katerina Messner now.'

Felix chuckled. 'Ah. So you liked living with them after all.'

Kat nodded, her eyes faraway. 'I loved them. Herr Messner – well, at first he and Magda tried to get me to learn the things that other little girls learned, cooking, sewing, mending, but... I didn't like those things. I wanted to do what Hob and Gus did. I wanted to go out with Herr Messner and learn how to shoot rabbits, and follow trails, and kill beastmen.'

Felix looked at her. A hardness had come into her voice.

'They thought it was because of what I had seen in Kleindorf, and in the raid on Flensburg, and they hoped that I would forget it in time.' She gave a sad smile. 'It *was* because of that, because I never wanted to let anything like that ever happen again.' She shrugged. 'But I didn't forget it. It never left me. And when Herr Messner realised that I wouldn't change, he didn't try to turn me away from it any more. He took me out with Hob and Gus and taught me everything he knew.'

'He seems to have taught you well,' Felix said.

'Aye,' she said. 'He was a good man.'

Felix paused at the past tense. 'He's... he's dead, then?' asked Felix.

'Aye,' said Kat, her voice suddenly dull. 'They all are.'

Felix's eyes widened. 'All of them?'

Kat sighed. 'Flensburg was destroyed by beastmen, another great herd. There were just too many.'

'How terrible,' said Felix. 'Was this during the invasion?'

Kat shook her head. 'No. Long ago. I was seventeen. I was already part of the duke's rangers by then, and was out on a long patrol when it happened.' She hung her head. 'I should have been there.'

Felix opened his mouth, about to say something trite like, 'There was nothing you could have done,' then closed it again. No one was ever really comforted by that. 'I'm sorry,' he said instead.

She shrugged. 'After that I quit the rangers and went out on my own.'

'Why?' asked Felix.

'The rangers are good at what they do,' said Kat. 'But they have their duties. They must visit such-and-such a town once a month, and that town and then the next town. They must keep the roads clear and report bandits and catch outlaws. I only wanted to hunt beastmen.' She bared her teeth. 'So many times I would find a hoof print trail and want to follow it to the beasts' camp, but the patrol had to move on and I couldn't.'

She looked up at Felix. 'I wanted to be able to track them wherever they went, whether on the duke's land or not, and for however long it took. I was sure that was the only way to really get rid of them. You couldn't just kill a hunting party here and a warband there, you needed to find their secret places, where they lived, and bred, and destroy them utterly with fire and sword!'

Felix blinked, unnerved at her sudden fury. 'Er, yes,' he said.

'The first herd I tracked down was the one which had killed Papa and Mama and my brothers. I lived in the woods for months while I followed them. Never went near a town or a road until finally I found the camp and worked out a way that an army could surround it so that none of them could escape. Then I went to Magnusdorp, which was the nearest castle, and showed the lord my maps.' She glowered at a memory. 'He laughed at me. He didn't believe me. He didn't think a little girl could have found such a place.'

'Well,' said Felix carefully. 'You can't really blame him for that. You're a bit of an exception to the rule.'

Kat sniffed, dismissive. 'So I snuck back to the camp and cut off the head of a gor, then brought it back to him.'

'A gor?' Felix asked, confused.

'A beastman,' she said. 'The big ones, with the heads and legs of beasts, are called gors. The smaller, more human ones, are called ungors.'

Felix nodded. 'All these years fighting them and I didn't know. Sorry. Go on. You brought the head of one of the beasts back to the lord of Magnusdorp?'

'Aye.' She grinned, showing a lot of teeth. 'He listened to me then.' Her eyes grew dreamy and faraway, as if she were talking about attending a dance. 'His men wiped out the herd entirely. Their herdstone was crushed to dust.'

Felix swallowed. Kat was as driven as a Slayer. It was a bit intimidating. 'So, uh, you've been tracking beastmen ever since?' he asked.

Kat nodded. 'Until Archaon's invasion. Then I thought it would be better if I helped the soldiers.' She straightened proudly. 'I was a scout for Count von Raukov from Wolfenburg all the way to Middenheim, spying on the hordes, scouring the woods during the retreat, bringing the army information on enemy positions.' She laughed. 'There were times when I was so close to the Kurgan that I could have patted them on the head, but they never found me.'

Felix shook his head. The girl didn't seem to know any fear at all – at least while she was in the woods.

She frowned again. 'I will go back to hunting beasts soon, but right now there are still too many people in the Drakwald who shouldn't be here – all these refugees and soldiers trying to get home. I will guide them until they are gone, then I will return to my true purpose.'

Felix swallowed, suddenly emotional, his depression at the sorry state of mankind lightening. Here was the counter to the greed and the corruption that had sickened him in Bauholz – the selflessness of a girl whose only thought was to help people return home and make the world a safer place. 'You are doing great work, Kat,' he said at last.

She blushed and tucked her nose down into her scarf. 'I am doing what I can.'

After they had walked a little while in silence, Felix spoke again. 'Is Bauholz your home now, then?' he asked. 'Do you live with Doktor Vinck?'

She shook her head. 'I haven't lived in a town since... since Flensburg was destroyed,' she said. 'I go to Bauholz and to other towns for supplies, but I live here.' She waved a hand around at the forest. 'This is my home.'

And welcome to it, thought Felix, staring around uneasily at the thick wall of trees on either side of the path.

'Doktor Vinck sewed me up a few years ago when a beastman gored me with its horns,' she continued. 'I would have died without his help, so I always try to look after him, and Bauholz.' She snorted bitterly, a great cloud of steam rising before her face. 'I wish I had dealt with Ludeker as I deal with the beasts.' She spat. 'I *should* have, but Herr Doktor said there are laws, and that the law should deal with him.' She looked back at the Slayer with a sly smile. 'I'm glad Gotrek thought otherwise.'

For five days Felix, Gotrek, Kat and Ortwin continued north and west through the deep forest, marching at a slow but steady pace. Their rate of travel was helped because the path they were on was the route by which supplies and reinforcements were brought to Fort Stangenschloss, and was therefore relatively clear and well maintained. Had they been travelling in any other direction, they might have measured their day's travel in yards rather than miles, for the forest to either side of the path was an almost impenetrable undergrowth of brambles and intertwined tree roots.

Ease of travel, however, was countered by the fact that such a well-marked path was a target, watched by those who would prey upon those who used it. This had been why Kat had wanted to join the supply train that was to have left Bauholz two days after their arrival. A well-manned, well-guarded convoy would be a less attractive target than four travellers on foot. Twice in those five days she had asked them to wait, then disappeared into the woods in order to investigate further along the trail. The first time it had been bandits, waiting in the brush at a place where the path dipped down to go through a swift stream. The second time it had been mutants, hiding in overhanging trees for the unwary.

Both times, Gotrek had wanted to go fight the ambushers, and Ortwin had concurred, and both times it had fallen to Kat and Felix to discourage them. Felix reminded them that Sir Teobalt had charged them with finding the lost templars, not to fight random villains on the road. Kat had reminded them that Doktor Vinck was days behind them and the fort days ahead of them, and that even if they were victorious they would undoubtedly incur wounds that they might die from before they reached help.

Gotrek and Ortwin had reluctantly bowed to this combination of duty and cold logic, and had allowed Kat to lead them into the woods and around the ambushes, and they had escaped undetected.

At night, they made camp just off the path, hidden from it by a screen of brush. Kat always stopped before the sun went down, so that by the time it got dark their fire would have died down and the pulsing embers could warm them without bright flames giving away their position. As Felix, Gotrek and Ortwin made up their bedrolls and gathered firewood,

Kat would vanish into the trees and return a half-hour later with rabbits or pheasants or a fox, each shot neatly through the skull with a steel-tipped arrow. These she would skin and gut with practiced precision and cook over the fire. They never went hungry.

On the night of the second day, the falling snow grew heavier, and they woke up the next morning with their bedrolls covered in two inches of dry powder, but with blue skies overhead. This distressed Kat, and not because it would slow them – the build-up was hardly enough to cover Felix's boots.

'We will leave tracks that will be easy to follow,' she said. 'It would be better if the snow continued, so it would cover them again.'

Later that day, they came to a place where the forest had been burned and saw signs that some great battle had occurred in the midst of the charred trees. Under the thin cover of snow, the ground was burned black, and ash-covered bones and dented, soot-blackened armour littered it like broken teeth.

Felix, Gotrek and Ortwin stared at the devastation.

'What happened here?' asked Ortwin, stunned.

Kat spat. 'This was the path of the army of Strykaar, one of Archaon's lieutenants. They say there were more than five thousand in his train.' She indicated the burned area with a sweep of her arm. 'Men from Stangenschloss met them here. They waited in ambush – archers and spearmen and men-at-arms. They wanted to strike and retreat into the woods, then continue to harry the marauders' line as they moved west.' She shook her head sadly. 'But Strykaar had things of Chaos with him, whispery things that could move through the woods like wind, dogs with skin like red scales, flying things. The men's first attack was their last. They could not retreat far enough or fast enough. They were hunted down and killed like vermin. Only a few made it back to Stangenschloss to tell the tale.'

Felix shivered as he pictured desperate men scrambling through the thick wood, running from silent, loping shadows.

'But their deaths were not in vain,' Kat continued as they started across the ugly burn. 'Their attack killed many of Strykaar's champions, and slowed his advance, giving Middenheim and the forts further east more time to prepare.'

Gotrek cursed and kicked the distorted skull of a dead Kurgan. 'Another worthy doom missed,' he muttered as it bounced across the snow. 'Damned weak-willed Kurgan. They couldn't have held on another two months.'

For the rest of the day the Slayer was in a foul mood, cursing under his breath and speaking to no one.

* * *

Just after noon on the fourth day, they found the remains of a much more recent fight.

Kat, as usual, was scouting far out in front, and saw it first. Felix saw her go on guard, crouching and drawing her axes from her belt, then creep forwards steadily around a bend in the path.

'On guard, manling,' said Gotrek, and pulled his axe from his back.

Felix and Ortwin drew too, and they all moved quickly ahead, staring and listening all around them. As they came around the bend they saw what Kat had found.

She stood looking down at the ground beside a twisted line of smashed wagons, some of which had been tipped on their sides, all of them missing their horses and the supplies they had carried. As Felix got closer he saw that there were bodies lying by the carts, each covered in a thin white blanket of snow. Broken spears and bent swords littered the ground, and arrows stuck from the surrounding trees. But Kat was looking at none of it, only staring at a body at her feet – a middle-aged man in the colours of Averland.

'You know him?' asked Felix, approaching her.

'He was my friend,' she said, nodding listlessly. 'Sergeant Neff. He was a quartermaster for Stangenschloss. They left Bauholz a few days before you arrived.'

Sergeant Neff's left arm lay a few feet from the rest of him, and both he and it had been partially eaten by some forest predator. His face hadn't been touched, however, and looked up at Felix from under a cap of snow with an accusatory stare.

'I'm sorry,' said Felix.

Kat shrugged. 'It's what happens in the Drakwald,' she said. But as she turned away, Felix could see tears glittering on her cheeks.

'Did beastmen do this?' asked Ortwin, looking angrily around at the white-cloaked carnage.

'Kurgan,' said Gotrek. He held up a horned helmet that had a sword cut through it.

Felix swallowed and looked around at the woods at the mention of the northmen. Even in the middle of the day the shadows beneath the trees were impenetrable, and they might hide anything. He shivered as he imagined the mad red eyes of crazed barbarians staring at him from their depths. It took an effort of will to turn away from the trees and return his attention to the wagons.

As he walked around them, he counted seven bodies. It didn't seem enough. 'How many men guard these convoys?' he asked.

'Twenty, and two ostlers for each wagon,' said Kat.

'Then where are they?' asked Felix.

'Taken,' said Kat. 'For slaves.'

'Your friend was lucky, then,' said Gotrek.

Kat shuddered. 'Aye.'

'Do we go after them?' asked Ortwin.

Kat shook her head. 'This happened before it snowed, three days ago. They could be fifty miles from here, and the snow will have covered their trail.' She sighed and turned north again. 'I only hope someone got away to warn the fort.'

'Shouldn't we at least bury them?' asked Ortwin, as Kat started away from them. 'It goes against Morr's law to leave them here for the wolves.'

Kat turned on him, eyes dark. 'There is no time for things like that here. The ground is too frozen to dig, and we have too far to go.'

Ortwin looked for a moment like he was going to protest again, but then finally joined Gotrek and Felix as they followed the heavily bundled little figure north again.

The rest of the day passed without incident, and they made camp as usual just a few paces off the trail, collecting firewood and starting a fire as the light of the day began to turn from gold to red. A little while later, Kat brought them two squirrels, a rabbit and a pigeon, and set to cleaning and skinning them.

'Another day to Stangenschloss,' she said as she flensed the fur from the rabbit with quick, deft strokes of her hunting knife. She was always careful with these, because she sold the pelts of every one she ate. 'I wish I wasn't bringing bad news.'

'Another day still?' asked Ortwin. He looked around at the encroaching forest. 'I would have thought we'd have been in the Chaos Wastes by now.'

'That's because you've never left Altdorf,' said Felix with a smile.

'That's not true!' said Ortwin. 'I went to Carroburg once.'

Felix chuckled at that, but just then Gotrek rose from his seat and held up a hand.

'Quiet,' he said.

Everyone froze and looked around. Felix strained his ears. At first he heard nothing but the usual sounds of the forest – the crackling of the fire, the wind in the branches, the cries of wild animals in the distance. But then he heard it – a clash of steel, very faint, then another, and then an angry cry.

'Fighting,' said Ortwin.

'North and east,' said Kat. 'Deeper in the woods.'

'Shut up!' growled Gotrek.

They listened again. More clashes and clangs, then a howl of pain and a hoarse roar of triumph.

Gotrek pulled his axe off his back and turned in the direction of the sounds. 'That was a dwarf,' he said.

'Follow me,' said Kat, drawing her bow and diving into the woods.

Gotrek and Ortwin were right behind her. Felix snatched a burning branch from the fire for a torch, then hurried after them.

Running through the untamed forest was nothing like walking along the trail. The ground was a lumpy tangle of roots, creepers and dead branches that caught their feet and tripped them constantly. Thick undergrowth grew shoulder-high in places, but Kat led them unerringly around the worst of it, and they never had to stop or turn back. Still, thorns and nettles caught at them like claws and branches whipped their faces. The light of Felix's makeshift torch was almost more disorientating than it was helpful, for its bobbing, flickering light caused the shadows to dance, making it seem that the trees were looming out at them and jumping in their way.

Creatures of the night skittered away from them, screeching and yipping. An owl shot up in front of Felix, wings battering him as it tried to get away – and behind the crashing and thudding of their passage, still the ring and roar of distant battle.

Kat danced through it all without a mis-step, as if she had run this exact path a thousand times and knew every inch of it by heart. The others were not so nimble. Ortwin put a foot wrong and staggered to the side, slamming into a tree. He recovered and hurried on, weaving slightly. Felix jolted down into a hidden hollow, snapping his teeth shut and putting his foot into freezing mud. Gotrek hacked through the underbrush with his axe, clearing away great masses of black vines and leafless shrubs and shouldering on implacably.

Seconds later they could see an orange glow ahead, segmented by the vertical black bars of trees – a fire. They pounded on, and with each tree they passed, the light got brighter and the noise of battle louder, until, after dodging around the trunk of an ancient oak, Felix could see naked flames and surging shadows in a clearing up ahead, and make out individual voices in the torrent of sound.

'Stay together, curse you!' bawled an Empire voice. 'Hold your line!'

'Down here, you painted ape!' rasped a dwarf voice.

Kat paused at the edge of the clearing, laying an arrow to the string of her bow. Gotrek, Felix and Ortwin stopped around her, readying their weapons and catching their breath as they stared at the mad battle before them.

On the far side of a huge fire, a dozen or so Empire spearmen stood in a curving line before a clump of towering Kurgan marauders, who drove them back towards the trees with swipes from massive swords and axes. On the near side of the fire, two dwarf Slayers fought back to back in the centre of four more Chaos warriors. To one side, horses bucked and screamed against their tethers and chained prisoners huddled together, the fire reflecting in their terrified eyes as they watched the fight. The ground was littered with the corpses of both men and marauders, all horribly mutilated.

'On, on,' said Ortwin, between gasps. 'Before another man falls.'

'Do not help the Slayers,' said Gotrek, starting forwards. 'They will not thank you.'

There was a thrum at Felix's ear and one of the Kurgan who faced the spearmen barked in pain, an arrow sprouting from his back.

'Go,' whispered Kat. 'Go!'

Gotrek, Felix and Ortwin charged out of the trees, running low as more of Kat's shafts whistled past their heads. The Kurgan howled and turned as the shafts pin-cushioned them. Felix grimaced. They were hideous – impossibly muscular gargantuans in furs and rusty armour – but their bearded faces were painted up like fright masks. Felix hurled his flaming branch at one with striped cheeks and purple eyelids, then slashed at him with his sword. Ortwin dodged a blow from one with black lips and pink matted hair. Gotrek smashed through the shield of one who fought entirely naked, but with so many iron rings piercing his flesh that he looked like he wore chainmail.

The Empire spearmen cheered as they saw their enemies flanked, and the line pressed forwards with renewed energy.

'On them!' shouted a captain. 'Keep the advantage!'

The eyes of the painted Kurgan shone with berserk frenzy, and though the arrows had caught their attention, they didn't seem to have slowed them down. Felix blocked an axe blow from his opponent that nearly shivered Karaghul from his hands. Ortwin's blade bit deep into the pink-haired one's sword arm, but the giant only moaned as if in ecstasy and struck back savagely, knocking the boy to the ground with a blow that sent his helmet bouncing across the trampled earth. Felix cursed. He had forgotten how hard to kill the Kurgan were. They had hides like iron, and when their battle-madness was upon them, they seemed to feel no pain.

Gotrek killed the pierced one with a chop under the ribs that sunk to his spine, then backhanded the one who had flattened Ortwin, shearing through his pitch-smeared armour and biting into his back.

Felix stabbed his painted opponent through the leg, but he didn't even flinch, and Felix had to leap back ungracefully to avoid being gutted by his double-headed axe. As the huge weapon whipped by, Felix gashed the madman across the back of the wrist, cutting him to the bone. That the Kurgan felt. He howled and dropped his axe, but then drew two daggers the size of short swords and leapt again at Felix, still screaming wordlessly. Felix stabbed him in the sternum, trying to keep him at a distance, and felt Karaghul grate against thick bone. The marauder came on, pressing his breastbone against the tip of the sword and forcing Felix back with his weight as he swiped at him with his daggers, just out of range.

Suddenly Kat screamed up beside Felix and hacked the painted berserker in the shoulder with one of her hatchets. He swung a dagger at her face.

'No!' cried Felix, but the girl ducked it neatly and slashed at the marauder's knees.

The berserker jumped back and Kat and Felix advanced, pressing him back towards the Empire spearmen.

'Come on, then!' shouted Felix, trying to keep his attention fixed forwards.

It worked. The berserker didn't hear the spearmen behind him, and as he raised his axe to strike at Felix, a spearhead burst from his abdomen. He turned, roaring in pain and fury, and Felix jumped forwards and decapitated him with a whistling slash. The Kurgan's painted eyes stared with surprise as his head tumbled from his slumping body.

The head rolled to a rest against Ortwin just as the boy was sitting up and looking around. He yelped as it hit his leg and scrambled up, kicking at it.

Felix and Kat turned, searching for more opponents, but there were none. The spearmen had capitalised on the Kurgan's confusion and had slaughtered the rest while they were distracted. On the far side of the fire, however, the battle between the two Slayers and their massive opponents still continued.

The spearmen turned towards it.

'Leave them be,' said Gotrek, holding out a warning hand.

'Not to worry, Slayer,' said the captain, a long-jawed veteran with a battered helmet and a bloody face. 'We know the rules.' He grinned at Kat, throwing her a jaunty salute. ''Lo, Kat. Might have known. It is proof of Sigmar's grace that you found us in time.'

'It was Gotrek that heard the fight, Captain Haschke,' said Kat, humbly, then turned to watch the Slayers fight.

Two of the marauders were down, one with his bald head cleft down to the neck, the other with his guts spilling out of his stomach and sizzling in the fire, but though the two Slayers still stood and fought strongly, Felix could see they had paid for their victories.

The shorter, broader Slayer, who wore his scarlet beard woven into two long thick plaits, and whose two side-by-side crests arced over his bald head to match, had a huge lump on the right side of his head and seemed to be having trouble remaining upright. He swung furiously but unsteadily at his enemy with a double-bladed axe, his head tilted at an odd angle. The taller, rounder Slayer, who had a braided crest and a beard like an orange haystack, was bleeding freely from the stumps of two missing fingers on his right hand, and had a diagonal gash on his scalp that was flooding his eyes with blood. He could barely see to swing his long-hafted warhammer.

Still, both seemed to be in high spirits.

'Take a rest, Argrin,' said the double-crested Slayer. 'I can take 'em both.'

'And give you my doom?' scoffed the braid-crested Slayer. 'No fear, Rodi.'

Felix could see the spearmen inching forwards, wanting to help the dwarfs, but apparently their captain had schooled them, for they held back, though he could see it pained them to do it.

'Be ready if the Slayers fall,' murmured Captain Haschke.

Then, abruptly, it was over. Rodi, the double-crested one, weaved drunkenly out of the way of an axe swing and found himself standing almost under the legs of his towering opponent. He hacked savagely at the marauder's inner knee with his axe, but overbalanced and cut off the Kurgan's foot instead.

The giant screamed and tried to take a step, but collapsed when he put his weight on his stump and crashed into the other Kurgan, sending him stumbling into the path of Argrin's warhammer. The massive weapon caught the second marauder in the ribs, knocking him flat. Argrin jumped up onto his chest and crushed his skull with a sickening pop, just as Rodi planted his axe deep in the chest of the first marauder, sending up a fountain of gore.

The spearmen cheered. The Slayers didn't seem to notice. They were too busy complaining to each other.

'See now, Rodi Balkisson?' said Argrin, turning to Rodi, who was decapitating the footless Kurgan, just to be sure. 'You interfered in my fight. You've cost me another doom.'

Rodi sneered as he wiped his axe on his Kurgan's furs. 'You've a way to go before you reach the number of times you've cost me *my* doom, Argrin Crownforger. Nine times! I've kept count.' He turned to survey the rest of the clearing. 'Now where did...' He broke off as he saw Gotrek. 'Another Slayer!' he said.

Argrin wrapped a cloth around the stumps of his two missing fingers and peered around. 'Where? Oh, so there is. By Grimnir, where did he come from?'

'No idea,' said Rodi. 'But where's old Father Rustskull? I lost track during the fight.'

'There he is,' said Argrin, pointing to a heap of dead Kurgan who lay piled on top of each other near the fire. Felix looked closer and saw that there was a pair of short, thick legs sticking out from under them.

The two Slayers limped forwards and grabbed the dead marauders by the arms and legs.

Rodi beckoned to the others. 'Hoy. Help us shift these fat pig Kurgan.'

Gotrek, Felix and Ortwin and some of the spearmen came forwards to help. The Kurgan were unbelievably heavy, as if they were made of oak, not flesh, but finally, working together, they succeeded in rolling them off the dwarf who lay at the bottom of the pile, unmoving, his eyes closed.

Felix stared, stunned. The unconscious dwarf was a Slayer with a huge white beard, an enormous warhammer held slack in one gnarled hand, an oft-broken nose, a cauliflower ear on one side of his head, no ear at all on the other, and a crest made of dozens and dozens of big iron nails, all rusted to a dirty brownish orange.

'Snorri Nosebiter,' said Gotrek softly. 'As I live and breathe.'

SEVEN

'I think he's dead,' said Argrin.

'The lucky bastard,' said Rodi. 'Found his doom at last.'

Gotrek grunted. 'He's not dead. He's out cold.' He slapped Snorri's cheek. It sounded like a pistol shot. 'Wake up, Nosebiter.'

Snorri didn't move.

'Maybe we should give him some air,' said Felix, stepping back.

'Aye,' said Rodi. 'He's been breathing Kurgan's armpit for the last ten minutes. That would kill anybody.'

'Chafe his wrists,' said the captain of the spearmen.

'Lift his legs,' said one of his men.

'Maybe we should give him a drink,' said Kat, reaching for her canteen.

'Snorri thinks that is a very good idea,' said Snorri.

'Ha!' said Argrin, as Snorri's eyes flickered open. 'He's alive!'

'The poor bastard,' said Rodi. 'Another doom missed.'

Gotrek helped Snorri sit up. The old Slayer reached shakily for Kat's canteen and upended it over his mouth, guzzling greedily.

Then suddenly he was spitting it all out again, covering them all in spray and hacking and gasping so much that his eyes turned red. 'What... was that?' he sputtered.

'Only water,' said Kat, looking a little alarmed.

Snorri made a face. 'Snorri didn't like that at all.'

Argrin crossed to a pack with a small wooden keg strapped to the bottom of it. He brought it back and handed it to Snorri.

Snorri upended it like he had the canteen, but this time he drank smoothly and happily. After a very long pull, he lowered the keg, sighed happily and licked the foam off his white moustaches. 'That was much better.'

He handed the keg back to Argrin and looked around at everybody, ending on Gotrek. He blinked, a look of confusion on his face.

Gotrek grinned. 'Well met, Snorri Nosebiter.'

Snorri frowned. 'Snorri knows you,' he said slowly. 'Snorri knows he knows you.' He turned curious eyes to Felix. 'And you too.'

Gotrek's grin collapsed. 'Gotrek, son of Gurni,' he said quietly.

'And Felix Jaeger,' said Felix.

'It's only been twenty years,' said Gotrek. 'You don't remember?'

Snorri nodded. 'Snorri knows Gotrek Gurnisson and Felix Jaeger. They are his old friends.' he said. 'Are you them?'

Felix and Gotrek exchanged a glance. Felix wasn't sure if he had ever seen Gotrek look more unsettled.

'Please, sirs,' came a woman's voice from behind them. 'Please, can you free us from these chains?'

Everybody stood and turned. Felix flushed, ashamed. They had been so busy hovering over Snorri that they had forgotten the prisoners.

The Slayers and the spearmen hurried to them and began breaking them loose. They were a pitiful lot – a flock of shivering half-naked men and women, all huddled around the tree they had been shackled to. The women wore the remnants of Shallyan robes, and some still had dove pendants hanging from their necks. They wept and thanked the spearmen for their release. The men wore the same uniform as the spearmen – those that wore anything at all – but they reacted almost not at all to being freed, only stared unseeing at their unshackled wrists or looked about them with dark, haunted eyes, murmuring under their breath.

Kat pressed her lips together as she looked at them. 'Neff's men,' she said. 'The guards of the supply caravan. What can have done that to them to make them like this?'

Felix shuddered. He didn't want to know.

Kat turned to the spear captain. 'Captain Haschke, how did you find them?'

Haschke grimaced. 'The Kurgan bastards attacked the Shallyan hospital wagons two days ago, while they were on the way south to Bauholz. One of their guards escaped and got back to the fort. He led us to the place where they were attacked, and we followed their trail here.' He nodded sadly at the supply train guards. 'I guess the Kurgan have been watching the trail.'

'Aye,' said Kat. 'We found the supply train earlier. Neff's dead. About seven others.'

Haschke sighed and shook his head. 'Ah, that's bad. I'll be sorry to tell Elfreda.'

'I... I'll tell her,' said Kat.

Haschke looked relieved.

Once they had freed all the prisoners and did what they could to get them up and moving – and put those who couldn't move on the backs of the stolen horses – Kat invited everyone back to the camp she had made by the road. The Kurgan camp was a charnel house, and not fit to stay the night in.

The undergrowth it had taken Kat, Gotrek, Felix and Ortwin two minutes to run through earlier took half an hour to lead the horses and the staggering victims through, but finally they made it back and got everyone around the fire and settled.

Gotrek watched Snorri as the old Slayer nodded off, then crossed to Argrin and Rodi, who were cleaning and wrapping their wounds and combing out their beards and crests.

Gotrek nodded to them politely as Felix and Kat watched from nearby. 'Gotrek, son of Gurni, at your service,' he said.

The two dwarfs stood and bowed in return.

'Rodi, son of Balki, at yours,' said the short, double-crested Slayer. He had arched black eyebrows and a sly look on his sharp-featured face.

'And I am Argrin Crownforger,' said the bigger Slayer, whose braided crest was now unwound and hanging down over the left side of his square, lumpy face.

Gotrek acknowledged their names and they all sat again. Gotrek looked back at Snorri. 'How long has he been this way?' he asked. 'His memory.'

'Since we've known him,' said Argrin.

'Though that hasn't been long,' said Rodi. 'We met him at the siege of Middenheim, a few months back.'

Felix saw Gotrek's shoulders tense. 'You were at the siege?'

'Aye,' said Rodi, his powerful chest swelling with pride. 'Slew a daemon.'

Felix could hear Gotrek's knuckles crack over the popping of the fire. 'Did you?' he rumbled.

'It wasn't a daemon,' grunted Argrin, as if they had had this argument before. 'Not a real one.'

'It breathed fire and vanished into pink smoke when I hit it,' said Rodi, sticking his fork-bearded chin out.

'And it was the size of a cat,' said Argrin.

'Don't lie, curse you,' snarled Rodi. 'It was bigger than that! It was easily as big as–'

'A dog,' interjected Argrin.

'A wolf!' protested Rodi. 'It was as big as a wolf! A big wolf!'

Gotrek cleared his throat meaningfully. 'So, you don't know when Snorri Nosebiter started to lose his memory?'

The two Slayers broke off their argument and shook their heads.

'He's always been that way,' said Rodi. 'As far as we know. We sometimes have to remind him who we are, and he sees us every day.'

'Too many bumps on the head,' said Argrin.

'Too many *nails* in the head,' said Rodi.

Argrin shrugged sadly. 'He remembers long ago like it was yesterday, and yesterday not at all.'

Gotrek cursed under his breath.

Argrin gave Gotrek an odd look. 'He certainly tells enough stories of you, Gotrek son of Gurni.'

'Aye,' laughed Rodi. 'And if they're all true, then you're the worst Slayer of all time.'

'What was that?' growled Gotrek, balling his fists.

Kat sucked in a breath. Felix sat up, watching warily. This could be bad. His doom was a subject upon which the Slayer was notoriously touchy.

'Easy,' said Rodi, holding up his palms. 'A joke, that's all. I just mean that you must be too good. You should have been dead a dozen times over in the years you were with Snorri, and yet you defeated everything you met – daemons, dragons, vampires – and now it's twenty years later and you still live.'

'Do you question my dedication to seeking my doom?' said Gotrek, rising, his one eye flashing in the firelight.

Rodi stood too, chest to chest with Gotrek. 'Are you putting words in my mouth? I didn't say that.'

Felix put a hand on his sword. Kat looked from one Slayer to the other. The spearmen from Stangenschloss were turning their heads.

'Then what *did* you say?' said Gotrek.

'Come now, lads,' said Argrin, rising and trying to step between them. 'Let's not fight over nothing.'

'My honour is not nothing, beardling,' said Gotrek, snarling at him.

Felix stepped forwards anxiously. 'I can confirm that the Slayer hasn't let a day go by in the last twenty years without actively seeking his doom.' Except for those months in Altdorf where he tried to drink himself to death, he thought, but he kept it to himself.

'Stay out of this, manling,' said Gotrek.

Argrin put a hand on Rodi's shoulder. 'Apologise, Rodi. Come now.'

'But, I didn't…' said Rodi.

'It doesn't matter,' said Argrin. 'A Slayer's doom is between him and Grimnir, not anyone else. You shouldn't even have brought it up. Now apologise.'

Rodi made a sulky face, but finally bowed to Gotrek. 'Forgive me, Gotrek, son of Gurni, I should not have asked after that which is not my business. Please accept my apology.'

Gotrek hesitated, looking like he still wanted to punch the young Slayer in the nose, but then nodded curtly. 'Accepted,' he said, and returned to Felix, still muttering under his breath.

* * *

Slowed as they were by the Shallyan sisters and the rescued men, all of whom were wounded and half-starved, it took two further days to reach Stangenschloss. Nothing happened on the journey, but it was still a difficult trip, at least for Gotrek and Felix. Felix spent the two days watching Gotrek watch Snorri, saddened to see the Slayer at such a loss.

Snorri was as cheerful as he had ever been, and seemed no less intelligent – and no more intelligent – than he had been before, but there was definitely something wrong with his mind. He greeted Gotrek and Felix as strangers each morning, and when they reminded him who they were, he would laugh and say of course they were and remember for the rest of the day, but at the same time, he would tell them stories of his old friends Gotrek and Felix, as if they were two completely different people from the man and the dwarf who walked beside him.

Gotrek nodded as Snorri told the stories – most of which were terribly mixed up and wrong – but his face was set in a grim scowl, as if he was trying to work out a puzzle. It hurt Felix to see it. This was not Gotrek's sort of problem. It was not a thing to be solved with an axe, or a daring rescue. There was nothing the Slayer could do to help his friend, and Felix could see it pained him. What should have been a joyous reunion with lots of drinking and property damage, had been instead an awkward and heartbreaking non-event.

Gotrek, being both a dwarf and a Slayer, wasn't one to moan in the face of tragedy, however. Instead, Felix could see him getting angrier and angrier, and at the same time more frustrated that he had nothing to lash out at. Felix could hear him grinding his jaw as they walked, and he was constantly clenching and unclenching his fists. Given that they were going ever deeper into the Drakwald, it was inevitable that the Slayer would come across some evil that needed to be killed and he would finally find some release.

For Gotrek's sake, Felix hoped it would come soon.

Stangenschloss wasn't quite as impressive as Felix had expected. He had been picturing some grim, monolithic bulwark against the forces of Chaos, its towering stone walls lined with massive engines of war and bristling with spearmen, swordsmen and handgunners. In reality, it was smaller than Bauholz, and though its walls were of stone, they weren't much taller than the village's wooden palisade, and had been knocked down in places. The garrison was less than five hundred men, most of them gaunt from hunger and weary from a hard year of war, and there were no catapults or trebuchets that Felix could see.

Captain Haschke caught him looking around as they crossed the yard and smiled grimly. 'It's better than it was.'

'You must have seen some fierce battles here,' said Felix.

'Not us,' said Haschke. 'At least not here. We were further north, with von Raukov. This place was garrisoned by a Lord von Lauterbach. They were overrun, killed to a man and the fort destroyed.'

'So how did you come to be here?' Felix asked.

Haschke grinned. 'Another of my lord Ilgner's brainstorms,' he said. 'We were returning south after the end, and came across this fort. It was abandoned, and all the nearby settlements ravaged by the loose ends of Archaon's army who had melted into the forest instead of back north. Well, Lord Ilgner can't stand to see a fly hurt, and so he says we must stay here until these horrors have been rooted out and the people can live in peace again.'

'A most noble sentiment,' said Ortwin, piping up.

'Aye,' said Haschke. 'Though many of the men didn't think so. They'd been fighting all year, and wanted to see their families in Averland again. There was a lot of grumbling at the first, I don't mind telling you.'

'Is he not well liked, then?' Felix asked.

'Oh no, they love him,' said Haschke. 'He gives 'em victories and keeps 'em fed – for the most part – and he has a way of making even the most mercenary soldier feel like he's part of a noble cause. We're proud of him, and proud to be holding the line. We're just a bit… tired, that's all.'

After he had found them a place to drop their packs, Captain Haschke brought Gotrek, Felix, Kat and Ortwin to Lord Ilgner, the commander of the fort, to give him the details of their encounter with the marauders. Abbess Mechtilde, the senior sister of the Shallyans, came too.

They found Ilgner sitting at a desk made from a heavy wooden door laid across two sawhorses. It was next to a little camp stove in a curtained-off portion of the keep's dining hall that served him as both office and sleeping quarters. The upper storeys of the keep had been shattered during the war and not yet rebuilt, so even the officers had to make do in the common areas.

Like his fort, Ilgner was not what Felix had expected. He had thought to find some ironclad giant of a man with a dour expression and the strength of ten. Instead Ilgner was short and bustling, and looked as if he would have tended towards the pudgy side if conditions at the fort hadn't been so dire. His hair was dark and thinning on top, his eyes were bright, and his teeth even brighter when he smiled, which was often.

'Sigmar preserve us,' he said when Haschke presented them. 'Another Slayer. Y'don't drink like the other three, do you? As much as we have welcomed their prowess these last weeks, they have near to drunk us out of beer.'

'Slayers drink,' said Gotrek, shrugging.

'And not a little,' grinned Ilgner. 'They keep saying they're going off to find their doom, but they keep coming back, much to my cellarer's dismay.' He looked up at Haschke. 'They did come back again, didn't they?'

'Aye, my lord,' said Haschke. 'They're having a pint even now. Claim it helps their wounds heal faster.'

Ilgner sighed, then nodded respectfully to Gotrek and Felix and Ortwin. 'Well, you're all welcome here nonetheless. We can use all the proven veterans we can find.' He turned to Kat, his face growing suddenly sober. 'So, Neff's dead then?'

'Aye, my lord,' she said. 'A third of his men as well. And the supplies taken. I'm sorry.'

'And those that survived…' said Haschke, then bit his lip. 'Well, they were captured by the Kurgan, and… and they ain't themselves.'

'What's wrong with them?' asked Ilgner.

'They're… broken, sir,' said Haschke. 'Won't speak. Won't hardly eat. No life to them.'

'They were most cruelly abused, my lord,' said the abbess. She hesitated as all attention turned to her. Her face turned red. 'The marauders told us that they were taking me and my sisters to… to breed with, to make more of their kind, but the men, they used them as… as pets, or toys. That is–'

'No need to go on, sister,' said Ilgner, blushing. 'I understand your meaning. The villains were followers of the god of pleasure. They did as they do.'

Haschke put his hand on his sword hilt. 'My lord, I beg you to let me take a force of men and find the rest of these degenerates. We slaughtered those we found to the last man, but they were only a raiding party. I know the main body of their force must be somewhere near, with our supplies.'

Ilgner sat down at his desk wearily. 'Would that I could, captain. But I fear we have a more pressing problem that must be dealt with first.'

'What's that, my lord?'

Ilgner shoved aside the papers and mugs and dinner plates on his desk until he uncovered a map of the Drakwald. He tapped it with a finger. 'We have reports of a great herd of beastmen, as big as anything we saw in the war, coming south out of the Howling Hills, destroying villages and settlements as they go.' His finger trailed down the map. 'We don't know where they're going, or what they want, but they're heading this way, and they must be stopped.'

Felix and Gotrek exchanged a look at this. Ortwin was holding his breath.

Felix stepped forwards. 'Forgive me, Lord Ilgner. We have come north seeking news of the templars of the Order of the Fiery Heart. Do you know if this is what they went to meet?'

Ilgner pursed his lips, nodding. 'Aye. The village they left to protect was the first hint of this trouble. The day they rode forth we received five more messenger pigeons begging for our aid – all from villages and timber camps on the edges of the hills.'

'Have you had word of the templars, sir?' blurted Ortwin.

Ilgner shook his head sympathetically. 'I'm sorry, lad. No one we have sent north has returned, and the refugees that stream south just babble with fear. I've heard nothing.' He returned his attention to the map, moving his finger again. 'Calls for help come from new villages every day, and each one further south than the last.' He looked around at them all. 'My estimate is that the herd is six days from here now. I am going north at dawn tomorrow to see for myself its size and nature.'

Haschke snapped to attention. He saluted. 'My lord, I would be at your side in this. Please allow me to accompany you.'

Ilgner chuckled. 'No, Haschke. You've only just returned from a desperate fight. You're wounded. You'll stay here. I'm only taking a few men anyway. It's a reconnaissance mission, not a war party.'

Haschke looked crushed.

Ilgner turned to Kat. 'Kat, if you're well, I'd have you as scout.'

'Of course, sir,' she said.

Ortwin stepped forwards, then went down on one knee. 'My lord Ilgner, my friends and I have vowed to discover the fate of the Templars of the Fiery Heart. We would be most grateful to be allowed to join you as you go north, and seek our answers there.'

Ilgner raised his eyebrows, seemingly amused at the boy's formality. He turned to Kat. 'And do you vouch for these noble seekers, scout?'

'Aye, my lord,' she said, her eyes bright. 'They are the finest warriors and bravest, most honourable friends I have ever known. And the boy can fight too.'

Ortwin glared at her as Ilgner grinned.

'Well then,' he said. 'It seems we'd better have them, hadn't we?'

After they left Lord Ilgner, the companions split up. Felix got a bucket of hot water from the cook and scrubbed himself clean behind the barracks, then went to the place that Haschke had found for them – a second-floor room in a half-demolished tower – and had a short nap, for it had been a gruelling trip from Bauholz.

He was plagued by dreams of skulking forms moving in shadows, and his father screaming curses as clawed hands ripped at his flesh. But his curses weren't directed at his torturers, but at Felix, who looked in at the window and shrank back as his father's bleeding eyes turned accusingly towards him, as he jerked at the bell rope by his bed, futilely ringing for help that would never come.

Felix woke to the jangling clang of a distant dinner bell and the smell of boiled cabbage. It was not the most appetising odour in the world, but it was a relief after the horrors of his nightmare. The dream lingered unpleasantly as he pulled his boots on, and he could still feel his father's eyes glaring at him as he started down to the dining hall, silently demanding to know why he had taken Sir Teobalt's quest and abandoned the vengeance that he was owed.

As he was crossing the muddy courtyard, Felix saw Kat standing by the kitchen door with a woman in an apron. The woman was looking down, her shoulders slumped, and Kat held one of her hands, patting it awkwardly. Felix slowed, struck by the seeming sadness of the scene. What had happened, he wondered? He realised he was staring and made to continue – he didn't want to intrude on someone else's misery – but then he saw Kat step back and say some final word to the woman, and he paused again. The woman nodded at Kat's words, but didn't look up, and after an awkward moment, Kat turned and walked away, her head down too.

Felix hesitated between withdrawing and going to her, and in that instant she looked up and saw him. She paused for a moment, then dropped her head again and continued towards him.

'Hello, Felix,' she said, not slowing as she reached him.

'Are you all right, Kat?' he asked. 'Who was that woman?'

Kat paused, then continued around him towards the dining hall, still not looking up. 'Neff's wife, Elfreda,' she said. 'She bakes our bread. I... I told her–' Her words cut off short and she broke into a sudden trot. 'Ex... excuse me.'

'Kat!' Felix hurried after her and caught her by the elbow.

She struggled for a moment, but when he turned her around she fell against his chest, knocking her forehead on his breastbone and sobbing silently. Felix wrapped his arms around her and held her tight. She clung to him, the front of his jerkin balled in her fists as her tears soaked the cloth.

'I'm sorry, Felix,' she mumpfed. 'It's only... only...' and then she was off again.

Felix patted her back and shushed her gently, marvelling again at her contrasts – so savage in battle, so sure of herself in the wild, so courageous in the face of death, and yet still so human beneath it all.

She head-butted his chest, angry. 'Why can I look at Neff's corpse without a tear, but when I go to tell 'Freda...' She sobbed again.

Felix stroked her filthy hair and decided not to remind her that she *had* cried then, if only silently. Instead he said, 'I suppose it's because the dead are past suffering. It is those who survive them who feel the pain of death.'

She nodded, still weeping. 'She wanted him to go south before winter locked them in, but he... but he was too loyal to Ilgner. He wouldn't go! Poor 'Freda.'

There were fresh sobs after that. Felix let her cry herself out, wrapping her in his red Sudenland cloak and looking sadly down at the top of her head. She weeps here because it is safe, he thought. In the Drakwald there is no room for tears. She has to be alert and on guard at all times. Emotion would kill her, so she saves it up until she is out from under the trees. He was oddly pleased that she felt safe enough in his arms to let herself go like this.

After a while her sobs subsided and she lay against him, sniffing. Finally she raised her head and looked up at him with a lopsided smile.

'I'm sorry, Felix,' she said. 'I think... I think I've ruined your jerkin.'

He chuckled. 'Tears are hardly the worst things that have stained this rag,' he said.

They stood that way for a moment, wrapped in each other's arms, smiling fondly at each other, but then, without anything changing, something changed, and Felix's heart lurched. One second, the embrace had been innocent, a brother hugging a sister, and then, without warning, it was innocent no longer.

It wasn't that Felix was suddenly overcome with lust. It was just that he had all at once remembered that he was a man and Kat was a woman and that it felt very nice to hold her like this. He paused, heart pounding, and felt Kat tense too. She had become aware of it as well.

Their eyes met, and for the briefest second an electric understanding passed between them, then they broke free of each other, practically leaping apart, suddenly unsure where to look.

'Er...' said Felix, apparently very interested in what was going on across the yard. 'Well, we'd best get to dinner then, eh?'

'Aye,' said Kat, intently rewrapping her scarf. 'Aye, dinner. Yes.'

They turned and hurried towards the dining hall, both looking straight ahead.

Things continued uncomfortably at dinner. While Gotrek listened to Snorri's mixed-up stories of the siege of Middenheim, and Rodi and Argrin laughed and shared stories with their friends among the Stangenschloss garrison, Felix and Kat ate quietly, not speaking to one another, and shying away from eye contact. Every once in a while Felix would look up and find Kat staring at him, only to look away when he caught her. And at other times he would find himself staring at her, only to look away when she caught him.

Felix cursed himself each time. What was wrong with him? It wasn't right! The girl was almost half his age!

On the other hand, he told himself, she was older than Claudia, and he had allowed himself to be seduced by her. But he hadn't known Claudia when she was seven! Nor had he cared for Claudia the way he did for Kat. Claudia had been a manipulative fool who had wanted to use him as a way to rebel against the strictures of her cloistered life, and in a weak moment he had been ready to use her in return.

Kat was different. Felix felt responsible for her. He had shaped her past, and was concerned for her future. He didn't want to hurt her through some callous, casual lovemaking. She was no tavern girl or courtesan who gave her favours easily and often. She was... Kat, still in his mind the solemn little girl who had waved and cried when he and Gotrek had left her to go to Nuln all those years ago.

If he and Kat came together – and the brief electric look they had exchanged had made him unable to think of anything else – it would have to mean something. It would have to be as lovers, and not just as friendly sparring partners. And that, he feared, was impossible, for a number of reasons.

First were their oaths. Kat was bound to the Drakwald by her vow to rid it of beastmen. Felix was bound to Gotrek by his vow to follow him and record his doom. He could never tell one day to the next where he would be. Nothing he and Kat shared could last for long, for Gotrek never kept still.

Second was their ages, something that hadn't mattered so much with Claudia, who would have never been more than a momentary affair. It would be different if he remained with Kat. No matter what Max said about Felix's longevity, he would still be in his sixties when she was forty. It would be fair to neither of them.

Third, and now that he thought of it, most important, was the stark fact that he wasn't sure if he was in love with her. He loved her, certainly, but it was the tender, protective love one has for family, rather than the soul-piercing, heart-enflaming love that one had for... for...

Ulrika.

Felix cursed when he thought of her. Was he always going to be comparing other women to her? It would never be a fair test. They had been a perfect match of temperament and inclination. Restless wanderers who struck sparks off each other like flint and steel. Beside her, Claudia was a spoiled, snivelling brat, and Kat was a sweet-natured but unworldly yokel. It was hopeless. Neither woman could hold a candle to her, and yet love with them was possible, if he wanted it, where it never would be with Ulrika. Ulrika had been made a vampire. She no longer lived by the laws of the living. There could be nothing between her and Felix that would not lead to death or destruction for one or both of them. He had to forget her. It was imperative. Someday he would have to give up and settle for his second choice.

He looked at Kat again. He knew Ulrika would not begrudge him taking up with the girl. It had been she after all who had said that they must find solace among their own kind. But what solace could be had when he would be taking Kat's love without being able to return it in full? The guilt would kill him. She deserved more than what he could give.

She looked up, and again there was that arcing spark of attraction between them. He looked away quickly, pretending to look for more beer. He bit his cheek hard to drive away the flicker of lustful images that flared up before his eyes, then laughed at himself. So full of noble sentiments. He only hoped they would stand when put to the test.

Beside him Gotrek had turned away from Snorri and was staring at a soldier who sat across the table from Rodi and Argrin.

'Empty?' Gotrek was saying. 'Do you mean all dead?'

Felix turned to listen as the soldier shook his head. 'No, herr dwarf. The man said "empty". Him and his fellows is trappers, and they was out in the deep woods when the big herd passed by. They never saw 'em, but when they got back to Weinig they could see that them beasties had been to call and no mistake. The whole place was mashed flat – gate, houses and temple – just as you'd expect. But the weird part...' The soldier leaned in and lowered his voice for effect. 'The eerie part, was that there was no people. Not a man, woman or child. They was all gone, and precious few corpses neither.'

Rodi shrugged. 'The beastmen took them,' he said. 'For food or for slaves.'

'No,' said Kat. 'You don't know them.'

Rodi's eyes widened to be challenged so bluntly by a woman, but Kat continued without looking at him.

'They might have taken some for food,' she said. 'But not many. They don't carry their larders with them. They eat as they go. And they don't take human slaves, because they can't keep up.'

'Then where did they go?' asked Argrin. 'The men, I mean.'

Kat shrugged. 'I don't know.'

'Neither did the trapper,' said the soldier, eager to get the attention back on himself. 'But he found the same thing in Bohrung and Grube further south. All vanished, like they was sucked up into the sky by a whirlwind.'

'Mayhap yer trapper was mad, Pfaltz,' said another soldier, laughing. 'A herd of beastmen that makes people disappear? Sounds like a tall tale to me.'

'Or a good doom,' muttered Gotrek, his one eye shining with the fire from the torches of the hall as the others laughed and insulted the storyteller.

Felix shivered. When Gotrek smelled a good doom, he knew trouble was sure to follow. He did not look forward to the morrow.

For three days Lord Ilgner's party pushed ever deeper into the trackless heart of the Drakwald, a terrifying green vastness that seemed to Felix, his imagination fuelled by the stories of the tale-spinning soldier, to be one giant malevolent organism that watched them through half-slumbering eyes like some listless cat – too comfortable for the moment to bother going after the mouse that has entered its territory, but secure in the knowledge that its prey was trapped, and that it could reach out its paw and crush it any time it chose – or make it vanish.

There were no roads north of Stangenschloss, not even the meagre tracks that had served as such between Bauholz and the fort, and so the expedition travelled single file along faint game paths. Kat scouted the way far out in front, while Snorri, Rodi and Argrin – who had insisted on accompanying them despite their wounds – marched before Ilgner and ten picked knights leading their horses. Finally came Gotrek, Felix and Ortwin, bringing up the rear and keeping an eye out for anyone who might be following them.

Felix was relieved that Kat was taking point. She seemed to have regained her composure again swiftly, and had greeted him with a cheery and non-committal hello on the morning they had set out, but he found that he was still having difficulty keeping his eyes off her when she was around, and so welcomed anything that took her out of his sight.

Each day out of Stangenschloss the terrain grew hillier than the last, with much struggling up steep, brush-covered ridges, or pushing through thickly wooded ravines. Several times they came to places where they had to hack down the undergrowth to make a passage for the horses. Despite the bitter cold, the effort of the march made them sweat so much that they steamed.

On the third day they woke up to ominous clouds and whistling winds. Gusts of driving sleet lashed their faces as they broke camp and shouldered their packs. Felix wondered if Ilgner might give the order to return to Stangenschloss due to the threat of a storm, but the general didn't even discuss it, and they continued north as before.

'One advantage to travelling in the thick of the forest,' he said cheerily. 'Keeps the weather off!'

His knights laughed at that. Felix didn't find it particularly funny, or particularly true. Being under the trees did keep the wind and the sleet out of their faces, but the melting ice dripped from the needles and down the back of his neck, and turned the forest floor into a mouldy mulch of leaves and mud that made walking more like sliding and froze his feet through his boots.

Just before noon they at last found evidence of the mysterious herd's passage. It wasn't hard to miss. The party wormed their way down a densely wooded pine slope and discovered Kat at the base of it, squatting and staring at a river of crushed underbrush, hoof prints, beast-dung, gnawed animal bones and branch-shorn trees so wide that the far side of it was beyond the distance they could see into the wood. Her expression was dark and thoughtful.

'What troubles you, Kat?' asked Lord Ilgner. 'Is it a very big herd?'

She nodded, her mouth a flat line. 'I don't know if I've seen bigger, but that's not all of it.'

She beckoned them forwards, cutting across the beastmen's trampled path. As they went on, the murky leaf-shrouded light brightened, until, after twenty paces, they stepped out into a strange gap in the forest where the trees had been chopped down in a long straight line that followed the beastmen's line of march, and the sleet beat down at them from roiling grey sky above.

Felix shielded his eyes and looked up and down the line of felled trees. It went as far as he could see in both directions – like a furrow cut into the forest by some unimaginably large plough. It was not wide – no more than five or six paces from edge to edge – but there were fallen trees and ragged stumps all along it, the axe cuts that had felled them so fresh that thick sap welled up out of them like pus from a septic wound.

'This,' said Kat. 'This is unnatural. The beastmen don't travel like this.'

'Is it perhaps marauders instead?' asked Ilgner.

'Doesn't smell like marauders,' said Argrin.

Kat agreed. 'There are only hoof prints. No boots. It was a herd that did this, but I have never seen a herd cut down trees on the march. They are creatures of the forest. They move through trees like we move in the open. I don't understand it.'

'Perhaps they have a cannon,' said Felix.

Rodi laughed. 'Beastmen don't have cannon!' he said. 'They don't even have bows and arrows.'

'Listen to the beardling,' said Gotrek under his breath. 'He knows everything.'

'Those that lead the beasts sometimes have cannon,' said Felix, remembering the hellish weapon that the Chaos champion Justine had brought with the herd that had attacked Flensburg.

'It might be a cannon,' said Kat doubtfully. 'But where are the tracks of the wheels?'

'Unnatural or not,' said Ilgner, waving her on, 'we have found our quarry's spoor, and it does not appear to be hard to follow. Let the hunt begin.'

EIGHT

Whatever the beastmen's reasons for clearing a path through the forest, Ilgner was right, it made them exceptionally easy to follow, and also allowed the party of knights and Slayers to nearly double its speed. By mid-afternoon they had covered the same distance they had travelled the whole of the previous day, and Kat said that they were coming very near to catching up to the herd, for the dung and the half-eaten carcasses that littered the trail were still fresh. After that, they went with weapons drawn, and Ilgner and his knights stayed mounted, their helmets on and crossbows loaded and ready.

Felix was so focused on looking and listening to the front, worried that at any minute they were going to run into the back of the herd, that when trouble came from behind them, he failed to hear it. Only when Gotrek stopped and looked back did he hear the distant thudding of heavy hooves below the moaning of the wind and the rattle of the freezing rain. He followed Gotrek's gaze, wiping his eyes and peering through the slanting sleet, but the sound was coming from over the last ridge and there was nothing to see yet.

'Beastmen?' asked Ortwin, his voice wavering between anxious and eager.

'Aye,' rumbled Gotrek, his eyebrows dripping. 'Though not nearly enough.'

Even one beastman was more than Felix cared for, but he let it go. He ran up the line to Ilgner. 'Beastmen behind us,' he said. 'Gotrek thinks it's a small party.'

Ilgner looked back, cursing, then turned to his men. 'Into the trees to the left. We'll let them pass.' He looked down at Felix again. 'Herr Jaeger, if you would be so kind as to go ahead and tell the Slayers and Kat.'

'Aye, general,' said Felix, and trotted forwards as the knights began leading their horses into the woods.

The Slayers didn't like it.

'Hide from beastmen?' said Argrin. He looked genuinely shocked.

'We didn't join this squig chase to hide,' said Rodi, indignant. 'You want to rob us of a doom.'

'Ilgner came to scout the big herd,' said Felix, struggling for patience. 'Not die before he found it. If you want a doom, stay behind and fight the whole herd after we've returned to Stangenschloss.'

The two Slayers grunted unhappily, but made for the trees. As Felix hurried forwards to find Kat, he heard Rodi mutter, 'Humans,' in a disgusted voice.

Kat looked grim when he told her.

'Foragers,' she said. 'A herd on the move has outriders that range for miles in all directions, hunting for food.'

They ran back and joined the others, who had disappeared into the trees on the left side of the ragged path. Lord Ilgner had ordered the knights not just out of the open cut, but beyond the edge of the wider swathe of flattened undergrowth that the herd had trampled on either side of it. They buried themselves in the heavy brush, the knights with their cloaks and hoods drawn over their armour and helmets so that they would not betray themselves with any stray reflections. They waited with shields on their arms and cocked crossbows in their sword hands.

Felix looked back at the path as he and Kat crouched down next to Gotrek and Ortwin in the bushes. It could be seen only in little slivers between the black silhouettes of the intervening trees. The sounds of the approaching beastmen were louder now – the clump, clump, clump of hooves on earth, the bawling and braying of their inhuman speech.

'Will they see our tracks?' whispered Felix.

'They might,' said Kat, laying an arrow on the string of her bow. 'But our prints will blend in with all of theirs, so they likely won't notice.'

'Let us pray they don't,' said Ilgner.

Rodi and Argrin snorted at that. Ortwin however seemed to be taking the general at his word, and was mumbling over his clasped hands, his head bowed.

As the sounds got louder, the horses began to shift nervously, but the knights held their bridles and murmured soothing words to them and they remained quiet.

Soon Felix saw flashes of movement between the trees, like glimpses through the cracks in a plank fence. A big beastman – a gor, Felix remembered – with a head like an antlered bear lumbered down the treeless path with a club over one shoulder, its hairy torso covered in rags and scraps of rusty armour. Four more big gors followed behind it in twos, each pair carrying a pole between them from which was hogtied the corpse of a giant boar. Behind these came a score of the smaller, more man-like beasts – those Kat had named ungors – all armed with spears, and some leading dogs – or things that might once have been dogs – on ropes.

Now it was the Slayers' turn to get restless. Felix could hear them muttering.

'Dibs on the big one.'

'I called him first.'

'Abominations.'

'Snorri could use a good fight just now.'

'Quiet, sirs,' hissed Ilgner urgently. 'Their hearing is as good as their sense of smell.'

'We can only hope,' said Rodi, but the dwarfs' murmuring stopped.

Felix and the others watched in silence as the hunting party plodded along, snarling at each other and the weather and shaking the wet sleet from their fur. All Ilgner's party had to do was wait. Another minute and the beasts would be out of sight. A minute after that they would be out of earshot.

One of the dogs raised its tusked snout, sniffing, and Felix and the others held their breath. Had it scented them? It stopped and strained towards the trees. Its ungor master jerked its leash and cursed it. The dog barked and kept looking at the woods. The knights and the Slayers white-knuckled their weapons. Kat raised her bow, though Felix doubted even she could hit a target through that thick screen of trees.

The dog barked again. The ungor snarled and kicked it, dragging it on. It growled at the abuse, then at last gave up and padded on.

Felix, Ortwin, Kat and the knights sighed with relief. The Slayers cursed.

Gotrek sneered. 'Dogs on both ends of that leash–'

He was cut off by a crashing and a thudding at their backs. Everybody turned, peering into the depths of the forest with eyes blinded from staring towards the relative brightness of the path. Out of the shadows came two of the ungors, filthy, half-naked savages with tiny horns and pointed teeth. One had a brace of rabbits over its shoulder, the other carried a dead fox by the hind leg. They were running right for the hidden party.

'Kill them,' snapped Ilgner. 'Swiftly!'

The two ungors pulled up short as they saw the knights and the Slayers standing before them in the darkness. Their eyes bulged and they opened their mouths to scream.

The one with the fox never got a chance. An arrow appeared in its throat and it toppled backwards without a sound. The other, however, lived a second longer, and spent it screaming and trying to run.

Two of Ilgner's men fired their crossbows. The two bolts vanished into the ungor's back and it went down thrashing and shrieking. Another shot from Kat silenced it, and everybody turned back to the path. Had the hunters heard over the wind?

There was a sound of bestial voices raised in the distance, and then the tread of heavy hooves coming nearer.

'They heard,' said Kat.

'Damn and blast,' said Ilgner.

'Grimnir be praised!' said Rodi and Argrin.

Ilgner started forwards, motioning for the rest to follow. 'Back to the open path. Hurry. They'll murder us in here. No, curse you! Leave the horses!'

The knights and the Slayers shouldered through the maze of trees towards the cleared strip, but before they had made it halfway, a handful of the ungors came back down the path, dogs straining at their leashes as they peered into the woods and called out questions. Then one of them shouted and pointed directly at Felix – or so it seemed to him – and it and its comrades charged baying into the tree line, their massive dogs bounding before them.

'At them!' roared Ilgner. 'Push them out! Don't let them trap us in here!'

The knights shouted a battle cry and ran forwards, shields up and swords back. The Slayers were just behind, axes and hammers high, roaring with joyous rage. Felix, Kat and Ortwin ran with them, screaming along with the rest.

The two sides crashed together just inside the tree line, swords and axes singing and blood flying. Felix grinned with grim pleasure as he saw that this would be no repeat of the fight around the ale wagon. The ungors were outnumbered and outfought. They weren't attacking hired bravos and old men this time, but well-trained, well-armoured men, and berserk, battle-hardened dwarfs, and they were getting the worst of it.

Felix cut down a dog with scales for skin, then gutted an ungor with bat ears and two rows of pointed teeth. Ortwin and Kat killed another dog. All around them axes fell and swords flashed and the ungors shrieked and died. Then they were stumbling out onto the cleared path with all the rest – and straight into the thundering charge of the five big beastmen and the rest of their ungor followers. Three of the knights went down instantly under the crushing blows of spiked clubs and crude axes.

'Dress ranks!' shouted Ilgner. 'Dress ranks!'

But it was too late. The gors were already in their midst, swinging in all directions as their smaller followers circled and struck from without. Another knight fell. Ilgner's visor was ripped away by a spiked club, and blood sprayed from his helmet like sweat as he fought the beastmen's bear-headed leader.

Then the Slayers shoved to the fore, howling for blood. Gotrek's axe bit into a beastman's club and he wrenched the weapon out of its hands. Felix and Ortwin hacked the monster down then turned to fight the ungors that tried to flank them as Gotrek challenged another gor. Snorri elbowed Ilgner aside and crashed his hammer down on the bear-headed beastman's kneecap, shattering it. The big gor fell on its side and Ilgner and two of his knights stabbed it to death. Rodi and Argrin struck a beastman at exactly the same time and it crashed down onto its back.

'Mine!' cried Argrin, as he finished it off.

'No, mine!' roared Rodi, doing the same.

All around the melee, the ungors fell squealing as arrows whispered out of the woods and feathered their backs and sides. Good old Kat. Felix looked up as he stabbed a fallen ungor through the heart. The tide had turned. Now it was the beastmen who were surrounded and the Slayers and the knights who were on the offensive. They were winning. It would be over in seconds.

But then, from the centre of the melee, Ilgner bellowed and pointed. 'Stop them! They'll warn the herd!'

Felix turned. Three of the ungors were running as fast as they could down the cleared path. Already they were hard to see through the sheets of slashing sleet. Two of the knights broke away and ran after them, but in their plate armour they were too slow. The dwarfs would be no better. Ortwin was still engaged. With a resigned grunt, Felix realised it would have to be him.

He charged down the path, slipping and slewing in the mud, but before he'd taken five steps, one of the ungors dropped with an arrow in its back. Felix looked around and saw Kat at the tree line, her feet braced wide as she nocked another arrow and drew back the string. He kept running just in case.

Another of the ungors fell, an arrow sticking from its arse like a tail, but the third one showed some intelligence and swerved for the woods. An arrow followed it and took it in the leg. It stumbled but ran on, vaulting over a felled tree and disappearing into the shadows.

Felix cursed. If they lost the thing they were doomed. The herd would know they were following them. The only sane option at that point would be to turn back – and Felix knew that was an option neither Ilgner nor the Slayers would take. At least the man-beast was wounded. Felix had some chance of catching it.

He ran into the trees, glad that the herd's passage had made the area to either side of the cleared path marginally easier to navigate. All the undergrowth had been mashed flat and pounded into the earth, but the trees were still so closely spaced that it was impossible to see more than a dozen paces ahead. The ungor was out of sight, but Felix could still hear it, thudding and thrashing ahead of him.

Then there were footsteps behind him too. He looked back. Kat was darting through the trees towards him.

'Run!' she said as she passed him.

'I am… running,' he gasped. But not like Kat, he thought. She ran like a deer, as if she had no weight at all. He surged on, struggling to keep up with her.

A second later they dodged around an ancient tree and spied the ungor ahead of them, running with a hopping limp through the pines. It was a vile-looking thing, as lean as a starving wolf, with long greasy hair that flapped behind it as it ran. It had torn Kat's arrow out, and blood ran down its bare leg and soaked into its filthy buskins.

Kat drew an arrow and tried to fit it to her bow while she ran. The ungor looked back and shrieked, its black horse-eyes wide with fear, then dived into the thick brush at the edge of the trampled area, thrashing and kicking to get through.

Kat cursed and ran to the place it had entered, plunging in without slowing. Felix was right behind her. They shouldered together through brambles and bushes as the forest got darker around them. Felix could hear movement from in front of him, and could see the shaking of branches, but he had lost sight of their quarry.

After a moment they pushed out into a slightly more open area and Kat stopped, looking and listening. Felix could hear nothing over his own breathing and the rattle of the sleet on the overhanging needles, but apparently Kat had keener ears.

'This way,' she said, and started to the left.

They ran on, leaping gnarled roots and ducking overhanging branches as they raced up a slick, wooded hill. Felix had no sense of where the ungor was now.

They broke onto a narrow game trail and Kat followed it further up the hill, putting on more speed. At the crest of the hill, the ungor flashed through a shaft of grey light then disappeared beyond the ridge. It was lurching with every step.

'Ha,' said Kat. 'It's slowing.'

'Good,' said Felix. He felt like his throat was made of hot sand. 'So am I.'

They pounded after it, Felix slipping as they reached the top of the rise. Finally, as they came around a bend, it was before them, weaving wearily as it staggered down the path. Felix and Kat charged it. It screeched and dived into the thick brush again, like a rabbit into a hedgerow.

'After it,' shouted Kat.

They plunged in, fighting through the heavy growth as it struggled ahead of them. Then, with a surprised cry, it dropped out of sight, and they heard a heavy thud.

'It's fallen!' said Felix, and pressed forwards eagerly.

'Felix, wait!' barked Kat.

Felix burst through a screen of bushes and stumbled forwards into the clear, then back-pedalled desperately. There was a ravine directly in front of him, dropping down a rocky cliff to a tree-hemmed stream below. His foot slipped at the muddy edge. He fought for balance. Pebbles pattered away under his boot.

Then, just as he knew he was going to fall, Kat clutched his flailing hand and hauled him back. He toppled against her then fell to his knees.

Without a word, Kat stepped past him to the edge of the slope, readying an arrow.

'Thank you, Kat,' said Felix as he got to his feet and joined her. 'Is it dead?'

'I don't know,' she said, peering down into the ravine intently. 'I hope... No, Taal curse it, there it goes.'

Felix looked down where she pointed and saw the ungor just limping under the screen of trees, splashing down the centre of the ice-rimmed stream.

Felix eyed the sheer face of the sleet-slicked cliff uneasily. With some rope they might have descended, but with just hands and feet it would be treacherous. 'I don't know if we can–'

'But we must!' said Kat, angrily. 'If I fail in this we are dead!' She cursed with frustration and began trotting along the edge of the cliff in the direction the man-beast had gone, looking at the thick covering of trees that hid the bottom of the chasm.

'You set yourself a high mark,' said Felix, following her. 'You killed two of the three that ran, and wounded this one–'

'It won't be enough!' she said. Then suddenly she skidded to a stop, staring out into the ravine. 'Ha!'

Felix followed her gaze, trying to see what she saw through the gusts of sleet. At first he couldn't make out anything that would draw her attention, but then he saw that there was a break in the trees through which he could see the glint of the swift-flowing stream.

Felix shook his head. The gap was a good fifty yards from where they were, and at this distance he could have hidden it by holding out his arm and covering it with his palm. The ungor would walk past it in three strides. Could Kat even loose an arrow before it passed? It seemed impossible, even without the wind and the sleet.

Nevertheless, she raised her bow and drew the arrow back to her ear, then stood as still as a statue while she waited.

Felix looked from her to the gap and back, not daring to speak for fear of ruining her concentration. How long could she hold the tension of the bow? How long could she keep her aim steady?

He scanned the trees before the gap, looking for some sign of the man-beast's passage, but the cover was too thick. He could see nothing until the break. He watched it like a cat watches a hole, trying not to blink.

Suddenly Kat loosed the arrow, and Felix gasped, thinking she had fired at nothing, but then, as he watched, astonished, the beast sloshed into the gap – and into the path of the arrow. The shaft caught it in the neck, betwixt shoulder and ear, and it splashed face first into the stream and lay there unmoving, its head and torso half under the water.

Kat let out a yelp of triumph and leapt into the air. 'Yes!' she said, then turned to the still-stunned Felix and hugged him, wrapping her arms around his neck.

Felix snapped out of his staring and burst out in astonished laughter as he hugged her back, lifting her off the ground. 'Well shot, Kat! Sigmar's hammer, what a shot! Never in my...'

His words trailed off as he realised that he was eye to eye with her, and that she was looking at him with the same strange intensity that she had when they had hugged before.

'Kat?' he said.

Suddenly she pushed her mouth to his and kissed him full on the lips, her tongue thrusting forwards to find his. For a moment he responded in kind, too shocked and too aroused to think what he was doing, and they grappled and crushed together like wrestlers.

But then his mind caught up with his body, and he pulled back from her, loosening his grip.

'Kat,' he said again. 'Listen. I... I don't think...'

She looked at him, blushing suddenly, and pushed out of his arms. 'I'm sorry,' she said, turning to hide her face. 'I... I didn't mean to do that. I just...'

She hurried to collect her bow, which she had dropped on the ground.

Felix stepped towards her. 'There's no need to apologise,' he said. 'You just... er, that is, I hadn't expected...'

'Forget it,' said Kat, not looking at him. 'Just forget it. I'm a fool.'

'You're not a fool,' said Felix, turning her around. 'I won't pretend I haven't felt the same... urges, but...' He paused, wondering if he should tell her all the things that had been roiling in his head since that first brief spark of awareness. Could he even articulate it? Better perhaps to keep it simple. 'I've known you since you were seven, Kat. It just feels... wrong.'

She looked up at him, then away again, nodding. 'I... I understand. Only...' She paused, looking as if she was going to continue speaking, but then just turned back the way they had come. 'We should get back to the others.'

She started into the bushes without a look back. Felix looked after her for a moment, wanting to say something to make her feel better, but still not knowing what that would be. He sighed and started after her.

After a while of walking together in silence he shook his head and laughed. 'I still don't understand how you made that shot. You loosed the arrow before the beast appeared.'

'It was walking in the stream,' she said, her voice dull. 'I shot when I saw the ripples of its steps. I knew it would follow behind them.'

* * *

By the time Felix and Kat made their way back to the others, the wind had become stronger and the sleet had turned to snow – great fat flakes that whirled before the gale to stick to their clothes and melt into the mud.

They found Ilgner and his knights and the Slayers tending to their wounds in the midst of the bodies of the fallen beastmen.

'Excellent news,' said the general when Felix told him the runners were dead. 'Then we may proceed.' He had a bloody gash across his nose and cheeks that one of his knights was stitching up with needle and thread.

The sewing knight looked uneasily at the sky. 'This doesn't look like letting up, my lord,' he said. 'We could be in for a bad storm.'

Ilgner shrugged, seemingly entirely unaffected by the terrible cut on his face. 'We're stuck in it no matter if we go forwards or back, so... onwards.'

As the party hurried to finish binding their wounds, Felix noticed Ortwin off to one side, kneeling in the mud beside one of the beastmen, his head bowed mournfully.

Felix crossed to him. 'Everything all right, Ortwin?' he asked. 'Did you not find this battle as glorious as the others?'

Ortwin raised his head. There were tears in his eyes. 'It isn't that, Herr Jaeger,' he said. 'It is this.' He indicated the dead beastman he knelt beside.

Felix blinked in surprise as he realised that the rusty, dented breastplate that the monster wore strapped around its powerful furred torso was emblazoned with the heraldry of the Order of the Fiery Heart.

NINE

'I fear we have reached the end of our quest, Herr Jaeger,' said Ortwin with a break in his voice. 'I fear we have discovered the fate of Sir Teobalt's brother templars.'

Felix sighed, his shoulders slumping. It wasn't as if he hadn't expected this all along – it had almost been inevitable that they would find that the templars had been killed by the beastmen. Still it was one thing to expect a tragedy, and another to learn that it had actually occurred. The tiny spark of foolish hope he had carried with him from Altdorf guttered and went out. He might win Karaghul now, for he had done what Teobalt had asked of him, but there would be no joy in it.

'I'm sorry, Ortwin. Truly. At least we know they died fighting bravely,' he said, noting the battered state of the stolen breastplate. To his mind that was poor compensation, but it seemed to comfort Ortwin.

The young squire nodded and said, 'Aye. They would have wished for no better end than to die fighting the enemies of mankind. May Sigmar welcome them to his halls.'

Felix nodded and stood a moment in silence, then turned and left the boy to his prayers.

Three of Ilgner's knights had to be left behind. One had been crushed to death by a beastman's mace, his armour so crumpled that he could not be removed from it. Another had a cracked skull and could not see straight, while the third had a shattered pelvis and could not walk or sit on a horse, let alone fight. Ilgner left the two wounded men with the corpse and some food and a fire, and said they would come back for them once they had seen what there was to see.

It seemed a polite abandonment to Felix, and he didn't doubt that the knights knew it. Even if Ilgner's party met no mishap while scouting the herd, it might be days before they returned, and both men were in need of immediate attention. Indeed, had Ilgner turned around and returned to Stangenschloss right then, it would still have been unlikely that the wounded knights would have survived the journey. Felix was impressed by how calmly the men accepted their fates, and it seemed the Slayers were too.

Argrin left them his keg of ale – which was admittedly nearly empty, but still had enough for a few drinks each – and Rodi said he would pray to Grimnir for them.

He shook his head as the rest of the party got underway. 'I hope when it comes, my doom is clean,' he said. 'Starving to death is no way to die.'

'Maybe some more beastmen will come,' said Snorri.

'Aye,' said Argrin. 'That would be best.'

'Dying well no matter the circumstance – that is what is best.' said Gotrek. 'No one gets to choose their doom, only how they will face it.'

The other Slayers nodded gravely at this. Even Rodi had no comment to make.

The party wasn't long on its march before the snow started sticking, turning the muddy track into dirty slush, and mantling the shoulders of the forest's green pines with epaulets of white. It fell so thickly and fiercely now that Felix found it impossible to see more than a few steps ahead, and he huddled inside his old red cloak and wished it had a hood. Fortunately, the path of the herd remained as easy to follow as ever – a raw gash of severed stumps that wound up and down wooded hillsides and between towering boulders through which the wind howled and the snow danced.

An hour on and the snow was covering even the muddy trail. An hour after that, in an open valley of scattered pines between high crags, Kat found hoof prints in the snow – a very different thing than finding snow in hoof prints. It meant that the herd had passed by so recently that the swiftly falling flakes had not yet had time to cover them.

'They are close, my lord,' she said to the general. 'Only minutes ahead.'

'Go find them and report back,' said Ilgner. 'We will follow slowly.'

Kat saluted and hurried off into the snow, disappearing almost instantly behind the slashing curtain of white. Felix shivered to see her going off into such danger, and glared at Ilgner for sending her on so blithely. Then he snorted angrily at himself. It was her job after all, and he had seen her do it before without worrying for her. Foolish how an unexpected spark and an unintended kiss had made him suddenly protective of her.

His mind continued to churn with thoughts of her. Damn the girl, why had she kissed him like that? The wildness of it! The sweet hunger of it! The urgent strength of her arms as she grappled herself to him! It made him dizzy just thinking about it.

He tried to calm himself. The reasons why being with her would be a bad idea were still as valid as they had been before, but now he found himself hunting for arguments that would poke holes in them. She wasn't *that* much younger than him, was she? And maybe it wasn't necessary that he love her. Perhaps she didn't love him. Perhaps all she wanted was a few nights together while they continued on the trail of the beasts.

He looked around at Ilgner and his knights, and Ortwin and the Slayers. No. That wouldn't be such a good idea. He didn't want a repeat of the embarrassment he and Claudia had endured on board the *Pride of Skintstaad*. Whatever he decided, he would have to wait until they got back to civilisation. Perhaps by then his fever for the girl would have cooled somewhat and he would be able to think rationally again.

He breathed a sigh of relief and returned his attention to their surroundings, pleased to have defused his trouble, at least for now.

The knights and the Slayers were following the beastmen's trail at a walk, not wanting to accidentally stumble into the tail of the herd. Here in this more open area, with only a few twisted pines dotting the valley floor, the true breadth of the herd's trail could be seen at last. The swathe of snow blackened by their passage was more than a hundred paces wide, and had been churned up by thousands of hooves. It was an intimidating sight.

Felix looked over to Ortwin to see how he was doing. He was worried about him. The boy had been praying constantly since Felix had left him to it back at the site of the fight with the foragers. Not only that, before they had resumed their hunt, Ortwin had stripped the breastplate with the insignia of the Order of the Fiery Heart from the dead beastman, and now wore it instead of his own.

'All right, Ortwin?' Felix asked.

'Yes, Herr Jaeger,' said Ortwin, breaking off his verses. 'Perfectly all right, thank you.'

'Not blaming yourself for the death of the templars or anything like that are you?'

'No, sir,' said Ortwin. 'It was the beastmen who slew them. And the order shall have its vengeance upon them, sir.'

'Of course they will,' said Felix. 'Of course they will.'

Less than an hour later, just as the grey day was darkening to a murky charcoal twilight, Kat's little bundled figure trotted out of the snow and waved them down. Felix and Gotrek and the others gathered around as she stood at Ilgner's stirrup to make her report. Her eyes were wide and fearful.

'I found them,' she said.

'And?' asked Ilgner, when she didn't go on.

'My lord, there are thousands of them. Thousands. I could not guess how many. I ran along the side of them for a quarter of an hour and still did not see the front of the herd. It wound away through the hills for... forever.'

'And did you see any champions among them? Any fiends of the Wastes?' Ilgner asked.

Kat shook her head. 'I didn't, my lord, but I did not reach the head, so did not see the leaders.'

Ilgner nodded, thinking, then sighed. 'There's no help for it. I must see them. I must know what we face.' He looked to Kat again. 'Can you bring us to the front of their line undetected?'

'I believe so, my lord,' said Kat after a moment. 'They are making their way over the hills by the broadest valleys. It takes them out of their way a bit. I think I may find a straighter line through smaller passes and get ahead of them, but it will be dangerous. They will have scouts and outriders moving before them and beside them. In this weather we won't know they are near us until they are on top of us.'

'Still we must risk it,' said Ilgner. 'It is that or risk doom for all the towns south of Stangenschloss.' He waved a gauntleted hand. 'Lead on, Kat. Lead on.'

And so they followed Kat's footprints up into the hills through narrow valleys and tree-choked canyons, all white and soft with snow that was now up to Felix's knees. It was hard slogging, and though the wind bit at his nose and cheeks, sweat was running down his back and ribs. The snow dragged at their legs and made it hard for them to judge their footing. More than once Felix slipped and fell and had to accept Gotrek's hand to stand again.

By the time they had reached the top of the hills, the snow had eased off somewhat, though the wind did not. It blasted straight over the crest, driving the flakes into their faces so hard that they felt more like sand than snow.

Rodi looked up as ragged clouds streamed across the sky, shredding like carded wool and revealing the sickly green light of Morrslieb behind them.

'Be easier to see them now,' he said.

'And easier for them to see us,' said Felix unhappily. Thousands of beastmen, Kat had said. A herd that went on forever. It seemed just the sort of doom Gotrek would be unable to resist – leagues from nowhere, in knee-deep snow, so that even if Felix wasn't killed by the beastmen who killed the Slayer, he would likely die from exposure before he made it back to civilisation. Wonderful.

They tucked their heads and started down the other side of the hill, and for another hour continued to go up and down smaller hills and in and out of wooded valleys until at last, just as it was becoming full dark, Gotrek lifted his head and inhaled.

'They're close,' he said. 'I can smell them.'

'No,' said Snorri, waving a hand behind him. 'That was Snorri. Sorry.'

'Unless you ate a wet fur coat,' said Rodi, 'it isn't just you. I smell them too.'

Just then Kat came back, appearing out of the trees to their left like a white ghost. 'They're coming,' she said, panting a bit. 'Down the length of the next valley.' She pointed back behind her. 'There is a stand of trees on the other side of this ridge. You may spy on them from there without being seen, my lord.'

'Excellent,' said Ilgner. 'Good work, Kat. Now we shall see what we shall see.'

They heard them before they saw them.

It was a quarter of an hour later. Felix was hunkered down at the edge of a pine wood that stretched down from the crest of the low hill behind them. He gazed with the others into a wide valley of jutting boulders and sparse, new-growth pine as the wind tore at his cloak and the steady snow slanted down ceaselessly from the charcoal sky and piled on his shoulders. It was full night now, but the white of the snow that blanketed the valley and the occasional light of Morrslieb piercing the torn and scudding clouds gave the scene the dim, colourless phosphorescence of a cave mushroom.

Despite his cloak, Felix was aching from the cold. His hands were stiff with it, and his face raw with it. Kat's hat was pulled down so low, and her scarf so high, that only her eyes were visible, flicking up and down the valley anxiously while Ilgner and the knights shuffled and stamped their feet to keep warm. Ortwin shivered, his teeth chattering as he continued his ceaseless praying. Only the Slayers didn't seem to mind the cold. They squatted there shirtless, their eyebrows, beards and moustaches dusted with snow and crusted with ice, and didn't even shiver.

'Snorri forgets why we're here,' said Snorri after a while.

'Beastmen, Nosebiter,' said Gotrek. 'We hunt beastmen.'

'Ah,' said Snorri. 'Now Snorri remembers. Did Snorri ever tell you about the time he fought beastmen with his friends Gotrek and Felix?'

Gotrek grunted, but said nothing.

Then it came – a distant chanting brought on the wind, the sound of a thousand savage voices raised in unison.

Everyone looked up at once, then turned towards the north end of the valley. There was nothing to see yet, but the noise grew steadily louder, and was soon joined by a steady rumble that they could feel through the ground. The vibration was slow and rhythmic, like that of marching feet, but Felix knew the beasts didn't march – they shambled along in a disorganised mob – so what was it? The chanting kept time with the thudding rhythm – a single phrase, repeated over and over in the beasts' crude tongue, a vile gargle of harsh syllables and guttural grunts. And layered over it all were louder noises – whip cracks and roaring, wailing and smashing, and sounds of titanic tearing and snapping.

'What are they doing?' Felix wondered aloud.

No one had an answer for him.

Then, after minutes of staring, with the snow and the moonlight playing tricks on his eyes and making him see all sorts of things in the swirling flurries, Felix blinked and shook his head, for it seemed to him that the white distance was glowing yellow, like a candle set inside a porcelain bowl.

When he looked again the glow was brighter, and he knew it wasn't a trick of the eye.

'They're here,' whispered Kat.

Soon the silhouettes of young pines could be seen against the yellow light, and the snow flakes danced and glowed before it like fireflies, while the chanting and the thumping got louder, as did the syncopation of thuds and roars and cracks.

It seemed to take forever for the glow to get closer, and Felix wondered why. He knew from experience that beastmen could travel very quickly through the woods when they wanted to, but this herd seemed to be moving at a crawl. Even dwarfs marched faster.

Then, as Felix and the rest stared, one of the silhouetted trees shivered and thrashed like it was in a cyclone, then slowly toppled, accompanied by a horrendous splintering crash. Another tree fell the same way a moment later, and then, after a pause, another. It was as if some gigantic foot was crushing them to the earth.

Felix looked around at the others, his heart racing.

Ilgner's knights were wide-eyed and staring. Kat was shrinking back like a rabbit. The Slayers were grinning with savage anticipation. Ortwin was still praying, his eyes closed.

'By all that's holy,' said Ilgner. 'What can flatten a tree like that?'

Felix looked back to the valley. The yellow light was brighter still, and had a shape now – long and sinuous, like some impossibly large glow-worm inching through the trees. The end of it faded into the snow-shrouded distance. It might have gone on forever.

More trees fell as the light crept ever closer. Felix began to see individual torches, and monstrous shadows moving around them, and now he could hear axes at work, which was almost a relief – for it was a much more mundane explanation for the toppling trees than the mad phantasms that had welled up unbidden in his mind.

"Ware the scouts,' said Kat.

Felix and the others looked where she pointed. Ahead of the crawling glow, dark shapes moved through the slender pines. Huge hunched shadows with giant axes and clubs in their hands, wading ponderously through the snowdrifts and looking all around them. Felix crouched lower instinctively as he saw them, but they continued on.

Then, finally, as more trees snapped and fell, through the swirling white veil of the snow came the column itself, and all Felix could do was stare.

First came the ungors, all carrying aloft burning brands to light the way. Just behind them lumbered a vanguard of huge, horn-headed gors, all in armour and carrying terrible weapons, which they raised over their heads and shook in time to the incessant chanting. There were hundreds of them, striding forwards in one ragged rank that stretched from just below Ilgner's position across to the far side of the valley for as far as Felix could see.

Behind them the trees fell. Felix squinted to make out the details in the bobbing lights of a moving mass of torches. The little shadows of hunched ungors scurried around the fallen trees, dragging them towards the sides of the valley, then running back for more as whip-wielding gors roared and lashed out at them.

Two more pines shivered and crashed to the ground with splintering screams, and four enormous horned shadows loomed through the gap they had made.

Kat gasped when she saw them, and Felix was afraid he had too. They were gigantic things, towering over the gors as the gors towered over the ungors, with shaggy, bull-shaped heads and heavy curling horns that stretched wider than a man might spread his arms. Each of them carried an axe taller than a beastman, with a double-bladed head that a dwarf could have hidden behind.

As the ungors hooked the branches of the fallen pines with chains and dragged them aside, the four great bulls strode to the next trees that stood in their way and hacked at their bases with slow, methodical strokes – one two, one two, one two. The trees were young and thin. It took no more than four bites of the massive axes for them to fall, then the bulls were onto the next group, with no more interest or emotion than a machine. It looked as if they had been doing this forever, and that they could go on doing it forever, never tiring, never slowing, never looking up from their work.

'Now they,' said Argrin, under his breath, 'would be a good doom.'

'For you?' said Rodi. 'Not if I reached 'em first.'

'Snorri thinks there is enough doom here for everybody,' said Snorri.

Felix wondered if the addled Slayer had ever spoken a truer word.

Gotrek just grunted and watched.

'But I don't understand why they're doing it,' muttered Ilgner, seemingly to himself. 'Have they been cutting this path since the Howling Hills? What for?'

Two columns of ungor torchbearers filed from the gap that the terrible minotaurs had cut in the trees. Between them capered a throng of wild-looking beastmen, all masked and bedecked with feathers and bones and strange fetishes – but otherwise entirely naked – and all shaking long staves capped with human and beast skulls and bits of crystal and brass that glittered and bounced in the torchlight. The dancing beastmen roared a guttural chant and thrust up their totems to the ponderous thudding rhythm, which continued to grow louder with each passing second. Some of them tore their flesh in ecstasy. Some of them burned themselves with torches, or butted heads with their fellows, their horns clashing with deafening cracks. Some fell, and scurrying ungors dragged them to the side, while new revellers jumped in to take their place.

And every few paces, following some rhythm Felix could not perceive, all of them would turn and bow behind them, wailing and shouting, then leap up again to dance on as before.

What comes now? Felix wondered anxiously. Are they bowing to some god? Has some champion of Chaos inspired this frenzy in them? If beasts as large as the minotaurs were toiling as lumberjacks, how terrible must the leader be?

Then Felix gasped again, as did all the other men, while the Slayers swore in surprise.

For an instant, as it came out of the trees, Felix thought that his mad imagining had been true, and that it *was* a giant glow-worm that crawled among the herd, for the thing was long and round like a worm and had many legs, but then, as he focused through the blaze of torches that surrounded it, he saw that what he thought were the thing's legs were actually beastmen, all walking in file and in step, with heavy wooden yokes across their shoulders that carried what Felix had thought was the body of the worm, but which was in reality the largest henge stone Felix had ever seen.

'Sigmar's blood!' breathed Ilgner, as they watched it emerge from the trees. 'What is it?'

'It… it is a herdstone,' said Kat. 'The totem of the tribe. But… but it's too big. And they never move them.'

'They do now,' said Gotrek.

The stone was laid on its side, and was as long as the mast of a Bretonnian galleon. Its rune-daubed dark grey granite had been crudely shaped, starting narrow at the top, but thickening as it went along until it was perhaps eight feet in diameter near the centre. Jagged veins of quartz twisted through it, pulsing from within with a weird blue light in time with its bearers' chant.

Several of Ilgner's knights made the sign of the hammer as they stared down at the thing, and Felix understood why. It radiated fell power like an evil sun. He didn't just *see* the pulses of blue light, he felt them on his skin like a warm wind, and within his mind, like a whisper heard in a nightmare. It made him want to run away, but also to run to it, to throw down his weapon and join in the revellers' frenzied dance. It took an effort of will to remain where he was and only watch.

'Slayer Gurnisson,' said Ilgner. 'Your axe. Hide its glow.'

Felix turned to see Gotrek taking his axe off his back and burying the head in the snow at his feet. Its runes were blazing almost as brightly as a torch. Even through the snow Felix could see their glow.

Gotrek grunted, annoyed, then laid the axe flat and sat on it. The light disappeared.

Felix shared an amused smile with Kat, then turned back to the procession below.

Double columns of beastmen marched under the sturdy yokes on either side of the stone, all striding in unison to the rhythm, and shaking the ground with each ponderous step. There were at least two hundred of the monsters, a hundred per side, and more milled along beside them, chanting as well, their weapons out, the fur of their faces painted with blue stripes and symbols – an honour guard perhaps.

As the base of the stone appeared from between the trees, Felix and the others at last saw the leaders of the herd. The first was an enormous beastman, almost as large and muscular as the minotaurs, though leaner, who paced up and down on top of the stone, roaring at those who carried it. He had the blunt head and thick curling horns of a ram, but his teeth, when he snarled, were those of a predator, and his eyes glowed with the same blue light that pulsed from the stone.

The thick fur that covered his rippling muscles was coal-black, and criss-crossed with the white scars of a hundred battles. Over this natural armour he wore a suit of steel and bronze armour that fitted him perfectly, yet looked far beyond any beastman's ability to make. The axe he carried also bore the mark of the same sophisticated hand. It was a weapon as tall as Felix, crowned with a huge, single-bladed head with a deep notch in the cutting edge shaped so that it looked like the open beak of some screaming predatory bird. Fist-sized blue gems gleamed on each side of the axe like angry avian eyes.

'There now,' said Rodi, chuckling. 'I'll have a go at *him*.'

'I thought you wanted the bulls,' said Argrin.

'They'll be for afters,' said Rodi.

While the war-leader prowled up and down the stone, urging on his followers with hoarse bellows, the stone's other passenger stood stock still upon it, a gnarled staff raised high as he lifted his goatish head to exhort the heavens in a keening, high-pitched wail. He was half the size of the other, and appeared to be some sort of bestial holy man, grey of fur and gaunt with age, and dressed in long dirty robes, stitched over with crude symbols. On his cadaverous head he wore a leather mask with a sinuous blue symbol painted on the brow, and a crest of blue feathers that arced over his head and ran all the way down his back. One of his horns was bent at an odd angle, as if it had been damaged when he was young. The strangest part of his aspect, however, was the hundreds of severed bird claws that dangled from every part of his costume at the ends of strings and leather thongs. Eagle claws served him as earrings, crow feet as braid-locks in his straggly goat beard. Hawks' talons clutched every finger of his scrawny hands and shrivelled chicken feet fringed the arms of his robes. Even the head of his leather-wrapped, fetish-woven staff followed the motif, for it appeared to be the powerful fore-claw of a griffon, which clutched a pulsing blue orb.

'A shaman,' hissed Kat. She made a curious sign by hooking her thumbs and spreading her fingers so that her hands looked like antlers, then thrust them angrily in the robed beast's direction. 'Taal wither you, fiend. Rhya poison your fodder.'

'Is it a crusade of some kind, then?' asked Ilgner, again to himself. 'Do they do the bidding of their foul gods?'

The stone-bearers plodded slowly on, coming parallel with Ilgner's party's hiding place, with the main body of the herd appearing at last behind them. Felix stared as he watched them shamble out of the snow. For all the eldritch fear that the stone and its riders had inspired in Felix's heart, this was perhaps the most terrifying sight he had yet beheld.

The beastmen came down the valley like a slow brown tide, thousands upon thousands of them, an endless winding river vanishing into the opaque distance, and filling the valley from edge to edge so that the nearest beasts lapped halfway up the hill that Ilgner's party hid upon. Every single one of them croaked the shaman's chant, so that the air throbbed with it. Felix edged further back into the pines for fear of being seen. Not since his journey with Gotrek and Malakai over the Chaos Wastes had he seen so many of the monsters in one place.

Ilgner too seemed impressed. 'This beggars belief,' he whispered. 'Kat, have you ever seen the like?'

She shook her head. 'There are more here than all the herds I have spied upon combined.'

'But what is their purpose?' asked Ilgner again. 'Where do they go with the thing? What do they mean to do with it?'

'Whatever it is,' said Kat, 'they are heading south, into the lands of men. They must be stopped.'

'Aye,' said Ilgner. 'Aye.' And Felix could tell that he had left unspoken the simple question, 'How?'

For the Slayers the question wasn't how, but when? They could barely contain their eagerness to be at the monsters. They shifted restlessly and toyed with their weapons.

Gotrek turned to Felix, Ilgner and the rest, a wild light in his single eye. 'You'd best get away,' he said. 'Return to the fort and prepare for what is to come. This is a true doom, a final doom at last. We four will die here.' He looked at Felix. 'Manling–'

But whatever he had been about to say was cut off as, behind him, Ortwin stood abruptly from his fevered praying and drew his sword, then stepped to the edge of the pines and held it aloft.

'The Order of the Fiery Heart shall have its vengeance!' he cried, and plunged down the hill, wading through the knee-deep snow straight towards the herdstone, as ten-score beastmen turned their heads his way.

For a stunned second, everyone just stared, and then they were all scrambling at once.

'Stop him!' hissed Ilgner.

'Kill him!' barked Rodi.

'Run!' whispered Kat.

Felix and some of the knights stood and started forwards, but hesitated at the edge of the woods. Kat half-drew an arrow, then stopped, uncertain. Only Gotrek acted. He scooped up some snow between his hands, packed it and hurled it. It caught the squire square on the back of the head and pitched him face first into the snow.

'Mad infant,' grunted Argrin.

'Forget him,' said Ilgner, staring at the beasts, more and more of which were turning and looking in their direction. 'We must go. Now!'

Felix was in hearty agreement, but he hesitated. Sir Teobalt had entrusted the boy to his care. He couldn't just leave him behind. With a curse, he ran down the hill, lifting his knees like a Kislevite dancer so that the snow wouldn't slow him.

'Felix! No!' called Kat.

Ortwin was just picking himself up when Felix reached him.

'Come on, you little idiot,' he snapped, and grabbed the squire's arm, pulling him back towards the top of the hill. The nearest gors and ungors were starting towards them, roaring and raising their weapons, and the ripple of turning heads had reached the herdstone.

Ortwin struggled to get away. 'No, I must avenge my masters!'

Felix cuffed his ear. 'What kind of vengeance is suicide? Come *on*!' He hauled on Ortwin's arm and the boy reluctantly allowed himself to be dragged up the hill.

Behind them, more of the beastmen were breaking from the column, their howls getting louder. At the crest, Kat was crouching and beckoning them on as Ilgner and his men backed away and the Slayers readied their weapons.

'Hurry!' she cried.

Then a hair-raising shriek split the night and froze them all in their tracks. Felix turned as it echoed away down the valley, and saw that the beast-shaman was looking their way, his staff raised, and that the whole herd now stood staring at them, unmoving and utterly silent as the snow fell around them. The skin crawled on the back of Felix's neck as he looked at them. He could see the hate boiling in their glittering animal eyes, their hands tensing on the hafts of their weapons, but they remained where they were. Even the ones who had been chasing them stopped and fell silent.

'What are they doing?' asked Ortwin.

'I have no idea,' said Felix. 'Just keep moving.'

He turned up the hill as the shaman's voice rang out a second time, this time in a high chant, different from the one before, faster and more urgent. Then, like the murmur of thunder, the herd began to echo him, getting louder and more insistent with each repetition.

Felix could feel the air tingle around him, and the falling snow began to dance in wild eddies that bore no relation to the direction of the wind.

'Run!' he shouted, and shoved the boy ahead of him.

There was a crack like a pistol shot and Felix glanced back, fearful. The shaman was slamming the head of his orb-clutching griffon-claw staff against the herdstone in time to the new chant, and with each strike, the veins of quartz that ran through it flashed blue and bright.

'Faster!' Felix shouted.

At the top of the hill, Ilgner and his knights had recovered from their surprise and were scrambling to mount their horses. Kat was backing away, open-mouthed, the flashes of blue reflecting in her white-rimmed eyes. The Slayers were snarling and striding forwards, ready for battle.

Felix looked back again. The flashes from the stone were getting brighter and brighter as the old shaman struck harder and the chant got louder. The blue light lanced out in knife-sharp shafts, like bars of sunlight cutting through a dark room.

One shaft cut across the snow to Felix's right, turning it a blinding white. He pressed on, blinking and wincing as he herded Ortwin before him, then gaped when he saw that the snow where the light had touched it was melting, steam rising from it in wispy curls.

'Sigmar, he's aiming for us!' he said. He waved a wild hand at the knights on their horses. 'Down! Down! The light!'

Another crack came from behind them, and Felix threw himself to the snow, trying to knock Ortwin down with him, but the boy only stumbled and turned, reaching out a hand.

'Herr Jaeger, take my–'

'Ortwin! Curse you, get–'

A jagged bar of blue-white light flashed across Ortwin's eyes and he fell back with a cry, throwing his hands over his face. Felix looked away, expecting to hear the sizzle of cooking meat, or the crackle of charring skin, but it didn't come.

'My eyes!' wailed Ortwin. 'My eyes!' Another shaft of light shot up the hill past them and Felix heard Ilgner and his knights cry out. He grabbed Ortwin's hand and dragged him on. Only a few more steps, a few more plodding, slogging steps.

Ortwin stumbled along blindly behind him, wailing, 'It burns! Oh,

Sigmar protect me, it burns!' and dragging behind horribly. Did the boy want to die?

Felix turned, angry. 'Move, damn you! Pick up your–'

He stopped, staring, utterly stricken. 'By the gods,' he murmured. 'Your face.'

'What's wrong?' the boy asked. Then he shrieked in agony as he was wracked with convulsions.

Felix stumbled back from him, horrified. The boy was changing before his eyes. Hair grew on his cheeks and spread like fire to his hairline. His nose was lengthening and his chin receding. His ears were growing points. Lumps were beginning to form on either side of his brow.

Ortwin reached out trembling hands towards Felix as another spasm shook him. 'Please, Herr Jaeger. Help me! What's happening to me?'

Claws tore out through the fingers of the boy's gloves. Stubby horns burst from his forehead in sprays of blood, and his irises swelled to fill his whole eye.

The boy was becoming a beast.

TEN

The squire's yellow claws clutched at Felix's legs. 'Hllp me, Hrrr Jaegrr,' he pleaded. His voice was no longer human – more like the bleating of a goat. Felix could barely understand him.

'Ortwin,' said Felix in a whisper. 'I'm sorry.'

He kicked the boy in the chest, sending him tumbling down towards the herd, then turned and ran up the slope, his mind jagged with grief for the boy and fear for himself. What would he tell Sir Teobalt?

Fresh screams made him look up, and he moaned with despair. At the top of the hill, Ilgner's knights were writhing and falling from their rearing horses as Gotrek and the other Slayers backed away from them. One of the knights was clawing at his face. Another was tearing at his breastplate, shrieking, 'Bees! Wasps! Get them off!' as fur grew from the joints of his armour. A third looked up from where he had fallen and Felix saw to his horror that he had a snout where his mouth had been, and the black, shining eyes of a goat. A warhorse danced in a circle, hooves flying as tusks grew from its mouth and bony spines rose from its mane.

'Slayers!' roared Gotrek. 'To work!'

Kat knelt over Lord Ilgner, who was curled and shaking in the snow. 'My lord,' she cried. 'My lord, are you all right?'

Lord Ilgner howled with pain and the back of his cuirass split down the middle. A sable-furred ridge like that of a boar ripped out from it. He turned, snarling from a bestial mouth, and swiped a gauntleted paw at her, knocking her onto her back.

Her eyes went wide with shock as the thing that had been Ilgner rose and advanced on her. 'Oh no, my lord,' she wept. 'Not you. Not you!'

Felix reached the crest of the hill and charged the general, sword high, but Gotrek was there first, his axe a blur. Ilgner's wolf-like head dropped from his shoulders in a shower of blood and thudded to the snowy ground between Kat's legs.

Felix groaned with misery. If the knights had only stayed low like Kat and the Slayers, the fatal blue light would have flashed over their heads. 'The poor man,' he mumbled.

'No time for pity, manling,' said Gotrek, as a beast-knight charged him. 'Defend yourself.'

Felix turned just in time to take the sword of one of the changed knights on Karaghul's edge. Felix's arm stung as the force of the blow staggered him back. The thing's muscles had burst its armour and the sword looked like a plaything in its ham-hock hands. Behind it, he could see Snorri, Rodi and Argrin battling armoured monsters and slavering hell-horses in a mad scrum.

Felix slashed back at his opponent, cutting through the furred hide of its leg. It howled and attacked again.

Beside him, Kat chopped at it with her axes, weeping as she did. 'I know them,' she sobbed. 'I know them all.'

Felix ran the changed knight through and stole a glance down the hill as it fell.

Through the ever-swirling snow he could see that the beast-shaman and the war-leader had turned away from them as if they were of no more concern, and the giant herdstone was on the move again, as was the herd that followed behind it. Unfortunately, a dozen or so of the blue-painted honour guard had detached themselves from the rest, and were wading through the snow in their direction. Of Ortwin he could see no sign.

He turned back just as a horse with a mouth like an Arabyan crocodile lunged and snapped at him. He stumbled aside and the thing shouldered him to the ground.

'Gotrek,' gasped Felix, trying to recover his breath. 'More coming.'

'I see them, manling,' said Gotrek.

'We have to get away!' said Kat. 'We have to warn the fort! We have to warn the villages!'

'Aye,' said Felix. He lurched up and faced the horse as it turned and charged again. He dodged away as it kicked at him with its forelegs, then darted in again and gored it in the belly. Kat cut the hamstrings of its back legs with her axes. It collapsed to the ground, screaming, still sounding much too much like a horse. Felix shivered with revulsion.

He and Kat looked around. The melee was over. The Slayers stood shoulder-deep in a ring of dead horses and knights, but the blue-painted beastmen were halfway up the hill.

'Snorri has never killed a horse before,' said Snorri, sounding sad.

'Those weren't horses,' said Argrin.

'Now let's get the real beasts,' said Rodi, striding eagerly towards the edge of the hill.

'No,' said Gotrek grimly. 'This doom must be deferred.'

The two young Slayers turned on him, staring.

'Are you mad, Gurnisson?' asked Rodi.

'This is a great doom,' said Argrin.

Felix looked down the hill. The blue-daubed beastmen were closing fast.

'It is a selfish doom,' said Gotrek. 'If we take it, the fort will not be warned. Thousands will die.'

Rodi snorted. 'A doom is a doom.'

'Aye,' said Gotrek. 'But a great doom makes a difference.'

'We're all doomed if we don't go now,' said Felix, exasperated. This was not the time to be arguing the finer points of Slayer doctrine.

'We're doomed whether we go or stay,' said Rodi. 'The beasts are too fast. We might as well fight now as later.'

'We have to try,' said Kat. 'Please! Let's go!'

'There is one great doom here,' said Argrin solemnly. 'For the one who stays behind.'

'I'll stay!' said Rodi.

'No,' said Snorri. 'Snorri will stay.'

'There's no time for this!' said Felix.

'Let the Slayer who suggested it stay,' said Gotrek. He nodded to Argrin approvingly. 'May Grimnir welcome you to his halls.'

Snorri shrugged. 'That seems fair to Snorri.'

Rodi looked about to burst, but then cursed and spat. 'Fine,' he said. 'But I will have the rear guard.' He bowed to Argrin. 'Die well, Argrin Crownforger.'

Argrin bowed back. 'We shall drink together at Grimnir's table.'

'Goodbye, Argrin,' said Snorri.

'Hurry!' said Kat.

Gotrek, Snorri and Rodi started into the pines without another look back as Argrin stepped to the edge of the hill and readied his steel-headed warhammer.

'Come on, you cow-faced dung piles!' he roared. 'I'll cut you into chops and cook you on Grungni's forge!'

Felix and Kat turned away and hurried after the Slayers as they heard the beastmen bellow in response. Felix was afraid it was all for naught. Argrin wouldn't hold the beastmen for long, and even in the dark and through the whirling flakes, they would have little trouble following the party's footprints in the snow. They were only postponing the end.

'We're not going to be fast enough,' he said when he and Kat caught up to the Slayers. 'They'll follow our footsteps and catch us.'

'Then another will stay behind to stop them,' said Gotrek. 'Until we have all met our doom.'

'If we can reach the deepest woods it might be possible to lose them,' said Kat. 'There are places where the snow never reaches the–'

She was cut off by the roaring of beasts and the clash of steel on steel, rising out of the wail of the wind in the trees.

Rodi paused and turned, but Gotrek shoved him on.

'Keep moving,' he growled.

They hurried up the hill through the darkness, silent and grim, following the footsteps they had made on the way here, and listening to the snatches of the fight that the wind brought them – screams and curses, clashes and thuds – and then, much too quickly, the triumphant howl of the beastmen.

The sound brought a lump to Felix's throat. He had barely known Argrin, but the young Slayer had made a great sacrifice for them, and the fact that it had been very likely worthless just made it all the sadder.

'Lucky bastard,' snarled Rodi, with a rasp of emotion in his voice.

'Snorri is jealous,' said Snorri.

As they reached the top of the ridge and started down the other side, Felix strained his ears behind him. He could hear nothing. The wailing wind covered everything. Had the beastmen given up? Had they decided it was too much bother to give chase, and gone back to the herd? It was impossible to know.

The pines were thicker on this side of the hill, and the darkness beneath them was almost complete. Only the white of the snow gave some light, but not nearly enough. Felix followed Gotrek more by sound than sight. The crackle of branches and the slap of a twig against his cheek told him they were entering another tangle of brush before his eyes did. Felix would have loved to light a torch, but light would be their doom.

Six steps into the thicket, Kat hissed. 'Stop! Turn left!'

Gotrek obligingly turned left, and Felix followed, Kat, Rodi and Snorri crunching in behind him. The bracken grew even thicker here, and the faint light faded entirely. They might have been in a cave.

'Some trouble?' Gotrek asked.

'No,' Kat said. 'But deeper in the bracken, they might not see we've turned off our old path.'

'Ah,' said Gotrek. 'Smart.'

For a few minutes it seemed that the ruse had worked. As they broke out of the brush and continued along the steep shoulder of the hill they heard nothing behind them but the wind. It felt as if they might be entirely alone in the wood.

But then, as Felix followed Gotrek's steps through densely packed trees, feeling his way like a blind man, there was a distant crashing behind them, as of something big wading through bracken, just audible above the moan of the trees.

'Found us again,' called Rodi from the back.

Gotrek cursed and quickened his pace. Felix tried to do the same, flinching at the darkness that loomed up at him with every step. He could hear Kat picking up the pace behind him.

'Find an open space, Gurnisson,' Rodi called again. 'I'll need some room to swing my axe.'

They sped on, Felix stubbing his fingers and barking his knuckles on the trunks of trees he couldn't see, then pushing past. He shivered at the thought of fighting beastmen in the pitch dark. It would be short at least. And he wouldn't see it coming.

A guttural howl echoed from behind them, the baying of a beast that has caught the scent. Felix looked back – a stupid thing to do, since he could no more see behind him than in front. He turned back, and ran smack into a tree, cracking his head on some knot of wood. The world spun around him and he staggered, hissing in pain, then caught himself and felt his way around the tree one-handed as he massaged his temple with the other. There was blood, and a lump was rising. Touching it made his legs go wobbly and he had to steady himself again, fighting nausea.

He started on again, but after a few steps he realised he wasn't hearing Gotrek ahead of him any more. He paused. The noise of the others was off to his left, only a few feet. He edged in that direction, but ran into dense undergrowth. There was no way through. For an instant he thought about working his way back to where he had left the trail, but he didn't dare. The beastmen were in that direction. He'd have to keep going and angle back after the brush thinned.

'Felix?' came Kat's voice.

'Coming,' he called over the wind. 'Sorry.'

He pushed on faster, trying to go straight, but having to go out wider and wider to his right around the tangled brush. He fought for balance as the angle of the hill got steeper under his feet.

Then behind him he heard the thud of hooves and a garble of inhuman voices.

'Hurry, Felix,' Kat hissed. 'They're coming!'

'Move, girl!' shouted Rodi.

Felix shoved at the brush but it wouldn't give. He sidestepped desperately, trying to find a way through. His ankle banged into something hard and immovable on the ground. He fell sideways, flailing with his arms for purchase. His fingers caught at twigs but they snapped, and he was tumbling down the hill in a flopping sprawl of limbs, upside down, then right side up, then crashing into invisible tree trunks, rocks and bushes before slamming hard on his side at the bottom of the slope and cracking his head on another invisible obstacle.

The only thing he could see was stars.

He woke again to the sound of distant fighting. For a long moment he had no idea where he was, or what the sound meant, or why he couldn't see, or what had caused the horrible throbbing in his head. He only knew that lying there in the dark was infinitely preferable to moving in any way. Moving hurt like a hangover, and he didn't care for it. Besides, the wind and the patter of snowflakes on his face were comforting somehow.

Then bubbles of memory began to float up through the mud of his brain and burst one by one on the surface. He had fallen. From where? A hill. Why had he been on a hill? There had been some desperate reason to get somewhere. At that memory his heart filled with dread, though he couldn't remember the cause. He had been trying to reach someone. Who? He knew he had to help them. Had to save them. A girl. She was running from...

Suddenly it all flooded back and he sat up with a gasp. At least he tried to. Really he flopped over on his side and vomited – while his brain smashed around inside his skull like an iron mace that might shatter it from the inside.

On a second try he made it to his hands and knees, which made it very convenient to vomit again – so he did. He was tempted to stay that way for a while, but the sounds of the fighting were still going on. Gotrek and Kat and the others still lived. He had to help them.

He forced himself to his feet with the aid of a tree. It was so black around him that he could see nothing at all – not the snow, not the sky, nothing. For all he knew the crack on the head might have blinded him. But he could hear the fight, above him and off to the left, some distance away.

He staggered forwards, wading through the snow and the blackness with his hands out in front of him. Every step hurt. He had bruises from head to toe, and he had smashed his left knee and twisted his right ankle. At least nothing seemed broken. He stumbled on at a snail's pace, feeling with both his hands and his feet. He wanted to run, but he wasn't sure he'd be able to get up if he fell again.

After a few more steps, the trees thinned out and the ground sloped down a little before him. This was encouraging. He might be able to make better speed in the clear. At the bottom of the little slope the ground under the snow became very flat and smooth. He took another step and his heel shot out to the side. He was on ice!

He scrambled to catch his balance, but his other foot went and he fell backwards. There was a loud crack and the ice gave beneath him. His heart stopped, as the image of plunging into some frozen lake or river and sinking to the bottom in his chainmail flashed through his mind.

Nothing so dramatic happened. He landed flat on his back in a foot of snow, and for a moment thought that he hadn't broken through the ice after all. Then he felt freezing cold water seeping though the seat of his breeches and the back of the leather jerkin he wore under his mail.

With a curse he fought to sit up. Soaking wet in the middle of a snowstorm was not good at all. He put his hand down on the ice to lever himself up. It broke through. His hand hit bottom almost instantly, his sleeve soaked to the elbow. He must be in some frozen pond or stream. He tried to be cautious, but no matter where he put his weight, the ice broke under it, and by the time he dragged himself to the edge he was soaked to the skin from the waist down. His cloak and both sleeves were wet through too.

'This is bad,' he murmured. And then he realised something worse.

He couldn't hear the fight any more. He paused and strained to listen over the howling and moaning of the wind, but there was nothing.

No. There it was. A clash.

He stood and started towards it. No. That way was the water. He'd have to go a little further down to the left. He stumbled on, his teeth chattering and his feet and leg joints aching with cold as his wet breeches slapped around them. His pack felt as if it weighed as much as Gotrek.

He listened again. 'Come on, curse you!' he muttered. 'Keep fighting! Let me hear you!'

He laughed as he realised that all of a sudden he was hurrying to the fight to be rescued, rather than to be the rescuer.

Another clang. He reorientated himself and started ahead again. At least he thought he was moving in the right direction. The wind made it hard to pinpoint the sound. After a few more steps he braved a move to the left and found the stream again. This time he shuffled across as cautiously as an old man – though to be honest, his wet clothes and his muscles were so stiff now he could hardly do anything else.

He reached the opposite bank without incident and listened again. He heard nothing. He moved a little further on. Still nothing. Had he got turned around? Shouldn't he have come to the hill by now? He pressed on, shivering as the wind pressed his ice-crusted clothes against his skin. Another ten steps. Still nothing. Was he even going in a straight line? He couldn't tell.

'Gotrek!' he called. 'Kat! Snorri!' But his voice came out in a plaintive whisper that was whipped away in the wind. He could hardly hear it over the ceaseless chattering of his teeth. And in this wind, he doubted his friends could have heard him even if he had shouted at the top of his lungs. Was that why he couldn't hear them? Or perhaps they were all dead, killed by the blue-painted monsters. Perhaps he was all alone in the Drakwald but for the beastmen – the only living man for a hundred miles.

It came to him then that he was going to die there – that his corpse would be buried in the snow, frozen to the marrow until the spring, when it would thaw and rot, to become food for the beetles and worms of the forest. Maybe some scout or forester would find his bones and wonder who they had belonged to. Just another victim of the war, they would say. And all because he had walked the wrong way around a tree and lost the others. It seemed an impossibly silly reason to die.

A sob lodged painfully in his throat as he thought of all the things he had left unfinished. He would never witness Gotrek's doom or complete his epic. He would never have vengeance upon the skaven sorcerer who had ordered his father's death. He would never see Ulrika again. He would never–

He shook himself. Sigmar, he was having brain fever! He had to stop ruminating and do something or he would die indeed. He had to make a fire and get warm. But, no, if he made a fire, the beastmen would find him. He shrugged. He didn't care. He would rather die warm than frozen. Besides, if Gotrek and the others had won the fight, the light might lead them to him.

He stopped and struggled to take his pack off. He was shaking so violently now he could hardly get his arms out of the straps. Finally he got it off his shoulders and it thudded to the ground behind him. He turned and felt around until he found it. His heart sank. No wonder it had felt so heavy. The leather was wet and crackled with ice. The bedroll and blanket that he had strapped to the bottom of it were soaked through.

He groaned in despair. A wet blanket, no dry clothes to change into. He really was going to die.

He fumbled for the buckles of his pack with fingers so numb that he couldn't feel what he was touching. It seemed to take him an hour to get the straps loose and the flap open – an hour when the cold from his ice-hardened clothes seeped into his skin to the bone. He felt made of lead – cold lead. It was almost impossible to move his arms.

He dug painfully through the contents of the pack, all wet and ruined, until he found his flint and steel and tinderbox. The box was smashed, probably during his fall, and the little pine shavings wet and limp.

'It's not fair!' he said, sobbing, then was glad that no one had been there to hear him.

Pushing to his feet hurt more than a sword wound. It felt like he had Altdorf's temple of Sigmar on his back – like all his joints were wrapped tight with leather straps. He staggered around until he found a bush, then snapped twigs off it until he had a shaking fistful. He turned and went back to where his pack was. It wasn't there. He whimpered and started feeling around. He'd lost it in the dark. It was probably a foot from him and he'd lost it. He found it at last behind him, and knelt beside it, breathing a shuddering sigh of relief and sweeping away the snow in front of him so he could pile the little handful of twigs on the bare ground. Then he found the flint and steel again and struck them together. At least he tried to. His fingers were so stiff, and his shaking so violent, that he missed. He tried again. This time they clashed together, but they were too wet to strike a spark.

With a grunt of frustration he slipped them down between his jack and his shirt, the only place on him that was fully dry. The cold steel against his chest made him flinch, but it had to be done. After a second he fumbled them back out and tried again. A spark!

It flew away on the wind, never coming close to the twigs. He shifted around so that his back was to the gale and tried again. Still the spark flew. He sobbed. Every muscle in his body was cramping with cold. He felt made of wood now. His arms could barely hold their position. His fingers couldn't hold the steel. It slipped out of his hand and fell on the snowy ground. He struggled to pick it up again. It was like trying to grab something with one's elbow. He could only push it around.

At last he got the little bar trapped against his leg and fumbled it up into his grip. He struck it against the flint again, and again, and again. The sparks hopped onto the twigs and died – snuffed by the ice or blown out by the wind.

He paused. He was tired. He couldn't lift his arms any more. He needed to rest. Yes, that was it – a little rest and he would try again. He laid his arms on his knees and bowed his head. All he needed was a few minutes and he would get his strength back. Just a few minutes. He closed his eyes. That was better. He was feeling better already. Warmer even. A gentle heat seemed to be flowing through his veins. He felt cosy. Maybe he would just lie down for a bit. Yes, that was best. A little nap.

He eased over on his side, letting the flint and the steel fall from his fingers and curling into a ball. All was well. A cosy little nap and everything would be fine.

But then, just as he was drifting off into a drowsy dream of hearths and warm brandy, there was a noise in the darkness. His heart lurched. Something was coming for him. He tried to open his eyes, tried to move his arms and legs, to force himself to sit up, to draw his sword. He couldn't. He was pressed to the ground by weariness and petrified with stiffness. His body would not answer his call.

The thing in the darkness got closer. He could hear it behind him. He could hear it breathing.

ELEVEN

'Felix! Felix, wake up!'

Someone was shaking him. It hurt. His muscles screamed. He tried to shrug the person off, tried to complain, but he couldn't move, couldn't stop his jaws from trembling long enough to speak. The person stepped in front of him and held a slotted lantern to his face. Though the light was dim, after so long in the dark it blinded him. He cringed away.

'Rhya be praised.' said the person. 'You're alive!'

Felix knew the voice. A voice from the distant past. A girl he used to know. Kirsten? Ulrika? Was he dreaming? He couldn't tell.

A warm hand touched his face and felt at his neck.

'Gods, not by much. Wait here.'

He heard the person set down the lantern and move away. He squinted against the light, looking around only with his eyes, for he couldn't move his head. Through a screen of slashing snow he saw a little bundled-up form was bustling in and out of his field of vision, taking off her pack, looking though his.

Kat. It was Kat. He wasn't sure if he was disappointed or relieved.

'All wet,' she said to herself. 'Felix, what happened? How did you do this to yourself?'

There was a sharp scraping noise and a flash, and then after a moment, the space in front of him got brighter. Kat moved away and he saw she had started a little fire. It almost made him cry. How had she done it so easily? Why had it been so hard for him? He saw her digging away the snow around him as if she were a dog burying a bone, then she vanished again for a moment. Something was laid over him, and then Kat was kneeling beside him, raising it on sticks. She was making a tent around him.

Then she vanished again, and for long enough that he grew worried. Had she left him? Had something grabbed her?

Finally she stepped back in front of him, a big bundle of dead branches and twigs in her arms. She dropped them beside the little fire and then began to lay them carefully on top of it. The heat of it was reaching his face now. It stung like ice.

When she had built up the fire, she placed her canteen and his next to it, then crawled into the tent and spread out her bedroll beside him, then turned to him and pulled off his cloak, which was stiff and heavy with ice. She threw it out beside the fire, then started on the wool coat he wore over his chainmail.

'Wh... wh... what are you doing?' he managed.

'Your clothes are killing you,' she said. 'They are wet and frozen and taking your heat. You must get out of them or you will die.'

He tried to protest, but more for form's sake than anything else. He knew she was right, it was just that, though he had more than once pictured her taking his clothes off, it hadn't been like this. Not with him helpless as a baby. Not when it was a matter of life or death.

She had terrible trouble with his chainmail, but he could do little to help her. She had to raise his arms so that she could tug it off over his head, for he couldn't move them himself. At last, after much grunting and cursing, she dragged it off him and threw it aside. The rest came much easier, and soon he was lying naked under the tent with all his clothes drying around the fire.

Still he couldn't move except to shiver. Also, though he shook so much that he thought he would break his teeth with their chattering, he was burning up. He felt like he was back in the desert of Khemri, dying in the sun. With a grunt of effort, Kat rolled him onto her bedroll and pulled the blanket over him, then started taking off her hat and coat and scarf.

'Don't do that,' said Felix. 'You'll freeze too.'

'I am going to lie with you. The blankets are not enough. You need true warmth.'

Felix was alarmed. Again, he had dreamed of this, but not like this! 'But... but I'm too hot already.'

'You are not,' said Kat, unbuckling and shucking her leather armour. 'You're as cold as a fish. You only think you're hot. It is the madness that comes before the end.'

'M-madness?' stuttered Felix as Kat pulled her wool undertunic off over her head and revealed her naked torso.

She was as lean and wiry as a greyhound, but most definitely a woman. She shucked her boots and breeches, then reached out of the tent and grabbed her canteen from beside the fire. She hissed as it burned her fingers, then pulled it into the tent by the strap. When she had it, she quickly rolled under the blanket with him and wrapped an arm around him, while she gingerly unscrewed the cap of the canteen.

'Kat,' he said. 'I... this...'

'Shhhh,' she said, and lifted the canteen to his mouth. 'Drink this.'

He jerked back, yelping, as the water scalded his lips. 'It's too hot! I can't!'

'You must. You must warm your insides. Drink!'

Felix opened his mouth again and did his best to swallow as she poured it into him, though it felt as if the water were blistering his mouth and throat as it went down. Finally she relented and set the canteen aside, and he lay back, panting and gasping.

She rested her head on his chest and hugged him hard. It felt remarkably good, but Felix remained rigid. He wasn't sure if he should return the gesture, or if he wanted to, or even if he could.

'Listen, Kat...' he said, then couldn't think of what to say.

'Forget it, Felix,' she said. 'I remember what you said. Just rest.'

From the way that she said it he could tell it still stung her. He grunted, frustrated. He didn't want her thinking that he didn't love her. It wasn't that. It was... His mind was too jumbled with the cold and the warmth and the dizziness from drinking the hot water so fast. He gave up. He dragged his lumpish, unresponsive arms up and put them around her. She remained tense for a moment, but then relaxed and nestled her head under his chin, very like a cat indeed. It was such a sweet, cosy gesture he almost cried.

'Damn it, Kat,' he sighed, his words slurring a little with drowsiness. 'What is the matter with you?'

'What do you mean?' she murmured.

'Why do you like me? And don't say you're in love with the hero I was to you when you were young. You're smarter than that, and I was never that hero anyway.' He snorted. 'It was you who saved me that day, not the other way around. And...' His shivers overcame him again for a moment and he had to stop. 'And here you've done it again, so it can't be that.'

Kat was silent for a long time, and Felix wondered with mixed feelings if he had actually convinced her of her folly and that she would say, 'You're right, Felix. It was my memories of you I loved. I've been a foolish girl.'

But after a moment she squeezed him again and said, 'You *are* a hero to me, Felix. Not for killing that woman, but for trying to stop her even though you knew she would kill you. But...' She paused again. 'But it isn't that – not just that.' She stared out of the tent at the fire. 'There are many men I know who accept me as a scout, but not as a woman.' Her eyes narrowed. 'They call me she-beast, or tom-cat, or... other names.' She paused again, and Felix could feel angry tension in her arms, then she continued. 'And there are other men, like Milo, who would accept me as a woman, but not as a scout.' She turned her head and looked up at him, her brown eyes liquid in the glow of the fire. 'You accept me as both. That...' She swallowed, then buried her head against his chest again. 'That doesn't happen very often.'

A heart-sized lump welled up in his chest. 'Ah, Kat,' he said, and pulled her tighter against him. Why hadn't it occurred to him that all the time she spent alone in the forest might not have been entirely self-imposed? 'Ah, Kat.'

A snap of a twig from outside the tent brought her head up again, snapping his teeth shut as she cracked his chin with the top of her skull. Felix cursed, then tried to turn his head to look into the night.

Gotrek, Snorri and Rodi were stepping out of the darkness towards the fire. They were covered in minor cuts and bruises, but seemed otherwise whole.

Gotrek snorted when he saw Felix and Kat in the tent. 'Found him, then, did you?'

'I... I...' said Kat, pulling the blanket higher.

'It's... it's not what you think,' said Felix.

'It never is, manling,' said Gotrek. 'It never is.'

Rodi snickered.

Snorri shrugged. 'Snorri doesn't know what he thinks it is.'

'Don't let it trouble you, Father Rustskull,' said Rodi. 'But come spread your roll on this side of the fire. Give the poor skinny things some privacy.'

Felix groaned with embarrassment. 'It really isn't what–'

Kat stopped him with a shake of her head. 'Never mind, Felix,' she said. 'And it's time for you to drink again.'

He sighed. More torture. But now that he came to notice, he wasn't shivering nearly as much as before, and suddenly he felt very, very sleepy.

The next day, Felix woke alone. Kat was outside the tent, sitting with the Slayers, cooking rabbit over the fire. Felix's stomach growled at the smell of it and he tried to sit up. He hissed with pain. Everything hurt – his head, his joints, his muscles, but at least the terrible shaking and the frightening inability to think or move were gone.

After a few minutes of grunting and groaning, he got himself dressed and crawled out of the tent. The snow was piled high all around them, but the storm had stopped and it was a bright morning. He was greeted by a nod from Gotrek, a sly smirk from Rodi and a vacant grin from Snorri. Kat smiled at him, then looked away shyly.

'All right, manling?' asked Gotrek.

'I'll be fine,' said Felix, sitting down gingerly at the fire and warming his hands.

'Frozen stiff, were you?' asked Rodi.

'Nearly,' said Felix.

The young Slayer chuckled. 'Nice for the girl then, eh?'

Felix jumped to his feet, though his muscles shrieked with complaint. 'Leave Kat out of this.'

Kat looked from one to the other of them, her eyes nervous.

Gotrek held up a hand. 'Easy, manling,' he said, then turned and gave Rodi a look with his one cold eye. 'He won't do it again.'

Rodi looked put out. 'Only making a joke.'

'A joke at the expense of my friends,' said Gotrek. 'There have been names penned in the book for less.'

Rodi glared at the Slayer sullenly for a moment, then had to look away. 'Aye, aye,' he said. 'Fair enough.'

'Snorri doesn't get the joke,' said Snorri.

Thankfully nobody tried to explain it to him.

As Felix and the Slayers ate, Kat took down her tent and folded it into her pack.

'I'm leaving for Stangenschloss,' she said, when all was packed away. 'And then on to Bauholz. They must be warned before the herd arrives, and I can make better time on my own.'

'Aye,' said Gotrek. 'A good plan.'

Felix opened his mouth to object. She would be out in the wilderness on her own, without anyone to protect her! Then he paused, flushing. Who had saved who last night, exactly? And after what Kat had said as they lay together, about him being one of the few to accept her as both a scout and a woman, it wouldn't do to tell her he didn't want her to go. He closed his mouth.

'Can you find your way there without me?' Kat asked.

Rodi and Snorri shook their heads.

'Too many trees,' said Rodi. 'They all look alike.'

Felix wasn't sure he could get there either. After twenty years of wandering, he had learned quite a bit about travelling by the sun and the stars, but that was difficult under the forest canopy, and it helped to know where one was starting from. He had no idea where they were, or what direction they had travelled during the snowstorm the night before.

'We'll follow the herd,' said Gotrek.

Kat nodded sadly. 'Aye, I'm afraid the fort is exactly where they're heading.' She stood and shouldered her pack. 'Well, luck to you. See you there.'

The Slayers grunted non-committally.

Kat turned to Felix. 'Goodbye, Felix,' she said.

Felix stood. 'Goodbye, Kat,' he replied. He wanted to go to her and embrace her, but he felt Rodi's eyes upon them, and didn't.

Kat waited for an awkward second, then turned away abruptly and headed into the trees.

Felix cursed himself inwardly as he sat down again. Was he really so concerned about what the dwarf thought, or was it that he still didn't know what he thought about her, and had been afraid that she would read too much into it if he had gone to her?

The girl was driving him mad.

They found Argrin Crownforger's corpse on the way back to the wide valley that the herd had passed through the night before. It was buried by a deep layer of snow, a white hump surrounded by bigger humps, and they might not have found it at all had they not seen the haft of a beastman's spear sticking up out of the soft cover.

When they cleared it away they found that the spear was sticking up out of Argrin's chest, the point buried to the shaft between his ribs. All the snow around and below him was red crystals, and there were five dead beastmen surrounding him, as stiff and lifeless as he was.

Rodi tried to pry Argrin's warhammer from his hand, 'to return it to his kin,' but found that he couldn't. Argrin's death grip was too tight. He would have had to cut off Argrin's hand to do it.

'Leave it,' said Gotrek. 'And leave him. Let the beasts of this accursed forest see who killed their brothers. Let them see what a Slayer can do.'

Rodi nodded, and he and Gotrek and Snorri bowed their heads over Argrin's body for a moment, then turned and started down the hill towards the herd's trail.

As they started along the beastmen's trail, Felix was afraid they would catch up to them again as they had before, and that the Slayers might not this time be able to resist charging in to their doom. He needn't have worried. Though the storm had passed, it had left three feet of snow behind. Rodi was up to his fork-bearded chin in it, while Gotrek and Snorri were up to their chests and, strong as they were, it was still slow, weary work ploughing through it, with many stops to restore their strength. Felix doubted if they made ten miles that first day.

'This is rubbish,' snarled Rodi just after noon. 'Wading through leagues of snow to chase the doom we might have had last night.'

'A selfish doom,' rasped Gotrek. 'As I said before.'

Rodi snorted. 'I see now why you haven't found your doom in twenty years, Gurnisson.'

Gotrek turned a dangerous eye on him. 'What do you mean by that, beardling?'

'You are too choosy,' said Rodi. '"It must be an honourable doom, a great doom," says the great Slayer. Bah! Those things mean nothing. A doom is a doom is a doom. It is the dying in battle that counts with Grimnir. Nothing else.'

Gotrek grunted and started forwards again. 'Grimnir asks only for death. Others ask for more.'

Rodi stared after him. 'What do you mean by that? A Slayer answers only to Grimnir. He renounces all else.'

But Gotrek wouldn't answer him.

Felix followed wide-eyed. He had never heard the Slayer say anything like this before and he didn't know what it meant any more than Rodi did. Who were these others? What did they ask of Gotrek? Had the Slayer been the subject of some king all this time and never mentioned it to Felix? Did he worship some other god? Did it have something to do with the great shame that had made him a Slayer in the first place? Felix grumbled with frustration. He might never know. Gotrek never spoke of these things and Felix knew better than to ask. Perhaps Rodi would goad it out of him as he had this. Felix would just have to keep his ears open.

A few minutes later, as if to change the subject, Gotrek turned to Felix. 'What happened to the squire, manling? I was fighting the knights and didn't see.'

'He changed,' said Felix. 'Along with the rest.'

'Did you slay him?'

Felix shook his head. 'I... I didn't have the heart.'

'It would have been kinder if you had.'

Felix sighed. He knew it was the truth. If the boy retained even a small portion of his mind, the life of a beastman would be torture to his Sigmarite soul. The thought brought Felix up short, for suddenly, with a sickening sinking of his stomach, he knew that the templars of the Order of the Fiery Heart had not died at the hands of the beastmen like Ortwin had thought. They had become beastmen themselves. The beastman that Ortwin had killed, who had worn the breastplate with the insignia of the order upon it, had not stolen it, it had been his all along.

'The templars didn't die, did they?' he said after a moment.

Gotrek shook his head. 'No, manling. But if we find them, I will give them peace.'

Felix nodded in agreement. It was the best that they could do for them. Next time he would not falter.

But as they continued on, a new thought gave Felix pause. How many of the massive herd had once been human? How many had been changed into monsters by the light flashing from the shaman's herdstone? The reports of empty villages that the soldier at Stangenschloss had spoken of – had the people all been slain? Had they all fled? Or had they changed as the blue light caught them, and followed obediently in the shaman's wake?

He shivered with fear. How could an army stand against such a thing? They might charge the herd as knights and spearmen and greatswords, but before they reached them, the blue light would sear their eyes and they would fall twisting and screaming, only to rise again as beastmen and turn on their fellows. It was something out of a nightmare, and if the nightmare were true, then Stangenschloss would be lost – and every village and town between it and the Talabec. Could even Talabheim or Altdorf repel such a threat? The wizards of the colleges would have to be mustered at once and the stone destroyed, before the herd numbered not thousands, but tens of thousands.

He slogged on, numb with the horror of it.

On the second day, they came to the place where the herd had been when the snowstorm had stopped, and they found the snow on the path trampled to a blackened inch-thick crust that made travel easier. Felix again became afraid that they would catch up to the beastmen and that the Slayers would do something rash, but on the morning of the second day they woke to their tents being ripped from the ground by another screaming gale, and the snow came down heavier than ever, once again blotting out the trail.

Felix began to wonder why he had ever longed to return to the land of his birth.

Out of the blue on the morning of the fourth day, as they were making their slow way through an area of enormous oaks with the wind still blowing snow in their faces, Snorri chuckled and said, 'This reminds Snorri of fighting beastmen in the snow with his old friends Gotrek and Felix.'

Felix looked to Gotrek at this, and saw him wince.

'Snorri,' said Felix. 'We *are* your old friends Gotrek and Felix.'

Snorri looked at Felix with a puzzled frown, then smiled. 'Snorri knows that,' he said. 'But this was before. Snorri and Gotrek and Felix and their friend Max had just killed a vampire and then they were attacked by beastmen in the snow. Then Gotrek and Felix went through the door and never came back.'

'Snorri, listen to me,' said Felix, losing patience. Why couldn't the old Slayer make the connection between then and now?

'There's no use telling him,' said Rodi. 'Poor Father Rustskull is a few bricks shy of a–'

'What happened after that, Nosebiter?' Gotrek interrupted. 'Where did you go?'

'Max and Snorri went back to Praag to fight the hordes of I-can't-remember-his-name,' said Snorri. 'But the cowards ran away as soon as they got there.' He paused. 'After that… After that…'

'After that you went beastman hunting with someone named Rag Neck Ruchendorf,' said Rodi impatiently. 'And killed a beast-lord in the forests of Ostermark.'

'Aye, that's right,' said Snorri. 'Now Snorri remembers.'

Felix looked at Rodi. 'You were there?'

'Nah,' said Rodi. 'But he's told it before. Sometimes he remembers. Sometimes he doesn't.'

'Rag Neck was a good man,' said Snorri, his eyes faraway. 'Drank almost as much as Snorri, which Snorri thinks is pretty good for a human.' The old Slayer laughed. 'He made a contest with Snorri. Told him if he could take as many beastman heads as all of his men together he would give Snorri a keg of Karak Norn ale. Snorri killed ninety beastmen in three days – some big ones too – and won by fifteen kills!' He smiled.

'You still don't see it,' Rodi sighed. 'Your friend Rag Neck must have been collecting bounty for those heads. He robbed you of your share and fobbed you off with beer.'

'It was good beer,' protested Snorri.

Rodi shook his head, giving up.

'And after that?' asked Gotrek.

Snorri's heavy brows pulled together thoughtfully. 'Snorri was many places after that, slaying many things – orcs, beastmen, trolls, skaven. He even fought a dragon once, with his friends Gotrek and Felix.'

'No,' said Felix. 'That was before.'

'Oh yes,' said Snorri. 'That was before.'

He seemed troubled by that for a moment, then laughed uproariously. 'Did Snorri ever tell you about the time he was put in jail for killing beastmen?'

'Yes,' said Rodi grimly.

'No,' said Gotrek and Felix.

Snorri laughed again, then scratched among the nails of his crest and continued. 'Snorri was in some town of men – he can't remember the name. He and some others had been hired by the townsfolk to protect them from beastmen, and he had killed many. The night after he had driven the beastmen away, Snorri went to have a drink, then after ten or twenty beers he decided to go back to the army camp, which was in a field outside the village. On the way, Snorri saw a whole herd of beastmen standing in a meadow, looking towards the village. Snorri realised that the treacherous beastmen had come back, so he took out his axe and slew them all. Snorri took more than fifty heads that night.'

That sounded like an exaggeration to Felix. Still, it might have been twenty. 'But why did they arrest you for that?' he asked. 'Surely you had done them a great service.'

Snorri snorted. 'The mayor of the town told Snorri that they hadn't been beastmen, but cows, and put him in jail.' Snorri laughed. 'If they had been cows, then why would Snorri have slain them? There is no glory in slaying cows.'

'They *were* cows, you cloth-head,' said Rodi. 'They must have been. And you're lucky the mayor didn't hang you. You robbed the people of all their milk and meat. Half the town probably went hungry that winter because of you.'

Snorri shook his head. 'Snorri is pretty sure they were beastmen.'

Felix saw Gotrek shake his head at this, but he said nothing.

'So you've been fighting orcs and beastmen and trolls for twenty years and still haven't found your doom,' said Felix. It seemed amazing to him, but then, Gotrek had been fighting orcs and beastmen and trolls for twenty years, and he hadn't found his doom either.

Snorri nodded slowly. 'Snorri is sad about that. He has met many Slayers, and they have all found their dooms, but Snorri has never found his.' He glared around at the woods with uncharacteristic anger. 'Snorri thinks it is the old lady's fault.'

Felix and Gotrek exchanged a look at this, then looked to Rodi. The young Slayer shrugged and rolled his eyes.

'What old lady?' asked Gotrek.

'Snorri saved an old lady in the woods,' said Snorri. 'Spiders were attacking her. Big spiders, like the goblins ride. Snorri killed them all, but they bit him many times, and he got dizzy and couldn't walk. The lady took him to her house – Snorri thinks she lived in a tree – and she fed him and gave him terrible-tasting beer.' His brow furrowed in confusion. 'Snorri thinks he was there for a long time, but he can't remember, but when he left, the lady told him that he should have died from the spider bites. She said she gave him some medicines, but she was too late, and he should have died.'

'Well, she was obviously wrong, wasn't she?' said Felix.

Snorri nodded. 'Snorri wishes she would have been wronger. She said she looked at Snorri's stars and saw that he would not meet his doom for many years. She said Snorri had a great destiny.' He snorted, his anger returning. 'Snorri thinks the lady cursed him. Snorri thinks her stars have stopped him from finding his doom.'

Felix blinked at this. Snorri Nosebiter had a great destiny? Who would have thought it?

'Human nonsense,' said Rodi.

'Snorri wishes it was,' said Snorri. 'He has tried to prove her wrong many times, but he is still alive. Snorri is very angry with that lady.'

Gotrek frowned deeply at this.

Felix thought about trying to explain to Snorri that foretelling didn't work like that, and that he had it the wrong way around, but if the old Slayer still believed that a herd of cows had been a herd of beastmen, the nuances of prophecy would undoubtedly be lost on him.

'Did the old lady say what this destiny was?' asked Gotrek.

'No,' said Snorri. 'But Snorri hopes it doesn't come soon.'

Gotrek turned, fixing Snorri with a hard stare. 'What? Why is that? Do you no longer seek your doom?'

A look of shame came upon Snorri's ugly face. He hung his head. 'Snorri shouldn't have said anything.'

Gotrek stopped walking and faced the old Slayer, his one eye boring into him like an auger. 'Snorri Nosebiter, if you have renounced your vow to Grimnir, we will no longer walk together.'

'It isn't that, Gurnisson,' said Rodi. 'He–'

Gotrek held up a hand. 'I would hear it from his own mouth.'

Snorri continued to stare at the ground, a look of such lugubrious misery on his face that it was almost comic. 'Snorri has a great shame,' he said at last. 'A new great shame.'

'What shame is this?' growled Gotrek.

'Snorri...' The old Slayer swallowed, then continued. 'Snorri has forgotten why he became a Slayer.'

TWELVE

Gotrek blinked, a look of blank shock on his hard face. 'When did this happen?'

'Snorri doesn't know,' said Snorri. 'He tried to remember after the fighting at Middenheim but nothing came to his mind. There was nothing there.'

'Too many nails in the head,' muttered Rodi under his breath.

'It's shameful for a Slayer to forget his shame?' asked Felix, confused.

'It is worse than shameful, manling,' said Gotrek, not taking his eye off Snorri. 'It is a crime against Grimnir.' He sighed. 'A dwarf becomes a Slayer to atone for a great shame. If he forgets that shame, then he cannot atone for it. If he dies without remembering, he will not be admitted into Grimnir's halls. He will have no peace in death.'

It took a moment for the immensity of Snorri's plight to sink in, but then Felix saw that it was a terrible thing, the equivalent of a devout follower of Sigmar discovering that he was growing a tentacle or a third eye. Snorri was being denied salvation and forgiveness.

'Snorri is making a pilgrimage to Karak Kadrin,' said Snorri. 'To pray at the Shrine of Grimnir. He will ask Grimnir to give him his memory back so he can have his doom.'

Gotrek nodded. 'That is the right thing to do, Snorri Nosebiter. May Grimnir grant your boon.'

'But if you are afraid to meet your doom before you get your memory back,' said Felix as a thought came to him, 'why are you still fighting? Isn't it a terrible risk?'

Snorri shrugged. 'The old lady said that Snorri had a destiny, so he is safe until he finds it. And also,' he grinned, sheepish, 'when there are things to slay, Snorri gets excited and forgets that he has forgotten.'

'Forget his head if it wasn't attached to his shoulders,' said Rodi.

Gotrek shot the young Slayer a hard look, then turned and started shouldering through the snow again. 'Come on,' he said. 'We have a long road ahead of us.'

A while later, when Rodi and Snorri had fallen a little bit behind, Felix turned to Gotrek and lowered his voice.

'Gotrek, don't you know why Snorri became a Slayer?' he asked. 'Couldn't you tell him and relieve him of his misery?'

Gotrek shook his head. 'A Slayer does not tell of his shame,' he said. 'Not even to another Slayer. He has not told me. And even if I did know, I would not tell him.'

'Sigmar, why not?'

'It is a Slayer's responsibility to keep his shame firmly in mind,' Gotrek rumbled. 'If Snorri Nosebiter has forgotten his, then it is his burden to bear, and his problem to solve. To tell him would be as wrong as killing him to give him his doom. There is no easy path to Grimnir's hall.'

Felix thought this was cruel and unfair, but then, much of what passed for dwarf philosophy seemed harsh to him. He sighed and pushed on, suddenly depressed. Poor Snorri. He had never expected to feel sorry for the happy-go-lucky old Slayer – he hadn't really thought Snorri had the capacity for sadness – but it seemed that the grimness of the Old World was great enough to touch even the most oblivious. It was too bad.

On the fifth day, the second storm cleared off, and by the middle of the sixth day they came again to flattened snow, which told them that the herd was no more than a day ahead. Felix began to worry about Stangenschloss. Even if Kat had made it in time to warn them, what could the fort do to prepare for the oncoming herd? Would the soldiers abandon it? Would they send south for a wizard? Would they hope that the herd would pass them by? Would they even believe Kat's story?

In the late afternoon of the seventh day, they saw the first signs of battle – a soldier's helmet tossed to one side, a trail of red in the snow, the scattered skeleton of a horse, scraps of meat still sticking to its bones. A little further on they found a headless corpse wearing the uniform of Ilgner's company. After that, the Slayers readied their weapons and went more cautiously. Felix did the same. The herd might be just around the next bend, or the one after that.

An hour later, as the setting sun was turning the snow as red as the spilled blood, they came to the fort at last. The beastmen's trail led right to it, entering the cleared fields that surrounded it from the rear.

Felix and the Slayers paused before stepping out into the open area and surveyed the fort. The walls still stood, and there was no column of smoke rising from it, but there were also no signs of life – no glint of helmets from the walls, no kitchen smoke, no sound.

'Have they deserted it?' asked Felix.

'We'll see,' said Gotrek.

They started around the edge of the clearing, keeping within the tree line. The ground along the side of the fort was littered with a score of dead beastmen, all with arrows sticking from them, but no other signs of a battle. The walls were undamaged, and there were no dead soldiers.

Felix began to wonder if the herd had tramped past and not bothered to assault the fort, but when they could see around the corner tower, his heart sank, capsized with a flood of dread. The gates were wide open and no sentries stood before them.

'Look,' said Rodi.

Felix turned and followed his gaze with the others. On the far side of the cleared fields, a gap had been cut in the forest, just like the one they had entered from.

'The beastmen have moved on,' said the young Slayer.

'But have they taken the garrison with them?' asked Gotrek.

Panic surged in Felix's chest. 'Kat,' he said, and he had to forcibly hold himself from racing towards the fort to look for her. If she were dead or changed it would have happened hours, maybe days ago. No mad charge now could change it.

He and the Slayers crept warily towards the entrance, passing more arrow-studded beastmen as they went, and eyeing the battlements every step of the way. No arrows came from them, however, nor any spears or stones or shouted challenges.

Finally they reached the open gates and looked in. The courtyard was still and silent, but only because it was too cold for there to be flies. There were corpses everywhere – men and beastmen all hacked to gory pieces, some still locked in the struggle that had killed them, and bright blood mottling the snow between them like red islands in a frozen sea.

'Snorri missed a fight,' said Snorri.

'Not much of one,' said Rodi. 'There are barely a score of men dead here.'

'Two score,' said Gotrek.

Rodi snorted. 'Your eye is failing you, Gurnisson. I don't count more than–'

'Look at the beastmen,' said Gotrek. 'They wear the same uniform as the men they fought.'

Rodi turned and Felix followed his gaze. It was true, all the beastmen in the yard wore torn jerkins and dented breastplates, all marked with Ilgner's colours and device.

'The stone,' Felix groaned.

'Aye,' said Gotrek. 'It has done its evil work.'

Felix thought again of Kat and this time he could not restrain himself. 'Excuse me,' he said. 'I must...' and he ran off across the courtyard.

'Manling,' barked Gotrek. 'Wait.'

Felix hurried on, ignoring him, and looking fearfully at each beastman he passed to see if it wore a scarf and a hat and a heavy coat of wool.

As he turned the corner into the stable yard he saw a little figure in silhouette kneeling over a corpse and his heart gave a great leap, but then he saw that it was a boy, dressed in peasant rags, and that he was tugging at the rings on the hand of a dead knight.

'You, boy!' called Felix.

The boy looked up, eyes wide, then bolted for the kitchen yard, which was around another corner of the keep.

'Come back here!' called Felix and ran after him. He might have news of Kat!

He saw the boy disappear into a wooden storage barn built against the outer wall, and slowed to a trot. There was no exit from the shed. He was trapped.

'All right, then,' he said, stepping into the wide doorway. 'Come out. I only want to talk–'

He cut off abruptly when he saw that he was facing a bristling thicket of daggers and spears and clubs, with a gang of frightened-looking rustics behind them.

'This be our spoils,' said the one in front, a slope-shouldered fellow with a thatch of dirty yellow hair sticking out from under a stocking cap. 'Go find yer own.'

The boy was peeking out from behind him, glaring at Felix with angry eyes.

Felix looked past the men and saw that they had been loading bags of flour and jars of cooking oil onto a cart with a bony old plough horse hitched to it. He stepped back, lowering his sword and raising his free hand.

'Easy,' he said. 'I don't want your spoils. I... I only want to ask what happened here.'

The men looked at each other, then back at him, still suspicious. 'It weren't our doing,' said the leader. 'You can't blame us for what happened.'

'Of course not,' said Felix, as soothingly as he could. 'It was the beastmen. I just–'

'The blue light!' wailed a voice from a corner. 'The blue light!'

Felix's hair stood on end at the eerie sound. He turned with the others. Another peasant sat in the corner, hugging his knees. He was a big man, a smith's apron strapped around his barrel torso, but his face had the wide-eyed fear of a child woken from a nightmare. 'The blue light!' he said again.

'Quiet, Wattie,' snapped the leader. 'They're gone now, I told you.'

'And where's Hanna, Gus?' cried the big man. 'Where's Hanna gone?'

'She...' Gus looked over at a canvas tarpaulin that had been draped over something by the door. A cloven hoof, small for a beastman, stuck out from under it. 'She went on to Leer, Wattie. I told you. Now be quiet.'

Gus turned back to Felix. 'You best just go on yer way, mein Herr. We don't want–' He broke off as footsteps crunched across the snow from outside.

The peasants' spears and daggers thrust back into guard.

'Who's that?' snarled Gus. 'Who's with you?'

Felix saw the shadows of the dwarfs stretch across the straw of the barn floor as they stepped into the door behind Felix.

'What's this, now?' asked Rodi.

Gus stared, then dropped his spear and stepped forwards. 'Master Rodi, you've come back!' Then, shooting a nervous look at the wagon full of plunder, 'Er, is m'lord with you?'

'No, master cook,' said Rodi. 'Lord Ilgner's dead. Argrin too. Killed by the beastmen.'

Gus's face fell. 'Aw, that's bad that is.'

The other peasants groaned.

'What happened here?' asked Rodi.

Gus sighed, and his shoulders slumped. 'Don't know, exactly. When the little forester girl brought word the beasts were coming, some of us was afraid and we went to hide in the old bandit caves.'

'So she made it here!' cried Felix.

'Aye,' said Gus. 'Though much good her warning did, as ye can see. Only Wattie stayed behind, but he won't say what happened. Something terrible though,' he said, glancing again at the form of the little beastman under the tarpaulin.

'The blue light,' moaned Wattie from his corner.

'When did this happen?' asked Gotrek.

'We hid in the caves last night,' said Gus. 'When we come back this morning, it was like this.'

'The girl who brought the news,' said Felix anxiously. 'Do you know what became of her?'

Gus and the others shook their heads.

'Saw her talking with Captain Haschke before we went to the caves,' said Gus. 'But not since.' He turned back to Rodi. 'Y'won't tell on us, will ye, Master Rodi? We're only fending for ourselves.'

Rodi shrugged. 'Who is there to tell?'

Felix's panic was returning. He backed out of the barn. 'I must see if she's here,' he said, and ran off again.

He searched the fort from battlements to dungeon, torn between fear of finding Kat, and the frustration of not knowing what had happened to her. Every new body he found quickened his heart and tightened his shoulders. Every fallen beastman he came to made him cringe in anxious anticipation. At last, as the purple sky blackened to full night, he gave up. She wasn't there, at least not that he could find, or in a condition he could recognise. Had she continued on to Bauholz? Had she gone out to fight the herd and died on the field or in the woods? He had to find out.

He ran back down to Gotrek, Snorri and Rodi, who were rolling a keg of beer up from the cellars as Gus and his followers prepared a meal.

'We have to leave for Bauholz,' said Felix. 'Now.'

'It's too late in the day, manling,' said Gotrek. 'We'll start in the morning.'

'We can't wait until morning,' cried Felix. 'We have to get to Bauholz before the herd does.'

'And we will,' said Gotrek, setting the barrel on its end. He nodded at Rodi. 'The beardling has bought the cook's horse and cart. We'll take it by the forest road while the beasts carve their way through the trees, foot by foot. We'll be ahead of them in a day.'

'But we should gain as much of a lead on them as possible!' Felix insisted. 'It will take some time to get everyone away.'

'Relax, Herr Jaeger,' said Rodi. 'A night under a roof will give us more stamina for the road. Besides, I'm hungry for a real meal.'

'And Snorri is thirsty for real drink,' said Snorri.

Felix growled with frustration, but he knew the dwarfs were right. A night wouldn't make much difference, but it just felt wrong not to be moving, not to be doing something to find Kat – and help Bauholz, of course.

It was a tortuous trip. Felix was cursing with impatience every minute of the five days it took. The bony old plough horse might have been quicker than the dwarfs on foot, but it was not fast enough. Every bump, every stop to ease the cart over a frozen rut, every time they had to tromp tracks in the heavy snow so that the wheels would not get stuck, drove Felix to nail-biting frustration. He wanted to run ahead and leave the Slayers behind, and there were times when he almost gave into the urge and told them goodbye, but he knew it was folly. Without their protection he was prey to everything that lurked in the woods, and he would die not knowing if Kat lived. With them, as slow as they were, he was much more likely to get to Bauholz in one piece and be able to do something useful once he got there.

When at last, at noon on the fifth day, the snow-covered fields and timber walls of the little town hove into sight, Felix breathed a huge sigh of relief. The chimney smoke rising in little grey ribbons from its roof tops told him that the beasts had not touched it. He jumped down from the cart, unable to control his anxiety any longer, and jogged ahead to the gates.

'I'll just, uh, let them know we're coming,' he said over his shoulder as he ran.

'Aye, manling,' said Gotrek.

Rodi chuckled slyly.

The palisade walls were acrawl with villagers, retying the ropes that bound the logs together, setting new logs in the long-unrepaired gaps, building wooden mantlets at the tops to hide behind while firing bows. Felix nodded with surprised approval. It seemed that Noseless Milo had actually taken seriously his vow to protect the town when he took it over. Felix would not have thought it of him, though of course it would do no good in the end. Even without the foul stone, the shaman's massive herd could overrun the little village without breaking stride. The people should be leaving, not preparing to fight.

A pair of gaunt peasants were guarding the front gate, and only stared at him as he ran through. As he started down the main street, he saw that the village was as busy within as without. The townsfolk were doing what they could to strengthen their meagre houses – boarding up the windows, fitting the doors with crossbars and braces, making barricades to block the streets. Felix looked around for any sign of Milo or his men, and saw none. Were they all on the walls, helping with the defences? Or had the bandit failed to defeat Ludeker's soldiers after all? But Felix saw no Wissenland uniforms among the villagers either. Strange.

He ran to the *Powder and Shot*, the old Sigmarite temple turned beer hall, and stopped in wonder as he saw two men on ladders taking down the crudely painted tavern sign in preparation for replacing the gilded wooden hammer that had hung there before.

A gaunt old man stood on the steps of the temple, watching the proceedings, and Felix recognised him as Doktor Vinck.

'Herr Doktor!' he called as he ran towards him.

The old surgeon looked up, then smiled as he recognised Felix. 'Herr Jaeger, is it? Well met, sir. I confess I didn't expect you to return.'

'What are you doing here?' Felix asked. 'Are you working for Noseless Milo now? Is Kat here with you?'

Doktor Vinck's smile faded. 'I'm afraid the answers to all those questions are linked, my boy. I am here because Milo and his cronies left town as soon as Kat brought word that the beastman herd was coming this way. They have taken all the stolen supplies that Ludeker had gathered, put them on carts and headed south. We face our destiny with nothing but a few pitchforks and hunting bows.' He laughed and looked at the tavern sign, with its depiction of bullets and blackpowder barrel. 'The powder and shot is gone, and so we must put our trust in Sigmar.'

'But Kat,' said Felix impatiently. 'What of Kat?'

Doktor Vinck sighed. 'Milo took her with him.'

'What?' cried Felix. 'She went with that... filth?'

'Not willingly, I assure you.' The surgeon looked away, shame colouring his face. 'They took her while she was sleeping in my tent. Bound and gagged her and dragged her out. There... there was nothing I could do.'

THIRTEEN

Felix stared at the doctor, fear and rage rising in him like a boiling flood. 'When did they leave? How long ago?'

'Only a few hours ago,' said Doktor Vinck. 'No more than three.'

Felix turned and ran back towards the gate without another word. Halfway across the village's only intersection he heard a shout from his left and looked around. Sir Teobalt was limping up from the docks, leading a troop of peasants with makeshift spears over their shoulders. He seemed to have made an almost complete recovery.

'Herr Jaeger!' he called. 'You have returned.'

Felix stumbled, gulping with nervousness. Sir Teobalt was the last person he wanted to see at that moment.

'What news have you?' the old knight asked, coming on. 'Did you find my brothers? Did my squire acquit himself honourably?'

'I…' said Felix, edging sideways. 'I'll tell you later, sir. I must go.'

He sprinted away again, the templar's confused cries following him as he ran.

The Slayers were just leading the cart through the village gate when he reached it.

'Gotrek, turn about,' said Felix, beckoning to the Slayer. 'We must go out again.'

'What's happened?' Gotrek asked.

'Milo has fled town and kidnapped Kat. They're three hours ahead of us.'

Gotrek looked around at the frantic efforts of the townsfolk to strengthen their walls. 'He's the only one with any sense. These people will all die if they stay here.'

'Then I will stay too,' said Rodi, his eyes lighting up. 'You get the girl and continue south to warn the armies of men. I will stay here and do my best to convince these fools to leave, and if they do not...' He smiled grimly. 'Then I will die defending them.'

'Snorri will stay too!' said Snorri, his eyes dancing with anticipation.

'No, Nosebiter,' said Gotrek, jumping down from the cart. 'You will not. You will come with us.'

'But Snorri wants to fight beastmen.'

Gotrek's jaws bulged under his beard. 'Have you forgotten your pilgrimage?'

Snorri frowned, then looked downcast. 'Yes, Snorri forgot. He will come with you.'

Gotrek turned and bowed to Rodi as Felix ground his teeth, impatient to go. 'May you find your doom, Rodi Balkisson.'

'And you as well, Gotrek Gurnisson,' said Rodi, bowing in return. He saluted Snorri too. 'May Grimnir favour you, Father Rustskull.'

'Goodbye, uh, what's-your-name,' said Snorri.

And with that eloquent farewell, Felix, Gotrek and Snorri turned and trotted south down the road.

Knowing that Milo had a three-hour head start, Felix was afraid he and the Slayers might never catch him, but to his surprise, only an hour later they heard curses and harsh voices coming to them across the silence of the snowbound forest.

Felix stopped and drew his sword, listening. Gotrek and Snorri stepped to either side of him and drew their weapons as well.

'Hold those horses still, curse you!' came a shout that Felix thought he recognised as Noseless Milo's. 'Anders, Uwe, lift together on my count. The rest of you lack-wits get behind and push.'

Felix and the two Slayers started forwards again, moving slowly and quietly towards a bend in the track.

'It's hopeless, Milo,' whined another voice. 'We'll have to leave some of the loot behind. We'll never get it over this damned road.'

'You're a damned fool, Heiko!' barked Milo. 'This is our fortune! If we sell all this in Ahlenhof we never have to work again. I'm not leaving a stick behind.'

'Then it's you who's the fool, Milo,' said Heiko's voice. 'Because at this rate we'll have beastmen crawling up our fundaments before we get ten miles.'

There was a scrape of drawn steel, and Milo's voice raised to a shout. 'Are you challenging me, you mewling little turd?'

Gotrek chuckled darkly. 'They'll do our work for us.'

'Snorri hopes not,' said Snorri.

They were almost at the bend now. Felix craned his neck to the left, trying to see around the intervening trees.

'I'm only asking you to see sense, Milo,' came Heiko. 'I don't want to–'

He was cut off by a heavy thud and a shout of surprise. Someone cursed, and then came a babble of voices.

'She's loose, damn it!'

'I've got her!'

'Ow!'

'Damn the bitch!'

'She's breaking for the woods!'

Then Milo's angry roar. 'Get her! Get my wife!'

Felix could wait no more. He charged around the bend with the two Slayers thundering at his heels. The scene that met his eyes was a frenzy of struggle and motion. Four wagons, heavily loaded with blackpowder kegs, crates, beer barrels and all manner of plunder – including Sir Teobalt's warhorse, Machtig, hitched to the last – sat in a crooked line along the trail, the first with its front right wheel down in a ditch and its back left raised like a dog cocking its leg to piss.

A dozen filthy men were breaking from the wagons and swarming after a little figure who plunged barefoot through the knee-high snow, dressed in nothing but a night shirt, her eyes burning with the savage desire for freedom. Felix's heart lurched. It was Kat, her wrists tied behind her back and a rope around her neck that dragged in her wake like a leash, and he knew at that moment that he loved her with all his heart and soul.

Just then the lead man leapt forwards and caught the end of the rope, jerking it tight. Kat's legs flew out in front of her and she went down flat on her back, yelping.

'No!' roared Felix, and bounded towards the man, the thudding footsteps of Gotrek and Snorri as they followed him barely registering through his rage.

The bandits turned at his yell.

'Ranald's luck,' spat Milo. 'It's the boyfriend. Stop him!'

Felix swung Karaghul around in a wide circle and it chimed off a half-dozen blades as he tried to break through the gangsters to Kat. He didn't get very far. Milo's men were well armed with swords, spears and rapiers that they must have taken from better men, and Felix could tell that some of them had been soldiers once, for they handled themselves well.

Felix parried two swords, but then had to jump back as a spearman stabbed at him from the second rank – proper military training.

None of that mattered once Gotrek and Snorri reached the fight. Swords shattered and men screamed as the Slayers waded in, weapons blurring. Felix shoved past a man who was clutching the stump of his wrist, and aimed a slash at the man who was dragging Kat away from the melee by the rope around her neck.

A movement at the corner of his eye made him duck and something clipped him a glancing blow across the top of the head. Felix hit the ground and floundered in the snow, his head smarting and the world spinning around him. Noseless Milo was trudging towards him, a woodsman's axe in one hand, and a length of chain in the other.

'Come on, ye pretty little Altdorf milksop,' he snarled, raising the axe. 'Let's see how much she likes you when you've got a nose like mine!'

Felix threw up his sword just as the axe came down, and staggered to his feet as it shrieked down the length of his blade. Milo's chain cracked him on the side of the face, then whipped around the back of his head and snapped against his other ear.

Felix howled with pain and stumbled away, his sword up blindly behind him as Milo came on. He needed a second to shake it off. He didn't have it. Milo swung with the axe and chain again and Felix lurched aside once more. Out of the corner of his eye he saw Kat on her feet, kicking in the teeth of the man who held her rope.

The stinging ebbed enough for Felix to recover himself. He heard the axe and chain whistling behind him and spun and ducked at the same time, Karaghul lashing out high. The rune sword sheared through the haft of the axe and the heavy head bounced hard off Felix's shoulder. The chain wrapped around Karaghul and held it tight.

Milo laughed and yanked hard, hoping to pull Felix off balance. But Felix was ready and went with it, lunging forwards to slam into Milo's chest and knock him to the ground. The bandit swung his headless axe at Felix's legs, but Felix kicked it out of his hand and wrenched Karaghul from the coils of the chain. He raised the blade high for the death stroke, but suddenly a little figure blurred in from his right and shoved him aside.

'No!' cried Kat. 'He's mine!'

She kicked Milo in the face, then dropped down with both knees on his chest. Her hands were still tied, but somehow she had them in front of her now, and they held a bloody dagger.

'Kat...' said Felix.

There was no stopping her. She stabbed down with the little blade, plunging it into Milo's neck, and then his eye, and then his screaming mouth. 'No man ties me!' she hissed. 'No man holds me!'

Felix blinked, stunned by her fury. Milo was long past hearing her, but still she stabbed.

'Kat,' Felix said again, then, 'Kat! He's dead!'

The girl looked up at him with the wild eyes of an animal, her teeth bared in a feral snarl. Felix stepped back, unnerved, but after a moment her face softened and she came back to herself. She lowered the dagger, and hung her head.

'I'm sorry, Felix. He...' she paused, then shook her head. 'I'm sorry.'

'That's all right,' said Felix, still a little shaken. 'I'm sure he deserved all of it.'

He looked around. The battle was over. Gotrek and Snorri stood in the centre of a ring of dead bodies and red snow, while a handful of bandits legged it for the trees.

Felix knelt by Kat and took the dagger from her hands, then used it to saw at the ropes on her wrists. She was trembling so hard he was having difficulty not cutting her.

'He... he took my boots,' she said. 'So I wouldn't run. But I... I ran anyway.' A big sob erupted from her, then, and as he parted the last strand of rope she threw her arms around him and wept on his neck. Felix paused, bewildered by her sudden change from feral fury to frightened girl, but then he took off his cloak and wrapped it around her.

'It's all right,' he said, holding her and murmuring into her hair. 'It's all over now. We're going south to Ahlenhof to spread the word of the herd's coming. You'll come with us. Everything will be all right.'

She looked up at that, snuffling back her tears. 'But, but no. I can't go. I have to stay and protect Bauholz. I won't let another village fall.'

'But, Kat,' said Felix, as gently as he could. 'It's inevitable. The herd is ten thousand strong if it's a hundred. Stangenschloss fell before it. How can you expect Bauholz to stand? Rodi has stayed behind to convince everyone to leave.'

Kat shook her head. 'The herd will miss the village,' she said. 'The beastmen have gone due south from Stangenschloss. I've been watching them. If they stay on course, they will pass fifteen to twenty miles to the east of Bauholz. It is only the foragers we must worry about.' She stood and padded back to the wagons in her bare feet. 'And they may not come.'

Felix followed her. 'Even so,' he said, as she pulled her boots and clothes out from under the buckboard and started pulling them on. 'If the foragers come in force, you don't stand a chance. A bunch of starved peasants, one old knight, one Slayer–'

'Three Slayers,' said Gotrek, stepping up to him.

Felix turned on him, sighing. 'Come, Gotrek, you said that we must go south to warn the Empire.'

'That was before,' said the Slayer. 'When the town's doom was certain. This is a fight we can win.'

'You might survive it,' said Felix. 'But what about the villagers? Even a small force of beastmen will kill too many of them.'

'Perhaps not,' said Gotrek, stroking his beard and looking speculatively at the heavily loaded wagons with his single glittering eye.

It took almost two hours for them to turn the wagons around and ride them back to Bauholz, and by then the day was guttering down to a dull grey twilight.

'Sigmar be praised!' said one of the guards at the gate. 'You've brought the weapons back,' and waved them through the gates.

Rodi swaggered up to them as they led the wagons towards the centre of the village. 'So, you're not running away after all,' he grinned.

'We heard you crying and came back,' said Gotrek.

'Any more word of the herd?' asked Kat.

Rodi nodded, his face growing serious. 'A scout came an hour ago to say that they continue due south, but that a band of foragers was heading straight for us.'

'How many?' asked Gotrek. 'And how soon?'

'The scout reckoned about a hundred, and a few hours at most.'

'Snorri doesn't know if he can wait that long for a hundred beastmen,' said Snorri.

'Kat! You're safe!' came Doktor Vinck's voice.

The old surgeon was hobbling out of the temple of Sigmar, now properly fitted with its gilded hammer. Sir Teobalt walked beside him, tall and proud despite his limp. Felix avoided his eye.

'And you've brought back the wagons too,' said Vinck as he stepped up to them. 'My prayers to Sigmar have been answered.'

Kat hopped down from the first wagon and embraced the doctor as the others pulled to a halt.

Doktor Vinck returned the hug, but then pulled back and looked sadly at her. 'Though you should have kept going south and forgotten about us. It will end badly here, I think, despite your return.'

'Not necessarily,' said Gotrek. 'I have an idea.'

Doktor Vinck turned to him. 'If it is that we should leave the village, like your fellow Slayer suggested, we will not do it. We have bowed before violence and savagery for too long. We will do so no longer.'

Gotrek shook his head. 'Not that. I have another way.' He turned and looked at the barrels stacked on the cart. 'We will put this looted black-powder to its proper use at last.'

Sir Teobalt and Doktor Vinck frowned at him, confused.

'But we have no cannons,' said Sir Teobalt.

'And few guns,' said Doktor Vinck.

'We don't need them,' said Gotrek. 'All we need is all the drink in the village.'

FOURTEEN

As Gotrek began to outline his plan, Sir Teobalt finally caught Felix's eye and gestured for him to step into the temple of Sigmar with him. Felix's heart shrivelled in his chest as he did so. The moment had come to tell the old templar what had happened to Ortwin and the other brothers of the Order of the Fiery Heart, and he dreaded it.

Teobalt limped to the newly refurbished altar and turned, stiff. Felix noticed that, beneath his armour, his arm and shoulder were still wrapped with bandages. 'As you have returned,' he said, 'I wonder if you have time now to speak with me of the fate of my squire, Ortwin, who I see is not with you.'

'Yes, Sir Teobalt,' said Felix. 'I apologise for not telling you sooner, but…' He motioned back towards the door.

'It was a matter of great urgency, aye,' said Teobalt, his eyes never leaving Felix's. 'But now it is finished. So…'

He left it hanging. Felix nodded, but still hesitated. Should he lie? Should he tell the knight that Ortwin and the other templars had died nobly in battle fighting the beastmen? It was an attractive idea. It would be so simple, and so kind. It would ease the old man's heart and make him proud. But what if he should learn the truth? Ortwin and the templars couldn't tell, but Gotrek and Snorri had been there. They knew, and Slayers never lied. Besides, Teobalt had asked for the truth. No matter how much of a kindness, to lie to him would not be honourable. It would not be a fitting way to win Karaghul. Felix would cringe at the taint of it for the rest of his life.

'Very well, Sir Teobalt,' he said at last. 'I will tell you. You... you heard from Kat how the herdstone that the beastmen carry changed Lord Ilgner and his men into beastmen?'

'I heard this from Doktor Vinck,' said Teobalt. 'Who heard it from her. A foulness. Did Ortwin die fighting these abominations, then?'

'No, sir,' said Felix lowering his head so he wouldn't have to meet Teobalt's eyes. 'He... he changed too. He became a beastman.'

There was silence from Sir Teobalt.

Felix swallowed and continued. 'And I fear that this is what happened to the Knights of the Fiery Heart as well. We killed a beastman wearing armour with the order's insignia upon it. At first we thought that the beast had stolen the armour, but having seen Ortwin change–'

Sir Teobalt's palm cracked Felix hard across the cheek, staggering him sideways. Felix caught himself and looked up, clutching his face.

Sir Teobalt advanced on him, his eyes blazing like blue suns. 'Lies!' he cried. 'Damned lies!'

'Sir Teobalt,' said Felix. 'I swear to you–'

'Will you perjure yourself in the house of Sigmar?' said the old templar. 'Cease, sir, lest his hammer strike you down!' He grabbed Felix by the front of his mail. 'The knights of the Order of the Fiery Heart were true followers of Sigmar. Devout, strong in their faith, and perfect in the observance of their duties. It is impossible that such as these could be corrupted by the foul touch of Chaos. I will not believe that they fell prey to such weakness of the flesh!'

'I'm sorry, Sir Teobalt,' said Felix, cringing away. 'But it's the truth.'

'It is not. You lie like a knave.'

'But why should I?'

'I know not. Perhaps to hide some fault of your own. Perhaps you failed to protect Squire Ortwin and now seek to blame him for your lapse. It matters not. You have betrayed my trust. And I will not have you by my side hereafter. Return the sword that you have taken unjustly and go from me.'

The knight held out an imperious hand. Felix hesitated, trembling with frustration. He wanted to try again to get the old templar to listen, but he knew that it would be fruitless. He doubted that even the testimony of Gotrek and Kat and Snorri would change his mind. What Felix had told him had broken the laws of Sir Teobalt's view of the world, and he would not believe it no matter what.

'Come, varlet,' barked Sir Teobalt, beckoning impatiently. 'Will you rob me as well as lie to me? Give me the sword or defend yourself with it.'

After another long moment, Felix sighed and began unbuckling the sword belt from around his waist. 'I have told the truth, Sir Teobalt,' he said. 'But since I cannot convince you, I will honour our agreement.' He pulled the belt free and wrapped it around the scabbard, then took a last look at the clawed crossguard and dragon-headed pommel of the ancient rune sword. He would miss it. With a catch in his throat, he held it out to the templar.

Sir Teobalt took it and pressed it against his breastplate. He nodded solemnly to Felix. 'You have honour at least in this, Herr Jaeger,' he said. 'Now go. I would pray.'

Felix bowed as the templar turned to the rebuilt altar, then he sighed and started for the door, his heart sick with regret.

He should have lied.

Two hours later, under a sky of stars and scudding clouds, Felix leaned against the raw pine trunks of the battlements, above and to the right of the village gate, looking dully out at the black wall of the forest that waited in the darkness beyond the flickering bonfires the villagers had set in their fields. The beastmen were out in that darkness somewhere, and as much as he hoped that they would somehow pass them by and leave the village in peace, he also wished they would show up quickly and end the nervous tension that always came with waiting and vanished with action.

Kat sat cross-legged on the narrow walkway beside him, waxing her arrowheads with a candle stub and cutting the feathers at the ends of her shafts so that they were all even. Two nervous village boys knelt near her, watching intently and trying to copy what she did.

'Why do you wax the points?' asked one of the boys. 'Do they fly faster that way?'

Kat shook her head. 'They slip through skin and armour better. Important with beastmen, as they have tough hides.'

The boys' eyes widened at this, and they fell to waxing their own arrows with more vigour than skill.

Felix smiled down at her, and it was all he could do to not pull her up to her feet and kiss her then and there. He thought back to the moment when he had seen her fleeing Milo's wagons, her bare legs flashing as she pounded desperately through the snow. He wasn't sure why everything had changed then, but it had. All his worries, all his confusion about what he felt had evaporated, and he had known that despite it all, he loved her.

Unworldly yokel she might be, tied to the forest by her vows to save it, and too young for him by a decade. None of it mattered. What did matter was that she was neither a fool nor a manipulator like Claudia had been, nor did she constantly measure him and demand tests of his loyalty and worthiness like Ulrika had done. She neither overvalued or undervalued him, or loved some idea of him concocted from her memories and his unearned fame. Instead, to his confoundment, she seemed to accept him for who he was, and loved him for it.

She looked up at him, as if she could feel his eyes upon her, and gave him a lopsided smile that went through him as if it were the arrow she held in her hand.

He smiled back, then shook his head as she returned to showing the boys how to cut their fletches. It seemed complete madness to him, but when he looked in her eyes he found that he was ready to love her for as long as the world allowed them both to live, no matter what obstacles might get in their way.

Of course, he thought, looking out towards the vastness of the forest with a sigh, that might not be for very long at all. In fact, it was highly probable that they would both die tonight, no matter how well Gotrek's strategy worked.

When Felix had returned to the others after giving Karaghul to Teobalt, he had helped them put the plan into action. It had been fairly straightforward. They were making a beastman trap, and baiting it with alcohol. The idea was this. They would hide three of the wagons, leaving in the main intersection only the one that was loaded with barrels of blackpowder. These they would hide under barrels of beer, brandy and gin. When the beastmen came, they would lure them into the centre of the village, let them attack the wagon and try to steal the liquor, then – from a safe distance – fire the powder and blow as many of them as they could to smithereens.

If there were any survivors, Gotrek, Felix and the Slayers, as well as Teobalt and whatever villagers they could muster, would finish them off before they recovered from the blast.

Felix was afraid that the blast would blow up the town as well, for Ludeker had amassed quite a little stockpile of powder during his tenure as 'protector' of Bauholz, and Milo had crammed every barrel of it onto the wagon. Gotrek assured him that all would be well. The two structures closest to the intersection were the old strong house and the temple of Sigmar. Both made of stone and, in the Slayer's words, 'solid – at least by human standards.'

A shallow groove had been dug in the frozen earth of the intersection and match cord laid in it from the wagon to the strong house, where the Slayers would be hiding. Then a line of planks was laid over the groove, to stop the beastmen from accidentally kicking or tripping over the cords and pulling them from the barrels.

When all had been prepared, Sir Teobalt and Doktor Vinck had directed the townsfolk in their duties. Those who could pull a bow would man the walls. Those that could fight would lie in wait in the temple of Sigmar, and those that could do neither would hide on the second floor of the strong house, with instructions to lock the bottom door and pray once the fighting started.

Gotrek gave Felix and Kat special duties, and sent them to the walls to wait with the archers. Felix could tell that Sir Teobalt wished that Felix would have left town entirely and not participated in such a noble enterprise, but the templar had said nothing, only pretended that Felix wasn't there.

Felix looked along the wall in the torchlight, sizing up the archers he could see. They didn't look like much. Their bows were new and well made, taken from the wagons along with their swords and helmets, but they themselves were mostly not of the same quality – a handful of village boys, a dozen refugees from the camp across the river, so starved that their bow staves seemed thicker than their wrists. But among them were a few old soldiers, trapped in town like the rest by recent events. From what Kat had said, the moment she had brought news of the herd, anyone with money or connections or a boat had taken to the river and sped south as quickly as possible, leaving only the poor and desperate behind.

The soldiers looked hardly more well fed than the refugees, but at least they knew their business. One of them, a hunched little man by the name of Weir, who sported a week's growth of beard and his own bow, had taken charge of the troops on this section of the wall, and was walking up and down the walkway with a profound limp, calling encouragement and cheerful abuse to his ungainly recruits.

'Keep yer bowstring away from the snow, ye daft bug,' he told a boy, 'If it gets wet ye won't be able to shoot five paces,' and, 'Can't bend yer bow, laddie? Are ye a maid? Here now, step through it and bend it across your hip. See it? Strength of Sigmar now, hey?' and, 'Don't stick 'em in the wood, ye lummox! Look ye, that won't cut yer beard now, will it? How's it to get through a beastman's scalp? Sharpen 'em again! Sharpen 'em again.' And on and on, keeping their minds away from the waiting and the fear of what was to come.

Felix sighed with uneasy impatience and put his hand on the pommel of his sword, then jerked it away again, surprised once more that he didn't feel the familiar serrated shape of the dragon head under his palm. He must have done this twenty times already, and still it alarmed and depressed him every time.

He had tried out a score of the swords that had been part of the plunder Milo had loaded on the four wagons, swinging them around and testing their balance, and had finally selected this one as the best of the lot, though really it felt just as wrong in his hand as all the others. He would have to get used to it though, or find a better sword if he ever made it back to civilisation. Karaghul wasn't his any more.

It was a very strange feeling. He had had the rune sword almost as long as he had known Gotrek, and in that time it had come to feel as much a part of him as his arm. He felt naked without it – almost amputated. It seemed unfair to have it taken from him like this. He had told the truth. He had done the right thing, and he had been punished for it. And yet there was nothing he could do. Sir Teobalt wasn't going to give the sword back to him – not unless he changed his mind, and that seemed unlikely. The old templar was hide-bound and stubborn. His faith, and his belief in the incorruptibility of his fellow knights, had blinded him more surely than the loss of his eyes might have done.

From the west wall of the village came a murmur of frightened voices. The archers all turned their heads and whispered questions at each other, then, after a moment, the news worked its way around the corner and the archers stood, snatching up their bows in nervous excitement.

'They're here!' said one. 'The boys on the west wall say they're circling in the woods.'

'But I'm not done waxing!' bleated another.

'Steady now, steady now,' said Weir. 'No need to rush. All the time in the world. String yer bows now, lads. Nice and easy. That's the way.'

Those that hadn't, strung their bows, while the rest craned their necks to watch to the west, waiting to see movement beyond the edge of the corner platform.

Felix watched with them as Kat calmly strung her bow and slipped her arrows into a leather quiver at her hip. The glare of the fires in the fields made it hard to see beyond them, but after a moment he thought he saw a suggestion of movement against the black of the woods – a glint of reflected flame, a ripple of shadow on shadow.

The archers saw it too, and their voices raised to a babble again. Weir, bless him, knew just what to say to calm them.

'There they are, lads. Have ye ever seen such big targets in yer lives? Sigmar, even bug-boy here ought to be able to hit something that size, eh?'

The boys chuckled and their babble subsided.

Felix, on the other hand, was growing uneasier by the second. The beastmen had come a little more into the light as they circled around to the south side of the village, and he could see their numbers now. There were scores of them! The scout had said a hundred. It looked to Felix like there were double that, but perhaps he was letting fear get the better of him.

The beasts were arcing in towards the gate now, and he could see that the first twenty or so carried something heavy between them. For a moment Felix's heart lurched at the idea that they were bringing some offspring of the giant herdstone to the village and were going to turn them all into beastmen after all, but then he saw that it was only a huge pine-tree, its branches trimmed to hand-hold stubs, and sharpened at its base.

He laughed a little wildly. What a state to come to when you were relieved that the beastmen coming to attack you were carrying *only* a battering ram.

The fires may have helped those on the wall see the beastmen, but they also made the fiends look more hellish then they already were, painting their fur blood-red and highlighting their cruel horns, their glittering eyes, and the curving teeth in their slavering black mouths.

The village boys whimpered at the sight, and a few of them put arrows on strings and raised their bows, but Weir barked angrily at them. 'Not yet, ye damned yokels! Have ye got so many arrows that ye can waste 'em? Wait! Ye see the fires? Well, do ye?'

The archers nodded sullenly, like schoolboys.

'Them fires are set at the edge of bow range,' he scolded. 'Ye fire now and ye'll hit naught but snow. Wait until they come past 'em, and then go on my word, aye?'

'Aye,' murmured his charges in return.

'Good,' said Weir. 'Now start to pick out yer targets. Pick a big one. The biggest one ye can see. These beasts, ye see, they follow the strongest. And if ye kill the leaders, the rest are lost and that much easier to beat. Have ye got a target?'

'Aye,' said the archers, more confident now.

'Good!' cried Weir. 'Then keep an eye on him, and listen for my call.'

The archers watched the beastmen in silence as they came. They were halfway between the tree line and the line of bonfires now, and coming fast, a jostling swarm of hulking monsters that strung out behind the ram-carriers in a long fanning tail.

'Wait for it!' cried Weir. 'Wait for it.'

Felix felt Kat's hand slip into his and give it a squeeze. He looked around at her and found her smiling up at him. He smiled back and returned her squeeze, then turned away. The thought that it might be the last smile he ever received from her nearly choked him, and he didn't want her to see the fear in his eyes.

Finally the beastmen carrying the felled pine trotted between two of the bonfires.

'Fire!' bellowed Weir. 'Cut them down!'

The archers raised their bows and loosed their arrows. It was a pathetic volley. Only Kat and Weir and a few of the other soldiers hit their marks. Most of the refugees and the village boys put their shafts in the snow. Some of their arrows failed to leave the bow, and they howled from stung fingers and wrists.

'Clumsy fools!' shouted Weir. 'Take it slow. Nock. Draw. Aim. Fire. And aim for their heads if you would hit their chests. Now fire!'

The boys tried again as Kat and the other trained archers fired at will, loosing five shafts to every one of theirs. Kat was concentrating on the gors carrying the battering ram, and had dropped the front three in six shots. More ran up to take their places and she rained shafts on them as well.

The biggest of the beastmen had fallen as well, pin-cushioned by a dozen arrows.

'All right, lads, all right,' said Weir, laughing. 'He's down. Now pick another.'

Kat grinned. 'The only good thing about beastmen,' she said to Felix out of the side of her mouth, 'is that they don't fire back. Imagine these boys trying to fire while ducking.'

Felix smiled, though he was secretly glad no one had asked him to take up a bow. She would be laughing at *him* then.

As they continued to shoot, the village boys got more confident and their aim improved. Now at least their arrows were falling among the beastmen and not in front of them.

Unfortunately, the gors came so swiftly that the lads hadn't time for more than a few volleys before they were at the gates, and despite the help of Kat and the other trained archers, less than a score had fallen.

'Fall back!' called Weir, as the ram boomed against the great wooden doors. 'To your second positions!'

The boys and the refugees lowered their bows and scurried for the ladders as Kat and a few of the other archers took final shots, sinking arrows to the fletching in necks and the tops of bestial heads as they shot straight down.

'Come on, Kat,' said Felix nervously. 'We've got a job to do, remember.'

'Just one more,' said Kat, then 'Ha!' as she let fly a final time.

Then they were dropping down the ladders after the other archers and pounding up the street to the barricade that the villagers had built between the first two houses of the village.

As they took up their places behind it, Felix could hear the splintering of the flimsy bar Gotrek had ordered set across the doors of the gate. The bar was weak on purpose, because they wanted the beasts to succeed in coming through. The success of Gotrek's plan depended on all the beasts moving together, and it would fail if they were spread out around the walls, all trying to climb over at different spots.

'Arrows on strings, lads,' said Weir, as they watched the wooden doors shudder and flex in the torchlight. 'Two volleys and run again. No heroes here, aye?'

A splintering crack drowned out the archers' response. The bar had snapped and the beastmen were surging in, shouldering the doors aside and roaring in triumph. Felix's stomach churned as they raced towards him, and he suddenly feared that the plan wasn't going to work. What could stop such a savage onslaught?

It seemed that the archers felt the same way, for only Kat and a few others fired. The rest just sat and stared, like rabbits before a wolf.

'Loose, curse you! Loose!' roared Weir, shooting into the stampede.

The villagers and refugees snapped out of their funk and fired, but poorly, and there was no time for a second volley. They had left it too long.

'Run!' shouted Weir.

The archers needed no further encouragement. They turned and fled down the street as fast as they could. Felix and Kat snatched up torches placed at the barricade just for the purpose and ran after them. Felix almost choked as he took a breath. The street reeked of spilled brandy – the breadcrumbs that would lead the gors to the trap if all else failed.

It seemed unnecessary at the moment. As Gotrek had predicted, the beastmen chased the fleeing villagers with murder in their savage eyes, leaping the barricade and closing the gap with frightening speed.

As they neared the village's main intersection, Weir looked back and waved his arms. 'Scatter! Scatter! To your third positions!'

Now was Felix and Kat's moment. As the archers broke left and right, dodging into the shadowed yards between the little houses, Felix and Kat continued forwards, waving their torches and shouting insults over their shoulders. It was imperative that the gors follow them and not split up to hunt down the fleeing archers.

Felix looked back, worried. A few were breaking off, but the majority were continuing after him and Kat. Good. He laughed hysterically. Again – what a state to come to when you were relieved that there was a herd of beastmen thundering after you.

Felix and Kat ran into the intersection, straight for the wagon that was parked in its centre. They jumped up onto its tailgate and clambered to the top of the barrels, then turned and waved their torches at the oncoming monsters. The brandy reek was even stronger here, for the casks had been opened so that the smell would be unavoidable. Felix was afraid his torch would light the fumes.

'Come on, you filthy scavengers!' Felix shouted.

'Catch me if you can!' shrilled Kat.

The beastmen did as they were ordered and surged forwards, straight for the wagon. From his high vantage point, Felix could see that the tail of the herd was only now coming through the gate. There were still so many of them! Too many! The powder couldn't possibly kill them all.

As the gors rushed to the wagon, Felix and Kat flung their torches at them, then leapt down and sprinted for the door of the strong house – praying now that the beastmen *didn't* follow them, and that they would be enticed by the trap they had set for them.

At first he thought they had failed, for he heard hooves clattering up the wooden steps behind him and heard the Slayers curse as he and Kat dived through the door into the darkness of the stone house.

Three huge gors burst through the door behind them, but the Slayers cut them down before they knew they were being attacked, and no more followed.

Felix and Kat caught their breath and joined the Slayers at the door, where a savage joyful hooting was coming from outside. The first beastmen were surging around the cart, climbing on it and fighting each other to get to the brandy and beer, and more and more of them were pouring into the square and pushing forwards for their share. One gor had a brandy keg raised over its head and was pouring it down its throat.

'Well done, Gurnisson,' said Rodi. 'They've taken the bait.'

Gotrek only nodded, his eye never leaving the mob outside.

'Stupid beasts,' chuckled Snorri. 'Distracted by beer.'

Rodi laughed. 'That would never happen to you, Father Rustskull.'

'Snorri doesn't know what you mean,' said Snorri.

'Er, Gotrek,' said Felix. 'Shouldn't you light the fuse now?'

'Not yet,' said Gotrek.

'But what if they find the blackpowder?'

'They'll probably drink that too,' said Rodi.

Felix waited, tension gripping his shoulders as he watched the beastmen flood into the intersection and crowd around the wagon. The edges of the pack were starting to reach the sides of the street. It was a close game Gotrek was playing. If he waited too long, the gors on the periphery would lose interest and turn to other prey. They might also smell the blood of their fallen brothers in the strong house and come to investigate.

Finally, just as the urge to take the torch from Gotrek and light the fuses himself was becoming overwhelming, the Slayer lowered it to the ends of the bundled match cords on the floor. They flared to life and the flame crawled down their lengths towards the door, spitting as it went.

'Stand clear,' said Gotrek, and waved the others back.

Everybody stepped back, but not so far that they couldn't watch the flames' progress. It was too mesmerising.

Then, disaster.

Two gors were trying to carry a beer keg away from the rest, punching and kicking and butting as others tried to steal it from them. A clawed hand caught the top of the keg and pulled it down. The two gors lost their grip on it and it smashed down on its side. A wave of golden liquid poured from the smashed-in top.

The beastmen quickly righted the barrel, but not quickly enough. As they continued fighting over it, the spill of beer foamed towards the covered groove that the dwarfs had dug to protect the match cords. Unfortunately, the planks were no protection against liquid, and the beer bubbled down into the cut.

Felix and the others stared, stunned. Gotrek said something in Khazalid that Felix was glad he didn't understand.

'Right,' said Rodi, raising his axe. 'Give me the torch, Gurnisson. It's time for me to meet my doom.'

'No,' said Snorri. 'Snorri wants the torch.'

'It was my plan,' said Gotrek. 'It will be my–'

'Rhya's tits!' snapped Kat, and before any of them knew what she intended, she snatched the torch from Gotrek's hand and raced out the door with it.

'Kat!' screamed Felix, and charged out after her.

Kat dodged through the surging, brawling herd like a rabbit through a country dance, ducking elbows and skipping out of the way of heavy hooves. Felix wasn't quite so small or nimble and was knocked hither and thither by oblivious beastmen, still trying to reach the barrels of liquor.

As he stumbled on, he saw Kat run past the spill of beer and flip up one of the planks nearer the wagon with the toe of her boot. A gor saw her and let out a bellow. It was lost in the general uproar.

'Kat! Look out!' shouted Felix.

She was too intent. She didn't hear. More beastmen turned as she stabbed the torch down into the groove. Sparks shot up from it, racing towards the wagon between a gor's wide-spread hooves.

Another beastman grabbed Kat by the back of her coat and lifted her off the ground. Felix shoved between two big monsters and slashed at the gor's arm with his new sword. Karaghul would have had it off at the elbow, but the new blade lacked weight. He only bit to the bone.

Still, it was enough. The gor roared and dropped Kat to turn on Felix. Felix ducked a swipe of its tree-stump club and pulled Kat up.

'Run!' he roared.

She was already running, her axes in her hands. Felix turned and hurried after her, desperate to get her to safety. More of the gors were aware of them now, reaching and swinging for them, calling to their brothers. Kat danced away from every swipe, backhanding the beasts she passed with deft hacks. Felix chopped at them as they turned after her, then plunged through them as they howled and staggered aside.

Finally they broke out of the pack and ran up the stone steps of the strong house. A few of the gors chased them, and Felix felt the wind of a giant mace fan the back of his neck as he and Kat raced, side-by-side, over the threshold.

Then, just as Felix was letting out a sigh of relief, there was a deafening thunderclap and something hit him so hard in the back that he was thrown to the far end of the room and slammed against an interior wall. For a long black moment he thought that the gor had connected with its mace and sent him to some hellish afterlife, for he seemed to be in a world of darkness and flame and noise and could not tell up from down or cold from hot. His body seemed at once numb and on fire. His head spun as if he'd been in a drinking contest with Snorri Nosebiter.

Then his vision returned and he was even more confused. A ball of fire seemed to be coming from the ceiling and rising to the floor. The walls swayed as if they were made of mattresses. Heavy wet things thudded all around him like rotten fruit. A huge weight pressed on his shoulders. Finally equilibrium reasserted itself and he realised that he was propped head-down against the wall, his neck bent and all his weight on his shoulders with his arse sticking up in the air. The ball of fire was receding through the door, and there were bits and pieces of beastman lying around him like the leavings on a butcher's shop floor. A leg with a cloven hoof lay beside him, oozing blood, while a beastman's head hung from the wall above him, one horn impaling the plaster. Dust rained down from above.

There was a little moan from his right. He turned his head and his body slid down the wall and slumped to the floor in a painful heap. He grunted and sat up. Kat lay curled in a ball next to him. His heart turned to ice. Had the explosion killed her?

'Kat?' said Felix. 'Are you all right?'

Kat pried open one eye. 'Are we dead?'

Relief flooded through him like a river through a burst dam. 'No.'

'Then I'm fine–'

'Slayers!' roared Gotrek from the door. 'Attack!'

Felix looked up to see Gotrek, Snorri and Rodi charging through the door, weapons at the ready.

Kat slowly levered herself up, using the wall for balance. She was shaking like a leaf. 'Come on, Felix,' she said. 'There is slaying to be done.'

Felix stood as well. He felt as if he was made of matchsticks and rusty hinges. 'Aye,' he said. 'But you're to do yours from the roof, remember?'

'But I want to fight by your side,' she said.

And I want you to live, thought Felix, but he knew that wouldn't fly. Instead he said, 'No, Kat. The archers need you. You saw them on the wall. Go to them. Show them how it's done.'

She looked up at him with her lopsided smile. 'Is this how you make Gotrek do what you want?'

Felix opened his mouth, but before anything came out she laughed and started unsteadily up the steps to the upper floor.

Felix watched her go, then turned and hurried for the door, where the sounds of slaughter were rising.

The intersection was a charnel house. The pulped remains of scores of beastmen were piled up against the walls of the houses facing the street like drifts of crimson rubbish. Of the powder wagon there was no sign, only a smoking patch of earth where it had stood, surrounded by melting red snow, but bits of timber and barrel staves stuck out of the wattle-and-daub houses like straw blown by the wind.

And yet, astoundingly, some of the beastmen still lived. Felix saw Gotrek and Snorri and Rodi laying into them at the south end of the intersection – three squat whirlwinds wading into two score beastmen. And they weren't alone. Sir Teobalt, Karaghul in hand, fought at the head of a small group of soldiers, refugees and villagers, all armed with Ludeker's stolen weapons.

'Men of the Empire,' cried the templar in a high warble. 'Destroy the enemies of man! Defend your homes!'

As Felix ran – or rather staggered – towards the fight he saw beastman after beastman fall, and not all from the exertions of the dwarfs and men.

From every rooftop shot flashing shafts that buried themselves in beastman fur, and he could hear Weir shouting from somewhere above and behind him, 'That's the way, lads! Stick to the edges. Don't want to kill our own, do we?'

Felix ploughed into the fight, swinging high and low, and cutting down a beastman with almost every stroke. It was a dream of a battle – the kind of battle he had imagined being the hero of when he had read the old sagas as a little boy. Thus had Sigmar slain a thousand orcs at Black Fire Pass. Thus had Magnus smote the forces of Chaos before the gates of Kislev. The beasts practically fell over before he hit them, and Felix's allies were faring just as well, killing beastmen as if they had been lambs.

Of course it wasn't a fair fight and Felix knew it. The blast had dizzied the beastmen as it had him, only more so, as they had borne the brunt of it. They reeled as if drunk, and could barely hold on to their weapons. Some of them had smoking bits of timber sticking out of them. Still, it felt magnificent, a glorious vengeance for all the violence and misery the gors and the Drakwald had inflicted upon him and his companions since he had left Altdorf.

Only one thing marred the fight. Only one thing kept it from being the perfect battle – the paltry and unfamiliar sword with which he fought. It should have been Karaghul. Without it, nothing felt right. His blocks and parries were off, his attacks lacked force – in fact, it was a fortunate thing that the beasts were so disabled, for at full strength and with their wits unscrambled, he wasn't sure he could have prevailed against them with the new blade.

He glared at Sir Teobalt across the battle in between fighting. He supposed the templar had a right to take the blade from him, but it still stung. It still seemed unfair. He almost wished... but no, that was an unworthy thought. He pushed it away.

After only a few moments, the last few beastmen broke and ran for the gate. Felix and the Slayers and Teobalt's ragtag company chased them all the way, cutting down all but the quickest. Only three remained when they reached the gate, and they quickly outdistanced their shorter-legged pursuers.

Gotrek heaved his axe at them as they ran across the field. It caught the slowest one in the left leg and it went down with a screech. The other two didn't look back, only sprinted for the black wall of the forest as quickly as they were able.

Felix and the others stopped just outside the gates of the village as Gotrek stumped forwards to retrieve his axe. Last came Sir Teobalt, limping and grimacing and wheezing like a bellows as he leaned against the gatepost and caught his breath.

'Well... well done, men,' he said to his troops. 'It was bravely fought. And well done to you as well, sons of Grimnir,' he added, turning to the Slayers. 'Your plan worked in all particulars.'

Felix noticed that the old templar didn't mention him in his congratulations.

Teobalt turned to one of the soldiers. 'Anselem, close the doors, and place the heavy bar. They may come again–'

'Srr,' came a strange voice from the shadows beside the gate. 'Srr, pleese.'

Felix and the others turned at the sound. A horrible crouching figure shuffled out of the darkness. It was one of the ungors, with little sprouting horns and a furred face, but features still mostly human. It had been terribly abused, with great gashes and bruises on its face and shoulders, and its wiry arms were clutched around its belly, trying to keep in the intestines that threatened to slither out of a gash that slit it from privates to breastbone. It looked as if it could barely stand.

'A beast!' shouted Sir Teobalt. 'Kill it!'

His men stepped forwards, but Snorri and Rodi got there before them, raising their weapons.

The ungor staggered back, crying out, a look of fearful pleading on his half-human face, and suddenly Felix recognised him.

'Stop!' he shouted. 'It's Ortwin!'

FIFTEEN

Sir Teobalt stared.

The two Slayers paused, but Gotrek, returning from retrieving his axe, did not. He pushed through them, preparing to strike. 'Not any more it isn't.'

The changed squire fell on his back, raising one hand in supplication. 'Pleese, no. I msst speek. I msst tell you.'

Gotrek stepped over him, axe high.

'Wait, Gotrek,' said Felix. 'Let him speak.'

'He is a beast,' said the Slayer. 'He must die.'

'Death is all I wssh,' mumbled Ortwin through his fangs. 'But I msst speek frrst.'

'It looks like he's going to die anyway,' said Felix.

Gotrek lowered his axe. 'Speak quickly then, beast,' he growled. 'My axe is impatient.'

Ortwin moaned with relief. 'Blsss you, Slayrr.'

Sir Teobalt stepped past the Slayers and looked down at his former squire. Felix had never seen the old knight look so stricken or sad. 'Ortwin, is it truly you?'

The changed youth cringed away from the knight's gaze. 'Frrgive me, mastrr. Sigmar have mrrcy on me.'

Sir Teobalt's shoulders slumped, and he covered his eyes with a shaking hand. 'Sigmar have mercy on us all.'

The crunching of snowy footsteps came from the village. Felix turned to see Kat and Doktor Vinck leading forwards a crowd of nervous villagers.

'Are they all dead?' asked Doktor Vinck. 'Have you chased them all–'

He choked when he saw Ortwin. There was an angry murmur from the crowd.

'Keep them back, doctor,' said Felix. 'There is no need to fear.'

The doctor obligingly waved the villagers back, but Kat came forwards, staring wide-eyed at the dying squire.

'Is it...?' she asked in a trembling voice. 'Is it...?'

Felix nodded, then took her arm. Her hand circled his waist.

'Go on, Ortwin,' he said, turning back. 'Tell us.'

Ortwin nodded weakly and took a laboured breath. 'I know whrrr they... take the stone,' he wheezed. 'I know what they will... do with it. I came... to wrrn you but they caught me, and...' He looked down at the horrible wound in his belly. 'At leest it will be over soon.'

'Sooner than you expect if you don't speak quickly,' said Gotrek. 'Tell your tale, beast.'

Ortwin fought to focus. 'They go to hills in the south,' he said. 'Acrrss the Talabec. Thrrr is an old crrcle. They will raise the stone. On... on Witching Night – Hexensnacht.' He grimaced with pain.

'To what purpose?' asked Sir Teobalt.

'A crrimony,' breathed Ortwin. 'Urslak Cripplehorn was granted a vssion by the brrd-headed god. Thss crrimony, on thss niight... will trrn all men undrr the shadow of the forest to beestmen, like me.'

The men and dwarfs stared at him in disbelief.

'All men?' said Felix uncertainly. 'Everyone? He has the power to do this?'

'The stone givss him the powrr,' said Ortwin. 'His god givss him the powrr. His beesthrrd giivess him the powrr.'

'Which forest?' asked Doktor Vinck. 'The Drakwald? The Great Forest? The Reikwald?'

'To the beestmen,' said Ortwin, 'all frrests arr one.'

Felix and the others looked around at each other.

'This is dread news,' said Teobalt.

'It's bunk,' said Rodi. 'It's not possible. No beast has such power.'

'Can you say that with the evidence before you?' asked Doktor Vinck, indicating Ortwin.

'Changing a handful of men isn't the same as changing thousands, over hundreds of miles,' replied Rodi.

'Does it matter?' asked Gotrek. 'If this shaman can do a tenth of what he claims it will be too much. He must be stopped.'

'He must,' agreed Kat.

Rodi nodded. 'Aye. And there is a great doom to be had, win or fail.'

'Snorri wants it to be Witching Night now,' said Snorri.

The comment brought Felix up short. 'Wait,' he said. 'What day is it?'

Sir Teobalt looked up. 'It is the twenty-first of Vorhexen – fasting day of Walhemar the Valiant.'

Felix did a quick calculation in his head. 'Then there are fourteen days until Hexensnacht. I don't know where the beasts are going below the Talabec, but at the rate they're moving they'll never make it in time. It took us ten days from Ahlenhof, and we went by roads. They're cutting every step through the deep woods.'

Kat nodded. 'It's impossible.'

'Nno,' moaned Ortwin.

They turned back to him. The snow around where he lay was crimson with his blood.

'Evrry changed man Urslak adds to the hrrd adds knowing,' said the squire through bubbles of red phlegm. 'He sees our minds. He knew I would trry to come to you. He knows how to use the rrver.'

'How to use the river?' said Sir Teobalt. 'I don't understand.'

'The timbrr camp,' said Ortwin. 'On the rivrr.'

'Aye, I remember it,' said Teobalt, nodding. 'We passed the night there.'

'What has a timber camp got to do with it?' asked Rodi. 'The beast has stopped making sense.'

Felix gasped as understanding came to him. 'Logs!' he cried. 'Rafts! We saw them!'

'What are you saying, manling?' asked Gotrek.

Felix grunted with impatience. Dwarfs seemed to have a blind spot for the uses of trees. 'The shaman means to float the stone down the river,' he said. 'A few of those rafts we saw bound together, and he can move it at twice his speed. Maybe three times as fast. They'll tow it down the Zufuhr like a barge.'

'Yss,' said Ortwin from the ground. 'Yss.'

'But beastmen don't know how to make boats,' said Rodi. 'They can barely tie a rock to the end of a stick and call it a mace.'

'Beestmen do not,' whispered Ortwin. 'But beests who wrrr once men do. Urslak is...' He coughed, spilling blood down his furred chest. 'Urslak is... lrrrning.'

Felix stared dully as Ortwin fell silent. A beastman who learned was a nightmare – the doom of the human race. It had been the beasts' savagery and lack of discipline, more so than the superiority of the defences of man, that had stopped them from taking over the world. If the monsters began to learn to use wagons and boats and developed organisation and tactics, there would be no stopping them.

'Anything else, beast?' asked Gotrek, looking down at Ortwin.

The changed squire looked up through dimming eyes. 'Bewrre... bewrre the axe of Gargorath the God-Touched,' he said. 'It... it eats what it kills.'

'That is all?'

Ortwin nodded and sank back. 'I am rredy.'

Gotrek raised his axe, but Sir Teobalt stepped forwards.

'Wait, Slayer,' he said. 'It should be I that does this.'

Gotrek nodded and stepped back as the old templar stood over his former squire. 'I can offer you no salvation, squire,' said Teobalt. 'A beast is beyond Sigmar's mercy. But... but I give you my thanks. Though you have fallen, you sacrificed your life to return and warn us. It was a brave thing, bravely done.'

'Thank you, srr,' said Ortwin, and there seemed to be tears in his bestial eyes – though it might only have been blood. 'Sigmrr blsss you.'

Sir Teobalt lifted Karaghul with both hands. 'May you find in death the peace you lost in life.'

The changed boy closed his eyes. The sword came down. Kat turned away and pressed her face against Felix's chest as the shaggy horned head dropped softly into the snow. He pulled her close, stroking her hair as he grieved.

The squire had been a fool sometimes, and too concerned with honour and doing heroic deeds for his own good – or the good of his companions on more than one occasion – but at the same time that honour had proved stronger than the animal instincts that had come with his new shape, and he had died to maintain it. It was doubtful that anyone would write any ballads about a youth that turned into a beast, but he was a hero nonetheless. He might very well have saved the Empire. That is, he might have if the rest of them could warn Altdorf in time.

'I must go south at once,' said Sir Teobalt.

'Not alone, you won't,' said Gotrek.

'Aye,' said Rodi. 'We're coming too.'

'Snorri is ready,' said Snorri. 'Where are we going?'

'Is there a boat?' asked Felix. It seemed the only way to catch up to the beasts.

Doktor Vinck shook his head. 'There is not. They were all taken by the soldiers and the refugees when news of the herd reached us.' He frowned. 'There is one at the lumber camp, or there was. Perhaps the beasts have taken it.'

'Unless they haven't reached it yet,' said Kat, lifting her head from Felix's chest. 'If we take the river road, we may beat them.'

'We must try it!' said Sir Teobalt. 'We will leave immediately.'

Felix, Kat, Sir Teobalt and the three Slayers left an hour later on a wagon to which they hitched four horses for greater speed – with Teobalt's Machtig tied behind. Though all were weary from the long day of preparing and defending the village, there was no alternative. They had to get ahead of the beastmen, and waiting until morning might make it impossible for them to catch up.

Doktor Vinck thanked them profusely for saving Bauholz, and gave them food and drink for the road. He begged Kat to be careful, and reminded Sir Teobalt to apply the ointment he had given him three times a day to his wounds, which were not yet fully healed, then waved goodbye to them until the wooden doors of the gate closed with a hollow boom.

Felix and Kat sat side by side in the back of the wagon as they rode out of town, alone – or at least nearly alone – for the first time since he had rescued her from Milo. Sir Teobalt, saying that he had done the least in the recent battle and would therefore take point, had unhitched Machtig and rode well ahead of the wagon, and the three Slayers sat on the buckboard, Gotrek driving the horses while Rodi and Snorri kept watch.

Felix took a deep breath. This might be the best opportunity they would have for days.

He put a hand on her leg. 'Kat,' he said.

She turned and smiled up at him, and all the words went out of his head. He just stared.

Kat stared back, and, as the silence stretched and the seconds ticked by, she covered his hand with hers, then lifted it and pulled it over her shoulders so that she could lean against him underneath it. He pulled her tight and all at once they were kissing, long and deep, and the freezing night was suddenly as warm as a Tilean spring.

After a moment Felix pulled back, holding her away from him. 'Wait, Kat,' he said, panting. 'Wait.'

She scowled at him. 'Does it still feel wrong to you, then, Felix? I am no longer seven.'

'I know,' he said. 'I know. That's... that's not what I was going to say.'

'Then what?' she asked, her chin thrust out.

He hesitated again, not sure how to begin, but finally he spoke. 'I realised, when we were fighting Milo, that... that I cared more for you than I have for anyone for a long long time, and that all my... misgivings were gone.'

Kat dropped her eyes at that, smiling shyly.

'But...'

She looked up again, her brow lowering once more. 'But?' she said, warningly.

Felix sighed and sat back. 'Kat, I don't have a proper life. I have no employment, no home, no money. I follow the Slayer into certain death time and time again, and my vow to him means I'll keep doing it until he dies.' He looked sideways at her. 'I've got nothing to give you. Not even the certainty that I'll be here tomorrow.'

Kat smiled and let out a relieved breath. 'Is that all?' she said.

'Isn't that everything?' he asked.

'It's nothing, Felix. Nothing.' She leaned against him, resting her head on his chest. 'When Papa trained me to be a scout, he taught me the first rule of the Drakwald – the rule that every woodsman and beast-hunter lives by.'

'What rule is that?' asked Felix.

'Today is all there is,' she said. She circled her arms around him, looking out over the tailgate of the cart. 'We are all like you, Felix. No home, no money, and death always only an eye-blink away. None of us knows if we'll be here tomorrow, so we live by that rule.'

'Today is all there is,' Felix repeated.

'Yes,' she whispered, and raised her head and looked into his eyes, her lips parting. 'Today is all there is.'

Felix lowered his mouth to hers, closing his eyes. He could feel her breath on his lips. He could feel her straining upwards.

'Easy, Machtig!' said Sir Teobalt's voice.

Felix and Kat jerked apart guiltily and looked up. The old templar was pulling Machtig around the back of the wagon and trying to dismount while the horse skittered sideways. He smiled at them. 'Wilful beast. He has been too long without a bit in his mouth.'

Felix and Kat untangled themselves as Sir Teobalt let himself down and tied the warhorse to the tailgate, then climbed up into the wagon between them. 'I am too weary after the day's events to remind him of his training,' he said, unbuckling his breastplate. 'No matter. I will have plenty of opportunity in the days ahead.'

'No doubt,' said Felix, cursing the knight inwardly. Today might be all there was, but if Sir Teobalt was going to make himself a fixture, Felix and Kat would still have to wait until tomorrow.

The old templar looked from him to Kat and back with an odd expression on his gaunt face, then removed his breastplate and set it on the floor of the cart. 'Sigmar watch you whilst you rest, friends,' he said, then laid back on the breastplate like it was a pillow, folded his hands across his chest and closed his eyes.

Felix sighed and gave Kat an exasperated look. She smirked back at him across Sir Teobalt's body and stifled a laugh, then shrugged.

'Well, goodnight, Felix,' she said. 'Pleasant dreams.'

'I doubt it,' growled Felix, then flopped down and pulled his cloak tighter around his shoulders as the old knight began to snore.

Felix dozed on and off, but unsurprisingly, he did not truly sleep. The bumping of the wagon and Teobalt's snoring, and Felix's frustrated thoughts of what might have been had the damned interfering old buzzard not been there didn't allow it. Towards morning, a particularly hard jolt woke him from a dream of Kat skinning out of her furs and stretching naked beside him, to find Sir Teobalt looking at him with thoughtful eyes.

Felix blinked at him sleepily. He was a jarring sight after his thoughts of Kat.

The templar kept staring.

'Are... are you well, Sir Teobalt?' Felix mumbled, as politely as he could manage.

'I have done you a disservice, Herr Jaeger,' he said after a long hesitation.

You certainly have, thought Felix, but all he said was, 'Have you?'

'I would have spoken of it earlier, but…' The templar looked over his shoulder at Kat. 'It is a private matter between us.'

'I'm not sure what you mean,' said Felix.

'You know of what I speak, Herr Jaeger.' Teobalt sighed and lowered his eyes. 'I could not allow myself to believe you when you told me of Ortwin's fate and the fate of my fellow templars. I… I see now that you told the truth.'

'It was a hard thing to believe,' said Felix.

'Aye.' The templar's brow furrowed. 'It pains me to think that such good men fell so far from the true faith that they could be twisted like this.'

Felix paused. Teobalt still didn't seem to understand. He was still looking to place blame. 'Forgive me, sir,' he said finally. 'But I'm not sure it is a matter of falling from faith. I think perhaps the shaman's power is just too strong. I wonder if even an arch lector could resist it.'

'You say this to hearten me,' said the templar. 'To allow me to think better of my brothers.'

'I say it because I believe it,' said Felix. 'I have seen the power of the stone. Lord Ilgner was a good man. He had fought the hordes and the herds with all his heart, and yet he changed with the rest.'

'Perhaps you are right,' said Teobalt, still not looking up.

He sank into a long silence, and Felix began to drift off again, thinking that the conversation was finished.

Then just as his head began dropping to his chest, the knight spoke again.

'You are an honourable man, Herr Jaeger,' he said.

Felix raised his eyes again and blinked. 'I am?'

'Aye,' said Sir Teobalt. 'You have done what I asked of you. You have discovered the fate of the templars of the Order of the Fiery Heart and, though you knew that I would not care to hear it, you told me the truth of that fate.'

Felix opened his mouth to speak, but the templar held up a hand.

'There still remains the task of recovering the regalia of the order, but I wonder if it is not lost forever. Or perhaps we will find it when we find the beastmen again. I know not.' He sat up, hissing and grimacing at his stiffness. 'Nevertheless, you have been true to your promise, and you do not deserve the punishment I meted out to you.'

He reached down and picked up Karaghul, which he had laid beside him as he slept, then held it out to Felix. 'Your sword, Herr Jaeger,' he said. 'And whether we find the regalia or not, you may carry it, as I had promised. You have already earned it.'

Felix's eyes moved from Teobalt's face to the sword and back. He almost didn't dare to reach for it, for fear it would be some kind of strange joke and the templar would pull it back. It was not a joke, and when Felix held out his hands, Teobalt laid the sword in them and inclined his head.

'Wear it with honour, Herr Jaeger,' he said. 'As I know you have until now.'

'Thank you, Sir Teobalt,' said Felix, shaking as he laid the sword at his side and ran a fond hand along its hilt. 'I will not disappoint you. I promise.'

When Felix next awoke, it was to dwarfen cursing.

He sat up, groaning and stiff, and looked around as Kat and Sir Teobalt yawned and grumbled beside him. It was the dark grey of dawn, and a heavy mist swirled about the wagon. Nevertheless, he could see why Gotrek and Rodi were cursing.

They all climbed down stiffly from the wagon and looked around as they shook out their arms and legs. They were in the middle of the logging camp they had stopped at on their way north with Reidle the merchant, but the camp wasn't there any more. It had been levelled – the walls, the tents, the short docks that had once stuck out into the river like stubby thumbs, all crushed and shaken down by the hooves of ten thousand beastmen. The rafts and stacks of logs were gone – either taken by the beastmen or fallen into the river and washed away. For as far as the eye could see in every direction the muddy snow was covered by their heavy black prints. It looked like a parchment written over and over with letters by some mad author who couldn't stop his hand.

'They've been and gone,' said Kat, staring around bleakly.

'Aye, and only hours ago, by the smell of it,' said Rodi, spitting.

'Snorri thinks they could have waited,' said Snorri.

'There's our boat,' grunted Gotrek, nodding down the river.

Felix followed his gaze. Through the mist he could see a little riverboat sunk to its gunwales in the water just south of the timber camp. It had crashed into a big rock that rose from the side of the stream and shattered its prow. He wondered if the timber men had tried to escape in it, or if the beasts had made some ham-fisted attempt to pilot it. Whatever the case, it was beyond repair.

'Get back on the wagon,' said Gotrek. 'We won't be sailing.'

'Thank Grungni for that,' said Rodi with a shiver. 'Boats are for elves.'

SIXTEEN

The trail of the herd was one of destruction and desolation. The road that paralleled the river was churned into a soup of mud and snow and the dung of ten thousand beastmen, and littered with abandoned wagons, mutilated corpses and half-eaten carcasses. The village of Leer was a shattered ghost town, its walls knocked flat and its buildings torn down, and entirely empty. There were a few corpses, but too few. Felix hoped they had fled into the woods, but he doubted it. More likely they had become the latest victims of the stone's mutating magic and had joined the herd, adding another few hundred to the shaman's endless train of followers.

He dreaded what would happen when the beastmen reached more civilised areas. He didn't see how anything could stop them, and as the wagon neared Ahlenhof after several days of hard, hurried travel, Felix feared the worst.

But when they came around the bend in the river and saw the town on the opposite bank, it appeared untouched. As they got closer, they saw why. The bridge that had spanned the Zufuhr had been demolished. Only the jagged stumps of the stone piers stuck up out of the water, all the rest had collapsed.

Hunching against the downpour of a cold, heavy rain, teams of labourers were hard at work fishing giant blocks of granite out of the freezing water and winching them up the banks to where foremen and engineers surveyed the damage on a promontory turned to a muddy hill by a million gouging hoof prints. A long line of carts and wagons and carriages that had come up the river road from Altdorf was stopped at the fallen span, and the drivers and passengers were milling about in the pouring rain, complaining to guardsmen from Ahlenhof and arguing amongst each other.

'What happened here?' Felix asked a young guard as they pulled up near the other wagons. 'Did the herd tear the bridge down?'

The guard shook his head. 'No,' he said wearily. 'The city did, for protection.' He pointed to the line of stopped traffic. 'If you want to cross to Ahlenhof, you'll have to go to the end of the queue. We've set up a ferry. Move along please.' It sounded like he'd been saying the same thing all day.

'We shall cross to Ahlenhof immediately, guardsman,' said Sir Teobalt, stepping down from the back of the wagon and limping forwards with his head high. 'I have news of greatest import for your mayor and for Emil von Kotzebue, your baron, concerning the herd.'

The guard blinked at the templar as if he'd sprouted from the ground, then bowed reflexively. 'Sorry, m'lord,' he said. 'Next ferry won't come for an hour.'

Teobalt pointed down to the bank of the river, where a long boat with eight oars was pulled up on the mud. 'Then I will take that,' he said.

The guard looked down at the boat, then hesitated. 'Er, I'll ask my captain.'

'At once, please,' said Teobalt.

Felix smiled as the guard scurried off. He didn't have much use for the noble classes as a rule, but they were handy to have around when one wanted to get things done in a hurry.

'Damned shame, isn't it?' said a halfling pushing a pie cart, nodding at the bridge. 'But it was the only way. Mined the pilings and blew it to pieces, they did. Fancy a hot pie?'

'Snorri doesn't want a pie,' said Snorri. 'Snorri wants a beer. He hasn't had a drink in a week.'

'Ah, you'll be wanting to speak to my darling wife then,' said the pie-seller. 'Hoy, Esme! These gentlemen would like a drink!'

A halfling woman further down the line waved to him and turned a wheelbarrow around, in the bed of which was an enormous barrel of ale. Gotrek, Rodi and Snorri licked their lips.

'And we was lucky,' said the halfling, leaning against his cart as he waited for his wife. 'For if the beasts had truly wanted the town, blowing up the bridge wouldn't have stopped them.'

'Why not?' asked Gotrek.

The halfling snorted. 'Well, they crossed the Talabec didn't they? Just jumped in and swam.'

Felix turned and looked at the wide, rushing river, more than a half-mile across here where the Zufuhr joined it. 'They swam the Talabec?' he said, unbelieving.

'Aye,' said the halfling. 'Or most of them did at any rate. Went across in a big clump, all clinging to each other, like. A lot of them still drowned. Hundreds, I hear. Swept away. Still, enough made it ashore to wipe Brasthof off the map. Trod it flat and kept on south like they was following a star.' He shivered. 'They say Brasthof's not there no more. Just... gone.'

Felix grimaced at the thought, but before he could ask the halfling any more questions, the guard returned with his captain, a round-faced, round-bodied fellow with a pointed beard and a nervous smile.

'Ah, m'lord,' he said, bowing to Sir Teobalt. 'Nesselbaum says you want to borrow our boat.'

'I wish to report to your mayor and your lord something of grave import concerning the beastman herd.'

'Thank you, m'lord,' said the captain. 'But a messenger was sent to Baron von Kotzebue yesterday, informing him of their passage.'

'It is not of their passage that I wish to inform him,' said Sir Teobalt, going a bit red in the face. 'He must hear of the threat the monsters pose, and of the danger involved in facing them. Is the baron on his way?'

'Er, no, m'lord,' said the captain. 'The mayor sent another messenger after the first telling him it wasn't necessary.'

'What?' The templar's eyes blazed. 'For what reason, in Sigmar's name?'

'Well, m'lord,' said the captain, shrinking back uneasily. 'They swam the river into Talabecland late last night. So they were no longer a threat to us.'

Felix stared, alarmed, as the veins bulged in Sir Teobalt's forehead and neck. He was afraid the old templar's heart was going to explode with fury.

'No longer a threat!' bellowed Sir Teobalt. 'Listen to me, you small-minded provincial buffoon. Has the late war taught you nothing? The Empire is strong only when it stands together! Had Middenland helped Ostland from the first, the invaders would have been stopped before they began!' He tugged off his riding gloves angrily, and Felix was afraid he was going to slap the fat captain with them, but after a moment he collected himself and took a deep breath.

'The leader of the beasts,' he said, speaking as one would speak to a small child, 'means to unleash a magic upon the Empire that will turn half of its citizens into beastmen and set them raging upon their neighbours. The spell will not stop at provincial borders. It will not respect the boundaries of any lord's land. It will touch anyone living under the shadow of the Empire's forests, be they in Talabecland, Reikland, Hochland, Middenland or anywhere else. Do you understand me?'

The captain's mouth opened and closed several times, but nothing came out.

'Now,' said the templar, 'you shall give this message to your mayor and tell him that he will send a third rider after the first two, and respectfully request Baron von Kotzebue come to the aid of his Talabecland neighbours before he and all his vassals start sprouting horns and hooves.'

'Ah... aye, m'lord,' said the captain, bowing convulsively. 'Right away, m'lord. But...' he hesitated, afraid to provoke the old knight's wrath any further.

'But?' said Teobalt, dangerously.

'But a military force must have permission from the ruling lord before entering his lands, m'lord. Baron von Kotzebue commands four thousand men. Talabecland would see it as an invasion. An invitation would have to be sent, and the baron surely wouldn't move his army before he had it.'

Sir Teobalt fought to control his temper. 'Then your messenger shall tell the baron that you have such an invitation already.'

'You ask us to lie to the baron?' said the captain, white as a sheet.

'It will not be a lie,' said the old knight. 'For you will this moment transport me and my companions across the river to Talabecland, so that I may speak to the lord there and procure the invitation you require.'

The captain hesitated, practically vibrating with fear at being the instrument that would carry a falsehood to his liege, but finally he bowed to Sir Teobalt. 'Very good, m'lord,' he said. 'I will find the oarsmen and have the boat prepared for you momentarily.' And with that he scurried off towards the riverbank, shouting for his subordinates.

Sir Teobalt let out a long sigh and sagged against the wagon, exhausted from his anger.

Rodi chuckled. 'That was telling him,' he said.

'Aye,' said Gotrek.

Felix put a hand on the knight's shoulder. 'Are you all right, sir?'

'I am fine, thank you, Herr Jaeger,' said Teobalt. 'I only hope I did some good. The message may yet fall foul of fools.'

Felix nodded and looked around. The halfling and his wife – who had come up during Teobalt's tirade – were staring open-mouthed at them all.

'Pardon, your worships,' said the pie-seller. 'Was all that true that you said just now? About everybody turning into beasts and killing each other?'

Felix hesitated and looked at the others. He could see the same thought in all their eyes. If this news were to spread there would be a terrible panic, and the halfling couple were just the ones to spread it, taking food, drink and gossip up and down the line of wagons, which would then travel to the ends of the Empire. It was a recipe for riot and rampage.

Gotrek fixed Felix with his single eye and gave him an almost imperceptible shake of the head.

'Nah. Not a word of it,' said Felix. 'Just something to get old Kotzebue moving a little faster.' He leaned in with what he hoped was a conspiratorial smile. 'Though don't tell the captain that. It'll spoil everything.'

The halfling and his wife grinned with relief.

'Not a word, squire,' said the little man. 'I know when to keep mum.'

'Thank you, sir.' said Felix, and then just to seal the deal, 'A pie and a pint all around while we wait for our boat.'

'It would be our pleasure, sir,' said the halfling.

The mayor of Esselfurt, the village almost directly across the Talabec from Ahlenhof, listened patiently as Sir Teobalt explained it all again. He was a big man, with a barrel chest, a booming voice and a chain of office around his neck that probably weighed more than Karaghul.

Felix almost dozed off in the middle of it. Esselfurt's council hall was warmed by a roaring fire, and he was basking in it. The crossing of the Talabec in a small boat had not been a pleasant experience. The battering wind had cuffed water off the waves and sprayed it in their faces. Felix, Kat and Sir Teobalt had hunched under their cloaks in the back of the boat, cold, wet and miserable, while Gotrek, Snorri and Rodi spent their time leaning over the side, giving their recently consumed pie and beer to the waves.

Now all was warmth and peace and the smell of wet wool drying by the fire – that is until Teobalt finished his tale and the mayor pounded the table he stood behind with a meaty fist, snapping Felix out of his nap.

'By Sigmar, Sir Teobalt,' he said. 'That's bad. A bad business. And Esselfurt stands behind you in your effort to defeat this terrible threat to our beloved Empire.'

'I thank you, Mayor Dindorf,' said the templar, relieved. 'Then you will send to your lord, and ask him to bring troops to face the herd before Hexensnacht?'

'Word was sent last night when the beasts crossed the Talabec, m'lord,' said Mayor Dindorf. 'And I will send messengers with this new information. But, er...'

'Is there a difficulty?' asked Sir Teobalt dangerously, as Dindorf faltered.

'Well, you see,' said the mayor, 'I'm not sure who will come. Or how soon.'

'I don't understand,' said the templar, his face clouding. 'Who would come but your lord?'

The mayor scratched the back of his head. 'Well, it's like this, m'lord. Count Feuerbach, the Elector of Talabecland is our liege here, but he hasn't returned from the fighting in the north. It is rumoured he might be dead. Most of the lords who would answer in his place are away in Talabheim, petitioning Countess Krieglitz-Untern to be his successor.'

'So you have sent to them there?' Sir Teobalt's shoulders sagged. 'Talabheim is days away. They will never return in time.'

'Word has also been sent to their castles, my lord,' said the mayor. 'But, well, there is no one at them but their sons and wives. I don't know who of them will answer.'

The templar sighed. 'Is there no one who can raise an army quickly?' he asked. 'We face the end of all things.'

'There is the Temple of Leopold in Priestlicheim,' said Mayor Dindorf, 'which trains warrior-priests. And the Monastery of the Tower of Vigilance further south. They're said to be a martial order, but they don't come out of the cloister much.'

Sir Teobalt nodded, though Felix could see that he was downhearted. 'Then I beg you, mayor, to send to them as well, and muster what militia you can from your people. Tell them to come to Brasthof. We will follow the herd's trail from there.'

'Aye, my lord,' said the mayor. 'I will do what I can.'

Felix wondered unhappily how much that might be.

Sir Teobalt was torn between depression and fury as they made their way west along the south bank of the Talabec towards Brasthof in the driving rain, and it pained Felix to see it.

'Sigmar, I am sickened,' said the old knight, his eyes dull as he rode along on the horse that he had commandeered from Mayor Dindorf. He'd had to leave Machtig behind in Ahlenhof – the warhorse had been too big for the boat. 'These puffed-up popinjays fight over the holdings of Count Feuerbach like so many thieves, while the Empire is being lost behind their backs.' He sighed. 'Perhaps we deserve our fate. Though we have pushed back the hordes from the north there is still much wickedness abroad in the land. Perhaps it is right to wipe the slate clean and start again.'

Felix was more inclined to put it down to bad luck and human nature, but he didn't want to further upset the old templar with argument, so he said nothing.

As the pie-seller had said, there were huge shoals of dead beastmen floating in the river and washed up on the muddy banks all along the road to the village – Felix couldn't even have begun to count how many, but it was hundreds, not dozens – all bloated and grey from being long in the water, and stinking to the gushing clouds.

In Brasthof, however, there were no bodies. The town was Stangenschloss and Leer and the timber camp all over again – shattered and empty except for a few looters, with the same unnerving lack of corpses they had seen before – proof that there had been no slaughter, just the terrible magic of the stone, replacing those who had drowned with the changed.

It had been a small town – bigger than Bauholz, smaller than Leer – but like Leer it had been sorely damaged by the herd's passage. It looked as if the beastmen, frustrated because the stone's transformative power left them with no enemies to fight, had taken out their rage on the buildings instead. Little flattened cottages lay with their thatched roofs on top of them like scratchy blankets, stables and smithies torn apart, shops set on fire. Gaping holes had been smashed in the front of the one tavern. The few survivors sat among the ruins, weeping and calling out to loved ones who were no longer there, and likely no longer human.

The temple of Sigmar seemed to have seen special attention from the beasts. It had been daubed with faeces and all its symbols torn down and smashed. In front of it, Felix saw a corpse in the robes of a priest. Up close they could see that the man had died halfway through changing into a beastman. It looked as if he had stabbed himself in the neck to stop the transformation.

As they made their way around the piles of rubble, Gotrek stopped and held up a hand. Felix and the others paused, listening. From behind the temple came the clank and rattle of armour and heavy steps. Felix and Sir Teobalt drew their swords. Kat pulled her bow from her back. The Slayers readied their weapons.

Then, around the corner crept four halberdiers in breastplates, morions and mustard-coloured uniforms slashed with burgundy. They stopped when they saw Teobalt's party and went on guard.

'Who are you?' asked the one in front. 'Scavengers?'

Sir Teobalt nudged his horse forwards a step. 'I am Sir Teobalt von Dreschler, templar of the Order of the Fiery Heart. I and my companions seek the doom of the beastmen.'

The men relaxed when they heard Teobalt speak, and the first one bowed. 'Soldiers of Lord Giselbert von Volgen, m'lord. You have knowledge of these beasts?'

'We have been following them for weeks,' said Teobalt.

'Then you had better speak to our master.'

The soldiers led them out the other side of the village to a windmill around which about a hundred mustard-uniformed soldiers stood at ease while a hard-faced, beardless young lord in a suit of fluted plate armour sat upon a barded warhorse and spoke to a huddled collection of villagers who stood beside him. The lord had a handful of other knights with him, and they hemmed in the villagers on all sides. A tall, powerfully built captain of halberdiers held the reins of the lord's horse.

Felix was heartened to see so many uniformed men. It wasn't an army, but after the excuses and disappointments at Ahlenhof and Esselfurt, to find a band of fighting men of any size on the trail of the beastmen was a welcome surprise.

'Damn it, Thiessen,' the square-jawed young lord was saying as Felix and the others approached. 'Make them stop blubbing and talk sense. I don't understand a word they're saying.'

'Aye, lord,' said the big captain, then turned to the villagers. 'Come now,' he said kindly. 'We won't get it straight if you keep weeping. Take a breath and tell it again.'

'They changed, I tell you!' wailed a woman dressed only in a muddied shift. 'Before my eyes they changed. My husband, my son, my... my beautiful little Minna. Horns and hooves and teeth! They... they turned on me. My Minna bit me!' She burst out in fresh tears.

'It is true, my lord,' said an older man in torn clothes that had once been of fashionable cut. 'The whole town became beasts. Blue lightning flashed and they changed, then attacked all they had loved.'

The young lord stared down at the man, a flat look on his cold face. He turned to his knights, obviously annoyed. 'It must be nonsense,' he said. 'They are lying. It's not possible.'

'It is possible, my lord,' said Sir Teobalt, as the soldiers led them close. 'And they do not lie. I have seen the evidence of it with my own eyes.'

The young lord looked up at him with angry eyes as his knights turned their heads to stare. 'Who interrupts?'

Seeing him full-on at last, Felix guessed he might be twenty-two, and with the look of a young man with something to prove.

The soldier who had brought Teobalt and the rest saluted. 'My lord, this is Sir Teobalt von Dreschler, a templar, and his companions. They have been on the trail of the beasts for weeks.' He turned to Teobalt and bowed. 'My master, sir. Lord Giselbert von Volgen, heir to these lands.'

Von Volgen's face relaxed somewhat when he heard Sir Teobalt's title, and he inclined his head respectfully. 'Well met, templar,' he said. 'So this madness they speak of is true?'

'It is, my lord,' said Sir Teobalt. 'And there is worse.'

And so the old knight began to tell it all again, to fresh horror and shock, but before he had got very far, more of von Volgen's soldiers ran towards the windmill from the town.

'My lord,' called one. 'A column approaches! Fifty men!'

The soldiers by the mill straightened and looked to their weapons.

Von Volgen wheeled around. 'Who is it?' he barked. 'Friend or foe?'

'It is your cousin, my lord,' said the soldier. 'Lord Oktaf Plaschke-Miesner, come from Zeder.'

Von Volgen's face twisted into a cold sneer. 'Foe then,' he said.

As those by the windmill watched, a double file of knights rode out of the village with a column of spearmen at their back. Leading them was an exquisite vision in red, black and gold. He rode a midnight horse with gold trappings, and was dressed head to foot in red garments of the finest quality, over which he wore a gleaming golden breastplate that looked like it belonged on the wall of a prince's dining hall rather than upon the torso of a fighting soldier. His red doublet and puffed velvet breeches were slashed with cloth of gold, and he wore a yellow feather in a broad black hat.

When he saw von Volgen, he spurred his horse to the mill, his eyes flashing.

'What is this, cousin!' he cried, drawing up. 'Have you forgotten what side of Priestlicheim Brasthof lies on?' His voice was high and clear and matched his overly refined features and long blond hair perfectly. If he hadn't been horribly plagued with spots, he would have been as beautiful as a girl. Felix guessed him to be seventeen – possibly sixteen.

Von Volgen looked the youth up and down contemptuously. 'I do not ride for the house of Volgen, Oktaf,' he said, 'but for Count Feuerbach. I do my duty.'

'It is your duty to invade my lands?' said Plaschke-Miesner.

'It is my duty, as it is yours, to protect the lands of our liege,' said von Volgen. 'Had you been doing your duty, I would not be here.'

'Am I not here?' said Plaschke-Miesner, putting a beringed hand to his breastplate.

'Aye,' said von Volgen. 'An hour after me, when Zeder is half as far as Volgen. But then,' he added with a sneer, 'you weren't coming from Zeder, were you? How long is the ride from Suderberg, cousin?'

Plaschke-Miesner snarled and drew his sword at that, crying, 'Longer, it seems, than the one from Count Feuerbach's grave!'

'You dare, you dog?'

Von Volgen's blade sang from its scabbard as, all around them, knights and soldiers from both sides rushed forwards shouting, 'My lords! My lords!' and Felix's head spun with all the names.

He felt like he'd come in during the middle of a performance.

SEVENTEEN

Felix, Kat, Teobalt and the Slayers stepped back as horses reared and soldiers and knights called out for calm. Von Volgen and Plaschke-Miesner were having none of it.

'Leave off, curse you,' called Plaschke-Miesner, waving his men back with a gold-hilted sword. 'He insults me on my own lands! I will have his blood.'

'Away,' roared von Volgen. 'I will not have my loyalty questioned!'

Suddenly Sir Teobalt pushed forwards, his face red with fury. 'My lords, there is no time for this! The threat of the beastmen–'

'Stay back, templar,' said von Volgen. 'This is a matter of honour.'

'It is indeed a matter of honour!' cried Teobalt. 'And you both dishonour your Empire and your names by–'

A sidestepping horse knocked him back. Felix and Kat jumped to catch him before he hit the cobblestones.

'Are you all right, Sir Teobalt?' asked Felix.

'Insolent little fighting cocks,' rasped the templar. He could hardly catch his breath.

Felix and Kat helped him away from the whirlwind that swept around the two nobles. Gotrek was growling under his breath as they passed him.

'Do you deny that you have come from Middenland, then?' called von Volgen, trying to control his plunging horse. 'Do you deny that you mean to marry a von Kotzebue and give your lands to the Middenlanders?'

'Love knows no borders, cousin,' shouted Plaschke-Miesner in return.

'Do you deny that your father is fitting himself for Feuerbach's mantle before it is certain that he is dead?'

'We only protect his lands in his absence,' said von Volgen. 'As we have for generations!'

'Liar,' shrilled Plaschke-Miesner, swiping wildly at von Volgen.

'Traitor!' bellowed von Volgen, slashing back.

'Enough!' roared Gotrek and, shoving forwards through the press of horses and men, he raised his axe then slammed it down between the two lords' horses with such force that it shook the ground and buried itself up to the heel in the hard-packed earth.

'If you want to tear each other to pieces,' said the Slayer into the sudden silence, 'wait until Witching Night, when you can do it with horns and hooves. Now stop this manling foolishness and listen to the templar or I'll give you a real fight!'

The knights and soldiers erupted in outrage at this.

'Kill the dwarf!' cried one. 'He threatens our lord!'

'Arrest them all!' said another.

'You shall hang for this, villain!' said a third.

'Come and try it,' growled the Slayer, pulling his axe from the earth in a spray of pebbles.

'And try me as well,' said Rodi, standing at Gotrek's shoulder.

'And Snorri too,' said Snorri.

Felix groaned. The Slayers were going to end up killing the people they needed most. He stepped forwards, raising his arms and his voice.

'Friends! Don't do this! We must all save our strength to fight the beastmen.'

'Stand aside, vagabond,' said the burly captain. 'Our lords have been threatened.'

'Your *lands* are threatened!' cried Felix, feeling some of Sir Teobalt's righteous rage infecting him. 'The beastmen will take everything! Your homes, your families, your souls! Don't you understand? If you do not put aside your differences and unite now, you will have nothing left to fight over! We will all become beastmen! There will be no Middenland, no Talabecland, no lands for you to inherit – just one great forest where beasts who were once men fight each other over rocks and dirt and scraps of meat.'

The knights and soldiers started to shout him down, but both von Volgen and Plaschke-Miesner waved for silence.

'No Talabecland?' said von Volgen. 'There will always be a Talabecland.'

'And what do you mean, "we will all become beasts"?' said Plaschke-Miesner.

Sir Teobalt stepped forwards again. 'The beast-shaman who leads this mighty herd goes south to perform a vile ceremony that is meant to turn all men who dwell within the shadows of the Empire's forests into beastmen. If he succeeds, all of the north will be affected, from Middenland to Ostermark, and you can be sure that great herd of changed men will not stay in the forests. They will come south, into Wissenland, Averland and the Reik. No part of the Empire will be untouched.'

The two lords and their retinues stared, dumbstruck. Someone at the back giggled.

'But... but surely it's impossible,' said von Volgen.

'Aye!' said Plaschke-Miesner. 'A fairy tale. No beast of the forest ever had such power. This "shaman" of yours won't succeed.'

Sir Teobalt nodded gravely. 'Perhaps not. But will you allow him to try?' He swung his arm to encompass the ruins of Brasthof. 'Think wisely, my lords. For this is what awaits all of the Empire if he succeeds.'

The two lords hesitated upon their horses for a long moment, alternately looking around at the devastation and glaring at each other.

Finally von Volgen snorted and swung off his horse. 'Thiessen, find a hovel in this wreckage that still has some furniture and make it fit for company.' He turned to a knight. 'Albrecht, be so kind as to invite our cousin Oktaf to join me with his advisors for a discussion of the situation.'

Plaschke-Miesner rolled his eyes and turned to one of his knights. 'Creuzfeldt,' he said. 'Please inform our cousin's emissary that we accept his invitation and will be delighted to attend.' He shot a look at Teobalt. 'And ask the templar and his odd sorts if they will join us as well, since they seem to know so much of the matter.'

Felix and Teobalt and Kat let out long-held breaths. The Slayers just grunted.

As they settled down on some nearby steps to wait for a meeting place to be prepared, Felix saw an old man in long dirty grey robes watching everything from the far side of the market square, but more particularly watching Gotrek.

Felix was about to say something to the Slayer, but just then the old man seemed to feel him watching and turned. For the briefest second, Felix felt their eyes meet, and he was jolted by the intensity of his stare. Then the man ducked back around the corner and the feeling faded.

Half an hour later everyone gathered around a long table in the tavern with the demolished front, von Volgen and four of his knights sitting on one side, Plaschke-Miesner and four of his knights sitting on the other, Gotrek, Felix and Sir Teobalt taking up the ends. Kat, Rodi and Snorri had declined to be there so that they could scavenge for food. Felix wished he had gone with them. Picking his way through unstable buildings searching for week-old meat would have been infinitely preferable to listening to the two young lords snipe at each other and protest every suggestion just for the sake of protesting.

The meeting was nearly over as soon as it began. Sir Teobalt started it by recounting their journey so far, and when he told of asking that Emil von Kotzebue and his army come aid in the fighting of the beastmen, Lord von Volgen jumped from his seat.

'By Sigmar, it is a plot after all!' he cried, hammering the table with his fist. 'These beastmen are a mere excuse to allow that damned Middenlander to cross the river with his army while we are undermanned! I'll warrant he stirred up the beasts just for this.'

Sir Teobalt controlled his temper with an effort. 'Baron von Kotzebue would not be coming at all had I not invited him. Indeed, if we are unfortunate, he still may not come. But you are thinking only of yourself again, my lord. Can you not understand that we fight for the survival of the Empire itself?'

'Aye, with von Kotzebue as Elector Count of Talabecland, no doubt,' snarled von Volgen.

'You want the title for yourself perhaps?' sneered Plaschke-Miesner, throwing his blond hair back from his face.

Von Volgen was about to retort when Gotrek cleared his throat and both young men fell silent.

'It is a matter of numbers,' said Teobalt. 'Not politics.' He held up his fingers. 'The beastmen herd numbers between five and ten thousand. How many troops do you both command?'

'I can muster a thousand from Volgen within a day,' said von Volgen. 'Seasoned cavalry and spearmen just back from the war, as well as a few hundred militia.'

'I can bring seven hundred,' said Plaschke-Miesner. 'Swords, spears, handgunners, and my father's two Gunnery School cannons.'

'Then we are outnumbered by at least three to one,' said Sir Teobalt. 'It will not be enough. This is why we need von Kotzebue. He can bring four thousand men to the field.'

'It is too many,' growled von Volgen. 'We won't be able to fight him if he turns on us.' He glared at Plaschke-Miesner. 'Particularly not if he is joined by turncoats.'

'You have little choice,' said Sir Teobalt before young Oktaf could respond. 'Unless you know of some other lord who can muster the necessary troops by Hexensnacht.'

Von Volgen turned to his knights and they muttered amongst themselves, but none of them could think of anyone close enough who had enough men to make a difference, so at last, after more such convincing, the grim-faced young lord agreed that von Kotzebue's help was needed, and they were finally able to turn the discussion to where they would fight the beasts and how.

When Teobalt related what Ortwin had told him about the ceremony being performed in a stone circle atop a hill, one of Plaschke-Miesner's knights suggested that the herd must be heading for the Barren Hills, which was known to be littered with such remnants of the old religion.

Plaschke-Miesner was pleased to hear it. 'For it gets them out into the open where we can use our cavalry and artillery against them.'

'And my militia can rain a cloud of arrows down upon them,' said von Volgen.

The two lords agreed to set a combined force of scouts on the herd's trail while they gathered their forces and led them by road to the Monastery of the Tower of Vigilance, where the scouts would bring them word of the herd's final position. Then they would wait until von Kotzebue arrived with his army, at which point all would advance to do battle with the beastmen.

'And if the baron doesn't come?' asked von Volgen.

Plaschke-Miesner laughed musically. 'Oh, you want him to come now? There's a new tune.'

'If von Kotzebue fails to arrive,' said Sir Teobalt, 'then your fathers shall hail you as the heroes who saved the Empire with your brave sacrifice.'

Felix saw young Plaschke-Miesner pale at that, but von Volgen's chin raised, and there was a sudden fire in his eye.

'Of more concern than von Kotzebue's arrival, however,' said the old templar, 'is the stone that the beastmen carry. With it, they are nigh invincible, since all who charge against them are in danger of changing into beasts themselves, and turning on their fellows.'

Now von Volgen paled as well. 'How can we defend against such a thing? Should we summon priests? Shall I raise the brothers of the Temple of Leopold?'

'Can it be destroyed?' asked Plaschke-Miesner.

'We don't have to destroy it,' said Gotrek.

Everyone turned to him.

'What's this, Herr Slayer?' asked Sir Teobalt, hopefully. 'You have some way to protect us? Some ancient dwarf rune of warding?'

Gotrek shook his head. 'The stone does nothing itself,' he said. 'Only when the shaman strikes it does the blue lightning flash. If the shaman dies, it is no longer a danger, and your armies may attack.'

The two lords looked at each other, frowning.

'But how can we kill the shaman without going to battle against the herd?' asked von Volgen.

Gotrek smiled a terrifying smile. 'Leave that to me,' he said.

And me, thought Felix with a resigned sigh. It was always the way.

'One moment,' said Plaschke-Miesner, licking his lips nervously. 'If this dwarf can render the stone harmless on his own, then what need is there to bring the herd to battle?'

He shrank back as everyone turned cold eyes on him.

'I will assume that it is out of concern for the lives of your men, rather than your own life that you ask this,' said Sir Teobalt stiffly. 'But there are several reasons. First, stone or no, your land has been invaded by thousands of the vilest enemies of man, and left to their own devices, they will spread wrack and ruin amongst your people. Second, though the death of the shaman will take the stone out of the battle, it is still a thing of great and fell power and must be destroyed before another shaman rises, or its evil influence spreads. We cannot destroy the stone without first destroying the herd.'

The youth hung his head and thrust out his bottom lip. 'Very well,' he said. 'It was only a question.'

In the end it was decided that Gotrek, Rodi and Snorri would join von Volgen's and Plaschke-Miesner's scouts, and once the scouts found the beastmen's location, the three Slayers would – no one was really certain how – infiltrate their camp and kill the shaman. Once this was done, the scouts would report back to the armies and the battle could commence.

Of course, where Gotrek went, Felix must follow, so he was going, and when Kat heard this, she said she wouldn't be left behind, so she was joining them as well.

Only Sir Teobalt was not coming. Instead he would be travelling with von Volgen and Plaschke-Miesner and their armies as military advisor. Felix was glad to hear the old man would be looking after them, for if the rivals' command of tactics was anything like their command of tact, the battle might go very poorly indeed.

Of course, if von Kotzebue's four thousand troops didn't show up, it would go even worse.

The scouts assembled before dawn the next day – four from von Volgen's force, and four from Plaschke-Miesner's – with Felix, Kat and the Slayers yawning sleepily among them. Two of the lords' men held swift ponies, which they would use to bring messages to their masters once they had discovered the herd's position.

As they started south on their way out of town, a hunched silhouette stepped out of the swirling grey fog and approached them, bobbing its head submissively.

'Greetings, my masters, greetings,' it said in a high, wavery voice. 'I hear you go to the Barren Hills.'

The party stopped and looked around. Felix frowned. It was the old man in the dirty grey robes who he had seen watching them so intently the day before, though he couldn't imagine why he had earlier thought him sinister and suspicious. This morning he only looked harmless and slightly batty.

Gotrek, however, didn't seem to agree. 'Who are you?' he growled, reaching for his axe.

The old man shied back, cowering behind his hands. 'Please, your worships,' he wailed in a trembling voice. 'I mean you no harm! Please don't kill me!'

'Who are you?' repeated Gotrek, as cold as before.

'Only Hans the hermit, my masters,' said the old man. 'Who deals in rags, bones and trinkets.'

Felix stepped back and covered his nose as the man sidled closer. He certainly smelled like a scavenger. Kat waved her hand in front of her face and edged upwind.

'And what d'ye know about where we're going?' asked Plaschke-Miesner's sergeant of scouts, a lean, clean-shaven man named Huntzinger.

The hermit tittered. 'Soldiers talk, my master. Soldiers talk. I heard you go to fight the beasts that brought ruin to Brasthof.'

'What's that to you?' asked Felke, a ginger-moustached tough who was von Volgen's scout sergeant.

'Glad tidings is what it is!' cried the hermit, bobbing his head again. 'I hate them beasties. I want 'em dead. If you go to kill 'em, I want to help.'

The scouts guffawed at this, and Felke grinned.

'And what can you do, y'old bag of bones? Are ye hiding a sword under those rags?'

The hermit shrieked as if that was the best jest he'd ever heard. 'Oh no, your worship, old Hans can't fight,' he said, slapping his matchstick knees. 'But he does know the Barren Hills, and for a few coins, he would be pleased to serve your worships as a guide.'

Felke rolled his eyes. 'Ah, now we come to the real issue. A few coins.'

Huntzinger sneered. 'What need have we of a guide? We're all scouts here, old fool.'

'And the trail's as wide as a temple and straight as a pike,' added Felke. 'Be off with you, beggar.'

He turned and motioned his men forwards, and the party started off again. But the ancient was not to be denied. He stumbled after them, bleating piteously.

'But, my masters, please!' he cried. 'I know the hills. I know their dangers. I can keep you safe!'

Gotrek turned at this, though he did not slow. 'What dangers are these, old man?'

'Oh, Herr dwarf,' chuckled the hermit, hobbling along beside him. 'The hills are a cursed place, withered by Morrslieb's glance, and filled with all manner of barrows and circles and stones of ancient and evil power. Why, a single mis-step, a wrong turn, and one might find oneself falling into an old tomb, trapped forever with nothing but dusty old skelingtons for company. But with me to guide you, naught will befall you. Oh yes, old Hans will see you right, so he will.'

'And how do you know so much about it?' asked Rodi, sounding as if he didn't believe a word of it.

The hermit giggled. 'Why, the hills is where I find all my things. The trinkets and bits that I sell to the city men. I know them barrows like I know my own fingers and toes.'

'A grave robber,' spat Gotrek. 'Robbing from your own ancestors.'

Felix smiled at the Slayer's disgust. There had been more than one occasion that the two of them could have been accused of the same thing, but maybe Gotrek put robbing someone else's ancestors in a different category from robbing one's own.

'A recoverer of beauty,' said the old man proudly. 'Gold, gems, wondrous swords. What need have the dead for these things? I rescue them from their selfish grasp and return them to those who can appreciate them.'

'Aye, aye,' said Huntzinger dismissively. 'A turnip is still a turnip, no matter what y'call it. On yer way.'

'Just a minute,' said Felke, pausing and turning back. 'What's the harm in it? I don't want t'be falling down no holes. If he knows the lay of the land down there, why not bring him along?'

'Because the smell of him'll spoil our food,' said Rodi.

But Huntzinger was fondling his chin, thinking about it. He looked towards the hermit. 'How much d'ye want, grandfather?'

Old Hans smiled, showing the stumps of half a dozen teeth. 'Only a few pennies, my masters. Ye'll be doing me a service, so you will, if y'chase them beasties away from my hunting grounds. I'll not be able to go about my business 'til they're gone.'

Gotrek crossed his arms over his broad chest and shook his head. 'I don't want him,' he said.

'Snorri doesn't want him either,' said Snorri. 'He smells like cheese.'

'We don't need him,' said Rodi. 'Dwarfs know all about holes and barrows.'

'Aye,' said Huntzinger. 'But we ain't all dwarfs, are we?' He fished in his belt pouch and tossed the old hermit a few coins. 'Come along, grandfather,' he said. 'But stay at the back until we get to the hills, far to the back.'

Hans caught the coins and bowed and giggled with excitement. 'Oh, thank you, my masters. Thank you. Old Hans won't steer you wrong, no he won't.'

Gotrek growled as the scouts started forwards again, clearly unhappy. Felix felt the same. The old hermit unnerved him somehow. He didn't want him along either, but they weren't the leaders of the party, so there was nothing they could say.

He took a last slantwise look at the filthy old man, who was kissing each of the coins as he pocketed them, then turned and followed the rest as they started into the gaping wound that the beastmen had cut into the forest.

The scouts were as amazed and unsettled by the scar as Felix and Kat had been, and cursed aloud when Snorri told them how it had been made. They were wary of it too, for though they could make good speed on it, it left them exposed, and they posted men far ahead and far behind, and wide to the east and west as well, to keep an eye all around.

And it was well that they did, for halfway through the first day, one of von Volgen's scouts, a bearded, buckskinned woodsman with a Hochland long-rifle slung across his back, trotted up from the rear, a grim look on his face.

'They ain't all before us,' he said, jerking his thumb over his shoulder. 'I spotted fifty a'coming from the west, and Gillich saw twenty or so on a southbound tack t'other side of Bekker Ridge, just to the east. Seems the local herds are joining their friends from up north.'

After that Kat volunteered to scout as well, and they posted her and the two rear scouts even further behind them so they would have plenty of warning to find cover before the beastmen arrived.

The first day, however, passed without incident, and they made camp well off the cut, just in case any beastmen came down it during the night.

Despite the constant patrolling of the scouts, Felix had felt the whole day that something was watching them – a squirmy tingle between his shoulder blades that made him constantly look behind him. This was a different feeling than he'd experienced when they had travelled north into the Drakwald. Then it had seemed as if the forest itself was watching them, like some half-slumbering nature spirit irritated by their intrusion into its domain. The feeling he had now was of some sinister entity that was following them through the forest but was not *of* the forest – but no matter how hard he had stared into the shadows or listened for footsteps, he had seen nothing and heard nothing.

The sensation only increased as the twilight faded and the night closed in around their camp. With the fire banked low and the blackness of the forest as close as a smothering blanket, he felt as if the presence was hovering directly over him, near enough to breathe in his ear.

Kat rolled over as he raised his head to look around once again.

'Do you hear something, Felix?' she asked.

'No,' he said. 'Just… just a feeling, that's all.'

She nodded. 'I feel it too.'

He lay down again and forced a smile. 'Maybe it's just old Hans's stench. I wish he'd sleep a little further away.'

Kat giggled. 'He's already out beyond the pickets.'

Felix edged his bedroll closer to hers until they were shoulder to shoulder. They grinned like guilty children. He felt better already.

'Goodnight, Kat,' he said.

'Goodnight, Felix.'

But despite her warm, soothing presence, when he finally slept, his dreams were full of formless terrors and half-heard whispers, and he awoke morose and out of sorts the next morning.

More than once on the second day they had to move off the path in order to let small groups of beastmen pass them by. The Slayers hated this, but bowed to the necessity of staying alive until they had the opportunity to try to kill the shaman – at least Gotrek and Rodi did. Snorri had some difficulty comprehending why they should wait.

'But Snorri wants to kill *these* beastmen,' he muttered again as they listened to the grunting and tramping of a passing band.

'These aren't important, Father Rustskull,' said Rodi. 'And besides, there's only thirty of them.'

'Snorri will share,' said Snorri.

'When we get to the big herd there won't be any need to share,' said Rodi. 'There will be hundreds for each of us.'

'But why can't Snorri fight these, and then fight those?'

Rodi rolled his eyes and gave up.

The next night, as before, they made camp a good distance from the path, and banked their fire before it got dark. Felix was still plagued with the feeling of being observed, but he was weary enough from their long days of marching that when he bundled down next to Kat, sleep took him relatively quickly and returned him to his unquiet dreams.

He was awakened some time later by urgent whispers. He blinked open his eyes as Kat, the Slayers and the scouts all sat up and looked around.

In the dim light of embers, Felix saw one of Plaschke-Miesner's scouts kneeling next to Huntzinger, panting heavily. 'More than two hundred,' he was saying. 'And spread very wide.'

'How far away?' asked Huntzinger.

The scout swallowed uneasily. 'No more than a half-mile.'

The sergeant frowned. 'How did they come so close?'

The scout hung his head. 'I... I must have dozed.'

Huntzinger cuffed his ear. 'You damned fool!'

Everyone stood and started talking at once.

'Cover the fire!'

'We'll have to run for it.'

'Damn you, Skall, you've killed us all!'

At the far edge of the camp, Hans the hermit listened with wide eyes.

Felke stepped past Huntzinger and grabbed the scout's jerkin. 'Can we get to one side of them?'

Huntzinger pushed Felke away. 'Lay off. He's my man, I'll question him.'

'Then, do it, curse you!' shouted Felke. 'We've got to move.'

Huntzinger turned to the scout. 'Well? Can we get around them?'

The scout shook his head. 'They're spread too wide. Foragers on either side.'

'Can we run?' asked one of von Volgen's scouts.

The scout sergeant looked down at the Slayers' short legs. 'I don't think so.'

'We'll hide in the trees,' said another.

'Dwarfs don't climb trees,' growled Gotrek.

'They will scent us anyway,' said Kat. 'It is too late.'

'Sigmar's blood,' said another scout. 'We're doomed.'

'Good,' said Rodi.

Gotrek shot a grim look at Snorri at this pronouncement and grunted savagely. Then he shrugged and started throwing logs on the sleeping fire, so that it began to burn bright again.

'What are you doing?' cried Huntzinger and Felke simultaneously.

'There's nothing to do but fight,' said Gotrek, turning to them. 'Face the woods with the fire behind you and be ready.'

The scouts babbled at this, terrified, but finally they followed the Slayer's example and lined up facing the direction the beasts were coming from with the rekindling fire at their back so that it wouldn't blind them, and waited.

Felix found himself shocked by the suddenness and the stupidity of it – not that he could say he was surprised. He had known the Slayer's doom was going to come sooner or later. He had just expected it to be grander and have more meaning. He had imagined that Gotrek would die fighting some eldritch monster from the dawn of time, not just perishing because of simple human error, which was all this was. Because of the scout's lapse, they could not outrun the beastmen, or outflank them. Instead, they were going to face them, and not even Gotrek, Snorri and Rodi could defeat two hundred beastmen. They would die here in the middle of nowhere, for the most foolish of reasons, with nothing accomplished – the shaman undefeated, the stone undestroyed, the Empire unsaved. It felt wrong. It wasn't fitting. Felix wouldn't have written it that way in a million years.

Off in the distance they could hear the beastmen coming – the heavy tread of their hooves, the crashing and lowing as they pushed through the brush.

A scout whimpered. The Slayers growled low in their throats and readied their weapons. Felix looked around and saw that the hermit had vanished – no doubt trying to run.

Kat took Felix's hand and squeezed it. 'At least we won't have to see our friends turned into beasts,' she said. 'At least we won't see the end.'

Felix swallowed. It was small compensation.

EIGHTEEN

The sounds of the approaching beastmen got louder. Kat took her hand from Felix's and fitted an arrow to her bow. Snorri chuckled happily. Rodi slapped himself in the face a few times and snorted like a bull. Gotrek ran his thumb along the edge of his axe, drawing blood. The scouts shifted nervously, eyes darting hither and thither.

Felix readied Karaghul, then paused and looked at Kat. She stared into the wood, anxious but unafraid, her sharp chin firm. On a sudden impulse, he caught her shoulder and pulled her to him, then kissed her hard. She was stiff with surprise for a brief moment, but then relaxed into him and returned the kiss in full.

For a moment, there was nothing in the world but the pleasure of holding her and tasting her and feeling her push against him, but then after a moment he heard Rodi's dirty chuckle and they broke off. A few of the scouts were staring at them.

Felix smiled at Kat, embarrassed. 'I... I just didn't want to leave that undone,' he said.

She grinned and nodded, not quite able to look at him. 'Aye. Good thinking.'

They turned back to the woods. Moving yellow lights flickered in the depths – the torches of the beastmen. The scouts murmured and shifted, watching for the first of them to appear.

'Steady,' said Sergeant Huntzinger. 'Wait for your targets. We'll take as many of them with us as we can.'

Now Felix could see horned shadows rippling across the trunks of trees, grotesquely stretched. They were almost within sight. The time had come. Time to fight and die, after all these years. Strangely, there was no fear, only a sudden, almost overwhelming melancholy. He wanted to weep for all the things he would miss.

A banshee wail split the night right above their heads, rising like a steam whistle, and an icy, unnatural wind swept through the camp, snuffing out the fire and throwing them into instant darkness. The scouts jumped and cried out, and Felix was afraid he had too. The eerie shriek made his hair stand on end. Kat mumbled a prayer to Rhya.

'What is that?' cried Sergeant Felke from somewhere to Felix's left.

Felix could see nothing. The woods were pitch-black. The light from the beastmen's torches had vanished as well, leaving not even the glow of embers behind, but Felix could hear them thrashing and howling in the distance. They seemed as scared as the men.

Felix didn't blame them. The ear-splitting wail continued rising – a sound like a soul being ripped asunder by daemons – and a dread presence filled the wood. Felix felt flensed by it – as if the bones had been sucked from his body, leaving him as limp as a dead jellyfish. He couldn't move, couldn't think, could only hunch there next to Kat, quivering and twitching and staring about as the noise went on and on.

After a moment a dim red light gave Felix back his sight – the glow of the runes on Gotrek's axe. The Slayer glared, uncowed, up into the trees, with Snorri and Rodi at his side, as the men trembled all around them. There was nothing to see but shadows and mist drifting through the branches.

Out in the darkness the herd was running. Felix could hear their screams and their hooves thundering past to the right and left of them, and he saw a few shadows flicker past, but strangely none of the beastmen came through the camp. Whatever the evil thing was that had snuffed their torches, they were terrified of it and would not come near it. It felt to Felix like he stood on a stone in the middle of a river and watched the waters split to his left and right.

Then a single beastman did run into the camp, bellowing and stumbling wildly as it crashed through the bracken. It ran directly at the leftmost scouts, but didn't seem to see them, for when they dived out of the way it didn't turn on them, only staggered off into the trees again, clutching its head and screaming as if it were being chased by the contents of its nightmares.

For a few more minutes the sounds of the beasts passing them by continued, while the shrieking echoed from the branches above them and the enervating terror pinned Felix and the scouts to the ground. But then, as the last heavy hoof beats diminished into the distance, the hideous wail trailed off and the feeling of dread dissipated into a sense of trembling relief.

The runes of Gotrek's axe dimmed as the others recovered themselves and muttered prayers to Sigmar.

'Get that fire lit,' said the sergeant.

Felix let out a shaky breath as one of the scouts fumbled with his flint and steel to rekindle the flames. 'What *was* that?' he asked.

Gotrek glared up into the branches of the trees above them, his one eye searching. 'Something vile.'

'But it protected us,' said Kat. 'It chased the beastmen away.'

'Protected us?' snorted Rodi. 'It robbed us of our doom.' He spat on the ground.

'Aye,' said Gotrek. 'Why?'

'Maybe it wanted the beastmen for itself,' said Snorri. 'Snorri thinks that's greedy.'

Felix doubted that was the reason, but he couldn't think of a better one.

Just then, a rustling at the edge of the camp made everyone turn and go on guard again. Old Hans the Hermit poked his head out from behind a tree, his eyes as big as eggs. 'Is it over, my masters?' he quavered.

Everyone grunted with disgust and relief and settled back down to their bedrolls as the scouts who were on duty headed back out into the woods to continue their patrols. Felix doubted, however, that anyone except the Slayers got any sleep. Felix certainly didn't. The memory of the shrieking and the cold, evil presence was too fresh. He knew if he closed his eyes they would return.

The next day, the ground began to rise and break up into rolling hills and winding valleys, all covered in oak and elm, and there was less undergrowth. The herd's axe-hewn trail twisted through the lumpy terrain like the path of a snake, avoiding the largest trees, which must have been too much bother to cut down, and sticking to riverbeds and areas of new growth.

After noon, the trees too began to grow more sparse, and those that remained had turned twisted and strange. The elms, which in the morning had been straight and tall, were now stunted and sickly, while the great spreading oaks had become black, tangle-rooted monsters with deformed branches and trunks that bulged with growths like bark-covered goitres. The beastmen's path grew straighter then, as they had fewer trees to fell, and veered to the south-east, cutting across the grain of the rise and fall of the hills.

A few hours later the trees gave out entirely, and they came at last to the northern edge of the Barren Hills. Felix thought they could not have been more aptly named. The land stretched out in an endless sea of low, mist-swathed ridges, mangy with dead winter grass and leafless thorn bushes, and bare of trees but for an occasional wind-bent pine hunched upon a rocky crest, like an old witch in a tattered cloak surveying her domain.

No birds sang here, and Felix saw no animal tracks in the patches of snow that hid in the shadowed valleys. Even the light that came through the grey clouds seemed thin and sickly, as if not even the sun could bear to look directly upon such dismal desolation. It seemed a blighted land, nearly as lifeless as the deserts of Khemri. At least the herd's trail was still clear. The tread of ten thousand hooves had churned up a wide swathe of the hills' dry, powdery earth, and it wound away towards the horizon for as far as the eye could see.

'Long ago it was a lovely place,' said Hans, looking wistfully out over the stark landscape. 'The Green Hills, men called them, all meadows and lakes and the like. But then old Morrslieb spat a nasty green gob down in the middle of it, and everything for leagues around twisted and died – never to recover. Too bad, too bad. All dead.' He giggled suddenly. 'Though that's good for my business, isn't it?'

'Morrslieb spat?' Felix asked, sceptical.

'Aye,' said the hermit. 'A great flaming gobbet. Straight out of the sky.' He made a gesture like an arrow falling to earth.

'You sound as if you saw it,' said Kat.

Hans tittered. 'Oh, dearie me, child. Do I look as old as that?'

Huntzinger shrugged, making a face. 'Might have been beautiful once,' he said. 'But it's ugly now.'

'At least there aren't any trees,' said Rodi, cheerily.

'And no cover either,' said Kat with a shiver.

Felix turned and saw that she was eyeing the vast space before her like a mouse peeking out from its hole. It occurred to him that, living from girlhood in the Drakwald, she might never have seen so open a place in her whole life. He reached out and squeezed her arm reassuringly as they started forwards again.

'Not to worry,' he said. 'They don't have any cover either. We'll see them from miles away.'

She gave him a grateful smile in return, and they followed the others, walking side by side.

Despite doing his best to reassure Kat, Felix was far from being at ease himself. He had hoped that once they left the forest, the itchy feeling of being watched would cease, and he would be able to relax again, but it failed to go away. Even more so than before he felt that malevolent eyes were upon him, watching his every step, but when he looked around, he still saw nothing. It was impossible that anyone was following them or spying on them. As Kat had said, there was nothing to hide behind, and yet every time he turned his head he felt as if someone had just ducked out of sight a second before. Nor was the lack of trees a relief from the hemmed-in feeling of the forest. What with the grim grey sameness of the bleak hills below and the dull charcoal sky like a lowering ceiling above, Felix felt crushed between two vast millstones, and he found himself hunching his shoulders like he was carrying a heavy burden.

* * *

They saw the smoke of the beastmen's camp on the afternoon of the next day. It looked at first like the smoke from the chimneys of a small city – hundreds of narrow grey ribbons rising above the low hills – and Felix fancied they might find some mundane town there, Barrensburg, perhaps, with a wall and a gate and tavern named after the local landmark – but he knew he would not. There were no towns in this terrible place.

They went more cautiously then, looking for scouts and hunting parties and taking advantage of what meagre cover they could find. The land here was littered with the burial mounds and standing stones of long-forgotten races – lumpy grass-covered barrows like tumours rising from the turf, and lichen-blotched menhirs sticking up like rotting teeth bursting from an abscess – and the scouting party did their best to keep in their shadows, despite the miasma of ancient menace that seemed to emanate from them.

At last there was only one more ridge, and they crept up it through the dry snow and brittle grass on their bellies until they reached the crest and could look down the other side into a Slayer's dream come true.

A diamond-shaped valley lay below them, perhaps a mile long and a half-mile wide, and narrowing at each end between the swelling flanks of the rolling hills, and it was filled from end to end and side to side with beastmen. Felix swallowed and shrank back at the sight. When he had seen the herd before, the forest had hidden its true size. Here, spread across the valley floor, its numbers were staggering. There had to be nearly ten thousand of the beasts – one vast camp made up of hundreds of smaller camps, each with a bonfire and a grisly standard stuck into the ground to let the others know who held sway there.

'Snorri thinks Rodi Balkisson was right,' said Snorri. 'There are enough beastmen for everybody.'

'So many,' murmured Kat, staring wide-eyed.

'Aye,' said Rodi, unusually subdued. 'This will do.'

'A certain doom,' said Gotrek, his eye gleaming.

Felix had to agree. It would doom all of them, and more than likely all the troops that von Volgen, Plaschke-Miesner and von Kotzebue could bring against them as well. He hadn't seen so many beastmen in one place since he and Gotrek and Snorri had flown over the Chaos Wastes in the *Spirit of Grungni*. There were beastmen fighting, beastmen feasting and drinking around the fires, but mostly there were beastmen facing towards the middle of the valley and shaking their weapons and raising their voices in a guttural chant that sounded like the song of the end of the world.

Felix turned to see what was holding their attention.

Out of the centre of the vast herd rose a single low hill, long and steeply sloped on its sides like a whale's back rising from the sea. Upon it, at the place where a whale would spout its steam, jutted an ancient stone circle, its rough black menhirs weathered with age and capped with snow. It was to this that the beastmen had carried their sacred stone from the depths of the Drakwald. Indeed, they were bringing it to the circle even as Felix and the others watched.

The hill was aswarm with beastmen, all thronging around the huge herdstone as it crawled up its flanks, borne upon the backs of its chosen carriers. The scene looked to Felix like ants carrying a dead grasshopper up their mound to the opening of their hole, but the stone did not vanish when it reached the top of the hill. Instead, the beastmen carried it into the centre of the stone circle, and then, with nothing but brute force and sheer numbers, pushed it upright.

Felix prayed to Sigmar that the evil thing would slip from their grasp and shatter upon the menhirs of the ring, but that prayer went unanswered. In the space of ten minutes the beastmen had righted and secured the stone, and the whole valley erupted in a howl of triumph that Felix thought must have been heard in Altdorf. He shivered as the implications of his thoughtless exaggeration sank home. If the Slayers and the three armies failed here, the beastmen's triumph would certainly be *felt* in Altdorf.

And it seemed inevitable that the men and dwarfs would fail. Even the Slayers seemed to have no illusions about that.

'It will be a grand doom,' said Rodi. 'But…'

Gotrek cocked his one eye at him. 'But? What happened to "A doom is a doom is a doom", Balkisson?'

Rodi grunted morosely. 'You've infected me with your pride, Gurnisson. Because of you, I want my doom to mean something. And this…' He shrugged. 'We may kill many, but we will never reach the shaman. Not by fighting, at least, and I was never any good at sneaking.'

'Not even the best scout in the world could sneak through that,' said Kat. 'They are too close together. Even if they didn't see us, they would smell us.'

'Can we wait until they're asleep?' asked Felix.

'They will likely carouse all night,' said Kat.

'And the ones on the hill will never sleep,' said Gotrek. 'You can be certain of that.'

Felix looked again to the central hill. There was a camp within the camp there – Urslak Cripplehorn's true herd – more numerous and tightly packed than the rest of the herds at the gathering. Felix could see patrols of massive beastmen circling the camp and the base of the hill, and more standing guard on its slopes. At the top of the hill, still more danced around and within the stone circle, waving torches and weapons.

'We may win the first charge,' said Gotrek. 'But once the alarm is raised, they will all come.'

'Snorri thinks that's a good idea,' said Snorri.

'Aye, Nosebiter,' said Gotrek, nodding. 'We'll have our doom then, but the stone will stand.'

'What is the date?' asked Felix.

'The thirtieth of Vorhexen,' said Sergeant Felke.

Felix sighed and rested his chin on his crossed arms. 'We have three nights then, to find a way.'

The hermit giggled behind them. 'Oh, my masters, have y'forgotten about me so soon? Don't worry yourselves so. Old Hans knows a way. Of course he does.'

NINETEEN

The party turned to face the hermit, staring.

'What's this?' asked Gotrek.

'A way to the hill!' Hans cackled. 'Without a beastman the wiser!'

'How?' asked Rodi, looking curious in spite of himself.

The old man cackled again and looked sly. 'Ye sons of earth may call me grave robber if you like, but if I weren't, you'd be in a pickle, eh? I know the barrows around these parts like the back of my hand, and the tunnels that link 'em too.'

'Tunnels,' said Gotrek, interested at last.

'Aye,' said the hermit, lowering his voice to a whisper. 'The old kings, they built not just for the dead, but for the living.' He turned and pointed down the hill, where old mounds snaked through the dead valleys like veins under the skin. 'Each barrow was an escape, and a place to hide in times of trouble. All led through secret doors to the old keep, built around yon sacred circle.' He turned back and nodded in the direction of the hill with the stone circle. 'Tarnhalt's Crown they called it then. Named for the last king that lived there.' He giggled again. 'His walls are fallen now, as do all works of men, the stones taken by folk for other things – all but the ring stones, which none dared touch – but the tunnels and cellars of the keep still sit under the hill. And there is a way out to the surface. A hidden way, not ten paces from the circle.'

The Slayers had gathered around the old man now, drawn by his words, their eyes eager.

'Show us the way, hermit,' said Rodi.

'Bring Snorri to the beastmen,' said Snorri.

'Aye, grave robber,' said Gotrek. 'Lead us to these tunnels.'

The old man's eyes narrowed with sudden suspicion. 'You will remove the beasts, yes? You'll smash their stone. You won't rob old Hans of his treasures, will you?'

Rodi sneered. 'Do you think we've come all this way to steal from *you*?'

'What do dwarfs care for human treasures?' said Gotrek. 'Your pathetic hoard is safe from us.'

Hans hesitated a moment, stroking his stringy white beard, but at last nodded. 'Very well, I will risk it. The beasts must go.' He turned and started down the hill at a sprightly pace that belied his age, lifting the skirts of his robe as he went. 'Follow me! Follow me!'

Felix and Kat looked to Gotrek as the scouts muttered amongst themselves.

The Slayer shrugged. 'It's worth a try.'

Huntzinger and Felke looked less than happy, but finally shrugged, and the party turned and followed the old hermit as he led them down the slope and along the base of the hills until he came to an overgrown old barrow mound that stuck out from one like a blunt finger. Dry old bracken covered the front of the tomb, but it wasn't growing from the earth. It had been placed there. The old hermit pulled it all aside and revealed a small black hole behind it, low to the ground, and so narrow Felix wasn't sure the Slayers would be able to get their wide shoulders through it.

'There, your worships,' he said gleefully. 'There is the hole that will lead you to the hill. Now, if you can give poor Hans a pen and paper, he will draw you a map of the way.'

Gotrek snorted. 'Dwarfs need no maps for tunnels, grave robber. We will find the way.'

'No no no!' said Hans, his eyes suddenly wide with alarm. 'A map is best, my masters. You don't want to go where you shouldn't.'

Everyone paused at that, and Gotrek gave him a dead-eyed stare.

'What's this?' he asked.

'What are you hiding in there?' asked Sergeant Felke.

'Are there ghosts?' asked Huntzinger, biting his lip.

'Traps?' asked Felix.

The old man shrank back, eyes darting from one to the other. 'No no! No traps, my masters. Not if you go where I say. I... I only fear that you... that you will try to take my things. I have protected them, and they–'

'They're trapped,' said Felix.

'Lead us, then,' said Gotrek.

'Aye,' said Rodi. 'That's the best plan. That way we'll stay out of mischief, and so will you.'

'No!' said the old man, suddenly frantic. 'I cannot! I have tarried with you long enough. I must continue my work! I must go!'

'I thought the beasts were keeping you from your work,' said Felix, getting more suspicious by the second.

'There are other barrows,' said Hans. 'I work all over these hills.'

'It'll wait,' said Gotrek. 'You're staying.'

The others encircled the old man. He shrunk away from them, trembling and shielding his head, and for the briefest second, Felix thought he saw a look of pure hatred flash in his eyes, but it was gone before he could be sure, and then Hans was smiling meekly again.

'Very well, your worships,' he bleated. 'I will stay. I will stay.'

With old Hans in tow, the party scouted the valleys around the beastmen's gathering place until they found a suitable site to stage the armies of the three nobles when, and if, they arrived. Then von Volgen's and Plaschke-Miesner's messengers readied their horses for their run back to their masters at the Monastery of the Tower of Vigilance so that they could tell them that the Slayers had found a way to reach the shaman and kill him, and that it would be safe to engage the herd.

'We will wait as long as possible,' Gotrek said. 'But if the armies are not here by sunset on Hexensnacht's eve, we start without them.'

Felke held up the hunter's horn he had slung around his neck. 'I will blow a blast when the shaman is killed,' he said. 'That will be their signal.'

Felix stepped forwards. 'And be sure to tell them not to attack before they hear it, or...' He shivered, remembering Ortwin's face changing before him. 'Or it may not go well.'

The messengers nodded, then mounted their horses and galloped away across the bare hills. At least, thought Felix, they will make good speed on such open ground, and with luck, the armies will make good speed back. The question was, would it be only von Volgen and Plaschke-Miesner, or would von Kotzebue and his four thousand men arrive with them?

'Right,' said Huntzinger, turning away. 'Now to find a place to lay low until the time comes.'

'The hermit's barrow,' said Gotrek without hesitation.

Huntzinger stared at him. So did Felke. Their men murmured uneasily.

'You can't be serious,' they said in unison.

Gotrek scowled. 'I am. It's warm. It's out of the wind. It's close to the beasts' camp, and they'll never find us there. It's perfect.'

'But... but it's a tomb,' said Huntzinger. 'We can't stay in a tomb.'

'Why not?'

'The old kings,' Huntzinger continued. 'They don't like being disturbed. They'll wake up and kill us in our sleep.'

'Aye,' said Felke. 'I'll go in at the end, to get to the beasts, but I'll not make camp there. I'll not sleep there.'

Their men murmured in agreement.

Gotrek rolled his eyes. 'Are you more afraid of a pile of dusty old bones than of ten thousand beastmen?'

Huntzinger and Felke exchanged a glance, then looked back towards Gotrek.

'Aye,' said Huntzinger. 'We won't do it, and that's that.'

'There are some things a man won't do,' said Felke.

Gotrek snorted with disgust, then shrugged his massive shoulders and turned away. 'There are some things a coward won't do,' he said under his breath.

Rodi and Snorri nodded in agreement.

Felix glanced at Huntzinger and Felke, afraid they'd heard the Slayer. From the scowls on their faces, it appeared they had, but it also appeared that they didn't look prepared to do anything about it.

After an hour of searching, the scout captains found a deep gorge about a half-mile from the valley that held Tarnhalt's Crown, and announced that this was where they would make camp. The dwarfs' silence on the matter was eloquent, as was the fact that they laid out their bedrolls as far from the scouts' tents as possible. They didn't go so far, however, as to not take part in the protection of the camp, and stood their watches without complaint.

Felix kept his mouth shut too. As much as he understood the dwarfs' view that going underground would be the best way to keep out of the way of the beasts, he wouldn't have relished spending a long period of time in the burial chambers of some ancient king either. He had done that once before. It hadn't gone well.

The scouts didn't dare start a fire until after dark for fear that smoke rising above the hills would give away their position. This meant a long day of shivering and stamping their feet, trying to keep out of the steady, ceaseless wind, and glaring at the Slayers, who paced around the camp bare-chested, seemingly as comfortable as if they were in a warm tavern.

For their part, Gotrek and Rodi were restless and irritable. They knew their doom was only a few valleys away, and it appeared to be testing their patience to wait for it. Only Snorri seemed at ease, following the other two Slayers around and telling them stories about his days with Gotrek as if Gotrek wasn't the one the events had happened to. Felix saw the Slayer's shoulders hunch at each new tale, but he never snapped at Snorri, only nodded and grunted non-committally, his brow furrowed and his mouth set in a grim line.

Felix did his best to ignore all the tension, and sat in the shelter of a big boulder, updating his journal with shivering hands, and wondering if he would be able to decipher the shaky lines he had written when he reread them later. He wished he could have waited out the day bundled in a tent with Kat – a much warmer and more pleasant way to pass the time – but she was doing her duty with the rest of the scouts, patrolling on a wide perimeter and keeping a constant eye on the herd, so he hardly saw her.

After a meagre dinner cooked over the low fire, Felix did his turn at watching on the lip of the gorge, looking and listening for approaching beasts, and watching as Morrslieb chased Mannslieb up the sky and then passed it by, so close that the edges of the two moons seemed to almost touch, before racing on and leaving its bigger, more distant brother in the dust of stars.

At midnight, with Mannslieb directly above and Morrslieb already setting over the eastern hills, his time was done, and he picked his way back down into the gorge to the camp and shook Gotrek by the shoulder.

'Your turn, Gotrek,' he said.

The Slayer sat up, awake instantly, and looked around. Then he stood and grabbed his axe.

'Where is the hermit?' he asked.

Felix looked to where they had leashed the old man to a stunted tree to make sure he didn't slip away. The rope that had gone around his wrists lay on the ground, but of Hans himself there was no sign.

Felix cursed. How had the hermit escaped? He looked around. Sergeant Huntzinger was on watch, the same man who had cuffed his scout for letting the beasts creep up on them. He crossed to him as Gotrek stepped to the empty leash.

'You let the old hermit go,' said Felix. 'Were you asleep?'

'What's this?' said the sergeant, standing and turning. He cursed as well. 'How can it be? I looked at him just before you came down the slope. He was lying there, asleep.'

Their voices were waking the rest of the camp, and sleepy questions followed them as they crossed to Gotrek, who was looking down at the leash. The sergeant made the sign of the hammer, for the knots that had tied the rope around Hans's wrists were intact.

'Sorcery,' said Huntzinger.

A scrap of parchment was rolled up in the loops. Gotrek picked it up and unrolled it. It was a crudely drawn map, showing rooms and corridors, and done apparently in blood.

'Or the ropes weren't tight enough,' said Sergeant Felke, sneering as he joined them. 'Looks like you're just as lax as your men, Huntzinger.'

'I tied those ropes myself,' protested Sergeant Huntzinger. 'He could not have escaped them.'

'But he did,' said Gotrek.

Felix looked over the Slayer's shoulder at the map. 'It looks like he still wants us to go after the beasts.'

'Or walk into a trap,' said Rodi, joining them and looking too.

Felix swallowed. Was that it after all? Was Hans's whole reason for joining him as their guide just a ruse to trick them into entering some underground trap? Perhaps he wasn't a grave robber after all. Perhaps he preyed on grave robbers. Perhaps the gold and trinkets he sold were stolen from the bodies of his victims rather than the tombs of the old kings.

Gotrek handed the map to Felix and turned away. 'Spread out and look for him,' he said. 'But watch for beasts.'

Huntzinger and Felke looked affronted at this casual assumption of command, but only turned to their men and chose who would go and who would stay.

Felix, Kat, Gotrek, Rodi and the four chosen scouts spread out on different headings, leaving Snorri – who couldn't be trusted to remember what he was searching for – and the rest to guard the camp. It was a fruitless search. Felix staggered back after two hours, half-asleep and two-thirds frozen, with nothing to report. The others came in soon after him with the same report. Hans had vanished. He was not to be found.

'Probably gone to ground in another barrow,' said Kat.

'Will he try anything?' asked Huntzinger.

Rodi shrugged. 'What could an old man do?'

'He could lead the beasts down on us,' the sergeant replied.

Felix frowned. 'I don't know about that. He seemed genuinely angry with them. And he left the map. I think he truly wants us to drive them away, though I can't guess what else he might want.'

'Do we still use the map, then?' asked Felke.

'What choice do we have?' said Rodi. 'There is no other way to get to the shaman.'

'We use it,' said Gotrek. 'But not blindly.' He nodded to Rodi and Snorri. 'We will scout the tunnels tomorrow so that we find no surprises on the night.'

The next morning, Felix, Kat and the three Slayers made their way back through the hills to the barrow that old Hans had shown them. As they approached it, Felix had the sudden irrational fear that they would find the hole into the crypt gone as if it never was, like some mysterious door in a hill in a fairy tale, but when they pulled away the bracken it was still there, an irregular black shadow in the face of the mound. Felix wasn't sure if he was relieved or not.

'I'll go first,' said Rodi.

'No, Snorri will,' said Snorri.

'I will,' said Gotrek, and stepped in front of them before they could stop him.

Felix didn't know how the Slayer was going to fit – his shoulders looked wider than the hole by a foot – but Gotrek didn't even hesitate. He knelt down, stuck his head and his axe arm in, then twisted and propelled himself through with his feet. A rattle and hiss of pebbles and dirt rained down after his passage and for a second Felix thought the opening was going to collapse, but then the rain eased up and Gotrek's voice echoed hollowly from within.

'It's safe.'

Snorri went next, widening the hole even more as he shoved through it, then Kat, who didn't even touch the sides.

'After you, Herr Jaeger,' said Rodi.

Felix took a breath, then knelt and crawled forwards. There was an awkward moment when his hands couldn't feel any floor and his legs were hemmed in by the sides of the hole, but then strong hands were pulling him out and setting him on his feet in utter darkness.

Felix stood and cracked his head on something above him. He hissed and hunched down, rubbing his crown.

There was a sharp scraping from nearby and then a torch kindled and glowed in Kat's hands, just in time to show Rodi crawling out of the hole like an ugly, crested mole.

'Ah,' said the young Slayer as he picked himself up and dusted himself off. 'Nice to be underground again.'

'Aye,' said Gotrek.

Felix looked around. They were in a long, low chamber – so low in fact that he could not stand straight in it. It seemed to have been built by people of Kat's stature. The stone walls were carved with crude wolf's heads and skulls, as well as angular intertwining runes and symbols. Against the long walls were four stone biers, old bones in rotting, dusty clothes scattered upon them, but not a single piece of armour or weaponry or jewellery. If old Hans wasn't a grave robber, someone else certainly had been.

Felix turned to the back of the barrow, where Hans had said the entrance to the tunnels would be. His heart sank. There was nothing but a stone wall with a crumbling relief of a running wolf. He was about to curse Hans for misleading them when Rodi laughed.

'The old man calls that a secret door?' he said. 'A blind elf could find that.'

'Snorri thinks a dead elf could find it,' said Snorri.

Felix closed his mouth again, chagrined, and followed the others to the back wall, thanking Sigmar he hadn't spoken.

Gotrek reached out and pulled a stone from the wall that looked no different to Felix than any other stone, and reached into the hole that resulted. He pulled at something inside the hole, and there was a grating of iron on stone. Then he pushed at the wall with the running wolf on it with his other hand and a narrow door swung open, revealing blackness behind.

'Come on then,' said Rodi, shoving in first.

Gotrek and Snorri gave him dirty looks, then followed after, and the three of them set off into the darkness without hesitation. Felix and Kat hurried after them, looking around warily in the light of Kat's torch. The tunnel beyond the door was as low as the barrow, and nothing more than a raw hole in the rock and dirt, kept from collapse by heavy wooden beams and posts. It smelled of mould and damp earth and decay. Spider webs hung like shrouds from the ceiling and fluttered in a constant moaning breeze. Felix hunched his head and kept one hand out to tear them down before he walked into them.

After no more than ten paces, Gotrek's steps slowed and he looked down at the floor. He stamped the floor with his boot heel, then did it again.

'There are many levels below us,' he said.

'Aye,' said Rodi, nodding in agreement. 'At least six.' He sniffed the air. 'And they touch bedrock.'

'What were they used for?' asked Felix.

'Burying the dead, by the smell of it,' said Rodi.

Felix shivered, the idea of countless ancient corpses flaking to dust in the silent tombs below him giving him a sudden chill.

As they continued on, they passed other tunnels that intersected with theirs, black maws yawning in the rock walls that seemed to swallow the light of the torch, and from which Felix imagined he heard soft scuttlings and whisperings. He tensed at each one, fearing that some trap or ambush would spring out at them, and that they would hear old Hans's mad titter echoing from the distance.

The dwarfs took lefts and rights without pausing, never once consulting Hans's map or conferring amongst themselves. They seemed to know the way by heart, despite never having been here before.

At one intersection, wider than the rest, Gotrek looked at some symbols carved in the wooden support posts. He spat, disgusted. 'These tunnels weren't only used for escape. Vile things were done here.'

He took his axe off his back and shaved away some of the symbols with the razor-sharp blade. 'Foolish manlings,' he growled.

They walked on, Felix even more uneasy than before. Perhaps the dead in the halls below weren't in tombs after all. Visions of crowds of weeping captives driven to mass sacrifice in some deep chamber came unbidden to his mind, and he found it hard to banish them.

A little later, Gotrek held up a hand and they stopped. The dwarfs cocked their ears to the ceiling. Felix listened too. There was a faint tremor in the air, and a distant muffled thumping that never ceased.

'We are under the herd now,' said Gotrek.

A short while later, they came to a place where the walls and floor became mortared stone. These halls were painted with browns and blues and yellows – crude faded murals of men in horned helmets and long beards fighting orcs and beastmen in great battles, and other murals of the same men on their knees, offering meat and drink to a white wolf with a moon over its left shoulder and the sun over its right.

'The catacombs of Tarnhalt's castle,' said Rodi. 'Not the best painters, were they?'

After a few more turnings, they came to an ancient stairwell. Air poured down from above, bringing with it the reek of animal fur and wood smoke. The constant vibration of the walls and ceiling was echoed by far-off roars and wails. It sounded like there was no door between them and the herd.

Gotrek stopped. 'The circle is above us.'

'Looks like the old man led us true after all,' said Rodi.

'Praise Taal for that,' said Kat.

Snorri raised his head and inhaled at the bottom of the stairs. 'Snorri smells beastmen,' he said. 'Time to go fight them, aye?'

'No, Nosebiter,' said Gotrek. 'Time to turn around and go back.'

The sudden sadness on Snorri's face was so comical that Felix had to turn away to keep from laughing.

The rest of the day was as cold and boring as the previous one had been – more endless grey hours without news or incident. Felix had known they would hear nothing from von Volgen and Plaschke-Miesner. It was impossible that the messengers could ride to the monastery and the armies advance to the herd's position in a single day, and yet the waiting still set his teeth on edge and tightened his shoulders into knots. When would the armies come? How many would come? Would they come at all? Having had a sample of their bickering, he knew it was entirely possible that the two young lords had fought again and that one or the other or both had decided not to come as a result.

There was also the nagging worry that – despite the encouraging evidence of the map – old Hans was lurking in the background somewhere, planning some revenge on them for holding him against his will. Felix could not imagine that the frail old man's vengeance would be anything but petty spite, but even something seemingly insignificant might inadvertently alert the beasts to their presence and bring them crashing down upon them.

Felix made more notes in his journal, and watched again as Snorri followed Gotrek and Rodi around, babbling cheerfully. But this time he noticed that Gotrek was shooting hard, surreptitious glances at the old Slayer when he wasn't looking, and once, when Snorri had gone off to relieve himself away from the camp, Felix saw Gotrek talking earnestly with Rodi as the young Slayer nodded gravely, fingering his plaited beard. When Snorri returned, the two stepped apart, for all the world like guilty schoolboys, and greeted him with painfully affected false cheer.

From this, Felix was certain that they had been talking about the old Slayer behind his back, but as to the nature of their conversation, he hadn't a clue.

Von Volgen's messenger returned at last at dawn on Hexensnacht eve with news that the two lords' armies would be in position by noon.

'How many men?' asked Gotrek.

'Lord von Volgen says that he has found fifteen hundred men, Herr

Slayer,' said the messenger. 'Mostly spearmen and archers, but with three hundred mounted men-at-arms, and Lord Plaschke-Miesner brings almost a thousand, two hundred of them knights, as well as two cannon.'

Felix winced. It was more than the lords had promised, but it was still far from enough. The beasts would slaughter them all. 'Any news of von Kotzebue?' he asked.

'Aye sir,' said the messenger. 'And good news at that. The baron has sent a messenger forwards to say that he crossed the Talabec with more than four thousand men two days behind my lord's march, and he is pressing south as quickly as he may.'

Felix exchanged looks with Gotrek, Rodi and Kat. Kotzebue's four thousand men would be welcome – even though they would still not put them at even odds with the beasts – but if they were two days behind at the outset, would they be here in time? It didn't seem likely.

'My lord and Lord Plaschke-Miesner beg you to wait as long as you dare to begin your mission,' the messenger continued, 'in order to give Lord von Kotzebue time to get into position.'

Felix didn't wonder at the request. Without von Kotzebue's troops backing them up, any attack the two young lords made would be nothing more than suicide.

'We will wait,' said Gotrek. 'But if he doesn't show by full dark, we will wait no more.' He turned to Sergeant Huntzinger and Sergeant Felke and their scouts. 'Go back with the messenger. The time for scouting is done. Better to die with your comrades than with us.'

The scouts paled at this malediction, but lost no time gathering up their gear.

As they watched them pack, Felix bit his lip and turned to Kat. 'You should go with them,' he said.

She looked like he had hit her. 'I'll not leave your side, Felix.'

'But, Kat–'

'I will not take the woman's part in this,' she continued, cutting him off. Felix could hear her fighting to control her voice. 'I... I thought you understood.'

The hurt in her eyes was like a dagger in his heart. 'I do,' he said. 'I don't ask it because you are a woman. I ask it because...' He looked around at the staring scouts and lowered his voice. 'Because I love you, and I don't want you to die.'

'I am not afraid,' she said, lifting her chin.

'It's not a question of that.' He sighed, then took her arm and led her away from the others. 'Kat, I know you are brave, but this...' He shook his head. 'It is impossible that any of us will survive. I have made a vow that I will follow the Slayer and witness his death, and I know I will die doing it. But you... you don't need to die here. You have so much life ahead of you.'

She glared at him. 'You forget I have a vow too.'

'I know you do,' he said. 'But there will be other herds, and other fights, fights where your help will make a difference.'

He knew as he said it that it was the wrong thing to say.

Kat's eyes got colder still and she drew herself up. 'You doubt my skills?' she asked, stiffly.

Felix ground his teeth. 'That's not what I meant, and you know it. The time for scouts is done, just as Gotrek said.' He nodded towards Felke and Huntzinger's men, who were lining up in preparation to march. 'I only want you to do what they are doing.' I only want to save your life, he cried inwardly, but did not speak it.

Kat hung her head and nodded. 'You are right, Felix. This is no place for scouts. I should go.'

Felix let out a sigh of relief. At last she was seeing sense.

'But,' she said, and all of Felix's tension returned as if it had never left. 'But still I cannot leave you.'

'Sigmar's blood, why not?' Felix cried.

She looked up at him with liquid brown eyes. 'Because I do not want you to die either.'

'But Kat,' he said, exasperated. 'I *will* die! There is no question.'

She shook her head. 'I have heard your stories. You have faced certain death before, and always there has been one little thing that saved you.' She swallowed and put her hand on his chest. 'What if, this time, I am that one little thing?'

Felix choked down a wave of emotion. The girl didn't want to die by his side. She wanted to protect him. It broke his heart. 'It's impossible,' he said. 'There's no chance. None.'

She stepped closer to him. 'How many times have I saved your life?'

He coughed. 'Er, twice? Three times? More than that?'

She looked directly into his eyes. 'There is always a chance, Felix. Always.'

Felix sighed, despairing that he had failed to convince her, but at the same time overwhelmed by how much she cared for him.

Their men assembled, Felke and Huntzinger stepped forwards and saluted Felix, Kat and the Slayers.

'Luck to you,' said Felke. He took off his hunting horn and passed it to Kat.

'And to you,' said Kat, taking it.

'Give our regards to Sir Teobalt,' said Felix.

The Slayers just nodded.

A few hours later, Felix stood watch again at the lip of the ravine, his mind still so full of worry for Kat and self-loathing that it was doubtful that he would have spotted a beastman unless it had trodden on his foot.

It was just after noon and the day had so far been torture. While the

Slayers had paced and griped and waited for news of the armies, Felix's mind had churned ceaselessly, trying to think of new arguments that would send Kat to safety, but failing again and again. He knew she would not leave, no matter what he said, and he watched her come and go from her patrols in a bitter, brooding melancholy. She was such a strange, unique creature – so fierce and bloodthirsty and confident, and yet so shy and good and uncertain at the same time – that it seemed a tragedy beyond all measure that she should be snuffed from the world like this, and he had spent the morning despising himself for not being able to think of a way to avert that tragedy.

Pebbles rattled behind him, waking him from his unhappy reverie. He turned to see Gotrek climbing up the steep slope to join him.

'Something wrong?' he asked as the Slayer pulled himself up the last few feet and stopped beside him, dusting his palms.

'Aye,' said Gotrek.

Felix expected him to continue, but the Slayer just stood there, looking out across the endless hills. Felix frowned, wondering if he was supposed to guess the trouble. Had Hans the Hermit returned? Had beastmen found a way into the ravine? Had something happened to Kat?

Finally the Slayer spoke. 'Snorri Nosebiter will not find his doom here,' he said.

Felix raised his eyebrows. This sounded like prophecy. 'How can you be certain of that?' he asked.

'I'm going to *make* certain,' said Gotrek. 'He will not die without remembering why he took the Slayer's Oath.'

'Ah,' said Felix. 'I see.' He was quietly shocked at this pronouncement. Gotrek rarely thought of anything other than his own doom. To see him actively concerned about someone else's troubles, even another Slayer's, was rare. Felix recalled that Gotrek had helped Heinz when the *Blind Pig* had burned down, but he suspected the Slayer had felt partially responsible for the fire. This was different. Gotrek hadn't caused Snorri to lose his memory. This was an actual, unasked for, act of kindness.

The Slayer kicked distractedly at the ground, his head low. 'I am releasing you from your vow, manling. You do not have to witness my doom, nor write of it. Instead, you will stay with Snorri Nosebiter, out of the battle, and when it is done, you will see him to Karak Kadrin and the Shrine of Grimnir. Then you are free.'

Felix choked, stunned. He couldn't believe what the Slayer was saying. 'Are… are you sure?'

Gotrek raised his head and glared at him with his single angry eye. 'Would I say it if I wasn't?'

And with that he turned and stumped back down into the gorge.

Felix stared after him, blinking with shock. His mind whirled with a hundred questions and emotions, all fighting for his attention at once. Gotrek had released him from his vow – or rather he had given

Felix a task that would give it a definite ending. He was so surprised that he wasn't sure how he felt about it. Was he elated? That he knew he wouldn't die beside the Slayer was a relief, he supposed, and finally putting an end to the uncertainty of when his long, mad journey would be over was a weight off his shoulders, but he couldn't say either thing made him happy.

Did he feel angry? Not precisely. Cheated perhaps? To have dutifully followed the Slayer for more than twenty years, waiting for him to die, only to be told at the end, 'never mind, you don't have to record it after all,' rankled a bit.

But thinking about that made him realise the true enormity of the Slayer's decision. Since Felix had known him, Gotrek had wanted only two things out of life – a good doom, and an epic poem to immortalise his legend and bring it to the world. That desire for fame was why he had asked Felix to join him on his quest for death all those years ago. It was, in a way, the Slayer's greatest weakness – a flaw of the ego that at once drove him headlong into impossible danger, and held him back from less worthy dooms. That he was now willing to give up that dream of glory, to go to his doom without any record of it being made, to die anonymously and alone, was proof to Felix of how deeply he cared for Snorri Nosebiter. He was sacrificing the fame he had spent more than twenty years accumulating in order to try to safeguard Snorri's afterlife, and without any certain knowledge that it would work. Felix was sure that Gotrek knew as well as anyone that Snorri's prayers might be unanswered at Grimnir's shrine, and yet he was willing to forego his remembrance for that faint, forlorn hope.

Understanding this, all of Felix's initial misgivings vanished. He was not angry that Gotrek had dismissed him. He did not feel cheated. Instead his chest swelled with pride, for that dismissal meant that Gotrek trusted him enough to put Snorri's salvation – a thing apparently more precious to him than his own fame – in Felix's hands. It was the greatest honour Felix had ever been given.

He swore then and there that he would see it through without fail. He would hide Snorri during the upcoming battle, he would see him safely through the Worlds Edge Mountains to Karak Kadrin, he would accompany him to the shrine, and then…

Felix paused, frowning.

And then… what?

And then he would be free of his vow to Gotrek for the first time in his adult life. He would have… a future.

A new thought exploded in his head as that sank in. Gotrek had asked him to sit out the battle and stay with Snorri for the duration. If he would not be in the battle, then Kat would not be in the battle! She would live! They both would live!

Suddenly his mind was ablaze. A future! He and Kat could be together!

They could *live* together, have normal lives together – well, no, not that. He still had his vow to take vengeance upon the skaven sorcerer who had brought about his father's death, and she still had her vow to vanquish the beastmen of the Drakwald, but why couldn't they travel the Empire and the forests together for the rest of their lives, hunting skaven and beastmen and sleeping in Taal's bower, living the simple life of the wanderer and the woodsman? It wasn't as if he would have to change his life much. He would still be a vagabond, as he had been for the last two decades. Only now he wouldn't be sharing the road with a surly, monosyllabic dwarf, but instead with a sweet, beautiful girl with whom he could also share his bed.

That brought him up sharp. He was actually looking forward to Gotrek's death! And the honour of bringing Snorri to Grimnir's shrine had become a mere stepping stone to his selfish dreams of happiness. He cringed with shame. What kind of friend was he? He should be mourning the Slayer's imminent passing and praying for Snorri's recovery, not gleefully planning the life he and Kat would have once he was free of both of them. How could he betray such lifelong friendships so callously? It wasn't right.

On the other hand, Snorri wasn't the sort to deny another person happiness because he couldn't find his own, and Gotrek was a Slayer. He wanted to die. He wouldn't want his death mourned. He would want it celebrated. Of course, dancing on his grave before he was even dead probably wasn't exactly what the Slayer had in mind.

Felix sighed, conflicted. There was no question that he would mourn the Slayer's passing – *and* celebrate it. Gotrek had often been hard to understand, and harder to like, but their friendship, though rarely expressed, had been real, and Felix would miss it when it was gone. But he could not pretend that he wasn't pleased and relieved that his life after Gotrek's death, which he had often feared would be an empty and meaningless shuffle to the grave, would instead be full of love and life and joy.

He was suddenly impatient for his watch to be over. He couldn't wait to tell Kat the news.

'This isn't a trick, is it, Felix?' Kat asked warily. 'You're not still trying to send me away?'

'It's no trick. I promise you.' Felix looked over his shoulder to where the three Slayers were sitting around the cold fire pit, cleaning their weapons for what must have been the fifth time that day. They were all out of earshot. He turned back to Kat. 'Gotrek doesn't want Snorri to find his doom until he has recovered his memory, so he has excused me from the battle so that I can bring him to Karak Kadrin to pray at the Shrine of Grimnir. I will not be fighting. You'll have no need to protect me.'

'And when you have brought Snorri to the shrine?' asked Kat.

'I'll be free to do as I please,' said Felix, smiling. 'And what I please, is to be with you.'

Kat shivered and shook her head. 'I'm sorry, Felix. I want it to be true, but I can't let myself believe it yet. It seems impossible.'

Felix chuckled and pulled her close. 'Not to worry,' he said. 'I understand. There is nothing worse than hope. Forget it. We won't speak of it until it has happened.' He kissed her on the forehead, then pulled back and gazed into her worried eyes. 'Just remember something that someone said to me not long ago.'

'What's that?' she asked.

Felix grinned. 'There is always a chance.'

A slow smile broke through Kat's cloudy demeanour and she hugged him hard. 'Aye,' she said. 'Always.'

Just as the last crimson sliver of the sun sank behind blood-coloured hills, a messenger finally arrived from the armies. Felix knew the news was not good when the man saluted from his horse, but did not dismount.

'Lord von Volgen and Lord Plaschke-Miesner's compliments,' said the messenger as they gathered around him. 'And they regret to inform you that no sign of Baron von Kotzebue's army has yet been sighted.'

'Then they will have to go without him,' said Gotrek.

'No, Herr dwarf,' said the messenger. 'My lords have determined that the risk is too great. If von Kotzebue does not arrive before your signal, they will retire.'

Gotrek snorted and turned away. 'So much for the courage of men.'

'This is madness,' said Kat. 'They must attack. They must!'

Felix stepped up to the messenger. 'I thought they understood that it was vital to attack the herd while it was all in one spot. If they let them disperse, the beasts will pillage the countryside for hundreds of miles in every direction, and they will be almost impossible to root out. If von Volgen and Plaschke-Miesner retreat, they are dooming Talabecland to years of raids and slaughter.'

The messenger nodded, very stiff. 'My lords are aware of this, and will go therefore to look to their own lands and strengthen the defences of their keeps.'

Rodi spat on the ground. 'Tell them from me that they are cowards, and deserve the fate that this tail-turning will bring them.'

The messenger bowed in the saddle. 'I will do so.'

And with that he wheeled his horse around and galloped off into the crimson twilight.

Morrslieb and Mannslieb were again rising together over the hills as Felix, Kat and the three Slayers crawled towards the top of the ridge again. The guttural chanting of ten thousand savage throats floated over the summit and raised the hairs on the back of Felix's neck. That such a huge herd of beastmen, a race famous for their fractiousness and infighting, should be in such accord that they could all chant in unison, was a terrifying thing. If this Urslak could continue to keep them unified and fixed on a single objective they would be unstoppable.

The five companions reached the top of the ridge and went forwards on knees and elbows until they could look down into the valley of Tarnhalt's Crown. The camps of the outlying herds were deserted, their bonfires dark. All the beastmen were pressing close around the base of the central hill from all sides, a shifting, undulating carpet of horned heads and hairy shoulders, with here and there torches sticking up to cast a ruddy glow on spear-tips and broad, armoured backs.

The hill itself was ablaze with yellow light. Roaring bonfires had been set all around the towering herdstone, causing the monoliths of the stone circle to cast thick black bars of shadow down the hill and across the swarm of beastmen that thronged it. A ring of blue-daubed guards protected the circle, lashing out at the teeming, chanting mob with blazing firebrands, keeping them back.

'Sigmar preserve us,' said Felix. It was like a scene out of the Chaos Wastes, transported to the centre of the Empire.

'He'd better not,' said Rodi.

'Snorri thinks it's nice of them to stay so close together,' said Snorri. 'Saves running after them.'

Felix, Gotrek and Rodi exchanged a look, but said nothing. Felix felt strangely guilty in the wake of that look, like he was in some conspiracy to murder Snorri, rather than save him.

Kat's keen eyes saw through all the flickering chaos to the centre. 'The shaman has already begun his ceremony,' she said.

Felix peered towards the circle again. He couldn't see the hunched old beastman, but he could see, through the haze of smoke and roaring flames, the occasional pulse of blue light from the jagged veins of the herdstone.

'It's time, then,' said Gotrek, then turned and started back down the hill.

Felix followed him with the others, fighting down waves of conflicting emotions. The time of Gotrek's doom was fast approaching. After all these years, he found it hard to imagine that it would really happen this time, but it was harder to see how it wouldn't.

Felix once again felt a chill of dread as they squirmed, one at a time, through the hole in the hill that led to the ancient burial chamber and the tunnels beyond. But though the fear of some strange vengeance by old Hans made him turn anxiously at every rustle and rattle that echoed in the dark as they hurried through the subterranean labyrinth, nothing happened. They came without incident to the catacombs of Tarnhalt's castle, and then to the ancient stairwell that led to the surface and the stone circle where the beasts performed their dread ceremony.

Kat passed her torch to Felix and drew her bow off her back as the dwarfs started up the square stone spiral. Felix followed her up, holding the torch to one side. The stairs crackled with dead leaves and dry twigs, blown down by the winds of ages, but as they got closer to the surface, the noises from above began to drown out all else – the stamping of thousands of hooves in unison, the hoarse chanting, now quickening to a frenzied pitch, the high wail of the old shaman rising above it all.

Felix found himself clutching his sword in a death grip, and his teeth were locked together like a vice. He had to keep reminding himself that he wasn't going out to fight the herd. He was going to stay hidden with Snorri and Kat while Gotrek and Rodi went to kill the shaman and meet their doom. It still felt unlikely. Would things really be different this time?

They turned up a final flight and saw a square of night sky above them. Torchlight flickered off the stairwell's crumbling walls. Gotrek slowed his pace and crept to the top, raising his head cautiously, then beckoning the rest up after him. They came out in the midst of a dense thicket of brambles that grew over and around broken knee-high walls – all that remained of the tower that had once surrounded the stairs.

Over their heads, Mannslieb and Morrslieb stared down, casting double shadows, and were even closer together tonight than they had been the night before, and from all around came bestial voices and the light of many fires. Felix and the others crouched down and peered through the criss-cross screen of thorny twigs to the scene beyond. Felix's heart pounded in his chest as he saw how close they were to the circle and the beasts.

The ring of stones rose only twenty paces away, and the circle of torch-wielding, blue-painted gors that guarded it was only ten paces away. The mob that the guards were holding back was even closer. In fact the stairwell was within their front ranks. The mob stretched out to both sides of it and behind it all the way down the hill to the valley floor. Only the mass of bushes and the tower's broken walls had stopped the beastmen from standing directly on top of it.

Felix heard Kat whispering frightened prayers to Taal and Rhya, and he did the same to Sigmar, all the while trying to keep his knees from shaking. It wouldn't take more than a cough or a loud sneeze to alert the beasts to their presence, and then they would be dead in seconds.

Gotrek pushed a little way forwards through the bushes, peering more closely at the circle. The others crept cautiously after him. Through the gaps between the standing stones Felix could see the blue quartz veins of the massive herdstone pulsing like a heart in time with the rhythm of the herd's chant, and before it, the twist-horned shaman, Urslak, standing in supplication, arms outstretched, his bird-claw robe flapping in an eldritch wind as he wailed a profane prayer. For a moment Felix thought he saw enormous blue-feathered wings sprouting from the shaman's shoulders, but then they vanished, and he decided it had only been a trick of the flames that surrounded him.

There were two ranks of beastmen between the Slayers and the shaman. The closest rank were the blue-daubed guardians. They were widely spaced, and faced out towards the herd, brandishing torches to keep them back. The massive war-leader – who Ortwin had named Gargorath the God-Touched – stood with them on the east side of the circle, his powerful arms folded as he looked down on the sea of upturned goat-like faces that stretched away from him to the base of the hill and beyond into the camp. The second rank of beastmen stood just within the monoliths, blue-robed initiates that faced in towards the shaman, chanting and shaking strange fetishes over their heads – bones, feathers, gnarled staffs and skulls of different animals and races. Felix remembered them. They had been the dancers that had preceded the stone when it was on the march.

'It is possible,' muttered Gotrek.

'Aye,' said Rodi, nodding. 'Only a handful to kill before we reach the old goat – if we're quick. After that…' He shrugged and smiled savagely.

'Snorri is ready,' said Snorri eagerly. 'Snorri thinks this is going to be a good fight.'

Gotrek and Rodi exchanged another glance, then backed towards the stairs, beckoning to Snorri to follow.

'Come here, Snorri Nosebiter,' said Gotrek, looking uncomfortable. 'I want to speak of your part in this.'

A look of impatience passed over Snorri's ugly face, but he followed Gotrek, stepping past Rodi, who hung back behind him.

'Why waste time talking?' said Snorri. 'Snorri knows what to–'

With a sound like a cannon ball hitting a wooden floor, Rodi struck Snorri with the heavy iron pommel of his axe, just below the lowest nail on the back of his skull. The old Slayer's eyes rolled up into his head and he sank to his knees, then pitched forwards, flat on his face. Rodi looked down at him, shame and sadness mixing in his eyes.

'Sorry, Father Rustskull,' he said. 'It had to be done.'

'Have…?' said Kat. 'Have you killed him?'

'Do you think a little tap like that could kill Snorri Nosebiter?' asked Gotrek.

But nevertheless, the Slayer felt Snorri's pulse, then he and Rodi lifted his limp body and rolled him down the stairs.

The two Slayers stood for a long moment, looking down into the darkness at their friend, then Gotrek turned to Kat.

'You have the horn?'

She unslung it from where it hung at her waist and held it up.

'Good,' said Gotrek, then looked to Felix and fixed him with a hard bright eye.

'And you know what to do?'

'Aye, Gotrek,' said Felix. 'I do.'

Gotrek nodded, then turned with Rodi towards Tarnhalt's Crown, running his thumb down the blade of his axe so that it bled, but then, after a step, he paused and turned back. He crossed to Felix and held out his hand. Felix took it, a lump suddenly constricting his throat.

'Goodbye, manling,' said Gotrek. 'You have been a true dwarf-friend.'

'Thank... thank you, Gotrek,' said Felix, hardly able to speak. 'I–'

But Gotrek had already turned away and joined Rodi as he pushed towards the edge of the thicket.

Felix looked at his hand. There was a streak of blood across the back of it where Gotrek's sliced thumb had pressed it. He blinked his eyes and turned away, emotion threatening to overwhelm him, only to find himself facing Kat, looking up at him with sad eyes. He turned from her too, afraid she was going to say something comforting, but she seemed to know better. She only put her hand on his back and kept silent.

'Now!' came Gotrek's harsh whisper.

Felix looked up in time to see Gotrek and Rodi streaking out of the bushes fast and low, straight for the two outer circle guards who stood between them and the stone circle.

The noise of the chanting and the darkness near the bushes covered the Slayers' approach, and the gors were dead before they even knew they were being attacked. Gotrek cut the legs out from under his, then chopped off its head as it hit the ground. Rodi gutted his with the leading blade of his double-headed axe, then severed its spine with the back blade as he shouldered past it.

The Slayers ran on. Felix looked around. It seemed none of the other beastmen had noticed them yet. He clenched his sword in anxiety. They just might make it. If they could get through the robed beastmen that stood within the stones–

A roar from the right brought his head around. One of the outer guardians had seen the Slayers and was running after them, calling to its comrades.

Kat sent an arrow at it. The gor stumbled but kept going. More were following him. She drew another arrow.

Gotrek and Rodi reached the circle and slammed into the backs of the chanting initiates who danced in the gaps between the stones. Three went down instantly, taken completely by surprise, but three more turned and gave battle, striking out with staves and sickle-shaped daggers. Bellows of anger came from those in nearby gaps as they saw what was happening to their fellows, and a few surged towards the Slayers, but the old shaman in the centre was too focused on his ritual to notice, and most of the chanters were, so transported by the frenzy of their invocation that they continued on, oblivious.

The two Slayers were making short work of the robed beastmen, but not short enough. The blue-painted guardians were coming swiftly behind them and would reach them before they were clear. Kat poured more arrows into the guards and a few fell, but she was only one archer. Most did not.

'They're not going to make it,' she said.

Felix knew it, and he fought the urge to rush out and help them. It was wrong for him not to be at the Slayer's side. He felt guilty and ashamed, but Gotrek had told him to stay with Snorri, and he had sworn he would do so.

'Where are the dirty beastmen that hit Snorri on the head?' said a blurry voice behind them.

Felix and Kat turned to see the old Slayer standing at the top of the stairs, rubbing the back of his head with a meaty hand and weaving slightly as he blinked around.

'Ah! There they are!' he said, squinting ahead. 'And Snorri's friends are taking them all!'

The old Slayer started forwards, wading through the brush towards the fight, a lump the size of an apple on the back of his skull.

TWENTY

'Snorri, wait!' hissed Felix, dogging the Slayer's steps as he pushed through the brambles. 'You can't go, remember? You must recover your memory first.'

'Aye, Slayer,' said Kat, following on his other side. 'You won't be allowed into Grimnir's hall.'

'Snorri knows,' said Snorri. 'He'll take care of that just as soon as he sorts out these beastmen.'

'But the beastmen will sort you out!' said Felix, exasperated. 'You'll meet your doom here, Snorri!'

'And it will be too soon,' said Kat.

'But there are beastmen,' said Snorri, breaking through the last of the bushes.

Felix looked around to see if any beastmen had noticed them. They were all looking towards Gotrek and Rodi. He grabbed Snorri's arm as Kat caught the wrist of his hammer hand.

'Snorri, please!' said Felix.

Snorri shrugged off Felix as if he were a fly, then gently pried Kat's hand away, all without breaking stride. 'You don't have to hold Snorri back,' said Snorri. 'There are plenty of beastmen for all of us.'

Felix and Kat made another grab for him, but just then Snorri swept his hammer up over his head and charged forwards, bellowing a Khazalid war cry.

Felix groaned, all his dreams of escaping Gotrek's doom and starting a new life vanishing in an instant. The cheese-brained old idiot had ruined everything. He turned to Kat. 'I… I'm sorry. I have to protect him. I promised.'

Kat shrugged and gave him a sad half-smile as she settled her bow over her shoulders and drew her axes. 'And I promised to fight at your side.'

He wanted to tell her no, and send her back to the stairs, but there was no time for argument. If this suicide was going to mean anything, he had to help the Slayers reach the shaman. As one, he and Kat sprinted after Snorri into the fight, roaring and screaming and slashing at the backs of the blue-painted beastmen that surrounded Rodi and Gotrek. Felix was so full of rage that he cut down two beastmen in one savage stroke. He just imagined they were Snorri.

As the beasts fell, Felix saw Gotrek look up from slaying a beast-initiate to see Snorri fighting beside him. Gotrek snarled and looked around. He found Felix and glared at him with his one angry eye.

Felix shrunk from his displeasure. 'He woke up,' he called, ducking a huge club. 'I couldn't–'

Gotrek cursed and gutted another beastman with an unnecessarily vicious twist of his axe. Beside him, Snorri dashed out the brains of another, while Rodi head-butted a third between the legs. All at once they were through the initiates and stumbling into the middle of the stone circle. Gotrek, Rodi and Snorri turned to face the blue-painted guardians who had been fighting so hard to stop them from entering it, but the beastmen skidded to a stop at the line of standing stones, staring at the huge glowing herdstone in abject fear, and would come no further.

'Ha!' barked Gotrek. 'To the shaman!'

The runes on the Slayer's axe flared white-hot as he turned, and Felix didn't wonder why. Entering the circle of menhirs was like stepping into an arcane furnace. Chaos energy radiated from the blazing blue veins of the herdstone in great pulsing waves, making his skin itch as if he was being eaten by ants and filling his mind with chittering, bird-like voices.

Gotrek, Rodi and Snorri ran directly for Urslak, and Felix and Kat followed. There was no one to stop them. The crooked-horned shaman continued his invocation, entirely unaware of their presence. The rest of the chanting initiates remained transfixed as well, and the guardians remained at the edge of the circle, fearing to come in. Felix's heart pounded with unexpected hope. They were going to make it!

But then, into the circle charged Gargorath the God-Touched, the hulking black-furred, blue-eyed war-leader, with five blue-painted, heavily armoured gors at his back.

Gargorath roared a challenge at the Slayers, his hate-filled eyes glowing with the same fire that emanated from the herdstone as he raised his vulture-headed axe above his head. Felix heard the weapon scream – the high, harsh shriek of a bird of prey. He shivered as he recalled poor Ortwin's last words – the axe ate what it killed. He wasn't sure what that meant, and he hoped he would never find out.

The Slayers answered the challenge with roars of their own, and with a deafening crunch of steel and bone the two sides slammed together. Felix and Kat swung at a brass-armoured elk-man as Snorri, Gotrek and Rodi piled into the others. The elk-man smashed aside Felix's puny attacks with a crusty black iron mace that likely weighed more than Kat. Felix staggered back, his hands stinging from the impact. Kat leapt aside, one of her axes snapped in half, and before they could recover the elk-man was on them again, sending them diving away. Felix's palms turned slick with fear. The elk-man was stronger and more skilled than any other beastman he had ever faced – an actual warrior, rather than just a brawling animal.

The Slayers were having the same difficulty. Gotrek blocked Gargorath's strike but was driven back several feet by the strength of the blow, the vulture-headed axe screaming in his face. Snorri was bleeding from a deep cut on his arm and was backing away from two bellowing beasts. Rodi's face was a mask of blood as he fought two more. Red sprayed from his braided beard with every swing of his axe.

'Felix! Look out!'

Kat shoved Felix and he staggered aside just as the elk-man's club whistled past his cheekbone, so close it made him blink. He returned his attention to the fight, aiming a cut at the beastman's eyes as Kat swiped at its ankles. The gor jumped back before this coordinated attack, and they pressed forwards.

On the other side of the fight, Gotrek's and Gargorath's axes met blade to blade and Gotrek's axe was caught in the vulture-headed weapon's beak notch. Gargorath tried to twist Gotrek's axe out of his hands, but the Slayer reversed the twist, his muscles bulging, and Gargorath's axe spun past Snorri's head to land on the ground.

The Slayer aimed a cut at the defenceless Gargorath, but when the big beastman leapt aside, Gotrek charged past him, straight for the shaman.

Felix stole glances from his own fight as Gargorath chased after the Slayer. Gotrek swiped behind him with his axe, ringing it off the war-leader's leg armour, but the beast caught him by the neck and shoulder and lifted him over his head.

'Gotrek!' cried Felix. Then to Kat, 'We have to help him!'

He and Kat jumped back from the elk-man and ran to Gotrek's aid, but before they could take three steps, they saw the Slayer chop down wildly at Gargorath's head. His rune axe sheered off one of the war-leader's curling horns and part of his ram-like snout. The beast howled in agony and flung the Slayer from him as hard as he could – right at the herdstone.

'No!'

Felix and Kat chopped at Gargorath as Gotrek sailed over the chanting shaman's head to crash down hard at the base of the looming herdstone. Kat's axe glanced off the war-leader's steel and brass breastplate, not even scratching it. Karaghul bit into the armour but did not touch flesh. The massive gor flattened them both with a careless backhand, then ran to snatch up his fallen axe.

Felix struggled up, trying to block Gargorath's way, but the elk-man was on him again and he had to fall back, the mace shivering his blade and turning his arms to jelly. Behind him, Kat sat up, shaking her head woozily.

Gargorath roared by her, axe in hand, charging towards Gotrek and the stone as Felix parried another brutal blow from the elk-man.

Gotrek stood to meet the war-leader, beckoning with his off hand and swinging his arm back in preparation for a powerful slash. As he did, his rune axe grazed the herdstone – the merest touch – but there was a sudden sparking crack and a flash of pure white light, and the ground slipped sideways beneath Felix's feet.

Felix caught himself before he fell and blinked his eyes to clear the after-images that danced before them. He looked around, his head throbbing. Gotrek was doubled up, his right arm cradled against his chest, while his axe lay smoking at his feet. Everybody else – man, dwarf and beastman – stood frozen, looking up at the herdstone. It was steaming and hissing, and little crumbling shards were flaking from it and raining down on the ground while the blue quartz veins that ran through it flickered and flashed like a torch in a windstorm.

The first to recover his composure was the beast-shaman, Urslak, who backed away and pointed a clawed finger at Gotrek, shrieking for his blood. The ring of robed initiates heeded his call, casting down their fetishes and drawing crude weapons as they surged forwards, braying their rage. Gargorath and his lieutenants added their voices to the howl and charged for the Slayer, but Rodi and Snorri had recovered as well, and leapt to stop them.

'Unfaithful beasts!' roared Rodi. 'You are *my* doom!'

'And Snorri's!' called Snorri.

Felix and Kat joined the Slayers, slashing at Gargorath and the elk-man and trying to keep them from Gotrek until he recovered, but the war-leader was too strong. He knocked Felix aside and he and the elk-man bounded over Kat towards the stunned Slayer while Snorri and Rodi engaged the others.

''Ware the leader, Gotrek,' called Felix from the ground.

But Gotrek paid Gargorath and his followers no attention. Instead, as he shook off his shock, he looked from his axe to the herdstone and back again, a cunning glint kindling in his single eye.

Felix knew that look of old, and it never boded well for anybody in the vicinity.

'Gotrek, that is a very bad idea,' he shouted, picking himself up.

Gotrek snatched up his axe and dodged Gargorath's charge, laughing darkly. 'No, manling,' he laughed. 'It is a very *good* idea.'

Gargorath and the elk-man slashed down at the Slayer with their weapons. Gotrek knocked both attacks aside with a whistling backhand, then swung upwards, decapitating the elk-man's mace and tearing through its armour and flesh like a plough through soft earth. As the beast toppled to the ground in an explosion of blood, Gotrek aimed another cut at Gargorath. The beastman desperately threw himself back to avoid the strike and it clashed off his breastplate, raising sparks and knocking him flat on his back.

Gotrek did not follow up. Instead, he turned to the herdstone again and swung his axe at it with all his might.

For a brief second Felix thought the world had ended. The thundercrack flash of the strike blinded and deafened him, and he lost all sense of up or down. He opened his eyes to find himself sprawled on the ground, along with all his friends and foes. The beasts lay everywhere, writhing and clutching their horned heads. The shaman was shrieking as if he'd been stabbed in the eyes. Kat was curled in a ball. Gotrek was flat on his back, spread-eagled, his eyebrows and the ends of his beard and crest smoking, ten feet from the stone. His axe lay beside him, the head glowing as if it had just left the forge.

The herdstone was shaking itself to pieces. Large chunks were breaking off and crumbling to dust as they fell, and the quartz veins were starred with fissures, like thick glass under pressure. Felix felt an unnatural wind blowing – not from the stone, but towards it – and he saw that the dust and pebbles that were falling from the stone were being sucked into the cracks in the quartz.

Gotrek groaned and sat up, as stiff and slow as an old man. He took up his axe and used it to lever himself to his feet. 'One more ought to do it,' he grunted.

'Wait, Gotrek!' shouted Felix over the wind and the rising hum of the stone. 'You'll kill us!'

'Then you'd better run, manling,' said Gotrek, and he limped towards the stone as if his legs were made of lead.

Felix cursed as he forced himself to his feet – nor was he the only one less than happy with Gotrek's course of action. Gargorath and his remaining lieutenants were rising and staggering towards him, and Urslak, the shaman, was raising his arms and snarling out a vile incantation as the claw-clutched blue orb at the top of his staff began to glow and pulse. Felix noted with horror that all the bird-claw fetishes that dangled from his robes were clutching and unclutching their talons in time to his chant.

'Hurry,' said Felix, lifting Kat to her feet and urging her forwards. 'Run.'

'Is he really going to...?' she asked, looking back.

'Without a doubt,' said Felix.

He and Kat turned and ran as Rodi and Snorri lurched up to intercept Gargorath and his warriors, and Urslak stalked towards Gotrek, who was still limping doggedly towards the stone.

The initiate beastmen had recovered now, and were charging forwards again too. Felix and Kat lashed out at them as they came, but the gors hardly paid them notice. All their attention was focused on Gotrek and the stone.

A crazy hope flared in Felix's heart as the way cleared before them. The stair to the tunnels was only a few paces beyond the stone circle. If they were lucky, and the rest of the beasts ignored them as well, they might just survive this mad folly after all.

Felix looked back. Beyond Rodi and Snorri's battle with the beastmen, Urslak swung his staff at Gotrek, the blue orb glowing like an azure sun. Gotrek hacked the staff in two, then gutted the shaman and kicked him back before the claw-held orb had stopped bouncing across the rocky ground.

The Slayer spat on the dying shaman, then turned back to the herd-stone, raising his axe.

'Faster!' said Felix, and sprinted with Kat for the ring of monoliths.

They weren't fast enough.

With another deafening crack, he and Kat were knocked flat again by a jolt stronger than all the others. It felt as if a giant had hit him in the back with an enormous shovel, knocking the wind out of him and pushing him to the brink of unconsciousness. He thought of trying to move, but it seemed too much effort. Easier to just lie there. Then Kat whimpered beside him. The thought of her galvanised him. He had to get her to safety.

As Felix fought to regain his senses, gasping and groaning and blinking the glare from his eyes, he became aware of a thunderous roaring behind him, and of a hard wind battering his face. He raised himself on shaking arms and looked back – then froze at what he saw.

The towering herdstone was rising from the ground and expanding – the jagged lines that had been the seams of quartz now widened into gaps between huge floating shards of granite that moved outwards from the core of the stone. And through these gaps shone a terrible blue light that bathed the inside of the stone circle in a harsh sapphire glow.

The impossible wind blew towards the widening cracks from all directions, as if they were chimney flues sucking smoke from a fireplace. Felix's hair streamed towards it. Leaves and branches whirled towards it. The wind tore at the floating granite shards of the herdstone too, crumbling their edges and sucking in the pebbles so that they shrank even as the gaps between them grew ever wider.

Felix squinted into the light that streamed from the expanding cracks, and a sickening dread swallowed all his other fears as he saw its source. Hanging within the core of the fragmenting herdstone was a hole in the world, a gash in reality that looked into some other place. Blue swirls of every shade wove a hypnotising dance inside the rift, blue swirls that looked at him with fierce intelligence, and begged him to join them in their search for ultimate knowledge.

Kat whimpered again beside him. 'It's… it's beautiful.'

Felix turned and clapped a hand over her eyes. 'Don't look!' he cried. 'It will take your mind.'

He fought to his feet, the unnatural wind pulling at him, then dragged her up too. 'Come on. Turn away from it. Run!'

And yet, even as he followed her, pushing hard against the rising wind, Felix found it impossible not to look back himself.

The beastmen were running from the stone, the initiates screaming with fear as the sucking wind dragged them back, Gargorath and his surviving lieutenants trampling them and hurling them aside in their eagerness to get away.

Chasing them came Gotrek, Rodi and Snorri, all roaring insults over the shrieking gale.

'Come back, you cowards!' called Gotrek.

'Are you afraid of a little wind?' bellowed Rodi.

'Snorri has seen squirrels with more courage!' shouted Snorri.

Felix could feel the wind trying to lift him off the ground as he leaned against it, and it was getting worse. It was going to suck him into the rift! Only two more yards to the menhirs, but it might have been two miles. He put Kat in front of him to shield her and they pressed on, fighting for every inch. More debris whipped past them, flying towards the vortex. One of the beasts they had killed as they fought their way into the circle rolled by, flopping loosely, over and over.

Finally they reached the ring of monoliths and Felix pushed Kat into the shadow of one, where the wind was less, then struggled to pull himself behind it as well. Kat caught his arms and hauled with all her strength. With a final grunt of effort he stumbled behind the stone and collapsed against it, breathing heavily.

The shadow of their stone shelter was as sharp as a knife in the harsh light of the vortex, and stretched away with the shadows of the other stones down the sloping sides of the hill to the valley below. Nothing could be seen within the shadows, but the light that blazed from between the stones illuminated a roiling sea of beastmen backing away from Tarnhalt's Crown with naked terror showing in their glittering black eyes. Felix couldn't blame them. If he could have run, he would have been over the hills and gone long ago.

'Are we safe even here?' asked Kat.

Felix shrugged weakly. 'I don't know. But I can go no further.'

A movement in the corner of his eye made him turn his head. Gargorath and his lieutenants had escaped the circle and were straining to reach the slope down into the valley as the gale tore at their armour and their fur.

Felix put his head around the corner of the standing stone, looking into the circle for Gotrek, Snorri and Rodi. The three Slayers were ploughing on, slowly but steadily, against the wind, cursing lustily all the while.

Behind them, the initiate beastmen weren't doing as well. Felix saw one fall backwards and roll head over heels towards the howling stone. Another was lifted bodily and spun away through the air to be sucked into the fissures between the shards – breaking up into its component parts as it went. The wind was too loud to hear its screams.

Then Felix saw a lone figure rise before the stone. It was Urslak. It seemed impossible for him to be alive, after the evisceration Gotrek had given him. It seemed even more impossible that he was able to stand steady so close to the stone and the vacuum of the vortex. And yet he did. Though buffeted cruelly by the wind, he straightened his hunched form and spread his arms wide, calling out some incantation that was lost in the roaring rush of air. His claw-festooned robe flapped and fluttered around him like a living thing, and his intestines, which had spilled through the cut made by Gotrek's axe, streamed out in front of him, drawn towards the glowing void and waving like some grisly banner.

Felix wasn't sure if the old shaman was trying to repair the damage that Gotrek had done, or was simply praying to his god. Whatever the case, neither the wind nor the light diminished. In fact both grew stronger, rising to an unbearable intensity as the granite shards began to crumble away to mere slivers.

The Slayers were on their hands and knees now, crawling with their heads down away from the herdstone. Gotrek was in the lead, only two strides away from Felix, but Felix was afraid they wouldn't make it.

'Come on, Gotrek!' shouted Felix. But he doubted the Slayer could hear him. He couldn't hear himself.

More of the initiate beastmen fell back and flew away, vanishing into the vortex in flashes of blue-white. Felix felt the massive monolith he leaned against shift under his shoulder as the wind pulled at it. Sigmar! The rift was going to suck in the whole world! It would swallow everything.

Finally, after a handful of lip-chewing seconds, as the wind shrieked louder and the light grew still brighter, Gotrek and Rodi dragged themselves behind the monolith just to the left of the one Felix and Kat hid behind. Only Snorri remained in the light. He looked back over his shoulder and shook his hammer at the vortex, shouting something Felix couldn't hear. But then big hands reached out of the shadow and jerked him back, and he vanished into the blackness behind the stone.

Felix was sure it wouldn't matter. They would all be pulled into the glittering void – all their hopes and dreams for the future ended here in a blinding flash of blue. He looked back towards the stone, shielding his eyes from the glare, and saw Urslak still standing there, a black silhouette against the bright blue, his arms wide, chanting ceaselessly as the wind tore at him.

The shaman grew thinner as Felix watched. The light was eating him. He was disintegrating, his flapping intestines and his flesh tearing away in chunks and vanishing into the swirling core, leaving at last nothing but his skeleton, and then that went too, flaking away like ash until there was nothing left.

Felix pulled back behind the monolith, unable to look any more as the light blazed from blue to white and the wind rose to an apocalyptic shriek. He wrapped Kat in his arms and hugged her tight, certain that these were their last moments together, and content – or nearly content – that his life should end that way.

Faces flashed before him like wreckage in the wind. Gotrek, Snorri. They were here. At least he was with them at their end. But there was no Max. No Malakai. No… no Ulrika. He cursed himself for thinking of her. Kat was here. Kat who loved him, and who he loved. He should be content. He should be ready.

A clap like thunder shook the ground and made him slap his hands to his ears. It felt as if his head was going to implode. Kat did the same, screaming inaudibly.

And then, utter silence. Utter blackness. Utter stillness. He lay in it a moment, stunned into motionlessness. Had the thunderclap broken his eardrums? Had it killed him? Was this some empty afterlife? He tried to feel his arms and legs, but he wasn't sure he even had any any more. 'Is this death, then?' he whispered, looking around at the impenetrable darkness. 'Is this the endless sleep of eternity?'

'What did you say?' said a voice from nearby. 'Snorri can't hear a thing.'

Felix frowned. He was pretty certain that the endless sleep of eternity wouldn't have Snorri Nosebiter in it. Then Kat shifted against him and he realised that he was alive.

After another moment of quiet contemplation, he finally found the wherewithal to sit up. The blackness, which had seemed absolute after so much light, was now penetrable, showing stars above and far-off torches and fires down in the valley, and the faint glow of the moons that showed Felix the line of Kat's cheekbone and the white streak in her hair.

'What happened?' she asked.

'I don't know,' said Felix.

To their left, Gotrek, Rodi and Snorri were grunting to their feet. Felix and Kat did the same, groaning and weaving dizzily. Felix felt like he was on a ship in heavy seas. The ground wouldn't stay still under his feet.

After a moment with his head down, he straightened and followed the dwarfs as they stepped out from behind the monoliths and looked into the circle.

The vortex was gone, and so was the herdstone. No trace of it remained. It had been sucked into the rift.

'What happened to it?' Felix asked. 'I thought it was going to swallow us all.'

'Things of Chaos are unstable, manling,' said Gotrek. 'It swallowed itself.'

'Then the Empire is safe,' said Felix with a relieved sigh. 'The shaman is dead. The herdstone is gone. The people of the Drakwald will not become beasts–'

'Taal and Rhya, look at the menhirs,' breathed Kat, interrupting him.

Felix and the others turned to look at the ring of monoliths. They were all leaning in towards the centre of the circle, like fingers closing, or like old crones whispering to each other. He shivered. The vortex had nearly succeeded in pulling the massive slabs of stone from the ground – and if they had gone, Felix and the others would have been quick to follow.

'Never mind the stones,' said Rodi. 'Look at the bodies.'

Felix looked where the young Slayer pointed. On the ground close to the centre of the circle, the bodies of a few beastmen remained, fallen where they had dropped when the vortex closed. There was nothing left of them but skeletons, but the skeletons were odd. They did not gleam white in the light of the two moons. They gleamed yellow – golden yellow.

'Gold, by Grungni!' cried Rodi, stepping forwards, his eyes gleaming with dwarfish lust. 'And of the purest too, by the look of it.'

'Snorri sees sapphires too,' said Snorri, stepping closer and pointing to a golden skull.

Felix stared at the thing, amazed. The horns and claws and hooves of the skeleton were indeed deep, star-crossed sapphire, polished as if by a master jeweller.

Gotrek put his arms out and held Snorri and Rodi back. 'You want nothing to do with that gold, nor that sapphire,' he said.

'But why not?' said Rodi, his eyes glazed with desire. 'It will solve everything. I can go back. I can pay the debt. I can…'

Gotrek slapped him hard across the cheek. Rodi snarled and doubled his fists.

Gotrek just glared at him, his single eye as cold as ice. 'It has already made you forget your oath,' he said. 'And you haven't yet touched it. Can you not see it for what it is?'

Rodi remained with his fists up for a long moment, then at last he sighed and lowered his hands. 'You are right, Gurnisson. Gold born of such an abomination could only ever bring misery. Forgive me.'

'Snorri still thinks it's pretty,' said Snorri.

Gotrek grunted and turned to Kat. 'It is time to blow your horn, little one,' he said, then looked to Felix and Snorri, his brow lowering. 'And it is time for you–'

He was interrupted by a bright tantara of rally horns blaring from the north. Everyone turned. The thunder of guns and cannons echoed off the stones around them, and the roar of angry beasts filled the valley.

'The armies!' said Kat. 'They're attacking!'

TWENTY-ONE

Felix, Gotrek and the others ran out of the circle to the north end of the hill. By the torches and fires of the beastmen, and by the light of the two moons rising side by side in the black sky, they could see the surging movements of the forces in the valley below them.

The whole of the herd was pressing forwards towards the narrow north end of the valley where regimented ranks of cavalry and infantry were stabbing into their milling mass. Felix's heart leapt at the sight.

'Hurrah!' cried Kat, throwing up a fist. 'They have come! The beasts are smashed!'

Gotrek grunted. 'Not with that force, they're not.'

'Aye,' said Rodi. 'Nor those tactics.'

Felix looked again, and his elation at the arrival of the armies faded. The Slayers were right. Everything was wrong.

It was difficult to tell in the uncertain light how many troops were cutting into the herd's side, but there were certainly not seven thousand. For some reason, despite their earlier statements, it seemed Plaschke-Miesner and von Volgen had attacked without waiting for von Kotzebue to arrive. Worse, Felix saw that Gargorath the God-Touched and his lieutenants had escaped the herdstone's implosion, and were at the forefront of their followers, urging them on and wreaking terrible damage in the human army's front ranks.

'What are they doing?' Felix asked. 'The lords said they wouldn't engage without Kotzebue's reinforcements.'

'And they were to wait for the horn,' said Kat.

'It seems they found their courage after all,' said Gotrek. 'Though not their wits.'

It was true. The two lords' armies were driving forwards so strongly that they were losing all advantage of terrain. If they had stayed in the narrow end of the valley and let the beasts come to them, they could have kept them all on their front, with their cannons, handguns and crossbows positioned on the steep hills to either side to keep the beasts from flanking them. Instead, the armies had stabbed so deeply into the mass of the herd that already the beastmen were curling around the ends of their lines to encircle them, and the cannons and guns were forced to fire at the edges of the herd so as not to hit their own troops. The lords had lost tactical superiority – the only advantage they had – within the first minute of the attack.

'It's madness!' said Felix. 'They've killed themselves, and taken all their men with them.'

'Aye,' said Rodi. 'They're acting like Slayers. A thing only Slayers should do.'

Snorri chuckled and smacked the haft of his hammer into his left hand. 'Snorri thinks this will be a proper fight,' he said, then plunged down the hill, bellowing a savage war cry.

'Nosebiter, stop!' shouted Gotrek.

It was too late. Snorri was already halfway down and didn't hear him. Gotrek growled.

'We better go keep him alive,' said Rodi, grinning.

'Aye,' said Gotrek.

And with that they charged after Snorri, roaring war cries of their own.

Felix wanted to call out after them, but knew it would not change their minds to remind them that they had already done their part – that they had killed the shaman and destroyed the stone and could retire from the field with honour for those accomplishments. That was not the Slayer way. By the Slayers' logic, having saved the day, they were now free to die gloriously.

With sudden shock, Felix realised that he was miraculously free *not* to die gloriously. By some mad mischance, he had ended up in a position where he wasn't in danger of being swallowed by Gotrek's doom. He was up above the fray while the Slayer ran towards it. He could observe from here and then slip away with Kat to the barrow tunnels and to freedom where he could record Gotrek's doom later at his leisure. He would have fulfilled his vow and lived to tell of it, and he could take Kat with him. He could have a life beyond his travels with Gotrek.

He turned to Kat, opening his mouth to tell her to come away with him, but then paused.

It felt wrong. He knew that he had vowed to Gotrek only to record his death, not die himself, but it still felt disloyal not to be fighting at the Slayer's side at the end. Their relationship, whatever it was, had become more than just that of Slayer and rememberer. It wasn't that they were friends in any way most men would recognise. They did not share their thoughts and inner turmoil with each other. They did not profess bonds of undying loyalty to each other. To the outside observer, and sometimes even to Felix himself, they seemed little more than master and servant. If Felix wanted to go somewhere and Gotrek didn't, they didn't go. It was not an equal partnership.

And yet, it *was* a partnership. They relied on each other, and trusted each other more than most so-called friends ever did. They knew each other better than they knew themselves, and certainly better than either of them knew anybody else. Like it or not, he and the Slayer were bound to each other by a bond not easily broken.

'You want to go with them,' said Kat, looking at him.

'I don't *want* to,' said Felix. 'But…'

Kat nodded. 'But you have to.'

Felix grunted, angry with himself. 'It's ridiculous. I don't understand it. I should be running away with you.'

'You have known the Slayer for a long time,' said Kat, smiling sadly. 'You can't leave him now.'

'But…' But, nothing. She was right. As stupid as it was, she spoke the truth. Felix sighed. 'Go back to the stairs,' he said. 'Get away from here. This is a fool's death.'

Kat shook her head. 'My life began with you, Felix,' she said, looking at him steadily. 'It will end with you.'

'Kat,' said Felix. 'Don't be an ass. Live your life–'

But she was already screaming down the hill after the Slayers.

'Kat!'

She did not slow. With a groan he charged down after her, but he cried no war cry.

In the minute since they had first looked down upon the battle it had become even worse. Plaschke-Miesner's and von Volgen's combined forces were completely surrounded by the herd, and the firing of the cannons and handguns was even more sporadic, as the gunners tried to aim around the central melee. But despite the insanity of the position the two young lords had put them in, Felix had to admit that their troops were maintaining good discipline. The wings of their formations had folded back and around as the beasts had swarmed them, and the army was now a neat square, bristling with spears on all four sides, with the sea of beastmen breaking against it and falling back as if it were a stone pier. Unfortunately, this formation had completely hemmed in the knights and mounted men-at-arms, making them almost useless. Felix saw a wedge of them struggling to reach Gargorath and his lieutenants on foot, their warhorses left with their squires in the centre of the square. At this rate, the army could not hope to last – and of course, the Slayers were driving right towards it.

With their longer legs, Felix and Kat caught up to Gotrek, Rodi and Snorri just as they reached the edges of the herd. The beastmen were facing away from them, all pushing north to get at the soldiers who had dared to attack them, and thus the Slayers' first charge was more murder than melee. Gotrek's and Rodi's axes severed spines and hamstrung legs as Snorri's warhammer crushed skulls and rib cages. Felix and Kat stabbed and chopped to their left and right.

But as the beastmen in the last ranks died, those before them turned, enraged, and fell upon the dwarfs in a frenzy. The Slayers laughed and pushed forwards to meet them, axes and hammer blurring as they blocked and countered a score of strikes. Felix and Kat stayed at their backs, guarding their flanks from the beasts that pressed in from the sides.

Gotrek looked over his shoulder as Karaghul deflected a spear tip meant for his neck. He glared at Felix.

'You shouldn't have followed, manling,' he said.

'I know, Gotrek,' said Felix.

The dwarf nodded and carried on fighting. No more needed to be said.

As the Slayers pressed deeper into the herd, more beasts swept in behind them, cutting off their retreat. The Slayers had done exactly what Plaschke-Miesner and von Volgen had done, but as Rodi had said, they were Slayers. This is what they did.

Unfortunately, Felix and Kat were with them, and for a moment it seemed that they would be slaughtered as the beasts surrounded them. But then Rodi and Snorri turned and stepped in front of them, cackling as they slashed at the flankers. Felix and Kat edged back gratefully, and found themselves in the centre of a moving triangle formed by the three Slayers. In this way the five companions fought slowly through the beasts – a three-headed snapping turtle crawling through a pack of wild dogs, with Felix and Kat stabbing out from within the Slayers' protection wherever they were needed. Felix shivered at the turtle metaphor, for he knew that, without the hard shell that Gotrek, Snorri and Rodi provided, the soft middle that was Kat and himself would die instantly. His chainmail and Kat's light leather armour would be no protection against a full-on strike from one of the gors' massive weapons.

After that there was no time for thought. Felix fell into the clanging rhythm of the battle, letting his eyes and ears tell him where his sword needed to be and taking his mind out of the equation – a block, a parry, a stab, a slash, a hop to the right, a twist to the left, over and over. Kat and the Slayers did the same. No one spoke a word. They worked together silently – a ten-armed threshing machine.

It was a precarious business. Despite the Slayers' prowess, if the beastmen had mounted one concerted rush at them they would have been dead in seconds, knocked flat by the sheer mass of the gors' huge bodies, and then run through before they could recover. Fortunately, the beastmen didn't seem capable of such united effort. Instead, in their eagerness to kill, they fought each other almost as much as they fought the enemies in their midst – pushing, shoving and getting in each other's way – and the five companions were thus able to fight them in ones and twos, rather than as a single overwhelming unit.

Another thing that helped keep Felix, Kat and the Slayers alive – though it terrified Felix almost more than the beasts themselves – was the sporadic firing of Plaschke-Miesner's mortars. His gunnery crews had found their range and were lobbing shots over the encircled army into the mass of beasts pressing towards them – in other words, they were aiming right where the five companions were fighting.

Every few moments a huge iron shell would whistle down out of the sky, then explode with a thunderous boom, splashing broken beastmen in every direction. One of these explosive rounds landed so close to the companions that the shock of the blast jarred Felix to his knees and threw Kat to the ground. Fortunately, the wall of beasts took the brunt of the impact and they had time to recover. Another time, a thrown beastman crashed into Felix and Kat's opponents and knocked them in all directions. Kat cut the throat of one before it stopped rolling, and Felix beheaded two more – then it was back to the endless dance as more rushed in to take their place.

That was the terrible, inescapable truth that gnawed at the back of Felix's mind. It didn't matter how many beasts they killed. There would always be more. Felix, Kat and the Slayers would eventually be ground down by weariness and exhaustion and die not because the gors could out-fight them, but because they could outlast them. Already Felix's arms were tired. Already his legs ached. Already his breath was harsh in his throat, and they had not killed a thousandth of the beastmen who filled the field.

Strangely, he was content. There was no fear any more, and no regret. If he died here, he died among friends, in a fitting conclusion to his life. He could have wished that there were others at his side – Max, Ulrika, Malakai – but it was selfish to want them to die here too just so that his circle could be complete, so he did not begrudge them their absence. This was a good death. They had already done a great thing today, no matter what else they had accomplished, and to go down fighting by Gotrek's side felt fitting. He would be complete here. The notes from his journal – if it was ever found – all led up to this battle, and the rest could be filled in by some other chronicler, and the more exaggerated and legendary they made it, the better, Felix thought. A grand finish to a mad life.

He welcomed it.

A moment later they chopped their way through to von Volgen and Plaschke-Miesner's lines, and were nearly attacked by the terrified spearmen who faced them. Felix could see by the men's faces and their ragged line that their initial discipline was fading fast. If there had been anywhere to run, they would have broken. There wasn't, so they fought on, but hopelessly, mechanically, knowing – as Felix knew – that they were only prolonging the end.

Desperate fights raged to either side of them as the five companions slipped through the spear ranks to the inside of the square. To the left, Felix could see Lord von Volgen leading his knights, his eyes mad with battle lust as he wheeled his horse and slashed at Gargorath. To the right, Lord Plaschke-Miesner, his helmet gone and his pretty face hideously marred by a cut that showed his back teeth, fought a pack of blue-daubed beastmen with a half-dozen young knights at his back. Further on, one of the towering, tree-felling minotaurs was sweeping its man-high axe through the ranks of a sword company and killing handfuls with every swing.

Gotrek started towards Gargorath, growling low in his throat. 'Time to finish what I started,' he said.

'Snorri wants to fight the big one,' said Snorri, turning towards the massive minotaur.

'Not if I get there first,' said Rodi, hurrying after the old Slayer and trying to get ahead of him.

Felix knew where he should be, and followed Gotrek. Kat came too. But as they moved down the back of the spear line to reach von Volgen, Felix saw a familiar figure fighting at the head of a sword company that was retreating hastily before a press of beastmen.

'Sir Teobalt!' Felix cried.

The gaunt knight was unable to fall back as fast as his terrified companions, and he was in danger of being surrounded. Felix and Kat pushed through the ranks of the fleeing swordsmen and ran to him.

The old templar was wheezing terribly as they fell in to either side of him, and seemed to be favouring his right leg. A heavy axe blow from a beast splintered his shield, sending him stumbling back, and he barely turned a spear thrust from another with his sword.

Felix stabbed at the axe-wielding gor while Kat swung at the head of the second. Felix's beastman turned on him, snarling, and the axe blade crashed against Karaghul's crossguard, nearly driving the sword back into his face.

It was reprieve enough. Teobalt thrust forwards with his long sword and drove it through the beastman's neck. Felix hacked through its ribs. It fell and he turned to the other beast.

Kat had left her axe in its back, and was dodging away from the questing point of its spear. Teobalt backhanded the thing with an off-balance slash and Felix sliced through its hamstrings. It fell shrieking, and Kat rolled aside and retrieved her axe.

The old templar fell against Felix, sucking air in great gasps. 'Thank… thank you, Herr Jaeger,' he said. 'I… have not the… breath I once had.'

'Keep your feet, sir,' said Felix, trying to walk him back to the sword line as he lashed out at encroaching beasts. 'We must get you to safety.'

Kat put Sir Teobalt's sword arm over her shoulder and they carried him back through the line, shoving the swordsmen aside.

Sir Teobalt groaned as they set him down behind. 'There is no safety. We will not... leave this place, thanks to those two... young fools.'

'Why did they attack like this?' asked Kat, opening her canteen and giving it to him. 'It was madness.'

'Madness?' said Teobalt after he had taken a drink. 'More like possession. I've never seen the like. One moment they stared at the flashes on the hill, biting their hands in fear like the poltroons they are. Then, when the bright light went out and the thunderclap came, they started raging like berserks, screaming for the attack to be sounded and howling for the blood of the beasts.' He shook his head. 'I urged them to wait for von Kotzebue, or at least hold to a defensible position, but they would have none of it, and led their knights in at a gallop, leaving all the rest to follow as they might.' He spat on the body of a dead beastman. 'Never have I seen lords show such flagrant disregard for the lives of their troops.'

To the west, Felix heard Gotrek's roar and looked up. The Slayer was charging Gargorath's retinue from the rear as the black-furred war-leader continued to trade blows with von Volgen. Gargorath looked back as his lieutenants screamed and fell, and von Volgen took advantage, hacking at the war-leader's neck with all his might. Had Gargorath stood still, it would have been a clean strike, but the beast lunged at the Slayer, enraged, and von Volgen's blade only glanced off his steel and gold armour, leaving the young lord half off his saddle and overbalanced.

With an annoyed bray, Gargorath lashed out behind him with the bird-headed axe. Von Volgen was fighting to stay on his horse and could not defend himself. The evil weapon ripped through his armour and bit deep into his chest. Felix shivered as he heard the axe scream like a vulture and saw its sapphire eyes glow bright blue. Von Volgen shrieked and clawed the air as the notched beak of the axe seemed to inhale the life out of him. The young lord's eyes collapsed into their sockets like dried peas and his face grew hollow and gaunt.

'Sigmar preserve us,' said Teobalt, making the sign of the hammer.

'It eats what it kills,' whispered Kat, her eyes wide with horror.

'And feeds its master,' gagged Felix, staring aghast.

As they watched, the blue glow from the axe's eyes spread across Gargorath's body and his myriad wounds knit together as if they had never been. Only the gash on his snout and the severed horn that Gotrek had given him did not heal, but all the rest were gone. He appeared at full strength again.

'Filthy magic,' Felix heard Gotrek shout as he swung at the huge war-leader. 'I'll give you a cut you won't recover from.'

Gargorath ripped the vulture-headed axe from von Volgen's chest and blocked Gotrek's attack with a deafening clang. The fight was on. Behind them, von Volgen toppled from his horse, nothing more than a parchment-covered skeleton in armour, as his knights wailed and cursed and called his name.

'I must go to Gotrek,' said Felix, standing.

But before he could take a step, a handful of beastmen broke through a line of spearmen to their left, roaring in triumph and attacking a company of unprepared archers who had been firing over the spear company's heads.

'Shore up! Shore up!' came a sergeant's cry, and Felix and Kat started forwards to help close the hole before any more gors could enter the square.

But Sir Teobalt stopped Felix and pointed at the beastman who led those who had smashed the line – a huge goat-headed gor that fought in a battered breastplate and a filthy loincloth made of some heavy material. Not so different than the rest, but what set the monster apart from ten thousand others was its weapon, a thick wooden club with a sword stuck sideways through it like a spike. Felix blinked. The sword was on fire, its flames blackening the wood of the club.

'The beast wears the armour of Baron Orenstihl, the grand master of the Order of the Fiery Heart,' said Teobalt. 'And that which it has driven through its club is the Sword of Righteous Flame. And the cloth belted around its waist is our banner.' The old templar fought to his feet and stood tall, readying his sword and shield. 'If the beast has stolen these things, I will have my revenge upon it. If the beast is Baron Orenstihl himself, I will put his poor tortured soul to rest.'

And with that, Teobalt charged at the gor and its followers as they pressed the archers back against the nervous mass of abandoned cavalry mounts that strained and squealed behind them.

'Wait, Sir Teobalt!' called Felix, racing after the limping knight with Kat at his side. 'We will help you.'

'No!' said Teobalt. 'This is my fight alone.'

Felix gave Kat a look and she nodded in agreement. They continued after Teobalt. The old templar was going to get their help whether he liked it or not.

'Grand Master Orenstihl!' cried Teobalt as they neared the melee.

The big gor turned from the retreating archers, its black eyes glaring, though Felix couldn't tell whether it recognised the name or was just responding to the noise.

'If it be you that wear yon sacred banner,' said the old templar, striding towards it, 'then lower your club and let me free you from your curse.'

The beastman cocked its head, as if confused, and dim recognition clouded its goatish face.

'It *is* you,' quavered Teobalt. 'Sigmar save us.'

'I prayed to Sigmrr,' snarled the beastman as Teobalt came on. 'He wss weak! He did not save me!' He raised the club with the burning sword stuck through it. 'The changrr is strongrr!'

'We shall see,' said Teobalt, and rushed to meet him, bellowing a prayer.

Orenstihl roared a response and a few of his gors turned from pursuing the archers to see what threatened their leader. Felix and Kat ran to block them as Teobalt and the bestial templar slammed together, swinging hard. The gor's sword-pierced club smashed against the old knight's blade with the force of an avalanche, and Felix thought the fight was over before it had begun. But Teobalt had been a knight for more years than Felix had been alive. He knew something of swordplay. He gave way before the blow, letting it take his sword around, then came up over the top of his shield and hacked down into Orenstihl's shoulder, chopping through his pauldron and finding flesh.

The other gors howled with fury and surged forwards to help the corrupted templar. Felix blocked a spear thrust aimed straight for Teobalt's head. Kat hamstrung a beast who was raising a mace.

Felix cast a swift look around as he and Kat fought to keep the knight from being flanked. Things looked grim. Beastmen were pushing back a spear company to their right, as their captain screamed, 'Hold the line! Hold the line!' as his soldiers tossed away their weapons and fled. Beyond that, a dozen gors tore Lord Plaschke-Miesner from his saddle as he slashed weakly at them. Near him, Rodi stood over the body of Snorri Nosebiter, defending it against a circle of beastmen. Was the old Slayer dead? The massive corpse of a minotaur lay beside him, its skull a red crater, so if he was, he had gone as a Slayer should. To the left, Gotrek cursed as Gargorath's axe fed on another soldier and restored its master's wounds once again.

The crunch of a heavy impact brought Felix's head around. Sir Teobalt was staggering back, his shield split in two, as Orenstihl advanced on him. With a curse, Felix disengaged from his opponent and lunged at the beast-templar, gashing his shoulder. He grunted and swiped the sword-pierced club at him without turning from Teobalt. Felix threw himself to the ground, the flaming blade flashing an inch above his head.

'Felix!' cried Kat.

Orenstihl's gors stabbed down at him. He flung himself aside inches ahead of their points. Kat hauled him to his feet and they danced back, blocking desperately as the beasts hacked at them.

'Hold on, Sir Teobalt!' Felix cried, trying to edge around the gors and get back to the templar.

Suddenly a handful of arrows thwacked into the beastmen and they screamed and twisted. The archers had rallied!

Kat cheered, and she and Felix cut down two of the pin-cushioned beasts before they could recover. Kat shattered the teeth of a third with her axe and it fell back spitting blood.

Together she and Felix leapt the dying gors and ran for Sir Teobalt. They were seconds too late. With a sickening thud, the beast-templar slammed his club into the old knight's breastplate and folded him up like a rag doll.

'Sir Teobalt!' cried Felix.

The knight's sword fell from his limp fingers as Orenstihl lifted the club, and Teobalt with it. Felix gaped, his stomach churning as he saw that a foot of flaming steel jutted from the back of Teobalt's cuirass. The beast had impaled him on the club's sword-spike, and was now raising it to shake him off.

'Sir Teobalt!' cried Kat. 'No!'

Felix charged forwards with her and slashed at Orenstihl's head as she hacked at his knees. The changed templar stumbled back, wrenching the club's burning blade from Teobalt's body, and nearly decapitating Kat with a backswing. She ducked and dodged behind his legs.

Felix shouted to the archers. 'Shoot it! Shoot the beast!'

But unfortunately the corrupted templar was too closely engaged with Kat for them to shoot. In fact, the damned girl had leapt on the beast-man's back, and was clinging to his breastplate with one hand while trying to bury her remaining axe in his skull with the other!

Orenstihl roared and reached for her. She hacked at his fingers and sent one spinning. The beast howled, but still caught her wrist and flung her down on the ground in front of him. She landed hard on Sir Teobalt's body and bounced to the dirt, dazed, her axe flying from her hand as the beastman raised his terrible club to strike her.

'No, you cursed goat!' cried Felix, running forwards and slashing for the thing's unprotected waist.

Orenstihl turned his swing and the flaming sword-spike whipped towards him like the point of a scythe. Felix blocked the blade, but the end of the club glanced off his shoulder and slammed him to the dirt beside Kat.

'Are…?' he said, unable to draw a breath to finish the question.

'I'm…' She stopped and nodded, also unable to breathe.

They crabbed back from the beast-templar as he advanced, then scrambled to their feet as he swung at them.

'Now!' shouted Felix, glancing towards the archers. 'Shoot it!'

But the bowmen had turned to fire on another fight and didn't hear.

Kat made a desperate lunge for Orenstihl's ankles, but his club swung down and she dived aside, crying out.

'Kat!' called Felix. Was she hurt? 'Keep away from her!' He slashed at the beast-knight, trying to keep him from turning to finish her.

It worked too well. Orenstihl gave Felix all his attention, swinging the pierced club at him in an impenetrable X pattern that smashed away Felix's every attempt to stab through. Each blow felt like it was breaking his arms, and forced him back and back.

Then, just as Felix felt he couldn't raise his sword to meet another strike, the corrupted templar cried out and stumbled, throwing his left arm out to one side for balance. Felix took the opening, and stabbed him in the armpit through the gap between his vambrace and his breastplate. Orenstihl howled and raised his club for a last strike, but something flashed between his legs from behind and buried itself in his crotch with a sickening *chunk*.

Felix pulled his sword from the monster's ribs and jumped back as he whimpered, then toppled forwards onto his face. Kat was standing behind him, barehanded. Her axe was sticking up from beneath the beast-templar's loincloth like a wooden tail.

'Well struck,' said Felix, swallowing. It was the first time he had ever felt sympathy for a beastman.

She gave him a weary grin as she recovered the axe.

They hurried to Teobalt, and Felix was surprised to see that the old templar still clung to life.

He lifted his trembling head, looking blindly around. 'Is... is it slain?'

'Aye, Sir Teobalt,' said Felix. 'It is dead.'

'And the banner? The sword?'

Felix looked back, grimacing. The banner was soaked in gore and caked in filth. The sword was stuck up to the hilt through a heavy wooden club and bent halfway along the blade. A more degraded set of regalia Felix could not imagine. Nonetheless, he went back and cut the belt that held the banner to the beastman's body, while Kat grasped the heavy club that held the sword and dragged it back.

'I'm afraid they are... beyond repair,' said Felix, returning to kneel beside the dying templar. He held the banner out to him as Kat turned the club so that the hilt of the sword was at his side.

Teobalt shook his head as he clutched the banner and gripped the sword. 'That matters not. They are returned. The honour of the order is restored.'

He coughed wetly, spraying blood, then drew a painful breath and looked up at Felix with his pale blue eyes. 'The Order of the Fiery Heart is... grateful, Herr Jaeger. You have done well. You are... worthy of Karaghul.' He patted Felix's arm with a delicate hand. 'All is well,' he said. 'All is well.'

Then he laid his head back on the hard ground, folded his arms across the banner, and allowed himself to die.

Felix and Kat bowed their heads over him.

'Morr watch over you, sir,' said Kat.

'Sigmar welcome you,' said Felix.

A thunder of bestial hooves interrupted their prayers. A company of spearmen had broken, and a rush of beastmen was charging into the square. Felix and Kat jumped up, then tried to lift Sir Teobalt's body and drag it back. There was no time. The beasts were too swift. Felix and Kat turned and ran with the fleeing archers in amongst the herd of screaming, rearing cavalry horses behind them.

Felix looked around as he shoved between the surging beasts. The square was close to collapsing on all sides. The two young lords were dead. The companies were shattered, and the beasts were breaking through everywhere. The day was lost. It would be over in minutes now. He searched for Rodi again and could only see a heap of beastman corpses taller than Kat. He turned in Gotrek's direction and saw the Slayer still battling Gargorath while a scrum of beastmen and von Volgen's men-at-arms fought all around them. The black-furred war-leader was staggering from a dozen wounds. The Slayer looked little better.

'We must help him,' said Kat.

Felix shook his head. 'He will want no help. But I'd like to be at his side at the end.'

'Then let's go to him,' said Kat.

Felix looked at her smiling, bloodied face, then out at the roiling sea of slaughter that was between them and the Slayer. They would die in the attempt – but on the other hand, they would die standing here just as certainly.

He smiled back. 'Aye, let's.'

He pulled her to him and kissed her as they were knocked this way and that amid the surging horses. Though tinged with blood and dirt, it was as sweet as any kiss he had ever tasted.

They broke apart.

'See you in Sigmar's halls,' said Felix.

Kat grinned. 'I'll race you there.'

With twin battle cries they charged from between the horses and dived into the press of beasts and men, sword and axe whirling. Felix cut through a beastman's neck on his first stroke, and gutted another on his second. Kat severed the spine of a third. It was easy to fight when you had no fear, when you knew the outcome was inevitable, no matter what you did. A strange, savage joy welled up in Felix's chest as he fought on. Perhaps, he thought, this is what the Slayers felt. Perhaps this was why they longed so fiercely for battle.

Ahead of him, through the mad jumble of murder that the battle had become, Felix saw Gargorath knock Gotrek back with a brutal blow, then sink his axe into the back of one of his own gors. The surprised beastman screamed, but not as loudly as the vulture-headed axe, which drew its life force from it and fed it to Gargorath.

As Felix and Kat stole horrified glances through their own fights, the war-leader's wounds once again closed up, and he was as whole as he had been at the start of the fight. Gotrek staggered up to face him again, as weary as Felix had ever seen him, and bleeding from a half-dozen deep wounds, but his single eye still blazing with fury. Gargorath was his exact opposite – for though his body was once again unmarked, and he still fought with unnatural energy, as he strode forwards, his glowing blue eyes registered fear and uncertainty. It was clear that he had expected the fight to be over long ago.

Then, with alarming suddenness, it *was* over. Felix caught a flash of inspiration in Gotrek's eye as he blocked another of Gargorath's brutal slashes. The Slayer backed away, feigning weakness, then, as the warleader slashed again, Gotrek turned his axe so that the blade met the haft of the daemon weapon edge on. With an inhuman shriek and a blinding flash of blue light, the head of the vulture-headed axe was severed from its haft and spun away to bite the bloody ground with its glowing eyes fading to black.

Gargorath was left holding a sizzling stick.

With a triumphant roar, Gotrek charged in, bringing his axe up in an overhand swing that bit into the beastman's gold and steel breastplate so deeply that the rune-inscribed head disappeared entirely. Gargorath grunted and staggered back, tearing the axe from Gotrek's grip. He looked down at the weapon, blinking stupidly, then, with the slow majesty of a stone tower collapsing, toppled backwards to land flat on his back.

Gotrek chuckled, than stepped up onto the dead beast's massive chest, levered his axe free and spat in his face. 'Heal that, you overgrown sheep,' he rasped.

The other beasts had fallen back from Gotrek at the death of their invincible leader, but now they surged in again, howling for his blood. He roared in response and rushed to meet them.

Kat and Felix raced to him and fought at his side, still in the blissful trance of nothing-left-to-lose – though Felix was slightly sad for the Slayer. He almost wished that Gargorath had killed the Slayer, for it was certainly a grander doom to die fighting a great leader then to be laid low by the faceless numbers of the endless herd. He also grieved for Snorri, who would not now be supping in Grimnir's halls, but instead would wander as a forlorn ghost for the rest of eternity. But these were passing concerns, as all his being was taken up with the sheer physical joy of block and parry, strike and counterstrike. He took a terrible cut on the leg, but didn't feel it. A club numbed his off hand. He didn't feel that either. He was content to go down fighting in the middle of the great swirl of battle, knowing that he went with his friends at his side.

Then, at the edge of his consciousness, he heard a boom, and then another boom, and then a blare of horns and a roar of voices all raised in unison. He killed a beastman who looked away from him, craning its neck to find the source of the sounds.

For a moment, Felix could not conceive of what was happening. Since he had raced down into the battle from Tarnhalt's Crown, the scope of his world had been no more than the beasts around him and the short time he had to fight them, so this strange intrusion of distant sounds was as alien to him as air would be to a fish. But then, above the rising roar, he finally understood the words the far-off voices were shouting.

'Von Kotzebue! Von Kotzebue! The Empire! The Empire!'

TWENTY-TWO

It struck Felix as funny how quickly all his fear and pain and worry for the future came back with the knowledge that help had arrived. Hope was an evil thing. Without hope he had been at peace, knowing that his death was inevitable. With hope, suddenly he was desperate to stay alive and keep alive those that were nearest and dearest to him. Suddenly his heart was hammering with anxiety, and his limbs aching with fatigue. Could he stay alive long enough for von Kotzebue's army to reach them? Could he protect Kat? Could Snorri be saved? Was the old Slayer still alive?

The wounds that hadn't troubled him when he knew that they were only momentary precursors to death now nearly crippled him with their agony. He felt faint and sick and weak, and wasn't sure he could continue to fight – something that hadn't mattered in the least only seconds before.

Over the horned heads of the beastmen that surrounded him and Kat and Gotrek, Felix saw columns of ranked cavalry pouring down over the hills to the east and west, with wide ranks of spearmen racing down after them, snare drums rattling and banners waving as cannons and mortars belched fire over their heads. A great cheer rose from the throats of the beleaguered men in the centre of the thronging beastmen at the sight, and Felix and Kat raised their voices as well.

Felix couldn't see the impact when the two prongs of von Kotzebue's army slammed into the flanks of the herd, but he could feel it and hear it – a heavy shuddering crash that shook the ground and sent a ripple through the beastmen, like a boulder being thrown into a swamp.

All around Felix and Kat, von Volgen's and Plaschke-Miesner's soldiers and sergeants were calling encouragement to each other and fighting with renewed vigour.

'Hold on, lads!' cried one. 'Help's on the way!'

'Saved, by Sigmar!' called another.

'Look sharp, now!' shouted a third. 'Don't want those damned Middenlanders seeing us look beat, do we?'

'All be over soon,' said a fourth.

Of course, there was a lot more fighting to be done before it was all truly over, but at least the tide had turned. Felix and Kat and Gotrek lined up with a company of swordsmen, and they presented a united front against the panicking beasts.

For a time, the gors fought savagely against the three fronts that were ranged against them, and hundreds of Von Kotzebue's men fell after the initial charge, as well as hundreds more in the deteriorating square of troops trapped in their centre, but after less than a quarter of an hour, as withering volleys of arrow fire ate away at their edges, and the spears of the infantry and the lances of the knights pressed in on them on both sides, the beasts finally could take no more and turned and fled south, clawing and killing one another in their desperation to be away.

After that it was butchers' work, with von Kotzebue's lances riding down fleeing packs of beasts, while his infantry closed the jaws of their pincer movement to catch the rest in the middle. It was not easy work, however. In fact, this was the hottest fighting of the battle for the survivors in the remains of the square, for the beastmen in their terror fought with the frenzy of trapped rats, and tried to tear a hole through the Empire lines in a desperate attempt to escape. There were a terrible few minutes where many men who had thought salvation was at hand were felled by flailing horns and clubs and axes. But finally von Kotzebue's men cut down the last few gors and the rescuers met the survivors in the centre of the blood-soaked and eerily silent field.

'Well met, cousins,' said a greatsword captain in blue and grey who stood beneath von Kotzebue's banner.

'Aye,' said a Talabecland sergeant. 'If a little late.'

The captain ignored his comment and looked around. 'Do Lord von Volgen and Lord Plaschke-Miesner still stand?'

'Yer a bit late for that too,' said a voice from the ranks.

'But too soon for me,' muttered Gotrek under his breath, as the conversation between the armies continued. 'Another few minutes and I would have found my doom.'

Felix rolled his eyes. 'I'm sorry you were disappointed.'

Then his pain caught up with him and he groaned and looked for a place to sit and bind his wounds. Kat did the same, as did the rest of the army. All around them the soldiers sank down in weariness and pain, calling for surgeons and drinking from canteens and flasks. The cries of the wounded and dying were pitiful to hear.

Then a deeper voice boomed over the rest. 'Gurnisson! Here!'

Gotrek, Felix and Kat looked up. Rodi was waving a torch at them from beside the pile of beastman corpses he and Snorri had made. He held Snorri's warhammer in his hands. Gotrek grunted, then stumped heavily towards him. Felix and Kat exchanged a look, then rose again and limped after him. Felix was certain they would find Snorri dead, and was saddened by it. What a terrible irony that only the one who could least afford to die had perished.

'Is he dead?' asked Gotrek, as they approached.

Rodi shook his head and Felix breathed a sigh of relief.

The young Slayer was covered in gashes from head to foot, the worst being his left cheek, which was opened to the bone, but he seemed to be unbothered by any of them. 'He lives,' he said. 'But I broke my axe on a beastman's skull, and have need of yours.'

Without further explanation he turned and crawled up and over the ring of dead beastmen, using Snorri's hammer to balance himself. They followed, wobbling on the loose and uncertain ground.

In the centre of the ring lay Snorri, alive, but only barely. He was whiter than any dwarf Felix had ever seen, and bruised and cut all over.

He grinned weakly when he saw them. 'Snorri got the big bull,' he said.

'Aye, Father Rustskull,' said Rodi, pointing with the head of the warhammer. 'But the big bull got you too.'

Felix blanched as he looked where Rodi indicated. Snorri's right leg was a mangled mess from just below the knee – a tangle of shredded meat and shattered bone. His foot was missing entirely. A tourniquet had been tied above the knee to stop the flow of blood, but there was already too much on the ground.

'The minotaur hit him with its axe,' said Rodi. 'But it was dull from chopping trees. He needs a good, clean cut.'

Gotrek nodded. Felix winced, though he knew it had to be done.

Gotrek wiped his axe as clean as he could on the shirt of a dead soldier, then took Rodi's torch and held it under the cutting edge until both sides were black with carbon, then handed the torch to Kat.

'Sit on him,' he told Rodi. 'And hold the leg.' He looked at Felix. 'Manling, hold the good leg aside. Little one, bring the torch close.'

Felix nodded and squatted to grab Snorri's left boot as Rodi sat on the old Slayer's stomach and pressed down on his upper leg, just above the knee, while Kat, looking slightly queasy, lowered the torch.

'Snorri is ready,' said Snorri, closing his eyes.

Gotrek stepped up and raised his axe, sighting down with his one eye to line up his swing.

Felix pulled Snorri's left leg away from his right, then turned his head so he wouldn't have to see. There was a swish and a thud, and Snorri grunted and jerked, then lay still.

Felix opened his eyes again and looked. The damage had been cut away, leaving a clean, straight cut through bone and muscle that looked disturbingly like an uncooked steak. Because of the tourniquet there wasn't much blood, which somehow made it even worse. At least he lives, Felix thought. At least Snorri still has a chance to recover his memory before he meets his doom.

Rodi stood and turned, looking pleased with Gotrek's work. 'All right, Father Rustskull?'

Snorri opened his eyes and nodded, though he looked even paler than before. 'Snorri is fine, but he would like a drink soon.'

'And Snorri shall have his drink,' said Rodi. 'Just as soon as we find a surgeon with some hot pitch.'

Gotrek wiped his axe clean again, then found two discarded spears and crossed them. He and Rodi lifted Snorri onto the spears, then picked them up like stretcher ends and carried the old Slayer out of the ring of beastman corpses and across the field in search of a surgeon, with Felix and Kat following behind.

Felix shook his head as they walked, amazed that they had all survived. The battle he had been certain would be the Slayers' doom had ended, and they were all still alive. Maybe they truly were fated for some great destiny. It seemed the only explanation for their continued existence.

A cold wind blew through the valley as they walked past the place where Gargorath and his headless axe lay on the ground. Felix shivered and pulled his old red cloak closer around him. The wind stank of death and moaned like a tormented soul. Then he paused, the hair rising on the back of his neck, and looked around.

Though the moaning and the chill and smell continued unabated, nothing moved in the wind. Felix's hair didn't flutter around his face. His cloak didn't flap around his legs. The banners of the armies didn't lift in the breeze.

He turned to the others. They had stopped too. All around the field, conversations stalled and the cries of the wounded died away.

Kat's eyes were as wide as saucers. 'Something... something is wrong,' she said.

Gotrek and Rodi set Snorri's litter down and readied their weapons warily.

'The light,' said Gotrek, frowning. 'It's the light.' He looked up.

Felix and the others followed his gaze, and a collective gasp escaped their throats.

The moons were colliding, directly over their heads. Morrslieb was eclipsing Mannslieb, sliding across it like a dirty coin covering a freshly minted one. As they watched, the Chaos moon occluded its fairer sister entirely, and Mannslieb's clean white light vanished, to be replaced by a sickly green luminescence that spread across the battlefield like a plague, making the wounded and the dying appear not only maimed, but diseased as well.

All over the valley, soldiers stared up into the sky, cursing and praying to their gods.

'It's the end!' cried a man. 'We have sinned and this is our punishment!'

'Sigmar save us!' wailed another.

A rustling from behind him made Felix turn. A wounded beastman was trying to rise, though it only had one hand. Gotrek kicked it in the head and it fell over. Felix blinked. The beastman had no intestines either. They had fallen out through the hole in its abdomen. Felix shivered. How was the thing alive?

Another beastman twitched and tried to stand. And another. Beside them, an archer with an axe through his chest and a missing arm opened unseeing eyes and sat up.

Felix stepped back and backed into Kat, who was looking at a drummer boy with no legs squirming on the ground and trying to turn over.

'What is happening?' she asked.

Felix only shook his head, unable to form an answer.

A heavy thudding and shifting to their left made them all turn. Kat gasped. Rodi cursed. Gotrek grunted. Felix stared, his heart pounding double time in his constricted chest. Gargorath was getting to his feet. Though Felix could see the monster's shattered ribs through the gaping hole Gotrek had smashed in his breastplate, the war-leader was somehow still alive.

'It's impossible,' Felix said.

All over the battlefield, broken figures were standing, both man and beastman, while soldiers cried out in dismay and fear.

Kat clutched Felix's arm. 'What is happening?' she asked again, an edge of panic creeping into her voice.

'It is midnight on Hexensnacht,' said a weird, shrill voice behind them.

They turned. A tall thin figure in plate armour was clanking stiffly towards them, its head cocked at an uncomfortable angle. 'The year has turned,' it said. 'The age of the Empire of man has passed.'

Felix stumbled back as he saw that the knight was Sir Teobalt, the blood still running sluggishly from the fatal wound the bestial templar Orenstihl had given him. His face, as he approached them, showed no animation. His eyes stared fixedly above them and to the left, and though his jaw moved, it was jerky and stiff, and not quite in time with his words. 'The age of the Empire of the dead has begun.'

'Grungni!' said Rodi. 'What's happened to him?'

'What has happened to him,' said the thing that had been Sir Teobalt, 'is what will happen to you all.'

Felix frowned. The voice wasn't Teobalt's, but he recognised it all the same. How did he know it? He couldn't think.

'My necromancy could not work with the herdstone present,' said the same voice from beside them. They turned and saw that Gargorath's jaws were moving too. 'But I knew your axe could destroy it,' the beast said. 'So I showed you the way to smash it.'

'And smash it you did,' said the same voice again from yet another direction.

Felix and the others spun around.

Lord von Volgen and Lord Plaschke-Miesner were lurching towards them, von Volgen no more than a paper-skinned mummy, and both dead from terrible wounds. 'Then I whispered in the ears of these young lords,' the corpses said together. 'Telling them to attack. Telling them of the glory to be found in death.'

As the dead youths continued speaking, the same high eerie voice began to echo from the mouth of every dead beastman and every risen soldier on the field. 'Now,' it chorused. 'Now I invite you to join them in that glory.'

The corpses of the men and beastmen laughed in shrill unison as they lumbered towards Gotrek, Felix, Rodi and Kat, raising their weapons in their stiff hands, and though Felix had failed to recognise the voice that rattled from their dead throats, he suddenly recognised their laughter.

It was the mad giggle of Hans the hermit.

ZOMBIESLAYER

'There was no end to the horror. No sooner had we felled the beast-shaman and sundered the stone that might have destroyed the Empire, than a new threat arose, deadlier and more gruesome than the last, an army of the living dead, ten thousand strong.

'In the dire days that followed, when madness and despair were our constant companions, it seemed certain that his doom had found Gotrek at last, though in a form no Slayer would ever wish for. But despite the danger and hardship and the threat of an unworthy death, Gotrek's most painful challenge came not from our enemies, but from his oldest friend. To save the soul of Snorri Nosebiter, Gotrek's sacred oath to Grimnir would be tested as never before, and I could not be sure which would break first, the friendship or the vow.'

– From *My Travels with Gotrek*, Vol VIII, by Herr Felix Jaeger
(Altdorf Press, 2529)

ONE

Felix Jaeger stared in horror as eerie laughter echoed in unison from the dead throats of the encroaching zombie horde. Dead man and dead beastman alike, they all laughed with the same voice.

'Hans,' he said, edging back. 'Hans the Hermit is behind this.'

Gotrek Gurnisson hefted his rune axe. 'Should have gutted him the first time I saw him,' he growled.

Kat wiped her blood-grimed brow with the back of a bruised hand. Her skin, in the sick green light of Morrslieb, looked as dead as that of the walking corpses. 'We just killed them,' she groaned. 'Now we have to do it all over again?'

'Good,' said Rodi Balkisson, smoothing his braided Slayer's crest. 'Maybe this time we'll find our doom.'

'You may, Balkisson,' said Gotrek. 'But Snorri Nosebiter will not.'

The Slayer turned and helped Snorri up from the makeshift stretcher he and Rodi had carried him on after Snorri had lost his right leg. He slung Snorri's arm over his shoulder as Rodi did the same with Snorri's other arm, and with Felix and Kat following, the three dwarfs stumped towards Baron Emil von Kotzebue's troops, who were closing ranks and lowering spears against the undead army in the centre of the narrow valley.

'Snorri wouldn't mind slaying a few more beastmen, actually,' said Snorri, looking over his shoulder at the shaggy undead monsters that groped and stumbled after them.

'Sorry, Father Rustskull,' said Rodi. 'No slaying for you until you make your pilgrimage, remember?'

'Oh, yes,' said Snorri mournfully. 'Snorri forgot.'

As rally horns blasted bright tantaras and cannons roared from the hills, weary handfuls of spearmen and knights fought through the dead towards the relief column from every corner of the battlefield – cutting down corpses that wore the same uniforms as themselves.

That was the worst of it, thought Felix. Though half the zombies that threatened the living were risen beastmen, the other half were men he and the rest of the Imperial force had been fighting alongside not a quarter of an hour before. All around, valiant soldiers who had ranked up with their brothers in desperate besieged squares against the raging sea of beastmen, now instead lurched along with those same horrors and attacked their old comrades with blank-eyed ferocity – in death becoming traitors to their own kind.

Felix parried a blow from the corpse of Sir Teobalt von Dreschler, who, until he had died in Felix's arms, had been a noble templar of the Order of the Fiery Heart. Now he was a horrible, animate cadaver, with a dangling jaw and a glistening red wound in the middle of his caved-in chest. Kat hesitated when she could have hamstrung the old knight, and nearly lost a hand when he lashed out at her.

'How can I strike him?' she moaned. 'He was our friend.'

'Who he was is gone,' said Gotrek, cutting down a beast-corpse. 'Kill it.'

With a sob, Kat buried her hatchet in Sir Teobalt's knee as Felix hacked off his head with Karaghul, a relic of the old templar's order which Teobalt had bequeathed to Felix only days before.

'With his own sword,' said Felix bitterly as the old man fell.

Felix was so battered and tired as they pushed on that he could barely lift the blade against the dead that stumbled towards them. An hour ago, he and Kat and the three Slayers had charged into the circle of standing stones atop the hill known as Tarnhalt's Crown and attacked Urslak Cripplehorn, a powerful beast-shaman, attempting to stop him from completing a ceremony that would have turned every human within the Drakwald into a beastman. Half an hour ago, with Urslak dead, they had raced down into the valley below the Crown to join the armies of Viscount Oktaf Plaschke-Miesner and Lord Giselbert von Volgen in their ill-advised attack on the shaman's ten thousand-strong herd. Ten minutes ago, the forces of Baron Emil von Kotzebue had thundered into the valley and slammed into the flanks of the beastmen, and the young lords' doomed armies had been saved – though it was too late for the young lords themselves. One minute ago, Morrslieb, the Chaos moon, had eclipsed its fairer sibling, Mannslieb, at precisely midnight on Hexensnacht, the last second of the old year and the first second of the new, and all the dead on the battlefield, both man and beastman, had risen together in undeath and turned their dull, staring eyes upon the living. Felix had not stopped fighting in all that time.

The hulking corpse of Gargorath the God-Touched, the war-leader of Urslak's massive herd, staggered in front of the Slayers, moaning and swinging the cloven-hoofed leg of another beastman as if it were a club. The hole that Gotrek's rune axe had made in the beastman's chest when the Slayer had earlier killed it did not appear to be troubling it in the least.

'You want to die twice?' rasped Gotrek as he, Snorri and Rodi ducked the meat-club.

The stumbling beast-zombie turned after them, but Gotrek left Snorri to Rodi and swung his rune axe in a high arc behind him. The blade *chunked* into the side of Gargorath's black-furred neck and severed its spine.

'So be it.'

The dead beast toppled forwards as Gotrek wrenched his axe free and stepped back under Snorri's arm. They hurried on, falling in with other survivors and hacking in every direction. Fortunately, the zombies were still only rising in ones and twos, and it did not seem that Hans the Hermit yet had full control of their limbs. They jerked and twitched, and fell as often as they walked, or wandered off in the wrong direction, but with each passing second, their movements grew more certain and their attention more focussed – all turning towards von Kotzebue's besieged column like blind mosquitoes attracted by the scent of blood.

The closer Felix, Kat and the Slayers fought to the column, the thicker the mass of zombies became, until it was a solid wall through which Felix could see almost nothing.

'Dress ranks! Square up! Square up!' shouted a sergeant from somewhere beyond the corpses.

'Wounded on the carts! Them as can walk, carry them that can't! Move!'

'We will retreat in good order, curse you! If you want to fear something, fear my boot, or you'll get it up your backside!'

'Heads, necks or legs, gentlemen! Heads, necks or legs! All other strikes are worthless!'

This last came from a splendid-looking old knight in the colours of Middenland, who Felix saw over the heads of the zombies, lashing about vigorously with a long sword from the back of a heavily barded charger. His close-shaved head was bare, and he shouted his orders through the largest, whitest and most magnificent moustaches Felix had ever seen. This must be von Kotzebue, Felix thought – their saviour. Fighting beside him was a thick-necked, broad-chested nobleman, with a pugnacious bulldog face that Felix almost recognised. He wore a surcoat of mustard and burgundy over his plate, and the crowned eagle of Talabecland on his shield.

'My son!' the Talabeclander was shouting. 'Find my son!'

Hearing that, Felix recognised the face at last. It was a middle-aged mirror to that of Giselbert von Volgen, one of the young lords who had led his tiny army against the overwhelming might of the beastmen. This must be Giselbert's father, and he was shouting in vain. Giselbert was dead now, alas, killed by Gargorath, and raised again like all the other corpses on the field. He would not hear his father's cries.

Ten yards from the column, Felix, Kat and the Slayers found their way blocked by a supply cart, stranded amidst the swarming undead. Its driver and cargo men fought for their lives atop its load – the neatly stowed canvas and sticks of a score of officers' tents – as their horses kicked and screamed.

'Help us!' shouted the driver towards the troops.

But with a ragged blast of bugles and a roar of 'Company, march!' the knights and foot soldiers began to push their way south, fighting for every step.

Gotrek nodded Rodi towards the cart as the driver wailed with dismay.

'Here,' said the Slayer, hooking a zombie aside with his axe and shouldering his way to the tailgate. 'Up, Nosebiter.'

He and Rodi shoved Snorri up onto the pile of canvas, then fanned back the zombies and climbed up after him. Felix kicked back a corpse that had him by the leg, then pulled himself up as Kat clambered up beside him, panting.

'Drive!' Gotrek called to the driver as he and Rodi swiped back at the undead beasts and men that closed in after them. 'We'll hold them.'

'Oh thank you, sir dwarf,' said the man. 'Thank you!'

He took up the reins as Gotrek, Rodi, Felix and Kat joined his cargo men along the sides of the wagon and began hacking and kicking at the encroaching horde.

'Manling, little one,' barked Gotrek. 'Keep them off the horses.'

Felix groaned with fatigue, but crawled past the driver with Kat, then hopped awkwardly onto the backs of his carthorses. The terrified animals bucked and shrieked as Felix and Kat clung to their backs and slashed at the clawing zombies, but when a path had been cleared, they took it, and strained slowly towards the retreating column through a fetlock-deep swamp of twice-dead corpses.

Then a voice rose above the din of battle. 'My son! Stop! We must go back!'

Felix looked up. Lord von Volgen was pointing directly at the wagon, his eyes wide.

'Von Kotzebue!' he cried. 'Stop the column! My son!'

His son? Felix looked back, frowning. A figure in beautifully crafted armour was pulling itself up onto the tailgate of the cart at the head of a throng of undead. It wore the same mustard and burgundy as Lord von Volgen, but its face under its dented helmet was as withered and lifeless as when Felix had last seen it – when it and the corpse of its cousin,

Oktaf Plaschke-Miesner, had moments ago shambled towards him in a horrible mockery of life.

Gotrek and Rodi brained and decapitated the young lord's corpse, then kicked it back into the rest.

A wail of anguish rose from the column. 'Giselbert! No! My son!'

A claw raked Felix's arm, and he had to return his attention to the zombies around his horse, slashing and hacking and kicking them away as Kat did the same on the second horse. The strikes of the dead were clumsy and easy to block, but they were so many, and so relentless, that it was all she and Felix could do to keep them at bay and stay on their mounts.

After what seemed an hour, the cart reached the column, and the line of spearmen who were desperately staving off the shambling horde parted and let them through. Once behind their ranks, Felix and Kat flopped across the necks of their horses and just lay there, panting. Felix was as exhausted as he had ever been, and now that his limbs were at rest, the pain began to seep into the dozens of wounds he had taken during that long, long night. He was cut, bruised, scraped and battered from head to foot. There was nowhere on his body that didn't hurt.

'Well, that's that, then,' said Rodi, behind him. 'We can go back and find our dooms now.'

'You can,' said Gotrek. 'I stay with Snorri Nosebiter until the column wins clear.'

'But…'

Felix looked back as Rodi turned from the sea of zombies to glare at Snorri, who lay in the middle of the cart, tightening the tourniquet that was wrapped around his severed leg.

'All right,' Rodi grunted at last. 'I owe him that, but afterwards, no more waiting. There is a great doom here.'

'Aye,' said Gotrek. 'No more waiting.' He jumped down from the cart and started towards the left flank of the column. 'Come on, beardling. We'll warm up with these.'

Rodi hopped down after him, grinning. 'Good. The sooner these manlings get away, the sooner we have the rest to ourselves.'

The two Slayers shouldered forwards to join the sidestepping line of spearmen who stabbed mechanically into the surging mass of undead as the column marched out of the valley.

'Heads, necks and legs!' roared Rodi, bashing around at the zombies with his hammer.

The spearmen cheered and echoed his call. 'Heads, necks and legs!'

Gotrek didn't join in. He was too busy slaying.

'We should help them,' said Kat, rising wearily from her horse's neck.

'Aye,' said Felix, 'we should.'

But when he tried to push himself upright, his arms shook so much he knew he would be useless on the front line. He would only add himself to the dead, and he didn't fancy Gotrek slaying him for becoming a zombie. Still, there was other work that needed to be done.

Felix saw that the surgeons' assistants were overwhelmed by the number of wounded and dead falling back from the flanks and the rearguard. They were carrying them to the baggage carts as fast as they could, but men were still being left behind for want of bearers to carry them.

He dismounted and beckoned to Kat. 'Come on,' he said. 'This we can do.'

A great cheering arose and Felix and Kat looked up from laying another wounded spearman on the cart that had brought them there. It was following von Kotzebue's ragged column of knights, spearmen and halberdiers up through a low pass between two hills at the southern end of the valley of Tarnhalt's Crown, and all the men were shaking their weapons and roaring and thrusting up two-finger salutes back towards the battlefield.

Felix blinked. He and Kat had been so focussed on carrying the wounded that they hadn't noticed the column's progress. There were no zombies around them. The shambling dead were all further down the slope, funnelled together by the constricting hills and held back by a rearguard of spearmen that blocked the narrow pass – a noble sacrifice that would allow the rest of the army to escape.

'We – we won free,' said Kat, staring.

'And now we're going back,' said Gotrek, as he and Rodi joined them at the tailgate.

Felix's heart thudded in his chest. This meant that he and the Slayer were parting ways at last. He didn't know what to say.

But as he opened his mouth in the vain hope that something appropriate would fall out, a cold wind, reeking of death and earth, blew up from the valley and made the brave cheering falter and die. Lightning flashed above them, and thunder followed it, a deafening crack that went echoing across the endless Barren Hills.

Felix and the others looked up with the rest of the column. The two moons were now hidden behind a pale scrim of clouds, and had pulled apart from their earlier eclipse. Now they looked like the glowing eyes of a warp-dust addict gleaming through a mask of dirty gauze. And before them, stepping out of a fading cloud of shadow at the crest of the hill above the pass, was the twisted figure of Hans the Hermit, laughing maniacally.

'Yes,' he hissed, as the soldiers shivered and stared. 'Flee to your masters. Tell them I am coming. Tell them that every castle and town between here and Altdorf will fall before me. Tell them their dead will become my army. Tell them I will take Altdorf with a hundred thousand corpses, and that the Empire of Sigmar will become the Empire of the Dead.'

Pistols and long guns cracked at the hermit, and Kat unslung her bow and sent an arrow speeding his way, but he paid them no heed, and none of the missiles seemed to find its mark.

'You may outrun the tide now,' the hermit said. 'But soon the sea of death will overlap your walls and drown you. Then you will rise and walk with us. All will die. All will be one. All will be mine.'

The spearmen and knights roared defiance at this pronouncement, breaking ranks to start up the steep slope of the hill, and Gotrek and Rodi followed, bellowing dwarf curses, but before any of them could take more than three steps, mist and shadows coalesced around the hermit and he was gone as suddenly as he had appeared, and the ridge was empty.

Felix shivered and pulled his red Sudenland wool cloak tighter around his shoulders as the men whispered prayers of warding at this sorcerous disappearance. He hoped Hans's words were only boasting, but after seeing how the supposed hermit had tricked him and Gotrek and the others into destroying Urslak's herdstone so that he could work his dark magic, he wasn't willing to bet on it. Whoever he was, Hans was a powerful and cunning necromancer, and Felix feared they had only seen a fraction of his power.

'Come on, Gurnisson,' said Rodi. 'The manlings have picked a good place. We'll be able to hold the corpses there for a good long time.'

Gotrek nodded. 'Aye.'

'Snorri could help if he had a crutch,' said Snorri, sitting up in the cart.

Gotrek turned and scowled at him. 'You are going to Karak Kadrin, Nosebiter. This is not your doom.'

Snorri hung his head. 'Snorri forgot again.'

Felix and Kat stepped to the Slayers.

Felix swallowed. 'So... so it's goodbye at last,' he said, inanely.

'Aye, manling,' said Gotrek, and though he tried to be solemn, Felix could see he was finding it hard to keep the eagerness from his voice. 'Remember your pledge. Bring Snorri Nosebiter to the Shrine of Grimnir and you are free.'

'I'll get him there,' said Felix.

'Goodbye, Gotrek,' said Kat. 'Goodbye, Rodi. May Grimnir welcome you to his halls.'

Felix held out his hand, but as Gotrek made to clasp it, a thunder of hooves shook the ground. A score of knights were galloping down the column, Baron von Kotzebue and Lord von Volgen at their head, and pulled up at the back of the wagon, making a ring of horseflesh and pistols and naked swords around Gotrek, Felix, Kat and Rodi.

'There!' said von Volgen, pointing at the Slayers with his broadsword. 'There are the inhuman berserkers that murdered my son!'

TWO

Felix stared at von Volgen as Gotrek and Rodi went on guard. What was the lunatic talking about? Hadn't he seen his son's withered face? Hadn't he seen him attacking the Slayers with the other zombies?

'You will die here, dwarfs,' choked von Volgen.

'Aye, we will,' said Gotrek, looking past him into the valley, where the zombies were starting to push back the rearguard. 'If you get out of our way.'

'You stand between us and our doom,' growled Rodi.

The two Slayers started straight for the two lords. 'Kill them!' shouted von Volgen, waving at his men. 'Execute them for the murder of my son!'

'Come and try,' said Gotrek, still striding ahead.

'Wait, my lord,' called Felix, running forwards as von Volgen's knights dismounted. 'The Slayers did not kill your son! He was already dead!'

Von Volgen turned, glaring. 'What foolish lie is this? I saw it with my own eyes! My son was trying to escape the undead, and these wretched dwarfs cut him down without a second glance.'

The knights were stepping forwards to encircle the Slayers. There would be bloodshed any second.

'He wasn't escaping the undead,' said Felix desperately. 'He *was* undead! He died fighting the beastmen before you arrived and was raised with the others!'

'It's true,' said Kat, stepping up beside Felix. 'Please. I saw him die. It was a hero's death, but–'

'You question my eyes, peasant?' Von Volgen's face was purple with rage. He turned to his men. 'Stand back from the dwarfs, or die with them!'

'Somebody help Snorri stand,' said Snorri, from the cart. 'He wants to die with his friends.'

'Hold!' called von Kotzebue, and such was the command in his voice that the knights paused.

Von Volgen was furious. 'You order my men? You are in Talabecland now, sir. You have no authority here.'

'Perfectly correct,' said von Kotzebue, bowing from the saddle. 'But it occurred to me that, as both you and the dwarfs want the same thing – namely their deaths – you should let them do it slaying our common enemy, rather than getting into a fight that will wound, and likely kill your own men.'

Von Volgen scowled. 'How is it punishment to give them what they desire? If they wish to die, then it will be by execution!'

'Very well, my lord,' said von Kotzebue. 'But by my recollection, execution only comes after a trial, and it seems–'

'There is no time for a trial!' cried von Volgen, flinging out an arm to indicate the encroaching undead. 'We are about to be overwhelmed!'

'Precisely,' said von Kotzebue. 'Which is why I recommend you let the Slayers go to their doom and let us be on our way.'

Von Volgen chewed his lip, his angry eyes shifting from von Kotzebue to Gotrek and Rodi to the zombies and back. Felix didn't know who was more insane, the lunatic who wanted to kill them, or the madman who seemed perfectly happy to debate points of law while an army of zombies bore down upon them.

'No,' said von Volgen at last. 'We will take them with us and have your damned trial once this is over.' He motioned to his knights. 'Arrest them!'

Gotrek and Rodi raised their weapons as the knights began to move in again.

'Try it and you'll have your murder,' said Gotrek.

'Gotrek, please,' whispered Felix. 'These are men of the Empire. They are our allies.'

'Not if they try to arrest us, they aren't,' said Rodi.

'Aye,' said Snorri, dragging himself onto the tailgate. 'No one stands between a Slayer and his doom.'

'Noble dwarfs!' called von Kotzebue. 'If you are reluctant to spill the blood of men, hear me out. We travel to Castle Reikguard, six days to the south-west, to bolster its defences and send warning to Altdorf. If you accompany us there without violence, I will guarantee two things. One, a fair trial within its walls, and two, this shambling horde will be only days behind us. If you prevail in your trial, there will be ample opportunity to find your doom when they arrive. What do you say?'

'Since that one has already decided our guilt,' said Rodi, nodding at von Volgen, 'we say nay.'

Felix groaned, but drew his sword and stood beside the dwarfs. He didn't want to fight Empire men, but nor would he watch while Gotrek was attacked. Kat pulled her hatchet from her belt and crouched beside him.

'If you fight, Gotrek,' she said, 'I fight.'

'And so does Snorri' said Snorri, balancing on one leg.

Gotrek grunted, then, with a Khazalid curse, he lifted his head and levelled his one eye at von Volgen. 'Stop,' he said. 'We will go.'

Rodi turned, stunned. 'We will?'

'We will,' said Gotrek, not looking away from von Volgen. 'We will wear your chains and submit to your trial.'

Felix and von Kotzebue let out relieved breaths. Von Volgen's eyes gleamed.

'Arrest them,' he said. 'Take their weapons and shackle them to the cart.'

Rodi bristled at that and went back on guard, but Gotrek let his axe thud to the ground, his face cold and impassive. Rodi stared at him, as did Felix.

'Drop it,' said Gotrek, turning on the younger Slayer. 'Or I drop you. You too, manling. And you, little one.'

Felix shrugged and unbuckled Karaghul, then laid it next to the Slayer's axe. Kat threw down her hatchet as well, but Rodi stood defiant for a long moment, trying to withstand the baleful glare of Gotrek's glittering eye, then he cursed and tossed his hammer beside the rest.

Von Volgen's men stepped forwards with chains and led Felix, Kat and the Slayers to the wagon, then urged them onto it. When they were seated, the men chained them to the gunwales, even Snorri. They gave the key to the driver and told him and his cargo men that they had the care and feeding of them, then returned to their masters.

'Gotrek Gurnisson,' said Rodi as von Volgen and von Kotzebue galloped away. 'I want an explanation. You have robbed me of my doom.'

'And myself as well,' the Slayer said, then turned his eye on Snorri, who was looking back towards the valley, oblivious. 'Never involve yourself in another Slayer's doom,' he muttered, and that was all.

As they got under way again, the last of the rearguard fell, and the zombies welled up after them through the pass like pus bubbling from an open wound.

It was a grim march. Though most of the men were wounded and painfully weary from fighting two terrible battles back to back, there could be no stopping to rest and bind their cuts with the undead horde so close at their heels. They had to limp on, shambling like zombies themselves, through the long dark hours of the night, and then far into the day, without proper rest and eating from their packs at dawn before trudging on again over the endless wasteland of the Barren Hills.

As he slumped in the back of the open cart, the hood of his cloak pulled low against the ever-present wind, Felix had to smile at the favour von Volgen had done them. If the lord had let the Slayers go to their doom and allowed Felix, Kat and Snorri to march with the army, they would be slogging along beside the cart with the others, mile after mile. Instead, as prisoners, they rode where the others walked, and slept when they could.

Felix's mood was soured, however, as he saw men wounded far worse than he die on their feet around him. Over the course of the day dozens toppled to the ground in mid-step as their exhaustion caught up to them, or bled white while carrying the stretchers of comrades worse off than themselves. Still more died on the carts before the surgeons could get to them – and when they died, there was no time to bury them properly, nor could they be granted the dignity usually accorded the dead.

At first, to be sure they did not rise again, the heads of the fallen were cut off and wrapped in their shirts so they could be buried together later. Unfortunately, that procedure had to be abandoned after all the severed heads started talking in unison, whispering from their bags that the men should give up, that they should just lie down and let the sweet release of death come to them. After that, the heads were all smashed with hammers and left behind as the armies plodded on.

Von Volgen and von Kotzebue finally called a halt in the early afternoon and let their troops rest until nightfall. Word came down the line that, for the rest of the march, the force would be allowed to nap during the day, when the zombies were at their weakest and it was easiest to see them coming. The march would resume at nightfall to keep ahead of them.

During that first daylight halt, weary pickets patrolled the perimeter and wearier field surgeons worked straight through, trying to save the lives of knights and spearmen and handgunners whose wounds had been left too long. Because they were prisoners, the surgeons passed Felix, Kat and the Slayers by, but the driver, Geert, and his two cargo men, still grateful to them for saving their life and cargo, browbeat a surgeon until he consented to see them, and their wounds were cleaned and bound. The surgeon even found some hot tar to cauterise and seal Snorri's severed leg.

Kat shook her head as she looked at the Slayer's black stump. 'We fought so hard for nothing.'

'Not nothing,' said Felix, scratching under the bandage the surgeon had wrapped around his upper arm. 'Didn't we stop a great evil that might have caused the downfall of the Empire?'

'Yes,' she said, bitterly. 'And another sprang up in its place before it breathed its last breath. Will there never be peace?'

'Never,' said Gotrek, who was also looking at Snorri's leg. 'We will never win.'

'Then why bother to fight?' asked Kat.

'So we don't lose.'

Kat frowned. 'I don't understand.'

'It is a lesson the dwarfs learned of old,' said Rodi, lifting his head. 'We fight to hold ground. In some battles we win back a hold or a hall. In others we are driven back. But if we stopped fighting...' He shrugged.

Kat slumped against the side boards, not liking it. Felix reached out to put a hand on her shoulder and found his chains wouldn't let him.

'Snorri thinks this is good,' said Snorri from where he lay. 'It means Snorri will never run out of things to fight.'

Gotrek turned away at that, and glared out at the endless hills, and Rodi glared at Gotrek, while Snorri closed his eyes and went back to sleep, blissfully ignorant of the turmoil he was causing amongst his fellow Slayers.

Gotrek and Rodi had been at silent war since they were chained up, and the tension between them felt like a sixth person on the back of the cart – a sleeping ogre so large that it crowded the rest of them into the corners and made them unable to look at each other. Despite the discomfort, Felix did not try to talk the two Slayers out of their anger. He knew better. Dwarfs were stubborn, and Slayers the most stubborn of dwarfs. And what could he say anyway? The problem of Snorri seemed insoluble.

A dwarf became a Slayer to make penance for some great shame, swearing to Grimnir that he would die in battle against the most dangerous of enemies as recompense. If he died in some other fashion, or if his courage failed him, or if he gave up his quest, he would not be welcomed into Grimnir's halls, and would spend eternity as a miserable outcast spirit, wandering through the dwarfen afterlife. Snorri had done none of these forbidden things. He had never turned from his quest and he remained brave to the point of foolhardiness, but despite this, because he had lost his memory, he was in grave danger of dying without Grimnir's grace, and facing eternal damnation.

The trouble was that a Slayer was also required to die with his shame firmly in mind, and Snorri could not remember his. Too many blows to the head, too many nails pounded into his skull to make his rusty Slayer's crest – whatever it was, Snorri had trouble remembering even Gotrek, who had been his friend for over fifty years. He would regale Gotrek with tales of his old friend Gotrek, and not remember him as the same dwarf who sat next to him now. But the worst of this forgetting was his shame, which he last remembered remembering before the siege of Middenheim, but now could not recall at all.

The news had struck Gotrek hard. Snorri was one of his greatest friends, and Felix could see that the thought that the old Slayer would be denied entrance to the dwarfen afterlife pained Gotrek more than any wound he had ever taken. Indeed, it had caused him to free Felix from his vow to record his doom in an epic poem so that Felix could instead escort Snorri on his pilgrimage to the Slayer Keep of Karak Kadrin to pray at the Shrine of Grimnir, the Slayer god, for the return of his memory. Once Felix completed this task, he would be free from his vow, and able to live his life as he chose for the first time in more than twenty years.

Unfortunately, Gotrek was finding that keeping Snorri alive was interfering with his own doom, and worse, had caused him now to interfere with Rodi's as well. Felix knew Gotrek had not liked telling Rodi he couldn't fight von Volgen's men, but if the fight had happened, Snorri might have been killed, and that was unthinkable. And so, until the problem of Snorri was somehow resolved, Rodi glared at Gotrek, and Gotrek glared at Snorri, while Felix and Kat tried to rest and ignore the slumbering ogre of their anger as best they could.

There were no attacks during that brief afternoon stop, at least not from outside the camp, but men who had laid down to sleep barely alive later woke up dead and attacked their tent mates. Felix was twice jerked awake by sudden screaming before the orders came down that any man in danger of dying before he woke was to be tied into his bedroll and gagged so he couldn't bite.

But even when the screaming stopped, Felix found it hard to sleep, for he kept hearing the distant howling of wolves, and when he did at last doze, the howling invaded his dreams and he thought he heard something snuffling under the cart. Needless to say, it was not an easy rest, and he breathed a sigh of relief when, just as the sun was setting, the ragged army got under way again, leaving behind them a roaring pyre of burning, headless corpses – and limping south all night over the grey, changeless landscape.

Though the wolves howled all night long, and the half-heard flapping of wings had the men looking into the sky at every step, the column saw nothing of the undead that night, and fought only the icy wind that blew stiff and cold and ceaseless from the east. Felix's shackles froze his wrists and ankles. His fingers went numb. Kat curled up inside her heavy wool clothes and hid her face in her scarf. The Slayers didn't even shiver.

The morning brought relief from the wind, but none from fear or cold, for a thick fog smothered the hills, filling in the valleys and bringing with it a wet, seeping chill that made bones ache and teeth chatter. It was so dense that Felix could barely make out Rodi where he sat in the far corner of the cart, and flapping wings could be heard in its depths, while the howling of the wolves seemed even closer than it had been at night.

Von Kotzebue and von Volgen kept the men marching long past dawn in hopes that the fog would lift and they would be able to see when they made camp, but when it had failed to dissipate by noon, there was nothing they could do but call a halt. The men were too tired to go on.

The commanders ordered double pickets, set a ring of fires around the perimeter, and had their knights make constant long-range circuits of the camp.

None of these measures reassured Felix in the least. The fog was somehow more terrifying than the night. It couldn't be pushed back with torches, and it played tricks with the ear, making some sounds seem closer, while hiding others entirely. He stared out into it, unable to sleep, his eyes shifting from place to place, searching for unseen movements and shadows that weren't there.

A hoarse cry echoed from the camp.

'Another dead man waking?' asked Kat, looking up.

'I don't know,' said Felix.

He craned his neck but could see no further into the fog. Another cry came from the left, and then another from behind them.

'Wolf! Kill it! Kill it!'

Horns blared from every direction and sergeants bellowed.

'Companies, assemble!'

'Out of those tents! Up! Up!'

Running footsteps thudded past very close by.

Felix and Kat swivelled their heads towards each new sound, straining on their chains, but Gotrek, Rodi and Snorri only stared into the fog, unmoving.

'How can you just sit there?' Felix asked. 'We're being attacked.'

'*We're* not being attacked,' sneered Rodi. 'They are.'

'And if they turn on us?' insisted Felix. 'I thought you submitted to these chains to keep Snorri safe.'

'Snorri doesn't want to be safe,' said Snorri.

'Snorri Nosebiter will not meet his doom here,' growled Gotrek, wrapping the slack of his chains around his fists. 'No matter what happens to the humans.'

Felix heard movement and voices from Geert's tent, only a few paces away, and turned towards it.

'Geert! Release us! Give us weapons!'

But the driver and his cargo men ran out and into the fog, swords and cudgels drawn, calling to their comrades.

'Bastards,' grunted Kat.

An angry snarl brought their heads around. A young spearman ran out of the fog, panting and wide-eyed, and turned to sprint past the cart, but a huge black shape hurtled through the air and brought him down.

Felix and Kat drew back, sickened, as blood and limbs flew. The beast was twice as big as it should be, with rotting muscle showing through mangy crawling fur and a skinless skull for a head.

Another spearman appeared and charged, his spear raised.

'Hoff! Hang on!'

He struck the wolf's shoulder and it whipped around, snarling, to take a second thrust in the chest. The spear snapped, and the wolf slammed the spearman to the ground right next to the cart, tearing his throat out with its skeletal jaws.

Felix and Kat held their breath as it finished him off, wincing at the sound of crunching bones. Go away, thought Felix. Go back to your masters. There's no one else here. There's nothing left to hunt. The monster raised its head, sniffing the wind, then turned its red eyes straight towards him.

'Bugger,' said Felix.

He heard the sharp snap of breaking chains and turned. Gotrek and Rodi were standing and flexing their wrists.

Snorri had broken his chains too, and was struggling to sit up. 'Snorri will–'

'Snorri will stay where he is,' said Gotrek.

The wolf was padding towards them now, circling to come around the back of the cart.

Rodi took up the slack of his broken chain and held it tight between his fists. 'I'll hold it,' he said. 'You kill it.'

Gotrek nodded.

The wolf sprang.

Rodi ran to meet it, and beast and dwarf slammed together in mid-air, then dropped out of sight behind the tailgate as Gotrek leapt the side boards and snatched a spear from one of the dead spearmen. Violent thuds shook the cart and the monster heaved up again with Rodi on its back, choking it with his chain.

The wolf rolled, trying to crush him, but Gotrek leapt at it, spear high, and stabbed its exposed throat with such power that the point punched out the back of its neck and nearly put Rodi's eye out.

The wolf went limp and Rodi pushed it off. 'Are you trying to make me like you, Gurnisson?'

Gotrek let the spear drop and climbed back into the cart. 'You'll never be like me.'

'Grimnir, I hope not,' said Rodi, following him. 'Still chasing my doom twenty years from now? No thanks.'

A twinge of anger flashed across Gotrek's face as they sat down again, but he said nothing, only picked up the sprung link of his broken chain, slipped both ends into it, then twisted it closed. Snorri chuckled and did the same, and Rodi followed suit.

Kat stared in wonder at this casual display of strength and was about to say something when Geert and one of his cargo men limped out of the fog, their faces bruised and their clothes torn. The other cargo man wasn't with them.

'Sigmar's blood!' cried Geert when he saw the dead spearmen. 'Here's two more!'

He and the cargo man ran to the dead boys, then saw the wolf and cursed again. Geert looked from the dead beast to his prisoners and back, glaring suspiciously.

'Show me yer chains!'

Felix, Kat and the Slayers obligingly lifted their chains. Geert grunted to see them whole.

'Then who killed this here wolf?' he asked.

Rodi nodded to the dead spearmen. 'They did.'

'And who killed them?'

'The wolf did,' said Gotrek.

Geert and the cargo man looked dubiously from the wolf to the spearmen and back.

'And how did they kill each other when they was so far apart?'

'It was something,' said Felix, getting into the spirit. 'You should have seen it.'

Kat stifled a laugh and Geert glared at her, but after a moment he just shook his head and stomped off to his tent with the cargo man following.

'Snorri wishes there had been another wolf,' said Snorri. 'So he could have fought one too.'

Gotrek grunted at this, but said nothing, only glared into the distance and twisted his chains. Rodi in turn glared at Gotrek and stroked his braided beard, while Snorri lay back, oblivious, humming an off-key tune. The same tortuous round again, Felix thought as he looked at the Slayers. The same irresolvable tangle. He sighed and sat back and returned to watching the fog for loping black shapes.

For two more days, the pattern remained the same – a pyre of the day's dead as they broke camp at nightfall, a dull march across the featureless landscape during the hours of darkness, and shadowy hit-and-run attacks all through the fog-bound day. It was impossible to tell what progress the army was making when every mist-shrouded hill and valley looked the same as the one before, but to Felix it seemed the column was marching slower and slower, the sleepless, terror-filled days and nights taking a toll of weariness and despair.

And perhaps the column truly *had* slowed, for, two hours before sunset on the evening of the fourth day, a squad of von Volgen's knights came thundering into the camp, shouting that the zombies were not more than an hour away.

As their troops scrambled to dress and pack and get into march order, von Kotzebue and von Volgen and their captains convened at the north edge of the camp, looking into the grey fog as if they might see the encroaching horde from there. They talked near where Geert had left his cart, and Felix could hear them plainly.

'They have marched night and day,' said von Volgen, 'while we have only marched nights.'

'Yes,' said von Kotzebue. 'It is as I feared. Slow as they are, they never stop. We will not outrun them before we reach Castle Reikguard. At least...'

'At least the foot soldiers won't,' said von Volgen when the baron trailed off. 'Yes?'

Von Kotzebue nodded. 'I have less than three thousand foot troops left, and most of them wounded, starving and exhausted. The horde must number more than ten thousand. If my men stand and fight, they will die, and do nothing but add to the necromancer's ranks. If they run, it is the same. Your two hundred knights, however–'

'We will not abandon you, my lord,' said von Volgen, drawing himself up.

Von Kotzebue tilted his head, and Felix thought he saw him smile through his enormous moustache. 'I was thinking more that we would abandon you.'

Von Volgen frowned. 'I don't understand.'

'It is this way,' said the baron. 'The necromancer says he is driving for Altdorf, and plans to take the towns and castles in his way to bolster his troops. Castle Reikguard must be his first target, for it has the largest garrison, and he cannot afford to have it at his back. But to take it, he must act swiftly, before a concerted defence can be brought against him. Therefore, I believe if our infantry were to turn away from his line of march, he could not afford to follow. He could not spare the time.'

He looked west. 'We are almost due east of Weidmaren here. If I were to march west and bolster their garrison, while you and your knights raced south-west to do the same at Castle Reikguard, we would starve him of fresh troops, and make two of the strongholds he absolutely must take that much harder to win.' He turned back to von Volgen. 'What say you?'

Von Volgen stroked his heavy chin. 'I see the sense of it, but I wonder if Graf Reiklander will welcome an armed force of Talabecland men within his walls.'

'In the face of an enemy such as this necromancer, my lord,' said von Kotzebue, 'surely Empire must come before province.'

'Aye, baron,' said von Volgen. 'I only hope my lord Reiklander sees it that way.' He shrugged. 'Well, if you will take my foot troops and my wounded as well, I and my knights will speed south-west as you suggested.'

Von Kotzebue bowed. 'Of course. I will give my sergeants their orders.'

The two lords and their captains turned from the fog-shrouded vista, but before they had taken more than a few steps into the bustling camp, Rodi raised himself up in his chains and called after them.

'Hoy, lordling!' he barked. 'Aye, you. The one who can't tell the dead from the living. If you're running away, why not free us instead? We wouldn't want to slow you down.'

Von Volgen's brutish brow lowered into a scowl, and he turned his eyes to Geert. 'Make your cart ready to go,' he said. 'And find some extra chains.'

Geert saluted and the lords walked away.

'At this rate, beardling,' said Gotrek without looking around, 'you'll live long enough to learn when to shut your mouth.'

For the next two days, von Volgen and his two hundred knights rode hard to the south-west, with Geert's cart rattling along behind the other supply wagons. At noon on the first day, they plunged into the dark forest that bordered the Barren Hills. The narrow track they followed was old and often overgrown, and for all von Volgen's urgings that they make haste, sometimes the servants and cargo men were forced to stop and shoulder the carts over thick roots that humped up out of the path, or to guide them across rushing streams.

Each time this occurred, the dwarfs would watch from the cart, smug, as the men did the heavy work because von Volgen refused to unchain them. Felix was too uneasy to enjoy the irony. Whenever they slowed, he would stare into the depths of forest, fearing that at any moment undead horrors would lurch out of the shadows and attack. Adding to his nerves was the fact that von Volgen had sent his field surgeons along with his wounded to join von Kotzebue's train, so if an attack did happen, there would be no one to patch them up.

But no attack came. Not that day, nor that night when they made camp in a cramped glade not far from the track. Felix dreamed again of wolf howls and black wings, but when he woke, sweat freezing on his brow, he heard nothing, and there were no alarms from von Volgen's sentries.

The next day was the same as the first, except with freezing rain. The forest was so thick over their heads that even though the winter trees were bare of leaves the raindrops did not reach them, only great fat drips from the black branches that nonetheless soaked them to the bone. Felix tried to drape his cloak over himself and Kat, but they were chained just too far apart, and neither of them were fully covered. The dwarfs still showed no discomfort, except for wringing out their beards and flipping their drooping crests out their eyes. Snorri's crest of nails made little red rivulets of rust that dripped off the end of his bulbous nose like blood.

The next morning, the rain stopped, though the clouds remained. Unfortunately, the downpour had made a mud bath of their track, and there were many stops to pull the wagons out of wheel-sucking ruts, but at last, in the middle of the afternoon, the column came out of the forest and into a wet patchwork of dreary farmland, the fields black and brown and bare under stone-grey clouds.

Felix sighed with relief to be out of the woods, and it seemed the knights shared his mood. They had been almost entirely silent for the last two days, talking only when necessary, and laughing not at all, but now they began to chat and joke amongst themselves.

Geert stood up on the buckboard of the cart and pointed ahead. 'That'll be Castle Reikguard, or I'm a goblin,' he said to his surviving cargo man, Dirk.

'Soon be warm and dry now,' said Dirk, nodding.

'And on trial,' said Rodi, without looking up.

Gotrek didn't raise his head either, but Felix and Kat stood as high as they could in their chains and craned their necks. A dull gleam, far in the misty distance, was the Reik, snaking north and west towards Altdorf – and rising from it, like some massive, high-prowed stone ship, was a towering castle, heavy walls of dark granite circling a craggy hill to surround a stern old keep. A great tower jutted from its black slate roof, rising so high its pennons were lost in the lowering clouds.

Felix had seen the castle often as a boy travelling with his father on business. It had been a familiar landmark to be watched for on the way to Nuln, and he was surprised what a sense of nostalgia and comfort he felt seeing it again. The castle was the hereditary seat of the Reikland princes, and also Karl Franz's summer home, as well as the home of the garrison that had guarded the Reikland's north-eastern border since before Magnus the Pious. He felt, suddenly, that after his long trek through the wild and dangerous Drakwald, he was back in the civilised heart of the Empire. This was where his people were their strongest. This was home.

A thudding of hooves behind them made him turn his head. One of von Volgen's rearguard knights was galloping towards them down the forest road, his horse's flanks flecked with foam and his eyes wide and staring.

'My lord!' he cried as he reached the tail of the column. 'My lord! They're coming!'

The knight thundered on towards the vanguard before Felix could hear who was coming, and he and Kat and the Slayers looked back towards the forest, as did Geert and Dirk.

'What did he mean?' babbled Geert. 'Not them corpses? They couldn't have caught up with us so fast, could they?'

The knights were turning too, wheeling their horses around to face the woods, now a half-mile behind them, and a moment later von Volgen and his captains cantered back to stand with them and stare at the distant wall of trees.

'You are certain?' asked von Volgen, when nothing happened.

'Yes, my lord,' said the knight, panting along with his horse. 'And the wolves with them. They–'

Then they appeared.

From the dark of the forest came a swift, roiling blackness, shot through with flashes of white and steel and bronze, like shooting stars in a turbulent sky. Then the flashes resolved themselves. The white was bone – skull-faced riders leaning low over the necks of bone-shanked horses. The steel was swords and axes and lance-tips, held in gauntleted hands. The bronze was helms and breastplates and greaves of ancient design. And as the skeletons rode, the clouds in the sky above them lowered and blackened, so that the green fire that flickered in their empty eye sockets glowed brighter.

Felix swallowed, fear clutching at his insides. This was no shambling mob of clumsy corpses, mindless and unarmed. These riders were charging towards them in a disciplined line, as fast as smoke before a strong wind. A spike-helmed warrior in full plate led them, a black sword held high in one gauntleted fist, while the low black forms of dire wolves loped between their steeds like silent shadows.

'About eighty, my lord,' said one of von Volgen's captains, fighting to keep the fear out of his voice. 'Perhaps a hundred.'

Von Volgen's heavy jaw tightened and he wheeled his horse around. 'Make for the castle,' he said. 'Now!'

He galloped for the front of the column with his captains bawling orders to the wagons and the knights as they raced behind him.

Geert called up a prayer to Taal and slapped the reins over the backs of his horses as the column started forwards. 'Come on, Bette! Come on, Countess!'

The cargo man, Dirk, drew a hatchet out from under the driver's bench and made the sign of Sigmar.

Felix watched, mesmerised, as the undead riders surged closer behind them and von Volgen's knights and the other wagons pulled away ahead of them. Weaponless aboard the slowest of the wagons, he and Kat and the Slayers were worse off than they had been against the wolves in the fog. The skeletal knights would ride them down before they were halfway to Castle Reikguard.

THREE

'Will you allow *this* doom, Gurnisson?' asked Rodi, sneering. 'Does it meet with your approval?'

Gotrek glared back at the encroaching riders. 'It does not,' he said, then snapped his chains and stood.

Rodi and Snorri took that as a sign and broke theirs too, while Gotrek freed Felix and Kat.

'Thank you, Gotrek,' said Kat, rubbing her wrists.

'Then what are you doing?' asked Rodi. 'Are you going to fight?'

'I am going to see that Snorri Nosebiter reaches the manling castle,' Gotrek said, and pulled up one of the tightly rolled lengths of canvas tenting that lay on the bed of the cart.

Rodi snorted. 'We could do that by jumping off and facing them.'

'Do what you will,' said Gotrek, and heaved the first roll off the cart.

'Snorri doesn't want to go to a castle,' said Snorri, trying to stand on his one leg. 'Snorri wants to fight.'

Rodi shot an angry glance at the old Slayer, then cursed and started throwing off the canvas as well. Felix and Kat joined him.

Geert looked back, alarmed, as he heard the canvas rolls splat behind them on the muddy road. 'Hoy! What are y'doing free? And those are my tents!'

'You want to go back and get them?' asked Felix as he and Kat pitched another roll off the back.

Geert groaned unhappily, but only turned back and cracked the reins again.

The cart flew faster with every canvas they unloaded, and was soon bouncing and lurching in a terrifying fashion, but it was still not fast enough. They had caught up with the other carts, but von Volgen's knights were pulling further ahead, and the undead riders kept gaining.

Kat bent to shove off some of the tent poles that lay stacked in the centre of the cart, but Gotrek stayed her arm.

'Wait until they'll make a difference,' he said.

Felix looked back at the riders. Now that they were closer, he saw that not all were ancient skeletons. Some still had flesh on their bones, and wore the colours of Plaschke-Miesner or von Kotzebue or von Volgen. He stared, shocked. They must have been knights who had fallen at Tarnhalt's Crown, but like their bronze-clad comrades, their movements were swift and sure, not the vague stumblings of zombies. Was the necromancer controlling them like puppets, or had he somehow found a way to let them retain the skill they had possessed in life?

'How does a mad beggar like Hans have such power?' Felix mumbled.

The cart boomed over an ancient stone bridge that crossed a wide, winding stream. Felix looked around. The castle was closer now, and he could pick out details such as spear-tips glinting on the battlements and the yawning arch of its main gate, but it was still too far.

Behind him, the dead riders bounded over the broad stream as if they had wings, then touched down in a spray of mud and surged closer, pushing before them an icy, foetid wind that made Felix shiver with more than just cold.

Gotrek picked up one of the tent poles, nearly as long as a pike and heavier, then stepped to the back of the cart and heaved it like a javelin, straight at the spike-helmed warrior at the front. The rider danced its bone horse to the left and avoided the pole, but it bounced and knocked another dead knight from the saddle. The rest swerved around him and came on.

Snorri laughed. 'That looks like fun. Snorri wants to try.'

'Not with one leg, you won't,' said Rodi as he and Gotrek picked up more poles. 'You'll fall off the cart.'

Snorri sulked. 'Snorri never gets to do anything.'

Gotrek hurled his next pole low and to the left, and Rodi did the same to the right. They bounced in front of the lead riders, hitting their horses at knee height and sending them crashing neck-first to the turf in an explosion of armour and bones. More crashed down behind them as riders dodged and slammed into each other, but the fallen swiftly vanished behind the blurring hooves of the others, and the dread warriors closed ranks and came on.

Gotrek and Rodi bent to take up new poles, and Felix did the same, grunting at the weight. The long length of oak was an awkward, unwieldy weapon, and he marvelled again at the strength of the dwarfs to have pitched theirs with such ease and accuracy.

As he raised his to vertical the cart bounced and he overbalanced, falling against the side boards. Kat yelped as the pole banged down on the driver's bench between Geert and Dirk, and Felix lost his grip.

'Hoy!' said Geert. 'Watch it!'

'Leave it, manling,' said Gotrek, hurling his pole and bending for another.

Snorri snorted. 'Snorri could do as well as *that*.'

Felix recovered, flushing, and drew the pole back, letting the weight rest on the bench.

'Ah!' he said. 'That's a better idea.'

'What?' asked Kat. 'Not falling off?'

Felix ignored the dig and slid the pole out to the side of the cart, resting the weight of it on the side boards like it was an oar.

'Ah!' said Kat. 'I see now.'

The skeletal riders leapt a low stone wall and came parallel with the cart. Gotrek and Rodi swung their poles left and right at them, denting bronze helmets and knocking them out of their saddles.

Felix lowered the end of his close to the ground and swept it at the knees of a skeletal horse as Gotrek bashed at the rider. The pole ripped from his hands as it got tangled in milling forelegs, but the horse went down and the rider fell under the wheels, armour crumpling and bones snapping.

'Good work,' said Gotrek as Felix bent for another pole.

'Now *this* Snorri can do,' said Snorri.

The old Slayer grabbed a pole and came up on his knees, then hung it out over the right side of the cart while Felix did the same on the left, but by the time they were in position, most of the dead riders had already passed by, converging on the head of the column. Only a few of the loping wolves remained behind, dodging the Slayers' swipes and trying to leap up onto the cart.

Snorri punched one in the eye with the butt of his pole and sent it stumbling into a tree trunk. Gotrek knocked another off the tailgate and lanced a third, but the knights were faring less well. The undead riders cut them down at the gallop, but when the knights slashed back, their swords rang harmlessly off the skeletons' armour. Only a knight with a warhammer did better, shattering skulls and femurs, but he went down too, brought low by a dire wolf that tore his horse's left hind leg off with its exposed jaws.

Another knight went down right in front of a supply wagon, sending it vaulting into the air as its right wheel bounced over the falling corpse. The wagon crashed down on its side, pulling its draught horses with it and throwing its driver and cargo men into a field. The wagons behind it barely swerved aside in time, and Geert nearly ran into the ditch.

'Pull up! Pull up!' roared von Volgen as his bugler blared distress calls. 'Form a square!'

The lord might be a blind man who couldn't tell his son from a corpse, but Felix had to admire his courage and tactical sense, and the training of his men. When it was clear they wouldn't outrun the undead cavalry, he did not panic and keep fleeing. He ordered a defence, and his men obeyed neatly and without question, despite their mortal terror of the enemy they faced.

The echo of von Volgen's order had not died away before the column of knights had split – two files to the left, two to the right – and pulled up smartly, allowing the surviving wagons to slot between them so they were soon in the middle of a hollow square of knights, all facing out and fighting for their lives.

Geert and Dirk let out relieved breaths as they pulled the cart to a stop, but then Geert turned on Gotrek, Felix and the others. 'You shouldn't have broke them chains! I told you I'd...' He sighed. 'Well, I'm glad you did, though. Saved our bacon and no mistake. But I'm begging ye,' he added as he and Dirk took up their weapons, 'stay on the cart. If von Volgen sees you free, it's my hide.'

Gotrek shrugged. 'It's your hide if we do nothing.' He turned to Rodi. 'You seek a doom, Rodi Balkisson? Now is the time.'

'I don't need your permission, Gotrek Gurnisson,' snapped the young Slayer.

The two Slayers jumped from the cart and started towards the head of the column.

'Aw, now, gentles,' whined Geert after them. 'Don't do this to me. Haven't I done my best for ye?'

'And we go to do our best for you,' said Felix, heading after the Slayers with Kat.

'Snorri wants to come,' said Snorri.

'You can't walk, Snorri,' said Kat. 'Defend the cart.'

Felix and Kat hurried on, edging between the wagons and the shifting, surging battle line of knights and warhorses as Geert and Dirk called after them and the blasts from von Volgen's bugler were finally answered by an echoing horn from the castle.

Felix looked up at the noise. Help was coming, but would it be soon enough? On every side of the hollow square, knights were falling to the ancient swords of the undead riders. Von Volgen's men might outnumber them three to one, but the skeletons fought with a relentless mechanical savagery that knew no pain or panic, while the cold wind of fear that breathed from them paralysed the knights and made them falter. It would be mere minutes before the formation collapsed completely.

The Slayers found von Volgen at the far end of the square, cursing and standing over a dead horse as his chosen knights held back the undead riders and his squires scrambled to bring him a remount.

'Lordling!' barked Gotrek. 'Return our weapons if you want to live!'

Von Volgen glanced over his shoulder as his squires led a horse forwards. 'Go back to your chains, murderer,' he said, swinging into the saddle.

Gotrek's brow lowered and Rodi balled his fists. Felix could see they were an inch from returning to the cart and sitting on their hands while the knights died all around them. Felix couldn't stand by and let that happen. He stepped forwards.

'My lord,' he called. 'Will you let good men die while we sit safe behind them?'

Von Volgen drew his sword and turned his horse back towards the melee, and Felix wondered if he had heard or cared, but then, as he made to spur forwards, he looked along his line and saw how close it was to collapse. His lantern jaw clenched and he called towards the wagon that carried his baggage. 'Merkle. Give them their weapons.'

And with that, he sank his spurs into his horse's flanks and punched back into the line, severing the head of a recently-dead knight in black and gold as he shouted a challenge to the spike-helmed warrior who led the riders.

Gotrek and Rodi grunted with satisfaction, then turned with Kat and Felix as the driver climbed into the back of the wagon and unlocked a chest. He threw back the lid and tried to lift something out, then tried again.

'Leave it,' said Gotrek.

He climbed onto the wagon, then reached into the trunk and pulled out his rune axe with as little effort as it took Felix to lift a pen. He slung it over his shoulder, then handed down Rodi's hammer, Felix's sword and Kat's hatchet, bow and quiver. Felix felt emboldened as he strapped Karaghul on again. Now he was ready to fight.

Without another word, the Slayers shouldered through the stamping, side-stepping warhorses of von Volgen's line, and plunged swinging into the mass of skeletal riders. Kat watched as they were buffeted this way and that by the maelstrom of surging bone and horseflesh, and shook her head.

'I wouldn't last a minute in all that,' she said.

'Nor would I,' said Felix, looking around. A few yards away was a steed that had lost its rider. 'Here!'

He ran to it and pulled himself into the saddle, then hauled Kat up behind him and drew Karaghul as she drew her hatchet. The warhorse seemed to know where its duty lay and plunged into a gap between two knights with only the lightest touch of the heel, and Felix and Kat found themselves suddenly in the middle of the swirling, clattering melee.

A dire wolf snapped at the horse's neck. Felix chopped through the beast's spine, then decapitated a bronze-helmed rider that trampled over it to lunge at him. Kat shattered the skull of another rider with her hatchet, but it got caught in its helmet, and as she tried to yank it free, a second wolf clamped its jaws around her wrist and almost pulled her from the horse.

'Kat!' shouted Felix, slashing awkwardly at the thing.

Kat pulled against its teeth, trying to free herself, and stabbed left-handed at its skull with her skinning knife, popping one of its eyes. Felix finally twisted around enough to get a strike at its neck, and half-severed it. It fell away, twitching, and Kat righted herself behind the saddle.

'Are you all right?' asked Felix, looking back.

She nodded, hiding a wince as she slashed at another rider. 'It got mostly coat, I think.'

Felix nodded, hoping she wasn't being brave, and they fought on.

To their left, Gotrek and Rodi were hewing like woodsmen through a forest of bone and flesh horse legs. Despite their recent arguing, the Slayers were an effective team. Rodi would smash through the forelegs of a horse with his hammer, bringing it crashing to the ground, and Gotrek would chop off the rider's head, then on to the next. They were getting kicked and kneed and crushed by both sides, but they just took the pummelling and kept on killing.

Then, with a tantara of horns, two score knights appeared, galloping over the fields, the white and red banner of Castle Reikguard cracking above them in the wind. Von Volgen's knights gave a great cheer at the sight, and renewed their attacks on the dread riders. Von Volgen himself, however, didn't look like he would live long enough to be saved. He was in desperate trouble. The heavy black sword of the spike-helmeted skeleton had cut his plate to ribbons, and he was reeling in the saddle.

But then, just as the dread knight knocked von Volgen's sword from his hand and raised its black blade for the killing stroke, its skull-headed horse shuddered beneath it and staggered sideways. The sword missed von Volgen by a hair's breadth and the dead rider turned to aim a cut at something below it.

The strike never landed. Instead, the bone horse toppled forwards and the ancient warrior fell with it, vanishing under the seething combat. Felix saw an orange crest of hair bob up and an axe-head flash down, and a shout of triumph burst from von Volgen's men.

It was immediately echoed by the war cries of the Reikland knights as they slammed into the flanks of the dead riders, lances lowered. A score of ancient warriors went down under the charge, smashed from their horses and ridden over in a splash of shattered bones. Felix and Kat surged forwards with von Volgen's knights, yelling and slashing at the dead riders from the front as the Reiklanders bashed at them from behind.

In the face of this double assault, the ancients turned and raced back the way they had come, but not like any living troops Felix had ever seen. They didn't break in ones and twos, nor throw their weapons away in panic. Instead, it was as if an unheard voice had whispered a single order for, as one, they and the wolves wheeled and fought free of the melee to race away without a backwards glance or any attempt to rescue their fellows who had been laid low behind.

Felix exhaled grimly and slid from the borrowed horse, then helped Kat down as all around them von Volgen's captains called for perimeters to be set and for the wounded and dead to be counted and collected.

'How is it?' asked Felix, as he saw Kat pressing her arm.

Before she could reply, Rodi's booming voice rose from nearby. 'By Grimnir!' he shouted. 'Do humans have no honour at all?'

Felix and Kat exchanged a glance, then hurried around a knot of knights to find von Volgen, his powerful frame hunched with pain, supporting himself with the aid of his sword and standing before Gotrek and Rodi while his men moved in to surround them. Rodi was sputtering with fury, while Gotrek was staring at the wounded lord with cold, silent menace, his rune axe at the ready.

'Curse them,' said Felix, then hurried forwards with Kat running beside him.

'You are still my prisoners,' von Volgen was saying as they reached the confrontation. 'You will not be allowed your weapons.'

'You don't trust our word,' growled Gotrek, 'after we saved your life?'

'I don't trust your restraint,' said the lord. 'You might kill anyone in your frenzy.'

Gotrek's eye got colder still, and Felix's heart lurched. He had to say something before there was bloodshed, though he had no idea what.

'My lord!' he called, pushing through von Volgen's men. 'My lord, I–'

He stumbled over the body of a knight in red, black and gold and glanced down to step around it. The knight's severed head lay staring up at the sky from under his left arm. Felix stopped. He knew the knight's face, and all at once knew what he would say to von Volgen as well.

'My lord,' he called. 'If you intend to try my companions for the murder of your son, then perhaps you should submit yourself to trial as well – for the murder of your nephew, Viscount Oktaf Plaschke-Miesner.'

All heads turned his way.

'What is this nonsense, vagabond?' the lord snarled, wincing as he turned to face Felix. 'I haven't killed my nephew. I was told he died at Tarnhalt's Crown.'

'And yet he is here, my lord,' said Felix, indicating the body over which he stood. 'And cut down by your hand, if I recall, only moments ago. Perhaps he didn't die at Tarnhalt after all. Perhaps he was trying to escape these skeletons when you struck him.'

Von Volgen paled and stumped forwards to stare down at the boy in black armour. He wrinkled his nose. Oktaf smelled like a week old corpse, which of course he was. His blond hair was matted with filth and his beautiful face marred by a terrible wound, black and rotting at the edges, that showed his back teeth. Flies crawled around his lips.

'You did not recognise him when you cut off his head, my lord?' Felix asked. 'You didn't wait to be sure he wasn't still alive? From where I fought, it looked like he was coming to help you, not kill you. Were you so certain he was a zombie? Will you be able to look his mother in the face and tell her–'

Von Volgen's fists clenched. 'Enough, curse you! You've made your point!' He glared at Felix, his bulldog face flushed. 'I concede that my son may have... that he might possibly have been...'

'He *was*, my lord,' said Kat, stepping up beside Felix. 'He was dead before you arrived at Tarnhalt. We saw him die, killed by the beastmen's war-leader.'

Von Volgen turned his terrible eyes on her, and Felix gripped his sword, ready should the lord try and strike her, but instead he turned away, shoving his men aside to limp on his own back towards his horse.

Gotrek and Rodi and the knights remained on guard as he lurched unsteadily across the muddy, trampled harrows, then, halfway to the horse, he staggered to a stop and closed his eyes.

'Release them,' he rasped.

The knights relaxed, lowering their swords and hammers, and Gotrek and Rodi nodded, smug.

'But, hear me!' cried von Volgen, turning and standing straight. 'I will have my vengeance! Before Sigmar and Taal, I swear the foul necromancer who defiled my son's corpse and disturbed his eternal rest will die for his depredations, and all his works shall be cast down!'

His men cheered, raising their swords high. 'Death to the necromancer! Long live Lord von Volgen!'

'Well spoken, my lord,' came a new voice. 'But please tell me what trouble you have brought into the domain of Graf Falken Reiklander.'

Von Volgen and the others looked around to see two armour-clad noblemen in red and white approaching on a pair of sturdy warhorses. The one who had spoken was a tall, trim knight of middle years, with a jutting black beard and fierce brows, who rode ramrod-straight in his saddle. At his side was a florid, heavyset older man, whose breastplate bulged over his saddlebow to accommodate his belly, and whose face and neatly-trimmed beard were running with sweat. The rest of the Reikland knights gathered behind them.

'You are Reiklander, then?' asked von Volgen.

'I am General Taalman Nordling,' said the black-browed knight, bowing from the waist in his saddle. 'Acting commander of the castle until Graf Reiklander can resume his position.'

The red-faced lord mopped his jowls. 'The graf is recovering from wounds he received during Archaon's invasion,' he said, then bowed as well. 'Bardolf von Geldrecht, his steward, at your service. And to whom do I have the honour of speaking?'

'I am Rutger von Volgen, vassal of Count Feuerbach of Talabecland,' said von Volgen, returning the bow. 'And I thank you, my lords, for your timely intervention.' He looked around at the wounded and the dead and the skeletons that littered the field, then sighed. 'I did not wish to bring you trouble, but to warn you of its coming. These are but the vanguard of an army of the undead some ten thousand strong, which is led by a necromancer of great power who marches on Altdorf, and means to swell his ranks with the corpses of every garrison in his way.'

Nordling blinked. The knights around him murmured amongst themselves. Von Geldrecht's red face paled a little.

'Ten thousand?' he asked. 'You are certain?'

'Perhaps more,' said von Volgen. 'Many of my men now walk with them, turned against me in death. They are less than two days behind us, perhaps only one. We–'

He cut off as a spasm of pain made him wince and he nearly fell. His men rushed to him and steadied him.

Felix saw von Geldrecht whisper to Nordling as von Volgen recovered himself, and wondered if the men were going to turn them away, but finally General Nordling turned back to von Volgen and bowed.

'Forgive me, my lord, for ignoring your wounds,' he said. 'You and your men are welcome to Castle Reikguard. Enter and bring your wounded. The graf will be informed of your grave news.'

Von Volgen waved weakly, and his retinue picked him up and carried him to his baggage wagon while his knights and servants gathered their wounded and dead. Felix and Kat helped, guiding or carrying maimed men to their horses or the wagons, and the Slayers did the same, picking up fully armoured men with ease. Gotrek and Rodi also cut off the heads of those knights who had been killed in the battle. Von Volgen's men, long since aware of the necessity, did not object, but Steward von Geldrecht was outraged.

'What are you doing, you horrible savages?' he said, trotting up on his horse. 'You defile the bodies of my men!'

Gotrek glared up at him as he moved to the next body. 'Better now than later.'

'I don't know what you mean,' insisted von Geldrecht, and turned his horse to block Gotrek's way. 'By Sigmar, I should have you slain on the spot.'

Gotrek growled and readied his axe.

'He means,' said Felix, hurrying to them, 'that when the necromancer comes, he will raise the dead, foe and friend alike. If we don't do this now, my lord, we will be facing these same men in battle later.'

Von Geldrecht sputtered, his red face growing redder, but with the evidence of Plaschke-Miesner's corpse and the rest of the recently risen knights, there was no argument he could make.

'If it must be done, it must be done,' he said at last. 'But we will tend to our own. Leave them alone.'

Gotrek shrugged and returned to helping the wounded, and Felix and Kat did too. But Kat nearly lost her grip on the first knight they helped, and hissed as she clenched the arm the dire wolf had bitten. The cuff of her wool coat was black with blood.

Felix cursed. 'I thought you said it got mostly coat.'

'Aye,' said Kat. 'Mostly, but not all.'

Felix wanted to tell her there was no need to play the hero, but he resisted. She had long ago made him promise not to coddle her. Instead he followed as she went in search of more wounded, and helped her carry a handful of knights to the column – but he made sure he did the bulk of the lifting.

Finally, they could find no more, and returned to Geert's cart, where things had not gone well. Snorri was fine, and had crushed a dread rider with another tent pole, but Geert was binding a deep cut on his leg, and Dirk was dead, lying across the driving bench with an axe wound in his chest.

'I'm sorry,' said Felix, as he and Kat climbed aboard.

Geert shrugged. 'If you'd stayed in yer chains it would have been all of us.'

They laid Dirk beside Snorri, and Felix closed his eyes while Kat whispered prayers to Taal and Morr over him, then pried the hatchet from his rigid hand and slipped it into her belt. Felix smiled as he sat down next to her. Respect and pragmatism – the marks of a veteran.

At the head of the column, von Volgen signalled the company forwards, and the last of the wounded were hurried to the wagons as the captains and sergeants relayed the order down the line.

As they moved out Gotrek returned and pulled himself up onto the tailgate. Rodi appeared a moment later and did the same.

'You're not leaving, Balkisson?' asked Gotrek as Rodi sat. 'You're free now. And doom waits in the wood.'

Rodi shot Snorri a glance, then shook his head. 'Doom will come to the castle too, Gurnisson. I can wait.'

FOUR

Men cheered from the walls of Castle Reikguard as von Volgen's and Nordling's knights rode over the drawbridge and under the arch of its massive gatehouse. Felix looked around at the defences as the wagons followed them in. The moat over which the drawbridge lay churned with swift-flowing river water, diverted from the Reik, which looked as if it could sweep away any attacker smaller than a giant. The high stone walls that surrounded the courtyard were thick, strong, and in good repair, and the inner keep, looming above the courtyard on top of a steep rocky hill and reachable only by a narrow and easily defended stair, looked even stronger – a square, brutish fortress of massive granite blocks.

The courtyard contained all the things a castle was expected to have – a smithy, a stables, a temple of Sigmar and half-timbered residences butted up against the inside of the exterior walls – but it also had a more unusual feature: a small harbour. The castle was built right on the bank of the Reik, and a water gate, almost directly opposite the main gate, opened to the river to let boats in and out. There were several boats moored at the wooden docks – two big sloops, kitted out with cannons and swivel guns, as well as a few smaller oar boats. There was also a warehouse and a two-storey barracks at the quayside.

What the place did not seem to have, at least not in any great abundance, was men. Felix had expected to see companies of spearmen ready to march out in aid of the knights. He expected scores of grooms standing by to receive their horses. He expected dozens of field surgeons and scores of servants rushing out to help the wounded. Instead, there was one surgeon, a hunched little crow of a man with a meagre handful of assistants, and a plump old Sister of Shallya with a few very young-looking initiates to help her. There were no more than a dozen grooms, and though the spearmen who manned the main gate looked hale enough, too many of the fighting men who hurried from the outbuildings and down from the walls to greet the returning knights were wounded and maimed.

There were spearmen on crutches, handgunners with slings on their arms, greatswords with bandaged heads, artillerymen with missing hands and legs. They limped and hobbled forwards along with their more whole comrades to help the battered knights off their horses with admirable selflessness, but they were hardly better off themselves. A chill came over Felix as he watched the scene. The garrison of Castle Reikguard didn't look ready to stand up to an army of ten thousand undead.

Von Volgen, being helped from his baggage cart by his men, must have noticed this as well, for he rounded on Nordling, who was handing off his lance to a squire and swinging down from his horse.

'General, what is this?' he asked. 'Where are the rest of your troops? Is your graf undefended?'

Nordling lifted his black-bearded chin, glaring. 'The majority of Graf Reiklander's troops are likely where many of yours are as well, in northern graves. Talabecland was not the only province to march against the invaders.'

'I did not say–' said von Volgen, but Steward von Geldrecht interrupted him.

'The Reikland too gave of its best and bravest, Lord von Volgen,' he puffed, stepping up beside the general. 'My lord Reiklander marched north in support of his cousin, the Emperor Karl Franz, at the head of three-quarters of Castle Reikguard's strength. Only a month ago he returned with less than one-quarter still with him, and many of those gravely wounded. Because of this, we are at less than half strength.'

Von Volgen's jaw clenched. 'That is... unfortunate. I– I had hoped Castle Reikguard would be a bulwark against this necromancer's hordes.'

'It will be, my lord,' said Nordling, hard. 'We may not be at full strength, but we will not falter for that.' He turned to von Geldrecht. 'Lord steward, consult with the graf. I will gather the officers and we will meet in the temple to hear his will.'

'At once, general,' said von Geldrecht, bowing, and hurried towards the stairs to the keep.

Nordling looked back at von Volgen. 'My lord, if you are well enough, perhaps you will join us and tell us what you know of this threat.'

'Of course,' said von Volgen. 'Once my wounds are bound, I am at your service.'

Felix watched, frowning, as Nordling bowed and strode towards the barracks, while von Volgen's men helped him onto a stretcher and started to remove his armour. If Nordling was in command of the castle until Graf Reiklander recovered his wounds, why was it Steward von Geldrecht's job to consult with the graf?

'There will be a good doom here when the necromancer comes,' said Rodi approvingly as they all started to get down from Geert's cart.

Snorri nodded. 'Snorri thinks so too.'

'Aye,' said Gotrek heavily.

Gotrek put his shoulder under Snorri's arm and helped him as they crossed to where the wounded knights were waiting for the castle's surgeon and Sister of Shallya to see them. They sat, and Kat shrugged out of her big wool jacket, then unlaced the sleeve of her hardened leather jerkin. Felix winced as she peeled it back. There was a dark, U-shaped bruise from the dead wolf's jaws on her forearm, half a dozen bloody puncture wounds perforating it like rubies on a purple ribbon.

'Wait here,' he said. 'I'll get some water.'

'I'll go too,' said Gotrek.

Snorri laughed at him. 'Water? What does a dwarf need with water? Snorri thinks you should get beer instead.'

Felix too thought it was strange that Gotrek wanted water. The Slayer almost never drank the stuff, and hardly ever washed, but as Felix filled his canteen at the castle's well, the reason was revealed.

'You and the little one will take Nosebiter away tomorrow morning before the necromancer comes,' said Gotrek, looking back at Snorri.

'Aye, Gotrek,' said Felix. 'As I promised. To Karak Kadrin. Though… though it feels strange that I won't be here to record your doom.'

Gotrek shrugged. 'My epic is long enough.' He spat on the ground and started back to the others. 'Too long.'

Felix finished filling his canteen and followed the Slayer.

'It will wait,' said the pinch-faced little surgeon, glancing briefly at Kat's bite before stepping to the knight who lay beside her.

The plump priestess of Shallya and an assistant followed behind him, making notes in a ledger.

Felix stared after them, then stood, angry. 'Surgeon, the wounds are likely poisoned or diseased. Haven't you some ointment, or–'

'What I have,' snapped the surgeon, rounding on him with a beaky black glare, 'is a courtyard full of wounded *fighting men*, who will have to fight again, soon. Peasants, women and vagabonds will have to wait until those who contribute to our defence are seen to.'

'How do you think she got that?' asked Felix, pointing to the wound.

'Aye,' said Rodi. 'The girl's a match for any two of your *fighting men*.'

'It's all right,' said Kat. 'He'll see me when he can.'

'No it isn't,' said Felix levelly.

The priestess of Shallya looked over her shoulder, guilty, but the surgeon continued on, ignoring them, until Gotrek stepped in his way and folded his arms over his bearded chest.

The surgeon glared and opened his mouth, but Gotrek just kept staring at him, and whatever he had intended to say withered in his throat. Finally he snorted and turned back. 'Very well. Very well.'

He crossed to Kat and pulled her arm straight with more force than was necessary. She stifled a hiss, then sat stoic and grim as he prodded and squeezed the bite.

'A job for you, Sister Willentrude,' the surgeon said at last. 'Whatever poisons the beast carried are already in the bloodstream.' He looked back at his assistant. 'Fetterhoff, let the sister make her prayers, then salve it and bind it.' He stood and started back to the wounded knight. 'And be quick.'

'Yes, Surgeon Tauber,' said the assistant.

Felix and the Slayers watched him go with sullen eyes as the priestess and the assistant got to work. The sister took Kat's arm in gentler hands than Tauber's, and murmured over it while touching each of the punctures with her plump fingers. The assistant opened a leather case and took out a pot of salve and a length of gauze.

'Where is the mess in this place?' Rodi asked the assistant. 'All that fighting made me hungry.'

'And thirsty,' said Snorri.

Before the assistant could answer, Sister Willentrude finished her prayers and smiled. 'The mess hall is in the underkeep,' she said, pointing to a pair of tall iron-bound doors set into the rocky hill upon which sat the keep. They were swung wide, revealing a shadowy interior. 'Evening mess is at sunset, but there's always food for valiant fighters at Castle Reikguard.' She smiled over her shoulder as she started after the surgeon and the assistant started salving Kat's arm. 'And beer as well.'

The Slayers brightened considerably at this, and Gotrek and Rodi helped Snorri up, then put his arms over their shoulders. But before they could take a step towards the underkeep, a young knight in the mustard and burgundy of von Volgen's troops hurried towards them and made a tight bow, blocking their way.

'Your pardon, mein Herren,' he said. 'Lord von Volgen requests your presence in the temple of Sigmar. His son's scouts say you have some knowledge of the necromancer behind all this.'

The Slayers glared at him and kept walking.

'We don't know any more than he does,' said Gotrek.

'Nevertheless,' said the young knight, backing up before them. 'I'm afraid I must insist.'

'Will there be beer?' asked Snorri.

'Will there be food?' asked Rodi.

The young knight scowled. 'This is a council of war, mein Herren.'

'Who has a war council on an empty stomach?' asked Rodi. 'Come see us after we've eaten.'

The young knight was turning red in the face. 'But – but, mein Herren...'

Felix grunted. 'I'll go,' he said, then stood and looked down at Kat, who was waiting as the assistant tied off her bandage. 'I'll find you in the mess.'

She smiled up at him. 'I'll make sure they save you some beer.'

The temple of Sigmar was just to the right of the main gate – a squat, sturdy stone building with a simple wooden hammer hung above heavy wooden doors. Felix followed the young knight into the stark, unadorned interior and made to stand behind the other men who were gathered there, but von Volgen, leaning wearily against the heavy stone altar next to Nordling and von Geldrecht, beckoned him forwards with a splinted hand. Despite his wounds, or perhaps because of them, he looked even more of a brute out of his armour than in, his battered head growing out of his shoulders without a hint of neck, and his broad chest swathed in bandages under his open doublet. Wounded, thought Felix, but in no way weak.

'Mein Herr, welcome,' he barked. 'Now, tell us what you know of this cursed necromancer.'

Felix stepped to the altar, then turned, feeling awkward with all eyes upon him. The men were a hard-looking bunch, as befitted the officers of one of the great castles of the Empire, but also hard-used, with many a fresh scar and bandage among them. He saw no one he thought might be Graf Falken Reiklander.

'Well,' he said. 'We first saw him as we were leaving Brasthof, on the trail of the beast herd. He said his name was Hans the Hermit, and he offered himself as a guide who knew the Barren Hills. He seemed... a bit mad, but he knew his business. He led us to the beasts, and then showed us tunnels – old barrows – that led under their camp to Tarnhalt's Crown. He said he was a grave-robber.' Felix smirked ruefully. 'And he is at that, I suppose.'

Nobody laughed, so he continued. 'We – we should have known he was more than he seemed. He smelled of death, and slipped out of shackles that he shouldn't have been able to escape.'

'Did he speak?' asked General Nordling. 'Did he betray any weaknesses, any schemes?' Without his helmet, the black-browed knight revealed a ring of short black hair around a bald head.

'Not before he raised the dead,' said Felix. 'But after... after, he spoke through the corpses as they closed on us, all of them talking in unison. He said the beast-shaman's magic had interfered with his own, and he had led us to them because he knew Gotrek's axe could destroy their herdstone, which was the source of their power.' He turned to von

Volgen. 'I'm afraid that's all I know of him. You were there for the rest, my lord. He set the dead against us and threatened to sack Altdorf.'

Von Volgen nodded, then looked around at the others. 'Have any of you heard rumour of such a villain? Have any fought him before?'

The officers all mumbled and shook their heads, but then a gravel voice spoke from the back.

'What did he look like, this necromancer?'

Felix looked up and saw a long-jawed old priest of Sigmar sitting on a stool behind the others. He might once have been a powerful man, but he was frail now, and blind. There was a rag wrapped around his eyes and he held a cane instead of the traditional hammer. A skinny Sigmarite acolyte stood at his left shoulder, and the plump old sister of Shallya stood at his right. Another woman stood beside her – a noblewoman of about forty years, with braided blonde hair coiled tightly to her head. She was beautiful and richly dressed, but carried a sadness in her eyes that was painful to look upon.

'He looked like a beggar,' said Felix to the priest. 'A wild-eyed old madman with a long dirty beard and filthy robes. No one wanted to touch him, let alone stand downwind of him.'

'Do you know him, Father Ulfram?' asked von Geldrecht.

The priest frowned, wrinkling the bandage over his eyes. 'No, no. That is not the description I feared to hear. This man is unknown to me.' He sighed. 'There are so many wicked men now. So many turn away from Sigmar and... and...' He trailed off, staring blindly at a point over the altar, his mouth still open. Felix stared. How did such a feeble old man come to be priest for a garrisoned castle? Why wasn't there a warrior priest here?

After an uncomfortable second, his acolyte patted Father Ulfram on the shoulder and the old priest subsided, muttering, 'Thank you, Danniken. Thank you. Was I saying something?'

'Yes, Father Ulfram,' murmured the acolyte. 'And well said it was. Very well said.'

A sturdy handgunner captain with a short brown beard and a plain, open face stood and coughed. 'Lord general,' he said. 'I don't know about the others, but if this fellow can raise ten thousand corpses, it doesn't matter if he's mad. We haven't enough men now to stop him.'

'I'm with Hultz,' drawled a scrawny, sandy-haired spear captain who slouched against a pillar. Despite a recent scar that puckered the whole left side of his face, his eyes glinted with the sly humour of a barracks tale-teller. 'I went north with four hundred. I came back with seventy. We've done our bit. Let somebody else take the first charge for a change.'

The handgunner captain and a short red-cheeked, red-headed man in the canvas breeks and jacket of a boatman murmured their approval, but a tall young greatsword captain with a bushy blond beard stood and rounded on the spearman.

'Our "bit" never ends, Zeismann!' he barked. 'We are soldiers of the Empire. We never shirk our duty.'

'Easy, Bosendorfer,' said Zeismann. 'I didn't say my lads wouldn't fight. I just think we should do it from a better position.'

'That is not an option,' said General Nordling, then nodded to von Geldrecht. 'The steward has informed me of Graf Reiklander's decision. We are to defend Castle Reikguard to the end.'

Von Volgen grunted, clearly unhappy. 'Forgive me for speaking plainly, my lords, but I fear you are just not equipped to hold here. If – if you were to allow me to speak to Graf Reiklander, perhaps–'

'You may not,' said Nordling, cutting him off.

Von Geldrecht was more polite. 'I'm afraid the graf is extremely ill from his wounds,' he said, 'and must not be unduly disturbed. Is that not the case, Grafin Avelein?'

The blonde woman at the back nodded dully. 'Yes, steward. It is so.'

Von Geldrecht leaned towards von Volgen, embarrassed. 'She lets no one but myself see him,' he whispered. 'I suppose because I am a cousin.' He shrugged. 'It is an awkward situation. Please forgive it.'

'I– I see,' said von Volgen, glancing from Avelein to von Geldrecht to Nordling. 'I did not know his wounds were so grievous. Forgive me.'

'The fault is ours for not telling you earlier.' Von Geldrecht turned to the officers and raised his voice again. 'But the graf was adamant. He said that it matters not that we are at less than full strength. This is the ancestral seat of the Reikland princes. It is Karl Franz's family home. It is the Reikland's eastern bastion. For both strategic and symbolic reasons, it must not fall.'

'The question, then,' said General Nordling, 'is not whether we should defend the castle, but how? I have sent ten messenger pigeons to be certain that one reaches Altdorf. Once the message is received, it will take at least six days for a relief force to arrive, if one can be assembled quickly. We must therefore be prepared to hold out for a week or more.' He nodded to von Geldrecht. 'The lord steward tells me we have enough food and fresh water for three months of siege. Now I wish to hear from each of you the status of your forces – men, supplies, weapons, ammunition.' He turned to von Volgen. 'My lord, if you would begin.'

Von Volgen winced and pressed a hand to the bandages around his ribs, then nodded. 'I had roughly two hundred knights when I left the Barren Hills,' he said. 'I lost more than a dozen to harrying attacks along the way, and many more during the fight today. I cannot say how many, but I would guess twenty or more dead, and as many wounded. So, perhaps one hundred and fifty ready to fight, though I'm afraid their kit is not of the best at the moment.'

'Thank you, my lord,' said Nordling. 'My knights will be happy to supply you with anything you need. Zeismann?'

The spear captain touched his forelock with a hand that was missing its two middle fingers. 'As I said, general, seventy men fighting fit. Maybe twenty more could fill in if things got desperate. The rest...' He showed his mutilated hand. 'They got worse than I did, and can't hold a spear with both hands no more. Our kit's in good shape, though. We've more spears than men, sad to say.'

Nordling nodded. 'Hultz?'

The handgunner captain saluted. 'Not many of my boys left, as you know, general,' he said. 'Too many buried at Grimminhagen.' He shrugged. 'Fifty-two, counting me, but six of them in the sick tent. Our guns are in good order, and we have plenty of powder, but...' He shot a glance at the man beside him, a gaunt artillery captain with one white eye and one blue, and waxy burn scars all over his bald head. 'But Captain Volk tells me...'

Volk straightened. The burn scars made him look like a half-melted daemon, but he talked like an Ostermark farmer. 'We're low on shot, m'lord,' he said, 'fer cannon and hand weapons both. Firing stock fell low up north and the new order from Nuln tain't arrived yet.'

'How soon is it meant to?' asked Nordling.

'Any day now,' said Volk. 'But I hear they been slow filling orders lately. Lot of folk looking to restock just now.'

'Exactly how much shot have we left?'

Volk pursed his lips. 'Enough for a few small engagements, m'lord, but if we was to be asked to keep up a steady rate of fire...' He scratched his scarred chin. 'Three hours or so with all seven cannons going. Less for the handguns, if all fifty o' Hultz's boys was firing away at speed. Maybe two hours.'

'That is grave news,' said the general. 'And your crews? Have you men for all seven cannon?'

'Oh aye,' said Volk, then made a face. 'Well, enough for five, at least. But these corpses won't be sailing up on boats, will they? So we can likely leave the riverside guns cold.'

'We can but hope,' said Nordling. He turned to the greatsword captain. 'Bosendorfer?'

The young man snapped a sharp salute. Too eager by half, thought Felix. 'Yes, general,' he said. 'Thirty men fighting fit and eager to serve. Our kit is polished and in good repair, and our Zweihunders sharp.'

'Any wounded?'

'Eight, my lord,' said Bosendorfer, 'but recovering quickly. I did not include them in my count.'

'Thank you, Bosendorfer. At ease.' Nordling turned to the red-headed boatman. 'River Warden Yaekel?'

The man saluted, but chewed his lip before answering. 'You know we didn't go north, general. Our duties on the river kept us here same as Steward von Geldrecht here. So we have a full complement – two fully armed and stocked river sloops, twenty-man crews for each, and a few skiffs and longboats, but – but, my lord, I have to agree with Zeismann and Hultz. There ain't no point in staying here. We'll never hold for so long. We have to retreat.' He took an involuntary step forwards. 'Please, let me and my men sail to Nadjagard and arrange things for your coming. We will–'

'No, Yaekel,' sighed Nordling. 'You won't be going anywhere. No one will. The graf has spoken.' He turned to the last man in the group, a hangdog-looking fellow with greasy brown hair spilling from his cap. He wore a doublet that proclaimed he was a Nordland forester, but breeches that suggested he was an officer of the Nuln city guard. 'And you, Captain…? Captain…?'

'Captain Draeger, m'lord,' said the man in a voice that announced him as a native of Altdorf's slums, and therefore not likely to have won any part of his uniform legitimately. 'Beggin' yer pardon but this ain't our posting. My lads are on their way home to the old city and just stopped for the night – thank you kindly fer the hospitality. But if it's all the same to you, we'll be on our way again.'

Nordling glared at him. 'It is *not* all the same to me,' he said. 'You're Reikland militia, are you not?'

'Aye,' said Draeger. 'Altdorf muster. Gallows Lane's finest.'

'No doubt,' murmured the general. 'Well, Captain Draeger, the Reikland still needs you. You will stay. How many men in your company?'

'Er, about thirty,' said Draeger, his eyes widening. 'But – but, m'lord, we was demobbed in Wolfenburg. They gave us our pay and sent us home. We–'

'Don't try it, my son,' said Zeismann. '"We done our bit" won't fly for you any more than it did for us.'

'It most certainly will not!' said Nordling. 'You have officially re-enlisted, captain. And fear not,' he said, as Draeger began complaining again, 'you will be paid.'

'Rather be gone than paid,' muttered Draeger, and folded his arms.

Nordling ignored him and stroked his black beard, thinking. 'Well then,' he said. 'Combined with the graf's knights – at least those who are fighting fit – we have roughly five hundred men, and when all the tenant farmers are brought in from the graf's lands, we will have another five hundred or so bowmen to add to our complement, making it an even thousand.'

'Against ten times as many,' said Yaekel bitterly.

Nordling turned hard eyes on him. 'Enough, river warden. The walls of Castle Reikguard have never been taken. I have every confidence we will survive.'

He turned and surveyed the others. 'Now, are there any further questions? Any further objections?'

No one said anything.

'Very well,' he said. 'Steward von Geldrecht will take the information you have given and consult with the graf as to strategy. In the meantime, you will inform your men of our situation and prepare for imminent attack, understood?'

The men all grunted their assent.

'Very good,' said Nordling, then saluted the others. 'You are dismissed. Long live the Emperor and may Sigmar protect us all.'

'Long live, Sigmar protect,' came the answering murmur, and the men began to talk amongst themselves as they started for the door.

Felix watched them as he followed them out. Except for the river warden, Yaekel, and Draeger, the militia captain, he thought the defence of the castle seemed in good hands. Bosendorfer was young and excitable, but full of fire, and von Geldrecht was a pompous ass, but he only looked after the stores. All the rest seemed hard, seasoned men.

'Herr Jaeger,' said a rough voice behind him.

Felix turned. Von Volgen was limping up behind him.

'My lord?' said Felix warily.

Von Volgen read his expression and scowled, embarrassed. 'I– I wanted to apologise, mein Herr,' he said. 'I treated you and your friends abominably on our journey here. I hold the rule of law sacred above all things, and do my best to live by it, but the death of my son... deranged me for a time, and I let anger rule instead of logic. Please forgive me for the lapse.'

Felix blinked, surprised. The lord's gruff manner had not prepared him for such a speech. He inclined his head. 'I understand, my lord. It must have been a great shock. But it wasn't me you swore to kill. You should speak to the Slayers as well.'

'I will,' he said. 'And I thank you for your understanding.' And with that he bowed, and strode out through the temple door and into the courtyard.

Felix watched him go, bemused. He had expected the bulldog to act like a bulldog. Strange to find him a nobleman after all.

As he started to follow von Volgen out, he heard voices behind him and looked back. Avelein Reiklander was kneeling before the altar, head bowed to the hammer, while Sister Willentrude hovered behind her.

'Grafin,' the sister whispered, 'are you sure you wouldn't like me to look at your husband? Shallya has been known to work miracles.'

The grafin finished her prayer then stood, shaking her head. 'Thank you, Sister Willentrude, but my husband needs nothing but rest and peace. He will recover.'

The sister looked doubtful, but only bowed her head as the grafin turned for the door. Felix turned too, and hurried out, not wanting them to have caught him eavesdropping, and also wondering just what sort of wounds the graf had taken in the north.

* * *

'You are welcome to stay in any empty room you find,' said Captain Zeismann as he handed Felix and Kat bowls of stew from the mess line. 'And there's plenty empty. Most of the former occupants are sleeping in the ground north of Grimminhagen now.' He waved a magnanimous hand. 'Take some of the knights' rooms. Y'don't want to bunk with the likes of us. Filthy peasants, all of us.'

This got a laugh from his men, who stood in line as well. They were in the cavernous underground mess, just one of the many chambers of the labyrinthine underkeep, which also contained barracks, store rooms, kitchens and workshops, as well as Tauber's surgery and a Shallyan shrine. The mess hall was loud with a hundred conversations, and warm from the heat of a huge fireplace at one end of the hall and the kitchens at the other.

'Very generous of you,' said Felix. 'But shouldn't we ask the knights first?'

Zeismann scowled towards the household knights, who sat all together at a dozen tables on the right edge of the room. 'Nah,' he said. 'They'll only say no if y'ask. But no one'll say anything if y'just take 'em.'

Felix smirked. 'Well, if they do, I'll tell 'em it was you who told us we could.'

Zeismann laughed. 'You do that.'

'Snorri thinks your bowls are too small,' said Snorri, looking dubiously at what the serving girl had handed him.

'Are you sure your stomach isn't too big, Father Rustskull?' asked Rodi.

'Come back for seconds if you like,' said Zeismann. 'We're always well stocked at Castle Reikguard.'

'Aye,' said Artillery Captain Volk. 'Till the war, the biggest danger the castle garrison ever faced was gettin' fat.' He grinned down at his skinny frame. 'Be a while 'fore we get some meat back on our bones after our long winter's jaunt, though.'

'Worry not, Captain Volk,' said Zeismann. 'At least ye'll be safe from the zombies. They'll think yer one of them!'

Everybody laughed, then started for the tables.

Felix scanned the room as he, Kat and the Slayers followed. The various companies seemed to stick to their own kind, the handgunners at one table, the spearmen at another, the river wardens closest to the kitchens, while the household knights sat at the tables closest to the right wall. Bosendorfer, the towering, blond-bearded young captain, was laughing with his greatswords at a table near the fire. They were all big, broad-shouldered fellows like himself, and all wearing slashed doublets and hose and the most elaborate facial hair they could manage. It seemed they were having a contest to see who could spit into the flames from where they sat.

Von Volgen, as a noble guest, was dining with Nordling and von Geldrecht in their private quarters in the keep, which left his eight-score

Talabeclander knights to eat here, sitting in a huddled crowd to one side, not quite comfortable in a room full of Reiklanders. The castle's other guests, the slovenly free-company captain, Draeger, and his motley militiamen, sat whispering over a table as far from the others as they could find, and looking often over their shoulders.

Felix, Kat and the Slayers crowded in with Zeismann's spearmen at their table as they shoved aside to make room. They seemed a cheerful bunch, but Felix noticed a gauntness of cheek and hardness of eye among them that he had seen in other soldiers returning from the fighting in the north. Some, at the edges of the group, didn't join in the jokes and jibes at all, only stared dull-eyed at horrors hundreds of miles away and months in the past. Felix had seen that look before too.

'All dwarf work,' said Gotrek, looking up at the arched stone ceiling as he shovelled stew. 'All this underwork. And better built than that human pile that sits atop it.'

'Reikguard is the finest human-made castle in the Empire,' said the artillery captain, Volk.

'*Human*-made, aye,' said Rodi dryly.

There were some glares at that, but Zeismann spoke up before things could get uncomfortable. 'The Slayer is right, though,' he said. 'All this down here was built some eight hundred years ago, back when Gorbad Ironclaw was on his rampage. Emperor Sigismund ordered it to be converted into an Imperial fortress. It had to be turned from the Reikland princes' family seat into a citadel capable of holding a thousand soldiers and staff, and there was no one he trusted more than the dwarfs to do the job. They carved this little hill into a honeycomb, and built the harbour and outer walls too.'

'Trust dwarfs to put all our living quarters underground,' grumbled Volk. 'The knights' quarters have windows, air, the sun.'

'Wooden shacks,' said Rodi, between swallows. 'They'll fall down if you fart in them. You're safer here.'

'You haven't smelled Captain Volk's farts,' said one of the artillerymen.

Everybody laughed along with him, even Volk, and the tension eased. But as Felix took a swig from his mug, Kat trod on his toe under the table. He looked around and she nodded for him to bend down to her.

Felix frowned and looked around the hall as he leaned in. Had she spotted something strange? Was something wrong?

'What is it?' he whispered.

'We are leaving tomorrow with Snorri, yes?' she asked.

'Aye.'

'And Zeismann says we can have a private room tonight?'

'Aye,' Felix said again. 'If we want one, we are welcome–'

His eyes widened as he followed her train of thought to its conclusion. Though they had admitted their attraction to each other weeks ago, on the night she had saved him from freezing to death in the Drakwald, they had not, in all the time since, had any time to be alone together. Privacy had been fleeting on the trail, and being chased by beastmen was not particularly conducive to a romantic mood. The abject terror tended to get in the way.

But now, though a horde of undead was marching ever south towards them, they were for once in no immediate danger, and they would not be sleeping with only a thin sheet of canvas between them and their travelling companions.

'Ah,' he said. 'I see.'

Suddenly he couldn't finish his stew fast enough.

But though they practically raced across the courtyard – now filling up with the tenants coming in from Graf Reiklander's outlying farms – when they had finally found a room and closed the door behind them, they were strangely shy to begin.

For almost a full minute, Felix stood by the simple, neatly made soldier's bed, stroking Kat's hair and shoulders.

'Are – are you having second thoughts?' Kat asked at last.

'About you?' Felix laughed. 'Gods, no. It's only, having waited so long, I'm afraid we might have built up so great a mountain of expectation that... that we might not be able to get over it.'

Kat smiled shyly. 'You mean, "Now that we can, can we?"'

'Aye,' said Felix. 'Exactly.'

Kat shrugged. 'Well, there's only one way to find out.'

And with that, she tugged down on his collar until he bent to her, then went up on her tip-toes to kiss him. They came together hesitantly at first, but then Kat's lips parted and their tongues met. Filled with the strength of it, Felix crushed her to him, lifting her off her feet, and they toppled slowly to the bed.

FIVE

Felix and Kat walked together on a forest path. They were only a mile or so from Bauholz, where they were going to visit old Doktor Vinck. Felix was happy. It was an early spring day, still cold in the shade of the trees, but with a warm sun finding his face every now and then as they passed through a clearing, and he hadn't a care in the world. Gotrek wasn't there. Snorri and Rodi weren't there. Only he and Kat walked the path, and they were in no hurry, nor under any obligation.

Felix squeezed her hand. She squeezed back, and they stopped under the budding branches of an ancient oak, but as they leaned in to kiss, a distant cry reached Felix's ears – a bird of prey perhaps. He ignored it and bent closer, but Kat pulled back and looked around.

'Screaming,' she said.

'It's only a hawk,' said Felix.

'No.' Kat stepped away from him, back onto the trail. 'Can't you hear it? People are being killed.'

She started towards Bauholz again, jogging now.

'Kat, come back. It's nothing.'

She ignored him and ran on. He grunted in annoyance and started after her. The day was too perfect for trouble. He wanted her to come back and kiss him.

They ran out of the trees. The log walls of Bauholz rose beyond the fields before them, black smoke drifting in a cloud above them. The screams were clearer now. They were coming from the village.

Then they were at the gates, though Felix didn't remember running to them, shouting and pounding on the rough logs. Cries of terror and rage and the sharp reek of burning came from within.

Kat kicked the door. 'Get up!' she bellowed. 'Arm yourselves! We are under attack.'

Felix thought it was a very strange thing for her to say.

Felix blinked around, disorientated. He was not at the gates of Bauholz. He was in a dark room, lying in a cramped cot, his right side warmed by Kat and his left freezing where it pressed against the wall. But though the dream was fading, the shouting and pounding were getting louder and closer.

'Up, Reiklanders!' came the harsh low voice, and Felix wondered how he could have thought it was Kat's. 'To the walls!'

He raised his head and groaned, a terrible crick in his neck. Kat was sitting up beside him, naked and pushing her hair out of her face. The white streak in the middle of her dark brown tresses gleamed green in the light filtering through the room's diamond-paned windows. It looked like the castle had sunk beneath a sea of poison.

'What's going on?' Kat mumbled.

'I don't know.' He tried to sit up, then winced. His left leg was completely asleep.

The door slammed open and one of Nordling's knights leaned in. 'Up and out! The dead–' He stopped when he saw Felix and Kat. 'What in Sigmar's name are you doing here? These are our quarters!'

He waved an impatient hand and ran on, banging on the next door down the hall.

'The dead?' echoed Felix.

He and Kat looked at each other, then scrambled to their feet and started grabbing for their armour and weapons.

Spearmen, greatswords and knights hurried past them as Felix and Kat climbed the stone steps to the top of the castle wall. Torches glinted off their swords and spear-tips as they ran to their positions, and gleamed on the gun barrels of the handgunners who crouched between the crenellations, but the flames couldn't blot out Morrslieb's sickly green glow, which made the lowering clouds look like fat phosphorescent maggots, and turned everyone's skin a pasty grey.

To the right as they reached the parapet, Felix saw von Volgen talking earnestly with his knights, while to the left, Gotrek, Snorri and Rodi peered down over the battlements. Snorri had acquired a peg leg from somewhere, freshly sawn off at the bottom to fit his short frame, and had his hammer back, while Rodi had a new axe of dwarfen make to replace the one he had broken at Tarnhalt's Crown. Felix wondered where it had come from. A gift of the garrison?

'Snorri wants to go down and fight them,' Snorri was saying as Felix and Kat crossed to stand beside the Slayers.

'Don't worry, Father Rustskull,' said Rodi. 'They'll come to us soon enough.'

'Too soon,' said Gotrek, shooting a grim glare at Snorri.

Kat and Felix leaned out over the walls to see what the Slayers were looking at. The wan moonlight confused Felix's eyes, and at first he saw only twisted shadows lurching through the winter grass, but after a moment the shadows resolved themselves into walking corpses, both beast and man, hundreds of them converging slowly but inexorably on the castle. Already a thick crowd of them milled restlessly at the edge of the swift-flowing moat, while more and more stumbled forwards to join them, a moving carpet of the undead that stretched into the night for as far as he could see.

Gotrek was right. The dead had come too soon. Felix and Kat had planned to leave with Snorri the next morning, and be well on their way to Karak Kadrin before the horde arrived. Now they were trapped in the castle with everyone else. Gotrek must be furious. He had denied himself and Rodi a certain doom at Tarnhalt's Crown in order to get Snorri away from the undead, and now it was all for naught. Snorri was in worse danger than before, and Gotrek had done nothing but make an enemy of Rodi.

On the other hand, this wasn't necessarily the end of everything. Felix had fought the undead before and survived. He knew he was more than a match for any ten of them, and Gotrek was more than a match for a hundred. Still his stomach sank and his mouth went dry just looking at their lifeless, upturned eyes. And it wasn't just the dread of something dead returning to a travesty of life that chilled his blood, though that was horrible enough. It was the sheer, mindless inevitability of them. They were like ants, or water. A raindrop or a single ant was no threat. He could flick them away without effort. But a million ants, or a flood of water, those would find cracks in any wall, would spill over any barrier, would pull a man down and drown him in sheer numbers.

That was the true horror of the walking dead. They couldn't be reasoned with, couldn't be panicked into running away, couldn't be bought off or convinced to change allegiances. They were an unnatural force, as relentless as time or tides, and like time and tides, they would eventually wear you down, as mountains were worn down into hills and dead cattle were slowly stripped to the bone by thousands of tiny jaws. Zombies were as inevitable as death, for they were death.

'Look at 'em all,' said a spearman, his eyes dull. 'Endless. Endless.'

'And there's beasts among them,' said a handgunner, making the sign of the hammer. 'Sigmar, if that necromancer can make zombies of them monsters, what chance have we?'

'We must all pray to Morr,' said an artilleryman, touching a pin in the shape of Morr's raven on his cap. 'He will settle them and set us free.'

'Less of this talk!' cried General Nordling. 'We are Reiklanders! We fear nothing!' He was striding along the wall at the head of six household knights, with Steward von Geldrecht, and blind Father Ulfram and his acolyte, Danniken, following behind.

The men turned as the general stepped up into a crenellation and faced them, his back to the zombies. Felix could see that he was pale behind his jutting black beard, but he kept the fear out of his voice.

'Yes, our enemy is terrifying,' he said, as more men gathered around him. 'Yes, it is legion. But you are the strongest of the strong, the bravest of the brave, forged in battle against the Empire's greatest foes. Did we not hold the line together at Wolfenburg? Did we not drive back the fiends at Grimminhagen?'

'Aye!' cried the men. 'For the Empire! For the graf!'

Von Volgen and some of his men filed in at the back of the crowd, listening as Nordling continued.

'Neither do you stand naked and alone in the field against these horrors!' shouted the general, slapping the stones of the wall. 'You are protected by the defences of the finest castle of the Empire. Ogres could not ford our moat without being swept away. Dragons could not tear down our walls, so what chance have these poor corpses? Our battlements are dwarf-built and woven with powerful wards against the undead. They have endured for eight hundred years. Never has Castle Reikguard fallen, and never will it fall!'

The men cheered again, until Nordling raised his hands again. 'Quiet now for Father Ulfram, who will lead us in a prayer to Sigmar to give us strength for the coming–'

Something black and swift swooped out of the sky and slammed into him before he could finish, smashing him into Father Ulfram and knocking him off his feet.

'General! Father!' cried von Geldrecht, ducking and running to them as the black thing swept into the air again on leather wings.

'Kill it!' shouted a handgunner, pointing.

'Shoot it!' shouted a spearman.

Then the rest came.

Felix could not count the number of black shadows that streaked down out of the dim green sky and slammed into the defenders. It seemed as if the night had shattered and fallen in upon them. All along the walls, people were knocked to the courtyard, armour crushed and flesh torn, while others twisted and flailed as the things rode their backs, looking for all the world like lunatics dancing in flapping black cloaks. More were attacking the refugee farmers who had set up their meagre tents around the harbour. The peasants ran screaming as the ragged shades shredded their shelters and snatched up men, women and children to drop them to the flagstones or into the dark water of the harbour.

Felix ducked a swooping silhouette and drew his sword as Kat fired an arrow after it.

'Sigmar! What are they?'

Gotrek sheared the wing off one and it crashed at their feet in a spray of maggots and clotted bile. Felix recoiled at its rotting, snoutless face.

'Bats,' said the Slayer.

'Giant bats!' said Snorri, delighted.

'Giant *dead* bats,' said Rodi, wrinkling his bulbous nose. 'Grungni, what a reek.'

'So much for wards against the undead,' grunted Gotrek.

He and Rodi clambered onto the battlements and slashed around like whirlwinds as more black bodies dived at them. Snorri tried to follow, but couldn't manage with his new peg, and so stood guard with Felix over Kat as she continued loosing arrows.

A bat flew straight at Felix's face. He slashed with Karaghul and opened its chest to the bone, but momentum drove it into him, and it scrabbled at his chainmail shirt with diseased claws as teeth like black coffin nails snapped an inch from his cheek.

He retched, nauseated, and shoved it away, then cleaved its decaying head with his sword. It spun down over the wall, and Kat sent another after it, the fletching of her arrow sprouting from its eye. Felix made to turn back, but Kat laughed and pointed down towards the moat.

'Look at them!' she cried. 'Come on, you bone bags! More! More!'

Felix followed her gaze and saw that the undead, apparently stirred by the fighting over their heads, were pushing towards the walls – and toppling straight into the moat, where they were swept away by the roiling current. Dozens were floating downstream, and dozens more were falling.

Kat smiled grimly. 'At this rate the whole horde will be washed away!'

Gotrek chopped a bat out of the air directly above her head. 'Forget them, little one,' he rasped. 'Fight what you can hit.'

Kat scowled and she and Felix turned back to the bats on the walls, dropping them with sword and bow as they wheeled and swooped.

All along the parapet, the handgunners, knights and spearmen had rallied around their officers and were now fighting off the black shadows in good order, but they had already suffered terrible losses, and more fell every moment – punched from the parapet by the heavy bodies of the bats and torn apart by their claws. On Felix's right, the greatswords were sweeping their huge blades in wide circles over their heads, protecting Captain Bosendorfer as he pulled one of their number back onto the battlements. On his left, General Nordling had recovered, and was forming a square with his retinue around Father Ulfram and his acolyte while Steward von Geldrecht, bleeding badly from a wound on his leg, limped after them. Further on, Lord von Volgen and his men were fighting their way down the far stairs while the bats slammed down into them like black meteors.

In the courtyard Captain Zeismann and his spearmen were trying to herd the peasants towards the wide double doors of the underkeep as their tents burned down around them, but the farmers were being picked off as they ran, and many spearmen fell as well.

Then, with a sound like windmill blades turning in a gale, something huge swept over the wall, blotting out the sky. Felix ducked, and the thing skidded to a landing on the parapet beyond him, ploughing through Nordling's knights and knocking them flat with its enormous wings, as the armoured warrior on its back swept around it with an ugly black axe.

The beast was a wyvern – or perhaps a crude patchwork of several wyverns. It had a wyvern's vast leathery wings and whipping tail, and a cruel, horned head that snapped at the end of a long neck, but its scaly skin was ten different colours, the wings black, the head green, the body grey and red and brown, and in ten different stages of decay, with thick scars and stitches holding it all together; but as gruesome as it was, the rider mounted athwart its hulking shoulders was more terrifying still.

He looked more than a yard taller than Felix, and was encased in scarred black armour of ancient design. A heavy-browed skull, etched with age, glowered out from under a horned helm, green flames kindling in his empty eye sockets. He swung from the wyvern's saddle and waded into Nordling's retinue, his black axe trailing a glittering cloud of dark specks like the tail of a comet. Three knights died instantly as the fell weapon shredded their armour like parchment, and the rider trod their corpses underfoot to stride towards Nordling and Father Ulfram as von Geldrecht crabbed out of the way, gibbering with fear.

Gotrek, Rodi and Snorri stared. The ancient rune of power on the head of Gotrek's axe was glowing red.

'Mine,' he said.

'No, mine,' said Rodi.

'Snorri's!' shouted Snorri.

The three Slayers charged as Nordling raised his sword and stepped in front of the skeletal warrior to protect Father Ulfram. The rider's flaking axe snapped the general's sword in half and smashed him off the parapet to bounce down the roof of the temple of Sigmar and into the courtyard.

'Face me, wight!' roared Gotrek, chopping into the wing of the undead wyvern as he dodged past it. The wyvern shrieked at the wound and leapt into the air as Rodi and Snorri ran under it.

'Face *me*!' called Rodi.

'Face Snorri!' bellowed Snorri.

'Come on,' said Felix, hacking at the swooping bats and starting forwards. 'We're safer near them than away.'

Kat dropped another bat point-blank, then followed, shouldering her bow and drawing her hatchets.

Gotrek reached the armoured wight first, and slashed for his knees just as he was turning from von Geldrecht to see what the commotion was.

The dread warrior roared and blocked, and a choking cloud of obsidian dust shivered from his black axe as it clanged haft to haft with Gotrek's, covering the Slayer in black grit. Rodi struck next, but his blow glanced off the ancient black armour without leaving a mark. Snorri's hammer did no better. The wight seemed hardly to feel their attacks, and hacked back at them.

'Stand aside, Gurnisson!' shouted Rodi. 'You owe me this doom for that which you denied me at Tarnhalt's Crown!'

'I owe you nothing!' barked Gotrek. 'Take it if you can.'

Kat and Felix fell in behind the Slayers, then turned as the wyvern *whumped* down again behind them, snapping and shrieking. Felix cursed and dodged right as Kat dived left, almost falling off the narrow parapet. Trapped with the Slayers between the beast and its master. Oh yes, much safer. What had he been thinking?

Kat buried her hand-axe in the beast's scaly neck, and it whipped around, crushing her against the wall.

Felix slashed, and Karaghul sheared off one of the wyvern's heavy horns. It roared and snapped, and he fell back into Snorri as the Slayer was dodging back from the wight. They went down in a heap and the wyvern raised up, its fanged jaws distending as it snapped down at them.

Snorri swung his hammer up and knocked the scaly head aside. Its snout slammed into the parapet inches from Felix's shoulder, shattering the stone, and he and the old Slayer scrambled up – only to have the wyvern's wing sweep them off the wall.

Felix froze, certain he was about to be smashed to a bloody pulp on the cobbles of the courtyard, but the impact came sooner than he expected, and he found himself rolling down the slanted roof of the temple of Sigmar in a scree of broken slates. He slid to a stop inches from the edge, then grunted as Snorri crashed on top of him.

Kat leapt down to the roof as the wyvern's jaws clacked shut inches behind her. She skidded to a stop beside him.

'Are you all right?'

'Aye,' wheezed Felix as he and Snorri untangled themselves. 'You?'

'Snorri is fine,' said Snorri. 'He landed on something soft.'

They scrambled up the slant again, dodging and swiping at bats as Snorri's peg leg slipped on the broken slates. Above them, the tide of the battle had turned. Rodi was driving back the undead wyvern, his axe making gruesome cuts in its head, neck and breast, while Gotrek was backing up the armoured wight and matching him strike for strike as his axe traced rune-red swipes in the air.

But as Gotrek blocked a blow to his head, the champion turned his swing and cut at the Slayer's legs instead. Gotrek dodged back instinctively, but not quite quick enough, and the blade of the black axe grazed his thigh, cutting through his striped trews and slicing into his flesh.

The wound only seemed to anger the Slayer, and his next strike was so strong that it nearly knocked the undead champion over the parapet, and left him fighting for balance. Gotrek chopped at his flailing left arm and sheared through it at the elbow. The wight's armoured forearm bounced away along the parapet and became nothing but a lifeless bone rattling inside a battered vambrace.

He staggered back, as Gotrek pressed his advantage, denting his armoured legs and torso. The undead warrior had had enough. He jumped back from Gotrek, then barged past Rodi and leapt into the saddle of the reeling wyvern, spurring it savagely. The two Slayers raced after him, but were too late. The wyvern flared its massive wings and knocked them back, then dived over the battlements and away.

'Come back, you coward!' bellowed Gotrek.

'How can the dead be scared to die?' shouted Rodi.

'Snorri missed the fight,' said Snorri.

'There are still plenty to fight, Snorri,' said Felix, helping Kat back onto the parapet.

But all at once, there weren't.

As if an order had been given, the bats flapped clear of their combats and flew after the dead wyvern and its malefic rider. Within a matter of heartbeats, the battle was over but for the groaning of the wounded and the weeping of the peasants in the courtyard.

While officers called orders and soldiers called for the surgeon, Gotrek and Rodi turned from the battlements, their faces hard and angry. The wound in Gotrek's thigh had drenched his trews red to the knee, but he paid it no mind. Instead he crossed to the severed forearm of the undead champion and picked it up. It began to disintegrate as soon as he touched it, the armour rusting away in brown flakes and the radius, ulna and finger bones within it crumbling to dust.

Gotrek crushed it in his meaty hand and looked out over the walls. 'A worthy doom,' he said.

'Aye,' said Rodi, glaring at him. 'For me, Gurnisson.'

Gotrek turned on the young Slayer. 'I did not rob you of your doom at Tarnhalt, Balkisson. You put down your hammer for the same reason I put down my axe.'

Rodi snarled and stepped closer to him. 'You forced me to it.'

'You were free to defy me,' said Gotrek. 'As you were free to walk into the wood today.'

Rodi's hands balled into fists, and his face, already red, turned a deep vermillion. Gotrek put his axe on his back and waited, hands at his sides, meeting Rodi's furious glare with his single contemptuous eye.

'Snorri thinks he would have found his doom tonight,' said Snorri, trying to climb back onto the parapet as Kat helped Felix up, 'if some coward hadn't pushed him.'

Gotrek and Rodi held their staredown for another second, then broke off to take the old Slayer's hands.

'Lucky for you, you didn't,' said Rodi.

He and Gotrek pulled Snorri onto the wall and Felix breathed a sigh of relief. Snorri couldn't have done it on purpose, but he had intervened at just the right time. The last thing Castle Reikguard needed just now was a pair of Slayers brawling across the ramparts.

'Dwarfs!' gasped von Geldrecht, limping forwards on the arm of a knight, and followed by Father Ulfram and Danniken. 'Dwarfs, I owe you my life, and I thank you. You, more than anyone, drove that hellish wight away and saved me from its axe. But – but did you not tell us the leader of the undead horde was a mad old man?'

'That wasn't Hans the Hermit, my lord,' said Felix, shivering. 'I don't know who it was, or what. I have never seen it before.'

'It was Krell,' rasped Gotrek.

Von Geldrecht blinked. 'Who? Who is Krell?'

'Krell the Holdbreaker,' said Gotrek. 'The Lord of the Undead.'

'The Butcher of Karak Ungor,' said Rodi. 'The Doom of Karak Varn.'

'Whose name is written a hundred times in the Book of Grudges,' said Gotrek.

'Who so hated dwarf-kind that he returned from the dead to seek vengeance upon us,' said Rodi.

'My doom,' said Gotrek.

'*My* doom, said Rodi.

Gotrek glanced at the young Slayer and gave him a vicious smile. 'He may well be, beardling,' he said, then wiped blood from his wounded leg and looked at his hand. 'But he has already killed me.'

SIX

Felix frowned, certain he couldn't have heard the Slayer correctly. 'Killed you?' he said. 'Gotrek, it's just a scratch. You've taken worse. Far worse.'

'No, manling,' said the Slayer. 'I have not.' He held out his hand. The blood that dripped from his thick fingers was peppered with tiny black flecks. 'The Axe of Krell leaves behind splinters of obsidian. They burrow to the heart and bring slow death.' He smiled again, a grim flat line. 'I have found my doom at last.'

Felix's heart lurched. His head swam as he tried to take it in. Could he have already witnessed Gotrek's doom without knowing it? It seemed impossible. The Slayer couldn't die in such a sad, inglorious way.

'Gotrek,' he said, stepping forwards. 'You have to clean the wound. You can't let this happen.'

'Of course he can't!' said von Geldrecht, limping forwards. 'Sigmar's beard, Herr Slayer, you must see our surgeon immediately. These splinters must come out!'

Gotrek turned a cold eye on the steward. 'Is it my doom that worries you, lordling? Or your own?'

Rodi laughed at this, while Von Geldrecht's red face got even redder.

'Certainly, Slayer, you are a great boon to our defences,' he said. 'But you mistake me. I am merely concerned for your wellbeing–'

'A Slayer's "wellbeing" is his own business,' growled Gotrek, and started for the stairs to the courtyard with Rodi and Snorri following. 'And it doesn't matter. The slivers are already at their work. There's no getting them out now.'

Felix swallowed and stepped after him. 'Surely it's worth trying, Gotrek. Poison is no death for a Slayer.'

Gotrek waved him off and continued. 'Leave me be, manling. I need a drink.'

Kat put a hand on the Slayer's arm as he passed her. 'Gotrek. Please. It might let you live long enough to face this Krell again.'

The Slayer stopped and looked at her for a long moment. 'Aye. It might,' he said at last. He nodded. 'Very well.'

As they started for the stairs again, Felix shot Kat a relieved glance, and von Geldrecht let out a breath.

'Thank you, fraulein,' he said, limping after them. 'You have done us a great service with this–'

She stopped and snarled back at him. 'I didn't do it for you!'

Felix turned away so von Geldrecht wouldn't see him smirk at his stunned expression.

'I'm sorry, Felix.' said Kat. 'He doesn't give a damn about Gotrek's "wellbeing".'

'Don't apologise,' said Felix. 'I'd have done the same if I had any guts.'

Rodi growled as they started across the ruined courtyard towards the underkeep. 'Two thousand years of grudges crossed off in the book when Krell died,' he said.

Kat looked at him, amazed. 'You have fought him for two thousand years?'

'Aye,' said Rodi. 'Ever since he gave himself to the Blood God and came for our holds.'

'Karak Ungor and Karak Varn both suffered beneath his axe before that pup Sigmar killed him,' said Gotrek.

'And now he lives again,' spat Rodi. 'And all those grudges must be written back into the book as unavenged.'

Gotrek nodded, his one eye distant. 'Aye, but the Slayer who gives him a true and final death would be remembered in the histories forever.'

'Aye,' said Rodi, thumping his chest with his fist. 'Rodi Balkisson, Slayer of Krell.'

Gotrek shot him a hard look. 'We will see about that.'

'Snorri thinks Snorri Nosebiter, Slayer of Krell, sounds better,' said Snorri.

Rodi grunted at that, and Gotrek ground his teeth, and they stumped on in silence. Felix shook his head at the dwarfishness of it all. Cut by an axe that seemed certain to kill him, and Gotrek was still more concerned with wrongs done to his ancestors thousands of years before – and of course by how he would be remembered by the dwarfs who would come after him. It seemed sometimes that dwarfs lived more in the past than they did in the present.

As they continued across the courtyard, however, Felix's grim amusement faded, to be replaced by a growing sense that something was terribly wrong in the castle. The dead and dying were of course everywhere, and the air was filled with the stench of burnt tents and roasted flesh, but there was something else, something worse behind it all, though he couldn't put a finger on what.

Dead knights, farmers, spearmen, greatswords, handgunners and river men lay where they had died, their faces and necks shredded to red ruin, and their bones smashed by falling from the walls. There were corpses burning amidst the smouldering tents, and bumping against the hulls of the boats in the harbour, and the wounded looked hardly better, howling and sobbing with deep claw marks in their backs and their limbs crushed and bent.

Zeismann's spearmen and von Volgen's knights helped the farmers pick through the carnage, dragging the living to one side, and piling the dead on the other. The tenants wept pitifully when they found loved ones, and some could not continue. A mother hugged her child to her breast, the blood from his torn throat drenching her tunic. A young girl shrieked ceaselessly for her parents.

The men of the castle gathered their wounded as well, carrying them into the underkeep on stretchers as they moaned and wailed.

The wailing.

Perhaps that was it.

Felix couldn't tell if it was his imagination, but the screaming of the wounded seemed even more agonised than was usual after a battle. Even the cleansings and salvings of the Shallyan initiates and Surgeon Tauber's assistants appeared to hurt them beyond bearing, as if they were being bathed with fire instead of water, and it got worse as Felix and Kat followed the Slayers into the underkeep.

Wounded men were laid out in the mess hall and along the corridor leading to the surgery, all in incredible pain. There was a smell about them too – a sick, sour reek of neglect that Felix associated with overcrowded poverty wards. He would have expected such a smell if the soldiers had lain here for weeks, but not so soon. Their wounds were fresh – minutes old. The place should smell of blood and burnt flesh, but not the charnel house. Not yet.

Captain Zeismann stood from lowering a spearman into a cot, and gave Felix, Kat and the Slayers a weary salute.

'Well done, friends,' he said. 'Y'did heroes' work up on them walls tonight. Saved old Goldie's bacon for him and no mistake.'

'Goldie?' asked Felix.

'Von Geldrecht,' said Zeismann. 'He ain't much, but–'

A roar of anger from the surgery cut him off, followed swiftly by the crash of overturning furniture and bellowed accusations.

'Murderer!'

'Poisoner!'

'You're in league with the necromancer!'

'Yer tryin' to turn us all into zombies!'

'Please!' cried a higher voice. 'It's got nothing to do with me!'

Felix recognised the voice as Tauber's, strained to breaking with fear.

'Aw, what's all this now?' groaned Zeismann, and hurried for the surgery door, which was clogged with knights and foot troops, all shouting and trying to get in at once.

Felix, Kat and the Slayers followed as Zeismann shoved and elbowed at the back of the mob, raising his voice to a parade-ground bark to be heard.

'Step back! Step back! What's the trouble?'

The three Slayers bulled through the crowd as if it weren't there, and Zeismann followed gratefully in their wake, with Felix and Kat taking up the rear.

Inside, Greatsword Captain Bosendorfer and a semi-circle of men had backed Tauber and his assistants into a corner. Tauber shrank from them, a scalpel in his shaking hand. His assistants wielded stools and buckets and mops. It smelled worse in there than in the corridor.

'You may have killed us, you traitor,' said Bosendorfer, 'but we'll take you with us.'

'And take your head off too,' said a spearman. 'You'll not be joining your zombie brothers.'

'Hoy, now!' said Zeismann. 'What's this about?'

'I haven't poisoned anyone,' cried Tauber. 'It must be something else! The claws of the bats!'

'A liar as well as a traitor,' sneered Bosendorfer. He pointed to one of his men, sweating on a cot like he was in an oven and clutching an arm wound that glistened with oozing green pus. 'Pulcher was cut by falling slates. Those horrors never touched him!'

'Then I don't know what it is!' said Tauber. 'But I've got nothing to do with it.'

'That's just what you would say,' said Bosendorfer, starting forwards. 'Grab him! Bring him out to the yard where I can make a proper swing. And fetch out his minions too.'

'Wait, now, Bosendorfer! Wait!' shouted Zeismann, getting in the greatsword's way. 'I know you don't like old Tauber, but these are serious charges. Let's take it to General Nordling.'

Bosendorfer shoved the spearman into Felix. 'Stay out of it, Zeismann! You don't outrank me!'

The greatsword charged at Tauber with the mob barging in behind him, fists flying.

'This is bad,' said Kat. 'Gotrek needs him.'

'We all need him,' said Felix, setting Zeismann on his feet. Tauber might be a pinched little man with the bedside manner of a mollusc, but he had patched up nearly a hundred wounded the day before and none had sickened – not even Kat, not even after Felix had threatened him. Whatever his crimes, Felix doubted this present evil was one of them.

He caught Bosendorfer's arm as he started to drag Tauber out of the room. 'Wait, captain! Are you really going to kill the only man who can patch you up?'

'Aye,' added Zeismann, stepping beside him. 'Are y'daft?'

Bosendorfer glared down at them from his impressive height, and looked like he was going to shove them aside, but the Slayers moved in behind them and he only snarled.

'He's not patching us up,' he said. 'He's murdering us, like he did up north!'

'He didn't murder anyone up north, Bosendorfer,' said Zeismann, exasperated. 'That's all been sorted out. He just couldn't save everyone. You know that.'

'I know nothing of the sort!' snapped the greatsword. 'I said then he was with the Kurgan, and now I say he's with this necromancer, trying again!'

Felix blinked, confused. The warrior sounded mad. 'If he's with the necromancer,' he said, as calmly as he could, 'then why didn't he poison everybody yesterday after the fight?'

Bosendorfer's cheek twitched as he locked eyes with Felix. 'Who are you, that we should listen to you? Are you with the necromancer too? Are you, Zeismann? Get out of our way! We've a traitor to kill!'

The men roared in agreement, and this time Bosendorfer did shove Felix and Zeismann, but as he started to drag Tauber between them, Gotrek, Snorri and Rodi stepped in his way.

'If you insult the manling,' said Gotrek, 'you insult us.'

Bosendorfer paused at this, looking uneasily from Slayer to Slayer. 'I– I didn't insult him. I only told him to get out of the way.'

'You said he was with the necromancer,' said Rodi.

'Snorri doesn't know any necromancers,' said Snorri. 'And neither does young Felix.'

Felix could see that Bosendorfer would have liked to back down in the face of three so fearsome opponents, but the men behind him were shouting insults at the dwarfs and egging him on. He was trapped, and it made him angry. 'I don't care who you know or who you are!' he shouted. 'You have no authority here! I am Graf Reiklander's captain of greatswords. I order you to get out of my way!'

The Slayers said nothing, only raised their fists. Felix and Kat did the same as the mob roared and Zeismann called for calm. But then, over all the noise, came a bellowing from the hall.

'Surgeon Tauber! Clear your table!'

Felix recognised von Geldrecht's voice, and so did the rest, for they all stopped shoving as the steward limped through with two household knights behind him. He was using a cane to walk.

'Tauber!' he gasped. 'You must see to General Nordling at once. He has a pestilence in his–' He stopped as he saw the scene before him. 'Bosendorfer, what is this? Unhand our surgeon!'

'My lord,' said Bosendorfer, saluting. 'It is Tauber who has caused the pestilence. Look!' He flashed a hand around at the wounded, all moaning and putrefying in their cots. 'Look at their wounds. He has poisoned them!'

'You don't know that, Bosendorfer!' said Zeismann.

Von Geldrecht cringed as he looked from horror to horror, then turned back to Tauber, a frightened look in his eyes. 'Is– is this true, surgeon?'

'No, lord steward,' said Tauber. 'I don't know what has caused it. I swear to you.'

'He's lying!' shouted Bosendorfer. 'He's killed us all!'

'My lord,' said Felix, 'I don't think he has. If he was responsible, wouldn't he have tried to slip away? He has been at his post, tending the wounded.'

'He has been sickening them!' cried Bosendorfer.

'How d'ye know it was him that did it?' said Zeismann. 'It could be anyone!'

Everyone began shouting at once, with von Geldrecht bellowing over them all for silence, but then, into the room pushed four household knights with General Nordling on a stretcher between them, and the cacophony died away to a whisper of murmured prayers and indrawn breaths.

The general, so straight and proud when Felix had first seen him, now lay on the stretcher like a victim of famine. His limbs, under the bloody shirt that was his only cover, were bone-thin and swollen at the joints, and his face was gaunt and grey. His breath came shallow and fast, like a panting dog. Felix saw only one wound on him, but it was terrible. A spike of broken bone jutted out of his left leg above the knee, and the gash through which it stuck was black and bubbling with green pus, and stank of death.

Zeismann choked as the knights put Nordling on a table. 'Sigmar, what happened to him?'

A frightened field surgeon who had trailed in behind the knights shook his head. 'He was well enough after he fell from the chapel roof. Just the broken leg, and he made jokes about it as we carried him to the barracks, but only moments after we cleaned the wound he was like this. I don't understand it.'

Von Geldrecht turned to Bosendorfer and motioned to Tauber, who was still pinned in the greatsword's iron grip. 'Release him. Let him work.'

Bosendorfer reluctantly let go, and Tauber stood erect, his limbs shaking.

'Thank you, lord steward,' he said, bowing to Von Geldrecht.

'If you are responsible,' said von Geldrecht, putting his hand on his sword, 'you will reverse the poison. If you are not, you will cure him, or it will be the worse for you.'

Tauber swallowed, and a look passed between the two men that Felix could not read. 'I– I will try.'

The surgeon motioned to his assistants and approached the table as they began to prepare his implements.

'Tell me everything you did,' he said to the field surgeon as he checked Nordling's pulse and pulled back his eyelids. 'Omit no detail.'

'We did only what we always do,' said the man. 'We removed his armour and clothes, examined him thoroughly, then washed his wounds clean of dirt and gave him strong wine to drink so that he would feel it less when we put the bone back. But… but we never got so far as that. He sickened too fast. He wasted away before our eyes!'

Tauber frowned, seemingly baffled, then looked back uneasily at von Geldrecht, who gripped the hilt of his sword with white knuckles. 'I am not sure what to do, my lord,' he quavered. 'He appears to be dying of dysentery, but to reach such an advanced stage of the disease should take days, not minutes.'

'I care not what it is,' said von Geldrecht. 'Only heal him.'

'But, my lord, to heal a man in this condition takes days – weeks. He will not get better in a matter of moments, no matter what I do.'

Von Geldrecht said nothing, only drew his sword, his face white. Tauber sighed and turned his assistants. 'Wash his wounds clean of pus and spoon-feed him water,' he said. 'After I salve the wound we will set the bone.'

The assistants nodded. One dipped a cloth in a basin beside the table, then began dabbing at the black meat of the wound as the other tugged Nordling's mouth open and began tipping water into it from a spoon, one drop at a time. Tauber crossed to a shelf and began pulling down pots and vials. But as he laid them out on a tray, there was a commotion in the hall and a woman's voice, high and strained.

'Let me through! By all mercies, let me through!'

The soldiers at the door parted and Sister Willentrude pushed in between them, her round face red and shiny, and her heavy chest heaving like a sail. Her eyes widened when she saw Nordling on the table, and she shot out a hand.

'Stop!' she cried. 'Do not touch him with that cloth! Take away that spoon!'

The assistants cringed back and Tauber turned, staring at her.

'What is this, Sister Willentrude?' he asked. 'Is there something–'

'The water,' she gasped as she tried to catch her breath. 'The lower well has been poisoned. And every jug, canteen and horse trough I have checked.' She turned to von Geldrecht. 'My lord, you must tell everyone. Do not drink or wash with water until we can test it all.'

'You see!' cried Bosendorfer, turning back to Tauber as von Geldrecht stared. 'The traitor has poisoned us all.'

SEVEN

Von Geldrecht turned on Tauber, eyes filled with fear and questions. 'Surgeon–'

Tauber stumbled back. 'My lord steward, I assure you! I have not done this thing. I haven't any such power. I am just an ordinary man. You know that.'

'Don't listen to him!' shouted Bosendorfer. 'He's poisoned me before!'

'Please, lord steward,' said Sister Willentrude. 'I can't believe it could be Tauber. He is a fine surgeon, a dedicated man of medicine! It couldn't be him!'

'Can you prove it wasn't?' asked Bosendorfer. 'Can you prove he is innocent?'

Von Geldrecht said nothing, only stared at Tauber as Bosendorfer and the sister continued to argue.

Felix couldn't take it any longer. He stepped forwards and shouted at von Geldrecht. 'Steward! Are you going to stand here while the men of the castle are still drinking and bathing in tainted water? Give the order!'

Von Geldrecht's eyes snapped around to Felix, hot with anger, but then he stopped, paling with realisation. He turned to the men. 'On my order,' he said. 'Speed to every corner of the castle. No one is to drink or touch water until I say. Go! Spread the word.'

The men, cowed by the horror of Nordling's condition, hurried out of the surgery without argument, yelling to everyone in the hall and leaving von Geldrecht and his knights, Bosendorfer, Zeismann, Felix, Kat and the Slayers standing around Tauber and his assistants, who looked shaken and sick.

'Water,' Tauber mumbled. 'How was I to know? How was I–'

A breathy rattle interrupted him and everyone looked at General Nordling. His shallow panting had stopped, and he lay absolutely still. Tauber went white and stepped to him, taking his pulse again and listening to his chest. He closed his eyes and murmured a prayer, then stood.

'He– he is dead, my lord steward.'

The household knights groaned and lowered their heads, but Bosendorfer spun to von Geldrecht.

'Kill him, my lord,' he said. 'Kill him as you said you would!'

'No!' cried Kat. 'He must see to Gotrek! Tauber has to clean the Slayer's wound!'

'My lord, you mustn't kill him,' said Sister Willentrude. 'Without water, we will have to find other ways to clean and dress wounds. We will need his expertise.'

'His expertise is in death,' snarled Bosendorfer. 'Hang him! Or the men will do it for you!'

Von Geldrecht had said nothing through this storm of argument, only held eyes with Tauber, but at this last he shot a sharp look at Bosendorfer.

'With General Nordling's death,' he said, cold and quiet, 'I am now acting commander until Graf Reiklander recovers. And as commander, I will not allow a man to hang without trial, nor will I allow him to be subject to barracks justice.' He turned to the household knights. 'Classen,' he said to a young knight sergeant with tears in his eyes. 'Lock up the surgeon. He will stay in the dungeon until we get to the bottom of this.'

'But, my lord,' said Sister Willentrude. 'That is no better. How will he do his work from a cell?'

'How will he clean Gotrek's wound?' asked Kat.

'Until I know where his loyalties lie,' said von Geldrecht, 'he remains under lock and key. Take him away, Classen. And his minions too.'

The young knight nodded, then motioned to the others to arrest Tauber and his men.

'Now,' said von Geldrecht, sighing. 'We will check the stores. I want to see if anything else was tainted.'

Kat looked like she was going to protest Tauber's arrest again, but the Slayer shook his head.

'Forget it, little one,' he said. 'It's all part of the doom.'

Felix gagged as Gotrek knocked in the top of a barrel of salted meats with his axe. Fat maggots crawled all over bubbling beef and the stench of rotting flesh burned his eyes. Kat cut open a sack of beans, then choked as clouds of mildew spores billowed up from it. In other parts of the vaulted cellar von Geldrecht and the rest were finding similar horrors. Sister Willentrude was opening a sack of onions that had become black balls of slime. Bosendorfer was picking distastefully through apples and turnips gone brown and runny while Zeismann was cringing away from the hard sausages that hung from the beams, their casings split and giving birth to a swarm of flies.

From the far side of the room came a dismayed dwarfen shout. 'Not the beer, too!'

Felix and Kat looked around. Rodi was standing on tip-toe staring into a keg almost as tall as he was, his hands white-knuckled on the lip. Snorri was staggering back, awkward on his peg leg, waving a big hand in front of his bulbous nose.

'Snorri thinks that's the worst beer he's ever smelled.'

Von Geldrecht blinked at the two Slayers, then turned and hurried to a long rack of dusty wine bottles. He grabbed one and broke the top off by knocking it against the wall, then inhaled over the open neck. He coughed and winced, holding the bottle away from him and covering his face in the crook of his arm.

'This flour might be saved,' said Zeismann.

The rest came over to look at the sack he had split open. The flour that spilled from it was crawling with tiny beetles, but did not appear rotten.

Von Geldrecht looked revolted, but nodded. 'It will have to be sifted, but it seems we have flour at least.'

'Yes,' said Bosendorfer. 'Though no water to mix it with, thanks to Tauber.'

'Mmmm,' said Zeismann, rubbing his skinny belly. 'Dry flour, with bugs.'

Sister Willentrude shook her head. 'The necromancer has nearly defeated us in a single night,' she said. 'The bats killed scores of men. The poisoned water has killed scores more, and hunger and thirst will finish the rest. It is impossible that the castle can still stand.'

Von Geldrecht glared at her. 'It *must* stand! We must hold until our relief gets here.'

'But how?' asked the sister. 'A man might live a week on biscuit, though he will be as weak as a child, but a week without water? Impossible. Four days at the most, and much less if he is forced to fight.'

'And we *will* be forced to fight,' said Felix.

'Can't you pray to Shallya?' asked Bosendorfer, holding up a disintegrating apple. 'Can't you make it all wholesome again?'

'The food is fouled beyond redemption,' said Sister Willentrude. 'But prayers to Shallya might purify some water, though how much I couldn't say.'

'What about taking water from the river?' asked Felix. 'Surely the necromancer can't have poisoned the whole Reik?'

'He don't have to,' sighed Zeismann. 'We're downstream from the

Reiker Marshes. The water for miles below that stinking swamp ain't fit to drink unless it is boiled.'

'So start boiling,' said Gotrek.

Von Geldrecht swallowed, looking as pale and sick as one of the poisoned defenders. His first moments as acting commander of the castle had not been auspicious ones. 'Yes,' he said. 'Start boiling. And pass word to the men that the food has been poisoned as well. I... I will consult with the graf.' And with that, he turned and limped out of the room.

As they left the store room and Bosendorfer and Zeismann went to tell the castle about the spoiled food, Kat stepped after Sister Willentrude.

'Sister,' she said, 'can you look at Slayer Gotrek's wound? It must be cleaned or he may die.'

The sister turned, smiling patiently. 'Child, I must begin my prayers. The danger we face is bigger than the wounds of one dwarf.'

'But he isn't only a dwarf,' pleaded Kat. 'He is a Slayer. Who else is strong enough to fight the wight king if he comes back?'

Rodi snorted. 'You'd think he fought the bastard alone,' he said under his breath.

Gotrek ground his teeth. 'I told you to forget it, little one.'

But Sister Willentrude was frowning, considering. She looked at Gotrek. 'I saw you fight on the walls, Herr dwarf. You are indeed worth a score of men. But where is this grievous wound? I see only the scratch on your leg.'

'That is it,' said Felix quickly. 'It was made by Krell's axe, which leaves poison splinters that seek the heart and kill in time.'

'And it is too late to remove them,' growled Gotrek, impatient. He turned and started for the courtyard. 'There are worse wounded, priestess. See to them.'

'No, Herr Slayer,' Sister Willentrude called after him. 'You are key to our defence. For the sake of the castle, if not your own, I will ask you to come with me.'

Gotrek kept walking, but Kat caught up to him and put a hand on his massive arm.

'Please, Gotrek,' she said. 'Let her try.'

Gotrek walked for a few more steps, but at last he stopped. 'For you, little one,' he said, 'I will go.'

The sister smiled as he turned back to her. 'Thank you, Herr Slayer. Follow me.'

She led them back towards the surgery, talking over her shoulder as she went. 'It isn't just for your fighting skill that I wish to keep you among the living. You lot have cool heads, and with General Nordling dead now, we will be needing all of those we can lay our hands on, I'm thinking.'

They entered the surgery, where Sister Willentrude's initiates were tending to the moaning rows of wounded, and followed her to a pantry-sized shrine of Shallya at the back.

She pointed Gotrek to a bench as she gathered forceps, lens, jug and cloth, and pulled a stool up in front of him. 'General Nordling ran the castle well,' she sighed. 'But with him dead and the graf unwell, that leaves von Geldrecht, and I fear old Goldie isn't up to the task.'

The sister took up the jug of water and began praying over it as Felix and Kat watched and the Slayers waited at the door, Rodi still muttering about Gotrek not being the only one to have fought Krell. The Slayer's gash was not deep, but it was grimed with little black flecks.

Finishing her prayer, Sister Willentrude tasted the water, then, satisfied, poured it liberally over the wound and sponged it with the cloth. The flecks lessened, but did not vanish. Next she took up the lens and the forceps.

'Yes,' she said, prodding the wound. 'There are slivers well buried in the muscle. Many of them.'

Gotrek sat stoic, his jaw set, as she gripped and pulled with the forceps, removing splinter after splinter from his flesh and wiping them onto the cloth.

'So, Graf Reiklander is confined to his bed?' asked Felix as she worked. 'He is that ill?'

Sister Willentrude sniffed. 'I know not. I saw him once, the day he returned with his troops, and he was gravely wounded, but since then the Grafin Avelein has not seen fit to let me see him, only Tauber. Only he and von Geldrecht are allowed into his rooms, and they tell me nothing other than, "his lordship is recovering".'

'Is that why von Geldrecht would not allow Bosendorfer to string Tauber up?' asked Felix.

'Very likely,' she said. 'Thick as thieves the steward and the surgeon have been since Graf Reiklander returned.' She shook her head bitterly as she removed another sliver. 'I wish the graf were well again – or that his son would return from university in Altdorf. The graf was an able commander, wise and strong, and Dominic a sharp-minded lad. Neither would have locked Tauber up for fear of Bosendorfer. They would have locked Bosendorfer up for insubordination. Now I must do double duty as physician and sister, and spend time and strength I don't have praying for pure water. Hopefully von Geldrecht will come to his senses. Besieged like this we cannot survive long without a real surgeon.'

'Is Tauber a good surgeon?' asked Kat.

The sister chuckled without looking up from her work. 'Felt the lash of his tongue, have you? Well, he's never been a friendly sort, and going north only made that worse. So many men dead. So many men he couldn't save. It left him bitter, but you'll find no more talented bone-cutter in the Empire. He treats Karl Franz himself when he summers here.'

With a sigh she sat back and mopped her brow. 'Well, I've removed all I can see,' she said. 'But there are more. I'm certain of it.' She pushed to her feet and stepped to her cupboard again, where she began pulling down pots and jars. 'I will prepare a poultice that will, Shallya willing, draw out more, but I don't know if even that will get them all.'

Gotrek shrugged as she began to mix ingredients in a bowl. 'As long as I live long enough to face Krell again, I don't care.'

'Don't think I'll back off because of this, Gurnisson,' said Rodi. 'You'll still have to beat me to him if you want him.'

'Don't worry, Balkisson,' said Gotrek. 'I will.'

Thick smoke was rising into the pink sky of pre-dawn as Felix and Kat stepped wearily out of the underkeep with the Slayers. A great pyre of headless bodies burned in the middle of the courtyard, and the air was filled with the queasy smell of sweet pork. Father Ulfram and his acolyte stood in front of the pyre, chanting, the blind priest holding his warhammer unwaveringly above his head and clutching the holy book to his chest unopened. In a circle around the pyre, their heads bowed in silent prayer, the survivors of the battle stood – the household troops, the knights, von Volgen's men, the servants and refugee farmers who had thought the castle would protect them.

In the front row, their faces carved into stark, flickering relief by the glow of the fire, were the various commanders and captains – von Volgen, with new bandages to add to the one around his chest, von Geldrecht leaning on his cane, Bosenndorfer glaring at the fire as if it were the enemy, Zeismann chewing his lip and shuffling his feet, Yaekel, the river warden, asleep on his feet, and Draeger with his thumbs hooked in his belt, looking like he'd rather be anywhere else.

Many of the farmers and servants wept. Many more just stared dully, shocked by the suddenness and savagery of the attack. The knights and household troops, veterans of the war in the north, only looked tired and resigned. Felix knew the look. He had seen it many times before, in the faces of those he had fought beside over all his long years with Gotrek. The loss of comrades in battle was never easy, but for the professional soldier, it was a familiar pain, and caused neither shock nor anger, just a weary sadness they locked away where it would not interfere with their work. The pain would be let out later, when all was safe, and would escape as drinking and fighting and whoring and the singing of raucous songs. But it was hidden now, and would not show itself while the threat of further battle remained.

Felix and Kat started across the courtyard towards the pyre, but the Slayers were talking amongst themselves and didn't follow. Felix paused, wondering if they were still arguing about Krell, but it was something else entirely.

'Pay your respects, manling,' said Gotrek. 'We want to have a look at these so-called ward-woven walls.'

'"Enduring",' sneered Rodi. 'Aye. As enduring as an elf's honour.'

Felix nodded and he and Kat joined the mourners as the dwarfs stumped off in the opposite direction. After seeing the squabbling between Bosendorfer, Tauber and von Geldrecht, Felix was a bit envious of the Slayers' ability to put aside their animosities and work for the common good. He knew that Gotrek and Rodi were still angry with each other, but they wouldn't let it get in the way of what was important. If only humans could learn that skill.

When Father Ulfram's chanting ended and everyone had murmured a last 'Sigmar preserve us', the crowd broke up – the surviving refugees returning to clear away their blackened tents, the household troops to begin repairing the defences, but the officers gathered around von Geldrecht and Father Ulfram, who were talking together in low tones. Von Volgen joined them too.

Felix edged closer with Kat, wanting to hear whether Graf Reiklander had told von Geldrecht to hold or retreat, but it was Father Ulfram who was speaking.

'No, I can't be certain,' he quavered. 'But I fear it must be. In the histories, they are always mentioned in the same breath. If the dwarf spoke true, and it was Krell he fought on the walls, then the necromancer is who I feared he was from the first – Heinrich Kemmler, who raised Krell from a thousand-year slumber to serve as his champion.'

The name seemed to mean little to most of the officers, and it stirred only vague memories from university lectures in Felix, but von Volgen knew it.

'It can't be Kemmler,' he said. 'He was slain over twenty years ago, in Bretonnia.'

'It might be,' said the priest, nodding. 'It might be, but the deaths of necromancers are often greatly exaggerated. And if it is he, we face a terrible threat. Terrible. Kemmler was said to be one of the greatest necromancers since Nagash, defeating the most powerful magisters and priests of his age. If he is returned, then dark days have befallen the Empire. Dark days.'

Zeismann snorted. 'And that's a change, is it?'

Von Geldrecht smiled and clapped Zeismann on the shoulder. 'Thank you, captain,' he said, with forced cheer. 'That is the true Empire spirit. Knowing the name of our enemy changes nothing. We have faced worse before, and spat in their eye. We will do the same now.' He turned to the others. 'Now, gentlemen, your reports. Bosendorfer?'

The men all looked at each other, clearly not fully confident in their new commander, despite how hard he was trying – or perhaps because of it.

'Ten men dead, sir,' said the greatsword at last. 'Four from Tauber's poisons.'

The steward coughed. 'Enough about Tauber. How many can fight?'

'Thirteen,' said Bosendorfer, sullen. 'Only thirteen.'

'Zeismann?' asked von Geldrecht.

'Thirty-three dead or wounded,' said the spear captain. 'Thirty-nine fighting fit.'

'Thirty-seven knights dead,' said von Volgen. 'Fifty-five well enough to fight. Forty more are wounded or sick from the tainted water. I do not include the knights who died or were injured in yesterday's engagement.'

'Eight dead,' said Artillery Captain Volk. 'We'll have to drop to two-man crews if y'want all the cannon firing, my lord.'

'Eleven men dead, sir,' said Yaekel, 'And my barracks and the canvas on my sloops burned. My lord, I–'

Von Geldrecht held up a hand. 'Yes, Yaekel. You wish to retreat. So noted.' He turned to the handgunner captain. 'Hultz?'

'Twenty-eight dead, my lord,' said the man. 'Only – only eighteen left alive. Them bats, sir. They done for us something terrible.'

'I know, Hultz,' said von Geldrecht sadly. 'I know.' He nodded towards the slovenly free-company captain. 'And you, Captain… what is your name again?'

'Draeger, yer worship,' said the captain. 'Er, three dead and twenty-seven alive.'

Everyone's head turned.

Von Geldrecht glared. 'You didn't fight.'

Draeger squared his jaw. 'We guarded the stables, yer worship. Barred the door and watched them horses like they were our own.'

'The stables were never under attack!' roared Bosendorfer.

'Aye,' said Draeger, smug. 'Thanks to us.'

The other officers all started barking at once, but von Geldrecht held up his hands. 'Enough! Never mind! We will deal with this later.' He turned to the young knight sergeant who had wept at Nordling's death. 'Classen?'

Classen pulled his eyes away from Draeger and saluted. 'Thirty-two dead, sir,' he said, then swallowed. 'In-including General Nordling. Fifty still living and able.'

'And at least a hundred of the servants and farm folk dead,' said Father Ulfram. 'With more wounded and sick.'

Von Geldrecht sighed and stared into the fire. 'So,' he said. 'More than a third dead or incapacitated after one attack, and any reinforcements at least six days away – once they actually start their march. It… will be difficult.'

'It will be impossible!' cried Yaekel. 'Forgive me, my lord, but we have no chance here! We must take to the river and escape! There is no other way!'

'Be silent, Yaekel!' barked von Geldrecht. 'I have told you–'

Zeismann cut in before he could continue. 'Much as I hate to admit it,' he said, 'I'm afraid I've to side with Yaekel. We're too reduced now t'do any good. Let's fall back to Nadjagard where we can make a proper defence.'

'I agree,' said von Volgen. He bowed as von Geldrecht rounded on him. 'Forgive me, lord steward. I am your guest, and will follow your orders, but this attack was only a quick jab to test our mettle, and it killed a third of the garrison. When the necromancer brings his full strength to bear, what will be the cost then?' He shook his head. 'I fear the castle is a lost cause. We can do more good in Nadjagard.'

'Thank you for your opinion, my lord,' said von Geldrecht, very stiff. 'But though I see the wisdom of it, Graf Reiklander is adamant that Castle Reikguard be held to the last man, and I will not disobey him.' He turned to his captains. 'You will second men from each of your watches to help with the construction of hoardings and other defences, and–'

'But, my lord!' wailed Yaekel, interrupting. 'What will we eat? What will we drink? Even if the zombies don't get us, we'll die of thirst!'

'Sister Willentrude is purifying water to be used for the washing of wounds,' said von Geldrecht. 'And the kitchen staff are preparing fires to boil water for drinking and cooking. We will have water and a hearty meal of… of flat cakes very soon.'

'If I might make a suggestion, yer worship?' said Draeger.

'If it involves you running away, you can forget it,' growled Bosendorfer.

'Not at all,' said Draeger. 'Only, we're not completely cut off here, are we? Why don't we send out Warden Yaekel's boats on a foraging mission? Go downriver to some village where the zombies ain't, and bring back some food.'

Everyone looked around, taken off guard by the sensibleness of the idea. Von Geldrecht nodded.

'That is an excellent suggestion, Draeger,' he said. 'We will do just that.'

'Thank you, yer worship,' said Draeger. 'And if I might–'

'You will have no part in it,' said von Geldrecht, cutting him off, 'as I fear that you might somehow get lost while ashore.'

'Oh no, my lord,' said Draeger, his eyes wide. 'I assure you–'

'Enough!' said von Geldrecht. 'Zeismann, you will take fifteen of your men and escort Captain Yaekel and his crew downriver to requisition food and supplies from the villages there.' He paused as Yaekel's eyes lit up, then continued. 'And you will make sure that Captain Yaekel and his crew do not get lost either.'

Yaekel's face fell as Zeismann grinned.

'Yes, sir,' said the spear captain. 'There'll be no men overboard on this trip.'

Kat clutched Felix's arm as the conversation continued. 'Felix!' she whispered. 'This is our chance to get Snorri away!'

'Aye,' said Felix. 'Let's find Gotrek.'

* * *

They found the three Slayers at last in the narrow tunnel that ran under the castle's outer walls and connected its towers. They stood together, holding a lantern close to a square stone set in the wall, and staring at the angular dwarf rune that had been chiselled into it.

'Gotrek,' called Felix, as they approached. 'Von Geldrecht is sending out a foraging party by boat. We'll be able to get Snorri…'

He trailed off as he saw that the Slayers weren't listening. They just continued to stare at the rune.

'Is something wrong?' asked Felix.

Gotrek pulled his attention from the rune and looked at Felix. His one eye blazed with fury. 'It is broken.'

Felix and Kat stepped in and peered closer. A hairline crack split the stone from side to side, and cut through every arm of the rune.

'This is why the dead could cross the walls,' Gotrek rumbled. 'With this crack, the power forged into the rune has escaped.'

'And every rune we've found is the same,' said Rodi.

'But how did it happen?' asked Kat. 'An earthquake? Settling?'

Rodi shook his head. 'Since the Time of Woes, the dwarfs have made such runes impervious to natural wear. And this happened only days ago. A week at the most.'

'Snorri thinks it stinks of magic,' said Snorri.

'Aye,' said Gotrek. 'A hammer couldn't touch such a rune. A chisel couldn't make a mark. This was the work of sorcery.'

'So it was Kemmler's doing?' asked Kat.

'Kemmler?' asked Rodi. 'Who's Kemmler?'

'Father Ulfram says that if the wight is Krell,' said Felix, 'then the necromancer must be Heinrich Kemmler, who raised him from his tomb.'

'Never heard of him,' said Gotrek.

'Whoever he is,' said Rodi, 'if he broke the runes, he must have slipped into the castle himself.' He pointed to the floor of the tunnel, then to the stone again. 'You see where someone tried to brush away their footprints? You see the imprint of a hand there?'

Felix and Kat looked at the stone again. At the very centre, overlapping the broken rune, were a few smooth patches where it looked like the rough stone had been glazed. It reminded Felix of the shiny scars left on flesh by a branding iron, but the patches formed the shape of the palm and fingers of a hand.

Kat shivered. 'A touch that can crack stone?'

Rodi nodded. 'And the same marks are on every one we've found.'

Felix swallowed as a thought came to him. 'Kemmler wouldn't bother to wipe away his footprints. He wouldn't care. But someone who was afraid of being caught…'

Gotrek nodded. 'Aye, manling. The saboteur is in the castle.'

EIGHT

Felix groaned. On top of everything else, there might be a saboteur among them, and a powerful one – powerful enough to destroy centuries-old dwarf runes.

'We must tell von Geldrecht,' he said. 'We must find who did this.'

'Aye,' said Gotrek. 'And kill them.'

The Slayer walked towards the exit, then looked back as Felix, Kat and the other Slayers followed.

'You said something about a boat, manling?'

'Uh, yes,' said Felix. The revelation of the broken runes had momentarily knocked everything else out of his head. 'Von Geldrecht is sending a boat downriver to forage for food. It seems a perfect opportunity to get Snorri out and on his way to Karak Kadrin.'

'Why would Snorri want to go to Karak Kadrin when there are zombies to fight?' asked Snorri.

'You've forgotten again, Father Rustskull,' said Rodi. 'You're going to the Shrine of Grimnir to get your memory back.'

'Oh, right,' said Snorri. 'Snorri forgot he forgot.'

Gotrek shook his head. 'It won't work.'

Felix blinked. 'What do you mean? There are no zombies blocking the river gate. What would stop us?'

'I don't know,' said Gotrek. 'But the broken runes are proof the necromancer has planned this well. He would not forget the boats.'

* * *

The courtyard was a hive of activity as Felix, Kat and the Slayers stepped into it. Behind the pyre of the dead, still burning near the stables, carpenters and defenders were laying out lengths of wood and putting together the wooden roofs of hoardings, while more were winching pallets of blackpowder barrels and cannon shot up to the walls. Even the knights were bending their backs, von Volgen's Talabeclanders working side by side with the household knights. At quayside, Zeismann and his picked men were lining up as the river wardens made the largest of their sloops ready to sail. Von Geldrecht was giving Zeismann and Yaekel, the boat's captain, last-minute instructions as Bosendorfer and von Volgen waited to speak to him.

'As important as food is shot,' von Geldrecht was saying as Felix, Kat and the Slayers neared them. 'We must keep the guns firing. Take all you can.'

'My lord von Geldrecht,' called Felix. 'We have grave news.'

The steward broke off and turned, mouth pursed in annoyance. 'Everyone has grave news, mein Herr,' he said. 'It will have to wait.'

'It can't wait, my lord,' said Felix. 'It affects this foraging trip.'

Von Volgen and the three captains turned to listen.

Von Geldrecht's bearded jowls worked angrily. 'Very well,' he snapped. 'What is this desperately important news?'

'You have a traitor in the castle,' said Gotrek. 'Someone has destroyed your warding runes.'

'With magic,' said Snorri.

'Your walls wouldn't keep out an undead flea,' said Rodi.

Von Geldrecht, von Volgen and the officers stared, then looked around at their men nervously. But it seemed only they had heard.

The steward limped closer and lowered his voice. 'You are certain of this, dwarfs?'

'Certain as steel,' said Gotrek.

'But can they be repaired?' asked von Volgen. 'Can you fix them?'

Gotrek and Rodi snorted.

Snorri laughed. 'Snorri thinks you don't know much about runes.'

'A rune cannot be repaired,' said Gotrek. 'It must be replaced.'

'It takes a master runesmith years to make a single rune,' said Rodi. 'And we are not master runesmiths.'

'Someone in the castle?' von Geldrecht asked as he looked around at the soldiers and officers who were hard at work cleaning up the wreckage of the previous night's battle. 'Are you certain?'

'The footprints of he who did it were deliberately wiped away,' said Felix. 'Whoever did it had reason to hide.'

'Tauber!' cried Bosendorfer, triumphant. 'It was Tauber. He poisoned the water and destroyed the runes!'

Von Geldrecht blanched, but Zeismann just rolled his eyes.

'You've got Tauber on the brain, greatsword.'

'You think it's somebody else?' sneered Bosendorfer. 'Who, then?'

Von Geldrecht shushed them frantically as the men in the courtyard started to turn towards their raised voices. 'None of that! None of that! Let us have no unfounded speculation. We mustn't alarm the men.' He turned to Felix. 'I thank you, sir, and you, friend dwarfs, for your information. But please be quiet about this. I will take the necessary steps.' He turned away. 'Now, forgive me, I must see off Captain Zeismann and–'

'The boat won't come back,' said Gotrek.

Von Geldrecht's head jerked back around. 'I beg your pardon?'

Von Volgen and the three officers stared too.

'If this necromancer is cunning enough to plant a saboteur into your castle,' said Rodi. 'he isn't likely to have forgotten you could sail away, is he?'

'Yer saying he'll stop the boat?' asked Zeismann. 'How?'

Gotrek shrugged. 'It will be stopped.'

Von Geldrecht's head swivelled from Slayer to Slayer, eyes blazing, then he threw up his hands. 'This is mere supposition! How could he stop the boat? The sun is in the sky. Krell has gone. I see no bats. No, I am sorry, friends. We must eat or we will be too weak to fight. I must risk it.'

'My lord, please,' said Felix, stepping forwards. 'Gotrek is rarely wrong in these things. He–'

'Well, he is wrong now!' Von Geldrecht turned away and motioned to Zeismann and Yaekel, who, along with Bosendorfer and von Volgen, had been listening with uneasy expressions to the whole exchange. 'Go on,' he said. 'On board. Cast off. Just come back before sunset.'

'Lord steward,' coughed von Volgen, murmuring in von Geldrecht's ear. 'The necromancer has so far left nothing to chance. I fear–'

'There is no time for fear!' snapped von Geldrecht. 'Graf Reiklander orders me to act!'

'But, my lord–' said Zeismann, hesitant.

'Do you want to live on biscuit and water for seven days because you were too afraid to cross a river in broad daylight?' shouted von Geldrecht, his jowls quivering. 'Do you want our guns to stand cold when those horrors come for the walls? Get on the boat! I'm ordering you! Graf Reiklander is ordering you!'

Zeismann looked like he was going to make another objection, but then only saluted. 'Aye, my lord,' he said stiffly. 'Very good, my lord.'

The spear captain gave Felix, Kat and the Slayers a curt nod of farewell, then turned and marched onto the sloop with his men following behind. Yaekel hesitated at the foot of the gangplank, looking suddenly less than eager to depart.

Von Geldrecht fixed him with a glittering stare. 'Have you some complaint, captain?' he growled.

Yaekel swallowed and shook his head. 'No, my lord.'

'Then cast off! Open the river gate!'

'Aye, my lord!'

Yaekel ran onto the sloop and shouted at his boatmen as they pulled in the gangplank and took up their oars. The pilot at the stern turned the wheel, then raised a horn and blew a loud blast. In answer, there was a clattering and creaking from the towers on either side of the harbour gate, and the heavy iron lattices that served it as doors began to swing open. In the waist of the sloop, Zeismann made the sign of the hammer, then turned to his men.

'To the sides, lads,' he called. 'Spears at the ready, and keep your eyes on the water.'

As the sloop oared away from the quayside, Felix looked at the faces of the men who watched it go. Bosendorfer was pale, and von Volgen grim, but the most stricken of all was von Geldrecht, mopping his ashen brow with a trembling kerchief. For the briefest second he raised the cloth and Felix thought he was going to call back the sloop, but then he lowered it again and only wiped his mouth.

Gotrek shot a one-eyed glare him, then started towards the men who were assembling the hoardings. 'Come, manling,' he said over his shoulder as Rodi and Snorri followed him. 'There's work to be done.'

Felix looked from the Slayers to the sloop. 'What work?'

'If the wards are broken,' said Gotrek, 'then hoardings are the best defence. Smartest thing the manlings have done yet.'

Felix glanced again at the sloop, which was pulling in its oars and unfurling its sails as it neared the water gate, then looked questioningly at Kat.

'I have to see,' she said. 'I have to.'

Felix turned back to the Slayers. 'We'll find you.'

The dwarfs only grunted and kept on.

Felix and Kat hurried for the closest stair. Von Geldrecht and von Volgen were ahead of them, climbing in uneasy silence. The steward was met at the top by Captain Hultz of the handgunners.

'All quiet, my lord,' he said, saluting.

'I hope so,' said von Geldrecht and stepped past him with von Volgen to look over the battlements.

Felix and Kat found a spot a few paces to their left just as the sloop was passing through the water gate. Unnerved by Gotrek's warnings, Felix half-expected huge jaws or monstrous tentacles would rise out of the waves and drag it under, but nothing of the sort happened. The waters were undisturbed but for the sloop's bow wave, and though its passage was provoking movement amongst the zombies on the shore, they didn't appear to be any threat. The corpses shuffled clumsily in its direction like iron shavings being pulled upon by the influence of a lodestone, crowding the riverbank and pawing limply at the air as it passed, but that was all.

Von Geldrecht laughed and slapped the wall. 'You see? They can do nothing!'

Forbidding laughter wafted to them on the wind, an eerie echo of von Geldrecht's laugh.

Felix's heart clenched, for he knew that laugh. It was Hans the Hermit – or Heinrich Kemmler, if Father Ulfram was correct. Felix looked around, sweeping the horde of zombies with his eyes, but it was Kat who spotted him first.

'There!' she said, thrusting out a finger as she lifted her bow off her back.

Felix followed her gaze. A hundred yards downstream, a spindly figure in dirty robes, so like the army of corpses he had raised that he was nearly impossible to pick out, was moving from the bank onto a half-submerged outcropping of rocks and waving after the retreating sloop as it angled towards the opposite shore.

Quicker than Felix could follow, Kat had an arrow on the string and loosed it in Kemmler's direction. It went wide, but only just. She nocked another and fired again. The arrow seemed to curve away from the necromancer as it reached him.

'Fire at will, lads!' called Hultz, as his gunners raised their weapons.

'Yes!' shouted von Geldrecht. 'Kill him! A hundred crowns to the man who brings him down!'

But as the gunners sighted down at Kemmler, it became clear that the necromancer's arm-waving was not mere madness. Shadows blossomed around him, billowing from his dirty cloak to surround him in unnatural darkness until he vanished in a floating smudge of smoke.

The guns thundered, splintering the rocks around where Kemmler stood and sending up splashes in the shallows. Had they missed? Kat certainly did not. Her third arrow lanced straight through the heart of the smoke, precisely where Kemmler had been standing, but to Felix's dismay, it met no resistance, and stuck quivering in the ground beyond.

The darkness dissipated again, revealing nothing but empty rocks. Felix heard men running up the stairs behind him, drawn to the walls by the firing. He didn't turn. He was too busy searching the horde for Kemmler.

'Where's he gone?' cried von Geldrecht. 'Find him!'

'The boat,' croaked von Volgen, pointing.

Felix and Kat looked towards Yaekel's sloop as spearmen and greatswords crowded the battlements on either side of them. A swirl of shadow, almost impossible to see in the darker shadow of the sails, was coalescing behind the sloop's pilot. No one had seen it yet. Zeismann's spearmen were still following his orders and watching the waves. The crew were at their duties.

'The necromancer!' shouted one of Hultz's handgunners. "Ware behind you, boys!'

The crowd that now thronged the walls joined him, all waving and shouting at once, but the distance was too great. The men on the sloop stared back at them, uncomprehending, as the darkness clotted behind them and became opaque.

Finally, one of the spearmen – was it Zeismann? It was hard to tell so far away – turned to call to someone, and froze as he saw the patch of misty blackness that was spreading across the aft deck.

Though Felix heard nothing, Zeismann must have shouted, for all at once the other spearmen whipped around, and the crew turned and lifted their heads.

What followed seemed somehow more horrible to Felix because it played out in the silence of distance – a sad, sickening pantomime that he and Kat and the others on the wall were powerless to stop.

As the pilot fled before the spreading cloud, Zeismann and his spearmen crept towards it cautiously from all sides, spears extended. The river wardens closed from all corners of the ship, brandishing cutlasses and boarding pikes. A flash of red hair showed Felix that Yaekel was at their head, a pair of pistols at the ready.

Then, as Zeismann prodded nervously into the churning dark with his spear-tip, black tendrils of writhing smoke shot out from its centre in all directions at once, impaling the spearmen through their breastplates and bringing them up on their toes in a paralysing rictus.

The crowd on the wall gasped.

Kat cried out. 'Zeismann! No!'

Yaekel and his crew drew back in terror as the shadowy strands reeled the spearmen closer and closer to the spreading cloud while they squirmed like worms on hooks. Zeismann, with seemingly superhuman willpower, stabbed convulsively into the dark as it drew him into its embrace, but his attacks did nothing, and he vanished with the rest.

Felix tore his gaze from the horror and stepped to von Geldrecht and von Volgen.

'Lord steward!' he said. 'Send the other boat. Let us on it! We must save them!'

'Aye, my lord,' said Hultz. 'Something must be done!'

The others on the wall echoed him, begging to be sent to the rescue, but von Geldrecht shook his head, his eyes never leaving the sloop.

'It's too late. Too late.'

'Not for vengeance!' said Kat. 'Let us go. We will kill the necromancer for the deaths of your men.'

'Aye!' said a spearman who had stayed behind. 'Zeismann must be avenged.'

The steward didn't answer, but von Volgen coughed.

'I'm afraid the lord steward is right,' he said. 'We must not be drawn. The rescuers will only die and the castle will lose its second boat.'

Felix groaned, and the others cursed as they turned back to watch again. The lord was undoubtedly right, but it was hard to swallow.

With no one at the wheel, the sloop's rudder flopped free, and it turned with the current, its sails loose and snapping. Beneath them, Yaekel, with more bravery than Felix expected of him, was waving his crew back and advancing on the black cloud alone. The darkness now covered all of the aft deck and was curling down into the waist like a heavy ground fog. He aimed his pistols at it and shouted something, but clearly didn't get the response he'd hoped for, for he shouted again.

A figure emerged from the pall and Yaekel jumped back, frightened, but then, as it came into the light, it was revealed as a spearman, staggering like a drunk, his spear clutched in his hands. Yaekel spoke again, but this time seemingly in relief, and stepped forwards, lowering his pistols. The spearman stabbed him in the chest, burying his spearpoint between his ribs.

The river wardens cried out as Yaekel fell, and the distant pops of pistols carried across the water as they fired at his killer. The spearman twitched in the volley of lead, but did not fall, only jerked his spear free of Yaekel and stumbled down to the waist. More spearmen followed him out of the black mist, all with the same lurching gait, and fell upon the river wardens with ungainly savagery.

'Not our lads,' murmured the spearman who had spoken before. 'Not the captain.'

The crew fought valiantly, but the outcome was inevitable. Only seconds after his death, Yaekel rose again and turned to join the spearmen as they tore at his erstwhile men. And more and more of the river wardens followed him – falling as their guts were pierced by spears, only to rise again almost instantly, lifeless slaves to Kemmler's will, and leaving the living swiftly out-numbered.

Then, as the slaughter came to its grisly conclusion, the black cloud vanished from the deck and reappeared on the shore at the edge of the zombie horde, dissipating to reveal Kemmler, who once again laughed and waved to the sloop. In response, the newly risen zombies turned and staggered to the gunwales, then toppled into the water one after the other until there were none left on board, and the sloop drifted away down the river, unmanned.

'And that's that, then,' said a handgunner, staring hollow-eyed. 'Good men dead and drowned by the hand of that filthy grave-robber. May Morr watch over them.'

But that wasn't it, for as Felix, Kat and the others watched, there was a churning in the shallows near where Kemmler stood on the shore, and a cluster of helmed heads and armoured shoulders broke the waves, streaming water and blood. In ones and twos, the spearmen and river wardens from the sloop rose up and walked out of the river, then shambled past Kemmler to merge with the endless anonymity of the ten-thousand-strong horde as the necromancer's laughter again drifted to the castle on the wind.

Kat turned her head. 'Poor bastards. Poor Zeismann.'

'Aye,' said Felix, glaring at von Geldrecht. 'Damned short-sighted fool.'

The steward stood beside von Volgen, staring blankly after the receding sloop. The men around them wore the same expression, as if all hope had been pulled out of them in a single instant.

Suddenly, Draeger, the free-company captain, turned on von Geldrecht, his eyes blazing with fury. 'Y'fat bastard, y'trapped us! We could've got out yesterday but you wouldn't! If we all die here, I'm hanging it 'round your neck! It's you who've killed us, and nobody–'

Von Geldrecht slapped him across the face. 'Pull yourself together, captain!' he snapped. 'Or I'll have you in the gaol! There is no room for such an outburst here.'

Draeger balled his fists as the men on the wall held their breath, but at last Draeger just turned on his heel and stalked off.

Von Geldrecht glared after him, then seemed to remember he was supposed to be the commander, and drew himself up. 'Back to your duties!' he said. 'Back to your posts! If you want vengeance for this terrible loss, then shore up our defences. Sharpen your weapons, build the hoardings, carry shot and powder to the walls so that they are there when our gunners need them. There is no need to go to the enemy. The enemy will come to us, and when they do, we will make them pay tenfold for what they have done today!'

The men cheered this speech and broke up in better spirits, but as they filed past Felix and Kat towards the stairs, Felix heard some grumbling as well.

'If I wanted vengeance,' muttered a spearman, 'I'd baste ye in butter and send *you* out to forage, y'fat ham hock.'

'Two captains dead,' said another, 'and nothing to show for it. Nothing. Go back to the counting house, Goldie.'

'My lord steward,' said von Volgen, as the last of them left the walls. 'If I might make a suggestion?'

Von Geldrecht stiffened. 'What is it?'

Von Volgen nodded towards the river gate. 'We have seen now that zombies don't drown. I am therefore concerned that there might be a gap between the bottom of the lattice doors and the river bed. If the corpses were to find it...'

Von Geldrecht paled. He looked overwhelmed. 'Good thinking,' he murmured. 'Thank you. I will ask if a solution can be– Ack!'

Von Geldrecht ducked and flinched as something swooped out of the sky and squeaked and flapped around his head. Von Volgen drew his sword and Kat had an arrow on the string in an instant, but what fluttered around the steward's head was not a bat, but the strangest bird Felix had ever seen. It looked something like a pigeon, with a round body and smooth head, but its feathers glinted like metal and it whirred and clicked like an angry insect.

'Hold!' cried von Geldrecht, waving Kat down. 'It is a messenger pigeon.'

Kat held fire, but kept her bow at half-draw, staring as von Geldrecht raised his arm and the thing settled on his wrist.

'It… it is a machine,' she said, wonderingly.

Felix stared too. Now that it was standing still, he could see that it was indeed mechanical. The wings were made of steel and brass, the legs and claws hinged with screws, and the eyes made from glass lenses. He shook his head. He didn't remember the Empire having anything like this before he had left it for parts east. Engineering had come a long way in twenty years.

Von Geldrecht twisted the cap off the end of a brass tube affixed to the bird's chest and withdrew from it a twist of paper. He uncurled it with nervous fingers and peered at it.

'From Altdorf, my lord?' asked von Volgen.

Von Geldrecht nodded and let out a sigh, though Felix couldn't tell if it was one of relief or worry. 'Yes,' he said. 'The Reiksguard are coming, and as many state troops as they can recruit along the way. Graf Reiklander's son, Master Dominic, is returning with them. They left late yesterday.'

'Praise Sigmar,' said von Volgen.

'Aye,' said von Geldrecht, his eyes distant. He crumpled the paper. 'And pray his deliverance isn't too late.'

NINE

The rest of the day was hard labour, with no one exempt. Even the knights worked, falling in beside the handgunners, spearmen and artillerymen to proof the castle as best they could against the undead. Directed by Reikguard's master carpenter, Anders Bierlitz, half the garrison cut, nailed together and fit wooden hoardings to the tops of the walls, while nearly as many worked just as furiously dismantling the stables, the privies and whatever other wooden structures could be spared, in order to provide usable wood for the builders to build with.

Gotrek, Rodi and Snorri, meanwhile, set to dismantling the officers' residence for its stone. There had been much argument earlier about the best way to prevent the zombies from crawling under the water gate, with some wanting to sink the remaining riverboat in front of it, and others wanting to drive the gates down into the mud of the river bottom, but at last it was decided that the surest plan was to pile up heavy stones below the gates to plug the gap. Unfortunately, the castle wasn't a quarry, and taking them from the exterior walls was obviously not an option.

And so all day the Slayers used hammers, chisels and their bare hands to dismantle the corner tower of the officers' residence from top to bottom and tumble the stones down to river wardens, who then winched them onto oarboats and rowed them the short distance to the gate to dump them over the side as close to the iron doors as they could manage.

Felix and Kat, being neither capable carpenters nor stonemasons, went to work with the demolition gangs, and pried apart the weathered planks of the hayloft then pulled out every nail that could be salvaged. Even on a freezing late winter day, it was hot, dusty work, and they were soon working in their shirts, steam rising from their shoulders into the chilly air.

Ordinarily, this kind of labour would not have worn Felix out. Years of wandering and fighting had left him in good shape, and he was used to hardship, but even the toughest man could not go long without water, and there wasn't nearly enough to go around. Every vat and pan and pot in the kitchen was busy boiling water for drinking, but the process wasn't quick, and the rationing was severe. Every man got a ladleful to go with their single biscuit in the morning, and another in the afternoon, and some got less than that. Both times the crews were called to the mess, the water ran out before everyone got their share.

Gotrek, Rodi and Snorri never drank, though whether that was because they didn't need to, or out of sheer stubbornness, or just because it wasn't beer, Felix wasn't certain. Regardless, they each did the work of ten men, and never complained or showed any sign of weakness.

The same could not be said for the men. There were fights at the water barrel when some tried to drink more than their share. Others passed out or vomited from dryness. Felix was nearly one of them. By the late afternoon, he was staggering, and almost fell through a hole in the floor he was prying up. Only a swift grab by Kat stopped him from breaking his neck. Hunger and thirst weren't entirely to blame, however. Part of his clumsiness stemmed from his inability to keep his mind on the work. He couldn't stop wondering who the saboteur was.

All day long he watched his fellow defenders, wondering which one hid the power to shatter a dwarf rune – which was in league with Kemmler. Was it Tauber, like Bosendorfer believed? That would be tidy, for Tauber was already locked up, but somehow Felix doubted the castle was that lucky. But then who? It couldn't be anybody who had travelled with von Volgen, since the runes had been broken before his force arrived. Was it von Geldrecht? Had he ordered the garrison to hold the castle just so Kemmler could kill them all and swell his ranks with their corpses? Was it Bosendorfer, sowing discord by accusing others of crimes he himself was committing? Was it Father Ulfram? Was his blindness and seeming senility a cover for corrupt power? Was it Sister Willentrude, hiding an evil nature behind a kindly smile? Was it perhaps Graf Reiklander himself, or the Grafin Avelein, hiding in the keep and manipulating the rest of the castle for Kemmler's gain?

But why did it have to be one of the leaders? It could be anyone – a knight, a spearman, a groom, a scullery maid. There were too many choices, and too little to go on. It was maddening.

At least von Geldrecht was following through on his promise to take the necessary steps. As the day wore on, Felix saw him quietly pull aside each of his remaining officers and whisper in their ears, after which those officers began to look suspiciously around at their comrades. Felix supposed that removed von Geldrecht from the list of suspects, but perhaps not. What if he was telling his men to look for the traitor in order to throw them off the scent, or to create suspicion that would weaken the morale of the castle?

Felix cursed as his mind curled in on itself again, and forced himself to get back to the task at hand. Ceaseless suspicion would not find the saboteur. What they needed was proof, but Felix had no idea what to look for.

Less than a third of the hoardings were in place by the time the sun vanished completely. The towers of the gatehouse and the sections of wall to the right and left of it had been covered, but that was all. Felix, with little knowledge of these things, thought it was a poor showing, and the Slayers grumbled about 'manling laziness', but Bierlitz, the castle's carpenter, seemed well pleased, saying that given the lack of food and water the men had accomplished more than he expected.

Nor did the construction stop with the coming of darkness. After Bierlitz dismissed Felix and Kat and the rest of the men who had worked all day, he commandeered men from the night watches to keep at it, and the Slayers of course continued without a break.

Felix left them to it, and stumbled with Kat into the underkeep as the mess bell clanged.

It was time for another biscuit.

'To Captain Zeismann and all our fallen brothers,' said a young sergeant of spearmen, standing and holding up his mug. 'He'd not relish being toasted with water, but until we have beer again, let us honour him as we can.'

The rest of the spearmen stood from their tables in the mess and raised their mugs as well, and Kat, Felix and the other men in the room joined them.

'To Captain Zeismann and the spearmen,' said the crowd, and everyone knocked back their meagre ration of water in a single slug.

As they all sat again, a burly river warden stood from among his comrades and raised an empty hand. 'And as that was all to drink till morning,' he said, 'I ask that you salute Captain Yaekel and his crew with a pledge.' He closed his hand into a fist. 'Vengeance!'

The whole room raised their fists, and the walls echoed with their pledge.

'Vengeance!'

The warden inclined his head and sat again, but before everyone could lower their fists, Bosendorfer sprang up onto the table where he had sat with his greatswords.

'I ask a pledge as well,' he cried. 'In the name of greatswords Janus

Meier and Abel Roos, and the score of other men who died last night and today from the poisoned wounds that murdered them in their beds.'

He raised his fist in the air and the room followed suit, with many a 'hear hear' and 'well said'.

'Death to the poisoner,' said Bosendorfer. 'Death to Surgeon Tauber.'

Felix and Kat paused at that, and they weren't the only ones. Though many of the men joined in wholeheartedly, just as many were murmuring and lowering their fists instead of making the pledge. Even some of Bosendorfer's own men looked uncomfortable.

Bosendorfer glared around, his eyes blazing. 'What is this? Will you not honour my fallen men as you honour Zeismann and Yaekel?'

Captain Hultz stood from his handgunners. 'With a will, captain, if you choose a different pledge,' he said.

Bosendorfer sneered. 'You do not wish the death of our enemies, Hultz?'

'We don't all think it was Tauber who done it,' said Hultz. 'Choose another enemy and we will pledge.'

'Sigmar's hammer, I will not!' shouted Bosendorfer. 'I will honour my dead as I see fit, and if you will not join me, then be damned with you!'

Men stood all over the hall now, choosing sides and shouting at each other, as Bosendorfer continued to rave.

Felix shook his head and leaned to Volk, whose table he and Kat were sharing. 'Why does he hate Tauber so? I remember he spoke of Tauber murdering people during the fighting up north. Was the surgeon accused of worshipping Chaos?'

Volk shook his head sadly. 'Only by Bosendorfer,' he said, then sighed. 'When we marched north, the boy was only a sergeant. His brother Karl was the captain of m'lord's greatswords. But at the end, during the battle of Sokh, one of them Norse shamen blasted our whole left flank with purple fire, and afterwards, some of the men... well, they started to change. Bosendorfer's brother was one of 'em. His hands – they grew teeth, and other things.'

The artillery captain swallowed, then went on. 'It was standard procedure when that happened, to kill the man on the spot – for his own good, you understand – and Captain Karl was in the sick tent with a broken arm when he started to show, so–'

'So Tauber did it?' asked Felix.

Volk nodded. 'As gentle as possible. Laudanum, then poison. He just... fell asleep. But young Bosendorfer wouldn't believe it. He claimed it was Tauber who had made his brother's changes come, and that he'd killed Karl when he wouldn't pledge to the Ruinous Powers.' He looked over at the greatswords' table. 'Graf Reiklander himself talked to Bosendorfer, and got him to agree it wasn't true. Gave him Karl's commission too, which might not have been wise, as Bosendorfer ain't the man his brother was, not by a long shot, but it was a nice gesture, and the greatswords appreciated it, so...'

'But Bosendorfer doesn't seem to have really believed Tauber was innocent,' said Felix.

Volk shook his head. 'He's kept quiet about it till now, but no.'

Felix watched as Bosendorfer continued to rant. He could see the grief behind the young man's wild anger now, and felt sorry for him, but one could feel sorry for a savage dog that had been abused, and still not want to be trapped in the same room with it for days – or weeks.

He finished his last few crumbs of biscuit and turned to Kat. 'Shall we?'

She nodded, glaring at the greatsword captain. 'Aye, Felix,' she said. 'I'm starting to get an earache.'

They walked out of the underkeep and into the courtyard where, under the yellow light of flickering lanterns, Gotrek, Rodi and Snorri continued to knock apart the officers' residence, while the boatmen dumped another load of building stone at the river gate, and the carpenters and the men from the night watches kept on framing the hoardings and carrying them up to the walls.

Kat looked at all their industry, then shook her head. 'None of this is going to matter, is it? We won't stop them.'

'Not for long,' said Felix. 'But maybe long enough.'

A cold wind whistled down over the parapet, bringing with it the stench of corpses and the howling of wolves. Felix shivered and put his arm around Kat, and they hurried into the knights' residence and up to their borrowed room. By the time they had pulled their boots off and lay down on the narrow bed, they were too tired and hungry to do more than curl together and close their eyes.

Seconds later – or so it seemed – Felix was jerked awake by shouting and cursing and heavy boot steps shaking the residence building.

Kat came awake too, and blearily reached for her weapons. 'That's on the floor below,' she mumbled. 'What's going on?'

Felix crawled to the window and looked out. It was still night, and he could see little but the shadows of men running to the door of their residence and going in. Three slower, heavier shadows followed them, walking along with their weapons out.

Felix grunted. 'We'd better go down.'

He threw on his padded jack and squirmed into his chainmail as Kat pulled on her leathers and the shouting continued. When they were ready, they hurried down to the ground floor, but the shouting was now coming from the cellar, so they continued down and, after following the cacophony through a series of cramped stone passages, came at last to a small round room that was filled with a jumble of machinery, and far too many shouting men.

The room appeared to be the base of one of the circular towers that rose at the corners of the castle walls, and a great brass and iron contraption of gears and levers and pistons that had a very dwarfish look to it rose in the centre of it. It also looked very broken, with one of the main gears cracked in half, and a piston ruptured and bent.

Cowering in the lee of the machine were Captain Draeger and his militiamen, while surrounding them were von Geldrecht, his bulk wrapped in a nightshirt and brocade robe, von Volgen, and a crowd of knights and foot soldiers, all holding lanterns and torches and shouting questions while the Slayers watched from one side, their brawny arms folded across their beards.

'I swear to you, m'lord,' Draeger was saying. 'It wasn't us! We heard something suspicious and came looking, and found someone tampering with it. Sigmar be my witness it's the truth.'

Von Geldrecht laughed, and then waved a hand for quiet. 'So, you heard something suspicious, did you?'

'That's right, m'lord,' said Draeger. 'Woke us up. And–'

'You were sleeping in the underkeep and heard something suspicious in the cellar of the knights' residences *on the far side* of the courtyard,' continued von Geldrecht.

'Well, m'lord...'

The steward barged on. 'And so, you decided you would investigate this noise, with *all your men*?'

The knights and foot soldiers all laughed at this. Even von Volgen allowed himself a flat smile.

'Er, well,' stammered Draeger, sweating now. 'I know it seems strange on the face of it, m'lord, but–'

'It seems traitorous on the face of it!' bellowed von Geldrecht. 'By Sigmar, captain, if you've done what I think you've done here, you will die where you stand.'

Draeger cringed back. 'No, m'lord. Honest. We never touched it. It was the man we found tinkering with it. He wrecked it!'

Von Geldrecht rolled his eyes. 'One man wrecked this? Don't lie to me, captain. You have committed this sabotage, and you will pay for it with your life.'

'But we haven't!' cried Draeger. 'I swear to you!'

'Then why *did* you come here?' asked von Geldrecht, then sneered. 'And don't tell me you heard a noise.'

Draeger lowered his head and slanted a look to his men, then sighed. 'We... we was looking for a way out. A secret passage, like.'

Von Geldrecht stared. Someone in the back laughed.

'You were trying to escape,' said von Geldrecht.

'Aye, m'lord,' said Draeger, his chin going up with sudden defiance. 'We told you from the first we was already demobbed. This ain't our fight. We're free men.'

That brought another round of laughter, and a combined snort from the Slayers.

'Kill the lot,' said Gotrek, disgusted. 'We don't need cowards.'

Von Geldrecht inclined his head to him. 'Would that we had the luxury to choose who fought beside us, Herr dwarf. But alas, it cannot be.' He turned back to Draeger. 'No, your punishment, captain, is to fight for your life with the rest of us.' He snapped his fingers at the young sergeant of spearmen who had toasted Zeismann earlier in the mess. 'Sergeant Abelung, lock these men up. They are only to be let out to fight, yes?'

'Aye, my lord,' said the sergeant.

But as he began to herd them towards the exit, von Volgen looked Draeger in the eye.

'One question, captain,' he said. 'The man who was tinkering with the machine. Was he another lie?'

Draeger shook his head, glum. 'No, m'lord. We saw him, right enough.'

'And what did he look like?' asked von Volgen.

Draeger frowned. 'I didn't get a good look, m'lord. He wore a robe. Covered him head to toe. Couldn't see his face, or anything about him. Not a big man, though, and went like a rabbit.'

Von Volgen nodded and stepped back, and Sergeant Abelung led the militiamen to the door, but as they filed out, there were running footsteps in the passage beyond, and a handgunner squeezed past them into the room.

'My lord,' he said, panting as he crossed to von Geldrecht. 'It is as you feared. The dike locks have been closed and the moat is dry. The zombies have already crossed it, and are at the walls.'

Von Geldrecht cursed as the crowd of soldiers and knights murmured in dismay and began to hurry out. 'And until the lock mechanism is repaired,' he said, looking at the wrecked machine with a sigh, 'we cannot flood it again. Our saboteur is very thorough.'

Von Volgen turned to the Slayers. 'Can you fix this, dwarfs?'

Gotrek stepped forwards, shaking his head. 'The same hand that shattered the runes shattered this.' He pointed to a hole in the side of the crumpled piston. It was in the rough shape of a hand, and the steel all around it was cracked and brittle – more like glass than metal. Gotrek poked it with his finger. It shattered and fell away.

'It would take a team of dwarfs with a proper forge a month to replace all these parts,' said Rodi.

'Snorri would guess two months,' said Snorri.

Von Geldrecht groaned. 'The walls, the moat. The villain is peeling away our defences like an onion. He must be found and–'

Gotrek held up a hand, cutting him off, and cocked his head.

Von Geldrecht looked around, nervous. 'What is it?'

'Quiet,' said the Slayer, then crossed to the wall of the round room and put his ear to it.

Rodi and Snorri did the same. Felix and Kat exchanged a puzzled glance with von Geldrecht and von Volgen.

After a moment, Gotrek lifted his ear from the wall and turned to von Geldrecht. 'There is digging being done,' he said. 'Somewhere beyond this wall.'

Von Geldrecht's eyes widened. 'Digging? But what for?'

Rodi snorted. 'Maybe the corpses are planting a garden.'

Snorri frowned. 'Snorri doesn't think that's likely, Rodi Balkisson,' he said. 'Snorri thinks they're going to sap the walls.'

TEN

'So close,' said von Geldrecht, clutching his robe tighter around him. 'And yet so far away.'

Felix and Kat stood with the steward and von Volgen and the Slayers on Castle Reikguard's wind-whipped battlements, staring out at the stone-flanked, oak-doored canal-lock dike that gleamed dully in the light of the two moons about fifty yards upstream from the castle's easternmost corner. Until less than an hour ago, the lock could be opened to let the river spill into the moat, and closed to allow for cleaning and repairs. Now, with the destruction of the lock mechanism, the saboteur had closed it permanently, leaving the moat dry, and the sea of zombies which the moat had kept at bay now reached all the way to the castle, pawing futilely at the huge granite blocks of the sturdy walls.

Von Geldrecht sighed and shivered, then turned to the Slayers. 'And where is this digging?'

They led him back along the wall and pointed out and down. Felix, Kat, von Volgen and the steward leaned as far as they could over the wall, peering into the night. Felix couldn't see anything but zombies.

Von Geldrecht shook his head. 'I still don't see.'

'Snorri thinks humans have terrible eyesight,' said Snorri.

'They are in the moat,' growled Gotrek. 'Digging into the inner bank, straight for your walls.'

Felix looked again and finally, behind the shifting jumble of zombies that pawed at the walls, he thought he saw movement in the channel.

Von Geldrecht groaned. 'If only we could open the dike again, we could drown them out.'

'You couldn't, my lord,' said von Volgen. 'If you recall, zombies don't breathe.'

'And you don't want to open the dike again until that hole is filled in,' said Rodi. 'Or you'll have your moat in your cellar.'

'Snorri thinks that would bring down your walls faster than the zombies could,' said Snorri.

Von Geldrecht cursed and struck the wall with his fist. 'So how are we to stop them? We can't send men out to the digging. They'll be overwhelmed before they get there.'

'We dig to them,' said Gotrek. 'Then mine their tunnel and collapse it before it reaches the walls.'

Von Geldrecht stared at him. 'But... but is there time?' he asked. 'How long would it take to dig such a tunnel? I don't know if I have men enough to spare from strengthening our defences, nor if they will have enough strength.'

Gotrek held up a hand. 'Tell your men to finish blocking the river gate. We'll do this. Humans would only get in the way.'

The steward let out a sigh of relief and bowed to the Slayer. 'Thank you, Herr dwarf! You ease my mind. It will be as you say.'

Felix saw von Volgen wince at this unleaderlike display of emotion and look away, only to catch Felix looking at him. They exchanged a guarded look, then von Volgen turned and walked off as von Geldrecht began giving orders to his men.

The zombies started climbing the walls less than an hour later.

After they left von Geldrecht, Kat and Felix helped Gotrek, Rodi and Snorri search through the castle's stores for picks and shovels, then carted dirt away as the Slayers began digging down into the basement of the captains' residence – which was the point in the castle closest to where the zombies were digging. But weariness soon overcame them again and they returned to their room to try and sleep until morning. It was not to be, however – at least not for Felix.

Tired as he was, Felix could not quiet his mind. Draeger's description of the saboteur kept repeating in his head, and he couldn't stop comparing it to those he knew in the castle. A small man in robes, Draeger had said. And quick. Not much to go on, but it did rule out quite a number of suspects. With his wounded leg, von Geldrecht was neither small nor quick. Bosendorfer was a giant of a man, and the old priest, Ulfram, might have been gaunt, but he was tall too. He could rule out Sister Willentrude as well, who had the figure of a well-fed barnyard hen. Who did that leave? Tauber was a small man, but Tauber was locked up – wasn't he? Hultz of the handgunners was not large either, though he was broad in the shoulder. It could have been Grafin

Avelein, hiding her sex, or even the graf himself. Felix had never seen him, and had no idea what he looked like. But then, what if the villain was a master of illusion as well as a shatterer of runes? What if his small size and quickness were only a guise? After too much of that, it was almost a relief when the rally horns sounded and confused shouting echoed through the courtyard.

This time Felix and Kat hadn't bothered to strip out of their armour before lying down, and were therefore quick to the walls to see the zombies' new trick. Under cover of darkness the undead had brought tall, crudely made ladders to the castle and leaned them against all the land-side walls, and were now pulling themselves up towards the battlements in droves.

This wasn't much of a threat – at least not on its own. The zombies were terrible climbers and fell often, and the handgunners found it easy enough to use a pike to lever the ladders away from the wall and topple them to the ground. The problem was, they never stopped. It didn't matter how many times the defenders pushed the ladders back and sent all the zombies smashing into the moat, they just got up again, righted the ladders and resumed climbing, single-minded and untiring.

The handgunners were quickly joined by spearmen and river wardens sent by their captains to relieve them, but even with reinforcements, the men on the walls were run ragged, hurrying from ladder to ladder in a never-ending foot race. Unfortunately, it was even more pointless to try to kill the dead who mounted the ladders, for Kemmler would never run out. No matter how many the defenders might decapitate, or shoot through the head, there would always be more zombies to take their place.

Felix and Kat joined in the dizzy dance of run and push, run and push, run and push until the sky began to turn grey in the east, when they were finally both so tired they could no longer handle the pikes they had been given, and collapsed panting against the crenellations, legs as weak as twigs.

Captain Hultz, who looked no less weary than they, took the pikes and shooed them away. 'Go and sleep,' he said. 'You've done the work of ten tonight, the both of you, and the morning watch comes on any minute. Away. Away.'

Felix saluted and helped Kat up, and they staggered down the stairs, arm in arm, towards the knights' residence. But as they stumbled along the quayside, Kat stopped suddenly and blinked at two boatmen who were using boat hooks to manoeuvre a stone from the dismantled captains' residence under their winch so they could lower it into an oarboat.

'What is it?' Felix asked, frowning.

'Boat hook,' said Kat.

'What?'

The girl was gibbering from fatigue.

'Just a minute,' she said, then shrugged out from under his arm and crossed to the men.

'I need that,' she said, pointing.

The boatmen looked at her askance.

'The stone?' said one. 'What d'ye want a stone for?'

'The hook,' said Kat. 'I want the hook. And some rope. A lot.'

The boatmen looked at her again, and Felix did too. He had no idea what she was on about. Still, it was clear she'd had some sort of idea.

'If you can spare it,' he said politely, trying to make up for Kat's almost dwarfish brusqueness.

The boatman who had spoken shrugged, then went back onto the sloop and returned a moment later with a third boat hook and a coil of rope.

'I'll need all this back, mind,' he said, but Kat was already hurrying back to the stairs, tying the end of the rope around the T-shaped handle of the hook.

Felix stumbled up the stairs after her, still baffled, as she found Hultz and held out the hook and rope to him.

'Here,' she said, weaving slightly where she stood. 'This will stop them.'

Hultz blinked. 'And what is it supposed to be? A weapon? Am I to hook the corpses' guts out with it?'

'Not the corpses,' said Kat. 'The ladders. They can't climb without the ladders.'

Felix goggled at her. So did Hultz.

'Sigmar,' he said at last. 'Sigmar, it might work.'

He took the roped hook from her and called to his men. 'Lanzmann, Weitz, Sergeant Dore, take the end of this.'

Felix and Kat followed him and looked out as he let the hook drop down the wall. Just to their left, a mob of zombies was laboriously righting a fallen ladder and angling it towards the battlements.

'Perfect,' said Hultz, and sidestepped until he was above them.

The ladder bounced as it slapped against the wall, just a few feet below the crenellations, then steadied as the first of the zombies started to mount it.

'Quickly now, quickly now,' Hultz muttered to himself as he flicked the hook towards the rungs of the ladder. 'Before they all pile on.'

He got it on the second try and pulled it tight. 'Now, lads, now!' he shouted. 'Haul away!'

The three handgunners pulled on the end of the rope, gathering up the slack, then began to drag the ladder up the wall. There were two zombies at the bottom of it, but as it started to rise, one lost its grip and fell away. The other came up with the ladder, and clung to it as the gunners grabbed it and pulled it up hand over hand.

Hultz was waiting for it, and stove its head in with a flanged mace as the bottom of the ladder reached the top of the wall. The corpse fell away and the handgunners tossed the ladder down into the courtyard with a cheer.

Hultz turned to Kat with a grin. 'Girl, I do believe you have saved us a whole lot of bother.'

'And given us a nice supply of firewood,' said one of the gunners. 'Nice of that necromancer to provide for our cook fires.'

'Now all we need is food,' said Hultz, then turned to his men again. 'Lanzmann, Weitz, go tell them river pirates we need all the hooks and rope they have, and be quick about it!'

As they started back towards the stairs, Felix looked out over the wall at the fields beyond. The sun hadn't crested the horizon yet, but there was enough light to see all the way to the black line of forest, and a flurry of seething movement there caught his eye.

'What is that?' he asked, slowing.

Kat followed his gaze and they stepped to the wall for a better look. A tall, crooked shape was rising from the mist in front of the trees. It looked like a mummified giant, or an enormous cocoon, white and lumpy and asymmetrical, with a huge gaping mouth yawning and black at the top – and it was crawling from top to bottom with a constantly moving skein of zombies.

With growing horror and fascination, Felix realised that they were building the thing as he watched, like wasps constructing a hive, though instead of wood pulp and mud, they were using dead trees and bones and stretched skin. Angular black branches stuck out at random from the structure's mottled sides, and its base was affixed to giant curved tusks that looked like they had come from the skeleton of some long-dead leviathan.

'Taal and Rhya protect us, it's a siege tower,' said Kat.

Felix shuddered. That was precisely what it was. The curved tusks were skids so the thing could be dragged over the fields, and the hideous yawning mouth at the top would disgorge swarms of undead troops onto the walls. And another was just beginning to rise beside it.

'And look there!'

Kat pointed to the left of the towers, where two lower, wheeled constructions crouched in the shadow of the forest like monstrous insects – a heavy-timbered trebuchet and a catapult, as strangely constructed as the towers.

'Siege engines too,' said Felix, his stomach sinking. 'They've been busy.'

No one else seemed to have noticed the things. They were all too consumed with the task of hooking or pushing away ladders, but at Kat and Felix's words, the men on either side of them looked up to see what they were talking about.

'Sigmar's blood!' said one. 'Look at that!'

'Captain Hultz!' cried another. 'The wood! Look to the wood!'

Hultz looked up from trying to hook another ladder and cursed, but then raised his voice to shout down the babble of fear that was spreading like fire along the wall as the rest of the men began to notice the towers and the engines.

'Easy, lads! Easy!' he cried. 'They ain't moving yet. And plenty of time to prepare when they do. Keep on them ladders for now and we'll see to the rest when they get here.' He turned to his sergeant. 'Dore! My respects to Steward von Geldrecht, and if he could come have a look-see when he has a moment.'

Sergeant Dore saluted and trotted off to the stairs, and Felix steered Kat after him.

'And we'd better tell the Slayers,' he said.

The distance Gotrek, Rodi and Snorri had dug overnight was astonishing. They had bored down through the floor of the captains' residence cellar to a depth of about eight feet, then tunnelled east through the earth under the castle walls, and were already a few paces beyond them. A steady stream of squires and kitchen boys went in and out of the hole, carrying out buckets full of dirt and mounding it up all over the room. Off to one side, Volk, the artillery captain, was directing his gunners as they packed blackpowder into sections of clay drain pipe and affixed fuses to them. He gave a grin and a salute as Kat and Felix lowered themselves into the hole.

Felix had to bend almost double to enter the tunnel, for the Slayers had shaped it to dwarf proportions, and it was very low. A lamp was pegged into the wall at the far end, and he could see Gotrek and Rodi's broad muscled backs gleaming in its glow as they swung their picks at the workface. Snorri was a little bit behind them, shovelling the dirt into buckets for the squires to take away.

Felix was pleased to see that Gotrek and Rodi were still working side by side without growling at each other. The truce that had existed since they had discovered the broken runes of warding seemed to be holding. Felix only hoped it would stay that way.

'Slayers,' he called, picking his way down the tunnel. 'Kemmler's undead are building siege towers and siege engines. It looks like they will try the walls tonight.'

Gotrek nodded without breaking his rhythm. 'We will reach the corpses' tunnel soon after sunset,' he said. 'We will return to the walls once... once it is collapsed.'

Felix frowned. It sounded as if Gotrek was out of breath. That was almost unheard of. Felix had seen him fight a whole day and spend hours digging through solid rock and hardly do more than breathe hard, but now he was gasping.

'Gotrek?'

The Slayer cleared his throat and spat. 'I'm fine. Just dust.'

Rodi shot a look at Gotrek at that, but said nothing. Felix swallowed, unnerved by Gotrek's ragged voice and Rodi's glance.

'Ah,' he said. 'Dust.' He hesitated, wanting to say more, but then just nodded. 'Send word when you're nearly through. We'll return.'

'Aye,' said Gotrek.

Felix and Kat exchanged a look as they made their way back out of the tunnel, but neither spoke what they were thinking. Was it truly dust, or was it the slivers from Krell's axe doing their evil work? Could the vile specks really kill Gotrek? And if so, how long did the Slayer have?

As Felix and Kat stepped back into the courtyard they saw a very bleary Steward von Geldrecht limping down from the walls and stroking his beard with nervous fingers.

'Hultz must have shown him Kemmler's towers,' said Kat.

Felix nodded. The man looked overwhelmed. His face was grey and slack, and he limped unseeing through the sawhorses and timber stacks of the hoarding crews as he headed for the stairs to the keep. Before he reached them, however, Sister Willentrude saw him, and stepped from where she had been praying before the ever-burning pyre of the dead. Her habit and apron were covered in blood, and she looked like she hadn't slept since Felix had seen her last – which was likely true.

'My lord steward!' she cried after him. 'I demand you release Tauber and his assistants!'

Von Geldrecht turned towards her, blinking like a sleepwalker, as all around him the construction crews raised their heads. 'Sister?'

'Twenty-two men died last night, my lord,' she said, her eyes flashing. 'Twenty-two men that would have lived with a surgeon's care. I and my initiates can keep disease and infection at bay with our prayers and purified water, but we are not adepts of the knife and the needle. We cannot stop men from haemorrhaging to death, or drowning in their own bile.' She raised an accusing finger to the steward. 'You have killed these men, my lord. By locking Surgeon Tauber away, you doomed them to unnecessary–'

Von Geldrecht caught the sister by the arm and started to drag her towards the keep, a ghastly smile plastered to his face. 'Let us discuss this in *private*, sister,' he hissed. '*In private!*'

Felix smiled grimly to himself. He hoped she gave him even more of an earful in private, for she was right. When von Geldrecht had caved in to Bosendorfer's threats against Tauber, he had endangered the lives of every man in the castle. If there was anyone other than Kemmler to blame for the fix they were in, it was the steward and the greatsword captain.

Quite a few of the men in the courtyard, however, didn't seem to see it that way. They stared after von Geldrecht and Sister Willentrude as

Felix and Kat stumbled through them, murmuring amongst themselves.

'Does the old cow think Tauber would save us?' scoffed one. 'After he poisoned all the rest.'

'I don't know,' said another. 'I would have died after Grimminhagen if not for him. He saved my arm and no lie.'

'Men can change,' said a third. 'He wouldn't be the first who came back south a different man than marched north.'

'Bosendorfer says he was a bad'un *before* he went north,' said the first man. 'A poisoner from the start.'

Kat shook her head angrily as she and Felix entered the knights' residence. 'Sometimes,' she said, 'I think words are more poisonous than poison.'

When Felix and Kat woke again that afternoon, they found that Kemmler's second siege tower and another trebuchet had been completed at the edge of the woods, assembled by the ceaseless, swarming industry of the undead. More unnerving, the zombies who surrounded the castle had learned their lesson, and were no longer throwing their ladders up against the walls to have them stolen by the defenders' hooks. Instead, they held fresh ladders at their sides and stared up at the battlements with dead blank eyes – waiting.

And while the dead waited, the defenders scrambled to finish all their tasks before the storm broke. Men were levering apart the last stones of the officers' residence tower and winching them onto the oarboats for their last trips to the water gate. The powder monkeys were laying out the powder and shot beside the cannons that faced the land side of the castle, and the carpenters were cobbling together rickety hoardings out of the last few scraps of usable wood and sending them up to the walls to be fitted into place.

Felix and Kat joined the men on the walls, muscling the sides and roofs of the hoardings into place, while more skilled men made final adjustments and nailed them together. It was heavy, nervous work, done with one eye always glancing over the battlements to make sure the horde hadn't started its advance, and Felix therefore jumped a while later when a polite young voice piped up behind him.

'Herr Jaeger?'

Kat looked up as Felix turned.

A dirt-smeared squire was hovering near the work gang. 'Slayer Gurnisson's compliments,' he said, bowing. 'He and the others are almost through to the zombies' tunnel.'

'Thank you,' said Felix. 'Tell him we're coming.'

He and Kat turned to the lead carpenter as the boy scurried off.

'All right?' asked Felix.

'On your way,' said the man. 'And give 'em hell.'

* * *

Artillery Captain Volk and four of his men stood around the hole in the floor of the cellar. Each of the men held a pipe charge in his arms, and had picks, trowels, even metal spoons tucked through their belts, as well as lines of matchcord that snaked away behind them like tails, while more pipe charges were piled at their feet. In the centre of them, hunched over a spindle upon which all the match cords were wound, was Volk himself. He grinned when he saw Felix and Kat, his fire-scarred face forbidding in the light of the tinder pot that glowed at his side.

'Your mates are nearly through,' he said, stepping aside so they could get to the hole. 'Can hear the zombies through the dirt now – leastwise, they can. I can't hear nothing. Too many years around the guns.'

Felix nodded as Kat started down the ladder into the hole. 'Is there a plan?'

'Oh aye,' said Volk. 'You and the dwarfs push them dead bastards back to the mouth of their tunnel. We work in behind you and set the charges. When we're primed all the way to the far end, I call "fire in the hole" and y'run like blazes back to here, then...' He spread his fingers wide, eyes dancing with glee. 'Boom! The tunnel caves, the zombies are squashed, the castle is saved.'

Felix swung onto the ladder and started down. 'And we'll be able to get clear in time?' he asked.

'Aye,' said Volk. 'The Slayers've rigged a door in their tunnel that'll close behind them and cut off the blast. Should go as smooth as silk.'

Kat glared as they turned to go into the low passage. 'That was a jinx if ever I heard one,' she muttered.

'Aye,' said Felix, and crossed his fingers. He wasn't normally a superstitious man, but there was no sense tempting fate.

As they ducked into the tunnel, footsteps clattered down the stairs from above and six spearmen entered the cellar.

'Sergeant Abelung reporting,' he said. 'Steward sent us to help. Where do we go?'

Volk pointed at Felix and Kat. 'With them.'

Felix looked the spearmen over as they climbed down the ladder. They looked as tired as he felt, and no wonder. They had been working all day on the defences as well.

'Hope this doesn't take too long,' said Abelung, hunching into the tunnel after Felix and Kat. 'The zombies will be coming over the top soon.'

'I think you'll get your fair share down here,' said Felix.

As they all crouched along towards the distant ringing of picks on hard earth, Felix felt a tension in his chest that had nothing to do with the prospect of fighting zombies in cramped quarters. After a whole day and night of digging, would Gotrek's problem be worse? Would he be able to fight? Would he retire if he couldn't? Felix knew the answer to that, and it worried him.

After passing three lanterns, they saw the Slayers in the distance, still swinging away. Now it was Snorri and Rodi at the workface, and Gotrek behind, shovelling the dirt into a barrow. Felix eyed him uneasily, but to his relief, the Slayer's earlier breathlessness seemed to have passed.

About five paces back from the workface Felix and Kat came to a strange arrangement of logs and rope that Felix surmised must be the Slayers' blast door. A sturdy log that looked like it had once been a dock piling stretched across the top of the tunnel, with both ends well set into the walls. Hanging from it by means of heavy ship's cables was a thick wooden door propped open by a spear. The contraption reminded Felix of the sort of trap a hunter made by propping up a heavy rock with a stick and placing food under it, hoping that an animal would nudge the stick and bring the rock down on itself.

'Nothing could possibly go wrong here,' Felix muttered, edging around the precarious spear.

'Oh no,' agreed Kat. 'Perfectly safe.'

Abelung laughed like a cat being strangled as he and his men squeezed in behind them.

There was a clink and clatter of falling stone, and suddenly a freezing, foetid wind blew in Felix's face. He and Kat and the spearmen choked at the smell.

'That's done it,' said Rodi. 'We're through.'

Tattered grey hands were reaching through a ragged black hole in the workface and clawing at the dirt from the other side. Not all were human. Some were the huge, gnarled claws of beastmen.

Rodi and Snorri put down their picks and picked up their axe and hammer as Gotrek tossed aside his shovel and took up his rune axe. Felix and Kat drew as well, watching as the hole got rapidly larger.

Gotrek looked over his shoulder. 'Stay back and make sure the ones who fall down stay down.'

The zombies must have heard them talking, or smelled them, for their clawing became suddenly frantic, and there was a mournful groaning from the other side of the workface. One of the spearmen flinched back.

'Steady,' said Abelung, licking his lips.

A huge impact rocked the tunnel, and a beastman's horned head smashed through the workface in an explosion of dirt, making a big hole. Snorri caved in the beast-corpse's skull with his hammer as Rodi cut it off at the knees. It toppled forwards and a tide of zombies surged through the hole to crawl over its back into the narrow tunnel, groaning and swiping with claws and broken swords.

The three Slayers slammed into them with axe, hammer and shoulder, and quickly drove them back into their tunnel, then followed them in. Rodi was first, cutting down a dead knight without breaking stride, then Snorri and Gotrek followed, smashing aside a beast and a bowman, and vanished into the darkness beyond.

'Right,' said Felix, taking a breath. 'In we go.'

He pulled a lantern from a hook and stepped to the hole with Kat while the spearmen crept hesitantly after. The zombies' tunnel was at least four times as wide as the Slayers' narrow one, more than twice as high, and was filled wall to wall, for as far back as Felix could see, with dead men and beastmen.

In the lantern's flickering light they jumped into sharp relief as they swarmed forwards – a vision out of a nightmare, their teeth and claws flashing yellow, their shadows raking the walls and ceiling behind them as they attacked. Maggots crawled from holes in their faces and chests, and flies buzzed around their heads. Their eyes were wilted grapes, and their hair and fur was falling out in patches, while rips in their skin showed decaying, pus-leaking meat. The smell of them was like a hammer to the face, quite literally staggering.

Kat retched, then tied her scarf over her nose and mouth to block the smell. Behind her some of the spearmen were vomiting, though they spewed only water. There was nothing else in their stomachs.

The Slayers spread out across the width of the tunnel as they butchered their way into the shambling throng, but without the wall at their backs, the zombies started to edge around their flanks, and the spearmen saw their duty.

'Come on, lads,' Abelung quavered. 'Fill in their line.'

'Not too close,' said Felix, holding up a hand. 'Slayers sometimes, ah, *forget themselves* in battle.'

Abelung's eyes widened. 'Much obliged, mein herr. Right then, lads, stay back and keep them spearpoints busy.'

The spearmen stepped behind the Slayers and began stabbing between them, finding eyes, necks and knees. Felix and Kat capped their line at either end, closing off the space between the Slayers and the sides of the tunnel, and killing the zombies that tried to edge around. Against living opponents, the flashing spears would have been devastating, crippling and blinding them and making them defenceless against the Slayers' attacks; but even against the unfeeling dead they did enough, blocking the zombies' flailing claws and making them stumble, so the Slayers never had to worry about defending themselves, only attacking – sending withered limbs and heads and rotting organs spinning away from them like they were red whirlwinds.

It was a glorious slaughter, thought Felix, but how long could it continue? The Slayers would never tire, of course, but the spearmen were as exhausted as he and Kat. Would they have the stamina to fight all the way to the end of the tunnel? It looked like it went back more than fifty feet!

The Slayers took another stride forwards, their boots sinking ankle-deep in rotting entrails as they tromped through the dismembered dead to smash another rank of groaning corpses, and Felix, Kat and the spearmen paced forwards with them. A moment later, two artillerymen ducked through the door behind them, laying matchcord along the walls as they went, then digging holes close to the ceiling of the tunnel. Felix looked back and saw them casting uneasy glances at the undead throng that moaned and flailed only yards away from them, but they kept to their work, and once they had dug their holes, they wedged the pipe charges into them, spliced the matchcord to them and ran back towards the cellar for another load.

They continued in this fashion for what seemed an eternity, Gotrek, Rodi and Snorri carving through more zombies, and Felix, Kat and the spearmen advancing behind them as artillerymen came and went behind them, planting their charges. After a while, Felix felt like he was part of a plough being dragged the length of a farmer's field by a trio of scarred old plough horses. The Slayers were tilling the ground, while the artillerymen, like bloodthirsty farmers, were sowing bombs in the furrow, which would later sprout into beautiful red and yellow explosions on harvest day.

A gasp from Abelung snapped Felix from his delirious fancy. The young sergeant was fighting spear to spear with a corpse that had somehow stumbled between Gotrek and Rodi unscathed, and he suddenly staggered back, eyes wide.

'Captain?' he quavered. 'Captain Zeismann?'

ELEVEN

Felix looked around as Abelung's comrades cried out. It was true. The zombie Abelung fought was the corpse of Captain Zeismann, still recognisable though his ready smile had become a lipless grimace, and his kindly eyes were birthing maggots. And he had brought his men with him. They were pushing through to the front, their spears stabbing erratically at the Slayers. Some instinct, perhaps burned into their sinews through training, had kept them together and following their leader, even in death.

'Captain,' whimpered Abelung, edging back. 'Please, captain, don't–'

The zombie that had been Zeismann stabbed forwards, and Abelung, frozen by shock and grief, did not block in time. The spear point glanced off his breastplate, then skidded up and punched through his throat. He collapsed, wide-eyed, clutching at Zeismann's spear as blood bubbled from his neck.

'Damn you, sergeant!' shouted Felix, and leapt for Zeismann as the other spearmen shrank back.

The zombie captain thrust straight for Felix's heart, but though his aim had survived his death, his speed hadn't, and Felix swept the point aside, then hacked off Zeismann's head.

The living spearmen moaned as their old captain's body collapsed, and continued retreating as more of their dead comrades staggered past the hard-pressed Slayers.

'Don't be fools!' shouted Felix, trying to hold back all the dead spearmen by himself. 'You must kill them to free them! Cut them down! Let them truly die!'

Still the spearmen hesitated, on the tipping point between fight and flight, as Felix decapitated another zombie spearman and dodged three more.

'On!' he shouted desperately. 'For Abelung! For Zeismann! On!'

The names did it. With tears in their eyes and sobs in their throats, the spearmen fell in beside him. 'For Abelung!' they shouted. 'For Zeismann! For Zeismann!'

Their spears flashed forwards, stabbing their dead comrades in the chests, and after a wild few moments, the hole was plugged and their line restored and Felix was able to stagger back to his position behind Gotrek, panting and out of breath.

But as he did, he realised that his wasn't the only breathing he could hear. Though Gotrek fought on beside his fellow Slayers as tirelessly as ever, and had lost no strength or speed that Felix could see, his breath was once again raw and thick, as if fluid filled his lungs. And while he seemed in no way impaired by the constant rasping, his face was even redder than usual, and his single eye angrier, as if he was furious at his body's sudden betrayal.

Again the image of the black slivers burrowing through the Slayer's organs forced its way into Felix's mind and he couldn't push it out again. He suddenly feared that Gotrek's next strike or block might be the one to jar the flecks through his heart and kill him. He wanted to tell the Slayer to step back, to let him fight at the front for once. But Gotrek would never allow that. Nor would he care about the slivers. If they killed him in the middle of battle, so be it. He would have died a Slayer's death, and all would be well.

Felix glanced ahead and grunted with relief as he saw that the tunnel mouth was only a few paces ahead. They were almost there. He shot a questioning glance at Kat, on the far side of the tunnel. She gave him a weary nod and took another step through the reeking swamp of decapitated corpses, but as Felix did the same, a deep rumbling shook the tunnel, jarring him sideways and nearly knocking Kat and the spearmen off their feet.

'What is it?' asked Kat, as the noise grew louder and the shaking more violent.

'The siege towers,' said Gotrek. 'The attack has begun.'

From behind came footsteps and shouting.

'Slayers! Spearmen! Fall back!' called an artilleryman. 'We are needed at the cannons! Sappers, plant your last charges! We are lighting the fuses now!'

Gotrek and Rodi nodded to Felix, Kat and the spearmen as the artillerymen holding the last two charges shoved them hastily into their holes and hurried back down the tunnel.

'Start running,' said Gotrek. 'We will follow.'

'But there are still zombies,' said Snorri.

'Plenty more on the walls, Father Rustskull,' said Rodi.

Felix and Kat backed away with the spearmen, leaving the three Slayers alone against the roiling wall of zombies, then turned and ran – although 'running' was perhaps too fine a term for what they were doing. They were so weary from fighting, and the floor so littered with butchered zombies, that they stumbled and swerved like drunks passing through a slaughterhouse.

A young spearman crashed down behind his comrades, tripping on the crushed skull of a beastman and twisting his leg. Felix and Kat hauled him up and he limped on, hissing and lame.

From the direction of the cellar came a distant cry. 'Fire in the hole! Fire in the hole!'

Felix got the boy's left arm over his shoulder and Kat did the same with his right and they staggered after the rest towards the narrow hole to the Slayers' tunnel. Two sparking flames raced out of the hole as the spearmen squeezed through it, and Kat cried out in alarm. Two of the matchcords that were laid along the walls of the tunnel were sizzling towards their charges.

'That bastard Volk!' cried the spearman. 'He's blowing us up too!'

Felix's heart lurched with fear, but the matchcords burned past the first charges and sparked towards the end of the tunnel.

'No,' he panted. 'He's lit the furthest ones first.'

'Still cutting it damned fine,' said the spearman.

Kat and Felix helped him through the hole as two more sparks sizzled past them. A shout and heavy thud boomed down the tunnel from the direction of the cellar. Felix couldn't see what had happened. The tiny space was filled with the sulphuric smoke of burning matchcord, but someone was screaming.

They stumbled on and the haze thinned, and Felix could see that the heavy log-built blast door had fallen closed, pinning a spearman to the ground. Shouts and pounding came from the other side of the door, and three more spearmen were trying to lift it from this side, but it wasn't moving.

Felix, Kat and the limping spearman hurried to help them, and all of them together lifted the door enough to get it off the pinned man's back. Someone pulled him clear, but they couldn't raise the door any further. Two more flames hissed under their feet and sped down the tunnel towards the bombs.

'You on the other side!' called Felix. 'Heave on my count. One, two, *three*!'

Muffled groans came from beyond the door, and Felix could feel pressure from the other side adding to their lift. They had it up to their knees.

'Go, Kat,' said Felix. 'Get under.'

'I won't,' she said. 'Not alone.'

'Damn you, girl! There's no reason–'
'Stand aside, manling.'

Felix looked around. The three Slayers were striding up the narrow tunnel in single file, Gotrek at their head. Felix shifted aside and Gotrek lifted the door over his head as if it weighed no more than a window sash.

'Run,' he said.

Kat, Felix and the spearmen all ducked gratefully under the logs and staggered along the tunnel as fast as they could go. Felix looked back and saw Rodi and Snorri side-step past Gotrek through the door as calmly as if they were squeezing through a crowded market. Then the Slayer stepped forwards and dropped the door behind him.

The logs banged closed and the world turned upside down. It was as if the slamming door had struck a trigger, for just as it hit, the tunnel shook and a battering-ram of hot air punched Felix off his feet. He and Kat and the spearmen tumbled down the tunnel like leaves before a wind as an enormous boom battered his ears and made everything else go silent.

He came to rest on top of Kat with the spearmen on top of him, and someone's knee in his kidneys. The tunnel was swirling with grey smoke. He looked back along it. He couldn't see the Slayers.

'That… was loud,' said Kat.

Felix coughed and rolled off her, then pushed to his feet. 'Gotrek? Rodi? Snorri?'

Nobody answered him. He limped down the tunnel, afraid of what he would find. A squat body lay on the floor.

'Gotrek?'

The body coughed and sat up, shaking its nail-studded head. It was covered head to toe in grey dust. 'What was that, young Felix?'

'Nothing, Snorri,' said Felix. 'I thought you were Gotrek.'

'Say again? Snorri can't hear you.'

Felix edged past him, peering into the smoke.

'Gotrek? Rodi?'

Two short, sturdy silhouettes staggered out of the cloud, slapping dust off themselves. One was waggling a finger in his ear.

'Why are you whispering, manling?' asked Gotrek.

'Do you hear bells?' asked Rodi.

A muffled tantara of rally horns and the thunder of cannon echoed from above. The two Slayers cocked their ears and looked up. They could hear *that* well enough.

'Come, manling,' said Gotrek, sucking in a breath and striding past with Rodi. 'Time for some real fighting.'

Felix, Kat and the spearmen followed the Slayers out of the officers' residence and into hell. In every direction was noise, flames and confusion.

Lobbed missiles arced out of the night sky to crash down all over the courtyard – boulders, flaming corpses and dead cattle that exploded in showers of rotting entrails. Fires roared wherever Felix looked. The upper storey of the knights' residence was ablaze, as was the remaining river boat, and the hoardings were catching too. On the parapet, the knights, spearmen and handgunners fought off an endless tide of zombies that poured over the battlements as swooping bats slashed at any who tried to shove or steal their ladders away. And under all the shouting and shrieking, under the crack of the guns and the boom of the cannons, came the deep rumble of the approaching siege towers.

Gotrek was looking at none of it. Instead, his one eye swept the sky, glaring at it as if demanding an answer.

'Where is he?' he rasped. 'Where is the coward?'

'Don't be picky, Gurnisson,' snorted Rodi, brushing by him with Snorri and starting for the stairs. 'There are plenty of dooms here.'

Gotrek grunted and started after them, still looking at the sky. 'I already have my doom.'

Felix scanned the walls to see where they were most needed as he, Kat and the spearmen followed the Slayers across the courtyard and up the stairs. On the far side of the main gatehouse, the westernmost section of the wall was thick with the mustard and burgundy surcoats of von Volgen's Talabeclanders, fighting in a tight line at the battlements, with spearmen detachments ranked behind them and stabbing over their shoulders. On the eastern walls, von Geldrecht called encouragement to Castle Reikguard's household knights, who were lined up like the Talabeclanders, with ranked spearmen backing them up, while closest to the gatehouse, Bosendorfer and his greatswords had staked out a section of wall for their very own, and were slashing wildly at the zombies with no spearmen to back them up. And on the towers, Volk's crews, shirtless and sweating, were loading, priming and firing the castle's great-cannons while Hultz's handgunners clustered around them, blasting away at the giant bats that harried them and tried to ruin their aim. Even Draeger's militiamen were on the walls, dragged out of their cells as von Geldrecht promised, but apparently not entrusted with weapons. They ran amongst the others, wielding hooked ropes and boarding pikes to steal and shove back the ladders of the zombies all along the wall.

Felix nodded with grim satisfaction. For all the fire and noise and crashing stones, all seemed to be going well. The hoardings were protecting the defenders from the bats and the blazing barrage that Kemmler's catapults and trebuchets were raining down upon them, and the defenders were holding their lines and making short work of the corpses that managed to make it to the walls.

Unfortunately, it looked as if all that was about to change.

As Felix, Kat and the Slayers and spearmen squeezed onto the parapet behind the surging lines of knights, the deep rumble that had churned their guts since they had stepped into the courtyard grew so strong that it shook the castle walls, drowning out the shouts of the captains as they bellowed orders to their troops. Felix craned his neck to see over the battlements, and saw at last the source of the sound.

'Sigmar,' he breathed.

The towers had been frightening enough seen at a distance, when he had watched them being constructed at the edge of the woods. Now, lurching out of the night and crawling with nightmare crews, they were enough to make him want to turn and run. Up close, he saw they had been covered with the shaggy skins of beastmen, stretched across a twisted framework of dead trees, the hides crudely stitched together and the empty bags of head skin flapping and ballooning in the wind so that it looked like the eye and mouth holes were blinking and trying to say something.

More revolting still, the tower was being pulled by the dead beastmen that had been flayed to make it. Hundreds of skinless beast-corpses were harnessed to the towers, pulling them forwards by ropes that pierced them through their chests and strung them together like grisly fetishes on a shaman's braid. The bestial zombies trudged forwards as one, straining against the thick knots that pressed against their sternums as the towers skidded slowly over the uneven ground, swaying and shaking like they were in a high wind.

The boarding crews were just as hideous – naked, white-skinned ghouls with clawed hands and filed teeth. They hung from the fighting tops by the score, gibbering and howling for human flesh, and shaking shin-bone spears and thigh-bone clubs.

'Corpse-eaters,' moaned Kat, shuddering.

Felix fought down nausea as the reek of death and defecation washed over them. 'Gods,' he choked. 'The smell alone will kill us!'

The spearmen gave Felix and Kat a farewell salute, then hurried to rejoin the ranks of their comrades. Felix and Kat returned the salute, then followed the Slayers as they went left, heading for where the nearest tower was trundling towards the wall.

But as it loomed closer, hope swelled in Felix's chest. It looked like the crew of the menacing tower were going to drag it straight into the empty moat, where it would tip forwards and crash flat before it reached the wall – and the further tower seemed about to do the same.

'That's it, you brainless puppets!' shouted Captain Hultz from where his handgunners blazed at the ghouls. 'Do our work for us!'

'They're going to crush their own crews!' laughed a spearman.

The cat-calls died away, however, as the long trains of zombies that had been following the towers all at once surged ahead and began throwing themselves into the moat in front of them.

'What are they doing?' asked a knight. 'They'll be flattened!'

'Oh, Sigmar,' moaned a handgunner. 'They're making a bridge.'

And as he and Kat stared, Felix saw the man was right. The zombies kept piling into the moat in their hundreds until, just before the harnessed teams of beast-corpses reached them, they were level with its banks.

At first the dead beastmen lost their footing on the uneven surface of their comrades' stacked bodies, but then they recovered, digging their hooves into the faces and ribcages and guts of the undead bridge and using them for traction. The skids of the towers had less trouble. They slid across the mound of crushed corpses as if they were greased, and the towers picked up speed.

Cannons belched smoke from the castle walls, and the top of the further tower smashed to splinters, sending the ghouls that clung to it spinning away to their deaths, while the cannonball from the right-hand gun crashed through the waist of the nearer, snapping timbers and braces within before punching out the far side.

The men on the walls cheered, but though smashed and sagging, the towers kept coming, screeching ghouls swarming up from their depths.

Rodi and Snorri stopped behind Bosendorfer and his greatswords, who readied themselves at the place where the nearer tower would strike the wall.

'Here,' said Rodi, hefting his axe.

Gotrek shot a last disappointed look at the sky, then fell in beside him. 'Aye,' he said.

'Snorri wishes these humans would get out of the way,' said Snorri.

'Here it comes,' said Kat.

'Not one step back, greatswords!' yelled Bosendorfer.

'Not a step, lads!' shouted his sergeant, a hulking veteran with a grizzled beard. 'Not a step!'

With an impact that shook the whole castle, the hellish tower struck and the ghouls launched forwards, straight onto the sword-points of the greatswords – but they didn't come alone. As the first wave died screaming and tumbling off the battlements to crash amongst the skinless beast-zombies below, a cold wind exhaled from the maw of the tower and a shrieking spectre burst forth, shadows flapping around it like a shroud. An eyeless female face stared from the centre of the darkness as claws like sabres reached for the greatswords.

The hairs stood on Felix's neck as the thing came forwards, and he took an involuntary step back. Every fear he had ever had – of the dark, of losing his mother, of illness, death and tortures beyond the grave – all welled up in him at once as he looked into her empty eyes, and every fibre of courage he possessed dried up and crumbled in the scathing wind of her shriek. He wanted to turn and flee – to hide in a corner and weep.

And perhaps he would have, but Kat stumbled back too, bumping into him, and somehow, that contact, and the opportunity it gave him to put his hand on her shoulder and reassure her, reassured him too, and the panic passed.

The greatswords, unfortunately, had no one to reassure, and were edging back and dying as the ghouls took advantage of their terrified paralysis, raking out their eyes and ripping out their throats. Bosendorfer swung his two-hander at the ghostly horror, but his blade passed right through it without touching and it came on, swiping with its claws.

They impaled him through the chest, and though they seemed to do no physical damage to him or his armour, their touch made him stagger and shriek.

'Fall back!' he cried, flailing with his sword. 'Fall back, we cannot prevail!'

The greatswords, already on the point of breaking, followed this order with a will, and fled down the wall, Bosendorfer in the lead and the sergeant taking up the rear, as a score of ghouls flooded onto the parapet unopposed after them.

'Cowards!' growled Gotrek, and charged forwards into the corpse-eaters with Rodi and Snorri milling at his sides, and Felix and Kat following behind.

'At least they got out of the way,' said Snorri.

The banshee howled at the Slayers as they slaughtered the ghouls, but one swipe of Gotrek's axe and she dissipated into fading curls of mist, her miasma of fear fading with her. The Slayers pressed on, but they were like a boulder in a wide stream. Though they cut down ghouls with every swing of their weapons, without the greatswords to hold their flanks, many more spilled around them and swarmed down the wall, attacking the lines of the knights and spearmen from the rear. The ranks were crumbling and falling back in confusion, allowing the zombies to top their ladders and gain a foothold on the wall. The greatswords needed to come back!

'Bosendorfer!' shouted Felix, hacking down a ghoul. 'Turn about! She's gone!'

A few of the greatswords looked back, but Bosendorfer didn't seem to have heard. Felix cursed, then filled his lungs. It had worked with the spearmen in the tunnel. Perhaps it would work here.

'Greatswords!' he shouted. 'To me! Hold the wall! Hold for Castle Reikguard!'

A few of the greatswords slowed and turned, and then called more of their comrades back. The grizzled sergeant hesitated, looking towards Bosendorfer, then back to Felix again.

'To me!' shouted Felix again. 'We can hold them here!'

The words seemed to galvanise the sergeant, and he started back along the wall. The others followed, and fell upon the ghouls that had got behind the knights and spearmen.

'That's it!' cried Felix, as they worked their way back along the wall. 'For Graf Reiklander! For the Empire!'

With the greatswords pushing back the ghoul incursion, the Slayers pressed forwards to stem the tide at its source. They cut a bloody path to the battlements, then leapt from them to the siege tower and battled through the ghouls towards the maw from which they spewed.

Felix and Kat watched their progress uneasily as they and the greatswords fought to hem in the ghouls that still swarmed past the Slayers to the wall. The tower was listing decidedly to the left and creaking noisily as the skinless beast-zombies, no longer needed to pull it forwards, climbed its sides, still strung together on their long ropes.

'Don't the brainless things know it's broken inside?' cried Kat. 'They're going to pull it down!'

'Aye,' said Felix. 'And the Slayers with it.'

A roar from above brought Felix's head up. He cursed. Hurtling out of the sky on the back of his undead wyvern was Krell, aiming straight for the three dwarfs.

'Slayers!' shouted Felix.

Gotrek, Rodi and Snorri dived aside as the patchwork monster slammed down on the precarious tower and nearly rocked it off its runners. Ghouls and skinned beasts spun away to the ground as the Slayers clung like limpets, and more ominous crackings and grindings sounded from within.

'Mine!' roared Rodi as Krell dismounted and slashed at him with his black axe. The gauntleted hand and forearm Gotrek had previously severed seemed to have completely regrown.

'Find your own doom, Balkisson!' roared Gotrek, throwing himself forwards. 'This is mine!'

'Take it if you can, Gurnisson!' laughed Rodi and charged in as well.

Krell blocked both attacks with a scrape of steel, but Gotrek shouldered into his legs and sent him crashing back into his wyvern. The ugly beast flapped into the air, shrieking, and left the wight king lying at the edge of the tower as the Slayers advanced.

'Snorri wants it to be his doom!' called Snorri, limping after them.

A skinned beastmen pulled itself up onto the fighting top and lurched in Snorri's way as Krell and the Slayers clashed. Snorri crushed the beast-corpse's head with his hammer, only to find more of the hulking horrors pulling themselves up all around him, all still linked together like some grisly charm bracelet come to life.

'Get out of Snorri's way!' shouted Snorri.

Felix cursed. This was bad. He had to get Snorri off the tower before he found his doom. Unfortunately, there were more than a score of ghouls in the way.

'Drive them back!' he shouted to the greatswords. 'Drive them off the walls!'

The greatswords cheered, and the grizzled sergeant echoed him. 'Aye, lads! Drive 'em back to the graveyard!'

The greatswords fell upon the ghouls like a single man, their weapons rising and falling as one, and doing terrible damage to heads, shoulders and necks as Felix and Kat fought in their centre. Still, Felix wasn't sure they would be quick enough.

On the leaning tower, Snorri fought in the centre of a handful of skinned beasts, roaring joyously, while Gotrek and Rodi chopped at Krell from opposite sides. The wight king turned and slashed in their centre, his obsidian axe making a choking cloud of grit all around him. Rodi caught a mouthful and stumbled, coughing, and Krell struck him a blow so strong that, though he blocked it, it knocked the young Slayer to the very edge of the fighting top.

'Ha!' snarled Gotrek, charging in. 'Now we'll see whose doom it is!'

Krell backed from Gotrek's blurring axe, and his ancient black armour was quickly scored with a dozen metal-bright scars, but the surge was taking its toll on Gotrek too. His ragged breathing had returned, and his face glowed like a hot coal.

Rodi struggled to his feet and started up the slant again, but the skinned beast-corpses were surrounding him as well. 'Wait, Gurnisson!'

Gotrek coughed as he drove Krell to the edge. 'A Slayer doesn't wait!'

The undead champion's boot-heel slipped on the uneven lip of the fighting top, and Gotrek took advantage, hacking a huge divot out of his right greave. Krell threw himself to the side to avoid another strike and Gotrek turned after him, blowing like a steam tank.

At the same moment, Felix, Kat and the greatswords finally chopped down the last of the ghouls and leapt up onto the battlements to hack at the ring of skinless beasts that surrounded Snorri – only to find the old Slayer in a terrible predicament.

His peg leg was wedged between two planks at the very edge of the slanted platform, and he couldn't get it out. He swung mightily with his warhammer as the dead beasts pressed him from all sides, but he could not move or dodge, and they were clawing him to pieces.

Felix, Kat and the greatswords charged in, chopping at the ring of beasts, but there were too many, and they were too big. They weren't going to make it before Snorri was driven over the side.

'Gotrek!' shouted Felix. 'Snorri!'

Gotrek looked to the old Slayer as he smashed Krell's legs out from under him and sent him crashing down the slant. He hesitated, and Felix read his expression. If he went after the wight king, he could finish him, and cross out a thousand grudges in the dwarfs' ancient book. He could be known forever as the Slayer of Krell the Holdbreaker. But if he did, Snorri would fall to his death.

With a savage snarl, Gotrek charged at Snorri, and slammed into the wall of beasts around him, hamstringing one with his axe and shoving it over the edge. It jerked to a stop and swung like a hanged man as the rope that connected it to its fellows pulled taut. The next in the string staggered sideways at the jerk and Gotrek shoved it too. That did it. As the second beastman pitched over the side, its weight, combined with the weight of the first beastman and the steep angle of the platform, pulled all the rest off one after the other in rapid succession. It was like watching a string of ugly sausages slip over the edge of a cliff.

But as the last beast-corpse toppled, it impaled itself upon a dead tree branch that jutted out through the stretched skins of the tower's side, and stopped dead. All at once, all the weight of all the beasts on the string jerked the crippled tower hard to the left, and something vital broke within it.

Gotrek cursed and stumbled to Snorri, ripping his trapped peg from the planks as the tower began to sink slowly but inexorably to the side.

'Fall back, Nosebiter,' he wheezed, and shoved him at Felix and Kat, who dragged him back towards the battlements.

'Where did the beastmen go?' asked Snorri.

'Forget the beastmen, Snorri,' snapped Kat.

Gotrek turned back to Krell. Rodi was already there, driving him back across the tipping fighting top with brutal cuts as the wight king roared at the sky. Gotrek plunged after them, panting and rasping, but before he could reach them, the wyvern flashed down, flaring its wings, and Krell vaulted into the saddle.

Gotrek and Rodi rushed at him, but they were too late. The wyvern launched forwards and plunged away out of sight, and the tower tilted drastically under their feet.

'Coward!' roared Gotrek.

'Come back and fight!' bellowed Rodi.

'Slayers!' called Felix. 'Get off it!'

'Hurry!' cried Kat.

The Slayers stood for an agonising second, staring after Krell, then turned and walked back onto the battlements just as the collapsing tower finally sank away beneath them. Gotrek's face was hot and his chest heaved, but his single eye was as hard and cold as Felix had ever seen it.

Along the wall, the men pushing back the ladders and fighting the zombies cheered as the tower crashed to the moat, crushing scores of zombies and ghouls, and the cheer was echoed from the right as the second tower went down as well, burning like a kite in a furnace, but the Slayers did not seem in a celebratory mood.

Snorri, bleeding from a dozen claw wounds, was frowning at Gotrek as he struggled to stand. 'Snorri doesn't think it was right of you, Gotrek Gurnisson, to stop him from–'

'And Gotrek Gurnisson doesn't give a damn what Snorri thinks!' Gotrek bellowed in the old Slayer's face. 'Until he remembers his shame, Gotrek doesn't want to hear another word out of Snorri's mouth!'

Felix, Kat and Rodi stepped back as Snorri blinked, stunned by

Gotrek's outburst. The greatswords didn't seem to know where to look.

'And what if Snorri thinks he'd like to punch Gotrek Gurnisson's ugly face in?' asked Snorri, his fists balling.

Gotrek's brows lowered, but before he could gather enough breath to reply, von Volgen and a pair of knights shoved past him, running towards von Geldrecht.

'Lord steward!' called von Volgen. 'The harbour! Look to the harbour!'

Felix, Kat and the Slayers turned and looked down into the harbour, searching for what von Volgen was speaking of. Felix frowned. The sloop was still burning, and rocks and flaming corpses were still splashing down all over it, but he saw no new threat.

'What is it?' he asked. 'I don't see anything.'

'There!' said Kat, pointing towards the water near the quayside.

Felix followed her gaze. The water was filled with bobbing heads and thrashing hands as men tried to climb out onto the quayside.

No. Not men.

'Zombies,' rasped Gotrek. 'From under the river gate.'

TWELVE

'Sigmar's blood!' cursed Felix. 'How have they got in? We blocked it!'

The zombies were pulling themselves onto the docks in a mass now, like sludge-covered crabs crawling over each other to escape a roiling stew pot. The massive forms of dead beastmen heaved up amongst them, water pouring from their filthy fur, and they staggered towards the doors of the main gatehouse while the human corpses shuffled for the stairs to the walls and clawed up the sides of the burning riverboat as the river wardens hacked at them and shoved them back.

'So many,' moaned Kat. 'What do we do now?'

Felix turned to ask Gotrek the same question. The Slayer was walking after von Volgen with Snorri and Rodi following. Felix shot an uneasy look at Snorri, afraid he might still be angry at Gotrek, but the old Slayer's face was as placid as it always was – as if his oldest friend hadn't just shouted in his face. Felix sighed. That was one advantage to Snorri's memory problems, he supposed. He forgot an insult as quickly as he forgot anything else.

Felix saluted the greatsword sergeant as he and Kat turned to follow the Slayers. 'Thank you, sergeant.'

The big man gave him a sheepish smile. 'Thank you, mein Herr,' he said. 'Thank you for bringing us back.'

'You are thanking him, Sergeant Leffler?' rang a voice behind them. 'For countermanding my order?'

They all looked around. It was Bosendorfer, his eyes blazing.

'If I tell you to fall back, you fall back,' he said, stepping forwards. 'If I tell you to hold the walls, you hold the walls, is that clear?'

'Yes, captain,' said the sergeant. 'Very clear.'

'Good,' said Bosendorfer, then pointed to the now-empty battlements. 'Hold the walls!'

The men hesitated, and Leffler glanced at Felix as if to ask his permission. Felix nodded automatically, then saw that Bosendorfer had witnessed the exchange, and was rigid with rage.

The sergeant saluted hastily, then led the others back to the battlements.

Felix stepped back, feeling like he should say something, then turned away with Kat, growling. He felt Bosendorfer's eyes on him the whole way as they followed the Slayers down the wall.

'I don't think I've made a friend there,' he said.

'Who wants a coward for a friend?' sneered Kat.

They found the Slayers on the top of the easternmost tower, waiting impatiently as von Geldrecht gave orders to his officers while von Volgen stood at his side, whispering advice.

'One in every five men on the wall shall descend and defend the gatehouse!' called von Geldrecht, then turned to von Volgen, frowning. 'One in five? Are you sure? Will the walls hold?'

'With the towers down,' said von Volgen calmly, 'the zombies on the ladders can be contained. The harbour breach is your greatest threat, lord steward. It must be stopped and the gatehouse held, for if it falls, you will have to retire to the keep – and that will involve a great loss of life and treasure.'

'But how are we to stop the hole?' said von Geldrecht, and Felix could see he was an eye blink from panic. 'I thought we had already blocked it.'

'Leave that to us,' said Gotrek, his breathing slowly returning to normal. 'You keep the corpses out of the gatehouse, and we'll plug your hole for you.'

Von Geldrecht breathed a sigh of relief. 'Thank you, Slayers. You shall have all the assistance you require.'

'Rope, lamp oil, pipe charges and matchcord,' grunted Gotrek. 'Also an oarboat, and some men to keep off the zombies while we work.'

'It shall be done,' said von Geldrecht. 'And you will have Bosendorfer's greatswords to defend you.'

Felix coughed. 'Uh, no need to trouble them,' he said quickly. 'Perhaps some spearmen instead.'

'Certainly, certainly,' said von Geldrecht, then turned back to von Volgen as Felix, Kat and the Slayers started for the stairs. 'And you will see to the defence of the gatehouse, my lord?'

Von Volgen bowed. 'Of course, lord steward. We will hold it to the last man.'

Felix thought he did a remarkable job of keeping the contempt out of his voice.

* * *

A few minutes later, Felix, Kat and Snorri were prowling back and forth along the embankment of the harbour, fending off the giant bats that wheeled down out of the sky and chopping at any zombies that dared rear their heads above the waves while Rodi tied a rope around Gotrek's waist, and Gotrek chained his rune axe to his wrist. They were all tucked into the furthest corner of the harbour, behind the stairs that rose to the keep, and beside the river gate. The spearmen Gotrek had requested were posted between the stairs and the embankment, blocking any zombies that shambled towards them from the courtyard. That didn't stop the ones who tried to climb out of the water, however, and Felix, Kat and Snorri had their hands full.

'Sure you have enough breath?' asked Rodi, pulling the rope tight.

'It won't take much,' said Gotrek.

Felix swallowed. He could think of no more unpleasant experience than jumping into a dark harbour full of undead men and beastmen, but it would be impossible to patch the hole until they knew how big it was, and the only way to learn that was to sink down and look. Gotrek also wanted to know how the zombies had made it. Had they pushed aside the stones? Had they dug through the mud? How could they have done it in such a short time?

Rodi tied off the rope, then ducked aside as a great boulder smashed down next to them, shattering the flagstones and bouncing away, proof that the battle had not stopped so that they could carry out their investigation. Indeed, it had become worse. On the towers, Volk's cannons continued to blaze away, trying to knock out Kemmler's catapults and trebuchets, which still bombarded the courtyard with filth and stones and flaming death. On the walls, von Geldrecht's knights and spearmen kept up their never-ending battle to push back the zombies' ladders. And in the courtyard, von Volgen and his company of chosen men guarded the gatehouse doors against the ever-growing swarm of zombies that continued to surge up out of the harbour in a never-ending tide and attack them with mindless focus.

Unless Gotrek found some way to block the hole in the river gate, the outcome of that battle was inevitable. Von Volgen's men were holding up well, but faced with a force that would not break or tire or diminish, they would eventually die of attrition, and the gatehouse would fall. Then the zombies would open the gates and the rest of the horde would pour in. The lower courtyard would be lost, and likely the keep too. Castle Reikguard would be in the hands of Kemmler, and the relief force, when it at last arrived, would take the role of besieger, rather than rescuer.

Gotrek stepped to the edge of the embankment.

'Leave off, Nosebiter,' he said. 'It's time.'

Snorri put his hammer on his back and wrapped the end of Gotrek's rope around his massive fist. 'Snorri is ready.'

'Ready,' said Rodi, taking up a jug of lamp oil and a torch.

Gotrek nodded, then dived into the water, his axe in one hand. As soon as he vanished beneath the waves, Rodi cracked the jug of lamp oil on the stone embankment and let the contents spill onto the water, then touched the torch to the spreading sheen.

With a sudden *whump*, the oil went up in a ball of flame, then burned brightly on the waves, snaking like it was alive through the ripples and splashes.

A zombie came up in the middle of it and tried to climb onto the bank as the flames clung to its head and shoulders. It didn't seem to notice, and reached for Kat with a burning hand. She dodged back, then split its skull with one hatchet, and its throat with the other. The thing fell back, clawing weakly and fizzling as it sank beneath the waves.

A second later, the flames burned themselves out, and a second after that, Gotrek's rope began wildly jerking and thrashing in the water.

'Pull, Snorri!' shouted Rodi. 'Pull!'

The old Slayer heaved mightily on the rope, and began to reel it in fist over fist, but there was a lot of resistance. Rodi joined him and they pulled together as Felix and Kat stepped close to the edge, weapons raised.

The water churned at their feet, and then a shaven head and broad shoulders shot backwards up out of the waves, followed instantly by the horned goat head of a dead beastman, and the rotting, thrashing limbs of human zombies. Gotrek was infested with them. The beast-corpse had its ursine teeth clamped around his left shoulder, and the humans clung to his legs and torso, all clawing and biting as he swung his rune axe and roared sputtering defiance.

Felix struck the goat-headed monster a glancing blow. It was enough of a distraction for Gotrek to bury his axe under its jaw, and it fell away. Kat severed the spine of one of the men, and Gotrek peeled off the other two with his axe, then flopped on the embankment, coughing violently, as Felix and Kat drove the rest under the waves.

'Well?' said Rodi, throwing down the rope.

Gotrek sat up, still coughing, and slicked his crest back out of his eyes. 'Big enough for a beastman,' he said. 'But no bigger. And right through the gate.'

He opened his left hand to reveal a stub of metal bar. Felix and Kat looked at it over their shoulders. It was a broken piece of the iron lattice that made up the river gate doors, but it had a curious brittle look to it, and when Rodi poked his finger at it, it crumbled away like chalk.

'The saboteur,' he grunted. 'I thought Lord Lard-Guts was going to "take steps".'

Gotrek grunted and pulled himself to his feet. He had deep bite marks in his left shoulder, and claw marks everywhere. 'Forget the saboteur. We have to close the hole.' His eye focussed on the temple of Sigmar across the harbour. 'And that is the patch.'

* * *

'You can't take my door!' cried Father Ulfram, as his acolyte, Danniken, cowered in the background. 'This is a temple of Sigmar! You are committing sacrilege!'

The Slayers ignored him, just continued banging at the hinges of the huge iron-bound door with their hammers and chisels.

'I'm sorry, father,' said Felix, 'but it's the only way. It is strong enough and big enough, and–'

'You've prayed to Sigmar to protect us, haven't you, priest?' interrupted Kat, an edge to her voice.

'Of course I have,' said Ulfram. 'Constantly.'

'And what if this is his answer?' Kat asked.

The priest opened his mouth to retort, then paused, his brows furrowed behind the rag that hid his eyes. 'Here it comes,' said Rodi, and stepped back as the massive door suddenly dropped from its hinges, then toppled forwards to crash down on the temple's front steps with a deafening boom.

Ulfram wailed at the sound and turned towards the altar at the back of the temple, making the sign of the hammer on his sunken chest. 'O Sigmar, if this be your will, then grant me–'

'We'll be back for the altar,' said Gotrek.

'What!' cried Ulfram. 'No! At this I draw the line! You cannot–'

But the three Slayers had already picked up the heavy door and were walking it out to their commandeered longboat.

By the time the boatmen had pushed the heavy-laden longboat away from the quay and started rowing towards the river gate with Gotrek, Felix, Snorri, Rodi and Kat crouching on top of the precariously balanced door and altar, it was clear to Felix that Kemmler had figured out what they were doing and was trying to stop it.

The zombies that emerged from the waters of the harbour were no longer shambling towards von Volgen's beleaguered square of defenders before the gatehouse. Now they were bobbing up on all sides of the longboat and reaching for its sides with their water-bloated claws, while at the same time, every giant bat in the sky was now streaking down and trying to smash them all into the water.

It was a nightmare. Felix, Kat and Rodi crawled up and down the boat, slashing at the zombies in a frenzy, as Gotrek and Snorri stumped back and forth and fought off the bats that clattered and shrieked above them, while the terrified river wardens prayed to Manann and spent as much time bashing zombies with their oars as they did rowing.

Felix feared every second that the overloaded boat would capsize and they would sink into the roiling stew of zombies, but somehow – by Sigmar's grace? – they reached the river gate with only a foot of water in the bottom and only two of the oarsmen pulled to their deaths.

Gotrek lashed the boat length-wise to the iron bars of the gates, which allowed the boatmen to abandon their oars and take up their cutlasses and join Kat, Felix and Snorri in the defence, while Gotrek and Rodi bent to their work.

Felix had never been in so hectic a fight. It was a non-stop onslaught from water and air, a whirling madness of arms and wings and claws and snapping teeth, with the boat rocking and bumping under his feet. A bat clawed his forehead and he fought on blinded by blood. A zombie bit his ankle, and its jaws remained locked around it even after he had cut its head off. Kat weaved like she was drunk, her whole left side covered in black slime. The boatmen fought like cornered rats, snarling with rabid fear.

In the few brief over-the-shoulder glances he managed, Felix saw the two Slayers working feverishly – fixing the door to the gate with long chains looped around its hinge posts, then tying ropes around the massive altar, and doing the same to it.

By then the boat was wallowing so low in the water that Felix feared that a single zombie laying its hands on its gunwales would send it sinking to the bottom.

'Any time, Gotrek,' he hissed through clenched teeth. 'Any time.'

'Nearly there, manling,' said Gotrek.

He and Rodi turned to the bow where two of Volk's tunnel charges sat half-submerged. They took lengths of slow-burning gunner's match from their belts then turned to the boatmen.

'The blast will stun the zombies in the water and knock back any coming through the hole,' said Gotrek. 'It will also sink the boat.'

'Sink the boat!' cried a boatman. 'You didn't say–'

'You should have time to swim to the bank before the zombies recover,' smirked Rodi. 'But if you don't, well, at least you died saving your mates.'

The boatmen wailed at this, but there was little they could do. Gotrek and Rodi touched the gunner's match to the matchcord of the charges then pitched them towards the centre of the harbour where they splashed into the water. Felix had been a little sceptical of this part of the plan, but he changed his mind as he saw the sparking flame of the matchcord still burning as it sank towards the bottom.

The zombies, being zombies, paid no attention and just kept on attacking, as did the bats, but Felix's heart raced in his chest as he waited for the bang to come. How big would the explosion be? What if it smashed them all into the gate?

A dull thud, felt as much as heard, punched the soles of his feet and rocked the boat violently beneath him, then a geyser of water, smoke and zombie parts erupted in the middle of the harbour, spraying them all and sending a great mounded ring wave spreading in all directions.

'Here it comes!' shouted a boatman, dropping his cutlass.

The swell lifted them high, and as Felix had feared, banged the boat against the gates, but then the water passed through the bars and dropped again. The boat went with it, wallowing, then slipping out from under the chained temple door and roped altar to sink into the water.

The boatmen swam frantically for the embankment through a sargasso of floating, unmoving zombies, but Felix and Kat remained clinging to the bars of the gate and slashing at the wheeling bats as the last pieces of Gotrek's plan literally fell into place.

As the boat sank, the heavy temple door swung down on its chains until it vanished under the water and Felix felt it clang flat against the river gate.

'So,' said Felix, ducking as a bat smashed into the gate. 'That seals the hole?'

'Aye,' said Gotrek, then slapped the bulky stone slab of the altar, which still hung from its ropes, half-submerged, against the gate. 'And this is the lock. Not even a beastman could shift the door with this wedged behind it.' He raised his axe and turned to Rodi and Snorri. 'Ready, Balkisson? Nosebiter?'

'Snorri is ready,' said Snorri, pulling himself around so that he held the outer edge of the altar.

'Aye, Gurnisson,' said Rodi, lifting his axe.

As one, he and Gotrek cut the ropes holding the stone table, and it sank swiftly into the water.

The Slayers went with it, holding its sides to guide it, and disappeared beneath the dark water. Felix looked around – the floating zombies were beginning to twitch and groan.

'We'd better swim for it,' he said, sheathing his sword.

Kat nodded and they struck out for the embankment, only a few yards away. The boatmen helped them out of the water then looked back towards the gate.

'Have they done it?' asked one.

'It doesn't seem possible,' said another.

But as the Slayers' heads broke the surface again and they began swimming for shore, Felix noticed that all the bats banked away from them and began to attack von Volgen's men again, harassing them from the air as they defended the gatehouse against the huge mob of zombies that surrounded it.

'Aye,' said Felix. 'They did it. Kemmler has given us up for another target.'

The three Slayers heaved themselves out of the water and turned towards the battle at the gatehouse.

'Come on,' said Gotrek, wheezing as he started forwards with Rodi and Snorri. 'Only a few left now.'

Felix exchanged a weary look with Kat. It felt like they had been fighting forever, but the Slayer was right. Patching the hole would be pointless if the zombies that had already got in broke through the front gate. He drew his sword and Kat drew her hatchets, and they slogged after the Slayers.

When it was all over, when the last trapped zombie had been decapitated and thrown on the pyre, when the fires in the residences had been put out and the handgunners on the walls had stolen so many of the zombies' ladders that they could no longer continue their assault, von Geldrecht and von Volgen approached the Slayers with Captain Hultz and Father Ulfram and Danniken in tow. They all inclined their heads respectfully.

'Thank you, Slayers,' said von Geldrecht. 'If not for your quick thinking, we would have been overwhelmed. Castle Reikguard owes you a debt of gratitude it cannot repay.'

'Even if it cost us a temple door,' said Father Ulfram.

'But how did they get in?' asked von Volgen. 'Did they burrow under the stones? Were they not piled high enough?'

Gotrek caught his breath, then spoke. 'The gate was shattered. Like the lock mechanism. Like the runes.'

Von Geldrecht closed his eyes and groaned. 'The saboteur.'

Von Volgen turned grim eyes on him. 'You have learned nothing more of him, lord steward?'

'My captains assured me they would report any suspicious goings-on,' said von Geldrecht, shaking his head. 'But they have given me no reports.'

Felix saw von Volgen's jaw clench with suppressed anger. 'My lord, rooting out such a powerful traitor is of utmost importance. You – you must do more.' He turned to Father Ulfram. 'Cannot the good father discover the identity of this warlock through his prayers?'

Von Geldrecht coughed as everyone looked at the priest. 'I have asked,' he said. 'But–'

'But I am not what I was,' said Ulfram, raising his bandaged eyes towards von Volgen. 'The fight with the pestilent champion I slew at Grimminhagen was not won without sacrifice. It took my sight and – and the strength of my prayers. Danniken here has done his best to help me recover, but I am much diminished, and Sigmar has not seen fit to answer me in this matter.'

Von Volgen bowed, chagrinned. 'Forgive me, Father. I did not know.'

Felix looked wonderingly at Ulfram as he nodded and looked down again. The frail old man had slain a champion of the dark powers? Did that mean he had been a warrior priest during the war? It hardly seemed possible, looking at him now.

'Nonetheless, it was a worthy suggestion, Lord von Volgen,' said Von Geldrecht. 'And you are right. I must do more. I – I had thought to keep the sabotage quiet until the fiend could be apprehended, but – but I see now that drastic measures are required.' He sighed and stared at the ground for a long moment, then looked up, his sagging face haggard. 'Hultz, inform the officers, and you von Volgen, tell your men. I will address the whole of the castle in the courtyard tomorrow after morning mess. Everyone who is not on duty will attend – knights, foot soldiers, servants and staff. Everyone. I will expose this villain before them once and for all.'

'My lord,' said von Volgen, uneasy. 'What do you intend?'

'It is better that no one know in advance.' Von Geldrecht turned to Ulfram. 'Father, if I could see you in the temple.'

'Of course, lord steward,' said the priest. 'Come with me.'

Danniken took Ulfram's arm and led him towards the now doorless temple as von Geldrecht limped beside him, talking in low tones. Felix was amazed at the contrast between his memories of the cheerful and robust von Geldrecht he had met only days before, and the frail old man who shuffled away from him now.

Hultz gave Felix, Kat and the Slayers a salute as he turned to start back to his men. 'Well done, tonight, friends. When we have beer again, the first round's on me.'

'Hultz,' said von Volgen, calling him back. 'One moment.'

'Aye, my lord.'

Von Volgen shot an uncomfortable glance at the retreating von Geldrecht, then lowered his voice. 'It is not my place to order you, but perhaps someone should put a guard on the river gate so this does not happen again.'

Hultz too looked after von Geldrecht, then nodded. 'Aye, my lord. A very good suggestion. I'll put someone on it right away.'

He started away again and von Volgen turned to Felix, Kat and the Slayers. 'I know we did not start well, and I expect no friendship from you after having locked you up for something you didn't do. But I wish you to know that I value your presence here as much as I value that of my own knights. Thank you.' He clicked his heels together and bowed, then turned and strode off, ramrod-straight, and did not look back.

'He's still a blind fool that can't tell his own son from a corpse,' said Rodi, snorting.

Gotrek spat. 'He's not the fool that worries me,' he said, then looked after von Geldrecht, who was just entering the temple with Ulfram and Danniken. 'You don't catch saboteurs with speeches. You catch them in the act.'

'A trap?' asked Kat.

Gotrek looked around the courtyard. 'A watch on his next target.'

'You know where he'll strike next?' asked Felix.

'Well, it won't be the river gate,' said Kat. 'Not if Hultz guards it like he said.'

'The hoardings,' said Rodi. 'He's already taken away the wards, the moat, the river gate – what else is left?'

Gotrek nodded, then turned for the stairs to the walls. 'Find places to hide. We'll watch until the rat comes out of his hole. Then we spring.'

Felix groaned. He was weary beyond description. 'Tonight?'

'Aye, manling,' said Gotrek. 'Tomorrow could be too late. And tell no one what you're about. I trust no one in this madhouse.'

As they spread out, looking for likely vantage points, Felix felt eyes on him and turned to see Bosendorfer leading his greatswords into the underkeep and looking over his shoulder at him. The hate in his eyes almost singed Felix's hair.

Kat found a shadowed spot on the roof of the temple of Sigmar from which to watch the courtyard, while Snorri and Rodi chose places in the ruined stables, and half-burned residences respectively. Felix and Gotrek chose a dark section of wall on the river side of the castle, far from where the hoardings had been placed, but offering a view of all of them.

Now that he had stopped fighting and running and swimming and shouting, all of Felix's weariness and hunger and pain caught up to him, and he sagged against the battlements like an empty sleeve. He had cuts and bruises from head to toe, a loose tooth, a missing thumbnail – neither of which he could account for – and was covered in a grimy patina of smoke, sweat and harbour water.

How long had he been fighting? How long since he had more than a swallow of water and a single biscuit at a sitting? How long since he had more than a few hours of sleep at once? He was too tired to work out any of the answers. He was too tired to keep his head up, but at the same time, when he closed his eyes, his mind scuttled about like a nervous cockroach, and wouldn't let him sleep.

Who was the saboteur? What madness was von Geldrecht planning for tomorrow? What would happen with Bosendorfer? But the image his mind returned to more than any other was Gotrek bellowing in Snorri's face. The friendship between the two Slayers had had its ups and downs in the time that Felix had known them, but never anything like this.

Snorri had now cost Gotrek at least two certain dooms, and had forced him to bully Rodi into turning from a doom as well. The price of Gotrek's vow to make sure that Snorri reached Karak Kadrin was getting unbearably high, and if things progressed as it looked like they were sure to, it could only get higher.

'You can't blame him, you know,' he said, lifting his head from the wall.

'Can't blame who?' rumbled the Slayer, his one eye continuing to scan the hoardings.

'Snorri,' said Felix. 'You can't blame him for not remembering things.'

'Can't I?' growled Gotrek. 'If Nosebiter had found his doom twenty years ago like a proper Slayer, none of this would be necessary.'

Felix glared at the Slayer's hypocrisy. 'Isn't that the pot calling the kettle black?'

Gotrek spat over the wall. 'Leave it alone, manling.'

Felix shrugged then laid his head back down on the wall. 'I don't know why you bother, anyway. None of us is getting out of here alive. Not you. Not me. Not Snorri. Not Kat or Rodi. None of us will make it to Karak Kadrin.'

Gotrek shrugged. 'A vow is a vow,' he said. 'And a dwarf doesn't give up a vow just because it's impossible.'

THIRTEEN

'Wake up, manling,' whispered Gotrek.

Felix jerked his head up. He didn't remember going to sleep, but apparently he had. It was still night, though the first hints of a red dawn were smudging the sky above the trees to the east, and all seemed quiet. Handgunners were patrolling the walls, spearmen were standing guard on the embankment by the river gate, night watch crews were dragging debris out of the partially burnt residences and repairing other wounds the castle had suffered in the battle, and the pyre of dead zombies and defenders was still burning in the courtyard.

'What is it?' he croaked. 'Did he not show?'

'He's here,' said Gotrek, and nodded towards the hoardings that covered the easternmost corner of the castle. 'There.'

Felix squinted, trying to see into the blackness under the hoarding, but then his eye was caught by movement on top of it. A grey shadow, almost the same shade as the shingles that covered the slanting roof, was crawling along on hands and knees, as delicate and careful as a spider, and as Felix watched, it paused and reached over the side for perhaps the space of five heartbeats, then crawled on again.

'He'll hear if we try for him,' said Gotrek. 'But he won't hear an arrow.' He looked towards the temple of Sigmar. 'Go to the little one. Point him out. She can't see him from where she is. Then go and block the underkeep door.'

Felix looked down at the courtyard then back up to the hoardings. 'He'll see me.'

Gotrek shrugged. 'Lots of people about. You'll only be one more. Just don't look at him.'

Felix nodded, and crept off. He took the internal stair down through the left-hand river gate tower, then sauntered as casually as he could along the front of the knights' residence around the harbour to the courtyard. It was almost impossible not to glance in the direction of the shadow on the hoardings.

Instead, he focussed on the roof of the temple of Sigmar, and as he neared it, he saw a movement in the shadows where it butted up against the charred wall of the officers' residence, and Kat's face appeared, looking at him questioningly.

Felix nodded his head in the direction of the figure on the hoarding, twice, then, as casually as he could, brought his hand up to his chest and made a small drawing and firing motion, as if he were pulling back on a tiny bow.

Kat seemed to get the idea, for she nodded and ducked back into the shadows to lift her bow off her shoulders and draw an arrow from her quiver.

Felix turned away from the temple and crossed to the entrance to the underkeep. The big doors were shut, but the little inset door was open. He stopped beside it, then leaned against the sturdy oak, as if just getting some air while watching the comings and goings of the courtyard.

Now he allowed himself a glance up at the hoarding, and saw that the crawling shadow was still there, and still obliviously at its work, whatever that might be. It stopped again at a point just parallel to the officers' residence, reached down over the outer edge of the roof, paused for a few seconds and continued slowly on.

Unbeknownst to the shadow, however, forces were moving against it. From the ruins of the stables to Felix's left came Snorri, walking towards the stairs to the wall in the west corner as if he hadn't a care in the world. The squat silhouette of Rodi crept out the front door of the half-gutted knights' residence and started for the stairs in the east. Gotrek trudged along the parapet, looking out over the battlements as if the zombie horde was the only thing on his mind. And on the peaked roof of the temple of Sigmar, Kat crept up the slant until she could see over the officers' residence, then ducked back down and drew her bow to full extension.

Felix held his breath as Kat stepped out, pivoted and fired all in one fluid motion. It was too dark to see the shaft fly, but the there was no question that it had flown true. With a squawk like a frightened goose, the shadow on the hoarding reared up, clutching its shoulder, then crashed down on the shingles and rolled towards the edge.

Freed from the need of caution, the Slayers sped forwards, Snorri barging through the upper room of the gatehouse then bursting out the other side, Rodi pounding up the stairs, Gotrek rounding the east corner and passing him. Kat stood and drew back another arrow, but before she could fire, the shadow dropped off the edge of the hoarding.

Felix expected it to crash down dead on the roof of the officers' residence, but to his surprise, it hit on all fours like a cat, and though the fall had definitely hurt it, it kept moving, scrambling down through a blackened hole in the slates that had been made by the fires.

All three Slayers jumped from the walls after it, then stomped down the roof to the hole and dived in.

By now, men all over the courtyard were looking up at the noise, and as Kat swung down from the temple roof and ran for the residence's door, several fell in with her, drawing swords and daggers as she drew her hatchets. Felix stayed at the underkeep door with difficulty, wanting to be in on the action, but he had to stay where he was. In a game of cat and mouse, one had to guard all the holes.

From inside the half-burnt residence came thuddings and crashings and the roaring of dwarfs.

'Snorri has him!' shouted Snorri, and a second later, 'No he doesn't!'

Then Gotrek's voice, enraged. 'Stay in your rooms! Close your doors!'

And Rodi's. 'Get out of the way!'

A second later, the residence's door burst open and a black shadow shot out. Kat leapt at it first, swinging both hatchets, but somehow it slipped past her and drove through the crowd, knocking them left and right. The men fell all over themselves trying to catch it, but it fought through and broke away, then ran for the underkeep.

Felix stepped in front of the small door and raised his sword, smiling grimly. He had done right staying at the hole – the wise cat who would get the mouse when all the others had failed.

The shadow came on, neither slowing or swerving, as Kat and the Slayers and the men of the castle ran after it. Felix raised Karaghul even higher as it ran straight at him, then swiped down, aiming for the clavicle, and connected... with nothing. The blade cut through the shadow as if it wasn't there, and yet a second later it had shouldered him in the sternum hard enough to knock him flat, then ran over him into the underkeep.

Felix sprang up again, coughing and sucking air, and plunged in after it. It ran straight down the main hall, past the mess and the stores in the direction of the barracks at the end. If it reached them it would find plenty of places to hide within, and clothes to change into to disguise itself. Felix couldn't let that happen. He surged on, pumping his legs as fast as he could, and wonder of wonders, he gained on it.

Halfway down the hall he sprang forwards and made a diving tackle at its legs. It was only as he was flying through the air that he noticed that the figure had no arrow sticking from its shoulder.

He grabbed at the figure's berobed legs and they went down together, but something felt very wrong. Felix didn't feel legs under the robes. Indeed the robes didn't feel like robes.

They hit the floor as one, but as the figure slapped down, it exploded into a swarm of squeaking black shapes that fluttered around his face then up into the air. Felix clutched at them wildly and crushed one in his hand. It sank needle-sharp claws into his index finger as it stilled – a tiny little bat, but rotten with mould and decay.

The rest of the swarm looped up and around and shot for the door just as Kat and the Slayers and the rest of the men pushed through. They shielded their faces as the little beasts battered past them and vanished into the night.

'Where is he?' growled Gotrek, walking towards Felix.

Felix stood and held out his hand to show the mangled bat corpse. 'Here,' he said. 'And the flock that flew out the door.'

Kat shook her head. 'No,' she said. 'I hit a man. I heard him yelp. This was a decoy.' She started running towards the door. 'Back to the officers' residence! Quickly!'

Rodi shook his head. 'He won't be there. He sent us chasing in here so he could slip away.'

Gotrek nodded, disgusted. 'We lost him.'

'But we haven't,' said Felix. 'We just have to look for a man with a wounded shoulder.'

Gotrek raised a shaggy eyebrow. 'How many men in Castle Reikguard *don't* have a wounded shoulder?'

Felix's heart sank. The Slayer was right. After all the fighting, everyone in the castle was hurt in some way. Even if they found a man with a puncture wound, how would they prove it had been Kat's arrow that made it?

'Do you have a better plan?' Felix asked.

'Aye,' said Gotrek, walking away. 'Kill everybody. Then we're sure to get him.'

The steward, when he was roused from his bed and given the news, seemed close to tears. 'Again?' he said, pacing before the underkeep doors. 'Again?'

He stopped suddenly and turned to his officers. 'Wake everyone,' he said. 'Assemble them before the temple of Sigmar. I will not wait until after morning mess to speak. We will begin now. This will end today!'

'My lord,' said von Volgen, who had followed von Geldrecht down from the keep like a dour shadow, 'as the Slayer says, everyone is wounded. It will be difficult–'

The steward waved that away. 'There will be no need to check for wounds,' he said. 'I have a better way. We will find him out, you can be certain of that.'

But as he watched von Geldrecht limp away, Felix thought von Volgen didn't look very certain at all.

* * *

While the people of the castle began to gather in the courtyard for von Geldrecht's speech, Felix, Kat and the Slayers went up to the walls and looked at the sections of the hoardings that the traitor had visited during his shadowy prowling, and it was Felix who found the first sign of sabotage – and nearly died for it.

Remembering that the saboteur had stopped and reached over the outer edge of the hoarding roof at regular intervals, Felix climbed out onto the battlements and began to examine the shingles and walls from the outside, though he wasn't sure what he was looking for. He saw nothing on the shingles, nor anything on the shoulder-high panels that protected the defenders from airborne attacks and enemy fire, but as he looked at one of the support posts that held up the roof, he saw a strange black squiggle drawn on the wood.

At first glance, Felix took it for a carpenter's mark, made in charcoal, but something about the shape of it looked wrong. He grabbed the post to pull himself closer for a better look, but the wood around the mark splintered and gave way and the post slipped sideways under Felix's weight. Only a frantic scramble and a wild grab at the panels kept Felix from falling backwards off the walls to the sea of zombies below.

'Felix!' cried Kat, from the roof.

'All right, manling?' asked Gotrek, looking up.

Felix's heart was pounding so loud as he clung to the panel he almost didn't hear them. With infinite care, he pulled himself back onto the solid stone of the crenellations, then let out a breath.

'I believe,' he said, 'I may have found something.' He pointed a trembling hand at the next post. 'Look there, near the top. But don't put your weight on it. It won't hold.'

Kat and the Slayers stepped to the next post, and when Felix could get his legs working again, he joined them, and saw that it too had a squiggle drawn upon it. It was most definitely a symbol of some kind, but not one a carpenter ever made. It had the look of the kind of arcane glyphs he had seen carved upon ancient tombs and other places of unfathomable evil that his travels with Gotrek had led him to, and it hadn't been made in charcoal, but in blood, now dried and brown.

The wood around the symbol was a different colour than the rest of the post, pale and grey, as if it had been exposed to the elements for centuries. Gotrek grunted when he saw the discolouration, then pinched the wood between his finger and thumb. It crumbled like dry cheese.

Kat shook her head, dismayed. 'Taal and Rhya, had he marked every post…'

'The hoardings would have collapsed entirely,' said Felix.

'But likely not until the start of the next battle,' said Rodi, grinning. 'A nasty little trap.'

'See how many he marked,' said Gotrek.

But before they were able to check more than a few, a horn blared, and Classen's voice rang from the courtyard.

'Fall in! Fall in! Lord Steward von Geldrecht will speak!'

Gotrek ground his teeth and glared down at the assembled crowd. 'There are things to be done.'

'Aye,' said Rodi. 'Replace these posts. Open the dike and flood the moat again...'

'Kill more zombies,' said Snorri.

But the three Slayers turned and started for the stairs nonetheless, and Felix and Kat followed them down into the crowd.

The mood of the men as they squeezed through to the front was sullen at best. Soldiers who had only a few hours ago killed off the last of the river gate zombies were grumbling about not being allowed to sleep nor getting to eat or drink before lining up. Men from the morning watches, whose job it was to repair the damages incurred in the battle, grumbled about not being able to get on with their work. The servants grumbled about being dragged away from preparing the biscuit and water. Felix felt for them all. He and Kat hadn't had a minute's rest since he didn't know how long – nor did it look like they would get another minute anytime soon.

But they were hardly the worst off in attendance. Even the wounded had been trundled out to the courtyard and lay or sat or slumped where they had been put, while Sister Willentrude and her initiates stood wearily among them, looking angrier than everyone else in the audience combined.

When everyone had quieted, von Geldrecht walked up the steps of the temple of Sigmar and turned to stand with Sergeant Classen, Lord von Volgen and Grafin Avelein Reiklander. Father Ulfram and his acolyte waited behind them, while Bosendorfer and his greatswords flanked the steps, their huge blades drawn and point down at parade rest. What was the reason for that, wondered Felix?

'Defenders of Castle Reikguard,' called von Geldrecht, his haggard face stark in the light of the still-burning corpse-pyre. 'I have gathered you here today in Graf Reiklander's name...'

He inclined his head to Grafin Avelein at this, but she did not acknowledge it, only stared glassy-eyed into the middle distance, a strange half-smile on her lips.

Von Geldrecht coughed and began again. 'I have gathered you in Graf Reiklander's name, I say, in order to broach a serious matter – and to end it!' His voice cracked as he tried for emphasis, and his eyes, as he glared around at them all, glittered wildly. 'There is a traitor among us, a sorcerous saboteur who is weakening our defences!'

A murmur rose at that, but von Geldrecht waved it down with a weary arm.

'Yes!' he cried. 'A traitor! A collaborator with that foul necromancer who hides in the woods and sends his filthy corpses against us. It is this traitor who shattered the runes of warding that protected our walls, he who drained the moat, he who tore the hole through the river gate. But his reign of sabotage ends today! This morning – here and now – we will flush him out!'

The murmuring of the crowd grew louder as von Geldrecht turned to Father Ulfram.

'Father,' he said, 'let us begin.'

Father Ulfram hesitated, seemingly reluctant, then signalled to Danniken. The gaunt young man bowed, then stepped to a rough wooden table set to one side. On it was something wrapped in sable fur. He hesitated and seemed to pray, then gathered up the bundle in his arms as carefully as if it were a bomb, and returned with it to Ulfram. As the priest bowed before it, Danniken delicately unfolded the bundle to reveal a gold-filigreed, jewel-encrusted warhammer of incredible workmanship, gleaming red at the edges in the light of the pyre.

'Behold!' said von Geldrecht, holding out a hand to it. 'The Hammer of Judgement, first carried by Frederick the Bold, the great-grandfather of our beloved Emperor, Karl Franz. Long has it sat in the family vaults of Castle Reikguard, but whenever there is evil to be vanquished, it is brought forth, for its very touch destroys the unrighteous, and burns them with the holy fire of Sigmar's twin-tailed comet.'

Danniken's hands trembled as he held out the massive sacred hammer to Father Ulfram in its bed of furs. 'It is here, father.'

The blind priest reached out until he touched it, then lifted it with one hand and began a prayer as he held it over his head. He might be a shadow of his former self, thought Felix, but he must have retained some of his strength to lift a weapon like that. It looked as if it were made of solid gold.

As Father Ulfram prayed, von Geldrecht surveyed the crowd with too-bright eyes. 'Each of you,' he said, 'will come forwards, one at a time, and lay hands on the hammer. Our traitor will be the one whose impure flesh burns at the touch of so holy a relic! At which time...' He nodded to Bosendorfer and the greatswords. 'We will kill him immediately. He who refuses this test will *also* be killed immediately.'

Felix turned uneasily to Gotrek as the courtyard burst into anxious whispering. 'Do you think this will work?' he asked. 'Do you think the hammer has the powers he says it has?'

'That doesn't matter,' Gotrek grunted. 'The traitor won't touch it.'

'But von Geldrecht said everyone has to touch it,' said Kat.

Before Gotrek could answer, an angry voice called out from among the wounded. 'You have forgotten some suspects, my lord! Shouldn't Tauber and his assistants take the test as well?'

The whole courtyard turned to see Sister Willentrude glaring at von Geldrecht with haggard eyes.

Felix looked around, his anger rising. Was she right? Was Tauber not there? Had von Geldrecht forgotten him? Or had he left him out on purpose? Was this another sign of the strange connection between the two men that had caused von Geldrecht to hide him away from Bosendorfer – and keep him from his duties? His anger boiled over, when he saw that Draeger and his militiamen had been brought out from their cells, but not Tauber.

'Yes!' Felix cried. 'Where is Tauber? Let him prove his innocence so he can get back to work.'

'And if he burns?' muttered Gotrek.

Felix's heart lurched. He hadn't thought of that, but if Tauber was a traitor after all, then that was all the more reason for him to take the test.

'We already know what Tauber is,' called the steward, looking nervously from Felix to the sister. 'There is no need to test him.'

'Then you lied before, lord steward!' cried Willentrude. 'You said you were holding him until you could determine his guilt. If you know he is guilty, why haven't you killed him? Bring him out!'

The courtyard began to murmur in agreement, some because they wanted Tauber to burn, some – mostly the wounded – because they wanted him freed, but all seemed to agree he should be tested.

Von Geldrecht looked like he was going to explode. 'This is not about Tauber!' he said. 'This is about finding a further man!'

'But what if Tauber is the only one?' said Felix. 'What if he has the power to slip through his bars like mist? Or a swarm of bats?'

Von Geldrecht opened his mouth to make another argument, but voices were crying out from all around the yard now, drowning him out.

'Test Tauber!'

'Let him burn!

'Free him!'

Von Geldrecht's eyes darted around, frightened. Felix smirked. The steward would have to bring Tauber out now, or he'd have an insurrection on his hands. But then Felix glanced towards Bosendorfer, and saw that his eyes were gleaming with excitement, and his hands were clenched around the hilt of his two-handed sword.

'Very well!' shouted von Geldrecht over the cries of the crowd. 'Very well! Tauber will be tested!' He turned to two of his household knights and gave them a key. 'Bring the surgeon and his assistants.'

Felix groaned as the knights saluted and trotted to the stairs to the keep. 'Sigmar,' he said. 'We've signed his death warrant.'

'Whose?' asked Kat. 'Tauber's? You think he's guilty?'

Felix shook his head. 'Look at Bosendorfer. Do you think he'll wait for Tauber's guilt to be proved before he strikes?'

Kat's eyes widened. 'Shallya's mercy.'

'Now,' rasped von Geldrecht, leaning heavily on his cane. 'If there are no further interruptions, we will begin.' He turned to Grafin Avelein. 'Grafin, if you will go first, we will keep you no longer.'

Avelein woke from her daze and nodded. Bosendorfer's men tensed and the whole courtyard held its breath as she stepped up and without hesitation laid both hands on the sacred hammer, bowing her head in prayer. When she failed to burst into flames, the crowd let out their breath.

'Thank you, Grafin,' said von Geldrecht.

She curtseyed to him, then drifted off towards the stairs to the keep, the half-smile still on her face. Felix watched her curiously, her behaviour breaking through his anxiety about Tauber and Bosendorfer. What had happened to her earlier sadness? Was the graf recovering?

'Spearmen,' called von Geldrecht. 'Step forwards.'

The spearmen marched forwards, led now by a sergeant Felix didn't know. There were less than twenty of them now. The crowd quieted again as the sergeant reached out and touched the hammer, and again let out a breath when nothing happened. As the rest of the spearmen advanced and laid their hands on the hammer one by one without incident, the tension before each touch lessened, but still, no one looked anywhere else.

After the spearmen had finished, Bosendorfer's men pointed them to the big open doors to the underkeep, and sent them inside to wait. This was to make sure that no one who hadn't yet taken the test could slip in amongst those who had.

Halfway through testing Hultz's handgunners, the two knights who had run off returned, leading a sad, shuffling coffle of filthy men. It took Felix a moment to recognise the skinny, unshaven figure at their head as Tauber. The surgeon's superior sneer and the sharp eyes were gone, replaced by a dull, slack-mouthed stare.

Felix watched Bosendorfer as Tauber was brought to the front of the crowd, afraid he was going to attack then and there, but the greatsword only stared at the surgeon, hard and cold, and stayed at his post.

Felix thought von Geldrecht would test Tauber immediately and get it over with, but he did not. Instead he called up Classen and the household knights, and had them touch the hammer while Bosendorfer and his greatswords stood ready to strike them down, then he had Bosendorfer and his greatswords touch the hammer while Classen and his knights stood ready to strike *them* down. No one burst into flames.

After that came Sister Willentrude and her initiates and then the wounded, while Tauber and his assistants continued to stand and wait. Why was von Geldrecht doing it this way, Felix wondered? Was he saving the best for last? Was he afraid Tauber wouldn't burst into flames, and wanted to delay the inevitable anticlimax? Then it came to him. He wasn't afraid nothing would happen. He was afraid Tauber would actually burn.

'He thinks Tauber's guilty!' he whispered. 'And he doesn't want him to be.'

'Aye,' said Kat. 'You're right. But why?'

Felix shrugged. He had no idea.

It took almost a half-hour for the wounded to be tested, for many had to be carried up and lifted so that they could touch the hammer. Some were so weak they had to have their hands placed upon it for them. Some had no hands.

'How is a man like that supposed to have crawled across the hoardings?' growled Kat. 'Von Geldrecht is a fool.'

The servants came next – cooks, menials, maids, grooms, the blacksmith, carpenter and all the rest, and then the refugee farmers and all the other 'guests' of the castle.

Von Volgen and his Talabeclanders went first, as dignified as they could, under the circumstances, then Draeger and his militiamen, as sullen as ever, and then it was Felix's turn. He scowled as he put his hand on the hammer, but made no complaint, only gave von Geldrecht a withering look as he stepped aside to wait for Kat and the Slayers. Kat slapped the hammer contemptuously and made the horns of Taal right after. Gotrek turned the hammer by the head and squinted at it.

'Not bad for human work,' he said.

'Better than elvish at least,' said Rodi, running a thumb along the gold scrolling.

'Snorri thinks it sounds hollow,' said Snorri, tapping it with a thick forefinger.

As they reached the door to the underkeep, Felix turned to watch as von Geldrecht called the men off the walls one at a time and then sent them back. Then, finally, there was no one left but Tauber and his assistants.

Von Geldrecht glared and chewed his lip, then motioned for them to be brought forwards. He was almost cringing as they approached, and his brow was beaded with sweat.

Felix shot a glance at Bosendorfer. The greatsword's eyes were gleaming and his sword was rising. Felix's heart thudded. He was going to do it! And no one would see until it was too late. They were all too busy looking at Tauber.

'Bosendorfer!' he cried. 'Will you strike before you know?'

The shout snapped the greatsword around, and turned every head towards him and Felix. Bosendorfer froze in the glare of their scrutiny, his sword still held high, ready to strike, and rage and guilt quickly reddening him to the roots of his hair. He turned on Felix, snarling.

'You seek to embarrass me with a lie? I do not disobey orders, mein Herr!'

Felix held his eye for a moment, then bowed. 'Forgive me, captain. I must have been mistaken.'

Bosendorfer didn't look like he wanted to forgive, but von Geldrecht stepped forwards and banged his cane. 'Captain! Your duty!'

Bosendorfer pulled his eyes away from Felix with difficulty, then turned back to Tauber and his assistants and went on guard. Felix let out a relieved sigh. Now that he knew everyone would be watching him, Bosendorfer wouldn't dare strike Tauber without cause.

Von Geldrecht had the surgeon's assistants touch the hammer first – still delaying whatever it was he feared – but at last it was Tauber's turn. The crowd in the underkeep doorway became absolutely silent, staring intently as the surgeon reached out his trembling hand towards the hammer. Felix's eyes flicked ceaselessly from Tauber to Bosendorfer to von Geldrecht.

Tauber touched the hammer.

He didn't burst into flames.

Felix let out his breath as Bosendorfer only stared, his greatsword trembling in white-knuckled hands, but he did not strike. He seemed genuinely surprised that the surgeon had passed the test.

The surgeon stepped dully back, then turned and shuffled for the underkeep door with his assistants as von Geldrecht let out a sigh of his own. He seemed more relieved than Tauber himself.

The steward motioned weakly for Father Ulfram to put the hammer away, but before Danniken could step forwards with the furs, someone behind Felix called out, 'And yerself, lord steward?'

Von Geldrecht glared towards the speaker, but then stepped to the hammer and laid both hands on it, bowing his head over it like Grafin Avelein had. He didn't burst into flames either.

There was a snickering from the crowd in the underkeep door as Father Ulfram laid the hammer back into the furs and Danniken folded them up.

'And what exactly did that prove, Goldie?' shouted another voice from the back.

Von Geldrecht turned and snarled at them, his face salmon-red. 'Out!' he roared. 'Out of that hole and fall in! I will address you all!'

Everyone groaned and cursed, but no one refused, and all shuffled out to stand before von Geldrecht again as he paced the top of the temple steps.

'It seems our traitor is wilier than I thought,' he said. 'Either he has used his dark powers to protect himself from the great hammer's purity, or he has hidden himself where we cannot find him. So it seems I must appeal, again in Graf Reiklander's name, to your love of your Empire and your fellows.'

He straightened and looked around, his eyes flashing from man to man. 'One of you must step forwards and save us all, for one of you knows who the traitor is!'

This raised a confused muttering, and Felix could hear some angry whispers as well.

'I do not mean that you are also a traitor,' said von Geldrecht against the ugly drone. 'I do not mean anyone is intentionally hiding this villain from the rest of us. I mean that one of you, perhaps more than one, has seen a comrade do something, something strange or out of character, something that made you frown for a moment, but which you then dismissed as nothing. You told yourself you must not have seen correctly. It must have been some harmless gesture or innocent eccentricity. Well, it was not!' Von Geldrecht brought his voice to a cracking roar. 'It was witchcraft! And though you knew it not, you saw it! What was it? Who was it? I want each one of you to think back and remember. Where were you? Who were you with? What did they do? Was it a strange twist of the hand? A whisper in a foreign tongue? Did they lurk in certain places for too long with no reason?'

The whispering grew louder. The men started glaring around at each other while their sergeants barked for order. Von Volgen stared at the steward like he wanted to kick him down the stairs.

'Fat fool,' muttered Gotrek.

'Aye,' said Felix. 'They'll be burning each other at the stake before he's done.'

'And when you remember,' continued von Geldrecht, 'when those seemingly innocent actions are revealed in your mind for what they truly were, come to me. Not to anyone else! Not to your captain, not to your comrades. Only me. I will do what must be done.' Von Geldrecht spread his arms and bowed his head. 'Now, I thank you for your patience. You are dismissed. Return to your duties.'

But as the steward, the priest, von Volgen and Classen turned to talk amongst themselves, the crowd did not disperse. Instead they clumped together in little knots and began to argue amongst themselves, with many a wary glance over their shoulders at everyone else.

Felix groaned to see it.

Kat shook her head. 'How are they going to fight together when none of them trust each other?'

'Aye,' said Felix. 'He's–'

But he cut off as he saw the household knights falling in around Tauber and his assistants and motioning them back towards the keep along with Draeger and his men. What was this? He started forwards, but Sister Willentrude beat him to it.

'My lord,' she shouted, pushing towards von Geldrecht, 'are you going to lock Surgeon Tauber up again now that he has passed your test? Surely if he has touched the Hammer of Judgement of Frederick the Bold and not burst into flames, that is proof that he is innocent, and if he is innocent, you must free him so that he can care for the wounded.'

Von Geldrecht turned on her again, looking as sick as a mutant confronted by witch hunters, but then he composed himself as the whole crowd quieted to listen.

'The test was inconclusive,' he said, lifting his bearded chins. 'Since it proved no one's guilt, it did not prove Tauber's innocence. I cannot allow him to go free.'

There were murmurs at this. One of the wounded shouted, 'Free him!' Another shouted, 'Put Bosendorfer in his place! Let him rot!'

'Then will you lock the rest of us up?' shouted Felix, stepping forwards to stand with the sister. 'As it didn't prove our innocence either?'

Von Geldrecht's eyes flared. 'Herr Jaeger, if you speak another word, I will certainly have *you* locked up! Now, disperse, all of you. Tauber remains our prisoner. That is an end to it!'

He turned away, limping angrily towards the keep as the men of the castle watched after him, muttering and whispering dangerously.

'I'm beginning to think we should do it Gotrek's way, and kill everybody,' said Kat, then turned to follow the Slayers, who were crossing the yard to tell Carpenter Bierlitz about the weakened hoardings.

Felix nodded, distracted, but continued to stare after von Geldrecht. There was most definitely something between the steward and Tauber. That was the only way to explain his actions. He had been deathly afraid Tauber would burst into flames, and relieved when he didn't. Yet he would not release him. Why?

Perhaps later Felix could get von Geldrecht alone and get an answer out of him, but not just now. He didn't seem in the mood for talking at the moment. Felix sighed and made to follow Kat, but instead found himself chest to chest with Captain Bosendorfer, who was staring at him with pure hatred blazing from his ice-blue eyes.

FOURTEEN

Felix stepped back, his hand dropping to his hilt. 'You wish to speak to me, captain?'

'I wish to have your head, mein Herr,' Bosendorfer snarled. 'You have been a disrupting presence since you entered these walls, countermanding my orders to my men, and now accusing me of dishonourable conduct, and I demand satisfaction.'

Felix sighed. Did this have to start now? He was so tired. Too tired to argue. Too tired to fight. He just wanted to walk past the captain and go to sleep.

Bosendorfer's eyes widened. 'Do you sneer at me, Herr Jaeger? Was that a laugh?'

Felix rolled his eyes. 'That was a sigh, captain. A weary sigh. I have been awake a full day now, and have done a little fighting along the way. So–'

'And you suggest that I haven't? That I have less reason to be weary than do you?'

'Of course not, captain,' said Felix. 'We have all fought hard. I just want to go to sleep, that's all.'

'Not before you apologise for your actions,' he said. 'Not before you admit your accusations of dishonourable conduct are false.'

Out of the corners of his eyes Felix saw Kat and the Slayers turning back to see what the matter was on one side, and Bosendorfer's greatswords moving in on the other. All over the yard, people were turning their heads.

'I never accused you of dishonourable conduct, captain,' said Felix, rubbing his forehead. 'I may have warned you against it just now, but I am willing to believe you never intended it. And, on the wall?' he shrugged. 'I apologise for calling orders to your men, but there seemed no other way to get them back after they had fled–'

Bosendorfer slapped Felix across the cheek. It nearly knocked him to the ground. Kat cried out and ran forwards, drawing her skinning knife, with the Slayers striding in after her. Felix caught her arm as she made to put the blade to Bosendorfer's throat.

'No, Kat!' he shouted. The sting of the slap was making him tear up. 'Slayers, stay back!'

'You lie, mein Herr!' cried Bosendorfer. 'We did not flee! Not for an instant!'

Felix held Kat back as the three dwarfs ranged around to his left, ready to join in at his word. The greatswords were on guard on his right, but one, the grizzled sergeant who had fought beside Felix against the ghouls from the siege tower, was stepping to Bosendorfer and putting a hand on his shoulder.

'Captain, please,' he said. 'What's to fight about? We broke, and we came back. No one will say–'

'I did not break, Leffler!' shouted Bosendorfer, knocking the sergeant's hand aside and turning on him. 'I retreated in good order for your safety, and we would have taken up a new position had not Herr Jaeger, against all standards of military conduct, countermanded my orders and usurped my authority!'

The sergeant looked uncomfortable. 'That's as may be, captain. But we don't need to be fighting each other over things that happened in the heat of battle. Not when there's ten thousand dead bastards out there and we need every man in here. Herr Jaeger–'

'Are you defending him, Leffler?' cried Bosendorfer. 'Against your own captain?'

'No, captain, no,' said Leffler, holding up his hands. 'I'm only saying, if you want to challenge him, why not wait until we're clear of this? Until we can do it proper. Until you're all rested and ready.'

Bosendorfer looked at the sergeant for a moment, his eyes level and cold, then dropped his gaze to himself. He looked as battered at Felix felt – his armour dented, crusted rimes of blood on his arms, neck and chin, and a bandage around one hand that was stiff and black.

'Very well,' he sighed at last. 'Very well, when we are clear.' He turned on Felix again, eyes blazing as fiercely as before. 'But I *will* have satisfaction, and if you insult me again, or come between me and my men, I will not wait. We will resolve it between us then and there!'

Felix inclined his head. 'Very good, captain.'

Bosendorfer snorted and stalked away, head high.

Sergeant Leffler started after him, then looked back to Felix with an apologetic shrug. 'He's a good lad, mein Herr,' he murmured. 'But younger than his brother was.'

Felix nodded wearily, then let Kat out from the prison of his arms.

'You should have let me kill him,' she said, curling her lip. 'And done us all a favour.'

'Aye,' said Rodi. 'That one will never be old enough to be a captain.'

Gotrek shrugged. 'Don't worry,' he said. 'No one here will get much older.' He nodded to Felix. 'Get some sleep, manling. When you wake, we'll see about the moat.'

Felix nodded again, and it almost carried him over. He caught himself against Kat, and they staggered towards the residences.

'Let's hope,' said Kat, 'our room isn't one that burned.'

When Felix woke again, the day had already tipped past noon, and Kat was not beside him. He lifted his head up, afraid she had answered some call to action that he had slept through, but all that came through the room's shattered window was the normal hammering and thudding of repairs, and he sagged back, groaning. His muscles were so stiff it felt as if he had been dried on a rack like hard-tack, his head throbbed like he had a hangover and his mouth tasted like he had eaten a muddy shoe. He desperately needed a drink of water, but felt too tired to get out of bed. This was the time when one needed a servant. A servant would bring one water at the pull of a rope.

He looked up over the bed. There was no pull rope. There was hardly a ceiling. Though the room had not, as Kat feared, burned, one of Kemmler's trebuchets had dropped a boulder through it sometime during the battle last night. The boulder had missed the bed by inches, and now lay where the chair had been. Ah, well. He would just have to get the water on his own, then.

He levered himself up out of the bed, hissing and barking with pain, then pulled on his padded jack and chain shirt and strapped on Karaghul. The sky, when he stepped out into the courtyard, was low and grey, and the air wet and cold. He looked around for Kat and spotted her at last up on the parapet, leaning against the battlements and looking out over the walls near where Bierlitz and his men were replacing the hoarding posts that the saboteur had weakened with his sorcery. The Slayers were down at the far eastern corner of the walls, looking down towards the closed dike and talking amongst themselves.

Felix stepped into the underkeep and waited in line for his swallow of water and his single biscuit, then came back out to the courtyard and crossed the stairs to the wall. Around him teams of men were continuing the seemingly endless task of piling decapitated bodies on the eternal pyres, while others fished bloated corpses out of the harbour with boat hooks. The river wardens were all by the river gate in their remaining oarboats, adding to the makeshift patch that Gotrek and the Slayers had made last night and making it more permanent, while everywhere the men sharpened their weapons and repaired their kit in preparation for the battle that was sure to come with the sunset.

Despite all this activity, the mood of the castle could not have been more poisonous. The aftermath of von Geldrecht's speech was just what Felix had feared. The men of the various companies all whispered amongst themselves and shot suspicious looks at all the other companies, looking for signs of sorcerous behaviour. Some were muttering about freeing Tauber and bringing him back to the surgery. Some were muttering about breaking into his cell and murdering him.

Father Ulfram and Danniken shuffled from group to group, apparently trying to ease the tension, but it didn't seem to be working. Whoever they talked to just pointed fingers at one of the other groups or told them to go preach at von Geldrecht and Bosendorfer.

When he reached the top of the stairs, Felix crossed to where Kat was staring out over the misty fields and the sea of zombies, her chin in her hands. Felix leaned beside her and followed her gaze. Off by the tree line, new bone-and-skin siege towers were being erected, three this time, as ugly as the others, and more ballistae and trebuchets were growing as well. He groaned as he saw them.

'We'll have it to do all over again, eh?' he said.

Kat didn't answer.

'At least this time we can be fairly sure they won't get into the harbour.'

She still didn't answer.

Felix looked at her. 'Something wrong?'

Her jaw bunched and her brow lowered. 'I hate them,' she said.

'The zombies?'

'Not the zombies.' She glared over her shoulder at the yard. 'Them. The men. The knights and spearmen and gunners. All of them.'

Felix frowned. He was feeling less than charitable towards them himself, just then, but he didn't know why she should be. 'If this is about Bosendorfer, forget him. I've already put him out of my mind. He hasn't been giving you trouble, has he?'

Kat blew out a breath. 'It doesn't have anything to do with him. It's all the whispering, and the backbiting and the... I don't belong here, Felix.' She pointed out to the dark band of the forest. 'I belong there, in the wood, doing what I'm good at. I just don't understand these... these... Why do we help them when they're so awful?'

She turned to face him, her eyes glistening. 'I have sworn to rid the Drakwald of beastmen and protect the Empire, but when I come into the towns, or to a castle, people are just... vile! They cheat each other, they fight each other, shout at each other. They might join together when things are at their worst, but as soon as the trouble is over, they're back to blaming each other for what went wrong and trying to take more than their share!'

Felix shrugged, feeling helpless. 'That's just human nature, Kat. We've always been a–'

'Then I don't want to be human!'

Felix looked around to see if anyone had heard her outburst. That was not the sort of thing one said in a land of witch hunters and mutants. He turned her around to face him, meaning to speak, but she clung to him suddenly, hanging her head.

'I'm sorry, Felix,' she said. 'I don't mean it. Not really. I just – sometimes I wish I could go into the forest and never come out again.'

Felix sighed and stroked her hair. 'I know how you feel,' he said. 'There are times when I wish Gotrek and I had never come back to the Empire. But there are other times,' he kissed the top of her head, 'when I wish I had come home sooner.'

'I wish you had too.' Kat smiled up at him. 'I will be better when we get free of this place – if we get free. I'm always better when I am moving.'

Felix wondered if that was the case with him too. It had been so long since he had stayed in one place for any length of time that he had no idea how he would fare settled down.

A curse from down the wall drew their attention to the Slayers, and they broke from their embrace.

Gotrek was still leaning out over the battlements and chewing his thumb with a distracted air, while Snorri appeared to be trying to spit on as many zombies as he could, but Rodi was pounding the battlements with his fist.

'And why not?' he bellowed. 'It would be a glorious doom.'

Felix and Kat started down the wall towards them and heard Gotrek reply without looking around.

'You can go over the side anytime you want, Rodi Balkisson, but I'm not wasting so much blackpowder on a glorious failure.'

'It won't fail!' said Rodi. 'You think I can't cut my way through a pack of corpses with a few kegs of blackpowder on my back? Do you think I'm some weak human?'

'Look at it, Balkisson,' said Gotrek, pointing down at the dike with a stubby finger. 'Blowing yourself up in front of it would hardly splinter the wood.'

Felix and Kat leaned through the gap in the hoardings and looked where Gotrek was pointing. The dike was set into heavy stone ramparts built at an angle to the riverbank, so that when its doors were open, the water would rush easily into the moat like it was a branch of the river. When the doors were closed, however, as now, the water smashed into them in a constant foaming crest, angry at being denied its natural path. They therefore needed to be strong – and they were. Each of the foot-thick oak and iron titans looked to Felix to be about twenty feet high, and they were held closed against the pounding water by two great oak beams that slotted out across them from the stone banks, one near the top, and one near the bottom.

'At least four charges must be set,' said Gotrek. 'Two behind each beam, and fuses laid to blow them all as one.'

'What of it?' said Rodi. 'I can do all that.'

Gotrek snorted, then nodded towards the scores of zombies that milled around on the stone banks of the dike. 'And can you also keep the corpses from ripping out one fuse while you set the next? Or knocking the charges loose?'

Rodi opened his mouth, still defiant, but had no answer.

'There are some things even a Slayer cannot do alone,' said Gotrek, then looked back down at the dike. 'We wait for tonight's attack, when the necromancer's attention is on the walls. Then we will go.'

Rodi turned away, disgusted, but Snorri wiped the spit from his beard and looked up.

'Snorri likes this plan,' said Snorri. 'Snorri has been growing a little tired of staying inside this castle.'

'You will stay on the walls, Nosebiter,' said Gotrek. 'Only I, Balkisson and the manling will go.'

Snorri's face fell. 'Snorri doesn't like this plan.'

'Neither does Kat,' said Kat, sullen.

Gotrek looked at her. 'You will keep us safe from spying eyes, little one,' he said. 'Flying eyes.'

Kat nodded as she realised what he meant, but Felix could see that she was still disappointed. Snorri wasn't the only one tired of staying inside the castle. Felix, on the other hand, would have been perfectly happy to remain on the walls.

With a sigh he pulled his head back through the hoarding, but as he did, something caught his eye. On the support post next to him was a familiar little squiggle, and the wood around it was withered and dry. Felix frowned and looked down the wall. Bierlitz and his men were replacing a post about fifty paces along.

'Have the carpenters not got to this post yet?' he asked.

Gotrek turned to him. 'They replaced it this morning. Why?'

Felix pointed to the symbol as his guts sank. 'Then when could this have been done?'

Kat and the Slayers stepped closer and looked at the post. Gotrek touched the blood with his finger. It smeared. It hadn't fully dried yet.

'Today,' he said. 'Within the hour.'

Rodi scowled. 'We've been talking almost that long. Did the bastard do it while we were standing here?'

Gotrek stumped to the next post with the others following. It too had been marked, and its blood not yet dry.

'Snorri remembers they replaced that one too,' said Snorri.

All of them looked around, scanning the people in the courtyard and on the covered parapet. Felix cursed. It was impossible. There were too many, and it could be anyone – one of the men who was clearing rubble with the work gangs, one of the Shallyans carrying another body to the pyre, one of the handgunners who stood at their posts on the wall. It could be von Geldrecht or von Volgen or Classen or Volk or Bosendorfer, all of whom were peering out towards the zombies' new siege towers. Then there was Bierlitz and his crew putting up the new posts – was the old carpenter putting the mark on them as he erected them? Or was it Father Ulfram walking the walls with Danniken and giving encouragement to the men?

'We should tell the steward,' said Kat, looking towards von Geldrecht and von Volgen, 'though Bosendorfer will likely accuse us of it just for spite–'

'Wait,' said Felix. 'Wait!'

Kat and the Slayers looked at him.

He nodded towards Ulfram and Danniken. 'Watch the acolyte,' he said. 'Watch Danniken.'

The others turned. Felix bit his lip. Was he right? Was he seeing what he thought he was seeing? It was hard to tell in the shadow of the hoarding roof.

The gaunt acolyte took Father Ulfram's elbow as the priest finished talking to a group of handgunners, then walked him along the wall to the next group. As Ulfram hailed the men and began asking them questions, Danniken stepped back demurely and leaned against a support post, as if waiting for Father Ulfram to finish, but as he waited, he idly took out a little knife and cleaned his fingernails, then, accidentally – or so it seemed – cut the tip of his index finger.

He hissed and squeezed it, then circled his hand around the outside of the post and traced his bloody finger back and forth across the wood, never once looking at what he was doing.

'Clever,' said Rodi.

'But how– how can he...?' stuttered Kat. 'He held the Hammer of Judgement and did not burn! When all the others were ordered to touch it, he brought it to Ulfram and–'

'He didn't!' said Felix, remembering suddenly. 'It was wrapped in furs! He never once touched it with his bare hands!'

'Enough talk,' said Gotrek. 'He dies now.'

'Wait,' said Felix. 'We must tell von Geldrecht. We don't want anyone crying murder.'

Gotrek grunted with impatience as Felix hurried down the wall to where von Geldrecht, von Volgen, Classen, Bosendorfer and Volk still watched the zombies and talked amongst themselves. He checked the post next to von Geldrecht. It too had been marked, and was already rotting.

'My lord steward,' he whispered.

Von Geldrecht and the others looked around.

'What is it now, Herr Jaeger?' asked the steward, witheringly. 'Do you wish to upbraid me again?'

Felix pointed to the flaking post. 'New marks.'

'What!' he cried, and stepped forwards with the others crowding in.

Von Volgen sighed when he saw the rotting wood. Von Geldrecht cursed and slapped the wall.

'Quietly, my lord,' said Felix, glancing back at Danniken and Ulfram. 'We have found the traitor.'

'What? Who?' said von Geldrecht.

'Watch Danniken,' said Felix. 'Watch his hands.'

'Danniken?' said the steward, again louder than he should. 'What has he–'

Felix gripped his arm to quiet him, and nodded in the direction of the acolyte and the warrior priest. Von Geldrecht turned and watched with the rest as Danniken led Ulfram to the next group of men, then retired to lean against another post. Again, he followed the same routine, taking out his knife, paring his nails, reopening the cut on his finger, then drawing with his blood on the outside of the post.

'But...' said Bosendorfer. 'But, but...'

'Sigmar's beard!' breathed von Geldrecht. 'The acolyte! A man of the cloth!'

'A vile saboteur,' snarled von Volgen.

Classen started forwards, reaching for his sword. 'Come, let us show him Sigmar's mercy.'

Von Geldrecht held him back. 'No! I wish to interrogate him.'

'Yes!' said Bosendorfer, his eyes glittering. 'We must learn who his associates are!'

'No good comes from waiting to kill warlocks,' said Gotrek, coming up with Kat, Snorri and Rodi.

The steward ignored him and motioned to Classen. 'You and Bosendorfer go down and come up behind him, through the gatehouse. We will trap him from this side. There will be nowhere for him to go.'

'Aye, lord steward,' said Classen and Bosendorfer in unison, then started for the stairs.

Von Geldrecht beckoned to the others. 'Come,' he said. 'Let us take a stroll around the walls.'

'He has his back to us,' grumbled Kat as they started forwards. 'Why can't I just shoot him?'

Felix and the other humans made horrible attempts at miming casualness, but the dwarfs just walked along at their normal pace, glaring ahead with undisguised loathing. Felix almost said something, but then realised that they always looked like that, so were unlikely to raise Danniken's suspicions.

Something did, however. Perhaps it was Classen and Bosendorfer's wary posture as they came out of the gatehouse on his left, or the fact that eight people were bearing down on him from the right, or perhaps his dark powers warned him, but as von Geldrecht got within twenty paces of him, the acolyte's head came up and his eyes darted left and right, widening.

'He's on to us,' said Rodi.

Gotrek, Rodi and Snorri pushed past von Geldrecht and von Volgen, taking their weapons off their backs, as Felix, Kat and Volk fell in behind them. On the far side of the acolyte, Classen and Bosendorfer hurried forwards as well.

With a wild look, Danniken leapt to Father Ulfram and pulled him in front of him, putting his little knife to the priest's neck as the handgunners cried out in surprise.

'What's this?' barked Ulfram. 'Who's that? What's happening?'

'Kill me and I kill him!' said the acolyte.

'Fair enough,' said Gotrek, still walking forwards with Snorri and Rodi as everyone else stopped.

'Dwarfs! Hold!' cried von Geldrecht. 'We cannot risk Father Ulfram's life.'

'What is going on?' said Ulfram, turning his bandaged head this way and that as the Slayers reluctantly stopped. 'Danniken, is that you?'

'Your acolyte is the traitor, father,' said von Volgen. 'The foul warlock who closed the moat and weakened our defences.'

'And did you also poison the water, villain?' asked von Geldrecht. 'And ruin the food?'

'Who are your accomplices?' barked Bosendorfer. 'Is Tauber in league with you?'

Danniken's face split into a maniacal grin. 'Yes, I spoilt the food!' he cackled. 'And the water! And blinded Father Ulfram's witch sight as I treated his eyes after Grimminhagen.'

'You whelp!' cried Ulfram, struggling. 'I'll–'

Danniken pressed the knife deeper into the priest's throat, drawing blood. 'And yes, Tauber is in league with me,' he continued. 'And dozens of others. We are legion, my lords! Legion! You will never root us out!'

'Who?' asked von Geldrecht, his jowls quivering. 'Who are they? Tell me their names!'

'You are all traitors!' said Danniken. 'Your bones are traitors, lurking within your flesh, waiting only for death to betray you! And I will free them!'

And with that he tipped his head back and began keening in an ancient and arcane tongue.

The handgunners cowered back in superstitious fear, and Felix, Kat and the other humans hesitated, afraid to endanger Father Ulfram's life, but the Slayers had no such compunctions. They started forwards, raising their weapons. Father Ulfram, however, acted first.

'Hammer of Sigmar give me strength!' roared the old priest, and drove the back of his head into Danniken's jaw, snapping his teeth shut and cutting off his chant. The acolyte staggered against the battlement, spitting blood and pulling the priest with him.

'Well done, father!' cried von Geldrecht.

As the others surged in, the priest turned and threw blind fists at Danniken, shouting, 'Heretic! In Sigmar's name I cast thee out!'

A wild blow knocked the acolyte flat between two crenellations, but Ulfram overbalanced and fell on top of him, his head and shoulders over the wall.

'Stop them!' called von Geldrecht. 'Catch them!'

Bosendorfer reached them first and grabbed for Ulfram's ankles, but Danniken, with surprising strength, bucked under Ulfram, dragging the priest another foot over the edge, and the greatsword's hands were kicked away in the flailing.

Gotrek shoved Bosendorfer aside and grabbed Ulfram's long white surcoat, but too late. The priest and the false acolyte flipped over the side, still fighting and bellowing, and the Slayer was left holding a long strip of white cloth.

Felix and Kat pressed to the edge with everyone else and saw the two bodies smack into the thick mud of the empty moat amongst the milling zombies. For a long second, they and the others just stared as the bodies lay there, unmoving, but then, amazingly, the old priest coughed and gasped and flailed an arm.

'Father Ulfram!' called von Geldrecht. 'Father, are you all right? A rope, someone! A rope!'

It was Danniken, however, who rose first, pushing up from the priest's body, broken and bedraggled. He looked up at the parapet and laughed, his mouth full of mud and blood, then hauled Ulfram up by the collar and raised his little knife high as the priest pawed feebly at Danniken's legs with broken hands.

Danniken stabbed him in the chest. 'At last I am free to join my master!' he cried, striking again. 'As you will all join my master, to march with him on–'

An arrow appeared in his mouth, buried halfway to the fletching like some sword-swallower's trick. The acolyte's words cut off in a gargle of blood and his eyes showed white all around. Felix looked to his right. Kat's bowstring was still quivering. Her eyes blazed.

Danniken fell slowly backwards to lie beside Ulfram, who sprawled face down in the mud, blood spreading out below him in a red pool.

Gotrek grunted and glared at von Geldrecht. 'Should have done that at the start.'

The steward didn't seem to have heard. He just continued to stare down at the priest. 'Volk,' he said quietly, 'ask Bierlitz to rig a rope and harness. We will recover Father Ulfram's body, and give him the proper rites. We will also sever Danniken's head and search his body for–'

He paused as Father Ulfram's body twitched and he tried to get his hands under him.

'Father – Father Ulfram!' he cried. 'Father, do you still live? Sigmar be praised! Volk, the ropes! Quickly!'

Volk ran off towards Bierlitz, but as Father Ulfram pushed himself unsteadily to his feet in the ankle-deep mud, Danniken sat up beside him, staring straight up because the arrow through his mouth wouldn't let him lower his head.

'Blood of Sigmar!' swore von Geldrecht as the acolyte stood. 'Danniken lives too. Shoot him again, archer, before he does Father Ulfram further harm!'

Kat dutifully put another arrow to the string, but Danniken did not attack Ulfram. Nor did Ulfram attack Danniken. Instead, the two of them turned as one, and began to shuffle together into the milling horde of zombies all around them. By the time Volk had come back with Bierlitz, Felix had lost them in the horde. It had swallowed them whole.

Von Geldrecht leaned against the battlements and let his head sink down until it touched the stone. 'Forgive me, Bierlitz,' he said in a tired voice. 'There is nothing for you to do here. Continue replacing the damaged posts. Classen, Bosendorfer, Volk, spread the word. Our traitor has been found – and he is dead.'

Classen and Volk nodded, but Bosendorfer stayed where he was. 'And what shall we do about the other traitors, my lord? Tauber, and the scores of others Danniken mentioned.'

Von Volgen snorted.

Von Geldrecht closed his eyes and pushed himself upright. 'Don't be an ass, greatsword. There are no other traitors. He only said it to sow discord among us. Go and do as I have ordered.'

Bosendorfer glowered, but saluted and went off with Classen without another word. The Slayers fell in with Volk, asking him about blackpowder and fuses, but Felix hesitated near von Geldrecht and von Volgen.

'Er, my lord steward,' he said, 'I apologise for bringing it up again, but if you believe Danniken was the only traitor, then do you believe Tauber is innocent?'

Von Geldrecht frowned, then sighed. 'Yes, Herr Jaeger,' he said. 'He is most likely innocent.'

'So, you'll release him?'

'Sadly, I cannot.'

Von Volgen grunted, anger flaring in his eyes. 'My lord, why not? The man is needed.'

The steward looked from Felix to the lord, then turned away, his face haggard and glum. 'I am sorry, but it is Graf Reiklander's decision, not mine. Please let it lie.'

He started to limp for the stairs, but von Volgen stepped in his way, his jaw set. 'My lord, I would like to hear this order from Graf Reiklander's own lips. It is not only the lives of the men of Castle Reikguard that are at stake. Many of my knights have died these past days for want of care. I would like to hear from him the reasons why.'

Von Geldrecht's face reddened. 'That is impossible,' he said. 'The graf is too sick to be disturbed.'

'Aye?' asked von Volgen. 'And perhaps too sick to give orders?'

The steward froze, glaring. 'What are you implying, my lord? Speak plainly.'

Von Volgen held his gaze for a moment, then coughed and looked down. 'I do not blame you, lord steward. I think it only natural that, with command thrust upon you as it has been, you would use the graf's name to add authority to your orders... regardless if the graf was giving them or not.'

Von Geldrecht looked like he was going to explode, then he too looked away. 'Your suspicion is understandable, my lord,' he said. 'But Graf Reiklander does still rule here, and he wishes Tauber to remain imprisoned. I am sorry. You will have to take my word on it.'

And with that he turned away, limping to the stairs and cracking his cane angrily with every step.

Von Volgen's fists clenched and it looked like he was going to call after him, but he restrained himself, and turned back to the wall to stare out over the zombie horde.

Felix looked at von Volgen for a long minute, then stepped away from Kat to lean beside him. 'My lord,' he whispered, 'why don't you take his place?'

FIFTEEN

Von Volgen turned from the wall, eyes hard. 'I don't know what you mean, mein Herr.'

Felix grunted, impatient, and looked over his shoulder as Kat joined them. 'Yes you do, my lord. Von Geldrecht is no general. You know that. He isn't much more than a jumped-up quartermaster, and he is leading us to ruin! You could lead us to victory – or survival at least.'

Von Volgen fixed him with a cold stare. 'You speak of mutiny.'

'I speak of saving men's lives!' Felix blurted, then lowered his voice again. 'He has already killed half of us with his hesitations and his refusal to free Tauber. Will you sit and watch while he kills the rest? You could save us! You *want* to save us!'

'Yes, my lord,' said Kat. 'Please.'

The knuckles of von Volgen's hands were as white as bone, and the veins in his neck stood out like ropes. Felix was afraid he was going to hit him, but when he spoke, his words were quiet and measured.

'Herr Jaeger, I thank you for the high opinion you have of my abilities,' he said. 'But it doesn't matter what I want. I have no authority here. I may advise. I may suggest, but it would be mutiny, indeed, treason, for me to try to wrest command from the man the rightful lord of this castle has given it to, and I will not commit treason.'

'But your men may die!' whispered Felix. '*His* men may die! Sigmar's beard, if Kemmler takes Castle Reikguard and leads us all to Altdorf, it might be the Empire that dies! Isn't that a greater treason?'

Von Volgen turned and looked back out over the endless army of corpses, his brow furrowed. 'You make a compelling argument,' he said at last. 'But I cannot agree. Law is the strength of our Empire, Herr Jaeger. More than strength of arms or faith in Sigmar, the laws that bind lord to lord and lord to peasant protect us. They allow us to trust one another, to unite and to know that the strong will not take advantage of the weak in times of crisis.'

'But you won't take advantage,' said Kat. 'You aren't that sort of ruler.'

Von Volgen cut her off with a raised hand. 'Today I am not,' he said. 'Today I usurp the rule of Castle Reikguard for the noble cause of saving the Empire. But what will tomorrow's excuse be? Will I take command of my neighbour's forces because he is losing a war against beastmen? Will I overthrow the elector count of Talabecland if he rules poorly?' He shook his head. 'A man may break the law with the best of intentions, but when he sees the ease of it, it becomes habit, and he is lost. I am sorry, friends. I will give Steward von Geldrecht what aid I can, but he rules here, and I will not change that. Nor,' he said, turning hard eyes on them, 'will I allow anyone else to try. Do you understand?'

Felix looked down to hide the anger in his eyes, and he heard Kat grunt beside him. He understood von Volgen's reasoning, but what did it matter what a man might be tempted to do far in the future when what he did now could save hundreds of lives? It was maddening! Unfortunately, there seemed no point in arguing it further. The lord had made up his mind.

'I understand, my lord,' said Felix at last. 'Forgive me for suggesting it. It seems all I can hope for now is that the lord steward listens to you.'

He started down to the courtyard towards the Slayers, who were still deep in conversation with Volk, and left von Volgen at the wall, still gazing out over the endless zombie horde.

'Not yet,' said Gotrek, as he looked down over the eastern battlements towards the dike. 'Not yet.'

'Don't leave it too late, Herr Slayer,' said von Geldrecht anxiously. 'We no longer have enough men to mount a proper defence.'

'And whose fault is that?' muttered Kat.

Felix shot her a warning glance, then looked out towards the woods. After a long day of repairs and preparations, dusk was falling, and the horde was coming, in force this time. The men along the walls were already snagging ladders and lopping heads as the zombies began their ceaseless climbing. Beyond them, Felix saw the three new towers being dragged forwards by fresh gangs of skinned beast-zombies, while five trebuchets pitched stones, burning zombies and putrid corpses over the walls. A new weapon was trundling forwards as well, a long low contraption that was aimed straight for the front gate. It was roofed like the hoardings, and wheeled like a cart, and a huge battering-ram swung on chains beneath it, capped at the front with what looked like the skull of some knobby, mutated giant, crested with a ridge of iron spikes down the centre.

'That reminds Snorri of something,' said Snorri.

'It reminds me of Snorri Nosebiter heading for the privy,' said Rodi.

'No,' said Snorri. 'That wasn't it.'

Felix shifted his gaze to the dike. Just as Gotrek had predicted, the zombies guarding it were beginning to drift towards the walls, drawn like moths by the noise and violence to join their dead brethren in climbing the walls.

'Now,' said Gotrek. 'Lower the charges.'

Volk nodded and signalled to two men who held a rope, at the end of which were looped four knapsacks, each bulging with blackpowder charges. A third man shoved the knapsacks off the battlements, and the men with the rope started lowering them down as Gotrek and Rodi tied other ropes around their waists and stepped to the wall. Snorri took up the slack in Gotrek's rope while three more of Volk's gunners did the same with Rodi's.

'Ready,' said Gotrek and Rodi together, and stepped backwards off the battlements as Snorri and the gunners began to pay out the ropes.

Felix held his breath for the duration of the Slayers' descent, and Kat put an arrow to her bow and scanned the sky for bats or other spying eyes, but they were not spotted. They reached the ground without incident, then untied themselves and drew their axes while the rope slithered back up the wall. Then it was Felix and Volk's turn.

'Don't worry, young Felix,' said Snorri, as Felix tied the rope around his waist and the old Slayer drew in the slack. 'Snorri won't drop you.'

'That is the least of my fears, Snorri,' said Felix.

He gave Kat a nervous little salute, then stepped back off the wall and began to walk his way down beside Volk as Snorri and the gunners let out their ropes hand over hand.

As he descended, Felix's eyes darted nervously from the sky to the ground to the dike, expecting any second to see the zombies stumbling back around the corner, or the bats wheeling out of the sky towards them. To be caught dangling halfway down the wall by those flying slashers would be a nightmare. But despite his fears, he and Volk made it safely to the narrow strip of bulrushes beside the rushing Reik, and sank to their ankles in cold mud.

Volk hooked a flickering glass storm lantern to his belt, then grunted one of the packs onto his shoulders and held the other out to Felix.

'Here y'are, Herr Jaeger,' he said, grinning. 'Yer very own bundle o' joy.'

Felix smiled weakly as he stuck his arms through the straps and humped the thing up high between his shoulders. He was never at his most comfortable with explosives strapped to his back. It made him itch.

'Stay low. Stay quiet,' said Gotrek, and turned and strode into the river.

Felix, Rodi and Volk slipped in after him. The water was freezing and the current strong and very swift, even so close to the bank, but the bulk of the zombies were just on the other side of the sawgrass-covered mound that ran parallel to the river, and if the men and the Slayers didn't want to be seen, they had to remain as low as possible for as long as possible.

They trudged east along the river for about forty paces, but as they neared the dike, the bank began to narrow further, while the shallows grew steeper and the current swifter, until they came at last to the heavy stone flanks of the dike, looming up out of the water like the entrance to some massive, algae-covered mausoleum. Here the shallows fell away completely and the muddy bank disappeared into a roaring roil of crosscurrents.

Unable to continue in the river, Gotrek, Felix, Rodi and Volk climbed out onto the sloping stone shoulder and raised their heads just high enough to look over it. Felix shivered.

Seen from the ground, the panorama of Kemmler's horde on the move was even more horrific than when looked down upon from the walls. Thousands upon thousands of undead staggered forwards in an endless shambling mass, while the twisted hive towers lurched and swayed above them like living things, and the ghouls howled from their tops. The towers were halfway to the castle now and closing fast, and the covered battering-ram was moving even faster, and would reach the main gate in mere minutes. And while the rest of the undead army surged ahead, the trebuchets had hunkered down like spiders crouching to spring and launched stones and flaming corpses towards the walls with clockwork regularity. How could Castle Reikguard's beleaguered garrison hope to stop such a vast and terrifying host? Felix found it hard to imagine that even the combined might of the Empire could do it.

'Work fast,' said Gotrek. 'We'll be in plain sight.' He pointed at Volk. 'You and the manling will set your charges behind the top beam. Balkisson and I will set the lower, then pass our fuses up to you. You will bring them back here, to the bank, out of view.'

'Aye, Herr Slayer,' said Volk.

Gotrek held his eye. 'And you will not light them until I say.'

Volk swallowed, then nodded. 'Understood, Herr Slayer.'

'Then, go,' said Gotrek.

And with that, he and Rodi ran left to drop down into the moat. Felix and Volk scrambled up the stone bank to the top, keeping as low as they could, then looked down into the channel at the big oak doors. Up close, they were even more impressive than they had appeared from the castle. They were so thick Felix could have walked across the top of them to the far bank without narrowing his stride, and so tall a giant couldn't have looked over them, while the reinforcing bands of iron that crisscrossed them and bound the oak timbers together were inches thick.

Nor did any of the dike's strength or thickness seem less than necessary. The water beat against the doors with a constant deafening thunder that drowned even the rumble of the siege towers as they approached the castle. Felix could feel the power of it through the soles of his boots.

Volk pointed down to the upper of the two beams that held the doors closed. The bottom one stretched across the doors at a height of about five feet from the floor of the moat, while the upper one lay across them about five feet below the top. Both were as big around as tree trunks, and slotted firmly into holes in the stone banks.

'How do ye fancy dropping down to that while I pass ye the charges?' Volk asked.

Felix swallowed. The crossbeam might be thick, but balancing on it while trying to manoeuvre explosives into place didn't sound very appealing. 'Fancy would be too strong a term,' he said, taking off his pack. 'But it's what I came for.'

Felix gripped the top of the door and lowered himself to the beam. The wood thrummed under his hand with the rush of water behind it, and as his feet touched the beam, he could feel it flex as the doors pressed against it. He shivered. This would not be the place to be when those doors finally opened.

He glanced towards the horde again as he reached up to Volk, but none of the undead seemed to be looking their way. All the zombies were trudging towards the castle or crowding around the ladders, and the ghouls that swarmed the tops of the siege towers were too far away. A glance at the sky unfortunately told him nothing. It was too dark to see any circling bats.

Volk looped a coil of matchcord around his wrist, then leaned down with a pipe charge. 'Go to the middle and wedge it tight as you can between the door and the beam. Then come back for the second.'

Felix nearly overbalanced as he took the thing. It was heavier than he expected. He righted himself with a wild flail, then leaned back against the door and began sidestepping towards the centre, heart pounding, as the matchcord paid out behind him.

When he reached the middle of the doors he knelt and set the charge behind the beam in a gap between two of the iron bands. He pushed down on the charge to wedge it tight. Below him, the Slayers were doing the same. Rodi had climbed up onto the lower beam, while Gotrek lifted the charges up to him.

When his charge was as well seated as he could make it, Felix crossed back to Volk, who handed him down the second charge.

'It seems a small amount of powder,' said Felix, cradling it more carefully this time, 'to break such big doors.'

Volk gave him a hideous half-melted smile. 'Ah, well, the water's doing most of the work, y'see. All the charges need to do is make a little crack, and the water will bust 'em wide.'

Felix carried the second charge back along the beam and set it beside the first, then looked down as he heard a hiss from below.

'Manling. Here.'

One at a time, Gotrek tossed up the two coils of matchcord that ran from the bottom charges. Felix caught them and slipped them onto his right arm, then walked to Volk.

'Well done, mein Herr,' said Volk as he took the fuses. 'Them dead bastards won't know what hit 'em.'

He added the Slayers' coils to the two from the top charges, then helped Felix onto the stone bank, and together they crept back down to the riverbank, Volk paying out the four lines of matchcord behind him.

The Slayers joined them a moment later, then crawled up on hands and knees to watch over the embankment. Behind them, Volk braided the ends of the four fuses together into a single rope, then unhooked the storm lantern from his belt and set it beside them. Its flame flickered brightly inside its glass chimney.

'Ready when you are, Herr Slayer,' he said.

'Not yet,' said Gotrek.

Felix edged up beside the Slayers and looked out over the field. The siege towers and the battering-rams were close enough now that the castle's cannons were taking shots at them. A ball punched through the nearest tower, and an explosion of earth and flying zombies erupted near the battering-ram, but not near enough. The thing crawled on, and a shot from a third cannon missed too.

'Damned bats!' growled Volk, glaring up at the swarms that clattered around the gun positions. 'Spoiling our aim.'

'They should save their shot,' said Gotrek.

'You're so sure, mein Herr?' asked Volk.

Gotrek didn't answer, only watched the siege towers with unblinking intensity as they neared the dry moat. The zombies were doing the same thing they had done during the previous attack, swarming forwards to fill the dry ditch so the towers and their gangs of skinned beasts could use them as a bridge to cross the gap. More were doing the same for the battering-ram.

'Get ready,' said Gotrek as the first of the beast-zombie teams stepped out onto its bridge of corpses.

'Aye,' said Volk, and backed down the slope. 'Ready.'

Felix held his breath. The battering-ram was starting across its corpse bridge now, and the tower beyond it was nearly at the moat, while the middle tower was just beginning to cross. But as Gotrek raised his arm, the closest tower suddenly slowed as its team stumbled and became bogged down in its bridge of piled bodies.

Gotrek cursed. 'Hold,' he said.

There was a hollow boom from the gates. The ram had struck. Ghouls were locking off its wheels and driving long stakes down into the bank of the moat to hold it in place, while huge dead beasts swung the ram forwards and back on its chains in a ponderous rhythm – *boom... boom... boom...*

'Pull, you laggards,' Rodi growled as the near tower slowed even further. 'Pull!'

'Slayers,' said Volk, 'do we dare wait? They're knocking down our gates!'

'They'll hold a while,' said Gotrek, not looking around. 'I want them all.'

'Gotrek,' said Felix, grinding his teeth. 'You won't get any of them if you wait too long–'

A giant bat slammed down face first right in front of him, an arrow jutting from the back of its broken neck.

SIXTEEN

Felix and Volk flinched back as the Slayers looked up. Another bat jerked sideways in the sky above them and pinwheeled to the ground, an arrow in its eye, but there were more coming, screeching and swooping down at them, wings furled. They had been spotted.

'Now, gunner!' barked Gotrek, drawing his axe as Rodi and Felix drew as well. 'Now!'

'Aye,' said Volk.

He turned to lift the glass from the lantern, but as he bent, a bat crashed into him and knocked him flailing into the river.

'Volk!' cried Felix.

He sprang up, slashing, but two more bats slammed into him, driving him over the brink, and he too plunged into the waves.

The cold shock of it froze him for a second, but then he was smashed into the bank by the current and came up gasping as the water dragged him along, his knees scraping the rocky mud. Before he could find his feet, heavy wings flashed overhead and dropped towards the Slayers as he finally got purchase.

'Krell!' he croaked, and tried to pull himself out, but then something grabbed him from behind and jerked him back into the water.

Felix turned and kicked and raised his sword before he realised it was Volk, thrashing and panicked. The captain clutched his arm and Felix pulled him close, kicking for the bank. After being dragged along the muddy bottom again, he got his feet under him, and hauled Volk up after him. Though they had been only a few seconds in the water, the powerful current had carried them almost back to where they had descended from the castle.

Felix looked back towards the moat as he stood. Gotrek and Rodi were surrounded by a cloud of bats and fighting toe to toe with Krell and the patchwork wyvern, who stood between them and the fuses – which remained unlit next to the storm lantern. Felix choked and started running back. This was bad. The charges had to blow *now*, while the siege towers were still crossing the moat!

The bats wheeled at him, shrieking and battering him with wings and claws as he ran for the fuses. He slashed through them desperately, but a glance towards the castle told him he was going to be too late. The furthest tower was already nearly all the way across the moat. The closest was halfway, and the battering-ram was continuing its relentless *boom... boom... boom...*

Gotrek smashed Krell's wyvern back and it flapped up in the air, its leg hanging by a string of sinew. The Slayer ducked under it with Rodi, hacking for Krell, but the wight king knocked them both back with a sweep of his black axe. The Slayers weren't going to reach the fuses in time either.

A flash of flame shot down from above and struck behind Krell. For a second, Felix thought it was some new terror of Kemmler's, but then he saw it was an arrow, point down next to the lamp, a little flame just behind its head quickly fizzling out in the mud.

Felix blinked as he kicked a bat aside and gutted another. Who was shooting flaming arrows at them? And why? Then all at once he knew, and his heart surged.

A second arrow zipped down and quivered between the fuses and the lamp. So close!

'Come on, Kat!' Felix roared, chopping at the bats as Gotrek and Rodi exchanged ringing strikes with Krell.

Then the bats were gone from around him, flitting away and squealing. Sigmar! They were after the fuses!

A third arrow streaked down through the cloud of wings, and shattered the glass lantern, spraying its reservoir of oil in all directions and setting it alight. The bats flapped up, some of them on fire, and the little pool of flame spread. Then, all at once, there was a sparking and popping, and four lines of spitting flames began to crawl swiftly towards the dike. The fuses had lit!

'Slayers!' shouted Felix, backing away. 'Fire in the hole!'

The Slayers, however, did not seem to hear. As the bats dived and snapped futilely at the sizzling fuses like crows trying to catch speeding centipedes, Gotrek and Rodi drove Krell back towards the dike with single-minded intensity, cutting deep gashes in his black armour and sending chunks of it spinning away. It seemed that, for this brief moment at least, they had both abandoned thoughts of individual glory, and were working in tandem to take the champion apart piece by piece.

Krell took another step back from the Slayers' onslaught, and faltered on the edge. Rodi ducked in and smashed his axe into the wight king's knee in a burst of shattered iron and splintered bone. Krell fell sideways, and Gotrek leapt forwards and hacked at his neck with his glowing rune axe. The blade smashed through Krell's bevor, but before it could sever his neck, the champion toppled backwards into the moat and disappeared from Felix's sight.

The two Slayers stepped to the edge, and Felix was certain they were about to leap in after him, but as they tensed, the four sparking fuses burned between their feet and vanished over the lip. Rodi laughed and stepped back, but Gotrek remained where he was, blowing like a bellows and still poised to jump.

'That isn't death in battle, Gurnisson,' said Rodi, turning back to him. 'That's just death.'

Gotrek growled. 'My doom does not require your approval, Balkisson.'

'No,' said Rodi. 'Only Grimnir's.'

And with that, the young Slayer turned and ran back towards the bank. Felix held his breath, not daring to blink and miss the Slayer's last moment, though it might mean being caught in the blast himself, but after an interminable second, Gotrek cursed and raced after Rodi.

With a relieved breath, Felix sprinted for the corner of the castle, more than happy to use his long human legs to their fullest advantage, but even with his greater speed, he didn't quite make it.

As he neared the wall, he looked back to see how the Slayers were coming, and the world behind him suddenly turned black and orange and yellow. One second, the bats were wheeling above the dike, and Krell's wyvern was flapping down into the moat the next second, all of them were eclipsed by a billowing fireball that rose above the dike like a phoenix. The air was suddenly as hot as the Desert of Araby, and lifted Felix off his feet as a sound like the sundering of the world battered his ears.

He slammed down again ten feet further on, blind and concussed, and felt heavy thuds strike on either side of him. Then, through the ringing in his ears and the clouds in his head, came a new noise – a roaring, crashing tumult. He opened his eyes and rolled over. He was lying between the two Slayers, who were both looking back towards the moat and grinning like daemons. Felix followed their gaze and saw, frothing through the gap where the doors of the dyke had been, a rushing wall of water, twenty feet wide and twenty feet high, thundering down the moat like a stampede of white bulls.

Felix looked along the front of the castle, following the water's progress. The first tower was halfway across the moat now, its crew of skinned beasts obliviously straining at their ropes, but the ghouls clinging to the top had seen the wave coming and were shrieking and gibbering and trying to climb down. They were too late. The wall of water shot up over the bridge of zombies and hit the tower on its leading edge, lifting it and knocking it sideways and back. Screaming in terror, the ghouls rode the thing to the ground as it smashed to pieces in the ravaged fields.

The zombie mound was swept away like leaves in a gutter and the water rushed on towards the second tower. This one had almost reached the castle side of the moat. The flood slammed into its back edge, the froth climbing halfway up its height, and toppled it sideways, crashing it down right on top of the covered battering-ram and smashing it to pieces.

After that, the tide was spent, and it only rocked the third tower slightly as it streamed around its base before reconnecting with the Reik on the far side of the castle. Nevertheless, a huge cheer went up from the walls as the defenders saw the undead horde's attack reduced to a single tower, and the chances of the ram getting through the main gate reduced to zero.

Rodi laughed and pushed himself to his feet. 'We did it!' he said. 'We slew Krell and broke the back of Kemmler's army in one stroke.' He grinned at Gotrek. 'Not a bad night's work, was it, Gurnisson?'

Gotrek walked past him towards the ropes without a word, his chest working and his face as hard and cold as an anvil.

The eager hands of Bosendorfer's greatswords helped Gotrek, Felix, Rodi and Volk over the battlements and back onto the parapet, then slapped them jovially on their backs.

'Well done!' said Sergeant Leffler. 'Saved our bacon, mein Herr!'

Von Geldrecht limped towards them through the surging ring of well-wishers, his eyes wide. 'You did it, Slayers,' he said, wonderingly, 'Krell dead, the towers fallen, the moat restored, a thousand zombies crushed and swept away, the battle over before it's begun–'

'The battle's not done,' rasped Gotrek, his face still hard.

He pushed roughly through the men and continued down the wall, towards where Snorri and von Volgen and his knights were holding off the ghouls who spilled from the last remaining tower. Rodi followed him, but Felix stopped and looked for Kat.

She was at the wall, watching him as she shouldered her bow.

'That was quite a shot,' he said, crossing to her and giving her a squeeze. 'Where did you find flaming arrows?'

Kat held up her thick wool scarf, which now had rough holes torn in the end of it. 'This and some naphtha from Volk's cannon crews.'

Felix laughed. 'Well done. The whole castle is in your debt. They owe you a new scarf, at least.'

Kat showed her teeth. 'I'll settle for a beast-hide coat.'

Felix looked after the Slayers. 'If that's what you want, I think I can oblige you. As Gotrek says, "the battle's not done".'

Kat snorted at his pathetic imitation of the Slayer's sandstone rasp, and drew her hatchets. 'Lead on.'

As they started squeezing through the back-slapping greatswords, Felix felt someone's eyes on him, and glanced back to find Bosendorfer once again staring at him with undisguised loathing. Felix growled and hurried on. Was the greatsword angry that his men had offered Felix their congratulations? Ridiculous.

He hurried on with Kat, but by the time they had caught up with the Slayers, the fight was over. The cannon crews had set fire to the last siege tower, and Snorri and von Volgen's knights had held off the ghouls until it had burned out from under them and crashed back into the moat in a hissing cloud of steam and smoke. As Felix, Kat, Rodi and Gotrek arrived, the knights were all cheering and wiping the sweat from their eyes, and Snorri was limping out from among them, his face covered in blood and his warhammer over his shoulder at a jaunty angle.

'Gotrek Gurnisson! Rodi Balkisson!' he boomed as he saw them. 'There you are! Snorri thinks you missed a good fight!'

Gotrek balled his fists at this, and Rodi shot him a wary glance, but Gotrek only turned and stalked off again, pushing past Felix and Kat unseeing.

Rodi shook his head as he stared after him. 'Poor cursed bastard,' he said.

Felix frowned at him. 'What do you mean?'

Rodi looked up, seemingly surprised to have been heard. 'I shouldn't have spoke,' he said.

'Aye,' said Felix. 'But you did. What did you mean by it?'

The young Slayer looked uncomfortable. He shrugged. 'Don't tell him I said it,' said Rodi, 'but I fear Gurnisson is cursed. He will never find his doom.' He slanted a glance at Snorri. 'He needs the intercession of Grimnir more than Nosebiter does.'

An hour later, Felix stared at the broken ceiling of his room as Kat slept soundly beside him, Rodi's words turning over and over in his head.

He had always thought of Gotrek as unlucky – at least as Slayers thought of luck. He had survived encounters no one should have survived, and slain opponents he shouldn't have had a hope of defeating. Felix had also come to believe that the Slayer was partly culpable in his continued survival. Not that he ever shied from a fight or turned from danger, but as Rodi had said once before, he was sometimes choosy about his doom. He wanted it to be epic. He wanted it to have meaning. Dying in some pointless bloodbath was not the doom Gotrek envisioned for himself. He wanted to die saving the world.

But did his inability to find his doom stem from more than just bad luck and pride? Was the Slayer actually cursed? Had some god or daemon or mortal sorcerer somehow caused his quest to be endless? If so, why? What had the Slayer done to deserve such a fate? Was it tied in with the fate the daemon he had fought in the depths of the dark elves' black ark had spoken of? The vaporous being had said that Gotrek was to die fighting one greater than itself. Did this mean that the Slayer was being saved for some great destiny? Did it mean that nothing could kill him until that destiny manifested itself?

Felix grunted and shifted uncomfortably in the cot. There seemed to be precious little difference between 'destiny' and 'curse'.

The morale of the castle, so high after the restoring of the moat and the destruction of Kemmler's siege engines the night before, crashed down again with the coming of the dawn and the revelation that their great victory had been all for naught, and every gain the defenders had made had been cancelled out under cover of darkness.

Felix and Kat were pulled from sleep by cries of horror and dismay, and after struggling into their armour, made their way up to the walls under a lowering grey sky to find half the defenders huddled against a cold wind and staring silently down over the battlements.

The zombies were swarming near the ruins of the blasted dike, and like ants carrying bits of dirt to make an ant hill, they were carrying heavy rocks to it and throwing them into the water. Unlike ants, however, they were throwing themselves in as well – for the rocks were tied around their necks, and they were sinking to the bottom. Already the mound of weighted bodies had drastically constricted the flow of water through the channel, and the moat was half the depth it had been when it had swept away the siege towers.

'Is there nothing you can do, Captain Volk?' asked von Geldrecht from where he, von Volgen and his officers stood with the artillery captain further along the wall.

'Shooting at 'em might slow 'em a while,' said Volk, shrugging. 'But we're almost out of shot. And dropping pipe charges into the moat might shift a few, but they'll just pile more on.' He shivered. 'Look at 'em all. They're endless.'

Felix did just that, sweeping his eyes across the misty fields beyond the walls. Despite the thousands of undead that the bursting of the dike had swept away the night before, there seemed just as many zombies surrounding the castle now as there had been before, perhaps more. And at the tree line, three more towers were rising, and another battering-ram was taking shape.

'They don't need to eat,' said Kat. 'They don't need to sleep. They never run out of supplies. They don't care how many times we knock down their towers. They just keep making more.'

Von Geldrecht turned to Gotrek, who stood with Rodi and Snorri next to him at the wall, and held out his hands, pleading. 'Herr Slayer, you saved us last night. Is there nothing you can think of to fix this? Have you no clever trap to destroy them again?'

Gotrek grunted, his single eye never looking away from the zombies filling the moat. 'Sorry, lordling,' he said. 'There is nothing to do but fight.'

'That sounds good to Snorri,' said Snorri.

Von Geldrecht groaned, sagging as if something had broken within him, and turned back to the wall as his officers stared at him in dismay. Von Volgen grimaced and leaned in to speak to him again, then glanced up as he felt Felix looking at him.

Felix turned away. The mixture of fury and regret in the lord's eyes was too painful to see.

Though the hopelessness and the four days with little water and less food, had made the men of the castle listless, sick and weak, far worse for morale was the fact that there was no longer anything to do but wait for the end. The hoardings were all built and repaired, the river gate was patched, the saboteur had been caught and killed, the cannons supplied with all the remaining shot, and every weapon sharpened and polished until it shone.

Von Volgen kept his knights busy with exercise and wall patrols, but after his too-public display of despair, von Geldrecht disappeared into the keep without passing along any orders or words of encouragement, and his officers seemed to have decided to follow his example. They gave no orders, nor demanded any drill, just stood their watch when it was their time, and retired to their quarters when they were done. Consequently, their men did nothing as well, and sat huddled in little groups, griping and moaning and inventing rumours of more traitors. Even the weather added to the lassitude. Heavy clouds lowered over the castle, growing darker and more oppressive as the day went on and filling the air with a thick, undersea tension.

The mood was summed up perfectly by a spearman who Felix passed as he paced the walls. 'What's the point of doing anything,' he asked another spearman, 'when there's nothing to be done?'

There was a brief flurry of excitement in the middle of the afternoon, when von Geldrecht came out of the keep briefly to talk with Sister Willentrude, and von Volgen accosted him afterwards as he hurried back to the stairs.

'Lord steward,' he called, 'when may we expect to see you among us? Your presence is needed.'

Von Geldrecht waved him away and continued up the stairs. 'Not now, not now,' he said. 'I have pressing business.'

Von Volgen stopped at the bottom of the stairs, glaring. 'What business could be more pressing at this time than the morale of your men? You must order them, my lord.'

Von Geldrecht turned, his eyes feverish and his beard unkempt. 'The graf summons me!' he snarled. 'And it is his orders I obey, *my lord*, not yours!'

He hurried up the stairs and vanished once again into the keep, and after a few minutes of murmured speculation about the incident, the men returned to their lethargy, and the day continued as before.

The Slayers, being pragmatists, slept while they waited for the battle to come, but Felix and Kat were too restless, and wandered the castle ceaselessly, helping out where they could, but mostly just walking or staring out at Kemmler's siege towers as they grew like toadstools sprouting after rain. The swarm of activity around the looming constructs was as hypnotising as the gaze of a cobra before it strikes.

Another restless soul was Bosendorfer, who sat with his greatswords on the steps of the temple of Sigmar as they pounded out the dents in their armour and replaced damaged straps and buckles. Though he never moved from the spot, Felix felt Bosendorfer's eyes following him wherever he and Kat went, and all day long his talk was full of loud comments about honour and cowardice and disruptive outsiders – at which his men laughed uncomfortably.

Felix did his best to ignore it all, but then, towards the end of the afternoon, the tension, like the heavy clouds that were gathering over the castle, could no longer hold its burden, and burst into open conflict.

It started when one of Sister Willentrude's assistants came out of the underkeep and said something to Bosendorfer. The captain and his men rose and followed her inside, and taking advantage of their absence, Felix and Kat came down off the walls and warmed their hands at the ever-burning pyre.

A short while later, Bosendorfer and the greatswords came back out of the underkeep in double file, carrying a corpse between them on a stretcher. Bosendorfer was at the back of the procession, carrying a two-handed sword outstretched in his hands and chanting a prayer, while Sergeant Leffler was at the front, the doublet, breeks and morion helm of a greatsword's uniform held neatly folded in his arms.

Felix and Kat stepped back as the procession shuffled to the pyre and the greatswords laid down the dead man and made the sign of the hammer over him.

'Best to make yourself scarce, mein Herr,' said Leffler out of the corner of his mouth, then nodded at the corpse. 'That's Hinkner, who was wounded when we was fighting them ghouls with you. Captain blames you for his dying. Says he'd still be alive if we hadn't come back to the wall at yer call.'

Felix sighed. 'Very well, I'll retire. Thank you for the warning–'

'I told you not to speak to my men!'

Felix turned. Bosendorfer was striding towards them angrily, the sword he had held in reverence now gripped at the hilt and ready to strike.

Kat whipped out her skinning knife, but Felix held her back. 'He was just telling me to get out of the way, captain,' he said.

Bosendorfer laughed, harsh. 'Get out of the way? You could not go far enough unless you left the castle!' His hands shook as he pointed the sword at Felix's throat. 'That you are alive to witness the funeral of a man you killed is a travesty! It should be you on this pyre, not Hinkner.'

Felix knew he should back away. He knew he should say nothing and leave the captain and his men to their funeral, but that last jab had been too much, and his anger boiled over at last.

'I am indeed sad to witness the funeral of a brave man wounded in battle,' he said, as cold as he could manage. 'But if you want to throw someone on the fire for his death, captain, then it should be you who walks into the flames.'

'What!' cried Bosendorfer. 'What do you say?'

Felix stepped closer to him as men all over the courtyard turned to listen. 'The other night when we were raising toasts, you asked us all to pledge death to the man who had murdered the wounded who'd died in their cots. Do you remember?'

'Of course I remember!' said Bosendorfer. 'What has that to do with this?'

'Nothing, but the fact that you are the murderer,' said Felix. 'You are the one who killed those men. You are the one who killed Hinkner.'

Bosendorfer raised the two-handed sword over his head, snarling, but there was a cast of unease in his eyes, as if he feared he faced a madman. 'What are you saying? I've killed no one!'

'Haven't you?' asked Felix. 'Who forced von Geldrecht to hide Surgeon Tauber away for fear of his life? And how many men would still live had he been free to care for them? Hinkner didn't die in battle. He died from his wounds because Tauber couldn't see to them. You killed him, captain. You killed all of them. And if you wish to fight me over it, I am ready.'

He drew Karaghul and saluted, then stepped back into guard as the gathering crowd murmured and stared.

Bosendorfer glared at him, then answered his guard. 'Men may have died, but I saved the rest from worse. Tauber would have poisoned us all.' He raised his chin. 'When you are ready, mein Herr.'

Kat remained crouched, her knife out, looking like she wanted to intervene, but finally she stepped back. This was an affair of honour now. It was between just Felix and Bosendorfer.

Or it would have been, had not a higher power intervened.

'Hold! Both of you!' cried von Volgen, striding across the courtyard at the head of his knights. 'There will be no fighting among us!'

Bosendorfer shifted around to face the Talabeclanders and his greatswords put their hands on their weapons.

'You are not my commander,' said Bosendorfer stiffly. 'You cannot order me.'

'It is not a matter of orders and command,' said von Volgen, stopping before them. 'It is a matter of survival. We must kill the enemy, not each other.'

'But he has accused me of killing my own men!' shouted Bosendorfer.

'You did!' called someone in the crowd.

'It matters not,' said von Volgen, his eyes blazing. 'You are *both* needed to defend Castle Reikguard.' He turned to Felix. 'Apologise, Herr Jaeger, for the good of the Empire.'

Felix curled his lip, defiant. Why should he apologise for speaking the truth? But after a second in the heat of von Volgen's withering stare, he sighed. The Talabeclander was right. Fighting each other was insanity. He bowed to Bosendorfer. 'Forgive me, captain,' he said. 'I spoke out of turn.'

Bosendorfer sneered. 'That is all? You lied as well! You–'

Von Volgen turned on him, cutting him off with a gesture. 'Enough, greatsword! Accept the apology.'

'Damned if I will!' said Bosendorfer, stepping forwards. 'He has lied! He–'

Von Volgen barred his way with his sword. 'Accept it' captain,' he said, 'and continue with your funeral.'

'Who are you to order my troops!'

Felix, Kat and the others turned and saw von Geldrecht lurching down the stairs from the keep at the head of Classen and a handful of household knights, his sagging face crimson and quivering with anger.

Von Volgen bowed to him as the mob quieted. 'Forgive me, my lord, but would you have me let them murder each other?'

'I would have you leave the ordering to me,' von Geldrecht snarled, limping forwards. 'You have no authority here, no matter what your rank!'

'Nor do I seek it,' said von Volgen. 'But if you are absent when trouble starts, what choice have I?'

'You have the choice of leaving the castle if you dislike the way I am conducting its affairs,' said von Geldrecht.

Von Volgen paused at this, his square jaw clenching, and Felix waited for the explosion. Here, he thought, was the breaking of the Talabeclander's principles. Here was where the axe fell. In the face of such arrogant incompetence, could von Volgen really demur once again and let von Geldrecht continue to rule? Could he really let such stupidity pass without comment? Felix certainly hoped not.

Von Volgen bowed, as stiff as a board. 'Thank you, lord steward, but I will stay. We must remain united if Castle Reikguard is to stand. I only ask – I only ask that you return to us as soon as possible, and prepare us for the battle ahead.'

Felix grunted, disappointed. The man's moral code was going to doom them to von Geldrecht's leadership, which would doom them to destruction.

The steward, however, did not seem pleased with von Volgen's answer. 'You are ordering me again, Lord von Volgen!' he cried. 'You are telling me what to do!'

'No, my lord,' said von Volgen through clenched teeth. 'I am asking to be ordered. I am asking you to take command!'

Von Geldrecht's face turned red with fury, and he looked like he was going to lay into von Volgen, but then a cunning look came into his eyes and he raised his chins. 'Very well, my lord. Then I command you to surrender your sword to me, and turn over the leadership of your men to Sergeant Classen. You will be the guest of the keep until we are relieved.'

Von Volgen stared, stunned, and didn't seem to know what to say, but his men were not so dismayed. One of his captains drew his sword, and the others followed suit.

'He will not take you without a fight, my lord,' said the captain.

Von Geldrecht stepped back at this show of aggression and waved at Classen and Bosendorfer. 'Knights, greatswords,' he said, 'arrest them.'

The two captains hesitated, then stepped forwards with their men lining up behind them. Von Volgen watched them come, and Felix could see him weighing his options. Did he defend himself? Did he surrender? Did he order his men to attack?

Felix looked at Kat. She nodded, and they fell in on either side of von Volgen as the courtyard looked on, and Bosendorfer and Classen continued forwards with their troops.

'We are yours to order, my lord,' murmured Felix. 'We will do as you ask.'

Von Volgen grunted, his fist white-knuckled on the grip of his sword, then at last he raised his bulldog head and made to speak.

A loud rumble from above interrupted him, and the flagstones shook beneath everyone's feet. The lords and their men froze and looked to the walls, but the handgunners had raised no alarm. The sound had come from the sky. The low clouds over the castle had grown dark and pregnant while the drama below had unfolded, and lightning now flashed in their depths. The men stared, rooted to the spot, swords hanging slack in their hands, and then someone said what they were all thinking.

'Rain! It's going to rain!'

'Fresh water!' called a spearman.

'Get a wash tub!' cried a handgunner.

All over the courtyard men turned and ran for their quarters, the confrontation between von Geldrecht and von Volgen forgotten. Even their own troops were staring at the sky.

But as men began setting out pans and tubs and buckets, von Volgen returned his eyes to von Geldrecht, who looked back to him as well, and their men went on guard again. Felix held his breath as von Volgen clenched his jaw and raised his sword – then reversed it and held it out.

'My lord steward,' he said, 'I will not shed the blood of Empire men. You may do with me as you will.'

Von Geldrecht slumped in relief, and motioned Bosendorfer and Classen forwards again, but they stopped as von Volgen put up a hand.

'But,' he said, with a flat smile, 'I would be forever in your debt, if you would wait to take me to my cell until I had a drink of water.'

Von Geldrecht, who had stiffened when von Volgen spoke again, now relaxed and smiled. 'But of course, my lord. I would not be ungracious.' He bowed. 'You have the freedom of the courtyard until it rains.'

Von Volgen nodded his thanks and turned to his knights. 'Fetch your kit,' he said. 'Buckets, helmets, anything that will hold water. Go.'

The knights did not listen. They clustered around him, protesting his arrest, but he waved them down and told them to do as he ordered, and Felix let out a breath as they broke up and ran to collect their pots and pans.

He would have stood with the Talabeclanders, but the idea of fighting Empire men was just as abhorrent to him as it was to von Volgen, and he was glad it hadn't come to that – though it was a pity von Geldrecht was still in command.

'An ill wind,' said Kat, echoing his thoughts.

Felix nodded and looked up at the clouds, as Classen and Bosendorfer dismissed their men to find pots as well. It was going to be a brutal storm. He had rarely seen thunderheads so menacing. But was it his imagination, or did the lightning seemed tinged with red?

SEVENTEEN

All over the courtyard, the men not on wall duty feverishly laid out every receptacle they could find. In addition to bowls, pots and buckets, they were setting down helmets, wine glasses, tankards, even chamber pots and empty powder kegs. Some genuflected towards the temple of Sigmar to thank him for the blessing. Sister Willentrude knelt and prayed to Shallya. Von Volgen's and von Geldrecht's men, who only moments ago had been ready to kill each other for their commanders, laughed and rubbed elbows as they set out their rain-catchers.

Felix, however, was finding it hard to get into the festive mood, and continued to shoot uneasy glances at the burgeoning clouds. Their bellies were now the bruised purple of an over-ripe plum, and the lightning that flickered through them still left a crimson after-image on the backs of his eyes when he looked away. A thick fog had risen too, oily and cold, washing up against the walls of the castle like a grey sea, then spilling down into the courtyard so it was hard to see across to the opposite walls.

The thunder had woken Gotrek, Rodi and Snorri, and they had joined Felix and Kat by the harbour to scowl at the sky with suspicious eyes.

'Something's not right,' said Gotrek.

'Can Kemmler have poisoned the clouds?' asked Kat.

Rodi shrugged. 'Necromancers are tricky.'

'Snorri doesn't think it smells like rain,' said Snorri.

Felix inhaled, but couldn't smell anything but unwashed bodies, smoke and over-ripe dwarf.

'Double water rations!' called one of the cooks from the door to the underkeep. He and the rest of the kitchen help were rolling out handcarts with open water barrels on them. 'Steward von Geldrecht has declared two ladles for everyone!'

A great cheer rose up, and the knights and foot soldiers started streaming towards the barrels, snatching up cups and glasses from the ground as they went.

Kat stared after them. 'But... but what if it doesn't rain?'

With unease slithering through his chest, Felix started across the yard with Kat at his side, searching for von Geldrecht, and found him in the door to the underkeep, watching the throng around the barrels like a benevolent lord on a feasting day.

'My lord,' he said, lowering his voice as he stepped up to him, 'this is a grand gesture, but are you sure it's wise?'

Von Geldrecht turned cold eyes on him. 'You think I am interested in anything you have to say, Herr Jaeger? You stood against me with von Volgen.'

Felix swallowed, then shrugged. There was no denying it. 'I did,' said Felix, 'but that doesn't change–'

'What can be wrong with giving my men something they desperately need?' snapped the steward.

'Nothing, my lord,' said Kat through gritted teeth. 'Unless it doesn't rain.'

The steward gave them a comical scowl. 'Really, Herr Jaeger. You and your...'

His voice trailed off as an icy wind whipped through the courtyard, swirling the fog and flickering the torches that were set at either side of the underkeep door. There was a moaning on the wind that sounded like the cries of the wounded after a battle, and as it grew louder, the last purple tint of twilight faded from the heavy clouds and darkness fell in an instant.

All over the courtyard men looked up, shivering at this unnatural advent of night, but then, in the very next second, there was a blinding flash of lightning and a huge peal of thunder directly overhead, and the clouds let go at last.

Whoops of joy echoed from every corner of the castle as a deluge of fat drops rained down on them, battering their faces and drenching their clothes. Men ran around with their arms outstretched and heads tilted back, laughing hysterically. Felix couldn't help himself. Despite his worries, he joined them. He closed his eyes and spread his arms, letting himself get soaked to the skin, but as he opened his mouth to let the drops fall on his tongue, he smelled a strange but familiar metallic odour and wrinkled his nose.

The rain felt thicker than it should too, and slick, almost greasy. Felix opened his eyes and turned to Kat, who was looking down at her cupped hands. He choked. In the yellow light of the torches, it almost looked like she was covered in–

'Blood!' screamed someone. 'Sigmar have mercy on us all, it's raining blood!'

All over the courtyard the defenders were coming to the same realisation, and it stopped them in their tracks. Some only stared uncomprehendingly up at the clouds, letting the red rain splash on their faces. Others shook and vomited, utterly repulsed, or threw themselves in the harbour to try to cleanse themselves, but the vast majority just raged and wept, the crash of disappointment after their hopes for salvation had been raised so high too much for them to bear.

A servant holding a soup pot in shaking hands stared at the blood pooling in it. 'It's not right. It's not right.'

'What are we to drink?' asked a greatsword, wiping at his face. 'It's got into everything.'

Then, from beyond the walls came the now-familiar rumble of Kemmler's siege towers, and the gibbering of the ghouls.

'They're coming!' bellowed a handgunner from the walls. 'To the walls! To the walls!'

Kat and the Slayers started immediately for the stairs, while captains and sergeants shouted at their men and tried to pull them together, knocking pots out of their hands and hauling them to their feet, but as Felix started after his comrades, von Volgen stepped past him to von Geldrecht and saluted.

'It seems I won't be getting my water, my lord,' he said, holding out his sword. 'So I am your prisoner.'

Von Geldrecht pulled his eyes away from the haemorrhaging clouds and stared at him, blood-rain streaming down his face. 'Are – are you mad?' he choked. 'Get to the walls! Lead your men!'

Von Volgen inclined his head, his face impassive. 'Very good, my lord. Thank you. And may I suggest you do the same?'

Von Geldrecht glared after von Volgen, enraged all over again, as the Talabeclander turned and hurried to his men, but the goad seemed to have worked, for as Felix ran after Kat and the Slayers, he heard the steward shouting behind him.

'To the walls, Reiklanders!' he roared. 'For Castle Reikguard! For the graf!'

The zombies were already coming over the battlements as Felix, Kat and the Slayers mounted the walls. Rotting claws and maggot-spewing jaws swiped and snapped at the defenders as they raced to drive back the dead and throw down their ladders. But the corpses were only the first wave. Beyond them, emerging out of the fog like the ghosts of lurching, shrouded giants, came Kemmler's siege towers, their gangs of skinless beast-corpses marching over bridges of the dead, and their fighting tops crawling with shrieking, red-eyed ghouls. As before, two of the towers were aiming for either side of the gatehouse, while the third groaned towards the corner nearest the blasted and replugged dike, and all three were going to hit before the men of Castle Reikguard could mount a solid defence. There was no way they would keep the dead from gaining a foothold on the walls.

'We will defend the gatehouse until the humans clear the parapet,' said Gotrek, bulling for the door into the gatehouse's upper floor. 'Snorri Nosebiter, you and Rodi Balkisson hold this door,' he said. 'The manling, the little one and I will hold the opposite door.'

'Are you ordering me, Gurnisson?' snarled Rodi, pulling up.

Gotrek didn't look back. 'Do as you will, Balkisson.'

'Snorri doesn't need any help, Rodi Balkisson,' said Snorri. 'He can hold the door himself.'

Rodi shot an angry glance at the old Slayer, then strode on with the others. A handgunner was just pushing the door closed. Gotrek stopped it with a hand.

'Let us through.'

The gunner cursed and stepped aside. 'Hurry, then,' he snapped. 'They're here.'

Felix looked back as the wall shook under their feet. The middle siege tower had slammed into the battlements and ghouls were diving under the hoarding roof and tearing at the defenders with teeth and claws and sharpened bones.

'In,' said Gotrek.

Felix and Kat stepped through the door after him as Snorri and Rodi turned to defend it.

'Snorri will see you in Grimnir's halls, Gotrek Gurnisson,' said Snorri over his shoulder.

Gotrek whipped back, glaring. 'You are not going to Grimnir's halls, Snorri Nose–'

The handgunner slammed the door shut, cutting him off, then dropped a stout iron bar across it and led them across the small room as Gotrek cursed. In the centre of the room was the mechanism that raised and lowered the drawbridge and portcullis, and opened the gates. This was the reason the gatehouse must be defended at all costs. If the ghouls broke in there would be nothing to stop them from throwing open the main gate and letting the whole ten thousand zombies pour through and swarm the castle.

Another impact shook the room as they reached the opposite door, and the handgunners who crouched at the arrow slots looked up, uneasy.

'Let us out,' said Gotrek.

The handgunner paled as he looked through the slot next to the door. 'But they're coming! They're on the wall!'

Gotrek fixed him with his single-eyed glare. 'Let us out,' he repeated.

The handgunner swallowed and unlocked the door, then pulled it open. 'Go! Go!'

The ghouls were indeed coming. As Gotrek, Felix and Kat strode out into the red rain and the handgunner slammed the door behind them, a gibbering white tide of them launched themselves off the siege tower into the thin-stretched knights and spearmen who defended the battlements.

The first wave drove them back from the battlements and the second wave swarmed left and right around them – half towards the defenceless cannon crew at the far end, and half bounding straight at Gotrek, Felix and Kat, shrieking like deranged apes.

It was a mad, miserable fight. The blood-rain was slashing in under the roof of the hoarding in nearly horizontal torrents, blinding them and making the stones of the parapet slick and uncertain. Felix hacked at the ghouls as if on ice, his feet slipping and skating out from under him and hampering his attacks and blocks. His weakness didn't help either.

It had been four days since he had eaten anything other than a biscuit, and he felt hollow inside. His head spun. The wall and the hoarding and the sky reeled around him, refusing to stay in their proper places. Beside him, Kat weaved and staggered like she had drunk a whole keg of brandy. The only reason either of them was still alive was because the space was narrow and Gotrek was taking the brunt of the attacks – but Felix was beginning to wonder how much longer the Slayer would last.

As he fought, the Slayer's wheezing and coughing came back worse than before, and his face grew as red as a poker. Even so, his mighty arms never stopped moving and his axe remained a flashing steel streak that chopped tirelessly at the encroaching horde. The ghouls fell before him in pieces – heads, arms and legs flying every which way – and their bodies toppled left and right. Their blood added to the blood that fell from the sky and ran in the gutter along the battlements to pour out through the rain spouts.

The cannon crew at the far end of the wall unfortunately had no Gotrek to protect them, and Felix saw them go down under a swarming mass of pale flesh, defending their gun to the last, then the ghouls were hurtling down the far stairs and into the courtyard. Felix's blood chilled as he glanced after them. They were not the only undead who had made it over the walls.

Zombies were everywhere, left to crawl unopposed over the battlements as the men tried to deal with the more desperate threat of the siege towers and the ghouls. But the ghouls had fought their way in too. The knights on the eastern wall were overrun, and the horrors were scrambling over their corpses to leap to the roofs of the residences and drop to the harbour-side. More were loping towards the knights who had gathered to defend the gatehouse's lower doors, and billowing black shapes floated amongst them – shades and banshees that drove the defenders back with their unearthly shrieks.

'Gotrek, they're in,' said Felix. 'And they'll be through the gatehouse's lower doors before they get through us.'

The Slayer nodded and started forwards, his axe blurring. 'To the stairs, then,' he wheezed.

Felix and Kat crept along behind him, stabbing and swiping over his shoulders as he cut down the fiends in a whirlwind of blood and steel. The ghouls' claws and bone daggers could not stab past his flashing blade, nor could they defend themselves against it, and after a handful were reduced to meat and splattered brains, the rest fled in terror, but the way was not yet clear. There were zombies behind the ghouls now, spewing up out of the bowels of the siege tower and clogging the wall in a mindless mass.

Gotrek ploughed into them like a bull crashing through a cornfield, and they died dismembered, headless and trampled underfoot. Before he and Felix and Kat fought halfway down the wall, however, a cry and splintering crash from below told Felix it was all for naught.

The banshees had sent the knights fleeing in terror from the gatehouse's lower doors and a hulking beast-corpse was ramming its way through the left-hand one, using horns like a balled fist to splinter the wood. Bosendorfer and von Volgen and the other remaining defenders ran across the courtyard to stop them, but they were too late. The ghouls swarmed around the beast-zombie as the door caved in, and poured through the door like terriers down a rat hole.

Gotrek cut down the last of the zombies and reached the stairs only a second later, and he, Kat and Felix plunged again into the bloody downpour and down to the courtyard to join the others. A huge hollow boom rocked them as they got close, and the portcullis shot up in a clattering whine of gears and chains. Felix cursed. The ghouls had done it. They had killed the handgunners and reached the mechanism. The drawbridge was down, and the main gate was swinging open.

'Fall back!' shouted von Geldrecht from somewhere across the courtyard. 'Up the stairs! To the keep!'

From much closer, von Volgen countermanded the order. 'Hold! Hold! Block the gate!'

Both were drowned out by the rumble of hooves pounding across the drawbridge. Felix looked around. Thundering through the gate four abreast were the armoured skeletal riders that had chased down von Volgen's column as they had raced for Castle Reikguard five days earlier. They had a new leader, a skeletal, unarmoured wight with long blonde hair fixed to its skull by a golden crown and the decaying kirtle of some barbarian queen around its pelvis. The dead war queen rode a flame-mouthed black horse and held aloft a flanged mace that burned with viridian fire.

She and her riders smashed through von Volgen's hastily assembled line like it wasn't there, trampling knights under their flashing hooves and fanning out across the courtyard to ride down fleeing men as a black tide of dire wolves flowed in after them to tear out the throats of the fallen.

Gotrek set his eye on the queen and started through the red rain with a growl as she dashed out a spearman's brains with her mace. Felix and Kat followed as the Slayer cut down everything between him and her – zombies, ghouls, wolves and the mounted wights that slashed at him as they galloped by.

Before the gatehouse, von Volgen was bowing to the inevitable as he picked himself up and looked around. His line had been smashed and the gates could no longer be held. The zombies were spilling through after the wolves a thousand strong to spread like grey, slow-moving lava across the courtyard.

'Fall back!' he called. 'Bring the wounded! Protect the inner gate!'

His knights rallied around him and moved in a well-formed square for the stairs that rose to the keep. The household spearmen and knights and handgunners, abandoned by von Geldrecht – who was nowhere to be seen – rallied to von Volgen too, and began to retreat in good order.

Bosendorfer and his greatswords were not retreating. In a mad display of courage, they were plunging into the heart of the dead riders' ranks, their greatswords carving synchronised figure-eights in the air before them like the blades of some oversized threshing machine.

Gotrek ploughed into the ancient warriors' centre from another angle, shattering bone horse legs and ripping through bronze armour with each swing of his axe. Kat and Felix staggered and fought at his flanks and were soon joined by Snorri and Rodi, who were head to toe in blood, brains and bile.

'Snorri thinks we guarded the wrong doors,' said Snorri, chopping through the neck of a skeletal horse.

Gotrek decapitated a wing-helmed rider and took another step towards the wight queen, who was sowing crimson death amongst a knot of spearmen only a few paces away. 'They would have got in wherever we weren't.'

'Aye,' said Rodi. 'If we'd had a Slayer at each door, the gates would still stand.'

Beneath the blood that covered him, the young Slayer looked as pale as an elf, and he weaved as if drunk as he fought. He had a knight's surcoat tied around his middle that bulged, wet and red, just above his belt.

'Rodi,' said Kat, 'you're hurt.'

Rodi shrugged. 'A ghoul got lucky. Hooked my guts out. Had to stuff them back in.'

Felix and Kat blanched at this revelation, but Rodi fought on undisturbed.

Gotrek brought down another rider and the ancient queen was at last before him, slashing around with her mace as her flame-mouthed mount kicked in heads with its hooves and crimson rain flung from her golden hair.

'Turn, bone hag!' roared Gotrek. 'Turn and die!'

But as the queen wheeled to face him, Bosendorfer and his greatswords chopped through the riders on her right and crashed into her from the side, their two-handed swords rising and falling. The war queen shrilled with fury and swung her flaming mace, shattering a handful of long blades and clubbing Bosendorfer to the ground. Her riders and her wolves surged around her, slashing and snapping at Bosendorfer and his men.

Gotrek roared and bulled ahead, as if angry at being upstaged, and Kat, Felix and the Slayers slogged after him, smashing through the riders to the queen. She swung down at Gotrek with her mace, and he slashed up with his rune axe to meet it. The evil weapon shattered as if it had been made of ice, flaming green chunks spinning everywhere, and she fell back with an unearthly wail.

Gotrek's next blow took the queen's arm off at the elbow, and she turned her horse, trying to flee, but Snorri and Rodi cut the legs out from under it and the three Slayers chopped her into dust as she fell to the ground.

Her riders howled, and fell upon the Slayers and the greatswords in a frenzy.

'Protect the captain!' shouted Sergeant Leffler, standing over Bosendorfer, who lay unconscious on the red wet ground, his breastplate crushed and his leg a bloody ruin.

Felix looked around as he and Kat fought their way to them and the Slayers traded blows with the ring of riders. They were almost the last men in the courtyard. Von Volgen and his knights were protecting the bottom of the stairs that rose to the keep, while Classen and the household knights were escorting Sister Willentrude and a line of limping wounded from the underkeep. Almost everyone else had retired.

'Get him up,' said Felix to Leffler. 'Make for the keep.'

'Aye, mein Herr,' said the sergeant. 'I don't know what got into him, but it was brave work. Damn brave.'

Felix turned to Gotrek, Rodi and Snorri. 'Slayers, lead us to the stairs.'

Gotrek nodded and Rodi smiled.

'Aye,' he said. 'Then we hold them – to the death.'

'To the death!' repeated Snorri.

Gotrek shot the old Slayer a glowering look at this, but said nothing, only stepped in front of the greatswords with Felix and Kat at his sides, and began cutting a path through the riders and the wolves and the rain towards the stairs. Snorri and Rodi took up rearguard positions and the greatswords started forwards in double file, guarding the flanks as Leffler carried their fallen captain between them.

Ahead, Sister Willentrude was guiding the last of the line of wounded up the stairs as Classen's knights joined von Volgen's in protecting their retreat. A surging mass of undead crushed in on them from all sides – zombies reaching and groaning, wolves lunging, ghouls slashing, shades shrieking, dead beastmen looming above and swinging ponderous claws, while bats flashed down from above and the skeletal riders charged in with spears lowered, trampling the living and the dead alike in their homicidal desire to reach the knights.

Into the back of this murderous fray slammed Felix, Kat, the greatswords and the Slayers, axes and swords and Zweihanders flashing and spraying blood as they severed spines and necks and crushed heads and chests. On the walls, under the hoardings, the greatswords had not been at their best, but here, in the open, where they had room to swing, their effectiveness was astonishing. Nothing could reach inside the great sweeping arcs of their cuts, and they mowed down zombie and ghoul and beast-corpse alike without breaking step.

The knights around von Volgen and Classen cheered to see them coming and fought with renewed vigour, cutting a hole in the undead's front line for them to pass through.

Von Volgen clapped Felix on the shoulder as he stumbled out of the melee after Gotrek. 'Up you go, mein Herr,' he said, grinning through bloody teeth. 'I believe you are the last.'

'*We* will be the last,' said Gotrek, turning back to the wall of undead as the greatswords carried Bosendorfer through the lines with Snorri and Rodi following. 'Tell your men to retire, lordling. We will hold the rear.'

Von Volgen nodded. 'Very good, Slayer,' he said. 'A good doom to you.' Then he raised his voice and began shouting orders to his troops.

Gotrek turned to Felix. 'Go with them, manling, and take Snorri Nosebiter with you. Rodi Balkisson and I will hold until the gate is closed – and after.'

Snorri turned, looking confused. 'Snorri wants to hold the gate too.'

'Snorri has to go to Karak Kadrin before he finds his doom, remember, Father Rustskull?' said Rodi.

'Yes,' said Snorri sullenly. 'Snorri remembers.'

'Come, Snorri,' said Felix, and started for the stairs with Kat. 'Guard the greatswords' retreat.'

Snorri scowled, but took up the rear as Felix and Kat led the greatswords up the narrow, curving stairs to the gatehouse of the keep. Though the zombies could not reach them on the steps, they were open to the sky, and the huge bats swooped down at them in roiling clouds as they climbed. Felix must have cut half a dozen out of the air by the time they reached the top step, and Kat had done the same, while two greatswords had been torn from the steps by their claws, and the rest were bleeding.

More bats were attacking the gatehouse as they turned towards it, and Felix saw Sister Willentrude and a handful of tattered spearmen fending them off as the tail end of the column of wounded men limped in behind them.

'Foul beasts!' cried the sister, waving a broken spear. 'Get away!'

Cursing, Felix and Kat ran to help, but just as they reached her, a bat slammed into the sister's back, smashing her face-first into a pillar that flanked the gate, and biting her neck.

'No!'

Felix slashed at the thing, half-severing a wing. It flailed, shrieking, and ripped away from Sister Willentrude to flap at him, clawing his forearm. Felix shoved it back as it tore mail and flesh. It was too close to hit with his sword. Then it was gone, its head caved in by Snorri's blurring hammer, and flopping to the ground.

Felix let out a breath and wrung his bloodied arm. 'Thank you, Snorri.'

Kat helped Sister Willentrude to her knees as the greatswords filled in all around them. Blood was pumping through the Shallyan's fingers as she pressed them to her neck.

'Get her in!' said Felix to the spearmen who fought off the bats. 'And take Captain Bosendorfer. We will hold the gate! Snorri, greatswords, form a line!'

The spearmen looked relieved, and gladly took Bosendorfer and the sister as the greatswords and the old Slayer turned to defend the gate. It wasn't until he and Kat had ranked up with them and begun hacking at the bats that Felix realised he had likely overstepped his bounds.

He glanced at Leffler, fighting at his side. 'My apologies. I didn't mean to order you, sergeant.'

Leffler grinned. 'Why stop now, mein herr? Yer just gettin' good at it.'

Felix laughed uncomfortably and fought on, swinging at the clattering bats as von Volgen's men topped the stairs and ran for the shelter of the gate. The wounds in his forearm, which Felix had hardly felt when the bat had clawed him, were throbbing now, and his arm was stiffening like it had been beaten. Blood was running down his wrist and slicking Karaghul's hilt.

He glanced down to the steps. A double file of armoured wights was halfway up, hacking at Gotrek and Rodi, who were backing up, one step at a time, and protecting Classen's knights as they retired.

Felix allowed himself a tiny sigh of relief as he killed another bat. Thanks to von Volgen and the Slayers, the retreat into the keep was going as smoothly as could be hoped. There had been terrible casualties, of course, but after the initial panic, von Volgen's orders and the Slayers' impenetrable defence had stopped it from being a complete slaughter. It could have been much worse.

Kat's shriek brought his head around and snapped him from his optimistic daydream. A huge shadow swept overhead, cutting off the rain for an eyeblink, then banked and shot down straight at the gate – straight at him.

Felix and Kat and the greatswords dived aside as Krell's wyvern landed hard in front of the gate, its claws scraping trenches in the flagstones, and Krell flung himself out of the saddle to stand before them, slashing with his axe.

Felix stared, stunned. Krell shouldn't be standing there. Felix had seen him fall into the moat just before the doors exploded. His mount too. The fireball had engulfed them, and yet here they were. Krell looked none the worse for wear. Indeed all the great gashes that Gotrek and Rodi had chopped into his armour when they had knocked him into the moat were gone as if they had never been. His wyvern, however, looked more patchwork than ever, with fresh stitches holding together the disparate hides that made up its torso, and its head and neck were burned black and showed skull and vertebrae through the charred meat.

Two of the greatswords died by Krell's axe before they could stand again, but the rest attacked the towering wight king as one, their long blades whirling in their customary synchronisation. Snorri led the charge, bashing at Krell's knees with his hammer and driving him back towards the wyvern.

'Stand back, manlings!' he roared. 'Snorri needs some room to swing!'

'No, Nosebiter! You will not fight!'

Felix looked up as he and Kat joined the greatswords' line. Gotrek and Rodi were elbowing through Classen's knights to the top of the stairs, axes high.

'Leave him to us, Father Rustskull!' shouted Rodi.

The surcoat he had wrapped around himself had come loose, and his entrails were hanging out of his belly. He didn't seem to notice.

Krell turned from Snorri and the greatswords as Gotrek leapt on the wyvern from behind and severed its long neck with a single blow, then ran on with Rodi. Krell roared and swiped as they launched themselves at him, gashing Rodi's shoulder with his axe and cutting two inches off Gotrek's crest.

The two Slayers rolled past him to come to their feet before the gate while Classen's knights swarmed after them and surrounded him.

Gotrek waved them on. 'Go in,' he growled. 'Close the gate. This is our doom.'

'Aye,' said Snorri, stepping out from the greatswords' line to join him and Rodi. 'This is Slayers' work.'

Krell slashed at them and nearly took Snorri's head off, but the old Slayer got his hammer up in time, and the cut only knocked him off his feet.

'Curse you, Nosebiter!'

Gotrek charged forwards with Rodi to drive Krell back from Snorri, and Classen and his knights took advantage and ran for the gate. Felix and Kat hesitated as they ran past. The greatswords waited with them.

'Will you stay?' asked Kat, as Snorri picked himself up and the oak and iron doors of the gatehouse began to swing slowly closed.

Felix chewed his lip. The armoured wights were topping the stairs now, and surging in to support Krell, while Snorri hefted his hammer and started forwards again. Which vow did Felix honour? Gotrek had told him to keep Snorri safe, but after so many years fighting beside Gotrek, it seemed wrong to turn away.

'Go in, manling,' shouted the Slayer as Krell and the wights knocked him back and drove Rodi towards the gate. 'And take Snorri Nosebiter with you.' Snorri kept walking ahead. 'Snorri doesn't want–'

'I don't care what Snorri doesn't want!' roared Gotrek as he blocked and backed away. 'Go in!'

Snorri snorted, but then stopped, fists bunched, and watched as Gotrek and Rodi fought in the centre of Krell and the wights.

Felix looked back towards the doors. The gap between them was getting awfully narrow. 'Uh, Snorri...?'

With an enraged snort, the old Slayer turned and walked through the gate, as angry as Felix had ever seen him. Felix and Kat breathed a sigh of relief and followed him in as the greatswords filed in behind them. Once inside, Snorri turned and glared back through the closing doors. Felix and Kat joined him, staring as Krell and the ancient wights battered Gotrek and Rodi inexorably back towards the gate.

A tremor of realisation went through Felix as he watched. This was it. This was Gotrek's doom at last. He faced too many opponents. He would never survive. At least it was a good doom – certainly better than dying from slivers in the heart – and if he killed Krell, then the Slayer's fame was assured. He would be remembered as one of the greatest heroes of dwarf history. Felix's eyes brimmed. And what a poem it would make! A last stand. A closing door. Two rivals united against deathless evil, fighting shoulder to shoulder.

But then, with the doors almost too narrow for a dwarf to pass through, Rodi suddenly dropped his shoulder and slammed into Gotrek from the side, surprising him and knocking him off balance, then shoved him back through the gap.

'Sorry, Gotrek Gurnisson,' called the young Slayer as Gotrek crashed down inside the doors. 'You will not rob me of another doom!'

Felix and Kat and Snorri stared in shock as Gotrek bounded up and tried to squeeze back through the gap, but it was too small now and he couldn't get between the doors.

'Treacherous beardling!' Gotrek roared, pulling desperately. 'We'd both have had our dooms!'

'No, Gurnisson, we would not!' cried Rodi as he slashed at Krell and the armoured wights. 'Even here, even with a belly wound, even with the doors closed, we would have survived! You are cursed, Gurnisson! You will never find your doom! Nor will anyone around you! Grimnir mocks you, and I will not be part of the joke!'

Gotrek pulled with all his might, but at last he had to snatch his hands from the gap to keep them from being crushed. He turned on Classen as the doors boomed shut.

'Open them!' he shouted. 'Let me out!'

The knight sergeant edged back in the face of the Slayer's fury, but shook his head. 'No, Herr dwarf. I will not risk the keep for your personal wishes.'

Gotrek glared at him for a long moment, breathing heavily, then grunted and turned back as the muffled clash of steel against steel rose to a feverish tempo beyond the doors, and a whoop of fierce joy sang above the tumult – then was cut short.

After that, all that could be heard was the hiss of the crimson rain and the chop of axes and swords against the oak and iron of the doors. Gotrek's shoulders slumped and he stood facing them, head bowed, while Classen called for men to man the murder holes and drive Krell and the wights away with gunfire and boulders.

Kat and Snorri bowed their heads too, and so did Felix, though he wasn't sure how he felt. Rodi had been a sharp-tongued companion, and hot-headed as well. Nonetheless, Felix had liked him. He had been quick and funny and brave, but now that he had stolen a doom from Gotrek, those memories were beginning to sour.

'Cursed,' said Gotrek, then turned and started into the keep's courtyard.

Felix and Kat fell in behind him, with Snorri hobbling along after them, mumbling under his breath.

EIGHTEEN

'How many still live?' asked von Geldrecht, then amended his question as he looked around. 'How many can still fight?'

Felix looked around too. He, Gotrek and Kat stood with the steward, von Volgen and the remaining officers at the side of Bosendorfer, who lay wincing upon a cot in the back corner of a large cellar room within the keep. In normal times the room was a chapel belonging to Karl Franz's personal retinue of Reiksguard knights. Now it was carpeted with the wounded and the dying, and the prayers were to Shallya, not Sigmar.

Felix had made a fair number of prayers to the Lady of Mercy himself since the retreat to the keep. Kat had cleaned and bound the claw wounds on his forearm as best she could, but the bat's talons must have been diseased, for the arm was now stiff and hot, and the edges of the gashes red and painful to the touch. Still, he could hold a sword, and he could walk, and in this company, that ranked him among the able. Most of von Geldrecht's remaining officers were no better off, and some were worse – with splinted arms, seeping head wounds, missing fingers and missing eyes.

At least Bosendorfer's mad anger seemed to have bled out with the blood they had all lost. The steward seemed in no danger of sending von Volgen to the dungeon, and Bosendorfer hadn't even looked at Felix since he had woken from unconsciousness. They were all too weary for such nonsense now.

'Six,' said the greatsword captain, glancing to where Sergeant Leffler and his greatswords sat, binding each other's wounds. 'But there would be seven if someone would see to this leg. Where's that damned sister?'

'She is in need of a sister herself,' said von Geldrecht. 'Lord von Volgen?'

'Fourteen,' said von Volgen. 'Though even the fittest can barely stand in his armour.'

'There's only me,' said an artilleryman Felix didn't know. 'But all the powder's down in the underkeep where we can't get to it, and there's no shot for the top guns anyway.'

Looking at him, Felix realised almost all the officers were unfamiliar to him now. Volk was dead, Hultz of the handgunners was dead, and Felix was too numb to mourn their loss, or remember if he had seen them die. Even the young spearman who had taken the place of Abelung, who had taken the place of Zeismann, had been replaced by an even younger spearman. The boy had peach fuzz on his chin and a thousand-yard stare. Only Bosendorfer and von Volgen were left of those who had commanded before the fighting began, and the wound in Bosendorfer's leg that he had taken from the wight queen's mace would be the death of him.

The boy from the spearmen wiped at his cheek. It was caked in blood. All the men were, from head to foot. Drying, it looked like they were iron statues, gone to rust. 'Eleven, my lord,' said the boy. 'Eleven. Eleven.'

'I don't know,' said a young river warden. 'The rest took shelter in the underkeep. I couldn't get to them, so I came up here. There – there was fifteen before the battle.'

'They will be dead by now,' said von Geldrecht blankly. 'Handgunner?'

'Nine,' said the handgunner. 'And we've no powder or shot either.'

Classen had to be nudged awake.

'Eh?' he said, looking around.

'How many of your company can still fight, knight sergeant?' asked von Geldrecht.

'Nineteen,' said Classen. 'Though it'll be less by morning.'

Von Geldrecht swung his head around to Gotrek, Felix and Kat. 'And we are less one Slayer, yes?' His eyes glittered angrily. 'Died outside the gate when he could have backed through the doors and fought again.'

'A Slayer's doom is no one's business but his own,' rasped Gotrek.

'Even when he may have doomed the rest of us with it?' asked Bosendorfer. 'We may die tonight for want of his axe.'

'We will all die tonight,' said Gotrek. 'Rodi Balkisson's axe would make no difference.'

Von Geldrecht looked at him sourly. 'Less of that talk, dwarf. Would you have us give up hope? Would you have us give up fighting?'

Kat snorted. 'You certainly did,' she muttered, but fortunately only Felix heard her.

'I will fight,' said Gotrek. 'The dwarfs would have died out long ago if we only fought when there was hope.'

'Aye,' said von Volgen. 'We must fight. There may be no hope for us, but we are still the hope of the Empire. We fight now to slow Kemmler as long as possible, and give Karl Franz time to prepare for his coming.'

'Well said,' said von Geldrecht, looking as if he wished he'd been the one who had said it. 'Though I'd hoped we might survive at least one more night.' He looked around at them all. 'Is that impossible?'

Classen raised his chin. 'We will try, my lord. We will die fighting to make it...'

A figure moving towards them caused him to trail off in mid-sentence. The others looked around. Sister Willentrude was shuffling through the ranks of the wounded, the makeshift bandage that had been wrapped around her terrible neck wound as blood-soaked as her once-white Shallyan robes. She was staring at von Geldrecht with a look of dull despair on her ravaged face.

'Sister,' said von Geldrecht, 'you should not be up from your bed. What is the matter? Is there some new calamity?'

'She's come to look at my leg,' said Bosendorfer. 'Let her through.'

But Sister Willentrude didn't look at him, only raised her arms as if she wished to be comforted and stumbled on towards the steward, moaning.

Von Geldrecht stepped back, eyes widening, as the others began to stand. 'Sister? Are you well?'

'Draw your sword, fool!' shouted Gotrek, pushing forwards. 'She is–'

Before he could finish, the sister fell upon von Geldrecht, her hands clawing at his chest and her jaws snapping at his neck. The steward barked in terror and shoved her back, and Gotrek's axe bit deep into her side, then severed her head as she sprawled to the floor.

Von Geldrecht and the other leaders looked down at the headless corpse in stunned silence, as from all over the room, the wounded shouted and tried to stand.

'The dwarf killed the sister!' cried one.

'Kill him!'

'Lord steward, arrest him!'

Von Geldrecht held up his hands as some of the men started lurching towards them, balling their fists.

'Go back to your beds,' he said. 'She was already dead. She – she had turned.'

The angry looks turned to masks of grief and disbelief. The fists lowered.

'Not the sister,' said one. 'Not her.'

Beside Felix, Kat sobbed quietly. 'But we saved her,' she murmured. 'We *saved* her.'

He put his arm around her shoulder. She didn't seem to notice.

Von Geldrecht stared at the sister's headless body, then sighed again. 'Thank you, gentlemen,' he said. 'I will go inform Graf Reiklander of our numbers and our prospects. Please begin your preparations for tonight's attack. I will rejoin you soon.'

He turned and limped away, leaning heavily on his cane, as the others began to disperse and Bosendorfer stared at the corpse of Sister Willentrude.

'But who's going to look at my leg?' he asked.

Felix glared at him, and had to restrain himself from leaping up and throttling him. The man most responsible for the deaths of the wounded since the siege began, and now he was moaning about his leg not being seen to? It would be the most poetic of justice to see him die for want of a surgeon, but... but he wasn't the only one wounded, was he? There was a whole chapel full of hurt men. And Felix's arm needed attention as well.

Felix grunted to his feet and started after von Geldrecht.

'My lord steward,' he said as he caught up to him. 'I know you must be weary of my asking, but with Sister Willentrude dead, I must try again. Will you release Tauber and let him do his job?'

Von Geldrecht turned, and Felix was afraid he was going to get another earful, but instead the steward just stared at him for a long moment, and then nodded. 'Very well, Herr Jaeger,' he said. 'Very well.' He pulled his ring of keys off his belt and unhooked the clasp, then selected an age-blackened skeleton key and drew it off. 'I'm afraid I've left it too late,' he said, holding it out. 'And for that, I apologise. But as your dwarf friend says, just because there is no hope, doesn't mean one should stop fighting.'

He dropped the key in Felix's outstretched hand, then turned and started off again. 'Good luck, Herr Jaeger.'

Felix and Kat followed an old servant down narrow steps as he held up a lantern. 'Steward said I wasn't to let no one down here,' he said. 'Not on no account. But as you have the key...'

He stepped from the stairs into a cramped corridor then led them through a barred door into a rectangular room lined with sturdy iron-banded doors, each with a tiny window and a slot at the bottom for food.

'Herr Doktor is in this one,' he said, pointing. 'His assistants in that.'

Felix and Kat started to the door he indicated, but then a scuffling noise brought their heads around. There were noises coming from another cell.

'Who's that?' came a sharp voice. 'Are y'zombies?'

A hang-dog face appeared at the window of a door on the opposite wall. More crowded in behind it.

'Draeger!' said Kat.

'The dwarf-lover and his cat, is it?' asked Draeger. 'What's happened? We heard fightin', but nobody came for us – not that I'm complainin', mind.'

'The lower courtyard's been lost,' said Felix. 'We're all in the keep now.' He turned to the servant. 'Will this key open this cell?'

'Aye,' the servant said. 'Opens all of 'em.'

'Hang on!' said Draeger. 'Who says we want t'come out?'

Felix shrugged. 'Stay if you want, but next time it'll be the dead who come knocking.'

Draeger bit his lip and turned, and there was a whispered conversation behind the door, then he turned back. 'Let us out, then. We'll go down with our swords in our hands, thanks.'

Felix nodded and opened the cell. Draeger and his militiamen staggered out wearily, and blinked around.

'Much obliged, mein Herr,' said Draeger, touching his brow, then started for the guard room. 'Our kit's this way, lads. Come on.'

As they filed out, the servant crossed to Tauber's cell and held up his lantern so that Felix could put the key in the lock.

'You have visitors, Doktor Tauber!' he called.

There was no response from within.

The key shrieked and stuck as Felix twisted it, but turned at last and the bolt shot back. He pulled on the handle, then peered in with Kat as the door creaked open. At the back of the cell was a low cot, and lying upon it, face to the wall and arms hugging his knees, was a filthy, emaciated figure.

Felix lit a candle from the lamp and gave the key to the footman. 'Let out his assistants, please.'

'Yes, mein herr.'

As the man shuffled away, Felix stepped in. 'Doktor Tauber?' he said. 'Doktor Tauber, are you awake? I have water for you.'

There was still no response. Kat drew her skinning knife and crept forwards at Felix's side. Felix understood her caution. If Tauber had died, he might well rise and attack them.

Felix reached out and shook his shoulder as Kat held the blade ready. 'Doktor Tauber?'

The man jerked and grunted, and Kat and Felix stepped back, wary, but when he turned his head to look at them, there was intelligence in his blinking, squinting eyes.

'So,' he said, in a voice like dry paper. 'Von Geldrecht is gone then?'

Felix smiled. 'No, Herr doktor, he still lives. But he has relented at last. He wants you to see to the wounded.'

Tauber frowned at this, then rolled back over and closed his eyes again. 'Let them rot.'

Felix sighed. He had been afraid of this. 'Doktor, they need you.'

'What could they possibly need a warlock for?' croaked Tauber. 'Are they begging for poison now?'

'You are no warlock,' said Felix. 'You didn't poison anyone.' He pulled the stopper from a jug he had found with half an inch of water in it. 'Here. I have water.'

Tauber didn't look around. 'Bosendorfer certainly thought I did,' he said, sneering. 'Or *wished* I had. And the rest believed him. Why should I help the fools who wanted me killed?'

'For the good of the Empire,' said Felix. 'We have to hold back Kemmler's force as long as we can.'

Tauber rolled over and looked up at him, smiling thinly. 'Mein herr, I may have been locked down here, but even I know that the castle will fall no matter what I do – and soon.' He chuckled. 'Would you like to try again?'

Felix opened his mouth, but he didn't know what other argument to make. Maybe he should try threatening the man. Maybe he could force him to work.

Kat laid a hand on Tauber's shoulder. 'Because you are a doctor,' she said. 'If you are to die, it should be doing what you do.'

Tauber stared at her for a long moment, his brows lowering as if he was going to snarl at her, but then he closed his eyes. 'You... you said there was water?'

Felix held out the jug as Kat helped him to sit up. He seemed to have lost nearly half his weight, and looked more than ever like a starved crow with a bad disposition.

He took the jug in clawed hands and drank, but only in sips, moaning and shivering with relief. Felix shot Kat a grateful look over his head. Why hadn't he thought of that argument? She shrugged, embarrassed, then steadied Tauber as he lowered the canteen with a gasp and opened his eyes.

'Help me up,' he said. 'I am ready.'

Tauber stopped just before the door of the Reiksguard chapel, making Felix and Kat and his assistants jolt to a stop behind him. He peered through at the men who lay in groaning rows on its polished stone floor, and his hands clenched at his sides.

The hate in the doctor's eyes made Felix swallow, and he wondered if he had made a terrible mistake. Tauber may not have been a poisoner when Bosendorfer and the others had accused him of it, but what if his unjust imprisonment and their loathing of him had made him one? What if Tauber went into the chapel and proceeded to kill everyone he touched?

'Don't let them turn you into what they think you are, doktor,' he said.

Tauber gave him a ghastly smile. 'Fear not, Herr Jaeger. I have too much pride for that.'

The doctor straightened his shoulders and took a deep breath, then strode into the room with something approaching his old hauteur. As Felix and Kat followed him in, Felix saw the men look up at him, and winced at the fear and mistrust that flashed in their eyes. Tauber paid their reactions no mind.

'Who is most grievously hurt?' he asked, raising his voice. 'Who is closest to death?'

There was a chorus of pleading at this, but as Tauber raised up his hands for order, Sergeant Leffler stepped next to Felix and whispered in his ear.

'Please, mein Herr, I know he won't like to do it, but if you could ask him to look at the captain?'

Felix grunted. Tauber likely wouldn't like it at all, considering, but Leffler was right. Bosendorfer would be dead within the hour if his leg wasn't seen to.

'This way, doktor,' he said, and led him to the cot where Bosendorfer lay as Leffler murmured his thanks behind him.

The greatsword turned pale as he saw the doctor approach, and gripped the sides of the cot as if he wanted to flee.

Tauber smiled down at him like a wolf. 'Don't worry, captain,' he said. 'It will be my greatest vengeance to make you whole again.'

Felix sat against the chapel wall, trying to stay awake long enough for Tauber to get around to him, but it was a struggle. Despite the throbbing pain in his arm, sleep pulled at him like an anchor, dragging his head down to his chest. He was so tired from the five days of endless fighting and rebuilding and fighting and rebuilding that he felt encased in lead. Beside him, Kat looked as weary as he felt, staring at nothing while Gotrek and Snorri snored thunderously next to her.

A few minutes later, Tauber finally hissed down before Felix, and gave him a weary smile. He was moving like a man twice his age, but despite that, he seemed almost cheerful. Kat had apparently been right. There was no greater tonic than letting a man do what he did well.

'Now, Herr Jaeger,' he said, 'what can we do for you?'

Felix folded back his sleeve to show the makeshift bandage Kat had tied around the claw wounds. Tauber snipped through the cloth with a pair of scissors and pulled it away. His smile faded.

A cold lump formed in Felix's chest. 'Is it that bad?' he asked.

Tauber sighed. 'Were Sister Willentrude still alive, you would be in little difficulty, for her prayers would have driven out the infection and the wounds would have eventually healed on their own. As it is, they are too far gone. I can only wash and bandage them and tell you to pray.'

'There's nothing else to be done?' asked Kat.

Tauber pursed his lips. 'If you were strong enough, your body might fight off the infection, but none of us is at our strongest at the moment, eh?' He looked over his shoulder at the rows of wounded. 'They are all in the same fix. A proper field hospital, with water and Shallyan prayers and food, and most of them would live. Here, despite my best efforts, most will die within a day – perhaps sooner.'

Felix swallowed, his stomach sinking, and Tauber saw it.

'I'm sorry, Herr Jaeger,' he said. 'My bedside manner leaves something to be desired, I know. Forgive me. You will have perhaps a little longer. You may even pull through, for you have a good constitution, but unless you receive proper attention soon, your chances are slim.' He shrugged, then snapped his fingers at the assistant who stood behind him with a satchel full of bandages and makeshift implements. 'But here, let us do what we can do. Even a little attention may help, no?'

When Tauber had moved on, Kat and Felix sat silent for a long while, leaning against each other and holding hands. The crippling weariness that had dragged at Felix still weighed him down, but now sleep would not take him. Tauber's words had struck too hard.

'I hadn't really given up hope until now,' said Felix at last. 'Gotrek and I have been in helpless situations so often, and we've always cut our way out somehow, but... but you can't fight sickness with axe and sword.'

Kat nodded. 'What day is it? How long before the relief is supposed to come?'

Felix tried to think back. It was difficult. It all seemed like one long, miserable night. 'Four days since von Geldrecht sent the pigeon?' he said. 'Five?'

'And seven days to get here from Altdorf,' said Kat.

Felix nodded. 'They will get here too late.'

'Then this may be our last day alive,' said Kat. 'Our last day... together.'

Felix looked at her and swallowed, then forced a smile. 'Don't be ridiculous, Kat. We'll be together forever, marching side by side behind Kemmler's banner.'

Kat's eyes widened, but then she laughed and circled his arm with hers. 'As long as it's side by side, Felix, I am content.'

Felix blinked up out of a dream in which he had got into a contest with Gotrek over who could keep their arm in a roaring fire the longest. Gotrek had been laughing and sneering at Felix as he held his hand uncaring deep within the flames, while Felix had sweated and gritted his teeth even though he had only held his arm at the very edge of the fire.

The dream faded as he took in the murmuring hubbub that was going on around him, but the throbbing heat in his arm did not. He looked down at his wound and saw that the sick red of infection had spread beyond his bandages now. His head seemed to pulse with it too, and his vision was blurry and doubled.

'What's happening?' murmured Kat. 'Another attack?'

'I don't know,' said Felix.

'It's not an attack,' said Gotrek, sitting up beside Snorri, who snored on, undisturbed.

Felix squeezed his eyes shut then opened them again and the double vision went away, though the blurriness remained. At the far end of the room, beyond where Draeger and his militiamen had made their berth, the officers were again gathered around Bosendorfer's cot, and appeared to be arguing.

'But he can't!' Bosendorfer was saying. 'He's a Talabeclander.'

'He is also a lord,' said Sergeant Classen.

'Come on, manling,' said Gotrek, standing.

'Stay here, Kat,' said Felix. 'We'll see what it is.'

She nodded, and Felix pushed himself up from the wall, then had to hold himself there as the world did somersaults around him. When at last everything stopped moving, he stepped over Snorri and stumbled after the Slayer.

'You haven't asked if I want it,' von Volgen was saying as they joined the circle around Bosendorfer.

'Well, do you?' asked the handgunner.

The lord looked around at them all, ending on Bosendorfer. 'If I am asked, I will do it. But I will not ask it for myself.'

'What's going on?' asked Gotrek.

Classen looked up at him. 'Lord Steward von Geldrecht has disappeared,' he said. 'He is nowhere in the keep.'

NINETEEN

'Small loss there,' grunted Gotrek.

'You insult our commander?' snapped Bosendorfer. 'Have a care, Herr dwarf!' The greatsword seemed much recovered, his leg wound neatly bound and his eyes alert. Tauber had been as good as his word.

'What happened to him?' asked Felix.

'No one knows,' said Classen. 'And until we find him, we need a new leader.'

'Has anyone gone to speak with Graf Reiklander?' asked von Volgen.

'I asked to see him when we found von Geldrecht gone,' said Classen. 'But Grafin Avelein turned me away. She said the graf was too sick to speak.'

'He was never too sick to speak to von Geldrecht,' muttered the spearman.

'Does this mean no one has been in the graf's apartments?' asked von Volgen. 'Could the steward be within?'

'The grafin said he was not,' said Classen.

Felix suddenly remembered his last encounter with the steward, and a sinking suspicion iced his guts. 'When was von Geldrecht discovered missing?' he asked.

'No one has seen him since he went to tell the graf our situation,' said Classen. 'I assumed he retired to his rooms afterwards, but he is not there now, and no one has seen him since he entered the keep.'

'I think he has escaped,' said Felix.

Every head turned to him.

'Escaped?' said Bosendorfer.

'How?' asked Classen. 'We are trapped.'

'Why do you think this, Herr Jaeger?' asked von Volgen. 'Did he speak to you?'

'It – it wasn't so much what he said, but...' Felix frowned. 'It was when he gave me the key to Tauber's cell. He said he was afraid he'd left it too late, and he apologised, then – then he said "good luck".' He looked around at the others. 'It didn't occur to me at the time, but now that I think back on it, it sounded like he was saying goodbye.'

A dark laugh came from behind them and they turned. Tauber was limping towards them, an evil smile wrinkling his pinched face.

'That is exactly what he was saying, mein Herren,' he said. 'Lord Steward von Geldrecht has fled, and left you all behind.'

'What?' barked Bosendorfer. 'And how would you know this, locked in your cell?'

'Because he asked my help to do it,' said Tauber.

'What do you mean?' said everyone in unison.

'Why would the steward want to leave?' asked von Volgen.

Tauber laughed. 'Don't you want to leave, my lord? I certainly do.'

'Answer the question, curse you!' barked Bosendorfer.

'I would imagine he left,' said Tauber, shrugging, 'because he finally convinced the grafin to give him the last of her husband's gold.'

'Are you saying,' asked von Volgen as the others murmured in surprise, 'that von Geldrecht was stealing from the graf?'

'For years,' said Tauber. 'And he might have gone on indefinitely except that the graf had the temerity to die – which complicated everything.'

The men stared, stunned, at this casual pronouncement, but Bosendorfer jolted up, struggling to rise from his cot.

'What lie is this?' he cried. 'The graf isn't dead, you villain! The steward has given us his orders every day since we came back!'

'Indeed,' said Tauber. 'And who but the steward has seen him since then?'

The men looked around at each other, waiting for someone to speak, but then Classen cried out.

'His wife!' he said. 'The grafin never leaves his side!'

'Yes!' said Bosendorfer, turning on Tauber. 'The grafin! If the graf was dead, don't you think she would have said something?'

'Aye, the grafin,' said Tauber, nodding sadly. 'It was for her sake that I became part of this.'

'Part of what?' asked von Volgen. 'Tell it from the beginning.'

Tauber nodded, then pulled up a stool and hissed down into it, grimacing. 'I'm sorry, gentlemen,' he said. 'It is too long a story to tell standing.'

'Just get on with it,' said Classen.

Tauber inclined his head politely, then began. 'As I said, von

Geldrecht had been embezzling from the graf for years, and when Archaon invaded, von Geldrecht was well pleased to stay behind when the graf marched north, for with everyone away, his thieving could be even bolder. Unfortunately for him, the graf took a terrible wound at Sokh, and though I did my best, and kept him alive all through our long march back from the north, he died of it within a week of returning to Castle Reikguard.'

The men groaned at this, and Bosendorfer cursed.

'I don't believe it,' he said.

Von Volgen waved him silent and motioned for the surgeon to continue.

Tauber sighed. 'When von Geldrecht found the graf dead in his bed, he came to me before he went to the grafin. He said the lady was nearly mad with grief over the graf's suffering, and he didn't want to push her over the edge by telling her he had died. He begged me to tell her instead that he was comatose, and that with rest and care, he would recover.' Tauber scowled. 'I thought this was foolish, but eventually allowed myself to be convinced. Unfortunately, while I was lying to the grafin, von Geldrecht was lying to me. The real reason he wanted her to think her husband was still alive was greed. With the death of the graf, Castle Reikguard would pass to his son, Dominic, a much more suspicious fellow than his father, and von Geldrecht feared his embezzlement would be discovered.'

He coughed, then continued. 'Von Geldrecht therefore decided to leave before Dominic returned, but, greedy fool that he was, he didn't want to go without taking all he could, and the most valuable, portable, untraceable treasure in the castle was a chest of dwarf gold locked away in a secret chamber in the graf's rooms. The difficulty was, Von Geldrecht couldn't open it. Both the key and lock were cunningly hidden, and only two people knew their secret – the graf and the grafin – and the graf was dead.'

'So he went to work on the grafin,' said Felix.

'Very good, Herr Jaeger,' said Tauber. 'He did indeed. He told her her husband could be brought out of his "comatose state" by a great physician in Altdorf, but that the man charged a fortune to perform his miracles. He told her she would need all the gold in the secret chamber to pay him.' He smiled. 'I learned all this when von Geldrecht came to me a second time. The grafin had grown suspicious of his story, so the steward asked me to back him up, and was willing to give me a share of the gold for my cooperation.'

'Which you gladly took,' said Bosendorfer, glaring.

Tauber curled his lip. 'I did not. The graf was a good master and a true nobleman, and I had no intention of helping that fat villain rob him, but he reminded me that I had already lied to the grafin about the graf, and he threatened to tell her I had killed him.' The surgeon looked down. 'I – I should have still said no. But I feared the noose. So, in the end, I agreed to do as he said, but–'

He laughed suddenly. 'But even with my "learned" opinion backing up his lies, the grafin still hesitated. She said she'd had visions of a kindly old wise man who told her that if she waited and prayed to Sigmar, her husband would rise from his bed again.'

'And she believed this?' asked von Volgen.

Tauber nodded. 'I believe her fears for her husband twisted her mind.' He chuckled. 'And wasn't von Geldrecht vexed to find that he suddenly had a rival in a mad woman's visions? He did his best, telling her the dreams were false visions sent by some evil sorcerer, but she would not be dissuaded, and would not give him the gold.'

He shrugged and looked around at them all. 'Then, as you know, Kemmler's horde surrounded the castle, and von Geldrecht's departure grew even more complicated. Fortunately, he knew of an escape tunnel built by Karl Franz's great-grandfather, but despite his dire warnings to the grafin that the graf would be killed when Kemmler conquered the castle, she still refused to give up hope that the kindly old wise man would come and save him.'

Tauber nodded to Felix. 'This is the real reason von Geldrecht had me locked up, mein Herr, and why you could not convince him to let me go. He had me visit the grafin every day, telling the poor lunatic that the graf's condition was worsening, and that he must get away swiftly to Altdorf with all the gold.' He shook his head. 'The ruse still failed when last we tried it, but it seems he finally got her to do it – or perhaps he decided he couldn't wait any longer, and fled without the gold. Either way, he is gone. And now,' he said, standing with a groan, 'I must be getting back to my patients. Good day to you, gentlemen.'

He inclined his head to them all, then turned and limped to the next cot in the row.

The men looked around at each other, stunned.

'It must be lies,' said Bosendorfer. 'It must be.'

'And if it isn't?' asked the handgunner. 'If the steward's fled and Graf Reiklander is dead, is there any reason to stay here? Let's find this secret passage and go meet the relief column.'

'Aye!' said the young spearman. 'Now *that* is a plan.'

Von Volgen glared at them both. 'The reason for staying is the same as it ever was. We stay to slow Kemmler's hordes and allow a force to be assembled against him. No one will be taking that passage.'

Gotrek grunted his approval, as did Classen.

'I nominate Lord von Volgen as commander,' he said. 'Talabeclander or no, he is the wisest and most experienced of us.'

'Seconded,' said the artilleryman.

Classen looked around at the rest of them. The spearman and handgunner nodded, but Bosendorfer looked truculent.

'We must see if Graf Reiklander is truly dead first,' he said. 'I'll not give over command of the castle if our lord still lives.'

Von Volgen nodded. 'On this I agree,' he said. 'Let us go to the graf's apartments and discover the truth of the surgeon's story.'

Felix, Gotrek and the officers rose stiffly while Sergeant Leffler came forwards to help Bosendorfer to his feet, then tucked his shoulder under his arm. As they all followed von Volgen towards the door, Kat left Snorri snoring and joined them.

'What happened?' Kat whispered.

'Von Geldrecht has fled,' said Felix, 'and we go to see if the graf still lives.'

'He fled?' she asked, surprised.

'Aye,' said Felix. 'He had been waiting all this time while he tried to get some gold out of the grafin. We don't know if he got it, or gave up, but he is gone.'

They stepped from the Reiksguard's residence and blinked in the dreary light of an overcast afternoon. On the walls, the few remaining spearmen and handgunners shuffled through their patrols, while a mixed force of Reikland and Talabecland knights piled stones and barrels and whatever else they could find against the main gates to block them. Felix shivered. It would be night again soon, and the end would come at last.

A few moments later, after they had climbed to the middle floor of the keep, von Volgen knocked on the oak doors of the graf's quarters.

'My lord!' he called. 'Grafin Avelein, are you there?'

There was no answer. Felix and Kat and the others looked around at each other as they waited. Gotrek only stared at the door, arms folded across his massive chest.

Von Volgen knocked again. 'Grafin Avelein, if you do not open the door, we will be forced to break it in for fear of your safety.'

There was still no answer. Von Volgen sighed and drew his sword, but Gotrek pulled his axe from his back.

'Let me,' he said.

Von Volgen stepped aside, and Gotrek smashed the lock plate, then kicked in the double doors.

A gust of hot cloying air boiled out of the dark room, and everyone choked and covered their noses. Felix's eyes teared up. It smelled strongly of cinnamon and cloves and Estalian incense, but underneath all the spice was another, more worrying smell.

Felix and Kat followed Gotrek, von Volgen and the others into the dim interior. There were no lamps lit. The only light came from cracks between the drawn curtains, and was barely enough to see by.

'My lady Avelein?' called von Volgen, as he crossed the entry hall. 'Are you here?'

A sobbing came from somewhere further inside the apartments. Von Volgen started towards it and the rest followed, edging uneasily through an arched doorway into a larger room. The incense was stronger here, as was the second, underlying stench, which Felix could no longer deny was the reek of rotting flesh. Von Volgen crossed to a window and threw back the drapes, letting the light of the overcast afternoon illuminate a strange sad scene.

The room was a grand and richly furnished bedchamber, with panelled walls and a massive canopied bed in the centre, and slumped beside the bed, head down, was Grafin Avelein Reiklander, her vermillion dresses spreading across the Araby rugs like a pool of velvet blood. Her right hand was stretched out to hold the shrivelled claw of a corpse that lay propped up amidst tasselled pillows upon the bed – and there was no doubt it was a corpse. The face was sunken and gaunt, its lips pulled back from its teeth and its eyes withered in hollowed sockets. A wound on its neck had been sewn shut, but the edges had pulled away from the stitches, revealing dry, black meat within. There were flies everywhere.

Bosendorfer stared, pole-axed. 'He was telling the truth,' he mumbled. 'Tauber was telling the truth.'

He let go of Leffler's shoulder and sank, still staring, into a chair. Felix didn't wonder at his reaction. The greatsword had erected his tower of rage against Tauber upon the belief that he was a villain and liar in all things, but here was proof that the story the surgeon had told of Graf Reiklander was true, and if that much was true...

Von Volgen stepped to the grafin and hovered above her, uncomfortable. 'My lady–'

She flinched at his voice, but did not otherwise move. 'Go away,' she sobbed. 'Leave us alone!'

'Lady,' he said again. 'I apologise for intruding upon your grief, but with your steward apparently fled, we had to learn if Graf Reiklander was dead so that–'

'He is not dead!' she shrieked, raising her head to glare at him with red-rimmed eyes. 'He is only sick! Very sick!' She had a purpling bruise under one eye.

Von Volgen looked back at the others, his square, bulldog face a mask of discomfort, but no one else seemed inclined to speak up. He clenched his jaw, then turned back to her.

'Grafin,' he said, 'I understand von Geldrecht and the surgeon, Tauber, told you that your husband lived, but... but they lied. He is dead, lady. I am sorry.'

Avelein stood, eyes blazing, and slapped him hard across the face. 'He is not dead!' she cried. 'I have been promised! He will rise from his bed! He will return to me!'

'Who promised you this?' asked von Volgen. 'Von Geldrecht? Has he–'

Avelein turned away from him. 'Von Geldrecht betrayed me!' she snapped. 'I knew I shouldn't have trusted him! I knew the old man was telling the truth.'

'Von Geldrecht betrayed you?' asked Classen. 'How?'

Avelein put her hand to her bruised cheek and closed her eyes. 'He said the necromancer's hordes would overrun the castle before the old man could revive my lord, and he promised to take us away and use my lord's gold to heal him in Altdorf, but...' She gestured to the wall. 'But when I opened the secret chamber, he – he struck me and stole it all.'

Sobs overcame her again and von Volgen stepped forwards to comfort her, putting awkward hands on her shoulders.

'I am sorry, lady,' he said. 'His deceptions have hurt us all.'

Felix glanced towards where Avelein had gestured. A panel on the far wall was not quite flush. He crossed to it with Gotrek and Kat as the grafin continued to weep.

'I should never have listened,' she said. 'I knew he was lying. But he told me the outer walls had fallen.'

Felix pulled on the panel. It was heavier than he expected, and as it swung out he saw it was affixed to a door of stone a foot thick. Inside was a small closet with jewellery and jewelled weapons on shelves, and in the middle, an iron-bound chest, its lid thrown back and entirely empty.

'I only I hope I haven't offended the old man by losing faith in him,' continued the grafin as Felix blinked at the empty chest. 'I only hope he still comes, now that I have opened the door for him.'

Von Volgen and the others froze at these words, and Felix, Kat and Gotrek looked around. Opened the door? What door? Suddenly the grafin's fancy of the old man sounded more concrete, and more threatening. The image of Kemmler in his guise as Hans the Hermit flashed through Felix's mind. If the necromancer could wear one guise, he could undoubtedly wear another. Had he been appearing to the impressionable grafin in her dreams?

'My lord,' said Felix, starting back towards the bed with Gotrek and Kat. 'My lord, I fear I may know–'

Von Volgen waved him down and leaned towards the grafin, forcing a smile. 'Forgive me, Grafin, but I was not listening closely before. Please tell me more of this old man, and the door you have–'

He broke off as footsteps clattered in the corridor. Everyone turned, hands falling to their weapons, but it was no undead host striding in, but Captain Draeger and his militiamen, with a few of the castle's spearmen and handgunners skulking at the back – more than twenty men in all. Only Bosendorfer did not look up at their entrance, just continued to slump in his chair, staring at nothing.

Von Volgen glared at Draeger. 'What is this, captain?'

'Aye,' said Classen. 'You scum aren't allowed in here!'

Draeger snorted. 'Way I see it, everything's allowed now. It's every man for himself.' He jerked his thumb at his chest. 'And this man wants to leave, so where's this escape tunnel, then?'

Felix groaned. Apparently their discussion about von Geldrecht had been overheard.

Von Volgen's face grew hard and cold. 'There is no escape tunnel. No one will leave this castle. We will fight to the end or until we are relieved.'

'Very brave of you, m'lord,' said Draeger. 'But I think I like the steward's way better. Now–'

One of his lieutenants grabbed his arm and pointed towards the hidden closet, the door of which was still ajar. 'Captain!' he cried. 'The passage!'

Draeger's eyes lit up and he started towards it. 'Good eye, Mucker. This way, lads!'

'That is not the passage!' barked von Volgen. 'Get away from there!'

He and Classen tried to block the way, but the militiamen swarmed past them, laughing and jeering, and Draeger hauled open the door to the closet. The laughing stopped as they looked in. Draeger cursed, and his men grumbled.

'You see, fool,' said von Volgen, pushing to him. 'Only a closet. Now get back to your posts.'

Draeger ignored him and turned, laughing, to his men. 'No tears, lads,' he said. 'It ain't a way out, but I do see our back-pay, eh?' He reached into the closet, grinning. 'Look at all them sparklers.'

Von Volgen grabbed Draeger and threw him back into his men, then stepped in front of the panel. 'Back to your posts.'

Gotrek, Felix, Kat and the young officers joined him and blocked the closet. Only Bosendorfer and Sergeant Leffler remained where they were, the captain still and unseeing in his chair and Leffler kneeling beside him.

Draeger snarled and drew his sword as his men went on guard. The officers reached for their weapons and Gotrek raised his fists, but von Volgen held up a hand.

'No blades, gentlemen,' he said. 'These men must be fighting fit when we are done here.'

'Oh, we will be,' said Draeger. 'Killing unarmed men is easy.'

A horrendous crash boomed overhead, jarring both sides from their fighting stances, and everyone looked up at the ceiling. Heavy mailed footsteps clanked across it – dozens of them.

'What is that?' asked Classen.

Grafin Avelein rose from her husband's death bed and lifted her hands to the ceiling as if in welcome. 'He has come,' she said. 'The old man has come through the door.'

TWENTY

Before anyone could stop her, the grafin ran out of the bedchamber, calling joyously. 'Old man! Thank Sigmar you've come! My husband awaits you!'

'Grafin! Stop!' barked von Volgen, and hurried after her.

Gotrek was right behind him, pulling his axe from his back, and Felix, Kat and Classen swiftly followed. The other young officers fell in behind them, the handgunner and artilleryman drawing their backswords, and the spearman brandishing his spear with trembling hands. Draeger, however, stayed where he was, staring at the ceiling with wide eyes while his men huddled around him. In his chair, Bosendorfer continued to stare at nothing as Sergeant Leffler whispered urgently in his ear.

'The escape tunnel,' murmured Classen as they trooped into the entry hall. 'The madwoman has let them through Karl Franz's escape tunnel.'

As Gotrek and von Volgen strode for the broken doors, a rank wind blew in at them, carrying with it a graveyard stench that overpowered the room's incense and made Kat and Felix choke and retch.

'Old man!' came Avelein's voice from the corridor. 'Old man, this way–'

Then suddenly her glad cries became a wail of abject terror, which was immediately eclipsed by a high, crazed laugh. Felix groaned as he heard it, all his fears confirmed. But as he and the others followed Gotrek and von Volgen into the corridor, it wasn't Hans the Hermit that was waiting for them, but a figure infinitely more terrifying.

Grafin Avelein lay shrieking at the base of the flight of stairs that led up to Karl Franz's private apartments as more than two dozen enormous, barbarically armoured wights clanked down towards her in a verdigrised tide, and a sinister figure on the landing above laughed like a jackal.

The figure looked nothing like the old hermit who had led them from Brasthof to the Barren Hills. His grin was not toothless, his shoulders were not hunched, nor were his robes and beard black with filth. Instead a tall, cadaverous sorcerer in a peaked hat and long grey robes grinned down at them, a gnarled, skull-topped staff clutched in one taloned hand. Gone was Hans the Hermit's sagging scabrous flesh. Gone were his weak, watery eyes. In their place was skin like scarred leather stretched over bones as sharp as blades, and eyes like black pits of hate, five hundred years deep. Only his voice was the same.

'Greetings, my masters!' he said. 'Are you not pleased to see old Hans again? Do you not like the bits of bone and bronze I found in those old tombs?'

Half the armoured wights trampled over Grafin Avelein and continued down the stairs to the ground floor, but the other half charged straight for Gotrek and the others, green-fired eye sockets blazing. Gotrek roared a wordless challenge and sprang to meet them, and his first axe swing sheared through the armour and bones of the leader like they were so much cheese and chalk. His second cut the legs out from under two more.

The Slayer couldn't fight them all, however, and too many surged past him for von Volgen, Felix, Kat and the officers. Felix and Kat fell back instantly, the axe blows of the wights as heavy as a house falling, and the others were in trouble too. The young spearman was backing away, the head of his spear sheared off, and the handgunner and artilleryman were retreating with him, their backswords no match for the corroded axes. Von Volgen and Classen fought shoulder to shoulder, but staggered with every impact. Even Gotrek was having difficulty holding his ground, and his breath was again coming ragged and raw.

Felix glared back towards Reiklander's apartments as he ducked a vicious swipe. 'Draeger! Get out here! Fight for once in your miserable life!'

But it wasn't Draeger and his militiamen who charged out of the door, but Bosendorfer, arm in arm with Sergeant Leffler, and lurching like they were in a three-legged race. Both had their side weapons out – a long sword for Bosendorfer and a mace for Leffler – and they threw themselves into the fray like men possessed. The sergeant shattered the skull of the wight that threatened the handgunner, and Bosendorfer knocked back another with a wild strike, then fell and dragged Leffler down as his bad leg buckled under him.

Cursing, Felix and Kat kicked back a wight and hauled the greatsword to his feet.

'Fall back, captain,' said Felix. 'You can't fight on one leg!'

'I tried to tell him, mein Herr,' said Leffler, getting under Bosendorfer's arm again.

'No, I must!' cried the greatsword, lunging forwards again. 'I must do the work of the men I killed.'

Felix and Kat fought forwards with them, protecting their flanks as wights came in from all sides. Felix had a lump in his throat. Confronted at last with Tauber's innocence, Bosendorfer had finally realised what he had done by keeping the surgeon from his work, and had decided he must die for it.

Nor was Bosendorfer the only one with regrets. At the same time as he flailed at the wights in suicidal fury, Grafin Avelein stood and shouted at Kemmler, tears streaming down her bruised cheeks.

'You promised me!' she cried. 'You promised me my husband would rise from his bed. You promised me he would take me in his arms again!'

'And so he shall, dearest heart,' said Kemmler. 'Indeed he comes to you even now. Look!'

Avelein turned towards the apartments and wailed, bringing everyone's heads around. Staggering stiffly through the desperate melee came Graf Reiklander, a stained night shirt hanging loose about his shrunken limbs.

Felix and Kat stared at the graf as Classen and the younger officers fell back in superstitious horror, but Gotrek and von Volgen knew no fear and swung for his neck as he passed.

The wights blocked their strikes and crowded them back, allowing the graf to shamble on, and Avelein flew to him, weeping.

'Grafin!' called Felix. 'Beware!'

'Oh, Falken,' she sobbed, throwing herself into his arms. 'I knew you weren't dead. I knew it!'

Graf Reiklander tore her throat out with his teeth.

As she slumped in his bony arms, artery spurting, Gotrek at last broke through the wights, but he didn't attack the zombie graf. Instead, with a roar of fury, he charged straight up the stairs for Kemmler, the rune on his axe flaring bright.

Kemmler cried out in fear and raised his staff, and the landing was all at once choked with mist and shadows that blossomed like flames from his cloak. The Slayer plunged into the swirling darkness, axe high, but a second later the cloud dissipated again and revealed him slashing around at nothing, alone on the landing.

At the same time, as Felix and Kat fell back another step before the wights' attacks, tendrils of darkness began to curl around Graf Reiklander and Avelein, who now stood on her own, dead-eyed, as blood streamed down her neck. Kemmler appeared out of the mist behind them, then opened his cloak and enveloped them in its black folds.

'Come, children, we have work to do,' he said, then raised his voice to the wights. 'Finish them, then join your brothers at the gate.'

Gotrek bellowed and thundered back down the stairs, but the graf and the grafin and the necromancer vanished into the cloud of smoke, and by the time he reached it, it had dissipated into nothing and a trio of howling wights was turning to surround him with slashing bronze axes.

Felix and Kat tried to fight to him, but they could make no headway. Nor could any of the others. Indeed they were being driven back on all sides. Von Volgen was fighting one-handed now, his left mangled and missing fingers, and the young handgunner and spearman fought back to back above the butchered body of the artilleryman. Beside them, a wight dashed Sergeant Classen's brains out, and his body crashed into Bosendorfer and Sergeant Leffler. Bosendorfer stumbled at the impact and dropped his guard, and the wight's verdigrised axe bit deep into his guts.

With a cry of rage and grief, Leffler crushed the wight's skull, then dragged Bosendorfer back out of the way.

Felix and Kat surged forwards to guard their retreat and ended up beside von Volgen, who was falling back before two other wights.

'Do you hear it?' he asked, blood spraying from his lips. 'There is fighting at the inner gate. We must go. We must defend it.'

Over the clash and clang around him, Felix did hear it – a faint roaring and clashing from outside. He laughed bleakly, and was going to make a remark about not being able to defend themselves, but the words died as, in a single stroke, a wight cut down the young spearman and handgunner, chopping them both nearly in two, and Kat had to twist aside to avoid being butchered too. Felix cursed and shoved forwards to protect her, driving it back in a flurry of strokes, but as it stepped back, Gotrek suddenly flew back and crushed it flat as he crashed to the floor, a bloody gash across his chest.

The three wights strode after him, raising their axes, and he scrambled up again and leapt at them as fiercely as ever, but his breath was whistling like a bellows with a hole in it, and his crimson face was running with sweat.

This was the Slayer's doom, thought Felix, as wights slashed at them from every direction and anger began to boil in his guts. What a misery! It might be better than dying from poisoned slivers, but not by much. Instead of the doom he should have had, instead of dying a grand death at the hands of Krell the Holdbreaker, the Lord of the Undead – a truly fitting end to an epic life – the Slayer was going to be overwhelmed by nameless wights in a pointless skirmish, as the final battle for the gates of Castle Reikguard happened offstage. It didn't seem right. The only consolation Felix could find was that when the Slayer died, he would die too, and wouldn't have to write such an anticlimactic finale.

A deafening bang punched Felix's ears, and the skull of the wight he and Kat fought exploded in a spray of bone shards. Another bang, and a hole appeared in the breastplate of one that was driving back von Volgen.

'At 'em, lads!' cried a voice from behind. 'They're between us and the tunnel!'

As Felix stumbled back from the collapsing wight, Draeger's men flooded past him, hacking at the ancient warriors in a frenzy and cutting their way to Gotrek.

Kat blinked around in wonder. 'They're fighting.'

'Even a rat will fight when cornered,' grunted von Volgen.

Draeger strode past them, sword in one hand, smoking pistol in the other. His pockets were overflowing with necklaces, and he had a jewelled sword strapped around his waist. 'That's the way, lads! Through them and we're free!'

Felix, Kat, von Volgen and Sergeant Leffler lurched after the militiamen and joined their line. With escape so close at hand, the men fought with a will Felix had not seen in them before. Even so, they were letting Gotrek do most of the work, but the Slayer didn't seem to mind. With his flanks protected, he chopped through the wights like a vandal smashing statues, shearing through ancient breastplates and shattering bones in clouds of dust and bronze shrapnel as he drove them onto the landing. He kicked one back through the stair-rail to smash on the floor below. A half-dozen more followed as the militiamen crowded in around them, and finally there were none left, and Gotrek stood at the broken rail, panting and hawking noisily.

'Down!' said von Volgen, limping for the stair and beckoning the others to follow. 'We cannot rest yet. There are more at the inner gate!'

But the militiamen stopped where they were, and Draeger, who hadn't done much during the fight other than wave his sword about, did so again now.

'Well done, lads!' he cried. 'Now up and away! Karl Franz's bolt hole awaits!'

The militiamen cheered and turned to scramble up the stairs as von Volgen turned towards Draeger, furious.

'You may not leave!' he barked. 'You are needed at the gate! We may yet hold out!'

Draeger backed away, smirking. 'Sorry, m'lord. As I said all along, this ain't our posting. Best of luck to yer.'

And with that, he turned and ran after his men. Von Volgen cursed and staggered after him, but he was too winded and hurt to catch him.

'Forget them,' Gotrek grunted as he gulped in reedy swallows of air. 'You don't need cowards. Let's go.'

Felix mopped his brow and turned to the stairs with the others, but a weak voice stopped them.

'Sergeant. Jaeger.'

Bosendorfer was raising himself up on one elbow. Felix winced as he turned to see the man's guts spilling through a hole in his breastplate.

He crossed to him with Leffler and knelt beside him.

'I wasn't leaving you, captain,' said the sergeant. 'I–'

Bosendorfer waved him silent. 'You must. I go to Sigmar's halls, to beg forgiveness of the men I sent there.' He turned fevered eyes on Felix and gripped his arm. 'Jaeger. You led my men better than I. If–' He stopped as bloody coughing racked him, then continued. 'If they will have you, lead them now.'

Felix swallowed, not knowing what to say. It wasn't a duty he wanted, but he couldn't deny a dying man. 'If they will have me, captain,' he said.

Bosendorfer nodded, seemingly content, then lay back, clutching his chest with a gauntleted hand. 'Sigmar, that hurts.'

It was the last thing he ever said. With a mechanical rattle, his last breath escaped him and his arms slumped to his sides.

Felix and Kat bowed their heads as Sergeant Leffler covered his face.

'May Sigmar welcome you, greatsword,' whispered Kat, closing his eyes. 'May Morr keep you from Kemmler's clutches.'

Von Volgen coughed from the stairs. 'Come. There will be time later to grieve,' he said, 'if we live.'

All was darkness and clamour as Gotrek, Felix, Kat, von Volgen and Sergeant Leffler ran out into the keep's courtyard. The screams and clashings of battle filled the night, and the sickly green light of Morrslieb, glowing through the clouds like warpstone at the bottom of a pail of soured milk, glinted on the thrashing of armoured limbs and the wet red of bloody weapons.

The four humans and the Slayer hurried towards the action along a trail of butchered bodies – spearmen, knights, ghouls and wights – that led across the courtyard to the inner gatehouse, where the last of von Volgen's men and the few remaining household knights guarded the doors of the gatehouse from a surging ring of ghouls, zombies and towering bronze-armoured wights that hacked and clawed at them with tireless savagery.

To the left of the gatehouse, a handful of greatswords were holding the parapet stairs against a stream of corpses that poured down them, while on the walls above, a weary crew of spearmen and handgunners ran back and forth along the battlements, trying to drive back and topple the ladders of the zombies and ghouls that were climbing over at a dozen points.

But though these were all desperate battles, it was the fight that raged on the top of the gatehouse, silhouetted against the moon-bright clouds, that made Felix's guts sink and Gotrek grunt with anger. Snorri Nosebiter, his booming laugh echoing loud across the courtyard, was going toe to toe with Krell, the Lord of the Undead.

'Curse you, Nosebiter,' growled Gotrek, and veered for the stairs at a run.

Felix was about to follow, but then remembered the greatswords. He turned to Leffler.

'Sergeant,' he said. 'Forgive me. I cannot lead you. I am oathbound to the Slayer, and must follow him. You are their leader now.'

Before the sergeant could answer, however, von Volgen turned to both of them.

'Take the greatswords with you, Herr Jaeger,' he said. 'I and the knights can hold the doors, I think, but not if the dead keep pouring in from above. Hold them at the battlements until we can finish the wights, and we just may have a chance.'

'Yes, my lord,' said Felix.

But as he ran after Gotrek with Kat and the sergeant, and von Volgen ran towards the gate, Felix wondered if they did have a chance. The men were weary and starving and desperately outnumbered, and even if they could stop the wights and hold the doors closed, Kemmler was already somewhere inside. What hope had they against him? The necromancer had taken the graf and the grafin and said they had work to do. What would be the fruit of that labour? Felix shivered with anticipatory dread.

'Make a hole, lads!' cried Leffler as Gotrek raced up behind the greatswords who held the base of the stairs. 'Let the Slayer through!'

The greatswords glanced back, then parted as Gotrek shoved to their front line and slammed into the clot of undead at the bottom of the stairs.

From Felix's vantage, it looked like an orange-crested bomb had hit them. A shockwave of force ripped through them, knocking down zombies and ghouls further up the steps, and limbs and heads and trailing viscera flew in all directions.

'Follow the Slayer!' shouted Felix. 'To the walls!'

The greatswords glanced around from their fights, wary, as he and Kat pushed through after Gotrek.

'Where's the captain?' asked one.

'I'll not go against him again,' said another.

'The captain fell to the wights,' called Leffler. 'He told Herr Jaeger to lead us.'

'I'll not order you,' said Felix, looking back at them. 'I haven't earned that. But I'd have you with me if you'll come.'

And with that he turned with Kat and hurried after Gotrek, not looking back to see if they followed.

'To the walls!' roared Sergeant Leffler, and to Felix's surprise, the cry was echoed tenfold.

'To the walls!'

Gotrek was halfway up the stairs, corpses and fiends toppling before him in a rain of butchered flesh and body parts. Felix and Kat fell in behind him, severing the heads of those that Gotrek had only wounded, and Felix stole a glance to the wall.

Krell was driving Snorri back towards the river side of the castle, knocking him around like a bear slapping at a pit dog. The old Slayer got up and charged back in every time, but Krell just knocked him down again and took another step forwards. Felix tried to see if Snorri had taken a cut from Krell's axe, but he was covered in cuts from head to toe, and there was no way to tell what had made which.

'Manling,' coughed Gotrek, as they fought on. 'You will take Snorri Nosebiter to the escape tunnel.'

'Aye, Gotrek,' said Felix, then looked unhappily around at the battle. 'But–'

'The castle will fall,' said Gotrek. 'No matter how hard we fight. Fulfil your vow. Bring Nosebiter to Karak Kadrin.'

'Aye, Gotrek.'

The Slayer smashed a beast-corpse from the top step and he, Felix and Kat surged onto the parapet as the thing toppled to the courtyard below. The greatswords followed behind as they started towards Snorri's fight, and they all moved along the wall like some centipedal killing machine – Gotrek, Felix and Kat at the front, carving a path through the dead that were climbing over the battlements, and the greatswords at the sides, their two-handed blades scything down anything they missed.

A great cheer went up from the beleaguered spearmen and handgunners, and they took advantage of the greatswords' clean sweep to stave off and knock down a dozen ladders while the walls were clear. But as Felix looked back, he saw that without reinforcements, the reprieve would only be temporary. Already new ladders were slapping up against the wall and new zombies climbing them.

Felix turned to the greatswords. 'Leave me,' he said. 'Spread out on the walls. Hold back the zombies.'

The greatswords looked unhappy at this, and stayed in formation.

'Damn you!' Felix shouted. 'Now I *am* ordering you! The Slayer needs no help! Defend the walls!'

'You heard him!' roared Leffler. 'Face left! Spread out! Drive the bastards back!' And as the men slowed and turned, he gave Felix a smile and a sharp salute. 'On yer way, captain. They'll do you proud, I promise.'

Felix nodded, embarrassed. 'Thank you, sergeant,' he said, and almost added 'goodbye,' but decided that was too pessimistic. 'Sigmar watch over you.'

He turned and ran after Gotrek and Kat, who were charging towards the tower above the river where Krell had driven Snorri.

'Back off, Nosebiter! He's mine!' roared Gotrek as Snorri picked himself up and flung himself at Krell again. 'Turn, butcher! It's me you want to fight!'

Krell turned as Gotrek leapt, and the Slayer's axe, its rune blazing, sliced through his breastplate, opening a ragged hole that showed bone beneath. Krell bellowed and fell back, swiping his axe in wild desperation. Gotrek ducked the swing and came in again, chopping at the undead champion's legs and forcing him back.

Snorri whooped and charged in too, swinging his warhammer in a blurring arc, but Gotrek stiff-armed the old Slayer and sent him stumbling back.

'Enough, Nosebiter,' growled Gotrek. 'Your pilgrimage starts now.' He shoved Snorri towards Felix and Kat. 'Get him out. Go.'

'Aye, Gotrek,' said Felix, shocked at the suddenness of it. 'Then I guess this is good–'

But the Slayer was already charging Krell again, his rune axe raised over his head. The wight king roared in to meet him, and sparks and grit flew as their axes struck and counter-struck in a hurricane of rune-glow and obsidian.

Felix put a hand on Snorri's shoulder. 'Come, Snorri,' he said. 'We'd better go.'

The old Slayer politely removed Felix's hand without looking away from the fight. 'No thank you, young Felix. If Gotrek Gurnisson meets his doom, Snorri must avenge it.'

Felix clenched his jaw. 'But Gotrek doesn't want that, Snorri. He wants you to go to Karak Kadrin.'

'Snorri knows,' said Snorri. 'He will go after this.'

Felix groaned and glanced down to the courtyard, then back along the wall – the way they would have to go to get to the escape tunnel. His guts filled with ice. Von Volgen's strategy was failing. There weren't enough defenders left to make it work. At the gate, von Volgen and the last few knights fought with their backs to the doors, the wights and ghouls and zombies eight deep around them. On the battlements, the greatswords and the spearmen and the handgunners were being overwhelmed as more and more ladders rose and more and more zombies and ghouls crawled over the crenellations to surround them. If Felix didn't get Snorri away soon, there would be no leaving.

'Snorri,' said Kat, touching his arm. 'Please. Are you willing to give up going to Grimnir's halls to avenge Gotrek? Do you want to wander forever in the afterlife?'

Snorri continued to watch as Gotrek and Krell battered each other, but his jaw set, and his face grew harder than Felix had ever seen it. 'Gotrek Gurnisson is my friend.'

Kat bit her lip, and a lump formed in Felix's throat. Both the Slayers were willing to die for each other – *more* than die! To save Snorri's afterlife, Gotrek was prepared to dismiss Felix and allow his doom to go unremembered, and to avenge Gotrek's death, Snorri was prepared to give up his afterlife. Who would dare interfere with a bond as strong as that? And yet, a vow was a vow, so Felix must.

He wondered if he should try to knock Snorri unconscious and drag him away, the way Rodi had done at the battle of Tarnhalt's Crown, but he feared it wouldn't work. If a Slayer couldn't hit Snorri hard enough to keep him under, Felix doubted he could do it.

A blood-chilling shriek of victory brought Felix's attention back to the courtyard, and he groaned. The last of the knights were falling under the crush of the undead, and the ghouls and wights were pouring through the smashed-in doors of the gatehouse. Felix saw von Volgen hack off the skull of an armoured ancient before being gored and trampled by a beast-corpse with the horns of a bull.

A second later, there was a ratcheting clatter and the heavy doors of the inner gate began to swing ponderously open, letting in a spreading mass of shambling undead. The inner court was breached. Castle Reikguard had truly fallen.

He looked back to the walls. The defenders were dying there too, the spearmen and handgunners and greatswords disappearing beneath a tide of zombies and ghouls that poured over the walls. Sergeant Leffler was the last still on his feet, reeling and whirling his two-handed blade around his grizzled head, but as Felix watched, a ghoul leapt on his back and bore him down, and the rest fell upon him like swarming rats. He had held to the end.

The lump in Felix's throat became a brick.

'Well,' said Kat, edging back as the zombies began staggering their way and the ghouls started loping out ahead of them. 'There's no leaving now.'

Felix went on guard. 'So it seems.'

As the ghouls bounded forwards, Gotrek bellowed with rage behind them, and Felix and Kat glanced around. While they had been watching Castle Reikguard fall, Krell had got the upper hand on the Slayer, and was bashing him back towards the battlements in a storm of strikes.

Snorri growled in his throat as he watched Gotrek stumble and weave, and his hands clenched his hammer convulsively.

'Behind you, Snorri,' said Felix. 'Turn around!'

Snorri whipped around, still growling, but his eyes went wide as he saw the swiftly oncoming ghouls.

'Snorri's!' he roared.

Felix and Kat charged in behind the old Slayer as he slammed into the leaping fiends, and for a brief moment, they made a good account of themselves. Kat's hatchets severed fingers and shattered kneecaps, while Felix's sword lopped heads and severed arms, and the heavy head of Snorri's hammer was everywhere at once, cracking skulls, breaking legs and crushing chests in a whistling blur, but there were just too many facing them, and the weight of the zombies lumbering ever forwards at the back of the ghouls drove them back, foot by grudging foot, until they found themselves fighting shoulder to shoulder with Gotrek as Krell pressed him from the other side.

Felix laughed bitterly as their enemies closed in around them. When Gotrek had freed him from his oath to witness his doom, and told him that all he had to do was get Snorri to Karak Kadrin and his vow would be fulfilled, Felix had thought he was getting off easy. He'd had wild dreams of freedom, of future, of a life of peace at Kat's side. Well, those dreams were dead now. Indeed, all of them would lose what they most wanted here. Snorri would die without memory or peace, Kat would die far from the forests that she loved, Felix would die without having had a chance at a normal life and, with his death, Gotrek's saga would never be written. The Slayer would die unheralded and forgotten.

Felix saw Gotrek glance back at Snorri as they crowded together. The Slayer didn't look good, and he sounded worse. He was cut in a score of places, his one eye was nearly swollen shut and his breathing sounded like two bricks being rubbed together. Krell aimed a cut at his head, and he blocked it like he was being held up by a drunken puppet master.

A roar turned Felix back around. A huge beast-corpse was crashing through the crowd of ghouls for Snorri, swinging a club the size of a man. The old Slayer easily ducked the swipe and swung up sharp with his warhammer, burying the head deep within its prodigious gut, but though he killed it, the beast felled him too, for with a gush of gelatinous black entrails, it toppled forwards, smashing Snorri to the parapet as the ghouls shrilled and surged around him.

Kat and Felix hacked desperately to keep them back, but without Snorri's steadfast hammer, the fiends swiftly drove them back. Felix took a cut on the arm, and Kat kicked to shake grasping claws from her leg as more ghouls clambered towards them over the dead beast. But then it shook, staggering the ghouls, and flopped to the side.

Snorri roared up from beneath it, covered in guts and slime and swinging his hammer – and went down again immediately, his peg leg snapped off at the stump. The ghouls pounced as he fell, piling on and weighing down his arms so that he couldn't swing his hammer as more clawed for his neck and eyes.

Felix and Kat cried out and fought forwards to protect the fallen Slayer, but Felix knew they wouldn't last long. Already one had Kat by the hair, and another was throwing itself on Felix's sword so the others could drag him down.

Then something red and bloody and blowing like a blast furnace shoved past them and smashed back the clutching horde. It was Gotrek, breath ragged and blazing rune axe slicing through ghouls in every direction.

The ghouls fell back, shrieking, and Gotrek hauled Snorri up to his one leg. The old Slayer grinned through a crimson river that was pouring from his scalp as Felix and Kat fell in beside them and Krell roared in from the left.

'Well met, Gotrek Gurnisson,' said Snorri, spitting blood. 'Snorri thinks we have found our dooms at last, eh?'

'No,' gasped Gotrek, levering himself up onto the battlements and pulling Snorri after him. 'We... have not.'

And with that, he shoved Snorri off the wall.

Felix and Kat stared as the old Slayer dropped out of sight towards the river, flailing and howling in surprise.

'Gotrek!' cried Felix. 'You–'

Gotrek ducked Krell's axe, and pulled Felix up too.

'After... him... manling,' he wheezed, pushing Felix towards the drop. 'Little one... too.'

Krell's axe swept again towards Gotrek's head, trailing its black cloud of grit. Gotrek blocked with the rune axe, but the blow was so powerful it drove the haft of it back into the Slayer's cheek and smashed him into Felix.

For one brief, sickening moment, the two of them tottered on the very edge of the battlements, scrabbling at the stones, then gravity won out, and they too plunged from the wall.

Felix gaped as the scene on the parapet receded and the wall shot up beside him. Kat appeared on the battlement, screaming his name and bracing to jump, but Krell swung his axe at her and she fell back out of sight.

'Kat!' Felix screamed.

The river hit him in the back like a giant's club and he plunged into its depths, the cold waves closing over him and blocking out everything that meant anything to him in the whole world.

TWENTY-ONE

After an eternity of sinking blackness, Felix's feet touched bottom and he kicked up as hard as he could, fighting the weight of his chainmail and the rushing water and the ringing numbness of his body. He broke the waves for just a second and caught a ragged breath, then went down again, but this time he touched bottom almost instantly, though he was dragged along it by the current, and couldn't stand.

He kicked up again, flailing and straining to find the top of the castle walls against the night sky. Was Kat alive? Had Krell killed her? Had she jumped? He couldn't see anything! Already he was far down the river, and the castle was receding fast.

'Kat!' he shouted. 'Kat! Jump!'

Nothing.

'Kat!'

His chainmail pulled him down again, and the current dragged him on. He sheathed Karaghul and floundered for the bank, but just as he got his feet under him, he saw moving figures on it, lurching and turning towards his splashes. The fields were still crawling with zombies.

He sank back and looked around, searching the moon-rimmed waves.

'Gotrek? Are you there?' he whispered. 'We have to go back! Kat is still in the castle!'

There was no response. Where was the Slayer? Had he already gone back?

'Gotrek?'

A pale shape bobbed near him. He blinked water from his eyes and saw it was the Slayer's broad, muscled back, blood welling from a score of wounds. He was face down in the river, unmoving.

'Gotrek!'

Felix splashed to him and tried to lift his head out of the water, but they were still being dragged sideways by the current and he couldn't get leverage. He cursed and tried again, catching Gotrek's heavy wrist and pushing for the shore. Something sharp bumped his knee as he kicked, and he felt under the water. It was Gotrek's axe. The Slayer still clutched it in an iron grip.

'Is that you, young Felix?' came a voice from nearby.

'Snorri!' Felix cried, staring around. 'Snorri, come here!'

A dark shape with nails sticking from its head sloshed up out of the waves beside him.

'Snorri thinks Gotrek Gurnisson shouldn't have pushed him like that,' said Snorri. 'That was a good fight.'

'Snorri, help me. Gotrek is drowning.'

Snorri snorted. 'Gotrek Gurnisson can't drown. Snorri has seen him swim many times.'

Nonetheless, the old Slayer caught Gotrek's shoulders and rolled him over in the water so that he was face up. Gotrek's head hung to the side, and a trickle of water flowed from his mouth. Felix couldn't hear him breathing.

Felix's heart lurched at the sight, then he looked back towards the dark silhouette of the castle, dwindling further into the distance with every passing second. What did he do? He had to go back for Kat, but he couldn't leave Gotrek. Or could he? He could leave him with Snorri and head back alone, but how was he to storm the walls and fight Kemmler and Krell and the wights by himself? It was impossible. He'd be torn apart by the zombies before he even reached the castle. As shameful as it was to admit it, Felix needed the Slayer's help.

'Wake up, Gurnisson,' said Snorri. 'Snorri wants to go back and finish that fight.'

'Gotrek's hurt, Snorri,' said Felix. 'And you've lost your peg leg.'

'Oh,' said Snorri. 'Snorri forgot.'

'We'll go back as soon as Gotrek wakes up,' said Felix, staring towards the disappearing castle. 'We *have* to.'

A mile or so down the river, they came upon a small village, so dark Felix would not have noticed it but for the little dock sticking out into the river that he banged his head on. No light burned among the low cottages, nor did Felix hear any sounds of movement. He feared that they had not travelled beyond Kemmler's sphere of influence, and that the place might be populated with zombies, but the cold of the river had penetrated all the way to his heart now, and his teeth were chattering uncontrollably. He could wait no longer.

'H-h-here, Snorri,' he whispered. 'Help me pull him onto the beach.'
'Aye, young Felix,' said Snorri.

Together they dragged Gotrek out of the water onto a narrow strip of mud. This was not easy, as Snorri had to do the whole thing on his knees, but finally they managed it and rolled Gotrek on his side. More water spilled from his mouth, but Felix still could not tell if he was breathing. He put an ear to the Slayer's chest and heard it at last, a faint, thready whisper. There was a heartbeat too, but it was soft and uneven, like waves sluicing over a broken wall. Felix swallowed, hardly relieved.

He slapped the Slayer's cheek and whispered in his ear.

'Gotrek, wake up!'

There was no response. Snorri frowned, concerned.

'Let Snorri try,' he said, then slapped the Slayer so hard it sounded like a pistol shot.

Felix cringed and glanced around, afraid the noise might attract attention, then turned back to Snorri.

'I-I don't think that's going work, Snorri. Gotrek is... sick or-or, I don't know.' He shivered as the night wind nosed through his wet clothes, then looked towards the town. 'We have to get him someplace warm and dry. Can you...' He paused and looked at Snorri's stump. 'No, of course you can't. I'll go look for a cart.'

'Snorri doesn't need a cart,' said Snorri, and pushed unsteadily up onto his one leg, then tucked the head of his warhammer under his arm.

The old Slayer grabbed Gotrek's wrist, then pulled. Felix stood and helped and, with a lot of grunting and cursing, they got Gotrek onto his feet, then Snorri bent and put his shoulder against Gotrek's belt buckle and heaved him onto his shoulder.

Felix cursed as Snorri swayed alarmingly under Gotrek's weight, but then the old Slayer steadied, bracing with the hammer-crutch as Gotrek's head and arms hung limp down his back, dripping water. Felix noticed that, even though he appeared completely unconscious, Gotrek still had a death-grip on his rune axe, which dragged on the ground.

'Lead on, young Felix,' said Snorri, turning towards the village. 'Snorri hopes they have beer.'

Felix doubted it. There were lines and grooves on the muddy beach that showed where small boats had been, but they were gone now, and he had the feeling the people of the village would be gone too.

He drew Karaghul and they started forwards into the middle of the dark huddle of cottages, Felix as quiet as a thief, and Snorri as quiet as an ogre fist-fight, stumping and thudding and hitching and grunting with every step. If there was anything hiding there, it would certainly hear them coming, but perhaps it would be frightened away.

Felix couldn't see any damage to the village, nor any bodies on the ground, but at the same time, the place didn't look or sound occupied. In a normal village, he would have heard the clucking of hens in their roosts and the shifting of livestock in their pens. There would have been carts and barrows at the backs of the cottages, and the dull red of banked hearths showing through the shuttered windows. There was none of that here. The carts were gone, the windows were dark, and it was as quiet as a graveyard.

To the left a cottage door was hanging open, the interior as dark as a cave. The tiny tavern across the way, however, was boarded up tight, heavy planks nailed across the front door and all the windows.

Felix stopped just outside the open cottage, peering uneasily into the darkness until his eyes adjusted, then went in. It was empty. He beckoned to Snorri.

'Lay him by the hearth,' he said. 'I'll make a fire.'

Snorri hobbled in as Felix dried off his flint and steel and found some tinder.

'Snorri thinks Gurnisson has gained some weight,' said Snorri as he settled Gotrek to the dirt floor in front of the fireplace, then peeled his stiff fingers off his rune axe and leaned it beside the hearth.

After a few damp strikes, Felix finally knocked a spark from the flint and it kindled the tinder, then found a stack of chopped wood to one side of the hearth, and built it up around the tiny flame.

A few minutes later, once the fire was going nicely, he went and shut the door to hide the light, then looked around. The shack was a lot like the village as a whole – undamaged, unoccupied and stripped. The few cupboards along the walls were empty of plates and cups. The crude table was bare, and the bed stripped of linen and blankets. The people must have fled when Kemmler's hordes arrived. The question was, had the necromancer's unnatural blight spread this far? Was the food rotten and the water poisonous?

Felix crossed to a row of jars, his stomach suddenly howling. He tore off their lids, hoping for anything – flour, lard, honey. There were dried traces of something in the last one. He scraped at them with a finger, then stuck it in his mouth. Mustard, as crumbly as chalk.

Still, it tasted like mustard, with no mildew smell or sour reek of rot. In fact, to his starved tongue, it tasted better than grilled beef. Sigmar, he was hungry!

He turned to Snorri, who was wringing out his beard by the fire. 'Snorri, see if you can get into the tavern. Look for food and drink.'

Snorri grinned. 'That is the best idea you've had in a long time, young Felix.'

He gave his beard a final twist, then started out the front door as Felix went out the back. The garden was little more than a bare-earth dog run, but there was a tiny vegetable plot at the back and the wooden hatch of a cold cellar next to a chicken coop. Felix stumbled to the coop and threw open the door. Empty. He fumbled through the stinking straw at the bottom. Not even an egg. He pulled up the hatch of the cold cellar and looked in, then gave a glad cry – two small carrots and a head of cabbage that had seen better days.

He pulled them out and stuffed one of the carrots in his mouth immediately. It was dry and rubbery and covered in dirt, but still good – not rotted through like all the food in Castle Reikguard had been. He chewed it noisily as he crossed to the vegetable patch, and moaned as the juices ran down the back of his throat. In other times he would likely have thrown the thing aside as not fit for pig fodder, but these were not other times. This was the best carrot nature had ever grown!

The vegetable patch was a disappointment. It was barely spring, and nothing had sprouted yet. Still, the carrot and the cabbage were better than nothing, and the rest of the cottages would have cold cellars too.

He heard a splintering crash from the street and crouched, on guard, then realised it was only Snorri breaking into the tavern. He went back inside and sat down by the fire next to Gotrek, then began to stuff the cabbage leaves in his mouth, groaning with happiness. He eyed the other carrot lustfully, but put it aside. He couldn't be greedy. Snorri would be hungry too. And Gotrek as well.

'Gotrek,' he said, shaking the Slayer's shoulder. 'There's food.'

The Slayer didn't move. He lay sprawled where Snorri had laid him, eye closed. Felix stared at him uneasily, certain now that Gotrek's unconsciousness had no external cause. It hadn't been the fight, or the fall or the water. What was causing this had been in him for days – the poisoned black slivers from the axe of Krell.

The door of the cottage slammed open and Snorri limped in on his hammer-crutch, a keg on one shoulder and a mouldy sausage on a string dangling from his mouth. He spit it out, letting it fall to the dirt, and beamed.

'Beer, young Felix! Beer!'

Felix was more interested in the sausage, mouldy as it was, but he stood and helped Snorri lower the keg gently to the ground, then went and collected two of the empty jars from the side board.

Snorri knocked in the top of the keg with his hammer, then took one of the jars from Felix and plunged it in.

'Careful, Snorri,' said Felix as the old Slayer made to down the jar in one go. 'It might be spoiled like the stuff in the castle.'

Snorri paused, then took a cautious sip as Felix watched. A broad smile spread across his ugly face. 'No, young Felix,' he said. 'It's fine – for human beer at least.'

And with that, he tipped the jar back and drank it off, almost, it seemed, without swallowing. Felix dipped his own jar into the keg and filled it up. He inhaled as he brought it to his face, and the yeasty smell of the hops almost, brought tears to his eyes. He put it to his lips. Felix didn't know what Snorri was talking about. It was the best beer ever brewed, better by far than the best carrot ever grown.

He drank a few delicious swallows, then lowered the jar and let out a satisfied sigh. After starving for so long, he would be drunk in seconds from the beer, but he didn't care. It tasted too good.

A thought came to him and he looked at Gotrek. The Slayer had not been tempted from unconsciousness by a cabbage. Then again, who would be? But beer had been known to perform miracles of resuscitation upon dwarfs. Hadn't Felix seen Snorri sit up out of the depths of a concussion at the mere mention of the word?

Felix knelt beside Gotrek and raised the jar. Snorri saw what he was doing and joined him, holding up Gotrek's head as Felix tipped the jar and let a dribble of beer spill between his slack lips.

They waited.

Nothing.

Felix poured more beer into Gotrek's mouth. It spilled out again and sank into his beard.

Snorri's face, which until that moment had still worn the remnants of the smile the beer had placed upon it, fell with worry. 'Snorri has never seen Gotrek Gurnisson spit out beer before,' he said quietly. 'Snorri thinks something may be wrong.'

Felix nodded and sat down with a thump. 'Snorri isn't the only one.'

There had been times in Felix's life when he had thought that there was nothing that could make a man more miserable than fighting for his life. At other times he had felt that the moments before battle, when dread and anticipation filled a man's guts with cold fear, were the worst, and at still other times he had believed that nothing could make a man more miserable than regret, but now he knew that none of those miseries could even come close to the feeling of powerlessness that came when a man knew his friends were dying and in danger and there was nothing he could do about it.

With a stomach full of not very much sausage, but quite a lot of beer, he had managed at last to fall asleep near dawn, but it was not an easy sleep. It was full of dreams of running for Castle Reikguard to save Kat, but never getting there no matter how fast he ran, and other dreams of Gotrek getting up out of his sick bed, but not being Gotrek – not being alive at all – and turning on him with dead eye and axe glowing green. In some dreams, he reached Castle Reikguard at last, then ran through its halls, chambers and cellars, calling Kat's name, but never finding her. In other versions, he did find her, but she was shuffling with the other undead, pointing stiff, grey fingers at him and whispering, 'You did this. You left me behind.'

Sometimes he fled from her, ashamed. Other times, he ran to her, begging her forgiveness.

'I will forgive you,' she said in a hollow, faraway voice. 'But you must let me feed.'

In the depths of his guilt, Felix agreed, and offered her his arm, which she accepted, and began to gnaw on with needle-sharp teeth, and hot, foetid breath. The pain was excruciating, but it was only what he deserved.

'Wake up, young Felix,' said Snorri. 'Snorri thinks you're having a bad dream.'

Felix blinked slowly awake, and Kat's sad grey corpse-face was eclipsed by Snorri Nosebiter's ugly pink one. Grey daylight was streaming through the cracks in the shutters, and there was birdsong in the distance. He hadn't heard birds in… Sigmar, it felt like years.

'Thank you, Snorri,' he said.

He levered up onto his elbow, then hissed and nearly vomited as agony stabbed through his arm. The pain of Kat chewing on him had continued after the rest of the dream had faded, and he looked down. The bandage Tauber had wrapped around his wounds was now brown with dried blood and crusted with river mud, and the skin around it purple and bulging. He drew his dagger and cut off the gauze, then felt nauseous all over again. The deep gouges left by the bat's claws were like volcanic fissures that spewed a lava of stinking pus, and there was a network of black lines spreading under the inflamed skin around them. The volcano analogy was apt in another way too, for it felt as if his forearm had a molten core – as if his bones were white-hot – and were radiating heat like a stove.

Snorri clucked like a hen. 'Snorri thinks that might be infected.'

'Possibly,' said Felix. 'Yes.'

Felix turned to Gotrek, who lay unmoving beside him. The Slayer looked paler than Felix had ever seen him, and his lips had a faint bluish tinge.

'Is… is he…'

Snorri shook his head. 'No, young Felix. But he still won't drink any beer.'

Felix sat up, wincing and fighting dizziness as he moved his arm, then put his ear to the Slayer's chest again. The faint slushy sound of his heartbeat was still there, but even weaker than before, and he couldn't hear the Slayer's breathing at all.

Felix groaned and lay back. After his years of fighting and hard travel he could dress a wound well enough, even set a bone if he had to, but he had no idea how one fixed glassy slivers that crept through the heart and lungs. He was helpless to save Gotrek, just as he was helpless to save Kat. He doubted he could even save himself.

Still, he had to try. With a grunt he pushed himself unsteadily to his feet. 'Come, Snorri,' he said. 'We have to find food.'

But as he took a step towards the door, nausea and dizziness overcame him again and he found himself face-first on the floor, the world going black around him.

'Stay here, young Felix,' said Snorri out of the darkness. 'Snorri will find the food.'

After that, Felix was unable to follow the passage of time. He drifted restless and uneasy between consciousness and unconsciousness, between waking nightmares and nightmares that seemed reality.

He woke to find Snorri standing over him, waving something in his face. 'Look, young Felix. A turnip!'

He woke to sunlight stabbing him in the eyes and the worst thirst of his life. The jar of beer was a mile away. He spilled it when he reached it.

He woke to find his fever gone and Gotrek healed. Under cover of darkness, they and Snorri went back to the castle to rescue Kat, dodging zombies and killing ghouls before slipping across the dry moat and stealing a siege ladder. Felix led the Slayers over the walls and they found Kat bound for sacrifice in the defiled temple of Sigmar. Felix killed Kemmler while Gotrek and Snorri killed Krell, and they were all reunited until he woke again and found it was still day, and Snorri had brought him another carrot.

He woke to throbbing agony. The bruised lines in his forearm had spread to his neck and chest, and his pulse boomed in his ear like an orc war drum, shaking him with every beat. He was as hot as the jungles of Lustria, sweat beading on his brow and pouring down his neck, and yet, at the same time, as cold as he'd been that night he'd fallen through the ice in the Drakwald and nearly frozen to death. His teeth chattered like dice in a gambler's cup and he couldn't hold the jar of beer Snorri gave him, and had to let the old Slayer pour it into him with a patient hand.

He woke to his brother limping into the cottage with his gold-handled walking stick and *tsk*ing over him.

'Well, you've certainly made a mess of things this time,' he said, his chins wobbling with disapproval.

'Aye,' said his father, who lay beside him, his face torn with terrible scratch and bite marks. 'Just the sort of end I expected you to come to, you ne'er-do-well.'

Ulrika knelt down beside him and took his arm in her cool white hands. 'Let me kiss you, beloved,' she said, 'and we can live together forever, with no pain, and no partings.'

Felix looked up at her and thought she was the most beautiful woman he had ever seen. He wanted to open his mouth to say yes, but then Kat was at his other side, also dead, but not nearly as well preserved.

'Will you live on after I've died, Felix?' she asked. 'Weren't we to die together?'

Then, across the room, Gotrek got up and slung his axe over his shoulder. 'Come on, manling,' he said, glaring back at him. 'I've got a doom to find.'

Felix stared after the Slayer as he stumped out the door. He tried to rise. He tried to speak – tried to tell Ulrika and Kat that he couldn't go with them. He still had his vow to Gotrek to see to its finish – but he couldn't speak, couldn't move, couldn't even turn his head.

TWENTY-TWO

'Another nightmare, young Felix,' said Snorri, shaking his shoulder.

Felix peered up at him, having difficulty separating Snorri from the dream. He looked more unreal than the phantoms that had been surrounding him. He was at once too close and far away – his ugly face was glaring inches from his own, but the hand that touched his shoulder was at the end of a long arm that stretched from across the room. Felix looked away, unsettled, but got no relief elsewhere. The walls of the cottage were breathing in and out, and with each inhalation closing in a little closer – and it was blistering hot.

'Snorri,' he gasped. 'What are you playing at? Put out the fire. You're roasting us alive!'

'There is no fire, young Felix,' said Snorri. 'Snorri hasn't built it up yet.'

Felix looked past him to the fireplace and saw it was true. The fire was down to ashy embers, and pink light was seeping through the shutters. It was morning – though which morning, Felix had no idea.

He rubbed his greasy brow with the back of his hand. 'I... How is Gotrek? Has he...?'

'Still asleep, young Felix,' said Snorri. 'Snorri doesn't know if he'll wake up again.'

Felix shivered, then tried to sit up. His head swam and his arms wouldn't support him. The wounded one, which had hurt him so much the day before, now felt numb and distant, but at the same time as fat and full as an overstuffed sausage. His fingers were black, and so thick he couldn't close them.

Snorri gently helped him to his feet and held him there. 'Do you need to go to the privy, young Felix?'

Felix shook his head. 'Take me to Gotrek.'

The old Slayer dutifully put Felix's arm over his broad shoulders and crutched him over to where Gotrek lay by the hearth. Felix lowered himself unsteadily to the ground beside him, then once again put his ear to the Slayer's chest.

At first he could hear nothing but his own pulse pounding in his ear, but once he had listened past that, his overheated heart grew cold, for it seemed he could hear nothing at all. He pressed harder with his ear, hoping for anything, no matter how faint.

His heart flared with hope as he heard something at last, very soft, and hardly a beat at all, but something. He listened again to be sure. Yes, it was there, a low continuous vibration, like the roll of a snare drum, or surf, or distant thunder, or–

'Snorri thinks he hears horses coming,' said Snorri.

Felix looked up at him, marvelling. He could barely hear Gotrek's heart with his ear pressed to his chest, and Snorri could hear it standing a pace away. Truly, the senses of the dwarfs were... Then he heard it too – the same sound he had heard while listening for Gotrek's heart – the rumble of many horses on the move, but coming muffled through the walls of the cottage.

He looked at Gotrek again. What did this mean? Had he heard nothing? Was Gotrek dead? Or had the sound masked Gotrek's pulse? And how could he listen again if the horses were going to keep getting louder?

Wait.

Wait a moment.

Horses?

Getting louder?

'Snorri!' he said. 'Help me up!'

'All right, young Felix.'

The old Slayer reached down and set him on his feet with one hand, then draped his arm again around his shoulders.

'Out,' said Felix. 'Out to the road.'

Snorri hitched forwards on his hammer crutch and hobbled Felix forwards. Slow and unsteady, they stumbled out the door to the muddy road which ran through the town. Felix looked west, in the direction the sound was coming from. The road turned through a stand of trees beyond the west end of the village, and he could see nothing, but the rumble was getting louder, and birds flew up from the wood.

'Take cover,' said Felix, pointing to the side of the village's last house, 'until we see who it is.'

Snorri obligingly crutched him to the house and they watched from behind it as the source of the rumble finally appeared from behind the trees. First came ten pistoliers on swift horses, cantering out and surveying the village and surrounding land while woodsmen with longbows crept out of the trees to either side of the road, scouting for dangers in the brush. Then a great company of knights and magisters and warrior priests followed on colourfully barded horses, pacing majestically towards the village, banners flying and lances high.

The relief force had come at last!

'Come on, Snorri,' said Felix, urging the old Slayer forwards. 'We must go meet them. No time to spare.'

'All right, young Felix,' said Snorri. 'But it's only some humans.'

They lurched out from behind the house and started weaving towards the army like a pair of drunks heading home from the tavern. Felix waved and the pistoliers spotted him and galloped forwards, drawing their weapons.

'Who in Sigmar's name are you?' asked a young fellow with a dashing moustache as they thundered up and surrounded them, guns at the ready. 'Do you live?' The boy couldn't have been more than eighteen.

Felix threw up a hand in a limp approximation of a salute. 'Felix Jaeger and Snorri Nosebiter,' he slurred. 'The last defenders of Castle Reikguard.'

The pistoliers looked at each other, and the first one spoke again. 'Defenders?' he said. 'What do you mean, peasant? Y'don't seem to be defending a damned thing.'

'I mean,' said Felix, with elaborate precision, 'you have come too late, pistolier. Castle Reikguard has fallen.'

The pistoliers cried disbelief at this, and the dashing boy glared at him.

'What nonsense is this?' he snarled. 'Castle Reikguard has never fallen!'

Felix opened his mouth to argue with him, but realised it was pointless. 'If you would take me to your leader, I will tell him everything that has befallen.'

The pistolier scoffed. 'Take you, you sick old beggar? To see Horst von Uhland? How do we know you're not some pawn of Chaos, sent to give him the pox?'

Snorri gripped his warhammer at this, and raised it into a fighting position while balancing on one leg. 'Snorri Nosebiter is no pawn of Chaos!' he growled as Felix struggled to stay upright. 'And he'll fight any foolish human who says so!'

The pistoliers edged their horses back and thumbed back the hammers of their pistols, but before things could get out of hand, more hoof beats sounded, and Felix saw another contingent of riders trotting out from the main force.

'Easy, gentlemen,' called a white-bearded knight in the surcoat of the Reiksguard. 'Questions first. Shooting later.'

'My lord general,' said the young pistolier. "Ware, please! They may be the undead. Or cultists. Or–'

The general barked a laugh. 'A Trollslayer and a cultist? You need to see more of the world, lad.'

He pulled up in front of Felix and Snorri as his retinue of knights and companions reined in behind him.

'Now then,' he said, looking down at Felix and Snorri with a bright-eyed glare. 'Who are you? And where have you come from? Be quick.'

The eager pistolier saluted. 'They say they are the last defenders of Castle Reikguard, my lord. They say the castle has fallen.'

The general scowled at him. 'Why don't you let them tell–'

'Felix Jaeger!' cried a voice from behind him. 'And Snorri Nosebiter! As I live and breathe!'

Felix frowned and looked past the general. One of his companions, a tall man in a hooded beige travelling cloak, was getting down from his horse and hurrying forwards.

The general and the others looked around at him, surprised.

'You know them, magister?'

The man pulled back his hood, revealing a silver mane of hair and a lined, worried face. 'I do, general,' he said. 'Though I barely recognised them. Felix, Snorri, you look nine-tenths dead.'

It was Max Schreiber.

Felix's heart surged. He almost wept. He let go of Snorri's shoulder and stumbled forwards, reaching out to him.

'Max!' he said. 'Gotrek. Kat. I...' The world started to spin and dim. His legs wobbled. 'I think the Slayer has met his doom at–'

'Felix!'

The ground raced up and smacked Felix in the face. Far away, people were shouting, but he didn't care. The darkness was closing in around him again. It was warm and soft and lovely.

'He's coming around,' said someone.

'Thank you, sister,' said someone else. 'Now return to the others.'

Felix didn't want to open his eyes. The darkness had been too comforting, and he knew that leaving it would hurt, but already it was fading of its own accord, and he couldn't follow it. It was leaving him behind.

He lifted his eyelids and looked around, and for a moment was confused. He knew the roof beams above him from earlier wakings. He was back in the cottage. Had the coming of the relief force only been another dream? Had Max been a dream?

A balding, white-bearded man hove into his field of vision and looked down at him, his eyes hard, then Max stepped in to his right, followed by an anxious, dark-haired young man in armour, and... and... Felix blinked, thinking he was still hallucinating. Two men stood at Max's side, one in the black robes of a priest of Morr, the other in the midnight-violet robes of a wizard of the Amethyst College, but they both had the same long, sad face and shaved skulls. They were identical.

'Herr Jaeger,' said the white-bearded man, who Felix now recognised as the Reiksguard general without his helmet – von Uhland, the pistolier had called him. 'Are you well enough to talk? We have little time.'

Felix pulled his eyes from the unsettling twins and did a mental check of how he felt. Disorientated, certainly. In pain, oh yes, quite a bit, but not so much as before. And the freezing, fevered sweating had stopped, so, relatively speaking, not so bad.

'Yes,' he said.

'Good,' said the general, and sat, then motioned for the others to do the same.

Felix looked around as they did. He was lying in a military cot, his arm neatly bandaged and his fingers nearly returned to their normal size and colour. In the background, a Sister of Shallya was moving about, and through the door he could see that the village was teeming with soldiers. Gotrek's axe was propped near the hearth where Snorri had set it, but the Slayer wasn't there. Felix's heart thudded with sudden panic.

'We'll try to be as brief as possible,' said the general, as a scribe at his shoulder began to make notes in a big book. 'But we must ask you some–'

'Where is the Slayer?' asked Felix. 'Gotrek. Is he–'

Max leaned in, cutting him off. 'He's with the surgeons, Felix. They're doing everything they can.'

'No,' said Felix, heart thudding. 'You don't know. *They* don't know. The axe. Krell's axe. It struck him. It left poisoned slivers in the wound. They're killing him!'

The sombre twins raised their heads, and Max's eyes widened.

'Poisoned slivers?' he asked.

Felix nodded. 'The Slayer said they burrow to the heart. I fear they have already reached it.'

Max paled and turned to the general. 'My lord, if you would excuse me.'

'Go,' he said. 'We will make record of our conversation here.'

Max stood and hurried from the cottage. Felix wanted to get up and go with him. He should be with Gotrek, not here, talking.

General von Uhland turned back to him. 'He will be well taken care of, Herr Jaeger. I promise you. Now, we had the story from your friend with the – the nails in his head, but it was a bit confused. We'd like you to–'

'My father and mother,' broke in the dark-haired young man, leaning forwards with anxious eyes. 'Do they still live?'

Felix looked at him, bewildered. 'I– who are your father and mother?'

'This is Master Dominic Reiklander,' said the general. 'Son of the graf and grafin.'

Felix's face fell as he remembered the last time he saw them, when the undead graf had torn his wife's throat out. The boy read his expression and looked away before he could speak.

'I'm sorry. They...' Felix didn't want to go into details. 'They didn't survive.'

Dominic nodded, then stood abruptly and crossed to the hearth to stare into the fire.

Von Uhland looked at him, then turned back. 'This Krell you mentioned. He is the leader of the undead?'

Felix shook his head. 'Krell is a lieutenant. The necromancer who raised the horde is named Kemmler. I know little about him, but he is capable of raising thousands of undead, and blighting food and drink, and–'

'I know of him,' said the general, grim. 'Though I had heard he was dead, killed by Duke Tancred of Quenelles in Bretonnia.' He cursed, then looked back at Felix. 'And his plans? The message General Nordling sent said the fiend meant to march on Altdorf. Do you know his numbers?'

'I would guess more than eight thousand,' said Felix. 'Perhaps as many as ten. Men and beastmen alike, as well as picked troops of ancient warriors, giant bats, ghouls, spirits. And...' He looked apprehensively at Dominic's back. 'And, I fear he has some further plans for the graf and grafin.'

The young lord turned, dark eyes flashing. 'What? What do you say?'

Felix swallowed, wishing he didn't have to go on. 'He raised them, my lord, but I fear that was only the beginning...'

The young lord looked stricken, and had to sit down, but then looked up and fixed Felix with a hard eye. 'Tell me.'

Felix shrugged. 'I wish I knew more to tell. He raised them and took them away, saying they had "work to do". What that could have been, I don't know. But it kept him from the final battle.'

Dominic buried his head in his hands. 'He will pay,' he said. 'No matter what he's done. Their deaths and desecration cannot go unavenged.'

The sad-eyed priest of Morr cleared his throat. 'This does not bode well,' he said.

Von Uhland looked at him. 'You know what he intends to do, Father Marwalt?'

The priest shook his head, but it was his brother who answered.

'Not precisely,' said the Amethyst magister. 'But if he is using the graf and grafin in his ritual, it may mean that he is preparing something that will affect all of the Reikland.'

Von Uhland frowned. 'I don't understand, Magister Marhalt,' he said. 'How could their corpses help him?'

'In magic, there is power in name and place,' intoned Father Marwalt. 'Castle Reikguard is the ancient seat of the Reikland princes, the place from which the province was once ruled, and still the sometime home of the ruler of us all, Karl Franz.'

'And the graf and grafin are the rulers of Castle Reikguard,' continued

Magister Marhalt. 'Therefore, symbolically at least, the rulers of the Reikland.'

'A ritual performed in Castle Reikguard, upon the rulers of Castle Reikguard, could be used to affect all the lands that make up its domain,' finished Father Marwalt.

Von Uhland stared at them. 'What could he do?' he asked. 'What would this ritual be? Could he raise all the dead from here to Altdorf?'

The priest and the magister shrugged their narrow shoulders simultaneously. 'Who can know?' they said in unison. 'It might be anything.'

'And how long?' asked von Uhland, licking his lips. 'How long would such a spell take?'

The twins shrugged again.

'A ritual that powerful might take days or weeks,' said Magister Marhalt.

'And it has already been days,' said Father Marwalt.

Von Uhland paled and stood. 'No more time can be lost,' he said, turning to the door. 'I will survey the position, and then we will move.'

'I will come with you,' said Dominic, stepping to him. 'I know the castle as I know my hands, and the secret ways in and out as well.'

Felix thought of Kat, and struggled to push up from the bed. 'I'll come too,' he said. 'I must return to–'

Von Uhland put a hand on his shoulder and pressed him back. 'Rest, Herr Jaeger. The Reiksguard has the situation in hand. But thank you for your insight and information.'

'But…' said Felix.

The general was already walking out the door with Dominic Reiklander on his heels. Felix glared after them. Who was Uhland to tell him to rest? He wasn't going to idle in bed when Kat was in danger. He threw off the covers and pushed himself to a sitting position, then clutched the edges of the cot while the room spun around him.

Felix took deep breaths until the sensation passed. He wanted desperately to lie down again, but he wouldn't. He had to go with von Uhland and Dominic. He shifted his legs over the side of the cot and wobbled to his feet, then paused for the spinning to fade again, and started for the door.

Max appeared in it before he reached it. 'Felix,' he said, his face grave. 'Gotrek is dying. Come with me.'

TWENTY-THREE

Max led Felix through the red-bordered door of the sick tent, then stood aside. The Slayer lay on a cot against the back wall, his one eye closed, and his arms, legs and torso covered in bruises, bandages and stitches. Snorri stood beside him, a new peg on his stump, and stared down at him silently. Off to one side the Sister of Shallya was helping a surgeon pack up his scalpels, needles and thread.

'We did all we could, Felix,' said Max. 'The surgeon cleaned and patched every wound he could find, while the abbess prayed to Shallya to heal the damage done to Gotrek's internal organs. I performed every spell of cleansing and healing I know, but... but there has been no change. It seems we were too late.'

Felix nodded dully, then crossed to the cot and stood beside Snorri. Gotrek lay as if asleep, his brows furrowed, but his chest did not seem to rise and fall. He made no movement at all.

'He still lives,' said Max, 'but not for long. It is only a matter of time.'

Felix knelt beside the cot and leaned in. 'Gotrek,' he said. 'Please. Don't let your doom be a few specks of glass. Krell lives. Go back and finish him. Get your revenge and help me rescue Kat.'

There was no change in the Slayer's face. Felix hadn't really expected one, but it still hurt when it didn't come. He hung his head, then stood again, his fists balling at his sides.

'He should have his axe,' he blurted. 'He shouldn't die without his axe.'

'Snorri will get it,' said Snorri heavily, then turned and walked out of the tent.

Max coughed from the door. 'If there is anything you need, Felix,' he said.

Felix shook his head. 'Just– just some time.'

Max nodded and motioned to the surgeon and abbess, then stepped to the door as they filed out. 'I'll see you're not disturbed.'

Rage boiled in Felix's chest as he looked down at the Slayer. This was not how it was supposed to end. The Slayer was not supposed to die in bed. He was not supposed to go quietly. He was supposed to go down fighting, bleeding from a hundred cuts and torn to pieces by the death throes of the monstrous enemy he had just slain. This was pathetic, the worst end for Gotrek's saga that he could imagine. He would never have written it like this. Never!

Twenty years and more of travelling with the Slayer, fighting beside him, weathering his moods and sharing his triumphs – it had all seemed like it was building to something. He had felt that the epic would have a finish worthy of its chapters. Curse Krell! Curse him for a cheat and poisoning coward! And curse Rodi too, for robbing Gotrek of a true Slayer's death while he was still well enough to take it.

Felix turned away, snarling. Everything was wrong now. Everything! The Slayer had died poorly, and though, because of that, Felix was now free of his vow to him, what did that freedom hold? Nothing. It was meant to have been a new beginning for him – a new life with Kat, where they would go where they liked and do what they wanted, alone together at last, but it had been at least two days since he and Snorri and Gotrek had fallen from the walls of Castle Reikguard. There was no way Kat could still be alive after all that time. He would of course go with General von Uhland and find out for himself, but he already knew the answer. She was dead, and with her death, his dream of a better future died as well.

Snorri limped back into the tent and held out Gotrek's rune axe. 'Here it is, young Felix,' he said.

Felix stepped to him and took the weapon, and almost dropped it. It was unsettlingly heavy. With a grunt, he heaved it up and crossed to Gotrek's cot, then laid it on the Slayer's bearded chest and crossed his heavy hands over it.

'There, Gotrek,' he said, standing. 'You'll need that in Grimnir's halls.'

Snorri stood on the opposite side of the cot and bowed his head. 'May Grimnir welcome you, Gotrek son of Gurni,' he said.

This at least was right, thought Felix – that he and Snorri were there, and that the right things had been said. He decided he would stay and stand vigil over Gotrek until the sisters told him he was dead. He had vowed to the Slayer that he would witness his end, and if this sad, silent passing was it, then he would not fail that vow. If only he didn't feel like he was going to fall over at any second.

Felix looked around and saw a camp chair off to one side. He dragged it to the cot and sat. He would sit vigil then. It would be the same.

* * *

Felix snapped awake, panic seizing him. How long had he been asleep? He looked to the door. Red twilight filtered into the tent. No! It hadn't been noon when he'd sat down in the chair. How had this happened? How had he let himself fall asleep?

He turned to Gotrek's cot.

It was empty.

The panic in Felix's chest turned to cold dread, then crushing guilt. Gotrek had died. Snorri had taken him away to be buried, and Felix had missed it. He had not witnessed the Slayer's end. He had not been by his side in his final moments. He had failed in the duty that he had sworn to keep for twenty years. Now anger surged up to join the guilt. Damn Snorri! Why hadn't he woken him? Why hadn't he warned him when the end was drawing near?

Felix struggled up out of the chair and nearly fell on his face. He was much recovered from his wounds, and his arm no longer throbbed, but the dizziness still lingered, and he was so hungry he could barely stand.

He recovered and pushed unsteadily into a maze of tents. In the short time they had been here, the relief force had transformed the little village into a bustling camp, and one that was preparing for war. Knights and squires and grooms hurried by, carrying armour and saddles, and the harsh cries of sergeants echoed from every direction.

Felix took a right, heading – he hoped – for the main road through the village. He had to find Max or Snorri or the abbess of Shallya and ask them what had happened – and they would get a piece of his mind for letting him sleep through the death of his dearest friend.

After another turning, he found the road, and looked both ways. A large tent with the banner of the Reiksguard knights flapping above it sat beyond the shack he and Snorri had sheltered in. That would be the command tent. He started towards it, but before he had taken more than five steps, an intoxicating smell nearly stopped him in his tracks. Someone was roasting pork, and there was gravy too.

He turned towards the delicious scent just in time to hear a familiar voice say, 'Snorri would like more beer, please.'

Felix's heart lurched and he stumbled forwards. The old Slayer sounded very calm. Did he not know what had happened to Gotrek? Or had he forgotten already? Sigmar, that would be a terrible thing! The mess tent was just ahead on the left. Felix ducked through the canvas flaps, scanning for the old Slayer.

'Snorri,' he said. 'There you are. I–'

He cut off as the scene in the tent came into focus. Snorri sat at a long mess table in the middle of the room, with a feast of food before him and a huge mug of beer in his fist, and across from him, head down and fork shovelling food into his mouth like some sort of machine, was Gotrek.

'Hello, young Felix,' said Snorri, waving a well-stripped bone.

Gotrek raised his single eye to Felix, scowling. 'Finally awake, manling?' he asked. 'Now's not the time to sleep. There's work to be done.'

'Gotrek!' said Felix, but then a lump rose up in his throat and he found he couldn't say anything else, which was just as well, really. It would have only been something sentimental, and Gotrek would have thought him weak.

'Aye?' said the Slayer. 'What?'

He was not quite his old self. He looked as strong as ever, and he ate with his usual relish, but his movements were somewhat stiff, and he was uncharacteristically pale, while his face had lines and scars upon it that hadn't been there before they'd come to Castle Reikguard. But how was he alive at all? Max had said all their prayers and spells and surgery hadn't worked. Had they only taken some time to take effect? Had the Slayer recovered by sheer force of will? He thought of asking, but Gotrek would likely have snorted at that too.

'Nothing,' Felix said at last, forcing down the lump. 'It… it's good to see you, that's all.'

'Herr Jaeger,' called someone. 'Come here. Eat while we talk. We must be moving soon.'

Felix turned and saw General von Uhland. Indeed, now that he had got over finding Gotrek alive he saw that there was quite a gathering in the tent. General von Uhland and Lord Dominic Reiklander, still dressed for scouting, sat with a small circle of officers, while Max Schreiber, Father Marwalt and his twin, Magister Marhalt, sat beside them.

Felix sat and stabbed a few slices of ham from the platter, then slathered a slice of bread with butter. So this was how generals ate, he thought. No wonder they all got fat, no matter how much campaigning they did. Well, he was all for it now, and stuffed his mouth full with both hands. Sigmar, it was good! The juice of the ham ran down his throat like the elixir of life. He never wanted to stop eating.

'We have a challenge ahead of us, Herr Jaeger,' said General von Uhland as he ate. 'Kemmler's undead are dismantling Castle Reikguard. Already all of the buildings of the lower courtyard have been put to the torch, and the exterior walls have lost most of their crenellations.' He gave a grim smile. 'Were we to wait long enough, he would tear down the walls entirely, and we could ride in and attack, but we cannot wait. We cannot allow Castle Reikguard to become indefensible. We must win it back as whole as we can.'

'But how are we to get in without smashing down the gates or the walls?' asked one of the general's officers. 'Can we climb in?'

'It would be a slaughter,' said another man. 'The dead would tear us apart as we topped the walls.'

'With luck, it won't come to that,' said von Uhland. He nodded to Dominic. 'Lord Reiklander knows of a secret way into the castle that comes out in Karl Franz's apartments. A picked squad of men–'

'Kemmler knows that route,' said Felix. 'He used it. It will be guarded.'

Dominic's head came up. 'How? How did he learn of it? Who betrayed the secret?'

Felix hesitated. He was fairly certain it had been Dominic's mother who had told Kemmler the way in – thinking she was inviting in the kindly old man who would cure her husband. 'I – I don't know,' he said.

'It doesn't much matter how he knows,' said von Uhland. 'The question is, how well will it be guarded?'

Gotrek raised his head from his shovelling and swallowed noisily. 'That doesn't matter either,' he said. 'Nothing will stop me from facing Krell again.'

'Same goes for Snorri,' said Snorri.

Gotrek shot the old Slayer an angry look, but Snorri didn't seem to notice.

'I was hoping you would say that, Slayer Gurnisson,' said von Uhland. 'Someone must get in and open the gates for us, someone who knows the castle and who has the ability to reach the lower gatehouse. Someone who is quite prepared to die.'

'A Slayer is always prepared to die,' said Gotrek.

'I will go too!' said Dominic.

The general pursed his lips. 'My lord Reiklander, I cannot of course forbid you, but with your father dead you are the last heir of Castle Reikguard. It would be wiser if you stayed with the main force, and fought in the storming.'

'No!' said Dominic, his jaw clenching. 'Reikguard is my castle. I will not have it handed to me by my uncle's honour guard. *I* will take it. *I* will lead the infiltration!'

The general looked like he wished to say more, but at last only nodded. 'As you wish, my lord.'

'I will come as well,' said Max. 'You will need someone to shield you from Kemmler's sorceries and his witch sight.'

'As will we,' said the magister and the priest of Morr in unison. 'We are well used to dealing with the undead.'

'And I,' said Felix. 'I'm in.'

Gotrek looked from him to Snorri and back, his eye hard. 'You have made a pledge to me, manling. Do you forsake it?'

Felix looked down, unable to meet his gaze. 'Kat is there, Gotrek. If she lives, I must save her. If she is dead, I must avenge her. I am willing to die for it. I'm sorry, but–'

'Forget it, manling,' Gotrek grunted. 'I won't stop you.' He turned his eye back to Snorri. 'But there is one who will not go.'

As General von Uhland and his captains rose and left the mess tent to make ready to march, Max crossed to Gotrek's table and sat down beside Felix.

'I am glad to see you recovered, Gotrek,' he said. 'It seems a miracle.'

Gotrek shrugged and kept eating. 'Dwarfs have strong constitutions.'

'Even so,' said Max, 'not three hours ago, I counted you among the dead, and now you seem fully recovered.'

'Not yet,' said Gotrek. 'It'll take a few more beers.'

Max laughed then paused and turned to Snorri, smiling quizzically. 'Yes, Snorri?'

Felix looked around to see that Snorri was staring at the magister across the table, his brow furrowed.

'You look familiar to Snorri,' said the old Slayer. 'Does Snorri know you?'

Max raised an eyebrow. 'Max Schreiber, Snorri. You don't remember?'

'Snorri remembers Max Schreiber,' said Snorri. 'Do you know him?'

Max looked at Gotrek and Felix, confused. Gotrek just grunted and looked away.

Felix swallowed, and leaned in to speak in Max's ear. 'Snorri has some... difficulties with his memory.'

Max looked across the table to Snorri, then nodded, grim. 'I wondered if this might happen,' he murmured. 'There were already signs of it when last I saw him in Praag, twenty years ago. I had hoped he might find his doom before–'

Gotrek got up abruptly and strode off, batting out of the mess tent and into the night.

Max looked after him, confused. 'Did I say something wrong?'

Felix coughed, then drew Max further down the table. 'Snorri has forgotten his shame,' Felix said softly. 'According to Gotrek, he will not be welcomed into Grimnir's halls until he remembers it, which means that–'

'That he cannot die until he regains his memory,' broke in Max, nodding sadly. 'He cannot act as a Slayer should.'

Snorri looked up at them, puzzled. Apparently they hadn't moved far enough to escape his keen dwarfen hearing.

'Snorri doesn't know what you're talking about,' said Snorri as Felix reddened. 'Snorri remembers his shame.'

Felix blinked, his heart thumping with sudden hope. 'You – you remember?' he asked. 'Truly?'

'Of course,' said Snorri. 'How could Snorri forget? It was...'

Felix and Max waited as the old Slayer's gaze turned inwards and he paused, his fork halfway to his mouth.

'It was...'

A look of panic began to spread over Snorri's cheerful, ugly face, and his eyes darted left and right, as if his memory might be hiding in some corner of the tent.

'It was...'

Snorri's hand slowly lowered, and he laid his forkful of meat back on his plate. Now his eyes stared off into some unimaginable distance. 'Snorri has forgotten his shame,' he said softly. 'This is bad.'

Felix winced. 'Snorri, you already knew this,' he said. 'You told us on the way to the Barren Hills. You're going to Karak Kadrin to pray for the return of your memory at the Shrine of Grimnir.'

Snorri stuffed the meat into his mouth and chewed angrily. 'Snorri remembers,' he said. 'He just forgot that he forgot for a moment.' But the pain on the old Slayer's face told Felix that he was lying. The loss was as fresh as the first time he had realised it.

Felix and Max exchanged another look, then Felix had to turn away. How horrible to have to experience over and over again the pain of learning that you had forgotten the most important thing in your life – the key to your only chance at redemption.

'Wizard, come here.'

Felix and Max turned. Gotrek was standing in the door of the tent, looking at Snorri, his face hard and closed. Max crossed to him, and Felix stood and went with him.

'What is it, Gotrek?' asked Max.

'Snorri Nosebiter will need a sleeping draught,' he said.

Max looked over his shoulder at Snorri. 'Now? But there is less than an hour before we start for the castle.'

'Now,' said Gotrek through gritted teeth. 'Snorri isn't going.'

Max frowned, then nodded. 'Ah. I see. Very well, Slayer. It will be done.'

Gotrek grunted and turned away again, walking off into the darkness. The pain behind his rage was almost harder to witness than Snorri's confusion. Gotrek was the most honest person Felix had ever met – not the kindest by any means, but he never lied or engaged in trickery – so to be forced to go behind Snorri's back and drug him so that he would stay behind and not seek his doom was obviously killing him – even though it meant saving his old friend's eternity.

TWENTY-FOUR

Max brought Snorri a huge stein of beer as he was having his third helping of sausages, and by the time von Uhland's army moved out for Castle Reikguard an hour later, he was snoring noisily, his head down on the table and his hand still clasped around the stein.

Felix didn't dare meet Gotrek's eye as they left the old Slayer behind and followed Max, Father Marwalt, Magister Marhalt, Dominic Reiklander and six picked Reiksguard knights out of the camp. Gotrek was as tensed as a bear trap, and Felix didn't care to get his leg bitten off. He hoped the others were smart enough to sense his mood as well, or there would likely be violence before they reached the castle.

While von Uhland's main force marched off due east along the main road, Lord Dominic led the infiltrators by the light of a slotted lantern through the trees to the woods north of the fields that surrounded Castle Reikguard, where he said the entrance to the secret tunnel was hidden. Felix grew wary as they got close, for these had been the woods from which Kemmler's horde had poured. The bats had risen from this wood, and the siege towers had been built at its edge. But now, it seemed, they were deserted. He neither heard nor saw any evidence of the undead, nor of any other being. No birds sang in the branches. No rabbit or fox or badger rattled through the undergrowth, and with the winter branches as yet unbudded, it was as if they moved through a dead world – as if they might be the last men alive in the Empire.

As he trudged along at the back of the line with Gotrek, Felix kept finding himself staring at the twin brothers, Father Marwalt and Magister

Marhalt, who walked side by side in the centre of the line, their heads together as if having a private conversation, but without speaking a word. Finally, his curiosity got the better of him, and he edged up to Max, who was just ahead of him in the line.

'Max,' he said softly, nodding ahead. 'The father and the magister, do... do they have some sort of connection?'

Max smiled slyly. 'Besides the obvious?' he asked. 'Yes, they can speak with only their minds. Indeed, that is partly how they came to choose their professions.'

He dropped back with Felix and continued, filling his pipe with tobacco. 'There was a third brother, Marnalt – another twin – and the three could speak to each other in this manner from birth, but then Marnalt was murdered by a necromancer, and used for foul experiments. After his death, however, the dead brother came to the living pair in their dreams, and they discovered that they could communicate together as they had when they were alive.' Max made a flame appear at the end of his finger and lit the pipe, then went on. 'Marnalt begged his brothers to find a way to free him from his ghostly unlife and let him pass on to Morr's realm, and so the brothers found their calling. Marwalt sought the answer to his brother's predicament in the teachings of Morr, while Marhalt entered the Amethyst College to seek a sorcerous solution, and in the process, each discovered that they had great natural abilities, which they have since used to fight necromancy in all its forms.'

'And did they free their brother?' asked Felix.

'Oh yes,' said Max. 'And exposed, ruined and destroyed the villain who had imprisoned his soul, and the souls of a thousand other children.' He smiled and started ahead again. 'They have been much in demand since then.'

A while later, with the moons both low in the sky, Lord Dominic slowed to a stop and pointed ahead.

'The passage is in front of us,' he said. 'About fifty paces.'

Max nodded. 'Go quietly then,' he said. 'There may be guards.'

Felix and Gotrek and the Reiksguard knights drew their weapons as Dominic closed his slotted lantern, and Max and the robed twins mumbled spells and invocations. When all were prepared, they crept forwards again, and after a minute came to a small clearing. There was a charcoal maker's hut to one side, long since burned to the ground and slowly returning to the forest. Creepers overgrew the exterior walls and dead weeds pushed up through the planks of the little porch.

'I sense no one,' said Max.

'Nor any necromantic construct,' said Father Marwalt.

'Nor spell of death,' said Magister Marhalt.

'On, then,' said Dominic.

They entered the clearing, and quickly saw that it had been recently visited. The brush was crushed flat, and there were footprints in the leaf mould, some made by bare feet, some by heavy boots, and some by feet made of only bones.

'The entrance is in the hut,' said Dominic. 'It was hidden, but...'

The Reiksguard captain took the lead and stuck his head in cautiously. After a quick look, he motioned the others on.

Felix followed Gotrek in and looked around. The interior was as dilapidated as the outside, roofless and weed-choked, but in one corner, the charred planks had been pulled up, revealing a square hole of masoned stone below, with steps descending into darkness. A stone hatch lay cracked into two heavy pieces beside it. Dominic grunted as he saw it.

'Softly, friends,' said Max. 'There may be guards in the tunnel.'

'I'll go first,' said Gotrek.

No one argued, and the Slayer walked towards the steps with Felix following after. Dominic Reiklander stepped in at his side and opened his lantern again, but the Reiksguard captain coughed.

'My lord,' he said, 'perhaps we should go ahead.'

Dominic shook his head, though his face was pale. 'No, Captain Hoetker,' he said. 'I will not be given my castle. I will take it.'

The captain looked unhappy, but could only incline his head respectfully and form up behind him. Max and the twins took up the rear, and the procession followed Gotrek into the dark.

The tunnel was two men wide, and went straight south for as far as Felix could see – which was admittedly not very far. Beyond the glow of the lantern it was pitch-dark, but it was clear that Gotrek could see well enough, for he stumped forwards unconcerned, his axe swinging at his side.

A few moments later, something glittered in the darkness ahead of them, and Felix could make out a big lump blocking the passage. Gotrek didn't slow, but everyone else did, going on guard and whispering to each other as they went on. In a few more steps, the glittering became a spill of gold coins, and the lump became a body, slumped against one wall, its eyes bulging and its hands to its chest.

'Von Geldrecht!' gasped Dominic.

It was indeed the steward, his every pocket bulging with gold, and with packs, pouches and sacks heavy-laden with the stuff strapped and slung all over his body.

'And your father's treasure,' said Felix. 'He tricked your mother into unlocking its hiding place.'

'The thief!' snarled the young lord. 'He always *was* too fond of gold.'

'Well,' said Max, squatting by the body and looking into its eyes, 'then you will be pleased to hear he died of it. The strain of carrying it was too much.'

Gotrek snorted. 'Pathetic.'

Dominic looked uncertainly at the spilled treasure, then motioned for them to continue. 'We will have to leave it for the moment. None of you will speak of this until it is recovered. Understood?'

There was a general murmur of assent, though some of the knights looked over their shoulders as they went on, and Felix frowned back at it, puzzled.

'Why wasn't he picked clean by Draeger and his men?' asked Felix. 'This was their escape route.'

'Then they didn't get this far,' said Gotrek.

And about a hundred paces further in, the Slayer's prediction proved true. The passage was clotted with dismembered bodies and broken weapons, and blood festooned the walls.

'Who were these?' asked Dominic as he picked his way fastidiously through the carnage.

'A militia captain and his men,' said Felix. 'They tried to escape after Kemmler and his wights came in.' He grimaced as he found Draeger amongst the bodies. He was in three parts, and partially eaten. 'It seems they met some stragglers.'

Dominic shivered, then continued on.

The passage ended at last against a wall of massive, dwarf-cut stone that Felix realised must be the foundations of Castle Reikguard's outer walls. There was a thick, iron-bound stone door set in the blocks, wide open.

'Hold,' said Father Marwalt and Magister Marhalt, as Gotrek approached it. 'There are wards here.'

The Slayer stopped and waited impatiently as Max and the twins muttered and probed the air before them with cautious hands, conferring all the while. Finally, Father Marwalt turned and spread his long-fingered hands. All the colour seemed to drain out of the air between his palms, and a cloud of grey mist billowed forth, rolling towards the dwarf and the men. It was as cold as the grave.

Gotrek growled and lifted his axe. 'Curse your sorcery, death priest,' he snarled. 'What is this?'

'What are you doing?' barked Dominic. 'Desist!'

Magister Marhalt held up a hand as his brother continued the spell. 'Fear not,' he said. 'It is an invocation called Morr's Mask. It is harmless, if unpleasant. It will hide our warmth and heartbeats and make us appear dead to the undead. It is oft used by paladins of Morr to get close to their prey.'

A clammy chill permeated Felix's clothes, leaving a sticky film of damp on his skin. His breath clouded, then grew too cold to make steam. The tips of his fingers were blue.

'You are making corpses of us,' said Dominic, revulsed.

'My lord, I promise you,' said Magister Marhalt, 'it is only a mask. With it, we should be able to walk past any undead, for they will believe us more of their own kind.'

Dominic and the knights whispered prayers and made signs of the gods as the cloud settled around them. Gotrek cursed in Khazalid and glared at the priest and the magister with one cold eye, but he stayed his axe.

A moment later Father Marwalt lowered his arms, then ducked his head apologetically. 'I'm sorry,' he said. 'I should have explained first. I am unused to fighting alongside those who are not of Morr's temple.' He motioned to the door. 'You may go in. The wards will not notice us now.'

Gotrek strode to the door and went in without pausing. The rest followed more hesitantly. Felix could feel nothing as they passed through except the cold mist of the priest's spell, which moved with them as they went. Inside, the passage turned right, following the castle wall until it ended at a narrow spiral stair. The stair was almost too thin for Gotrek to enter, and he had to turn sideways and hold his axe behind him in order to climb it. Felix couldn't imagine how the huge wights had done it – unless they had deformed themselves in some way.

The stairs went on and on, around and around and around until Felix thought he was in some horrible looping nightmare where he was forced to climb forever without getting anywhere. Finally, however, long after his knees were ready to give out and his mind ready to scream, the steps ended at a short corridor with one wall of stone, and one wall of wood. Rather, the corridor had once had a wooden wall, but it had been smashed through, as if by an explosion, and the panelling and struts and the remains of the secret door that had been set into it were now strewn across the carpeted floor of the ruins of a stately bedroom.

A canopied bed larger than the charcoal burner's shack through which they had entered rose against one wall, the initials KF picked out in gold on the headboard, and beautiful pieces of furniture and giant paintings of the Emperor's august ancestors lined the panelled walls, now all sadly smashed and slashed.

Gotrek brought his axe into guard and stepped through the splintered wall into the room, looking around, then motioned the others forwards. They ducked through behind him, swords and spells at the ready.

'Come,' said Dominic, shaking his head at the wreckage as he crossed towards the far door. 'The stairs are this way.'

They passed through an entryway lined with suits of armour, then through a shattered door to a landing that Felix recognised. It was there that Kemmler had appeared to them before taking the graf and grafin away in his cloud of shadows. Felix edged to the railing and looked down. Below was the door to Graf Reiklander's apartments, and the pile of bodies of the men who had died there – the young spearman, the handgunner, the artilleryman, Classen and Bosendorfer. At least, he thought with a glance at Dominic, the corpses of the graf and grafin were not among them.

Movement from further below drew his eye and he looked down

the well of the stairway. The ground floor was crawling with shuffling zombies, wandering aimlessly and bumping into each other, as well as a few ghouls, their heads twitching nervously this way and that as they hunched over dead bodies and sucked the marrow from their bones. Felix tried not to wonder if any of those bodies, or any of the zombies, was Kat. He must focus on the task at hand.

He turned away and prepared to follow Gotrek with the others, but the Slayer stopped and raised his axe. The rune upon its head was blazing as bright as Felix had ever seen it, and reflected red in Gotrek's single eye.

'The necromancer is here,' he growled.

'Yes,' said Magister Marhalt, his eyes half-closed. 'Below us, on the ground floor. We must be careful.'

Father Marwalt put a finger to his lips. 'Quiet from here on and move slowly,' he said. 'The undead will not notice us.'

'And remember,' added Max, shooting a hard glance at Gotrek and Felix, 'our aim is to open the gates for von Uhland, *not* to have any unnecessary fights. You may fight as you like *after* we have let the army in.'

Gotrek grunted, but made no complaint, and they all turned and started down the steps at a ponderous crawl.

It was like something out of a nightmare, thought Felix – walking through a castle full of the living dead as if invisible, and all the while fearing that one would come upon a loved one. With thudding heart, he scanned each pile of bodies they passed, looking for, but praying he wouldn't find, the tatters of a heavy wool coat, or a broken bow or hatchet, among the bones. He saw nothing, but that was no guarantee Kat still lived. She might have been eaten. She might be a zombie. She might have been chopped to pieces by Krell and left on the wall.

The ground floor as they reached it was thick with zombies and ghouls, and Felix found it difficult not to go on guard as they neared them. Some of the knights couldn't help themselves, and Max and the twins had to surreptitiously grasp their arms to remind them to lower their swords.

Felix clenched his teeth until they ached, expecting at any moment that one of the horrors would look up and see them as interlopers and groan warning to the others, but they didn't. Even the ghouls, who were living things, with almost human intelligence, gave them no more than a passing glance. Still, he couldn't help holding his breath, or gripping the hilt of his sword.

The keep's grand foyer was ten paces down a broad corridor – a high, marble-floored entry hall with the door to the courtyard around the corner to the right, and the open double doors of the great hall to the left, and as they shuffled towards it through the crowds of undead, Felix began to hear low murmurings and whisperings coming from within the dining hall.

'Eyes front,' whispered Max. 'He is there.'

But as they entered the foyer and turned towards the front door, Felix couldn't help but look back, and neither could any of the others – not Gotrek, not Dominic, not even Max or Father Marwalt or Magister Marhalt, who all slanted their eyes over their shoulders as they walked on.

Felix had had a brief glance at the dining hall once before, when he'd entered the keep with von Volgen and Classen and the others to confront Grafin Avelein, and he remembered it as a regal room with heraldic shields and tapestries on the walls, chandeliers hanging from the ceiling, long, richly set tables below a raised dais and tall windows looking out onto a formal garden.

It was regal no more.

The shields and tapestries had been torn down, and in their place, strange symbols were scrawled in blood on the bare stone walls. The chandeliers had been replaced by inverted corpses, headless and dripping black fluids from the stumps of their necks. The tables had been smashed and thrown to the corners to make room for an eldritch circle, burned and gouged into the polished wood floor. Ringing the circle at nine points were bronze braziers in which burned mounds of severed heads, hands and arms, the fat and the flesh of them popping and hissing in the flames.

And in the centre of it all was a scene so strange it made Felix stumble in shock. It seemed to have been arranged as a sick parody of some old harvest ritual, where the lord and lady of the land would give their blessing to their peasants' crops and toast the bounty of nature. There were two thrones in the circle, each carved with the eagle and crown of the Reikland, and squirming in those thrones were the undead corpses of Graf Reiklander and Grafin Avelein – dressed in the full regalia of the ancient princes of the Reikland. Sable robes with ermine cuffs were draped around their bony shoulders, jewelled crowns slipped sideways on their shrunken skulls, chains of office hung across their sunken chests, swords and sceptres were clutched awkwardly in withered claws, and around them, mounded up on all sides of the thrones, was a bounteous feast of famine that was decaying as Felix watched.

Sheaves of wheat gone rotten were crossed at the corpses' feet. Cadaverous hogs lay trussed on platters, so gaunt their ribs had broken through their crumbling skin. Baskets of apples and cabbages and leeks, black and shrivelled, collapsed between spilled sacks of wormy flour and mouldy grain. The skulls of cattle and the bones of sheep, goats and geese lay in heaps. And standing before it all, his robes whipping in an unnatural wind and his arms flung wide like a priest giving a benediction, was Kemmler, his skull-topped staff gripped in one hand as he keened a cacophonous incantation.

A black nimbus flickered around him, curdling the air, and he seemed to be drawing it from the dead graf and grafin, and from the foul offerings that he had gathered around them. With each syllable of his chant the corpses and the bounty seemed to wither more, while the crowns and swords and chains the graf and grafin wore rusted and blackened and crumbled to dust as the rippling energy around the necromancer grew darker and more tangible.

It was the spell of blight again, Felix was sure of it – the same evil pall that Kemmler had cast upon the castle, poisoning the water and ruining the food, the spell that had starved and weakened the defenders and made them easy prey for his minions. Now he was casting it again inside Castle Reikguard, upon the rulers of Castle Reikguard, and if what Father Marwalt and Magister Marhalt had said was true, it would affect all the lands that made up its domain – the blight would spread across all the Reikland. Every well would be poisoned. All the food would wither, rot and die. The people would starve. The army would die on its feet. With one spell, Kemmler would defeat the forces of the Empire before his undead horde marched a single step.

'Mother,' choked Dominic. 'Father!'

Felix clamped a hand over the boy's mouth and looked around, afraid he had been heard, but a second later Gotrek pushed past them both, stalking towards the great hall as he ran his thumb along the blade of his axe and drew blood.

Felix gaped, and made to call after him. Max beat him to it.

'Gotrek!' hissed the magister, grabbing for him. 'What are you doing? I said you weren't to fight!'

Gotrek shrugged him off without breaking step. 'No one does that to a Slayer,' he growled. 'No one!'

Felix had no idea what he was talking about. Slayer? Which Slayer? Was Snorri here? Had he somehow woken from his drugged stupor and beaten them here?

Then he saw what Gotrek had seen, and he paled. Rodi Balkisson stood at one of the flaming braziers, feeding a severed head into the fire from a bucket full of body parts that he held in his left hand. There was a terrible axe wound in his chest, and his lower jaw and beard were missing, leaving a crusted red hole in his face where they should have been. There was no mistaking the braided Slayer's crest or massive physique, however. It was Rodi, and he was dead, and yet he walked. Nor was he the only one. Kemmler had also raised others to be his servants – Tauber, Sergeant Leffler and von Volgen also held buckets and fed the grisly fires as well.

Max and Father Marwalt and Magister Marhalt tiptoed frantically after Gotrek, whispering after him to come back. The Slayer didn't heed them. He strode into the great hall and chopped off Rodi's head with a single slash of his glowing rune axe.

'Go to Grimnir, Rodi Balkisson,' said Gotrek.

TWENTY-FIVE

Kemmler turned, his incantation faltering, as Rodi's body and jawless head thudded to the floor behind him.

'You have dishonoured the dead of the dwarfs, necromancer,' said Gotrek, launching himself at him. 'You will die for it.'

Kemmler leapt back, crying out in fear, and vanished into a cloud of darkness that erupted from his cloak.

The Slayer skidded to a stop, glaring around, then roared and charged out of sight to the right, bellowing, 'Stand aside, wight! The defiler dies first!'

'The dwarf is insane,' whispered Father Marwalt and Magister Marhalt, as Felix and Max hurried for the door.

'He is a Slayer,' said Max over his shoulder. 'Sanity doesn't enter the equation.'

'Then I am a Slayer too,' cried Dominic, and charged after them, drawing his sword. 'My mother and father must be avenged!'

'But, my lord, the gates!' called Captain Hoetker. 'We must open the gates!'

The young lord didn't listen. He shoved past Felix and Max as they reached the door, and plunged on in the direction Gotrek had gone.

Felix blanched as he saw what the boy was running towards. 'Lord Dominic! Come back!'

The right end of the great hall was a raised dais – the place where the graf and grafin's thrones should have been. A curtained musicians' gallery rose above it, and a mural of Young Sigmar killing Blacktusk the

Boar was painted behind it. Now it was bare of furniture, and full of wights. Kemmler stood in the centre of a square of motionless skeletal warriors, crooning out another incantation while below him on the dais's broad stairs, Gotrek fought Krell, the Lord of the Undead.

Felix raced forwards, reaching after Dominic, but he was too far back. The young lord shouldered in beside the Slayer and started hewing at the wight king like a woodsman. Unfortunately, his sword strokes were wild and glancing and did nothing. He looked like a terrier trying to help a bulldog fight a bear, and quickly met a terrier's fate. As Krell slashed at Gotrek, Dominic got in the way, and was smashed backwards into the rotting bounty at the foot of his father's throne, his sword sheared in half and his armour crumpled at the shoulder.

Felix ran to him as the Reiksguarders thundered in. He was stunned, and groaning in pain, but thankfully seemed uncut by Krell's axe.

'He lives?' asked Captain Hoetker, hurrying past.

'Aye,' said Felix.

'Well, keep him back.'

The knights charged forwards to attack Krell, and were followed into the room by a tide of zombies and ghouls.

'Father!' shouted Max. 'Magister!'

The twins turned, and Magister Marhalt backed from the door, mumbling cantrips and pulling something from his sleeves, while Father Marwalt pulled a stick of charcoal from his robes and began to recite a prayer to Morr.

Below the dais, Krell whirled his axe in a wide arc as the Reiksguarders fell in with Gotrek to attack him. Two of the knights tried to turn the blow on their shields and crashed down, shields sundered and arms maimed and flecked with black slivers.

'Get back, fools!' growled Gotrek, and Max echoed him.

'Knights!' he shouted. 'Leave Krell to the Slayer! Kill the wights! Attack Kemmler!'

At the door, Magister Marhalt held out a gold-chased human skull towards the undead who were shuffling into the room and cried an arcane phrase. The skull's jewelled eyes emitted a violet light that went through them like a shockwave. They flew backwards into the entry hall, knocking back those behind and disintegrating as they fell – arms, legs and torsos breaking into rotting chunks.

With the doorway momentarily clear, Father Marwalt rushed to it and drew a thick black line across the threshold with his charcoal, then dodged back. The zombies and ghouls came forwards again, but when they tried to step over the line, their flesh blackened and cracked as if they were being consumed by invisible flames. They could not cross it.

Felix looked back to the dais. The Reiksguarders had done Max's bidding and were attacking Kemmler's protective square of wights, leaving Gotrek to fight Krell all on his own.

The Slayer was revelling in it, raining blows on the wight king with a maniacal smile twisting his face. This, at last, thought Felix, was the fight Gotrek had been looking for since he had first crossed axes with Krell on the walls of the castle seven days ago. There were no distractions now – no undead wyvern to get in the way or allow Krell to escape, no interfering rivals, no worries about keeping Snorri alive. There was only a fight to the finish with a worthy enemy.

The dwarf and undead warrior were so evenly matched that it seemed neither would ever gain an advantage. No matter how fast Gotrek's axe blurred, Krell's was there to meet it. No matter how powerful Krell's strikes, Gotrek returned them with equal force, and the air shivered with the ringing of obsidian on steel.

Felix hauled the semi-conscious Dominic out of the way as Gotrek sent Krell crashing into Kemmler's ritual circle, then leapt after him.

'My lord,' said Felix, as Krell surged up again and the battle roiled their way. 'Can you stand?'

The boy only groaned and Felix dragged him further back.

Behind his protective wall of wights, Kemmler's arcane incantation was rising to a crescendo, but Max and Magister Marhalt and Father Marwalt were casting spells of their own to counter it. Magister Marhalt trained the jewelled sockets of his golden skull on the necromancer and bathed him in its burning violet stare. Max scribed glowing words in the air with one hand while brandishing a round metal mirror with the other. A white-gold light poured from the disc as if it were reflecting the light of the sun, and the beam seared Kemmler's eyes. Father Marwalt held a flickering black candle and recited traditional Morrian burial prayers, meant to lay the dead to rest and keep them there – and it appeared to be working, for the verdigised axes of Kemmler's wights seemed to be slowing, and the swords of the Reiksguarders were bashing through their defences and striking bronze and bone.

But, though Max's light blinded him and Magister Marhalt's fire burned him, Kemmler managed to shriek the last words of his incantation and thrust his skull-topped staff out before him.

A ripple of shadow burst from the staff and Max and the twins gasped and staggered. Felix did too, a wave of dizzying weakness buckling his knees. The Reiksguarders were affected as well, and suddenly it was their swords that were faltering, and the wights that were smashing them back. Felix groaned. His arms were shaking and his heart beating fast but faint. It felt as if all the days of thirst and starvation he had experienced during the siege were happening to him now in the span of a minute.

Then, just as he felt he would collapse next to Lord Dominic, a shimmer of gold passed through him and the sick weakness lessened, though not entirely. He looked around. Max stood before the dais, braced as if against a high wind, his arms outstretched and shaking, pushing the walls of a sphere of golden light out to encompass them all.

Protected by Max's ward, the twins renewed their prayers and incantations, though their hands pushed though their ritual motions like they were neck deep in quicksand. Kemmler had also thrown up a shield – a whirlwind of spectral forms and half-seen faces that swirled around him, screaming and dying as they blocked the purple light.

The only ones apparently unaffected by all the prayers and spells and counterspells were Gotrek and Krell, who fought on, oblivious, to everything but their close-fought combat. Krell slammed Gotrek backwards into a jumble of tables, smashing them to splinters, then charged in as the Slayer rolled from the wreckage and slashed behind him with his axe. The strike tore away Krell's greave and boot, leaving him limping on a bare bone foot, but he came on regardless, and his next strike sent Gotrek crashing into the braziers that ringed the circle and sending burning hands, feet and heads flying everywhere.

Felix pulled Dominic out of the way again, and the boy finally stumbled to his feet.

'This way, my lord,' said Felix. 'Keep back.'

But as he drew Dominic away, he bumped into something behind him, and turned to find Sergeant Leffler swinging his two-handed sword at him.

Felix gasped and ducked, and the blade whooshed an inch over his head – and gashed Dominic's shoulder. From their left, the corpse of Surgeon Tauber lurched in, hands outstretched, and from their right, Lord von Volgen was stabbing at them with his long sword.

Dominic twisted aside and gashed von Volgen with his broken sword, but the wound didn't slow the corpse in the slightest, and it slashed at him again.

Felix parried the blow and kicked von Volgen back, then bulled into Dominic to get him out of the path of Leffler's Zweihander.

'Stay behind me,' he shouted.

Felix chopped Tauber's head off as the zombies crowded in, then smashed the heavy two-handed sword from the sergeant's hands and ran him through the neck. That left only von Volgen. The corpse of the lord lurched towards him, but as Felix raised Karaghul to hack at it, its sword arm dropped, a sad expression on its face.

Felix faltered, but instinct carried the blow and he cut von Volgen's head from his body. His heart hammered as the corpse fell. It had seemed as if the zombie had allowed itself to be killed, almost as if it had been begging for it. But that wasn't possible, was it? Had some portion of von Volgen's soul remained trapped in its undead cage?

A movement brought his head around and banished the thought. Dominic was staggering once again towards the battle between Gotrek and Krell, and trying to raise his broken sword with his battered arm. Felix stepped after him.

'My lord,' he said, 'leave it to the Slayer.'

The young lord waved him back. 'I must do something! I must have some part in–'

He stopped as he found himself face to face with his mother and father. The corpses were writhing in their thrones and Felix saw that they had been tied there. They strained against the ropes, snapping at Felix and their son with mindless hunger.

Dominic stared at them, then choked back a sob. 'This is what I must do. I must do as the Slayer did, and free them as he freed his friend.'

The boy threw aside his broken blade and instead drew from its scabbard the sword strapped to his father's side. The corpse tried to claw at him, but the rope held it and it couldn't reach.

Aged by Kemmler's death magic, the blade was spotted with rust, but still whole enough to do the job. Dominic raised it over his head, then faced the grafin with tears in his eyes.

'Go to Sigmar, mother,' he said, then swept her shrivelled head from her neck. She made no noise as she died, but behind his wall of wights, Kemmler screamed as if the sword had struck him.

'Foolish boy! You're ruining it!'

His cry of rage turned into a shriek of pain as Max and Magister Marhalt's spells lanced through his lost concentration, but almost instantly, his shadows billowed forth again, growing stronger than before.

'Spoiler!' he shrieked. 'Vandal!'

'Finish it, my lord!' shouted Felix, stepping between the boy and the expanding darkness. 'Strike while you can!'

Dominic raised his sword over his father. 'Go to Sigmar, father.'

Again he struck true, and the graf's head tumbled off his shoulders.

Kemmler howled, and with a silent thunderclap the boiling ball of darkness around him exploded outwards in all directions, and his enervating power blasted Felix and Dominic and the other living men to their knees.

All the weakness that Max's sphere of protection had momentarily mitigated returned again tenfold. Felix's limbs would not support his weight. His heart beat so fast he felt it might explode, but it seemed to be pumping bile, not blood. His head swam and his vision blackened at the corners. Dominic dropped his father's sword. Max and Father Marwalt and Magister Marhalt were the same, arms shaking and struggling to rise. The knights who had been fighting the wights had collapsed too, and the ancient warriors were chopping them to pieces. And at the door, the black line of charcoal was greying and the zombies were beginning to push through it.

Even Gotrek seemed to have been stricken by the spell. He staggered back from Krell as if on his last legs, his torso a mass of bruises and his rune axe hanging heavy in his hands. The undead champion howled in triumph and strode after him, raising his black axe for a savage blow. But as it swung down, trailing its choking cloud, Gotrek jolted forwards and chopped hard at the haft of it, then twisted savagely and up.

Krell bellowed in surprise as the black axe flew from his gauntleted grip and spun up to the ceiling to bite into one of the great hall's gilded beams. It stuck there, quivering, twenty feet over his head.

Gotrek laughed and sprang, slashing for his legs, as the towering wight stumbled back.

'Two thousand years of grudges,' growled the Slayer, 'crossed out in a single stroke!'

Gotrek hacked at the undead champion's exposed leg bone and chopped through it like dry wood. Krell toppled to the floor in a deafening crash, and the Slayer straddled him, swinging down with his rune axe blazing red.

'No!' cried Kemmler, from the dais, and began incanting a new spell.

There was no stopping the axe's deadly trajectory. It cleaved through the champion's breastplate and buried itself in his rib cage. Krell struggled to rise, but Gotrek kicked him in the teeth and wrenched his axe free, grinning wildly.

'A single stroke, butcher!'

He raised the rune axe over his head for the final blow to the neck, but on the dais behind him, Kemmler thrust forwards with his staff and the skull that topped it opened its mouth, puking out a stream of roiling black energy.

Gotrek grunted and went rigid as the darkness struck him in the back, his grin turning into a rictus grimace as every muscle in his body tensed. Felix stared. It was a rare thing to see the Slayer affected by magic at all, let alone paralysed by it, but as shocking as that was, that wasn't all it was doing to him. As Felix watched, the lines in the Slayer's face deepened, and his cheeks grew gaunt. His body was growing leaner as well, every detail of his muscles and veins standing out from his skin as if he had been flayed.

Nor was he the only one affected by the spell. The flesh of Felix's fingers was shrinking and his knuckle bones poked through his tightening skin like tent poles. Max and the twins were the same. Max's silver hair was turning white at the roots, and the magister and the father were ageing before Felix's eyes, their spells and invocations weakening and flickering out. Kemmler's withering blast was pressing them all into the grave – a hand like that of time itself, crushing them with the weight of years – while more and more zombies broke through Marwalt's ward and shuffled into the room.

The Slayer turned, inch by straining inch, as if frozen in ice, and raised his rune axe in a shaking hand, but he couldn't turn fast enough. He was weakening with every half-step. He would never be able to reach the necromancer before the spell turned him into a walking skeleton.

Felix struggled to his feet, as weak as a broken reed, and drew his dagger, but as he raised it to throw at Kemmler, something flashed down from above and stuck in Kemmler's shoulder.

Kemmler barked in surprise and fell back, his stream of black energy boiling away to nothing as he turned, looking for the source of the attack. There was an arrow in his shoulder, and as Felix stared, another flashed down and sprouted from the necromancer's leg. He screamed again and fell.

An arrow?

Felix's heart thudded like it was trying to escape his chest. An arrow!

At the opposite end of the room, Gotrek broke free of his paralysis and ran for the necromancer with a blood-curdling howl of rage. Kemmler saw him coming and raised his staff in a trembling hand, spitting out the beginning of another incantation, but before he could utter more than a few syllables, the Slayer bounded onto the dais, smashed his way through the necromancer's remaining wights, and slashed down at him with all his might.

Kemmler blocked with his staff and Gotrek's rune axe chopped it in two, sending its grinning skull spinning to the side as a chorus of screams, like the dying of a thousand souls, shook the room and weird half-seen entities burst forth and vanished into the shadows. Then the axe found flesh, and Kemmler screamed as well, a great stain of blood spreading across his abdomen to darken his grey robes.

'Now, necromancer!' roared the Slayer as he raised his axe again. 'You die for your desecrations!'

But as Gotrek lashed down, misty shadows boiled up from Kemmler's cloak and enveloped them both in swirling darkness, and when it cleared, Gotrek was alone, his axe buried in the splintered planks of the dais, and his one eye blazing with frustrated fury.

'Coward!' he shouted at the air. 'Defiler!'

He turned with a growl to where he had brought down Krell, and charged back across the room towards the wight's still-prostrate form, but even as he ploughed through the rotting rubbish around the Reikland thrones, shadows formed around the fallen champion and by the time the Slayer reached him he was gone as well – even his axe had vanished from the ceiling – and Kemmler's voice echoed through the hall, coming from everywhere and nowhere at once.

'You have not defeated me, fools,' he hissed, 'only delayed me. I have all the time in the world.'

Gotrek cursed as the necromancer's mad laughter faded away, and he lashed around with his axe at nothing.

'Cursed!' he roared. 'Cursed!'

Felix turned from him as he heard moaning and shuffling behind him, and found the horde of zombies that was spilling through the door nearly at his back. He caught Lord Dominic's arm and pulled him up, and they staggered back from the dead, raising their swords together. Gotrek fell in beside them, still grunting angrily, and Max and Father Marwalt and Magister Marhalt rose behind them, corpse-thin and shaking from Kemmler's withering, but preparing spells nonetheless.

But as the zombies shuffled towards them, rusty weapons raised and claws outstretched, their steps began to falter, and their arms to droop. A big one in the apron of a butcher tripped and fell on its face. A woman in the remains of a rich dress lost an arm, then her lower jaw, then collapsed entirely, her skin putrefying before their eyes. The corpse of a beastman crashed down, taking several smaller zombies with him. Some of the others struggled gamely on, but they didn't last long. They were dropping like flies – the ones outside in the entry hall too. Finally the last of them crashed to its knees in front of Felix, its clawed fingers scratching feebly across the toe of his boot before stilling forever.

'Kemmler is gone,' whispered Father Marwalt, dropping into a broken chair.

'And his influence goes with him,' said Magister Marhalt, sagging to the floor. 'It is over.'

'For now,' said Max, letting his hands fall to his sides. 'How long before he comes again?'

Nobody had an answer for him. The twins just shivered where they slumped, while Dominic Reiklander staggered to kneel before the headless corpses of his mother and father, and Gotrek cleaned his axe.

Felix could not yet rest. His hope wouldn't let him. He looked to the dais where Kemmler had been struck by the arrows, then turned, trying to figure out where the shafts had come from. Somewhere high up. They had shot *down* at Kemmler. There. The musicians' gallery above the dais. He stumbled towards it, his heart beginning to pound.

'Kat!' he called. 'Kat, was it you?'

There was no answer.

'Kat?'

Still nothing.

There was a door in the wall below the gallery. He threw it open. It was a water closet. He cursed and started for the door to the corridor, stumbling over the mounds of rotting corpses that choked it. The door to the gallery must be on the floor above. He limped down the hall to the stairs, feeling as frail and light as a bird skeleton from Kemmler's withering.

The stairs were almost too much for him, but he crawled up them at last, then made his way down the corridor. There was a small door on the left-hand wall. He stumbled to it and pulled on the knob. It was locked. He pounded on the panel, desperate now.

'Kat! Kat, are you in there?'

Nothing. He yanked at the door, then kicked it, but it was useless. He was too weak. He couldn't budge it. He couldn't break it. A sob escaped him.

'Stand aside, manling,' said Gotrek.

Felix looked up. He hadn't heard the Slayer approach, hadn't known he had followed him.

Gotrek chopped at the door with his axe, knocking a great hole in the panel, then reached through and turned the latch from the inside. He pulled it open and stood aside.

'Go on, manling,' he said.

TWENTY-SIX

Felix hesitated on the threshold, almost afraid to go on now that the way was clear. What if she wasn't there? Or it wasn't her? Or...

He swallowed and stepped through into the narrow, curtained balcony. At first he could see nothing but the silhouettes of chairs and stools set in rough rows, and the pale litter of sheet music scattered on the floor. But then in the lee of the balustrade, he saw a small form, slumped and still.

'Kat!' he cried, stumbling through the chairs.

She lay on her back, eyes closed, her bow in her hands and an arrow nocked on the string, but so thin Felix didn't know how she'd had the strength to draw it. Her face, already gaunt when last he'd seen her, was a sunken skull, her skin stretched across the bones drumhead-tight.

He put a hand on her shoulder. 'Kat,' he whispered. 'Do you live?'

She didn't respond, didn't even seem to breathe. The arrow slipped from the string and clattered to the floor. Panic thudded again in Felix's chest.

'Kat, hang on.'

He reached down and got his arms under her and lifted. She was so light that, even weak as he was, he could stand with her in his arms. He staggered back to the door and out into the hall.

'Gotrek, bring the Shallyans!' he cried. 'Bring food!'

'Bring her to Max, manling,' said Gotrek. 'The Shallyans will come when we open the gate.'

Felix nodded and started downstairs, rushing so fast that twice he tripped, and would have fallen if Gotrek hadn't steadied him.

'Max,' called Felix, as he carried Kat into the great hall. 'Help her. Look at her.'

Max and the twins looked up, then made room as Felix laid Kat down beside them on the floor.

'This is the archer, then?' asked Max, kneeling. 'Who turned the tide and saved us all?' He looked up at Felix. 'You know her?'

Felix nodded, his throat tightening. 'She – she is–'

Max nodded. 'Ah. I see.' He smiled sadly as he looked Kat up and down. 'You've always liked the brave ones, haven't you, Felix?'

Father Marwalt put his right hand over Kat's heart and his left on her forehead, then closed his eyes. Felix held his breath. Max seemed to as well. Gotrek stepped to Felix's shoulder and crossed his arms, glaring at Kat as if trying to shame her into surviving.

After a long moment, Father Marwalt sat back on his knees. 'She is not Morr's concern,' he said. 'She stands on the threshold, but she has not yet passed through his portal.'

Felix choked out a sob of relief, and the tears he had held back until now streamed down his cheeks. What a fool! To cry at good news. What was the matter with him?

Max put a hand on his shoulder, and Felix nodded his thanks, then looked around for Gotrek.

The Slayer was walking towards the door to the corridor.

'Come on, manling,' he rasped over his shoulder. 'It takes four hands to open the gates.'

Though of course relieved that he hadn't had to lose any men fighting against Kemmler's undead army, General von Uhland seemed almost disappointed that the infiltrators had done it all themselves and hadn't given him a battle. All the zombies and wights in the castle had dropped dead with the necromancer's retreat, and the ghouls had fled. There was no horde left to fight, and the general's troops were faced with the much less glamorous, but just as necessary, challenge of disposing of ten thousand mouldering corpses before they diseased the whole region.

Snorri, too, was less than pleased to have missed the climactic battle, and he was still muttering about it late that afternoon, as he and Gotrek sat on either side of Felix's bed in the room in the keep in which the general's surgeon had put him.

'Snorri blames himself,' said Snorri, scowling. 'He hasn't been that drunk in a long time.'

Gotrek said nothing, and seemed to be having trouble meeting his old friend's eye.

'Snorri has never had manling beer that had such a kick either,' Snorri continued, licking his lips. 'He wonders who makes it.'

There was another silence, and then Gotrek grunted angrily.

'I am to blame, Snorri Nosebiter,' he said, forcing the words out as if they were heavy stones. 'I had you drugged, so you would sleep.'

Snorri raised an eyebrow. It made him look like a confused dog. 'Snorri doesn't understand.'

Felix saw Gotrek clenching his jaw and balling his fist, and cut in to save him.

'You can't find your doom until you get your memory back, Snorri,' he said patiently. 'And we knew you would forget and want to come with us.'

Snorri blinked at him, still seemingly lost, then lowered his head. 'Yes,' he said. 'Snorri forgot. Snorri always forgets.'

There was an uncomfortable silence after that, and none of them seemed to know how to break it. Fortunately, it was broken for them when Max entered the room, walking with the aid of a staff.

'Are you able to stand?' he asked Felix.

Felix nodded. 'I think so.'

'Then come with me.'

With Gotrek's help, Felix levered himself out of the bed and tottered unsteadily after Max as the Slayers followed behind. He still felt like he was made of matchsticks and spit, and he was still as gaunt as one of Kemmler's ghouls, but food and drink and the healing spells and prayers of Max and the Shallyan Sister had for the most part banished the dizziness and nausea. Gotrek only had to catch him once on the way down the hall.

Inside another room, the Sister hovered over another bed, but as Felix and Max and the Slayers approached, she stepped back.

Lying on the bed, looking scrubbed and unfamiliar in a clean white nightshirt and her hair combed back from her skeletal face, was Kat. Her eyes were closed and her withered hands were folded over her chest, and for a terrible moment Felix thought Max had brought him to her to pay his last respects, but then, as he stumbled to the side of the bed, she opened her eyes and looked up at him – and smiled.

'Hello, Felix,' she said in voice like the memory of a whisper.

Felix eased himself down beside her. 'Kat,' he said. 'It – it's good to see you.'

She reached out and he took her hand. Her fingers were trembling, and terribly thin.

'I knew you would come back,' she said. 'I knew it.'

He frowned. 'How did you survive?' he asked. 'How did you stay alive for so long with Kemmler's dead all around?'

Her face crinkled into a grin. 'Reiklander's secret closet,' she said. 'I hid myself inside and waited. Then I heard fighting, and knew it was you.'

Felix closed his eyes, imagining Kat lying in the dark for two long days and nights, not knowing if she would ever be saved, and praying the zombies wouldn't find her first.

He leaned down and kissed her. 'I'm just glad we were here in time.'

There was a polite cough. Felix looked up. Everyone was very busy looking somewhere else, but the Sister was smiling down at them.

'She should rest, mein herr,' she said. 'I only called for you because she insisted.'

Felix nodded and turned back to Kat. 'I will visit you whenever you wish,' he said.

'I'll be up and about soon,' she said. 'I'm feeling better already.'

Felix swallowed at that. Feeling better than when he had found her wasn't much to crow about, and she still looked more dead than alive.

'Good,' he said. 'Then I'll see you soon.'

She nodded and closed her eyes again and he stood, then limped to the Sister of Shallya and drew her into the hall.

'Sister,' he murmured. 'Will she live?'

The sister looked at him, then pursed her lips. 'I don't know,' she said. 'She has come as close to starving as is possible without succumbing. And you have both been subject to the enervation of the necromancer's spells. Neither of you may recover your full strength.' She shrugged. 'At least you were both in vigorous health at the start. Perhaps that will count in your favour. Rest and Shallya's blessing are what is needed now, lots of rest.'

Felix nodded, distracted, as the sister bowed and started down the hall. He looked back through the door at Kat, chewing his lip. What if the two of them were enfeebled like this for the rest of their lives? It might not be so bad for him. After all his years on the road, after all the fighting and running and chasing, it wouldn't be so bad to live quietly, to read and write and think for a time. But for Kat? She was a child of the forest, a hunter. What would she do if she couldn't survive in the wild on her own? What if she were housebound or bedbound for the rest of her life? It would kill her. She would sicken and die, like a wolf in captivity.

He closed his eyes. If that was her fate, it might almost have been better that she had died.

'I am no doctor,' murmured Max, stepping though the door to join him, 'but my advice is, that while rest is indeed what is needed now, in the long run, you would both do better to go where Gotrek goes, despite the dangers.'

Felix looked up at him. 'I am bound to anyway,' he said. 'But Kat too? Why do you say that?'

Max nodded at Gotrek, who was following him into the hall with Snorri. 'I mentioned before that some of your unusual vitality seemed attributable to your remaining near Gotrek all these years. Whatever the cause of it, it seems that your association with him has kept you healthy and mended wounds that should have been the end of your adventuring.' He looked towards Kat, sleeping in her bed. 'I cannot say if this strange influence would work on Kat as well, but it certainly couldn't hurt,' he said, smiling. 'Also, I don't think you could keep her from following even if you chained her to her bed.'

A glimmer of hope stirred in Felix's heart. He hadn't been sure he believed Max's theories about his health when the magister had first shared them with him, and he still wasn't now, but if it *was* true! It could be the saving of Kat. It might make her well again!

'Sounds like rubbish to me,' Gotrek grunted. 'But no one ever got strong lying in bed. She can come if she wants.'

Max smiled at Gotrek. 'Excellent. And where do you go now, Slayer? What unspeakable abomination do you intend to throw yourself at next?'

Felix looked at the Slayer, as curious as Max was. Their most recent journey had begun when they had gone north to fight the beastmen at the behest of Sir Teobalt of the Order of the Fiery Heart, and they had become caught in the web of Kemmler's schemes after that, but now, as far as he knew, Gotrek had no goal other than his perennial quest to find his doom, and that might lead him anywhere.

But as Felix waited for the Slayer to speak, he saw him slide his one eye towards Snorri, and suddenly he knew the answer.

'We go,' Felix said, turning back to Max, 'to Karak Kadrin, to accompany Snorri Nosebiter on his pilgrimage to the Shrine of Grimnir.'

OTHER TALES

THE FUNERAL OF GOTREK GURNISSON

Richard Salter

Thunder rumbled in the overcast sky and the rain came down in sheets. It was as gloomy as dusk, yet the day had not reached noon. Felix Jaeger stood silently in the graveyard, his hair matted and his clothes drenched. The downpour bothered him not at all.

A priest approached and cleared his throat.

Felix looked up. 'Thank you for doing this at such short notice.'

The priest bowed his head.

'I am happy to help. I have never… officiated the funeral of a Slayer before. However… it was my understanding that a customary send off for one such as he would involve more of a…'

'Celebration?'

'Indeed, yes.'

'He did not die a hero's death,' Felix explained. 'Anything more would not be appropriate.'

'Very well.'

Six pallbearers carried the coffin towards the open grave. They stopped close by and placed the casket on iron stands. At such short notice, Felix had only been able to procure a human-sized casket and a cheap one at that. Its occupant would be mortified if he could see this dreary scene.

The priest began the incantation while Felix stood impassive. His eyes were downcast, water dripping from the end of his nose. Rain collected in the brim of his hat, occasionally overflowing like torrents of tears.

He had told nobody about the funeral. While word had a habit of getting out, it was unlikely anyone would reach here in time. There were many who would want to attend, either to mourn Gotrek's passing, or to dance on his grave.

Felix was aware of a figure standing beside him, someone who didn't fit into either category.

The tavern was packed with revellers when Gotrek and Felix dragged themselves inside. Neither of them felt like joining in the fun. They sat down at the only free table, in the corner, awash with spilled beer and other detritus. They ordered food and ale, and then fell into a silent funk. Felix watched everyone else having a good time with weary resentment.

'It feels like my feet have pounded every cobblestone in Kutenholz,' Felix said in an attempt to break the silence between them. He had to speak up to be heard over the background din.

Gotrek merely grunted. Thankfully their food, a tough, unidentifiable meat with day-old bread, arrived so they had an excuse not to talk. If Felix weren't so hungry he would already be in his room, collapsed on his bed with exhaustion. He suspected that the Slayer, despite his formidable stamina, felt much the same.

As soon as they were done eating, Gotrek drained his tankard, bid Felix a gruff goodnight and shuffled over to the stairs. Felix waited until the Slayer had disappeared from view and then stood up. He wanted to ask everyone here if they had seen anything strange these past few weeks, but he was too bone-tired. Their search for the cursed liche Pragarti had led them to this town, but then the trail had gone cold. It was frustrating to say the least. Perhaps tomorrow he and Gotrek should lay low and let trouble come to them. If history was any indicator, they shouldn't have to wait long.

For now, to bed.

Felix dragged himself up the stairs. Each step took more effort than the one before. Once at the top he stumbled to his door and struggled to get the key in the lock. He felt so disconnected, he was sure he must have been drugged. But no, the fog in his head was only due to fatigue. He locked the door behind him and fell onto his bed, not even bothering to undress. Sleep took hold almost immediately.

Felix awoke suddenly. He sat upright and listened. Had he dreamt the noise? Despite the gloom he saw nothing out of place. He was just about to lie down when another crash jolted him fully awake.

Felix jumped out of bed and grabbed his sword. The disturbance came from the next room. Gotrek!

He burst into the corridor and tried to open Gotrek's door, but it was still locked. Now he could hear shouting: Gotrek's gruff voice telling someone to stand still.

Felix assessed the door as best he could in the semi-darkness. The wood nearest the top hinge seemed fairly rotten as he probed it with a finger. He was about to kick the door in when he remembered he had no boots on. A broken foot wasn't going to help anybody.

Luckily, the innkeeper had been awoken by the noise. He shuffled his ample frame along the corridor, complaining the whole time.

'What is going on in there?' he demanded of Felix.

'Open the door and we'll find out.'

The landlord sifted through a huge brass ring holding enough keys to keep all of Nuln's gaols secure.

After what seemed an age he unlocked the door. Felix burst in. The window to Gotrek's small room was open and the furniture was smashed and tipped over. In the centre of the room, a black-clad assassin was struggling mightily to free his ankle from Gotrek's grip. The Slayer's eyes were closed and he didn't appear to be conscious.

'Sigmar's beard!' the assassin cried. 'Why won't you just die?'

Kicking hard, the killer managed to wrest his leg free.

Felix leapt over a toppled wardrobe and threw himself at the assassin, tackling him to the floor. The killer kicked and punched with painful accuracy but Felix clung on. Finally he managed to pin him down.

'Who sent you?' Felix growled.

'Like I'd tell you that,' the assassin spat. Felix grabbed his sword and pushed the blade against the man's throat.

'I'm guessing you didn't intend this to be a suicide mission, so I'll ask again. Who sent you?'

'I wasn't told a name. My employer just said you would meet at the dwarf's funeral.' The assassin stared past Felix and cried, 'He's on his feet again!'

Felix knew he'd been fooled as soon as he turned his head. Gotrek was still comatose. Too slow, he turned back as the assassin twisted and punched, connecting with Felix's jaw, sending him sprawling.

The man disappeared through the window before Felix could even get up.

With enormous difficulty, Felix dragged the prone body of Gotrek down the stairs. He cringed every time the dwarf's head bounced off each wooden step. His aching back and weary arms begged him to stop. Finally he reached the bottom. At this hour the tavern was empty and the chairs were stacked on the tables. The landlord had already stomped off to bed, ordering Felix to vacate the premises immediately.

Breathing hard, unable to believe just how heavy one dwarf could be, he dragged his companion across the wooden floor as fast as he could manage. It took him precious seconds to unbolt the door, his hands shaking from the exertion.

At last he was out on the street. He felt drizzle on his face, the slight sting of water helping to cool his overheated skin. The street was empty save for a couple of drunks engaged in a fight on the corner. Felix headed in the other direction, dragging Gotrek two doors down from the inn.

He banged on the door in front of him, then banged harder when there was no response. After a few agonising moments he heard someone inside. A small hatch in the door slid open to reveal a suspicious pair of eyes.

'What are you doing waking me at this hour?'

'Please, it's an emergency.'

'It had better be!'

'My friend,' said Felix, unsure if the apothecary could see the prone body lying in a puddle at the foot of the door. 'He's been poisoned. I need you to save him!'

The eyes shifted up, down, left and right, looking for robbers ready to pounce. Warily, their owner opened the door and peered out into the rain. Then he stood back, waiting impatiently while Felix struggled to bring the Slayer inside.

'You could help!' Felix said.

'I *am* helping. If you would rather go elsewhere, that's fine by me.'

Felix held his tongue.

The apothecary examined the prone Slayer. 'Hmm,' he said as he peered into Gotrek's eyes and checked his throat and neck. He felt for a pulse, a look of amazement on his face. 'Quite remarkable,' he said.

'What is it? Is he going to be all right?'

The apothecary chuckled. 'My dear fellow, it's a wonder he isn't dead already! I see the point of entry here on the arm, likely a poison dart.'

That explained how the assassin had been able to poison Gotrek. The Slayer was legendary for his ability to hear an attacker coming, even in his sleep. After being hit with the dart, Gotrek must have made it to the window, dragged the assassin inside before he could escape, then beat him up while trying to stay consciousness.

'Can you save him?'

'Yes, but it won't be easy.' The apothecary hurried to the back of his shop and pulled down various jars from a high shelf. 'Your friend has been poisoned with ragethar, a poison so potent that one drop could kill an ogre. Lucky for you, I have an antidote.' He peered through crescent-moon spectacles at another label. Felix willed him to hurry up. 'Ah ha! Here it is, yes.'

He shuffled back to the prone dwarf. Felix noticed he was carrying two jars.

'The poison needs two antidotes?' he asked.

'Hmm? Oh, no no. One of these is the antidote, but that won't work on its own. I need to slow your friend's heartbeat down to almost nothing or else the poison will spread faster than the antidote can stop it.'

The apothecary must have noticed Felix's unconvinced expression. 'Don't worry, my dear boy. He'll be sleeping for a week or so, but when he wakes he'll be right as rain. Hmm? Yes indeed.'

Felix couldn't shake the feeling he was heading down a path he'd rather not follow. But what choice did he have? He nodded.

Two minutes later, Gotrek appeared even closer to death than before. There was no sign of breathing, no shadow of life. Felix had never seen him so... helpless. The enormity of what had happened hit him like a mounted regiment. He knew it would be up to him to protect Gotrek while he recovered. Assuming he ever recovered. At the same time, he must find out who poisoned the Slayer.

And then Felix had an idea.

He stood in the pouring rain, listening to the priest pass last rites over Gotrek's coffin.

'You're out early,' Felix said to the woman standing beside him.

'It's my kind of weather,' she replied.

'I thought you couldn't stand the Slayer.'

Ulrika chuckled. 'I want to make sure he's really dead.'

'How did you hear?'

'A lady does not reveal her sources.'

'You are no lady. At least, not any more.'

They stood in silence. Felix was aware that his boots were sinking into the boggy ground. After a time he said, 'I'm trying to find out who killed him.'

'Do you have any suspects?'

Felix laughed loudly, drawing stares from the pallbearers and the priest. He cleared his throat and put on a solemn expression.

'Oh, you're serious. Where do I start? The most obvious suspect is Pragarti. She's here in Kutenholz, somewhere.'

'You know, the most obvious suspect is rarely the real culprit.'

Felix nodded. 'Aye. While the list of those with a motive might be long, the number of folk likely to be in the vicinity is much shorter.'

'As far as you know.' Ulrika was quiet for a moment, then she said, 'So we should start with Pragarti then?'

'You know of her?'

'Of course, I'm looking for her too. Why else do you think I'm in this Sigmar-forsaken town?' Ulrika stepped towards the casket, her lithe form conjuring thoughts in Felix's mind that were inappropriate at a funeral. 'Can I see the body?' she asked.

'Why? Are you thirsty?'

'No!' Ulrika seemed genuinely offended.

'A morbid sense of curiosity, perhaps?'

'I want to examine him for clues.'

'Fair enough.' Felix ushered the priest over and whispered in his ear. The holy man nodded and took a step back. Felix signalled to the pallbearers and, with some difficulty, they raised the lid of the casket. All six of them gasped and stood back.

Felix and Ulrika hurried forwards to peer inside.

The coffin was filled with books. Of Gotrek's body there was no sign.

'I don't know anything!' the mortician spluttered, trying to maintain his composure despite the hand clamped around his throat, pinning him to the wall.

Ulrika squeezed a little harder. Felix swore he could see the man's eyes popping out.

'I find that unlikely,' Felix said. 'Now, we can do this the easy way' – he drew his sword – 'or we can do this the fun way.'

Felix raised the weapon and rested it in the crook of his free arm. He lined the point up with the mortician's right eye and slowly inched it closer.

The man screamed and writhed, desperate to break free.

Felix was disappointed. 'I've not even started yet!'

The mortician was trying to say something. Ulrika released her grip just enough to allow him some air.

'All right!' he gasped. 'Please, I beg you. Let me go... I'll tell you.'

'Some people are just determined to spoil the fun, don't you think, Ulrika?'

She probed one of her fangs suggestively with the end of her tongue and then said, 'They can be a real *drain*.'

She released him. He crumpled to the floor and struggled to recover his breath. All the while he stared warily, not at Felix's sword but at Ulrika's teeth.

Felix sheathed his blade and hopped up onto an unoccupied slab, hoping it had been washed down since its last use.

'If there's something you're keen to tell us, out with it.'

The mortician lay wheezing with his back to the wall, his gaze still locked on Ulrika.

'A woman... dressed in robes... came with others... forced me... took the dwarf's body...'

'And where did they take him?' Ulrika asked.

'I don't know! I swear... I have no idea. They paid me... and left.'

She raised an eyebrow. 'Paid you?'

'A token amount... for my trouble.'

'Oh, you're going to need a lot more payment than that...'

Ulrika advanced on him, but Felix stopped her.

'Don't! He can't help us any further. It's obviously Pragarti who took Gotrek and I don't think he knows where she is.'

'Luckily, I do,' Ulrika said, heading for the door.

Felix stared at her in surprise. Not only was he in search of the same foe as Ulrika, but all this time she knew where the liche was hiding!

'You know, if you'd told us you were here earlier, we could have avoided all this,' Felix said as they left the mortuary. 'Gotrek might still be alive.'

Ulrika laughed. 'Oh Felix, I know he's not dead!'

As he struggled to keep up with her, Felix longed for a day when he knew something, anything, that was still a secret.

It took about half an hour to reach Kutenholz's traders' district. Ulrika passed by warehouse after warehouse, eventually stopping at a derelict site where an old building had collapsed in on itself. One wall had crumbled entirely and the entrance was blocked by fallen beams.

'Why are we here?' Felix asked. 'Gotrek and I searched this area already.'

Ulrika didn't say a word. She walked towards the nailed-shut doors and, without hesitation, stepped right through them as if they weren't there.

Felix was suddenly all alone. He glanced about, looking for anyone who might be able to assure him he had not gone mad.

Hesitantly, he followed. He reached the doors and held out a hand. It passed straight through the illusion. He closed his eyes and stepped forwards.

When he looked again he saw the wall of a perfectly intact, smaller warehouse. Ulrika was moving along the outside of the real building, looking for a way in. Felix glanced behind him and saw the fake, ruined shell. From this side he could see it shimmer and fizz. He could even make out the street beyond.

'Felix, come on!'

He turned just in time to see Ulrika disappear through a window she had forced open. Felix climbed in after her.

The warehouse was full of activity. Felix resisted the temptation to stand and stare. Instead he ducked down behind the same pile of boxes Ulrika used for cover. He peered out at the warehouse floor, watching the multitude of workers carrying lanterns, boxes, crates, pieces of metal and other, unidentifiable objects back and forth. They appeared to be constructing some sort of altar in the centre of the space on a raised dais. Supervising them were a smaller number of hooded figures in long grey robes – no doubt Pragarti's loyal disciples.

'Do you have any idea how long we spent looking for this place?' Felix hissed as he moved back out of sight.

'Aye. Now shut up.'

After all this was over, Felix was going to need a seriously long chat with the vampire, preferably before Gotrek recovered. Otherwise, there wouldn't be a lot of talking going on; just violence.

Felix had no idea how much time had passed, he might even have nodded off for a moment. He hadn't had much sleep last night, after all. Ulrika was tapping him on the shoulder.

'What? What is it?'

She pointed in the direction of the warehouse floor. 'The Slayer,' she said.

Felix peered around the boxes. There was a lot less activity now. The altar was complete and the workers had withdrawn. Only the hooded minions remained, standing solemnly in a circle around the dais.

Four of them came into view carrying a litter, upon which lay the body of Gotrek Gurnisson. Felix rose involuntarily, but Ulrika pulled him back down.

'Not yet!' she hissed.

'What are we waiting for?' Felix whispered angrily. 'Come to think of it, why didn't we grab Gotrek before they brought him in here?'

'Too many people about,' Ulrika replied. 'Plus, I want to see what happens.'

'Whatever's about to happen, it won't be good for Gotrek!'

'Relax, Felix.'

'Tell me what she's up to or I swear I will give us away right now.'

Ulrika sighed. 'Fine. Pragarti is planning a spell, a big one.'

'I know that!' said Felix. 'That's why Gotrek and I were trying to find her and stop her. She's been gathering ingredients and followers all across the Old World. We've been tracking her for months, but we have no idea what the spell is for.'

'It will kill every first-born child in the Empire.'

'Sigmar's beard!'

Ulrika continued. 'The final ingredient is the blood of a dead hero.'

'Gotrek? But he's not dead!'

'Exactly. Why do you think I'm waiting to see what happens?'

Felix fell silent and watched as Pragarti stepped onto the dais. She lifted her hood to reveal a hideous, skull-like head. Sunken eyes gazed down at the prone Slayer while boney fingers toyed with the crest atop his head. Her parched skin clung tightly to withered cheek bones and her ghastly teeth, no longer concealed by lips, chattered as she began an incantation.

Despite the risk to Gotrek, Felix was also curious to see what would happen. Hopefully it would involve Pragarti's pickled innards spread over a wide area.

'Get up!'

The voice was so loud, everyone in the vast space turned to look.

Felix and Ulrika rose slowly. There was a gasp from many of the assembled throng. The two men who had discovered the eavesdroppers were carrying pistols. Their faces were obscured by their grey hoods.

'Why am I being interrupted?' Pragarti snapped, her voice echoing.

'Supreme sorceress,' one of the men said, pushing his captors out into the open. 'We found these two watching the proceedings.'

As Felix approached, Pragarti's fury turned to humour.

'Herr Jaeger,' she said. 'And Ulrika Magdova! I'm so glad you could join us. Have you come to pay your last respects?'

'You'll regret poisoning the Slayer, Pragarti,' Felix said, matching her steely gaze.

'I would love to take the credit, Herr Jaeger, but I would be doing the real killer a disservice. It's true I wanted Herr Gurnisson dead, but I had not intended him to die for a week or so. But since someone went to so much trouble, I thought it best to take advantage of such delightful happenstance. Genuine heroes are hard to come by.'

At first, Felix assumed she was lying. But why wouldn't she take credit for the Slayer's death if she was responsible? With no reason to lie, she must be telling the truth. So, if not Pragarti, then who had sent the assassin?

Ulrika slapped Felix on the arm to get his attention. He followed her gaze to the far corner of the warehouse where a sewer grating had been flipped over.

Nobody else had noticed. All eyes were fixed on Pragarti.

The sorceress didn't seem to care that her prisoners weren't paying attention to her. 'I shall continue, then, if that's all right with you and your distinguished friend, Herr Jaeger.'

'Yes, please do,' Felix said, turning back. 'It's just a shame you won't get to finish the spell. I for one would love to have seen the results.'

Pragarti smiled – at least Felix assumed it was a smile, it was hard to tell.

He glanced once again at the grating in the far corner. Something was emerging. No, not something. *Somethings*. Dozens of them. Black, fast moving, rodent-like.

Oh no.

Now all eyes turned to the flurry of activity in the corner. Swords were drawn, pistols readied, cloaks and hoods shaken off.

Felix backed away, following Ulrika's pre-emptive retreat. Nobody stopped them. A surge of black fur, twitching whiskers and deafening squeaks was pouring out of the sewer. A large area was now filled with writhing ratmen. It was like watching a swarm of giant insects. The smell of them was overwhelming: musty and cloying.

'Gotrek!' Felix yelled to Ulrika, taking a step towards the dais.

'There isn't time,' Ulrika insisted, pulling him back with astonishing strength. 'We have to go or we'll be cut to ribbons!'

The skaven descended on Pragarti's followers like a waterfall of thick, black pitch. Screams of dying men filled the air, mixing with the cacophony of chittering and squawking.

The sheer number of skaven was enough to convince Felix to turn and flee. As he ran he glanced back at Pragarti. She seemed twice her usual size now. Fire and lightning crackled from her bony digits. Creature after creature fell in crisp, toasted heaps at her feet as one by one she deep fried them in their own fur. The unnatural skaven stench was joined by the sickly sweet smell of sizzling flesh and smoldering fur. Hundreds of the creatures were roasted by Pragarti or cut down by the swords and pistols of her followers. But they didn't stop; the torrent of black fur seemed endless. Felix had seen skaven attacks like this before, but still he couldn't tear his eyes away.

'How have you survived this long?' Ulrika said. She yanked Felix's arm again and led him out of the building. The terrible screams of the dying – human and ratkin alike – were instantly muted as they passed back through the false image of the derelict warehouse. The illusion of shattered commerce masked the terrible battle taking place within. Felix was glad of it.

'What now?' he asked.

'Now we wait.'

'For what?'

'I have a theory,' Ulrika said. 'Ragethar is a skaven poison. Perhaps they've come to collect Gotrek's body. All we need to do is wait until they win, then follow them.'

Felix stared at the ruined facade for a moment, lost in thought.

'Perhaps you're right.'

When they re-entered some time later, it was hard to breathe. Clouds of scalded fur made the air thick. Bodies, skaven and human, littered the floor. The dying could be heard moaning and whimpering. Felix ignored them all. There was only one body he was interested in.

He leapt up onto the dais but saw that it was empty. He searched for some sign, any evidence that the Slayer had been consumed. Thankfully there was none.

'They took him?' Ulrika asked, eyeing the dead and wounded like a hungry, fat man would ogle a banquet table loaded with fine meats and delicacies.

'Aye, I think so.'

She nodded. 'Stands to reason. So we go after them?'

Felix saw no other choice, though he wished for one. He must have spent a good quarter of his life in sewers and tunnels. He knew full well that Gotrek would never leave him down there with a bunch of ratmen. He placed a hand on his sword hilt to still his nerves and followed Ulrika to the corner of the room.

In their haste to retreat, the skaven had left the grate open. Patches of fur clung to the sides of the square entrance. Felix tried to avoid making contact with anything as he dropped down into the tunnel below. Ulrika landed silently beside him and pointed ahead.

'The skaven will go as deep as possible as quickly as possible. Come on.'

The smell down here was stomach-churning, though slightly more tolerable than that of the battle's aftermath in the warehouse. Felix sloshed through the town's detritus as quickly as his aching legs would carry him, hoping that none of the undesirable flotsam spilled into his boots. He found himself missing the wide sewers of Nuln with their ledges alongside the water channel. Kutenholz was a town just big enough to warrant a sewer system, but it wasn't extensive. Every now and then they would pass under a grating, which allowed some light to filter down into the tunnel.

After a time, Felix could hear the rush of flowing water some distance ahead. Presumably this was the sewer's outlet to the river. Instead of continuing on, Ulrika led him to a side tunnel. Felix realised it was in fact a large hole, gnawed into the stones lining the sewer walls. As they walked, all trace of light faded and the ground sloped downwards. Felix knew they were entering the skaven undertown. He was aware of labyrinthine nests hidden beneath the Empire's cities, but it disturbed him that even towns such as Kutenholz had their own secret hives of activity beneath the surface.

Felix only became aware that Ulrika had stopped when he walked into her. He could barely make her out and was grateful for her astonishing night vision. He stepped back and unsheathed his sword part of the way, as quietly as he could. But a moment later, she started up again so it must have been a false alarm.

After what seemed like a lifetime of walking, the tunnel opened out. Ulrika halted again.

'That way is a large chamber,' she whispered. Felix couldn't see where she was pointing. 'It will likely be full of skaven. I'm surprised we've not seen any yet.'

Felix could hear noises from the gloom: voices, squeaking, chattering.

'We should find another way in.'

'Aye. Let's go this way.'

Ulrika headed off. Felix struggled to keep up with her. His leg muscles burned.

Finally, light crept into the tunnel. The sound of a single skaven speaking, punctuated by roars and squeaks from a large audience, carried clearly to Felix. In time, the pathway opened onto an empty platform, set up high above a huge chamber. As they crept out onto the rickety balcony, they could see below them hundreds of skaven gathered in the large space. All those present, mostly clanrats with a few rat-ogres here and there, stared up at a single, grey-furred creature addressing them. Its robes and markings were familiar to Felix, but the skaven itself was not. This grey seer was young, eager, no doubt deadly. At its feet lay the prone body of Gotrek.

Clearly, all was not well with this skaven army. It was hard to tell since they spoke in their native tongue, but to Felix it seemed as though the chieftains were speaking out against their leader, questioning his motives.

One of them spoke louder than the rest in a series of squeaks and hisses.

To Felix's surprise, he could understand every word the irritated grey seer spoke in reply.

'Castle Reiksguard can wait. Capturing the Slayer's body is not waste of time-effort. The Council of Thirteen will reward us when they receive this gift. All of us will be rewarded, yes-yes?'

The reaction to this sounded more positive. In the enclosed cavern the noise was deafening.

'Why is he speaking Reikspiel?' Felix asked Ulrika in a whisper.

'He's showing off,' she replied.

Another chieftain spoke, this time in broken Reikspiel. 'Who is Slayer, Grey Seer Gnawklaw? Why Council care?'

Gnawklaw tapped his staff upon the stone floor impatiently, quieting the din that accompanied the chieftain's question. It was clear most of the assembled skaven didn't understand the exchange but were following their chieftain's lead.

'He is much-much valuable. This prize is far greater than anything Castle Reiksguard has to offer. Besides, we can go there later. We will take both prizes to the Council and all of us will share in this success. We will achieve what my predecessor could not.'

Something about the way Gnawklaw said 'predecessor' put Felix in mind of an old enemy. He shuddered.

'You risk first mission as grey seer, and all our lives on hunch?' the chieftain said.

'What guarantee do we have that you will not take all the glory for yourself?' another asked.

Gnawklaw rapped his staff on the ground again to quell the roar of agreement.

'I only need to present the Slayer's head to the Council. Perhaps I should divide up the rest and share amongst you? Then you too will have proof of your role in the death of the greatest skaven nemesis!'

These words received the biggest roar of approval so far, enough to make Felix's ears ring. Once the noise had calmed down, he whispered to Ulrika. 'They're going to chop Gotrek up! We have to get him out!'

'I don't think so,' she replied. 'Look.'

Once again, Ulrika's sharp eyes had spotted what Felix had missed. He peered again at the Slayer's corpse-like form. Was that a twitching hand he spied?

It couldn't be. Gotrek wasn't supposed to wake up for a week at least!

'We will not become great by scuttling around, stealing from mancastles in the dead of night. We will become great by delivering the body of our greatest enemy to the Council of Thirteen. We will achieve glory! Now, who wants a cut-slice of Slayer?'

Gnawklaw drew a wickedly sharp blade from his robes, and in one swift moment, took a chunk out of Gotrek's crest. Felix winced but saw no blood. Still, the Slayer was going to be angry. The grey seer tossed the handful of hair into the crowd and the skaven chattered and squeaked appreciatively.

'What's that? You want a piece of his body? How about a hand?'

A roar of approval.

'Ulrika!' Felix hissed, hand on his sword, making ready to jump from the platform.

The skaven blade swished towards Gotrek's arm, but to the grey seer's shock it didn't make contact. A hand clamped around his wrist.

Gnawklaw squeaked. He tore his arm free and spoke a very rapid incantation. A puff of smoke accompanied his hasty departure.

Panic struck in a ripple effect, from those skaven nearest the front all the way to the back, as the ratkin all tried to leave at the same time. Many were trampled to death by the confused rat-ogres. Some made it out. Others were cut down by the hacking and slashing of a very angry Slayer armed with the razor-sharp blade of a grey seer.

'Why are you running away?' Gotrek cried, his voice slicing through the terrified mob as keenly as the knife parted their flesh. 'I'm dead, remember?'

Bits of skaven flew in all directions as the Slayer took out his frustrations upon them.

'You want a piece of me?' he roared, slicing a startled clanrat in two.

Felix and Ulrika jumped down from the ledge, their weapons ready. A mass of fleeing skaven tried to change direction when they saw the danger ahead, but not fast enough. Ulrika was a whirr of motion, dead clanrats dropping at her feet like the faithful worshipping Sigmar himself. Felix did his fair share of damage, his sword gutting, stabbing and slashing at the hateful creatures as they tried to run.

It wasn't long before Ulrika and Felix reached Gotrek.

'I am not happy,' the Slayer grumbled.

'Good!' Felix said. 'Take it out on the vermin!'

Gotrek was only too keen to comply. The remaining skaven had rallied a defence of sorts, forming a barrier between the three comrades and the retreating chieftains.

'Did you bring my axe?' the Slayer asked.

'No,' said Felix. 'I didn't think you'd be needing it.'

Gotrek grunted. 'Looks like we will need to fight our way out of here, manling.'

'Wouldn't have it any other way.'

The two companions yelled an impromptu battle-cry and charged, smashing into the skaven front line like a two-man avalanche.

Ulrika rolled her eyes. 'Men,' she said. Then she too rushed to join the fight.

Felix emerged into the moonlight, grateful for the cool night breeze on his face and the feeling of freedom. They were some way from Kutenholz, on the banks of the river Delb. His eyes had grown so accustomed to the dark of the tunnels that here, outside, it might as well have been noon on a summer day.

Ulrika and Gotrek emerged from the tunnel. Both were covered in skaven blood. Felix assumed he was too. He collapsed by the river, lying on his back and drinking in the sky and the stars. It was a beautiful night by any measure, but it felt even sweeter to be alive and out in the open air again. He rolled to the water's edge and drank for a good while.

Gotrek flopped down beside him. 'Where's my axe, manling?' he demanded.

Typical Gotrek. Not, 'Why was I dead?' but, 'Where's my axe?'

'It's safe, don't worry.'

'And the assassin?'

'Just a mercenary.'

Gotrek grunted. 'I have not been poisoned for a long time. I heard the assassin but assumed he had come to slit my throat. Didn't see the dart until it was too late. I assume we know who hired him.'

'Not for sure,' said Ulrika.

'What is *she* doing here?' Gotrek asked, as if noticing her for the first time.

'I'm just helping to save your life,' Ulrika snapped.

'Unlikely,' said Gotrek.

Ulrika coughed. 'Excuse me! I fought Pragarti and the skaven today, risking my neck for you.'

'You have been busy,' Gotrek said.

Felix turned on his side and propped his head up with one hand. He tossed small stones into the river with the other.

'It's curious, though, Gotrek. Every step of the way, Ulrika's been several moves ahead of me.'

'Not that curious, manling. The vampire is as slippery as a buttered eel.'

'How dare–'

'And isn't it curious,' Felix continued, 'that Ulrika knew you'd been poisoned with Ragethar, even though I never mentioned it to her?'

'I talked to the apothecary,' she explained.

'Perhaps, or maybe you already knew which poison was used.'

Before Ulrika could say anything, Gotrek moved with surprising speed. He leapt at the vampire, forced her to the ground and held the skaven blade against her throat.

'Let me go!' Ulrika hissed, struggling to break free of the Slayer's iron grip.

'Bite me,' said Gotrek.

Felix stood up and walked over. He crouched down close to Ulrika's face.

'And then I thought about how unlikely it was that the apothecary just down the street from the inn would not only recognise the symptoms of an obscure skaven poison but also have the antidote handy. By your own admission, you wanted Pragarti to believe Gotrek was dead so her spell would backfire. That's why you had him poisoned. Am I right?'

'Damn *heroes*,' she spluttered. 'You were so painfully obvious, stomping around looking for Pragarti! I couldn't go near you without her spies seeing me, and I didn't want her to know I was on her trail. I wanted her spell to backfire because she thought the Slayer was dead. If I had told you what I was planning, she would have found out.'

'I hope for your sake the plan worked and Pragarti is dead,' Gotrek said, his face mere inches from Ulrika's. He pressed the blade against her neck, drawing blood.

'Damn skaven interrupted us. I don't know if she escaped or not.'

'A pity. So, vampire, why should I not kill you right now?'

'Felix will not let you!' Ulrika insisted.

Felix didn't relish this. He was mad at Ulrika for what she had put him and the Slayer through. But her heart – cold and unbeating as it was – was in the right place. The threat to the Empire *had* been averted.

'Let her go,' Felix said.

'You do not tell me what to do, manling!' Gotrek thundered.

'I'm not telling you, Slayer. I'm asking you.'

For a moment Gotrek seemed about to slice Ulrika's head clean off. Then he growled in frustration and released her. She was on her feet in a second, but smart enough not to draw her weapon. She touched the fine cut on her neck and then licked the blood from her fingers.

'You had best stay away from us in future,' Felix warned. 'Next time I may not ask Gotrek to spare you.'

Ulrika scowled at them, and then she was gone.

Gotrek and Felix sat by the river as the first rays of dawn crept across the forest floor.

'Next time, I will ensure your funeral is more fitting,' Felix promised the Slayer.

'Aye, manling. Though I wonder if I am capable of dying.'

'Let's never stop trying to find out, eh, Gotrek?'

'I'll drink to that.'

SLAYER'S HONOUR

Nathan Long

1

'What a cesspit,' said Gotrek Gurnisson.

Felix Jaeger had to agree. They had smelled it before they topped the last rise in the road – a heady reek of rotting garbage, raw sewage, burnt meat and stale beer. Now that they were walking through its weathered wooden gates, Felix thought the sight of the place as offensive to the eye as the odour had been to the nose.

Deadgate squatted at the end of a narrow valley in the shadow of the ruined dwarf hold, Karak Azgal, which loomed on a rocky eminence above it. To Felix, the settlement's spread of crude, shingled roofs and dirty streets looked like a crusty brown stain seeping down the slope from an ancient granite cistern.

This was near enough the truth, to hear Gotrek speak of it. When the dwarf lords who ruled Karak Azgal had stopped trying to win the hold back from the orcs and goblins and other monsters that had taken up residence in its depths, they had instead thrown it open to adventurers, letting them delve into it in search of its fabled treasures – for a fee, of course. Word spread of this great opportunity and, despite the fact that Karak Azgal lay far from civilized lands, deep in the remote southern tail of the Worlds Edge Mountains, the valley was soon crawling with fortune hunters, all hoping to come away with dwarf gold, ancient weapons of great power, and gems the size of apples. To service these newcomers, a human settlement had grown up outside the hold. At first it was just a trading post, selling food and supplies for those going underground, but places to spend what loot the adventurers brought back to the surface quickly sprang into being – taverns, fighting pits, gaming parlours, brothels, mortuaries – until it became Deadgate, not so much a town as a clapboard abattoir, designed to flense gold from pockets before their owners made it out of the valley.

Garish signs assaulted Felix's eyes as he and Gotrek walked down the muddy main street, all painted on the fronts of the buildings or swinging over their open doors – the Painted Lady, the Red Rooster, the Pit of Blood, the Palace – each with its bill of fare beneath it, whether this were beer, wine, gambling, fighting, or female companionship.

Below the signs, barkers in flashy clothes sang out those same bills of fare to the hard-faced men who wandered the streets, trying to entice them within, while in the street, costermongers, charm sellers and professional criers were all making their pitches at the top of their voices.

'Gold-hunting canaries! Take one into the deeps and it will lead you to treasure!'

'Pears from the Badlands! One fresh for two pfennigs! Ten rotten for one!'

A human man holding a banner with a rearing dragon emblazoned upon it was shouting the loudest. 'Thane Thorgrin Dragonslayer needs you to fight the greenskin menace! Apply at the hold to join his throng. One gold coin per day of fighting, and free access to the deeps for a month. Make your fortune and save the hold!'

As they walked past a gaudy tavern called the Grail, Gotrek and Felix were accosted by a smiling villain who bowed and scraped before them. 'Come right in, mein Herr and Herr dwarf. This way. It's a long, dusty road from the Badlands to the Worlds Edge Mountains. Why not wet those dry throats with a few mugs of real dwarf ale? Or if your navel is touching your spine, we can fill you up. We have sausages and pies and–'

'Dwarf ale?' asked Gotrek, stopping.

'Indeed, Herr dwarf,' said the tout. 'Bugman's Best. Six kegs, brought up through the pass just this morning.'

The Slayer glared at the man. 'If you are lying, I'll come back here and feed you the mug.'

'No lie, friend,' said the man, holding up his hands. 'We aren't so foolish as to try to fool those who know. Indeed, there's another of your kin within, and he can't get enough of the stuff.'

Gotrek grunted and pushed through the swinging double doors. Felix followed him into the smoky interior, looking around warily. It did not look like the sort of place that would serve Bugman's – and if it didn't, there would be trouble. It was decorated in a shoddy attempt at Bretonnian courtly style, with arched doors and heraldic tapestries and high-backed chairs – but the patrons did not look like they would be at home reciting chivalric poetry at the High Castle of Couronne. A harder, more scarred collection of sell swords and fortune hunters Felix had never seen. Nor did the thick-necked bruisers who manned the bar look like they had been hired for their knowledge of viticulture.

'Are you sure you want to die in a town this ugly?' Felix asked as he and Gotrek stepped around a pair of bouncers dragging an unconscious patron to the door.

'I won't die here,' said Gotrek, pushing to the bar. 'The spider is in the deeps, so that jeweller said.'

'Ah, the deeps,' said Felix. 'I'm sure they'll be much more attractive.'

'They will be dwarf halls,' said Gotrek. 'A fitting place for a Slayer to die.'

'Not so fitting for a poet, unfortunately,' said Felix with a sigh, then signalled the barman. 'Two Bugman's, please.'

They had first heard of the dread spider known as the White Widow in the dwarf hold of Ekrund, where they had ended up after their misadventures in the Black Gulf left them stranded south of the Dragonback Mountains. A dwarf jeweller there, Harn Taphammer, had told them of it as he was appraising the few gems they had salvaged from the shipwreck. He said a human adventurer had come to him to have a ruby the size of a knuckle bone set into a medallion. The man had no left arm and no ears, and walked with a limp – all wounds, he said, from the guardian of the treasure trove from which he stole the ruby, the White Widow, an albino cave spider the size of a hay wagon that made its nest in the deepest reaches of Karak Azgal.

Naturally, Gotrek had set off for the Worlds Edge Mountains the next day. Naturally, Felix had gone with him.

The barman set two froth-capped mugs down in front of them. 'A silver shilling each, please.'

Gotrek scowled, incredulous. 'You're selling Bugman's Best for only a shilling?'

'Aye, Herr dwarf. Good beer at fair prices, that's the Grail's motto.'

Gotrek slid two shillings across the bar then picked up his mug. His single eye glittered sceptically as he lifted the mug to his nose. He inhaled, then grunted, noncommittal, and stuck his flame-red moustache in the foam and drank. Almost immediately he choked and coughed and held the mug at arm's length, staring at it.

'Grungni,' he breathed. 'It *is* Bugman's.'

Felix blinked, surprised, and tried his. It was cool and clean and crisp, with a taste that brought to mind wheat fields and mild autumn days, and it went down his throat like golden light. It was quite possibly the best beer he had ever drunk.

'How does a hole in the wall tavern at the godforsaken arse-end of nowhere have Bugman's Best on tap?' he asked as he came up for air.

'Good, isn't it?' said someone at his shoulder.

Felix turned. A wiry man with dark hair pulled back in a ponytail stood beside him, waving to the barman. He had a nose like an axe blade and an engaging smile, and was dressed in stained, sturdy travelling clothes.

'Very good,' said Felix.

The man's blue eyes took in Gotrek then darted back to Felix. 'A Slayer and his rememberer, am I right?'

'That's right,' said Felix. The Grail was proving a place of wonders. First Bugman's Best at rotgut prices, and now this. Many men knew what a Slayer was, but few knew the position of rememberer. Felix was more used to explaining what he did than acknowledging it. 'I'm surprised you know the word.'

The man grinned. 'I've some little experience with it.' He took two fresh mugs from the barman, then nodded towards the fireplace. 'My companion Agnar and I have a table by the hearth. Would you care to join us?'

Felix followed his gaze and stopped, staring. At the table the man indicated sat a Slayer, staring into the fire, his three orange crests bright red in the light of the flames.

2

Gotrek stared too, and his brow lowered. Felix knew from experience that Slayers did not always relish the company of others of their kind. They were generally solitary types, brooding on their pasts and singularly focussed on making their futures as short as possible. Gotrek's closest comrades Snorri Nosebiter and Malakai Makaisson were Slayers, but there had been others of his kind to whom he had taken an instant dislike. Felix, on the other hand, had never met another rememberer before, and the prospect of talking to someone who understood what his life entailed was too tempting to pass up. Despite Gotrek's wary glare, Felix nodded to the dark-haired man.

'Lead on.'

In any other company, the grizzled Slayer sitting at the table would have been the most intimidating drinker in the tavern. He was old enough that grey roots were showing at the base of his three red-dyed crests and braided beard, and his oft-scarred, heavily-muscled arms were so covered with fading tattoos that they were nearly solid blue from thick wrists to broad, bulging shoulders. His face was like a wood knot – so gnarled and battered that Felix could barely see his eyes – and he had a drinker's nose in the centre of it as red and lumpy as a halfling's fist.

Compared to Gotrek, however, he was practically puny. Gotrek was the biggest dwarf Felix had ever met. Even without his foot-high Slayer's crest, he was nearly five feet tall – half a head taller than Agnar – and almost a foot broader in the shoulder, with arm muscles that writhed like mating pythons at his every move. A great red beard flowed down over Gotrek's broad chest to tuck into a wide leather belt, and a patch covered his missing left eye. The eye that remained was as sharp as an ice-pick, and as bright as the gleaming blade of his ancient rune axe. Felix had known raging drunks twice Gotrek's size to mumble apologies and quietly leave the room when confronted with the full power of that malefic gaze.

Agnar looked up at Gotrek as they approached with ill-concealed mistrust, but his rememberer was all smiles.

'Agnar Arvastsson, may I present to you...' He looked to Felix. 'Pardon me, who may I present?'

Felix inclined his head. 'Felix Jaeger and Gotrek Gurnisson, at your service.'

'A pleasure,' said the rememberer. 'And I am Henrik Daschke, late of Talabheim – and just about every other city in the Empire.'

Agnar eyed them anew at their names. 'I've heard of you,' he said in a heavy voice. It sounded like he'd put away quite a bit of Bugman's already. 'You went north into the Wastes. You found Karag Dum.'

'Aye,' said Gotrek, and took a seat opposite him.

'I heard also that you found your doom,' said Agnar. 'In Sylvania.'

'No,' said Felix, taking the seat to Gotrek's right as Henrik sat by Agnar and gave him his mug. 'We were–' He paused, not wanting to try to explain the tunnels of the Old Ones and Albion and all that had come after. 'We just got lost.'

'I remember now.' Henrik raised an eyebrow. 'But that was years ago. A long time to be a-slaying.'

Gotrek bristled. 'What do you mean by that?'

Henrik held up his hands. 'Nothing, Slayer. Only that you must be indomitable in battle.'

Gotrek grunted and took another long pull at his Bugman's.

Henrik turned to Felix. 'And I'm surprised *you* are alive at all,' he said. 'The lot of a rememberer is an uncertain one, is it not?'

Felix shrugged, uncomfortable. Henrik was right, of course. Like Agnar, Gotrek was a Slayer, sworn to redeem himself for some secret shame by dying in battle against the deadliest monsters he could find. Felix had become his rememberer when, in the middle of a drunken binge, he had vowed to immortalise his death in an epic poem. Since then he had found himself the victim of a precarious paradox. How was he to stay close enough to Gotrek to faithfully record the details of his doom, and at the same time escape that doom himself? It was a puzzle that he had thought about often since their travels began, but it felt strange discussing it in front of the Slayers. 'It has its moments,' he said at last.

Henrik laughed. 'Moments indeed. How many times have I followed

Agnar into some deadly melee in order to witness his last moments, only to find that they were likely to be mine too. It's enough to make one want to stay at the inn and make up a doom out of whole cloth, hey?'

He clapped Felix on the shoulder, and Felix smiled weakly, then shot a glance at Agnar to see how he was taking it. He was shaking his head, but did not look particularly put out.

'Always with the jokes, manling,' he said. 'One day you'll take it too far and I'll slay you.'

'Then who would do your remembering for you?' asked Henrik.

Agnar just chuckled and had another drink. Gotrek eyed him with an expression halfway between pity and disgust. Felix felt a similar emotion, and was going to make his excuses when Henrik turned to him again.

'And what brings you to Karak Azgal?' he asked. 'Going after some horror of the deeps?'

'A spider called the White Widow,' said Felix. 'We heard rumour of it in Ekrund. As big as a steam tank, they said.'

'You're here for the same?' asked Gotrek.

Henrik laughed. 'Fear not, Slayer. There are dooms for all in the halls of the Dragon Crag. No, we came hoping to fight a monster of Chaos it is said lurks in the very deepest part of the mines, but another menace has risen that prevents us from descending.'

'What's that?' asked Felix.

'Orcs,' said Agnar.

'Did you not hear old Thorgrin's criers in the street as you came in?' asked Henrik.

'"Make your fortune and save the hold"?' asked Felix.

'That's the one,' said Henrik. 'And it needs saving. Thorgrin is desperate. Apparently, a warboss by the name of Gutgob Stinkfoot has conquered all the orcs that live in the lower depths, and is stirring them up to make war on the hold above. Thorgrin fears Gutgob has the numbers to wipe out Karak Azgal and Deadgate both and he's recruiting everyone who can hold a weapon to help him make a stand.'

'The orcs stand between us and our dooms?' asked Gotrek.

'And Thorgrin,' said Henrik. 'He has forbidden entry into the hold until the greenskins are dealt with. The only way to get in is to sign up with his throng.'

Gotrek snorted. 'Let me hunt this spider, and I'll kill any orcs I find on the way.'

'He wants an army,' said Agnar, shaking his head. 'Anyone acting alone lessens the troops he can field.'

Gotrek growled and took another drink.

'But he'll let anyone who fights into the depths afterwards, without paying the treasure hunting licence?' asked Felix.

Henrik nodded. 'It's not a bad deal. But I know a better one.'
'What's that?' asked Gotrek.
Henrik jerked his thumb at the bar. 'Louis Lanquin, who owns this place, has got Thorgrin's go-ahead to raise a regiment of his own, to fight alongside the dwarfs. He's paying twice what Thorgrin is paying, and he'll pay the licence fee for any who are in at the kill.'
'And why would he spend all this coin?'
'A simple matter of economics, friend dwarf,' said an accented voice behind Felix.
Felix turned and saw a richly dressed man with oiled blond hair and lace at his throat and cuffs stepping towards the table. He had a paunch and a double chin, but the breadth of his shoulders and the scar that crossed his nose at the bridge spoke of a more vigorous past. His eyes too had the keen alertness of a fighting man, no matter that he tried to hide it with a merry twinkle.
'I am Louis Lanquin of Quenelles, at your service,' he said, bowing with a flourish of his hand.
Felix inclined his head politely. 'Felix Jaeger and Gotrek Gurnisson, at yours,' he said. 'And my compliments to your cellar. We were surprised to find Bugman's here.'
Lanquin quirked a smile. 'Another enticement to woo men – and dwarfs – to my cause. Those who sign with me will drink free in my establishment for the rest of their lives.'
'Why?' asked Gotrek again.
Lanquin put his hand to his breast. 'Thane Thorgrin is not the only one to have a stake in the survival of this town. The dwarfs may rob the treasure seekers coming and going with their tolls for entry and their taxes on what is taken from the hold, but there is still enough left in their pockets afterwards for a poor innkeeper to make a living. I do well here, and I would like to continue to do well, and I do not have the confidence that Thorgrin's few recruits will guarantee that. Thus–' He produced a stack of four gold coins between his fingers as if by magic, then set it on the table. 'I am willing to make a substantial outlay now, in order to assure continued return in the years to come.'
He divided the stack in two and slid two gold coins towards Gotrek, and two towards Felix. 'Monsieurs Agnar and Henrik have signed on. What say you join them? With warriors of your calibre in our ranks, we are sure to win.'
Felix looked to Gotrek. This was his to answer.
The Slayer stared at the gold with a dwarf's usual reverence, but at last he shook his head. 'A Slayer who finds his doom needs neither gold nor ale afterwards. Your reward is meaningless.'
Agnar blinked at this statement, as if he hadn't considered it that way before, and Lanquin looked as if he were going to make another

argument, but finally he shrugged and took back his gold.

'As you will, friend dwarf,' he said. 'Perhaps you will change your mind. Until then, drink your fill. It is on the house.'

Felix groaned. Giving free beer to a Slayer was sure to lead to fighting and property damage, and the prospect of paying more gold to Lanquin than he had offered in order to repair tables, chairs and broken windows loomed large before him, but to his surprise, Gotrek was practically abstemious for the rest of the night. He only drank ten mugs of Bugman's, and did little more than exchange war stories with Agnar. Felix did the same with Henrik, enjoying himself despite the mocking tone the man put into every tale he told. Henrik might be a blowhard, but he knew Felix's every concern and complaint. He laughed at jokes and stories that only another rememberer would understand. He had known the loneliness and the homesickness and the cold nights in the middle of nowhere. He had suffered through the rages and black moods of his companion. He had made the hair's breadth escapes and survived the wounds and fevers that were an inescapable part of following a Slayer. Henrik might not be Felix's friend, but he was his brother. That could not be denied.

3

After sleeping the night at the Grail, Gotrek and Felix woke to a light but steady rain that soaked them to the skin as they trudged up the muddy zigzag path to Skalf's Hold, the dwarfs' above-ground settlement built upon the ruins of Karak Azgal.

Walking with Gotrek through the dragon-mouthed gate in the thick stone walls at the top of the broad plateau, Felix was struck with wonder. There could not have been a greater contrast between the town on the hill and the town in the valley. Within the hold's walls was a tidy grid of neatly paved, rain-washed streets, all lined with squat stone houses and commercial buildings of dwarfish design, and all immaculately cared for. There was no trash in the gutters, and the only smell was that of someone baking bread. Felix had seen dwarf riches before – vast, gilded chambers deep underground – but this modest holdfast in the middle of the moonscape of the Worlds Edge Mountains struck him as more ostentatious than the most lavish guild hall. It was as if some nobleman had allowed his beautiful daughter to walk naked and unescorted through the worst slums of Altdorf. She might not show any outward display of wealth, but the noble's confidence in her safety spoke of great reserves of hidden power.

Gotrek grumbled under his breath as they walked towards the keep that rose in the centre of the town. 'Not proper. A dressed-up defeat.'

'What do you mean?' asked Felix.

Gotrek snorted. 'The kin of Skalf Dragonslayer lost Karak Azgal, and couldn't win it back. Instead they built a town on top of it and charged others to do their fighting for them.' He flashed a thick-fingered hand at the prosperous houses. 'All this was built not on mining or smithing. It was built on fees and taxes taken from the fools who come to seek their fortune below.'

Felix looked around again, seeing it in a new light. 'So it's no different than Deadgate.'

'Aye,' said Gotrek. 'A marble-walled cesspit instead of a clapboard one.'

The streets around the town's central keep were filled with heavily armed dwarfs with the dragon of Karak Azgal on their shields, as well as a more motley collection of mercenaries, adventurers and fighting men, all hunching stoically in the rain. The square to the north of the keep had been turned into a makeshift military camp, with tents of all shapes and descriptions lined up in ragged rows. Recruiters were out in force, offering Thane Thorgrin's coin to fight the greenskins, and ale and food sellers were carting their wares around in barrows and doing brisk business with the troops and applicants.

Gotrek ignored it all and strode through the open doors of the keep itself. A table had been set up under a tent in the middle of the courtyard, and would-be warriors were lined up to make their mark in the recruitment book. Gotrek ignored this too and stumped towards a door that led into the keep itself. The dwarf guards who stood on either side of it stepped in his way, and a dwarf veteran crossed to him, his hand on his axe.

'What's your business here, Slayer?'

'I want a licence to enter the hold,' said Gotrek. 'I seek the cave spider.'

'Licences are not being issued,' said the dwarf. 'Not until Stinkfoot's been dealt with. You want to go down, join up. You'll have plenty of fighting.'

'I don't care about your fight. I go to my doom.'

The grizzled dwarf's eyes went cold. 'You don't want to help your race? You don't want to help your brothers save their hold?'

Gotrek spat at his feet. 'You don't want to save the hold. You want to save your little sky-bare surface town so you can go on selling licences and candle stubs.'

'*What* did you say?' The veteran's eyes had gone from ice to fire in a blink.

Felix swallowed and dropped his hand to his hilt. If this came to blows it would be bad. Gotrek might find his doom at the hands of fellow dwarfs, or worse, he might slaughter half the settlement.

'If you saved the hold,' continued Gotrek. 'You'd lose all your business. You'd have to work for a living.'

'Get out,' said the dwarf through clenched teeth. 'Before I throw you out. We don't want help from the likes of you.'

'On the contrary,' said a voice from behind him. 'A Slayer is just what I need.'

The veteran looked around as a white-bearded dwarf in gromril plate stepped through the door into the rain, followed by a retinue of dwarf Hammerers. The guards all saluted him but he looked only at Gotrek. He had a bulging gut beneath a breastplate that had been custom-made to accommodate it, and a round, pink face under his white beard. He looked like a shop keep, but the fine armour and the deference of the guards said otherwise.

'Thane Thorgrin,' said the sergeant. 'I was just removing this–'

'Stand down, Holdborn,' said the thane, then nodded to Gotrek. 'Your assessment of the situation is harsh but accurate, Slayer. We have profited from the loss of the hold, but better that than abandon it altogether. The sale of all those candle stubs will one day allow us to raise an army strong enough to purge the depths once and for all.'

'And meanwhile you let greenskins nest in the halls of your ancestors and grant licences to fools to be eaten by them.'

The rotund thane smiled. 'I have often thought that it was much easier for a dwarf to be uncompromising when he intended to die at his earliest opportunity.'

Gotrek snorted and turned back towards the gates. 'I'll go back to the Bretonnian. At least he's an honest thief.'

'Go if you wish,' said Thorgrin as Felix started after the Slayer. 'But I can give you one thing the innkeeper can't.'

Gotrek kept walking.

'The lair of the White Widow,' called the thane. 'My scouts have found its location.'

Gotrek stopped, then turned back.

'Help us defeat the greenskins,' said Thorgrin. 'And I will tell you where it lives.'

'Where do I sign?' said Gotrek.

By the time Gotrek and Felix had penned their names in Thorgrin's book and received his coin, and been told to report back to the keep the next morning before sunrise for the thane's big push into the hold, the earlier light rain had become a downpour. It came straight down in sheets so thick it was impossible to see more than five paces in any direction, and the gutters of Skalf's Hold's cobbled streets were swift-running streams a foot deep.

Deadgate had no cobbled streets or gutters, and was consequently a swamp. By the time Gotrek and Felix had made their way down the zigzag path and passed through the settlement's eastern gate, they were slogging through knee-high mud, and the streets had emptied completely, the doors and shutters of the ramshackle inns and houses closed tight against the torrent. The place might have been a ghost town.

Even so, Felix was surprised when he started seeing ghosts. Out of the corner of his eye, he thought he saw a hooded figure hunched in the mouth of an alley to their right, but when he looked properly, it was gone. There was nothing but rain and a pile of barrels. Another figure appeared at the corner of a building, but it too vanished when he turned towards it.

Gotrek stopped in the middle of the flooded street and glared around, peering out from under his sodden crest, which had flopped down over his one eye. 'We are being hunted.'

'Haunted?'

'Hunted.' He lifted his rune axe from his back and readied it.

'Only two streets to the Grail,' said Felix, drawing his sword. 'Should we make a break for it?'

'We'll have to get through them first,' said Gotrek.

Felix followed the Slayer's gaze. Five hooded figures were appearing out of the obscuring torrent like spectres materialising from the ether. Unlike spectres, however, they were armed with very real looking swords. He heard a splash behind him and the scrape of steel. Four more were blocking their retreat, and more stepped from the alleys on either side.

Felix went on guard and raised his voice to be heard over the rain. 'What do you want?'

'To get paid,' said one.

And with that, they attacked.

4

Felix faced out behind Gotrek and braced for the ambushers' attack. The Slayer, however, didn't wait. He roared towards the charging men, churning the mud and whirling his axe around his head like the blade of a dwarf gyrocopter. Busy with his own assailants, Felix didn't see what happened next, but he heard the clang of steel meeting steel and the sick chop of steel meeting flesh, followed by the shrieks and gasps of butchered men, and knew Gotrek was faring well.

He, on the other hand, was in some difficulty. The men he faced were not great swordsmen by any stretch, but there were a lot of them, and they all had one target, while he had many. He flashed around with Karaghul and knocked aside two blades, but three more were sweeping towards him. He jerked back and left to avoid them, and nearly pitched face-first into the mud as it sucked at his boots.

A bright bite of pain flared above his elbow as one of the blades nicked him, and two more swords stabbed for his face as he stumbled. With a desperate swat, he batted them aside, then crashed into the men who had wielded them, more by accident than design.

The first went down under the impact, but Felix clung to the second and spun him around, just in time for him to take the blades of two of his comrades in the stomach. Felix shoved the gutted man forward, then slashed over his shoulder with Karaghul and caught one of the assassins in the neck and the other on the back of the hand. As they staggered back, the man who had fallen tried to push himself up under Felix's feet. Felix chopped down and he sank into the mud, red staining the brown.

The others came in again, more wary now, six of them, and Felix backed away, sword out, tearing off his cloak with his free hand. The heavy wool was saturated with water and made him feel as if he were being dragged down by the shoulders. He wrapped a few folds of it around his wrist for a buckler and held it out to the side.

'Come on, then,' he said.

But the men were staring past him, faces uncertain, and when he dared a glance over his shoulder, he knew why. One of Gotrek's attackers was toppling, headless, into the mud, and the bodies of five others floated face down in spreading pools of crimson. The Slayer was backing up two more, one of which was holding a bent sword in front of him and weeping, while the other was missing his left forearm and clutching the stump. Two more were fleeing into the rain.

Felix grinned savagely at the men who hesitated before him. 'Aye. And if you kill me, he'll *really* be mad.'

He had to give them credit. Three of them actually came at him again. Felix slapped the leftmost one with his drenched cloak, knocking him into the centre one, then parried the blade of the right-hand one and backhanded him across the arm.

The man stumbled away, hissing and dropping his sword, and Felix turned on the other two, whirling his cloak in their faces and stabbing under it. They leapt back, then kept retreating, staring over his shoulder.

Felix looked back and saw Gotrek slogging through the mud towards him, spattered in blood, with brains dripping from the blade of his axe.

Felix cursed and splashed after them. 'Stop!' he called. 'Stand where you are! Who sent you? Who is paying you?'

They turned and ran without answering and he splashed after them, but floundered in the mud and went to his knees as they vanished into the downpour. With a sigh he struggled to his feet and slogged back to Gotrek, who was turning the bodies of the fallen face-up in the mud and pulling back their hoods.

'Any left alive?'

The Slayer shook his head. 'Those we didn't kill drowned.'

Felix looked at the uncovered faces of their attackers. He recognised none of them. They were all of the type common to Deadgate – lean, scarred men who looked hungry enough to kill their own mothers for meat. Well, they were sated now.

'Any idea who they were, or what they wanted?'

Gotrek grabbed one by the ankle. 'No. But I know who might.'

He started down the swampy street towards the Grail, dragging one of the corpses through the mud behind him.

Louis Lanquin wrinkled his nose as he looked at the dead man lying in a spreading puddle of filth and blood in the middle of his tavern.

'He is no acquaintance of mine,' he said. 'And I wish you had asked me to come out to see him, rather than bringing him in and dirtying my floor.'

The place was crowded with patrons seeking shelter from the rain, and they were all staring at Felix, Gotrek and the corpse. Felix noticed that Agnar and Henrik were not among them. Maybe they were still sleeping it off. Agnar had outdrunk Gotrek three to one the night before.

'You didn't pay him to kill us?' growled Gotrek.

The Bretonnian laughed. 'My friends, if I had wanted to kill you, I could have poisoned your Bugman's last night, or murdered you as you were sleeping it off.' He signalled two bouncers and gestured to the body, then looked back to the Slayer. 'There are many factions here in Deadgate, and more in Skalf's Hold, and some of them do not want the dwarfs to win. If they thought your deaths would further their cause, they would not hesitate.'

With practiced speed, the bouncers brought a sheet of canvas, laid it beside the dead man and rolled him onto it. As they dragged him towards the door, a servant came in with a mop and bucket and began cleaning up the mud. Within a minute, all trace of the corpse's visit was gone.

'I bear you no ill will for suspecting me,' said Lanquin. 'They who have just fought for their lives are bound to look on the world with some mistrust.' He waved to the bar. 'Please. You are welcome to drink as before, on the house. Think of it as an apology for how shabbily my adopted town has treated you thus far.'

Felix looked at Gotrek. The Slayer shook his head.

'We would not presume upon your hospitality further, monsieur,' Felix said. 'You have already been too generous. Thank you all the same.'

Lanquin shrugged. 'As you will, and I wish you a more restful time wherever you go.'

He bowed as Gotrek and Felix strode to the door and splashed out into the rain again.

'He's lying,' said Gotrek. 'Those killers were his.'

'You can't know that,' said Felix.

'I don't have to know it, manling. I *know* it.'

'But why would he want us dead? Because we took Thorgrin's coin instead of his? That doesn't make sense. Don't they both want the same thing? Why would Lanquin kill *anyone* who aimed to fight the orcs?'

'Maybe he wants the orcs to win,' said Gotrek.

Felix looked at him askance. 'That makes even less sense. You heard him last night. It is a simple question of economics. He needs Deadgate to survive just as much as Thorgrin does.'

Gotrek shrugged. 'Sense or no sense, I sleep with one hand on my axe tonight.'

'Aye,' said Felix. 'Aye.'

After spending a night at an inn called the Palace, Gotrek and Felix woke, mildly surprised they hadn't been attacked in their sleep, and returned before sunrise to Thane Thorgrin's keep. They were not alone. The courtyard of the keep was packed with dwarfs of Karak Azgal's throng, neat blocks of axe-wielding warriors, thunderers with their handguns over their shoulders, and veteran Ironbreakers clad head-to-toe in heavy plate armour. Behind the dwarfs were a less orderly mass of human mercenaries – a mix of hardened adventurers, greedy treasure seekers and nervous shopkeeps, come to protect their properties and investments in Deadgate. They were divided into squads behind more seasoned captains, and were haphazardly armed and armoured. Nevertheless, there were a fair amount of them. Felix reckoned that, all told, there were roughly three hundred dwarfs, and two hundred mercenaries lined up and awaiting orders, and to his surprise, Agnar and Henrik were among them.

The grizzled Slayer kept his eyes on the floor and seemed to weave on his feet as Felix and Gotrek crossed to them, while Henrik gave them a chagrined look.

'Agnar took what you said about gold and free ale to heart,' he said. 'So we followed your example.'

'A Slayer who meets his doom doesn't need those things,' said Agnar, still not looking up. 'And I didn't trust the Bretonnian.'

'Aye,' said Henrik with a snort. 'Too nice by half. We'll fight for Thorgrin and let fate lead us, as we always have.'

'We're glad to have you at our side,' said Felix, though he wasn't sure he was speaking for Gotrek. The Slayer just grunted and glared into the middle distance with his single eye while they waited for orders. Of course, that was his expression whether happy, angry or indifferent, so it was difficult to tell.

A short while later, Louis Lanquin arrived with the troops he had recruited, a force of about a hundred men, and was directed by Thorgrin's lieutenants to squeeze them in on the left side of the courtyard. He bowed with stiff politeness to the Slayers, then kept his eyes forward. It seemed to Felix that the innkeeper had done better with his recruiting than the thane had. Though there were fewer of them, most of his troops looked harder and more experienced than the humans Thorgrin had managed to recruit, and better equipped. He seemed to have spared no expense in outfitting them with quality arms and armour.

'A substantial outlay to assure a continued return,' murmured Felix.

With a rumble, the doors to the inner keep opened, and Thane Thorgrin strode out onto the steps with his Hammerers and banner carrier behind him. He saluted the assembly, then raised his voice.

'Citizens and friends of Karak Azgal, today begins a great venture. With this great army of dwarfs and men, we will shatter the alliance of tribes that Gutgob Stinkfoot has bullied together, and beat back the greenskin menace for decades to come. The safety and security of the Dragon Crag will be assured, and we will all be able to get back to business as usual.'

Gotrek snorted, and a few of the surrounding dwarfs looked around at him, but none spoke.

'It will not be an easy fight, nor a pleasant one,' continued Thorgrin. 'But I am confident that our superior tactics and weaponry will win the day. We intend to lead the orcs into a slaughterhouse from which there is no escape, and you will be the butchers!'

There was a cheer, mostly from the dwarfs, and Thorgrin waved for silence.

'A word of warning, before we enter the depths, to those not of our throng,' he said. 'During this war, our laws pertaining to treasure hunting remain in effect. All volunteers leaving the hold will be searched, and any treasures found are subject to the usual taxes. Any treasures deemed to be important relics of Karak Azgal's history will be confiscated. Anyone attempting to hide treasures from the authorities will be imprisoned. You are already being paid handsomely, and given opportunities to search the depths not normally granted. We will not take kindly to those who attempt to take advantage of our generosity.'

There was a general grumbling, but nobody made any open complaint, and Thorgrin continued, outlining his battle plans and the responsibilities of each of his sub-commanders. Felix didn't get to hear most of it, however, for only a moment later, Holdborn, the dwarf veteran who had butted heads with Gotrek, stepped up to him and Agnar and gave a curt bow. 'Slayers,' he said. 'If you would come with me. Thane Thorgrin has a special duty he would like to give you.'

Gotrek barked a laugh. 'Does he want us to unclog his jakes?'

Holdborn gave him a cold smile. 'I only wish. It is a clearance hardly more pleasant, though. This way.'

5

Gotrek, Agnar, Felix and Henrik followed Holdborn through a side door into the keep, then down a narrow stair into an underground chamber surrounding a great shaft that slanted into the earth. A mechanism of pulleys and chains for hauling things up and down the incline hunched at the top of the shaft, and a crew of dwarfs was fixing a stout, wheeled cannon to a hook. As Holdborn crossed to them, they began to let out the chain and lower it into the depths.

Holdborn nodded to the leader of the crew, a burly dwarf in a leather apron with a tightly braided beard and a handkerchief tied around his bald head, then turned to Felix, Henrik and the Slayers.

'This is Engineer Migrunssun. He and his crew are tasked with bringing cannon to the old firing platform in the minehead of the eastern gem shafts. They will be part of our enfilade when the battle starts. Unfortunately, the minehead is overrun with ghouls. This is where you come in.'

Gotrek and Agnar nodded, pleased, while Felix swallowed. He noticed Henrik was looking pale as well.

'Thick as maggots on a week-old corpse,' said Migrunsson, grinning. 'And we'll need to clear them out completely. Can't have ghouls trying to eat you while you're aiming a field piece. Distracting.'

'You expect the orcs to come up through the mine shafts, then?' asked Henrik. 'You're training your guns on them?'

Holdborn shook his head. 'That is the other duty of the engineers. They will be caving in the shafts, among other passages. Sealing them off, so the greenskins can't come up behind us.'

'The firing platform looks two ways,' said Migrunsson. 'It's a fortified room above an archway between the minehead chamber and the Great Hall of the Guild of Jewellers, and it has gun ports into both rooms. Thorgrin plans to make the great hall his field of battle. We'll poke our muzzles through the windows up top and be able to rake the orc flanks from an untouchable emplacement.'

'Untouchable?' asked Gotrek. 'What's to stop the greenskins coming through the archway from the great hall?'

'Ah, well,' said Migrunsson. 'That arch is sealed off. Has been since the ghouls started congregating in the minehead. The orcs won't get through it. Not without a battering ram.'

'But with the arch sealed off,' said Holdborn, 'neither will you. You'll have to go the long way around.'

'Naturally,' said Felix under his breath.

Henrik grinned bleakly at him.

The dwarf cannon crews pushed a heavily laden wagon towards the slanting shaft. It was loaded with blackpowder barrels and crates of cannon shot. A smaller wagon rolled out behind it, piled with food, firewood and other supplies. Felix's eyes widened. How far was it to the eastern minehead?

Catching his look, Migrunsson chuckled. 'It's only a few hours' march, rememberer. But we might be waiting a long time for the greenskins to accept our invitation to dance.'

'I hope you find your doom, Slayer,' said Holdborn, saluting Gotrek. 'It'll save me seeing your face again.'

Gotrek growled at his back as he turned and strode off. 'It'll save your hide, watchman.'

The chain stopped rattling off the winch and then went slack. Migrunsson started winding it back up and nodded to Felix, Henrik and the Slayers.

'Head on down,' he said. 'Two more carts and we're off.'

Gotrek and Agnar started down the slant shoulder to shoulder. Felix and Henrik hesitated, then went after them.

'Once more, eh?' asked Henrik.

'At least,' said Felix.

The walls of the shaft closed in around him and a chill wind blew up from below. He shivered, though from cold or premonition, he could not tell.

Sturdy little mine ponies were hitched in teams of two to the cannons and the wagons once they reached the bottom of the incline, and soon the artillery train was under way. Gotrek, Felix, Agnar and Henrik went first, followed by Migrunsson and the cannon crews – three dwarfs to a gun – then the guns themselves, the powder wagon and supply wagon, each with a dwarf driver, and the last with a dwarf field surgeon, and lastly, a rearguard of six Thunderers, who would be adding musket fire to the heavy shot of the cannons when they reached the emplacement.

'The long way around' was long indeed, and treacherous. Engineer Migrunsson assured them that things were much worse further down, but Felix thought that this first 'civilized' level was bad enough to be getting along with. They went by way of service passages and side tunnels, which, being dwarf work, were still wide enough for six dwarfs to walk abreast, and three times as tall as Felix – at least they would have been had they been in good repair. Unfortunately, they were not.

In the light of the torches that swung from the wagons, Felix saw everywhere signs of battle and cataclysm. Walls were slumped into rubble around blackened craters. Huge stones had fallen from the ceiling. In some places, the ceiling had come down entirely and the train had to skirt the blockage by way of smaller tunnels. In other places, the floor had buckled so steeply that all the dwarfs had to get behind the cannons and push, to help the ponies get them over the hump.

Though Felix saw no orcs or ghouls or other horrors, their spoor was everywhere – gnawed human bones, piles of scat, mounds of rotting rubbish, a long streak of dried blood where a body had been dragged – and he heard strange moans and screeches echoing out of dark cross tunnels. There were signs of human intrusion as well – holes broken through walls with pickaxe or explosives, abandoned lanterns and gloves and canteens scattered about, dead 'gold-hunting canaries' in tiny wicker cages, messages scrawled at intersections in many different languages.

'Go not this way. Giant rats.'

'Anya, I waited, but they're coming. I love you.'

'Merde. Je tourne en rond.'

There was a place where the ceiling had bulged down to within six feet of the floor, as if melted by some terrible heat, and the drivers had to lead the ponies through for it was too low to ride on the wagons. Felix's hair rose on his scalp as he ducked under that bulge and he felt a sick prickling under his skin that made him want to scrub himself with lye.

Migrunsson led them through all of it as if they were going on a walk through a meadow, turning left and right without hesitation and humming a jaunty little marching song. Henrik sang too. Not the same song, but a tuneless little tune like a nursery rhyme, though so soft Felix couldn't make out the words. It began to grate on his nerves after a while, but he didn't want to start an argument, so he didn't say anything. Agnar walked in silence, drinking from a canteen that Felix was almost certain didn't contain water.

They walked until Felix got hungry, and quite a while after that, but finally Migrunsson put up a hand and slowed to a stop.

'Eat something and have a drink,' he said. 'We are close to the ghoul nest now. You'll need your strength.'

The cannon crews and drivers took biscuit and dried meat from their packs, and lined up for ale poured from a keg on the supply wagon.

'Ghouls started biding in the minehead twenty years or so ago,' Migrunssun told the Slayers as they knocked back a few mugs. 'Some master of the dark arts set up house there, stealing bodies of dead adventurers and performing weird rites upon them, but he didn't last long. A band of heroes led by a hammer priest went down there and caved his head in, then burned his body. Ever since then, though, ghouls seem to be drawn to the place. It's like they can still smell the black magic in the stones.'

'And you haven't tried to cleanse the place?' asked Henrik.

'Oh aye,' said Migrunsson. 'Many a time. But they always come back. Worse than roaches.'

When the dwarfs had finished their meat and drink, they drew their hand axes and jammed their helms down on their heads and murmured vows to their ancestors. The Slayers didn't pray, just rolled their necks and limbered up their arms in preparation for the fight to come.

Agnar's weapon was a long axe as tall as he was, with a sharply curved head and a vicious spike at the heel. He and Henrik drank one last mug of ale each, and Henrik refilled Agnar's canteen from the keg for him. When they were finished, Henrik drew a heavy broadsword and made the sign of Sigmar's hammer on his chest.

'I've never quite got over it,' the rememberer murmured to Felix as they went to stand behind the Slayers in the line of march. 'The nerves before a battle.'

'Nor I,' said Felix.

Engineer Migrunsson whistled the column forward and the Slayers strode ahead into the darkness beyond the wagon lanterns. Agnar was listing a little as he walked.

The smell came first – a faint sourness that wrinkled the nose and clung to the back of the throat. A minute later it was an eye-watering reek, equal parts rotting corpse and unwashed beggar, and as the flags of the tunnel became littered with bones, excrement and torn clothes, it swelled to a choking miasma of death that made Felix wish he had not eaten anything at their stop. Henrik turned and vomited against the wall, and the dwarfs soaked their kerchiefs in ale and tied them over their noses and mouths before continuing.

The glow of a fire flickered on the walls of the tunnel ahead, and a hunched form was briefly silhouetted. It raised a misshapen head towards the oncoming company, then darted into an open archway, gibbering warnings.

'Through there is the minehead chamber,' said Migrunsson, priming a flintlock. 'Their home sweet home.'

Ahead, the passage echoed with howls of rage and the slap of bare feet on stone. Felix's stomach slid into his guts as he watched churning shadows looming larger against the tunnel wall. Then they appeared. A seething tide of fish-white horrors poured out of the archway and bounded at the dwarfs: long-armed, crook-backed subhumans – males and females – their slavering mouths filled with sharp teeth and their eyes filled with nothing but hunger.

The nearest went down to Migrunsson's handgun, its head exploding in a crimson shower, but the rest vaulted its toppling body and surged ahead, clawing and shrieking and snapping their jaws. Gotrek and Agnar charged forward to meet them, and dismantled half a dozen into bloody chunks with their first swings, but the tunnel was too wide for the two Slayers to stop them all, and dozens more swarmed past to launch themselves at Felix, Henrik and Migrunsson's cannon crews.

Hook-clawed hands slashed at Felix's face and grabbed at his arms. Saw-toothed mouths shrieked at him, nearly overwhelming him with breath that smelled like putrid meat. He lashed out with Karaghul, gagging, and carved great wounds into the horrors, cleaving flesh and shattering bones and knocking them to the floor. Beside him, Henrik fought with a wide-eyed determination that showed both skill and terror. Felix guessed he looked about the same.

Around them, the dwarfs met the ghouls' crazed flailing with practised formation, spreading across the width of the tunnel and hewing with their hand axes like threshers advancing down a field. Felix and Henrik kept pace with them, content to take the protection of their flanks and let the Slayers do their butcher's work out in front of the line.

Watching them, Felix was once again stunned by the speed and savage fury of their kind. They spun like drunken tops, axes blurring and red crests whipping about, and the ghouls seemed to just fall apart around them. White limbs flew in arcs of blood. Scarred heads toppled from bony shoulders. Guts spilled from torn torsos. Agnar was not quite as fast or strong as Gotrek, but his long axe had a greater reach, and he whirled it around him like a fan blade, lopping heads and crushing skulls. Gotrek got in closer, shearing legs and splitting ribcages, and was soon crimson from head to toe.

With this red whirlwind at its head, the dwarf column chopped its way to the archway and through it into the minehead, a high, firelit staging room with a huge black opening on the west wall and a smaller on the north. On the east wall, a wide flight of steps rose to a door above a sealed arch – the firing platform. They had reached their destination.

Scores of ghouls were rising from where they crouched around feeble fires and loped across the filth-slicked floor for the dwarfs. Beyond them, the flames showed shoulder-high heaps of bones and clothing and broken implements piled in the corners, and crusted rag-mounds that Felix feared were beds. Bodies lay half-eaten near the fires – some human, some dwarf, some ghoul. The death reek wafting from them was so thick Felix could almost see it.

'Hold the cannons in the passage!' called Migrunsson.

The driver of the first cannon parked it side-on to the door as the dwarfs followed Gotrek and Agnar into the room. The other drivers ranked up in front of the cannon, protecting it, while the thunderers who had been the rearguard climbed on top of it, straddling the barrel, and began firing their muskets over the dwarf line into the ghouls with a steady, ceaseless rate of fire.

Without the walls of the tunnel to protect their flanks, the dwarfs were quickly surrounded, and fought in a tight square against the leaping, shrieking ghouls. Even so, and outnumbered two to one, the battle seemed a foregone victory for Migrunsson's troops. Not one dwarf had yet fallen, and the floor was littered with the dismembered corpses of ghouls. Between the dwarf line's steady winnowing, the thunderers' sniping, and the Slayers' mad slaughter, the gibbering fiends would soon fall.

Felix shattered a ghoul's clavicle with a heavy down-stroke then glanced at Henrik, fighting beside him in the dwarf square. The rememberer fought with a tight smile lining his face.

'Better once it starts, eh?' said Felix.

'Much,' said Henrik. 'Anticipation is always worse than–' His head lifted. 'What was that?'

Felix cocked an ear as he fought on. He didn't hear anything other than the shrieks of the ghouls and the butcher shop chop of steel cutting flesh – or did he? Was that a rumble he felt through his feet? The cannons weren't rolling. The dwarfs weren't charging. What was shaking the ground?

Then, above the rumble, he heard a roar. Not the shrill howling of ghouls, but a deeper, angrier sound.

'Retreat to the door!' called Engineer Migrunsson. 'Something's coming from the mines!'

Felix gutted another ghoul and stole a look back towards the great square portal of the minehead, beyond which a broad ramp descended into darkness – except the ramp was no longer dark. Fire moved in its depths now, and huge shadows loomed on its bare rock walls.

Henrik groaned. 'Sigmar's balls, one thing at a time!'

His prayer, if prayer it was, was not answered. As the dwarfs began an orderly retreat towards the door, up from the ramp poured a flood of armoured green brutes, all howling a savage battle cry.

6

'Waaagh!'

Two score orcs charged for the dwarfs in a foaming, yellow-eyed rage, huge cleavers and crude axes swinging from fists bigger than Felix's head. The ghouls scattered before them, shrieking in terror, as the dwarfs continued to retreat to the door. The Slayers, however, answered the greenskins' roar with one of their own, and chopped through the fleeing ghouls to meet them.

A massive monster with a crude helmet that seemed to have been nailed to his head broke from the pack and smashed down at them with a mace like a beer keg stuck on the end of a fence post. They dodged aside as it shattered the flagstones, and Agnar hewed at its elbow, splintering the bone. Gotrek leapt onto its forward leg and buried his rune axe in its skull, splitting its spiked helm and its face. The orc toppled backwards, dead, and Gotrek leapt from its falling body into the mob, slashing around in a frenzy. Agnar fell in beside him, matching him stroke for stroke and seeming no worse for the constant stream of drink he had poured into himself.

After that there was no time for Felix to look to anything but his own survival. More than half the orcs had swept past the Slayers, and Felix, Henrik and Migrunsson's dwarfs only had a second to form up in the door before they ploughed into their line like a green avalanche.

Felix ducked a swipe by a cleaver and stabbed the orc who wielded it with Karaghul, but the weight and momentum of the hulking savage drove him back into the hall until he crashed into the wheel of the gun carriage behind him. To either side of him it was the same. Henrik was flat on his back, an orc careening past him with its guts looping to the floor. Migrunsson was pressed against the muzzle of the gun, exchanging blows with an orc more than twice his height. Two of his dwarfs were dead, cut down and trampled under heavy, steel-shod boots.

Nevertheless, the line held. When the orcs' impetus ran out, the dwarfs were still standing, and still fighting, while the thunderers atop the first cannon fired into the faces of the orcs, sending them reeling back with shattered jaws and burst eyes.

Felix knocked aside a cleaver that would have split Henrik in two and hauled him to his feet.

'Much obliged,' Henrik gasped, and impaled the neck of an orc that was aiming for Felix.

'Likewise,' said Felix.

He cut the legs out from under the orc that Henrik had spitted, but as he spun to slash at the next, he heard the crack of a gun from inside the minehead chamber. He would have mistaken it for an echo from the dwarfs' muskets, except that he saw, through the orcs' flailing limbs, Gotrek stagger, and a blossom of blood appear on his broad left shoulder.

Felix choked in surprise as the Slayer recovered and fought on. Someone had shot Gotrek! But who? Orcs didn't use guns. Felix tried to see further into the minehead chamber, but the row of brawling monsters blocked his view.

'Curse you! Let me by!'

In a panic, Felix fought forward, stepping out from the dwarf lines and driving back the orcs before him. He chopped through the fingers of one, then shattered its knees as its cleaver fell from its stumps. He hacked open the skull of another that had taken a dwarf musket ball to the shoulder.

'You madman,' called Henrik. 'You're exposing your flanks!'

'Someone's shooting at the Slayers!'

As the next orc fell, Felix was afraid he would see Gotrek and Agnar with their heads blown off, but they were still fighting back to back in the centre of a dozen roaring greenskins, with a dozen more sprawled across the floor amongst the white corpses of the ghouls the Slayers had slain before.

Another shot came, and one of the orcs fighting Agnar stumbled, howling. Felix turned at the muzzle flash, an afterimage of a spindly, kneeling figure holding a long-barrelled gun etched into the backs of his eyes. The shot had come from the mine shaft. He tried to see into it, but it was too dark.

'Engineer Migrunsson!' he called. 'Someone's shooting from the minehead.'

Migrunsson looked, and apparently saw the gunner.

'Thunderers!' he barked. 'The minehead! Get that shooter!'

Two of the thunderers turned from blasting the orc line and fired on the ramp. Felix could not see the result, but they must have struck true, for no more shots came from the darkness.

Another dwarf fell at the line, his chest caved in by an orc axe, and the greenskins pressed for the gap. Three Thunderers jumped down to fill it, swinging their gun butts, but one died before his feet touched the ground, and the other two were driven back into the cannon.

'Close up!' called Migrunsson. 'Keep them out!'

An orc broke through the line and leaped onto the gun to smash the rest of the Thunderers. Felix thought it was the end, but just as the greenskins cut down the closest gunner, a high shrieking shivered the air and the ghouls, their courage restored, flooded back into the chamber, howling for vengeance.

They fell upon the orcs first, and their interference ended the battle. Attacked from front and back, the orcs quickly fell to the Slayers' axes and the steady murder of Migrunsson's line. Sadly, the thanks the ghouls received for this timely intervention was their extinction. With the orcs dead, Felix, Henrik and the dwarfs fell upon them and slaughtered them all. Even those that turned and fled were shot down by the Thunderers before they reached the doors.

As the dwarfs saw to their dead and Migrunssun called for the surgeon, Felix and Henrik looked to the Slayers. Agnar was on one knee, catching his breath and drinking from his canteen, while Gotrek was examining his shoulder wound, one of many he had received in the fight.

Henrik shook his head. 'Your Gotrek certainly slays his share, doesn't he? And then some.'

Felix glanced at him. It seemed an odd thing to say. 'He likes to fight, yes. As does Agnar, I see.'.

'A bit,' said Henrik, then crossed to the old Slayer. 'Another doom missed, Agnar. I'm sorry. Have a drink?'

Felix frowned after him for a moment then joined Gotrek. 'How bad is it?'

Gotrek shrugged. 'It passed through.'

'Did you see the gunner?' asked Henrik, looking uneasily towards the mine shaft.

'I saw him fall,' said Agnar.

He stood and started for the ramp. Gotrek, Felix and Henrik followed him. There was no body, but Gotrek found a spatter of blood on the stones, and then a trail of drops that went down into the darkness.

'Who do you think it was?' asked Henrik. 'Or what?'

Felix frowned and sniffed around the area where the blood drops were thickest. He couldn't smell anything. The reek of ghouls was too overpowering. Still...

'I only saw a silhouette,' he said. 'But something about it...' He shrugged. 'It didn't look human to me.'

'An orc?' asked Agnar, incredulous. 'A ghoul? They don't use guns.'

Felix shook his head. 'It was skinnier than that, and smaller, except for its head. I think it might have been–'

'A skaven,' said Gotrek.

Henrik laughed. 'A skaven? Ridiculous.'

Felix turned to him, raising an eyebrow. 'You don't believe in them?'

Henrik gave Agnar an amused roll of the eyes.

'Oh no,' said the rememberer. 'We've proof of their existence carved upon us. I can show you the scars. I only meant it is ridiculous that skaven would be helping orcs.'

'You think it was human, then?' asked Felix. 'Would that be any less ridiculous?'

'Not all humans love dwarfs,' said Henrik. 'Perhaps it was a servant of the Ruinous Powers, causing chaos where he might.'

Felix nodded. That made more sense than a skaven assassin, if only slightly, though it didn't explain how the shooter had come to be there. Was he following the orcs? Was he their ally?

'We should go after it and find out,' said Agnar, looking down the dark ramp.

Gotrek grunted agreement, but Henrik looked askance.

'We've agreed to help Migrunsson. We can't leave him now. He's lost five dwarfs.'

The Slayers nodded reluctantly and started back up to the chamber, but as Felix fell in with Gotrek he saw Henrik hold Agnar back and begin speaking to him in low tones. The old Slayer's brow lowered as he listened, and he scratched his beard and frowned after Gotrek. Felix wondered what Henrik was saying, and was going to mention it to Gotrek, but just then Migrunsson and the surviving cannon crews appeared at the top of the ramp, rolling blackpowder barrels and resting pickaxes on their shoulders.

'Well fought, Slayers,' said the engineer, as they started down the ramp. 'Your prowess saved us, and the cannons.' He gestured back to the chamber. 'Rest while we set the charges and place the guns. We should be on our way to the second spot in an hour or so.'

'Thank you, Engineer Migrunsson,' said Felix, then looked back at Henrik and Agnar. Whatever they had been talking about, they were done now, and Henrik gave him a cheery smile. Felix smiled back reflexively, then continued up the ramp into the chamber, unsettled without knowing why.

* * *

7

The Slayers did not rest. After allowing themselves to be patched up by the dwarf field surgeon, they went to help the cannon crews get the cannons up the stairs and into the enclosed firing platform, but they did not work together. When Gotrek joined one crew, Agnar joined the other. When Gotrek asked Agnar to pass him a pry bar, Agnar did it without looking Gotrek in the face, and answered him in monosyllabic grunts.

Felix would have taken this for typical dwarfish terseness, but for the fact that he had seen the Slayers conversing together before, and they had been practically chatty then. Gotrek seemed to notice this new tension as well, but being a dwarf, he made no mention of it, merely grunted in turn and got on with his work.

The stairs to the gun emplacement were wide, but the door was narrow, so the cannons needed to be dismantled and carried through it a piece at a time – first the barrel, then the wheels and pieces of the gun carriage – before being reassembled within. Also, the gun ports had been sealed up at the same time as the archway below, so they had to be reopened to make room for the barrels of the cannons. Felix helped with this, swinging a mattock to knock the bricks loose, then took the opportunity to look through one into the Great Hall of the Jewellers' Guild, which was Thane Thorgrin's chosen field of battle.

By the bright glow of the tall work-lamps that shone above the engineers and dwarf troops who were preparing the ground, Felix could see that the guild hall was an enormous room, handsomely decorated in the monumental dwarf style. Towering statues of dwarfs in guild vestments held up an arched roof that stretched over an open floor that looked to Felix to be as big as the Reikplatz in Nuln. It was longer going north and south than it was east and west, with large archways in the narrow ends. Felix saw teams of dwarfs preparing supplies and chalking off the dwarf lines at the north end of the hall, while other cannon crews placed guns on a balcony above the north arch.

Migrunsson mopped his gleaming scalp with his kerchief and leaned in the gun port next to Felix, pointing to the arch in the south wall. 'Thane Thorgrin's plan is that we close off all paths into the hall except that one. If the greenskins want battle, they will have to come through there – straight into those guns there. We'll leave them no way to flank us or sneak around behind.'

'And from here you'll be able to shoot into their sides as they charge,' said Felix.

'Aye,' said the engineer, grinning. 'It'll be a slaughter.' He pushed away from the port. 'But first we have to finish closing off the other paths.'

He gave Felix a friendly salute, then went to supervise the second team of dwarfs who were busy setting charges in the walls of the mineshaft.

Less than an hour later, they were ready to light the fuses. The dwarfs moved the carts and ponies well up into the passage to the north of the minehead chamber, playing out matchcord as they went, then, when everyone was clear, Migrunsson took up the fuses and bowed his head.

'It's a sad day when a dwarf must destroy the works of his fathers,' he said. 'But to save the body, sometimes a limb must be severed. Forgive us, ancestors, for this necessary sin.'

And with that, he touched flame to the fuse ends. Felix and the others watched them hiss and spark down the corridor.

Felix tensed as he saw the flames vanish into the minehead chamber, waiting for the roof to come down on his head, but the blasts, when they came, were surprisingly small – a quartet of heel-jarring thumps and a billow of smoke and flame that dissipated as it entered the passage.

Henrik looked up and took his fingers from his ears. 'That's it? Did all the charges go–'

A heavy rumble interrupted him, growing louder and shaking dust and pebbles from the ceiling, before tailing away again. Now a much thicker cloud billowed into the passage and rolled their way. Henrik blinked.

Migrunsson smirked. 'A true engineer knows it isn't the size of the blast, but the placement of the charges.' He pulled his kerchief up over his nose and started forward into the dust. 'It's done, I think. But best go back and have a look.'

The minehead chamber was entirely covered in a thin coating of grey granite powder. The corpses of the orcs and ghouls looked like stone statues of themselves, and the geometric designs on the floor were completely hidden. The mineshaft portal was still there. Indeed it had been blown wider and taller, and for a moment, Felix thought the dwarfs had failed, but then he saw that all the rock that had fallen from the ceiling and walls had tumbled down into the slanting shaft, choking it completely. It would take days to remove all the rubble, particularly if one were working from below.

Migrunsson nodded sadly as he examined the cave-in, then turned back to the north corridor. 'Well done, lads. On to the next.'

The next was a bridge.

Migrunsson led them down two levels to a wide natural chasm that cut east and west for as far as Felix could see – admittedly not very far – and dropped away to a glowing red line far below. An oven-hot updraft rose from it that had them all sweating in moments. The bridge that spanned the chasm was wide and solid, with statues of dwarf ancestors holding lamps set at regular intervals along its length, and stretched from an archway cut into the north side of the chasm to another arch in the south side.

Looking up, Felix could faintly see more archways in the sides of the rift, and the broken remains of other bridges, all fallen away, before the heights of the chasm swallowed them in darkness.

'This one's a bit trickier,' said Migrunsson. 'It would be easy enough to blow it up and be done with it, but...' He grinned. 'I'd rather take a few score greenskins with it, so we'll weaken it instead – and let them find out it's broken when they're falling towards the lava.'

Gotrek chuckled approvingly. Agnar seemed about to do the same, but then shot a look at Gotrek and only grunted.

'What do you want us to do?' asked Felix.

Migrunsson pointed to the south end of the bridge. 'Guard that arch. We don't want any greenskins discovering the surprise before it's ready.'

Henrik swallowed. 'Er, you're going to weaken the bridge, then ask us to walk back across it when you're done?'

Migrunsson laughed. 'The four of you could jump up and down on it from here to Valdazet and it wouldn't fall. It will take all the weight and stomping of a greenskin warband on the march to shake it down.'

Henrik nodded, but did not look entirely convinced. Nevertheless, he went with Gotrek, Agnar and Felix to guard the end of the bridge.

Though there was nothing to do but stand around while the dwarfs worked, Felix found it impossible to relax. The heat from the lava made him sweat inside his chainmail, and the thought of invisible assassins firing on them or orcs raging out of the darkness made the space between his shoulder blades itch as if someone had carved a target there with a poisoned thorn. For more than an hour, he did nothing but pace and check his weapons and watch Migrunsson and his crew don harnesses and drop over the sides of the bridge to chip away at the network of stone supports that made up its understructure.

Gotrek seemed entirely absorbed with the process, watching with arms folded and single eye intent. Agnar watched too – though he stood as far from Gotrek as he could manage – but Henrik soon grew bored, and once again began to sing his repetitive little melody while staring into the darkness of the tunnel.

Felix ground his teeth and tried to shut out the tune, but Gotrek was not so polite.

'Do you have do to that?' he asked over his shoulder.

Henrik sniffed. 'I only do it when I'm nervous.'

'So, all the time then,' said Gotrek, and turned back to watching the engineers.

'You'll take that back, Gotrek Gurnisson,' said Agnar, glaring at him.

'Take what back?'

Felix turned, wary. Now what?

'No one insults my rememberer,' growled Agnar. His voice was slurring a little with drink and anger. 'Particularly not an underhanded doom-stealer like you, Gurnisson.'

Gotrek raised an eyebrow. 'I've stolen no doom.'

'You have!' Agnar stepped towards the Slayer. 'You interfered with my fight. You killed greenskins that might have killed me. I saw you! Henrik saw you!'

'I killed every greenskin I could reach,' said Gotrek. 'You did the same. What of it?'

Felix looked at Henrik. His eyes were glittering. It was as if he *wanted* to see the Slayers fight. Felix flashed back to the aftermath of the fight with the orcs. Was this the nonsense that Henrik had whispered in Agnar's ear?

'You deliberately blocked attacks that were aimed at me. I might have found my doom but for you.'

Gotrek snorted, dismissive. 'I didn't stop to weigh which were yours and which were mine. I fought to kill.'

'You fought to keep me from finding my doom before you found–!'

Gotrek held up a hand. 'Stop.'

'I'll not stop, you cheating–'

'Be quiet. Listen!'

Agnar cut off and listened. Felix strained, but could hear nothing. Apparently Agnar could, however, for the anger vanished from his face, to be replaced by grim concentration. He and Gotrek drew their weapons and stepped silently onto the span, then craned their necks to look up at an archway above them that pierced the south face of the chasm. Felix and Henrik tiptoed after them.

The archway was more utilitarian than the ones that capped the bridge they were on, with little ornamentation, and a torn and twisted end of a mine cart rail-line dangling from it like the lolling tongue of some steel serpent.

'What is it, Gotrek?' asked Felix.

'Something moving in that rail tunnel,' said the Slayer.

'Aye,' said Agnar. 'Gone now though, I think.'

They all stood silent, but the noise of Migrunsson's crews tapping on the stone supports of the bridge drowned out all else.

'Engineer,' called Gotrek. 'Hold your work.'

Migrunsson waved his dwarfs silent and everyone stopped what they were doing and strained their ears.

At first Felix could hear nothing, but then a faint metallic keening reached his ears, like someone rubbing a rosined bow across a flexed saw blade.

'What is it?' he asked. 'It sounds like–'

'The rails,' said Agnar. 'The rails are singing. Something is coming down the track!'

* * *

8

'Clear the bridge!' roared Gotrek. 'Get off now!'

The gun crews scrambled to comply, but half were still busy under the span, weakening the understructure, and those on top did not abandon them. They hurried to the ropes and heaved mightily to pull their brothers up. Migrunsson fell in with the rest, holding down a hand to haul a gunner over the rail and then pulling at another rope.

Gotrek, Agnar and Felix started forward to help, but before they had taken a step, the singing of the rails rose in volume and a clattering rumble added to it. The whole chasm shook with the noise.

Felix looked up at the twisted ends of the rail-line. Dust was shivering from them and they twitched like insect antenna. The rumble became a roar, drowning out the hoarse cries of the dwarfs, and then, as if the cliff face had vomited a string of iron sausages, a long train of mine-carts shot out of the tunnel mouth and arched down in freefall, straight at the bridge.

Felix watched in horror as the carts, all filled to the brim with rocks and boulders, crashed down amongst the scattering dwarfs and punched through the bridge like a massive cannon ball, smashing it in two. Half the dwarfs fell instantly, dropping away with the shattered stones, or dragged over the edge as the carts snagged their ropes. The others scrabbled to get clear, but they had done their sabotage too well.

With the centre of the span gone, and the rest of the supports weakened, the remains of the bridge could not stand. As the dwarfs crawled for the ends or climbed their ropes, the stones fell out from under them, toppling after the broken centre like sand running out of an hourglass. The gunners, the cannon crews, and Migrunsson too, trying even to the last to push the others to safety, plummeted away towards the glowing red line, ropes and harnesses trailing after them, their howls of rage rising on the hot wind.

Gotrek stood at the broken end of the span, ten paces out from the wall of the chasm, clutching the railing with one hand, and gripping Agnar by the wrist with the other. The old Slayer was dangling over the abyss, his face as grey as river clay.

Gotrek gave him a nasty grin. 'Should I let you go, Agnar Arvastsson? I wouldn't want to rob you of a doom.'

'Pull me up, curse you,' rasped Agnar. 'You know falling is not a proper Slayer's death!'

Gotrek hauled Agnar up and dropped him on the broken flagstones beside him. The old Slayer grunted and pushed himself to his feet.

Henrik stepped forward to help him. 'Maybe Gurnisson's forgotten what a proper Slayer's death *is*,' he sneered. 'After all, he's been ten years searching for one.'

Gotrek's brow lowered and he balled a fist, but before he could use it, a shot rang out from above and a bullet struck between the three of them, spraying them with splinters of stone. The Slayers dodged left and right, and Henrik hunched back towards the archway with Felix. They looked up. The same spindly shadow was backing into the darkness of the rail tunnel, reloading as it went. Gotrek snatched up a chunk of rubble from the edge of the bridge and heaved it up after it.

The rock vanished into the arch and an angry squeal echoed from the hole. Gotrek, Felix and Agnar all looked at each other and backed under the lee of the arch.

'Skaven,' they said in unison.

'Hoy!' came a voice. 'Who still lives?'

They looked across the chasm. Two of the wagon drivers stood in the opposite arch, peering across at them.

'The Slayers and their rememberers!' called Felix. 'But take cover. There is a marksman above us.'

The drivers looked up, then stepped back into the tunnel. One shouted from the shadows. 'We have ropes and pegs. We can get you across.'

'Not with that gunner above us,' muttered Felix.

'We shouldn't go back anyway,' said Henrik. 'Thorgrin will want to know what part the skaven are playing in all this. We should find them and discover their plans.'

Felix laughed. The way he spoke of it, it sounded as simple as going to the baker for some bread, not making their way through trackless, troll- and orc-infested catacombs without guide or map. 'You know the way to their lair, do you? An hour ago you didn't think they were involved.'

Henrik raised his chin. 'Agnar is an excellent tracker. If we can find the trail of the assassin above us, he can find their lair.'

'Aye,' said Agnar. 'I'll find them. Let's go. There's no going back anyway.'

Gotrek didn't move. He was staring directly at Henrik. The rememberer caught the look square between the eyes and stumbled at its fierceness.

'Wh-what are you looking at?'

'You have twice questioned my dedication to seeking my doom, human,' said Gotrek. 'Do not do so a third time.'

'Or what?' growled Agnar, stepping up to him.

Gotrek looked him up and down. 'If a dog bites me, I beat the master for not teaching it manners.'

Agnar snarled and raised his fists. Felix jumped between him and Gotrek.

'Slayers, please!' he said. 'Save it for the skaven, eh?'

The Slayers stood nose to nose for a long moment, then Gotrek turned and stumped down the passage. Agnar and Henrik started after him, glaring at his back.

Felix sighed and looked across to the drivers. 'Go back to Thorgrin. Tell him he fights skaven as well as orcs. We're going further in.'

'Skaven?' called the drivers in unison.

'Aye,' said Felix. 'Skaven.'

'Very well,' said the first. 'If we make it, we will tell him. Good luck to you.'

'Thank you,' said Felix, then lit his slotted lantern and started down the passage after the others into the unknown. 'We'll need it.'

Felix and Henrik followed Gotrek and Agnar as they stumped forward, exploring side passages and debris-strewn stairways, looking for a way up to the rail-line tunnel and the trail of the skaven long-gunner. The whole party moved in a sullen silence, the recent squabbling suspended but most decidedly not forgotten. Felix could practically see the waves of anger pulsing between Agnar, Henrik and Gotrek. And he was fairly angry himself.

It seemed obvious to him that the rememberer was trying to provoke a fight between Agnar and Gotrek, but he couldn't figure out why. As far as Felix could remember, Gotrek had given Henrik no cause to be angry – at least no more cause than the brusque Slayer normally generated. The rememberer seemed to have developed his dislike for him in an instant. What was the reason for it? He couldn't truly think that Gotrek had denied Agnar his doom on purpose, could he?

After a lot of dead ends and backtracking, the Slayers eventually found their way up to the rail-line tunnel above the broken bridge, but the skaven gunner was long gone. Its spoor, however, was not. Tracks in the dust led back along the twisted rails and its greasy rodent stink lingered in the air.

They followed the tracks along the rails and through an ancient foundry. Ten great stone smelting furnaces squatted along the walls of a long, rubble strewn room – one of them had exploded some time in the distant past, and its stones were scattered all over. A dozen or so mine carts sat on the rails that ran past the smelters, or lay smashed and toppled on their sides.

In the centre of the room, they found a wide area of overlapping skaven tracks. Some were the usual, narrow dewclawed imprints, but some were bigger, with heavier claws. The prints went back and forth from the rails to the piles of rubble around the exploded smelter.

'Rat-ogres,' said Gotrek, pointing to the larger prints as Felix held up his lamp. 'The ratkin made them fill the carts with stones, then push them down the rails.'

'That would have taken all the time Migrunsson's crew were working on the bridge,' said Felix.

Gotrek nodded. 'They spied on us from the beginning.'

Agnar and Henrik added nothing to this conversation. Henrik just hummed his annoying tune. Agnar followed the skaven's trail out of the room to the west.

Gotrek fell in beside him, and the party followed the tracks down a broad stair to a lower level, then through a series of chambers that seemed to have been dwarf clan halls and common areas – galleries, meeting halls, feast halls – each larger and grander than the last. There was more ancient damage here – ceilings fallen in, walls crumbled. One room was charred black, and the stone pitted as if by acid. Another was filled with the skeletons of goblins, hundreds of them, all mounded at the edges of the room, as if they had died trying to escape something in the centre.

As they descended to the next level, the copper tang of recently spilled blood and the stench of skaven and acrid chemicals grew so strong that Henrik and Felix covered their mouths.

'We must be close to their lair,' said Felix, wiping tears from his eyes.

Gotrek shook his head. 'The stench of a burrow is much worse. This is… something else.'

They followed the smell to an ancient workshop – and discovered a scene out of a nightmare. Between the dusty work tables and forges lay the bodies of scores of human warriors, their faces and bodies twisted in attitudes of agonising rictus, and the lanterns they had carried still burning. Felix stepped into the room to examine them more closely, then stepped back, gagging. Whatever poison had killed the men still lingered in the air, and it burned his eyes and nose.

'This just happened,' said Gotrek, covering his nose. 'Not an hour ago. Their blood is still fresh.'

Felix squatted and raised his lamp, deciding it wisest to make his examination from the door. The eyes of the corpses bulged from their sockets, and bloated black tongues stuck from their mouths. The men's hands were at their throats, and some had clawed great wounds in their necks in their desperation. The blood was still pooling beneath them.

'Who are they?' he choked. 'And why didn't they flee?'

'They tried,' said Gotrek. 'Look.'

In the dim light of the dead men's lanterns, Felix could barely make out what he was indicating, but he saw it at last. Splintered wood on the other doors of the room. One still had an axe buried in it. The men had tried to cut their way out.

'They were locked in,' he said at last. 'A trap. What a horrible way to die.'

Agnar broke his silence at last. 'I know that one,' he said, pointing at a well-armoured man near the door. 'He took Lanquin's coin. As did that one. And him too.'

Felix turned to him. 'They are all Lanquin's mercenaries? But how did they come here?'

Henrik cleared his throat. 'He made us swear not to speak of it to any who did not sign up with him, but Lanquin did not think Thane Thorgrin's battle would win the day. He thought it would be better to take the fight to the orcs, and said he would send the best of his recruits to kill Stinkfoot in his lair.'

'And he didn't tell the thane?' asked Felix.

Agnar shook his head. 'The thane wouldn't have allowed it.'

'With good reason, it seems.' Felix shuddered. 'What a fool. To send his best men to die in a skaven trap. Who is left to fight in Thorgrin's battle?'

'The rank and file,' said Henrik. He shivered too. 'I warned him it was a mistake. He wouldn't listen.'

Gotrek turned back to the corridor.

'A mistake the ratkin saw coming,' he muttered, but only Felix heard him.

Another level down and things got more confusing. The area was a warren of clan burial chambers and treasure vaults, all mostly ransacked and desecrated. Tracks of all kinds wound through the halls – the boots of men, the hind-claws of skaven, the calloused feet of orcs, the paws of huge beasts – and Felix lost the trail of their particular skaven entirely, but Gotrek still seemed to be on the scent.

A while later the tracks of men, dwarfs and skaven all but vanished, and those of the orcs multiplied. The sour, fungal reek of the greenskins grew thick in the air, and rough symbols were daubed on the walls in blood and dung. These depicted fists, axes, skulls, but most of them had been crossed out, and a crudely drawn foot with wavy lines rising from it drawn on top.

'I guess the rumours about this Stinkfoot becoming boss are true,' said Henrik.

'And the skaven walk openly into his territory,' said Felix, looking at the skinny tracks that overlay the orcs' heavier prints in the muck of the corridor.

'Not openly.'

Gotrek turned at an intersection, then stopped at a narrow crack broken through the wall of the side corridor, studying it. 'They're sneaking in. This way.'

'And we're going to follow them?' asked Henrik, uneasily.

'You wanted to discover their plans,' said Gotrek.

He gripped the edges of the hole and pulled himself through. It was a tight squeeze, and he scraped his naked torso front and back before he called for the rest to come ahead.

Henrik swallowed and pushed his lantern through before him. 'At least we know the rat-ogres didn't go through this.'

Felix followed him, and Agnar brought up the rear. They found themselves on a narrow ledge, close to the ceiling of a looted vault. Dwarf ancestor faces looked down on smashed chests, heaps of trash, broken furniture and skeletons – dwarf, man, orc and skaven – that lay littered across the floor. A crude wooden ladder ran down to the mess from the ledge, but Gotrek disdained it and leapt to a stone statue of a prim dwarf maiden standing on a pedestal, then slid down to the floor. Agnar followed suit, but Henrik took the ladder and Felix followed him.

Looking around with his lantern, he saw that the skaven tracks crossed to a bigger hole knocked through the far wall. The doors of the vault were ajar, but the dust there was undisturbed. Felix could hear faint noises coming through it, however – the distant howling of orcs, the throb of their drums, and somewhat closer, a grunting and snorting that sounded like angry boars.

Gotrek started to the hole in the far wall, but before he got halfway there, orc shouting erupted in the near distance, and running boot steps thudded beyond the vault's partially open door. Gotrek and Agnar went instantly on guard, and Henrik and Felix drew their swords a second later, lining up behind them. The boot steps boomed closer, but ahead of them came a skittering clicking, then something scrawny and hunched scrambled through the vault doors and bolted for the ladder.

Gotrek and Agnar slashed at it as it went by, but it dodged past in a streak of brown fur, then ducked Felix's thrust and shot up the ladder to the ledge – the skaven gunner, hiding no more.

It grabbed the ladder in its disturbingly human hands and began to pull it up behind it, beady black eyes glittering malevolently. Felix lunged for the ladder, but just then the doors of vault slammed open and a crowd of orcs shoved in, shouting and holding up torches as they looked around. They pulled up short as they saw the Slayers in front of them, and raised their weapons, roaring. Felix let go of the ladder to face them as Henrik glared up at the skaven.

'Won't do your own dirty work, will you? Clever bastard.'

Its chittering sounded like laughter as it wormed through the hole, dragging the ladder after it.

Henrik turned back to the orcs and readied his sword. 'Well, we've killed this many before, haven't we, Agnar? We've killed ten times as many.'

Even as he spoke, the room shook with a heavy tread, and the orcs guffawed, grinning at the Slayers as if they had a secret. Felix looked uneasily to the door in time to see an ugly head the size of a beer keg duck under the lintel and look around, ears flapping like drooping flags.

'Sigmar's balls,' said Henrik. 'A troll.'

* * *

9

Agnar seemed considerably happier than his companion. 'I knew I would find a doom here.' He shot a hard look at Gotrek. 'Unless you rob me of this one too.'

'I robbed you of nothing,' growled Gotrek.

The troll stood to its full height as it came into the room, a looming, lumpy horror with skin the texture of lichen-blotched stone, muscles like ship's cables, and a reek that smelled like low-tide in high summer. It held no weapon. The massive, bone-knuckled hands at the end of its ape-like arms were weapons enough. Its lugubrious long-nosed face stared stupidly as the orcs prodded it forward, pointing at the Slayers.

'Prepare fire, rememberer,' said Agnar.

'Aye, Agnar,' said Henrik, unhooking his lantern from his belt and looking around.

Felix did the same, hunting for something to burn. He and Gotrek had fought a troll once before, in the crypts below Karak Eight Peaks, and had only defeated it by setting it aflame. Without fire, its flesh regenerated almost instantly. Even severed limbs grew back in time. But what to burn? The sundered treasure chests would provide some wood, but not enough for a big blaze. He supposed they could gather all the furniture and smashed chests, but– He stopped as he saw the solution. Hidden under a broken table was a pile of rolled up carpets, covered in dust.

'Henrik, here!'

They ran to the table and heaved it up as Agnar charged the troll, roaring a Khazalid battle cry. Gotrek, to Felix's surprise, charged the orcs. Was he letting Agnar have the glory? Was he avoiding the troll? Neither seemed likely, but what then?

The orcs seemed surprised as well, and stumbled back, wrong-footed, in the face of his fury. Gotrek opened up the first with a slash across its belly, then smashed the cleaver from the hands of the second and buried his axe in its spine as it turned to flee. It fell and he severed its leg at the hip, then flung it at the troll.

'Hungry, rock head?'

The leg smacked the troll in the side of the head, and the smell of blood and fresh orc meat made it lick its lips and turn for the treat. Agnar took advantage of this distraction and stepped in, swinging for its legs. His long-hafted axe bit halfway through the monster's left knee and it crashed down on its side, lowing like a lovesick moose.

As Felix and Henrik pulled at a heavy roll of carpet, the six remaining orcs roared to see their champion laid flat and charged in, attacking the two Slayers. Agnar ignored them, severing the troll's knee so the wound wouldn't heal, and paid for it. An orc with a cleaver took a chunk from his arm, spinning him around with the weight of the blow, but Agnar whipped his axe up in mid-turn and sank it into its bare green chest, then recovered and faced two more as blood poured down his forearm. Gotrek fought three more, a fourth dead at his feet. Behind him, the troll was pushing to its knees, its stump already closing.

'Come on!' called Felix. 'We've got to start the fire!'

Felix shouldered one carpet while Henrik grabbed another, and they ran them back. The troll was up, weaving unsteadily on its right knee and its severed left leg, and lashing around in a blind rage. It crushed the skull of Gotrek's last opponent with its stone-hard fist, and knocked Gotrek flying. The Slayer crashed headfirst into a sealed stone treasure chest, then slumped to the floor beside it, dazed and bleeding.

Unable to crawl after Gotrek on its mismatched legs, the troll picked up the stone statue of the dwarf maiden and threw it at him. Felix's heart thudded in alarm, for its aim was true, but at the last second the Slayer flung himself aside and the statue smashed into the wall, sending marble chips flying everywhere.

Gotrek staggered to his feet, off-balance, and charged the troll, roaring defiance. At the same time, Agnar finished the last of his orcs and ran at the troll from behind. The monster swiped at Gotrek, tearing tufts from his crest with its claws, but the Slayer ducked and hacked through its elbow, severing its right arm. Agnar swung for its right thigh and chopped its leg off. It fell back, howling, three limbs lost, and clawed for Agnar with the last. He dodged back and Gotrek stomped on the thing's wrist, pinning it, then sliced through its arm at the shoulder.

Felix had never felt sorry for a troll before, and likely never would again, but the sight of the monster lying helpless, armless and legless, like a turtle on its back, as it keened in pain and confusion, jolted him with pangs of unwanted empathy. Still, the limbs were already growing back, white spurs of bone extending from the severed tibias and fibulas, and strands of muscle beginning to form around them.

'Burn it,' said Gotrek.

Felix threw his carpet over the troll as Henrik did the same. Henrik then emptied the contents of his lamp's oil reservoir over everything and took up a torch from a fallen orc.

'Maybe next time you won't be so foolish as to be born a troll,' he sneered, then touched the torch to the carpets and stepped back as they started to burn.

He and Felix and the Slayers threw broken furniture and shattered chests onto the flames, then tossed the monster's severed limbs in the middle of it. Gotrek stepped to the troll's head and severed it with a swift chop. Felix breathed a sigh of relief as its frightened howls ceased.

After they were sure the thing was well and truly burning, and after Henrik had helped Agnar bandage the wound in his arm, Gotrek started again for the skaven's hole in the wall. Felix and Agnar made to follow, but Henrik held the old Slayer back and whispered in his ear, gesturing angrily at the burning troll.

Felix looked back, suspicious. 'Coming?'

Henrik stepped from Agnar and they started forward, the old Slayer shooting a hard look at Gotrek's back.

'Aye, coming.'

The skaven's hole in the wall led into what seemed to be a tight drainage pipe. It was covered with a crust of dry algae and the reeking residue of the passage of many skaven, and angled down to the left and up to the right. Gotrek examined the tracks, then started up on hands and knees with Felix following. It quickly turned left and levelled out, and Felix guessed that it was running above the corridor outside the vault.

A moment later, he was proved right, for he came to a tiny hole bored through the floor of the pipe that looked down into the corridor.

'Skaven spy holes,' he murmured. 'Have we been watched all along?'

As the party moved on, the pounding of drums began to echo loudly down the pipe ahead of them, and they heard the guttural grunting of arguing orcs. A few more yards and the pipe split left and right, and the drums boomed up from a wide hole in the floor of the left-hand pipe. Gotrek stuck his head through it, then lowered himself down. Felix, Agnar and Henrik followed, dropping one after the other into what appeared to be a pump room. A smaller pipe ran down one wall into a fat brass reservoir, and there were valves and levers sticking from it, and more pipes running from it. A narrow door, held open by a pile of garbage, led back into the corridor, and noise and light spilled in through the gap. It sounded as if the orc argument were reaching a crescendo.

Gotrek eased through the half-open door with the others following behind. To the east, the passage vanished into darkness, but just ten paces to the west, it opened onto a wide, pillared balcony that looked out over a vast dwarf-built chamber with a soaring cross-vaulted roof. The walls were pierced with balconies and galleries that rose in overhanging tiers above the smoky light of the fires that burned below, and echoed with the deafening howls of hundreds of orc warriors.

Gotrek, Felix, Agnar and Henrik crouched on the balcony and peered through the balustrade to the savage horde below.

Gotrek's single eye kindled eagerly at the sight. 'This is a worthy doom.'

10

The floor of the enormous chamber was crammed with a seething ocean of orcs, above which rose banners marked with dozens of crude symbols – glaring suns, red fists, grinning moons, cracked skulls and bloody axes. The green monsters were all shouting and shaking weapons and torches over their heads and looking towards the middle of the room where four big bonfires blazed.

There crowded the biggest mob of all, over three hundred orcs rallying around dirty green banners with the crude symbol of a stinking foot painted on them in white. Inside the area marked off by the four bonfires was a square of open floor, and two orcs lay dead within it, while two more circled each other.

'What's going on?' asked Henrik.

'A challenge,' said Gotrek.

One of the orcs was as big as any Felix had ever seen, head, shoulders and chest above the rest, and muscled like a mutated ape. He was dressed in heavy rusted armour, studded all over with spikes, and had a helm with an even bigger spike sticking straight up from the top of his head.

His opponent was shorter, and, though well-muscled and encased in crude plate, was not nearly as massive as Spike Helm. He also walked with a limp, his right foot bound up in dirty bandages. But there was a confidence to his stance, and a cunning in the turn of his head.

'The little one is Stinkfoot?' asked Henrik. 'He doesn't stand a chance.'

'Let's hope so,' said Felix. 'With him dead, the orc alliance falls apart, and we can all go back to the tavern.'

'Let's hope *not*, then,' said Agnar, shooting a sour glance at Gotrek. 'I still haven't been able to claim my doom.'

Spike Helm took a few exploratory swipes at Stinkfoot, all the while howling and gargling orcish insults, but Stinkfoot did not fight back. He just stared at the bigger orc and turned to keep him in front of him. Enraged by this behaviour, Spike Helm charged. Stinkfoot side-slipped and Spike Helm stumbled past, his spiked mace crushing only air, then turned again to face the warboss.

Across the circle, Stinkfoot raised his bandaged foot and thrust it at Spike Helm as if he was trying to kick him in the privates. He didn't come close. His opponent was six paces away from him, and yet, astoundingly, the huge orc went down anyway, toppling like a side of beef cut from a hook to sprawl on the floor, unmoving.

Felix stared as all the orcs in the room quieted in fear and awe. Had it been magic? Had it been a trick? Was the stink of Stinkfoot's foot so vile that it could kill an orc at six paces?

'That wasn't right,' said Agnar. 'How did he do that?'

Stinkfoot stepped up onto the huge barrel chest of his fallen rival and raised his bulging arms, roaring his dominance to the others. The orcs echoed his roar, shaking their weapons and headbutting each other in excitement. The chamber shuddered with the sound of it.

Over this clamour, Stinkfoot roared again, and pointed with his axe to a great archway on the north side of the chamber. The orcs howled in response, then gathered up and started forward.

'It begins,' said Agnar. 'They go to war.'

'And we're too late to warn Thorgrin,' said Henrik.

'But not too late to do what that dead orc couldn't,' said Gotrek. He nodded towards a balcony over the great arch through which Stinkfoot's army was flowing, and towards which Stinkfoot himself was slowly moving. It was connected to the one they were on by a columned gallery. 'If we run, we can jump down on the greenskin before he passes under that arch.'

Agnar's eyes glittered eagerly. 'Aye. Aye!'

The two Slayers hurried north into the gallery.

As Felix and Henrik started after them, Henrik cleared his throat. 'Slayer Gurnisson, ah, perhaps you should let Agnar jump first when we get there.'

'Why?' asked Gotrek without slowing.

'Er, well, you have robbed Agnar of two dooms already on this trek. To make up for it–'

Gotrek ground his teeth. 'I've robbed no one. If he wants to jump first, let him try.'

'You interfered. Twice,' insisted Henrik, raising his voice.

Felix cringed. 'Quiet! The orcs are right below us.'

Henrik ignored him. 'You blocked blows meant for Agnar during the minehead fight! And just now you distracted the troll when it was sure to have killed him! A Slayer's honour demands–'

Gotrek snorted. 'No manling can lecture me about a Slayer's honour. I warned you I would–'

'Then I will lecture you!' barked Agnar, and stopped to face him. 'Gotrek Gurnisson, you have left the way of the Slayer. A true Slayer could not follow the true path for ten years and still live.'

Gotrek stopped and stared at him with his single baleful eye for a moment, then turned and continued down the passage. 'There's no time for this. We must reach the arch.'

'Do you deny it, then?' asked Henrik. 'Do you call Agnar a liar?'

'What are you doing?' whispered Felix. 'Why stir trouble when they'll both find their dooms in that jump? Leave it be!'

Henrik carried on as if Felix hadn't spoken. 'Will you let him call you a liar, Agnar?'

'I will not!' Agnar stumped after Gotrek and spun him around with a hand on his shoulder. Gotrek shoved him back, sending him into the wall.

'Do not lay hands on me, Agnar Arvastsson.'

Agnar pushed off the wall and stepped again in front of Gotrek, blocking the way to the balcony. 'Why did you attack the orcs just now, when there was a troll before you?' He asked. 'A true Slayer should attack the most dangerous foe.'

'I killed the orcs to distract the troll with their meat,' said Gotrek, with surprising restraint. 'It made it easier to kill. Now let me by.'

'Easier to kill?' Agnar shook with rage. 'Easier to kill? A Slayer does not make his enemies *easier to kill*!'

'For Sigmar's sake, lower your voice!' said Felix.

Nobody paid him any attention.

'Does he not?' asked Gotrek. 'Why do you carry that axe?'

Agnar blinked, confused.

'If you wanted to make your enemies harder to kill,' said Gotrek. 'You would attack them unarmed, yet you don't.'

'An axe is a Slayer's weapon!' said Agnar. 'It is tradition. That's not the same as–'

'Grimnir asks of us that we fight our enemies with all our skill and strength,' said Gotrek. 'Anything less is suicide, which he disdains. Do you think he means us not to use our strength of mind? I fight with all the strength I possess.' He gave Agnar a withering look and stepped past him. 'It seems you do too.'

'I do!' shouted Agnar, thumping his chest. 'I fight with all my strength. Who says I do not?'

'Quiet!' whispered Felix again, but fortunately, the orcs were making too much noise and didn't hear.

'He's insulted you, Agnar,' called Henrik. 'He says you have no strength of mind!'

Felix shoved him, hissing. 'Do you *want* them to fight? You are keeping them from their doom!'

Henrik shoved him back. 'I am defending my friend's honour, which you and your friend seem determined to take from him!'

'Is that what you say, Gurnisson?' asked Agnar, getting in front of Gotrek again. 'Do you think me a fool?'

'You're both fools!' cried Felix, pointing over the balcony. 'Stinkfoot is getting away.'

Agnar looked up from glaring at Gotrek and blinked as if waking. 'Curse you. You've slowed me down!'

He raced down the galley again with Gotrek pounding after.

'*I've* slowed *you* down?'

'Agnar!' called Henrik, but this time the old Slayer was deaf to his words and continued on. Felix was glad of it. It meant he wouldn't have to shut Henrik's mouth for him.

Unfortunately, Agnar's belated hurry was too little too late. By the time they reached the balcony, the very tail of the orc army was filing through the arch below it, and Gutgob Stinkfoot was long gone.

Agnar punched the balustrade in frustration and glared at Gotrek. 'We might have made it if not for your arguing!'

'Aye,' said Gotrek. 'I shouldn't have argued. I should have knocked you out and been done with it.'

'Well, there's no time to argue now,' said Felix, trying to change the subject. 'We must find a way back to the first level and warn Thorgrin of their coming.'

Gotrek shook his head and turned away from Agnar, who was looking murder at him. 'First I want to see what killed the greenskin's challenger.'

Gotrek stumped to a broad stair that descended from the balcony to the floor of the chamber. Agnar glared after him, looking as if he might bury his axe in Gotrek's back, but then cursed under his breath and followed. Felix did the same, watching Henrik like a hawk. He still didn't know what the rememberer was up to, but whatever it was, he wasn't going to let him do it.

At the bottom of the stairs, Gotrek stepped onto the broad floor and started towards the four bonfires. As Felix followed his spine itched between his shoulder blades. He felt as exposed as a cockroach in the middle of a bare floor. Anybody could see them, but they could see nothing outside the fires' square of light.

As he reached the challenge ground, Gotrek knelt by the enormous, spike-helmed orc, examining his legs and torso, but found no mark or sign of sorcery. Neither was there any wound on his arms or face, but when he heaved the great brute over onto his front, Felix noticed something sticking from the back of its neck.

'A dart.'

He plucked it out carefully and showed it to Gotrek, who examined it. It was small and crudely made, and fletched with what looked like beetle wings. The rusty iron tip was crusted with some tarry greenish black substance.

'A ratkin dart.'

Henrik and Agnar examined the other two challengers. They had died in the same fashion.

'Stinkfoot's foot did not win the day after all,' said Felix.

'Does he know that?' asked Gotrek, then cocked his ear.

There was a whizzing sound, and the Slayer snapped out his hand and clamped it shut. When he opened it again there was another dart in it, poisoned like the others.

Felix and Henrik hit the floor, covering their heads, but the Slayers stood and drew their weapons, looking in the direction the dart had come from – the gallery on the south wall of the chamber. Four strange missiles arced out of the darkness after the dart, and Gotrek and Agnar braced to knock them out of the air, but they didn't fall upon the Slayers, but instead landed in the fires.

In the brief second before they struck, Felix saw they were little burlap bags, each trailing a tail of dust, and he feared they were blackpowder, but when they touched the fire they burst into clouds of blackness that put out the flames and left them in darkness but for the lamps at their belts.

In the dim light that remained, Gotrek hauled up one of the smaller dead orcs and held it up before him. Agnar followed his example, and not a moment too soon. Another dart thudded into his orc a second later. A third whizzed by Felix's ear.

Gotrek turned to him and Henrik. 'Darken your lanterns. They're shooting at the light.'

Felix and Henrik gulped and closed the slots of their lanterns, then crouched in the lee of the huge green corpse-shields as the Slayers started towards the south gallery. Henrik started his singing again, but this time Felix had had enough.

'Stop that,' he whispered. 'They'll hear you!'

'They already know we're here,' said Henrik. 'And it calms my nerves.'

'So does poison.'

The skitter of clawed feet in the darkness made Felix freeze. They were coming from all directions. Henrik fumbled for his lamp.

'Wait,' said Gotrek. 'Wait for my word.'

Felix put his finger on the lever that opened the slots, and held his breath. The skittering was closing in all around. It sounded like they were right on top of them. It took all his willpower not to open the lantern.

'Now!' said Gotrek.

Felix slapped open the slots, and the light streamed out, revealing a black-clad skaven in mid-leap. It squealed and shielded its eyes at the fire-glow, and Felix slashed with Karaghul, biting deep into its hip. It rolled off into the darkness, yelping, but there were more behind it.

Gotrek heaved his orc at two, flattening them, then shattered the legs of a third with his rune axe as it leapt the green corpse. Agnar shrugged his orc off his shoulders and swung his long axe at two that charged in at him, curved knives glistening green in the flickering light. The dead orc's back was pincushioned with throwing stars.

Henrik ducked another skaven as it leapt over his head, then slashed after it, but missed by a mile. Two more appeared at the edge of Felix's vision, hurling more throwing stars. He grabbed the edge of his red Sudenland cape and swept it in front of him, and felt them thud into the heavy wool.

The assassins sprung in after their stars, hooked steel claws strapped to their wrists. They were blindingly fast. Felix parried the claws of the first an inch from his neck, and only his chainmail saved him from those of the second. They cracked across his forearm like hammers, but did not break the rings.

He swept Karaghul in a backhand as they flitted past him, and caught one in the back, sending him sprawling and thrashing, but the second eluded the blow and tossed a glass globe over its shoulder.

'Oh, bol—'

Felix dove for the thing and caught it just before it shattered on the floor, then rolled up and hurled it into the darkness after the skaven who had thrown it. A tinkle of glass and a horrible retching told him he had found his mark.

Gotrek snatched another dart out of the air and threw it at a skaven that fought Henrik, then hurled his axe in the direction the dart had come from. There was a terrible squeal and then a thud, and all the other skaven suddenly froze, then turned and fled, leaving a stinking cloud of animal musk behind.

Felix coughed and spat and squeezed his burning eyes, then followed Gotrek as he strode into the darkness to retrieve his axe. On the floor lay a skaven with a blowgun in one hand and a long-barrelled gun strapped across its back.

'The one who shot you,' said Agnar, coming up behind them.

'Aye,' said Gotrek, pulling his axe from its chest. It had buried itself in its solar plexus. 'The one who knew we would be in the minehead chamber. The one who led the greenskins and the troll to us.'

Gotrek wiped his axe blade off on the skaven's black head-wrap, then noticed a roll of parchment sticking from a pouch on its belt. He pulled the parchment free.

'You shouldn't touch them,' said Henrik. 'They cover themselves in poison.'

Gotrek ignored him and unrolled the parchment.

'What is it?' asked Agnar.

Gotrek looked at it, then handed it to Felix. At first what was drawn upon it just looked like a jumble of squares and lines and arrows, but then he realized it was a map of the depths – part of them anyway – with portions marked in the claw-scratch script of skaven writing, but the ratmen weren't the only ones to have written upon the map. Notes had been scribbled upon it in a human hand, in Bretonnian. A cold chill went down Felix's spine as he saw them.

'Lanquin wrote this.'

'You can't know that,' said Henrik. 'He's not the only Bretonnian in the world. There's a whole nation of them.'

'What does it say?' asked Agnar.

Calling upon the meagre Bretonnian he had learned while studying poetry at the University of Altdorf, Felix struggled to decipher the words. '*Apportez votre rongeurs ici.* Uh, transport... no, bring, your rats... to here. *Nous allons laisser cette voie accessible.* We will allow... passage to... No, that's not right. We will let the path to be... unguarded!'

Felix looked at the map again and saw an arrow pointing to a small passage that led into what he recognised must be the Great Hall of the Jewellers' Guild. It opened up behind where the dwarfs intended to set their battle line. 'Blood of Sigmar! Whoever wrote this says he will let the skaven come in and attack the dwarfs from the rear!'

'Let me see that,' said Henrik, and snatched the map from Felix's fingers.

'It *must* be Lanquin,' said Felix as Henrik pored over the parchment. 'Who else would be in a position to promise them such an advantage? How does a man stoop so low!'

'He's already done worse,' said Gotrek.

'What could be worse than that?' snarled Agnar.

Gotrek motioned back the way they had come. 'The room with the poisoned men. The Bretonnian didn't send the best of his recruits into the deeps to kill Stinkfoot. He sent them to die – in a skaven trap.'

Felix stared at him. 'But – but why would he do that?'

Gotrek shrugged. 'To take them out of the fight. To weaken the thane's army so the orcs win.'

'That's insane! He can't want that! He–' Felix cut off as another thought blasted that one aside. 'That's why he wanted us to take his coin! He wanted us to sign up with him so he could send us to our deaths with the others!'

Agnar shook his head like a confused bull. 'All that Bugman's – a trap.'

Felix pointed to the parchment in Henrik's hands. 'We have a map. We must use it to find a way back to Thane Thorgrin as quickly as we can. We must warn him of this treachery before the battle begins.'

'Two of us must,' said Gotrek. 'The other two must attack the ratkin where they prepare their attack and slay all that can be slain.'

Agnar grunted in agreement, but Henrik rolled his eyes. 'And I suppose that'll be you and Jaeger, then. While Agnar and I run your errands for you.'

'What?' said Agnar, looking up. He turned hard eyes on Gotrek and hefted his axe. 'I'll be damned if I will.'

11

Gotrek snorted. 'Put it away, puppet. Your master pulls your strings again.'

'I am no one's puppet, Gotrek Gurnisson,' said Agnar, dangerously. 'Least of all yours. If you think to send me away while you go to your doom–'

'Your twister said that,' growled Gotrek. 'Not I. Come with me if you wish. The manlings can return to the thane.'

Henrik's eyes blazed. 'Now he would deny you your rememberer! He would have you die alone and forgotten, with no one to tell the tale of your last battle!'

Felix had had enough. Henrik's carping and accusations had worn him raw at last. He shoved the rememberer, sending him sprawling over the corpse of the black-clad rat.

'You're talking rubbish!' he barked. 'Gotrek denies Agnar nothing he doesn't deny himself!'

Henrik's eyes glittered with triumph as he looked up from the floor. 'Agnar, they lay hands upon us! They mean us harm!'

The old Slayer turned towards Felix, raising his long axe. 'No one touches my rememberer, human. Defend yourself.'

Gotrek snarled and knocked the axe aside with his own. 'Stand down, fool! You've listened to this jackal for too long!'

Agnar brought his axe back into guard, his eyes blazing and his arms trembling with rage. 'You strike me now, Gurnisson? You insult me to my face? Henrik is right. It is *you* I have listened to for too long!'

And with that, he charged, slashing wildly. Gotrek backed away, blocking the attacks, but made none of his own. Nonetheless, Henrik chose to see Gotrek's retreat as an act of aggression, and leapt at his back, his sword high.

'Die, coward!'

Felix cursed and whipped Karaghul from its scabbard just in time to block the strike. Henrik grinned like a skull as he turned to face him, slashing high and low.

'Ah, you show your true colours at last!' he hissed. 'All "hail-fellow-well-met" in the tap room, but it's knives in the back when we're too deep to call for help. I know your kind!'

Felix parried the blows with difficulty. Ordinarily he would not have called Henrik his equal as a swordsman, but whatever madness was possessing him had given him a frenzied strength and speed, jittery and unpredictable, and it was hard to know where he was going to strike next.

'You describe yourself!' said Felix, retreating before the torrent. 'You invite us to drink with you, you fight by our side, and now you attack us on the flimsiest of pretexts. I begin to wonder if you are a pair of rogues in disguise, or–'

Felix faltered as something clicked in his head. Henrik saw the opening and gashed his leg. It stung, but not as sharply as Felix's epiphany. Not a *pair* of rogues, no. Agnar was a true Slayer, of that there was no doubt. But Henrik? Who had suggested Gotrek and Felix take Louis Lanquin's coin? Who had shown a barely credible 'change of heart' when Gotrek and Felix joined Thorgrin's throng? Who had sung an annoying little tune before every appearance of the skaven?

'You're with Lanquin!' cried Felix, attacking Henrik with new vigour. 'You never changed sides! You joined Thorgrin's horde to keep an eye on us, to make sure we died in the depths! You are with the skaven!'

Henrik choked. 'The skaven? You're mad! No dwarf would side with the ratkin!' He glanced over his shoulder. 'Do you hear him, Agnar? Now he calls you a traitor to your–!'

He broke off with a yelp as Felix took advantage of his distraction and sliced open his arm above the elbow, then knocked his blade from his hands.

Agnar roared at this and tried to fight past Gotrek. 'Let me by!'

Felix advanced on Henrik, sword extended. 'I said nothing of Agnar Arvastsson, you conniver. You tricked him too. You're pitting him against Gotrek, hoping both will die.'

'Don't listen to him, Agnar!' cried Henrik. 'You know I am your truest friend. I would never–'

Felix put Karaghul to his throat.

'Talk, rememberer,' he said. 'What are Lanquin's plans? Why is he colluding with the skaven?'

Henrik put his hands up and opened his mouth as if to comply, then turned and fled across the huge room like a scalded dog. Felix cursed and pounded after him, but Henrik was younger, slimmer and less heavily armoured, and outran him with ease.

'Rememberer!' called Agnar. 'Where are you going?'

'Goodbye, Agnar,' Henrik called over his shoulder. 'I will sing the song of your doom in the taproom of the Grail. It will be the greatest doom ever remembered – hundreds of skaven, thousands! Men will weep to hear it.'

'But… but the skaven didn't kill me.'

'Oh, they will,' laughed Henrik as he sped for an archway on the western wall. 'That I promise you! They'll kill all of you.' And with that he began singing his annoying song again as loud as he could manage.

Felix slowed to a stop as Henrik ran under the archway into the corridor, and quickly vanished but for the bobbing glow of his lantern. Felix watched it dance out of sight, then sighed and started back towards the Slayers. They were no longer fighting. Agnar was staring at the archway with a look so blank and stunned that it would have been comical if it hadn't been heartbreaking. Gotrek put a hand on his shoulder, but had the decency not to say anything.

'Five years,' said Agnar. 'Five years, he was my rememberer.' His brow lowered. 'I must find him. I must slay him.'

'Aye,' said Gotrek. 'But his villainy must be stopped first. Time enough for vengeance after the skaven are slaughtered.'

Agnar hesitated, then nodded. 'Very well. But who will warn the thane?'

'I'll go,' said Felix, though he had no idea how he'd manage it. He didn't know where he was, he didn't know how to get to the Great Hall of the Jewellers' Guild, the place was crawling with orcs, skaven, trolls and Sigmar knew what else, and…

Felix groaned. 'Henrik has the map. That tricky little–'

Noises to the east brought his head up. Hunched shadows were moving in the darkness at the east end of the chamber, spilling out of the tunnels that fed into it. He swallowed. 'Maybe the map is the least of our problems.'

Gotrek and Agnar looked around, and Agnar started forward, growling under his breath.

Gotrek stopped him. 'We must make sure the manling gets away first.'

Agnar shot him a look that had some of his old animosity in it, but then nodded, and he and Gotrek started for the western end of the hall, jogging as fast as their short legs could carry them.

Felix struggled to shorten his pace so that he wouldn't swiftly outdistance them. 'Are they after us?' he asked, looking warily over his shoulder. He heard no squeals of challenge.

Gotrek shook his head. 'They head for the same shaft as we do. It is the quickest way to the upper levels.'

Felix stared at him. 'How do you know where they're going? How do you know where *we're* going?'

Gotrek shrugged. 'I read the map.'

There was a shriek of dismay behind them. Felix looked back, but all he could see was milling shadows.

'They have found the bodies of their assassins,' said Agnar, without looking back.

'*Now* they're after us,' said Gotrek.

Gotrek led Felix and Agnar through the corridors of the vault level with the shrill cries of the skaven growing steadily closer behind them. The passages were high and wide in this area, with few twists and turns, and it felt to Felix as if they were trying to outrun a cresting wave. At last he and the Slayers ran through a crumbling arch into a large square chamber that made Felix's skin prickle and his shoulders hunch with fear as soon as he entered it.

A ghostly grey glow illuminated a scene out of a builder's nightmare. It looked as if some drunk giant had constructed a house of cards within the chamber and hadn't been too neat about it. Scrap-wood scaffolding rose up in uneven layers along all four walls, and a precarious forest of supports held up portions of the mortared stone ceiling, which looked as if it might come down in a heap if someone sneezed. The walls behind the scaffolding showed signs of battle damage – shattered marble, scorched granite, and broken bas-reliefs – and it seemed the scaffolding had been erected to attempt repairs, but it must have all happened a long time ago, for the wooden joists were warped and sagging under the weight of stone they supported, and the whole thing was covered in dust and thick with spiderwebs.

It was from these webs that the light emanated, a pale putrid pearlescence that made the scaffolding look as if it were covered in spectral shrouds. Lumpy cocoons hung from the beams as well, tethered by thicker strands. Some were the size of dwarfs. Some were the size of orcs. All glowed like misshapen moons.

In the centre of the room, a more well-constructed structure rose amidst the cobwebbed scaffolding. It was a square column of iron latticework, roughly twenty feet to a side, that vanished up into darkness through a wide hole in the ceiling, as well as down into a corresponding hole in the floor. Felix had seen such cage-lifts in other dwarf holds, but none so elaborate or ornate. On this one, in addition to the metal cage enclosed within it, an iron stairway wound around the outside of the shaft, going both up and down.

The Slayers ran for the wide iron bridge that extended from the edge of the hole to the shaft, but as they got closer Felix saw they were too late. The lift cage was already rising.

Henrik's grinning face appeared between the bars as it rattled up towards the darkness. 'Weep not, Agnar! You are no worse a dupe than the fools who stand beside you, or Thorgrin and his kin, or the orcs who go to fight him. We duped them all! Duped the skaven into helping Stinkfoot become warboss so he would rise against the dwarfs. Duped the dwarfs into fighting back. And once they wipe each other out, it will be Lanquin and I who rule Skalf's Keep and collect the taxes, while our skaven partners rule the deeps. A mutually beneficial relationship.'

'If you believe that,' snarled Gotrek, 'you're more a dupe than any of us.'

'Rememberer!' roared Agnar. 'You will die by my axe for your treachery! I swear it!'

'Treachery?' called Henrik as he vanished through the roof. 'I have given you a certain doom! What more could a Slayer want from his rememberer?'

The rainstorm patter of hundreds of clawed feet behind them turned Felix and the Slayers around. The ratmen were spilling through the scaffolding-supported archway in a gibbering, chittering tide – spearskaven in rags and human-skin hoods; swordskaven in rusty armour and brass helms, towering, hideously mutated rat-ogres with crude weapons grafted to the stumps of their wrists and giant mutant rats the size of bulldogs, all spreading to the right and left to surround them.

Gotrek stepped to the base of the iron stairway and readied his rune axe. 'This is their route to the top. Manling, go to the thane. We'll hold them here.'

Felix looked up. The stairs were endless. He wondered if he would die from exhaustion climbing them. It was at least a less certain death than fighting a hundred skaven with his back to a bottomless precipice. He swallowed as he realised that he and the Slayer were parting ways at last. 'Are you sure, Gotrek? I will not witness your doom. My vow–'

'Your vow is fulfilled. You know what my doom will be,' said the Slayer. 'Write it well.'

'Write mine too,' said Agnar, snarling. 'And shove it down Henrik Daschke's throat.'

'I will,' said Felix. 'With pleasure.'

The skaven were edging in from all sides now, the rat-ogres wading through the smaller troops to the fore, and shots were being fired from the back. It was time to go.

'Farewell, Slayers,' said Felix, trying to keep any unseemly emotion out of his voice as he started up the iron stairs. 'Die well, and may Grimnir welcome you–'

The stairs shook violently, cutting him off. He clung tight and looked up. Was the cage coming down again? Was the scaffolding collapsing?

The skaven edged back from the shaft at the noise, and the Slayers looked around for the source of it. Then Felix saw it – not above, but below in the darkness, and rising swiftly.

It looked at first like the hand of a giant, though more slim and graceful, climbing up the latticed side of the iron lift shaft like a man might walk his fingers up his lover's arm. They weren't fingers, however. They were legs, bone white, and as hard and sharp as sabres, but longer than lances. There were eight of them, extending from a fat misshapen abdomen that glowed with the same grey glimmer as the cobwebs. Eight glassy black eyes looked up at Felix from a hard, hammer-shaped head under which twitched pincers that could have snipped him in half with one bite. There was something round and glowing rising from its carapaced back, but Felix couldn't quite see it, for a cloaked skaven sat in front of it, riding the gigantic horror as if it were a warhorse.

'Gotrek,' said Felix through lips suddenly dry. 'Your cave spider is here.'

12

Gotrek, Agnar and Felix dived away from the iron stairs as the White Widow pulled itself out of the hole and slashed its hooked forelegs at them. Its rider, an ancient black-robed skaven, shrieked orders at it and whacked the spider's carapaced head with an orb-topped brass staff.

Looking at it full on and standing before them, the cave spider was terrifying – a mountain of hard chitin, crusted white with what looked like bat droppings, its bulging abdomen looming twice Felix's height, and its graceful legs spreading as wide as a merchant ship's deck. The skaven troops feared it as well, and backed under the rickety scaffolding as it ticked delicately across the floor. Gotrek, however, nodded approvingly.

'This will be a fight,' he said.

'What is that on its back?' asked Agnar.

Felix looked again at the strange sphere that glowed behind the skaven. It was a barrel-sized globe of brass plates, bound to the White Widow's thorax with leather straps, and riveted together so poorly that sick green light seeped through the joins and glowing steam leaked from it in a fog. A short brass rod with a pulsing gem fixed to the end sprouted from it like a lightning rod, and a crude lever stuck up beside it.

'A bomb,' said Gotrek. 'A warpstone bomb.'

'But they'll kill themselves too,' said Felix.

'So long as they win,' said Agnar. 'Rat-lords care not if rat-troops die.'

The black-robed skaven shrilled orders at the hundred-strong mob of ratmen cowering under cover of the scaffolds, and they hesitantly began to edge behind the giant spider and run up the iron stairs as it held Felix and the Slayers off.

Felix cursed. 'They'll reach Thorgrin before my warning does.'

'At least you'll witness my doom,' said Gotrek.

'And share it,' muttered Felix.

The Slayer didn't seem to hear him. He charged the White Widow, roaring a dwarf battle cry. Agnar was only a split second behind him. The cave spider stabbed down at them with its scythe-like forelegs, shattering the stone floor as they dodged past and swung for its body with their axes. It scuttled back on its six other legs and they missed, then had to duck and weave as the forelegs slashed for them again.

On the White Widow's back, the skaven sorcerer chanted and raised his brass staff, causing flickers of green lightning to play about the orb that glowed at its end. Felix was ready to leave the fighting of the spider to Gotrek and Agnar. As they would say, it was 'Slayer's work', but he could certainly protect them from being brought low by magic when all they wanted was a good fight.

He scooped up a fist-sized rock from the rubble that was scattered across the floor and hurled it. It missed, but just barely, and the skaven flinched back, losing the rhythm of his chant. He chittered angrily and glared at Felix, then began again. Felix found another rock and flung it. This time it found its mark and mashed the skaven's furless nose.

With a shriek of rage, the ratman swatted its spider mount between its two rows of eyes, goading it towards Felix, who backed under a low course of scaffolding and searched for another rock.

Dancing under the White Widow's legs, Gotrek and Agnar struck home as it moved. Agnar's long axe sent splinters of chitin flying, but didn't crack its carapace. Gotrek, however, armed with his starmetal rune axe and considerably more muscle, broke through its left foreleg, biting into the meat inside. Black ichor sprayed him and the spider staggered sideways, trying to escape the pain of the wound.

With cries of triumph, the Slayers pressed their advantage, hewing like woodsmen at the shattered limb, trying to widen the break.

The White Widow's right foreleg stabbed at them, and Agnar did not dodge in time. It knocked him flying, and he skidded to a stop a foot from the edge of the lift hole, half-conscious, blood welling from the back of his head.

Gotrek spun away as the bladed leg swept in again, and chopped into a back leg instead. It was a brutal strike, half-severing the joint, and leaving the limb flopping loosely and trailing fluids. Felix had never heard a spider shriek before. Indeed, he hadn't known they could, but this one did – a high reedy sound, like violin bows rubbing together.

'Felt that, did you?' laughed the Slayer.

He pressed his advantage as the White Widow reeled sideways, its balance thrown. His axe slashed at the monster's other legs, splintering them and leaving star-shaped cracks with every impact. The spider swiped and snapped back at him in a frenzy, its forelegs blurring as they tried to lance its prey. Gotrek was swifter, however, and fought within its reach, almost under its belly, making it back up in order to see where he was.

Shrieking with frustration, the skaven sorcerer beat the White Widow mercilessly with his staff, but the monster continued to retreat from the thing that was causing it pain – and into disaster. Its massive abdomen backed into the scaffolding along the west wall, snapping supports and causing the whole structure to groan and shift.

'Sigmar save us,' said Felix, as the platform above the spider buckled and sagged.

After that, the outcome was inevitable. Felix had earlier compared the scaffolding to a house of cards, and like a house of cards, when the bottom card was pulled out, the rest went with it. A chain of collapses followed the first, all the platforms and ladders and cross braces slowly folding in and crashing down upon the White Widow and the shrieking skaven.

Gotrek backed away as the first boards and posts began to topple, then turned and ran as the rest came rumbling after. He sprinted to Agnar, just now picking himself up at the edge of the hole, and dragged him aside as the wreckage struck the floor and spread in a tide of wood that spilled all the way to the precipice and sent planks and boards spinning away into the darkness below.

Through the rising cloud of dust, Felix could see that, under the debris, the giant spider still moved, and he thought it might rise up and shrug it off, but then, with a thunderous cracking and splintering, the granite cladding of the ceiling, which the scaffolding had been holding in place, peeled from the roof and crashed down on top of it, burying it completely.

'Well,' he said, coughing. 'I think you got it.'

Agnar shook his head. 'It might still live. We should dig down and make sure.'

'There's no glory in killing a trapped beast,' said Gotrek. 'And no time. Thorgrin must still be warned of the skaven and the Bretonnian's treachery.'

Agnar scowled. 'The skaven must be halfway there already. We'll never catch them.'

Gotrek looked towards the lift. 'We'll beat them easily.'

'But the cage is gone,' said Felix. 'Henrik took it.'

Gotrek ignored him and walked out onto the iron bridge, now partially bent from the rocks that had fallen on it, and eyed the cluster of cables that stretched down one side of the shaft. Felix followed him out, his heart palpitating.

'Gotrek, I hope you're not thinking–'

'There's no faster way.'

'But how will we stop? If you cut the cable, the cage will drop and pull us up, I see that, but we'll be going too fast. We'll be pulled through the pulley at the top of the shaft. We'll come out like sausages!'

'The cage will stop here,' said Gotrek. 'And we will stop just short of the pulley.'

'How? Are you going to hook your axe into the wall as we fly past? Even you aren't that strong.'

Gotrek didn't answer; he just stamped on the iron bridge with a heavy foot as if to test it, then strode to the scaffolding that still stood above the archway through which they had entered the room, all the while craning his neck and looking up at the ceiling.

'What is he doing?' asked Agnar.

'I have no idea,' said Felix.

Gotrek remained before the scaffolding, stroking his beard for a moment, then at last hefted his axe and started chopping at a particular support post.

'Gotrek!' cried Felix.

'Into the passage, manling,' said Gotrek. 'And you, Arvastsson.'

Felix and Agnar hurried past Gotrek into the passage, as, in three deft strokes, he cut the through post and it snapped under the weight. Again the scaffolding above began to fold in on top of itself. Gotrek stepped into the passage to stand with Felix and Agnar as it all crashed down to the floor and spread out across it in a roaring cascade.

Suddenly unsupported, the braces that held up the ceiling fell after it, and huge chunks of masonry began to plummet down and smash the floor below – at first only a few, but then more and more, an ever widening collapse that sent arches and keystones and decorative corbels thundering down to shake the ground. And as they hit, they bounced off the drift of wooden refuse and avalanched towards the iron bridge. The great stones bounded across it and slammed into the front of the lift shaft, denting and tearing it, and the stones that followed the first caved it in even more, until, as the rain of masonry finally subsided, there was a great, concave bulge in the shaft, filled with rocks.

Felix stared as the dust subsided. 'You've pinched it shut.'

Gotrek nodded. 'Now the lift cage will hit the rocks and stop.'

'And the cable will stop short of the pulley,' said Agnar.

'And fling us against the walls of the cage to be crushed into jelly,' groaned Felix.

Gotrek shrugged. 'It might, but we'll beat the skaven.'

13

'I should have seen it,' growled Agnar, as he and Gotrek hacked through the iron latticework of the lift shaft with their axes. 'I should have known him for a rogue from the beginning.'

'Perhaps he wasn't one at the beginning,' said Felix, slotting a ladder taken from the wrecked scaffolding through the lattice. Wedged into a corner of the shaft, it made a makeshift platform they would be able to step on. 'A man might think being a rememberer a grand thing for the first few years, but come to regret it later.'

Gotrek looked around at him, cold-eyed. Felix squirmed under his attention, but went on.

'A man might get impatient, and want to get on with his life. He might want riches and comforts. He might want to settle down.'

Agnar chewed his lip through his beard as he swung again. 'He always joked about hoping I'd find my doom quickly, so he might spend all my gold while he was young. Perhaps it wasn't a joke.'

Felix frowned as he slotted a second ladder into the shaft about five feet below the first. 'What gold is this?'

'All I have collected over my years of slaying, I put in a dwarf bank in Talabheim. It is to go to my family, who I shamed before becoming a Slayer, but I granted Henrik a part of it.'

'And he will take all of it,' growled Gotrek.

With a final swipe of his axe, he finished the hole in the lattice, then squeezed through and crossed the ladder to the cables. Each was as thick as his leg and made of wound steel. He tapped them with the heel of his axe, listening to the tone, then nodded and scored one with the blade.

'Bring the rope, manling.'

Felix stooped through the hole, then edged out onto the ladder and crossed to the cables, clinging to the walls of the shaft for support. He handed Gotrek a coil of rope recovered from the collapsed scaffolding, and the Slayer proceeded to tie him tightly to the cable at the waist and under the arms so that he was facing out. The ropes were so constricting that Felix could hardly breathe, and he began to panic again about slamming into the walls when the cable was loosed, but there was nothing for it now.

When Gotrek finished tying him, he beckoned Agnar ahead. The old Slayer squeezed into the shaft with his own coil of rope over one shoulder, and let Gotrek tie him to the cable too, back to back with Felix. When that was done, Gotrek lowered himself down to the second ladder and took his axe from his back, then started hacking at the woven steel.

Felix closed his eyes in helpless terror as he felt the shuddering of it through his spine. The rune axe bit into the softer metal with ease, and the smaller strands parted with deep, heartstopping twangs.

After a moment, the chopping stopped, and Felix pried open his eyes and looked down. Gotrek was tying himself to the cable at the waist, leaving his torso free. Just below him, a few thin strands of the cable remained uncut, twanging and singing with the stress of holding so much weight. Once he had bound himself to his satisfaction, Gotrek used the leftover rope to tie his axe to his wrist so that even if he lost his grip it would not fall.

Finally he was ready, and raised the axe over his head. Felix wanted to close his eyes, but couldn't. If he was going to die, he wanted to see it coming.

Gotrek swung down between his legs, chopping into the remaining strands below his feet. One snapped and the rest groaned. He swung again.

Felix heard a bright twang and, with a jolting rush, his stomach dropped into his boots. The filigreed lattice blurred past at an alarming rate, inches from his eyes, and the upward force was so strong that he could not raise his arms against it or take a breath. At least the thing he had feared the most did not happen. Though the cable bowed out towards the side of the shaft and the struts flashed by less than an arm's length from his chest, he was not crushed against it.

A look below showed him why. The frayed end of the cable, less than a yard below Gotrek, was pressed against the side of the shaft, scraping off a cascading shower of sparks and making a deafening shriek as it rose, holding its passengers away from death with its rigidity. Gotrek, closer to the end than Felix, was even closer to the wall, and was sucking in his gut and holding down his beard to keep it from being ripped off at the roots. Over the screaming of metal on metal and the rattle of the shaking shaft, Felix heard a wild whooping. It took him a moment to realise it was the Slayers, howling with savage glee.

Chambers and rooms flicked by as they whipped past, separated by short intervals of black, and a few seconds later the plummeting cage shot by inches behind them, dropping so fast that Felix hadn't time to fear it crushing them before it was gone.

An eyeblink after that, Felix saw a flash of movement outside the cage, and caught a frozen picture of a gaping ratty face staring at him amongst a swarm of others. They had shot past the skaven troops, still labouring up the stairs that wound around the shaft one step at a time. Gotrek had been right. They were going to beat them to the first level – if they lived.

Only seconds later, the ride came to an end, and what Felix had earlier feared finally happened. As the boom of a huge impact echoed up from below, the cable jerked to a stop, snapping Felix's teeth shut, then slapped back and forth like a pendulum in a wind storm. Felix was crushed against the side of the shaft, and only great good fortune let his heavily bound chest take the blow and not his head. Even so, all the air was knocked out of him and his ribs felt like they had been hit with a sledgehammer. His knees too cracked against the steel, and he hissed in agony.

'All... alive?' he asked as the swaying stopped.

Behind him and below, the Slayers grunted in the affirmative, and he saw that they had taken some damage too. Agnar had blood streaming from his scalp where the front few inches of his Slayer's crest had been ripped away by some passing snag, and it looked like his nose had been broken. Gotrek had deep scrapes and bruises on his shoulders and forearms, and a great welt over one eye.

As he looked around, however, Felix feared that they had a greater problem than their wounds. They were dangling over a bottomless pit in the centre of the shaft, tied securely to the cable, and the door they had hoped to reach was more than thirty feet above their heads.

'Are you certain you thought this through, Gotrek?' Felix asked.

'Swing, manling,' said Gotrek. 'With me. You too, Arvastsson.'

Gotrek began to swing his arms, legs and rune axe back and forth in a slow, strong rhythm. Felix and Agnar did the same, moving as he moved. At first the effect of their motion on the heavy cable was negligible, and Felix feared it was all for naught, but after a while their feeble wiggle became a slight sway, and then, as the movement of the cable added itself to their momentum, their swings got longer and longer, until, finally, Gotrek was able to reach out and grab the lattice of the shaft.

The first time, it ripped from his hand, but the second time he was able to catch a crossbar with the hook of his axe and they stopped in mid-swing. Gotrek pulled himself hand over hand up the haft of the axe, then grabbed onto the lattice and clung there as he untied the rope that bound his waist to the cable. One end of this he retied to the lattice, then unwound the other.

'Gotrek!' Felix cried. 'You'll–'

The last few coils whipped off Gotrek like a chain going through a pulley and the cable sprang free again.

'All part of the plan, manling,' said Gotrek, as Felix and Agnar swung again to a stop in the middle of the shaft.

'I'm relieved to hear there *is* a plan,' said Felix.

Gotrek coiled up the loose rope and made to throw it at him. 'Catch it and pass it around you, then throw it back.'

Felix caught it with a wild grab, then passed it behind him to Agnar, who handed it back to him on the other side.

'Now lift it so it is above your heads,' said Gotrek as Felix heaved the remaining length back to him.

Agnar and Felix took the rope, which was at their waists, and edged it up over their shoulders and heads until it was wrapped around nothing but the cable.

Gotrek nodded approvingly, then threaded the loose end of the rope through the lattice and started hauling at it, winching them closer and closer to the side with every pull.

Finally, Felix was able to grab the lattice and pull himself closer. Gotrek swiftly tied off the rope, then used his rune axe to cut through Felix and Agnar's bonds, and they were all clinging like flies to the side of the shaft.

'To the door,' said Gotrek.

Though Felix's knees ached and his arms shook, and his head spun with vertigo, he climbed with the Slayers to the folding gate. It was closed, and locked with a geared hook, but one swing of Gotrek's axe and the lock fell away in pieces. Felix crawled gratefully out onto an iron bridge as the Slayers pushed the doors open, and into a room very similar to the one in which they had entered the shaft, except that this one was in better repair. He sighed with relief as he reached the floor. It felt good to have solid stone under his feet again.

The room had a large arch on its north wall, but it had been sealed up with granite blocks, and recently, if the footprints and blobs of dried mortar around its base were any indication. The sounds of a big battle came from behind it – the roar of orcs, the battle chants of the dwarfs, the clash of weapons and the thunder of cannons – all muffled, but still loud.

Gotrek grunted. 'They've already begun. Come on.'

He and Agnar started for a smaller open door in the west wall. Felix followed, confused. It looked hardly large enough for him to fit through, let alone a rat-ogre.

'The skaven are coming here?' he asked. 'I thought Lanquin had kept a passage open for them.'

'You didn't look at the map,' said Gotrek. 'They are exiting the stair one level down and coming up from the north, behind the thane.'

'Ah,' said Felix, chagrined. He had looked at the map, but he didn't have a dwarf's perfect recall of such things. 'I must have misread it.'

Gotrek stepped into the narrow passage. 'This funnels into the path Thorgrin left open for the greenskins. Part of the plan to make sure they could approach the battlefield from only one direction.'

Felix swallowed. 'So we'll be entering the great hall on the orc side of the battle?'

Agnar smiled, an evil glint in his eye. 'Aye. Right at their backs.'

14

After a few twists and turns in the dark, the passage opened into a grand promenade, fully thirty paces wide, and five times Felix's height. It was decorated in high dwarf style, with towering ancestor figures holding massive braziers in outstretched hands, and great battle scenes laid out in mosaic on the wall panels between them – and it reeked of orcs.

The signs of their passage were hard to miss – grimy footprints in the dust, greasy smears where their hands and shoulders had rubbed against the walls, discarded bones where they had eaten on the march – and the sounds of their advent came loud from the north.

Gotrek and Agnar started towards the noise at a trot and Felix followed, drawing Karaghul. Ahead, an arch as wide and tall as the promenade flickered with fire and movement, and as they jogged through it into the Great Hall of the Jewellers' Guild, it resolved into a scene of furious battle.

The dwarfs had set huge bonfires around the great hall to illuminate it for the battle, and in their hot orange light, Felix could see Stinkfoot's orc army swarming the tight dwarf front. As Engineer Migrunssun had pointed out to him before, Thorgrin had chosen his position carefully, lining up his dwarf and human infantry four-deep across the narrow end of the great hall with the walls at either end protecting his flanks. This limited the number of orcs that could face his dwarfs at one time, and left a lot of the greenskins crowded together behind their comrades, all scrabbling and shoving at each other to get to the front.

All in all it was as neat and tidy a battle line as Felix had ever seen, but unfortunately, he and the Slayers were on the wrong side of it, and there was no way to reach it except through the orcs. The closing off passages that had forced the greenskins to attack from the front had brought Gotrek, Agnar and himself to the same place – and there were more dangers than just rabid orcs in the way.

On the east side of the room, the cannons and gunners that Migrunsson had placed in the minehead firing platform had perfect position to rake these frustrated tag-alongs in the flank, and mangled orc bodies splashed up like green spray every time a cannon fired and the huge iron balls skipped through them. Felix looked at them askance as the Slayers advanced. He didn't fancy being blown to bits by cannons he had helped to place.

More cannons and muskets boomed behind Thorgrin's line, firing over the dwarfs' heads from a balcony above the archway that led to the stairs to the surface, while Lanquin's mercenaries – those he hadn't sent to the depths to die – held the west end of the line, keeping the orcs at bay with spears and swords.

As Felix scanned the mercenaries, he saw Henrik behind them, gesturing feverishly as he talked in Lanquin's ear. Agnar saw him too, and changed course towards their position.

'There you are, rememberer,' he growled and picked up his pace.

'Manling,' said Gotrek as they followed. 'When we're through the line, go to the thane. Tell him the ratkin will attack from behind his guns, from the balcony.'

'Aye, Gotrek.'

Ten paces on, the Slayers charged into the back of the massed orcs. The greenskins didn't hear them coming. All their attention was focused on the dwarfs and humans ahead of them, and the bite of Gotrek and Agnar's axes severing their spines was their first indication that they were flanked.

Five died before the rest even knew the Slayers were among them. Then flying blood and body parts alerted them and they turned, roaring, upon their whirling, slashing foes. It was then that Felix attacked, hacking at their necks and backs as they closed on the Slayers. He killed two in as many seconds, and hamstrung a third as he dodged through the press.

An orc with a rusty cleaver swung at his head. Felix ducked and Gotrek's rune axe arced up and smashed through the brute's lantern jaw from below. Felix sidestepped to avoid its falling corpse and stabbed over Gotrek's shoulder into the neck of another.

It fell, spraying blood from a severed artery, and they pressed on, carving a red swathe through the green tide, step by step, until only one last rank of orcs stood between them and Lanquin's mercenaries, and these, attacked from both in front and behind, died quicker than the rest.

'Who are you?' barked a dark-browed sergeant as Felix and the Slayers stepped over the corpses of the last orcs.

'We have news for Lanquin!' called Felix before the Slayers could say anything undiplomatic. 'News from the deeps.'

'Aye,' muttered Agnar as the man waved them impatiently past and the line closed up behind them. 'News of his death.'

Gotrek and Agnar pushed through the mercenaries and started immediately for Lanquin and Henrik. The two men stared in shock at the Slayers, then backed away, pointing and shouting. Felix grinned at their reaction as he turned and ran for Thane Thorgrin, who was fighting at the centre of the dwarf line. It was a fool's game betting on a Slayer's demise, as the two traitors were learning to their cost.

Thorgrin, for all Gotrek's grumbling that he was a soft-handed, surface-dwelling brigand who had grown fat by charging others to fight his battles for him, was still dwarf enough to lead from the front when forced to war. He stood upon a broad shield held aloft by two sturdy shieldbearers, and was hewing away at the front line of Stinkfoot's black orc retinue with a will. Stinkfoot, by contrast, was hanging back and kicking his rotting foot in Thorgrin's direction, but it seemed its magic had abandoned him, for the thane did not fall.

'Thane Thorgrin,' Felix called from the back of the ranks. 'You are betrayed. Louis Lanquin has sided with the skaven and is going to let them attack your rear! They will come from the balcony.'

The battle was too loud. Thorgrin didn't hear, but Holdborn was in the second row of the Hammerers who protected the thane's right side. He heard.

'What is that, rememberer?' he asked, stepping back from his troops. 'Where is Engineer Migrunsson? Where are the other engineers?'

'Killed by a skaven trap,' said Felix. 'Two survivors were to have come back and told you.'

Holdborn scowled suspiciously. 'No one came back to us. And what is this talk of skaven? We fight the greenskins.'

'The skaven manipulate the orcs, and Lanquin too, and–' He broke off with a curse. 'There's no time to explain! Tell Thorgrin that Lanquin has cleared a path for the skaven, they will attack from–'

'Fall back! Retreat! Retreat!'

Felix and Holdborn whipped around to see Lanquin and Henrik running for the archway that led to the surface and shouting over their shoulders for their mercenaries to follow. Gotrek and Agnar were in hot pursuit, but their short dwarf legs could not match the traitors' pace, and the two men were through the arch before the Slayers had crossed half the floor.

The mercenaries ran past them, breaking from the orcs all along the west flank and fleeing after Lanquin. Many died as the greenskins surged after them and cut them down, but just as many made the archway and vanished.

Holdborn cursed as a tide of orcs began to sweep around the now undefended west wing of the dwarf line and attack them from the rear. Felix groaned as a realisation struck him. The Slayers may have goaded Lanquin into running earlier than he had planned, but this retreat had always been part of his plan. He had always intended to take his troops to the surface and leave the dwarfs in the lurch. How else to ensure their destruction and leave himself the last man standing? His treachery was now complete.

Gotrek and Agnar abandoned Lanquin and Henrik and turned to stop the orcs, but though they fought like ten dwarfs, they were only two, and could not hold them all back.

'Thane Thorgrin!' roared Holdborn. 'We are flanked! We must shore up the west!'

Thorgrin looked around, and nearly died for it as the black orcs he was facing took advantage of his distraction. Fortunately, his shieldbearers did their job, and backed him out of the arc of the orcs' cleavers, and he returned to the fight a second later, calling out orders as he parried the greenskins' blows.

'Peel off the back rows of the Hammerers and Ironbreakers. Wheel and cap the flank! Tell the Thunderers to turn all their guns to the west!'

Holdborn bawled the orders to his troops and they stepped back and turned towards the new front with practised calm, marching at the crazed orc charge in a perfect line.

The sergeant next looked up to shout orders to the Thunderers on the balcony, but there was no need. They had already turned on their own initiative, and were firing down into the greenskins, while the cannon crews were starting to wheel their field pieces into position.

They died before they could finish the turn.

The closed door behind them smashed open and an enormous rat-ogre roared out, sweeping around with handless arms that ended in metal scythes, severing dwarf heads and impaling dwarf chests. From around the mutated monster a seething swarm of ratmen spilled onto the balcony, and the Thunderers and cannon crews fell to knives in the back and claws across the throat.

Felix cursed and ran for Gotrek and Agnar. 'Slayers! The skaven! The skaven are here!'

15

Gotrek and Agnar looked up to the balcony as one, then jumped back from their combats and ran for the balcony stairs as the Hammerers and Ironbreakers took their place and tore into the orc advance. The torrent of skaven flooded down the stairs and slammed into the Slayers on the bottom step, but Gotrek and Agnar crushed them back like a fist to the face, snapping brass-tipped spears and rusty swords and making red ruin of the furred limbs that wielded them. Felix fell in behind, hacking down those ratmen who tried to leap over the Slayers to swarm easier prey beyond. He knocked a spearrat out of the air with a swipe from Karaghul, then spitted the belly of another as it flew at him, a verdigrised scimitar clutched in its paws.

'Go back to the greenskins, Gurnisson,' said Agnar, as the Slayers battled step by step up the flight. 'This is my doom. Though I did not know it, my actions aided the skaven. I have lost honour a second time, and I will die for it here.'

'It will take more than you to close that door, Arvastsson,' said Gotrek. 'But I will give you the holding of it.'

Agnar nodded, and they fell silent, concentrating on mowing down the skaven and driving them back up the stairs. On the balcony above, the rat-ogre picked up one of the cannons and hurled it over the balustrade at the dwarf troops. It slammed down in the midst of a squad of Longbeards just to the left of Thane Thorgrin, crushing half of them before bouncing into the greenskin lines and flattening as many orcs.

'Leave off, you pea-brain rodent!' roared Agnar, as the rat-ogre bent to pick up another cannon. 'Fight me!'

The rat-ogre ignored him and got the second gun up to his chest. With twin bellows of rage, Agnar and Gotrek redoubled their attacks and surged up the stairs, making mincemeat out of the skaven that stood in their way.

They reached the top just as the rat-ogre got the gun over its head. It roared at Gotrek as he hove up before it, and made to drop the cannon on him, but Agnar darted behind it and hamstrung it. With a howl of pain, it fell, its legs buckling, and the cannon crashed down on its chest, pinning it.

Gotrek hacked its head off and pointed at the door, where a second rat-ogre was bursting onto the balcony at the head of a second wave of skaven. 'Go, Arvastsson. Hold it until I can seal it shut.'

'Aye, Gurnisson,' said the old Slayer, his eyes glittering. 'Take your time.'

And with that he charged.

The rat-ogre slashed at him with wrist-blades the size of scythes. Agnar dodged its left-hand blade and shattered the right with a chopping parry from his long axe, then followed up with an overhand smash. The rat-ogre dodged back to avoid having its head caved in and pressed into the skaven that followed it. They squealed in fear, but some squirmed by and sprang at Felix and Gotrek.

'How will you close the door?' asked Felix, slashing at the ratmen. 'It's smashed to bits.'

'Smash it some more,' said Gotrek.

Felix heard him grunt and risked a look back. The Slayer stood under the muzzle of the last cannon, and was pulling down on it with one hand as he swept his axe around at the skaven with the other. His efforts were tipping the cannon forward and lifting its back stock off the ground so it was balanced only on its wheels, and he was leaning on it with all his strength, urging it around.

'Keep… the rats… clear,' Gotrek rasped. The cords of his neck stood out like taut rope.

'Aye, Gotrek,' said Felix, and laid into the skaven, cutting them down and kicking them out of the path of the cannon's ponderous turning.

In the door, Agnar battered the rat-ogre back with furious blows, carving red trenches in its grey fur and shearing off its second wrist blade, but it gave as good as it got, rocking the old Slayer with bone-knuckled blows and rending his flesh with its chisel-shaped claws. Agnar was reeling on his feet, and sprays of blood flew from his beard with every swing of his axe.

The lesser skaven squeezed past this titanic battle in ones and twos, ducking the flashing steel and flying fists, and charged on. Felix thought he could hold them – at least until Gotrek got the gun around – but a quick glance to the floor of the great hall and he wondered if it would matter. The dwarfs were in dire shape, with the Hammerers and Ironbreakers who had been sent to stop the flank attack nearly overrun, and Thorgrin's retinue being pushed back almost to the balcony.

'The orcs are winning, Gotrek.'

'One… more… minute…' grunted the Slayer.

Facing back to cut down a pair of leaping skaven, Felix saw that Gotrek had turned the gun so it was pointing directly at the arch, and was now cranking the elevation screw vigorously and raising the barrel higher. Felix wondered if he meant to blow the rat-ogre's head off.

A second later, he saw there would be no need.

He heard a bellow, and looked over the heads of his chittering opponents. The beast had Agnar in its grip, its claws digging deep into his flesh and snapping his ribs as it lifted him off the ground. It tried to catch his fighting arm with its other hand, but Agnar fought through the pain and swatted at the snatching claw, severing two thick fingers, then chopped down at its neck, cutting though meat and bone and arteries. The monster hissed an airless roar and dropped him to clutch at its throat. Agnar swung again as he fell, gashing open its belly so that its bloated black intestines spilled to the floor. The steaming viscera entangled the old Slayer as the rat-ogre toppled. He tried to stand, but the floor was too slick. The monster's massive skull crashed down, headbutting him and knocking him flat on his back across the threshold of the door with the rat-ogre on top of him.

Immediately, the skaven that had been trapped behind the mutated behemoth flooded out, scrambling over its body and stabbing at Agnar with spears, swords and daggers. He swept at them with his axe and fist, but there were too many, and he was too stunned. Though a handful fell to his deadly flailing, twice as many buried their blades in his naked torso, then surged on as he twitched and gouted blood. And there were more behind them – many more.

'Gotrek!' cried Felix as he braced for their impact.

'Fire in the hole!' roared Gotrek.

Felix glanced behind and saw the Slayer putting a flame to the touch hole of the cannon, which was pointing directly at Felix's head!

He yelped and ducked away, cutting down skaven as he went, before a deafening boom shook the balcony and smoke and fire blinded him.

The shot was followed immediately by an even louder crack, like thunder directly overhead, and yet more shaking and booming.

Coughing and blinking, Felix looked through the smoke to see the arch of the door collapsing. Gotrek's shot had shattered the keystone, and with its removal, the door could not support itself. Huge blocks of masonry caved in on top of shrieking skaven, and the roof of the passage beyond the door followed suit like dominoes. In seconds it was filled to the ceiling with rubble and the shrill agony of dying ratmen. The skaven sneak attack was stopped.

But as he and Gotrek clambered over the rubble to finish off the ratmen who had escaped the collapse, Felix saw that, as he had predicted, it wasn't going to matter. The thin line of Hammerers and Ironbreakers was dead, trampled underfoot by five times their number of orcs, and now the rest of the dwarfs and men were pressed front and back by slavering greenskins.

Stinkfoot, either frustrated by his foot's poor showing as a weapon, or emboldened by the dwarfs' desperate situation, finally limped through his black orc bodyguards and closed with Thorgrin, swinging an axe that looked like it had been crusted with the grot from between his toes.

As he and Gotrek killed the last of the skaven, Felix looked down to see the warboss's vile weapon flash down like a grimy lightning bolt. Thorgrin flinched back, covering his nose with his free hand, and the axe only nicked his vambrace, but it didn't stop there. The greasy blade swept on to chop through the shield the thane stood on, splitting it in two and sending Thorgrin crashing to the ground as Stinkfoot slashed at his shieldbearers.

'Thorgrin's down, Gotrek,' said Felix. 'We better–'

With a Khazalid war cry, the Slayer vaulted the balustrade and leapt down at Stinkfoot, his axe high over his head. The warboss looked up just in time to take the keen blade of the rune axe right between his beady yellow eyes. Gotrek split his head like a melon, all the way down to his underbite, then hit him high in the chest with his knees and rode his body down to the ground to roll to his feet right in the middle of his retinue of black orcs.

'Come on, you snot heaps!' roared Gotrek. 'Avenge your leader!'

Felix's heart thudded, expecting the end as all the towering orc champions turned towards the Slayer, but they were looking as much at Stinkfoot's corpse as they were at Gotrek, and when one began to advance on the Slayer, raising its club, another shoved it and tried to get ahead of it. Within seconds, they were all fighting each other, fist and cleaver and headbutt, with Gotrek standing forgotten in their middle.

The Slayer roared, enraged, and hacked Stinkfoot's stinking foot off at the knee, then dug his fingers into the oozing meat of the cut to wrap them around the severed shinbone and raised it up like a club. With this foul instrument in one hand and his rune axe in the other, he laid into the brawling black orcs like a whirlwind, swatting them in the teeth with the rotting appendage, then hacking them to bits as they fell back, choking and retching.

The dwarfs and humans were not slow to take advantage of this turn of events, and rallied all along their lines, driving the orcs back and reforming into squares.

'Sigmar,' Felix breathed. 'Has he done it? Has he turned the battle–?'

Before he could complete the thought, the room shook from a great impact. The orcs and dwarfs were too engaged in their battle, and didn't seem to notice, but Felix had felt it and looked around, trying to see the source. He saw nothing out of the ordinary, and was about to start down the stairs to join Gotrek when it came again. This time he was able to pinpoint the source of the sound. It was coming from the far left end of the room. He stared into the dim distance and saw grey dust hovering near the sealed-up entrance to the lift chamber.

Another heavy boom and Felix saw the dust shiver from the arch as it shook from an impact. A fracture line appeared between the blocks of the barricade. Something was trying to smash through!

'Gotrek!' Felix shouted, but the clamour of battle was too loud. The Slayer didn't hear him.

'Gotrek!'

With a final thunderous impact, the wall that sealed up the entrance exploded outward in a jumble of heavy blocks, and a shape like a glowing white hand smashed through to stagger into the room.

The White Widow had returned from its rubble grave, and both the warpstone bomb that was strapped to its back and the wrinkled skaven who rode it appeared mostly intact.

16

As the White Widow made its unsteady way towards the battle on its seven good legs and one broken one, the ancient skaven leapt from its back and scuttled away to hunch in the shattered archway, where it began waving its scrawny arms and shaking its orb-topped brass staff. A dim green light glowed to life within the orb, and Felix saw a similar light begin to glow within the matching globe on the rod that sprouted from the bomb on the spider's back.

Felix's insides fluttered with moths of dread as he realised that the skaven sorcerer meant to use a spell to detonate the bomb from afar!

Felix hopped over the balustrade and jumped down on the pile of black orc corpses that Gotrek had left heaped there. It wasn't a pleasant landing, and he ended up covered in black blood and orc smell, but it was softer than the floor and quicker than the stairs. He rolled off the putrid bodies and ran through the battle, setting his sights on the White Widow and the skaven.

Two orcs slashed at him as he ran past. He ducked their blows and tried to run on, but they blocked the way. He snarled with frustration. He had to stop the sorcerer!

A rotting, bandage-covered foot hit the left orc in the face as Felix ducked its axe, and it stumbled back, gagging. Felix chopped it in the ribs, then flinched aside, his eyes watering, as the foetid foot bounced his way. Gotrek appeared next to him and finished the orc off with an axe to the chest, then turned on the second. It snarled as it swung at the Slayer, and Felix thrust Karaghul through its neck.

'Gotrek!' he gasped as he ran on. 'The White Widow! The bomb! The skaven–'

'Get the rat, manling,' said Gotrek, shoving the dying orc out of his way as he started forward again. 'I'll get the spider.'

Felix ran on, pounding across the endless marble floor as the green glow in the matching orbs grew brighter and brighter. If the warpstone bomb detonated here it would not only kill everyone in the Great Hall of the Jewellers' Guild, it would make all of the upper levels unlivable for anyone except for the skaven, who thrived on the vile stuff. For decades – perhaps centuries – to come, anything that descended into Karak Azgal would die from its eldritch emanations.

His heart thudded at the implications. Was that what the skaven had intended all along? Had they helped Stinkfoot unite the orcs and lead them against the dwarfs just so both sides would be all together in one place – an easy target for their bomb? It sounded like just the sort of thing the ratmen would do. Felix almost laughed to think of Lanquin and Henrik helping the skaven in the belief that they would share the depths with them. What had Henrik called it? A mutually beneficial relationship? The cracked and leaking bomb strapped to the back of the White Widow was proof that the ratmen wanted Karak Azgal all to themselves. Lanquin and Henrik were betrayed along with everyone else.

The skaven sorcerer backed under the broken arch as Felix sprinted at him, pulling a long bronze knife that buzzed with strange black energy. Just the drawing of it made the hair stand up on Felix's arms, and the hum it emitted drilled into his brain.

Felix slashed at the ratmage without slowing, trying to bear it down by sheer momentum, but it slipped left with jittery speed and he missed, while its buzzing blade flicked past less than an inch from his ear.

He flinched and spun to face the sorcerer, and the blade was again in his face. He parried desperately and felt a sick trembling as the blades touched and the knife's power crackled down Karaghul's length. In all this, the skaven had not stopped his chant, and his staff continued to glow brighter.

Over the ratmage's shoulder, Felix saw Gotrek hacking madly at the White Widow. The eight-legged monster slashed back just as furiously, stabbing down with its sabre-sharp forelegs and striking sparks from the marble floor. The Slayer dodged past the blows and tried to close with it, aiming for the soft underbelly of its abdomen, but it skittered in a nimble circle and kept him before it.

Beyond that fight, Felix could see the battle raging on, with the dwarfs now firmly back in command, while the orc army disintegrated into a dozen squabbling warbands. The various bosses who had bowed to the power of Stinkfoot's stinking foot, now realising that there was no leader, had all decided that *they* could be the leader, and all over the field, the bosses were ignoring their common enemy and turning on each other. The dwarfs were now sure to win.

It would not matter, however. It wouldn't even matter whether Gotrek killed the White Widow. If Felix didn't kill the skaven mage, the bomb would still blow, and all would be for naught. They would die from the blast, or worse, become twisted, mutated parodies of themselves. He had to finish it.

In desperation, he barged forward, slashing wildly, and deliberately left himself open. The skaven could not resist the bait. It stabbed at his chest.

Felix caught its stringy wrist and stopped the blade a half-inch from his chest. Hissing angrily, the mage swiped its only available weapon at him – its staff. This was what Felix had wanted. He parried the swipe with Karaghul, putting all the strength he could muster into the block, and bit deep into the brass shaft. A bright flash blinded him and leaping arcs of energy sizzled down Karaghul to paralyze his arm with stabbing shocks, but the glowing orb dimmed and fizzled.

The skaven sorcerer shrieked with rage and clubbed Felix's head with the staff, making suns explode behind his eyes and sending him reeling into the arch. With limp arms, he raised Karaghul to defend himself, but the ratmage was turning away from him, chanting and shaking the staff at the spider, which continued to battle Gotrek.

The globe on the staff flared bright for a moment, then died completely and fell off to bounce across the floor. Chittering with fury, the skaven hurled the rest of the staff away and scampered for the White Widow, its robes flapping like dirty wings. For a second, Felix thought the mage was racing to attack Gotrek, but instead it danced between the spider's legs and clambered onto its back.

In his stunned state, this seemed to Felix a bizarre and foolhardy thing to do. Gotrek was backing the White Widow up with every slash of his axe. He had sheared off the first yard of its left foreleg and caved in three of its eight eyes, and its thicket of mandibles was a splintered, oozing mess. But then Felix saw the skaven reaching for the lever beside the fading orb, and he realised its intent. It was going to trigger the bomb manually. It was going to blow itself up, and the rest of them with it.

Heart thumping in his chest, Felix pushed himself up and ran for the fight. 'Gotrek! The skaven! Kill the skaven!'

The Slayer was too focused to hear him, and it was too late anyway. The ratmage had grabbed the lever and was pulling on it. They were all going to die.

The lever didn't move.

While Gotrek laid into the White Widow, meeting its every leg-slash with a hack from his axe, the skaven hauled repeatedly upon the bomb's brass-handled switch, but nothing happened. Felix laughed with relief. The contraption must have been damaged when the roof fell in on it.

Squealing with frustration, the skaven bent closer to the mechanism, trying to find some way to unstick it and being jounced around like a flea on a hot skillet as Gotrek drove the White Widow into the lift room. Felix added his sword to the Slayer's axe, hope rising in his chest. If they could kill the spider before the skaven freed the switch, they might just have a chance.

Gotrek was bruised and running with gore from head to foot, and the little finger of his left hand was bent backwards at an alarming angle. Nevertheless, he attacked the beast in a wild fury, his one eye ablaze with savage joy, and his teeth bared in a bloody grimace.

'The bomb, Gotrek,' said Felix. 'We have to stop the skaven from setting it off.'

'Just as soon as I'm done with this spider, manling.'

'But–'

But what other course was there? It would be impossible to reach the skaven until the White Widow was dead. Unless….

Felix looked around for something to throw at the mage, as he had done before, but the blocks that had fallen from the arch when the spider had smashed through it were too large. There was nothing the right size.

Then, suddenly, there was.

As Gotrek and Felix slashed at the spider, it reared up to avoid a blow, and its flailing forelegs cracked against the broken arch above them. A fresh course of blocks tumbled down at the impact, and smashed those that had already fallen, sending Gotrek and Felix diving aside to avoid being crushed by rubble.

The White Widow pounced upon Gotrek as he struggled to rise, stabbing at him with its one remaining foreleg, but the Slayer rolled, and the sharp tip only tore his thigh instead of impaling it. Gotrek grunted and staggered up under the spider, his leg buckling, but right where he wanted to be, and he did not let pain stop him from striking true. He chopped upward with his rune axe and buried it deep in the monster's abdomen.

The White Widow reared up like a spooked stallion and backed away, ichor gushing from the wound, and for a second time, Felix heard it scream. Gotrek limped after it, slashing at the spider's legs where they connected to its body, and it cringed back to the edge of the lift hole, its back feet slipping off into thin air.

On the thing's back, the ratmage was continuing to yank on the lever, still to no avail. Felix picked up a turnip-sized piece of rubble and hurled it, but missed. The White Widow was scrabbling at the edge now, clinging on desperately in the face of Gotrek's brutal barrage, and the skaven was being jerked around like a puppet.

Gotrek's axe burst one of the spider's larger eyes, then crushed a mandible. 'Come on, you oversized louse!' he roared. 'Fight back! Slay me!'

The spider tried, but with the loss of an eye, its aim was off, and its strikes landed wide. Gotrek hacked off a leg and it jerked back, its fat abdomen hanging out over open space. Felix thought that would be the end of it, but its back legs found purchase on the filigree of the lift shaft, and it braced itself over the drop.

Felix saw the opening just as Gotrek did, and together they sprang forward to hack at the White Widow's three middle legs, spread wide on the lip of the hole. Gotrek sheared through one, Felix cracked another, then kicked it off the edge as it drew back.

The spider listed sharply as its props fell away, and stabbed down with its remaining foreleg to catch its weight, but Gotrek chopped through that one too and it collapsed, its hammer-hard head crashing against the edge, then slipping off. The hooks of its back feet tried to hold onto the lift shaft, but its weight was too great, and they lost their grip. The White Widow fell.

Felix stepped to the edge with Gotrek and looked down as it plummeted away, bouncing and jolting off the walls. The last thing he saw before the spider vanished into the darkness was the skaven sorcerer, still pulling feverishly on the lever of the bomb.

Gotrek spat after it. 'Interfering rats. Without the weight of that scrap yard contraption on its back, the spider might have beaten me.'

Felix nodded. 'It would have made a grand doom.'

'Aye,' said Gotrek, then turned and started back into the Great Hall of the Jewellers' Guild.

As Felix followed him, a huge shock jolted the room, bringing rocks and dust down from the high ceiling and stopping dead every combat on the field of battle as the dwarfs and orcs looked up and dodged falling rubble. Felix picked himself up from where the impact had knocked him off his feet, then scrabbled away as a giant block broke from the arch and bounced across the floor. He looked around, heart pounding. A hellish green glow was pulsing from the depths of the lift shaft.

'Wh-what was that?'

Gotrek shrugged and kept walking. 'The ratmage finally got that lever to work.'

17

Gotrek and Felix strode back towards the battle, but it was nearly over. Riven with infighting, the orcs had had enough, and were scattering for the promenade with the dwarfs and humans in hot pursuit. Those orcs left on the field were dead or dying under the dwarfs' thorough throat cutting.

Gotrek ignored it all and continued towards the balcony where Agnar had met his doom. To one side, Felix saw Thorgrin on his back, his helmet off, surrounded by a circle of concerned dwarfs. A dwarf surgeon was tending to his wounds. Gotrek ignored him too, and stumped up the balcony stairs. Agnar lay dead from a score of stab wounds amongst drifts of slaughtered skaven. His legs were buried under the massive corpse of the rat-ogre he had slain, and the rubble of the collapsed doorway, but his butchered torso was uncovered and his face, in death, had a look of peace that Felix had never seen upon it in life.

Gotrek pried Agnar's axe from his still-clenched hands, then cleared the rubble and the rat-ogre's corpse from his legs and lifted him up as if he weighed no more than a child.

'Bring his axe, manling.'

Felix grunted as he picked up the long-hafted weapon. It was twice as heavy as he had expected. He followed Gotrek down the stairs, then to the corridor that led to the stairs to the surface, where the dwarfs and humans were laying their dead. As Gotrek knelt and laid Agnar with the others, Thorgrin, now bandaged and splinted, limped forward with the assistance of his remaining shieldbearer.

'Well met, Slayer,' he said. 'I mourn that you did not find your doom as your comrade did, but I thank you for slaying the orc and the White Widow. I – we – are in your debt.'

Gotrek bowed his head over Agnar as if Thorgrin wasn't there. 'You have restored your honour, Arvastsson, and died as a Slayer should,' he said. 'May Grimnir welcome you to his halls.'

Felix stepped forward to lay Agnar's axe on his chest, but Gotrek took it. 'No, manling,' he said, standing and turning towards the door. 'That axe has a vow to keep.'

Thorgrin bowed and tried again to thank him. 'Is there any reward we could offer you? Two months' entry into the hold with the licence waived, perhaps? Lodgings at the Golden Mug?'

Gotrek stepped past him and through the door without slowing. 'Your war isn't over, brigand. There are still more rats to kill.'

* * *

The Grail appeared to be closed when Gotrek and Felix reached it. The front door was locked and barred, and the gate to the stable yard was chained shut. Sounds of frantic activity drifting over the high fence, however, suggested that it was not entirely empty.

Gotrek sheared through the chain with one swipe of his axe and pushed the gate open. In the yard, still soupy with mud from the recent rain, Louis Lanquin and Henrik Daschke were busily saddling and bridling a pair of horses and throwing heavy-laden saddle bags over their rumps. A pack mule was already loaded with satchels and trunks. They looked up at the noise of the gate and froze as they saw Felix and the Slayer sloshing towards them.

Henrik backed to his horse, scrabbling blindly for the reins with one hand and his sword with the other. 'Ride,' he said. 'Now. The dwarf is a maniac. We must not face him.'

Lanquin smiled. 'And we won't.' He drew a pair of heavy pistols from his saddle holsters and aimed them at Gotrek and Felix. 'You should have taken my gold, dwarf. You might have died as a Slayer should.'

Gotrek sneered. 'By poison gas? That is not a Slayer's death.'

Lanquin's cool amusement faltered as Gotrek kept walking towards him, undaunted. Henrik clutched the innkeeper's shoulder.

'Come on! Let's fly!'

Lanquin shook him off. 'I have more saddlebags to pack.' He thumbed back the hammers on the guns. 'Stand where you are, curse you!'

'A loaded gun is no threat to those who are ready to die,' growled Gotrek.

Felix wanted to remind him that some present were not quite ready to die, but at that moment Lanquin turned both guns on the Slayer.

'Then I shall unload them,' he said.

Gotrek hurled his axe as the Bretonnian squeezed the triggers. The axe hit first, smashing into Lanquin's shoulder, and the pistols went off at wide angles as he crashed to the mud, screaming in pain. Felix ran forward to kick the pistols from Lanquin's hands, but Henrik leapt in his way, slashing with his sword. Felix parried the blow, then raised Karaghul to riposte.

'Hold, manling,' said Gotrek.

Felix held, on guard, and glanced back at him. 'You want me to spare him? After all he's done?'

'Agnar Arvastsson swore that this betrayer would die by his axe. It would not be fitting to let a Slayer's last oath go unfulfilled.' Gotrek pulled Agnar's long axe from his back and stood before Henrik.

'Step aside, manling.'

'You're going to kill me in cold blood?' squealed the rememberer. 'That's murder.'

'You have your sword. Defend yourself,' said Gotrek.

Henrik stepped back, shaking.

'Defend myself? Against you? That's still murder! You know I can't win!'

'You should have thought of that before you betrayed the oath you took to your Slayer,' said Gotrek. 'Now fight.'

'No listen, Slayer,' whined Henrik. 'I was wrong, I know that. But you don't know–'

He stabbed for Gotrek's throat with his sword, trying to take him by surprise. The Slayer was too quick. He knocked the thrust aside with such force that the blade snapped, then buried his axe in Henrik's chest.

Henrik coughed blood all over Gotrek's hands as his body went rigid, then his head slumped forward and he sagged to his knees in the mud.

Felix heard splashing behind him as Gotrek pulled Agnar's axe free, and turned to see Lanquin staggering for the back gate, his left arm red to the wrist from Gotrek's axe cut, which had laid him open to the bone. Felix leapt after him and put himself between the Bretonnian and escape.

Lanquin held up his hands.

'Please, I beg you,' he sobbed. 'I only want to leave. Take my gold, all of it!'

'Why would we let you go when we killed Henrik?' asked Felix. 'You're the worst of the lot. You colluded with the skaven to kill the dwarfs. You sent men who had sworn loyalty to you to their deaths. You tried to have us killed in the street.'

'Yes, but what will you get if you kill me?' It was a cold day, but the sweat was pouring from Lanquin's brow like a river. 'Only what I have here. Spare me and I'll tell you where I have more. You may have it all. All my wealth!'

Gotrek retrieved his axe from where it had fallen in the mud, then stepped up to Lanquin and cleaned it on his fancy cape before sheathing it on his back beside Agnar's.

Lanquin swallowed, hope kindling in his terrified eyes. 'You – you're not going to kill me?'

'You don't deserve a quick death, innkeep,' rumbled the Slayer, then turned towards the stables. 'Hold him while I fetch some rope, manling. We'll leave him for the thane.'

Lanquin whined and complained, but a minute later they had tied him to a hitching post and were examining the contents of the saddle bags and trunks as he wept quietly behind them. There was a fortune of gold coins in the satchels, and a treasure trove of jewel-studded crowns, armour and weapons that looked like they had been worn by dwarf kings and princes in the mule's packs and trunks, items far too fine for the thane to have ever allowed to be taken from the hold.

'Hmmm,' said Felix, looking at a jewelled comb that might have bought a townhouse in Altdorf. 'Take the relics back to Thorgrin and keep the coin?'

Gotrek grunted. 'It's more than the brigand deserves, but who wants to lug all that around? Maybe just... this.'

He took a sturdy gold bracelet and slipped it around his wrist, then sealed the saddlebags and slung them over his shoulder. Felix shouldered the other set and grunted to his feet under its weight. He gave Lanquin a sly salute, then led the pack mule out of the stable after Gotrek – where they came face to face with Thane Thorgrin, Sergeant Holdborn, and a phalanx of dwarf constables. A rough crowd of mercenaries and treasure hunters had gathered behind the dwarfs to see what had brought the thane of Skalf's Keep to the stinking streets of Deadgate.

Thorgrin bowed politely as he looked past them into the yard. 'It seems we owe you another debt, Slayer. You have detained the villain who masterminded this whole false war.' He nodded to the saddlebags and the pack mule. 'And I see that you have already chosen your reward. Very good. For all that you have done, you deserve it.'

Gotrek just glared at him, so Felix bowed for the both of them. 'Thank you, thane. And we have also–'

'There is the small matter of the tax, however,' said Thorgrin, speaking over him. 'As you know, all treasures taken within the confines of Karak Azgal are subject to a ten per cent tax, and if they are of particular historical significance to the hold they may not be taken at–'

'You mealy-mouthed thief!' snarled Gotrek. 'We were bringing it back to you! Here. We don't want it!'

He took the reins of the mule from Felix and handed them to Thorgrin. 'It's all yours.'

The thane stared as the dwarf constables took down and opened the trunks and revealed the great treasures within, then turned back to Gotrek and Felix and bowed again. 'The return of such important relics is a fine and noble gesture, heroes, and I am humbled by it, but, may I ask, what do you carry in the other saddlebags?'

The veins in Gotrek's neck were throbbing, and his face was turning a dangerous red. Felix stepped ahead of him, speaking quickly.

'It is nothing from Karak Azgal. We took it from Lanquin. Gold coins. His profits from the Grail, I would guess.'

'No doubt,' said Thorgrin. 'And you are welcome to it, b-but–' He stuttered as Gotrek fixed him with his blazing single eye, then continued. 'But, you seem to be under a misapprehension about the boundaries of Karak Azgal. It is not just the deeps, but also Skalf's Keep and Deadgate. The tax applies to treasures found here as well. If you would allow us to count–'

Gotrek exploded. 'You cheap chiseller! I came here to seek my doom, not to hunt treasure.' He ripped open the saddlebags, then snatched Felix's from his shoulder and did the same to them. 'If you want your ten per cent, take it.'

And with that he hurled the open saddlebags over the heads of the thane and the constables and into the crowd. The gold coins flew everywhere, and the mob immediately cried out and dropped to their knees to scrabble in the mud for them.

As the constables strode into the confusion, bellowing for everyone to stop, Gotrek picked up the trunks carrying the ancient crowns and axes and armour and threw them too, spilling the 'important relics' into the muck, to the horror of Thorgrin, but the wild delight of the crowd.

Felix laughed as the thane sputtered and gaped. It was worth the loss of the gold to see the look on his face.

'Slayer!' Thorgrin cried. 'This is an outrage! You have deprived the council of its rightful–'

Gotrek pulled Agnar's axe off his back, and the thane stepped backwards, wary.

'Will you attack me now?' he cried. 'What do you want?'

Gotrek slashed down with the axe and planted its blade in the mud at Thorgrin's feet. 'I want you to bury that with the body of Slayer Agnar Arvastsson, the only dwarf or man I met in this cesspit who wasn't a thief.'

The Slayer turned away from the stricken thane and started for the town gate.

'Come on, manling. This place stinks.'

A GOTREK & FELIX GAZETTEER

A

Adelbert Wissen
Ward captain of the Neuestadt, in Nuln. He is handsome, always immaculate, and obviously of noble descent. Felix takes an immediate dislike to him.

Adolphus Krieger
A vampire. He was one of von Carstein's most trusted minions but vanished after the battle of Hel Fenn and von Carstein's defeat, only to resurface in Praag centuries later. Tall, dark and thin, he speaks with a noticeably foreign accent. He will also stop at nothing to get his hands on the Eye of Khemri, a deceptively powerful artefact.

Aethenir Whiteleaf
An elven scholar sent to Marienburg to look for a book that has been stolen from the library of White Tower of Hoeth. The book contains maps of the lost elf settlements in the Wastelands at the mouth of the Reik, on the northern coast of the Empire. As chance would have it, Aethenir's mission seems to coincide with Max and Claudia's expedition to investigate magical disturbances in the same area. His prim elven ways do not endear him to his travelling companions, particularly the crew of the *Pride of Skintstaad*.

Agnar Arvastsson
A Slayer who Gotrek & Felix meet on their trip to Karak Azgal to seek the White Widow. Agnar is old and grizzled, with three red-dyed crests and a braided beard. His adventuring companion is the rememberer Henrik Daschke.

Alberich
Prior of the Schrammel monastery.

Albericht Kruger
The Mutant Master. He was a mild-mannered mage who attended Altdorf University at the same time as Felix Jaeger but he has now become corrupted by the Dark Arts he practises.

Albion
Reputedly a land of perpetual rain and mists, very little else is actually known about it, mainly because it has always been surrounded by spells of great potency intended to ward it from the eye of outsiders.

Aldred Keppler
Known as 'Fellblade', a knight of the Order of the Fiery Heart. He journeyed to Karag Eight Peaks to retrieve the blade Karaghul.

Aldreth
One of the oldest servants of Teclis and his brother.

Altdorf
Greatest city in the Old World, Capital of the Empire, and seat of the Emperor Karl Franz II.

Ambrosio Vento
A Tilean merchant in possession of a magic amulet, coveted by the skaven.

Annabella Jaeger
Otto Jaeger's Bretonnian wife.

Ansgar Ernot
A hedge wizard who comes to a nasty end in a protracted bar brawl in Middenheim.

Anya Nitikin
A Kislevite woman, author of *Call of the South*, said to be one of the finest writers in the Empire. She is taking her younger sister Talia to the Kingdom of the Dragon searching for a cure for her out-of-control behaviour.

Arag
A strong drink made from anise, found in exotic lands far to the south of the Empire.

Arek Daemonclaw
A formidable Chaos Warrior who has succeeded in uniting the four different factions of the Dark Powers to march down from the Chaos Wastes and lay siege to Praag. He is superstrong, superfast and near invulnerable.

Argrin Crownforger
A dwarf Slayer who Gotrek & Felix meet while hunting for the missing Order of the Fiery Heart. He has a braided crest, and a beard like an orange haystack. He has a square, lumpy face and missing two fingers on his right hand.

Avelein
Wife of Graf Reiklander, she is beautiful, but carries a sadness in her eyes.

Aver Isle
A small island in the middle of the River Aver, at Nuln. It is here that the Engineering School test their devices, so as not to risk injuring innocent bystanders.

Axe of the Runemasters
Also known as the Axe of Valek. An ancient artefact of immense power, previously wielded only by the High Runemasters of Karag Dum.

B

Baldurach
A member of the Council of Truthsayers in Albion.

Banner of Baldemar
Sacred banner of the Order of the Fiery Heart, made from the cloak of the knight who founded the order.

Barak Varr
'Torrent Gate', the dwarf port lying on the mouth of Blood River. Being not only a lowland fortress but a haven for oceangoing vessels, more traditional dwarfs consider the locals a little touched.

Bardolf von Veldrecht
Steward of Castle Reikland.

Barren Hills
'Felix thought they could not have been more aptly named. The land stretched

out in an endless sea of low, mist-swathed ridges, many with dead winter grass, and leafless thorn bushes, and bare of trees but for an occasional wind-bent pine hunched upon a rocky crest...'
From *Shamanslayer*,
by Nathan Long

Baulholz
An Empire town situated about five days' travel south of Fort Stangenschlosse.

Bear's Milk
A strong alcoholic beverage popular with the knights of the Black Bear Order. It consists of fermented bears' milk mixed with vodka.

Belegar
Nominal ruler of Karag Eight Peaks, he led the expedition to reclaim the lost stronghold.

Belryeth Elvendawn
A distressed elf maiden who begs Aethenir's help in recovering a lost 'family heirloom'. However, her story is merely a ruse to co-opt the elf scholar into obtaining a special book for her.

Big Nod
A halfling 'trader' who plies his trade in the docks of Nuln. The epithet is, of course, entirely ironic.

Birgi
A dwarf slave aboard a dark elf black ark, and father of Farnir.

Birrisson
A dwarf engineer, based in Karak Hirn. He was obsessed with gyrocopters, and had a lab where he could tinker with his creations, linked to the main body of the hold by a secret passage.

Bjorni Bjornsson
Bjorni is a squat, muscular, repulsively ugly dwarf with a gruesome collection of warts on his face and a particularly huge and hairy one right on the end of his nose. He is crude, lewd and tells some exceptionally tall tales about his sexual conquests, though admittedly he does enjoy surprising success with women, a fact which never ceases to amaze Felix Jaeger. He is first encountered by Ulrika at Karak Kadrin and introduces himself by propositioning her. Though she rejects him, he joins the party on their quest anyway and is one of the seven Slayers who go to confront the dragon Skjalandir in its lair.

Black Ark
Monstrous floating island-fortresses employed by the dark elves to travel over the seas of the Old World. Each is a self-contained military unit, boasting a full complement of troops, slaves, beasts and associated vessels.

Black Coach
Unmarked coach that travels the Bögenhafen road on Geheimnisnacht, said to be driven by daemons.

Black water
A volatile, malodorous liquid that can be used to power dwarf gyrocopters.

Black Water, the
A vast lake located in the Worlds Edge Mountains, south of Zhufbar. It was formed when a meteor hit the earth in the far distant past. In the dwarf language, it is known as Varn Drazh.

Blind Alley
A disreputable tavern in Barak Varr.

Blind Pig, The
A tavern on Commerce Street, Nuln, owned by Heinz. Gotrek and Felix were employed as bouncers and it is here that the gutter runners stage their daring attack.

Blood-gold
A rare type of gold, much coveted by dwarfs.

Blutdorf
A small and particularly squalid village

located between Fredericksburg and Nuln.

Blutdorf Keep
Rundown castle overlooking Blutdorf, inhabited by the wizard Albericht Kruger.

Boneripper
Thanquol obtains a succession of unfortunate rat-ogre bodyguards from Clan Moulder, at great cost. Finally, he has a mechanical version constructed by a warlock-engineer, but even this proves unreliable.

Books
Possession of certain dangerous books is forbidden in the Empire; even to know their names can invoke censure from the authorities, notably the Templars of Sigmar, more commonly known as the witch hunters.

Borek the Scholar
Also known as Borek Forkbeard because he has a huge forked beard which reaches all the way to the floor before being looped back up into his belt.

He is the ancient dwarf scholar who organises an expedition to the Chaos Wastes to try and find the lost citadel of Karag Dum. It was Borek and his brother Vareg, who brought the last message from Karag Dum before it was swallowed by the Wastes, and though he tried to return at the time, the first mission failed and he was one of only three survivors.

Bounty Bay
Location where the combined fleets of Estalia finally defeated Redhand's pirate fleet. Redhand is believed to have escaped.

Bran Mac Kerog
The bear-like chieftain of the mountain men of Carn Mallog whose main passion seems to be greed.

Brocht
Huge circular stone tower.

Broken Pickaxe, The
Inn situated in the small town of Gelt. Gotrek, Felix and their party stay there en route to the Dragon Mountain.

Brotherhood of the Cleansing Flame
One of the many cults that proliferated in Nuln during the reign of Karl Franz. Their rallying cry veered between overthrowing the old order by violence, and burning away corruption with fire. Followers identified themselves with yellow masks and tabards, decorated with a crude symbol of a flame. The cult has its base in the Broken Crown, a multi-level tenement in the roughest part of Nuln.

Bugman's Best
A renowned dwarf beer.
'It was cool and clean and crisp, with a taste that brought to mind wheat fields and mild autumn days, and it went down his throat like golden light. It was possibly the best beer Felix had ever drunk.'
– From *Slayer's Honour*, by Nathan Long.

Bunk and Binnacle, The
An especially unpleasant inn in Marienburg. It is small, smelly and damp, and looks as if it might fall down at any moment.

C

Cabbage
A gnoblar in the service of the ogre Gutsnorter.

Canary
A little yellow coloured finch from the Southlands. They will cheep madly if taken anywhere near gold, which makes them a valuable accessory for treasure hunters. It is claimed that these birds will keel over at the slightest hint of gas, but this is plainly ridiculous.

Captain Ahabsson
Captain of the *Storm Hammer*. He has a

hook to replace his lost hand, and a Letter of Marque from Barak Varr.

Captain Doucette
Bretonnian captain of the *Reine Celeste*.

Captain Rion
Leader of Aethenir's elf bodyguard.

Carn Mallog
A settlement of brochts on a ridge top and home to Bran Mac Kerog's mountain men. They are massive structures designed to resist siege and are engraved with runes similar to the tattoo patterns which adorn the faces of the warriors.

Castle Reikguard
Ancestral seat of the Reikland princes, this large castle guards the eastern border of the Reikland. It is of great strategic and symbolic importance to the defence of the Empire, and cannot be allowed to fall. Located on the banks of the River Reik, it has its own docks area.

Caspian Rodor
Former grandmaster of the Order of the Black Bear. When he died, Rodor had his body sealed up in a cask of Wynters XVI. On the anniversary of his death, it became the tradition for every man in the order to take a ceremonial drink from his grave-cask.

Cauldron Lake
A lake in the southern end of the Grey Mountains, near the dwarf hold of Karak Hirn.

Cauldron of a Thousand Poxes
A hideously powerful artefact for brewing diseases. Reputedly stolen from a temple of the Plague God, Nurgle and reconsecrated to the service of the Horned Rat.

Chang Squik
Of Clan Eshin, the assassins. Trained for years in the delivery of silent death. Third Degree adept in the way of the Crimson Talon and black belt in the Path of the Deadly Paw. Pupil of the infamous skaven assassin, Deathmaster Snikch.

Chaos Wastes
A hellish land to the far north beyond Kislev and Blackblood Pass. The armies of the four ruinous powers of Chaos reside there.

Chimera
A fantastic beast with the head of a lion, the body of a goat, and a serpent's tail. They are sometimes captured and used as mounts, or to fight as beasts of war.

Claudia Pallenberger
A journeyman of the Celestial College. When Felix first meets her, she is about twenty years old, very slim and beautiful, with long fair hair and deep blue eyes. Claudia's special talent is her ability to see into the future, and her visions of the Empire's cities being destroyed lead to her and the wizard Max Schreiber being sent to the northern parts of the Empire, to investigate the source of the disturbance.

Despite her magical talents, at the time of this expedition she is not emotionally mature, and becomes infatuated with the good-looking poet, Felix Jaeger.

Count Andriev
Ulrika's distant cousin, a collector of antiques and curiosities. He hires the Slayer and his companions to protect his collection and in particular, the Eye of Khemri.

Countess Gabriella of Nachthafen
A beautiful woman of indeterminate age. Sister-in-law to Rudgar. She also appears to have a mysterious connection to Krieger. Latterly, she has taken up residence in Nuln, where she runs a prestigious 'boarding house' for young ladies, and has established herself as a sort of mother figure for Ulrika, both of whose parents have been lost.

Count Hrothgar
Nobleman and member of the Order. He wants the Children of Ulric dead.

Crannog Mere
A strange floating village built in the middle of a lake. The somewhat primitive houses appear to be either on stilts or situated atop small artificial islands and are linked by causeways of mud and logs. The only way of getting out to them is by way of a narrow, winding causeway, cunningly concealed just below the waterline so that it can only be seen from close at hand.

Crassik
Litter-brother of Siskritt the skaven.

Crimson Ones
Elite palace guard in the employ of the corrupt caliph of Ras Karim. They are not entirely human.

Culum
A massive and extremely well muscled Albion tribesman who challenges Gotrek to an arm wrestling competition. He is related to Murdo MacBaldoch in some way and married to Klara.

Cult of Slayers
Dwarf cult which has its spiritual home in Karak Kadrin, where the Shrine of Grimnir is located.

D

Darkstone Ring
Stone circle lying between Blutroch and the Standing Stones Inn, to the north of the Bögenhafen road.

Deadgate
A scrappy human settlement that has sprung up in the valley below Karak Azgal. It is here that adventurers and treasure hunters gather prior to their descent into the lost dwarf hold. Traders and tavern keepers do their best to fleece visitors before they head to the hold, as the likelihood is that they will never return anyway.

Detlef Sierck
Greatest playwright in the Empire, and known associate of the vampire Genevieve.

Dider Reidle
An ale merchant that Gotrek and Felix help on their way to Fort Stangenschloss.

Dieter
A stern, grey-haired man, who looks after the von Diehl entourage. He employs Gotrek and Felix as mercenaries.

Dog and Donkey, The
A tavern in Guntersbad, and the scene of Gotrek and Snorri's epic drinking contest.

Dominic Reiklander
A young Empire lord, son of Graf Reikland.

Dragon Crag
Another name for Karak Azgal.

Dragon Mountain
Under this peak, in an extensive cave system, is where the dragon Skjalandir has made his home.

Dragon Vale
The valley leading to the Dragon Mountain, which has been devastated by Skjalandir since it has made its home there.

Drakenhof Castle
A huge castle in Sylvania, it is said to be built on a particularly ill-omened site, a nexus of terrible dark energies, and is a sacred place to the Arisen.

Drexler, Doktor
A physician and scholar in Nuln. He studied medicine in Kah Sabar, Araby. Felix is referred to him by his brother when he starts displaying what could be possible symptoms of the Plague.

Druric Bodrigsson
Dwarf ranger of Blackfire Pass who joins the expedition to liberate Karak Hirn from the greenskins.

Duk Grung Mine
A dwarf mine in the mountains near Karak Hirn. A secret passage leads from here into a treasure vault in Karak Hirn.

E

Echter
A witch hunter Thanquol locks horns with when his mind is temporarily trapped in Boneripper's body.

Elissa
Barmaid at the Blind Pig in Nuln and Felix's love interest for a while.

Emperor's Griffon
Tavern in the Human quarter of Karak Kadrin.

Emil von Kotzebue
A baron of the Empire.

Engineer Migrunsson
A dwarf engineer who Gotrek & Felix meet when they take part in an expedition to clear the greenskins out of Karak Azgal. He is a cheerful, no-nonsense sort, with a leather apron and a tightly braided beard.

Enrik Kozinski
The Duke of Praag. A middle-aged man with greying hair, his tendency to see the works of Chaos around him has led to rumours that he shares his father's insanity. His curt manner and fiery temperament belie a gentle and caring manner.

Eye of Khemri
A small, oval-shaped pendant carved from obsidian with a central eye surrounded by odd pictograms of animal-headed people. The stone itself is gripped in a silver hand setting with pointed talons. Found in the rubble of Khemri and also known as the Eye of Nagash.

Eye of the Lord
A magical artefact, kept by Kelmain and Lhoigor. A gigantic crystal orb encased in metal, it is used to predict the future.

F

Father Rustskull
Rodi Balkinsson's affectionate name for Snorri, after the Slayer loses his memory.

Falhedar il Toorissi
The tyrannical caliph of Ras Karim. He controls his unruly subjects through use of the Serpent Crown, a magic artefact that allows him to subdue the wills of other men.

Falken Reiklander
Graf of Castle Reikland. Having been badly wounded in a Chaos invasion, the castle is currently under the control of General Nordling.

Faragrim
A senile dwarf prospector who Gotrek and Felix bump into in the Border Princes.

Farnir
An enslaved dwarf Gotrek & Felix meet when they are captives aboard a dark elf black ark. Being captured as a child, he has never known any other life than that of a slave.

Fedrich Gerlach
Innkeep at the Skewered Dragon, Middenheim.

Felix Jaeger
Born the younger son of a wealthy Altdorf merchant, Gustav Jaeger and his wife Renata, Felix Jaeger always had dreams of becoming a famous poet and scholar. Unfortunately, his promising career was cut short when he found himself expelled from University after accidentally killing a fellow student in a duel. He then became involved in the infamous Window Tax Riots where he met Gotrek Gurnisson under somewhat fortuitous circumstances, when the Slayer

pulled him out from under the hooves of one of the mounted cavalry officers sent in to break up the fray. Unfortunately, the Slayer then took exception to nearly being trampled himself, so set about breaking a few heads. Unsurprisingly, both soon found themselves wanted by the authorities.

Later that evening in the Axe and Hammer tavern, Felix heard of the Slayer's quest to find a worthy doom, and being slightly worse for wear at the time, swore a blood oath to follow the dwarf and record his demise in a suitably epic poem, never dreaming just what this would entail.

The duo's adventures have seen them journey extensively throughout the Empire, battling the forces of Chaos wherever they find them. Felix acquired the mystical dragon-hilted blade, Karaghul, in a troll's treasure hoard under Karak Eight Peaks and has used it to great effect against the numerous enemies he has fought since, particularly the dragon Skjalandir. Since teaming up with the Slayer, he has also thwarted a skaven invasion, an assassination plot and a great Chaos incursion, and battled true Terror in the lost dwarf city of Karag Dum. He has also found time to meet and fall in love with Ulrika Magdova Straghov, though the affair has been a bitter-sweet experience.

Tall, broad-shouldered and blond, probably the most notable thing about Felix's handsome features is the long, thin scar which mars his cheek, a legacy of his student duelling days. He wears a tattered, red Sudenland wool cloak and though his clothes are of good quality, they have all seen better days; much like the poet himself, in fact.

Ferga
A dwarf maiden of Karak Hirn; the beloved of Prince Hamnir.

Firgigsson
A dwarf guildmaster, and representative of the Dwarf Black Powder Guild. When black powder bound for Middenheim is stolen from the docks in Nuln, Gotrek and Felix become involved in the search to recover it.

Flanders Draahl
A knight of the Order of the Black Bear. A trained duellist, he carries a rapier rather than a longsword, and wears a hauberk of leather and ringmail rather than plate armour.

Forbidden Garden, The
A house of ill-repute in the port of Ras Karim.

Forgast Gaptooth
A Slayer acquaintance of Snorri who killed a troll in a most unusual way.

Fort von Diehl
Settlement founded by the von Diehl family and their retainers, following their exile from the Empire.

Frau Winter
Sorceress, part of the von Diehl entourage, and mistress to Kirsten.

Fredric Gerlach
Owner and barkeep of the Skewered Dragon.

Fredericksburg
Town in Averland, near Blackfire Pass.

Fritz von Halstadt
Head of Nuln's secret police and a chief magistrate. A tall, gaunt man, von Halstadt is a deadly swordsman and obsessed with the Elector Countess he serves.

G

Garg Gorgul
Huge ogre encountered by Gotrek and Felix below Karag Eight Peaks.

Gargorath the God-touched
A beastman champion. He wears armour of steel and bronze over his black

fur, and carries an enormous single-bladed axe that magically drains the life from its foes. Though the nominal leader of a massive beastman army, the brains behind the enterprise are Urslak Cripplehorn's.

Galin Olifsson
A dwarf engineer who accompanies Gotrek and Felix on their expedition to retake Karak Hirn.

Gam's Spire
The top of the Zhufgrim Scarp.

Geheimnisnacht
'Night of Mystery', considered extremely unlucky by citizens of the Empire. Both moons are full on this night.

Giselbert von Volgen
A lord of the Talabecland. He is young, beardless, and wears fluted plate armour.

Gnawklaw
Gotrek and Felix cross paths with this skaven grey seer while hunting the liche Pragarti under the streets of Kutzenholz.

Gnoblars
These malicious little greenskins are related to goblins, and indeed rather resemble them. They can be mostly found living alongside ogres, where they serve as servants, soldiers and (more often than they would like) food.

Golden Brotherhood
A secret order devoted to seeking Chaos and destroying it. Max Schreiber is a member.

Golden Gull
Katja Murillo's ship, sunk by Uragh Goldtusk while she was searching for Redhand's treasure.

Golden Hammer, The
An upmarket restaurant in Nuln which Otto Jaeger takes Felix to, and where Felix sees and recognises Fritz von Halstadt.

Gospodar Muster
A force of 5,000 mounted warriors, led by the Ice Queen herself, that go to aid Praag in its fight against the forces of Arek Daemonclaw.

Gotrek Gurnisson
Gotrek, son of Gurni was born and raised in the corridors of Karaz-a-Karak and like all citizens of the King's Council, did his military service in the depths below the Everpeak as a youth. Details of the intervening years between then and his meeting with Felix Jaeger are vague, though it is known that he was part of the first ill-fated attempt to find the lost city of Karag Dum. One of only three survivors to return from the Chaos Wastes, when he did so, he was carrying the awesome star-metal rune axe which never leaves his side.

After swearing blood kinship with Felix Jaeger and making him his rememberer, the pair set out on their travels, the Slayer actively seeking his doom, the man simply there to record it. Losing his eye in an epic battle against some greenskins at Fort von Diehl has been perhaps the most noticeable injury the Slayer has sustained and though there have been a few close calls, much to his chagrin, Gotrek inevitably lives on to fight another day.

A typical Slayer, Gotrek sports the bright orange crest and numerous tattoos which mark him as such. He is huge by dwarf standards and though he only comes up to his companion's chest, he outweighs him by a substantial margin, all of it muscle. A gold chain runs from nostril to ear and a leather patch covers his ruined eye. He can drink almost as well as he can fight, which is saying something indeed, and he hates trees, boats and elves with a vengeance.

> *'...there was no denying that the Trollslayer presented a formidable appearance. Although Gotrek only came up to Felix's chest, and a great deal of that height was made up of the huge dyed crest of red hair atop his shaved*

and tattooed skull, he was broader at the shoulders than a blacksmith. In one massive paw, he held a rune-covered axe that most men would have struggled to lift with both hands. When he shifted his massive head, the gold chain that ran from his nose to his ear jingled.'

From *Trollslayer*,
by William King

Gottfried von Diehl
Baron of the Vennland Marches, exiled after a conflict with their Sigmarite neighbours. He leads his people on a doomed expedition out of the Empire south into the Border Princes.

Grail, The
A tavern in the settlement of Deadgate. It is decorated in imitation Bretonnian courtly style, an oddity that can surely be traced back to the nationality of its owner, one Louis Lanquin.

Green Man, The
A fortified inn on the road to Drakenhof.

Greypaw Hollow
A small skaven settlement located under a forest.

Griffon, The
An inn in Latdorf where Gotrek and Felix stay for a couple of months recuperating after the crash of the *Spirit of Grungni*.

Grim Hogan
A Kislevite knight of the Order of the Black Bear.

Grimme
A dwarf Slayer, first encountered by Felix in the Shrine of Grimnir. He speaks very little, seeming to be too overwhelmed by some personal grief to allow any kind of connection with others. He is one of the seven Slayers who go to beard the dragon in its den.

Grudi Halfhand
Dwarf Slayer, son of Olgep Wynters, Master Brewer. He lost his left hand in an unnamed battle, and has a hook in its place. Grudi and Snorri join up with the knights of the Black Bear on their expedition to reclaim the Wynters Brewery.

Gulf of Araby
Expanse of water lying between the southern coast of Araby and the Southlands.

Grume of the Night Fang
A massive and foul-smelling Khorne warlord who is in league with the Tzeentch sorcerers, Kelmain and Lhoigor. He wants to kill Gotrek and claim his axe for his own, and carries the fearsome Skull Mace of Malarak to help him achieve his goal.

Guntersbad
A small town on the road to Talabheim.

Gurag
A monstrously obese orc shaman who pits his powers and his wits against Teclis, with surprising results.

Gustav Jaeger (i)
Otto Jaeger's son. A tall, thin, serious-looking youth, he studies theology and law at the University of Nuln.

Gustav Jaeger (ii)
Felix and Otto Jaeger's father, and head of the Jaeger's of Altdorf trading company, one of the richest merchant businesses in the Empire. From humble origins himself, he was determined that his two sons have the best education he could afford. Sadly, his younger son Felix showed no interest in the family business, and let himself be sucked into a life of 'adventure', at the beck and call of a renegade dwarf.

Gutgob Stinkfoot
An orc warboss who has conquered and unified the orcs in the lower depths of Karak Azgal, thereby making it impossible for adventurers to explore the ruined dwarf hold. As his name suggests, he has a very stinky foot!

Gutsnorter
An ogre, and relative of Vork Kineater.

H

Halim il Saredi
A revolutionary who wishes to overthrow the cruel caliph of Ras Karim.

Hall of the Well
The main hall housing Thangrim's people in Karag Dum. The settlement is protected by Runes of Concealment.

Hammer of Fate
The mighty magical warhammer used by King Thangrim, said to be one of the artefacts bequeathed to the dwarfs by the Ancestor-Gods.

Hanged Man, The
Inn located in Blutdorf, just as unpleasant as the rest of the village.

Hans Euler
A trader based in Marienburg. When his father, Ulfgang, dies, Hans comes into possession of incriminating documents which he tries to use to blackmail Felix Jaeger's father, Otto, into giving him a share of the family business, Jaeger and Sons.

Hans the Hermit
A strange old man in dirty robes who has often been seen lurking round the borders of Talabecland.

Hans Muller
The Divine One. A filthy, unkempt and quite, quite mad mage whose Spell of Translocation went wrong so he ended up the Ruined City in the Chaos Wastes where he meets Gotrek, Felix and Snorri.

Harbinger of Stromfels
Part shark, part octopus, totally monstrous, this horrific sea creature has been plaguing the port of Marienburg for centuries. It has not been seen since its defeat at the hands of the dwarf Slayer Gotrek Gurnisson.

Hargrim
Son of Thangrim Firebeard, a massive broad-shouldered dwarf and leader of the Tunnel Fighters at Karag Dum.

Harp of Ruin
A sinister-looking black harp, if played, this ancient elven magical artifact can make the earth move – or so the dark elves believe. Like many such artefacts created in ages past, it was too dangerous to use, yet too dangerous to destroy.

Haschke
Captain of a regiment of Empire spearmen patrolling the Drakwald forest.

Hate Child
A parable told by the monks of the Schrammel monastery. It concerns a noble count called Benoist, and the consequences of his liaison with a woman called Yvette.

Haunted Citadel
An abandoned slann fortress in the swamps near Crannog Mere.

Heart of Fire
A magical gem secreted in the depths of the temple where Redhand's treasure was hidden. It was believed to control the eruptions of the island's volcano.

Hef (i)
Trapper, hired by the von Diehl family to guide them across the Border Princes. Felix first encounters him in the trading post where Hef is harassing Kirsten.

Hef (ii)
One of two twin sewerjack knifemen who work with Gotrek and Felix in the Nuln sewers (see also **Spider**).

Heinrich Kemmler
Aka 'the Lichemaster'. This necromancer has plagued the Empire for hundreds of years. His already significant magic powers are complemented by the undead Chaos champion, Krell, who follows him, though the exact

relationship between the two is hard to determine.

Heinrich Lowen
A witch hunter based in Middenheim. Following a nasty run-in with a deviant, he has had some of his missing teeth replaced with metal studs.

Henrik Daschke
Human rememberer, late of Talabheim, companion to the Slayer Agnar Arvastsson. Gotrek and Felix make the acquaintance of this pair while visiting Karak Azgal. Despite his engaging smile, Henrik's motives and loyalties are not quite as clear as he pretends they are.

Heinz
Owner of the Blind Pig and an old mercenary friend of Gotrek. He spent ten years as a halberdier and rose to the rank of captain during Karl Franz's campaigns against orcs to the East. Sports a bad leg after being stamped on by a Bretonnian charger at the Battle of Red Orc Pass.

Henkin Warsch
A traveller who crosses paths with Gotrek and Felix at Schrammel, near the infamous monastery there.

Henrik Richter
A bandit chief who has forged the bands of outlaws together in a bid to defeat the invading horde led by Ugrek Manflayer.

Herman Faulkstein
A watch officer in Middenheim.

Heshor
A dark elf sorceress. If her plans to use the harp of ruin in the Sea of Manann come to fruition, the resulting seismic upheaval could have terrible consequences for Marienburg and the Empire.

Heskit One Eye
Master Warp Engineer of Clan Skyre, he leads the attack on Nuln's College of Engineering in an attempt to steal a steam tank.

Hieronymous Ostwald, Count
Secretary to Her Serene Highness, Countess Emmanuelle. Friend of Drexler's.

Hippogryph
A fabulous beast with the forequarters of a griffon, and the rear quarters of a horse, found in the wildest reaches of the Old World. They are occasionally captured and forced to fight in arenas, or tamed for use as riding beasts.

Hirhaz Helmgard
A dwarf thane who gets trapped in Karak Hirn when it is invaded by greenskins. He and his followers only manage to survive by barricading themselves inside their clan's inner hold.

Holdborn, Sergeant
An officious dwarf sergeant at Karak Azgal.

Horn Gate
The name of Karak Hirn's front gate. Recapturing the Horn Gate is the keystone of Prince Hamnir's plan for the dwarfs to regain entry to their lost hold.

Huntzinger
Plaschke-Miesner's sergeant of scouts.

I

Ilgner
Commander of the Empire soldiers garrisoned at Fort Stangenschloss.

Indestructible
Malakai's first flying ship. Big as a sailing ship, the fuselage was over a hundred paces long and the ship itself could fly at ten leagues an hour. It crashed and was destroyed utterly.

Iron Door, The
Tavern in Karak Kadrin. A reputed hangout for Slayers, renegades, and other lowlifes.

Iron Tower
Headquarters of the witch hunters in

Nuln, this forbidding tower is set on its own island on the Aver.

Issfet Loptail
Humble servant of grey seer Thanquol. He lost his tail in a raid on a human farm, hence the surname.

Ivan Stragov
Ulrika's father. A huge burly man with a long white beard and a shaved head except for a top knot. He is a Kislevite March Warden, in command of a thousand men.

Ivan took care of Borek, Gotrek and Snorri on their return from the Chaos Wastes on their first mission to find Karag Dum and thus earned their respect and friendship.

Ivory Road
A long trading road that runs between Barak Varr, the dwarf sea port, and Cathay, far to the east. It is a dangerous trip, not be undertaken without an armed escort.

Ixix
Goblin shaman, serving under Ugrek Manflayer, considered mad even by greenskin standards.

Izak Grottle
Obese Clan Moulder Packmaster, Grottle's appetite for food is rivalled only by his appetite for power.

J

Jilfte Bateau
A passenger boat that runs between Altdorf and Marienburg, down the River Reik. Through progress down the river is not fast, it is at least slow, steady and safer than the roads.

Johann Zauberlich
A wizard and companion to Aldred Keppler. When not adventuring, he is a lecturer at the University of Nuln.

Jules Gascoigne
A Bretonnian scout originating from Quenelles. He was hired by Aldred Keppler to guide their party to Karag Eight Peaks.

Julianus Groot
High Chancellor of the Imperial Gunnery School in Nuln. He is a cheerful, pot-bellied man with greying mutton chops and a nearly bald head.

Jurgen, Frater
Librarian of the Schrammel monastery.

Justine
A Chaos Warrior of Khorne, leader of the beastmen that destroyed Kleindorf.

K

Kaadiq
Court sorcerer of the caliph of Ras Karim. He has a magic silver flute, which enables him to charm beasts and animals to do his bidding.

Kagrin Deepmountain
A young dwarf who is part of the expedition to liberate Karak Hirn from its orc and goblin occupiers.

Karag Dum
Lost dwarfhold in the Chaos Wastes and formerly one of the greatest dwarf cities, the mightiest in the northern lands in fact. It fell during the last great incursion of Chaos before the reign of Magnus the Pious.

Karaghul
Magic sword, originally wielded by the Templar Raphael. It was discovered by Felix, in Thulgul the troll's treasure hoard.

Karak Eight Peaks
Ancient dwarf stronghold that fell to the goblins three thousand years ago.

Karak Azgal
The original name of this dwarf hold was *Karak Izril*, the City of Jewels, but

nowadays it is known as Karak Azgal – 'Hoard Peak'. The hold fell to orcs and goblins nearly five hundred years ago, and the dwarfs have never been able to drive out the invaders. These days, the dwarfs run the lost hold as a money-making enterprise, letting adventurers explore the depths... charging them a fee to enter, and a tax on any treasure they retrieve. The dwarfs still cling to the dream that one day they will be able to reclaim their lost territory, and the underground forges will once again ring with the merry sound of dwarf hammers.

Karak Hirn

Aka 'Horn Hold'. A dwarf hold at the far south of the Empire, where the bottom of the Grey Mountains meets the Worlds Edge Mountains, just north of the Border Princes. When it is overrun by goblins, its lord, Prince Hamnir, organises an expedition to reclaim it for the dwarf nation. The hold's symbol is a horn over a stone gate.

Karak Kadrin

'Slayer Keep', a dwarf stronghold that overlooks the Peak Pass in the Worlds Edge Mountains. Karak Kadrin has never fallen, partly due to the presence of the Shrine of Grimnir which attracts Slayers from across the Old World.

Karak Varn

A Dwarf steamship that sank in a tale told by Urli aboard the *Storm Hammer*. Nobody knows why it sank.

Karl-Franz

Leader of the most powerful human nation in the Old World, the Empire, he leads fearlessly leads his armies into battle against their enemies – greenskins, beastmen, and worse.

Kat aka Katerina Messner

A young girl with a distinctive white streak in her black hair. She was found by Gotrek & Felix in the ruins of Kleindorf. Kat's experiences as a young girl dictated the course of her life, and she became a hunter of beasts, vowing to clear the Drakwald of all beastmen. While sometimes she guides refugees from war-ravaged areas to safety, she also scouts out beastman camps for the Empire army. She is especially skilled with bow and arrows, her weapon of choice.

Katja Murillo

Captain of the *Golden Gull*, and captive of Uragh Goldtusk when she first meets Felix. Tall, with raven-black, curly hair that falls to her shoulders, and with a low, husky voice. Despite being somewhat attracted, Felix cannot help but be suspicious of her.

Kazad Varr

A sturdy dwarf fortress just outside the main entrance to Barak Varr, at the top of the Rising Road.

Kelmain Blackstaff

An albino Tzeentchian sorcerer of immense power, he is also the identical twin of Lhoigor. Both he and his brother served as advisors to Arek Daemonclaw and also had a hand in the corruption of the dragon, Skjalandir. Kelmain carries a staff of ebony and silver, which he found in ruins in the Chaos Wastes. He and Lhoigor are also responsible for opening the Paths of Old Ones and unwittingly putting the whole of the Old World in jeopardy by doing so.

Khimar

In the South Lands, a local term for a chimera.

Kingdom of the Dragon

A mysterious land – possibly mythical – rumoured to lie far, far to the east.

Kirgi Narinsson

A dwarf of the Ironskin clan, from Karak Hirn.

Kirsten

Indentured to Frau Winter, part of the von Diehl entourage. Felix rescues her from the attentions of Hef, Kell and Lars in the trading post and she becomes his first love.

Kislev
Reputed to be a land of ice and snow where winter never lifts. In actuality, it is a land of rolling plains and thick forests of pine which has a brief but intense summer and a long, cold winter. Famed for its horsemen.

Klara
Culum's pretty and somewhat inquisitive wife. Her attempt to wheedle information out of Felix only succeeds in earning him the enmity of her husband.

Kleindorf
Small village on the Flensburg road, deep in the Drakwald.

Knoblauch, Frater
Gatekeeper at the Schrammel monastery.

Krakul Zapskratch
An itinerant warlock engineer who at one time passes through the skaven outpost of Greypaw Hollow. It is here where he takes on a job for Grey Seer Thanquol – constructing a mechanical Boneripper.

> 'Had it been standing, the creature would have been three times the size of its master, a towering construction of steel, bone and wire fuelled by a warpstone heart and driven by the arcane mechanics of Clan Skryre techno-sorcery. In shape, it retained a morbid resemblance to a living rat-ogre, and the warlock-engineers had even used the bones of Thanquol's first Boneripper when assembling their creation.'
>
> From *Mindstealer* by CL Werner

Kregaerak
The location near where the *Karak Varn* was washed up.

Krell
Krell is a mighty lord of the undead, resurrected by Heinrich Kemmler. He is armed with a magic axe, the edge of which shatters upon impact, leaving tiny flecks of evil in his opponent's body.

L

Lady Hermione
A beautiful noblewoman of Nuln, and business rival of Countess Gabriella.

Landryol Swiftwing
A dark elf corsair captain encountered by Gotrek and Felix when they are held captive on a black ark.

Lars
Trapper. Felix manages to enamour himself of Lars by smashing his teeth during a fight in the trading post.

Leatherbeard the Slayer
A dwarf Slayer who joins Gotrek & Felix in their attempt to get into Karak Hirn 'the back way'. His head is covered with an intricate leather mask, to hide the shameful fact that he has no beard.

Lhoigor Goldenrod
A tall, vulpine albino sorcerer of immense power, he is evenly matched with his identical twin, Kelmain. Both Lhoigor and his brother come from the strange Weirdblood tribe and from birth they were marked by the favour of the Changer of Ways, by being born with teeth and claws so they could have meat as their first meal. Lhoigor carries a gold-sheathed staff which was unearthed in the Ruins of Ulangor in the Chaos Wastes.

Lonely Tower
Built on top of an old coal mine, this is the secret location where Malakai and his engineers build the *Spirit of Grungni*. It comes under attack by Grey Seer Thanquol and his minions as they try to steal the airship.

Lord of Dragons
One of the Undying Ones, ghostly elven

wizards who sacrificed themselves in order to save Ulthuan and their people. He and his brethren are mighty mages, responsible for maintaining the web of spells that keeps the island continent of Ulthuan afloat and it is he who brings the danger facing the island to Teclis's attention.

Lord Tarlkhir
Commander of the black ark that captures Gotrek and Felix and their party while they investigate magical disturbances in the Sea of Claw.

Lothar Kryptman
Alchemist, living in Fredericksburg. A weirdroot addict, he assists Gotrek & Felix after their encounter in the Sleeping Dragon.

Lothern
Great elvish harbour city where the Phoenix King holds court. Teclis and his brother Tyrion have a mansion built on the side of the highest hill overlooking the city.

Lothlahk
An ancient elf city, now submerged under the Sea of Chaos. It is believed that ancient treasures still lie hidden in its watery depths, there to be claimed by any with magic powerful enough to reach them.

Louis Lanquin
Originally from Quenelles, this Bretonnian is the owner of the Grail inn in Deadgate. He recruits his own regiment to fight alongside Thorgrin's in the doomed attempt to clear Karak Azgal of orks.

Ludeker
A corrupt soldier who runs the Empire town of Baulholz, having ousted its original mayor. He and his soldier cronies constantly demand 'taxes' from inhabitants and visitors for all manner of madeup 'infringements'.

Luipold Gunda
A reputable citizen of the Empire found murdered on the streets of Middenheim. The political activist Felix Jaeger is thought to have had a hand in his demise, but nothing has been proven.

Luitpold
A rat catcher, based in Middenheim. A servant of the Dark Powers, he met a well-deserved end at the hands of the witch hunters.

Lurkers Within
Ancient spider daemons who guard the Haunted Citadel in Albion. They are naturally resistant to magic.

Lurking Horror
A fantastic beast that is rumoured to be quite fantastical.

Lurk Snitchtongue
Thanquol's henchling and a former Clawleader. He has a warpstone-powered communication amulet hammered into his skull by his master and sneaks aboard the *Spirit of Grungni* at his master's command. An encounter with a warp-storm while onboard leaves him somewhat changed though.

M

Madame Mathilda
A female gang boss who rules the slums south of the river in Nuln, rumoured to be an associate of Lady Hermione and Countess Gabriella. She is voluptuous looking, in a rough way, and could have been beautiful were it not for the scar on the left corner of her mouth. It is said she keeps as her companion a large, black, vicious dog.

Magda Freyadotter
Cleric of Valaya, member of Belegar's expedition to Karag Eight Peaks. She warns Gotrek and his party of the dangers awaiting them beneath the Peaks.

Magdalena
Mysterious silver-haired girl with golden eyes, a captive of Count Hrothgar.

Magrig One Eye
The fearsome guardian of the Temple of the Old Ones. He was the mightiest of the giants of old before his brain became clouded and he acquired the lust for man-flesh. He lost an eye in a ferocious battle to the death with his brother and is worshipped as a god by the local orc tribes.

Magritta
City-state on the southern coast of Estalia. Built upon the Bay of Quietude, it commands one of the greatest fleets in the Old World, much to the chagrin of its Tilean neighbours.

Malakai Makaisson
Thought to be the best engineer who ever lived. He was drummed out of the Guild of Engineers after the first airship fiasco and became a Slayer. He built the *Spirit of Grungni* and is responsible for devising many other ingenious munitions and weapons also.

He is another shaven-headed dwarf, with the customary red dyed crest and a short white beard. When flying the airship, he wears a short leather jerkin with sheepskin collar, a leather cap with long ear flaps and a cut-out for his crest to fit through and thick optical lenses engraved with crosshairs.

Malakai appears to have been a prolific inventor, and well travelled, with devices allegedly invented by him turning up all over the Empire and the dwarf realms. The powered skiff used by the dwarfs of Wynters Brewery being a case in point.

He is originally from Dwimmerdim Vale, way up north – an isolated place, which is thought to account for his somewhat odd accent.

In later years, Malakai had an office in the College of Engineering at Nuln. Not being welcome in the dwarf holds, the humans were grateful for his assistance designing and making machines to help the Imperial war effort against the continued Chaos invasions.

Malgrim
Chief engineer of the *Storm Hammer*.

Mannfred von Carstein
The most cunning and dangerous of the von Carstein vampires.

Manfred von Diehl
Nephew and heir to Gottfried von Diehl, considered a brilliant, if blasphemous playwright among the cognoscenti of Altdorf.

Mattrak
An extremely old dwarf who acts as a guide on Gotrek and Felix's trip into Karak Hirn via the secret engineer's entrance. He has rheumy eyes and a wooden leg.

Maximilian Schreiber
Max is a powerful mage and as such, he has become an invaluable ally to Gotrek and Felix in their recent adventures. He was expelled from the Imperial College of Magicians for showing an unhealthy interest in Chaos but found a sympathetic sponsor for his research in the form of the Elector Count of Middenheim. A tall, good-looking man with a well-trimmed beard, he is about ten years older than Felix. He and the other man also share a mutual interest in the same woman, Ulrika Straghov, and this has led to a few complications recently. Max is also a member of the mysterious Golden Brotherhood, an order dedicated to fighting Chaos, though the details are vague.

Mead and Mazer, The
Schrammel's only inn.

Megalean Chain
A group of islands lying in or near the Gulf of Araby.

Meinhart Gessner, Father
Priest of a nameless village in the Mountains of Mourn. Gotrek and Felix pass through while acting as caravan guards on a journey to Skabrand.

Messenger pigeons
A tried and trusted way of sending

messages from one part of the Empire to another.

Middenheim
The City of the White Wolf. The central heights of this mountain top city are dominated by the Elector Count's Palace and the mighty Temple of Ulric. It started life as a fortress but then a fair sized community sprung up around the heights as well.

Migrunsson, Engineer
Dwarf engineer involved in the fight to reclaim Karak Azgal from the orcs.

Mikal's Ford
Site of the mustering of the Kislevite forces.

Mine code
A tapping code that dwarf miners use to speak to each other.

> 'A system for communicating through miles of tunnels with nothing but a hammer. The code was more jealously guarded than the dwarf language, for with it they could talk through walls and across enemy lines.'
>
> From *Orcslayer*,
> by Nathan Long.

Mistress Wither
A strange creature – nominally a woman – who haunts the streets of Nuln, often in the company of the Lady Hermione. She is tall, and appears to be skeletally thin under the hooded shroud which completely covers her body.

Mobi
Dwarf marine aboard the *Storm Hammer*. He is short even for a dwarf, and very wide.

Monastery of the Tower of Vigilance
A monastery in Talabecland.

Morakai
Thangrim Firebeard's other son who died out in the wastes in the cave surrounded by the bodies of the twenty beastmen he'd killed.

Morrslieb
One of the two moons of the Old World (the other being Mannslieb). Morrslieb is smaller than its brother, and characterised by a sickly green glow. It is generally considered to be a sign of ill omen.

Murdo MacBaldoch
The old but surprisingly tough chieftain of Crannog Mere. He is also a member of the Order of Truthsayers of Albion and a canny man. He wears trews and a pleated cloak of a tartan colour that blends into the undergrowth and sports the same strange tattoos that all his people do, tattoos that bear a marked resemblance to some of the engravings in the Paths of the Old Ones.

N

Naktit
Scout-rat in the employ of Warlord Pakstab.

Narli
Ancient dwarf marine aboard the *Storm Hammer*. His face was like a diseased prune and his beard came almost to his feet.

Narin Blowhardsson
A blond-haired, blue-eyed dwarf who joins the expedition to liberate Karak Hirn from its greenskin occupiers. Narin carries a sliver of the Shield of Drutti in his beard, as a reminder of his clan's grudge against Gotrek.

Noseless Milo
A miserable ruffian who 'runs' the refugee camp outside Bauholz. The man would be ugly even if he did have a nose. He is ambitious, and designs to oust Captain Ludeker from his position of town leader.

Nuln
Large city-state in the southern Empire

and former capital. Ruled by Countess Emmanuelle von Liebewitz.

O

Odgin Stormwall
Dwarf commander of Kazad Varr, the landside fortress of Barak Varr.

Ogham Rings
Great stone circles, which attract dark magical energy in Albion and somehow render it harmless.

Oktaf Plaschke-Miesner
An Empire noble, and cousin to von Volgen. He rides a black warhorse, and wears a gleaming gold breastplate. Oktaf is very young, under twenty, and his inexperience and fiery temper severely hamper the Empire's efforts to combat Gargorath's beastman invasion.

Olaf
Cultist sent to kill Felix in Praag. A short, stocky man with a high rasping voice. He accompanied Sergei and was considered the brains of the pair.

Old Ones
A race of gods older than the gods. Some claim they created the world, others that they never existed at all.

Olgar Olgersson
Also known as Olgar Goldgrabber because of his miserly tendencies. He funds the expedition to the Chaos Wastes.

Olgep Wynters
A dwarf master brewer.

Oracle of Truthsayers
A tall woman, sharp faced but still beautiful. She is a respected wise woman throughout Albion and lives with her guardians in sacred caves up in the mountains. She has been gifted with visions though had to pay a heavy price for the power. Teclis is told to seek her out and ask her advice on how to close the Paths of the Old Ones.

Order of the Black Bear
An order of Empire knights based in Averheim.

Orensthil
Grand master of the (now defunct) knightly order of the Fiery Heart. Sadly, when Teobalt finally finds his missing lord, he is not the man he used to be.

Ortwin
Squire to Sir Teobalt, a knight of the Order of the Fiery Heart. He is young and impressionable, and hero-worships the poet-adventurer Felix Jaeger.

Otto Jaeger
Felix's older brother, a prosperous trader who lives in Nuln. While Felix is away on his adventures, Otto takes it on himself to publish his brother's books… putting aside some of the costs to cover his own expenses, of course. Otto works for Felix's father's business, Jaeger's of Altdorf.

P

Pakstab, Warlord
The leader of the skaven settlement of Greypaw Hollow.

Paths of the Old Ones
An ancient network of strange interdimensional corridors with nexus points in places all over the world. A very dangerous place indeed.

Pavel
Tzeentchian cultist, sent to assassinate Enrik.

Pelican's Perch, The
An inn in Marienburg. Gotrek & Felix get thrown out after getting involved in a ruckus.

Petr
Malakai Makaisson's young assistant, who

assists him in his work for the College of Engineering at Nuln. Well-meaning and ever-busy, he is a bit of a klutz, constantly having little accidents. His short-sightedness doesn't help in this regard.

Pfaltz-Kappel, Lord
A rich noble based in Nuln. As a city official, he helps finance the Empire's war efforts to supply cannons and blackpowder for Middenheim.

Pigbarter
A filthy little port city on the estuary of the River Ruin, whose primary currency is swine.

Praag
City in northern Kislev on the River Lynsk. Kislev's second most powerful City State.

Pragarti
A cursed liche that Gotrek and Felix go hunting for, with little success. The trail leads them to the Empire town of Kutzenholz.

Pride of Skintstaad, The
A two-masted trading ship that the elf Aethenir hires to hunt for a valuable stolen book.

Priestlicheim Brasthof
A small town in Talaecland, razed by beastmen.

Prince Hamnir Ranulfsson
Prince of Karak Hirn, second son of its ruler. When the dwarfs are driven out of their hold by grobi, he invokes an old oath of friendship to force Gotrek to join a military expedition to recover the dwarfs' territory from the grobi invaders. A trader by profession, he finds leading a military endeavour challenging, but never gives up.

Q

Quadira
Citadel on the Gulf of Araby, where Gotrek and Felix board the *Storm Hammer*.

R

Ranagor
A renowned breeder of gryphons who raised Teclis's beast from an egg she found on the slopes of Mount Brood.

Ras Karim
A port some hundred leagues east of Copher. Historically, the caliph of this city has two crowns at his disposal – the maleficent Serpent Crown, and the more benevolent Lion Crown. The choice of crown says much about its bearer's style of rulership.

Rassmusson brothers
Three dwarf brothers – miners all – who go with Gotrek and Felix to break into Karak Hirn via a secret back way. Their names were Karl, Ragar and Arn, and they all look so alike it is hard to tell them apart.

Red Rose, The
Large brothel in Praag, visited by Felix, Gotrek and the other Slayers during their 'investigations'.

Redhand
Pirate captain and former scourge of the southern seas. At one time, Redhand's fleet sailed as they pleased and even stormed the walls of Magritta. Redhand's fate is unknown.

Reine Celeste
A Bretonnian trading ship that plies the seas of the southern Old World.

'Reliable'
One of Malakai Makaisson's more bizarre inventions, this device allows the bearer to 'float' safely down to the ground from great heights, for example a damaged airship or gyrocopter. Like all dwarfs, Makaisson is extremely protective of his work, and the only human known to

have used one is the poet adventurer Felix Jaeger... if one can in fact believe any of his claims.

Rememberer
Someone who travels with a Slayer to record the heroic manner of his death. For reasons that can only be guessed at, they are usually human.

Rising Road
A wide road that connects Barak Varr to Rodenheim Castle.

Riskin Tatterear
The Clan Skyre Warleader in command of the skaven burrows under the great port city of Marienburg.

Roche
Adolphus Krieger's hulking, pockmarked henchman. His family has served Krieger for generations.

Rodenheim Castle
A human keep near Karak Hirn. It is here that the exiled dwarfs of Karak Hirn gather their forces, prior to their attempt to retake the conquered dwarf hold.

Rodi Balkinsson
A Slayer. Short and broad, he wears his beard into two long thick plaits, and sports two crests on his head.

Rodrik
A huge, golden-maned knight and body guard to Countess Gabriella. Son of Rudgar.

Rudgar
Count of Waldenhof. A tall, florid aristocrat and brother-in-law to the Countess Gabriella.

Ruen
A white-bearded dwarf of Karak Hirn. He has fading blue tattoos on his wrist and neck.

Ruined City
An ancient city in the Chaos Wastes where everything is built on a giant scale. There is a massive ziggurat in the middle of it which is home to harpies and something far worse.

Rumblebelly
An ogre 'chef'.

Rutger von Volgen
A lord of the Talabec.

S

Schrammel
A small village somewhere in the isolated wildness of the Empire.

Schrammel Monastery
The site of this monastery – now in ruins – lies an hour's walk from the village of Schrammel, somewhere in the Empire. Supposedly run by the followers of Solkan, the God of Law, in reality the monastery's allegiance lay with a darker master.

Sentinels, The
A pair of towering rock formations that mark an unnamed trading post on the road between Barak Varr and Cathay.

Sergei
Cultist sent with Olaf to kill Felix in Praag. A tall, heavily built man with a deep voice. His lack of wits make him no less dangerous.

Shadowfang
A skaven assassin employed by Grey Seer Thanquol to kidnap Gotrek and Felix in one of his nefarious schemes.

Shield of Drutti
Ownership of this dwarf shield is subject to a grudge between the Ironskin and the Stonemonger clans of Karak Hirn... A dispute that Gotrek 'solves' in his own, special way.

Shienara
One of Teclis's female companions. She and her twin, Malyria, are courtesans.

Shrine of Grimnir

Located in the dwarf hold of Karak Kadrin, this shrine is dedicated to Grimnir, the most bloodthirsty of the dwarf ancestor gods. Once a dwarf has taken his Slayer oath, his name is carved into the great pillar in the temple – the pillar of woe – so all will know of their passing from life.

> 'You say Grimnir is bloodthirsty,' Ulrika asked. 'Does he accept living sacrifices then?'
>
> 'Only the lives of his Slayers. He takes their death in payment for their sins. And their hair.'
>
> Borek must have noticed the startled look pass across Felix's face, for he added: 'Most Slayers take their vow before the great altar of Grimnir down there, that is where they shave their heads, then they burn their hair in the great furnace. Outside is the street of the skin artists, where they have their first tattoos inked into their flesh.'
>
> From *Dragonslayer*,
> by William King

Siobhain

One of the Oracle's Guardians and an accomplished warrior. She is almost as tall as Felix and tattoos cover her face and arms in the style of her people.

Siskritt

A skaven sent on a mission to Sartosa to steal a magic talisman.

Skabrand

An ogre settlement located in the southern reaches of the Mountains of Mourn.

Skalf's Keep (or Hold)

The dwarfs' above-ground settlement built on top of the ruins of Karak Azgal. It is noticeably better constructed and cleaner than the adjoining human town, Deadgate, down in the valley. Presumably due to the comparative richness of the dwarfs.

Skaven

The existence of skaven is a closely-guarded secret within the Empire. For the good of the people – and to prevent widespread panic and despair – the authorities always refer to them as 'beastmen'.

Sketti Hammerhand

A dwarf. Deep Warden of Karak Izor.

Skewered Dragon, The

A bar in Middenheim.

Skitch

Izak Grottle's henchling. A hunchback who wears glasses, Skitch is reputed to be the best ratmaster of his day.

Skjalandir

A huge and ancient dragon, it is first encountered by the *Spirit of Grungni* whilst travelling to Kislev. Its long sleep had been disturbed by Kelmain and Lhoigor, who drove warpstone charms into its flesh, corrupting it. Skjalandir made its nest in a system of caverns below the Dragon Mountain along the Old High Road.

Skull Mace of Malarak

A weapon wielded by Grume of the Nightfang. Made of some odd metal, its head is shaped like the skull of a daemon and the empty eye-sockets glow with an infernal light. It freezes the limbs and chills the hearts of those who face it.

Sleeper, the

A terrible, ancient evil said to lurk in the depths below Karak Hirn. Its nature and purpose are unknown, and the few brave souls who encountered the creature are loath to speak about it except in whispers of dread. The poet Felix Jaeger claims that he and his companion the Trollslayer Gotrek Gurnisson bested the creature, but as we all know, his penny-dreadful tales – though entertaining – are pure fiction.

Sleeping Dragon, The

Tavern in Fredericksburg.

Snelli
Dwarf marine aboard the *Storm Hammer*. He volunteers to join the party that search for Redhand's treasure.

Snorri Nosebiter
Snorri is a massive, well-muscled and immensely stupid Slayer. His trademark 'crest' is made up of nails, which have been painted different colours and driven into his skull and this may account for his lack of wits. His beard is cropped short and his nose has been broken so many times that it's shapeless. One ear is cauliflowered, while the other one is missing altogether, leaving only a hole in the side of his head. He has a huge ring through his nose and is heavily scarred and tattooed.

He is one of only three survivors of the first ill-fated mission to find Karag Dum, and at some point in the past, there has been a tragedy involving a dwarf woman and child, which has led Snorri to take the Oath.

Snorri fights with a hammer and axe and enjoys the simple things in life – drinking and killing, and he is very good at both!

Sonnstill
The festival of the summer solstice, observed in and around the Empire and the surrounding lands.

Sphere of Destiny
Strange apparatus Teclis found in the ruins of an ancient Cathayan city nearly two centuries ago. A massive sphere of bronze, engraved with strange runes, he uses it to augment his powers when performing a particular spell of viewing.

Spirit of Grungni
The second airship built in secret by Malakai, it is even bigger than its ill-fated predecessor, the *Indestructible*. It is made up of two main parts: a massive, many skinned balloon full of lift-gas cells, and a smaller, heavily armed and armoured cabin suspended beneath it. There are weapons cupolas embedded into the fuselage of the main ship and it has many portholes and a massive glass window at the front helm to allow a good view from the command deck. Powered by 'black water' engines and a massive propellor at the stern, the airship is capable of flying over two hundred leagues per day. Malakai wanted to call it the *Unstoppable* but much to the relief of the many dwarfs who serve onboard, he was persuaded against it!

Spider
One of two twin sewerjack knifemen Gotrek and Felix work with in Nuln. He is distinguished from his brother by the spider tattooed onto his cheek (*see also* Hef II).

Standing Stones Inn, The
Coach house on the Bögenhafen road.

Stangenschloss
A fort in the Drakwald. Though it has been badly damaged by the forces of Chaos, the place is still kept garrisoned by Empire troops. Gotrek and Felix help the defenders repulse an attack by...

Steg
Dwarf Slayer, met by Felix and Gotrek in the Iron Door tavern. His shame lies in being caught as a thief, though he seems little concerned about further tarnishing his name.

Stew
The sewers beneath Nuln where Gotrek, Felix and the other sewerjacks patrol. The tunnels themselves are of Khazalid workmanship with high vaulted ceilings more reminiscent of a cathedral than a sewage system.

Storm Festival
A Marienburg festival held in honour of Manann, god of the sea, thanking him for sparing their ships from the harsh winter storms. The occasional disappearance during this time of celebration is put down to drunken revellers just falling into canals, rather than some sort of 'curse'.

Storm Hammer
Dwarf steamship which Gotrek and Felix take passage on to escape Araby.

Stromfels
A shark god – an evil mirror to Manann – worshipped by pirates up and down the coast of the Old World.

Stromfels' Heart
A bracelet made of woven gold wire, decorated with a sea-green gem the size of a walnut. This piece of jewellery is sacred to Stromfels' worshippers, who use it as part of their debased yearly ceremony to honour their god.

Stromfels' Reach
A low hill somewhere in the Cursed Marshes near Marienburg. A set of standing stones decorates to the top of the rise – an altar to the shark god Stromfels. It would be impossible to find the place without the aid of a native guide.

Submersible
A generic name for a sea-going vessel that can travel underwater. Such devices are rare and unique; even Gotrek and Felix have only travelled on two – a rickety skaven submersible in the Sea of Claws, and a rather more robust dwarf version out of Barak Varr.

Sulmander's tomb
Gotrek and Felix ransacked this tomb whilst in Araby.

Sword of Righteous Flame
A sacred relic of the knightly Order of the Fiery Heart. It is said that the weapon bursts into flame in the presence of unrighteous.

Sylvania
A forsaken region of the Empire, a nexus of death and evil. No sane man would ever wish to tread its soil, or penetrate its dark, gloomy forests. Nominally, it is part of Stirland, but its true lords are the vampire counts.

T

Taalman Nordling
Empire noble, and acting commander of Castle Reikland while its actual lord is discommoded.

Talia Nitikin
A Kislevite woman, younger sister of Anya. Following a fall, her behaviour has become so erratic and aggressive that she is danger of being labelled a follower of Chaos.

Tarhalt's Crown
A hill surmounted by a stone circle, located deep in the Barren Hills. It is a place of power, and it is here that the beastman army of Gargorach comes to enact their vile ritual on Hexensnacht.

Tasirion
An elf mage who broke elvish law by unlocking the Paths of the Old Ones. The venture ended in his ultimate madness and his fate is considered a warning to others who might attempt to do the same. He has left some documented accounts about the Paths which Teclis consults.

Tauber
A doctor who works at Castle Reikguard. He is unfairly accused by the terrified soldiers of being in league with the enemy.

Teclis
A mighty elven arch-mage and twin to Tyrion. In his youth, he was frail and sickly but then he learned to strengthen himself with spells and potions so now the only visible legacy of this former weakness is a slight limp in his left leg. He bears the War Crown of Saphery and the staff of Lileath, artefacts of considerable power.

His first encounter with Gotrek Gurnisson is within the Paths of the Old Ones and it is not an auspicious one.

Temple of Leopold
A temple that trains warrior-priests in Priestlicheim, in Talabecland.

Temple of the Old Ones
A massive stepped pyramid in Albion with seven huge levels, each level marked with ancient runes.

Teobalt von Dreschler
A knight of the Order of the Fiery Heart. When he finds Felix in Altdorf, he demands the return of the sword Kara-ghul, which was taken from the body of one of his order, some twenty years previously. Later, he makes a bargain with Felix that if he and Gotrek assist him in a quest – locating the fallen members of his order and recovering their banner – the knight will grant him stewardship of the sword.

Terror
The Great Destroyer, a Blutdrengrik, the Bane of Grung – a bloodthirster of Khorne!
A daemon of Chaos summoned by Skathloc in the last days of the siege of Karag Dum. Huge, more than twice the height of a man, it is winged with ruddy red skin and has the mark of the Blood God on its brow. It is armed with a whip and an axe.

Thangrim Firebeard
The leader of the dwarfs at Karag Dum. An old but still powerful dwarf with long red hair and beard striped with white, he carries the Hammer of Fate.

Thanquol
A skaven magelord and master schemer whose cunning plans always seem to be thwarted – usually by his own paranoia! Pre-eminent among the Grey Seers, the feared and potent skaven magicians who rank just below the Council of Thirteen itself, Thanquol is a mighty mage indeed, especially when he augments his powers by liberal use of the powdered warpstone snuff he keeps in a manskin pouch at his belt.
Pale-furred with pink, blind-seeming eyes, he sports the horns which signify his calling, and the favour of his master, the Horned Rat. Thanquol loathes and fears Gotrek Gurnisson in equal measures, and holds the Slayer and his human companion entirely responsible for all his recent setbacks. Still, he is determined to have his revenge, no matter how long it takes!

Thiessen
An Empire captain under the command of von Volgen.

Thorgig Helmguard
Friend of Kagrin Deepmountain, this young dwarf takes part in Prince Hamnir's attempt to free Karak Hirn from orc and goblin invaders.

Thorgrin Dragonslayer
Thane of Karak Azgal. He leads a force of dwarfs and human mercenaries into the ruined hold in an attempt to reclaim it, but the expedition fails due to betrayal.

Thulgul
A hideously mutated troll, the guardian of the lost hoard of Karag Eight Peaks.

Tialva
A beer-like drink that Gotrek and Felix first taste in Ras Karim. It is made from sorghum, rather than wheat.

Tobaro
Tilean city-state on the western coast of the Tilean Sea. Built upon ancient elven ruins, the city is protected both inland and along the coast by rugged natural defences.

Tobi
Young dwarf marine aboard the *Storm Hammer*.

Trollslayer's Doom
The alternate name Felix considered for his 'My Travels with Gotrek' journals.

Trees
'I hate trees. They're like elves, manling,' Gotrek said. 'They make me want to take an axe to them.'

From *Trollslayer*,
by William King

Trolls
Vile monsters that lurk in the dark, dank and largely forgotten corners of the world. They are huge and strong, and possess tremendous powers of recuperation that make them very hard to kill. They aren't very bright, but their savage nature more than makes up for this one failing. Fighting and killing trolls is a perfect test of skill and courage for dwarfs with a death wish.

Truthsayers
The order of wizards of Albion. The formation of the order of Truthsayers apparently dates back to the legendary times when the Old Ones walked the earth.

Twisted Paths
Spoken of by Tasirion, they are said to be where the work of the Old Ones intersect with bubbles of pure Chaos.

Tyrion
Teclis's twin brother. A handsome warrior and consort to the Everqueen. The deadliest elf warrior in twenty generations.

Tzarina Katarin
'The Ice Queen', ruler of Kislev. An accomplished mage and warrior, her nickname derives from her cool demeanour as well as her mastery of Ice Magic.

U

Ufgart Haginskarl
A dwarf of the Stonemonger clan, based in Karak Hirn.

Ugrek Manflayer
A massive orc who has united the greenskin tribes near Karak Kadrin. He is known as far as Altdorf, such is his reputation. He is said to skin his captives and make the skins into cloaks. He wields a magical cleaver.

Ulfram
A warrior priest of Sigmar. He is old, frail and blind, but well-versed in the myths and legends of the Empire.

Ulgo
A witch hunter and member of the Cult of Ulric. He accuses Gotrek and Felix of conspiring with Chaos.

Ulli Ullisson
A dwarf Slayer who joins Felix and Gotrek's quest to slay the dragon Skjalindir. His freshly shaven head suggests that he is only a recent convert to the Slayer cult, and his manner is that of a nervous braggart rather than a truly brave warrior.

Ulrika Magdova Straghov
A beautiful, blonde Kislevite and an expert swordswoman. Her father is March Warden of an estate bordering the troll country and she is the love of Felix Jaeger's life for a while. After an encounter with the sinister Adolphus Krieger, Ulrika's life takes an unusual and unforseen direction.

Ulthuan
The island continent of the elves, raised and held above the sea by potent magic.

Undgrin
The ancient underground dwarf road system that was built to link all the holds together. Sadly, much of it has fallen into disrepair, damaged by the dwarfs' enemies, or geographic upheaval.

Ungrim Ironfist
Slayer-king of Karak Kadrin. Due to the vow taken by his ancestor Baragor, Ungrim is bound both by his oaths as king and Slayer, and tries to balance both as best he can.

Unsinkable
Malakai's famous steamship and the biggest one ever seen. Two hundred paces long and weighing over five hundred tons, it could sail at over three leagues an hour and had steam-powered gatling turrets for protection. It hit a rock and sank.

Uragh Goldtusk
Orcish captain, and the most feared pirate in the Gulf of Araby. Remarkably agile and intelligent for an orc, he wields twin cutlasses.

Urli
Marine sergeant aboard the *Storm Hammer*. Known as Ugli Urli to his comrades, his face has been pock-marked by shrapnel.

Urslak Cripplehorn
A beastman shaman. Though old, and not big by beastman standards, he is extremely powerful. One of his horns is bent at and odd angle, and he is festooned with birds' feathers and claws. Urslak rides into battle on am immense herdstone, carried by beastman followers, which has the power to turn men into beasts with its vile magic.

V

Varek Varigsson
Son of Vareg of the Clan Grimnar and nephew of Borek Forkbeard.

Plump and civilised looking, his well-groomed beard reaches almost to the floor and he wears thick glasses. A scholar like his uncle, he diligently keeps a diary of all the events that take place. He is equipped with bombs made by Malakai, and the engineer also taught him how to fly a gyrocopter, a skill he uses to great effect when the *Spirit of Grungni* is attacked by a dragon.

Van Niek's Emporium
Shop in Nuln that specialises in rare and exotic books and other artefacts. Reputedly, it also serves as a government front as well.

Vermak Skab
Warlord of Clan Skab and Lurk's distant cousin. Sent to lead the attack on Nuln but tragically meets his end in a terrible accident involving a loaded crossbow and an exploding donkey!

Vilebroth Null
Low Abbot of the Plague Monks of Clan Pestilens who tries to bring about the downfall of Nuln by using the Cauldron of a Thousand Poxes to spread the plague.

Villem Kozinski
Younger brother of the Duke Enrik. His diplomatic manner makes him a more suitable candidate for the throne than his brother, and he acts as a foil to Enrik's abruptness.

Vinck, Doktor
Originally the mayor of Bauholz, he now ekes out a precarious existence as a physician in the refugee camp on the edge of the town. He is a thin old man with wispy white hair.

Volg Staahl
A Templar of the Order of the Black Bear. Impromptu leader of the expedition to reclaim the Wynters brewery – and the precious grave-cask of Grandmaster Rodor – from the greenskins. Sometimes called 'the Voluminous', he was a big man with an even bigger voice.

Voorman
Count Hrothgar's pet wizard and a member of the Order of Tzeentch.

Von Carsteins
The most infamous line of vampire counts. Based in Sylvania, they occasionally rise up and lead massive armies of undeath across the lands of the living, swelling their ranks with the freshly dead bodies of their victims. Of them all, the most dangerous is Mannfred von Carstein, who lives (if one can use that word for such a creature) to pose a constant danger to the human Empire.

Von Diehls
An ancient Empire family line, rumoured to be cursed.

Von Uhland
A general of the Reiksguard, who leads

the recapture of Castle Reikguard from the necromancer Heinrich Kemmler.

Vork Kineater
Leader of the ogre mercenaries employed in Skabrand by Zayed al Fahruk to protect his caravan. It's possible his name came from eating all his family. Kineater kidnaps Talia Nitikin, intending to marry her, an act which inflames the other ogres of his tribe against him.

W

Waldenschlosse
Castle which sits above Waldenhof and home to Rudgar, Count of Waldenhof.

Waldemar Lichtmann
A bright wizard who works in the Engineering School of Nuln alongside Groot and Makaisson, making war machines for the Empire troops to use against Chaos invaders who are menacing Middenheim. He is thin and tall, with reddish brown hair.

Warlord Pakstab
Warlord of the skaven settlement Greypaw Hollow.

Whisperer of Hayesh, The
A mythical monster that Gotrek has never been able to find.

White Boar, The
A tavern in Praag where Gotrek, Felix and the rest stayed during the Siege of Praag.

White Widow
A massive albino cave spider said to lurk in the haunted depths of the lost dwarf hold, Karak Azgal. Gotrek's desire to hunt down and slay this beast lead to the two adventurers taking part in a expedition to retake the hold. Needless to say, their quest turns out to be more complicated than they had originally envisaged.

Wildgans, Frater
An instructor at the Schrammel monastery.

Willentrude
A plump Sister of Shallya Gotrek and Felix encounter while they help garrison Castle Reikland from an undead army.

Witch
Grey seer Thanquol suffers an unfortunate consequence when he angers an unnamed strigany witch in a forest.

Wolfgang Krassner
Man killed by Felix in a duel, resulting in his expulsion from university.

Wolfgang Lammel
Decadent fop and Slaaneshi cultist. His father owns the Sleeping Dragon in Fredricksburg, where he hangs out with his equally unpleasant friends.

Worlds Edge Mountains
Immense range of mountains that mark the eastern boundary of the Empire and the Old World, believed in ancient times to be the edge of the world itself.

Wulf's
A private gentleman's club in the Handelbezirk district of Nuln. Its members wear a golden pendant in the shape of a shield, emblazoned with a wolf's head. Felix's brother Otto is a member.

Wynters Brewery
A dwarf brewery renowned for the quality of its beers, especially Wynters Own.

Y

Yhetee
A mythical creature rumoured to haunt the mountains of the Old World. These shy creatures are larger than men, clad in pale-coloured fur that lets them blend into the snowy scenery. Though roughly human-shaped, they are not much more intelligent than wild beasts.

Yuleh il Toorissi
A princess, and niece of a previous ruler of Ras Karim. She conspires with her

lover, Halim, to overthrow the current, corrupt caliph, Falhedar.

Z

Zayed al Mahrak
An Arabyan caravan master who plies the Ivory road between Barak Varr and Cathay. He employs Gotrek and Felix as caravan guards on one of his journeys.

Zarkhul
A prophet and the uniter of the orc tribes of Albion. He intends to lead them into the great Waaagh! to reclaim the Temple of the Old Ones.

Zhufgrim Scarp
A high, sheer-sided cliff in the mountains by Karak Hirn. At its foot lies the Cauldron Lake.

ABOUT THE AUTHORS

Nathan Long hails from Los Angeles, California, where he began his career as a screenwriter in Hollywood. He has written a wide selection of Warhammer fantasy novels, including the Blackhearts trilogy and the adventures of Ulrika the vampire. To many fans, he is best known for his work on the hugely successful Gotrek & Felix series, including five full-length novels and the first Black Library fantasy audio drama, *Slayer of the Storm God*.

Richard Salter is a British writer and editor living near Toronto, Canada with his wife and two young sons. He edited the short story collection *Short Trips: Transmissions* for Big Finish Productions and is now working on *World's Collider*, an apocalyptic anthology. He has sold over twenty short stories including tales in *Solaris Rising: The New Solaris Book of Science Fiction*, *Phobophobia* from Dark Continents Publishing and *Machine of Death 2*.

READ IT FIRST

EXCLUSIVE PRODUCTS | EARLY RELEASES | FREE DELIVERY

blacklibrary.com

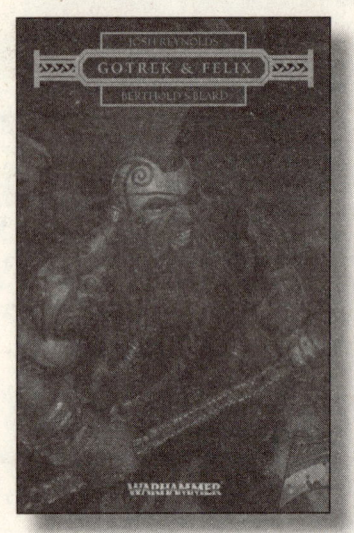

Download your copy of
Berthold's Beard from
www.blacklibrary.com

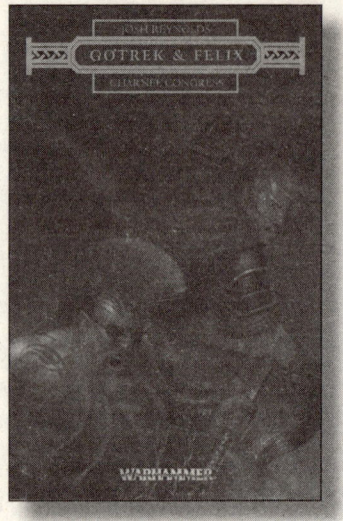

Download your copy of
Charnel Congress from
www.blacklibrary.com

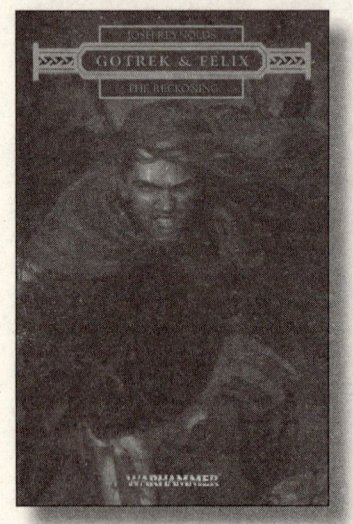

Download your copy of
The Reckoning from
www.blacklibrary.com

All titles exclusively
available from
www.blacklibrary.com